GARDNER ERLE STAN
LE STANLEY GARDNER
GARDNER ERLE STANL
LE STANLEY GARDNER
GARDNER ERLE STANL
LE STANLEY GARDNER
GARDNER ERLE STANL
LE STANLEY GARDNER
GARDNER ERLE STANL
LE STANLEY GARDNER
GARDNER ERLE STANL
LE STANLEY GARDNER
GARDNER ERLE STANL
LE STANLEY GARDNER
GARDNER ERLE STANL
LE STANLEY GARDNER
GARDNER ERLE STANL
LE STANLEY GARDNER
GARDNER ERLE STAN

ERLE STANLEY GARDNER

RLE STANLEY GARDNER

The Case of

The Gilded Lily

The Daring Decoy

The Fiery Fingers

The Lucky Loser

The Calendar Girl

The Deadly Toy

The Mischievous Doll

The Amorous Aunt

Heinemann/Octopus

The Case of the Gilded Lily first published in Great Britain in 1962
The Case of the Daring Decoy first published in Great Britain in 1963
The Case of the Fiery Fingers first published in Great Britain in 1957
The Case of the Lucky Loser first published in Great Britain in 1962
The Case of the Calendar Girl first published in Great Britain in 1964
The Case of the Deadly Toy first published in Great Britain in 1964
The Case of the Mischievous Doll first published in Great Britain in 1968
The Case of the Amorous Aunt first published in Great Britain in 1969

This edition first published in 1976 by
William Heinemann Limited
15–16 Queen Street, London W1

in association with
Octopus Books Limited
59 Grosvenor Street, London W1

ISBN 0 7064 0575 7

Printed in Great Britain by
Jarrold & Sons Ltd., Norwich

Contents

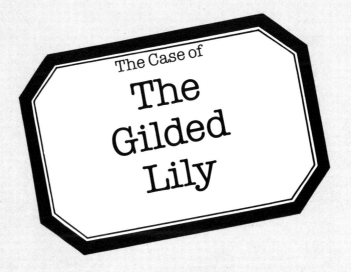

The Case of

The Gilded Lily

FOREWORD

My friend Dr Walter Camp is an outstanding figure in the field of legal medicine.

One of his greatest attributes is the calm, detached manner with which he approaches any scientific problem. It is impossible to think of Dr Camp ever being 'stampeded' so that he would lose his intellectual integrity on the one hand, or on the other hand let any personal or financial considerations colour his judgment.

Dr Camp is both an M.D. and a Ph.D., yet despite his intellectual and scientific achievements, and a brain which functions as unemotionally (and as accurately) as an adding machine, he remains a warm, friendly human being.

Dr Camp is one of the country's leading toxicologists. He is a Professor of Toxicology and Pharmacology at the University of Illinois and is Coroner's Toxicologist for Cook County, which includes the seething metropolis of Chicago.

For the past couple of years he has been Secretary of the American Academy of Forensic Sciences, and heaven knows how much time, energy and time-consuming effort he and his personal secretary, Polly Cline, have poured into that organization.

Dr Camp is no prima donna with a temperament, although his achievements and record would entitle him to develop all the idiosyncrasies of temperament; on the contrary, he loves to work with others, to become a member of a 'team', and then to minimize his own part in that team's achievement.

Such men, who have the ability to get things done, who have the executive qualities necessary to co-ordinate the work of others, and the stability necessary to work with others, are rare.

This year, the annual meeting of the Academy of Forensic Sciences was held under the guidance of Dr Camp, Secretary; Fred Inbau (Professor of Criminal Law at North-Western University), President; and Dr Richard Ford (head of the Department of Legal Medicine at Harvard University), Programme Chairman. Those of us who attended found it one of the most inspirational and informative Academy sessions ever to be held in an organization covering such a complex field. This was due mainly to the fact that these three men worked together as a team with such perfect co-ordination, such smooth co-operation, and such clockwork efficiency that many of us failed to realize the untold hours of planning, working, and almost constant consultation which made the extraordinary results possible.

Dr Camp has worked on many a spectacular case where anyone less cool, less objective in his approach would have been swept off his scientific feet. There was, for instance, the famous Ragen case where a man on the receiving end of a shot-gun blast was later claimed to have died because of mercuric poisoning. There was another famous case: that of a gangster awaiting execution in the electric chair who beat the executioner to the punch, reportedly with the aid of a lethal dose of strychnine.

Dr Camp, as a referee in these cases, handled himself in a manner which was a credit to the best traditions of forensic science. He refused to be influenced by rumours, the pressures of interested parties, or popular excitement. He approached the problems as a scientist and he solved them as a scientist.

And so I dedicate this book to my friend:

WALTER J. R. CAMP, M.D., Ph.D.

Erle Stanley Gardner

I

Stewart G. Bedford entered his private office, hung up his hat, walked across to the huge walnut desk which had been a birthday present from his wife a year ago, and eased himself into the swivel chair.

His secretary, Elsa Griffin, with her never-failing and characteristic efficiency, had left the morning paper on his desk, the pages neatly folded back so that Mrs Bedford's photograph was smiling up at him from the printed page.

It was a good picture of Ann Roann Bedford, bringing out the little characteristic twinkle in her eyes, the sparkle and vitality of her personality.

Stewart Bedford was very, very proud of his wife. Mixed with that pride was the thrill of possession, the feeling that he, at fifty-two, had been able to marry a woman twenty years his junior and make her radiantly happy.

Bedford, with his wealth, his business contacts, his influential friends, had never paid attention to social life. His first wife had been dead for some twelve years. After her death the social circle of their friends would have liked to consider Stewart G. Bedford as the 'most eligible bachelor', but Bedford wanted no part of it. He immersed himself in his business, continued to enhance his financial success, and took almost as much pride in the growing influence of his name in the business world as he would have taken in a son if he had had one.

Then he had met Ann Roann and his life suddenly slipped into a tail spin that caused a whirlwind courtship to culminate in a Nevada marriage.

Ann was as pleased with the social position she acquired through her marriage as a child with a new toy. Bedford still maintained his interest in his business, but it was no longer the dominant factor in his life. He wanted to get Ann Roann the things out of life which would make her happy, and Ann Roann had a long list of such things. However, her quick, enthusiastic response, her obvious gratitude left Bedford constantly feeling like an indulgent parent on Christmas morning.

Bedford had settled himself at his desk and was reading the paper when Elsa Griffin glided in.

'Good morning, Elsa,' he said. 'Thanks for calling my attention to the account of Mrs Bedford's party.'

Her smile acknowledged his thanks. It was a nice smile.

To Stewart, Elsa Griffin was as comfortable as a smoking-jacket and slippers. She had been with him for fifteen years, she knew his every want, his every whim, and had an uncanny ability to read his mind. He was very, very fond of her; in fact, there had been a romantic interlude after his first wife died. Elsa's quiet understanding had been one of the great things in his life. He had even considered marrying her–but that was before he had met Ann Roann.

Bedford knew he had made a fool of himself falling head over heels in love with Ann Roann, a woman who was just entering her thirties. He knew the hurt he was inflicting on Elsa Griffin, but he could no more control his actions than water rushing down a stream could stop on the brink of a precipice. He had plunged on into matrimony.

Elsa Griffin had offered her congratulations and wishes for every happiness and had promptly faded back into the position of the trusted private secretary. If she had suffered–and he was sure she had–there was no sign visible to the naked eyes.

'There's a man waiting for you,' Elsa Griffin said.

'Who is he? What does he want?'

'His name is Denham. He said to tell you that Binney Denham wanted to see you and would wait.'

'Benny Denham?' Bedford said. 'I don't know any Benny Denham. How does it happen he wants to see me? Let him see one of the executives who–'

'It's not Benny. It's Binney,' she said, 'and he says it's a personal matter, that he'll wait until he can see you.'

Bedford made a gesture of dismissal with his hand.

Elsa shook her head. 'I don't think he'll leave. He really intends to see you.'

Bedford scowled. 'I can't be accessible to every Tom, Dick and Harry that comes in and says he wants to see me on a personal matter.'

'I know,' she said, 'but Mr Denham . . . there's something about him that's just a little . . . it's hard to describe . . . a persistence that's . . . well, it's a little frightening.'

'Frightening!' Bedford said, bristling.

'Not in that way. It's just the fact that he has this terrible, deadly patience. You get the feeling that it would really be better to see him. He sits in the chair, quiet and motionless, and . . . and every time I look up he's looking at me with those peculiar eyes. I do wish you'd see him, S.G. I have a feeling you should.'

'All right,' Bedford said. 'What the hell! Let's see what he wants and get rid of him. A personal matter. Not an old school friend that wants a touch?'

'No, no! Nothing like that. Something that . . . well, I have the feeling that it's important.'

'All right,' Bedford said, smiling. 'I can always trust your intuition. We'll get him out of the way before we tackle the mail. Send him in.'

Elsa left the office and a few moments later Binney Denham was standing in the doorway bowing and smiling apologetically. Only his eyes were not apologetic. They were steady and appraising, as though his mission were a matter of life and death.

'I'm so glad you'll see me, Mr Bedford,' he said. 'I was afraid perhaps I might have trouble. Delbert told me I *had* to see *you*, that I had to wait until I saw you, no matter how long it took, and Delbert is a hard man to cross.'

Some inner bell rang a warning in Bedford's mind. He said: 'Sit down. And who the devil is Delbert?'

'He's a sort of associate of mine.'

'A partner?'

'No, no. I'm not a partner. I'm an associate.'

'All right. Sit down. Tell me what it is you want. But you'll have to make it brief. I have some appointments this morning and there's some important mail here which has to be handled.'

'Yes, sir. Thank you very much, sir.'

Binney Denham moved over and sat on the extreme edge of the chair at the side of the desk. His hat was clutched over his stomach. He hadn't offered to shake hands.

'Well, what is it?' Bedford asked.

'It's about a business investment,' Denham said. 'It seems that Delbert needs money for financing this venture of his. It will only take twenty thousand dollars and he should be able to pay back the money within a few–'

'Say, what the devil *is* this?' Bedford said. 'You told my secretary you wanted to see me about a personal matter. I don't know you. I don't know Delbert, and I'm not interested in financing any business venture to the tune of twenty thousand dollars. Now if that's all you–'

'Oh, but you don't understand, sir,' the little man protested. 'You see, it involves your wife.'

Bedford stiffened with silent anger, but that inner bell which had sounded the note of warning before now gave such a strident signal that he became very cautious.

'And what about my wife?' he asked.

'Well, you see, sir, it's like this. Of course, you understand there's a market for these things now. These magazines . . . I'm sure you don't like them any better than I do. I won't even read the things, and I'm quite certain, you don't, sir. But you must know of their existence, and they're *very popular*.'

'All right,' Bedford said. 'Get it out of your system. What are you talking about?'

'Well, of course, it . . . well, you almost have to know Delbert, Mr Bedford, in order to understand the situation. Delbert is very insistent. When he wants something, he *really* wants it.'

'All right, go on,' Bedford snapped. 'What about my wife? Why are you bringing her name in this?'

'Well, of course, I was only mentioning it because . . . well, you see, *I* know Delbert, and, while I don't condone his ideas, I–'

'What are his ideas?'

'He needs money.'

'All right, he needs money. So what?'

'He thought you could furnish it.'

'And my wife?' Bedford asked, restraining an impulse to throw the little man bodily out of the office.

'Well, of course your wife's record,' Denham said.

'What do you mean, her record?'

'Her criminal record, fingerprints, etc.,' Denham said in that same quietly apologetic manner.

There was a moment of frozen silence. Bedford, too accustomed to playing poker in business to let Denham see the slightest flicker of expression on his face, was rapidly thinking back. After all, what did he know about Ann Roann? She had been the victim of an unhappy marriage she didn't like to discuss. There had been some sort of tragedy. Her husband's suicide had been his final confession of futility. There had been some insurance which had enabled the young widow to carry on during a period of readjustment. There had been two years of foreign travel and then she had met Stewart Bedford.

Bedford's own voice sounded strange to him. 'Put your cards on the table. What is this? Blackmail?'

'*Blackmail!*' the man exclaimed with every evidence of horror. 'Oh, my heavens, no, Mr Bedford! Good heavens, no! Even Delbert wouldn't stoop to anything like that.'

'Well, what *is* it?' Bedford asked.

'I'd like an opportunity to explain about the business investment. I think you'll agree it's a very sound investment and you could have the twenty thousand back within . . . well, Delbert says six months. I personally think it would be more like a year. Delbert's always optimistic.'

'What about my wife's record?' Bedford's voice now definitely had a rasp to it.

'Well, of course, that's the point,' Denham said apologetically. 'You see, sir, Delbert simply *has* to have the money, and he thought you might loan it to him. Then, of course, he has this information and he knows that some of these magazines pay very high prices for tips. I've talked it over with him. I feel certain that they wouldn't pay anything like twenty thousand, but Delbert thinks they would if the information was fully authenticated and–'

'This information is authenticated?' Bedford asked.

'Oh, of course, sir, of course! I wouldn't even have mentioned it otherwise.'

'How is it authenticated?'

'What the police call mug shots and fingerprints.'

'Let me see.'

'I'd much prefer to talk about the investment, Mr Bedford. I didn't really intend to bring it up in this way. However, I could see you were rather impatient about–'

'What about the information?' Bedford asked.

The little man let go of the rim of his hat with his right hand. He fished in an inner pocket and brought out a plain Manila envelope.

'I'm sure I hadn't intended to tell you about it in this way,' he said sorrowfully.

He extended the Manila envelope towards Bedford.

Bedford took the envelope, turned back the flap, and pulled out the papers that were on the inside.

It was either the damnedest clever job of fake photography he had ever seen or it was Ann Roann . . . Ann Roann's picture taken some years earlier. There was the same daring, don't-give-a-damn sparkle in her eyes, the tilt to her head, the twist to her lips, and down underneath was that damning serial number, below that a set of fingerprints and the sections of the penal code that had been violated.

Denham's voice droned on, filling in the gap in Bedford's thinking.

'Those sections of the penal code relate to insurance fraud, if you don't mind, Mr Bedford. I know you're curious. I was too when I looked it up.'

'What's she supposed to have done?' Bedford asked.

'She had some jewellery that was insured. She made the mistake of pawning the jewellery before she reported that it had been stolen. She collected on the insurance policy, and then they found where the jewellery had been pawned and . . . well, the police are very efficient in such matters.'

'What was done with the charge?' Bedford asked. 'Was she convicted, given probation? Was the charge dismissed, or what?'

'Heavens! *I* don't know,' Denham said. 'I'm not sure that even Delbert knows. These are the records that Delbert gave me. He said that he was going to take them to this magazine and that they'd pay him for the tip. I told him I thought he was being very, very foolish, that I didn't think the magazine would pay as much as he needed for his investment, and frankly, Mr Bedford, I don't like such things. I don't like those magazines or this business of assassinating character, of digging up things out of a person's dead past. I just don't like it.'

'I see,' Bedford said grimly. He sat there holding in front of him the photostatic copy of the circular describing his wife–age, height, weight, eye colour, fingerprint classification.

So this was blackmail. He'd heard about it. Now he was up against it. This little man sitting there on the edge of the chair, holding his hat across his stomach, his hands clutching the rim, his manner apologetic, was a blackmailer and Bedford was being given the works.

Bedford knew all about what he was supposed to do under such circumstances. He was supposed to throw the little bastard out of his office, beat him up, turn him over to the police. He was supposed to tell him: 'Go ahead. Do your damnedest! I won't pay a dime for blackmail!' Or he was supposed to string the man along, ring up the police department, explain the matter to the officer in charge of such things, a man who would promise to handle it discreetly and keep it very, very confidential.

He knew how such things were handled. They would arrange for him to turn over marked money. Then they would arrest Binney Denham and the case would be kept very hush-hush.

But would it?

There was this mysterious Delbert in the background . . . Delbert, who apparently was the ringleader of the whole thing . . . Delbert, who wanted to sell his information to one of those magazines that were springing up like mushrooms, magazines which depended for their living on exploiting sensational facts about people in the public eye.

Either these were police records or they weren't.

If they were police records, Bedford was trapped. There was no escape. If they weren't police records, it was a matter of forgery.

'I'd want some time to look into this,' he said.

'How much time?' Binney Denham asked, and for the first time there was a certain hard note in his voice that caused Bedford to look up sharply, but his eyes saw only a little man sitting timidly on the very edge of the chair, holding his hat on his stomach.

'Well, for one thing, I'd want to verify the facts.'

'Oh, you mean in the business deal?' Denham asked, his voice quick with hope.

'The business deal be damned!' Bedford said. 'You know what this is and I know what it is. Now get the hell out of here and let me think.'

'Oh, but I wanted to tell you about the business deal,' Denham said. 'Delbert is certain you'll have every penny of your money back. It's just a question of raising some operating capital. Mr Bedford, and–'

'I know. I know,' Bedford interrupted. 'Give me time to think this over.'

Binney Denham got to his feet at once. 'I'm sorry I intruded on you without an appointment, Mr Bedford. I know how busy you are. I realize I must have taken up a lot of your time. I'll go now.'

'Wait a minute,' Bedford said. 'How do I get in touch with you?'

Binney Denham turned in the doorway. 'Oh, *I'll* get in touch with *you*, sir, if you don't mind, sir. And of course I'll have to talk with Delbert. Good day, sir!' and the little man opened the door a crack and slipped away.

2

Dinner that night was a tête-à-tête affair with Ann Roann Bedford serving the cocktails herself on a silver tray which had been one of the wedding presents.

Stewart Bedford felt thoroughly despicable as he slid the tray face down under the davenport, while Ann Roann was momentarily in the serving pantry.

Later on, after a dinner during which he tried in vain to conceal the tension he was labouring under, he got the tray up to his study, attached it to a board with adhesive tape around the edges so that any latent finger-prints on the bottom would not be disfigured, and then fitted it in a pasteboard box in which he had recently received some shirts.

Ann Roann commented on the box the next day when her husband left for work carrying it under his arm. He told her in what he hoped was a casual manner that the colour of the shirts hadn't been satisfactory and he was going to exchange them. He said he'd get Elsa Griffin to wrap and mail the package.

For a moment Bedford thought that there was a fleeting mistrust in his wife's slate-grey eyes, but she said nothing and her good-bye kiss was a clinging pledge of the happiness that had come to mean so much to him.

Safely ensconced in his private office, Bedford went to work on a problem that he knew absolutely nothing about. He had stopped at the art store downstairs to buy some drawing charcoal and a camel's-hair brush. He rubbed the edge of the stick of drawing charcoal into fine dust and dusted this over the bottom of the tray. He was pleased to find that he had developed several perfectly legible latent fingerprints.

It now remained to compare those fingerprints with the fingerprints on the criminal record which had been left him by the apologetic little man who needed the 'loan' of twenty thousand dollars.

So engrossed was Steward Bedford in what he was doing that he didn't hear Elsa Griffin enter the office.

She was standing by his side at the desk, looking over his shoulder, before he glanced up with a start.

'I didn't want to be disturbed,' he said irritably.

'I know,' she said in that voice of quiet understanding. 'I thought perhaps I could be of help.'

'Well, you can't.'

She said: 'The technique used by detectives is to take a piece of transparent cellophane tape and place it over the latent fingerprints. Then when you remove the Scotch tape the dust adheres to the tape and you can put the print on a card and study it at leisure without damaging the latent print.'

Stewart Bedford whirled around in his chair. 'Look here,' he said. 'Just how much do you know and what are you talking about?'

She said: 'Perhaps you didn't remember, but you left the intercommunicating system open to my desk when you were talking with Mr Denham yesterday.'

'The devil I did!'

She nodded.

'I wasn't conscious of it. I'm almost sure I shut it off.'

She shook her head. 'You didn't.'

'All right,' he said. 'Go get me some cellophane tape. We'll try it.'

'I have some here,' she said. 'Also a pair of scissors.'

Her long, skilful fingers deftly snipped pieces of the transparent tape, laid them over the back of the silver tray, smoothed them into position, and then removed the tape so they could study the fingerprints, line for line, whorl for whorl.

'You seem to know something about this,' Bedford said.

She laughed. 'Believe it or not, I once took a correspondence course in how to be a detective.'

'Why?'

'I'm darned if I know,' she admitted cheerfully. 'I just wanted something to do and I've always been fascinated with problems of detection. I thought it might sharpen my powers of observation.'

Bedford patted her affectionately. 'Well, if you're so darn good at it, draw up a chair and sit down. Take this magnifying-glass and let's see what we can find out.'

Elsa Griffin had, as it turned out, a considerable talent for matching fingerprints. She knew what to look for and how to find the different points of similarity. In a matter of fifteen minutes Stewart Bedford came to the sickening realization that there could be no doubt about it. The fingerprints on the police record were an identical match for the four perfect latents which had been lifted from the silver tray.

'Well,' Bedford said, 'since you know all about it, what suggestions do you have, Elsa?'

She shook her head. 'This is a problem you have to solve for yourself, S.G. If you once start paying, there's no end to it.'

'And if I don't?' he asked.

She shrugged her shoulders.

Bedford looked down at the silver tray which reflected a distorted image of his own harassed features. He knew what it would mean to Ann Roann to have something of this sort come out.

She was so full of life, vivacity, happiness. Bedford could visualize what would happen if one of these magazines that were becoming so popular should come out with the story of Ann Roann's past; the story of an adventurous girl who had sought to finance her venture into the matrimonial market by defrauding an insurance company.

No matter what the alternative, he couldn't let that happen.

There would, he knew, be frigid expressions of sympathy, the formal denunciation of 'those horrible scandal sheets.' There would be an attempt on the part of some to be 'charitable' to Ann Roann. Others would cut her at once, deliberately and coldly.

Gradually the circle would tighten. Ann Roann would have to plead a nervous breakdown . . . a foreign cruise somewhere. She would never come back–not the way Ann Roann would want to come back.

Elsa Griffin seemed to be reading his mind.

'You might,' she said, 'play along with him for a while; stall for time as much as possible, but try to find out something about who this man is. After all, he must have his own weaknesses.

'I remember reading a story one time where a man was faced with a somewhat similar problem and–'

'Yes?' Bedford said as she paused.

'Of course, it was just a story.'

'Go ahead.'

'The man couldn't afford to deny their blackmail claims. He didn't dare to have the thing they were holding over him become public, but he . . . well, he was clever and . . . of course, it was just a story. There were two of them just as there are here.'

'Go on! What did he do?'

'He killed one of the blackmailers and made the evidence indicate the other blackmailer had committed the murder. The frantic blackmailer tried to tell the true story to the jury, but the jury just laughed at him and sent him to the electric chair.'

'That's far-fetched,' Bedford said. 'It could only work in a story.'

'I know,' she said. 'It was just a story, but it was so convincingly told that it . . . well, it just seemed terribly plausible. I remembered it. It stuck in my mind.'

Bedford looked at her in amazement, seeing a new phase of her character which he had never dreamed existed.

'I never knew you were so bloodthirsty, Elsa.'

'It was only a story.'

'But you stored it in your mind. How did you become interested in this detective business?'

'Through reading the magazines which feature true crime stories.'

'You like them?'

'I love them.'

Again he looked at her.

'They keep your mind busy,' she explained.

'I guess I'm learning a lot about people very fast,' he said, still studying her.

'A girl has to have *something* to occupy her mind when she's left all alone,' she said defensively, but not defiantly.

He hastily looked back at the tray, then gently put it back in the shirt-box. 'We'll just have to wait it out now, Elsa. Whenever Denham calls on the telephone or tries to get in touch with me, stall him off if you can. But when he gets insistent, put the call through. I'll talk with him.'

'What about these?' she asked, indicating the lifted fingerprints on the Scotch tape.

'Destroy them,' Bedford said. 'Get rid of them. And don't just put them in a waste basket. Cut them into small pieces with scissors and burn them.'

She nodded and quietly left the office.

There was no word from Binney Denham all that day. It got so his very failure to try to communicate got on Bedford's nerves. Twice during the afternoon he called Elsa in.

'Anything from Denham?'

She shook her head.

'Never mind trying to stall him,' Bedford said. 'When he calls, put the call through. If he comes to see me, let him come in. I can't stand the strain of this suspense. Let's find out what we're up against as soon as we can.'

'Do you want a firm of private detectives?' she asked. 'Would you like to have them shadow him when he leaves the office and–'

'Hell, no!' Bedford said. 'How do I know that I could trust the private detectives? They might shadow him and find out all about what he knows. Then I'd be paying blackmail to two people instead of one. Let's keep this on a basis where we're handling it ourselves . . . and, of course, there *is* a possibility that the guy is right. It may be just a loan. It may be that this partner–this Delbert he refers to–is really a screwball who needs some capital and is taking this way of raising it. He may really be hesitating between selling his information to a magazine and letting me advance the loan. Elsa, if Denham telephones, put through the call immediately. I want to get these fellows tied up before there's any possibility they'll peddle that stuff to a magazine. It would be dynamite!'

'All right,' she promised. 'I'll put him through the minute he calls.'

But Binney Denham didn't call, and Bedford went home that evening feeling like a condemned criminal whose application for a commutation of sentence is in the hands of the Governor. Every minute became sixty seconds of agonizing suspense.

Ann Roann was wearing a hostess gown which plunged daringly to a low V in front and was fastened with an embroidered frog. She had been to the beauty parlour, and her hair glinted with soft highlights.

Stewart Bedford found himself hoping that they would have another tête-à-tête dinner, with candlelight and cocktails, but she reminded him that a few friends were coming in and that he had to change to a dinner-coat and black tie.

Bedford lugged the cardboard box up to his room, opened it, tore off the strips of adhesive tape which held the silver cocktail tray to the board, and managed to get the tray down to the serving pantry without being noticed.

The little dinner was a distinct success. Ann Roann was at her best, and Bedford noted with satisfaction the glances that came his way from men who had for years taken him for granted. Now they were looking at him as though appraising some new hidden quality which they had overlooked. There was a combination of envy and admiration in their expressions that made him feel a lot younger than his years. He found himself squaring his shoulders, bringing in his stomach, holding his head erect.

After all, it was a pretty good world. Nothing was so bad that it couldn't be cured somehow. Things were never as bad as they seemed.

Then came the call to the telephone. The butler said that a Mr D. said the call was quite important, and he was certain that Mr Bedford would want to be advised.

Bedford made a great show of firmness. 'Tell him that I'm not receiving any calls at the moment,' he said. 'Tell him he can call me at the office tomorrow, or leave me a number where I can call him back in an hour or two.'

The butler nodded and vanished, and for a moment Bedford felt as though he had won a point. After all, he'd show these damn blackmailers that he wasn't going to jump every time they snapped their fingers. Then the butler was back.

'Beg your pardon, sir,' he said, 'but Mr D. said the message is *most* important, that I was to tell you his associate is getting entirely out of control. He said he'd call you back in twenty minutes, that that was the best he could do.'

'Very well,' Bedford said, trying to keep up the external semblance of poise, but filled with sudden panic. 'I'll talk with him when he calls.'

He didn't realize how frequently he was consulting his wrist-watch during the next interminable quarter of an hour, until he saw Ann Roann watching him speculatively; then he cursed himself for letting his tension show. He should have gone to the telephone immediately.

None of the guests seemed to notice anything unusual. Only Ann Roann's deep slate eyes followed him with that peculiarly withdrawn look which she had at times when she was thinking something out.

It was exactly twenty minutes from the time of the first call that the butler came to the door. He caught Bedford's eye and nodded. This time Bedford, moving in a manner which he tried to make elaborately casual, started towards the door, said: 'All right, Harvey. I'll take the call in my upstairs office. Hang up the downstairs phone as soon as I get on the line.'

'Very good, sir,' the butler said.

Bedford excused himself to his guests, climbed the stairs hurriedly to his den, closed the door tightly, picked up the receiver, said: 'Yes, hello. This is Bedford speaking.' He heard Denham's voice filled with apologies.

'I'm terribly sorry I had to disturb you tonight, sir, but I thought you'd like to know. You see, Delbert talked with someone who knows the people who run this magazine and it seems he wouldn't have any difficulty at all getting–'

'Whom did he talk with?' Bedford asked.

'I don't know, sir. I'm sure I don't know. It was just someone who knew about the magazine. It seems that they do pay a lot of money for some of the things they publish and–'

'Bosh and nonsense!' Bedford interrupted. 'No scandal sheet is going to pay that sort of money for a tip of that sort. Besides, if they publish I'll sue them for libel.'

'Yes, sir. I know. I wish you could talk with Delbert. I think you could convince him. But the point is *I* couldn't convince him. He's going to go to the magazine first thing in the morning. I dare say that when they learn what he has, they'll offer him a very paltry sum, but I thought you'd like to know, sir.'

'Now look,' Bedford said. 'Let's be sensible about this thing. Delbert doesn't want to deal with that magazine. You tell Delbert to get in touch with *me*.'

'Oh, Delbert wouldn't do *that*, sir! He's terribly afraid of you, sir.'

'Afraid of me?'

'Yes, of course, sir. That's why I . . . well, I thought you'd understand. *I* thought we should tell *you*. I thought we owed you that much out of respect for your position. It was all *my* idea coming to you. Delbert, you see, just wanted to make an outright sale. He says there's certain disadvantages doing business this way, that you might trap him in something. He's . . . well, he doesn't want to do it this way at all. He wants to give the magazine a piece of legitimate news and take whatever they give him as legitimate compensation. He tried to keep me from going to you. He says there's every possibility you could trap us in some way.'

'Now look,' Bedford said. 'This man Delbert is a fool. I am not going to be told what to do and what not to do.'

'Yes, sir.'

'I'm not going to be terrified by anybody.'

'Yes, sir.'

'I also know this information is phony. I know there's something cockeyed about it somewhere.'

'Oh, I'm sorry to hear you say that, sir, because Delbert–'

'Now, wait a minute,' Bedford interrupted. 'Just hold your horses. I've told you where *I* stand, but I've also made up my mind that rather than have any trouble about it, I'm willing to go ahead and do what you people want. Now is that clear?'

'Oh, yes, sir. That's very clear! If I can tell Delbert that, it will make him feel *very* much different–that is, I hope it does. Of course, he's afraid that you're too smart for us. He's afraid that you'll lay a trap.'

'Trap, nothing!' Bedford said. 'Now, let's get this straight. When I do business, I do business on a basis of good faith. My word is good. I'm not setting any traps. Now, you tell Delbert to keep in line, and you call at my office tomorrow and we'll arrange to fix things up.'

'I'm afraid it has to be done tonight, sir.'

'Tonight! That's impossible!'

'Well, that's all right then,' Denham said. 'If you feel that way, that's–'

'Wait a minute! Wait a minute!' Bedford shouted. 'Don't hang up. I'm just telling you it's impossible to get things lined up for tonight.'

'Well, I don't know whether I can hold Delbert in line or not.'

'I'll give you a cheque,' Bedford said.

'Oh, good heavens, no, sir! Not a cheque! Delbert wouldn't ever hear to that, sir. He'd feel certain that was an attempt to trap him. The money would have to be in cash, if you know what I mean, sir. It would have to be money . . . well . . . money that couldn't be traced. Delbert is very suspicious, Mr Bedford, and he thinks you're a very smart business-man.'

'Let's quit playing cops and robbers,' Bedford said. 'Let's get down to a business basis on this thing. I'll go to the bank tomorrow morning and get some money, and you can–'

'Just a moment, please,' Denham's voice said. 'Delbert said never mind. Just let the matter drop.'

'Here, wait, wait! Hold on a moment!' Bedford said. Bedford could hear voices at the other end of the line. He could hear the sound of Denham's pleading, and once or twice he fancied he could hear a gruff voice; then Denham would cut in in that same apologetic drone. He couldn't hear the words, just the tone of voice.

Then Denham was back on the phone again.

'I'll tell you what you do, Mr Bedford. This is probably the best way of handling it. Now, tomorrow morning just as soon as your bank opens you go to your bank and get twenty thousand dollars in traveller's cheques. The cheques are to be one hundred dollars each. You get those cheques and go to your office. I'm awfully sorry I bothered you tonight, Mr Bedford. I knew we shouldn't have done it. I told Delbert that it was an imposition. But Delbert gets terribly impatient and he *is* suspicious. You see, this deal means a lot to him, and . . . well, you'd have to know him to understand.

'I'm just trying to do the best I can, Mr Bedford, and it puts *me* in a terribly embarrassing position. I'm terribly sorry I called you.'

'Not at all,' Bedford heard himself saying. 'Now you look here, Denham. You keep this Delbert person, whoever he is, in line. I'll see that you get the money tomorrow. Now don't let him get out of line. You stay with him.'

'Yes, sir.'

'Can you be with him all the time tonight? Don't let him out of your sight. I don't want him to get any foolish ideas.'

'Well, I'll try.'

'All right. You do that,' Bedford said. 'I'll see you tomorrow. Good-bye.'

He heard Binney Denham hang up, and reached for his handkerchief to wipe the cold sweat on his forehead before dropping the receiver into place. It was then he heard the second unmistakable click on the line.

In an agony of apprehension he tried to remember if he had heard the sound of the butler hanging up the receiver on the lower phone after he came on the line. He had no recollection of the sound.

Was it possible the lower phone had been open during the conversation? Had someone been listening?

Who?

How long had they had this damned butler anyway? Ann Roann had hired him. What did she know about him? Was it possible this whole thing was an inside job?

Who was this damned Delbert? How the devil did he know that there actually was any Delbert at all? How did he know that he wasn't dealing with Denham, and with Denham alone?

Filled with a savage determination, Bedford opened the drawer of his dresser, took out the snub-nosed blued steel ·38 calibre gun and shoved it in his brief-case. Damn it, if these blackmailers wanted to play tough, he'd be just as tough as they were.

He opened the door from the den, descended the stairs quickly, and then at the foot of the stairs came to a sudden pause as he saw Ann Roann in the butler's pantry. She had found the silver serving tray and was holding it so that the light shone on the back.

The silver tray hadn't been washed and there remained a very faint impression of charcoal-dusted fingerprints, of places where the strips of adhesive tape had left marks on the polished silver.

3

Stewart G. Bedford felt unreasonably angry as he signed his name two hundred times to twenty thousand dollars' worth of cheques.

The banker, who had tried to make conversation, didn't help matters any.

'Pleasure or business trip, Mr Bedford?'

'Neither.'

'No?'

'No.'

Bedford signed his name in savage silence; then, realizing that his manner had only served to arouse curiosity, added: 'I like to have some cash reserves on hand these days, something you can convert to cash in a minute.'

'Oh, I see,' the banker said, and thereafter said nothing.

Bedford folded the cheques and left the bank. Why the devil couldn't they have taken the money in tens and twenties the way they did with kidnap ransom in the movies? Served him right for getting mixed up with a damn bunch of blackmailers.

Bedford entered his private office and found Elsa Griffin sitting there waiting for him.

Bedford raised his eyebrows.

'Mr Denham and a girl are waiting for you,' she said.

'A girl?'

She nodded.

'What sort of a girl?'

'A babe.'

'A moll?'

'It's hard to tell. She's really something for looks.'

'Describe her.'

'Blonde, nice complexion, beautiful legs, plenty of curves, big limpid eyes, a dumb look, a little perfume, and that's all.'

'You mean that's really all?'

'That's all there is.'

'Well, let's have them in,' Bedford said, 'and I'll leave the intercom on so you can listen.'

'Do you want me to . . . to do anything?'

He shook his head. 'There's nothing we can do except give them the money.'

Elsa Griffin went out and Binney Denham came in with the blonde.

'Good morning, Mr Bedford, good morning. I want to introduce you to Geraldine Corning.'

The blonde batted her big eyes at him and said in a throaty, seductive voice: 'Gerry, for short.'

'Now it's like this,' Binny Denham said. 'You're going out with Gerry.'

'What do you mean, going out with her?'

'Going out with me,' Gerry said.

'Now look here,' Bedford began angrily. 'I'm willing to–'

He was stopped by the peculiar look in Binney Denham's eyes.

'This is the way Delbert says it has to be,' Denham said. 'He has it all figured out, Mr Bedford. I've been having a lot of trouble with Delbert . . . a whole lot of trouble. I don't think I could explain things to him if there were to be any variation.'

'All right,' Bedford said angrily. 'Let's get it over with.'

'You have the cheques?'

'I have the cheques here in my brief-case.'

'Well, that's fine! That's just dandy! I told Delbert I knew we could count on you. But he's frightened, and when a man gets frightened he does unreasonable things. Don't you think so, Mr Bedford?'

'I wouldn't know,' Bedford said grimly.

'That's right. You wouldn't, would you?' Binney said. 'I'm sorry I asked you the question in that way, Mr Bedford. I was talking about Delbert. He's a peculiar mixture, and you can say that again.'

Gerry's eyes smiled at Bedford. 'I think we'd better start.'

'Where are we going?' Bedford asked.

'Gerry will tell you. I'll ride down in the elevator with you if you don't mind, Mr Bedford, and then I'll leave you two. I'm quite certain it will be all right.'

Bedford hesitated.

'Of course,' Denham said, 'I'm terribly sorry it had to work out in this way. I know that you've been inconvenienced enough as it is, and I just want you to know that I've been against it all along, Mr Bedford. I know that your word is good, and I'd like to deal with you on that basis, but you just can't understand Delbert unless you've had dealings with him. Delbert is terribly suspicious. You see, he's afraid. He feels that you're a smart business-man and that you may have been in touch with somebody who would make trouble. Delbert just wants to go right ahead and make a sale to the magazine. He says that that's perfectly legitimate and no one can–'

'Oh, for heaven's sake!' Bedford exploded. 'Let's cut out this comedy. I'm going to pay. I've got the money. You want the money. Now let's go!'

Gerry moved close to him, linked her arms through his, holding it familiarly.

'You heard what he said, Binney. He wants to go.'

Bedford made for the door that led to the outer office.

'Not that way,' Binney said apologetically. 'We're supposed to go out through the exit door directly to the elevator.'

'I have to let my secretary know I'm going out,' Bedford said, making a last stand. 'She *has* to know I'm going out.'

Binney coughed. 'I'm sorry, sir. Delbert was most insistent on that point.'

'Now look here–' Bedford began, then stopped.

'It's better this way, Mr Bedford. This is the way Delbert wanted it.'

Bedford permitted Geraldine Corning to lead him towards the door. Binney Denham held it open and the three of them went out in the corridor, took the express elevator to the ground floor.

'This way,' Binney said and escorted them to a new-looking yellow car which was parked at the kerb directly in front of the building.

'Are you worried about women drivers?' Geraldine asked him.

'How good are you?' Bedford asked.

'At driving?'

'Yes.'

'Not too good.'

'I'll drive.'

'O.K. by me.'

'How about Denham?'

'Oh, Binney's not coming. Binney's all finished. He'll follow for a way, that's all.'

Bedford got in behind the wheel.

The blonde slid gracefully in beside him. She was, Bedford conceded to himself, quite a package–curves in the right places; eyes, complexion, legs, clothes–and yet he couldn't be sure whether she was stupid or putting on an act.

'Bye, Binney,' she said.

The little man bowed and smiled and bowed and smiled again. 'Have a nice trip,' he said as Bedford gunned the engine into life.

'Which way?' he asked.

'Straight ahead,' the blonde said.

For one swift moment Bedford had a glimpse of Elsa Griffin on the sidewalk. Thanks to the intercom she had learned their plans in time to get to the sidewalk before they had left the office.

He saw that she was holding a pencil and notebook. He knew she had the licence number of the car he was driving.

He managed to keep from looking directly at Elsa and eased the car out into traffic.

'Now look,' Bedford said. 'I want to know something about what I'm getting into.'

'You aren't afraid of me, are you?'

'I want to know what I'm getting into.'

'You do as you're told,' she instructed him, 'and there won't be any trouble.'

'I don't do business that way.'

'Then drive back to your office,' she said, 'and forget the whole business.'

Bedford thought that over, then kept driving straight ahead.

The blonde squirmed around sideways on the seat and drew up her knees, making no attempt to conceal her legs. 'Look, big boy,' she said. 'You and I might just as well get along. It'll be easier that way.'

Bedford said nothing.

She made a little grimace at his silence and said: 'I like to be sociable.'

Then after a moment she straightened in the seat, pulled her skirt back down over her knees and said: 'Okay, be grumpy if you want to. Turn left at the next corner, grouch-face.'

He turned left at the next corner.

'Turn right on the freeway and go north,' she instructed.

Bedford eased his way into the freeway traffic, instinctively looked at the petrol gauge. It was full. He settled down for a long drive.

'Turn right again and leave the freeway up here at the next crossroads,' she said.

Bedford followed instructions. Again the blonde doubled her knees up on the seat and rested one hand lightly on his shoulder.

Bedford realized then that she was carefully regarding the traffic behind them through the rear window of the car.

Bedford raised his eyes to the rear-view mirror.

A single car followed them off the freeway, maintaining a respectable distance behind.

'Turn right,' Geraldine said.

Bedford had a glimpse of the driver of that other car. It was Binney Denham.

From that point on Geraldine, seated beside him, gave a series of directions which sent him twisting and turning through traffic.

Always behind them was that single car, sometimes close, sometimes dropping far behind, until finally apparently satisfied that no one was following them, the car disappeared and Geraldine Corning said: 'All right, now we drive straight ahead. I'll tell you where to stop.'

They followed the stream of traffic out Wilshire. At length, following her directions, he turned north.

'Slow down,' she said.

Bedford slowed the car.

'Look for a good motel,' she told him. 'This is far enough.'

As she spoke, they passed a motel on the left, but it was so shabby Bedford drove on without pausing. There was another motel half a mile ahead. It was named 'The Staylonger'.

'How's this?' Bedford asked.

'I guess this will do. Turn in here. We get a motel unit and wait.'

'How do I register?' Bedford asked.

She shrugged her shoulders. 'I'm to keep you occupied until the thing is all over. Binney thought you'd be less nervous if you had me for company.'

'Look here,' Bedford said. 'I'm a married man. I'm not going to get into any damned trap over this thing.'

'Have it your way,' she said. 'We just wait here, that's all. There isn't any trap. Let your conscience be your guide.'

Bedford entered the place. The manager smiled at him, showing gold teeth. He asked no questions.

Bedford signed the name, 'S. G. Wilfred', and gave a San Diego address. At the same time he gave the story that he had hurriedly thought up' 'We're to be joined by some friends who are driving in from San Diego, We got here early. Do you have a double cabin?'

'Sure we do,' the manager said. 'In fact, we have anything you want.'

'I want a double.'

'If you register for a double, you'll have to pay for both cabins. If you take a single, I'll reserve the other cabin until six o'clock and then your friends can register and pay.'

'No, I'll pay for the whole business,' Bedford said.

'That'll be twenty-eight dollars.'

Bedford started to protest at the price; then, looking out at the young blonde sitting in the car, realized that it would be better to say nothing. He put twenty-eight dollars on the counter and received two keys.

'They're the two cabins down at the end with the double garage in between–numbers fifteen and sixteen. There's a connecting door,' the manager said.

Bedford thanked him, went back to the car, drove it down, parked it in the garage and said: 'Now what?'

'I guess we wait,' Gerry told him.

Bedford unlocked one of the cabins and held the door open. She walked in. Bedford followed her.

It was a nice motel–a double bed, a little kitchenette, a refrigerator, and a connecting door between that and another unit that was exactly the same. There was also a toilet and tiled shower in each unit.

'Expecting company?' Geraldine asked.

'That's your room,' Bedford said. 'This one is mine.'

She looked at him almost reproachfully, then said: 'Got the traveller's cheques?'

Bedford nodded. She indicated the table and said: 'You'd better start signing.'

Bedford zipped open his brief-case and was reaching for the traveller's cheques when he saw the gun. He had forgotten about that. He hurriedly turned the brief-case so she couldn't see in it and took out the books of traveller's cheques.

He sat at the table and started signing the cheques.

She slipped out of her jacket, looked at herself appraisingly in the mirror, studied her legs, straightened her stockings, glanced over her shoulder at Bedford and said: 'I think I'll freshen up a bit.'

She went through the connecting door into the other unit. Bedford heard the sound of running water. He heard a door close, a drawer open and close, then the outer door opened.

Suddenly suspicious, Bedford put down his pen, walked through the door and into the other room.

Geraldine was standing in her bra, panties and stockings in front of an open suitcase.

She turned casually and raised her eyebrows. 'All signed so soon?' she asked.

'No,' Bedford said angrily. 'I heard a door open and close. I was wondering if you were taking a powder.'

She laughed. 'Just getting my suitcase out of the trunk compartment of the car,' she said. 'I'm not leaving you. You'd better go on with your signing. They'll want the cheques pretty quick.'

There was neither invitation nor embarrassment in her manner. She stood there watching him speculatively, and Bedford, annoyed at finding himself not only aware but warmly appreciative of her figure, turned back to his own unit in the motel and gave himself over to signing cheques. For the second time that day he signed his name two hundred times, then went to the half-opened connecting door. 'Everybody decent?' he asked.

'Oh, don't be so stuffy. Come on in,' she said.

He entered the room to find Geraldine attired in a neat-fitting gabardine skirt which snugly outlined the curves of her hips, a soft pink sweater which clung to her ample breasts, and an expensive wide contour belt around her tiny waist.

'You have them?' she asked.

Bedford handed her the cheques.

She took the books, carefully looked through each cheque to make sure that it was properly signed, glanced at her wrist-watch and said: 'I'm going out to the car for a minute. You stay here.'

She went out, locking the door from the outside, leaving Bedford alone in the motel. Bedford whipped out a notebook, wrote the telephone number of his unlisted line, which connected directly with Elsa Griffin's desk. He wrote: 'Call this number and say I am at The Staylonger Motel.' He pulled a twenty-dollar bill from his wallet, doubled it over, with the leaf from his notebook inside, then folded the twenty-dollar bill again and thrust it in his vest pocket. He went to her suitcase, tried to learn something of her identity from an inspection of the contents.

The suitcase and the overnight bag beside it were brand new. The initials G.C. were stamped in gold on the leather. There were no other distinguishing marks.

He heard her step on the wooden stair outside the door and quietly withdrew from the vicinity of the baggage.

A moment later the girl opened the door. 'I've got a bottle,' she said. 'How about a highball?'

'Too early in the day for me.'

She lit a cigarette, stretched languidly, moved over to the bed and sat down. 'We're going to have to wait quite a while,' she said by way of explanation.

'For what?'

'To make sure everything clears, silly. You're not to go out–except with me. We stay here.'

'When can I get back to my business?'

'Whenever everything's cleared. Don't be so impatient.'

Bedford marched back into the other unit of the motel and sat down in a chair that was only fairly comfortable. Minutes seemed to drag into hours. At length he got up and walked back to the other unit. Geraldine was stretched out in the over-stuffed chair. She had drawn up another chair to use as a foot-rest and the short skirt had slid back to show very attractive legs.

'I just can't sit here all day doing nothing,' he said angrily.

'You want this thing to go through, don't you?'

'Of course I want it to go through; otherwise I wouldn't have gone this far. But after all, there are certain things that I don't intend to put up with.'

'Come on, grumpy,' she said. 'Why not be human? We're going to be here a while. Know anything about cards?'

'A little.'

'How about gin rummy?'

'Okay,' he said. 'What do we play for?'

'Anything you want.'

Bedford hesitated a moment, then made it a cent a point.

At the end of an hour he had lost twenty-seven dollars. He paused in his deal and said: 'For heaven's sake, let's cut out this beating around the bush. *When* do I get out of here?'

'Sometime this afternoon, after the banks close.'

'Now wait a minute!' he said. 'That's going too damned far.'

'Forget it,' she told him. 'Why don't you loosen up and be yourself? After all, I'm as human as you are. I get bored the same as you do. You've already parted with your money. You have everything to lose and nothing to gain by trying to crab the deal now. Sit down and relax. Take your coat off. Take your shoes off. Why don't you have a drink?'

She went over to the refrigerator, opened the door of the freezing compartment and took out a tray of ice cubes.

'Okay,' Bedford surrendered. 'What do you have?'

'Scotch on the rocks, or Scotch and water.'

'Scotch on the rocks,' he said.

'That's better,' she told him. 'I could like you if you weren't so grouchy. Lots of people would like to spend time here with me. We could have fun if you'd quit grinding your teeth. Know any funny stories?'

'They don't seem funny now,' he said.

She opened a new fifth of Scotch, poured out generous drinks, looked at him over the brim of the glass, said: 'Here's looking at you, big boy.'

'Here's to crime!' Bedford said.

'That's better,' she told him.

Bedford decided to try a new conversational gambit.

'You know,' he told her, 'you're quite an attractive girl. You certainly have a figure.'

'I noticed you looking it over.'

'You didn't seem very much concerned at the . . . at the lack of . . . of your costume.'

'I've been looked at before.'

'What do you do?' Bedford asked. 'I mean, how do you make a living?'

'Mostly,' she said smiling, 'I follow instructions.'

'Who gives the instructions?'

'That,' she said, 'depends.'

'Do you know this man they call Delbert?'

'Just by name.'

'What kind of a man is he?'

'All I know is what Binney tells me. I guess he's a screwball . . . but smart.

He's nervous–you know, jumpy.'

'And you know Binney?'

'Oh, sure.'

'What about Binney?'

'He's nice, in a mild sort of way.'

'Well,' he said, 'let's get on some ground we can talk about. What did you do before you met that character?'

'Co-respondent,' she said.

'You mean, a professional co-respondent?'

'That's right. Go to a hotel with a man, take my clothes off, wait for the raiding party.'

'I didn't know they did that any more.'

'It wasn't in this state.'

'Where was it?'

'Some place else.'

'You're not very communicative.'

'Why not talk about you?' she said. 'Tell me about your business.'

'It's rather complicated,' he explained.

She yawned. 'You're determinedly virtuous, aren't you?'

'I'm married.'

'Let's play some more cards.'

They played cards until Geraldine decided she wanted to take a nap. She was pulling the zipper on her skirt as Bedford started for the connecting door.

'That's not nice,' she said. 'I have to be sure you don't go out.'

'Are you going to lock the door?'

'It's locked.'

'Is it?'

'Sure,' she said nonchalantly. 'I have the keys. I locked it from the outside while I was out at the car. You didn't think I was dumb, did you?'

'I didn't know.'

'Don't you ever take a nap?'

'Not in the day-time.'

'Okay. I guess we'll have to suffer it out then. More cards or more Scotch–or both?'

'Don't you have a magazine?'

'You've got me. They didn't think you needed anything else to keep you entertained. After all, there are some details they couldn't have anticipated,' she laughed.

Bedford went into his room and sat down. She followed him. After a while Bedford became drowsy with the sheer monotony of doing nothing. He stretched out on the bed. Then he dozed lightly, slept for a few minutes.

He wakened with the smell of seductive perfume in his nostrils. The blonde, wearing a loose-flowing, semi-transparent creation, was standing beside him, looking down at him, holding a small slip of paper.

Bedford wakened with a start. 'What is it?' he asked.

'A message,' she said. 'There's been a hitch. We're going to be delayed.'

'How long?'

'They didn't say.'

'We have to eat,' Bedford said.

'They've thought of that. We can go out and eat. I pick the place. You stay with me–all the time. No phones. If you want to powder your nose, do it before we start. If there's any double cross, you've just lost your money and Delbert goes to the magazine. I'm to tell you that. You're to do as I say.

'They want you to be contented and not be nervous. They thought I could keep you amused. I told them you don't amuse very easy, so they said I could take you out–but no phones.'

'How did you communicate with them?' he asked.

She grinned. 'Carrier pigeons. I have them in my bra. Didn't you see them?'

'All right. Let's ride around awhile,' he said. 'Let's eat.'

He was surprised to find himself experiencing a feeling of companionship as she slid in the car beside him. She twisted around to draw up her knees so that her right knee was resting across the edge of his leg. Her hands with fingers interlaced were on his shoulder.

'Hello, good-looking,' she said.

'Hello, blonde,' he told her.

'That's better,' she said, smiling.

Bedford drove down to the beach highway, drove slowly along, keeping to the outside of the road.

'Well,' he said at length, 'I suppose you're getting hungry.'

'Thanks,' she said.

He raised his eyebrows in silent interrogation.

'You're thinking of me as a human being,' she explained. 'After all, I am, you know.'

'How did you get in this work?' he asked abruptly.

'It depends on what you mean by "this work",' she said.

There was a moment's silence. Bedford thought of two or three possible explanations which would elaborate on his remark, and decided against all of them.

After a moment she said: 'I guess you just drift into things in life. Once you start drifting, the current keeps moving more and more swiftly, until you just can't find the opportunity to turn and row against it. Now I suppose that's being philosophical, and you don't expect that from me.'

'I don't know what I am supposed to expect from you.'

'Expect anything you want,' she said. 'They can't arrest you for expecting.'

Bedford was thoughtful. 'Why start drifting in the first place?' he asked.

'Because you don't realize there's any current, and even when you do, you like it better than sitting still. Damn it, I'm not going to give you a lot of philosophy on an empty stomach.'

'There's a place here where they have wonderful steaks,' Bedford said, starting to pull in and then suddenly he changed his mind.

He looked up to see her eyes mildly amused, partially contemptuous, studying his features. 'You're known there, eh?' she asked.

'I've been there.'

'One look at me and your reputation is ruined, is that it?'

'No, that's *not* it,' he said savagely. 'And you should know that's not it. But under the circumstances, I'm not anxious to leave a broad back trail. I don't know who I'm playing with or what I'm playing with.'

'You're sure not playing with me,' she said. 'And remember, I'm to pick the eating-place. You pay the check.'

He drove up the road for a couple of miles. 'Try this one,' she said abruptly, indicating a tavern.

They found a booth in a dining-room that was built out over the water. The air was balmy, the sun warm, the ocean had a salty tang, and they ate thick filet mignon steaks with French-fried onions, Guinness stout, and garlic bread.

They had dessert, a brandy and benedictine, and Bedford paid the check. 'And this is for you,' he told the waiter, handing him the folded twenty with the message inside.

He scraped back his chair, careful to have Geraldine on her way to the door before the waiter unfolded the bill. He knew he was being foolish, jeopardizing the twenty-thousand-dollar investment he had made in a blackmail pay-off, but he had the feeling he was outwitting his enemies.

Only afterwards, when they had again started driving up the coast road, did he regret his action. After all, it could do no good and it might do harm, might, in fact, wreck everything.

Yet his reason told him they weren't going to any scandal magazine, not when they had a bonanza that could be clipped for twenty thousand dollars at a crack.

And the more he thought of it, the more he felt certain Delbert was only a fictitious figment. Binney Denham and the blonde were all there were in the 'gang'.

Was it perhaps possible that this acquiescent blonde was the brains of the gang? Yet now, somehow, he accepted her as a fellow human being. He preferred to regard her as a good scout who had somehow come under the power of Binney, a sinister individual beneath his apologetic mask.

The silence between Bedford and the girl was warm and intimate.

'You're a good guy,' she told him, 'when a girl gets to know you. You're a shock to a girl's vanity at first. I guess some married men are like that and are all wrapped up in their wives.'

'Thanks,' he told her. 'You're a good scout yourself, when a fellow gets to know you.'

'How long you been married?'

'Nearly two years.'

'Happy?'

'Uh-huh.'

'This deal you're mixed up in involves her, doesn't it?'

'If it's all the same with you. I'd rather not talk about her.'

'Okay by me. We probably should be getting back.'

'They'll let you know when everything is clear?'

'Uh-huh. It takes a little time to negotiate two hundred traveller's cheques, you know, and do it right.'

'And you're supposed to keep me out of circulation until it's done right, is that it?'

Her eyes flickered over him slowly. 'Something like that,' she said.

'Why didn't Binney do the job?'

'They thought you might get impatient with him.'

'They?' he asked.

'Me and my big mouth,' she told him. 'Let's talk about politics or sex or business statistics, or something that I can agree with you on.'

'You think you could agree with me on politics?'

'Sure, I'm broad-minded. You know something?'

'What?'

'I'd like a drink.'

'We can stop in one of these road-houses,' Bedford suggested.

She shook her head. 'They might not like that. Let's go back to the motel. I'm not to let you out of my sight, and I'm going to have to powder my nose. How'd you happen to get mixed up in a mess of this sort?'

'Let's not talk about it,' he said.

'Okay. Drive back. I guess you just drifted into it the same way I did. They start telling you what to do, and you give in. After that first time it's harder to resist. I know it was with me. But you have to turn against the current some time. I guess the best time is when you first feel the current.

'I'm spilling to you. I shouldn't. It's not in the job. They wouldn't like it. I guess it's because you're so damned decent. I guess you've always been a square shooter.

'You take me. I've always gone along the easy way. I guess I haven't guts enough to stand up and face things.'

They drove in silence for a while. At length she said: 'There's only one way out.'

'For whom?'

'For both of us. I'd forgotten how damned decent a decent guy could be.'

'What's the way out?' he asked.

She shook her head, became suddenly silent.

She cuddled a little closer to him. Bedford's mind, which had been working furiously, began to relax. After all, he had been a fool, putting himself in the power of Binney Denham and the mysterious individual whom he knew only as Delbert. They had his money. They wouldn't want any publicity now. Probably they'd play fair with him because they'd want to put the bite on him again–and again and again.

Bedford knew he was going to have to do something about that, but there would be a respite now, a period of time during which he'd have an opportunity to plan some sort of attack.

Bedford turned in at the motel. The manager looked out of the door to see who it was, apparently recognized the car, waved a salutation, and turned back from the window.

Bedford drove into the garage. Geraldine Corning, who had both keys, unlocked the door and entered his cabin with him. She got the bottle of Scotch, took the pack of cards, suddenly laughed and threw the cards in the waste-basket. 'Let's try getting along without these things. I was never so bored in my life. That's a hell of a way to make money.'

She went to the refrigerator, got out ice-cubes, put them in the glasses, poured him a drink, then poured herself one.

She went to the kitchenette, added a little water to each drink, came back with a spoon and stirred them. She touched the rim of her glass to his and said: 'Here's to crime!'

They sat sipping their drinks.

Geraldine kicked her shoes off, ran the tips of her fingers up her stockings, looked at her leg, quite plainly admiring it, stretched, yawned, sipped the drink again and said: 'I feel sleepy.'

She stretched out a stockinged foot, hooked it under the rung of one of the straight-backed chairs, dragged it towards her, propped her feet up and tilted back in the over-stuffed chair.

'You know,' she said, 'there are times in a girl's life when she comes to a fork in the road, and it all happens so easily and naturally that she doesn't realize she's coming to a crisis.'

'Meaning what?' Bedford asked.

'What do they call you?' she asked, '. . . your friends?'

'My first name's Stewart.'

'That's a helluva name,' she said. 'Do they call you Stu?'

'Uh huh.'

'All right, I'll call you Stu. Look, Stu, you've shown me something.'

'What?'

'You've shown me that you can't get anywhere drifting. I'm either going to turn back or head for shore,' she said. 'I'm damned sick and tired of letting people run my life. Tell me something about your wife.'

Bedford stretched out on the bed and dropped both pillows behind his head. 'Let's not talk about her.'

'You mean you don't want to discuss her with *me*?'

'Not exactly.'

'What I wanted to know,' Geraldine said somewhat wistfully, 'was what kind of a woman it is who can make a man love her the way you do.'

'She's a very wonderful girl,' Bedford said.

'Hell! I know *that*. Don't waste time telling me about that. I want to know how she reacts towards life and . . . and somehow I'd like to know what it is that Binney has on her.'

'Why?'

'Damned if I know,' she said. 'I thought I might be able to help her.' She put back her head and sucked in air in a prodigious yawn. 'Cripes! but I'm sleepy!'

For some time there was silence. Bedford put his head back against the pillows and found himself thinking about Ann Roann. He felt somehow that he should tell Geraldine something about her, something about her vitality, her personality, her knack of saying witty things that were never unkind.

Bedford heard a gentle sigh and looked over to see that Geraldine had fallen asleep. He himself felt strangely drowsy. He began to relax in a way that was most unusual considering the circumstances. The nervous tension drained out of him. His eyes closed, then opened, and for a moment he saw double. It took him a conscious effort to fuse the two images into one.

He sat up and was suddenly dizzy, then dropped back against the pillows. He knew then that the drink had been drugged. By that time it was too late to do anything about it. He made a half-hearted effort to get up off the bed, but lacked the energy to do it. He surrendered to the warm feeling of drowsiness that was sweeping over him.

He thought he heard voices. Someone was saying something in whispers, something that concerned him. He thought he heard the rustle of paper. He knew that this had something to do with some responsibility of his in the waking world. He tried to arouse himself to cope with that responsibility, but the drug was too strong within him and the warm silence enveloped him.

He heard the sound of a motor, and then the motor backfired and again he tried to arouse from a lethargy. He was unable to do so.

What seemed like an eternity later Bedford began to regain consciousness. He was, he knew, stretched out on a bed in a motel. He should get up. There was a girl in the room. She had drugged his drink. He thought that over with his eyes closed for what seemed like ten or fifteen minutes, thinking for a moment, then dozing, then waking to think again. *His* drink had been drugged, but the *girl's* drink must have also been drugged. They had been out somewhere. She had left the bottle in the room. Someone must have entered the room and drugged the bottle of whisky while they were out. She was a nice girl. He had hated her at first, but she had a lot of good in her after all. She liked him. She wouldn't have resented his making a pass at her. In fact, she resented it because he hadn't. It had been a blow to her vanity. Then it had started her thinking, started her thinking about his wife. She had wanted to know about Ann Roann.

The thought of Ann Roann snapped his eyes open.

There was no light in the room except that which came through the adjoining door from the other unit in the motel. It was quite dark outside and even the half-light in the motel unit hurt his eyes momentarily. He started to get up and became conscious of a piece of paper pinned to his left coat sleeve. He turned the paper so that the light struck it. He read: 'Everything has cleared. You can go now. Love, Gerry.'

Bedford struggled to a sitting position.

He walked towards the lighted door of the adjoining unit of the motel, his eyes rapidly becoming accustomed to the brighter light from the interior of the room. He started to call out: 'Everybody decent?' and then thought better of it. After all, Geraldine would have left the door closed if she had cared. There was a friendly warmth about her, and thinking of her, Bedford felt suddenly very kindly. He remembered when he had gone through the door earlier and had found her standing there practically nude. She really had an unusually beautiful figure. He had kept staring at her and she had merely stared back with an expression of amused tolerance. She had made no attempt to reach for her robe or turn her back. She had just stood there.

Bedford stepped into the room.

The first thing he saw was the figure lying on its side on the floor, the red pool which had spread out on to the carpet, the surface glazed over and reflecting the light from the reading-lamp in a reddish splotch against the wall.

The figure was that of Binney Denham, and the little man was quite dead. Even in death he seemed to be apologetic. It was as though he was protesting against the necessity of staining the faded rug with the pool of red which had flowed from his chest.

4

For a moment panic gripped Stewart Bedford. He hurried back to the other room, found his hat and his brief-case. He opened the brief-case, looked for his gun. The gun was gone.

He put on his hat, held the brief-case in his hand, closed the door into the adjoining unit, and by so doing shut out all of the light except a flickering red illumination which came and went at regular intervals.

Bedford pulled aside the curtain, looked out and saw that this light came from a large red sign which flashed on and off, the words: 'The Staylonger Motel,' and down below that a crimson sign which glowed steadily, reading: 'Vacancy.'

Bedford tried the door of the motel, shuddering at the thought that perhaps

Geraldine had left the door locked from the outside. However, the door was unlocked, the knob turned readily, and the door swung open.

Bedford looked out into the lighted courtyard. The units of the motel were arranged in the shape of a big U. There were lights on over each doorway and each garage, giving the motel an appearance of great depth.

Bedford looked in the garage between the two units which he and Geraldine had been occupying. The garage was empty. The yellow car was gone.

Faced with the problem of getting out where he could find a taxi-cab, Stewart Bedford realized that he simply lacked the courage to walk down the length of that lighted central yard. The office was at the far end, right next to the street. The manager would be almost certain to see him walking out and might ask questions.

Bedford closed the door of unit fifteen, walked rapidly around the side of the building until he came to the end of the motel lot. There was a barbed wire fence here, and Bedford slid his brief-case through to the other side, then tried to ease himself between the wires. These barbed wires were tightly strung; Bedford was nervous, and just as he thought he was safely through, he caught the knee of the trousers and felt the cloth rip slightly.

Then he was free and walking across the uneven surface of a field. The light from the motel sign behind him gave him enough illumination so he could avoid the pitfalls.

He found himself on a side road which led towards the main highway, along which there was a steady stream of automobiles coming and going in both directions.

Bedford walked rapidly along this road.

A car coming along the main highway slowed, then suddenly turned down the side road. Bedford found himself caught in the glare of the headlights. For a moment he was gripped with panic and wanted to resort to flight. Then he realized that this would be a suspicious circumstance which might well be communicated to the police and result in a prowl car exploring the territory. He elevated his chin, squared his shoulders, and walked steadily along the side of the road towards the headlights, trying to walk purposefully as though going on some mission–a business-man with a brief-case walking to keep some appointment at a neighbouring establishment.

The headlights grew brighter. The car swerved and came to a stop abreast of Bedford. He heard the door open.

'Stu! Oh, Stu!' Elsa Griffin's voice called.

She was, he saw, half hysterical with apprehension, and in the flood of relief which came over him at the sound of her voice he didn't notice that it was the first time in over five years she had called him by his familiar nickname.

'Get in, get in,' she said, and Stewart Bedford slid into the car.

'What happened?' she asked.

'I don't know,' Bedford said. 'All sorts of things. I'm afraid we're in trouble. How did *you* get here?'

'Your telephone message,' she said. 'Someone who said he was a waiter telephoned that a man had left a message and a twenty-dollar–'

'Yes, yes,' he interrupted. 'What did you do?'

She said: 'I went down to the motel and rented a unit. I used an assumed name and a fictitious address. I juggled the figures on my licence, and the manager never noticed. I spotted that yellow car–I'd already checked the licence. It was a rented car from one of the drive-yourself agencies.'

'So what did you do?' he asked.

'I sat and watched and watched and waited,' she said. 'Of course I couldn't sit right in the doorway and keep my eye on the cabin, but I sat back and had my door open so that if anyone came or went from that cabin I would see it, and if the car drove out I could be all ready to follow.'

'Go on,' he said. 'What happened?'

'Well,' she said, 'about an hour and a half ago the car backed out and turned.'

'What did you do?'

'I jumped in my car and followed. Of course, not too close, but I was close enough so that after the car got on the highway I could easily keep behind it. I had gone a couple of miles before I dared draw close enough to see that this blonde girl was alone in the car. I turned around and came back and parked my car. And believe me, I've had the devil of an hour. I didn't know whether you were all right or not. I wanted to go over there, and yet I was afraid to. I found that by standing in the bathroom, with the window open, I could look out and see the garage door and the door of the two units down there at the end. So I stood there in the bathroom watching. And then I saw you come out and go around the back of the house. I thought perhaps you were coming around towards the street by the back of the houses. When you didn't show up, I realized you must have gone through the fence, so I jumped in my car and drove around, and when I came to this cross street I turned down it and there you were.'

'Things are in quite a mess, Elsa,' he said. 'There's somebody dead in that cabin.'

'Who?'

'Binney Denham.'

'How did it happen?'

'I'm afraid he was shot,' he said. 'And we may be in trouble. I put my gun in my brief-case when I got that phone call last night. I had it with me.'

'Oh, I was afraid,' she said. 'I was afraid something like that might happen.'

'Now wait a minute,' Bedford said. '*I* didn't kill him. I don't know anything about it. I was asleep. The girl gave me a drugged drink–I don't think it was her fault. I think someone got into the cabin and drugged the whole bottle of whisky. She poured drinks out of that.'

'Well,' Elsa Griffin said, 'I have Perry Mason, the lawyer, waiting in his office.'

'The devil you have!' he exclaimed in surprise.

She nodded.

'How come you did that?'

She said: 'I just had a feeling in my bones. I knew there was something wrong. I rang Mr Mason shortly after you left the office and told him that you were in trouble, that I couldn't discuss it, but I wanted to know where I could reach him at any hour of the day or night. Of course, he's done enough work for you, so he feels you're a regular client and . . . well, he gave me a number and I called it about an hour ago, right after I returned from chasing that blonde. I had a feeling something was wrong. I told him to wait at this office until he heard from me. I told him that it would be all right to send you a bill for whatever it was worth, but I wanted him there.'

Stewart Bedford reached out and patted her shoulder. 'The perfect secretary!' he said. 'Let's go.'

5

It was after ten o'clock. Perry Mason, the famous trial lawyer, sat in his office. Della Street, his trusted confidential secretary, occupied the easy-chair on the other side of the desk.

Mason looked at his watch and said: 'We'll give them until eleven and then go home.'

'You talked with Stewart G. Bedford's secretary?'

'That's right.'

'I take it it's terribly important?'

'She said money was no object, that Mr Bedford had to see me tonight, but that she would have to get hold of him before she could bring him up here.'

'That sounds strange.'

'Uh-huh.'

'He married about two years ago, didn't he?'

'I believe so.'

'Do you know his secretary?'

'I've met her three or four times. Quite a girl. Loyal, quiet, reserved, efficient. Wait a minute, Della, here's someone now.'

Knuckles tapped gently at the heavy corridor door from the private office.

Della Street opened it.

Elsa Griffin and Stewart Bedford entered the office.

'Thank heaven you're still here!' Elsa Griffin said. 'We got here as fast as we could.'

'What's the trouble, Bedford?' Mason asked, shaking hands. 'I guess both of you know my secretary, Della Street. What's it all about?'

'I don't think it's anything to worry about,' Bedford said, making an obvious effort to be cheerful.

'I do,' Elsa Griffin said. 'They can trace S.G. through the traveller's cheques.'

Mason indicated chairs. 'Suppose you sit down and tell me all about it from the beginning.'

Bedford said: 'I had a business deal with a man whom I know as Binney Denham. That may not be his name. He seems to have got himself murdered down in a motel this evening.'

'Do the police know about it?'

'Not yet.'

'Murdered?'

'Yes.'

'How do you know?'

'He saw the body,' Elsa Griffin said.

'Notify anyone?' Mason asked.

Bedford shook his head.

'We thought we'd better see you,' Elsa Griffin said.

'What was the business deal?' Mason asked.

'A private matter,' Bedford explained.

'What was the business deal?' Mason repeated.

'I tell you it's just a private matter. Now that Denham is dead there's no reason for anyone to–'

'What was the business deal?' Mason asked.

'Blackmail,' Elsa Griffin said.

'I thought so,' Mason said grimly. 'Let's have the story. Don't hold anything back. I want it all.'

'Tell him, S.G.,' Elsa Griffin said, 'or I will.'

Bedford frowned, thought for a moment, then told the story from the beginning. He even took out the police photograph of his wife and her description and fingerprints. 'They left this with me,' he explained, giving it to Mason.

Mason studied the card. 'That's your wife?'

Bedford nodded.

'Of course you know it's her picture, but you can't tell about the fingerprints,' Mason said. 'After all, it may be a fake.'

'No, they're her prints all right,' Bedford said.

'How do you know?'

Bedford told him about the silver cocktail tray, the lifted fingerprints.

'You'll have to report the murder,' Mason said.

'What happens if I don't?'

'Serious trouble,' Mason said. 'Miss Griffin, you go down to a pay station, call the police department, don't give them your name. Tell them there's a body down in unit sixteen at The Staylonger Motel.'

'I'd better do it,' Bedford said.

Mason shook his head. 'I want a girl's voice to make the report.'

'Why?'

'Because they'll find out a girl was in there.'

'Then what do we do?' Bedford asked.

Mason looked at his watch, said: I now have the job of getting Paul Drake of the Drake Detective Agency out of bed and on the job, and I can't put it on the line with him because I don't dare to let him know what he's investigating.'

'What's the licence number of that automobile?'

'It's a rented automobile from one of the drive-yourself agencies and–'

'What's the number?' Mason asked.

Elsa Griffin gave it to him. 'Licence number CXY 221.'

Mason called Paul Drake of the Drake Detective Agency at his unlisted number. After he heard Drake's sleepy voice on the line, he said: 'Paul, here's a job that will require your personal attention.'

'Good Lord!' Drake protested. 'Don't you *ever* sleep?'

Mason said: 'Police are discovering a body at The Staylonger Motel, down by the beach. I want to know everything there is to know about the case.'

'What do you mean, they are *discovering* a body?'

'Present participle,' Mason said.

'Another one of those things,' Drake complained. 'Why can't you wait until the body becomes a past participle and give a guy a break?'

'Because minutes are precious,' Mason told him. 'Here's a car licence number. It's probably a drive-yourself number. I want you to find out just where that car is, who rented it, and if it's been returned I want to know the exact time of its return. Now then, here's something else. I want you to get some operative who is really above suspicion, someone who can put on a front of being entirely, utterly innocent, preferably a woman. I want that woman to rent that car just as soon as it is available.'

'What does she do with it after she rents it?'

'She drives it to some place where my criminalist can go over it with a vacuum-sweeper, testing it for hairs, fibres, bloodstains, weapons, fingerprints.'

'Then what?'

'Then,' Mason said, 'I want this woman to go up somewhere in the mountains first thing in the morning and get some topsoil for her garden, fill the car full of pasteboard boxes containing leaf mould, and pick up some frozen meat to take home to her locker.'

'In other words,' Drake said, 'you want her to contaminate the hell out of any evidence that's left.'

'Oh, nothing like that!' Mason said. 'I wouldn't *think* of doing anything like that, Paul! After all, there wouldn't be anything left to contaminate. We'd have a criminalist pick up all of the evidence that was in it.'

Drake thought that over. 'Isn't it a crime to juggle evidence around?'

'Suppose the criminalist removed every bit of evidence *first*?'

'Then what do we do with the criminalist?'

'Let him report to the police if he wants,' Mason said. 'In that way we know what he knows first. Otherwise, the police know what's in the car, and we don't find out until the district attorney puts his expert on the stand as a witness.'

'Then why all the leaf mould and frozen meat and stuff?' Drake asked.

'So some criminalist doesn't come up with soil samples, bloodstains and hairs, make a wild guess as to where they came from and testify to it as an expert,' Mason told him.

Drake groaned. 'Okay,' he said wearily. 'Here we go again. What criminalist do you want?'

'Try Dr Leroy Shelby if you get hold of the car.'

'Is he supposed to know what it's all about?'

'He's supposed to find every bit of evidence that's in that car,' Mason said.

'Okay,' Drake told him wearily. 'I'll get busy.'

'Now get this,' Mason said. 'We're one jump ahead of the police, perhaps just half a jump. They may have the licence number of that automobile by morning. Get Dr Shelby out of bed if you have to. I want all the evidence that's in that car carefully impounded.'

'They'll ask Shelby who hired him.'

'Sure they will. That's where you come in.'

'Then they'll come down on me like a thousand bricks.'

'What if they do?' Mason asked.

'Then what do I tell them?'

'Tell them I hired you.'

There was relief in Drake's voice. 'I can do that?'

'You can do that,' Mason told him, 'but get busy.'

Mason hung up the phone, said to Bedford: 'Your next job is to get home and try to convince your wife that you've been at a director's meeting or a business conference, and make it sound convincing. Think you can do that?'

'If she's already gone to bed, perhaps I can,' Bedford said. 'She isn't as inquisitive when she's sleepy.'

'You're to be congratulated,' Mason told him dryly. 'Be available where I can call you in the morning. If anybody asks you any questions about anything at all, refer them to me. Now, probably someone will want to know about those traveller's cheques. You tell them it was a business deal and that it's too confidential to be discussed with anyone. Refer them to me.'

Bedford nodded.

'Think you can do that?' Mason asked.

'I can do it all right,' Bedford said, and then added: 'Whether I can get away with it or not is another question.'

Bedford left the office. Elsa Griffin started to go with him, but Mason stopped her. 'Give him a few minutes head start,' he said.

'What do I do after I have called the police?'

'For the moment,' Mason told her, 'you get out of circulation and keep out of circulation.'

'Could I come back here?'

'Why?'

'I'm anxious to know what's going on. I would like to be on the firing-line. You're going to wait here, aren't you?'

Mason nodded.

'I wouldn't be in the way and perhaps I could help you with telephone calls and things.'

'Okay,' Mason told her. 'You know what to tell the police?'

'Just about the body.'

'That's right.'

'Then, of course, they'll want to know who's talking.'

'Never mind what they want to know,' Mason said. 'Tell them about the body. If they interrupt you to ask you a question, don't let them pull that gag and get away with it. Keep right on talking. They'll listen when you start telling them about the body. As soon as you've told them that, hang up.'

'Isn't that against the law?'

'What law?'

'Suppressing evidence?'

'What evidence?'

'Well, when a person finds a body . . . just to go away and say nothing about . . . about who you are–'

'Is your identity going to help them find the body?' Mason asked. 'You tell them where it is. That's what they're interested in. The body. But don't tell them who you are. You make a note of the time of the call.'

'But how about withholding my name?'

'That,' Mason told her, 'is information which might tend to incriminate you. You don't have to give that to anyone, not even on the witness-stand.'

'Okay,' she said. 'I'll follow your instructions.'

'Do that,' Mason told her.

She closed the door behind her as she eased out into the corridor.

Della Street looked at Mason. 'I presume we'll want some coffee?'

'Coffee, doughnuts, cheeseburgers, and potato chips,' Mason said, and then shuddered. 'What an awful mess to put in your stomach this time of night.'

Della Street smiled. 'Now we know how Paul Drake feels. This time the situation is reversed. We're usually out eating steaks while Drake is in his office eating hamburgers.'

'And sodium bi-carb,' Mason said.

'*And* sodium bi-carb,' she smiled. 'I'll telephone the order for the food down to the lunch counter.'

Mason said: 'Get the Thermos jug out of the law library, Della. Have them fill that with coffee. We may be up all night.'

6

At one o'clock in the morning Paul Drake tapped his code knock on the hall door of Mason's private office.

Della Street let him in.

Paul Drake walked over to the client's big, over-stuffed chair, slid into his favourite position with his knees over the arms and said: I'm going to be in the office from now on, Perry. I've got men out working on all the angles. I thought you'd like to get the dope.'

'Shoot,' Mason said.

'First on the victim. His name is Binney Denham. No one seems to know what he does. He had a safe-deposit-box in an all-night-and-day bank. The safe-deposit-box was in joint tenancy with a fellow by the name of Henry Elston. At nine-forty-five last night Elston showed up at the bank and went to the box. He was carrying a brief-case with him. Nobody knows whether he put in or took out. Police have now sealed up the box. An inheritance tax appraiser is going to be on hand first thing in the morning and they'll open it up. Bet it'll be empty.'

Mason nodded.

'Aside from that, you can't find out a thing. Denham has no bank account, left no trail in the financial world, yet he lived well, spent a reasonable amount of money, all in cash.

'Police are going to check and see if he made income tax returns as soon as things open up in the morning.

'Now, in regard to that car. It was a drive-yourself car. I tried to get it, but police already had the licence number. They telephoned in and the car is impounded.'

'Who rented it, Paul?'

'A nondescript person with an Oklahoma driving licence. The driving licence data was on the rental contract. The police have checked and it doesn't mean a damned thing. Fictitious name. Fictitious address.'

'Man or woman?'

'Mousy little man. No one seems to remember much about him.'

'What else?'

'Down at the motor court, police have some pretty good description stuff. It seems that the two units were occupied by a man and a babe. The man claimed he was expecting another couple. They got a double unit, connecting door. The man registered; the girl sat in the car. The manager didn't get a very good look, but had the impression she was a blonde, with good skin, swell figure, and that indefinable something that marks the babe, the chick, the moll. The man looked just a little bit frightened. Business-man type. Got a good description of him.'

'Shoot,' Mason said.

'Fifty to fifty-four. Grey suit. Height five feet nine. Weight about a hundred and ninety or a hundred and ninety-five. Grey eyes. Rather long, straight nose. Mouth rather wide and determined. Wore a grey hat, but seemed to have plenty of hair, which wasn't white except a very slight bit of grey at the temples.'

Elsa Griffin flashed Mason a startled glance at the accuracy of the description.

Mason's poker face warned her to silence.

'Anything else, Paul?' the lawyer asked.

'Yes. A girl showed up and rented unit number twelve–rather an attractive girl, dark, slender, quiet, thirty to thirty-five.'

'Go ahead,' Mason said.

'She registered; was in and out, is now out and hasn't returned as yet.'

'How does she enter into the picture?' Mason asked.

'She's okay,' Drake said. 'But the manager says he caught a woman prowling her place–a woman about thirty, thirty-one, thirty-two. A swell-looker, striking figure, one of the long-legged, queenly sort; dark hair, grey eyes. She was prowling this unit twelve. The manager caught her coming out. She wasn't registered at the place and he wanted to know what she was doing. She told him she was supposed to meet her friend there, that the friend wasn't in; the door was unlocked, so she had gone in, sat down and waited for nearly an hour.'

'Have any car?' Mason asked.

'That's the suspicious part of it. She must have parked her car a block or two away and walked back. She was on foot, but there's no bus line nearer than half a mile to the place, and this gal was all dolled up–high heels and everything.'

'And she was prowling unit number twelve?'

'Yes, that's the only suspicious thing the manager noticed. It was around eight o'clock. The woman in unit twelve had just checked in two hours or so earlier, then had driven out.

'The manager took this other woman–the prowler–at face value; didn't think anything more about it. But when the police asked him to recall anything at all that was out of the ordinary, he recalled her.

'Police don't attach any significance to her . . . as yet anyway.

'The manager remembered seeing the yellow car go out somewhere around eight o'clock, he thinks it was, and, while he can't be positive, it's his impression the blonde girl was driving the car and no one else was in the car with her. That gave police an idea that she *might* have left before the shooting took place. They can't be certain about the time of the shooting.'

'It was a shooting?' Mason asked.

'That's right. One shot from a ·38 calibre revolver. The guy was shot in the back. The bullet went through the heart and he died almost instantly.'

'How do they know it was fired from the back?' Mason asked. 'They haven't had an autopsy yet.'

'They found the bullet,' Drake said. 'It went entirely through the body and failed to penetrate the front of the coat. The bullet rolled out when they moved the body. That happens a lot more frequently than you'd suppose. The powder charge in a ·38 calibre cartridge is just about sufficient to take the bullet through a body, and if the clothes furnish resistance the bullet will be trapped.'

'Then they have the fatal bullet?'

'That's right.'

'What sort of shape is it in, do you know, Paul? Is it flattened out pretty bad, or is it–'

'No, it's in pretty good shape, as I understand it. The police are confident that there are enough individual markings so they can identify the gun if and when they find it.

'Now, let me go on, Perry. They got the idea that if the blonde took out alone it might have been because this man Denham showed up and he was having an argument with her boy friend. He used the name of S. G. Wilfred when he registered and gave a San Diego address. The address is phony and the name seems to be fictitious.'

'Okay, go ahead. What happened?'

'Well, the police got the idea that if this man, whom we'll call Wilfred, had popped Denham in a fight over the gal and then was left without a car there at the motel, he might have tried to sneak out the back way. So they started looking for tracks, and sure enough, they found where he had gone through a barbed wire fence and evidently snagged his clothes. The police got a few clothing fibres from the barbed wire where he went through–that was clever work. Your friend, Lieutenant Tragg, was on the job, and as soon as he saw the tracks going through the barbed wire he started using a magnifying-glass. Sure enough, he caught some fibres on the barbed wire.'

'What about the tracks?' Mason asked.

'They're having a moulage made of the footprints. They followed the tracks through the wire, across a field and out to a side road. They have an idea the man probably walked down to the main highway and hitch-hiked his way into town. The police will be broadcasting an appeal in the newspapers, asking for anyone who noticed a hitch-hiker to give a description.'

'I see,' Mason said thoughtfully. 'What else, Paul?'

'Well, that car was returned to the rental agency. A young woman put the car in the agency parking lot, started towards the office and then seems to have disappeared. Of course, you know how those things go. The person who rents the car puts up a fifty-dollar deposit, and the car rental people don't worry about cars that are brought in. It's up to the renter to check in at the office in order to get the deposit back. The rental and mileage on a daily basis don't ordinarily run up to fifty bucks.'

'The police have taken charge of the car?'

'That's right. They've had a fingerprint man on it, and I understand there are some pretty good fingerprints. Of course, they're fingerprinting units fifteen and sixteen down there at the motel.'

'Well,' Mason said, 'they'll probably have something pretty definite then.'

'Hell! They've got something pretty definite right now,' Drake said. 'The only thing they *haven't* got is the man who matches the fingerprints. But don't overlook any bets on that. They'll have him, Perry.'

'When?'

Drake lowered his eyes in thoughtful contemplation of the problem. 'Even money they have him by ten o'clock in the morning,' he said, 'and I'd give you big odds they have him by five o'clock in the afternoon.'

'What are you going to do now?' Mason asked.

'I have a couch in one of the offices. I'm going to get a little shut-eye. I've got operatives crawling all over the place, picking up all the leads they can.'

'Okay,' Mason said. 'If anything happens, get in touch with me.'

'Where will you be?'

'Right here.'

Drake said: 'You must have one hell of an important client in this case.'

'Don't do any speculating,' Mason told him. 'Just keep information coming in.'

'Thanks for the tip,' Drake told him and walked out.

Mason turned to Elsa Griffin. 'Apparently,' he said, 'no one has attached the slightest suspicion to you.'

'That was a very good description of the occupant of unit twelve,' she said.

'Want to go back?' Mason asked.

There was a sudden, swift alarm in her face.

'Go back? What for?'

Mason said: 'As you know, Bedford told me about your help in getting the fingerprints off that silver platter. How would you like to go back down to the motel, drive in to your place at unit twelve. The manager will probably come over to see if you're all right. You can give him a song and dance, then take a fingerprint outfit and go to work on the door-knobs, on the drawers in the dresser, any place where someone would be apt to have left fingerprints. Lift those fingerprints with tape and bring them back to me.'

'But suppose . . . suppose the manager is suspicious. Suppose he re-checks my licence number. I juggled the figures when I gave him the licence number of the car when I registered.'

'That,' Mason said, 'is a chance we'll have to take.'

She shook her head. 'That wouldn't be fair to Mr Bedford. If anybody identified me, the trail would lead directly to him.'

'There are too damn many trails leading directly to him the way it is,' Mason told her. 'Paul Drake was right. It's even money they'll have him by ten o'clock in the morning. In any event, they'll have him by five o'clock in the afternoon. He left two hundred traveller's cheques scattered around, and Binney Denham was getting the money on those cheques. Police will start back-tracking Denham during the day. They'll find out where some of those cheques were cashed. Then the trail will lead directly to Bedford. They'll match his fingerprints.'

'And then what?' she asked.

'Then,' Mason told her, 'we have a murder case to try. Then we go to court.'

'And then what?'

'Then they have to prove him guilty beyond all reasonable doubt. Do you think he killed Denham?'

'No!' she said with sudden vehemence.

'All right,' Mason said, 'he has his story. He has the note that was pinned to his sleeve, the note he found when he woke up saying he could leave.'

'But what reason does he give for not reporting the body?'

'He did report the body,' Mason said. 'You reported it. *He* told you to telephone the police. He did everything he could to start the police on their investigation, but he just tried to keep his name out of it. It was an ill-advised attempt to avoid publicity because he was dealing with a blackmailer.'

She thought it over for a while and said: 'Mr Bedford isn't going to like that.'

'What isn't he going to like about it?'

'Having to explain to the police why he was down there.'

'He doesn't have to explain anything,' Mason said. 'He can keep silent. *I'll* do the talking.'

'I'm afraid he won't like that either.'

Mason said impatiently: 'There's going to be a lot about this he won't like before he gets done. Persons who are accused of murder seldom like the things the police do in connection with developing the case.'

'He'll be accused of murder?'

'Can you think of any good reason why he won't?'

'You think I can do some real good by going down and looking for fingerprints?'

Mason said: 'It's a gamble. From what Drake tells me, you're apparently not involved in any way. The manager of the motel won't want to have his guests annoyed. He'll keep the trouble centralized in cabins fifteen and sixteen as far as possible. You have a cocktail and spill a little on a scarf you'll have around your neck so it will be obvious you've been drinking. Go into the motel just as though nothing had happened. If the manager comes over to tell you about a prowler in your cabin, tell him the woman was perfectly all right, that she was a friend of yours who was coming to visit you, that you told her to go in and wait in case you weren't there, that you got tied up on a date with someone you liked very much and had to stand her up.

'I'd like to have the fingerprints of whoever it was that was in that cabin, but what I'd mainly like is to have *you* remove all of *your* fingerprints. After you get done developing latent prints and lifting any that you find, take some soap and warm water and scrub the place all to pieces. Get rid of anything incriminating.'

'Why?' she asked.

'Because,' Mason said, 'if later on the police get the idea that there's something funny about the occupant of unit number twelve and start looking for fingerprints, they won't find yours.

'Don't you see the thing that's going to attract suspicion to you above all else is *not* going back there tonight? If your cabin isn't occupied, the manager will report that as another suspicious circumstance to the police.'

'Okay,' she said. 'I'm on my way. Where do I get the fingerprint outfit?'

Mason grinned. 'We keep one here for emergencies. You know how to lift fingerprints all right. Bedford said you did it from the cocktail tray.'

'I know how,' she said. 'Believe it or not, I took a correspondence course as a detective. I'm on my way.'

'If anything happens,' Mason warned, 'anything at all, call Paul Drake's agency. I'll be in constant touch with Paul Drake. If anyone should start questioning you, dry up like a clam.'

'On my way,' she told him.

7

Seven o'clock found Paul Drake back in Perry Mason's office.

'What do you know about this Binney Denham, Perry?' the detective asked.

'What do *you* know about him?' Mason countered.

'Only what the police know. But it's beginning to pile up into something.'

'Go on.'

'Well, he had that lock-box in joint tenancy with Harry Elston. Elston went to the lock-box, and now the police can't find him. That's to have been expected. Police found where Binney Denham was living. It was a pretty swank apartment for one man who was supposedly living by himself.'

'Why do you say supposedly?'

'Police think it was rather a convivial arrangement.'

'What did they find?'

'Forty thousand dollars in cash neatly hidden under the carpet. Hundred-dollar bills. A section of the carpet had been pulled up so many times that it was a dead giveaway. The floor underneath it was pretty well paved with hundred-dollar bills.'

'Income tax?' Mason asked.

'They haven't got at that yet. They'll enlist the aid of the income tax boys this morning.'

'Makes it nice,' Mason said.

'Doesn't it,' Paul Drake observed.

'What else do you know?'

'Police are acting on the theory that Binney Denham may have been mixed up in a blackmail racket and that he may have been killed by a victim. The man and the girl who occupied those two units could have been a pushover for a blackmailer.

'The police can't get a line on either one of them. They're referring to the man as Mr X and the girl as Miss Y. Suppose Mr X is a fairly well-known, affluent business-man and Miss Y is a week-end attraction, or perhaps someone who is scheduled to supplant Mrs X as soon as a Reno divorce can be arranged. Suppose everything was all very hush-hush, and suppose Binney Denham found out about it. Binney drops in to pay his respects and make a little cash collection and gets a bullet in the back.'

'Very interesting,' Mason said. 'How would Binney Denham have found out about it?'

Drake said: 'Binney Denham had forty thousand bucks underneath the carpet on the floor of his apartment. You don't get donations like that in cash unless you have ways of finding out things.'

'Interesting!' Mason said.

'You want to keep your nose clean on this thing.' Drake warned.

'In what way?'

'You're representing somebody. I haven't asked you who it is, but I'm assuming that it could be Mr X.'

Mason said: 'Don't waste your time assuming things, Paul.'

'Well, if you're representing Mr X,' Drake said, 'let's hope Mr X didn't leave a back trail. This is the sort of thing that could be loaded with dynamite.'

'I know,' Mason said. 'How about some of this coffee, Paul?'

'I'll try a little,' Drake said.

Della Street poured the detective a cup of coffee. Drake tasted it and made a face.

'What's the matter?' Mason asked.

'Thermos coffee,' Drake said. 'I'll bet it was made around midnight.'

'You're wrong,' Della Street said. 'I had it renewed a little after three this morning.'

'Probably my stomach,' Drake said apologetically. 'I've got fuzz on my tongue and the inside of my stomach feels like a jar of sour library paste. Comes from spending too many nights living on coffee, hamburgers and bicarbonate of soda.'

'Anybody hear the shot?' Mason asked.

'Too many,' Drake said. 'Some people think there was a shot about eight-fifteen, some others at eight forty-five; some at nine-thirty. Police may be able to tell more about the time of death after the autopsy.

'The trouble is this Staylonger joint is on the main highway and there's a little grade and a curve there right before you get to the turn-in for the motel. Trucks slack up on the throttle when they come to this curve and grade, and quite a few of them back-fire. People don't pay much attention to sounds like that. There are too many of them.'

Drake finished the coffee. 'I'm going down and get some ham and eggs. Want to go?'

Mason shook his head. 'Sticking around awhile, Paul.'

'Jeepers!' Drake said. 'Mr X must be a millionaire.'

'Just talking, or asking for information?' Mason asked.

'Just talking,' Drake said and heaved himself out of the chair.

Twenty minutes after he had left, Elsa Griffin tapped on the door of Mason's private office, and when Della Street opened the door, slid into the room with a furtive air.

Mason said: 'You look like the beautiful spy who has just vamped the gullible general out of the secret of our newest atomic weapon.'

'I did a job,' she said enthusiastically.

'Good!' Mason told her. 'What happened?'

'When I got there everything had quieted down. There was a police car in the garage and apparently a couple of men were inside units fifteen and sixteen, probably going over everything for fingerprints.'

'What did you do?'

'I drove into unit twelve, parked my car, went in and turned on the lights. I waited for a little while, just to see if anyone was going to show up. I didn't want to be dusting the place for fingerprints in case they did.'

'What happened?'

'The manager came over and knocked on the door. He was sizing me up pretty much–I guess he thought perhaps I had a wild streak under my quiet exterior.'

'What did you do?'

'I put him right on that. I told him that I was a member of a sorority and that we'd been having a reunion, that I came up to town for that and we'd had a pretty late party, that I was going to have to grab a few hours' shut-eye and be on my way in order to get back to my job.'

'Did he say anything?'

'Not about the murder. He said there'd been a little trouble, without saying what it was, and then he said that some woman had been in my unit and asked if it was all right, and I told him: "Heavens, yes," that she was one of the sorority members who was to meet me and I'd told her that if I wasn't there to go in, make herself at home. I said I'd left the door unlocked purposely.'

'Did he get suspicious?'

'Not a bit. He said there'd been some trouble and he'd been trying to check back on anything that had happened that was out of the ordinary; that he'd remembered this woman and he'd just wondered if it was all right.'

'Tell you about what time it was?' Mason asked.

'Well, he didn't know the hour exactly, but as nearly as I can figure she must have been in there while I was out chasing that blonde. I had to follow her for quite a ways before I dared to swing alongside.'

'And it *was* the blonde who was driving?'

'That's right, it was Geraldine Corning.'

'What about fingerprints?' Mason asked.

She said: 'I got a flock of them. I'm afraid most of them are mine, but some of them probably aren't. I have twenty-five or so that are good enough to use. I've put numbers on each of the cards that have the lifted prints and then I have a master list in my notebook which tells where each number came from.'

'Clean up the place when you left?' Mason asked.

'I took a washrag, used soap and gave everything a complete scrubbing, then I made a good job by polishing it with a dry towel.'

Mason said: 'You'd better leave your fingerprints on a card so I can have Drake's men check these lifted prints and eliminate yours. Let's hope that we've got some prints of that prowler. Do you have any idea who she might have been?'

'Not the least in the world. I just simply can't understand it. I don't know why in the world anyone should have been interested in the cabin *I* was occupying.'

'It may have been just a mistake,' Mason said.

'Mr Mason, do you suppose that these . . . well, these blackmailers became suspicious when I showed up? Do you suppose they were keeping the place under surveillance? They'd know me if they saw me.'

Mason said: 'I'm not making any suppositions until I get more evidence. Go down to Drake's office, put your fingerprints on a card, leave the bunch of lifted fingerprints there, tell Paul Drake to have his experts sort out all of the latents that are yours and discard them, and bring any other fingerprints to me.'

'Then what do I do?'

Mason said: 'It would be highly advisable for you to keep out of the office today.'

'Oh, but Mr Bedford will need me. Today will be the day when–'

'Today will be the day when police are going to come to the office and start asking questions,' Mason said. 'Don't be too surprised if they should have the manager of The Staylonger Motel with them.'

'What would that be for?'

'To make an identification. It would complicate matters if he found you sitting at your secretarial desk and then identified you as the occupant of unit twelve.'

'I'll say!' she exclaimed in dismay.

'Ring up Mr Bedford. Explain matters to him,' Mason said. 'Don't tell him about having gone back to cabin twelve and taken the fingerprints. Just tell him that you've been up most of the night, that I think it would be highly inadvisable for you to go to the office. Tell Mr Bedford that he'll probably have official visitors before noon, that if they simply ask him questions about the traveller's cheques to tell them it's a business transaction and he cares to make no comment. If they start checking up on him and it appears that they're making an identification of him by his fingerprints as the man who drove that rented car or as the man who was in the motel, or if they have the manager of the motel along with them, who makes an identification, tell Mr Bedford to keep absolutely mum.

'Have him put on a substitute secretary. Have her call my office and call the office of the Drake Detective Agency the minute anyone who seems to have any connection with the police calls at the office. Think you can do that?'

She looked for a moment into Mason's eyes and said: 'Mr Mason, don't misunderstand me. I'd do anything . . . anything in the world in order to ensure the happiness or the safety of the man I'm working for.'

'I'm satisfied you would,' Mason said, 'and that's what makes it dangerous.'

'What do you mean?'

'In case he was being blackmailed,' Mason said, 'it might occur to the police that your devotion to your boss would be such that *you'd* take steps to get rid of the blackmailer.'

'Oh, I wouldn't have done anything like *that*!' she exclaimed hastily.

'Perhaps you wouldn't,' Mason told her, 'but we have the police to deal with, you know.'

'Mr Mason,' she ventured, 'don't you think this Denham was killed by his partner? He mentioned a man, whom he called Delbert. This Delbert was the insistent one.'

'Could be,' Mason said.

'I'm almost certain it was.'

Mason looked at her in swift appraisal. 'Why?'

'Well, you see, I've always had an interest in crime and detective work. I read a lot of these magazines that publish true crime stories. It was because of an ad in a magazine that I took my detective course by mail.'

Mason flashed a glance at Della Street. 'Go on.'

'Well, it always seems that when a gang of crooks get a big haul, they don't like to divide. If there are three, and one of them gets killed, then the loot only has to be split two ways. If there are two, and one of the men gets killed, the survivor keeps it all.'

'Wait a minute,' Mason said. 'You didn't read that in the magazines that feature true crime stories.

'That gambit you're talking about now is radio, motion pictures and television. Some of the fiction writers get ideas about a murderer cutting down the numbers who share in the loot. The comic strips play that idea up in a big way. Where did you read this story?' Mason asked. 'In what magazine?'

'I don't know,' she admitted. 'Come to think of it, I have the impression that this story I referred to was in a comic strip.

'You see, I like detective works. I read the crime magazines and see the crime movies–I suppose you can say I'm a crime fan.'

'The point is,' Mason said, 'the authorities aren't going to charge any accomplice. They're going to charge Stewart Bedford. That is, I'm afraid they are.'

'I see. I was just thinking, Mr Mason. If a smart lawyer should get on the job and plant some evidence that would point to Denham's accomplice, Delbert, as the murderer, that would take the heat off Mr Bedford, wouldn't it?'

'Smart lawyers don't plant evidence,' Mason said.

'Oh, I see. I guess I read too much about crime, but the subject simply fascinates me. Well, I'll be getting along, Mr Mason.'

'Do that,' Mason told her. 'Go on home and make arrangements to be ill so that you can't come to the office. Don't forget to stop in at Paul Drake's office and leave your fingerprints.'

'I won't,' she promised.

When the door had closed Mason looked at Della Street. 'That girl has ideas.'

'Doesn't she!'

'And,' Mason went on, 'if *she* should plant some evidence against this Delbert . . . well, if she has any ideas of planting evidence against anyone, she'd better be damned careful. A good police officer has a nose for planted evidence. He can smell it a mile off.'

Della Street said: 'The worst of it is that if she *did* try to plant evidence and the authorities found it had been planted, they'd naturally think *you* were the one who had planted it.'

'That's a chance a lawyer always has to take,' Mason said. 'Let's go eat, Della.'

8

By the time Mason and Della Street had returned from breakfast, Sid Carson, Paul Drake's fingerprint expert, had finished with the lifted fingerprints that had been left him by Elsa Griffin and was in Mason's office, waiting to make a report.

'Nearly all of the prints,' he said, 'are those of Elsa Griffin, but there are four lifted latents here that aren't hers.'

'Which are the four?' Mason asked.

'I have them in this envelope. Numbers fourteen, sixteen, nine, and twelve.'

'Okay,' Mason said, 'I'll save them for future reference. The others are all Miss Griffin's?'

'That's right. She left a set of her fingerprints and we've matched them up. You can discard all of them except these four.'

'Any ideas about these four?'

'Not much. They could have been left by some prior occupant of the motel. A little depends on climatic conditions and what sort of cleaning the place had, how long since it's been occupied and things of that sort. Moisture in the air has a great deal to do with the time a latent fingerprint will be preserved.'

'How are these latents?' Mason asked. 'Pretty good?'

'They're darn good. Very good indeed.'

'Any notes about where they were found?'

'Yes, she did a good job. She lifted the prints, transferred them to cards, then wrote on the back of the cards where they were from. Two of these prints were from a mirror; two of them came from a glass knob on a closet door. She even made a little diagram of the knob, one of the sort of knobs that have a lot of facets so you can get hold of it and get a good grip for turning.'

Mason nodded, said: 'Thanks, Carson. I'll call on you again if we get any leads.'

'Okay,' Carson said and went out.

Mason contemplated the fingerprints under the cellophane tape.

'Well?' Della Street asked.

Mason said: 'Della, I'm no fingerprint expert, but–' He adjusted a magnifying glass so as to get a clearer view.

'Well?' she asked.

'Hang it!' Mason said. 'I've seen *this* fingerprint before.'

'What do you mean, you've seen it before?'

'There's a peculiar effect here–' Mason's voice trailed away into silence.

Della Street came to look over his shoulder.

'Della!' Mason said. His voice was explosive.

She jumped at his tone. 'What?'

'That card Bedford left with us, the card showing his wife and her fingerprints–get that card from the file, Della.'

Della Street hurried to the filing-case, came back with the card which Bedford had left with Mason, the card which the blackmailers had given him in order to show the authenticity of their information.

'Good heavens!' Della Street said. 'Mrs Bedford wouldn't have been there.'

'How do you know?' Mason asked. 'Remember what Bedford told us about getting the telephone call from Binney at his house while he was entertaining guests, that he wanted to talk in privacy, so he said he went up to his study and told the butler to hang up the phone as soon as he answered? Suppose Mrs Bedford became suspicious. Suppose she sent the butler on an errand, telling him that she'd take over and hang up the phone. Suppose she listened in on the conversation and knew–'

'You mean . . . found out about–'

'Let's be realistic about this thing,' Mason said. 'When was this crime of defrauding the insurance company committed?'

'Several years ago, before her first marriage,' Della Street said.

'Exactly,' Mason told her. 'Then she married, her husband committed suicide, she came into some money from insurance policies; then it was a couple of years before she married Bedford and a couple of years after the marriage before the blackmailers started to put the bite on Bedford.

'Yet, when the police went to Binney Denham's place, they found the floor carpeted with crisp new hundred-dollar bills.'

'You mean they'd been blackmailing her and–'

'Why wouldn't they?' Mason said. 'Let's take a look at these fingerprints. If she knew Binney was starting to put the bite on her husband . . . a woman in that situation could become very, very desperate.'

'But Mr Bedford said they took such great precautions to see that they weren't followed. You remember what he told us about how the girl had him drive around and around and Binney followed in his car, and then Bedford picked the motel?'

'I know,' Mason said, 'but let's just take a look. I've seen this fingerprint before.'

Mason took a magnifying-glass, started examining the fingerprints on the card, then compared the two lifted fingerprints with the prints on the card.

He gave a low whistle.

'Struck pay dirt?' Della Street asked.

'Look here,' Mason said.

'Heavens!' Della Street said, 'I couldn't read a fingerprint in a year.'

'You can read these two,' Mason said. 'For instance, look at this fingerprint on the card. Now compare it with the fingerprint here. See that tented arch? Count the number of lines to that first distinctive branching, then look up here at this place where the lines make a–'

'Good heavens!' Della Street said. 'They're identical!'

Mason nodded.

'Then Mrs Stewart G. Bedford was following–'

'Following whom?' Mason asked.

'Her husband and a blonde.'

Mason shook his head. 'Not with the precautions that were taken by the girl in the rented car. Moreover, if she'd been following her husband and the girl, she'd have known the units of the motel where they were staying and she would have gone in there.'

'Then who was she following?'

'Perhaps,' Mason said, 'she was following Binney Denham.'

'You mean Denham went to the motel to collect the money?'

Mason nodded. 'Possibly.'

'Then why would she have gone into Elsa Griffin's unit? How would she have known Elsa Griffin was there?'

'That,' Mason told her, 'remains to be seen. Get Paul Drake's office for me, Della. Let's put a shadow on Mrs Stewart G. Bedford and see where she goes this morning.'

'And then?' Della Street asked.

Mason gave the matter a moment of frowning concentration. 'If I'm going to talk with her, Della, I'd better do it before the police start asking questions of her husband.'

9

The woman who eased the low-slung, foreign-made sports car into the service station was as sleek and graceful as the car she was driving. She smiled at the attendant and said: 'Fill it up, please,' then, opening the car door, swung long legs out to the cement, holding her skirt tightly against her legs as she moved out from under the steering-wheel.

She gave her skirt a quick shake, said to the attendant: 'And we might as well check the oil, water, and battery.'

She turned and confronted the tall man whose slim-waisted, broad-shouldered figure and granite-hard features caused her to take a second look.

'Good morning, Mrs Bedford. I'm Perry Mason.'

'The lawyer?'

He nodded.

'Well, how do you do, Mr Mason. I've heard of you, of course. My husband has spoken of you. You seem to know me, but I don't recall ever having met you.'

'You haven't,' Mason said. 'You're meeting me now. Would you like to talk with me for a moment?'

Her eyes instantly became cold and wary. 'About what?'

'About five minutes,' Mason said, with a warning glance in the direction of the service station attendant who, while looking at the nozzle on the petrol hose, nevertheless held his head at a fixed angle of attention.

For a moment she hesitated, then said: 'Very well,' and led the way back over towards an open space where there were facilities for filling radiators and an air hose for tyres.

'Now I'll ask you again. What do you wish to talk about, Mr Mason?'

'About The Staylonger Motel and your visit there last night,' Mason said.

The slate-grey eyes were just a little mocking. There was no sign to indicate that Mason's verbal shaft had scored.

'I wasn't visiting any motel last night, Mr Mason, but I'll be glad to discuss the matter if you wish. The Staylonger Motel . . . it seems to me I've heard that name. Could you tell me where it is?'

'It's where you were last night,' Mason said.

'I could become very annoyed with you for such insistence, Mr Mason.'

Mason took a card from his pocket, said: 'This is the print of the ring finger of your right hand. It was found on the underside of the glass door-knob on the closet. Perhaps you'll remember that glass door-knob, Mrs Bedford. It was rather ornamental–moulded with facets that enable a person to get a good grip on the glass, but it certainly was a trap for fingerprints.'

She regarded the lawyer thoughtfully. 'And how to you know this is *my* fingerprint?'

'I've compared it.'

'With what?'

'A police record.'

She glanced away from him for a moment, then looked back at him.

'May I ask just what is your object, Mr Mason? Is this some sort of a legal cat-and-mouse game? I am assuming that your reputation is such that you wouldn't be interested in the common, ordinary garden variety of blackmail.'

Mason said: 'The afternoon papers will announce the discovery of a murder at The Staylonger Motel. Police are naturally very much interested in anything out of the ordinary which happened there last night.'

'And *your* interest?' she asked coolly.

'I happen to be representing a client, a client who prefers to remain anonymous for the time being.'

'I see. And perhaps your client would like to involve me in the murder?'

'Perhaps.'

'In which event I should talk with *my* lawyer instead of his–or hers.'

'If you wish,' Mason told her. 'However, that probably wouldn't be the first conversation you'd have.'

'With whom would I have the first conversation?'

'The police.'

She said: 'The attendant is finishing with my car. There's a hotel a few blocks down the street. It has a mezzanine floor, with a writing-room and reasonable privacy. I'll drive there. You may follow me, if you wish.'

'Very well,' Mason told her. 'However, please don't try any stunts with that powerful sports car of yours. You might be able to lose me in traffic, and that might turn out to be a rather expensive manœuvre as far as you're concerned.'

She stared at him levelly. 'When you get to know me better, Mr Mason–if you ever do–you'll learn that I don't resort to cheap, petty tricks. When I fight, I fight fair. When I give my word, I stay with it. Of course, I'm assuming you can move through traffic at a reasonable rate of speed without having a motor-cycling officer take your car by the fender and lead it across the intersections.'

With that she turned, walked over to sign the sales slip that the petrol attendant handed her, then guided the low-slung car out into traffic.

Mason followed her until she swung into a parking lot. He parked his own car, entered the lobby of the hotel, took the elevator to the mezzanine and followed her to a writing-table at which there were two chairs.

Everything about her appearance seemed to emphasize long lines. She was, Mason noticed, wearing long ear-rings; the carved ivory cigarette-holder in which she fitted a cigarette was long and emphasized the length of the tapering fingers of her left hand which held the cigarette.

Mason seated himself in the chair beside her.

She looked at Mason and smiled.

'All the way up here I tried my damnedest to think up some way that I could keep you from questioning me,' she said, 'and I couldn't do any good. I don't know whether you're bluffing about my fingerprints and the police record, but I can't afford to call your bluff, in case it is not a bluff. Now then, what do you want?'

'I want to know about the jewels and the insurance company.'

She took a deep drag from the cigarette, exhaled thoughtfully, then abruptly gave in.

'All right,' she said. 'I was Ann Duncan in those days. I have always had a hatred of anything mediocre. I wanted to be distinctive. I wanted to stand out. I had to go to work. I was untrained. Nothing was open except the sheerest kind of office drudgery. I tried it for a while. I couldn't make it. My appearance was striking enough so that the men I worked for didn't want to settle just for the mediocre office services, which were all they were willing to pay for.

'About all I inherited from my mother's estate was some jewellery. It was valuable antique jewellery and it was insured for a considerable amount.

'I needed a front. I needed some clothes. I needed an opportunity to circulate around where I'd be noticed. I was willing to take a gamble. I decided that if I could meet the right kind of people in the right way, life might hold a brighter future–a future different from the drab prospect of filing letters all day and having a surreptitious dinner date with the man I was working for after he'd telephoned his wife the old stall about being detained at the office.'

'So what did you do?'

'I went about it in a very clumsy, amateurish way. Instead of going to a reputable firm and having the jewellery appraised and making the right sort of a business transaction, I went to a pawnshop.'

'And then?'

'I felt that if I could get some money as a loan, later on I could repay the loan and redeem the jewellery. I felt that I could parlay the money I received into something worthwhile.'

'Go on.'

'I was living with a penurious aunt, a nosy busy-body. I shouldn't say that about her. She's dead now. But anyhow, I had to account for the loss of the jewellery, so I tried to make it look like a burglary, and then I pawned the jewellery.'

'And your aunt reported the burglary to the police?'

'That was where the rub came in.'

'You intended she would?'

'Heavens, no!'

'Then what?'

'I wasn't prepared for all the embarrassing questions. The jewellery was insured and my aunt insisted that I had to file a claim. She got a blank, made it out, gave it to me to sign. The police investigated. The insurance company investigated. Then the insurance company paid me the amount for which the jewellery was insured. It was the money I didn't want, but I had to take it in order to keep my aunt from finding out what I had done. I didn't spend it. I kept it intact.

'Then I told my aunt a whopping fib about going to visit some friends. I took the money I'd received from the pawnbroker, got myself some glad rags and went to Phoenix, Arizona. I registered at one of the winter resort hotels where I felt I stood a chance of meeting the sort of people I was interested in.'

'And what happened then?' Mason asked.

'Then,' she said, 'the police found the jewellery in the pawnshop. At first they thought they were just recovering stolen property. Then they got a description of the person who had pawned the jewels and began to put two and two together and . . . oh, it was hideous!'

'Go on,' Mason told her. 'What happened?'

'However,' she said, 'in the meantime I'd met a very estimable gentleman, an attorney at law, a widower. I don't know whether he would ever have been attracted to me if it hadn't been for the trouble I was in. He was a lawyer and I went to him for help. At first he was cold and sceptical, then when he heard my story he became sympathetic. He took an interest in me, helped straighten things out, saw that I met people.

'I had the most wonderful three months I'd ever had in my life. People liked me. I found that there is a great deal to the saying that clothes make the pirate.

'I met a man who fell for me hard. I didn't love him but he had money. He needed me. He was never sure of himself. He was always too damned cautious. I married him and tried to build his ego, to get him to face the world, to take a chance. I didn't do a very good job. He made a start, built up some degree of assurance, then got in a tight place, the old doubts came back and he killed himself. The pathetic part of it was that it turned out he won the battle he was fighting. The news came an hour after he'd fired the shot that ended his life. I felt terrible. I should have been with him. I was at a beauty parlour at the time it happened. In a fit of despondency he pulled the trigger. He was like that. After his death his doctor told me he was what was known as a manic-depressive. The doctor said it was a typical case. He said I'd really prolonged his life by helping to give him stability. He said they had suicidal compulsions in their moments of deep depression and that sometimes the fits came on them suddenly.

'My husband left me quite a bit of property and there was considerable insurance. I was moving in the right set then. I met Stewart Bedford.

'Stewart Bedford fascinated me. He's twenty years older than I am. I know what that means. There isn't a great deal of difference between thirty-two and fifty-two. There's a lot of difference between forty-two and sixty-two, and there's an absolutely tragic difference between fifty-two and seventy-two. You can figure it out mathematically, and you can't get any decent answer, no matter how you go at it. Stewart Bedford saw me and wanted me. He wanted me in the same way an art collector would want a painting which appealed to him and on which he had set his heart.

'I agreed to marry him. I found out that he wanted to show me off to his friends, and his friends move in the highest social circles.

'That was something I hadn't bargained on, but I tried to live up to my end of the agreement.

'And then this thing came up.'

'What thing?'

'My record.'

'How did it come up?'

'Binney Denham.'

'He blackmailed you?'

'Of course he blackmailed me. It was hideous. I couldn't afford to have it appear that the wife Stewart Bedford was so proud of had been arrested for defrauding an insurance company.'

'Then what?'

'Binney Denham is one of the most deceptive personalities you ever met. I don't know what to do with the man. He pretends that he is working for someone who is obdurate and greedy. Actually, Binney is the whole show. There isn't anyone else except a few people whom Binney hires to do his bidding, and they don't know what it's all about.

'A week ago I got tired of being bled white. I told Binney he could go to hell. I slapped his face. I told him that if he ever tried to get another cent out of me, I'd go to the police. And, believe me, I meant it. After all, I'm going to live my own life, and not go skulking around in the corners and shadows because of Binney Denham.'

'And did you tell your husband?' Mason asked.

'No. In order to understand this, Mr Mason, you have to know a little more about backgrounds.'

'What about them?'

'Before my husband married me he'd been having an affair with his secretary–a faithful, loyal girl named Elsa Griffin.'

'He told you that?'

'Heavens, no!'

'How did you find out?'

'I sized up the situation before I committed myself. I wanted to make certain that it was all over.'

'Was it?'

'Yes, as far as he was concerned.'

'How about her?'

'She was going to have her heart broken anyway, win, lose or draw. I decided to go ahead and marry him.'

'Did your husband know that you knew anything about this secretary?'

'Don't be silly. I played them close to my chest.'

'So you'd been paying blackmail, and you got tired of it?' Mason said.

She nodded.

'And what did you decide to tell your husband about it?'

'Nothing, Mr Mason. I felt that there was a good even-money gamble that Binney would leave me alone if he knew I was absolutely determined never to pay him another cent. After all, a blackmailer can't make any money publicizing what he knows.'

'Nowadays he can,' Mason said. 'There are magazines which like to feature those things.'

'I thought of that, but I told Binney Denham that if the thing ever became publicized I'd go all the way, that I'd tell about the blackmail I'd been paying to him and that I had enough evidence so I could convict him.'

'And then what?'

She avoided his eyes for a moment and said: 'I'm hoping that's all there is to it.'

Mason shook his head.

'You mean, he . . . he went after Stewart?'

'What makes you ask that?'

'I . . . I don't know. There was a telephone call night before last. Stewart acted *very* strangely. He went up to take the call in his room. The butler was to hang up the phone after my husband picked up the receiver upstairs, but the butler was called away because of an emergency and the downstairs phone was off the hook; I happened to be going by and I saw the phone off the hook and could hear squawking noises. I picked up the telephone to hang it up and they stopped talking just as I hung up the telephone. Over the receiver I thought I heard that whining, apologetic voice of Binney Denham. I couldn't distinguish words, just the tone of voice. And then I made up my mind it was just my imagination. I thought of asking my husband about the call, then decided to do nothing.'

Mason said: 'I'm afraid you're in a jam, Mrs Bedford.'

'I've been in jams before,' she said with cool calm. 'Suppose you tell me what you're driving at.'

'Very well, I will. You've had this secret hanging over your head. You paid out thousands of dollars in blackmail. Then all of a sudden you became bold and–'

'Let's say I became desperate.'

'That,' Mason said, 'is what I'm getting at. For your information, it was Binney Denham who was murdered last night at The Staylonger Motel down near the beach.'

Again her eyes gleamed with an indefinable expression. Then her face was held rigidly expressionless.

'Do they know who did it?' she asked.

'Not yet.'

'Any clues?'

Mason, looking her straight in the eyes, said: 'The manager saw a woman down there last night at about the time the murder was being committed, a woman who came out of unit twelve. She had evidently been prowling. The description the manager gave fits you exactly.'

She smiled. 'I suppose lots of descriptions would apply to me. Descriptions are pretty generalized anyway.'

Mason said: 'There are certain distinctive mannerisms you have. The manager gave a pretty good description.'

She shook her head.

'And,' Mason said, 'certain fingerprints that were lifted from cabin twelve were unmistakably yours.'

'They couldn't be.'

'They are. I just showed them to you.'

'Do the police know that you have them?'

'No.'

'I tell you I wasn't there, Mr Mason.'

Mason said nothing.

'You've done quite a bit of legal work for my husband?'

'Some.'

'Isn't there some way of faking or forging fingerprints?'

'There may be. Fingerprints experts say there isn't.'

'These prints you mentioned are in this cabin?'

'Not now. They were developed and lifted from the places they were found in the cabin.'

'Then what happened?'

'The cabin was wiped free of all prints.'

'Someone is lying to you, Mr Mason. Those can't be my fingerprints. There's some mistake.'

'Let's not have any misunderstanding,' Mason said. 'Didn't you follow Binney Denham down to that motel some time last night?'

'Mr Mason, why on earth would I follow Binney Denham down to any motel?'

'Because your husband was at that motel paying twenty thousand dollars' blackmail to Binney Denham.'

She tightened her lips. Her face was wooden.

'You didn't follow Binney down there, did you?'

'I'd rather be dead than have that slimy little blackmailer get his clutches on Stewart. Why, I'd . . . I'd–'

Mason said: 'That is exactly the reasoning the police will follow in trying to determine a motivation.'

'A reason why I should murder Binney Denham?'

'Yes.'

'I tell you I wasn't there! I was home last night waiting for Stewart and your information about him is erroneous. He never went near that motel. He was at some stuffy old directors' meeting and working on a deal so delicate he didn't dare to leave the room long enough to telephone me. You're sure Binney Denham is dead? There can't be any doubt about it?'

'No doubt whatever,' Mason said.

She thought that over for a moment, then got to her feet. 'I'd be a liar and a hypocrite, Mr Mason, if I told you I was sorry. I'm not. However, his death is going to create a problem you're going to have to cope with.

'The police will start checking Binney's background. They'll find out he was a blackmailer. They'll try to get a list of his victims in order to find someone who had a compelling motive to kill him. As the lawyer who handles my husband's problems, you're going to have to see the police learn nothing of Binney's hold on me. Stewart loves to take me out socially and . . . well, it's hard to explain. I suppose in a way it's the same feeling an owner has when he has a prize-winning dog. He likes to enter him in dog shows and see him carry off the blue ribbons. It's supposed to make other dog owners jealous or envious. Stewart loves to give me clothes, jewels, servants, background and then invite his friends to come in and look me over. They regard him as a very lucky husband, and Stewart likes that.'

'And underneath you resent it?' Mason asked.

She turned again and looked him full in the eyes. 'Make no mistake, Mr Perry Mason. I love it. And as Stewart's lawyer, you're going to have to find some way of saving him from a ruinous scandal. You'll have to find *some* way to keep from having my past brought to light.'

'What do you think I am–a magician?' Mason asked.

'My husband does,' she said. 'And we're prepared to pay you a fee based on that assumption–and for proving these fingerprints are forgeries and that I wasn't anywhere near that motel last night.'

With that she turned and walked away with long, steady steps, terminating the interview with dignity, finality, and in a way which left her complete mistress of the situation.

10

Perry Mason turned his car into the parking lot by his building. The attendant, who usually saluted him with a wave of the hand, made frantic signals as he drove by.

Mason braked his car to a stop. The attendant came running towards him. 'A message for you, Mr Mason.'

Mason took the sheet of paper. On it had been scribbled: 'Police are looking for you. Della.'

Mason hesitated a moment, thinking things over, then parked the car in the stall which was reserved for him and walked into the foyer of the office building.

A tall man seemed to appear from nowhere in particular. 'If you don't mind, Mason, I'll ride up with you.'

'Well, well, Lieutenant Tragg of Homicide,' Mason said. 'Can I be of some help to you, Lieutenant?'

'That depends,' Tragg said.

'On what?' Mason asked.

'We'll talk it over in your office, if you don't mind.'

They rode up in silence. Mason led the way down the corridor past the entrance door of his office, went to the door marked 'Private', unlocked and opened the door.

Della Street's voice, sharp with apprehension, said: 'Chief, the police are looking for . . . oh!' she exclaimed as her eyes focused on Lieutenant Tragg.

Tragg's voice was gravely courteous as he said: 'Good morning, Miss

Street,' but there was a certain annoyance manifest as he went on: 'And how did you know the police were looking for Mr Mason?'

'I just heard it somewhere. There isn't supposed to be anything secret about it, is there?' Della Street asked demurely.

'Apparently not,' Tragg said, seating himself comfortably in the client's chair and waiting for Mason to adjust himself behind the office desk.

'Cigarette?' Mason asked, extending a packet to Tragg.

'Thanks,' Tragg said, taking one.

Mason snapped his lighter and held the flame out to Tragg.

'Service!' the police lieutenant said.

'With a smile,' Mason told him, lighting his own cigarette.

Lieutenant Tragg, almost as tall as the lawyer, was typical of the modern police officer who is schooled in his profession and follows the work because he enjoys it, just as his associate, Sergeant Holcomb, who made no secret of his enmity for Perry Mason, typified the old school of hard-boiled, belligerent cop. Between Mason and Tragg there was a genuine mutual respect and a personal liking.

'Staylonger Motel,' Lieutenant Tragg said, looking at Mason.

Mason raised his eyebrows.

'Mean anything to you?'

'Nice name,' Mason said.

'Ever been there?'

Mason shook his head.

'Some client of yours been there?'

'I'm sure I couldn't say. I have quite a few clients, you know, and I presume some of them stay at motels rather frequently. It's quite convenient when you're travelling by auto. You can get at your baggage when you want it and–'

'Never mind the window dressing,' Tragg said. 'We had a murder at The Staylonger Motel last night.'

'Indeed?' Mason said. 'Who was murdered?'

'A man by the name of Binney Denham. Rather an interesting character, too, as it turns out.'

'Client of mine?' Mason asked.

'I hope not.'

'But I take it there's *some* connection,' Mason told him.

'I wouldn't be too surprised.'

'Want to tell me about it?'

'I'll tell you some of the things we know,' Tragg said. 'Yesterday afternoon a man who looked the executive type, with dark hair, iron grey at the temples, trim figure, well-tailored clothes, and an air of success, showed up at The Staylonger Motel with a woman who was quite a bit younger. The man could have been fifty. The woman, who was blonde and seductive, could have been twenty-five.'

'Tut-tut-tut!' Mason said.

Tragg grinned. 'Yeah! I know. Almost unique in the annals of motel history, isn't it? Well, here's the funny part. The man insisted on a double cabin; said they were going to be joined by another couple. However, after getting two units with a connecting door, the man apparently parked the blonde in unit sixteen and established his domicile in unit fifteen.

'The man was driving a rented car. They had drinks, went out, came back, and that evening the blonde drove away–alone.

'At around eleven last night the police received a call from an unknown woman. The woman said she wanted to report a homicide at unit sixteen in The Staylonger Motel, and then the woman hung up.'

'Just like that?' Mason asked.

'Just like that,' Tragg said. 'Interesting, isn't it?'

'In what way?'

'Oh, I don't know,' Tragg said. 'But when you stop to look at it, it has a peculiar pattern. Why should a woman call up to report a homicide?'

'Because she had knowledge that she thought the police should have,' Mason said promptly.

'Then why didn't she state her name and address?'

'Because she didn't want to become involved personally.'

'It's surprising the way you parallel my thinking,' Tragg said. 'Only I carry my thinking a step farther.'

'How come?'

'Usually a woman who wants to keep out of a thing of that sort simply doesn't bother to report. Usually a woman who reports, if she's acting in good faith, will give her name and address. But if that woman had been advised by a smart lawyer who had told her: "It's your duty to report the homicide to the police, but there's no law that says you have to stay on the phone long enough to give your name and address–" Well, you know how it is, Mason. It starts me thinking.'

'It seems to be a habit you have,' Mason said.

'I'm trying to cultivate it,' Tragg told him.

'I take it there's something more?' Mason asked.

'Oh, lots more. We made a routine check down at The Staylonger Motel. We get lots of false steers on these things, you know. This time it happened to be correct. This character was lying there in the middle of the floor with a bullet-hole in his back. The executive-type business-man and the curvaceous-type blonde and the rented car had completely disappeared.

'The blonde had driven away in the car. The man had gone through a barbed wire fence out the back way. He'd torn his clothes on the barbed wire. He evidently was in a hurry.'

Mason nodded sympathetically. 'Doesn't leave you much to work on, does it?'

'Oh, don't worry about a little thing like that,' Tragg said. 'We have *lots* to work on. You see, we had the licence number of the automobile. We traced it down. It was a rented automobile. We got hold of the automobile, and we've come up with some pretty good prints.'

'I see,' Mason said.

'Shortly after we phoned in the order to impound this automobile, we received a telephone call from the man who runs the car rental agency. He said that a woman came in to rent a car, inquired about cars that were available, wanted a car of a certain type, looked over the cars that he had, and then changed her mind. She had a slip of paper with a licence number on it. She seemed to be looking for some particular car.'

'Did she say what car?' Mason asked.

'No, she didn't say.'

Mason smiled. 'The manager of the car rental agency may have a vivid imagination.'

'Perhaps,' Tragg said. 'But the woman acted in a way that aroused the suspicion of the manager. He thought perhaps she might be trying to get hold of this particular car that had figured in a homicide. When she left, he followed her around the block. She got in a car that was driven by a man. The manager took down the licence number of the automobile.'

'Very clever,' Mason said.

'The automobile was registered in the name of the Drake Detective Agency.'

'You've talked with Drake?' Mason asked.

'Not yet,' Tragg said. 'I may talk with him later on. The Drake Detective Agency has offices here in the building on the same floor with you and does all of your work. You and Paul Drake are personal friends and close business associates.'

'I see,' Mason said, tapping ashes from the end of the cigarette.

'So I started making a few inquiries of my own,' Tragg said. 'Nothing particularly official, Mason. Just checking up.'

'I see,' Mason said.

'I notice that when Paul Drake is working on a particularly important case and stays up all night, he has hamburgers sent up from the lunch counter a couple of doors down the street. I probably shouldn't be telling you this, Mason, because it never pays for a magician to expose the manner in which he does his tricks. It has a tendency to destroy the effect.

'However, I dropped in to the lunch counter this morning, had a cup of coffee, chatted with the manager, told him I understood he'd been delivering quite a few hamburgers the night before, said I'd like to talk with the man who was on the night shift. Well, he'd gone home but hadn't gone to bed as yet, and the manager got him on the phone for me. I thought it would just be the same old seven and six of deliveries to Drake's office, but I hit unexpected pay dirt. I found that you and your secretary were up all night, and that you had hamburgers and coffee.'

Mason said thoughtfully: 'That's what comes of trying to get service. I should have gone down myself.'

'Or sent Miss Street for them,' Tragg said, smiling at Della Street.

'And so?' Mason said. 'You put two and two together and made eighteen. Is that it?'

'I haven't put two and two together as yet,' Tragg said. 'I'm simply calling your attention to certain factors which I haven't tried to add up so far.

'Now, I'm going to tell you something, Mason. Binney Denham was a blackmailer. We haven't been able to get *all* the dope on him as yet. He kept his books in some sort of code. We haven't cracked that code. We do have the fingerprints from that rented car. We have some cigarette stubs from the ash-tray. We have a few other things we aren't talking about just yet.

'Now if you happen to have a client who was susceptible to blackmail, if Binney Denham happened to be bleeding that client white and the client decided to get out of it by just about the only way you can deal with a blackmailer of that type, the police would be as co-operative as is consistent with the circumstances–if we received a little co-operation in return.

'What we don't know is just where this curvaceous blonde entered into the picture. There are quite a few things we don't know. There are quite a few things we do know. There are quite a few things we are finding out.

'Now, a good, smart lawyer who had a client in a jam of that sort might make a better deal with the police and perhaps with the D.A. by co-operating all the way along the line than by trying to hold out.'

'Are you speaking for the D.A.?' Mason asked.

Tragg ground out his cigarette in the ash-tray. 'Now there, of course, you've come to the weak point in my argument.'

'Your district attorney is not particularly fond of the ground I walk on,' Mason pointed out.

'I know,' Tragg conceded.

'I think, under the circumstances,' Mason said, 'a smart lawyer would have to play them very close to his chest.'

'Well, I thought I'd drop in,' Tragg said. 'Just sort of a routine check-up. I take it you don't want to make any statement, Mason?'

Mason shook his head.

'Keep your own nose clean,' Tragg warned. 'There are people on the force who don't like you. I just thought I'd give you a friendly warning, that's all.'

'Sergeant Holcomb going to be working on the case?' Mason asked.

'Sergeant Holcomb *is* working on the case.'

'I see,' Mason said.

Tragg got up, straightened his coat, reached for his hat, smiled at Della Street, and said: 'At times you're rather obvious, Miss Street.'

'I am?' Della Street asked.

Tragg nodded. 'You keep looking at that private, unlisted telephone on the corner of Mason's desk. Doubtless you're planning to call Paul Drake as soon as I'm out of the door. I told you this was a *friendly* tip. For your information, I don't intend to stop in at Drake's office on the way out and I don't intend to talk with him *as yet*.

'I would like to be very certain that nothing happens to put your employer out of business as an attorney, because then he couldn't sign your pay cheques, and personally it's a lot more fun for me to deal with brains than with the crooked type of criminal lawyer who has to get by by suborning perjury.

'I just thought I'd drop in for a social visit, that's all, and it might be a little easier for you to keep out of trouble if you knew that I'm going to have to report what I've found out down at the lunch counter about the consumption of sandwiches and coffee in the Mason office during the small hours of the morning.

'I don't suppose the persons who entered and signed the night register in the elevator would have been foolish enough to have signed their own names, but of course we'll be checking that and getting descriptions. I wouldn't be too surprised if the description of the man and the woman who went to your office last night didn't check with the description of the man and the woman who registered in units fifteen and sixteen at The Staylonger Motel. And, of course, we'll have a handwriting expert take a look at the man's signature on the register the elevator-man keeps for after-hours visitors.

'Well, I'll be ambling along. I have a conference with my zealous assistant, Sergeant Holcomb. I'm not going to mention anything to him about having been here.'

Tragg left the office.

'Hang it!' Mason said. 'A man will think he's being smart and then overlook the perfectly obvious.'

'Lieutenant Tragg?' Della Street said.

'Tragg nothing!' Mason said. 'I'm talking about myself. Having hamburgers sent up from that lunch counter is convenient for us and damned convenient for the police. We'll remember to keep out of *that* trap in the future.'

'Thanks to Lieutenant Tragg,' she said.

'Thanks to a very worthy adversary who is very shortly going to be raising hell with our client,' Mason said.

11

Mason carefully closed the doors leading to his private office, moved over close to Della Street, and lowered his voice. 'You're going to have to take a coffee break, Della,' he said.

'And then what?'

'Then while you're taking the coffee break, make certain that no one is in a position to see the number you're dialling. Call Stewart Bedford and tell him that under no circumstances is he to try to communicate with me, that I'll call him from time to time from a pay station; tell him that the police realize I'm interested in the case and may be watching my office.'

Della Street nodded.

'Now,' Mason said, 'we're going to have to be very, very careful. Lieutenant Tragg knows that Paul Drake is working on the case. Tragg is a deadly combination of intelligence, ability, and persistence.

'They've got hold of that automobile from the drive-yourself agency and they've developed fingerprints. They don't have any way of picking up Stewart Bedford from those fingerprints because they don't know whose fingerprints they are, but if they ever get a line on Bedford they can then take his fingerprints and *prove* that he was in the automobile.'

'What about Mrs Bedford?' Della Street asked. 'Aren't you obliged to tell Mr Bedford about her?'

'Why?'

'You're representing him.'

'As his attorney,' Mason said, 'I'm supposed to be looking out for his best interests.'

'His wife is mixed in it. Shouldn't he know?'

'How is she mixed in it?'

'She was down there at the motel. She had all the motive in the world. Chief, you know as well as I do that she went down there because she thought Binney Denham was putting the bite on her husband and she didn't intend to stand for it. There was only one way she could have stopped it.'

'You mean she killed him?'

'Why not?'

Mason pursed his lips.

'Well, why not?' Della Street insisted.

Mason said: 'In a case of this kind we don't know what we're up against until all of the facts are in, and by that time it's frequently too late to protect our client. In this case I'm protecting my client.'

'Just the one client?'

'Just the one client, Stewart G. Bedford.'

'Then aren't you obligated to tell him about . . . about his wife?'

Mason shook his head. 'I'm a lawyer. I have to take the responsibility of reaching certain decisions. Bedford is in love with his wife. It's quite probable that he's more in love with her than she is with him. Marriage for her may have been something of a business proposition. For him it represented a complete romantic investment in a new type of life.'

'Well?' she asked.

'If I tell him about his wife having been down there, about the fact that she may be suspect, Bedford will become heroic. He'll want to take all the blame in case he thinks there's any possibility she's guilty.

'I'm somewhat in the position of a physician who has to treat a patient. He doesn't tell the patient everything he knows. He prescribes treatment for the patient and does his best to see that the patient gets the right treatment.'

Della Street thought that over for a moment, then said: 'Will the police be able to locate Bedford today?'

'Probably,' Mason said. 'It's just a matter of time. Remember, Bedford is vulnerable on two or three fronts. For one thing, he bought a lot of traveller's cheques, counter-signed them and turned them over to the blackmailers. They cashed them. Somewhere along the line they've left a back trail that Tragg will pick up. Also remember that Bedford scribbled a note which he gave to the waiter at the cocktail lounge, asking him to call Elsa Griffin and give her the name of the motel. He didn't sign his name to the message, but after the newspapers begin to talk about the murder at The Staylonger Motel, the waiter will probably remember that that was the name of the motel he was to give Elsa Griffin over the telephone.'

'Do you suppose the waiter saved the message?'

'He could have,' Mason said. 'There was twenty dollars in it for him, and that was bound to have registered in his mind. He could very well have saved the note.

'About all we can do is try to stall things along while Paul Drake gets information about Denham's background and see if we can locate that blonde.'

'All right,' Della Street said, 'I'll take my coffee break and telephone Mr Bedford.'

'How are you feeling, Della?'

'As long as I can pour the coffee in, I can keep the eyes open.'

'You'd better go home early this afternoon and try getting some sleep.'

'How about you?'

'I'll be all right. I may break away this afternoon myself. Things are now where we have to wait for developments. I'm hoping Drake can come up with something before Tragg gets a line on our client. Get yourself some coffee and then go on home and turn in, Della. I'll phone you if anything comes up.'

'I'll stick it out a while longer. I wish you'd get some rest and let *me* stay on the job and call *you*.'

Mason looked at his watch. 'Wait until noon, Della. If Drake hasn't turned up something by that time, we'll both check out. I'll leave word with Drake's office where they can call me.'

'Okay,' Della Street said. 'I'll call Bedford right away.'

12

Mason stopped in at Paul Drake's office.

'You don't look bad,' Mason said to the detective.

'Why should I?'

'Up all night.'

'We get used to it. *You* look like hell!'

'*I'm* not accustomed to it. What are you finding out?'

'Not too much. The police are on the job, and that makes things tough.'

'This man Denham,' Perry Mason said. 'He had this blonde girl friend.'

'So what?'

'I want her.'

'Who doesn't? The police want her. The newspaper people want her.'

'What's the description?' Mason asked.

'The description the police have is a girl about twenty-five to twenty-seven, five feet three, maybe a little on the hefty side, slim-waisted, plenty of hips, and lots of chest.'

'What do they have from the rented car, Paul?'

'No one knows. The police keep that pretty much of a secret. They have *some* fingerprints.'

'And from the units at the motel?'

'They have fingerprints there, too.'

Mason said: 'I'll give you a tip, Paul. The police are wise that you're working on the case.'

'It would be a miracle if they weren't. You can't try to get information in a case of this sort without leaving a trail that the police can follow. I suppose that means they've connected me with you?'

Mason nodded.

'And you with your client?' Drake asked, watching Mason sharply.

'Not yet.'

'Be careful. They will.'

'It's just a matter of time,' Mason conceded. 'I want to find that blonde before they do.'

'Then you'll have to give me some information that they haven't got,' Drake said. 'Otherwise, things being equal, there isn't a whisper of a chance, Perry. The police have the organization. They have the authority. They have all the police records. I have nothing.'

'I can give you one tip,' Mason said.

'What's that?'

'In this business names don't mean anything,' Mason told him. 'But initials do. My client tells me this girl gave the name of Geraldine Corning. She had a new overnight bag and suitcase with her initials stamped in gilt–*G.C.*'

'You don't think she gave her right name to this client of yours?'

'I doubt it,' Mason said. 'But I have a hunch her initials are probably the same. The last name won't mean much, but there aren't too many first names that begin with *G*. You might try Gloria or Grace, for a start.'

'Blondes with first names of Gloria or Grace, are a dime a dozen,' Drake said. 'The city's full of them.'

'I know, but this was a girl who was hanging around with particular people.'

'And you know what happens when you ask questions about girls who are hanging around with people like that?' Drake asked. 'You run up against a wall of silence that is based on stark fear. You can open up any source of information and have things going good, and then you can casually mention: "Do you know a girl by the name of Grace or Gloria Somebody-or-other who was playing around with this blackmailer, Binney Denham?" . . . well, you know what happens. They clam up as though you'd pulled a zipper.'

Mason thought that over. 'I see your point, Paul. But a lot depends on this. We've simply *got* to get this girl located. She must have had a charge account some place that was paid by her sugar daddy or–'

'You know what would happen if we tried to get a line on all the blondes who have accounts that are paid by sugar daddies? We'd–'

'No, no, now wait a minute!' Mason said. 'I'm just trying to narrow the thing down for you, Paul. She must have had an account at a beauty parlour. She must have had contacts, perhaps not with Binney Denham but perhaps with this Harry Elston who had the lock-box with Binney. What can you find out about him?'

'Absolutely nothing,' Drake said. 'Elston visited the joint tenancy lock-box and faded from the picture. He's crawled into a hole and pulled the hole in after him.'

'The police want him?'

'Very much.'

Mason said: 'Blackmailers and gamblers. Gamblers go to race-tracks. Try covering the race-tracks. See if you can get a line on this blonde. She had relatively new baggage. It may have been bought for this occasion.

'I'm going out to my apartment and get some shut-eye. I'd like to have you stay on with this personally for another couple of hours if you can, Paul. Then you can turn it over to your operatives and get some sleep.'

'Shucks! I'm good for another day and another night,' Drake said.

Mason heaved himself out of his chair. 'I'm not. Call me whenever you get a lead. I want to find that blonde and interview her before the police do, and I have an idea things are going to get pretty rugged this afternoon. I want to be able to think clearly when the going gets rough.'

'Okay,' Drake said. 'I'll call you. But don't get too optimistic about that blonde. She's going to be hard to find, and in blackmailing circles the word will have gone out for everybody to clam up.'

13

Mason took a hot shower, crawled into bed, sank instantly into restful oblivion only to be aroused, seconds later, it seemed to him, by the insistent ringing of the telephone.

He managed to get the receiver to his ear and mutter thickly into the telephone: 'Hello!'

'Paul Drake's voice, crisp and business-like, said: 'The fat's in the fire, Perry. Get going.'

'What?' Mason asked.

'Police checking back on Denham's associates got on the trail of some traveller's cheques. It seems a whole flock of traveller's cheques were cashed. They bore the signatures of Stewart G. Bedford. Because of his prominence, the police were reluctant to start getting rough until they'd made a complete check.

'They got photographs of Bedford and took them out to Morrison Brems, the manager of The Staylonger Motel. Brems can't be certain, but he thinks from the photograph the police had that Bedford was the man who registered with the blonde.

'The police have–'

'Have they made an arrest?' Mason interposed.

'No.'

'Brought him in for inquiry?'

'Not yet. They're going to his office to–'

Mason said: 'I'm on my way.'

Mason tumbled into his clothes, ran a comb through his hair, dashed out of the apartment, took the elevator down, jumped into his car and made time out to Bedford's office.

He was too late.

Sergeant Holcomb, a uniformed officer, and a plain-clothes detective were in Bedford's office when Mason arrived. A rather paunchy man with a gold-toothed smile stood patiently in the background.

'Hello,' Mason said. 'What's all the trouble?'

Sergeant Holcomb grinned at him. 'You're too late,' he said.

'What's the matter, Bedford?' Mason asked.

'These people seem to think I've been out at some motel with a blonde. They're asking me questions about blackmail and murder and–'

'And we asked you nicely to let us take your fingerprints,' Sergeant Holcomb said, 'and you refused to even give us the time of day. Now then, Mason, are you going to advise your client to give us his fingerprints or not?'

'He doesn't have to give you a damn thing,' Mason said, 'If you want to get his fingerprints, arrest him and book him.'

'We can do that too, you know.'

'And run up against a suit for false arrest,' Mason said. 'I don't know anyone I'd rather recover damages from than you.'

Sergeant Holcomb turned to the paunchy man. 'Is this the guy?'

'I could tell better if I saw him with his hat on.'

Sergeant Holcomb walked over to the hat closet, returned with a hat, slapped it down on Bedford's head. 'Now take a look.'

The man studied Bedford. 'It looks like him.'

Sergeant Holcomb said to the man in plain clothes: 'Look the place over.'

The man took a leather packet from his pocket, took out some various coloured powders, a camel's hair brush and started brushing an ash-tray which he had picked up.

'You can't do that,' Mason said.

'Try and stop him,' Holcomb invited. 'Just *try* and stop him. I don't know anyone I'd rather hang one on than you. We're collecting evidence. Try and stop us.'

Holcomb turned to Bedford. 'Now then, you got twenty thousand dollars in traveller's cheques. Why did you want them?'

'Don't answer,' Mason said, 'until they can treat you with the dignity and respect due a man in your position. Don't even give them the time of day.'

'All those cheques were cashed within a period of less than twelve hours,' Sergeant Holcomb went on. 'What was the idea?'

Bedford sat tight-lipped.

'Perhaps,' Holcomb said, 'you were paying blackmail to a ring that was pretty smart. They didn't want you to be able to make a pay-off with marked or numbered bills, so they worked out that method so they could cash the cheques themselves.'

'And thereby left a perfect trail?' Mason asked sarcastically.

'Don't be silly,' Holcomb said. 'The way those cheques were cashed you couldn't tie them in with Binney Denham in a hundred years. We'd never even have known about it if it hadn't been for the murder.'

The plain-clothes officer studied several latent fingerprints which he had examined with a magnifying-glass. Abruptly he looked up at Sergeant Holcomb and nodded.

'What have you got?' Holcomb asked.

'A perfect little fingerprint. It matches with the little fingerprint on the–'

'Don't tell him,' Sergeant Holcomb interrupted. 'That's good enough for me. Get your things, Bedford. You're in custody.'

'On what charge?' Mason asked.

'Suspicion of murder,' Holcomb said.

Mason said: 'You can make any investigation you want to, or you can make an arrest and charge him with murder, but you're not going to hold him on suspicion.'

'Maybe I won't hold him,' Holcomb said, 'but I'll sure as hell take him in. Want to make a bet?'

'Either charge him, or I'll get habeas corpus and get him out.'

Holcomb's grin was triumphant. 'Go ahead, Counsellor, get your habeas corpus. By the time you get it, I'll have him booked and have his fingerprints. If you think you can get a suit for malicious arrest on the strength of the evidence we have now, you're a bigger boob than I think you are.

'Come on, Bedford. Do you want to pay for a taxi, or shall we call the wagon?'

Bedford looked at Mason.

'Pay for the taxi,' Mason said, 'and make absolutely no statements except in the presence of your attorney.'

'Fair enough!' Sergeant Holcomb said. 'I don't need more than an hour to make my case bullet-proof, and if you can get a habeas corpus in that time, you're a wonder!'

Stewart G. Bedford drew himself up to his full height. 'Gentlemen,' he said, 'I desire to make a statement.'

'Hold it!' Mason said. 'You're not making any statements yet.'

Bedford looked at him with cold, resolute eyes. 'Mason,' he said, 'I have retained you to advise me as to my legal rights. No one has to advise me as to my moral rights.'

'I tell you to hold it!' Mason said irritably.

Sergeant Holcomb said hopefully to Bedford: 'This is *your* office. If you want him out, just say the word and we'll put him out.'

'I don't want him out,' Bedford said. 'I simply want to state to you gentlemen that I *did* go to The Staylonger Motel yesterday.'

'Now, that's better!' Sergeant Holcomb said, pulling out a chair and sitting down. 'Go right ahead.'

'Bedford,' Mason said, 'you may *think* you're doing the right thing, but–'

Sergeant Holcomb said: 'Throw him out, boys, if he tries to interrupt. Go ahead, Bedford; you've got this on your chest and you'll feel better when you get rid of it.'

'I was being blackmailed by this character Binney Denham,' Bedford said. 'There is something in my past that I hoped never would come out. Somehow Denham found out about it.'

'Where was this?' Sergeant Holcomb asked.

Mason started to say something, then checked himself.

'A hit-and-run,' Bedford said simply. 'it was six years ago. I'd had a few drinks. It was a dark, rainy night. It really wasn't my fault and I was perfectly sober. This elderly woman in dark clothes was crossing the street. I didn't see her until I was right on her. I hit her a solid smash. I knew the minute I had hit her there was nothing anyone could do for her. I threw her to the pavement with terrific force.'

'Where was this?' Sergeant Holcomb asked.

'Out on Figueroa Street, six years ago. The woman's name was Sara Biggs. You can find out all about her in the accident records.

'As I say, I'd had a few drinks. I know very well what I can do and I can't do when I'm drinking. I never drive a car if I'm sufficiently under the influence of liquor to have it affect my driving in the slightest. This accident wasn't due in any way to the few cocktails I'd had, but I knew that I *did* have liquor on my breath. There was nothing that could be done for the woman. The street was, at the moment, free of traffic. I just kept on going.

'I made it a point to check up on the accident in the papers. The woman had been killed instantly. I tell you, gentlemen, it was her own fault. She was crossing the street on a dark, rainy night in between intersections. Heaven knows what she was trying to do! She was out there in the street, and that's all. As I learned afterwards, she was an elderly woman. She was dressed entirely in black. I didn't know *all* of these things at the time. All I knew was that I had been drinking and had hit someone and that it had been her fault. However, I'd had enough liquor, so I knew I'd be the goat if I'd stopped.'

'Okay,' Sergeant Holcomb said. 'So you beat it. You made a hit-and-run. This guy Denham found out about it. Is that right?'

'That's right.'

'What did he do?'

'He waited for some time before he put the bite on me,' Bedford said. 'Then he showed up with a demand that I–'

'When?' Holcomb interrupted.

'Three days ago,' Bedford said.

'You hadn't known him before that?'

'That was the first time in my life I ever met the slimy little rascal. He had this apologetic manner. He told me that he hated to do it, but he needed money and . . . well, he told me to get twenty thousand dollars in traveller's cheques, and that was all there'd be to it.

'Then he told me he had to keep me out of circulation while the cheques were being cashed. That was when he showed up yesterday morning. He had a blonde woman who gave the name of Geraldine Corning. She had a car parked in front of the building. I don't know how they'd secured that parking space, but the car was right in front of the door. Miss Corning drove me around until we were certain we weren't being followed; then she told me to pick out a good-looking motel and drive in.'

'*You* picked out the motel, or *she* did?' Sergeant Holcomb asked.

'I did.'

'All right. What happened?'

'We saw the sign of The Staylonger Motel. I suggested that we go in there. It was all right with her. I was already paying blackmail on one charge and I didn't propose to have them catch me on some kind of frame-up with a woman. I told the manager, Mr Brems–the gentleman standing over there who has just identified me–that I expected another couple to join us and therefore wanted a double unit. He said I could do better by waiting until the other couple showed up and let them pay for the second unit. I told him I'd pay the entire price and take both units.'

'Then what?'

'I put Miss Corning in one unit. I stayed in the other. The door was open between the units. I tried to keep rigidly to myself, but it became too boring. We played cards. We had a drink. We went out for a drive. We stopped in a tavern. We had a very fine afternoon meal. We returned and had another drink. That drink was drugged. I went to sleep. I don't know what happened after that.'

'Okay,' Sergeant Holcomb said, 'you're doing so good. Why not tell us about the gun?'

'I *will* tell you about the gun,' Bedford said. 'I had never been blackmailed in my life. It made me furious to think of doing business on that kind of a basis. I . . . I had a gun in my study. I took that gun and put it in my brief-case.'

'Go on,' Holcomb said.

'I tell you the last drink I had was drugged.'

'What time was that?'

'Sometime in the afternoon.'

'Three o'clock? Four o'clock?'

'Probably four. I can't give you the exact hour. It was still daylight.'

'How do you know it was drugged?'

'I could tell. I have never been able to sleep during the day. However, after I took this drink, I couldn't focus my eyes. I saw double. I tried to get up and couldn't. I fell back on the bed and went to sleep.'

'This blonde babe drugged the drink?' Sergeant Holcomb asked.

'I rather think that someone else had entered the motel during our absence and drugged the bottle from which the liquor was poured,' Bedford said. 'Miss Corning seemed to feel the effects before I did. She was sitting in a chair and she went to sleep while I was still awake. In fact, as I remember it, she went to sleep right in the middle of a conversation.'

'They sometimes put on an act like that,' Holcomb said. 'It keeps the sucker from becoming suspicious. She dopes the drink, then pretends she's sleepy first. It's an old gag.'

'Could be,' Bedford said. 'I'm just telling you what I know.'

'Okay,' Sergeant Holcomb said. 'How did it happen you used this gun? I take it the guy showed up and–'

'I *didn't* use the gun,' Bedford said positively. 'I had the gun in my brief-case. When I awakened, which was sometime at night, the gun was gone.'

'So what did you do?' Holcomb asked sceptically.

'I became panic-stricken when I found the body of Binney Denham in that other unit in the motel. I took my brief-case and my hat and went out through the back. I crawled through the barbed wire fence–'

'You tore your clothes?' Holcomb asked.

'I tore the knee of my pants, yes.'

'And then what did you do?'

'I walked across the lot to the road.'

'And then what?'

'Then I managed to get a ride,' Bedford said. 'I think, gentlemen, that covers the situation.'

'He was killed with your gun?' Sergeant Holcomb asked.

'How do I know?' Bedford said. 'I have told you my story, gentlemen. I am not accustomed to having my word questioned. I am not going to submit myself to a lot of browbeating cross-questioning. I have told you the absolute truth.'

'What did you do with the gun?' Sergeant Holcomb said. 'Come on, Bedford, you've told us so much you might as well make a clean breast of it. After all, the guy was a blackmailer. He was putting the bite on you. There's a lot to be said on your side. You knew that if you started paying you were going to have to keep on paying. You took the only way out, so you may as well tell us what you did with the gun.'

'I have told you the truth,' Bedford said.

'Nuts!' Sergeant Holcomb observed. 'Don't expect us to believe a cock-and-bull story like that. Why did you take the gun in the first place if you didn't intend to use it?'

'I tell you I don't know. I presume I thought I might intimidate the man by telling him I had paid once, but that I wouldn't pay again. I probably had a rather nebulous idea that if I showed him the gun and told him I'd kill him if he ever tried to shake me down again, it might help get me off the hook as far as future payments were concerned. Frankly, gentlemen, I don't know. I never did make any really definite plan. I acted on impulse, some feeling of–'

'Yeah, I know,' Sergeant Holcomb said. 'I know all about it. Come on through with the truth now. What did you do with the gun after the shooting? Tell us that and then you'll have got it all off your chest.'

Bedford shook his head. 'I have told you all I know. Someone took my gun out of my brief-case while I was sleeping.'

Holcomb looked at the plain-clothes officer, said to Bedford: 'Okay. We'll go talk with the D.A. You pay for the cab.'

Holcomb turned to Mason. 'You and your habeas corpus,' he said. 'This is one case that backfired on you. How do you like your client now, wise guy?'

Mason said: Don't be silly. If Bedford had been going to shoot Denham, why didn't he do it *before* he paid the twenty thousand and save himself that much money?'

Sergeant Holcomb frowned for a moment, then said: 'Because he didn't have the opportunity before he paid. Anyhow, he's smart. It would be worth twenty grand to him to give you that talking point in front of a jury.

'It's your question, Mason, and the D.A. will let you try to answer it yourself in front of the jury. I'll be there listening.

'Come on, Bedford. You're going places where even Perry Mason can't get you out. That statement of yours gives us all we need.

'Call the cab. We leave Mason here.'

14

Mason, bone tired, entered the offices of the Drake Detective Agency.

'Drake gone home?' he asked the girl at the switchboard.

She shook her head and pointed to the gate leading to a long, narrow corridor. 'He's still in. I think he's resting. He's in room seven. There's a couch in there.'

'I'll take a peek inside,' Mason said. 'If he's asleep I won't disturb him. What's cooking? Anything?'

'He has a lot of operatives out and some reports are coming in, but nothing important. He's trying to locate this blonde young woman you were so anxious to find. He's left word to be called if we get anything on her.'

'Thanks,' Mason said. 'I'll tiptoe down. If he's sleeping I won't disturb him.'

Mason walked on down the corridor past a veritable rabbit warren of small-sized offices, gently opened the door of number seven.

This was a small office with a table, two straight-backed chairs, and a couch. Paul Drake lay on his back on the couch, snoring gently.

Mason stood for a moment in the doorway, regarding the sleeping figure, then eased out and closed the door.

Just as the door latched shut, the phone on the table shrilled noisily. Mason hesitated a moment, then gently opened the door.

Paul Drake came up to a sitting position on the couch. His eyes were still heavy with sleep as he groped for the telephone, got the receiver to his ear, said: 'Hello . . . yes. . . . What is it? . . .' His sleep-sodden eyes looked up, saw Mason, and the detective nodded drowsily.

Mason saw Drake's expression suddenly change. The man galvanized into wakefulness as though he had been hit in the face with a stream of cold water.

'Wait a minute,' he said. 'What's that address? . . . Okay, what's the name? . . . Okay. . . . I've got it. I've got it.'

Drake scribbled rapidly on a pad of paper, then said into the telephone: 'Hold everything! Keep watch on the place. If she goes out, shadow her. I'll be out there right away–fifteen or twenty minutes. . . . Okay, good-bye.'

Drake banged the telephone, said: 'We've got her, Perry,'

'Who?'

'This Geraldine Corning babe.'

'You're sure?'

'Her name's Grace Compton. I have the address here. You had a correct hunch on the initials on the baggage.'

'How'd you locate her, Paul?'

'I'll tell you after we get started,' Drake said. 'Come on. Let's go.'

Drake ran his fingers through his hair, grabbed a hat, started down the narrow corridor with Mason pounding along at his heels.

'Your car or mine?' Mason asked in the elevator.

'Makes no difference,' Drake told him.

'We'll take mine,' Mason said. 'You do the talking while I'm driving.'

Mason and the detective hurried across the parking lot, jumped into Mason's car. Drake was talking by the time the car was in motion.

'The location of the car rental agency gave us something to work on,' Drake said. 'We started combing the classified ad directory for stores in the neighbourhood handling baggage. I've had five operatives on the job covering every place they could think of. One of them struck pay dirt. A fellow remembered having sold baggage to a blonde who answered the description and putting the initials *G.C.* on it. The blonde paid with a cheque signed "Grace Compton", and the man remembered the bank. After that it was easy. She's living in an apartment-house, and apparently she's in at the moment.'

'That's for us,' Mason said. 'Good work, Paul.'

'Of course, it *could* be a false lead. After all, we're just working on a description and slender clues. There are lots of blonde babes who buy baggage.'

'I know,' Mason said, 'but I have a hunch this is it.'

Drake said: 'Turn to the left at the next corner, Perry.'

Mason swung the car around the corner, then, at Drake's direction, turned back to the right after three blocks.

'Find a parking place in here some place,' Drake said.

Mason eased the car into a vacant place at the kerb. He and Drake got out and walked up to the front of a rather ostentatious apartment-house.

A man sitting in a parked car near the entrance to the apartment-house struck a match, lit a cigarette. Drake said: 'That's my man. Want to talk with him?'

'Do we need to?'

'No. Striking the match and lighting the cigarette means that she's still in there. That's his signal to us.'

Mason walked up to the directory, studied the names and saw that Grace Compton had apartment two-thirty-one.

'How about this door, Paul?' Mason asked, indicating the locked outer door. 'Do we sound the buzzer in her apartment, or can you–?'

'That's easy,' Drake said, looking at the lock on the outer door. He took a key from his pocket, inserted it in the lock. The door swung open.

'Let's walk,' Mason said.

They climbed the stairs to the second floor, walked back down the corridor and paused before the door bearing the number two-thirty-one.

'It's your show from here on,' Drake said. 'Of course, your hunch may be right and it may be wrong. All we have is a description.'

'We'll take a chance,' Mason said.

He pressed the bell button. A long, two shorts and a long.

They heard the quick thud of steps on the inside, then the door was swung open. A blonde in lounging pyjamas said: 'My God! You–' She stopped abruptly at the sight of the two men.

'Miss Compton?' Mason asked.

Her eyes instantly became cautious. 'What is it?' she asked.

'We just wanted to talk with you,' Mason said.

'Who are you?'

'This is Paul Drake, a detective.'

She said: 'You can't pull that line of stuff with me. I–'

'I'm Perry Mason, a lawyer.'

'Okay, so what?'

Mason said: 'Know anything about The Staylonger Motel, Miss Compton?'

'Yes,' she said breathlessly, 'I was there. I was there with one of the big-name motion picture stars. He didn't want the affair revealed. He just swept me off my feet. Now I'm suing him for support of my unborn child. How did you know?'

Mason said: 'Were you there with Mr Stewart G. Bedford yesterday?'

Her eyes narrowed. 'All right, if this is a pinch, get it off your chest. If it isn't, get out of here.'

'It's not a pinch. I'm trying to get information *before* the police do.'

'So you brought a detective along with you?'

'Private.'

'Oh, I see. And you want to know just what I did yesterday. How perfectly delightful! Would you like to come in and sit down? I suppose you expect me to buy you a drink and–'

'You knew Binney Denham?'

'Denham? Denham?' she said and slowly shook her head. 'The name means nothing to me. Am I supposed to know him?'

'If you're the one I think you are,' Mason said, 'you and Stewart Bedford occupied units fifteen and sixteen in The Staylonger Motel yesterday.'

'Why, Mr Mason, how you talk!' she said. 'I never go to a motel without a chaperon . . . never!'

'And,' Mason went on, 'Binney Denham was found sprawled out stone dead in the unit you had been occupying. A ·38 revolver had sent a bullet through his–'

She stepped back, her face white, her eyes wide and round. Her lips opened as though she might be going to scream. She pressed her knuckles up against her lips, hard.

Mason nodded to Paul Drake, calmly pushed his way into the apartment, closing the door behind him. He moved over to a chair, sat down, lit a cigarette, and said: 'Sit down, Paul,' acting as though he might have owned the apartment.

The girl looked at him for several long seconds, terror in her eyes.

At length she asked: 'Is this . . . is this on the up and up?'

'Ring up the police,' Mason said. 'They'll tell you.'

'What do *I* want with the police?'

'It's probably the other way around at that,' Mason told her. 'They'll be here any minute. Want to tell us what happened?'

She moved over to a chair, eased down to sit on the extreme edge.

'Any time,' Mason said.

'What's *your* interest in it, Mr Mason?'

'I'm representing Stewart Bedford. Police seem to think he might have had something to do with the murder.'

'Gosh!' she said in a hushed voice. 'He could have at that!'

'What happened?' Mason asked.

She said: 'It was a shakedown. I don't know the details. Binney has hired me on several occasions to do jobs for him.'

'What sort of jobs?'

'Keep the sucker out of circulation until Binney has the cash all in hand. Then Binney gives me a signal and I turn him loose.'

'Why keep him out of circulation?' Mason asked.

'So he won't change his mind at the last minute and so we can be certain he isn't working with any firm of private detectives.'

'What do you do?'

'I keep their minds on other things.'

'Such as what?'

'Am I supposed to draw diagrams?'

'What did you do with Bedford?'

'I kept his mind on other things . . . and it was a job. He's in love with his wife. I tried to get him interested, and I might as well have been an ice cube on the drain-board of the kitchen sink. Then after a while we really did get friends, and– Don't make any mistake about it. That's all it was. Just a good, decent friendship. I like the guy.

'I made up my mind then and there that that was to be my last play in the sucker racket. When I saw the way he felt about his wife, the way he . . . well, I'm young yet. There's still a chance. Maybe some man will feel that way about me some day if he meets me in the right way. He's never going to feel that way about me the way things are now.'

'So what did you do?'

'That,' she said, 'is where somebody gave us both a double-cross.'

'What happened?'

'I went out. I left a bottle of liquor on the table. Sombody must have doped the liquor. We came back and had a drink. I didn't even know I was drugged until I woke up sometime after dark. Bedford was still sleeping. I'd given him about twice as much whisky as I took. I felt his pulse. It was strong and regular, so I figured there hadn't been any harm done. I thought for a while it might have been knock-out drops, and those can be dangerous. I guess this was one of the barbiturates. It didn't seem to hurt anything.'

'And then what?'

She said: 'I took a shower and got dressed and put on some other clothes. I knew that it wouldn't be very long. The banks had closed and Binney should be showing up any minute.'

'And he did?'

'He did.'

'What did he tell you?'

'Told me that everything was clear and we could leave.'

'Then what happened?'

'Then I accused him of drugging the drink, and he denied it. I got a little hot under the collar. I thought he didn't trust me any more. I was mad anyway. I told him that the next time he had a deal he could just get some other girl to do the job for him. One thing led to another. I told him Bedford was asleep. We tried to wake him up. We couldn't wake him. He'd get up–to a sitting position–and then lurch back to the pillows. He was limber-legged.

'Okay, there wasn't anything I could do about it. He was just going to have to sleep it off. I was mad at Binney, but that wasn't putting any starch in Bedford's legs.

'I wasn't going to stick around there. He had money. He could get a cab and get home. I pinned a note on his sleeve, saying things were all right, that he could leave any time. Then I went out to my car.'

'Where was Binney Denham?'

'Denham was in his car.'

'Then what did you do?'

'I drove back and turned the car in at the rental agency the way I was supposed to. On a deal of that sort I'm not supposed to try and get anything back on the deposit. I just park the car in the lot with the keys in it, walk towards the office as though I'm going to check in, and then just keep on going. They find the car parked, with the keys in it. There's a fifty-buck deposit on the thing and only eleven or twelve dollars due. They wait awhile to see if anyone's coming back for the credit and then, after a while, some clerk clears the records, puts the surplus in his pocket and that's all there is to it.'

'Did you leave Binney behind?'

'No, he pulled out about the same time I did.'

'Then he must have turned around and gone back.'

'I guess so. Was his car there?'

Mason shook his head. 'Apparently not. What kind of a car?'

'A nondescript Chevy,' she said. 'He wants a car that nobody can describe, a car that looks so much like all the other cars on the road nobody pays any attention to it.'

'Was there any reason for him to have gone back?'

'Not that I know of. He had the money.'

'Was there anything he wanted to see Bedford about?'

'Not that I know. He had the dough. What else would he have wanted?'

Mason frowned. 'It must have been something. He went back to see Bedford for some reason. He couldn't have left something behind, could he–something incriminating?'

'Not Binney.'

'Do you know what the shakedown was?'

'Binney never tells me.'

'What name did you give?'

'Geraldine Corning. That's my professional name.'

'Planning on taking a trip?' Mason asked, indicating the new baggage by the closet door.

'I could be.'

'Make enough out of this sort of stuff to pay?'

She said bitterly: 'If I made a hundred times as much it wouldn't pay. What's a person's self-respect worth?'

'Then you can't help Bedford at all?' Mason asked.

'I can't help him, and I can't hurt him. He paid, and paid up like a gentleman. It was quite a shake-down this time–twenty thousand bucks. All in traveller's cheques.'

'What did you do with them?'

'I got him to sign them and I put them out in the glove compartment of the rented car. That was what we had agreed to do. Binney was hanging around there some place where he could see.

'We'd made arrangements so that we were sure we were safe. We knew we couldn't be followed. We just cruised around until we were dead certain of that. I doubled and twisted and Binney followed until we knew no one was tailing us. Then I let Bedford pick whatever motel he wanted. That gave him confidence, relaxed him.

'I locked him in so he couldn't get out, went to the phone booth, called Binney, told him where I was and told him the mark had signed the traveller's cheques.'

'Then what?'

'Then I left them in the glove compartment of the rented car. That was the procedure we'd agreed on. Binney took the cheques out and got them cashed.'

'Do you have any idea how he went about doing it?'

She shook her head. 'Probably he has a stand-in with a banker friend somewhere. I don't know. I don't think he put them into circulation as regular cheques. He just handled the deal his own way.'

'How about Binney? Did he have an accomplice?'

She shook her head.

'He referred to a man he called Delbert.'

She laughed. 'Binney was the smooth one! Suckers would get so infuriated at this fictitious Delbert they could kill him with their bare hands, but they always had a certain sympathy for Binney. He was always *so* sweet and *so* apologetic.'

'You were his only partner?'

'Don't be silly! I wasn't a partner. I was a paid employee. Sometimes he'd give me a couple of hundred extra, but not often. Binney was a one-way street on money. Getting dough out of that little double-crosser was–'

'Yes, go on,' Mason prompted as her voice died down.

She shook her head.

'He double-crossed you?'

'Go get lost, will you? Why should I sit here and blab all I know. Me and my big mouth!'

Mason tried another line of approach.

'So you made up your mind it was your last case?'

'After talking with Bedford I did.'

'How did that happen? What did Bedford say to you?'

'Damned if I know. I guess he really didn't say anything. It was the way he felt about his wife, the way he'd look right past me. He was so much in love with his wife he couldn't see any other woman. I got to wondering how a woman would go about getting the respect of a man like that . . . hell! I don't know what happened. Just put it down that I got religion, if you want to put a price tag on everything.'

Mason said: 'We only have your word for it. It was a sweet opportunity for a double-cross. You yourself admit you had decided to quit the racket. You could have told Binney you were quitting. Binney might not have liked that. You admit you and Binney were in their working with Bedford, trying to get him to wake up. You had undoubtedly gone through Bedford's brief-case and knew what was in it. When the party got rough you could have pumped a shot into Binney's back, gone through him to the tune of twenty thousand dollars, and simply driven away.'

She said: 'That's your nasty legal mind. You lawyers do think of the damnedest things.'

'Anything wrong with the idea?'

'Everything's wrong with it.'

'Such as what?'

'I told you I was quitting. I told you I'd got religion. Would I get moral and decide to quit a racket and then plan on bumping a guy off to get twenty grand? That'd be a hell of a way to get religion!'

'Perhaps you had to kill him,' Mason said, watching her with narrow eyes. 'Binney may not have liked the idea of you getting religion. He may have had ideas of his own. The party may have got rough.'

She said: 'You're bound to make me the fall guy, win, lose, or draw, aren't you? You're a lawyer. Your client has money, social position, political prestige. I have nothing. You'll throw me to the wolves to save your client. I'm a damn fool even to talk with you.'

Mason said: 'If you killed him in self-defence, I feel certain Mr Bedford would see that you–'

'Get lost,' she interrupted.

Mason got to his feet. 'I just wanted to get your story.'

'You've had it.'

'If anything happened and you *did* have to act in self-defence, it would strengthen your case if you reported the facts to the police. You should also know that any evidence of flight can be construed as an admission of guilt.'

She said sarcastically: 'You've probably got a lot of things on your mind, Mr Mason. I've got a lot of things on *my* mind now. I'm not going to detain you any longer and I'm not going to let you detain me.'

She got up and walked to the door.

The two men walked slowly back down the stairs. 'Have your operative keep her shadowed, Paul,' Mason said. 'I have a hunch she's planning on making a break for it.'

'Want to try and stop her if she does?'

'Gosh no! I only want to find out where she goes.'

'That might be difficult.'

'See that your operative has money,' Mason said. 'Let him get on the same plane that she takes. Go wherever she goes.'

'Okay, Drake said. 'You go get in the car. I'll talk with my operative.'

Mason walked over to his car. Drake walked past the parked automobile, jerked his head slightly, then walked on around the corner.

The man got out of the parked automobile, walked to the corner, overtook Drake, had a few minutes' brief conversation, then turned back to the car.

Drake came over to Mason and said: 'He'll let us know anything that happens, and he'll follow her wherever she goes; only the guy doesn't have a passport.'

'That's all right,' Mason said. 'She won't have one either. Your man has enough money to cover expenses?'

'He has now,' Drake said.

'We have to be certain she doesn't know she's being shadowed, Paul.'

'This man's good. You want her to run, Perry?'

Mason said, somewhat musingly: 'I wish she didn't give that impression of sincerity, Paul. Sure I want her to run. I'm representing a client who is accused of murder. According to her own story this girl had every reason to kill Binney Denham. Now if she resorts to flight I can accuse her of being the killer, *unless* the police find more evidence against Bedford. Therefore, I want her to have lots of rope so she can hang herself . . . but somehow she bothers me. The story she tells arouses my sympathy.'

'Don't start getting soft, Perry. She's a professional con woman. It's her business to make a sob-sister story sound reasonable. It's my guess she killed Denham. Don't shed any tears over her.'

'I won't shed any tears,' Mason said. 'And if she dusts out of here in a hurry I've just about got a verdict of not guilty in the bag for Stewart G. Bedford.'

15

Mason sat in the attorneys' room at the jail and looked across at Bedford.

'I presume,' he said, 'you had that hit-and-run thing all figured out so you could save your wife's good name and were willing to sacrifice yourself in order to keep her from becoming involved.'

Bedford nodded.

'Well, why the devil didn't you tell *me* what you were going to do?' Mason asked.

'I was afraid you'd disapprove.'

'How did you get the details?' Mason asked.

'I took care of that all right,' Bedford said. 'As it happens, it was a case that I knew something about. This old woman was related to one of my employees. The doctors had decided she needed rather an expensive operation. My employee didn't approach me on it, but he *did* tell the whole story to Elsa Griffin. She relayed it to me. I told her to see that the man was able to get an advance which would cover the cost of the operation, and then told her to raise his wages in thirty days so that the raise would just about take care of payments on the advance. Two nights later the old woman started to cross the street, apparently in sort of a daze, and someone hit her and hit her hard. They never did find out who it was.'

'Will your employee get suspicious?' Mason asked.

'I don't think so. The story was not told to me but to Elsa Griffin. Of course, that's one angle that I've got to take care of. Elsa will handle that for me.'

'Well, you've stuck your neck in the noose now,' Mason said.

'It's not so bad,' Bedford told him. 'As I understand it, a felony outlaws within three years, so they can't prosecute me on the hit-and-run charge because it's over three years ago. Don't you see, Mason? I simply *had* to have something that they could pin on me so there would be an excuse for me to be paying blackmail to Denham. Otherwise, the newspaper reporters would have started trying to find what it was that Denham had on me, and of course they'd have thought about my wife right away, started looking into her past, and then the whole ugly thing would have been out.

'In this way, I've covered my tracks in such a way that no one will ever think to investigate Mrs Bedford.'

'Let's hope so,' Mason told him.

'Now look, Mason. I think I know who killed Denham.'

'Who?'

'You remember that there was a woman prowling around the motel down there, a woman whose presence can't be accounted for.

'Now, I've got this thing figured out pretty well. Denham was a blackmailer. Someone decided that the only way out was to see that Denham was killed. The only way to kill him so that it wouldn't arouse suspicion and point directly to the person committing the murder was to wait until Denham was blackmailing someone else and then pull the job. In that way, it would be a perfect set-up. It would look as though the other person had done the job.'

'Go on,' Mason said.

'So, as I figure it, this woman was either shadowing Denham or had some way of knowing when Denham was pulling a job. She knew that he was blackmailing me. She followed Denham down to the motel. When he got the payment from me, she killed him.'

'With your gun?' Mason asked dryly.

'No, no, now wait–I'm coming to that. I tell you I've got the whole thing all figured out.'

'All right,' Mason said. 'How do you have it figured out?'

'Obviously she couldn't have followed Geraldine Corning and me down to the motel. In the first place, Geraldine took all sorts of precautions to keep from being followed, and in the second place, I was the one who picked the motel after she made up her mind that we weren't being followed. She said I could pick any motel I wanted, and I picked that one.'

'Okay,' Mason said. 'You're making sense so far.'

'All right. This woman knew, however, that Denham was getting ready to put the bite on another victim, so she started shadowing Denham. Denham drove down to the motel to pick up the money. She didn't have anything on him at that time. He went back and cashed the cheques. That was where this woman *knew* that Denham was on another job.

'So when Denham came back to tell Geraldine that the coast was clear, Geraldine left and the woman had her chance. She had to be hiding down there in the motel. Naturally, she couldn't hide right on the grounds, so she tried the doors of the adjoining units. It just happened that Elsa had left the door of twelve unlocked because she didn't have anything valuable in there. The woman slipped into unit twelve and used it as her headquarters. Then she must have killed Denham with *her* gun.

'After that she cased the place and found that I was lying there asleep, apparently drugged. My brief-case was on the floor. Naturally she got to wondering who I was and how it happened I was asleep, and she went through the brief-case. She saw the card giving my name and address in the brief-case and she found my gun in there. What better than for her to take out the gun and conceal it where it would never be found. In that way I would be taking the rap for Denham's murder.'

'Could be,' Mason said non-committally.

'Therefore, I want you to move heaven and earth to find that woman,' Bedford said. 'When we find her and get the *real* murder weapon, the ballistics experts can prove that it was the gun with which the murder was committed. Then we can find out what she did with my gun after the shooting.

'Can't you see the play, Mason? This woman prowler the manager saw in unit twelve is the key to the whole mystery.

'Now, I understand you sent Elsa back to the cabin to get fingerprints. Evidently our minds were working along the same lines. Elsa says she got some very good fingerprints of this woman, particularly a couple she got from a glass door-knob.'

'Of course, a lot of the prints were Elsa's,' Mason pointed out.

'I know. I know,' Bedford said impatiently. 'But some of them weren't. Elsa didn't even open the closet door. The two fingerprints on the knob simply *had* to be those of the woman.

'Now, this manager of the motel–whatever his name is–had a chance to talk with this woman. He saw her coming out of the motel, asked her what she was doing and all of that stuff. That makes him a valuable witness. I want you to have your men talk to him again and get the most minute description possible. Then you have these fingerprints to work on. Now damn it, Mason! Get busy on this thing and play it from that angle. It's a hunch I have.'

'I see,' Mason said.

Bedford said impatiently: 'Mason, I've got money. I've got lots of money. The sky is the limit in this thing. You get all the detectives in the city if you need 'em, but you find that woman. She's the one we want.'

'Suppose she did kill him with your gun?'

'She couldn't have. She shadowed Denham down there for one purpose, and only one purpose; she intended to kill him. She'd hardly intend to kill him with her bare hands.'

Mason said: 'Before we go all out on *that* theory, I'd like to be certain the murder wasn't committed with your gun. In order to prove that we need to have either the gun or some bullets that were fired from it. You don't know of any trees or stumps where you put up a target for practice, do you?'

'You mean so you can find some old bullets?'

'Yes.'

'No. I don't think I ever fired the gun.'

'How long have you had it?'

'Five or six years.'

'You signed a firearms register when you bought it?'

'I can't remember. I guess I must have.'

Mason said: 'I have another lead. I want you to keep it confidential.'

'What's that?'

'The blonde who was with you in the motel.'

'What about her?'

'She had the opportunity and the motive,' Mason pointed out. 'She is the really logical suspect.'

Bedford's face darkened. 'Mason, what's the matter with you? That girl was a good kid. She probably had knocked around but she wasn't the type to commit a murder.'

'How do you know?' Mason asked.

'Because I spent a day with her. She's a good kid. She was going to quit the racket.'

'That makes her all the more suspect,' Mason said. 'Suppose she told Binney Denham she was going to quit and he started putting on pressure. That left her with only one out. Binney must have had enough on her to crack the whip if she tried to get free.'

Bedford shook his head emphatically. 'You're all wet, Mason. Get after this woman in number twelve.'

'And,' Mason went on, 'we could convince a jury that the blonde would logically have taken the gun from your brief-case and used it, whereas any woman who was shadowing Binney, intending to kill him, would have had her own gun.'

'That's what I'm telling you.'

'So then, if you try to play it your way,' Mason went on, 'and the murder weapon does turn out to have been your gun, you're hooked.'

'You play it the way I'm telling you,' Bedford instructed. 'I have a hunch on this and I always play my hunches. After all, Mason, if I'm wrong it'll be my own funeral.'

'You may mean that figuratively,' Mason told him, getting up to go, 'but that's one thing you've said that's *really* true.'

16

Mason was yawning with weariness as he fitted a latch-key to the door of his private office and swung it open.

Della Street looked up from her secretarial desk, said: 'Hello, Chief. How's it coming?'

'I thought I told you to go home and go to bed.'

'I went home. I went to bed. I slept. I'm back and ready for another night session if necessary.'

Mason shuddered. 'Don't even think about it. One of those is enough to last me for quite a while.'

'That's because you're under such a strain. You can't relax in between times.'

'Today,' Mason told her, 'there haven't been any in-between times.'

'Paul Drake phoned while you were gone. He says he has something he thinks will prove interesting. He wants to come down and talk with you.'

'Give him a ring,' Mason said.

Della Street called Paul Drake, using the unlisted telephone, and not putting the call through the switchboard.

Mason tilted back in the swivel chair, closed his eyes, stretched his arms above his head and gave a prodigious yawn. 'The trouble with a case of this sort,' he said, 'is that you have to keep one jump ahead of the police, and the police don't go to bed. They work in shifts.'

Della Street nodded, heard Drake's tap on the panels of the door, and got up to open it for him.

'Hi, Paul,' Mason said. 'What's new?'

'You look all in,' Drake told him.

'I had a hard day yesterday, and then things really started coming pretty fast last night. How are the police doing?'

'The police,' Drake said, 'are jubilant.'

'How come?'

'They found some bit of evidence that makes them feel good.'

'What is it, Paul?'

'I can't find out, and neither can anyone else. They seem to think it's really something. However, that isn't what I wanted to see you about at the moment. I suppose you've heard that your client, Bedford, has made another statement.'

Mason groaned. 'I can't get back and forth fast enough to keep up with his statements. What's he said this time?'

'He told the reporters he wants an *immediate* trial, and the district attorney says that if Bedford isn't bluffing, he'll give it to him, that there's a date on the calendar reserved for a case which has just been continued. Because Bedford is a business-man and insists that his name must be cleared and all that stuff, it looks as though the presiding judge might go along with them.'

'Very nice,' Mason said sarcastically. 'Bedford never seems to think it's necessary to consult his lawyer before issuing these statements to the press.

'What about Harry Elston, Paul? Have you been able to get any line on him?'

'Not a thing, and the police haven't been able to,' Drake said. 'Elston opened that safe-deposit box about nine forty-five last night. He had a brief-case with him, and, as I said, no one knows whether he put in or took out, but police are now inclined to think he took out and *then* put in.'

'How come?'

'It was a joint lock-box in both names. Now there isn't a thing in there in the name of Harry Elston, but the box is jammed full of papers belonging to Binney Denham. They're papers that just aren't worth a hang, things that nobody would keep in a lock-box.'

'Some people keep strange things in lock-boxes,' Mason said.

'These are old letters, receipted statements, credit cards that have expired, automobile insurance that's expired, just a whole mess of junk that really isn't worth keeping, much less putting in a safe-deposit box.'

Mason pursed his lips thoughtfully.

'The point is,' Drake went on, 'that the lock-box is full–just so jam full that you couldn't get another letter in it. The police feel that the idea of this was to keep them from thinking anything had been taken *out*. They're pretty well convinced the lock-box was full of cash or negotiable securities, that Elston found out Denham was dead, cleaned out the box and put his stuff in it.'

'How'd he find out Denham was dead?' Mason asked.

'Well, for a while the police were very much interested in the answer to that one. Now they're not concerned any more. They think they have a dead open-and-shut case against Bedford. They think that any jury will convict him of first-degree murder. The D.A. says he hasn't decided whether he will ask for the death penalty as yet. He has stated that, while he will be ever mindful of the responsibilities of his office, he has never received any consideration from Bedford's counsel and sees no reason for extending any courtesies.'

Mason grinned. 'He wants to send my client to the gas-chamber in order to get even with me. Is that it?'

'He didn't express it that way in so many words, but you don't have to look too far in between the lines to gather his thought.'

'Nice guy!' Mason said. 'Anything else, Paul?'

'Yes. This is what I really wanted to see you about. I got a telephone call just before I came in here. The operative who was shadowing Grace Compton only had time for a brief telephone call. He's at the airport. Our blonde friend is headed for Acapulco, Mexico. I guess she wants to do a little swimming. My operative is keeping her under surveillance. He has a seat on the same plane. He didn't have time to talk. He just gave me a flash.'

'What did you tell him?'

'Told him to go to Acapulco.'

'When are they leaving?'

'There's a plane for Mexico City leaving at eight-thirty.'

Mason looked at his watch. 'And she's down at the airport already?'

Drake nodded.

'What the devil is she doing waiting down there?'

'Darned if I know,' Drake said.

'How has she disguised herself?' Mason asked.

'How did you know about the disguise?' Drake exclaimed. 'I hadn't mentioned it.'

'Figure it out for yourself, Paul. She knows that police have a pretty damn good description of her. She knows that they're looking for her. When the police are looking for someone, they're pretty apt to keep the airport under surveillance. Therefore, if Grace Compton was going to Acapulco, Mexico, the logical thing would be for her to stay in her apartment until the last minute, then dash out and make a run to get aboard the plane. Every minute that she's hanging around that airport makes it that much more dangerous for her. Therefore she must have resorted to some sort of disguise which she feels will be a complete protection.'

'Well,' Drake said, 'you hit the nail right on the head that time, Perry. She's disguised so that no one's going to recognize her.'

Mason raised his eyebrows. 'How, Paul?'

Drake said: 'I don't know the details. The only thing I know is that my man told me she was disguised, that if he hadn't followed her and seen her go through the transformation, he wouldn't be able to recognize her. You see, he had time for a flash but no details. He says she's waiting to take the plane to Acapulco, and that's all I know.'

'He'll call in again?' Mason asked.

'Whenever he gets a chance he phones in a report.'

'He's one of your regular operatives?'

'Yes.'

'Do you suppose he knows Della Street?'

'I think he does, Perry. He's been up and down in the elevator a thousand times.'

Mason turned to Della Street. 'Go on down to the airport, Della. Get a cab. Paul's operative will probably phone in before you get there. See if you can contact him. Describe him, Paul.'

Drake said: 'He's fifty-two. He used to have red hair. It's turning kind of a pink now and he's bald on top, but Della won't see that because he wears a grey hat with the brim pulled fairly well down. He's a slender man, about five foot seven, weight about a hundred and thirty-five pounds. He goes for grey, wears a grey suit, a grey tie, a grey hat. He has grey eyes, and he's the sort of guy you can look directly at and still not see.'

'I'll find him,' Della Street said.

'Not by looking for him,' Drake said. 'He's the most inconspicuous guy on earth.'

'All right,' Della said, laughing, 'I'll be looking for the most inconspicuous guy on earth. What do I do after that, Chief?'

Mason said: 'You get this girl spotted. Try to engage her in conversation. Don't be obvious about it. Let her make the first break if possible. Sit down beside her and start sobbing in a handkerchief. Be in trouble yourself. If she's frightened that may make her feel she has a bond in common with you.'

'What am I going to be sobbing about?' Della Street asked.

Mason said: 'Your boy friend was to have flown down from San Francisco. He's stood you up. You're waiting, watching plane after plane.'

'Okay,' Della said. 'I'm on my way.'

'Got plenty of money for expenses?'

'I think so.'

'Go to the safe and take out three hundred bucks,' Mason said.

'Gosh! Am I supposed to go to Acapulco too?'

'I'm darned if I know,' Mason told her. 'If she gives you a tumble and starts confiding in you, stay with her as long as she's talking. If that means getting on a plane, get on a plane.'

Della Street hurried to the emergency cash drawer in the safe, took out some money, pushed it down in her purse, grabbed her hat and coat, said: 'I'm on my way, Chief.'

'Phone in if you get a chance,' Mason said. 'Use the unlisted telephone.'

When she had gone, Mason turned to Paul Drake. 'Now let's find out about this girl's apartment, Paul.'

'What about it?'

'Did she give it up or simply close it and lock it?'

'Gosh! I don't know,' Drake said.

'Find out, and when you find out let me know. If she's given up the apartment, and it's for rent, get a couple of good operatives whom you can trust, a man and woman. Have them pose as a married couple looking for an apartment. Pay a deposit to hold the place, or do anything necessary so they can get in there and dust for fingerprints.'

'You want some of this girl's prints?'

Mason nodded.

'Why?'

'So I can show them to the police.'

'The best way to get them,' Drake said, 'would be to give the police a tip on what's happening.'

Mason shook his head.

'Why not?' Drake asked. 'After all, they have her fingerprints. They have them from the car and from the motel and–'

'And they're building up a case against Stewart Bedford,' Mason said. 'They wouldn't do a thing to this girl now. They'd think she was a red herring I was drawing across the trail. For another thing I want the prints of someone else who must have been in that apartment. However, the main reason I don't want the police in on it is that I don't dare risk the legal status of what's happening.'

'What's the legal status of what's happening?'

'A killer is resorting to flight,' Mason said.

Drake frowned. 'You got enough evidence to convict her of murder, Perry, even if you have evidence of flight?'

Mason said: 'I don't want to *convict* her of murder, Paul. I want to acquit Stewart G. Bedford of murder. See what you can do about getting fingerprints and be sure to tell your man to watch out for Della Street. I have a feeling that we're beginning to get somewhere.'

17

It was seven o'clock when Della Street made her report over the unlisted telephone.

'I'm in a booth out here at the airport, Chief. I haven't been able to get to first base with her.'

'Did you contact Drake's man?' Mason asked.

'Yes, that is, he contacted me. Paul certainly described him all right. I was looking all around for an inconspicuous man and not being able to find him, and then something kept rubbing against me, and it was the elbow of the man standing next to me at the news-stand. I moved away and then suddenly I looked at him and knew that was the man.'

'And you picked out Grace Compton?' Mason asked.

'He did. She'd have fooled me.'

'What's she done?' Mason asked.

'Well, she has on dark glasses, the biggest lensed, darkest dark glasses I've ever seen. Her hair is in strings. She's wearing a maternity outfit with–'

'A maternity outfit!' Mason exclaimed.

'That's right,' Della Street said. 'With a little padding and the proper kind of an outfit a girl with a good figure can do wonders.'

'And you couldn't get anywhere with her?'

'Nowhere,' Della Street said. 'I've sobbed into my handkerchief. I've made every approach I could think of that wouldn't be recognized as an approach. I've got precisely nowhere.'

'Anything else?' Mason asked.

'Yes. When she got slowly up and started for the rest-room, I made a point of beating her to it. I knew where she was heading, so I was in there first. I found out one reason why she's wearing those heavy dark glasses.

'That girl has had a beautiful beating. One eye is discoloured so badly that the bruise would show below the edge of the dark glasses if she didn't keep it covered. She stood in front of a mirror and put flesh-coloured grease-paint on her cheek. I could see then that her mouth is swollen and–'

'And you're not getting anywhere?' Mason asked.

'Not with any build-up I can think of. No.'

Mason said: 'Go out and contact Drake's man, Della. Tell him that you'll take over the watching job while he calls me. Have him call me on this phone. Give him the unlisted number. Tell him to call at once. You keep your eye on the subject while he's doing it.'

'Okay, I'll contact him right away, but I'd better not be seen talking to him.

I'll scribble a note and slip it to him.'

'That's fine,' Mason said. 'Be darn certain you're not caught at it. Remember, that's one bad thing about dark glasses. You can never tell where a person's eyes are looking.'

'I'll handle it all right,' she said, 'and you can trust Drake's man. He can brush past you and pick up a note without anyone having the least idea of what's happened. He looks like a mild-mannered, shy, retiring, hen-pecked husband who's out for the first time without his wife, and is afraid of his own shadow.'

'Okay,' Mason said. 'Get on the job. Now, Della, after this man telephones me and comes back out of the phone-booth, grab a cab and come on back to the office.'

'What a short-lived vacation!' she said. 'I was thinking of a two-weeks' stay in Acapulco.'

'You should have got her talking then. I can't pay out my client's money to have you sob your way down to Mexico unless you get results.'

'My sobbing left her as cold and hard as a cement sidewalk,' she said. 'I should have tried a maternity outfit and the pregnancy approach. I can tell you one thing, Chief, that woman is scared stiff.'

'She should be,' Mason said. 'Get Paul's man to phone, Della.'

Some five minutes later Mason's unlisted phone rang. The lawyer picked up the receiver, said: 'Hello,' and a man's voice talking in a low, drab monotone, said: 'This is Drake's man, Mr Mason. You wanted me?'

'Yes. How did she work the diguise?'

'She came out of her apartment wearing a veil and heavy dark glasses. She got in a taxi-cab, went to the Siesta Arms Apartment House. She went inside. I couldn't see where she went, but I managed to butt my car into the rear end of the waiting taxi, got out and apologized profusely, got the guy in conversation gave him five dollars to cover any damage that might have been sustained, which of course was jake with him because there wasn't any. He told me that he was waiting for a fare who had gone upstairs to pack up for her sister, that her sister was pregnant and was going to the airport to take a plane to San Francisco. This sister was to pick up the cab.'

'Okay, then what happened?' Mason asked.

'Well, I waited there at the apartment house, right back of the cab. This woman didn't suspect a thing. When she came out, I would sure have been fooled if it wasn't for her shoes. She was wearing alligator skin shoes when she went in, and despite all the maternity disguise, she was wearing those same shoes when she came out. I let the cab-driver take off, and I loafed along way, way behind, because I was pretty sure where they were going.'

'They went to the airport?'

'That's right.'

'And then what?'

'This woman got a tourist permit, bought a ticket to Acapulco, and checked the baggage. When she went down there she didn't have any more idea when the next plane was leaving than I did. She just sat down to wait for the next plane to Mexico City.'

'She isn't suspicious?'

'Not a bit.'

'Ride along on the same plane with her, just to make sure she doesn't try to disguise her appearance again. You'll be met in Mexico City by Paul Drake's correspondents there. You can work with them and they'll work with you. They know the ropes, speak the language, and have all the official pull they need. It will be better to handle it that way than for you to try and handle it alone.'

'Okay, thanks.'

'Now get this,' Mason said. 'This is important! You saw Paul Drake and me when we went up to call on Grace Compton?'

'That's right.'

'You saw her when she came out?'

'Yes.'

'She didn't come out and go anywhere between the time Drake and I left and the time she came out with the baggage and got the taxi-cab?'

'That's right.'

'How much traffic was there in and out of that apartment building?'

'Quite a bit.'

Mason said: 'Some man went in. I'd like very much to spot him.'

'Do you know what he looked like?'

'I haven't the faintest idea as yet,' Mason said, 'but I may have later. I'm wondering if you could recognize such a man if I dug him up. Could you?'

The expressionless voice, still in the same drab monotone, said: 'Hell, no! I'm not a human adding machine. I was there to watch that blonde and see that she didn't give us the slip. Nobody told me to–'

'That's all right,' Mason interrupted. 'I was just trying to find out. That's all.'

'If you'd told me, then I might have–'

'No, no, it's all right.'

'Okay, anything else?'

'That's all,' Mason said. 'Have a good time.'

For the first time there was expression in the man's voice. 'Don't kid yourself, I won't!' he said.

When Della Street returned to the office, she found Perry Mason pacing the floor.

'What's the problem?' she asked.

Mason said: 'I've got some cards. I've got to play them just right to be sure that each one of them takes a trick. I don't want to play into the hands of the prosecution so they can put trumps on my aces.'

'Do they have that many trumps?' Della Street asked.

'In a criminal case,' Mason said, 'the prosecution has *all* the trumps.'

Mason resumed his pacing of the floor, and had been pacing for some five minutes, when Drake's code knock sounded on the panel of the exit door.

Mason nodded to Della Street.

She opened the door. Drake came in and said: 'Well, you had the right hunch, Perry. The babe's rent was up on the tenth. She told them there had been a change of plans because her sister expected to be confined in San Francisco and was having trouble. She said she had to leave for San Francisco almost immediately. She left money for the cleaning charges and all that, and told the landlady how sorry she was.'

'Wait a minute,' Mason said. 'Was this a face-to-face conversation or–?'

'No, she talked with the landlady on the telephone,' Drake answered.

Mason said: 'Some fellow gave her a working over. I'd sure like to find out who it was.'

'Well,' Drake said, 'I put my operatives on the job and they tied up the apartment. They gave the landlady a fifty-dollar deposit, told her they wanted to stay in there and get the feel of the place for a while. She said to stay as long as they wanted.

'So they went all over the place for fingerprints and lifted everything they could find. Then they cleaned the place off so that no one could tell lifts had been made.'

'How many lifts?' Mason asked.

Drake pulled an envelope out of his pocket. 'They're all on these cards,' he said. 'Forty-eight of them.'

Mason shuffled through the cards. 'How are they identified, Paul?'

'Numbered lightly in pencil on the back.'

'Pencil?'

'That's right. We ink the pencil in afterwards before we go to court. But just in case there are two or three prints you wouldn't want to use, you can change the numbers when they're written in pencil. In that way, when you get to court your numbers are all in consecutive order. Otherwise, you might get into court and have prints from one to eight inclusive, then a gap of three or four prints, and then another set of consecutive numbers. That would be an invitation to opposing counsel to demand the missing fingerprints and raise hell generally.'

'I see,' Mason said.

'Well, that's it,' Drake told him. 'We've got our deposit up on the apartment. It won't be touched until the fifteenth. Now then, do you want the police to get a tip?'

'Not yet!' Not yet!' Mason said.

'With that babe down in Acapulco, you may have trouble getting the evidence you want,' Drake said.

Mason grinned. 'I already have it, Paul.'

Drake heaved himself up out of the chair. 'Well, I hope you don't get another brain storm along about midnight tonight. See you tomorrow, Perry.'

'Be seeing you,' Mason said.

Della Street looked at Mason in puzzled perplexity. 'You've got the expression of the cat that has just found the open jar of whipping cream,' she said.

Mason said 'Go to the safe, Della. Get the fingerprints that Elsa Griffin got from that motel unit number twelve.'

Della Street brought in the envelopes.

'Two sets,' she said. 'One of them the prints that were found to be those of Elsa Griffin, and the others are four that are prints of a stranger. These four are on numbered cards. The numbers are fourteen, sixteen, nine, and twelve respectively.'

Mason nodded, busied himself with the cards Drake had handed him.

'All right, Della, make a note,' he said.

'What is it?'

'Pencil number seven on Drake's list is being given an inked number fourteen. Number three on Drake's list given an inked number sixteen. Number nineteen on Drake's list given a number nine. Number thirty on Drake's list given the number twelve in ink. You got that?'

She nodded.

'All right,' Mason said. 'Take these cards and write the numbers in order on them–fourteen, sixteen, nine, and twelve. I want it in a woman's handwriting, and, while I wouldn't think of asking you to commit forgery, I'd certainly like to have the numbers as near a match for the numbers on these other cards as we can possibly make it.'

'Why, Chief,' Della Street said, 'that's–Why those are the numbers of the significant lifted prints from unit twelve down there at the motel.'

'Exactly,' Mason said. 'And as soon as you have these numbers copied on the cards, Della, you'll remember to produce them whenever I ask for latent prints on cards fourteen, sixteen, nine, and twelve.'

'But, Chief, you can't do that!'

'Why not?'

'Why, that's substituting evidence!'

'Evidence of what?'

'Why, it's evidence of the person who was in that cottage. It's evidence that Mrs–'

'Careful,' Mason said. 'No names.'

'Well, it's evidence that the person was actually in that unit.'

'How very interesting!' Mason said.

Della Street looked at him in startled consternation. 'Chief, you can't do that! Don't you see what you're doing? You're just changing things all around. Why . . . Why–!'

'*What* am I doing?' Mason asked.

'Why, you're numbering those cards fourteen, sixteen, nine, and twelve and putting them in that envelope and Elsa Griffin–Why, she'll take the numbers on those cards, compare them with her notes and say that print number fourteen came from the glass door-knob and . . . well, in place of the person who was in there being there, it will mean that this blonde was in there instead.'

Mason grinned. 'And since the police have a whole flock of the blonde's fingerprints they'd have the devil of a time saying they didn't know who it was.'

'But,' Della Street protested, 'then they would accuse Grace Compton of being the one who was in unit twelve when . . . when she wouldn't have been there at all.'

'How do you know she wasn't there?' Mason asked.

'Well, her fingerprints weren't there.'

Mason merely smiled.

'Chief, isn't . . . isn't there a law against that?'

'A law against what?'

'Destroying evidence.'

'I haven't destroyed anything,' Mason said.

'Well, switching things around. Isn't it against the law to show a witness a false–?'

'What's false about it?' Mason asked.

'It's a substitution. It's shuffling everything all around. It's–'

'There's nothing false about it,' Mason said. 'Each print is a true and correct fingerprint. I haven't altered the print any.'

'But you've altered the numbers on the cards.'

'Not at all,' Mason said. 'Drake told us that he put temporary pencil numbers on the cards so that it would be possible to ink in the numbers that we wanted.'

Della Street said: 'Well, you're practising a deception on Elsa Griffin.'

'I haven't said anything to Elsa Griffin.'

'Well, you will if you show her these prints as being the ones that she took from that unit number twelve.'

'If I don't *tell* her those were the prints that came from unit number twelve, I wouldn't be practising any deception. Furthermore, how the devil do we know that these prints are evidence?'

Della Street said: 'Chief, *please* don't! You're getting way out on the end of a limb. In order to try and save Mrs . . . well, you know who I mean if you don't want me to mention names. In order to save her, you're putting your neck in a noose and you're . . . you're *planting* evidence on that Compton girl.'

Mason grinned. 'Come on, Della, quit worrying about it. I'm the one that's taking the chances.'

'I'll say you are.'

'Get your hat,' Mason told her. 'I'll buy you a good steak dinner and then you can go home and get some sleep.'

'What are *you* going to do?'

'Oh, I may as well go to bed myself. I think we're going to give Hamilton Burger a headache.'

'But, Chief,' Della said, 'it's substituting evidence! Faking evidence! It's putting a false label on evidence! It's–'

'You forget,' Mason said, 'that we still have the original prints which were given us by Elsa Griffin. They will have the original numbers which she put on them. We've taken other prints and given them other numbers. That's our privilege. We can number those prints any way we want to. If by coincidence the numbers are the same, that's no crime. Come on. You're worrying too much.'

18

Judge Harmon Strouse looked down at the defence counsel table at Perry Mason, Mason's client, Stewart G. Bedford, seated beside him, and immediately behind Bedford a uniformed officer.

'The peremptory challenge is with the defence,' Judge Strouse said.

'The defence passes,' Mason said.

Judge Strouse glanced at Hamilton Burger, the barrel-chester, bull-necked district attorney whose vendetta with Perry Mason was well known.

'The prosecution is quite satisfied with the jury,' Hamilton Burger snapped.

Very well,' Judge Strouse said. 'The jurors will stand and be sworn to try the case.'

Bedford leaned forward to whisper to Mason. 'Well, now at least we'll know what they have against me,' he said, 'and what we have to fight. The evidence they presented before the grand jury was just barely sufficient to get an indictment, and that's all. They're purposely leaving me in the dark.'

Mason nodded.

Hamilton Burger arose and said: 'I am going to make a somewhat unprecedented move, Your Honour. This is an intelligent jury. It doesn't have to be told what I am going to try to do. I am waiving my opening statement. I will call as my first witness Thomas G. Farland.'

Farland, being sworn, testified that he was a police officer, that on the sixth day of April he had been instructed to go to The Staylonger Motel, that he had met the manager there, a man named Morrison Brems, that he had exhibited his credentials, had stated that he wished to look in unit sixteen, that he had gone to unit sixteen and had there found a body lying on the floor. The body was that of a man who had apparently been shot, and the witness had promptly notified the Homicide Squad, which had in due time arrived with a deputy coroner, fingerprint experts, etc., that the witness had waited until the Homicide Squad arrived.

'Cross-examine!' Hamilton Burger snapped.

'How did you happen to go to the motel?' Mason asked.

'I was instructed.'

'By whom?'

'By communications.'

'In what way?'

'The call came over the radio.'

'And what was said in the call?'

'Objected to as incompetent, irrelevant, and immaterial. Not proper cross-examination and hearsay,' Hamilton Burger said.

Mason said: 'The witness testified that he was "instructed" to go to unit sixteen. Under the familiar rule that whenever a part of a conversation is brought out in direct examination the cross-examiner can show the entire conversation, I want to know what was said when the instructions were given to him.'

'It's hearsay,' Hamilton Burger said.

'It's a conversation,' Mason said, smiling.

'The objection is overruled,' Judge Strouse said. 'The witness, having testified to part of the conversation, may relate it all on cross-examination.'

'Well,' Farland said, 'it was just that I was to go to the motel, that's all.'

'Anything said about what you might find there?'

'Yes.'

'What?'

'A body.'

'Anything said about how the announcer knew there was a body there?'

'He said it had been reported.'

'Anything said about *how* it had been reported?'

'He said an anonymous telephone tip.'

'Anything said about who gave the anonymous tip–whether it was a man's voice or a woman's voice?'

The witness hesitated.

'Yes or no?' Mason said.

'Yes,' he said. 'It was a woman's voice.'

'Thank you,' Mason said with exaggerated politeness. 'That's all.'

Hamilton Burger put a succession of routine witnesses on the stand, witnesses showing that the dead man had been identified as Binney Denham, that a .38 calibre bullet had fallen from the front of Denham's coat when the body was moved.

'Morrison Brems will be my next witness,' Hamilton Burger said.

When Brems came forward and was sworn, Hamilton Burger nodded to

Vincent Hadley, the assistant district attorney who sat on his left, and Hadley, a suave, polished court-room strategist, examined the manager of the motel, bringing out the fact that on April sixth, some time around eleven o'clock in the morning, the defendant, accompanied by a young woman, had stopped at his motel; that the defendant had told him he was to be joined by another couple from San Diego; that they wished two units; that the witness had suggested to the defendant it would be better to wait for the other couple to arrive and let them register, in which event they would be paying only for their half of the motel unit. However, the defendant had insisted on paying the whole charge and having immediate occupancy of the double.

'Under what name did the defendant register?' Vincey Hadley asked.

'Under the name of S. G. Wilfred.'

'And wife?' Hadley asked.

'*And* wife.'

'Then what happened?' Hadley asked.

'Well, I didn't pay too much attention to them after that. Of course, looking the situation over and the way it had been put up to me, I thought–'

'Never mind what you thought,' Hadley interrupted. 'Just tell us what happened, what you observed, what you saw, what was said to you by the defendant, or by others in the presence of the defendant.'

'Well, just where do you want me to begin?'

'Just answer the question. What happened next?'

'They were in there for a while, and then the girl–'

'Now, by the girl, are you referring to Mrs Wilfred?'

'Well, of course she wasn't any Mrs Wilfred.'

'You don't *know* that,' Hadley said. 'She *registered* as Mrs Wilfred, didn't she?'

'Well, the defendant here registered her as Mrs Wilfred.'

'All right. Call her Mrs Wilfred then. What happened next?'

'Well, Mrs Wilfred went out twice. The first time she went around to the outer door of unit fifteen and I thought she was going in that way, but–'

'Never mind what you thought. What did she *do*?'

'I know she locked him in, but I can't swear I saw the key turn in the lock, so I suppose you won't let me say a thing about that. Then after she'd done whatever it was she was doing, she went to the car and got out some baggage. She took that in to unit sixteen. Then a short time later she came out and went to the glove compartment of the car. I don't know how long she was there that time because I was called away and didn't get back for half an hour or so.

'Then quite a while later they both left the place, got in the car and drove away.'

'Now just a minute,' Hadley said. 'Prior to the time that you saw them drive away, had anyone else been near the car?'

'That I just can't swear to,' Brems said.

'Then *don't* swear to it,' Hadley said. 'Just tell us what you know and what you saw.'

'Well, I saw a beat-up sort of car parked down there by unit sixteen for a few minutes. I thought it was this other couple that had–'

'What did you *see*?'

'Well, I just saw this car parked there for a spell. After a while it drove away.'

'Now the *car* didn't drive out. Someone must have driven it out.'

'That's right.'

'Do you know the person who was driving that car?'

'I didn't then. I do now.'

'Who was it?'

'This here Mr Denham–the man who was found dead.'

'You saw his face?'

'Yes.'

'Did he stop?'

'No, sir.'

'He didn't stop when he drove his car out?'

'No, sir.'

'Did he stop when he went in?'

'No, sir.'

'All right. Now try to remember everything as you go along. What happened after that?'

'Well, of course I've got other things to do. I've got a whole motel to manage down there, and I can't just keep looking–'

'Just tell us what you saw, Mr Brems. We don't expect you to tell us everything that happened. Only what *you saw.*'

'Well, the defendant and this girl–'

'You mean the one who had registered as Mrs Wilfred?'

'Yes, that's the one.'

'All right. What did they do?'

'They were out for quite a while. Then they came back in. I guess it was pretty late in the afternoon. I didn't look to get the exact time. They drove into the garage between the two units–'

'Now, just before that,' Hadley interrupted. 'While they were gone, did you have occasion to go down to the unit?'

'Well, yes, I did.'

'What was the occasion?'

'I was checking up.'

'Why?'

'Well . . . well, you see, when couples like that come in . . . well, we have three rates–our regular customer rate, our tourist rate, and our transient rate.

'Now, take a couple like this. We charge 'em about double the regular rates. Whenever they go out we check the units to see whether they're coming back or not.'

'If they've left luggage, we look at it a bit if it's open. Sometimes if it isn't locked, we open it. Running a motel that way you have to cater to the temporary transients if you're going to stay in business, but you get high rates for doing it and usually a big turnover.

'Anyhow, it isn't the sort of trade you like, and whenever the people go out, you go in and look around.'

'And that's why you went in?'

'Yes, sir.'

'And what did you do?'

'I tried the door of unit fifteen and it was locked. I tried the door of unit sixteen and *it* was locked.'

'What did you do?'

'I opened the door with a pass-key and went in.'

'Which door?'

'Unit sixteen.'

'What, if anything, did you find?'

'I found that the girl . . . that is, this Mrs Wilfred . . . had a suitcase and a bag in unit sixteen and that the man had a brief-case in unit fifteen.'

'Did you look in the brief-case?'

'I did.'

'What did you see in it?'

'I saw a revolver.'

'Did you look at the revolver?'

'Only in the brief-case. I didn't want to touch it. I just saw it was a revolver and let it go at that, but I decided right then and there I'd better–'

'Never mind what you thought or what you decided. I'm asking you what you *did,* what you saw,' Hadley said. 'Now, let us get back to what happened after that.'

'Yes, sir.'

'Did you see the defendant again?'

'Yes, sir. He and this . . . this woman . . . this Mrs Wilfred got back to the motel along late in the afternoon. They went inside and I didn't pay any more attention to them. I had some other things to do. Then I saw a car driving out somewhere around eight o'clock, I guess it was. Maybe a little after eight. I took a look at it and I saw it was this car the defendant had been driving, and this woman was in it. I didn't get a real good look at her, but somehow I didn't think anybody else was in that car with her.'

'Had you heard anything unusual?'

'Personally, I didn't hear a thing. Some of the people in other parts of the motel did.'

'Never mind that. I'm talking now about you personally. Did *you* hear anything unusual.'

'No, sir.'

'And you so reported to the police when they questioned you?'

'That's right.'

'When did you next have occasion to go to either unit fifteen or sixteen?'

'When this police officer came to me and said he wanted to go in.'

'So what did you do then?'

'I got my pass-key and went to the door of unit sixteen.'

'Was the door locked?'

'No, sir. As a matter of fact, it wasn't.'

'What happened?'

'I opened the door.'

'And what did you see?'

'I saw the body of this man–the one they said was Binney Denham–lying sprawled there on the floor, with a pool of blood all around it.'

'Did you look in unit fifteen?'

'Yes, sir.'

'How did you get in there?'

'We went back out of the door of unit sixteen and I tried the door of unit fifteen.'

'Was it locked?'

'No, sir, it was unlocked.'

'Was the defendant in there?'

'Not when we went in. He was gone.'

'Was his brief-case there?'

'No, sir.'

'Did either the defendant or the woman who was registered by the defendant as his wife return to your motel later on?.

'No, sir.'

'Did you subsequently accompany some of the authorities to the back of your lot?'

'Yes, sir. You could see his tracks going–'

'Now wait just a moment. I'm coming to that. What is in the back of your lot?'

'A barbed wire fence.'

'What is the nature of the soil?'

'A soft, loam type of soil when it's wet. It gets pretty hard in the summer-time when the sun shines on it and it bakes dry. It's a regular California adobe.'

'What was the condition of this soil on the night of April sixth?'

'Soft.'

'Would it take the imprint of a man's foot?'

'Yes, sir, it sure would.'

'Did you observe any such imprints when you took the authorities to the back of the lot?'

'Yes, sir.'

'Are you acquainted with Lieutenant Tragg?'

'Yes, sir.'

'Did you point out these tracks to Lieutenant Tragg?'

'I pointed out the route to him. *He* pointed out the tracks to *me.*'

'And then what, if anything, did Lieutenant Tragg do?'

'Well, he went to the barbed wire fence right where the tracks showed somebody'd gone through the fence, and he found some threads. Some of the barbs on the barbed wire were pretty rusty and threads of cloth would stick easy.'

'Now from the time you saw Binney Denham, with his automobile which you have referred to as a rather beat-up car, near unit sixteen earlier in the day, did you see Mr Denham again?'

'Not until I saw him lying there on the floor dead.'

'Your motel is open to the public?'

'Sure. That's the idea of it.'

'Mr Denham could have come and gone without your seeing him?'

'Sure.'

'You may cross-examine,' Hadley said.

Mason said: 'As far as you know, Denham could have gone into that unit sixteen right after the woman you have referred to as Mrs Wilfred left, could he not?'

'Yes.'

'Without you seeing him?'

'Yes.'

'That's readily possible?'

'Sure it is. I look up when people drive in with automobiles and act like they're going to stop at the office, but I don't pay attention to people who come in and go direct to the cabins. I mean by that, if they drive right on by the office sign, I don't pay them any mind. I'm making a living renting units in a motel. I don't aim to pry into the lives of the people who rent those units.'

'That's very commendable,' Mason said. 'Now, you rented other units in the motel during the day and evening, did you not?'

'Yes, sir.'

'On the evening of April sixth and during the day of April seventh, did you assist the police in looking around for a gun?'

'Objected to as incompetent, irrelevant, and immaterial, not proper cross-examination,' Hadley said, and then, getting to his feet, added: 'If the Court please, we have asked this witness nothing of what he did on April seventh. We have only asked him about what took place on April sixth.'

'I think, under the circumstances, the morning of April seventh would be too remote,' Judge Strouse ruled. 'The objection is sustained.'

'Did you ever see that gun again?' Mason asked.

'I object to that as not proper cross-examination,' Hadley said. 'As far as the question is concerned, he may have seen it a week later. The direct examination of this witness was confined to April sixth.'

'I'll sustain the objection,' Judge Strouse ruled.

'Referring to the afternoon and evening of April sixth,' Mason said, 'did you notice anything else that was unusual?'

Brems shook his head. 'No, sir.'

Bedford leaned forward and whispered to Mason: 'Pin him down. Make him tell about that prowler. Let's get a description. We've simply got to find who she is!'

'You noticed Binney Denham at the motel,' Mason said.

'Yes, sir. That's right.'

'And you knew that he wasn't registered in any unit?'

'Yes, sir.'

'In other words, he was a stranger.'

'Yes, sir. But you've got to remember, Mr Mason, that I couldn't really tell for sure he wasn't in any unit. You see, this defendant here had taken two units and paid for them. He told me another couple from San Diego was coming up to join him. I had no way of knowing this here Denham wasn't the person he had had in mind.'

'I understand,' Mason said. 'That accounts for the presence of Mr Denham. Now, did you notice any *other* persons whom we might call unauthorized persons around the motel that day?'

'No, sir.'

'Wasn't there someone in unit twelve?'

Brems thought for a minute, started to shake his head, then said: 'Oh, wait a minute. Yes, I reported to the police–'

'Never mind what you reported to the police,' Hadley interrupted. 'Just listen to the questions and answer only the questions. Don't volunteer information.'

'Well, there *was* a person I didn't place at the time, but it turned out to be all right later.'

'Some person who was an unauthorized occupant of one of the motel units?'

'Objected to as calling for a conclusion of the witness and argumentative,' Hadley said.

'This is cross-examination,' Mason said.

'I think the word "unauthorized" technically calls for the conclusion of the witness. However, I'm going to permit the question,' Judge Strouse said. 'The defence will be given the utmost latitude in the cross-examination of witnesses, particularly those witnesses whose direct examination covers persons who were present prior to the commission of this crime.'

'Very well,' Hadley said. 'I'll withdraw the objection, Your Honour, just to keep the record straight. Answer the question, Mr Brems.'

'Well, I'll say this. A woman came out of unit twelve. She wasn't the woman who had rented the unit. I talked to her because I thought . . . well, I guess I'm not allowed to tell what I thought. But I talked to her.'

'What did you talk to her about?' Mason asked.

'I questioned her.'

'And what did she say?'

'Now there, Your Honour,' Hadley said, 'we are getting into something that is not only beyond the scope of cross-examination, but calls for hearsay evidence.'

'The objection is sustained,' Judge Strouse ruled.

'What did you ask her?' Mason asked.

'Same objection!' Hadley said.

'Same ruling.'

Mason turned to Bedford and whispered: 'You see, we're up against a whole series of technicalities there, Bedford. I can't question this witness about any conversation he had with her.'

'But we've got to find out who she was. Keep after it. Don't let them run you up a blind alley, Mason. You're a resourceful lawyer. Fix your question so the judge has to let it in. We've *got* to know who she was.'

'You say this woman who came out of unit twelve had not rented unit twelve?'

'That's right.'

'And you stopped her?'

'Yes.'

'And did you report this woman to the police?'

'Objected to. Not proper cross-examination. Incompetent, irrelevant, and immaterial,' Hadley said.

'Sustained,' Judge Strouse said.

'You have testified to a conversation you had with the police,' Mason said.

'Well, of course, when things got coming to a head they wanted to know all about what had happened around the place. That was after they asked if they could look in unit sixteen to investigate a report they had had. I told them that they were welcome to go right ahead.'

'All right,' Mason said. 'Now, as a part of that same conversation, did the police ask you if you had noticed any other prowlers during the afternoon or evening?'

'Objected to as incompetent, irrelevant, and immaterial, not proper cross-examination and hearsay,' Hadley said.

Judge Strouse smiled. 'Mr Mason is now again invoking the rule that where part of a conversation has been brought out in direct examination, the entire conversation may be brought out on cross-examination. The witness may answer the question.'

'Why, for the most part they kept asking me whether I'd heard any sound of a shot.'

'I'm not talking about their primary interest,' Mason said. 'I'm asking if they inquired of you as to whether you had noticed any prowlers during the afternoon or evening.'

'Yes, sir, they did.'

'And did you then tell them, as a part of that conversation, about this woman whom you had seen in unit twelve?'

'Yes, sir.'

'And what did you tell them?'

'Oh, Your Honour,' Hadley said, 'this is opening a door that is going to lead into matters which will confuse the issues. It has absolutely nothing to do with the case. We have no objection to Mr Mason making Mr Brems his own witness, if he wants to.

'He can then ask him any questions he wants, subject, of course, to our objection that the evidence is incompetent, irrelevant, and immaterial.'

'He doesn't have to make Mr Brems his own witness,' Judge Strouse ruled. 'You have asked this witness on direct examination about a conversation he had with officers.'

'Not a conversation. I simply asked him as to the effect of that conversation. Mr Mason could have objected, if he had wanted to, on the ground that the question called for a conclusion of the witness.'

'He didn't want to,' Judge Strouse said genially. 'The legal effect is the same whether you ask the witness for his conclusion as to the conversation or whether you ask him to repeat the conversation word for word. The subject of the conversation came in on direct evidence. Mr Mason can now have the entire conversation on cross-examination if he wants.'

'But this isn't related to the subject that the police were interested in,' Hadley objected. 'It doesn't have anything to do with the crime.'

'How do you know it doesn't?' Judge Strouse asked.

'Because we know what happened.'

Judge Strouse said: 'Mr Mason may have *his* theory as to what happened. The Court is going to give the defendant the benefit of the widest latitude in all matters pertaining to cross-examination. The witness may answer to the question.'

'Go on,' Mason said. 'What did you tell the officers about the woman in unit twelve?'

'I told them there'd been a prowler in the unit.'

'Did you use the word "prowler"?'

'I have the idea I did.'

'And what else did you tell them?'

'I told them about talking with this woman.'

'Did you tell them what the woman said?'

'Here again, Your Honour, I must object,' Hadley said. 'This is asking for hearsay evidence as to hearsay evidence. We are now getting into evidence of what some woman may have said to this witness and which conversation was in turn relayed to the officers. It is all very plainly hearsay.'

'I will permit it on cross-examination,' Judge Strouse ruled. 'Answer the question.'

'Yes, I said that this woman had told me she was a friend of the person who had rented that unit. She said she'd been told to go in and wait in case her friend wasn't at home.'

'Can you describe that woman?' Mason asked.

'Objected to as incompetent, irrelevant, and immaterial. Not proper cross-examination,' Hadley said.

'Sustained,' Judge Strouse ruled.

Mason smiled. 'Did you describe her to the officers at the time you had your conversation with them?'

'Yes, sir.'

'How did you describe her to the officers?'

'Same objection,' Hadley said.

Judge Strouse smiled. 'The objection is overruled. It is now shown to be a part of the conversation which Mr Mason is entitled to inquire into.'

'I told the police this woman was maybe twenty-eight or thirty, that she was a brunette, she had darkish grey eyes, she was rather tall . . . I mean she was tall for a woman, with long legs. She had a way about her when she walked. Sort of like a queen. You could see–'

'Don't describe her,' Hadley stormed at the witness. 'Simply relate what you told the police.'

'Yes, sir. That's what I'm telling–just what I told the police,' Brems said, and then added gratuitously: 'Of course, after that I found out it was all right.'

'I ask that that last may go out as not being responsive to the question,' Mason said, 'as being a voluntary statement of the witness.'

'It may go out,' Judge ruled.

'That's all,' Mason said.

Hadley, thoroughly angry, took the witness on re-direct examination. 'You told the police you thought this was a prowler?'

'Yes, sir.'

'Subsequently you found out you were mistaken, didn't you?'

'Objected to,' Mason said, 'as leading and suggestive, not proper re-direct examination. Incompetent, irrelevant, and immaterial.'

'The objection sustained,' Judge Strouse said.

'But,' shouted the exasperated assistant district attorney, 'you subsequently *told* the police you *knew* it was all right, didn't you?'

'Objected to as not proper re-direct examination,' Mason said, 'and as not being a part of the conversation that was testified to by the witness.'

Judge Strouse hesitated, then looked down at the witness. '*When* did you tell them this?'

'The next day.'

'The objection is sustained.'

Hadley said: 'You talked to the woman in unit twelve about it that same night, didn't you?'

'Objected to,' Mason said, 'as incompetent, irrelevant, and immaterial, calling for hearsay evidence, a conversation had without the presence or hearing of the defendant, not proper re-direct examination.'

'The objection is sustained,' Judge Strouse ruled.

Hadley sat down in the chair, held a whispered conference with Hamilton Burger. The two men engaged in a vehement whispered argument; then Hadley tried another tack.

'Did you, the same night, as a part of that same conversation, state to the police that after you had talked with the woman you were satisfied she was all right and was telling the truth?'

'Yes, sir,' the witness said.

'That's all,' Hadley announced triumphantly.

'Just a moment,' Mason said as Brems started to leave the stand. 'One more question on re-cross-examination. Didn't you also at the same time and as a part of the same conversation describe the woman to the police as a prowler?'

'I believe I did. Yes, sir, at *that* time.'

'That was the word you used–"a prowler"?'

'Yes, sir.'

Mason smiled across at Hadley. 'That's all my re-cross-examination,' he said.

'That's all,' Hadley said sullenly.

'Call your next witness,' Judge Strouse observed.

Hadley called the manager of the drive-yourself car agency. He testified to the circumstances surrounding the renting of the car, the return of the car, the fact that the person returning it had not sought to cash in on the credit due on the deposit.

'No questions,' Mason said.

Another employee of the drive-yourself agency testified to having seen the car driven on to the agency parking lot around ten o'clock on the evening of 6 April. The car was, he said, driven by a young woman, who got out of the car and started towards the office. He did not pay any attention to her after that.

'Cross-examine,' Hadley said.

'Can you describe this woman?' Mason asked.

'She was a good-looking woman.'

'Can you describe her any better than that?' Mason asked, as some of the jurors smiled broadly.

'Sure. She was in her twenties somewhere. She had . . . she was stacked!'

'What's that?' Judge Strouse asked.

'She had a good figure,' the witness amended hastily.

'Did you see her hair?'

'She was blonde.'

'Now then,' Mason asked, 'I want to ask you a question, and I want you to think carefully before you answer it. Did you, at any time, see any baggage being taken out of the car after she parked it in the lot?'

The man then shook his head. 'No, sir, she didn't take out a thing except herself.'

'You're certain?'

'I'm certain.'

'You saw her get out of the car?'

'I'll say I did.'

There was a ripple of laughter in the court-room

'That's all,' Mason announced.

'No further questions,' Hadley said.

Hadley called a fingerprint expert, who testified to examining units fifteen and sixteen of The Staylonger Motel for fingerprints on the night of 6 April and the early morning of 7 April. He produced several latent prints which he had developed and which he classified as being 'significant'.

'And why do you call these as being significant?' Hadley asked.

'Because,' the witness said, 'I was able to develop matching fingerprints in the automobile concerning which the witness has just testified.'

Hadley's questions brought out that the witness had examined the rented automobile, had processed it for fingerprints, and had secured a number of prints matching those in units fifteen and sixteen of the motel where the body had been found, that *some* of these matching fingerprints were, beyond question, those of the defendant, Stewart G. Bedford.

'Cross-examine,' Hadley announced.

'Who left the other "*matching*" print that you found?' Mason asked the witness.

'I assume that they were made by the blonde young woman who drove the car back to the agency and–'

'You don't *know*?'

'No, sir, I do not. I do know that I secured and developed certain latent fingerprints in units fifteen and sixteen of the motel, that I secured certain latent prints from the automobile which has previously been described as having licence number CXY 221, and that those prints in each instance were made by the same fingers that made the prints of Stewart G. Bedford on the police registration card when he was booked at police headquarters.'

'And you found the prints which you have assumed were those left by the blonde young woman in both units fifteen and sixteen?'

'Yes, sir.'

'Where?'

'In various places–on mirrors, on drinking-glasses, on a door-knob.'

'And those same fingerprints were on the automobile?'

'Yes, sir.'

'In other words,' Mason said, 'as far as your own observations are concerned, those *other* fingerprints could have been left by the murderer of Binney Denham?'

'That's objected to,' Hadley said. 'It's argumentative. It calls for a conclusion.'

'He's an expert witness,' Mason said. 'I'm asking him for his conclusion. I'm limiting the question as far as his own observations are concerned.'

Judge Strouse hesitated, said: 'I'm going to permit the witness to answer the question.'

The expert said: 'As far as *I* know or as far as my observations are concerned, either one of them could have been the murderer.'

'Or the murder *could* have been committed by someone else?' Mason asked.

'That's right.'

'Thank you,' Mason told him. 'That's all.'

Hamilton Burger indicated that he planned to examine the next witness.

'Call Richard Judson,' he said.

The bailiff called Richard Judson to the stand. Judson, an erect man with good shoulders, slim waist, a deep voice, and cold blue eyes which regarded the world with the air of a banker appraising a real estate loan, proved to be a police officer who had gone out to the Bedford residence on 10 April.

'And what did you do at the Bedford residence?' Hamilton Burger asked.

'I looked around.'

'Where?'

'Well, I looked around the grounds and the garage.'

'Did you have a search warrant?'

'Yes, sir.'

'Did you serve the search warrant on anyone?'

'There was no one home; no one was there to serve the warrant on.'

'Where did you look first?'

'In the garage.'

'Where in the garage?'

'All over the garage.'

'Can you tell us a little more about the type of search you made?'

'Well, there was a car in the garage. We looked over that pretty well. There were some tyres. We looked around through them, some old inner tubes–'

'Now, you say "we". Who was with you?'

'My partner.'

'A police officer?'

'Yes.'

'Where else did you look?'

'We looked every place in the garage. We looked up in the rafters, where there were some old boxes. We made a good job of searching the place.'

'And then,' Hamilton Burger asked, 'what did you do?'

'There was a drain in the centre of the garage floor–a perforated drain so that the garage floor could be washed off with a hose. There was a perforated plate which covered the drain. We unscrewed this plate, and looked down inside.'

'And what did you find?'

'We found a gun.'

'What do you mean, a gun?'

'I mean a .38 calibre Colt revolver.'

'Do you have the number of that gun?'

'I made a note of it, yes, sir.'

'That was a memorandum you made at the time?'

'Yes, sir.'

'That was made by you?'

'Yes, sir.'

'Do you have it with you?'

'Yes, sir.'

'What do your notes show?'

The witness opened his note-book. 'The gun was a blued-steel, .38 calibre Colt revolver. It had five loaded cartridges in the cylinder and one empty, or exploded, cartridge case. The manufacturer's number was 740818.'

'What did you do with that revolver?'

'I turned it over to Arthur Merriam.'

'Who is he?'

'He is one of the police experts on firearms and ballistics.'

'You may cross-examine,' Hamilton Burger said to Perry Mason.

'Now as I understand it, you had a search warrant, Mr Judson?' Mason asked.

'Yes, sir.'

'And what premises were included in the search warrant?'

'The house, the grounds, the garage.'

'There was no one home on whom you could serve this search warrant?'

'No, sir, not at the time we made the search.'

'When was the search warrant dated?'

'I believe the eighth.'

'You got it on the morning of the eighth?'

'I don't know the exact time of day.'

'It was in the morning?'

'I think perhaps it was.'

'And after you got the search warrant, what did you do?'

'Put it in my pocket.'

'And what did you do after that?'

'I was working on the case.'

'What did you do while you were, as you say, working on the case and after putting the search warrant in your pocket?'

'I drove around looking things over.'

'Actually, you drove out to the Bedford house, didn't you?'

'Well, we were working on the case, looking things over. We cruised around that vicinity.'

'And then you *parked* your car, didn't you?'

'Yes, sir.'

'From a spot where you could see the garage?'

'Well, yes.'

'And you waited all that day, did you not?'

'The rest of the day, yes, sir.'

'And the next day you were back on the job again?'

'Yes, sir.'

'Same place?'

'Yes, sir.'

'And you waited all that day?'

'Yes, sir.'

'And the next day you were back on the job again, weren't you?'

'Yes, sir.'

'Same place?'

'Yes, sir.'

'And you waited during that day until when?'

'Oh, until about four o'clock in the afternoon.'

'And then, from your surveillance, you knew that there was no one home, isn't that right?'

'Well, we saw Mrs Bedford drive off.'

'You then *knew* that there was no one home, didn't you?'

'Well, it's hard to *know* anything like that.'

'You had been keeping the house under surveillance?'

'We had been, yes.'

'For the purpose of finding a time when no one was home?'

'Well, we were just keeping the place under surveillance to see who came and who went.'

'And at the first opportunity, when you thought there was no one home, you went and searched the garage?'

'Well . . . I guess that's about right. You can call it that if you want to.'

'And you searched the garage but didn't search the house?'

'No, sir, we didn't search the house.'

'You searched every inch of the garage, every nook and corner?'

'Yes, sir.'

'You waited until you felt certain there was no one home, then you went out to make your search.'

'We wanted to make a search of the garage. We didn't want to be interrupted and we didn't want to have anyone interfering with us.'

Mason smiled frostily. 'You have just said, Mr Judson, that you wanted to make a search of the garage.'

'Well, what's wrong with that? We had a warrant, didn't we?'

'You said of the *garage*.'

'I meant of the whole place–the house–the whole business.'

'You didn't *say* that. You said you wanted to search the *garage*.'

'Well, we had a warrant for it.'

'Isn't it true,' Mason asked, 'that the only place you really wanted to search was the garage, and you only wanted to search that because you had been given a tip that the gun would be found in the garage?'

'We were looking for the gun, all right.'

'Isn't it a fact that you had a tip before you went out there that the gun would be found in the garage?'

'Objected to as incompetent, irrelevant, and immaterial, not proper cross-examination,' Hamilton Burger said.

Judge Strouse thought for a moment. 'The objection is overruled . . . if the witness knows.'

'I don't know about any tip.'

'Isn't it a fact you intended primarily to search the garage?'

'We searched there first.'

'Was there some reason you searched there first?'

'That's where we started. We thought we might find a gun there.'

'And what made you think that was where the gun was?'

'That was as good a place to hide it as any.'

'You mean the police didn't have some anonymous telephone tip to guide you?'

'I mean we searched the garage, looking for a gun, and we found the gun in the garage. I don't know what tip the others had. I was told to go look for a gun.'

'In the garage?'

'Well, yes.'

'Thank you,' Mason said. 'That's all.'

Arthur Merriam took the stand and testified to experiments he had performed with the gun which he had received from the last witness and which was introduced in evidence. He stated that he had fired test bullets from the gun, had examined them through a comparison microscope, comparing the test bullets with the fatal bullet. He had prepared photographs which showed the identity of striation marks on the two bullets while one was super-imposed over the other. These photographs were introduced in evidence.

'You may cross-examine,' Hamilton Burger said.

Mason seemed a little bored with the entire proceeding. 'No questions,' he said.

Hamilton Burger's next witness was a man who had charge of the sporting goods section of one of the large down-town department stores. This man produced records showing the gun in question had been sold to Stewart G. Bedford some five years earlier and that Bedford had signed the register of sales. The book of sales was offered in evidence; then, as a photostatic copy of the original was produced, the Court ordered that the original record might be withdrawn.

'Cross-examine,' Hamilton Burger said.

'No questions,' Mason announced, suppressing a yawn.

Judge Strouse looked at the clock, said: 'It is now time for the afternoon adjournment. The Court admonishes the jurors not to discuss this case among yourselves, nor to permit anyone else to discuss it in your presence. You are not to form or express any opinion until the case is finally submitted to you.

'Court will take a recess until tomorrow morning at ten o'clock.'

Bedford gripped Mason's arm. 'Mason,' he said, 'someone planted that gun in my garage.'

'Did you put it there?' Mason asked.

'Don't be silly! I tell you I never saw the gun after I went to sleep. That liquor was drugged and someone took the gun out of my brief-case, killed Binney Denham, and then subsequently planted the gun in my garage.'

'And,' Mason pointed out, 'telephoned a tip to the police so that the officers would be sure to find it there.'

'Well, what does that mean?'

'It means that someone was very anxious that the officers would have plenty of evidence to connect you with the murder.'

'And that gets back to this mysterious prowler who was in that motel where Elsa–'

'Just a minute,' Mason cautioned. 'No names.'

'Well, that woman who was in there,' Bedford said. 'Hang it, Mason! I keep telling you she's important. She's the key to the whole business. Yet you don't seem to get the least bit excited about her, or try to find her.'

'How am I going to go about finding her?' Mason asked impatiently. 'You tell me there's a needle in a haystack and the needle is important. So what?'

The officer motioned for Bedford to accompany him.

'Hire fifty detectives,' Bedford said, holding back momentarily. 'Hire a hundred detectives. But *find that woman*!'

'See you tomorrow,' Mason told him as the officer led Bedford through the passage way to the jail elevator.

19

Perry Mason and Della Street had dinner at their favourite restaurant, returned for a couple hours' work at the office, and found Elsa Griffin waiting for them in the foyer of the building.

'Hello,' Mason said. 'Do you want to see me?'

She nodded.

'Been here long?'

'About twenty minutes. I heard you were out to dinner but expected to return to the office this evening, so I waited.'

Mason flashed a glance at Della Street. 'Something important?'

'I think so.'

'Come on up,' Mason invited.

The three of them rode up in the elevator and walked down the corridor. Mason opened the door of the private office, went in and switched on the lights.

'Take off your coat and hat,' Della Street said. 'Sit down in that chair over there.'

Elsa Griffin moved quietly, efficiently, as a woman moves who has a fixed purpose and has steeled herself to carry out her objectives in a series of definite steps.

'I had a chance to talk for a few minutes with Mr Bedford,' she said.

Mason nodded.

'A few words of *private* conversation.'

'Go ahead,' Mason told her.

She said: 'Mr Bedford feels that with all of the resources that he has placed at your command, you could do more about finding that woman who was in my unit there at the motel. Of course, when you come right down to it, *she* could have kept those two units, fifteen and sixteen, under surveillance from my cabin and then gone over and . . . well, at the proper moment she could have simply opened the door of sixteen and fired one shot and then made her escape.'

'Yes,' Mason said dryly, 'fired one shot with Bedford's gun.'

'Yes,' Elsa Griffin said thoughtfully, 'I suppose she *would* have had to get into that other cabin and get possession of the gun first. . . . But she *could* have done that, Mr Mason. She could have gone into the cabin after that blonde went out, and there she found Mr Bedford asleep. She took the gun from his brief-case.'

Mason studied her carefully.

Abruptly she said: 'Mr Mason, don't you think it's bad publicity for Mrs Bedford to wear those horribly heavy dark glasses and keep in the back of the court-room? Shouldn't she be right up there in front, giving her husband moral support, and not looking as though–as though she were afraid to have people find out who she is?'

'Everyone knows who she is,' Mason said. 'From the time they started picking the jury, the newspaper people have been interviewing her.'

'I know, but she'll never take off those horrid dark glasses. And they make her look terrible. They're great big lensed glasses that completely alter her appearance. She looks just like . . . well, not like herself at all.'

'So what would you suggest that I do?' Mason asked.

'Couldn't you tell her to be more natural? Tell her to take her glasses off, to come up and sit as close to her husband as she can to give him a word of encouragement now and then.'

'That's what Mr Bedford wants?'

'I'm satisfied he does. I think that his wife's conduct has hurt him. He acts very differently from the way he normally does. He's . . . well, he's sort of crushed.'

'I see,' Mason said.

Elsa Griffin was silent for a few minutes, then said: 'What have you been able to do with those fingerprints I got for you from the cabin, Mr Mason?'

'Not very much, I'm afraid. You see, it's very difficult to identify a person unless you have a complete set of ten fingerprints, but as one who studied to be a detective, you know all about that.'

'Yes, I suppose so,' she said dubiously. 'I thought Mr Brems gave a very good description of that prowler who was in my cabin.'

Mason nodded.

'There's something about the way he describes her, something about her walk. I almost feel that I know her. It's the most peculiar feeling. It's like seeing a face that you can't place, yet which is very familiar to you. You know it as well as you know your own, and yet somehow you can't get it fixed with the name. You just can't get the right connection. There's one link in the chain that's missing.'

Again Mason nodded.

'I have a feeling that if I could only think of that, I'd have it. I feel that there's a solution to the whole business just almost at our finger-tips, and yet it keeps eluding us like . . . like a Halloween apple.'

Mason sat silent.

'Well,' she said, getting to her feet, 'I must be going. I wanted to tell you Mr Bedford would like very much indeed to have you concentrate all of the resources at your command on finding that woman. Also, I'm satisfied he would like it a lot better if his wife wouldn't act as though she were afraid of being recognized. You know, really she's a very beautiful woman and she has a wonderful carriage–'

Abruptly Elsa Griffin ceased speaking and looked at Mason with eyes that slowly widened with startled, incredulous surprise.

'What's the matter?' Mason asked. 'What is it?'

'My God!' she exclaimed. 'It *couldn't* be!'

'Come on,' Mason said. 'What is it?'

She kept looking at him with round, startled eyes.

'Are you ill?' Della Street asked.

'Good heavens, Mr Mason! It's just hit me like a ton of bricks. Let me sit down.'

She dropped down into a chair, moved her head slowly from side to side, looking around the office as though some mental shock had left her completely disoriented.

'Well,' Mason asked, 'what is it?'

'I was just mentioning Mrs Bedford and thinking about her carriage and the way she walks and . . . Mr Mason, it's just come to me. It's a terrible thing. It's just as though someone had crashed into my mind.'

'What is it?' Mason asked.

'Don't you see, Mr Mason? That prowler who was in my unit at the motel. The description Mr Brems gave fits her perfectly. Why, you couldn't ask for a better description of Mrs Bedford than the one that Morrison Brems gave.'

Mason sat silent, his eyes steadily studying Elsa Griffin's face. Abruptly she snapped her fingers.

'I have it, Mr Mason! I have it! You've got her photograph on that police card–her photograph and her fingerprints. You could compare the latents I took there in my unit in the motel with her fingerprints on there, and . . . and then we'd *know*!'

Mason nodded to Della Street. 'Get the card with Mrs Bedford's fingerprints, Della. Also, get the envelope with the unidentified latent prints. You'll remember we discarded Elsa Griffin's prints. We have four unidentified latents numbered fourteen, sixteen, nine, and twelve. I'd like to have those prints, please.'

Della Street regarded Mason's expressionless face for a moment, then went to the locked filing-case in which the lawyer kept matters to which he was referring in cases under trial, and returned with the articles Mason had requested.

Elsa Griffin eagerly reached for the envelope with the lifted fingerprints, took the cards from the envelope, examined them carefully, then grabbed the card containing Ann Roann Bedford's criminal record.

She swiftly compared the lifted latent prints with those on the card, looking intently from one to the other. Gradually her excitement became evident, then mounted to a fever pitch.

'Mr Mason, these prints are hers!'

Mason took the card with Mrs Bedford's criminal record. Elsa Griffin held on to the cards numbered fourteen, sixteen, nine, and twelve.

'They're hers, Mr Mason! You can take my word for it. I've studied fingerprinting.'

Mason said: 'Let's hope you're mistaken. That would *really* put the fat in the fire. We simply couldn't have that.'

Elsa Griffin picked up the envelope containing the lifted latents. 'Mr Mason,' she said sternly, 'you're representing Stewart G. Bedford. You *have* to represent his interests regardless of who gets hurt.'

Mason held out his hand for the latent prints. She drew back slightly. 'You can't be a traitor to his cause in order to protect . . . to protect the person who got him into all this trouble in the first place.'

Mason said: 'A lawyer has to protect his client's *best* interests. That doesn't mean he necessarily has to do what the client wants or what the client's friends may want. He must do what is best for the client.'

'You mean you aren't going to tell Mr Bedford that it was his own wife who, goaded to desperation by this blackmailer, finally decided to–'

'No,' Mason interrupted, 'I'm not going to tell him, and I don't want you to tell him.'

She suddenly jumped from her chair, and raced for the exit door of the office.

'Come back here,' Della Street cried, making a grab and missing Elsa Griffin's flying skirt by a matter of inches.

Before Della Street could get to the door, Elsa Griffin had wrenched it open.

Sergeant Holcomb was standing on the outer threshold. 'Well, well, good evening, folks,' he said, slipping an arm around Elsa Griffin's shoulders. 'I gather there has been a little commotion in here. What's going on?'

'This young woman is trying to take some personal property which doesn't belong to her,' Mason said.

'Well, well, well, isn't that interesting? Stealing from you, eh? Could you describe the property, Mason? Perhaps you'd like to go down to headquarters and swear out a complaint, charging her with larceny. What's your side of the story, Miss Griffin?'

Elsa Griffin pushed the lifted latents inside the front of her dress. 'Will you,' she asked Sergeant Holcomb, 'kindly escort me home and then see that I am subpoenaed as a witness for the prosecution? I think it's time someone showed Mr Perry Mason, the great criminal lawyer, that it's against the law to condone murder and conceal evidence from the police.'

Sergeant Holcomb's face was wreathed in smiles. 'Sister,' he said, 'you've made a *great* little speech. You just come along with me.'

20

Hamilton Burger, his face plainly indicating his feelings, rose to his feet when court was called to order the next morning and said: 'Your Honour, I would like to call the Court's attention to Section 135 of the penal code, which reads as follows: "Every person who, knowing that any book, paper, record, instrument in writing, or other matter or thing, is about to be produced in evidence upon any trial, inquiry, or investigation whatever, authorized by law, wilfully destroys *or conceals* the same, with intent thereby to prevent it from being produced is guilty of a misdemeanor."'

Judge Strouse, plainly puzzled, said: 'The Court is, I think, familiar with the law, Mr Burger.'

'Yes, Your Honour,' Hamilton Burger said. 'I merely wished to call the sections to Your Honour's attention. I know Your Honour is familiar with the law. I feel that perhaps some others persons are not, and now, Your Honour, I wish to call Miss Elsa Griffin to the stand.'

Stewart Bedford looked at Mason with alarm. 'What the devil's this?' he whispered. 'I thought we were going to keep *her* out of the public view. We can't afford to have Brems recognize her as the one who was in unit twelve.'

'She didn't like the way I was handling things,' Mason said. 'She decided to become a witness.'

'When did that happen?'

'Last last night.'

'You didn't tell me.'

'I didn't want to worry you.'

The outer door opened, and Elsa Griffin, her chin high, came marching into the court-room. She raised her right hand, was sworn, and took the witness stand.

'What is your name?' Hamilton Burger asked.

'Elsa Griffin.'

'Are you acquainted with the defendant in this case?'

'I am employed by him.'

'Where were you on the sixth day of April of this year?'

'I was at The Staylonger Motel.'

'What were you doing there?'

'I was there at the request of a certain person.'

'Now then, if the Court please,' Hamilton Burger said, addressing Judge Strouse, 'a most unusual situation is about to develop. I may state that this witness, while wishing the authorities to take certain action, did nevertheless conspire with another person, whom I shall presently name, to conceal and suppress certain evidence which we consider highly pertinent.

'I had this witness placed under subpoena. She is here as an unwilling witness. That is, she is not only willing but anxious to testify to certain phases of the case. However, she is quite unwilling to testify as to other matters. As to these matters she has refused to make any statement, and I have no knowledge of how much or how little she knows as to this part of the case. She simply will not talk with me except upon one point.

'It is, therefore, necessary for me to approach this witness upon certain matters as a hostile witness.'

'Perhaps,' Judge Strouse said, 'you had better first examine the witness upon the matters as to which she is willing to give her testimony, and then elicit information from her on the other points as a hostile witness, and under the rules pertaining to the examination of hostile witnesses.'

'Very well, Your Honour.'

Hamilton Burger turned to the witness.

'You are now and for several years have been employed by the defendant?'

'Yes.'

'In what capacity?'

'I am his confidential secretary.'

'Are you acquainted with Mr Morrison Brems, the manager of The Staylonger Motel?'

'Yes.'

'Did you have a conversation with Morrison Brems on April sixth of this year?'

'Yes.'

'When?'

'Early in the evening.'

'What was said at that conversation?'

'Objected to as incompetent, irrelevant, and immaterial,' Mason said.

'Just a moment, Your Honour,' Hamilton Burger countered. 'We propose to show that this witness was at the time of this conversation the agent of the defendant, that she went to the motel in accordance with instructions issued by the defendant.'

'You had better show that first then,' Judge Strouse ruled.

'But that, Your Honour, is where we are having trouble, that is one of the points where the witness is hostile.'

'There are some other matters on which the witness is not a hostile witness?' Judge Strouse asked.

'Yes.'

'The Court has suggested that you proceed with those matters until the evidence which can be produced by this witness as a friendly witness is all before the Court. Then, if there are other matters on which the witness is hostile, and you request permission to deal with the witness as a hostile witness, the record will be straight as to what has been done and where, when and why it has been done.'

'Very well, Your Honour.'

Hamilton Burger turned again to the witness. 'After this conversation did you return to The Staylonger Motel later on in the evening of April sixth?'

'Actually it was, I believe, early on the morning of April seventh.'

'Who sent you to The Staylonger Motel?'

'Mr Perry Mason.'

'You mean that you received instructions from Mr Mason while he was acting as attorney for Stewart G. Bedford, the defendant in this case?'

'Yes.'

'What did Mr Mason instruct you to do?'

'To get certain fingerprints from unit twelve, to take a fingerprint outfit and dust every place in the unit where I thought I could get a suitable latent fingerprint, to lift those fingerprints and then to obliterate every single remaining fingerprint which might be in unit number twelve, after that to bring the lifted fingerprints to Mr Mason.'

'Did you understand the process of taking fingerprints and lifting them?'

'Yes.'

'Had you made some study of that process?'

'Yes.'

'Where?'

'I am a graduate of a correspondence school dealing with such matters.'

'Where did you get the material necessary to lift latent fingerprints?'

'Mr Mason furnished it.'

'And what did you do after Mr Mason gave you those materials?'

'I went to the motel and lifted certain fingerprints from unit twelve as I had been instructed.'

'And then what?'

'I took those fingerprints to Mr Mason so that the fingerprints which were mine could be discarded, and thereby, through a process of elimination, leave only the fingerprints of any person who had been prowling the cabin during my absence.'

'Do you know if this was done?'

'It was done. I was so advised by Mr Mason, who also told me that all the latent prints I had lifted were my prints, with the exception of those prints contained on four cards.'

'Do you know what four cards these were?'

'Yes. As I lifted prints I put them on cards and numbered the cards. The cards containing the significant prints were numbered fourteen, sixteen, nine, and twelve.

'Fourteen and sixteen came from the glass door-knob of the closet door in the motel unit; nine and twelve came from the side of a mirror.'

'Do you know where these four cards are now?'

'Yes.'

'Where?'

'I have them.'

'Where did you get them?'

'I snatched them from Perry Mason last night and ran to the police as Mr Mason was trying to get them back.'

'Did you give them to the police?'

'No.'

'Why?'

'I didn't want anything to happen to them. You see by last night I knew whose prints they were. That is why I ran with them.'

'Why did you feel that you had to run?' Burger asked.

Judge Strouse glanced down at Perry Mason expectantly. When the lawyer made no effort to object, Judge Strouse said to the witness: 'Just a minute before you answer that question. Does the defence wish to object to this question, Mr Mason?'

'No, Your Honour,' Perry Mason said. 'I feel that I am being on trial here and that therefore I should let the full facts come out.'

Judge Strouse frowned. 'You may feel that you are on trial, Mr Mason. That is a matter of dispute. There can be no dispute that your client is on trial, and your primary duty is to protect the interests of that client regardless of the effect on your own private affairs.'

'I understand that, Your Honour.'

'This question seems to me to be argumentative and calls for a conclusion of the witness.'

'There is no objection, Your Honour.'

Judge Strouse hesitated and said: 'I would like to point out to you, Mr Mason, that the Court will take a hand if it appears that your interests in the case become adverse to your client and no objection is made to questions which are detrimental to your client's case.'

'I think if the Court Please,' Mason said, 'the opposite may be the case here. I feel that the answer of the witness may be strongly opposed to my personal interests but very much in favour of the defendant's case. You see that is the reason the witness is both a willing witness on some phases of the case and an unwilling witness on others. She feels that she should testify against me, but she is loyal to the interests of her employer.'

'Very well,' Judge Strouse said. 'If you don't wish to object, the witness will answer the question.'

'Answer the question,' Hamilton Burger said. 'Why did you feel that you had to run?'

'Because at that time I had identified those fingerprints.'

'You had?'

'Yes, sir.'

'You said that you had studied fingerprinting?'

'Yes.'

'And you were able at that time to identify these fingerprints?'

'Yes, sir.'

'You compared them with originals?'

'Well, enough to know whose they were.'

'Hamilton Burger turned to the Court and said: 'I confess, Your Honour, that on some of these matters I am feeling my way because of the peculiar situation which exists. The witness promised to give her testimony on the stand but would not tell me–'

'There is no objection,' Judge Strouse interrupted. 'There is, therefore, nothing before the Court. You will kindly refrain from making any argument or comments as to the testimony of this witness until it comes time to argue the matter to the jury. Simply proceed with your question and answer, Mr District Attorney.'

'Yes, Your Honour,' Hamilton Burger said.

Judge Strouse looked down at Mason. His expression was thoughtfully dubious.

'You yourself were able to identify those prints?' Hamilton Burger asked.

'Yes, sir.'

'Whose prints did you think they were?'

'Now just a minute,' Judge Strouse said. 'Apparently counsel is not going to object that no proper foundation has been laid and that this calls for an opinion of the witness. Miss Griffin?'

'Yes, Your Honour?'

'You state that you studied fingerprinting?'

'Yes, I did, Your Honour.'

'How?'

'By correspondence.'

'Over what period of time?'

'I took a complete course. I graduated. I learned to distinguish the different characteristics of fingerprints. I learned how to take fingerprints and compare them and how to classify them.'

'Is there any objection from defence counsel?' Judge Strouse asked.

'None whatever,' Mason said.

'Very well, whose prints were they?' Burger asked.

'Now just a minute,' Mason said. 'If the Court please I feel that that question is improper.'

'I feel the objection is in order,' Judge Strouse ruled.

'However,' Mason went on, 'I am not interposing the objection which perhaps Your Honour has in mind. I feel that this witness, while she may have qualified as an expert on fingerprinting, has qualified as a limited expert. She is what might be called an amateur expert. I feel that, therefore, the question should not be as to whose fingerprints these were, but in her opinion, for what it may be worth, what points of similarity there are between these prints and known standards.'

Judge Strouse said: 'The objection is sustained.'

Hamilton Burger, his face darkening with annoyance, asked: 'In your opinion, for what it may be worth, what points of similarity are there between these latents and the known prints of any person with which you may have made a comparison?'

Elsa Griffin raised her head. Her defiant eyes glared at the defendant, then at Mason, and then turned to the jury. In a firm voice she said: 'In my opinion, for what it may be worth, these prints have so many points of similarity I can say they were made by the fingers of Mrs Stewart G. Bedford, the wife of the defendant in this case.'

Hamilton Burger grinned. 'Do you have those fingerprints with you?'

'I do.'

'And how do you identify them?'

'The cards are numbered,' she said. 'The numbers are fourteen, sixteen, nine, and twelve, respectively. Also I signed my name on the backs of these cards at a late hour last night so that there could be no possibility of substitution or mistake. I did that at the suggestion of the district attorney. He wanted me to leave these cards with him. When I refused he asked me to sign my name so there could be no possibility of trickery.'

Hamilton Burger was grinning. 'And then what did I do, if anything?'

'Then you signed your name beneath mine and put the date on the cards.'

'I ask of the Court please that those prints be introduced in evidence,' Hamilton Burger said, 'as People's Exhibit under proper numbers.'

'Now just a moment,' Mason said. 'At this point, Your Honour, I feel that I have a right to a *voir dire* examination as to the authenticity of the exhibits.'

'Go ahead,' Hamilton Burger said. 'In fact, handle your cross-examination on this phase of the case if you want, because from here on the witness becomes an unwilling witness.'

'Counsel may proceed,' Judge Strouse said.

'You made this positive identification of the latent prints last night, Miss Griffin?'

'Yes.'

'In my office?'

'Yes.'

'You were rather excited at the time?'

'Well . . . all right, I *was* a little excited, but I wasn't too excited to compare fingerprints.'

'You checked all four of these fingerprints?'

'Yes.'

'All four of them were the fingerprints of Mrs Bedford?'

'Yes.'

Bedford tugged at Mason's coat. 'Look here, Mason,' he whispered. 'Don't let her–'

Mason brushed his client's hand to one side. 'Keep quiet,' he ordered.

Mason arose and approached the witness stand. 'You are, I believe, skilled in classifying fingerprints?'

'I am.'

'You know how to do it?'

'Very well.'

Mason said: 'I am going to give you a magnifying-glass to assist you in looking at these prints.'

Mason took a powerful pocket magnifying-glass from his pocket, turned to the clerk, and said: 'May I have some of the fingerprints which have been introduced in evidence? I don't care for the fingerprints of the defendant which were found in the car and in the motel, but I would like some of those other exhibits of the unidentified party, the ones that were found in the car and in the motel.'

'Very well,' the clerk said, thumbing through the exhibits. He handed Mason several of the cards.

'Now then,' Mason said, 'I call your attention to People's Exhibit number twenty-eight, which purports to be a lifted fingerprint. I will ask you to look at that and see if that fingerprint matches one on any of the cards numbered fourteen, sixteen, nine, and twelve, which you have produced.'

The witness made a show of studying the print with the magnifying-glass, shook her head and said: 'No!' and then added: 'It can't. These prints are the prints of Mrs Bedford. Those prints in the exhibits are the prints of an unidentified person.'

'But isn't it true that this unidentified person, as far as you know, might well have been Mrs Bedford?' Mason asked.

'No, that person was a blonde. I saw her.'

'But you don't know that it was the blonde who left the prints?'

'No, I don't *know* that.'

'Then please examine this print closely.'

Mason held the print out to Elsa Griffin, who looked at it with the magnifying-glass in a perfunctory manner, then handed it back to Mason.

'Now,' Mason said, 'I call your attention to People's Exhibit number thirty-four, and ask you to compare this.'

Again the witness made a perfunctory study with the magnifying-glass and said: 'No. None of these prints match.'

'None of them?' Mason asked.

'None! I tell you, Mr Mason, those are the prints of Mrs Bedford, and you know it as well as I do.'

Mason appeared to be somewhat rebuffed. He studied the prints, then looked at the cards in Elsa Griffin's hand.

'Perhaps,' he said, 'you can tell me just how you go about examining a fingerprint. Take this one, for instance, on the card numbered sixteen. That is one, I believe, that you secured from the under side of a glass door-knob in the cabin?'

'Yes.'

'Now what is the first characteristic of that print which you noticed?'

'That is a tented arch.'

'I see. A tented arch,' Mason said thoughtfully. 'Now would you mind pointing out just where that tented arch is? Oh, I see. Now this fingerprint which I hand you which has been numbered People's Exhibit number thirty-seven also has a tented arch, does it not?'

She looked at the print and said: 'Yes.'

'Now, using this print number sixteen, which you say you recovered from the closet door-knob, let us count from the tented arch through the ridges until we come to a branch in the ridges. There are, let's see, one, two, three, four, five, six, seven, eight ridges, and then we come to a branch.'

'That is right,' she said.

'Well, now let's see,' Mason said. 'We take this print which has been introduced by the prosecution as number thirty-seven and we count–let's see, why, yes, we count the same number of ridges and we come to the same peculiar branching, do we not?'

'Let me see,' the witness said.

She studied the print through the magnifying-glass. 'Well, yes,' she said, 'that is what you would call *one* point of similarity. You need several to make a perfect identification.'

'I see,' Mason said. 'One point of similarity could of course be a coincidence.'

'Don't make any mistake, Mr Mason,' she said icily. 'That *is* a coincidence.'

'Very well, now, let's look at your print number sixteen again, the one which you got from underneath the closet door-knob, and see if you can find some other distinguishing mark.'

'You have one here,' she said. 'On the tenth ridge.'

'The tenth,' Mason said. 'Let me see . . . oh yes.'

'Well, now let's look at thirty-seven again, and see if you can find the same point of similarity there.'

'There's no use looking,' she said. 'There won't be.'

'Tut, tut!' Mason said. 'Don't jump at conclusions, Miss Griffin. You're testifying as an expert, so let's just take a look now, if you please. Count up these ridges and–'

The witness gasped.

'Do you find such a point of similarity?' Mason asked, seemingly as much surprised as the witness.

'I . . . I seem to. Somebody has been tampering with these fingerprints.'

'Now, just a moment! Just a moment!' Hamilton Burger said. 'This is a serious matter, Your Honour.'

'Who's going to tamper with the fingerprints?' Mason asked. 'The fingerprints that the witness has been testifying to were in her possession. She said that she had them in her possession all night. She wouldn't let them out of her possession for fear they might be tampered with. She signed her name on the back of each card. The district attorney signed his name and wrote the date. There are the signatures on the cards. These other cards are exhibits which the prosecution introduced in court. I have just taken those exhibits from the clerk. They bear the file number of the clerk and the exhibit number.'

'Just the same,' Hamilton Burger shouted, 'there's some sort of a flimflam here. The witness knows it and I know it.'

'Mr Burger,' Judge Strouse stated, 'you will not make any such charges in this court-room. Not unless they can be substantiated. Apparently there is no possibility of any substitution. Miss Griffin?'

'Yes, Your Honour?'

'Kindly look at the card numbered sixteen.'

'Yes, Your Honour.'

'You got that card last night?'

'I . . . I . . . yes, I must have.'

'From the office of Perry Mason?'

'Yes.'

'And you compared that card *at that time* with the fingerprints of Mrs Stewart Bedford?'

'Yes, Your Honour.'

'That card was in your possession and under your control at that time?'

'Yes, Your Honour.'

'Now, speaking for the moment as to this one card, exactly what did you do with that card *after* satisfying yourself the print was that of Mrs Bedford? What did you do with it?'

'I put it in the front of my dress.'

'And then what?'

'I was escorted by Sergeant Holcomb to the office of Hamilton Burger. Mr Burger wanted to have me leave the prints with him. I refused to do so. At his suggestion, I signed my name on the back of each card. Then he signed his name and the date, so there could be no question of a substitution, so that I couldn't substitute them, and so that no one else could.'

'And that's your signature and the date on the back of that card?'

'It seems to be, but . . . I'm not certain. May I examine these prints for a moment?'

'Take all the time you want,' Judge Strouse said.

Hamilton Burger said: 'Your Honour, I feel that there should be some inquiry here. This is completely in accordance with the peculiar phenomena which always seem to occur in cases where Mr Perry Mason is defence counsel.'

'I resent that,' Perry Mason said. 'I am simply trying to cross-examine this expert, this so-called expert, I may add.'

Elsa Griffin looked up from the fingerprint classification to flash him a glance of venomous hatred.

Judge Strouse said: 'Counsel for both sides will return to their chairs at counsel tables. The witness will be given ample opportunity to make the comparison which she wishes.'

Burger reluctantly lumbered back to his chair at the prosecution's table and dropped into it.

Mason walked back, sat down, locked his hands behind his head and, with elaborate unconcern, leaned back in the chair.

Stewart Bedford tried to whisper to him, but Mason waved him back into silence.

The witness proceeded to examine the cards, studying first one and then the other, counting ridges with a sharp-pointed pencil. The silence in the courtroom grew to a peak of tension.

Suddenly Elsa Griffin threw the magnifying-glass directly at Perry Mason. The glass hit the mahogany table, bounced against the lawyer's chest. Elsa Griffin dropped all the fingerprint cards, put her hands to her eyes, and began to cry hysterically.

Mason got to his feet.

Judge Strouse said: 'Just a moment. Counsel for both sides will remain seated. The Court wants to examine the witness. Miss Griffin, will you kindly regain your composure. The Court wishes to ask you certain questions.'

She took her hands from her face, raised tearful eyes to the Court. 'What is it?' she asked.

'Do you now conclude that your print number sixteen is the same as the print which has been introduced in evidence, prosecution's number thirty-seven–that both were made by the same finger?'

She said: 'It is, Your Honour, but it *wasn't*. Last night it *was* the print of Mrs Bedford. Somebody somewhere has mixed everything all up, and . . . and now I don't know what I'm doing, or what I'm talking about.'

'Well, there's no reason to be hysterical about this, Miss Griffin,' Judge Strouse said. 'You're certain that this fingerprint number sixteen is the one that you took from the cottage?'

She nodded. 'It has to be . . . I . . . I *know* that it's Mrs Bedford's fingerprint!'

'There certainly can be no doubt about the authenticity of the Court Exhibit,' Judge Strouse said. 'Now apparently, according to the testimony of the prosecution's witness, the identity of these fingerprints simply means that the same woman who was in unit sixteen of the motel on April sixth was also in unit twelve of the motel on that same day, that this person also drove the rented automobile.'

Elsa Griffin shook her head. 'It isn't so, Your Honour. It simply can't be. It isn't–' Again she lapsed into a storm of tears.

Hamilton Burger said: 'If the Court please, may I make a suggestion?'

'What is it?' Judge Strouse asked coldly.

Hamilton Burger said: 'This witness seems to be emotionally upset. I suggest that she be withdrawn from the stand. I suggest that the four cards, each bearing her signature and the numbers fourteen, sixteen, nine, and twelve, be each stamped by the clerk for identification; that these cards then be given to the police fingerprint expert who is here in the witness-room and who can very shortly give us an opinion as to the identity of those fingerprints. In the meantime, I wish to state to the Court that I am completely satisfied with the sincerity and integrity of this witness. I personally feel that there has been some trickery and substitution. I think that a deception and a fraud is being practised on this court and in order to prove it I would ask to recall Morrison Brems, the manager of the motel, to the stand.'

Judge Strouse stroked his chin. 'The jury will disregard the comments of the district attorney,' he said, 'in regard to deception or fraud. This witness will be excused from the stand, the cards will be marked for identification by the clerk and then delivered to the fingerprint expert who has previously testified and who will be charged by the court with making a comparison and a report. Now in the meantime the witness Brems will come forward. You will be excused for the time being, Miss Griffin. Just leave the stand, if you will, and try to compose yourself.'

The bailiff escorted the sobbing Miss Griffin from the stand.

Morrison Brems was brought into court.

'I am now going to prove my point another way,' Hamilton Burger said. 'Mr Brems, you have already been sworn in this case. You talked with this so-called prowler who emerged from unit number twelve?'

'Yes, sir.'

'You saw that prowler leaving the cabin?'

'Yes, sir.'

Hamilton Burger said: 'I am going to ask Mrs Stewart G. Bedford, who is in court, to stand up and take off the heavy dark glasses with which she has effectively kept her identity concealed. I am going to ask her to walk across the court-room in front of this witness.'

'Object,' Bedford whispered frantically to Mason. 'Object. Stop this! Don't let him get away with it!'

'Keep quiet,' Mason warned. 'If we object now we'll antagonize the jury. Let him go.'

'Stand up, Mrs Bedford,' Judge Strouse ordered.

Mrs Bedford got to her feet.

'Will you kindly remove your glasses?'

'This isn't the proper way of making an identification,' Perry Mason said. 'There should be a line-up, Your Honour, but we have no objection.'

'Come inside the rail here, Mrs Bedford, right through that gate,' Judge Strouse directed. 'Now just walk the length of the court-room, if you will, turn your face to the witness, and–'

'That's the one. That's the one. That's the woman!' Morrison Brems shouted excitedly.

Ann Roann Bedford stopped abruptly in her stride. She turned to face the witness. 'You lie,' she said, her voice cold with venom.

Judge Strouse banged his gavel. 'There will be no comments except in response to questions asked by counsel,' he said. 'You may return to your seat, Mrs Bedford, and you will please refrain from making any comment. Proceed, Mr Burger.'

A grinning Hamilton Burger turned to Perry Mason and made an exaggerated bow. 'And now, Mr Mason,' he said, 'you may cross-examine–to your heart's content.'

'Now just a moment, Mr District Attorney,' Judge Strouse snapped. 'That last comment was uncalled for; that is not proper conduct.'

'I beg the Court's pardon,' Hamilton Burger said, his face suffused with triumph. 'I think, if the Court please, I can soon suggest to the Court what happened to the fingerprint evidence, but I'll be *very* glad to hear Mr Mason cross-examine *this* witness and see what can be done with *his* testimony. However, I do beg the Court's pardon.'

'Proceed with the cross-examination,' Judge Strouse said to Perry Mason.

Perry Mason rose to his full height, faced Morrison Brems on the stand.

'Have you ever been convicted of a felony, Mr Brems?'

The witness recoiled as though Mason had struck him.

Hamilton Burger, on his feet, was shouting: 'Your Honour, Your Honour!

Counsel can't *do* that! That's misconduct! Unless he has some grounds to believe–'

'You can always impeach a witness by showing he has been convicted of a felony,' Mason said as Hamilton Burger hesitated, sputtering in his rage.

'Of course you can, of course you can,' Hamilton Burger yelled. 'But you can't ask questions like that where you haven't anything on which to base such a charge. That's misconduct! That's–'

'Suppose you let him answer the question,' Mason said, and then–'

'It's misconduct! That's unprofessional. That's–'

'I think,' Judge Strouse said, 'the objection will be overruled. The witness will answer the question.'

'Remember,' Mason warned, 'you're under oath. I'm asking you the direct question. Have you ever been convicted of a felony?'

The witness who had been so sure of himself as he had regarded Mason a few short seconds earlier seemed to shrivel inside his clothes. He shifted his position uncomfortably. The court-room silence became oppressive.

'Have you?' Mason asked.

'Yes,' Brems said.

'How many times?'

'Three.'

'Did you ever use the alias of Harry Elston?'

The witness again hesitated. 'You're under oath,' Mason reminded him, 'and a handwriting expert is going to check your handwriting, so be careful what you say.'

'I refuse to answer,' the witness said, with a sudden desperate attempt at collecting himself. 'I refuse to answer on the grounds that to do so may incriminate me.'

'And,' Mason went on, 'on the seventh day of April of this year you called on your accomplice Grace Compton, who had occupied unit sixteen at The Staylonger Motel on April sixth under the name of Mrs S. G. Wilfred, and beat her up because she had been talking with me, didn't you?'

'Now just a minute, Mr Brems. Before you answer that question, remember that I had a private detective shadowing Miss Compton, shadowing the apartment house where she lived, noticing the people who went in and out of the apartment, and that I am at the present time in touch with Grace Compton in Acapulco. Now answer the question, did you or didn't you?'

'I refuse to answer,' the witness said, 'on the ground that to do so might incriminate me.'

Mason turned to the judge, conscious of the open-mouthed jurors literally sitting on the edges of their chairs.

'And now, Your Honour, I suggest that the Court take a recess until we can have an opinion of the police fingerprint expert on these fingerprints and so the police will have some opportunity to reinvestigate the murder.'

Mason sat down.

'In view of the situation,' Judge Strouse said, 'Court will take a recess until two o'clock this afternoon.'

21

Stewart Bedford, Della Street, Paul Drake, and Mason sat in Mason's office.

Bedford rubbed his hands over his eyes. 'Those damn newspaper photographers,' he said. 'They've exploded so many flash-bulbs in my face I'm completely blinded.'

'You'll get over it in an hour or so,' Mason told him. 'But you'd better let Paul Drake drive you home.'

'He won't need to,' Bedford said. 'My wife is on her way up here. Tell me, Mason, how the devil did *you* know what had happened?'

'I had a few leads to work on,' Mason said. 'Your story about the hit-and-run accident was of course something you thought up. Therefore, the blackmailers couldn't have anticipated that. But the blackmailers *did* know that you were at The Staylonger Motel because of blackmail which had been levied because of your wife. In order to get a perfect case against you, they wanted to bring your wife into it. Therefore, Morrison Brems, apparently as the thoroughly respectable manager of the motel, stated that he had seen a prowler emerging from unit twelve.

'When you and Grace Compton went out for lunch, Brems realized this was the logical time to drug the whisky, then kill Denham with your gun, loot the lock-box which had been held in joint tenancy, and blame the crime on you with the motivation being your desire to stop a continuing blackmail of you and your wife.

'For that reason, Brems wanted to direct suspicion to your wife. Elsa Griffin hadn't fooled him any when she registered under an assumed name and juggled the figures of her licence number. So Brems invented this mysterious prowler whom he said he had seen coming out of unit twelve. He gave an absolutely perfect and very detailed description of your wife, one that was so complete that almost anyone who knew her should have recognized her.'

'But, look here, Mason, *I* picked that motel.'

Mason grinned. 'You thought you did. When you check back on the circumstances, you'll realize that at a certain point the blonde told you the coast was clear and to pick any motel. The first one you passed after that was a shabby, second-rate motel. You didn't want that and the blackmailers knew you wouldn't.

'The next one was The Staylonger and you picked that. If you hadn't, the blonde would have steered you in there, anyway. You picked it the same way the man from the audience picks out a card from the deck handed him by the stage magician.'

'But what about those fingerprints? How did Elsa Griffin get so badly fooled?'

'Elsa,' Mason said, 'was the first one to swallow the story of Morrison Brems. She fell for it, hook, line and sinker. As soon as she heard the description of that woman, she became absolutely convinced that your wife had been down there at the motel. She felt certain that, if that had been the case, your wife must have been the one who killed Binney Denham. She wasn't going to say anything unless it appeared your safety was jeopardized.

'I sent her back down to unit twelve in order to get latent fingerprints. She was down there for hours. She had plenty of time not only to get the latent fingerprints, but to compare them as she took them. That is, she compared them with her own prints and when she did she found, to her chagrin, that she hadn't been able to lift a single fingerprint which hadn't been made by her. Yet she was absolutely certain in her own mind that your wife had been down there at the cabin. What she did was thoroughly logical under the circumstances. She was completely loyal to you. She had no loyalty and little affection for your wife. In spite of your instructions she had preserved those fingerprints which had been lifted from the back of the cocktail tray, so after she left the motel she drove to her apartment, got those prints, put numbers on the cards that fitted them in with the prints she was surrendering, and turned the whole batch in to me.

'She knew absolutely then that by the time her fingerprints had been eliminated there would be four prints of your wife left. She didn't intend to do anything about it unless the situation got desperate. Then she intended to use those prints to save you from being convicted.

'I will admit that there was a period when I myself was pretty much concerned about it. Elsa, of course, thought that your wife had worn gloves while she was in the cabin and so hadn't left any fingerprints. I thought that your wife was the one who had been in the cabin until I became fully convinced that she hadn't been.'

'Then what did you do?'

'Then,' Mason said, 'it was very simple. I had fingerprints lifted from Grace Compton's apartment. I placed four of the best of those in my safe. I put the same numbers on the cards that Elsa had put on her cards.'

Paul Drake shook his head. 'You pulled a fast one there, Perry. They can sure get you for that.'

'Get me for what?' Mason asked.

'Substituting evidence.'

'I didn't substitute any evidence.'

'There's a law on that,' Drake said.

'Sure there is,' Mason said, 'but I didn't substitute any evidence. I told Della Street to get me fourteen, sixteen, twelve, and nine from the safe. That's what she did. Of course, I can't help it if there were two sets of cards with numbers on them, and if Della got the wrong set. That wasn't a substitution. Of course, if Elsa Griffin had asked me if those were the prints she had given me, then I would have had to acknowledge that they weren't, or else have been guilty of deceiving the witness and concealing evidence, but she didn't ask me that question. Neither did she really compare the prints. Since she *knew* these prints she had given me belonged to Mrs Bedford she simply pretended to make a comparison, then she grabbed the prints and made for the door, where she had arranged to have Sergeant Holcomb waiting. Under the circumstances, I wasn't required to volunteer any information.'

'But how the devil did you *know*?' Bedford asked.

Mason said: 'It was quite simple. I knew that your wife hadn't left any fingerprints in the cabin because I knew she hadn't been there. Since the description given by Morrison Brems was so completely realistic down to the last detail and fitted your wife so exactly, I knew that Morrison Brems was lying. We all knew that Binney Denham had some hidden accomplice in the background. That is, we felt he did. After Grace Compton had been beaten up because she had talked with me, I knew there must be another accomplice. Who, then, could that accomplice be?

'The most logical person was Morrison Brems. Binney Denham wanted to pull his blackmailing stunts at a friendly motel where he was in partnership with the manager. You'll probably find that this motel was one of their big sources of income. Morrison Brems ran that motel. When people whose manner looked a little bit surreptitious registered there, Morrison Brems made it a point to check their baggage and their registration and find out who they were. Then the information was relayed to Binney Denham, and that's where a lot of Denham's blackmail material came from.

'They made the mistake of trying to gild the lily. They were so anxious to see that your wife was brought into it that they described her as having been down there. The police hadn't connected up the description, but Brems certainly intended to see that they did before the case was over. Elsa Griffin connected it up as soon as she heard it, and kept pestering you to get after me to find the woman who had been down there. When I didn't move fast enough to suit her, she decided to ring in the fingerprints.

'Because she knew they were fingerprints that had been taken from the silver platter and not from the motel where she said she found them, she only went through the motions of comparing them. She was so certain whose prints they were that she just didn't bother to look for distinguishing characteristics.'

'But,' Bedford asked, 'how did you know they were gilding the lily, Mason? How did you know my wife hadn't been down there?'

Mason looked him in the eyes. 'I asked her if she had been there,' he said, 'and she assured me she hadn't.'

'And you did this whole thing, you staked your reputation and everything on her word?'

Mason, still looking at Bedford, said: 'In this business, Bedford, you got to be a pretty damn good judge of character or else you don't last long.'

'I still don't see how you knew that Brems had a criminal record.'

Mason grinned. 'I was simply relying on the law of averages and of character. It would have been as impossible for Morrison Brems to have lived as long as he has with the type of mind he has without having a criminal record as it would have been for your wife to have looked me in the eyes and lied about having gone to that cabin.'

Knuckles tapped gently on the door of Mason's office.

'That'll be Ann Roann now,' Bedford said, getting to his feet. 'Mason, how the devil can I ever thank you enough for what you have done?'

Mason's answer was laconic. 'Just write thanks underneath your signature when you make out the cheque.'

RLE STANLEY GARDNER

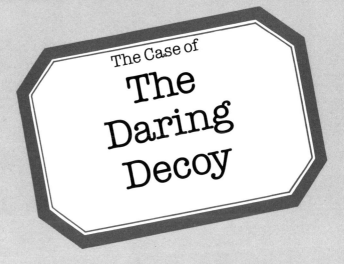

The Case of

The Daring Decoy

FOREWORD

For the most part I have dedicated my Perry Mason books to outstanding figures in the field of legal medicine. But this book is dedicated to a doctor of medicine; one of the kindest, most considerate men I have ever met. He reached the top of the ladder in his chosen profession, and then, in place of taking up golf or yachting, turned his razor-keen mind to a 'spare time' study of the problems of evidence, of law enforcement and the part the citizen could and should play in co-operating with the various law-enforcement agencies.

Merton M. Minter, M.D., is a Diplomat of the American Board of Internal Medicine, a member of the Board of Regents of the University of Texas, and, in fact, holds so many offices in the field of education, banking and medicine that there isn't room to list them here.

I am writing this because I wish more of the influential members of the medical profession would follow in Doctor Minter's steps. We need their sharp minds, their diagnostic skills, their seasoned judgement in the field of better law enforcement and the better administration of justice.

And so I dedicate this book to one of the most sympathetic, courteous, and thoughtful doctors in the world, a man who is rounding out his career doing good for his fellow man in the fields of medicine, education, law enforcement and justice, my friend,

MERTON MELROSE MINTER, M.D.

Erle Stanley Gardner

I

Jerry Conway opened the paper to page six.

There it was, just as it had been every day for the last week.

It was a half-page ad signed: PROXY HOLDERS BOARD OF SALVAGE, cleverly written, starting off with a statement that was manifestly true on the face of it:

> You stockholders of the California & Texas Global Development & Exploration Company invested your money because you wanted to make money. You wanted money for yourselves, your children, and your heirs.
>
> What are you getting?
>
> Aside from a stroke of pure luck, what has Jerry Conway done for you? He says he is 'pyramiding'. He says he is 'building'. He says he is laying a 'firm foundation'.
>
> That isn't the way the most expert operators in the business look at it.
>
> These people say Jerry Conway is laying an egg.
>
> 'You're entitled to a run for your money. You're entitled to action. You want to make a profit now, next year, and the year after, not ten years or twenty years from now.
>
> Mail your proxy to Gifford Farrell, care Proxy Holders Board of Salvage, and then, with Giff Farrell in the saddle, watch things begin to hum.
>
> Farrell believes in results, not promises. Farrell believes in action, not idle planning; in decisions, not day-dreaming; in performing, not hoping.

Conway closed the paper. It was, he admitted to himself, an ad that would get proxies. The ad also hurt.

According to the Proxy Holders Board of Salvage, it was simply a stroke of luck that the C. & T. Global Development & Exploration Company had been right in the middle of the Turkey Ridge pool.

After that pool came in, Jerry Conway could have declared big dividends, pushed up the value of the stock. Instead he had chosen to put the money into other holdings potentially as big as the Turkey Ridge pool.

Gifford Farrell had been a disruptive influence from the start. Finally there had been a showdown before the board of directors, and Farrell had been thrown out. Now he had started to fight for proxies. He was trying to wrest control of the company away from Conway.

Who was back of Farrell? What money was paying for the ads in the papers? Conway wished he knew. He wished he knew how to strike back.

Conway's over-all, master plan had to be carried out quietly. The minute he tried to blueprint his plans, he defeated his own purpose. Prices of properties he hoped to acquire would go up beyond all reason.

Conway couldn't explain publicly. He intended to address the stockholders' meeting. He was hoping that the stockholders who were there, and most of the big ones would be, would stand by him. But what about the smaller stockholders? The ones who had put in a few dollars here, a few dollars there? Stockholders who concededly wanted profits and actions?

Would these people stay in line, or would they send their proxies to Farrell?

An analysis of the books showed that there were enough small stockholders to take over control, if they acted as a unit. If Farrell could get their proxies, they'd act as a unit. If, however, Giff Farrell's clever ads didn't get more than 60 per cent of these smaller stockholders, and if Conway's personality could hold the larger investors in line at the stockholders' meeting, everything would be all right.

Those, however, were two great big ifs. And at the moment Jerry Conway didn't have the answer.

Jerry Conway folded the newspaper, switched out lights in the office, and was heading for the door, when the phone rang.

Jerry answered it. He was answering all phone calls now. He dared take no chance of offending some of the small stockholders who would want explanations, and, heaven knows, there had been enough of them who had called up! So far, these people had listened to his explanation that a company in the process of acquiring valuable oil properties couldn't blueprint its plans in the public Press. Stock that the investors had bought a year ago had more than doubled in value. Giff Farrell said that was due purely to a 'stroke of luck' with which Conway had nothing to do. Conway would always laugh when he quoted that. Stay with him and there might be more strokes of luck, he promised. Tie up with Giff Farrell's crowd, and the company would be looted for the benefit of insiders.

So Jerry picked up the telephone.

'Jerry Conway speaking,' he said.

The woman's voice was intriguing, and yet there was something about it that carried its own warning. It was too syrupy-smooth, and Conway felt he had heard it before.

'Mr Conway,' she said, 'I must see you. I have some secret information which will be of the greatest value to you.'

'I'll be in my office at nine o'clock tomorrow morning, and–'

'No, no. I can't come to your office.'

'Why not?'

'People are watching me.'

'What do *you* suggest?'

'I want to meet you privately, alone, somewhere where no one will know, somewhere where we won't be disturbed.'

'You have some idea?' Jerry asked.

'Yes, if you'll go to the Apex Motel out on Sunset tonight, register under your own name as a single, turn your lights out, leave your door unlocked, and wait until after midnight, I'll–'

'I'm sorry,' Jerry interrupted. 'That's out of the question.'

'Why is it out of the question?'

'Well,' Jerry equivocated, 'I have other plans for this evening.'

'How about tomorrow night?'

'No, I'm afraid I can't do it tomorrow night, either.'

'Is it because you're afraid of me?'

'I'm living in a glass house at the present time,' Conway said dryly.

'Look,' she said, 'I can't talk with you any longer. My name is–well, let's say it's Rosalind. Just call me Rosalind. I want to see you. I have information you should have, information that you *must* have in order to protect the stockholders, protect yourself, and save the company. Giff has a lot more proxies than you think he has. He's a very dangerous antagonist. You're going to have to start a counter campaign.'

'I'm sorry,' Conway said. 'There are certain matters I can't discuss over the telephone, and certain matters I can't discuss in the Press. After all, the stockholders must have some faith in someone. Otherwise, they'll wind up in the financial gutter. Their holdings have doubled in value during the past year under my management. I have every reason to believe they'll continue to climb, and–'

'Good heavens!' the voice exclaimed. 'Don't try to sell *me*. I *know*. Giff Farrell is a crook. He's trying to get control of the company so he and his friends can make a clean-up by manipulating company assets. I wouldn't trust him two feet away for two seconds. I want you to have the information that I have.'

'Can you put it in a letter?' Conway asked, curious.

'No, I can't put it in a letter,' she said impatiently, 'and if you knew as much as I know, you'd realize that I'm in danger just talking to you.'

'What danger?' he asked.

'In danger of getting killed,' she said angrily, and slammed up the telephone.

Jerry Conway sat at his desk for some minutes after he had dropped the receiver into its cradle on the telephone. There had been something about the voice that had carried conviction.

However, Jerry knew the necessity for caution. Half a dozen attempts had been made to frame him during the last two weeks. If he should go to a motel, leave the door open, have some young woman join him in the dark, and then perhaps a few minutes later there should be the sound of police whistles and–no, it was a chance Jerry simply couldn't take. Even a little unpleasant newspaper notoriety coming at this time could well turn the tide in the proxy battle.

Jerry Conway waited for fifteen minutes, then again switched out the lights, saw that the night latch was on the door, and went down in the elevator.

Rosalind telephoned the next day at a little after eleven.

Jerry Conway's secretary said, 'There's a woman on the line who gives the name of Rosalind and no other name. She says you know her, that she has to talk with you, that it's important.'

'I'll talk with her,' Jerry said. He picked up the telephone, said, 'Hell,' and again heard the smooth tones of Rosalind's voice, a voice that he felt he should recognize but couldn't.

'Good morning, Mr Conway.'

'Good morning, Rosalind.'

'Did you know you're being followed?'

Jerry hesitated. 'I have wondered if perhaps certain people weren't taking an undue interest in my comings and goings.'

'You're being tailed by a high-class detective agency,' she said, 'and that agency is being supplemented by a couple of thugs. Be very, very careful what you do.'

'Thank you for the warning,' Jerry said.

'But,' she went on, 'you *must* see me. I've tried to think of some way of getting in touch with you. One of the men who's shadowing you at the present time is a private detective. He's not dangerous. He's just doing a routine job of shadowing. However, there's another individual named Baker, whom they call Gashouse Baker. He's a one-man goon squad. Watch out for him! Are you armed?'

'Lord, no!' Conway said.

'Then get a permit to carry a gun,' she said. 'You shouldn't have too much trouble spotting the detective. Baker will be more difficult. At the moment, he's driving a beat-up, black car with a corner bent on the licence plate. Don't take any chances with that man!

'These people are playing for keeps and they don't intend to play fair. You're looking for a straightforward battle for proxies and you're planning everything along those lines. These people don't play that way.

'And don't ever mention to anyone that you have been in communication with me. I shouldn't have given you the name of Rosalind, but I wanted to put the cards on the table.'

Jerry Conway frowned thoughtfully. 'I wish you could tell me something of the nature of the information you have, something–'

'Look,' she said, 'I can tell you the number of proxies they hold, and if I have your assurance that you can protect me, I can give you the names of the people who have sent in proxies. However, if any of this information should get out, they'd know where it came from and I'd be in danger.'

'How much danger?' Jerry Conway asked. 'If it's economic security that you–'

'Don't be silly!' she interrupted sarcastically. 'I've seen one woman after Gashouse Baker worked her over. I–Oh-oh!'

The phone abruptly clicked and the connexion went dead.

Jerry Conway gave the matter a great deal of thought. That noon he drove around in a somewhat aimless pattern, carefully watching cars in his rearview-mirror. He couldn't be certain anyone was following him, but he became very uneasy. He felt he was in danger.

Conway knew that he was going to have to take a chance on Rosalind. If she had the information she said she had, it would be of inestimable value. If he knew the names of the persons who had sent in proxies, there would still be time to concentrate a campaign on those people.

Rosalind called shortly after two-thirty. This time there was a note of pleading and desperation in her voice.

'I *have* to get this information to you so you can act on it. Otherwise the company will be ruined.'

'Exactly what is it that you want?'

'I want to give you information. I want primarily to keep Giff Farrell and his crowd of goons from wrecking the company. I want to protect the honest investors, and I . . . I want to get even.'

'With whom?'

'Use your imagination,' she said.

'Now, look here,' Conway said, 'I can have a representative meet you. I can send someone in–'

She interrupted with a hollow laugh. 'The business that I have with you is with you personally, with the number one man in the company. I'm not taking any assurances from anyone else. If you're too cautious to meet me face to face to get this information, then I guess the things Giff Farrell is saying about you *are* true!'

Conway reached a sudden decision. 'Call me back in fifteen minutes,' he said. 'I'm not free to make arrangements at the present time. Can you call in fifteen minutes? Will you talk with me then?'

'I'll call,' she promised.

Conway summoned his secretary. 'Miss Kane, the young woman who has just called me is going to call again in fifteen minutes. She's going to make arrangements with me for a meeting, a meeting which has to be held in the greatest secrecy.

'I want you to listen in on the conversation. I want you to make shorthand notes of exactly what is said so that if the necessity should arise, you can repeat that conversation verbatim.'

Eva Kane never appeared surprised. She took things in her stride, with a calm, professional competence.

'Do you want shorthand notes of what *she* says, or shorthand notes of the entire conversation?'

'Notes of the entire conversation. Transcribe them as soon as you've taken them, and be in a position to swear to them if necessary.'

'Very well, Mr Conway,' Eva Kane said, and left the office.

When the phone failed to ring at the end of the fifteen-minute period, Conway began restlessly pacing the floor.

Abruptly the telephone rang. Conway made a dive for the desk, picked up the receiver, said, 'Yes?'

Eva Kane's calmly professional voice said, 'A young woman on the line who says you are expecting the call. A Miss Rosalind.'

'You ready, Miss Kane?' Conway asked.

'Yes, Mr Conway.'

'Put her on.'

Rosalind's voice came over the line. 'Hello, Mr Conway?'

'Rosalind?'

'Yes. What's your answer?'

'Look here,' Conway said, 'I want to talk with you, but I'll have to take adequate precautions.'

'Precautions againt what?'

'Against some sort of a trap.'

Her laugh was bitter. 'You're childless, unmarried, thirty-six. You aren't responsible to anyone for your actions. Yet you worry about traps!'

'Tonight at exactly five-thirty the private detective who is shadowing you goes off duty. Another one takes over for the night shift. They don't make contact. Sometimes the man is late. Perhaps it can be arranged for him to be late tonight. At precisely one minute past five-thirty leave your office, get in your car. Start driving west on Sunset Boulevard. Turn at Vine. Turn left on Hollywood Boulevard. Go to Ivar. Turn right, and then start running signals. Go through signals just as the lights are changing. Keep an eye on your rearview-mirror. Cut corners. Make certain you're not being followed. I think you can shake off your tail.'

'And after that?' Conway asked.

'Now, listen carefully,' she said. 'After that, after you are absolutely certain that you're not being followed, go to the Empire Drugstore on Sunset and LaBrea. There are three phone booths in that store. Go to the one farthest from the door, enter the booth and at precisely six-fifteen that phone will ring. Answer it.

'If you have been successful in ditching your shadows, you will be directed where to go. If you haven't ditched your shadows, the phone won't ring.'

'You're making all this seem terribly cloak-and-dagger,' Conway protested somewhat irritably. 'After all, if you have any information that–'

'It is terribly cloak-and-dagger,' she interrupted. 'Do you want a list of the stockholders who already have sent in proxies?'

'Very much,' he said.

'Then come and get it,' she told him, and hung up.

A few minutes later, Eva Kane entered the office with impersonal, secretarial efficiency, and handed Conway typewritten sheets.

'A transcript of the conversation,' she said.

'Thank you,' Jerry told her.

She turned, started for the door, paused, then suddenly whirled and came towards him. 'You mustn't do it, Mr Conway!'

He looked at her with some surprise.

'Oh, I know,' she said, the words pouring out in rapid succession as though she were afraid he might be going to stop her. 'You've never encouraged any personalities in the office. I'm only a piece of the office machinery as far as you're concerned. But I'm human. I know what you're going through, and I want you to win out in this fight, and . . . and I know something about women's voices, and–' She hesitated over a word or two, then trailed off into silence as though her vocal mechanism had been a motor running out of fuel.

'I didn't know I was so unapproachable,' Conway protested.

'You're not! You're not! Don't misunderstand me. It's only that you've always been impersonal . . . I mean, you've kept things on a business basis. I know I'm speaking out of turn, but please, please don't do anything as ridiculous as this woman suggests.'

'Why?' he asked.

'Because it's a trap.'

'How do you know it's a trap?'

'It stands to reason if she had any information she wanted to give you, she could simply put it in an envelope, write your name on the envelope, put a stamp on the envelope, and drop it in the nearest mailbox.'

Conway thought that over.

'All of this mystery, all of this cloak-and-dagger stuff, it's simply a trap.'

Conway said gravely, 'I can't take any chances on passing up this information.'

'You mean you're going?'

'I'm going,' he said doggedly. 'You said something about her voice?'

She nodded.

'What about it?'

'I've trained my ears to listen to voices over the telephone. I was a phone operator for two years. There's something about her voice . . . and–Tell me, do you have the feeling you've heard that voice before?'

Conway frowned. 'Now that you mention it, I do. There's something in the tempo, in the spacing of the words more than in the tone.'

Eva Kane nodded. 'We know her,' she said. 'she's someone who has been in the office. You've talked with her. She's disguising her voice in some way–the tone of it. But the tempo, the way she spaces the words can't be changed. She's someone we both know, and that makes me all the more suspicious. Why should she lie to you? I mean, why should she try to deceive you about her identity?'

'Nevertheless, I'm going to go,' Conway announced. 'The information is too valuable, too vital. I can't afford to run the chance of passing up a bet of that sort.'

Suddenly Eva Kane was back in character, an efficient, impersonal secretary.

'Very well, Mr Conway,' she said, and left the office.

Conway checked his watch with a radio time signal, started his car precisely on the minute, and followed directions. He went through a light just as it was changing and left a car which seemed to be trying to follow him hopelessly snarled in traffic with an irate traffic officer blowing his whistle.

After that, Conway drove in and out of traffic. At five minutes past six he was in the drugstore, waiting in the phone booth farthest from the door.

At six-twelve the phone rang.

Conway answered it.

'Mr Conway?' a crisply feminine voice asked.

'Yes. . . . Is this–this isn't Rosalind.'

'Don't ask questions. Rosalind must take precautions to get rid of the people who were shadowing *her*. Here are your directions. Are you ready?'

'Yes.'

'Very well. As soon as you hang up, leave the phone booth, and the drugstore. Get in your car. Drive to the Redfern Hotel. Park your car. Go to the lobby. Tell the clerk that your name is Gerald Boswell and that you're expecting a message. The clerk will hand you an envelope. Thank him, but don't tip him. Walk over to a secluded corner in the lobby and open the envelope. That envelope will give you your cue as to what you're to do next.'

She hung up without saying good-bye.

Conway left the phone booth, went at once to his car and drove directly to the Redfern Hotel.

'Do you have a message for Gerald Boswell?' he asked the clerk.

For a moment, as the clerk hesitated, Conway was afraid he might be going to ask for some identification, but the hesitation was only momentary. The clerk pulled out a sheaf of envelopes and started going through them.

'Boswell,' he said, repeated the name mechanically as he went through the envelopes. 'Boswell. What's the first name?'

'Gerald.'

'Oh, yes, Gerald Boswell.' The clerk handed Conway a long envelope, and for a moment Conway's heart gave a sudden surge. The envelope was of heavy manilla, well sealed, well filled. This could be the list of stockholders who had sent in their proxies, the list that would make all the difference in the world to him in his fight to retain the company management.

Conway moved over to a corner of the lobby, sat down in one of the worn, overstuffed chairs as though waiting for someone to join him.

Surreptitiously he sized up the other occupants of the lobby.

There was a middle-aged woman immersed in her newspaper. There was a bored, seedy-looking man who was working a crossword puzzle; a younger woman who seemed to be waiting for someone and who apparently had not the slightest interest in anything other than the street door of the hotel lobby.

Conway slipped his penknife from his pocket, slit open the envelope and slid out the contents.

To his disgust, the envelope contained only pieces of old newspaper which had been cut to size to fit into the envelope. Nor did these bits of newspaper clippings have any significance or continuity. The sections of newspaper had been cut crosswise and evidently used only to fill out the envelope.

Folded in with these pieces of newspaper, however, was a key attached to an oval brass tag carrying the imprint of the Redfern Hotel and the number of the room, 729.

His sense of prudence urged Conway to terminate the adventure then and there, but the mere thought of so doing gave him a feeling of frustration. The person who had dreamed up this plan had used applied psychology. Once persuaded to do a lot of unconventional things to avoid detection, Conway was conditioned for a step which he would never have considered if it had been put up to him at the start.

Conway pushed the strips of newspaper back into the envelope, put the envelope into the container for waste-paper and moved over towards the elevators. After all, he would at least go up and knock on the door.

The young woman who was operating the elevator seemed completely absorbed in her paperbacked novel. She gave Conway a passing glance, then lowered her eyes.

'Seven,' he said.

She moved the cage to the seventh floor, stopped it, let Conway out, and was dropping the cage back to the ground floor before Conway had more than oriented himself as to the sequence of numbers.

The hotel had an aura of second-class semi-respectability. The place was clean but it was the cleanliness of sterilization. The carpets were thin. The light fixtures were cheap, and the illumination in the corridor was somewhat dim.

Conway found Room 729 and tapped on the door.

There was no answer.

He waited and tapped again.

The key in his hand was an invitation. The thought of inserting it in the door and entering the room was only a little less distasteful than that of putting the key in his pocket, returning to the elevator and leaving for ever unsolved the mystery of the locked room and the possibility of obtaining the lists of stockholders who had sent in proxies.

Jerry Conway fitted the key to the door. The spring lock clicked smoothly, and Conway pushed the door open.

He found himself peering into the conventional sitting-room of a two-room hotel suite. The door that he judged would lead to the bedroom was closed.

'Anybody home?' Conway called.

There was no sound.

Conway closed the corridor door behind him, and gave the place a quick inspection. There was hope in his mind that this was part of an elaborate scheme to deliver the papers that he had been promised, a delivery that could be made in such a manner that he would have no contact with the person making the delivery.

He found nothing in the sitting-room and was thoughtfully contemplating the bedroom door, when the knob turned and a young woman wearing only a bra, panties and sheer stockings stepped out into the parlour, closing the bedroom door behind her. Apparently, she hadn't even seen Conway. She was humming a little tune.

Her head was wrapped in a towel. Her face was a dark blob, which Conway soon recognized as a mud pack that extended down to her throat.

The figure was exciting, and the underthings were thin, flimsy wisps of black lace which seemed only to emphasize the warm pink of the smooth skin.

Conway stood stock-still, startled and transfixed.

Then abruptly she saw him. For a moment Conway thought she was going to scream. Her mouth opened. The mask of the mud pack kept him from seeing her features. He saw only eyes and the red of a wide-open mouth.

'Now, listen! Let me explain,' Conway said, talking rapidly and moving towards the young woman. 'I take it you're not Rosalind?'

The figure answered in a thick voice due to the hard mud pack. 'I'm Rosalind's room-mate, Mildred. Who are you? How did you get in here?'

She might have been twenty-six or twenty-seven, Conway judged. Her figure was full, and every seductive curve was visible.

Standing there in the hotel suite confronting this young woman, Conway had a sense of complete unreality as though he were engaged in some amateur theatrical playing a part that he didn't fully understand, and confronted by an actress who was trying in an amateurish way to follow directions.

'*How* did you get in?' she demanded in that same thick voice.

'Rosalind gave me her key,' Conway said. 'I was to meet her here. Now look, Mildred, quit being frightened. I won't hurt you. Go get your clothes on. I'll wait for Rosalind.'

'But why should Rosalind have given you a key?' she asked. 'I–That isn't at all like Rosalind. . . . You can imagine how *I* feel coming in here half-nude and finding a strange man in the apartment. How do I know Rosalind gave you the key? Who are you, anyway?'

'I've been in touch with Rosalind,' Conway said. 'She has some papers for me. I was to pick them up here.'

'Papers?' Mildred said. 'Papers. Let me see.' She walked over to the desk with quick, purposeful steps, and again Conway had the feeling that he was watching an actress playing a part.

She pulled back the lid of the desk, put her hand inside, and suddenly Conway heard the unmistakable click of a double-action revolver being cocked. Then he saw the black, round hole of a barrel held in a trembling hand, the young woman's nervous finger pressing on the trigger.

'Hey!' Conway said. 'Don't point that thing at me, you little fool! That may go off!'

'Put your hands up,' she said.

'For heaven's sake,' Conway told her, 'don't be a fool! You've cocked that revolver, and the slightest pressure on the trigger will–Put that gun down! I'm not trying to hurt you!'

She advanced towards him, the revolver now pointing at his middle.

'Get your hands up,' she said, her voice taking on an edge of hysteria. 'You're going to jail!'

The hand that held the revolver was distinctly trembling, her finger rested against the trigger.

Conway waited while she advanced one more step, measured the distance, suddenly clamped his left hand over her wrist, grasped the gun with his right hand. Her hand was nerveless, and he had no difficulty forcing up the barrel of the revolver and at the same time pushing his thumb over the cocked hammer of the gun.

Conway wrested the gun from her limp grip, carefully lowered the hammer, shoved the weapon in his pocket.

'You little fool!' he said. 'You could have killed me! Don't you understand?'

She moved back to the davenport, seated herself and stared, apparently in abject terror.

Conway stood over her. 'Now, listen,' he said, 'get a grip on yourself. I'm not going to hurt you. I'm not here to make any trouble. I'm only trying to get some papers from Rosalind. Can't you understand that?'

'Don't hurt me!' she said. 'If you'll promise not to kill me, I'll do anything. . . . Don't hurt me! My purse is in the desk. Everything I have is in it. Take it all. Only please don't–don't . . .!'

'Shut up!' Conway snapped. 'I've tried to explain to you! Can't you understand? Can't you listen?'

'Just don't kill me!' she pleaded. 'I'll do anything you say if you just won't kill me.'

Conway abruptly reached a decision.

'I'm leaving,' he said. 'Don't go near that telephone for five minutes after I leave. Don't tell anyone that I was here, no one except Rosalind. Do you understand that?'

She simply sat there, her face a wooden mask.

Conway strode to the door, jerked it open, slammed it shut, sprinted down the corridor to the red light that marked the stairwell. He pushed open the door, ran down two flights of stairs to the fifth floor, then hurried over to the elevator and pressed the button.

It seemed an age before the elevator came up, then the door slid open and Conway stepped inside, conscious of his rapid breathing, his pounding heart.

The girl who was operating the elevator shifted her gum to the other side of her face. She held her book in her right hand. Her left hand manipulated the control which dropped the elevator to the ground floor. She didn't even look at his face, but said, 'You must have walked down two floors.'

Conway, mentally cursing his clumsiness, said nothing. The elevator girl kept her eyes lowered, raising them only for one swift glance.

Conway didn't dare to leave the key to Room 729 on the clerk's desk. Walking when he wanted to run, the revolver in his hip pocket, Conway moved rapidly across the lobby, out of the door of the hotel, and then hurried down the street to the place where he had parked his car.

He jumped inside, started the motor and adjusted himself behind the steering wheel. He became increasingly conscious of the bulge in his hip pocket.

He withdrew the ·38-calibre revolver, started to put it in the glove compartment, then just as a matter of precaution, swung open the cylinder.

There were five loaded cartridges in the cylinder, and one empty cartridge case bearing the imprint of the firing pin in the soft percussion cap.

Conway snapped the cylinder back into place, smelled the muzzle of the gun.

The odour of freshly burnt orange powder clung to the barrel.

In a sudden panic, Conway pushed the gun into the glove compartment, started the car, and drove away from the kerb fast.

When he came to a service station where there was a telephone booth, he parked the car and looked up the number of Perry Mason, Attorney at Law.

The directory gave the number of Mason's office. There was no residence phone, but a night number was listed.

Conway called the night number.

A voice came on the line and said, 'This is a recorded message. If you are calling the office of Mr Perry Mason on a matter of major importance, you may call at the office of the Drake Detective Agency, state your name, address, and business, and Mr Mason will be contacted at the earliest possible moment.'

2

The unlisted telephone in Perry Mason's apartment jangled sharply.

Only two persons in the world had that number. One was Della Street, Perry Mason's confidential secretary. The other was Paul Drake, head of the Drake Detective Agency.

Mason, who had been on the point of going out, picked up the receiver.

Paul Drake's voice came over the wire. 'Perry! I have a problem that you may want to work on.'

'What is it?'

'Have you followed the fight for proxies in the California & Texas Global Development & Exploration Company?'

'I know there is a fight on,' Mason said. 'I've seen ads in the paper for the last week.'

'Jerry Conway, president of the company, is waiting on another telephone. He's calling from a pay station. He's pretty well worked up, thinks he's been framed, and wants to see you at once.'

'What kind of frame?' Mason asked. 'Some sort of badger game, attempted bribery, or–'

'He doesn't know,' Drake said, 'but he has a revolver in his possession and the weapon has been freshly fired. Of course, I've just hit the high spots on the phone with him, but he's got a story that's sufficiently out of the ordinary so you should be interested, and he says he has money enough to pay any fee within reason. He wants action!'

'A revolver!' Mason said.

'That's right.'

'How did he get it?'

'He says he took it away from a woman.'

'Where?'

'In a hotel room.'

'Did he take her there?'

'He says not. He says he had a key to the room, and she came in and pulled the gun on him, that she had a nervous trigger finger, and he took the gun away from her. It wasn't until after he had left the place, that he noticed the gun had been freshly fired and now he's afraid he's being put on the spot.'

'That's a hell of a story!' Mason said.

'That's the way it impresses me,' Drake told him. 'The point is that if the guy is going to be picked up and he's relying on a story as phony as that, somebody should instruct him to at least tell a lie that will sound plausible.'

Mason said, 'They have to think up their own lies, Paul.'

'I know,' Paul retorted, 'but you could point out where *this* one is full of holes.'

'Can he hear your side of this conversation?'

'No.'

'Ask him if it's worth a thousand dollars for a retainer,' Mason said. 'If it is, I'll come up.'

'Hold the phone,' Drake said. 'He's on the other line.'

A moment later Drake's voice came back on the wire. 'Hello, Perry?'

'Uh-huh,' Mason said.

'Conway says it's worth two thousand. He's scared stiff. He thinks he's led with his chin.'

'Okay,' Mason said. 'Tell him to go on up to your office and make out his cheque for a thousand bucks. Get a couple of good men to stand by in case I need them. I'm on my way up.'

Mason switched out the lights in his apartment, and drove to Paul Drake's office.

Jerry Conway jumped up as Mason entered the room.

'I have a feeling that I've walked into a trap, Mr Mason,' he said. 'I don't know how bad it is. But . . . well, there's a lot of money involved in this proxy fight, and the people on the other side are willing to do anything. They'll stop at nothing!'

Drake slid a cheque across the desk to Perry Mason. 'I had Conway make out this cheque for the retainer,' he said.

'Got a couple of men lined up?' Mason asked.

Drake nodded.

Mason picked a straight-backed chair, spun it around so that the back was facing the centre of the room. He straddled the chair, propped his elbows on the back of the chair and said to Conway, 'All right, start talking.'

'There isn't much time,' Conway said nervously. 'Whatever has happened is–'

'There's no use running around blind,' Mason said. 'You're going to have to take time to tell me the story. Tell it to me fast. Begin at the beginning.'

Conway said, 'It started with a telephone call.'

'Who from?' Mason asked.

'A young woman who gave the name of Rosalind.'

'Have you seen her?'

'I don't think so. I don't know.'

'Why don't you know?'

'I saw a young woman tonight who said she was Rosalind's room-mate. I . . . I'm afraid–'

'Go on,' Mason interrupted. 'Get it over with! Don't try to make it easy on yourself. Give me the details.'

Conway told his story. Mason leaned forward, his arms folded across the back of the chair, his chin resting on his wrists, his eyes narrow with concentration. He asked no questions, took no notes, simply listened with expressionless concentration.

When Conway had finished, Mason said, 'Where's the gun?'

Conway took it from his pocket.

Mason didn't touch the gun. 'Open the cylinder,' he said.

Conway swung open the cylinder.

'Turn it so the light shines on it.'

Conway turned the weapon.

'Take out that empty shell,' Mason said.

Conway extracted the shell.

Mason leaned forward to smell the barrel and the shell. 'All right,' he said, still keeping his hands off the gun. 'Put it back. Put the gun in your pocket. Where's the key to the room in the hotel?'

'I have it here.'

'Pass it over.'

Conway handed the key to Perry Mason who inspected it for a moment, then dropped it in his pocket.

Mason turned to Paul Drake. 'I'll want you with me, Paul.'

'What about me?' Conway asked.

'You stay here.'

'What do I do with the gun?'

'Nothing!'

'Shouldn't I notify the police?'

'Not yet.'

'Why?'

'Because we don't know what we're up against yet. What about that woman in the room?'

'What about her?'

'Was she really frightened or acting?'

'Her hand was shaking and the gun was wobbling.'

'When she came out, all she had on were a bra and panties?'

'Yes.'

'Good-looking?'

'Her figure was all there.'

'Yet she didn't seem embarrassed?'

'She was frightened.'

'There's a difference. Was she embarrassed?'

'I . . . I would say just frightened. She didn't try to . . . to cover up.'

'How old?'

'Probably late twenties.'

'Blonde, brunette or red-headed?'

'She had a towel wrapped around her head. All I could see was from the neck down–and I mean all.'

'Eyes?'

'I couldn't see well enough to tell.'

'Rings?'

'I didn't notice.'

'Where did she get the gun?'

'Apparently out of the desk.'

'And after that?'

'She acted as though she thought I was going to assault her or something. She wanted to give me all of her money, and begged me not to hurt her.'

'Did her voice sound like Rosalind's voice over the telephone?'

'No. This mud pack seemed to have hardened. Her lips wouldn't move well. You know how those mud packs act. Her talk was thick–like a person talking while asleep. Rosalind's voice was different.

'I've heard Rosalind's voice before. I have the feeling that I've heard it quite a few times. It wasn't her voice so much as the spacing of the words, the tempo.'

'You don't think this girl in the hotel was Rosalind?'

'I don't think so.'

'You're not sure.'

'I'm not sure of anything.'

'Wait here until you hear from me,' Mason said. He nodded to the detective. 'Let's go, Paul.'

Mason crossed the office, held the door open.

'My car or yours?' Drake asked, as they waited for the elevator.

'Mine,' Mason said. 'It's out here.'

'You scare me to death in traffic,' Drake told him.

Mason smiled. 'No more. When John Talmage was Traffic Editor of the *Deseret News*, he followed all my cases and took me to task for the way I drove. He cited a few statistics.'

'Cure you?' Drake asked.

'Made a Christian of me,' Mason admitted. 'Watch and see.'

'I'm sceptical but willing to be convinced,' Paul told him.

Mason, carefully complying with all the traffic regulations, drove to the Redfern Hotel and found a parking space.

'Going to identify yourself?' Drake asked.

Mason shook his head. 'I'll keep in the background. You'll go to the desk, ask if there are any messages for Mr Boswell.'

Drake raised his eyebrows.

'In that way,' Mason said, 'we'll find out if the clerk remembers Conway coming in and asking the same questions. If he does, he'll look at you suspiciously and start asking questions. Then you can identify yourself and we'll start from there.'

'And if he doesn't remember?' Drake asked.

'Then,' Mason said, 'you talk with him long enough for him to remember your face. Then if anyone asks him to identify the person who came to the desk and inquired for messages for Boswell, he'll be confused on the identification.'

'Suppose there's a Boswell registered in the hotel. Then what do we do?'

'We first go to the room phones, say we want to speak with Gerald Boswell. Find out if he's registered. If he isn't, we go up to 729 and look around.'

'For what?'

'Perhaps we'll find the girl under that mud pack.'

The two men entered the Redfern Hotel and went to the house phones. Mason first asked for Gerald Boswell and was told he was in Room 729. There was no answer.

'Go on, Paul,' Mason said, handing him the key.

Paul Drake walked to the desk, stood there quietly.

The clerk looked up from some book-keeping he was doing, came over to the counter.

'Messages for Boswell?' Drake asked.

'What's the first name?'

The clerk moved over to the pigeon-holes, picked out a stack of envelopes from the one marked 'B', and started flipping them over.

Abruptly he stopped, looked at Paul Drake, said, 'You were in here earlier, weren't you, Mr Boswell? Didn't I give you an envelope?'

Drake grinned. 'Let's put it this way: I'm looking for a *recent* message.'

'I'm quite certain there isn't any,' the clerk said. 'I gave you that–Or was it you?'

Drake said casually, 'That envelope. What's come in since?'

'Nothing!'

'You're certain?'

'Yes.'

'Look it over again and make certain.'

The clerk looked through the file, then regarded Drake dubiously. 'I beg your pardon, Mr Boswell, but do you have any means of identification?'

'Sure,' Drake said.

'May I see it?'

Drake took the key to 729 from his pocket and tossed it on the counter in front of the clerk.

'Seven-two-nine,' the clerk said.

'Right,' Drake said.

The clerk moved over to the directory of guests, looked under 729, then became apologetic. 'I'm sorry, Mr Boswell. I was just making certain, that's all. If any recent messages came in, they would be in the key box. There's nothing . . . You didn't have anyone else come in this evening and ask for messages, did you?'

'Me?' Drake asked in surprise.

The clerk nodded.

'Don't be silly,' Drake told him. 'I'm able to get around. I take my own messages.'

'And I gave you a letter earlier?'

'There was a message in a brown manila envelope,' Drake said.

The clerk's face showed relief. 'I was afraid for a minute that I'd given it to the wrong party. Thank you very much.'

'Not at all,' Drake said and, picking up his key, moved over to the elevator.

Mason moved over to join him.

The girl in the elevator was reading her paperbacked novel. The picture on the cover depicted a good-looking woman in panties and bra, engaged in casual conversation with a man in evening clothes. The title was *No Smog Tomorrow*.

The elevator girl didn't look up. As Mason and Drake entered, and as the cage moved under their added weight, the operator closed the book, holding her forefinger to mark the page.

'Floor?' she asked.

'Seven,' Drake said.

She started chewing gum as though the book had been sufficiently absorbing to make her forget about the gum.

'What's your book?' Drake asked.

'A novel,' she said shortly, looking up for the first time.

'Looks spicy,' Drake said.

'Any law against my reading what I want?'

'None,' Drake said.

'You can buy it yourself at the news-stand for twenty-five cents, in case you're interested.'

'I'm interested,' Drake told her.

She flashed him a quick glance.

'But not twenty-five cents' worth,' the detective added.

She diverted her eyes, pouted, jerked the cage to a stop, said, 'Seventh floor.'

Mason and Paul Drake walked out and down the corridor.

The girl held the cage at the seventh floor. The mirror on the side of the elevator shaft showed her eyes as she watched the two men walking down the corridor.

'Go right to 729?' Drake asked Mason in a low voice. 'She's watching.'

'Sure,' Mason said.

'She's interested.'

'So much the better.'

Mason paused before the door of 729. He knocked twice. There was no answer.

Drake produced the key, glanced at Mason.

The lawyer nodded. Drake inserted the key, clicked back the latch.

The door swung back on well-oiled hinges.

There was no one in the room, although the lights were on.

Mason entered the room, closed the door behind him, called, 'Anyone there?'

No one answered.

Mason walked to the partially opened door leading into the bedroom. He knocked gently.

'Everybody decent?' he called, waited for a moment for an answer, then pushed open the door.

Abruptly he recoiled.

'All right, Paul, we've found it!'

Drake came to stand at Mason's side. The body of the girl was sprawled diagonally across one of the twin beds. Her left arm and the head were over the far edge of the bed, blonde hair hung straight down alongside the dangling arm. The girl wore a tight-fitting, light-blue sweater, and blood from a bullet wound in the left side of the chest had turned the sweater into a purplish hue. The right arm was raised as though to ward off a blow at her face, and remained stiffly grotesque. The short, disarranged skirt disclosed neat nylon legs doubled up and crossed at the ankles.

Mason crossed to the body, felt the wrist, and put slight pressure on the upturned right arm.

Puzzled, he moved around to the side of the bed and touched the left arm.

The left arm swung limply from the shoulder.

Paul Drake said, 'Good Lord, Perry, we're in a jam. We've *got* to report this. I insist.'

Mason, regarding the body in frowning concentration, said, 'Okay, Paul, we'll report it.'

Drake lunged for the telephone in the room.

'Not here! Not now!' Mason said sharply.

'We have to,' Drake said. 'Otherwise we'll be concealing evidence and making ourselves accessories. We've got to turn Conway in and let him–'

'What do you mean, we have to turn Conway in?' Mason interrupted. 'Conway is my client.'

'But he's mixed up in this thing!'

'How do you know he is?'

'He admits it!'

'The hell he does. As far as we know, there was no body in the room when he left. This isn't the girl *he* left here. If it is, she dressed after he left.'

'What do you intend to do?' Drake asked.

'Come on,' Mason told him.

'Look, Perry, I've got a licence. They can take it away. They–'

'Forget it,' Mason said. 'I'm running the show. You're acting under my instructions. I'm taking the responsibility. Come on!'

'Where?'

'To the nearest phone booth where we can have privacy. First, however, we give it a quick once-over.'

'No, Perry, no. We can't touch anything. you know that.'

'We can look around,' Mason said. 'Bathroom door partially open. No sign of baggage, no clothes anywhere. Conway said the girl was in undies and was supposed to be Rosalind's room-mate. This place doesn't look lived in.'

'Come on, Perry, for the love of Mike,' Drake protested. 'It's a trap. If they catch us prowling the place, we'll be the ones in the trap. We can claim we were going to phone in a report and they'll laugh at us, want to know what we were doing prowling the joint.'

Mason opened a closet door. 'I shouldn't have brought you along, Paul.'

'You can say that again,' Drake said.

Mason regarded the empty closet.

'Okay, Paul, let's go to the lobby and phone. This is a trap, all right. Let's go.'

Drake followed the lawyer to the elevator. The elevator girl had brought the cage back to the seventh floor. She was sitting on the stool, her knees crossed, good-looking legs where they could be seen.

She was looking at the book but seemed more interested in her pose than in the book.

She looked up as Mason and Paul Drake entered the elevator. She closed the book, marking the place with her right forefinger. Her eyes rested on Paul Drake.

'Down?' she asked.

'Down,' Mason said.

She looked Paul Drake over as she dropped the cage to the ground floor.

Drake, engrossed in his thoughts, didn't give her so much as a glance.

Mason crossed the lobby to a telephone booth, dropped a dime, and dialled the unlisted number of Della Street, his confidential secretary.

Della Street's voice said, 'Hello.'

'You decent?' Mason asked.

'Reasonably.'

'Okay. Jump in your car. Go to Paul Drake's office. You'll find a man there. His name's Conway. Identify yourself. Tell him I said he was to go with you. Get him out of circulation.'

'Where?'

Mason said, 'Put him any place, just so it isn't the Redfern Hotel.'

Della Street's voice was sharp with concentration. 'Anything else?'

'Be sure that he registers under his right name,' Mason said. 'Got that?'

'Yes, Chief.'

'All right. Listen carefully. He heard a woman's voice on the telephone. There was something in the spacing of that voice he thinks was familiar. The voice itself was disguised, but there was something in the tempo he's heard before.

'Now, it's important as hell that he identify that voice. Keep after him. Make him think. Hold his nose to the grindstone. Tell him I have to have the answer.'

'What shall I tell him about the reason for all this?' Della asked.

'Tell him you're following my instructions. *Make* him remember what it is about that voice that's familiar.'

'Okay. That all?'

'That's all. Get started. You haven't much time. Return to the office after you get him located. Be discreet. Act fast.'

'Where are you now?'

'At the Redfern Hotel.'

'Can I reach you there?'

'No. Don't try to reach me anywhere. Get this man out of circulation, then go to the office and wait.'

'Okay, Chief, I'm on my way.'

Mason hung up, dropped another dime, dialled police headquarters and said, 'Homicide, please.'

A moment later, when he had Homicide on the line, he said, 'This is Perry Mason, the attorney.'

'Just a minute,' the man's voice said. 'Sgt Holcomb's here. I'll put him on.'

'Oh-oh,' Mason said.

Sgt Holcomb's voice came over the line. 'Yes, Mr Mason,' he said with overdone politeness. 'What can we do for you tonight?'

'For one thing,' Mason said, 'you can go to the Redfern Hotel, Room 729, and look at the body of a young woman who's sprawled across one of the twin beds in the bedroom. I've been careful not to touch anything, but it's my opinion that she's quite dead.'

'Where are you now?' Holcomb asked sharply.

'In the telephone booth in the lobby of the Redfern Hotel.'

'You've been up in the room?'

'Naturally,' Mason said. 'I'm not psychic. When I tell you a body's there, it means I've seen it.'

'Why didn't you use the room phone?'

'Didn't want to foul up any finger-prints,' Mason said. 'We came down here and used the phone in the lobby.'

'Have you told anyone about this?'

'I've told you.'

Holcomb said, 'I'll have a radio car there in two minutes. I'll be there myself in fifteen minutes.'

'We'll wait for you,' Mason said. 'The room's locked.'

'How did you get in?'

'I had a key.'

'The hell you did!'

'That's right.'

'Whose room is it?'

'The room is registered in the name of Gerald Boswell.'

'You know him?'

'As far as I know,' Mason said, 'I've never seen him in my life.'

'Then how did you have the key?'

'It was given to me.'

'You wait right there,' Holcomb said.

Mason hung up the phone, said to Paul Drake, 'Well, we may as well wait.'

The lawyer seated himself in one of the overstuffed, leather chairs.

Drake, after a moment, eased himself into an adjoining chair. He was obviously unhappy.

The clerk behind the desk eyed them thoughtfully.

Mason took a cigarette case from his pocket, extracted a cigarette, tapped the end, held flame to the end of the cigarette and inhaled a deep drag.

'What the devil am I going to tell them?' Drake asked.

'I'll do the talking,' Mason told him.

They had waited less than a minute when the door opened, and a uniformed police officer hurried in. He went to the desk, talked briefly to the clerk.

The startled clerk pointed to Mason and Paul Drake. The officer came over to them.

'Are you the men who reported a body?' he asked.

'That's right,' Mason told him.

'Where is it?'

'Room 729,' Mason said. 'Do you want a key?'

The lawyer took the room key from his pocket, and handed it to the officer.

'Homicide says for you to wait here. I'm to seal up the room until they can get here.'

'Okay,' Mason told him. 'We're waiting.'

'You're Perry Mason?'

'That's right.'

'Who's this?'

'Paul Drake, private detective.'

'How'd you happen to discover the body?'

'We opened the door and walked in,' Mason said. And then added, 'Are you supposed to get our story now, or get up and see no one is in the room tampering with evidence?'

The officer said curtly, 'Don't go away!' He grabbed the key and hurried to the elevator.

The excited clerk was conferring with the girl at the hotel switchboard. A moment later she started making frantic calls.

Mason pinched out his cigarette in an ash-tray.

'They'll make us tell the whole story,' Drake said.

'Everything we *know*,' Mason said. 'We're not supposed to do any guessing for the police, only give them the evidence we have.'

'And the name of our client?'

'Not *our* client,' Mason said sharply. '*My* client. He's nothing to you. *I'm* your client.'

Mason walked over to the hotel desk, took an envelope from the rack, addressed it to himself at his office, put a stamp on the envelope, moved over to the mailbox.

Drake came to stand beside him.

Mason took Conway's cheque for a thousand dollars from his pocket, pushed it in the envelope, sealed the envelope, and dropped it in the mailbox.

'What's that for?' Drake asked.

'Someone might book me for something and search me,' Mason said. 'Even Sgt Holcomb would connect up a thousand-dollar retainer with our visit to the Redfern Hotel.'

'I don't like this,' Drake said.

'Who does?' Mason asked.

'Are we in the clear withholding Conway's name?'

'Why not? Conway didn't commit any murder.'

'How do you know he didn't?'

'He says he didn't.'

'He has the gun.'

'What gun?'

'The one with which the murder was committed!'

'How do you know it's the gun?' Mason asked.

'It has to be,' Drake said.

'I told you,' Mason told him, 'we're not supposed to engage in any surmises or jump to any conclusions as far as the police are concerned. We're supposed to tell them what we know, provided it isn't a privileged communication.'

Drake said, 'They'll sweat it out of us.'

'Not out of me, they won't,' Mason told him.

'They'll find Conway in my office.'

Mason shook his head.

'So that's it!' Drake said. 'That was the first telephone call you made!'

Mason yawned, reached for his cigarette case, said, 'You're not supposed to deal in surmises when you're talking with the police, Paul, only facts. That's all they're interested in.'

Drake cracked his knuckles nervously.

The clerk left the desk and came over to join them. 'Did you two report a body in 729?' he asked.

'Sure,' Mason said, as though surprised at the question.

'How did it happen you did that?'

'Because we found a body,' Mason told him. 'You're supposed to report to the police on things like that.'

'I mean, how did you happen to find the body?'

'Because she was there.'

'Dead or passed out?' the clerk asked.

'She looked dead, but I'm not a doctor.'

'Mr Boswell was with you when you found the body?' the clerk asked.

'Boswell?' Mason asked in surprise.

The clerk nodded towards Paul Drake.

'That's not Boswell,' Mason said.

'He claimed he was Boswell,' the clerk said accusingly.

'No, he didn't,' Mason said. 'He asked if there were any messages for Mr Boswell.'

'And I asked him to identify himself,' the clerk said indignantly.

'And he put the key to 729 on the counter,' Mason said. 'You went and looked up the registration and found it was in the name of Boswell. You felt that was all the identification you needed. You didn't ask him for a driving licence. You didn't ask him if his name was Boswell. You asked him for identification, and he put the key on the counter.'

The clerk said indignantly, 'I was led to believe I was dealing with Mr Boswell. The police aren't going to like this.'

'That's unfortunate,' Mason said, and then added, 'for you.'

'I asked him for identification as Boswell.'

'No, you didn't. You asked him for *some* identification.'

'That's a technicality, and you know it.'

'What's a technicality?'

'I meant that I wanted to know who he was. I wanted to see his identification.'

'Then you should have asked him for it and insisted on seeing it,' Mason said. 'Don't try to hold *us* responsible for *your* mistakes.'

'The room is registered in the name of Gerald Boswell.'

'Uh-huh,' Mason said.

'And this is the man who claimed to be Boswell earlier in the evening. He got an envelope from me.'

'You're sure?' Mason asked.

'Of course I'm sure.'

'You weren't so sure a moment ago.'

'I *was* sure.'

'Then why did you ask him for identification?'

'I wanted to be certain he was the same man.'

'Then you *weren't* certain.'

'I'm not going to let you cross-examine me.'

'That's what you think,' Mason told him, grinning. 'Before you get done, you'll be on the witness stand. Then I'll give you a *real* cross-examination.'

'Who are you?'

'The name's Perry Mason.'

The clerk was nonplussed. 'The lawyer?'

'That's right.'

Abruptly the door of the lobby pushed open, and Sgt Holcomb, followed by two officers in plain clothes, came striding across towards the elevators, saw Mason, Drake and the clerk, and detoured over to them.

'Good evening, Sergeant,' Mason said cordially.

Sgt Holcomb ignored the greeting.

He glared at Perry Mason. 'How does it happen *you're* in on this?'

'In the interests of my client, I went to 729 to look for some evidence,' Mason said.

'In the interest of whom?'

'A client.'

'All right,' Holcomb said, 'let's quit playing ring-around-the-rosy. This is murder. Who was the client?'

Mason shook his head and said, 'That information is confidential.'

'You can't withhold that,' Holcomb told him. 'You'll become an accessory, if you try to protect a murderer.'

'This man wasn't a murderer,' Mason said.

'How do you know?'

'I know. Furthermore, he's my client. I don't have to divulge the names of my clients to anyone.'

'You can't withhold evidence.'

'I'm not withholding any *evidence*. As soon as I entered the room, I found a body. As soon as I found the body, I notified you.'

The clerk said, 'Excuse me, Sergeant, but this man standing here is the client.'

Sgt Holcomb said disdainfully, 'Don't be silly. That guy's the private detective who does Mason's investigative work. Mason called him in after he knew there'd been a murder.'

'I'm sorry, Sergeant,' the clerk protested, 'but that isn't true in this case.'

'How do you know?'

'That's the man who got the key to the room in the first place. His secretary registered for him. He's been in several times asking for messages.'

Sgt Holcomb turned to Paul Drake. 'Hey! Wait a minute! Wait a minute! What's all this?'

Paul Drake said, 'The guy's nuts!'

'What's your name?' Holcomb asked the clerk.

'Bob King.'

'All right. Now, what's this about the room?'

'It was rented about two o'clock. A young woman came to the desk and said she was the secretary of Gerald Boswell, that Boswell wanted to have a suite in the hotel for one day, that he would appear later, and go to the suite, but that she wanted to inspect it and make sure it was okay, that since she had no baggage, she would pay the rent in advance and take the keys. She asked for two keys.'

'Say,' Holcomb said, 'you're giving out a hell of a lot of valuable information.'

'Well, you asked for it. What's valuable about that?'

Holcomb jerked his head towards Mason. 'He's drinking it in.'

'Well, you asked me.'

'All right. Now shut up. . . . Wait a minute. Tell me about Paul Drake here.'

'He showed up about six-thirty, asked for a message, gave the name of Boswell, and I went through the file and gave him an envelope.'

'An envelope containing a key?' Holcomb asked.

'Perhaps the key was in it, but as I remember it now, and it's beginning to come back to me, it was a big, heavy manila envelope, thick, and jammed with papers.'

'And it was Paul Drake here who got the letter?'

'I think so. . . . Yes, this was the man.'

'Then what did he do?'

'Went up to the suite. I didn't pay much attention. He seemed quiet and respectable, and the suite was paid for in advance.'

Holcomb whirled to Paul Drake and said, 'What about this?'

Drake hesitated.

'I can answer for Paul Drake,' Mason said. 'I think there has been a case of mistaken identity.'

'The hell there has!' Sgt Holcomb said. 'Drake went up there on some kind of job for you! This girl got herself bumped off in his room, and he sent out an SOS for you. He didn't stay in the suite, did he?' Holcomb asked the clerk.

'I don't know. I didn't pay attention. He came back this second time and asked for messages. That was when I had occasion to look at him particularly, because these two gentlemen were together and I asked this man, whom you say is Mr Drake but who gave me the name of Boswell, if I hadn't already given him a message.'

Sgt Holcomb said to Drake, 'We may not be able to make Mason kick through with the name of a client, but we can sure as hell make a private detective tell what he knows about a murder or bust him wide open.'

Mason said, 'I tell you, Sergeant, it's a case of mistaken identification.'

'Phooey!' Holcomb said. 'I'm going up and take a look at the place. We'll have a finger-print man up there. If we find your prints and–'

'We were up there,' Mason said. 'No one questions that. That's where we discovered the body.'

'Drake with you.'

'Yes.'

'You came in together?'

'That's right.'

'What about the story King tells about Drake going to the desk and asking for messages?'

'That part of it is true,' Mason said. 'We had reason to believe the suite was registered in the name of Boswell, and Drake, acting purely in an investigative capacity, asked if there were any messages for Boswell. He never said he was Boswell.'

Sgt Holcomb said, 'This thing sounds fishy as hell to me. You two stick around. I'm going up. Remember now, don't leave. I want to question you further.'

Holcomb strode towards the elevator.

Mason turned to Paul Drake, said, 'Get on the phone, Paul. Start locating more operatives. I want half a dozen men and a couple of good-looking women, if I can get them.'

'You can get them,' Drake said, 'but, if you don't mind my asking the question, just what the hell do you intend to do?'

'Protect my client, of course,' Mason told him.

'I mean about me,' Drake said.

'I'm going to get you off the hook,' Mason told him.

'How?'

'By letting you tell everything you know.'

'But I know the name of your client.'

'I can't keep him out of it,' Mason said. 'He's walked into a trap. All I can hope to do now is to gain time.'

'How much time?'

'A few hours.'

'What can you do in that time?' Drake asked.

'I don't know until I try,' Mason said. 'Get on the phone and line up some good operatives. Have them at your office. Come on, Paul. Let's go!'

Drake went to the telephone booth.

Mason lit a cigarette, paced the floor of the lobby thoughtfully.

A deputy coroner, carrying a black bag, two plainclothes men, a police photographer loaded with cameras and flash-bulbs entered the hotel.

Sgt Holcomb came back down as Drake finished with his telephoning.

'All right,' Holcomb said. 'What do you know about this?'

'Only what we've told you,' Mason said. 'We went to that room. We entered it. We found a corpse. We called you.'

'I know, I know,' Holcomb said. 'But how did you happen to go to that room in the first place?'

'I was acting on behalf of a client.'

'All right. Who's the client?'

'I can't tell you the name of my client until I get his permission.'

'Then get his permission.'

'I will, but I can't get it now. I'll get it first thing in the morning.'

'Well, you can't hold out on us in a case like this. It's one thing to be an attorney, and another thing to be an accessory.'

'I'm not trying to hold out,' Mason said. 'I can't betray the confidences of my client. My client will have to speak for himself. I need time to get in touch with him.'

'Tell me who he is and *we'll* let him speak for himself.'

Mason shook his head. 'I can't give you his name without his permission. I'll have my client at the district attorney's office at nine o'clock in the morning.

My client will submit to questioning. I'll be there. I'll advise him as to his rights. I can tell you this, Sergeant: To the best of my client's knowledge, there was no corpse in the suite when my client left it. I expected to meet someone there.'

'Who?'

'A woman.'

'This one who was killed?'

'I don't think so.'

'Look, we want to talk with this guy, whoever he is.'

'At nine in the morning,' Mason said firmly.

Holcomb regarded him with smouldering hostility. 'I *could* take *you* in as a material witness.'

'To what?' Mason asked. 'I've told you all I know about the murder. As far as the private affairs of my client are concerned, he's going to speak for himself. Now, if you want to start getting tough, we'll both get tough and I'll withdraw my offer to have my client at the D. A.'s office at nine in the morning.'

Holcomb said angrily, 'All right, have it your way. But remember this. We're not considering this as co-operation. You have your client there at nine o'clock, and he won't be entitled to one damned bit of consideration.'

'He'll be there,' Mason said, 'and we're not asking for consideration. We're asking for our rights. And I think I know what they are. . . . Come on, Paul.'

Mason turned and walked out.

3

It was shortly after eight-thirty that evening when Mason and Drake left the elevator and walked down the echoing corridor of the office building.

The lawyer left Drake at the lighted door in the office of the Drake Detective Agency and kept on down the corridor. He turned at a right angle, walked to the door marked: PERRY MASON, ATTORNEY AT LAW, PRIVATE, fitted his latchkey and opened the door.

Della Street was seated at her secretarial desk reading a newspaper.

She dropped the paper to the floor, ran towards Mason almost by the time he had the door open.

'Chief,' she said, 'what is it? Is it . . . a murder?'

Mason nodded.

'Who found the body?'

'We did.'

'That's bad!'

'I know,' Mason said, putting his arm around her shoulder and patting her reassuringly. 'We always seem to be finding bodies.'

'Who was it?'

'No one seems to know. Rather an attractive young woman sprawled out on a bed. What about our client?'

'He's taken care of.'

'Where?'

'Do you remember the Gladedell Motel?'

Mason nodded.

'The man who runs it is friendly, and it's close in.'

'Did you call on the manager personally?'

She shook her head. 'We drove down together. I had Mr Conway let me out a block and a half from the motel. Then he went in and registered by himself, came back, picked me up, reported and took me to where I could get a taxi-cab. He's in Unit 21. I came back by cab. I didn't want to use my own car. I was afraid someone might notice the licence number if I left it parked near the motel.'

'How much did you find out on the trip down?' Mason asked.

'Quite a bit.'

'Such as?'

'Jerry Conway's a very eligible bachelor. He seems to be really a grand person. He takes an interest in the people who work with him and seems to be on the up and up.

'Giff Farrell worked for Conway for a year or two, then Conway helped him get promoted to assistant manager. It took Conway a year to find it out, but Farrell was systematically trying to undermine Conway. He started rumours. He got confidential information from the files and used it in such a way that it would make things more difficult for Conway. In fact, he did everything he could to get Conway in bad. Finally Conway found out about it and fired him. Farrell took the matter to the directors and he had been preparing his case for months. He'd made careful note of all sorts of things that had happened, and I guess there was quite a scene at the directors' meeting.'

Mason nodded.

'Farrell almost made it stick. He might have done so, if it hadn't been for the loyalty of one of the secretaries. Conway was able to show that Farrell had been passing confidential information on to a competitive company, simply in order to discredit the programme Conway was carrying out. When that became apparent, the directors threw Farrell out. Farrell waited for an opportunity and then started this campaign trying to get proxies.

'Now then,' she went on, 'I worked on him all the way down to see if he could place the voice of the person who phoned him. He seems to think the voice was disguised as to tone, and it was the tempo that was hauntingly familiar. He just can't place it.

'I told him to keep working on it and phone Drake's office if he came up with any answers.

'His secretary, Eva Kane, used to be a phone operator and is accustomed to listening to voices on the phone. She feels positive the voice was that of someone they both know.'

Mason said, 'Well, I've got to go talk with Conway. You'd better go home, Della.'

She smiled and shook her head. 'I'll stay and hold the fort for a while. Phone if you want anything. I'll make some coffee in the electric percolator.'

Mason drove his car past the lighted office of the Gladedell Motel, stopped in front of Unit 21, parking his car beside Conway's car, and switched out the lights.

Jerry Conway opened the door of Unit 21, but didn't come out in the light. He stood back on the inside and said, 'Come on in, Mason.'

Mason entered and closed the door behind him.

Conway indicated a chair for Mason, seated himself on the edge of the bed.

'How bad is it?' he said.

Mason said, 'Keep your voice down. These units are close together, and the walls may be thin. It's bad!'

'How bad?'

'Murder!'

'Murder!' Conway exclaimed.

'Watch it!' Mason warned. 'Keep your voice down.'

'Good heavens!'

'You should have known,' Mason told him. 'I wouldn't have spirited you down here unless it had been serious.'

'I knew it was bad . . . but I hadn't–Who was killed? Farrell?'

'No, some woman.'

'A woman?'

'That's right, a young woman. Now, tell me if you've seen her, and I want you to think it over carefully. This is a woman about twenty-six or twenty-seven, blonde, with blue eyes and a good figure, but perhaps a little over-developed. The waist seemed slim, but she had curves above and below. She was wearing a light-blue sweater that probably matched her eyes.'

Conway thought for a moment, then shook his head. 'She means nothing to me–unless she was the girl I saw. She had black-lace underthings. I think her eyes were sort of light, but that black mud pack on her face would make her eyes seem light. I can remember how the whites of her eyes glistened.'

'How about young women you know?' Mason asked. 'Any of them fit that description?'

'Listen,' Conway said impatiently, 'we have fifteen or twenty girls working for us. I can't seem to place one of that description off-hand. You say she's good-looking?'

'Very!'

'Conway thought again, shook his head.

'Try tying it up with the voice?'Mason asked.

'I've been trying to.'

'Let's take a look at that gun.'

Conway handed Mason the revolver. Mason broke it open, looked at it, took down the numbers in his note-book.

'You're going to try to trace it?' Conway asked.

'That's right,' Mason said. 'C 48809. I'll try to trace it. What about this secretary of yours? Where does she live?'

'Eva Kane. Cloudcroft Apartments.'

Mason said, 'You're going to have to go before the D.A. tomorrow morning at nine o'clock and tell your story.'

'Do I have to?'

Mason nodded.

'What do I tell him?'

'I'll be with you,' Mason said. 'I'll pick you up at eight o'clock. We'll talk on the way in.'

'Here?'

'Here,' Mason said.

'How about going back to my apartment?'

Mason shook his head.

'Why not?' Conway asked. 'They won't be able to get a line on me this early.

I want to get some things: toothbrush, pyjamas, razor, and a clean shirt.'

Mason said, 'Go to an all-night drugstore. Buy shaving things and a toothbrush. You'll have to get along without the clean shirt.'

'Surely you don't think they'd spot me if I went to my apartment?'

'Why not?' Mason asked. 'Someone set a trap for you. We don't know when that someone intends to spring the trap. Perhaps he'd like to have you sit tight for four or five days before giving a tip-off to the police and having you picked up. By that time, your silence would have made it seem all the worse. On the other hand, perhaps he knows that I'm in the picture and has decided to tip off the police so they can pick you up before I'll have a chance to find out what it's all about and advise you what to do.'

'Well, *you* can't do anything between now and nine o'clock tomorrow morning,' Conway said.

'The hell I can't!' Mason told him. 'I'm going to have a busy night. You go to an all-night drugstore, get what you want, then come back here and stay here.'

'Do I keep the gun?'

'You keep it!' Mason said. 'And be damned sure that nothing happens to it!'

'Why? Oh yes, I see your point. If I should try to get rid of it, that would be playing right into their hands.'

'Right into their hands is right,' Mason said. 'It would amount to an acknowledgement of guilt. I want you to tell your story, tell it in your way up to the time you left the hotel, got in your car and drove away.'

'I stop there?'

'You stop there,' Mason said. 'Don't tell them where you spent the night or anything about it. It's none of their damned business. I told the police I'd have you at the D.A.'s office at nine o'clock in the morning, and you're going to be there.'

'You know what this means?' Conway said. 'Unless I can convince the police, it's going to put me behind the eight ball. If the police should detain me or accuse me of having fired the fatal shot, you can realize what would happen at the stockholders' meeting!'

'Sure!' Mason said. 'Why do you suppose a trap was set for you in the first place?'

'Somehow,' Conway said, 'I can't believe that it was a trap.'

'You can't believe it was a trap!' Mason exclaimed. 'Hell's bells! The thing sticks out like a sore thumb. Here was this girl in her undies pulling a gun on you, her hand shaking, and she walked towards you, *kept walking towards you!*'

'Well, what's wrong with that?'

'Everything!' Mason said. 'A girl half-nude getting a gun out of the desk would have been backing away from you and telling you to get out of the room. She didn't tell you to get out of the room. She told you to put your hands up and she kept walking towards you with the gun cocked and her hand shaking. You just *had* to take it away from her. She did everything but shove it in your hand.'

'You think it will turn out to be the murder weapon?'

'I know damned well it will be the murder weapon!' Mason said. 'And you'll probably find that the young woman who was murdered was someone who had this list of stockholders who had sent in their proxies.'

Conway thought that over for a moment. 'Yes, that part of it was a trap, all right. It had to be a trap. Yet somehow, Mason, I have the distinct feeling that there was an element of sincerity about that woman who called herself Rosalind. I think if we can ever get to the bottom of it, we'll find that–I wonder if that young woman who was killed was Rosalind.'

'Chances are about ten to one that she was. This girl told you that she was Rosalind's room-mate, and that was their suite. That suite has been stripped clean. There isn't so much as a pair of stockings in the place, no clothes, no baggage, nothing.'

'But won't that make it look all the more like a trap? Can't we explain to the D.A. that I was framed?'

'Sure we can,' Mason said. 'Then we can try to make it stick. A good deal depends on whether we can find something to back up your story. The way you tell it, it sounds fishy as hell!'

'But I'm telling the truth,' Conway said.

'I know,' Mason told him, 'but the D.A. is going to be cold, hostile, and bitter. He won't like it because you didn't go to the police instead of consulting an attorney. What's more, we don't know yet how much of a trap you've walked into.'

'You think there's more?'

'Sure there's more,' Mason said. 'But there are some things about it I can't figure.'

'Such as what?'

'If the idea had been to frame you for murder,' Mason told him, 'they'd have gone about it in a different way. If the Farrell crowd had been willing to take a chance on a killing, it would have been easier for them to have killed you and let it go at that.'

'The evidence seems to indicate that they'd been planting one kind of trap for you to walk into, and then something happened and they found themselves with a corpse on their hands. So then they worked fast and tried to switch things around so they had you on a murder rap. When they start moving fast like that, they can easily make mistakes. If they make just one mistake, we may be able to trip them.'

Conway said, 'I know that I look like a fool in this thing, Mason, but hang it! I can't get over feeling that this Rosalind was sincere, that she really had this information she wanted to give me, that she was in danger. She said herself that she might be killed if anyone thought she was going to turn over this information to me.'

'That makes sense,' Mason told him. 'If she wasn't tied up with Farrell in *some* way, she wouldn't have had access to the information you wanted. If she *was* tied up with Farrell and was going to run out on him, almost anything could have happened.'

Suddenly Conway's face lit up. He snapped his fingers.

'What?' Mason asked.

'I'm just getting an idea,' Conway said. 'Why should I have to wait here like a sitting duck while *they* start sniping at *me*? Why couldn't I double-cross them at this stage of the game?'

'How?' Mason asked.

'Let me think. I may have an idea.'

'Ideas are all right,' Mason told him, 'but let's be damned certain that you don't do anything that backfires. So far you've had things done for you. Let's keep it that way.'

Conway thought for a moment, then said, 'Hang it, Mason! Farrell is mixed up in this thing. He had to be the one who killed that girl. He–'

'Now, wait a minute,' Mason said. 'Don't start trying to think out antidotes until we're sure what the poison is and how much of a dose you've had.'

Conway was excited now. 'I tell you I'm certain. This girl Rosalind was sincere. She was terrified. She told me herself that she was afraid she'd be killed if anyone knew. . . . Farrell found out what she was doing and–'

'And you think Farrell killed her?'

'No,' Conway said, 'but I think this Gashouse Baker, or some of his thugs did, and then Farrell got in a panic and tried to blame it on me.'

'That checks,' Mason said. 'I'm willing to ride along with you on that, but so far it's just an idea.'

'Farrell tried to trap me,' Conway said. 'I–'

Abruptly he broke off.

'Well?' Mason asked.

'Let me think,' Conway told him.

'All right. Do your thinking,' Mason said, 'but don't start moving until you know where you are. In the meantime, ring up your secretary and tell her that I'm coming up to talk with her.'

'Shall I tell her anything about what happened?'

'Don't tell her what happened. Don't tell her where you are,' Mason said. 'Simply tell her that I'm coming up to talk with her, that I'm your attorney, that you want her to co-operate with me to the limit. Tell her nothing else.'

'Okay,' Conway said. 'I'd better get busy. I've got a lot of things to do.'

Mason looked at him suspiciously. 'Such as what?'

'Such as getting that phone call through, getting to an all-night drugstore and making my purchases.'

Mason regarded him thoughtfully. 'You're getting filled with energy all at once.'

'When there's something to be done, I want to get started.'

'All right,' Mason said, 'start in by calling your secretary. Tell her I'll be there in fifteen minutes.'

'And I'll see you at eight o'clock in the morning?'

'A little after eight,' Mason said. 'Be sure you have breakfast. You won't want to tackle what we're going up against on an empty stomach.'

4

Mason left the motel, stopped at a phone booth, called Paul Drake's office.

'Anyone found out who the corpse is, Paul?'

'Not yet.'

'I've got a job for you.'

'What?'

'I want that gun traced.'

'What's the number?'

'Smith & Wesson C 48809.'

'It won't be easy to get the dope on it tonight.'

'I didn't ask you if it would be easy. I said I wanted it traced.'

'Have a heart, Perry!'

'I'm having a heart. I told you to get your men lined up. Now put 'em to work.'

'Will I be seeing you?'

'In an hour or two.'

Mason hung up the phone, drove to the Cloudcroft Apartments, and tapped gently on the door of Eva Kane's apartment.

The door was almost instantly opened.

'Miss Kane?'

'Yes. Mr Mason?'

'That's right.'

'Come in, please. Mr Conway telephoned about you.'

Mason entered a typical one-room furnished apartment, wide-mirrored doors concealing the roll-away bed. Here and there were bits of individual touches, but for the most part the apartment adhered to the standard pattern.

'Do sit down, Mr Mason. That chair is fairly comfortable. Can you tell me what happened?'

'What do you mean, what happened?' Mason asked.

'You see, the last I knew Mr Conway was going out to keep that appointment. I begged him not to. I had a premonition that something terrible was going to happen.'

'It's all right,' Mason said. 'We're in the middle of a three-ring circus, and I'd like to start getting things unscrambled before too many people catch up with me.'

'But what happened? Is Mr Conway–? He told me he was not in his apartment, and he couldn't tell me where he was.'

'He's temporarily out of circulation,' Mason said. 'We're going to be at the district attorney's office at nine o'clock in the morning.'

'The district attorney's office!'

Mason nodded.

'Why?'

'Someone got killed.'

'Killed!'

Mason nodded. 'Murdered.'

'Who was it?'

'We don't know. Some young woman. Blonde hair. Blue eyes. Rather slender waist, but lots above the waist and quite a bit below. About–oh, somewhere along twenty-seven. Blue eyes. Tight-fitting sweater. . . . Does that ring any bell?'

'That much of it rings too many bells, Mr Mason. I know lots of girls that description would fit. 'How did it happen? Was she the woman Mr Conway was to meet, the one who called herself Rosalind?'

'We don't know,' Mason said. 'I haven't time to give you a lot of information. I have too many things to do between now and nine o'clock tomorrow morning. *You're* going to have to give *me* information. Now, about that voice. I understand there was something vaguely familiar about that voice, about the tempo of it?'

She nodded.

'All right. Let's think,' Mason told her.

'I've been trying to think. I . . . I'm so worried about Mr Conway, I'm afraid–Oh, I just had a feeling it was a trap.'

'You like him a lot?' Mason asked.

She suddenly shifted her eyes. Her face coloured. 'He's very nice,' she said. 'However, he doesn't encourage personal relationships at the office. He's always very courteous and very considerate but–Well, not like Mr Farrell.'

'What about Farrell?' Mason asked.

'Farrell!' she spat suddenly with dislike in her voice.

'What about him?' Mason asked. 'I take it he's different from Conway?'

'Very different!'

'Well,' Mason said, 'you're going to have to quit thinking about Conway, and start thinking about that voice, if you want to help him. You're going to have to try and place what it was about the voice that was familiar.'

She shook her head. 'I've been thinking and thinking, and somehow it just eludes me. Sometimes I feel that I almost have it and then it's gone.'

'All right,' Mason said, 'let's start doing some methodical thinking. Rosalind, whoever she was, promised to deliver lists of those who had sent in their proxies.'

She nodded.

'Therefore,' Mason said, 'she was either baiting a trap for Conway–and the way it looks now she was baiting a trap–or she was offering genuine information. In either event, she had to be someone who was fairly close to Farrell.

'If she was baiting a trap, then she was Farrell's tool, because the Farrell crowd would be the only ones who would wish Conway any bad luck. If, on the other hand, she was acting in good faith, then she must have had access to information that only some trusted employee of Farrell's would have.'

Eva Kane nodded.

'It was a woman's voice,' Mason said. 'Did it sound young?'

'I think so. I think it was a young woman.'

'Are many young women close to Farrell?'

She laughed and said, 'Mr Farrell is very close to many young women. Mr Farrell is a man with restless hands and roving eyes. He doesn't want any one woman. He wants women–plural. He doesn't want to settle down and have a home, he wants to satisfy his ego. He wants to play the field.'

'A little difficult to work for?' Mason asked.

'It depends on the way you look at it,' she said dryly. 'Some girls seem to like it. And to like him.'

'He's married?'

'Yes, he's married, but I understand they separated a month ago.'

'What kind of woman is his wife?'

'Very nice. She's–' Abruptly Eva Kane sucked in her breath. Her eyes became wide. 'That's it, Mr Mason! That's it!'

'What is?'

'The voice. Rosalind! It's Evangeline Farrell!'

'Now, wait a minute,' Mason said. 'You're certain?'

'Yes, yes! I knew all along there was something about it that–I've talked with her on the phone, when Mr Farrell was with us. She has that peculiar trick of holding on to one word for a beat and then speaking rapidly for five or six words, then pausing and speaking rapidly again.'

'She was trying to disguise her voice on the phone?' Mason asked.

'Yes. The voice was disguised. It was–Oh, very sweet and seductive and syrupy and–But that little trick of timing. That's distinctive. That was Evangeline Farrell.'

'She's not getting along with her husband?'

'So I understand. They've separated. It was–Oh, it's been a month or so ago. There was something in the paper about it. One of the gossip columnists had an article. She walked out on him and–I don't know what did happen. I don't think she's filed suit for divorce. Maybe she wants a reconciliation.'

'Do you know where she lives?' Mason asked.

'They had a rather swank apartment and . . . and I think she was the one who moved out. I think she left him.'

'No divorce?'

'Not that I know of.'

'Grounds?'

'There should be lots of them. Around us girls at the office he didn't even bother to be subtle about it.'

'Where can I get her present address?'

'I may have it in our address book. You see, she's a stockholder in the Texas Global. Because of the proxy fight, I've made lists of the names and addresses of all stockholders of record. There's one at the office, Mr Conway has one, and I have one.'

'Here?'

'Yes. I keep mine with me at all times.'

'How does it happen she's a stockholder?'

'Part of Mr Farrell's compensation while he was with us was in stock, and those shares of stock were turned over to his wife.'

'When he got them, or as a result of some property settlement?'

'When he got them. He likes to keep all his property in the name of some other person. But I think she wrote about them after the separation. I'm certain we had a letter giving a new address.'

'See if you can find that address,' Mason said.

She said, 'Pardon me,' went to a desk, pulled out a large address book, thumbed through the pages, then said, 'I have it. It's the Holly Arms.'

'I know the place,' Mason told her. 'She's living there?'

'Yes. Do you want to talk with her on the phone?'

He thought a moment, then said, 'No, I'd better surprise her with this. Thanks a lot, Miss Kane.'

'Is there anything I can do–to help?'

'You've done it.'

'If Mr Conway phones, should I tell him that I think I know the voice?'

'Tell him nothing,' Mason said. 'Not over the telephone. You can't tell who's listening. Thanks a lot. I'm on my way.'

5

Mason picked up the house telephone in the lobby of the apartment hotel.

'Mrs Farrell, please.'

The girl at the switchboard was dubious. 'I beg your pardon. It's after ten o'clock. Was she–?'

'She's expecting the call,' Mason said.

'Very well.'

A moment later a woman's voice said, 'Hello.'

Mason said, 'I'm an attorney, Mrs Farrell. I'd like to see you on a matter of some importance.'

'Are you representing my husband?'

'Definitely not.'

'When did you wish to see me?'

'Right away.'

'Right away? Why that's impossible! . . . What is your name, please?'

'Mason.'

'You're not–not *Perry* Mason?'

'That's right.'

'Where are you, Mr Mason?'

'I'm downstairs.'

'Are you–? Is anyone with you?'

'No.'

'May I ask why you want to see me?'

'I'd prefer not to discuss it over the telephone,' Mason said. 'I can assure you it's a matter of some urgency and it may be to your advantage.'

'Very well. Will you come on up, Mr Mason? I'm in lounging pyjamas. I was reading and–'

'I'd like to come right away, if I may.'

'All right. Come on up. You have the number?'

'I'll be right up,' Mason said.

Mason took the elevator, walked down a corridor, pressed his finger against the mother-of-pearl button beside the door of Mrs Farrell's apartment. Almost instantly the door was opened by a striking, red-headed woman who wore Chinese silk lounging pyjamas, embroidered with silken dragons. There was the aroma of Oriental incense in the apartment.

'Mr Mason?' she asked.

Mason nodded.

She gave him her hand. 'How do you do? Won't you come in?'

Mason found himself in the living-room of an apartment which had at least two rooms.

Lights were low, and there was an air of scented mystery about the place.

The brightest spot in the room was where a silk-shaded reading lamp cast subdued light on a deep reclining chair and foot-stool.

An opened book lay face down on the table near the arm of the chair.

'Please be seated, Mr Mason,' Mrs Farrell said, and then when Mason had seated himself, glided across to the easy chair, dropped into its depths with a snuggling motion and picked up a long, carved, ivory cigarette holder, which contained a half-smoked cigarette.

She took a deep drag, said, 'What is it you want to talk with me about, Mr Mason?'

'About Texas Global and the proxy battle.'

'Oh, yes. And may I ask why you're interested?'

'I'm representing Jerry Conway.'

'Oh!'

'Why did *you* want to talk with him?' Mason asked.

'Me? Talk with Mr Conway?'

'That's right.'

She chose her words carefully. 'I don't want to talk with him. I know Mr Conway. I like him. I have great confidence in his business management. I suppose you know, Mr Mason, that my husband and I have separated.

'I expected to file suit for divorce on grounds which–Well, frankly, Mr Mason, you're a lawyer and you understand those things. The grounds may depend somewhat on the type of property settlement which is worked out.'

'There is considerable property?' Mason asked.

'As to that,' she said, 'there are two ways of thinking. Gifford Farrell is a gambler and a plunger. There *should* be quite a bit of money, but Gifford's attorney insists that there is very little.'

'However, he has an earning capacity?' Mason said.

'Yes. He's accustomed to doing big things in a big way.'

'Therefore,' Mason pointed out, 'it would be very much to your interest to see that he wins out in this proxy fight.'

'Why do you say that?'

'Because then he would be in clover financially.'

She took a deep drag on the cigarette, exhaled, said nothing.

'Well?' Mason asked.

'I would say that was a fairly obvious conclusion, Mr Mason.'

She extracted the end of the cigarette from the ivory holder, ground it out in the ash-tray.

'May I fix you a drink, Mr Mason?'

'Not right now,' the lawyer said. 'I'm sorry I had to call at such a late hour. If you can give me the one piece of information I want, I can be on my way.'

'I didn't know I had any information that you wanted, Mr Mason, but–You say you're representing Mr Conway?'

'That's right.'

'And you're here on his behalf?'

'Yes.'

'What is it you want to know?'

Mason leaned forward in his chair. 'How it happens that, if you're trying to negotiate a property settlement with your husband and want to get the most you can out of it, you offered to give Jerry Conway information on the number of proxies that have been received to date by the proxy committee?'

'Mr Mason, what on earth are you talking about?'

'You know what I'm talking about,' Mason said. 'I want to know why, and I want to know why you disguised your voice and took the name of Rosalind.'

She sat perfectly still, looking at him with startled slate-grey eyes.

'Well?' Mason asked.

'Why, Mr Mason, what makes you think that I would do anything like that?'

Mason said impatiently, 'Come, come! You used a telephone. Calls can be traced, you know.'

Startled, she said, 'But I didn't use *this* telephone. I–'

Abruptly she caught herself.

Mason said nothing, continued to regard her with steady, penetrating eyes.

She said, 'Well, I guess that did it. I seem to have walked into your trap.'

Mason remained silent.

'All right,' she said suddenly. 'I'll tell you. I'm a stockholder of Texas Global. I have a fair block of stock in that company. I have a feeling that that stock is about all of the financial nest-egg I'm going to get, and if Gifford Farrell gets control of that company, I don't think the stock will be worth the paper it's written on within a period of two years. If Jerry Conway continues as president, that stock is going to be very valuable.'

'Therefore, you're for Conway.'

'I'm for Conway, but I don't dare let it be known. I don't dare do anything that could be seized upon by Gifford's attorneys and twisted and distorted into evidence that they could use against me. I–Mr Mason, how *did* you find that I made those calls?'

'That's quite a long story,' Mason said. 'Something has happened that makes it quite important to get at the facts in the case. Now, you sent Conway to the Redfern Hotel. Why?'

'*I* sent him to the Redfern Hotel?' she asked.

'That's right.'

She shook her head.

'Yes, you did,' Mason said. 'You had him running around so as to ditch persons who were supposed to have been shadowing him. Then you telephoned him at six-fifteen and told him to–'

'*What* did I tell him at six-fifteen?' she asked.

'You know,' Mason told her. 'You told him to go to the Redfern Hotel and ask for messages for Gerald Boswell.'

She picked up the ivory cigarette holder and began twisting it in nervous fingers.

'Didn't you?' Mason asked.

'I did not, Mr Mason. I don't know anything about the Redfern Hotel. I didn't tell Mr Conway to go there.'

'What did you tell him?' Mason asked.

She hesitated thoughtfully.

Mason said, 'I think it's going to be to your advantage to confide in me, Mrs Farrell.'

'All right,' she said suddenly, 'you seem to know enough. I'm going to have to trust to your discretion. You *could* place me in a very embarrassing position if you let Gifford know what I had done.'

'Suppose you tell me just what you did do.'

'I wanted to give Mr Conway some information I had. I had a list of the persons who had sent in proxies. I thought it was an accurate, up-to-the-minute list that would be of the greatest value to him. I wanted him to have that list.'

'Why didn't you mail it to him?'

'Because I was afraid someone knew that I had this list. If it was ever traced to me, and then my husband could prove that I had given it to the person he was fighting for control of the company, he'd use it to prejudice the court against me.'

'So what did you do?'

'I intended to give him a big build-up, send him out to a motel somewhere to keep a mysterious appointment, and then phone him and tell him that I'd planted the list in his car while he was waiting. I wanted it to be handled with such a background of mystery and all that he'd think I was very, very close to Gifford and terribly frightened. I wanted to do everything as much unlike myself as I possibly could. I wanted to cover my trail so thoroughly he'd never suspect me.

'I tried to arrange a meeting with him twice. Tonight he was to ditch the shadows, go to a public telephone in a drugstore that was a couple of blocks from here. I was to telephone him there at six-fifteen.'

'And you did?'

'I did,' she said, 'and he didn't answer.'

'Are you telling me the truth?'

'I'm telling you the truth.'

'You didn't get him on the telephone and tell him to go to the Redfern Hotel and ask for messages in the name of Gerald Boswell?'

She shook her head, said, 'I know nothing whatever about the Redfern Hotel. I've heard the name, but I don't even how where it is.'

Mason said, 'You'll pardon me, but I have to be sure that you're telling the truth.'

'I've told you the truth,' she said, 'and I'm not accountable to you. I don't propose to have you sit there and cross-examine me. I don't owe that much to Mr Conway and I don't owe that much to you.'

'Perhaps,' Mason said, 'you owe that much to yourself.'

'What do you mean by that?'

'For your information,' Mason said, 'a woman was murdered at the Redfern Hotel this evening. Conway was in the suite where the murdered girl was found. He was sent there by someone who telephoned the drugstore where he was to get his final directions and–'

'So *that's* it!' she exclaimed.

'What is?'

'I lost control of him. Someone must have called him there just a few minutes before I did. I called him a minute or two before six-fifteen, got a busy signal on the line. I called him at almost exactly six-fifteen, and there was no answer. I kept ringing and finally a man's voice answered. I asked if Mr Conway was there, and he said he was the druggist in charge of the store, and that no one was there. He said a man had been there a few minutes earlier, and had left.'

Mason took out his cigarette case, started to offer her one of his cigarettes.

'Thanks, I have my own,' she said.

Mason started to get up and light her cigarette, but she waved him back, said, 'I'm a big girl now,' picked up a card of paper matches, lit her cigarette, dropped the matches back on the table.

Mason snapped his lighter into flame, lit his cigarette.

'Well?' he asked.

She said, 'It's *his* phone that's tapped. It's not mine. I put in the calls from pay stations. You can see what happened. I was anxious to see that he wasn't followed. I didn't want anyone to know I had had any contact with him. Someone listened in on the conversation. What about that secretary of his? What do you know about her?'

'Very little,' Mason said.

'Well, you'd better find out,' she said, 'because someone beat me to the punch on that telephone call and sent him to the Redfern Hotel. I was going to tell him to meet me in a cocktail lounge about a block and a half from the drugstore, but I wanted to be certain he wasn't followed.'

'Do you now have an accurate list of the proxies, or–?'

'I now actually have such a list.'

'May I ask how you got it?'

She smoked for a moment in thoughtful silence, then extricated herself from the chair with a quick, lithe motion, said, 'Mr Mason, I'm going to confide in you.'

The lawyer said nothing.

She walked over to a bookcase, took down an atlas, said, 'When a woman marries, she wants a man for her very own. She wants security. She wants a home. She wants companionship on a permanent basis.'

Mason nodded.

'I should have known better than to have married Gifford Farrell in the first place,' she said. 'He's a playboy. He doesn't want a home, he doesn't want any one woman, and he can't give anyone security. He's a gambler, a plunger, a sport.'

Mason remained silent.

Mrs Farrell opened the atlas. She took out an eight-by-ten glossy photograph from between the pages and handed it to Mason.

Mason saw what at first seemed to be a naked woman, but after a moment saw she was wearing the briefest of light-coloured Bikini bathing suits.

Mason looked at the voluptuous figure, then suddenly started as his eyes came to focus on the girl's face. He moved over closer to the light.

Mrs Farrell gave a short laugh. 'I'm afraid you men are all the same,' she said. 'She's wearing a light-coloured Bikini suit, Mr Mason. She's not nude. She's *dressed!*'

'I see she is,' Mason said dryly.

'You have to look twice to see it.'

Mason nodded. 'I'm looking twice.'

The photograph showed a blonde young woman, with well-rounded curves, apparently the same young woman whom Mason had seen earlier in the evening lying dead on the bed in the Redfern Hotel.

'I take it,' Mason said, 'that you have some connexion with the woman shown in the photograph.'

Mrs Farrell laughed. 'I'm afraid the connexion is with my husband.'

Mason raised his eyebrows in silent interrogation.

Mrs Farrell handed Mason a piece of paper which was evidently a clipping from a popular magazine. The clipping illustrated a curvaceous woman clad in a Bikini bathing suit and across the top of the ad was printed in large, black letters: 'SHE'LL LOVE IT.' In smaller type appeared: '*And she'll love you for it.* Get these private Bikini bathing suits. A wonderful, intimate, personal present, for just the right girl.'

The ad went on to extol the virtues of the specially made Bikini bathing suit.

'Yes,' Mason said dryly, 'I've seen these ads.'

'Evidently my husband answered this,' she said, 'purchased a suit by mail, and persuaded this young woman to put the suit on.'

Mason studied the picture thoughtfully. 'This is a posed picture?'

'It is.'

Again Mason studies the picture.

Mrs Farrell said, 'For your information, Mr Mason, either the suit was donned for the occasion or–Well, I'll be charitable and say that the suit was donned for the occasion. . . . Do you find her so very attractive that you're completely engrossed?'

'I'm sorry,' Mason said. 'I was trying to make out the background.'

'Well, It's dark and out of focus. I'm afraid you can't get much from it, Mr Mason. However, if you'll notice the pattern of the rug beneath those high-heeled shoes, which are designed to bring out the shapeliness of her legs, you'll notice a certain very definite pattern. For your information, Mr Mason, that rug is in my husband's bedroom. Apparently, the picture was taken while I was in New York a couple of months ago.'

'I see,' Mason said.

'My husband,' she went on bitterly, 'is something of an amateur photographer. He took this picture and two others. Evidently he wanted something to remember the girl by.'

'And how did you get them?' Mason asked.

'I happened to notice that my husband's camera, which is usually kept in his den, was in a dresser drawer in the bedroom. There was a roll of films in the camera and three films had been exposed. I'm afraid I have a nasty, suspicious nature, Mr Mason. I slipped that roll of films out of the camera and replaced it with another. I turned the film to number four so that, in case my husband investigated, he wouldn't know there was anything wrong, and in case he had the films developed and found three perfect blanks, he would think something had gone wrong with the shutter, when he was taking these pictures.'

'I see.' Mason commented dryly. 'I take it that there were then two other exposed pictures on this roll, and the model was *well* exposed.'

Mason strove to keep his voice from showing undue interest. 'I wonder if you've been able to locate the model?' he asked.

'I have located the model.'

Mason raised his eyebrows.

'She is Rose M. Calvert, and in case you're interested, the "M" stands for Mistletoe, believe it or not. Her father, I understand, insisted on the name. It turned out to be quite appropriate.

'Rose Calvert was an employee in the brokerage firm which handles accounts for my husband, and, I believe, for some of the officials of the Texas Global Company. My husband has a roving eye, and Rose Calvert–well, you can see from the photograph what she has.'

'She's still working with the brokerage company?' Mason asked.

'Not Rose. Rose, I understand, is living on the fat of the land. She has an apartment at the Lane Vista Apartments, number 319, but I'm afraid that's just one of the perches where this young bird lights from time to time. Apparently, she drops in for mail, and to change her clothes. I've had the place under surveillance for a few days.'

'There are then two other pictures?' Mason prompted.

'Two others.'

Mason waited expectantly.

Mrs Farrell shook her head. 'I'm afraid not, Mr Mason. They're indicative of a progressive friendship. Evidently this young woman doesn't have the slightest compunction about exhibiting her charms to men or to cameras.'

'I'm shockproof,' Mason said.

'I'm not.'

Mason studied the face of the girl in the picture.

Mrs Farrell said, somewhat bitterly, 'You men are all alike. For your information, Mr Mason, those fine curves will be blanketed in fat in another ten years.'

'I'm afraid you're right,' Mason said, handing back the photograph.

'My husband likes them like this,' Mrs Farrell said, tapping the photograph.

Mason almost automatically glanced at the lounging pyjamas.

Mrs Farrell laughed and said, 'It's all right, Mr Mason. I don't make any secret of it. Now, how about a drink?'

'Well,' Mason said, 'I could be induced if you twisted my arm.'

'Hold it out,' she said.

Mason held out his arm.

Mrs Farrell took hold of the wrist, held the lawyer's arm tight against her body, gave it a gentle twist.

'Ouch!' Mason said. 'I'll take it! I'll take it!'

She laughed huskily and said, 'All right, sit down. I'll have to go to the kitchen. What do you like, Scotch or bourbon?'

'Scotch,' Mason said.

'Soda?'

'Please.'

'Make yourself comfortable,' she told him, 'but don't wear that photograph out while I'm gone. I am going to have use for it.'

When she had left the room, Mason hurriedly moved over to the atlas in which the photograph had been concealed. He riffled through the pages but was unable to find any other photographs.

Mrs Farrell entered the room, carrying a tray with two tall glasses.

Mason held his drink to the light. 'That looks pretty stout.'

She laughed. 'You look pretty stout yourself, Mr Mason. I may as well confess that you're one of my heroes. I've followed your cases with the greatest interest. I like your way of fighting.'

'Thanks!' Mason said.

She raised her glass.

'Here's to crime!' Mason said.

'Here's to us!' She touched the brim of her glass to his, let her eyes rest steadily on his as she raised the glass to her lips.

Mason waited until she had seated herself, then said, 'I am interested in how you were able to secure the information that you offered Mr Conway. The list of proxies.'

'Oh, that!'

'Well?' Mason asked.

She said, 'Quite naturally, Mr Mason, after I located this Rose Calvert, I became interested in her comings and goings. A couple of days ago, Rose Calvert was closeted in her apartment. It was one of the rare intervals when she was home for a fairly long period of time, and she was pounding away on a typewriter.

'I have a firm of detectives that seem to be very competent indeed. The man who was on duty managed to inspect the wastebasket at the end of the corridor from time to time, hoping that Rose Calvert would perhaps have made some false starts and he could find enough torn scraps to find out what she was writing. As it turned out, he did far better than that. Rose Calvert was evidently writing a very, very confidential document for my husband. She was instructed to make as many copies as possible and to use fresh carbon sheets with each copy.

'You know how a carbon sheet retains the impression of what has been typed, particularly if you can get the new carbon used in the first copy and there is nothing else on the sheet.

'The detective produced the sheets, and I found that I had a perfect series of carbon papers showing the typing that Mrs Calvert was doing for my husband.'

'*Mrs* Calvert?'

'That's right. She's married and separated. Her husband lives out in the country somewhere.'

'Know where?' Mason asked casually.

She shook her head. 'I've heard of the place. It's out towards Riverside somewhere. . . . Would you like to see the carbons, Mr Mason?'

'Very much,' Mason said.

She put down the drink and eased gracefully out of the chair. She walked over to a desk, opened a drawer and took out several sheets of carbon paper.

'As nearly as I can tell, these are the carbon papers used in making the first copy,' she said. 'She was making an original and seven copies. So, of course, there were a lot of duplicate sheets of carbon paper. I carefully segregated the different sheets?'

'Have you copied them?'

'I haven't had time. I've had them photostated. I intended to give Mr Conway one of these complete sets of carbon paper. Since you're here and are his attorney, I'll give it to you.'

'Thanks,' Mason told her. 'Thanks very much indeed.'

She glanced at him archly. 'Don't mention it. Perhaps you can do something for me some day.'

'Who knows?' Mason said.

'You'll have to protect me, Mr Mason. I don't want anyone, least of all Mr Conway, to know where those carbon copies came from.'

'You can trust my discretion,' Mason said. 'However, I'm going to have to ask a favour. I want to use your phone.'

'It's in the bedroom. Help yourself.'

Mason put down his glass, went to the bedroom, picked up the phone.

'Number, please?' the operator asked.

'Give me an outside line, please,' Mason said.

'You'll have to give me the number. I'll get it for you.'

Mason lowered his voice, gave the number of the Gladedell Motel. When the number answered, he said, 'Can you ring Unit 21?'

'Surely, wait a moment, please.'

Mason waited for several seconds, then the voice said, 'I'm sorry, that phone doesn't answer.'

'Thanks,' Mason said, and hung up.

He returned to the other room.

Mrs Farrell was stretched out on a chaise-lounge, showing up to advantage through the embroidered lounging pyjamas.

'Get your party?'

'No. He didn't answer.'

'There's no hurry. You can try again–later.'

Mason sat down, picked up his drink, took a hasty swallow, said, 'This is really loaded.'

He looked at his watch.

Her look was mocking.

'Now you're terribly impatient. You want to hurry through your drink. Now that you have the information you want, the documents you want, you are giving every indication of being in a hurry to be on your way. Am I that unattractive?'

Mason said, 'It isn't that. It's simply that I have a lot of work to do tonight.'

She raised her eyebrows. 'Night work?'

'Night work.'

'I was hoping that while you were here you would relax and that we could get acquainted.'

Mason said, 'Perhaps your husband is having your apartment watched. He might suggest that you were entertaining men in your apartment.'

Again she laughed. 'Always the lawyer! Now, please, Mr Mason, don't tell anyone about the identity of Rosalind. I'm leaving it to you to protect me.'

'And,' Mason said, 'I suppose I'm not to say anything about these pictures?'

'Not for a while,' she said.

'What are you going to do with them?'

She said, 'When I'm through, I'm going to see that Mrs Calvert has plenty of publicity. If she's an exhibitionist, I'll let them publish her picture where it will do the most good.'

'You seem rather vindictive,' Mason said. 'Do you feel that she stole your husband?'

'Heavens, no!' she said. 'But I'm vindictive just the same. I feel towards her the way one woman feels towards another who–I don't know–she cheapens all of us. Before I get done with her, she'll wish she'd never seen Gifford Farrell.

'All right,' she went on, laughing, 'don't look at me like that. I'm a cat! And I have claws, Mr Mason. I can be very, very dangerous when I'm crossed. I either like people or I don't. I'm never lukewarm.'

Mason said, getting to his feet, 'I'm sorry, but I have to leave.'

Abruptly she arose, gave him her hand. 'I won't try to detain you any longer. I can see you really don't want to stay. Good night.'

Mason stepped out into the corridor, carrying the sheets of fresh carbon paper in a roll.

'Good night–and thanks,' he said.

'Come again some time,' she invited.

6

Mason stopped at a telephone booth and called Paul Drake.

'Anything on the gun, Paul?'

'Hell, no! We're just getting started.'

'Any identification of the corpse?'

'None so far. The police are grubbing around the hotel and can't seem to get anywhere.'

Mason said, 'I'm on the track of something, Paul. I'm going to have to take a chance.'

'You take too many chances,' Drake told him.

'Not too many,' Mason said. 'I take them too often.'

'Well, that's the same thing, only worse.'

'According to the law of averages, it's worse,' Mason told him. 'Now look, Paul, I'm going out to the Lane Vista Apartments. I want to see a Rose Calvert who is in Apartment 319. For your information, she's probably going to be named as co-respondent in a divorce suit by Mrs Gifford Farrell.'

'What's the lead?' Drake asked.

'Probably more of a hunch than anything else right now,' Mason told him. 'The point is that there *may* be a private detective sticking around trying to get a line on her.

'Can you have one of your men get out to the Lane Vista Apartments, scout the territory and see if he can find someone who looks like a detective?'

'Sure. What does he do if he finds this guy?'

'I'll be out there,' Mason said, 'inside of thirty minutes. I can make it from here in about fifteen minutes, and your man should be able to make it in fifteen minutes. I'll give him fifteen minutes to case the place.'

'I can't guarantee anything,' Drake said. 'My operatives are pretty clever at spotting men who are waiting around like that, but you just can't tell what the set-up is, and–'

'I know,' Mason said. 'I don't want the impossible. I just want to know whether the place is being watched.'

'And if it is?' Drake asked.

'I want to find out about it.'

'All right,' Drake said, 'I'll have a man there in fifteen minutes. I have a man sitting right here in the office who's good. I'll put him on the job.'

'Does he know me?' Mason asked.

'He knows you by sight. He'll pick you up all right.'

'All right. I'll be there within thirty minutes. I'll park my car a block or two away and walk past the entrance to the apartment without looking in. Have your man pick me up and brief me on the situation. Can do?'

'Can do and will do,' Drake said.

'How long you going to be there, Paul?'

'Probably all night. At least until something definitely breaks.'

'Okay, I'll be calling you.'

'You'd better keep your nose clean,' Drake warned. 'If any good private detective is out there, *he'll* recognize *you* the minute he sees you.'

'That's why I want to know if he's there,' Mason said and hung up.

Mason looked at his watch, noted the time, drove until he found a hole-in-the-wall restaurant that was open, sat at the lunch counter and had two leisurely cups of coffee. He paid for the coffee, entered the phone booth, called the Gladedell Motel and this time got Gerald Conway on the line.

'Where have you been?' Mason asked.

'Nowhere. Why?'

'I called and you didn't answer.'

'Oh. I just ran out to a drugstore for shaving stuff and a toothbrush. What did you want?'

'I wanted to tell you I have what I think is a complete proxy list. It doesn't look too good. I'll see you tomorrow. Just sit tight.'

Mason hung up and drove to a point within two blocks of the Lane Vista Apartments, where he parked his car at the kerb, got out and walked along the sidewalk, walking directly past the entrance to the apartment house without hesitating.

Half-way to the next corner, a figure detached itself from the shadows and fell into step by Mason's side.

'Paul Drake's man,' the figure said without turning his head.

'Let's take a look,' Mason told him.

'All right. Around the corner.'

'Anyone sitting on the place?'

'Uh-huh.'

'Okay,' Mason said, and the two walked around the corner until they came to the mouth of an alley.

The man paused, took a folder from his pocket containing his credentials and a small, fountain-pen flash-light.

Mason studied the credentials, said, 'Okay, tell me about the stake-out.'

'I know the guy who's waiting,' the detective said. 'He's from the firm of Simons & Wells. They make a speciality of serving papers.'

'Did he notice you?' Mason asked.

'Hell's bells!' the man said. 'I walked right into it with my chin out.'

'What do you mean?'

'I know the guy who's sitting on the job. I started to case the joint. This guy was on stake-out. He knew me, and I knew him.'

'You talked with him?'

'Sure. He said hello, and wanted to know what I was out on, and I asked him if he was waiting to serve papers and he said no, he was just making a preliminary survey. I asked him if I could have one guess as to the initials of the party, and we sparred around for a while. Then he admitted he was there to tail Rose Calvert. Seems like her middle name is Mistletoe.' The operative chuckled. 'Some name!'

'Okay,' Mason said, 'what about Rose Calvert?' Is she in her apartment?'

'Apparently not. Hasn't been in all afternoon. She was reported to have been in yesterday. A little before ten today she called a cab, loaded a bunch of baggage and went away. She hasn't come back.'

'Dolled up?' Mason asked.

'Not too much.'

'Taking a powder?'

'She could have been taking a powder, all right. Quite a bit of baggage. There's a letter in the mailbox outside the apartment, according to what this guy tells me.'

'This operative has been ringing Rose Calvert's bell?' Mason asked.

'No. He found out she was out. He's waiting for her to show. However, he goes off duty at 1.30 a.m. He didn't start working until five-thirty this evening. There's no relief coming on.'

'You take a look at the letter in the mailbox?'

'No. My friend told me about it.'

'What did you tell your friend?'

'Told him I was interested in another case.'

'Did you give him any names?'

'No, but I don't think I fooled him any.'

'What about this letter?'

'It's in an envelope addressed to Rose M. Calvert and it's got a return address in the upper side from Norton B. Calvert. The address is 6831 Washington Heights, Elsinore.'

'You didn't take a peek at the letter?' Mason asked.

'Hell, no! I'm not monkeying with Uncle Sam. I didn't even touch the envelope. I got my data from my friend.'

'Stamp cancelled and postmarked?'

'That's right. Postmarked Elsinore yesterday.'

'How is the letter? Typewritten or ink?'

'Written in pencil.'

'From Norton B. Calvert, eh?'

'That's right.'

'Who is this Norton B. Calvert? Husband? Son? What?'

'I don't know. She's pretty young to have a son living away from home. Around twenty-seven, as I get the impression.'

'Know how she was dressed?' Mason asked.

'Yes, she was wearing a tight-fitting, light-blue sweater, straight matching blue skirt, and high-heeled shoes.'

Mason digested the information in thoughtful silence.

'That mean anything to you?' the operative asked.

'I think it does,' Mason said, looking at his watch. 'I'm going to play a hunch. What's that address in Elsinore?'

'6831 Washington Heights, Elsinore.'

Mason said, 'Let's see. It's about an hour to Corona and then about thirty minutes to Elsinore. That right?'

'I believe so. That won't miss it very far.'

'Ring up Paul's office,' Mason said. 'Tell Drake to stick around until he hears from me. Have him tell Della Street to go home. Do you think this detective connected you with me?'

'Sure he did. Naturally he's dying to find out what *my* angle is. When you came along, he would have been all eyes and ears. I let you go as far as I dared before I cut in on you, but I'm satisfied he was where he could watch us. He goes off duty at one-thirty, in case you want to call without being seen. She may be in by then.'

'Okay,' Mason said. 'Go back and watch the place so this detective can't say you quit as soon as I showed up. Try to give him a line before he leaves. Tell him you're going to be on duty all night as far as you know. When he quits at one-thirty, wait ten or fifteen minutes to make certain he's gone, and then high-tail it back to Drake's office.'

'Suppose she shows?'

'She won't.'

'You're sure?'

'Pretty sure. If she shows, it won't make any difference. I just want to keep from giving this private detective any blueprints of my plans.'

Mason swung away from the man, walked around the block, went to where he had parked his car, got in, filled the tank with gas at the nearest service station, and took off down the freeway.

From time to time he consulted his watch, and despite the last cup of coffee, found himself getting sleepy. He stopped at Corona for another cup of coffee, then drove on.

When he got to Elsinore, he found the town completely closed up. The police station and fire station had lights. Aside from that there was no light anywhere.

Mason drove around trying to get the lay of the town. He saw a car turn into a driveway. A family who had evidently been to one of the neighbouring cities at a late show got out of the car.

Mason drove up.

'Can anybody tell me where Washington Heights is?' he asked.

The man who was evidently the head of the family detached himself from the group, came over towards Mason's car.

'Sure,' he said. 'You drive straight along this road until you come to the first boulevard stop, then turn right, and climb the hill, the second street on the left is Washington Heights.'

'Thanks,' Mason told him, leaning slightly forward with his head to one side so his hat-brim would be between his features and the other man's eyes. 'Thanks a lot!'

Mason pushed his foot gently on the throttle, eased away from the kerb.

Mason located the 6800 block on Washington Heights, but missed 6831 the first time he went down the block. It was only after he turned and came back that he found a little bungalow type house sitting back from the street.

Mason stopped his car, left the parking lights on, and his feet crunched up the gravel walk leading to the house.

A neighbour's dog began barking with steady insistence.

Mason heard annoyed tones from the adjoining house telling the dog to shut up.

The lawyer climbed up on the steps of the small porch and groped for a bell button. Unable to find it, he knocked on the door.

There was no answer from within.

Mason knocked the second time.

Bare feet thudded to the floor in the interior of the house. The dog in the neighbouring house started a crescendo of barking and then abruptly became silent.

At length a porch light clicked. The door opened a crack, held from opening farther by a brass chain which stretched taut across the narrow opening.

A man's voice from inside said, 'Who is it?'

'I'm an attorney from the city,' Mason said. 'I want to talk with you.'

'What about?'

'About your wife.'

'My wife?'

'That's right. Rose Calvert. She's your wife, isn't she?'

'You better ask *her* whose wife she is,' the man said.

Mason said, 'I'm sorry. I don't want to discuss the matter out here where the entire neighbourhood can hear. I drove down here to see you because I feel it's important.'

'What's important?'

'What I want to see you about.'

'Now, you look here,' the man said. 'I'm not going to consent to a single thing. I'm hoping Rose will come to her senses. If she does, all right. If she doesn't, I'm not going to make things any easier for her or for that fellow who has her hypnotized, and that's final!'

He started to close the door.

'Just a moment,' Mason said. 'I don't want you to consent to anything. I just want to get some information.'

'Why?'

'Because it's important.'

'Who's it important to?'

'It may be important to you.'

The man on the other side of the door hesitated, then finally said. 'Well, all right. You can come in. But this is a hell of an hour to get a man out of bed to start asking questions.'

'I wouldn't do it if it wasn't urgent,' Mason said.

'What's urgent about it?'

'I'm not sure yet,' Mason said, 'and I don't want to alarm you until I am sure. I'm an attorney, but I'm not representing your wife in any way. I'm not representing anyone connected with the aspect of the case in which you're interested. I just want to get some information, and then perhaps I can give you some.'

'Well, come on in.'

The chain was removed and the door swung open.

The man who stood, tousle-haired and barefooted, in the entrance hallway was wearing striped pyjamas. He was nearly six foot tall, slender, about thirty-two, with dark, smouldering eyes and long, black hair which had tumbled about his head.

'Come on in,' he said, yawning.

'Thanks. I'm Perry Mason,' the lawyer told him, shaking hands. 'I'm an attorney and I'm working on a case in which it has become necessary to get some information about your wife.'

'We're all split up,' Calvert said shortly. 'Maybe you came to the wrong place.'

Mason said, 'I want to talk with you.'

'There's not much I can tell you about her, except that she wants a divorce.'

'There are no children?'

The man shook his head.

'How long have you been married?'

'Two and a half years. Can you tell me what this is all about? I'm sorry. I may have been a little bit short with you. I wake up kinda jumpy sometimes.'

Mason said, 'I have something to tell you, but I want to be pretty certain I'm right before I tell you. This may take a little time. Fifteen minutes or twenty minutes. Do you want to get some clothes on?'

'I'll get a blanket to wrap around me,' the man said.

He vanished into the bedroom, came back with a blanket and wrapped it around him.

'Sit down there in that chair by the table,' he told Mason.

Mason seated himself, said, 'This is a nice little bungalow you have here.'

The man made a little gesture of dismissal. 'I rent it furnished. After we broke up, I thought for a while Rose would come back to me, but now I've about given up.'

'Were you living together down here?'

'No, I moved down here about three months ago–that was right after we split up.'

'What's your occupation?'

'Running a service station.'

'Would you think me terribly presumptuous if I asked you to tell me about what happened in your marriage, how it happened you broke up, and–'

'I guess it's all right,' Calvert said. 'We got off to a good start. We had been going together a couple of months. She was in a brokerage office. I was a salesman. We sort of clicked and we got married.

'She didn't want children right at first. We decided we'd wait on that and that we'd both keep on working

'Then an uncle of mine died and left me quite a nest egg. Not too much. It figured about sixty thousand, by the times taxes were taken out of it. So then I felt we could start having a family.'

'How much of that nest egg do you have left?' Mason asked.

Calvert's lips tightened. 'I've got all of it left.'

'Good boy!' Mason told him.

'And if I'd listen to her, I wouldn't have had *any* of it left,' Calvert went on. 'That was one of the things that started the trouble. She wanted to live it up, to travel, to get clothes, to do all the things that take money.

'I wanted to save this money to invest in something. I wanted a business of our own. I didn't want her to keep on working. I wanted children.'

'Did she want children?'

'She couldn't be bothered.'

'All right, what happened?'

'Well, we got along all right, but I could see the novelty of marriage was wearing off and–Rose is a woman that men notice. She has a figure and she's proud of it. She likes people to notice it.'

'And they do?' Mason asked.

'They do.'

'Precisely what caused the final split-up?'

'A man by the name of Gifford Farrell.'

'With Texas Global?'

'That's right. He's fighting a proxy battle. There are ads in the Los Angeles newspapers. He's trying to get enough proxies to take over.'

'How long has he known your wife?'

'I don't know. I don't think it was entirely his fault, but he certainly was on the make and she fell for him.'

'How long had it been going on?' Mason asked.

'I tell you I don't know. I guess quite a while. I wanted to get ahead by plugging along and keeping my eye on the main chance.

'This Farrell is just like Rose. He's a gambler, a guy who shoots the works, rides around in high-powered automobiles, spends three and four hundred dollars on a suit of clothes, wouldn't think of looking at a pair of shoes that didn't cost over twenty dollars. He's a showman, likes to go out to night clubs and all of that.'

'And now your wife wants a divorce?'

'That's right.'

Mason took his cigarette case from his pocket. 'Mind if I smoke?'

'Not at all. I'll join you. I smoke a good deal myself. Here.'

The man passed over an ash-tray which was pretty well filled with cigarette stubs, said, 'Wait a minute! I'll empty that.'

He went out into the kitchen, dumped the ashes into a wood stove, came back with the ash-tray, inspected the cigarettes in Mason's cigarette case, said, 'Thanks, I have my own brand.'

He took a package of cigarettes from his pyjama pocket, extracted one, and leaned forward to accept the light which Mason held out as he snapped his lighter into flame.

The lawyer lit his own cigarette, said, 'Do you have any pictures of your wife?'

'Pictures? Sure.'

'May I see them?'

'Why?'

'I want to be absolutely certain that you and I are talking about the same woman,' Mason said.

Calvert looked at him for a moment, took a deep drag on the cigarette, exhaled twin streams of smoke from his nostrils, got up, walked into the other room and came back with two framed pictures and an album.

'These are pictures she had taken,' he said.

Mason studied the framed, retouched photographs. 'You have some snapshots?'

The man opened the album, said, 'This goes back to when we first met. She gave me a camera for my birthday. Here are some of the more recent pictures.'

Mason thumbed through the album. Within a half-dozen pictures he was virtually certain of his identification.

He closed the album and said, 'I'm sorry to have to bring you the news, Calvert. I can't be *absolutely* certain, but I'm *practically* certain that your wife was involved in a tragedy which took place a few hours ago.'

Calvert jerked bolt upright. 'An automobile accident?'

'A murder.'

'A murder!'

'Someone killed her.'

For several long seconds Calvert sat absolutely motionless. Then his mouth twitched downward at the corners. He hastily took another drag on his cigarette, said, 'Are you sure, Mr Mason?'

'I'm not absolutely sure,' Mason said, 'but I think the body I saw was that of your wife.'

'Can you tell me about it?'

'She was in the Redfern Hotel, lying on a bed. She was wearing a blue sweater, sort of a robin's-egg blue, and a skirt to match.'

Calvert said, 'That sweater was a Christmas present from me last Christmas. She likes tight-fitting sweaters. She's proud of her figure. It's a good one.'

Mason nodded.

'Have they got the person who . . . who did it?'

'No, I don't think so.'

Calvert said, 'She was pretty well tied up with this Farrell. She was afraid of Mrs Farrell.'

'Why?'

'I don't know. I think Mrs Farrell had threatened her at one time. I know she was afraid of her.'

'You had separated for good?' Mason asked.

'I never really gave up. I thought she'd come to her senses and come back. That's why I came down here. At present I'm running this filling station. I've got a chance to buy a store here. I think there's a good living in it, but I'm a man who goes at things like that pretty cautiously. I don't act on impulse. I wanted to look this place over at first hand. The service station I have is right next door to the store. I think maybe I'll buy it. . . . How can I find out for sure about my wife?'

'Someone will probably be in touch with you within a short time, if the body is that of your wife,' Mason said. 'It's hard to make an identification from photographs.'

Calvert pinched out the cigarette. 'How did you happen to come here?' he said. 'How did you find me?'

Mason said, 'There's a letter in the mailbox at her house. It had your address on the upper left-hand corner. I had to see some photographs. I thought perhaps you'd have them.'

'You saw . . . saw the body?'

Mason nodded.

Calvert said, 'I hadn't heard from her for six weeks, I guess. Then she wrote to me and told me she wanted to go to Reno and get a divorce.'

'Did she say that she and Farrell were planning on getting married?'

'No, she just said she wanted a divorce. She said that she could establish residence in Reno and get a divorce without any trouble if I'd co-operate.'

'What did she mean by "co-operate"?'

'She wanted me to file an appearance of some sort. It seems if I get an attorney and appear in court to contest the action, they can get around a lot of red tape in serving summons and save a lot of delay. She said she was willing to pay for the attorney.'

'And what did you tell her?' Mason asked.

'I told her that I'd co-operate if she was sure that was what she wanted,' Calvert said,' 'and then I've been thinking things over and–well, I just about decided to change my mind. When you came down here and got me up out of a sound sleep, I was mad! I made up my mind I wasn't going to fall over myself fixing it so she could get tied up with this man Farrell. He's a fourflusher, a woman chaser–and he's just no good!'

'Do you have the letter which your wife wrote?' Mason asked.

'I have it,' Calvert said. 'Just a minute.'

He kicked off the blanket, walked into the bedroom again, came back with an envelope which he handed to Mason.

The lawyer shook the letter out of the envelope, read:

Dear Norton,

There's no reason why either of us should go on this way. We're both young, and we may as well have our freedom. We've made a mistake which has cost us a lot of heartaches, but there's no reason for it to ruin our lives. I'm going to Reno and get a divorce. They tell me that, if you will get a lawyer, and make an appearance in Reno, that will save me a lot of time and a lot of money in having the case brought to trial.

So why not be a sport and give me a break? You don't want a wife who isn't living with you, and I don't want to be tied up by marriage. That's not fair to me and it isn't doing you any good.

I'm sorry I hurt you so much. I've said this to lots of people and I'll keep on saying it: You are one of the most thoughtful, considerate husbands a girl could ask for. You're sweet and patient and understanding. I'm sorry that I couldn't have been a better wife to you, but after all each person has to live his own life. Now be a sport and let me make a clean break, so we can both begin all over.

Yours,

Rose.

Calvert began twisting his fingers nervously. 'I just can't seem to picture her as being dead, Mr Mason. She's so full of life and vitality. You're sure?'

'No,' Mason told him, 'I'm not sure. But I *think* the woman I saw was your wife. She was blonde with blue eyes, and she was wearing this blue sweater which just about matched her eyes. The eyes were only partially open, and–well, you know how it is with a dead person. Sometimes it's hard to make a positive identification from photographs, but I think I'm right.'

'What was she doing at the Redfern hotel?'

'I don't know.'

'How does Gifford Farrell figure in this?'

'I don't know that. I don't even know that he figures in it.'

Calvert said with considerable feeling, 'Well, you can bet your bottom dollar he figures in it somewhere. I guess I could have got along without Rose all right, if I'd felt she was being happy with somebody, but this . . . this thing–it just sort of knocks me for a loop.'

Mason nodded sympathetically.

Abruptly Calvert got up. 'I'm sorry, Mr Mason. You've got the information you want and I . . . well, I'm just not able to keep on talking. I feel all choked up. I guess I'm going to take it pretty hard. I tried to pretend that I could get along without her, but I always had a feeling she was coming back, and–Just pull the door closed when you leave.'

Calvert threw the blanket into a crumpled ball on the floor, walked back hurriedly to the bedroom, kicked the door shut.

The house grew silent.

Mason switched out the lights, and felt his way to the door. Behind him he could hear harsh, convulsive sobs coming from the other side of the bedroom door.

The lawyer eased out of the house, tiptoed up the gravel walk. The dog in the adjoining house once more started a frenzied barking and was again calmed to silence by a man's authoritative voice.

Mason got in his car and drove back towards the city.

From Corona, Mason called Paul Drake.

'This is Perry, Paul. Any news?'

'Nothing important.'

'Body been identified?'

'Not yet. At least not as far as anyone knows.'

'Anything else new?'

'Sgt Holcomb rang up and wanted to know where you could be reached.'

'What did you tell him?'

'I told him I didn't know where you were, but I knew that you intended to be at the district attorney's office at nine o'clock in the morning.'

'What about Della?'

'I told her you said to go home, but she didn't go. She's sticking it out. She's got a percolator full of hot coffee. . . . What the heck are you doing down at Corona?'

'Running down a lead,' Mason said. 'Now look, Paul, here's something I want you to do.'

'What?'

'Cover the Redfern Hotel. Find out if there were any check-outs from the seventh floor between six and eight last night. If there were, I want those rooms rented by some of your operatives.'

'You can't ask for a specific room by number,' Drake said. 'It would make them suspicious. . . .'

'Don't be that crude,' Mason told him. 'Have operatives go to the hotel. They're just in from a plane trip. They don't want to get too high, but they want to be high enough to be away from the street noises, something on the seventh floor. Then start getting particular until they get the rooms we want.'

'Check-outs tonight? Is that right?'

'Well, it's yesterday night now,' Mason said, 'but I want any check-outs between–well, say between six and nine just to be safe.'

'You coming in here?' Drake asked.

'I'm coming in,' Mason told him. 'What have you found out about the gun? Anything?'

'Not yet. We're working.'

'Well, get some action,' Mason told him.

'Do you know what time it is?' Drake asked.

'Sure, I know what time it is,' Mason said. 'And I'll tell you something for your information. By tomorrow the police will be swarming all over us. If we're going to do anything at all, we're going to have to do it before nine o'clock this morning.'

'I've got ten men out,' Drake said. 'They should turn up something. Come on in and have a cup of coffee. I'll try to get a line on the hotel. I've got a couple of men in there already. They're buying drinks, tipping the bell-boys and trying to get them to talk.'

'What kind of a place?' Mason asked.

'You can get anything you want,' Drake told him.

'Who runs it? The clerks?'

'The bell captains run that end of it.'

'Well, we may want something,' Mason told him. 'I'm coming in, Paul. I'll be seeing you in an hour.'

7

Mason's steps echoed along the corridor of the silent building as he left the elevator and walked down to his office. He inserted his latchkey, snapped back the spring lock and opened the door.

Della Street, who was stretched out in the overstuffed chair, her feet propped on another chair, her legs covered with a topcoat, jumped up, blinking.

She saw Mason's face, smiled, and said, 'Gosh, Chief, I was asleep. I made myself comfortable and all of a sudden I went out like a light.

'There's coffee over there in the electric percolator. I'm afraid it's pretty strong and stale by now. I made it fresh about midnight.'

'Didn't Drake tell you to go home?'

'He told me you *said* to go home,' Della Street smiled. 'But I thought I'd wait it out, at least until you got in.'

'What have you got to go with the coffee?' Mason asked.

'Doughnuts. And they're pretty good. I went down to this doughnut shop just before it closed at midnight and got a bag of fresh doughnuts. . . . I'll bet I'm a mess.'

She shook out her skirt, put her hands to her hair, fluffed it out, smiled at Perry Mason.

'What's new?'

'Lots of things, Della. Give Paul Drake a ring and ask him if he wants to come down and have coffee, doughnuts and chitchat.'

Della Street promptly put through the call, said, 'He's coming right down.'

Mason opened the closet which contained the washstand, washed his hands and face in hot water, rubbed briskly with a towel.

Della Street produced three big coffee mugs and opened the faucet on the electric percolator. The office filled with the aroma of hot coffee.

Drake's code knock sounded on the door.

Della Street opened it.

'Hi, Paul,' Mason said, hanging up the towel with which he had been drying his face. 'What's new?'

'Not too much at this end,' Drake said. 'What's new with you?'

'They're going to have the body identified in about thirty minutes,' Mason said.

'How do you know?'

Mason grinned. 'I fixed a time bomb so it will go off just about on schedule.'

'How come?'

'The body,' Mason said, 'is that of Rose Calvert. Rose's middle name, believe it or not, was Mistletoe. Her dad thought she might turn out to be romantic. His hunch was right–poor kid.

'For your information, Rose's husband, Norton B. Calvert, lives in Elsinore, is running a service station, and was waiting from day to day in hopes that his wife would come back.

'Probably at about this time he's at the Elsinore police station, telling them that he has reason to believe his wife has been murdered, and asking the Elsinore police to find out about it. They'll call the Los Angeles police, and since there is only one unidentified body, at least so far, the police will ask for a description, and very shortly will have an identification.'

'But won't they find out that *you* were down there?' Della Street asked apprehensively.

'They'll find out I was down there,' Mason said, 'and they'll be mad. They'll feel that I held out on them in respect to an identification of the body.'

'Well?' Drake asked dryly. 'Wouldn't that be a natural conclusion under the circumstances?'

'Sure it will,' Mason said. 'So the police will decide to give my client the works. They'll check on Rose Calvert, and find out that during the last few weeks of her life she had been very, very much involved with Gifford Farrell. They will, therefore, jump at the conclusion that Farrell is my client. They'll descend on him, and they'll probably be rather inconsiderate and ungentle.

'Find out anything about that gun, Paul?'

'Not yet! That information is supposed to be available only during office hours, at least to the general public. However, I took it on myself to issue a gratuity of fifty dollars and I'm expecting–'

'Well, grab this coffee while it's hot,' Della Street said, 'and you can do your expecting right here.'

Drake said dubiously, 'I've been swigging down coffee all night.'

Mason picked up one of the big mugs, put in sugar and cream, stood with his feet apart, leaning slightly forward. He reached for a doughnut, then raised the coffee mug to his lips.

'How is it?' Della Street asked apprehensively.

'Couldn't be better,' Mason said.

'I'm afraid it's stale and bitter.'

'It's wonderful!'

Drake tasted his coffee, said, 'Well, you have to admit one thing, it's strong.'

'I need it that way,' Mason said. 'At nine o'clock I'm going to have to face an irate district attorney, and by that time the police are going to feel I've pulled at least one fast one on them.'

The telephone rang, and Della Street said, 'That's probably your office calling you now, Paul.'

Drake put down his coffee mug and picked up the telephone.

'Hello,' he said. 'Yes, yes, this is Drake talking. . . . How's that again . . . ? Hold the phone a second.' Drake looked up at Della Street and said, 'Make a note, will you, Della? Pitcairn Hardware & Sporting Goods. Okay. I've got it. What's the date? September second, three years ago. Okay.' Drake hung up the telephone, said, 'Well, we've got the gun located. I don't know whether this is going to do you any good or not, Perry.'

'What do you mean?' Mason asked.

'The gun was sold to the Texas Global for the protection of a cashier. The signature was that of the cashier, but the charge was made to the company itself on an order made by Conway.

'You can see what that does. It brings that weapon right home to Jerry Conway.'

Mason thought for a moment, then a slow grin suffused his features. 'That,' he said, 'brings the gun right home to Gifford Farrell. Gifford Farrell was with the company at that time, and was taking a very active part in the office management.'

'What do you think happened?' Della Street asked.

Mason stood holding his doughnut in one hand, his coffee mug in the other.

'What I *think* happened is that Gifford Farrell had a fight with his sweetheart and probably caught her cheating. He lost his head, pulled a gun and fired. Or it may have been that Rose Calvert found Gifford was cheating and committed suicide. In any event, Farrell must have had Conway's telephone tapped. He knew that Conway was going to a public telephone booth to get directions at six-fifteen. Farrell took a chance. He had a girl call in at six-twelve, and Conway was there a few minutes early waiting for the other call. So

Conway took the wrong message and was gone by the time the real message came in. Conway was just like a guided missile that's being directed by radio. When he got to a certain point, someone with another more powerful radio stepped in, took control and sent the missile off on an entirely new path.'

'Well,' Drake said, 'it's a two-edged sword. Remember that both Farrell and Conway could have had access to the fatal weapon.'

'It's all right,' Mason said, 'unless–'

'Unless what?' Della Street asked.

'Unless,' Mason said, 'Conway got smart and decided to–No, he wouldn't do anything like that. . . . However, I didn't take the number of the gun when he first showed it to us. It wasn't until after he was down at the motel I wrote down the number. . . . Anyway, it's all right. We'll go down to see the D.A. in the morning, and there'll be nothing to it. He can't make a case against Conway now, and he's going to be afraid to try. What did you find out about check-outs, Paul?'

'There was only one check-out at the hotel between six and nine from the seventh floor.'

'What time was that check-out, Paul?'

'About six-fifty.'

'Who was it?'

'A young woman named Ruth Culver.'

'The room number?' Mason asked.

'Seven-two-eight.'

'Where is that with reference to 729?'

'Directly across the hall.'

'Have you got that room sewed up?' Mason asked.

'I have an operative in it right now. He'll stay until we give him the word.'

'What have you found out about the Culver girl?'

'I've got men working on her. She's in her twenties with auburn hair, a fairly good-looking babe. . . . Here's the strange thing, Perry. She checked in about ten in the morning, then left just before seven that night.'

'Did she make any explanation as to how she happened to check out at that time?'

'She said she'd had a long-distance call. Her father who lives in San Diego is very ill.'

'Baggage?' Mason asked.

'Quite a bit of it.'

Mason said, 'Check the San Diego planes, Paul. Find out if one of them had a passenger named Ruth Culver, and–'

'Now look,' Drake interrupted, 'you don't have to do *all* my thinking for me, Perry. That's routine. However, the clerk thinks this girl said she was going to drive down.'

Mason finished his doughnut, held out his mug for a refill.

Della Street turned the spigot and let coffee trickle into the mug.

'What about your operative up in Room 728? Can I trust him?' Mason asked.

'You can trust him unless the police start putting pressure on him,' Drake said. 'None of these operatives are going to stand up to the police, Perry. They need the good will of the police to keep working.'

'What's the name of this operative in Room 728?'

'Fred Inskip.'

'Does he know me?'

'I don't think so.'

'Give him a ring,' Mason said. 'Tell him that I'm going to come up some time before noon. Tell him to leave the door unlocked. I want to take a look in there. . . . How about the police? Have they cleared out?'

'They've cleared out,' Drake said. 'They sealed up Room 729.'

Drake watched Mason as he picked up another doughnut, said, 'How I envy you your stomach, Perry! I've ruined mine sitting up nights living on soggy hamburgers and lukewarm coffee. Somehow when coffee is lukewarm, you drink four or five cups of it. If you can get it piping hot, you don't drink so much.'

'Why don't you get one of these big electric percolators?' Mason asked.

'Let me have Della Street to run it and keep house, and I will.'

Mason grinned. 'Don't talk like that, Paul. You could get yourself shot. Ring up Inskip and tell him to expect me around–oh, say ten or eleven.'

Drake put his coffee mug down on a piece of blotting paper, dialled a number, said, 'I want to talk with Mr Inskip in 728, please. Yes, I know it's a late hour, but he's not in bed. He's waiting for this call. Just give the phone the gentlest tinkle if you don't believe me.'

A moment later, Drake said, 'Fred, this is Paul. I won't mention any names, because I have an idea someone is monitoring our conversation, but a friend of mine is coming to see you around ten o'clock. Leave the door unlocked. . . . Okay.'

Drake hung up the telephone, said to Mason, 'Remember, Sgt Holcomb is looking for you. Are you going to try to get in touch with him?'

'He'll be in bed by this time,' Mason said. 'I wouldn't want to disturb his beauty sleep.'

'Now look,' Drake warned, 'remember this about Inskip. He isn't in a position to hold out on the police if they start asking specific questions. You've been around the hotel, and someone may recognize you.'

'It's all right,' Mason said. 'I don't care if they know I've been there after I've left. The only thing I *don't* want is to have some smart guy like that room clerk, Bob King, ring up the police and say that I'm there and am visiting someone in Room 728. That might be what you would call premature.'

'To say the least,' Drake said dryly. 'Della, please put those doughnuts out of sight. They tempt me, and I'd have my stomach tied up in knots if I tried to keep up with your ravenous employer.'

Mason said, 'I guess this just about winds things up, Della. How about getting in your car and driving home?'

'What are you going to do?'

'I'm going to run out to my apartment, shave, take a shower, and maybe get a couple of hours' sleep before I have to go pick up Conway.'

'All right,' she said, 'I'll go home.'

'Don't bother with straightening things up here now. You can do it in the morning. Come on, I'll go down with you and see that you get in the car. Pull that percolator plug out of the socket, and leave everything until morning.'

'The office looks a wreck.'

'What do we care.'

Mason held Della Street's coat for her. They switched out lights, and Mason, Della Street and Paul Drake walked down the corridor.

'You going to call it a day, Paul?' Mason asked.

'Gosh, no!' Drake said. 'I'm sitting in the middle of everything up there. I have to be where I can handle the telephones.'

'Can you get any sleep?'

'I don't think so. I'll keep right on.'

'You'll have some stuff to do tomorrow–that is, I mean later on in the day.'

Drake said, 'It's all right, Perry. I work right on through lots of times. That's what's wrong with my stomach.'

'Well,' Mason told him, 'I think we've got this case pretty much under control. We'll go up there and make an appearance at the D.A.'s office as a matter of form, but–Say, wait a minute, Paul. They should know who the corpse is by this time. Let's check.'

'All right. Step in my office,' Drake said.

They followed Drake into his office. Drake asked the switchboard operator, 'Anything new on that murder case at the Redfern Hotel?'

'Nothing except the calls I relayed down there.'

'They haven't identified the body?' Drake asked.

'Not as far as *we* know.'

Drake looked at Mason.

Mason said, 'That fellow was pretty well caved in. I sure gave him pretty much of a jolt, but I felt he'd have been in touch with the police long before this time.'

'It could have happened without our knowing it,' Drake said. 'I've got one of the newspaper reporters on the job. He telephones in to his paper first and then he'll give it to me second. If he got an exclusive scoop, he probably wouldn't want to trust me with the information until after the paper was on the street. But on anything routine that the other reporters would pick up, he'd call me just as soon as he'd finished talking with the rewrite man at the desk.'

'Well, they probably know by this time, but aren't announcing it to the Press,' Mason said. 'They've probably sent for the husband to come and make the identification. They'll sure be looking up the boy friend. Well, I'll put Della in her car and go on to my apartment. I'll be seeing you, Paul.'

Mason took Della Street's arm. They left the office, rode down silently in the elevator.

Mason escorted her over to the parking lot and put her in her automobile. 'I don't like to have you driving around the streets alone at this hour, Della.'

'Phooey! I'll go home like a streak. No one's going to bother me. I am out at all hours of the day and night on this job.'

'I know you are,' Mason said. 'And I wish you weren't. You take too many chances driving around a city at this hour of the morning.'

She patted his hand. 'Thanks for the thought, Chief, but I'm fine. Don't worry. I put the windows up, lock the doors, use the mechanical signal and don't stop until I get to the apartment. I'll be seeing you.'

'I'll follow you in my car, Della, see you safely home and–'

'You'll do nothing of the sort! You need every minute of sleep you can get. Good night!'

Della Street stepped on the starter, switched on the lights and drove out of the parking lot.

Mason got in his own car, gunned the motor to life and raced after her. He caught up with her five blocks down the street.

The brake lights on Della's car blazed red as she swung in to stop at the kerb. Mason drew alongside, rolled down the window on his car.

'Chief, you go home! I'm just as safe as can be. You shouldn't be–'

Mason rolled up his window, sat waiting with the motor running. At length Della gave up and pulled out from the kerb.

Mason followed her to her apartment house. She parked her car, came over to where Mason was waiting.

Again the lawyer rolled down his window.

'Chief,' she said in a low voice.

'Yes?' He leaned out to hear her better.

She said, 'Custom decress that when a man has taken a girl home, he is entitled to a token of thanks.'

Before he caught the full import of her words, she had kissed him full on the lips, then turned and ran up the steps of her apartment house.

'Thank you,' she called to him as she opened the door.

'Thank *you*!' Mason said.

8

It was five minutes after eight when Mason swung his car into the Gladedell Motel and drove to Unit 21.

Jerry Conway was waiting for him.

'All ready?' Conway asked. 'Shall I follow you in my car?'

'Wait a minute,' Mason told him. 'We're going to have to do some talking. I'll drive my car down the road for a couple of blocks then pull into the kerb. I'll park my car there and drive in with you.'

'How about having me go in your car?'

'No, the police will want to search *your* car.'

'I've searched it,' Conway said, 'and I've found something that bothers me.'

'You've *found* something?'

'Yes.'

'What?'

'It was under the front seat where a man ordinarily wouldn't look once in a couple of years. It was a neatly typed list of the stockholders who had sent in their proxies.'

'Let me look at it,' Mason said.

Conway handed him four typewritten sheets of paper neatly stapled together. He said, 'It was there under the front seat where it might seem I had tried to conceal it where it wouldn't be found. It was in a manila envelope.'

'How did it get there?'

'I don't know. It could have been put there any time.'

'While you were parked near the hotel?'

'While I was parked near the hotel, while I was parked in front of the drugstore where I was telephoning, while I was parked any place.'

'You keep your car locked?'

'No, I take the ignition key with me, of course, but the doors and windows are unlocked.'

'What about the list? Have you checked it?'

'As nearly as I can. There's one peculiar thing about it.'

'What?'

'It's almost *too* good.'

'What do you mean, almost too good?'

'Almost too reassuring. The people who have sent in proxies are, for the most part, the very small shareholders, and some of them I know were discontented, anyway. They'd have sent in proxies even if there hadn't been any advertising campaign.'

'On a percentage basis what does it figure?'

'As nearly as I can figure without having access to the books of the corporation, there's only about 17 per cent of the outstanding stock represented on this proxy list.'

'Any date on it?'

'Yes, it's dated only a couple of days ago. It's supposed to be right up to date.'

'How much have you handled it?'

'Handled it? Quite a bit. Why?'

'Then you've probably obliterated any chance of tracing it,' Mason said.

'What do you mean? You can't get finger-prints from paper, can you?'

'Sometimes you can,' Mason said. 'Using iodine fumes, you can quite frequently bring out latent finger-prints.'

'I didn't handle the envelope much. I've gone over the list pretty thoroughly.'

'I'm afraid it's part of the trap,' Mason said. 'Let's get started and I'll tell you about *my* information. You've had breakfast?'

'Sure, I had breakfast early this morning. I didn't sleep much last night.'

'Who did?' Mason asked.

'You were worried?' Conway asked in alarm.

'I was busy,' Mason told him. 'Come on, let's get started.'

'What about your list of stockholder proxies, and why do you think my list is a trap?' Conway asked.

Mason produced the sheets of carbon paper from his brief-case. 'Take a look at these and you can see for yourself.'

'Where did you get these?' Conway asked.

'Straight from the horse's mouth.'

Conway held the sheets of carbon paper to the light one at a time, studied them carefully.

When he had finished he said, 'If these are the straight goods, Mason, I'm licked.'

'That bad?'

'That bad.'

'These *could* be phony,' Mason said, 'but I don't think so.'

'What will I do with that other list, the one I found in my car?'

'You'll have to give it to the D.A. Tell him you found it when you searched your car. *You* don't know where it came from so you'll have to tell him the whole story. They'll be searching your car this morning.'

'Do I tell him anything about these sheets of carbon paper you have?'

'Not unless you want a one-way ticket to San Quentin.'

'You're damned mysterious, Mason I'm your client.'

'That's why I'm being mysterious. I'm going to get you out of this, but I'll do it my way.'

'That's a promise,' Conway said. 'Let me tell them I'm checking out. Then you drive your car down the street and I'll pick you up.'

'Okay,' Mason said. 'We've got lots of time.'

Mason drove a block before he found a parking space. He slid his car into the kerb, put the ignition keys in his pocket, took his brief-case and moved over to Conway's car.

Conway was preoccupied, thinking about the proxy battle. 'I'm afraid those ads have done more damage than I realized,' Conway said.

'Of course,' Mason pointed out, 'the ads have been running for a while, and most of the people who would be swayed by that type of reasoning would already have sent in their proxies. Don't throw in the sponge. . . . You have that gun with you?'

'Yes. . . . How *did* you get that list, Mason?'

'It's a long story,' Mason told him, 'and we haven't time to discuss it now. We're going to have to go to the district attorney's office, and you'll have to tell your story. You're going to be questioned, and the newspaper reporters are going to have a field day.'

'That will suit Farrell just fine!' Conway said bitterly.

'Don't be too certain,' Mason said. 'I think Farrell is having troubles of his own.'

'How come?'

'I planted a couple of time bombs on him,' Mason said. 'The police haven't made any public announcement as yet, but I think they've identified the corpse.'

'Who is she?'

'A Rose Calvert who worked in a brokerage office, and–'

'Rose!' Conway exclaimed.

'Do you know her?'

'Of course I know her. She works in the brokerage office that handles my accounts. That is, she did work there. I think she left two or three months ago. I haven't seen her for a while.'

'You used to talk with her?'

'Yes.'

'Kid her along?'

'Yes.'

'Ever date her?'

'You aren't kidding?'

'No.'

'She's married, Mason. It's *Mrs* Calvert.'

'And you never dated her?'

'No.'

'Never tried to date her?'

'No.'

'But you did kid her along?'

'She liked to kid. She was jolly and liked attention from the customers.'

'The masculine customers,' Mason said.

'That's right. She had a good figure and she knew it.'

'All right,' Mason said. 'Now, here's where you let your hair down and tell me the truth. Did you try to do any gun juggling?'

'What do you mean?' Conway asked.

'I know it was a temptation,' Mason said. 'You felt that you had been framed. You felt that Gifford Farrell was back of it. You didn't want to sit still and take it. You probably felt that if you could get rid of that fatal gun and substitute another gun in its place, there was no way on earth they could ever prove that it *was* the fatal gun that you had taken away from that girl.'

Conway said, 'You've probably been reading my mind.'

'All right,' Mason told him, 'what did you do about it?'

'Nothing. You're my lawyer. I followed instructions.'

'You didn't try to switch guns?'

'No.'

'You were tempted?'

'I thought of it.'

Mason said, 'In a case of this kind, you really can't tell what to do. If you switch guns, you've got the other people in an embarrassing position. They can't swear that the guns have been juggled without disclosing their own guilty knowledge.

'The whole crux of their frame-up depends upon getting *you* to tell a story that sounds improbable on the face of it, something that sounds like a desperate attempt to account for having the fatal gun in your possession, as well as a list of stockholders which somehow must have been taken from Rose Calvert. You add to that the fact that you asked for mail under an assumed name, went up to a room in which the body was subsequently found, entered that room with a key, and it builds up to a pretty darned good case of first-degree murder.'

'It gives me the creeps to hear you summarizing it,' Conway said.

'Well, don't worry too much about it,' Mason told him, 'because there's one weak point in the case.'

'What's that?'

'They had to force you to take the fatal gun,' Mason said. 'The weak link is that the fatal gun can be traced.'

'You've traced it?'

'Yes.'

'Who bought it?'

'You did.'

'What?' Conway shouted. 'What are you talking about?'

'You bought it,' Mason said. 'At least you authorized its purchase.'

'What are you talking about? I never saw this gun before in my life.'

'That may be,' Mason said, 'but apparently some three years ago the cashier convinced you that he needed a gun for protection, and you authorized the purchase of a weapon at the Pitcairn–'

'Heavens, yes! I remember it now,' Conway said, 'but I never even saw the gun. The voucher came through, and I put my okay on it. The cashier was the one who went down and bought it.'

'What happened to that cashier?' Mason asked.

'He died eight or ten months later.'

'While Farrell was with the firm?'

'I believe so.'

'And what happened to the gun?'

'That I don't know.'

'You didn't check it?'

'Good Lord, Mason, the Texas Global has options on potential oil land scattered half-way across Texas. I'm trying to figure where the oil deposits are, how much we can afford to pay, how deep we should go with our wells. . . . I had no time to go take an inventory of the property in the desk of a cashier who dies suddenly.'

'Exactly,' Mason said. 'That's the weak point in the scheme. Farrell had just as good access to the gun as you did, and when it comes to proving motivation or having connexion with the corpse, Farrell is in a *very* delicate position. He had been playing around with this young woman, had taken photographs of her in the altogether, and his wife was planning to name her as co-respondent in a divorce suit.'

'Oh-oh,' Conway said.

'So,' Mason told him, 'if *your* nose is clean, and if you didn't try to get smart by juggling weapons between the time you left Drake's office and the time I took the number off that gun, I think we can get you out of it. I know we can put you in such a position that the district attorney won't dare to proceed against you without more evidence.'

Conway drove for a while in silence, then said, 'Mason, don't underestimate Gifford Farrell. He is not a sound thinker, but he has a chain-lightning mind. He'll completely dazzle you. He'll reach some conclusion after seemingly brilliant thinking, and then, for some cockeyed reason or other, the conclusion will turn out to be unsound.'

'I know the type,' Mason said.

'Well, don't underestimate him,' Conway pleaded. 'He's clever, he's ingenious and he's utterly ruthless.'

Mason nodded.

'Now, what do I do at the district attorney's office?' Conway asked.

'You tell them the truth,' Mason said. 'Unless I stop you, keep on talking.'

'Tell them the *entire* truth?'

'The entire truth.'

'That might call for a little thought here and there.'

'It calls for nothing,' Mason said. 'You have no guilty knowledge of the crime. You know what happened, and your job is to convince the officers. The minute you start getting cagey and trying to withhold something, or emphasizing one fact and minimizing another, trying to spread gilt paint over the truth, they'll know exactly what you're doing. They've had so much experience with liars, they can just about tell when a man starts lying.'

'All right,' Conway said, 'I'll tell them the truth. But I'm worried about that gun.'

'I was at first,' Mason told him, 'but I'm not any longer. When it comes to a showdown, we can probably prove that Farrell took that gun out of the cashier's desk, or at least had more opportunity than you did.'

Conway thought things over for several minutes, then said, 'Mason, I'm afraid that you may be trying to over-simplify this thing.'

Mason lit a cigarette. 'Just quit worrying, tell the truth, and leave the rest to me,' he said.

9

Promptly at nine o'clock Mason held the door of the district attorney's office open for Jerry Conway.

'Perry Mason and Mr Conway,' he told the secretary at the other desk. 'I told the police I would be here at nine o'clock with my client to answer questions. We're here.'

The girl at the desk said, 'Just a moment!'

She picked up the telephone, put through a call, then said, 'You may go in, Mr Mason. Right through those swinging doors and all the way down the corridor, the office on the far left.'

Mason and Conway walked down the long corridor, opened the last door on the left.

Hamilton Burger, the big, barrel-chested district attorney, sat behind the desk facing the door. He was flanked by Lt Tragg, one of the most skilled investigators in the Homicide Department, a uniformed police officer, and Alexander Redfield, who did ballistics work for the authorities.

The spools of a tape recorder on the table were revolving slowly.

Hamilton Burger said, 'Good morning, gentlemen. I have decided that this interview should be recorded. I trust there is no objection?'

'None whatever,' Mason told him.

'Thank you,' the district attorney said sarcastically. 'I may also state for your information that there is a microphone in this office, and the conversation is also being monitored by a police shorthand reporter.'

'Quite all right,' Mason said. 'This is my client, Gerald Conway, gentlemen.'

'Sit down,' Hamilton Burger invited. 'What is your occupation, Mr Conway?'

'I'm president of the California & Texas Global Development & Exploration Company.'

'As I understand it, you had occasion to consult Mr Perry Mason some time last night?'

'Yes, sir.'

'Do you remember the time?'

'It was, I believe, shortly before seven o'clock.'

'And how did you get in touch with Mr Mason?'

'I looked up a night number in the telephone exchange, called it, was directed to the Drake Detective Agency, and so managed to get in touch with Mr Mason.'

'And what did you want Mr Mason to do?'

'I wanted him to advise me in connexion with a disturbing incident which had happened in the Redfern Hotel.'

Hamilton Burger glanced suspiciously at Mason. 'You're going to let him tell his full story?'

'I'm going to let him tell his full story,' Mason said.

'All right, go ahead,' Hamilton Burger said. 'Go right ahead.'

Conway told about the mysterious telephone calls, about the offers to give him the list of stockholders who had given proxies to Gifford Farrell's proxy committee. He told about his hesitancy, his final decision to have a meeting with the mysterious Rosalind.

He told about calling in his secretary to take down the conversation, about going out and following instructions to the letter, about the telephone call which had been received while he was waiting at the booth in the drugstore.

Conway then went on to tell about his trip to the Redfern Hotel.

Mason said, 'Just a minute. I want to interrupt for a couple of questions.'

'Later,' Hamilton Burger said. 'I want to get his story now.'

'I'm sorry,' Mason said, 'but you have to know a couple of things in order to understand the full import of that story. About the time element, Mr Conway, you had been told that the telephone would ring at six-fifteen?'

'That's right.'

'When *did* the telephone ring?'

'It was a few minutes earlier than that.'

'What difference does that make?' Hamilton Burger asked.

'It makes a lot of difference, as I will be prepared to show later on,' Mason said. 'Now, one other thing, Mr Conway, when that call came in, that is, the one you received at the drugstore, it was a woman's voice, was it not?'

'Yes.'

'Was it the same voice that you had heard earlier? In other words, was it the voice of the woman who described herself as Rosalind?'

'That's another point. I didn't think it was at the time, and the more I think of it, the more certain I am that it wasn't.'

Mason said, 'I don't think my client understands the full import of this, gentlemen. But the point is that the woman who described herself over the telephone as Rosalind was going to call Mr Conway at six-fifteen and tell him to go to a certain place to get the information he wanted. When she called the pay station at six-fifteen, there was no answer. The reason was that Mr Conway had already received his erroneous instructions and was then on his way to the Redfern Hotel.'

'Why would someone give him erroneous instructions?' Lt Tragg asked.

'You be the judges of that,' Mason said. 'Now, go on, Conway, and tell them what happened.'

Conway described his trip to the hotel, the envelope that he had received containing the key to Room 729. He told of going up to the room, knocking at the door, receiving no answer, then being tempted to retrace his steps, turn in the key, and call the whole thing off.

However, he pointed out, the prospect of getting the information which would be of the greatest value to him was too much of a temptation. He had used the key, had gone in. With dramatic simplicity he described in detail his adventure with the young woman who was clad only in the scantiest of apparel.

Then Conway described the panic which had gripped him when he realized the weapon he had taken from the young woman had been fired once, and recently. He decided he should consult Perry Mason.

'And what did Perry Mason advise you to do?' the district attorney asked.

Mason interposed with an urbane smile, 'At this point, gentlemen, my client's story ends, except for the fact that he found a paper containing a list of stockholders who had sent in their proxies in his car. This list which I now hand to you contains Conway's initials on each page, and also my initials are on each page.

'My client's car is parked downstairs, and I reported that fact to the police before we came up and suggested they would want to search the car.

'My client has nothing to say about anything that happened *after* he consulted me. I am perfectly willing to answer questions from that point on. However, you must realize that the advice of an attorney to a client is not anything which can be produced in evidence, and questions about it should not be asked.'

Hamilton Burger's face slowly purpled. 'As a citizen, you're bound by laws the same as anyone else. Whenever you try to conceal a weapon with which a murder has been committed–'

'A murder?' Mason asked.

'A murder!' Hamilton Burger shouted. 'A murder was committed with that weapon!'

'But I didn't know it! I didn't know there had been a murder. Conway didn't know there had been a murder. He only knew that he had taken possession of a weapon under circumstances which made the whole thing look suspiciously like a frame-up. He called on me to investigate. I investigated.'

'But as soon as you investigated,' Burger said, 'you went to that room and encountered a corpse.'

'That's right.'

'And then you knew that the gun was the murder weapon!'

'Indeed I did not!' Mason said. '*I* didn't know it was the murder weapon. I don't know it *now*.'

'The hell you don't!' Burger shouted. 'Anyone with the intelligence of a two-year-old would have known it, and you're not that big a fool. Where's the gun?'

Conway took the gun from his pocket and passed it across to Hamilton Burger. 'It's loaded,' he said.

Burger looked at the gun, handed it to Alexander Redfield.

The ballistics expert looked at the gun, swung open the cylinder, looked at the exploded shell, took a sharp, pointed engravers' tool from his pocket and etched on the shells the relative position which they occupied in the cylinder of the gun. Then he snapped the cylinder shut, and dropped the gun in his pocket.

'Now then,' Hamilton Burger said, 'I want to know what happened last night. I want to know where this man was all night.'

'What does that have to do with it?' Mason said.

'It has a lot to do with it,' Burger said. 'He resorted to flight.'

'To flight!' Mason said.

'You're damned right he did!' Burger said. 'Don't think the police are entirely dumb, Mason. We found out about Conway a short time ago, after we had identified the corpse. We found out that Conway had gone up in the elevator of your office building last night, that he had gone to Paul Drake's office, that an hour or so later your estimable secretary, Della Street, came up in that elevator, that shortly afterwards Conway went down and just a few moments later Della Street went down. I think the inference is fairly obvious.

You had telephoned Della Street to get your client out of circulation.'

'But why should I want him out of circulation?' Mason asked.

'So he couldn't be questioned.'

'Then why should I bring him here this morning?'

'Because now you've had time to concoct a story!'

'I'm sorry, Mr District Attorney,' Perry Mason said, 'but your suspicions are not justified by facts. There was no flight. Mr Conway simply felt that it would be inconvenient for me to consult with him during the night at his apartment. I was doing some investigative work, trying to find out the extent of what I felt was a frame-up. Therefore, I had Mr Conway wait at a place where he would be more available and where I could call on him at night without disturbing anyone or attracting undue attention.

'Mr Conway, for your information, gentlemen, was at the Gladedell Motel. He occupied Unit 21, and I'm quite certain you will find that he registered under his own name. It is certainly not flight for a person to go to a motel and register under his own name, driving in his own car, and registering the correct licence number of that car.'

'All right!' Burger shouted. 'Then why did you withhold this evidence until nine o'clock this morning?'

'What evidence?'

'This gun. The one that Redfield has. The murder weapon.'

'But I don't know it's a murder weapon,' Mason said. 'I knew that you wouldn't be at your office until nine o'clock in the morning. I made arrangements with Mr Conway to come here at the earliest possible hour this morning. We arrived just as soon as your office opened. In fact, I think an investigation would disclose that you are here unusually early this morning because you wanted to question my client.'

'That's just a run-around,' Hamilton Burger said. 'You should have given this weapon to the police last night and you know it.'

'Why?'

'Because a murder was committed with it.'

'Oh, I certainly hope not,' Mason said. 'Oh, I certainly *do* hope not, Mr District Attorney. That would complicate matters!'

'You mean you didn't have the slightest idea that this was a murder weapon?' Burger asked sarcastically.

'How would I know it was a murder weapon?' Mason countered. 'No one even told me how the young woman died. They told me to get out of the room and stay out of the room. The police didn't reveal the result of their investigations to me. Was she killed with a revolver?'

'She was killed with a revolver, and this is the murder weapon, the one which you folks were concealing from the police all night.'

Alexander Redfield cleared his throat. 'May I say something, Mr Burger?'

'Not now!' Burger said. 'I demand that Mr Mason give us an explanation.'

Mason said, 'There isn't any explanation because I am not prepared to concede the premise on which you are acting. *I* don't know that it's the murder weapon. I did feel that an attempt was made to frame my client with a gun which had been discharged somehow. I wanted to try and find out something about that gun and where it came from.'

'And you did?' Hamilton Burger asked.

'I did,' Mason said. 'For your information, that is a revolver which was purchased some three years ago by the Texas Global Company for the protection of its cashier.

'I can assure you, gentlemen, that I have been quite busy trying to get information in this case so that I could be of some assistance to you this morning.'

'You went to Elsinore last night!' Hamilton Burger charged.

'That's right. I did indeed!'

'Why?'

'Because I felt there was a possibility Mr Norton B. Calvert, who lives in Elsinore, could shed some light on the identity of the corpse.'

'All right,' Hamilton Burger said sarcastically. 'Now tell us just what intuitive reasoning made you think he could shed light on the identity of the corpse?'

Mason said, 'Mr Burger, I will answer that question if you tell me that you are asking that question in your official capacity, and that as a citizen and as an officer of the court it is my duty to answer.'

'What are you trying to do?' Hamilton Burger asked.

'I'm trying to protect myself,' Mason said. 'Do you tell me that such is the case?'

'I tell you such is the case. Answer the question.'

'Very well,' Mason said. 'I felt there was a great possibility that, if there had been a frame-up–and mind you, I say *if*, gentlemen, I am not stating that there was a frame-up. I am simply stating that if there had been a frame-up–there is always the possibilty that frame-up might have something to do with the Texas Global proxy fight.

'With that in view I did a lot of investigative work last night and I learned that Gifford Farrell had been taking a great interest in a Rose M. Calvert. I learned that the description of this young woman matched perfectly the description of the young woman whose body I had seen in the hotel bedroom. Therefore, I decided to go to see Rose Calvert's husband and see if I could find some photographs of his wife. I felt that perhaps such a trip would disclose important information.'

'And that is the reason you went to see the husband?' Lt Tragg asked, suddenly curious.

'That is why I went to see him.'

'How did you get his address?' Tragg asked.

'I was advised,' Mason said, 'that there was a letter in the letter box at the Lane Vista Apartments where Rose Calvert has her apartment, addressed to her and bearing the return address of Norton B. Calvert of 6831 Washington Heights, Elsinore.'

'How did you know that letter was there?' Hamilton Burger asked.

'I was advised it was there.'

'By whom?'

'By a detective.'

'And he looked at that letter?' Burger asked.

'No, sir. I don't think he did. I think he in turn was advised by another detective, who was shadowing the apartment at the request of still another party.'

'Mrs Farrell?' Lt Tragg asked.

'I didn't say that, Lieutenant. I didn't mention any names. I am simply trying to tell you how it happened I went to Elsinore. I have been ordered to answer that question and I am trying not to withhold information. I don't want you to think I am making any accusations. I am only exposing my mental processes.'

'Well, you seem to have had a remarkably brilliant flash of inspiration or intuition, or mental telepathy or psychic ability, or whatever you want to call it,' Hamilton Burger said sarcastically. 'The body was that of Rose Calvert, but *we* didn't know it until about six o'clock this morning. You evidently had the information some hours before we did, and did nothing about it.'

'I didn't have the information,' Mason said. 'I saw pictures and I noticed that there was quite a resemblance. I told Mr Calvert that I was very much afraid his wife had been the victim of a tragedy. I felt that if he wanted to pursue the matter further, he would get in touch with the police.

'However, you can appreciate my position. I certainly couldn't start saying that Rose Calvert had been murdered, and then have it appear the whole thing was a hideous mistake, and Rose Calvert would show up alive and well.

'Making an identification of a corpse whom you have seen only from snapshots is rather a ticklish matter as you, Lieutenant, undoubtedly realize.'

'You're being very conservative all at once,' Hamilton Burger said.

'I wanted to be sure,' Mason said.

'Moreover,' Burger went on, 'you aren't telling us the truth about how you secured the husband's address.'

'What do you mean?'

'There wasn't any such letter in the mailbox.'

'I was advised that there was.'

'Well, there wasn't.'

'I'm sorry,' Mason said, 'but that's how I got the address. . . . I was told the letter was there.'

Hamilton Burger turned to Redfield. 'Redfield,' he said impatiently, 'get to your laboratory and test that gun. Fire test bullets from it. Identify it as the fatal weapon. At least let's get that done. That's what you're here for.'

Redfield made no move to leave his chair. 'May I say something, Mr District Attorney?' he asked.

Hamilton Burger, his patience worn thin, shouted, 'Well, what the hell do you want to say? That's the second time you've made that crack.'

'And I was told not to say anything,' Redfield said.

'Well, if you have anything to say, for heaven's sake, say it and then start checking on that bullet.'

Redfield said, 'This is not the murder weapon. The fatal bullet which killed Rose Calvert was fired from a Colt revolver. A Colt has six grooves which are inclined to the left. This is a Smith & Wesson revolver and, for your information, it has five grooves which are inclined to the right.

'I knew as soon as Mr Conway passed over this gun that it couldn't possibly have been the murder weapon.'

'What?' Hamilton Burger shouted.

Lt Tragg half-rose from his seat, then settled back.

Mason strove to keep a poker face. He looked sharply at Conway.

Hamilton Burger seemed to be trying to get his ideas orientated.

Suddenly He said, 'So that's it! It's the same old razzle-dazzle. Mason has taken this murder weapon and switched it. He's had his client turn in this other gun, and is acting on the assumption that no one can disprove his story without producing the young woman from whom Conway says he took this gun. . . . And the minute that is done, there will be confirmation of Conway's story. . . .

This is a typical Perry Mason razzle-dazzle!'

'I resent that!' Perry Mason said.

'Resent it and be damned!' Hamilton Burger shouted. 'I've seen too many of your slick substitutions, your sleight of hand . . . your–'

'Just a minute,' Mason interrupted. 'Don't be foolish. I am perfectly willing to resort to some forms of unconventional action for the purpose of checking the testimony of a witness. However, I certainly would not be party to any substitution of a murder weapon and then have a client tell you a lie about it.'

'Poppycock!' Hamilton Burger said.

For a moment there was a silence. Everyone seemed to be at an impasse. Abruptly Burger picked up the telephone and said, 'Bring Gifford Farrell in here, please.'

The door from an anteroom opened, and Sgt Holcomb of Homicide Squad escorted a debonair individual into the district attorney's office.

'Mr Gifford Farrell,' the district attorney announced.

Farrell was in his thirties, a tall, broad-shouldered, thin-waisted, well-dressed individual. His face was bronzed with outdoor living. A hairline moustache emphasized the curve of his upper lip. He had smooth, dark eyebrows, dark, glittering eyes, so dark that it was impossible to distinguish the pupils. His hair was cut so that sideburns ran a couple of inches below his ears. He was wearing a brown plaid sport jacket, and gaberdine slacks.

'You know Mr Conway,' Hamilton Burger said.

Farrell's thin lips came away from even, white teeth in a smile. 'Indeed I do,' he said. 'How are you this morning, Jerry?'

'Good morning, Giff,' Conway grunted.

'And this is Mr Perry Mason,' Hamilton Burger said. 'He has just accused you of trying to frame his client, Mr Conway.'

Farrell's lips clamped shut, his glittering, dark eyes regarded Mason with cold hostility.

'I have done nothing of the sort,' Mason said smoothly. 'I have simply pointed out to the district attorney that I felt my client was the victim of a frame-up.'

'Well, you said that it was a frame-up over this proxy battle in Texas Global,' Burger said.

'I did indeed,' Mason said. 'And I am quite willing to state that I think the probabilities are–mind you, gentlemen, I say the *probabilities* are–that the attempted frame-up, was because of that proxy battle, and if there was a frame-up, then I believe there is a possibility Mr Farrell should be considered suspect.'

'There you are,' Hamilton Burger said.

Farrell kept his eyes on Mason and said, 'I don't like that.'

Mason surveyed the man from head to foot and said calmly, 'No one asked whether you liked it or not.'

Farrell took a quick step towards Mason. The lawyer made no move.

'Just a minute!' Hamilton Burger said.

Farrell stopped his advance.

Hamilton Burger said, 'Farrell, what do *you* know about a gun that was purchased by the Texas Global Company for the protection of its cashier? The gun was purchased three years ago.'

Farrell frowned in concentration, shifted his eyes from Mason to Burger, said, 'I'm afraid I know nothing, Mr Burger.'

'Now, think carefully,' Burger said. 'The gun was purchased, and I understand was turned over to the cashier who–'

'Do you know who okayed the invoice?' Farrell asked.

'Mr Conway has admitted that he probably did.'

'I said I thought I might have,' Conway corrected.

Once again Farrell's teeth flashed. 'Well, gentlemen, there's your answer!'

Mason said, 'I take it you knew the young woman who was found dead in the Redfern Hotel, Mr Farrell?'

Farrell's eyes were impudent. 'What if I did?'

'You knew her rather intimately, I believe.'

'Are you making an accusation?'

'I am asking a question.'

'I don't have to answer your questions. I'll answer questions asked by the police and by the district attorney.'

'This Rose Calvert was doing some work for you?' Hamilton Burger asked Farrell.

'Yes, sir. She was, She was doing some very confidential work. It was work that I didn't want to entrust to a regular stenographer. I wanted someone who was outside of the business, someone whom I knew I could trust. I chose Mrs Calvert.

'Now, I will say this, gentlemen. In some way it leaked out that she was doing this work, and an attempt was made to get her to deliver information to Mr Conway. Conway offered her five thousand dollars in cash for copies of the work she was doing, listing the stockholders who had sent in their proxies. She refused the offer.'

Conway said angrily, 'That's a lie! I never talked with her in my life–that is, about work. I didn't know she was doing it!'

Farrell said, 'I have her assurance that you did.'

The district attorney looked at Conway.

'That's an absolute falsehood,' Conway said. 'I never rang up Mrs Calvert in my life. I knew her only as a young woman who was in the brokerage office where I transacted my individual business and much of the business of the Texas Global. I used to chat with her, in the way one would chat with an employee under conditions of that sort. I didn't notice her otherwise.'

'How well did Farrell know her?' Mason asked.

'I'll conduct this inquiry, Mr Mason,' Burger said.

'In case you're interested,' Mason told him, 'Mrs Calvert's husband says that Gifford Farrell knew her quite well; in fact, too well.'

'And that is a falsehood!' Farrell said. 'My relations with Rose Calvert were a combination of business and friendship.'

'Ever buy any clothes for her?' Mason asked.

Farrell said, 'I did not, and anyone who says I did is a damned liar!'

'Then' Mason said, 'I have talked with a liar who says that you bought her a Bikini bathing suit. You sent a mail order to one of the magazines that advertises those things. However, there's no use questioning your word, because the mail-order records will show that.'

Farrell's face showed startled surprise. His eyes which had been glaring at Perry Mason suddenly shifted. He became conscious of the circle of men who were regarding him with keen interest, their trained eyes taking in every flicker of facial expression.

Farrell took a deep breath, then once more his teeth flashed in a quick smile.

'I'm afraid, Mr Mason, that you have been making a mountain out of a molehill. It is true, I did send away for one of those Bikini bathing suits. It was just a gag. I intended to use it as the basis for a practical joke in connexion with one of my associates.

'I can assure you that the suit had nothing to do with Rose Calvert.'

'Then how did it happen,' Mason asked, 'that she put the suit on?'

'She didn't!' Farrell snapped.

'Then how did it happen that you took her picture with the suit on, a picture which was posed in your bedroom while your wife was in New York?'

Try as he might, Farrell couldn't keep the dismay from his face.

There was a long period of silence.

'Well?' Hamilton Burger asked. 'We're waiting, Farrell.'

Farrell said, 'I don't know what the idea of this is. I came up here to do anything I could to help find the murderer of Rose Calvert. I didn't come up here to be cross-examined by some attorney who is trying to shield the murderer and drag a lot of red herrings across the trail.

'There has been a lot of talk about frame-up, and I guess perhaps I have been unusually naïve. I don't know who is trying to frame something on me, but if this question is going to hinge upon some Bikini bathing suit which I purchased as a joke, and some accusations in regard to pictures, I guess I had better get an attorney of my own.'

'Do you deny that you took such a picture?' Mason asked.

Farrell faced him and said evenly, 'Go to hell.'

Mason grinned at Hamilton Burger. 'The canary seems to have quit singing and started chirping.'

Sgt Holcomb said, 'I've had a long talk with Farrell, Mr Burger, and I'm convinced that he's all right. Perry Mason is just trying to use this business as a red herring.'

Hamilton Burger said abruptly, 'I see no reason for letting this interview degenerate into a brawl. Conway has appeared and has told his story. The gun which he has handed us and which he insists he took from the Redfern Hotel is quite obviously not the fatal gun.'

'Not the fatal gun!' Farrell exclaimed.

Burger shook his head.

'Then he's switched guns!' Farrell said.

'You don't need to point out the obvious to this office,' Hamilton Burger said with dignity. 'Mr Mason's legal ingenuity is too well known to need any comment from anyone.

'I desire to interrogate Mr Farrell further.

'Mr Mason and Mr Conway are excused. Just go on out and I will send for you again if there are any further developments.'

Mason took Conway's arm. 'Come on, Jerry.'

Mason opened the door. Conway and Mason walked out together down the long corridor and out through the folding doors into the district attorney's waiting room. The office was jammed with newspaper reporters. Flashbulbs popped in a dazzling array of blinding light flashes.

Reporters crowded around asking questions.

Conway tried to force his way through the reporters.

'Take it easy, Jerry,' Mason said. And then to the reporters, 'We'll make a statement to you, gentlemen. An attempt was made to frame a murder on my client, Gerald Conway. I don't know whether the murder was committed and then the murderer, in desperation, tried to involve Mr Conway, or whether the whole thing was part of a scheme to discredit Conway in connexion with his battle for proxies in the Global Company. I can only tell you gentlemen what happened, and assure you of our desire to co-operate in every way possible in cleaning up this case.'

'Well, what happened?' one of the reporters asked.

Mason turned to Conway and said, 'Tell them your story, Jerry.'

Conway frowned and hesitated.

'It's a damned sight better to let the newspapers have *your* version,' Mason said, 'than to get a second-hand garbled version from someone who was present in the district attorney's office–Gifford Farrell, for instance.'

Conway again related his story, while reporters crowded around making notes and asking questions.

10

Conway, driving Mason back towards the Gladedell Motel so the lawyer could pick up his car, said, 'That wasn't so bad! How did I do, Perry?'

'You did all right,' Mason told him. 'I think you made a good impression on the newspaper boys and that's going to mean a lot. Fortunately, you had a chance to tell the reporters your story first. By the time the district attorney gets done questioning Gifford Farrell and he has a chance to talk with the reporters, the story of your interview will have been written up.'

'It was worth a lot watching Giff Farrell's face when you sprang that on him about the Bikini bathing suit,' Conway said.

Mason nodded. 'Of course, Jerry, the fact that a man has been buying a Bikini bathing suit for a girl doesn't mean that he murdered her.'

'Well, he could have murdered her, all right.'

'And,' Mason went on, 'you have to remember that we don't *know* it was murder. She might have committed suicide. The thing I can't understand is about that gun.'

'What about it?'

'It wasn't the murder weapon.'

'Boy oh boy! Wasn't it a grand and glorious feeling when that expert spoke up?' Conway said. 'That let me right off the hook!'

'I'm not so certain,' Mason told him. 'It's a complication that I can't understand and I don't like it.'

'Why?'

Mason said, 'That woman *wanted* you to take that gun from her. She didn't intend to shoot you. She came out of the bedroom stripped down to the minimum in order to put you at a disadvantage. All she had to do was to start screaming, and you would have been at a terrific disadvantage. You realized that and wanted out of there the worst way. She drew that gun and then kept advancing towards you. Her hand was shaking. There's no question about it; she wanted you to take that gun!'

Conway said, 'Thinking back on it, I'm not so sure it wasn't just plain panic on her part.'

'She walked out of a room where there was a corpse.' Mason pointed out. 'She pulled a gun out of the desk and kept advancing on you, holding out the gun so that it was an invitation for you to grab it.'

Conway, feeling expansive with relief, said, 'She may have been nervous. Perhaps she got blood on her clothes in shooting her room-mate and wanted to change her clothes and get rid of the blood-spattered garments. She was in the process of doing that when I walked in the room. Naturally she was in a terrific panic.'

'So she pulled a gun on you?'

'That's right.'

'And what did she want when she pulled the gun?'

'She was afraid I was going to–Well, perhaps she was afraid I was going to take her into custody.'

'She didn't tell you to get out,' Mason said. 'She told you to hold up your hands. The thing just doesn't make sense.'

'Well, we're out of it now,' Conway said.

Mason remained silent.

Conway drove for a while in silence, then said, 'Well, here's your car.'

'Wait a minute,' Mason said, 'that's a police car parked up there in the next block. Let's see what they're doing. Drive on slowly, Jerry.'

Conway drove up to the next block.

'Oh-oh,' Mason said, 'they're searching the motel grounds with mine detectors.'

'What's the idea of that?' Conway asked.

'The idea of that,' Mason told him dryly, 'is they think you substituted weapons and disposed of the murder gun while you were down here at the Gladedell Motel. . . . Look over there to the left. Quick!'

One of the searchers had thrown down the mine detector and was calling excitedly to the others.

A group of people from two police cars converged around him. For a moment, as Conway drove by, Mason had a brief glimpse of a man holding a revolver out at arm's length. A pencil was placed down the barrel of the gun he was holding so that any finger-prints would not be smirched.

There was only the one brief glimpse of that scene, and then Conway's car had slid on by. Conway put a foot on the brakes.

'Keep going! Keep going,' Mason said.

'That man had a gun,' Conway exclaimed.

'Sure he had a gun,' Mason remarked, 'and what's more he dug up that gun from the yard in back of the motel where you admitted staying last night. Now then, Conway, suppose *you* tell *me* the truth.'

'What do you mean?'

Mason said, 'You got smart. You buried the gun they gave you. Then you went to your office and got this other gun. You substituted guns so you wouldn't have the fatal weapon in your possession.'

'I did no such thing!' Conway retorted angrily, slowing down.

'Keep driving!' Mason told him. 'Stop now and we're sunk.'

Conway said, 'I am not a fool, Mason. I put myself in your charge. I asked for your advice. I took it and–'

'All right! All right!' Mason said. 'Shut up. Let me think for a minute!'

'Where do you want to go?' Conway asked.

'Drive around the block,' Mason said. 'Take me back to my car, and–'

A siren sounded behind them.

'All right,' Mason said. 'Pull over to the kerb, and get a story ready. They've evidently recognized us.'

However, the siren was merely being used to clear the traffic. The police car coming from behind rocketed on past with steadily accelerating speed.

Mason said, 'They're rushing that gun to the crime laboratory for testing.'

'But how could Giff Farrell have known where I was going to be so he could plant that gun down here?' Conway asked.

Mason said, 'You took elaborate precautions to see that you weren't followed *to* the Redfern Hotel. But you didn't take precautions to see that you weren't followed *from* the Redfern Hotel.'

'There wasn't anybody there to follow me,' Conway said. 'I had ditched the shadows.'

'If it was a frame-up,' Mason pointed out, 'they would have been waiting for you at the Redfern Hotel and have shadowed you from there to Drake's office, then out. In that way they'd have known you spent the night at the Gladedell Motel. What a slick scheme it would be to have you take a gun which you actually thought was the murder weapon, go through all the agony of trying to decide what to do, tell your story to the district attorney, and then have it appear that *you* had switched guns during the night.'

Conway thought for a moment, then said bitterly, 'I told you this Gifford Farrell was ingenious.'

'That,' Mason said, 'makes a beautiful, beautiful frame-up.'

Conway turned the corner. 'All right. What do we do?'

'We sit tight, Mason said. 'We wait for the breaks, and if they've pulled that sort of frame-up on you, I'm going to have to use every ounce of ability and mental agility I can command to get you out of it.'

'Well, that's Gifford Farrell for you,' Conway said. 'That's a typical Farrell idea! I told you the guy was brilliant.'

Mason said, 'Get me to my car, Conway! I've got work to do.'

'Then what do I do?'

'Go to your apartment,' Mason told him. 'They'll drag you in for questioning as soon as they've tested that gun at ballistics. If it's the fatal weapon, you're going to have a charge of first-degree murder placed against you.'

'Hang it!' Conway said. 'I should have known Farrell wouldn't stop with a simple frame-up. That guy always does things with what he likes to refer to as the artistic touch.'

'There's one thing that Farrell didn't count on,' Mason pointed out. 'That's the roll of undeveloped film in his camera and the fact that his wife has those pictures. I can see now why that knocked him for a loop.'

'And what do I do if they charge me with first-degree murder?' Conway asked.

'You put the matter in my hands,' Mason said.

Conway abruptly slid his car into the kerb. 'I can't go any farther, Perry. I'm shaking like a leaf. I know now what's happened. I know what it means. Even if they don't convict me of murder, it will mean the end of Texas Global as far as I'm concerned. Proxies will be pouring in on Farrell like falling snowflakes.'

'Get yourself together,' Mason said. 'Pull out and drive up as far as my car. I haven't time to walk. Now, just remember one thing. If they bring you up and confront you with the murder weapon, and if they say they're going to charge you with first-degree murder, demand that they bring the case to trial before this stockholders' meeting. Insist that it's a frame-up on account of the proxy fight and demand vindication.

'Okay, now, get yourself together and start driving!'

11

It was nearly noon when Perry Mason parked his car near the Redfern Hotel.

He bought a paper, opened it and then walked rapidly to the door leading to the lobby.

As he pulled back the door, Mason held the paper in front of him as though engrossed in some article on the sporting page.

He walked at a leisurely, steady pace to the elevator.

'Seven,' Mason said, holding the paper so that he could see only the legs of the girl elevator operator, his face completely concealed from her by the paper.

The cage started upwards.

Abruptly she asked, 'Where's your friend?'

'How's that?' Mason asked.

'The one who was interested in my book.'

Mason lowered the newspaper, looked at the girl with interest. 'Oh,' he said, 'it's you. What are you doing here?'

'Running the elevator.'

'So I see. Do you work twenty-four-hour shifts?'

'Eight-hour shifts. We switch shifts every two weeks. This is shift day. I started at 5.0 a.m. and go off duty at one o'clock.'

'How did you recognize me?' Mason asked curiously.

'From your feet.'

Mason regarded his shoes thoughtfully. The elevator came to a stop at the seventh floor.

'What about my shoes?' Mason asked.

'Not your shoes. Your feet.'

'I thought you were interested in that book you were reading.'

'I was, but I notice people's feet and–well, I noticed your friend. Where is he now?'

'He's in his office–or he was the last time I saw him.'

'Is he married?'

'Not him.'

She said, 'I like him.'

'I'll tell him,' Mason said.

'No, no, don't do that! I didn't mean it *that* way. I meant . . .'

Mason laughed as her voice trailed off into silence.

'All right,' Mason said, 'what about my feet?'

'It's the way you stand,' she said. 'You keep your feet flat on the floor and evenly spaced like a man getting ready to slug somebody. Most people lounge around with their weight on first one foot and then the other or lean against the rail along the edge of the elevator. You stand balanced.'

'Thanks for telling me,' Mason said. 'I'll try to be more average after this.'

'Don't do that,' she said.

'Why not?'

She smiled at him. 'You're too distinctive the way you are.'

Mason regarded her thoughtfully. 'But you fell for my friend,' he said.

'Who said I fell for him?'

'Didn't you?'

She pouted a moment, then said, 'Well, perhaps a little. You're different. You're inaccessible. But your friend is more . . . well, more available. Now, if you tell him any of this, I'm going to put scratch marks all over your face.'

'Can I tell him you're interested?' Mason asked.

'No,' she said shortly.

'When did you quit last night?' Mason asked.

'Gosh, not only did I have to switch shifts this morning, but I had to work later last night because of the trouble. They wanted to question the other girls.'

'When you say the trouble, you're referring to the murder?' Mason asked.

'Hush! We're not supposed to even mention that word.'

The buzzer on the elevator sounded.

'Well, thank you,' Mason said, 'I'll tell my friend.'

She looked up at him impudently. 'Where are you going?'

'What do you mean?'

'Here on the seventh floor?'

The buzzer rang again.

'You'd better get the elevator back down,' Mason said.

She laughed. 'That's what I mean by being inaccessible. You've been talking to me, not because you were interested in *me*, but because you don't want me to know what room you're going to. You were stalling around waiting for me to start down. All right, smartie, I said you were inaccessible. Go ahead.'

She slid the elevator door closed, and took the cage down.

Mason walked down to Room 728 and turned the knob.

The door swung open. A man who was seated in a straight-backed chair which had been tilted against the wall, his stockinged feet on the bed, a cigarette in his mouth, looked up at Mason and nodded.

Mason kicked the door shut.

'You're Drake's man?' Mason asked.

The man said, 'Hello,' tonelessly, cautiously.

Mason walked over to stand by the individual who got to his feet. 'You know me. I don't know you,' Mason said.

The operative opened his wallet and showed his identification papers. 'How thoroughly have you gone over this place?' Mason asked.

'I've taken a look,' Inskip said. 'It's clean.'

'Let's take another look,' Mason told him. 'Got a flash-light?'

'In my bag there.'

Mason took the flashlight, bent over and carefully followed the edges of the worn carpet around the room. He gave a careful inspection to the washstand in the bathroom.

'You sleep here?'

'I'm not supposed to sleep until I get an okay from Drake. He told me you were going to be in this morning. I was looking for you earlier. I didn't want to go to sleep until after you'd been here. When you leave, I'll put a "don't disturb" sign on the door and get eight hours' shut-eye. However, I'll be available in case anyone wants anything.'

Mason said, 'On a check-out they'd make up the bed before they rented the room.'

'Sure!' the man said.

'Okay,' Mason told him. 'Let's take a look at the bed. You take that side, I'll take this. Just take hold of the bottom sheet and list the whole thing right off on to the floor. I want to look at the mattress.'

'Okay,' Inskip said, 'you're the boss.'

They lifted the sheets and blankets entirely off the bed.

Mason studied the mattress carefully.

'I don't know what you're looking for,' Inskip said, 'but I heard that the bullet didn't go clean through. Death was instantaneous and there wasn't any bleeding except a little around the entrance wound. That was all absorbed by the sweater.'

'Well, there's no harm in looking,' Mason said.

'You don't think anything happened here in *this* room, do you?' Inskip asked.

'I don't know,' Mason told him.

The lawyer moved the flash-light along the edge of the mattress.

'Give me a hand,' he said to Inskip. 'Let's turn this mattress over.'

They raised the mattress.

'Any stain on the mattress would have had to soak through the sheets, and blood-stained sheets would have been reported,' Inskip said.

'I know,' Mason said. 'I–Here! What's this?'

'Well, I'll be damned,' Inskip said.

They propped the mattress on its edge and looked at a small, round hole in the mattress.

'It looks to me,' Inskip said, 'as though someone had held a gun right up against the bottom of the mattress and pulled the trigger, holding the gun on an angle so the bullet wouldn't go all the way through.'

'Well, let's find out,' Mason told him.

'How are we going to do it?'

Mason pushed his finger in the hole, said, 'That won't do it. Let's see if we can get something to use as a probe.'

'There's a wire coat hanger in the closet,' Inskip said. 'I have a pair of pliers with wire cutters in my bag. I always carry pliers with me, because you never know what you're going to run up against in this business. Let me make a probe.'

Inskip cut a piece of straight wire from a coat hanger while Mason held the mattress.

The detective ran the wire up inside the hole in the mattress for a few inches, then said, 'Here is is. I can feel the wire hitting something hard.'

'Can you make a hook on that wire and get it out?' Mason asked.

'I can try,' Inskip said, 'by putting a loop on the thing and working it over. I'll see what I can do.'

Inskip used his pliers, then again put the wire probe in the hole in the mattress, manipulated it back and forth, up and down, said, 'I think I've got it,' then pulled. He pulled something back for a couple of inches, then the probe slipped loose.

'Have to get another hold,' Inskip said. 'I think I can widen that loop a little now.'

He again worked on the wire, then once more pushed it up in the hole, said to Mason, 'I've got it now.' He pulled back on the wire. A metallic object popped out of the hole and fell down between the springs.

Inskip retrieved it. 'A ·38-calibre bullet,' he said.

Mason stood motionless, his eyes half-slitted in thoughtful concentration.

'Well?' Inskip asked.

'Let's get the bed back into shape,' Mason said. 'Turn the mattress the way it was.'

'Now what?' Inskip asked.

Mason said, 'Take a sharp knife, take the pointed blade of the knife and make some kind of an identifying mark on that bullet so you can recognize it. Better put it on the base of the bullet. Try not to disfigure the bullet any more than possible.'

'Then what?'

'Keep that bullet with you,' Mason said. 'Don't let it out of your possession at any time, no matter what happens.'

'Now, wait a minute. *You'd* better keep it,' Inskip said.

Mason shook his head. 'I wouldn't want to be a witness in a case I was defending. I want you to keep that. And I want you to keep it with you. Don't let it out of your possession. Get some soft tissue and wrap it up so you don't destroy any of the striations on that bullet.'

'Then what?' Inskip asked.

'Then,' Mason said, 'we make up the bed and you can go to sleep.'

'But how the devil did that bullet get in that mattress?' Inskip asked.

'That,' Mason said, 'is one of the things we're going to have to find out.'

'Do we want to tell anyone about this?'

'Not now,' Mason said. 'The police would laugh at us and claim we were faking evidence.'

'Later on it'll be just that much worse,' Inskip pointed out.

'I know,' Mason told him. 'That's why I want you to keep the bullet. What's your background? How long have you been in this business?'

'Quite a while. I was deputy sheriff for a while, then I drifted up to Las Vegas, and worked there. I did some security work when Hoover Dam was going through. I've been with the government and now I'm working as a private operative.'

'Ever been in trouble?'

'No.'

'Nothing they can throw up at you? You're not vulnerable in any way?'

Inskip shook his head. 'My nose is clean.'

'All right,' Mason told him, 'save that wire probe so you can show it if you have to.'

'What's the significance of that bullet?' Inskip asked.

'I don't know,' Mason told him. 'That is, I don't know yet.'

'Okay, you can call on me any time.'

'You going to tell the police about this?' Mason asked.

'I'd like to, Mr Mason.'

Mason said, 'Hold it until ten o'clock tonight, anyway. I want first chance to tell the police about it. Then you can–'

'Let's not talk time schedules,' Inskip interrupted. 'Let's leave it this way: I suggest to you that I think the police should know about this, and you say that *you're* going to tell them. Okay?'

'Okay,' Mason said, 'we'll leave it at that. I didn't say when, did I?'

'No. You didn't say when. I told you to report to the police. You said you would. I assumed you meant right away. However, because of that assumption I didn't pin you down. That was my mistake. That's all it was, a mistake.'

'A mistake,' Mason agreed.

12

Judge Clinton DeWitt nodded to Hamilton Burger. 'Do you wish to make an opening statement, Mr Burger?'

Burger nodded, got up from the counsel table and lumbered over to the jury box.

'Ladies and gentlemen of the jury,' he said, 'I am going to make one of the briefest opening statements I have ever made. We expect to show that on the sixteenth day of October the defendant, Gerald Conway, was president of a corporation known as California & Texas Global Development & Exploration Company, usually referred to as Texas Global.

'Mr Conway was engaged in a proxy fight with a former official of the company, one Gifford Farrell. There were advertisements in the newspapers asking stockholders to send in proxies to a committee which was pledged to vote Mr Farrell into power. That stockholders' meeting, ladies and gentlemen, is now three days away. At the insistence of the defendant, this case has been brought to trial so that the issues could be clarified before that meeting.

'We expect to show that the decedent, Rose M. Calvert, was employed by Gifford Farrell in a confidential capacity to make an ultra-secret list of the proxies which had been received. She typed out that list and gave it to Mr Farrell.

'We expect to show that, in some way, the defendant found out the decedent was typing that list. When he found that he could not bribe her, he tried to take the list away from her at the point of a gun. She resisted and was shot.

'Thereupon, we expect to show that the defendant released to the Press and gave to the police an utterly fantastic story designed to account for his presence in the room where the murder had been committed. We expect to show that the defendant went to his present attorney, Perry Mason, and consulted that astute lawyer, long before anyone knew a murder had been committed. We expect to show that Perry Mason immediately started working out what he hoped would be a good defence for the defendant.

'The defendant was spirited to the Gladedell Motel where he occupied Unit 21 during the night.

'We expect to show, at least by fair inference, that during that night the defendant went out and buried the weapon with which the crime had been committed.

'This was a Colt revolver No. 740818, being of ·38 calibre and without any question, ladies and gentlemen of the jury, being the weapon that fired the bullet that took the life of Rose Calvert.

'We expect to show that the defendant went to the Redfern Hotel, entered the room where the murder was committed after giving the clerk a fictitious name so as to make the clerk believe that the young woman in the room was his secretary. We expect to show that the room where the murder was committed had been rented by the victim under this fictitious name. We expect to show, according to his own admission, that the defendant had a key to that room, that he entered that room, was there for an appreciable interval, and then left the room and went at once to consult an attorney. We will show that the defendant's attorney knew the identity of the murdered woman long before the police knew it, and that the only way he could have had this information was from the mouth of the defendant.

'Upon that evidence, ladies and gentlemen, we shall ask a verdict of first-degree murder.'

Hamilton Burger turned and walked with ponderous dignity back to the counsel table.

Judge DeWitt glanced down at Perry Mason. 'Does the defence wish to make an opening statement at this time, or do you wish to reserve your opening statement until later?'

Mason said, 'I wish to make it at this time, Your Honour.' He arose and walked over to stand in front of the jurors.

'May it please the Court and you ladies and gentlemen of the jury,' Mason said, 'I am going to make the shortest opening statement I have ever made in my life.

'The defendant is charged with first-degree murder. He is involved in a proxy fight for the control of the Texas Global, a corporation which has very large assets. We expect to show that an attempt was made to frame the defendant so that he would either be convicted of murder or in any event would be so discredited that it would be possible to wrest control of the corporation from him.

'In order to make a frame-up of this kind, ladies and gentlemen, it is necessary to use either one of two kinds of evidence, or to combine those two kinds of evidence: that is, perjured evidence or circumstantial evidence. We expect to show that both types of evidence were used in this case; that, under the law, wherever circumstantial evidence is relied upon by the prosecution, the Court will instruct you that, if the defence can advance any reasonable hypothesis other than that of guilt which will explain the circumstantial evidence, it is the sworn duty of the jurors to accept that hypothesis and acquit the defendant.

'You jurors have told us that you will abide by the instructions of the Court, and the Court will instruct you that that is the law.

'Under those circumstances, we shall expect a verdict of acquittal.'

Mason turned and had started to walk back towards the counsel table when Hamilton Burger jumped to his feet.

'If the Court please,' he said, 'I feel that the jurors should be advised that it is incumbent upon the defence to offer a *reasonable* hypothesis. It has to appeal to the *reason*, to the sound common sense of the jurors.'

'The Court will cover that matter in its instructions, Mr District Attorney,' the judge said. 'Proceed with your case.'

Hamilton Burger said, 'My first witness will be Sgt Holcomb.'

Sgt Holcomb came forward, was sworn and gave routine testimony as to the conversation with Perry Mason, going upstairs in the hotel, finding the body of a young woman sprawled out on the bed.

'Did you have some conversation with Mr Mason as to how he happened to discover the body?' Burger asked.

'Yes.'

'What did Mason say at the time?'

'Objected to as incompetent, irrelevant, and immaterial,' Mason said. 'The conversation took place outside of the presence of the defendant.'

'Did Mr Mason admit to you that he was acting in his capacity as attorney for some client when he discovered the body?'

'He did.'

'Did he say he was acting as attorney for this defendant?' Judge DeWitt asked.

'He didn't say so in so many words.'

'The objection is sustained, at least for the present.'

'You went up to Room 729?' Hamilton Burger asked.

'I did, yes, sir.'

'What did you find?'

'I found the body of a young woman.'

'Lying on the bed?'

'On the bed.'

'She was dead?'

'She was dead.'

'Can you describe the position of the body?'

'She was stretched out, half on her back, her right hand up in the air as though trying to protect herself and–'

'I move that part of the answer be stricken,' Mason said, 'as a conclusion of the witness.'

'That will be stricken,' Judge DeWitt said. 'The witness can testify to the position of the hand, but cannot give his conclusion as to why the hand was in that position.'

'Just indicate to the jury the position of the hand,' Hamilton Burger said, smiling triumphantly, knowing that the point had reached the jurors regardless of the judge's ruling.

Sgt Holcomb held up his hand.

'What time was this that you arrived at the hotel?' Burger asked.

'Approximately ten minutes to eight.'

'And you went up almost immediately to the room?'

'Yes, sir.'

'What time did you view the body?'

'I would say it was approximately eight o'clock. My notes show that I started looking around the suite at eight-four.'

'Cross-examine,' Hamilton Burger said abruptly.

'The right hand was held up above the face in the position you have indicated?' Mason asked.

'Yes.'

'The left arm was hanging down?'

'Yes.'

'Did you touch the body?'

'I touched the wrist to make sure there was no pulse.'

'The wrist of which hand, the right or the left?'

'The right.'

'You found no pulse?'

'No.'

'The hand was held up in the position you have indicated?'

'Yes.'

'It was not resting up against her face?'

'No, sir, it was not.'

'There was a space between the back of the hand and the face?'

'There was.'

'Yet the hand was up there and the woman was dead?'

'Certainly,' Sgt Holcomb snapped. 'The condition was that known as *rigor mortis*.'

'You know about *rigor mortis*?'

'Certainly.'

'What is it?'

'It's what happens after a person is killed and the body stiffens.'

'And the right hand was held up and *rigor mortis* had set in? Is that right?'

'Yes.'

'Now, what about the left arm?'

'It was hanging over the side of the bed.'

'Did you touch the left arm?'

'Yes, I touched the left arm.'

'You say it was *hanging* down from the bed?'

'Yes.'

'Do you mean by that the left was not rigid?'

'It was hanging down. It was hanging from the shoulder.'

'Did you move the left arm?'

'Slightly.'

'You could move it?'

'Certainly.'

'It was limp?'

'It was swinging from the shoulder. I didn't try to bend the elbow.'

'But the arm was swinging from the shoulder, is that right?'

'Yes.'

'Thank you,' Mason said. 'That's all. I have no further questions.'

'My next witness will be Gifford Farrel,' Hamilton Burger said.

Farrell had about him an air of hushed solemnity and grief as he walked quietly forward to the witness stand.

Some of the women jurors leaned forward to look at his lean, bronzed face. The men were more casual in their appraisal, but it was plain to be seen that the man's manner aroused interest.

Hamilton Burger turned the examination of Farrell over to his trial deputy, Marvin Elliott.

'Were you acquainted with Mrs Norton Calvert during her lifetime?'

'I was.'

'Her first name was Rose?'

'That is correct.'

'She was married?'

'She was married and had separated from her husband.'

'Do you know where Mrs Calvert is now?'

'She is dead.'

'Did you see her dead body?'

'I did.'

'Where?'

'At the morgue.'

'When?'

'On the seventeenth day of October of this year.'

'Do you know what if anything Mrs Calvert was doing at the time of her death?'

'She was working for me.'

'In what capacity?'

'I am engaged in a proxy fight for control of Texas Global. I have done extensive advertising in the newspapers, and Mrs Calvert was acting as my very confidential secretary, keeping tabs on the proxies which had come in.'

Elliott turned to Perry Mason, said, 'I show you a list containing the names of stockholders, the numbers of stock certificates, and a statement in regard to proxies which bears your initials and the initials of the defendant on each page. I believe you will stipulate this was a list which was turned over to the district attorney's office on the morning of October seventeenth.'

'I will so stipulate. I will further stipulate that this was a paper which the defendant found under the front seat of his automobile late on the evening of October sixteenth. I will state further that we handed this list to the district attorney on the morning of October seventeenth with the statement that it might be evidence in the case, and the further statement that the defendant had no knowledge as to how or when it had been placed under the seat of his automobile.'

'Very well,' Elliott said, 'we will stipulate as to the fact the defendant made this statement. We expect to disprove it.'

Elliott turned to Farrell. 'Mr Farrell, I show you this list and asked you if you know what it is?'

'Yes, sir.'

'What is it?'

'It is a list, dated the fourteenth of October, which purported to show the proxies that had been received to date.'

'Who had possession of that list?'

'Rose Calvert.'

'We ask that this list be received in evidence, Your Honour,' Elliott said.

'Just a moment,' Mason interposed. 'I'd like to ask a few questions concerning this list before it is received in evidence.'

'Very well,' Judge DeWitt said.

Mason said, 'My initials and the initials of the defendant are on that list. Is there any identifying mark of yours on that list?'

'No, sir, there is not.'

'Then how do you know it is the same list which Rose Calvert had in her possession?'

Farrell's smile showed that he had been anticipating this question. 'It is a completely phony list,' he said. 'It was purposely prepared and given to Rose Calvert, so that if anyone tried to force her to surrender the list she was making, she would have this phony list which was purposely misleading.'

'That list did not reflect the true situation at that time?' Mason asked.

'It did not!'

'Who prepared that list?'

'It was prepared at my dictation.'

'And you saw it in Rose Calvert's possession?'

'I did.'

Mason turned to Judge DeWitt and said, 'I think the statement that it was given to Rose Calvert to be surrendered in case anyone tried to take the list from her is completely incompetent, irrelevant and immaterial as far as this defendant is concerned. But because we are anxious to get at the truth of this case, we will not move to strike out that part of the answer. We have no objection to the list being placed in evidence.'

'Very well,' Judge DeWitt said, 'it will be marked as the Peoples' Exhibit and given the appropriate number by the clerk.'

Marvin Elliott said, 'I will now ask you, Mr Farrell, if you gave Rose Calvert certain instructions on the sixteenth of October as to what she was to do at the Redfern Hotel?'

'Just a minute,' Mason said. 'I object on the ground that that is incompetent, irrelevant and immaterial and not binding on the defendant. Unless it is shown that the defendant knew of this conversation or was present at the time it took place, it has no bearing on the case.'

'It is part of the *res gestae*,' Elliott said.

Judge DeWitt shook his head. 'The objection is sustained.'

Elliott said, 'I have no further question at this time.'

Mason said, 'That's all. I have no cross-examination.'

Elliott said, 'I'll call Robert Makon King.'

Robert King walked quickly to the witness stand and took the oath.

'What is your occupation?' Elliott asked.

'I am a clerk at the Redfern Hotel.'

'On the evening of October sixteenth did you have occasion to see a body in the hotel?'

'I did.'

'Who showed you that body?'

'Sgt Holcomb.'

'Where was the body?'

'In Room 729.'

'Were you able to identify that body?'

'Not by name, but as a guest in the hotel, yes.'

'You had seen that young woman during her lifetime?'

'I had.'

'Where and when?'

'She had entered the hotel and stated that she wanted a suite somewhere on the sixth or seventh floor, preferably the seventh. She stated that–'

'Never mind what she stated,' Mason said. 'I object on the ground that it's incompetent, irrelevant and immaterial.'

'This is very definitely part of the *res gestae*,' Marvin Elliott said. 'It accounts for certain facts which otherwise would be confusing.'

'I think I will sustain the objection to the conversation,' Judge DeWitt said. 'You may asked what she did as part of the *res gestae*.'

'Did she register for a room?'

'She did.'

'Under what name?'

'Under the name of Gerald Boswell.'

'I'm sorry,' Elliott said, 'that I can't ask you for the conversation. I will ask you if she paid for the suite in advance.'

'She did. Yes, sir.'

'You may cross-examine,' Elliott said.

'Did this young woman have any baggage with her when she registered?' Mason asked.

'I didn't see any.'

'Could there have been baggage which you didn't see?'

'It was the duty of the bellboy to take up the baggage.'

'But she did pay for the suite in advance?'

'Yes, sir.'

'And took it under the name of Gerald Boswell?'

'Yes, sir. She said he was her–'

'Just a minute,' Judge DeWitt interrupted.

'Your Honour, I'm going to withdraw my objection to the conversation,' Mason said. 'I'm going to let the witness relate it.'

'Very well,' Judge DeWitt said.

King said, 'She told me that she was the secretary of Gerald Boswell, that he wanted her to engage a suite for him, and that she would pay the rent in advance.'

'Did she say she would do that because she had no baggage?' Mason asked.

'Now that you mention it, I believe she did.'

'What time was this?'

'Sometime in the afternoon. I don't know just when. The records show it was just before two o'clock.'

'What time did you come on duty?'

'At twelve o'clock in the afternoon.'

'What time did you normally leave?'

'At eight o'clock in the evening.'

Mason thought the situation over for a moment. 'You're *certain* this was the young lady who rented the suite?'

'I'm certain.'

'Your memory for faces is rather poor, isn't it?'

'On the contrary, it is very good.'

'No further questions,' Mason said.

'That's all,' Elliott said. 'I will wish to examine this witness upon another phase of the case later on in the trial.'

'We object to the testimony being put on piece-meal,' Mason said. 'We feel that this witness should be interrogated at this time as to all the evidence which counsel intends to develop.'

'Oh, Your Honour,' Elliott said, 'it would mean putting on our case out of order. We have to introduce an autopsy report, we have to introduce photographs.'

'Well,' Judge DeWitt said, 'if the counsel for the defence wants the evidence to be presented now, I think it would save time, at least, to ask questions of this witness now.'

'Very well,' Elliott said. 'Did you deliver an envelope to anyone who asked for messages in the name of Gerald Boswell on the evening of October sixteenth?'

'I did.'

'To whom?'

'To the defendant.'

'The gentleman sitting next to Mr Perry Mason?'

'Yes, sir.'

'What time was that?'

'That was sometime around six-thirty. I can't give you the exact time.'

'And did you have any further conversation with the defendant?'

'Not with the defendant. With his attorney and a gentleman with him, whom I have since learned was Paul Drake, a detective.'

'And what was that conversation?'

'This detective, Mr Drake, asked for messages for Gerald Boswell. I asked him for some identification and he showed me the key to Room 729. Then he went to the elevator.'

'Carrying that key with him?'

'Yes.'

'You don't know whether he went to Room 729?'

'Only by what he said afterwards. He told me that he had.'

'In the presence of Mr Mason?'

'Yes, sir.'

Mason said, 'If the Court please, I am not objecting and because it is embarrassing for counsel to be a witness, I will stipulate that Mr Drake and I went to the Redfern Hotel, that Mr Drake asked for messages for Gerald Boswell, that he was told there were no messages, that he was asked for identification, that he produced a key to Room 729, that he went up to Room 729, that we discovered the body of this young woman on the bed, and that we notified police.'

'Very well, that will simplify matters,' Elliott said.

'Just a moment,' Mason said. 'I have a couple of questions on cross-examination.'

'When Mr Drake first asked for messages for Mr Boswell, Mr King, you told him that you had delivered a message to him earlier in the afternoon, didn't you?'

'Well, I was a little suspicious. I–'

'I'm not asking you whether you were suspicious. I'm asking you what you told him.'

'Yes, I believe I told him something to that effect.'

'Yet now you say it was the defendant to whom you delivered that message?'

'Well, I've had a chance to think it over.'

'And to look at the defendant?'

'Yes.'

'Yet on the sixteenth of October, when the occasion was more fresh in your mind, you stated to Paul Drake, the detective, that you had delivered the message to him, did you not?'

'I may have said so, yes.'

'And if you could have made a mistake in confusing Paul Drake with the defendant, isn't it possible that you could have made a mistake in regard to Rose Calvert and that it was some other young woman who rented the suite, 729?'

'No, sir. I am positive of my identification and I am not going to let you confuse me.'

'Thank you,' Mason said. 'That's all!'

'Call Dr. K. C. Malone,' Elliott said.

Dr Malone came forward, was sworn, identified himself as Dr Klenton

C. Malone, an autopsy surgeon who had performed the autopsy on the body of Rose Calvert.

He testified as to the single bullet wound, the direction and nature of the wound, the fact that death was instantaneous, that there had been little external bleeding, that the wound was a contact wound, meaning that the gun had been held directly against the body when the wound was inflicted.

'When was the time of death?' Elliott asked.

'I fixed the time of death at between six-fifteen and seven o'clock on the evening of October sixteenth.'

'Did you recover the fatal bullet?'

'I did.'

'And what did you do with it?'

'I turned it over to Alexander Redfield, the ballistics expert.'

'He was present when the autopsy was performed?'

'He was.'

'Cross-examine,' Elliott said to Perry Mason.

'When did you perform the autopsy?' Mason asked.

'It was during the morning of the seventeenth.'

'What time on the morning of the seventeenth?'

'About seven o'clock in the morning.'

'Is that the time you usually go to work, Doctor?'

'No, sir. I was called to perform this autopsy by the district attorney. I was asked to perform it as early as possible.'

'When were you called?'

'About ten o'clock in the evening.'

'Why didn't you perform the autopsy that night?'

'There was not that much urgency about it. The district attorney wanted to have certain information by nine o'clock in the morning. I started the autopsy so I could give him the information he wanted.'

'*Rigor mortis* had developed when the body was discovered?'

'I understand it had.'

'When does rigor develop?'

'That is variable, depending upon several factors.'

'Can you give me the approximate times during which rigor develops?' Mason asked.

'That I cannot,' the witness said. 'The authorities are in great dispute as to the development of rigor. Persons dying under conditions of excitement or emotion may develop rigor almost immediately. This is also true if death has been preceded by a physical struggle.

'I may state that there were conditions existing in this case which made it appear rigor had developed with considerable rapidity.'

'Did you consider *rigor mortis* in connexion with determining the time of death?'

'I did not. I determined the time of death from the contents of the stomach and intestines.'

'Did you know when the last meal was ingested?'

'I was told that time could be fixed with great certainty. I know that death occurred approximately two hours after the last meal had been ingested.'

'You were told when the meal was ingested?'

'Yes.'

'That was hearsay?'

'It was the best information I was able to get.'

'It was hearsay?'

'Naturally, Mr Mason. I wasn't with this young woman when she took her lunch. I had to rely on what was told me.'

'You didn't consider *rigor mortis* as an element in fixing the time of death?'

'I did not. There were indications that *rigor mortis* had set in almost immediately.'

'What about post-mortem lividity?' Mason asked.

'The lividity had apparently just began to develop. However, Mr Mason, I didn't see the body at the time it was found. The deputy coroner made those observations.'

'Now then,' Mason said, 'the wound in that body is as consistent with suicide as with murder, isn't it, Doctor?'

Dr Malone hesitated then finally said, 'No, sir, it is not.'

'Why?'

'From the position of the wound and the course of the bullet, it would have been virtually impossible for a right-handed woman to have held the weapon in exactly that position. And if the weapon was held in the left hand, the posture would have been cramped and somewhat unnatural. Moreover, Mr Mason, we made chemical tests on the hands of the decedent to see if there was any indication a weapon had been held in the decedent's hand. There was none.'

'You used the paraffin test?'

'Yes.'

'Thank you,' Mason said. 'That's all.'

Elliott called Dr Reeves Garfield, who testified that he was from the coroner's office, that he had gone to the scene of the crime within an hour after the body had been discovered. He had supervised the taking of photographs, and had made on-the-spot observations. He had assisted in performing the autopsy. He gave it as his conclusion that death had taken place sometime between six-fifteen and seven o'clock.'

'Cross-examine,' Elliot said.

'The body was clothed when you saw it?'

'Yes.'

'In rigor?'

'I will say this: It was partially in rigor.'

'What do you mean by that?'

'*Rigor mortis* begins at the chin and throat muscles and slowly spreads downward until the entire body is involved. Then rigor begins to leave the body in the same order in which it was formed.'

'And rigor varies as to time?'

'Very much. Much more so than many of the authorties would indicate. A great deal depends upon individual circumstances. I have known of one case in which rigor developed almost immediately.'

'What was the reason for that?'

'There had been a physical struggle, and an emotional disturbance at the time of death. I have known one other case where rigor was quite well developed within thirty minutes. And by that I mean a complete rigor.'

'Under ordinary circumstances, the onset is much slower than that?'

'Oh yes. Much slower.'

'You say the body had developed *rigor mortis* at least in part. Were you there when the body was moved from the hotel?'

'Yes.'

'And what was done with reference to rigor at that time?'

'The rigor was broken.'

'What do you mean by that?'

'When a person dies,' Dr Garfield said, 'the muscles are at first completely limp. The head can be moved from side to side with the greatest of ease. The limbs can be flexed. Then after a variable period of time, depending on circumstances, the rigor sets in, and when the rigor is completely developed, the body has become stiff.'

'How stiff?'

'Very stiff indeed.'

'Then what?'

'Then after a lapse of time as the muscles become alkaline again, the rigor leaves the body and the body once more becomes limp.'

'Now, what do you mean by saying that rigor can be broken?'

'You can forcibly move the limbs after rigor has developed and, once the rigor is broken, it does not return.'

Mason said, 'Isn't it a fact, Doctor, that when you saw the body, there was rigor in the right arm, but that there was no rigor in the left arm?'

'I won't say that,' Dr Garfield said, 'but I did notice that there was no rigor in the left shoulder.'

'But there was in the right?'

'The right arm and shoulder were in complete rigor. The right hand was held up so that it was perhaps an inch or so from the face, but was stiff enough to remain in that position.'

'Thank you, Doctor,' Mason said. 'Now I want to ask one more question: Isn't it a fact that it was possible for death to have taken place earlier in the afternoon?'

'Well . . .' Dr Garfield hesitated.

'Go ahead,' Mason said.

'There were certain conditions there that were puzzling. The development of the rigor, the post-mortem lividity, and a very faint discoloration of the left side of the body.'

'What was this discoloration?'

'I am not certain. I would prefer not to discuss it because we finally came to the conclusion that it was not significant.'

'But there was a discoloration?'

'Well, I wouldn't exactly call it a discoloration. It was just a faint tinge which was all but invisible except in certain lights. We decided, after discussing the matter, that it had no real significance. However, it had no significance because the contents of the stomach and intestines furnished a very accurate means of fixing the time of death.'

'You personally examined the contents of the stomach and intestines?'

'Oh, yes.'

'Can you determine when death occurred with reference to when the last meal was ingested?'

'I would say within a period of two hours to two hours and fifteen minutes.'

'Then you think that young woman had lunch at about four-thirty o'clock?'

'Apparently at exactly four-thirty.'

'How do you know that?'

'Room Service sent lunch up to the room at four-thirty. Potatoes au gratin had been sent up by Room Service, and those remnants were found in the stomach. Roast turkey was sent up by Room Service, and those remnants were found in the stomach, as well as remnants of other items on the hotel's turkey plate luncheon.'

'You have investigated this, of course?'

'Of course.'

'And checked with Room Service in the hotel?'

'Yes.'

'And what was your conclusion, Doctor?'

'As to the time of death?'

'As to the contents of the stomach.'

'As compared with the lunch sent up?'

'Yes.'

The witness hesitated.

'Well?' Mason asked.

'It is hard to answer that question without bringing in hearsay evidence,' Dr Garfield said. 'The hotel restaurant was able to check the order sent out–a regular plate dinner of roast turkey with dressing. The decedent also ordered asparagus. We found all those articles in the stomach.'

'Any other articles?' Mason asked.

'Yes.'

'What?'

'Green peas.'

'But there were no green peas on the luncheon sent up?' Mason asked. 'Those peas must have come from another source?'

'There *were* green peas on the luncheon,' Dr Garfield said positively. 'The hotel records show no peas listed on the check, but they were sent up. They had to be on that lunch tray. The hotel employees all admitted it was very possible the records were in error and the peas simply had not been put on the bill because of an oversight.'

'Did she sign the check for Room Service?'

'No, sir, she paid it in cash.'

Elliott said, 'We expect to show the contents of the last meal which was sent up by Room Service, and we expect to show that green peas were added by an inexperienced waiter who neglected to put them on the bill. There can be no question as to what actually happened.'

'If the Court please,' Mason said, 'I take exception to the statement by counsel that there can be no question as to what happened. Counsel is advancing his own conclusions.'

'I was merely trying to shorten the cross-examination of this witness, save the time of the Court, and keep from confusing the issues in the minds of the jury,' Elliott said.

Judge DeWitt said, 'Just a moment, gentlemen. Despite the short time spent in getting a jury, it has reached the hour for the afternoon adjournment. Court will take a recess until ten o'clock tomorrow morning. In the meantime, the jurors are instructed not to discuss this case with anyone or permit it to be discussed in their presence, nor to form or express any opinion concerning the matter until it is finally submitted for their consideration. I have previously admonished the jury on this point and I think they understand their duties. Court will recess until ten o'clock tomorrow morning.

'The defendant is remanded in custody.'

Mason turned to smile reassuringly to Conway. 'I think we've got them, Jerry,' he said.

Conway said, 'I don't see how you figure it. I think we're licked.'

'What do you mean?'

Conway said, 'Our only hope was in getting Giff Farrell to show himself in his true light before the jurors. He came off with flying colours.'

Mason grinned. 'You mean I didn't cross-examine him vigorously enough?'

Conway said, 'You're running the show, Mason. But you must be able to see for yourself what has happened. Farrell's testimony is now completely established and he hasn't even been embarrassed. Why didn't you ask him about his relations with the dead woman, about those photographs?'

'Because,' Mason said, 'if we ever get that far, I am going to force the district attorney to put Gifford Farrell on in rebuttal, and by that time I'm going to have him sketched as quite a villain. When I get done with him then, he's going to be an entirely different individual from the debonair man who occupied the witness stand this afternoon.'

'Well, I hope so,' Conway said. 'However, one thing is certain. I've completely lost control of Texas Global.'

Mason patted him on the shoulder. 'Take it easy, Conway,' he said. 'And remember people are watching you in the courtroom. Don't act discouraged. Act as though you felt certain right would triumph.'

'You can't smile in a situation like that,' Conway said. 'The bottom has dropped out and,–'

'Don't grin,' Mason said, 'simple look less overwhelmed.'

Conway straightened himself, gave Mason a smile.

Mason clapped him on the back, said in a loud voice, 'Okay. See you tomorrow. And by tomorrow night you should be out. Sleep tight.'

Mason picked up his brief-case and left the courtroom.

13

Mason, Paul Drake, and Della Street were gathered in the lawyer's office.

Mason said, 'What's new with Farrell, Paul?'

'Not a damned thing,' Drake said. 'He's keeping his nose so clean it shines.'

Mason frowned and said, 'Now look, Paul, whoever did this job *had* to have a female accomplice. She was rather young, good-looking, with a sexy figure that she wasn't averse to showing.

'This woman who left the hotel must have been the woman that Conway saw in Room 729. That's the woman who held the gun on him, who really holds the key to the whole plot.

'Now, Farrell has put himself entirely in the power of this woman. She must be someone who's infatuated with him. Farrell wouldn't dare let her be where she could cool off as far as he's concerned. He wouldn't dare let her conscience start bothering her. He *must* be seeing her.'

'But he isn't,' Drake said. 'Farrell has been 100 per cent circumspect. He has hardly gone out socially since this came came up. Apparently, he was pretty much broken up by the death of Rose Calvert. He must have been pretty much attached to her.'

'Phooey!' Mason said. 'He's seeing this other woman somewhere. . . . It must be one of the girls in his office.'

'We've got a line on every girl in his office,' Drake said. 'I've got a pile of stuff two feet thick, Perry. I can tell you so much about those girls that it would frighten them if they knew we knew it. One of them is married and living with her husband. One of them is engaged. One of them is going steady. The other is a good-looking babe that Farrell has been out with once or twice, but she's a girl who's built for speed, narrow hips and a light chassis. There's another one that Farrell probably had an affair with at one time, but she's a tall babe, one of these long, willowy gals.

'Conway says this woman who emerged from the bedroom and then held the gun on him had a figure and was of average height. . . . Don't worry, if Farrell starts trying to keep any female accomplice in line, we'll spot her.'

'He'll have to do it when the case gets a little hotter,' Mason said.

'How's it going, Perry?'

Mason said, 'Well, I'm getting my theory worked into the case so unobtrusively that the prosecution doesn't even know it's there. Tomorrow I'll spring it.'

'Your theory that the body was moved?'

'That's right,' Mason said. 'The body had lain on its left side. There had been just the start of that peculiar discoloration which is known as post-mortem lividity. *Rigor mortis* had probably set in rather soon. The right hand and right arm were doubled up and probably the left arm was sticking straight out. When the body was moved and placed on that bed, it was necessary for whoever did it to break the *rigor mortis* in the left shoulder so the arm would hang down somewhat naturally. If that left arm had been sticking out straight as a poker, it would have been a dead give-away and anyone would have known that the body had been moved. With the body lying on the bed, it became necessary for that left arm to be hanging down. so rigor was broken at the shoulder.

'That Bob King is a miserable liar. He's trying to bolster up the prosecution's case, but he's not doing a good job of it.

'How are you coming along with your elevator girl, Paul?'

'Swell!' Drake said grinning. 'That's one of the best assignments I ever had. She's a darned good scout, Perry, and is fun to be with, although at times I do wish she'd quit that everlasting gum chewing.'

'What have you found out from her?'

'I've found out all she knows. I can tell you enough stuff about the operation of the Redfern Hotel to make your hair curl. I can tell you things about the bell captains, about the clerks–and I can tell you this: The woman who went up to Room 729 definitely didn't have any baggage, and that's the reason she paid in advance.

'My elevator girl says that the bell captain was grumbling. He thought that the girl intended to muscle in on his racket, and he was determined that, if she started entertaining men in the room, he'd have her thrown out unless she decorated the mahogany with a cut.'

Mason paced the floor. 'There's something funny there, Paul. The position of the body on the bed was changed. Now, why would it be changed? Why did someone discharge a gun into the mattress in Room 728? The gun was pushed up against the mattress so it wouldn't make any loud noise.

'The noise made by a contact wound when a gun is held up against a body or when the gun is pushed up against a mattress of that sort isn't loud enough to attract attention. It's not much louder than exploding a paper bag.'

'But why change the position of the body?' Drake asked. 'Why juggle guns?'

'That,' Mason said, 'is something we're going to have to find out. Beginning tomorrow, I'm going to start getting some of this stuff in front of the jury, and then I'm going to needle the prosecution by asking it these questions. I'm going to start punching holes in the prosecution's theory of the case.'

'Enough to get an acquittal for Conway?'

'I think so,' Mason said. 'I'm not worried so much about that as I am that the public may take it as a Scotch verdict: guilty but not proven, and Conway will never be able to live it down.'

'He's not the kind who would try very hard,' Drake said.

'In some ways he's not a fighter,' Mason admitted. 'He gets discouraged and throws in the sponge. He'll fight like the devil on a business deal, but in a matter of this sort which affects his personal integrity, he feels completely crushed.

'You keep in touch with your elevator operator–what the devil's her name?'

'Myrtle Lamar,' Drake said.

'She isn't taking you seriously, is she?' Della Street asked. 'You aren't going to wind up breaking her heart, are you, Paul?'

'Not Myrtle!' Drake said, grinning. 'Her heart is made of indiarubber.'

'Those are the kinds that fool you,' Della Street said. 'Probably beneath that cynical exterior, she's extremely sensitive and–Don't you go destroying her illusions, Paul Drake!'

'You can't destroy them,' Drake said, 'because she hasn't got 'em. As a matter of fact, I get a kick out of being with her. She knows that I'm trying to pick her brains to find out something about the case that has eluded us so far, and she's doing everything she can to help. She's telling me every little thing she can think of about the operation of the hotel, about what happened that night and all that.

'My gosh! The gossip I can tell you about the things that go on in that hotel! And what a miserable little stooge this Bob King is! He'd do absolutely anything just to curry favour with the authorities.'

Again Mason started pacing the floor. 'The trouble is we're one woman short in this matter. That woman couldn't have disappeared into thin air. She couldn't have disappeared from Gifford Farrell's life. He wouldn't have let her.

'Tomorrow I'm going to start asking embarrassing questions. The prosecution isn't accustomed to trying cases against lawyers who know anything about forensic medicine. The average lawyer considers it out of his line, and doesn't bother to study up on it. In this case the medical testimony is of the greatest importance and has some peculiar angles.

'Moreover, we're missing that woman and–'

Suddenly Mason stopped stock-still in his pacing, paused in the middle of a sentence.

Della Street looked up quickly, 'What is it, Chief?'

Mason didn't answer her question for a matter of two or three seconds, then he said slowly, 'You know, Paul, in investigative work the worst thing you can do is to get a theory and then start trying to fit the facts to it. You should keep an open mind and reach your conclusion after the facts are all in.'

'Well,' Drake said, 'what's wrong?'

'Throughout this entire case,' Mason said, 'I've let my thinking be influenced by Jerry Conway. He's told me that this was a frame-up which was engineered by Gifford Farrell, that the line to his office had been tapped, and that he was suckered into this thing by Farrell.'

'Well, it stands to reason,' Drake said. 'We know that someone cut in on the programme Evangeline Farrell had mapped out for Conway. Mrs Farrell was going to make certain that he wasn't followed and then she was going to have him meet her where she could give him those papers.

'She was to call him at six-fifteen, but somebody beat her to the punch by a couple of minutes and–'

'And we've jumped to the conclusion that it was some accomplice of Giff Farrell!' Mason said.

'Well, why not? The whole set-up, the substitution of guns, the burying of the fatal weapon–all that shows a diabolical ingenuity and–'

Mason said, 'Paul, I've got an idea. Get your friend Myrtle Lamar and have her in court tomorrow. Sit there in court and have her listen. I want to have her beside you.'

'She has to work, Perry. . . .'

'I'll serve a subpoena on her as a witness for the defence,' Mason said. 'Then she'll have to be there. I'm beginning to get the nucleus of an idea, Paul.

'You say you've had trouble holding your man Inskip in line?'

'I told you we'd have trouble,' Drake said. 'He keeps feeling that he's withholding evidence that the police should have, and it bothers him. When you finally spring your idea and he's called as a witness, the police will want to know why he didn't give them the tip, and–'

'Let him give them the tip,' Mason said.

'What do you mean?'

'Get hold of Inskip,' Mason said. 'Tell him to go to the police. Let him tell the police that his conscience is bothering him and he can't hold out any longer, that he knows I have an ace in the hole, that we discovered this hole in the mattress in Room 728. Let him give them the bullet that we took from the mattress and let Redfield check that bullet with the Smith & Wesson gun Conway turned over to the police. The bullets will check.'

Drake said, 'That would be awfully nice from Inskip's viewpoint but it would leave you right out in the open, Perry. They would know exactly what you were trying to do.'

'That's okay,' Mason said. 'That suits my plans fine!'

'And then what'll happen?'

'Then tomorrow,' Mason said, 'the prosecution will feel they know what I'm leading up to and they'll want time to combat it. I think this Dr Garfield is a pretty fair sort of individual. I'll start laying the foundation, and Hamilton Burger will go into a panic. He'll start stalling for time.'

'But you've been the one who wanted to rush things along so you could have the case over before the stockholders'–'

'I know, I know,' Mason interrupted. 'There's still time. Go ring up Inskip. Tell him to go tell the police the whole story!'

'The whole story?' Drake asked.

'Everything!' Mason said. 'Then get your girl, Myrtle Lamar, and be in court tomorrow morning. I'm beginning to get the damnedest idea and I think it's predicted on sound logic.'

14

Judge DeWitt said, 'The jurors are all present. The defendant is in court. At the conclusion of yesterday's testimony Dr Reeves Garfield was on the stand. Will you please resume your place on the stand, Dr Garfield?'

Dr Garfield took his place in the witness chair.

'Directing your attention to this discoloration which you noticed on the left side of the body,' Mason asked, 'can you tell us more about the nature of that discoloration?'

'It was barely noticeable; only in certain lights could you see it. It was simply a very, very faint change in the complexion of the skin.'

'Would you say that it had no medical significance, Doctor?'

'I would never state that any phenomenon one may find in a cadaver in a murder case had no medical significance.'

'Was there a dispute as to whether this colour had any *real* significance or not?'

Hamilton Burger was on his feet. 'Your Honour, we object to that as being improper cross-examination. It calls for something which is incompetent, irrelevant and immaterial. It makes no difference whether there was a dispute or not, this Court is trying this defendant not for the purpose of determining what argument someone may have had, but for the purpose of getting the ultimate facts.'

'I will sustain the objection,' Judge DeWitt said.

'Was there a dispute between you and Dr Malone as to the significance of this slight discoloration?'

'Same objection,' Hamilton Burger said.

Judge DeWitt hesitated for a long, thoughtful moment, then said, 'The same ruling. I will sustain the objection.'

'Isn't it a fact,' Mason said, 'that this slight discoloration may have been due to the fact that the body lay for some appreciable interval after death on its left side, and that the slight discoloration marked the beginnings of a post-mortem lividity, which remained after the body had again been moved?'

'That is, of course, a possibility.'

'A distinct possibility.'

'Well, it is a possibility. I will concede that.'

'Now, did you ever know of a case where there had been a pronounced development of *rigor mortis* in the right arm and shoulder with no *rigor mortis* in the left shoulder, unless someone had broken the rigor?'

'I know of no such case.'

'Is it your opinion that the rigor in the left shoulder had been broken?'

The witness shifted his position on the witness stand, looked somewhat hopelessly at Hamilton Burger.

'That's objected to,' Hamilton Burger said, 'on the ground that the question is argumentative, that it calls for a conclusion of the witness.'

'The objection is overruled,' Judge DeWitt said. 'The witness is an expert, and is testifying as to his opinion. Answer the question.'

Dr Garfield said slowly, 'It is *my* opinion that the rigor had been broken.'

'And it is your opinion that the position of the body had been changed after death, and prior to the time you saw it there in Room 729 at the Redfern Hotel?'

There was a long period of hesitation, then Dr Garfield said reluctantly, 'That is my opinion.'

'Thank you,' Mason said. 'That is all.'

'No further questions,' Elliott announced.

Hamilton Burger seemed preoccupied and worried. He bent over and whispered something to his trial deputy, and then ponderously tiptoed from the courtroom.

Elliott said, 'My next witness will be Lt Tragg.'

Tragg came forward and was sworn. He testified in a leisurely manner that was hardly in keeping with Tragg's usually crisp, incisive manner on the stand.

He had, he said, attended a conference of officers on October seventeenth. The defendant had appeared. With him had appeared his attorney, Perry Mason.

'Did the defendant make a statement?'

'Yes.'

'Was the statement free and voluntary?'

'It was.'

Elliott asked him to describe what was said.

Slowly, almost tediously, Tragg repeated the conversation in detail, with Elliott glancing at his watch from time to time.

The morning recess was taken and Court reconvened. Tragg's testimony was still dragging on until at eleven-thirty he was finished.

'You may cross-examine,' Elliott said.

'No questions,' Mason said.

Elliott bit his lip.

His next witness was the uniformed officer who had sat in on the conference in the district attorney's office. The uniformed officer was still giving his testimony about what had happened when Court took its noon adjournment.

'What's happening?' Conway whispered. 'They seem to be bogging down.'

'They're worried,' Mason whispered back. 'Just keep a stiff upper lip.'

The jurors filed out of the courtroom. Mason walked over to where Paul Drake, Della Street and Myrtle Lamar, the elevator operator, were standing talking.

Myrtle Lamar shifted her wad of gum, grinned at Mason.

'Hello, big boy,' she said.

'How's everything?' Mason asked.

'Sort of tedious this morning,' she said. 'Why the subpoena? I'm supposed to be on duty tonight and I should be getting my beauty sleep.'

'You don't need it,' Mason told her.

'I will before I get done.'

Drake put his hand on her arm. 'We'll take care of you all right. Don't worry!'

'You don't know the manager up there at the Redfern Hotel. Women must have made a habit of turning him down. He loves to kick them around. He'd throw me out on my ear as easy as he'd snap a bread-crumb off the table.'

'You don't snap bread-crumbs. You remove them with a little silver scoop,' Drake said.

'You and your damned culture,' she said.

'Come on,' Mason told her. 'We're going out.'

'Where?'

'We're going visiting.'

'My face,' she said, 'has bad habits. It needs to be fed.'

'We'll get it fed,' Mason said.

'Okay, that's a promise!'

Mason shepherded them down in the elevator into his car, drove carefully but skilfully.

'Where?' Drake asked.

Mason looked at his watch. 'Not far.'

Mason stopped the car in front of the apartment house, went to the room telephones, called Evangeline Farrell.

When her voice came on the line, the lawyer said, 'Mrs Farrell, I want to see you at once on a matter of considerable importance.'

'I'm not dressed for company,' she said.

'Put on something,' Mason told her. 'I have to be back in court and I'm coming up.'

'Is it important?'

'Very!'

'It concerns the case?'

'Yes.'

'Come on up,' she told him.

Mason nodded to the others. They took the elevator.

Mrs Farrell opened the apartment door, then fell back in surprise, clutching at the sheer negligee.

'You didn't tell me anyone was with you,' she said.

'I'm sorry,' Mason told her. 'I overlooked it, perhaps. I'm in a terrible hurry. I have to be back in court at two o'clock.'

'But what in the world–?'

Mason said, 'You could buy us a drink. This is important.'

She hesitated for a long moment, then said, 'Very well.'

'May I help you?' Della Street asked.

'Oh, I'm sorry,' Mason said. 'I haven't introduced these people to you.'

Mason performed introductions, mentioning only names except for Della Street. 'My confidential secretary,' he explained.

'Come on,' Della Street said, 'I'll help you.'

Somewhat hesitantly Mrs Farrell moved towards the kitchenette. When she had gone, Mason said to the elevator operator, 'Have you ever seen her before?'

'I think I have. If I could get a better look at her feet, I'd be sure. I'd like to see her shoes.'

'Let's look,' Mason said. He walked boldly to the bedroom door, opened it, beckoned to Paul Drake who took Myrtle's arm, led her along into the bedroom.

The elevator operator tried to hang back, but Drake shifted his arm around her waist.

'Know what you're doing, Perry?' Drake asked, as Mason crossed the bedroom.

'No,' Mason said, 'but I have a hunch.' He opened a closet door.

'Take a look at the shoes, Myrtle,' Mason said. 'Do they mean anything to you? Wait a moment! I guess we don't need those. Take a look at this.' The lawyer reached back into the closet, pulled out a suitcase. It had the initials 'R.C.'.

'Just what do you think you're doing?' an angry, icy voice demanded.

Mason turned, said, 'Right at the moment, I'm checking the baggage that you removed from the Redfern Hotel, Mrs Farrell, and this young woman who is the elevator operator who was on duty the day of the murder is looking at your shoes to see if she recognizes the pair you wore. She has the peculiar habit of noticing people's feet.'

Mrs Farrell started indignantly towards them, then suddenly stopped in her tracks.

Mason said, 'Let's take a look inside that suitcase, Paul.'

'You can't do that,' she said. 'You have no right.'

'Okay,' Mason said, 'if you want it the hard way, we'll do it the hard way. Go to the phone, Paul. Call Homicide and ask them to send up some officers with a warrant. We'll stay here until they arrive.'

Evangeline Farrell stood looking at them with eyes that held an expression of sickened dismay.

'Or perhaps,' Mason said, 'you'd like to tell us about it. We haven't very much time, Mrs Farrell.'

'Tell you about what?' she asked, trying to get hold of herself.

'About renting Room 729 and saying you were the secretary of Gerald Boswell, and that he was to occupy the room for the night.

'Tell us about shooting Rose Calvert, who was in 728; about sitting there waiting, trying to figure out what you'd do, then taking the body across the hall. . . . Did you manage that alone? Or did someone help you?'

She said, 'You can't do that to me. You–I don't know what you're talking about.'

Mason walked over to the telephone, picked up the receiver, said to the operator, 'I want Lt Tragg at–'

'Wait!' Mrs Farrell screamed at him. 'Wait! You've got to help me.'

Mason said into the mouthpiece of the telephone, 'Never mind.' He dropped the phone into its cradle.

'All right,' she said. 'All right! I'll tell you. I'll tell you the whole story. I've been frightened stiff ever since it happened. But I didn't kill her. I didn't! Please, please believe that I didn't kill her.'

'Who did?' Mason asked.

'Gifford,' she said.

'How do you know?'

'He must have. He's the only one. He thought she was selling out. I guess he must have followed me to the hotel. He knew I was there.'

'Go on,' Mason said. 'You only have a minute or two. Get it off your chest. What happened?'

She said, 'I wanted to give Mr Conway the lists of stockholders who had sent in proxies. I wanted to do it under such circumstances that Gifford would think his little mistress had sold him out. She was at the Redfern Hotel. She had this room in 728. She was typing. You could hear her through the transom banging away on a portable typewriter like mad. I told you the truth about getting the used carbon paper.'

'Why did you do all this?' Mason asked. 'Why did you rent that suite?'

'I didn't want Jerry Conway to lose control of Texas Global.'

'Why?' Mason asked. 'I would think your interests would have been elsewhere. I would think that your only hope of getting money out of your husband depended upon letting him get in the saddle by–'

'I had to look at it two ways,' she interrupted. 'I've already told you. I felt that under Conway's management my Texas Global stock would be valuable. I wasn't so sure about Gifford's management. I figured that by the time this tramp he was running around with got hers, and when the next tramp he would be running around with got *hers,* my stock would be worthless.'

'All right,' Mason said, 'what did you do?'

She said, 'I knew that my husband was playing around with Rose Calvert. I followed her to the hotel. She registered as Ruth Culver.'

Mason's voice showed excitement. 'Had she registered that way before?'

'Yes. In two hotels.'

'I want the names of those hotels,' Mason said.

'I can give you the names, the dates and the room numbers.

'While she was at those other hotels, my husband was bringing her data, and she was typing out lists of proxy holders on her portable typewriter. Then one day she left a copy of the list in her car. The car was parked, and the doors weren't even locked. I realize now it was a trap. I didn't know it at the time. I reached in and got this list. That, of course, was a completely phony list that they were hoping would lull Conway into a sense of security. I walked right into that trap.'

'Go on,' Mason said.

'I wanted Conway to have that list, but I didn't want him to know where it came from. So I telephoned him, and disguised my voice. I told him to remember me by the name of Rosalind.'

'You told him a lot of things about being followed by detectives and goon squads?' Mason asked. 'Why was that?'

'That was just to protect my identity and make him cautious.'

'Actually you didn't know he was followed?'

'I didn't *think* he was. This Gashouse Baker was entirely a figment of my imagination.'

'All right. Go ahead. What happened?'

'Well, I decided I'd do a little amateur detective work. I thought I'd get down to where I could follow Rose Calvert from her apartment. I wanted to know exactly what she was doing and where she was going.

'On the morning of the sixteenth, she went to the Redfern Hotel and registered as Ruth Culver. She was given Room 728.

'Once or twice during the morning, I went up in the elevator and walked down the corridor. I could hear her pounding away like mad on her typewriter. She stopped once around twelve-thirty when Room Service brought her lunch.

'You see, I had all the advantage because I knew what she looked like, but she didn't know me when she saw me. I was just a complete stranger as far as she was concerned. I had pictures of her in a Bikini bathing suit. I had pictures of her in the nude. I had followed my husband to her apartment. I knew all about her, and she knew nothing about me.'

'What happened at the hotel?' Mason asked, looking at his watch impatiently.

'Well, about ten minutes to two, I guess it was, Rose came downstairs and went out. She tossed her key on the counter for the clerk to put away. The clerk was busy, and when he had his back turned, I just walked up and took the key to Room 728. And then just after I'd picked it up and before I could turn away from the counter, the clerk turned around and came towards the counter and asked me if there was something I wanted. That was when I had a brilliant inspiration. I told him that I was a secretary for Gerald Boswell, that Gerald Boswell had some work he wanted done, and had asked me to get a suite in his name. I told him that, since I didn't have any baggage, I would pay the price of the suite and Mr Boswell would move in some time that evening. I asked him if he would give me two keys to the suite, so that I could get in and so I could give one to Mr Boswell.

'The clerk didn't think anything of it. I suppose he may have thought it was a date with a married woman sneaking away to meet her lover, but things like that don't even cause a lifted eyebrow in that hotel–not from what I hear.'

'Go on,' Mason said. 'Never mind the hotel. We want to know what you did.'

'Well, I told the clerk I wanted something not too low down and not too high up, something around the seventh floor. He said he had 729 vacant and I took that. I didn't have any baggage so there was nothing to take up to the room. I took the key, and after a while I walked up and settled down to listen. My room was right across the corridor from 728. I left the door slightly open and sat there watching.

'About two-thirty Rose Calvert came back.'

'But you had her key?'

'Yes, but you know how those things are. Keys are always getting lost around a hotel. They have several keys for each room, and sometimes the clerk will put one in the wrong box, or a tenant will walk away with it, so they always have duplicates. I don't suppose Rose had any trouble whatever getting a key to the room. She simply said she'd left hers at the desk, and the clerk dug one out for her.'

'Then what happened?'

'Well, then she didn't do any more typing, and I began to realize that probably the list I had was either obsolete or else a completely phony list they wanted to use as a red herring.'

'So what did you do?'

'So I went down and telephoned Mr Conway. I took the name of Rosalind, and gave him the old rigmarole.'

'You didn't call from the room?'

'No, I didn't even call from the hotel. I walked a couple of blocks to a phone booth and phoned from there.'

'Go ahead,' Mason said.

'Well, I went down and put in this telephone call, then I went shopping for a few things. Then I phoned again and went back to the room.'

'Then what?'

'Well, I started watching again.'

'Now, wait a minute,' Mason said. 'Let's fix this time schedule. You were in your room at two-thirty?'

'That's right.'

'Rose Calvert was back in her room by that time?'

'Yes. That's when she came in.'

'Then you went out to telephone Conway?'

'Yes, twice. In between I walked around a little while getting some fresh air and doing some shopping.'

'What time did you get back?'

'I didn't look at my watch.'

'All right, go on. What happened?'

'Well, I sat by the door listening for a while, but couldn't hear anything. Then along about three-thirty I was in the bathroom. That was when I heard a peculiar sound which I thought was made by someone banging on my bedroom door.

'I was completely paralysed with fright. It was as though someone had given my door a good, hard kick. I felt certain someone had discovered that I was spying on Rose Calvert across the hall, and I didn't know what to do for a moment.

'So I went to the door of the suite, put on my most innocent expression and opened it. No one was there. I looked up and down the corridor. I can't begin to tell you how relieved I felt. Then just as I was closing the door, having it opened just a crack, I saw the door across the corridor start to open. So I glued my eye to the door and . . . and–'

'Go on,' Mason said, his voice showing his excitement. 'What happened?'

'Gifford walked out.'

'Gifford Farrell, your husband?'

She nodded.

'Go on,' Mason said. 'Then what?'

'I didn't think anything of it at the time, because he'd been calling on her when she had rooms in the other hotels. I don't think there was anything romantic about *those* calls. She had her portable typewriter with her, and I guess she was doing typing work, and they took all those precautions to keep anyone from knowing what was going on.'

'Go on,' Mason said. 'What happened?'

'Well, I closed my door tight and waited awhile, then I opened it awhile and listened, but there were no more sounds coming from the room across the hall.

'And then suddenly I began to wonder if Rose might not have gone out while I was out. I went downstairs and out to the phone booth, called the Redfern Hotel and asked to be connected with Room 728.'

'What happened?'

'I could hear the noise the line makes when there's a phone ringing and there is no answer. The operator told me my party was out and asked if I wanted her paged.

'I said no, that I'd call later.'

'And then?' Mason asked.

'Then, I went back in a hurry, took the elevator up to the seventh floor, and tapped gently on 728. When there was no answer, I used my key and opened the door.'

'What did you find?'

'Rose Calvert was lying there dead on the bed. And then suddenly I realized what that noise had been. My husband had shot her and he'd shot her with my gun.'

'What do you mean, your gun?'

'My gun. It was lying there on the floor by the bed.'

'Your gun?'

'Mine,' she said. 'I recognized it. It was one that the Texas Global had bought for the cashier to carry because the cashier lived out in the country. He was afraid to drive alone at night for fear someone would try to hold him up and get the combination of the safe. I guess he was getting a little nervous and neurotic. He died a few months afterwards.

'Anyway, the company bought him the gun, and after he died, Gifford took the gun and gave it to me.'

'You recognized the gun?'

'Yes.'

'How?'

'I used to sleep with it under my pillow. I dropped it once, and there was a little nick out of the hard, rubber handle. Then once I'd got some finger-nail enamel on it and there was just that little spot of red.

'Of course, I'd never have noticed it if I hadn't seen Gifford leave the room. Knowing he'd shot her, I suddenly wondered about the weapon. And then I knew it was my weapon.'

'How long had he had it?'

'I moved out on him, and like a fool I didn't take the gun with me. So it was there in the apartment. . . .'

'I see,' Mason said. 'What did you do?'

'Well, I decided to leave things just the way they were and quietly check out of the hotel, so I opened the door and started out into the corridor, and that was when I got trapped.'

'What do you mean?'

'The chambermaid was walking by just as I opened the door, and she looked at me, then suddenly did a double take, and said, 'Is *that* your room?'

'What did you do?'

'I had to brazen it through. She evidently had been talking with Rose, and knew that that wasn't my room.'

'Well,' Mason said, 'what did you do?'

'I thought fast. I told her no, that it wasn't my room, that it was my friend's room, and that she'd given me her key and asked me to go and wait for her, but that I couldn't wait any longer. I was going downstairs and leave a note for her.'

'Did you convince the chambermaid?'

'That's the trouble. I didn't. The chambermaid kept staring at me, and I know she thought I was a hotel thief. But she didn't say anything. Probably she was afraid of getting into trouble. That trapped me. I knew that the minute the body of Rose Calvert was found in that room, I'd be connected with the crime. I was in a panic. I walked down the corridor to the elevator, waited until the chambermaid had gone into another room, and then I walked back to 729, let myself in and sat there in a complete blue funk. I didn't know what the devil to do.'

'What did you do?'

'After a while I got the idea that I wanted. I couldn't afford to let Rose Calvert's body be found in 728, but if I could move the body over to 729, and then check out of 728 under the name of Ruth Culver, which was the name she had registered under, everything would be all right. If her body was found in 728, the chambermaid would have remembered all about my leaving the place, and given a description of me. Later on she'd have been able to recognize me. Of course, I knew police could trace the gun. But if I could have it appear that nothing unusual had happened in 728, but that the person who was murdered was the one who had checked in at 729, *then* I would be sending everybody off on a completely false trail.'

'Go on,' Mason said. 'What did you do?'

'I did some fast thinking. I wanted to make it appear that the crime had taken place much later than had actually been the case. I waited until I was certain the corridor was clear, then I hurried across and started packing all the baggage in the room. Rose had been using her portable typewriter and there were a lot of fresh carbon papers dropped into the wastebasket. I picked those up, and that was when I realized I had a very complete list of the work she had been doing. She had been making a whole lot of copies, and had used fresh carbon. I took the sheets of used carbon paper with me.'

'Go on,' Mason said.

'Then I went back to Room 729, telephoned Room Service and asked them what they had for lunch.

'They said it was pretty late for lunch, and I told them I needed something to eat and asked them what they had. They said they could fix me a roast turkey plate, and I told them to bring it up.

'The waiter brought it up, and I paid him in cash, and gave him a good tip so he'd remember me. But I kept my face averted as much as possible.

'Then I ate the dinner and asked him to come up for the dishes.'

'And then?'

'And then, all of a sudden. I realized Jerry Conway was going to start out to get that list.'

'Go on.'

'Originally, I'd intended to telephone him at the drugstore, and tell him to go and ask for a message which had been left for him at a certain hotel. So suddenly I realized that it might be possible to kill two birds with one stone, and really to pull something artistic.'

'So?' Mason asked.

'So,' she said, 'after I called Room Service, I had the waiter come and take the dishes, and then I went down to the drugstore and bought a jar of this prepared black mud that women put on their faces for massages. It spreads smoothly over the face and then, when it dries, it pulls the skin. The general idea is that it smooths out wrinkles and eliminates impurities from the skin and all that. It has an astringent effect and pulls the facial muscles. I knew it would make my face completely unrecognizable.'

'So you put that mud on?' Mason asked.

She nodded, said, 'I called up the pay station at the drugstore from the booth in the hotel, and I was even smart enough to call up a few minutes before six-fifteen so that it would look as though someone else had cut in on my programme. I had been using a very sweet, dulcet voice when talking to him under the name of Rosalind, and this time I used a voice that was lower pitched. I've always been good at changing my voice and mimicking people. . . .'

'Go on, go on,' Mason said, looking at his watch. 'We have only a few minutes.

'I take it you left the envelope with the key for Conway to pick up?'

'That's right.'

'Then what did you do?'

'I just framed that murder on him, Mr Mason. I felt that he could get out of it a lot better than I could. He had money for attorney's fees, he had position–'

'Well, tell me exactly what you did,' Mason said, 'so I can get it straightened out.'

'Jerry Conway would have recognized me. He had, of course, seen me a good many times. So I put all of this mud on my face and wrapped a towel around my head, and then I took my clothes off.'

'Why the clothes off?'

She smiled archly. 'Well, I felt that a man wouldn't concentrate so much on my face if he–if I gave him other things to look at.'

Mason grinned. 'As it turned out, that was pretty good reasoning. Was the body in 729 when Jerry came up there?'

'No, no, I didn't dare take that chance. I thought, of course, I could make him take the gun.

'He fell for my scheme hook, line and sinker. He entered the room, and then I came out and apparently was surprised to see him there. I told him I was Rosalind's room-mate, then pretended to get in a panic. I opened the desk and grabbed this gun and cocked it and let my hand keep shaking, and, of course, Jerry Conway did the obvious thing. He was too frightened to do anything else. He grabbed the gun and got out of there.'

'And then?' Mason asked.

'Then,' she said, 'I washed my face, I put on my clothes, I waited until the corridor was empty, and then I tiptoed in and picked up the body. . . . Mr Mason, it was terrible!'

'You could carry the body all right?' Mason asked.

She said, 'I'm strong, Mr Mason. The girl didn't weigh over a hundred and eighteen pounds, and I had had a course in first-aid as a nurse. I got the body as far as the door, and then was the most awful two or three seconds of my life. I had to take that body across the corridor and into Room 729. I just had to take a chance that no one would come up in the elevator, and of course there was a possibility someone might open a room door and come out into the corridor. I had to take that chance, but it was only a few feet, and–well, I made it. You see 729 is a suite, and the door of the bedroom was right opposite the door of 728. I just rushed the body in there, dumped it on the bed, then went back, kicked the bedroom door shut. Then arranged the body on the bed. After that I stepped out in the corridor and went across to 728 to make sure I hadn't overlooked anything.

'That was when I found the second gun.'

'The second gun?'

She nodded and said, 'It was under the bed.'

'What did you do?'

'I put it in the hatbox. And believe me, after that I went over every inch of that room just as carefully as could be, making certain I had everything cleaned out.'

'And then?' Mason asked.

'Then,' she said, 'I hurried back to put the finishing touch on things in 729. The body had started to stiffen pretty badly. She looked as though she had been dumped on the bed instead of lying the way she should. I just forced her left arm down so it dangled, and moved the head over so the hair was hanging down.

'Then I closed the door, went across the hall to Room 728, and very calmly telephoned the desk and told them to send up a bellboy, I wanted to check out.'

'And the bellboy came up?' Mason asked.

'The bellboy came up, and I walked down and checked out. Since Rose had rented the room in the morning, and I was checking out early in the evening, I had to make some explanation. So I told the clerk that my father was critically ill in San Diego and I had to go to him. I said a friend of mine was driving me down. That's all there was to it.'

'No, it isn't,' Mason said. 'What about that second gun?'

She said, 'You came here and asked me questions that night, and you remember you said you wanted to use my phone. That phone goes through a switchboard downstairs, and we are charged with calls.

'I was wondering what to do about that gun. After you left, I went downstairs and got the switchboard operator to give me the number you'd called. I called that number and, when the person answered, he said it was the Gladedell Motel. I did some quick thinking and asked him if a Mr Jerry Conway was registered there, and he said yes, in Unit 21, and did I want him called. I said no, not to call him, that I was just checking, and hung up quick before they could ask any questions.

'So then I waited until after midnight. I drove down to the motel. Jerry Conway's car was parked in front of Unit 21, and I slipped the phony list of stockholders' proxies under the seat of the car, then walked over to the back of the lot. I'd taken a little trowel with me, and I buried that second gun. By that time I didn't know *which* gun had been used in committing the murder. But I felt that if things got to a point where I needed to, I could give the police an anonymous tip, saying I was a woman who lived near the motel and that I'd seen someone burying some metallic object that looked like a gun out there in the lot.'

'So,' Mason said, 'you were willing to have Conway convicted of murder in order to–'

She met his eyes and said, 'Mr Mason, my husband framed me for murder, and, believe me, because of the way things went I *was* framed for murder. Don't ever kid yourself, I could have gone to prison for life, or gone to the gas chamber. I had every motive in the world. The murder had been committed with my gun. I had been seen leaving the room where the murdered girl lay. I was up against it. I felt that I could frame enough of a case on Jerry Conway so the police would quit looking for–any other murderer, and I felt absolutely certain that a clever lawyer could keep Jerry Conway from being convicted. I suppose I've been guilty of a crime, and now you've trapped me. I don't know how you found out about this, but I'm coming clean and I'm throwing myself on your mercy.'

Mason looked at his watch and said, 'All right, I can't wait any longer. Paul Drake is serving you with a subpoena to appear as a witness for the defence. Serve the subpoena on her, Paul.'

Della Street, who had been taking surreptitious notes, looked up and caught Mason's eye. He raised his eyebrows in silent question, and she nodded, indicating that she had the statement all down.

'All right,' Mason said to Drake, 'come on, we've got to get back to court.'

'You're forgetting one thing,' Myrtle Lamar said.

'What?' Mason asked.

'My face,' she said. 'It's got to be fed.'

15

Driving back to the courthouse, Mason said to Paul Drake, 'Paul, this is a damned good lesson in the importance of circumstantial evidence.'

'What do you mean?'

'Circumstantial evidence is the best evidence we have,' Mason said, 'but you have to be careful not to misinterpret it.

'Now, look at the circumstantial evidence of the food in the stomach. Doctors are prepared to state that death took place within approximately two hours of the time the food was ingested. Because they know that the woman in Room 729 had food delivered to her around four-thirty, and presumably started eating when the food was delivered, they placed the time of death at almost exactly six-thirty-five to six-forty-five, the exact time that Jerry Conway was there.

'The only difference is the waiter didn't think there were peas on the dinner menu but peas were found in the stomach of the murder victim. Everyone took it for granted that it was simply a slip-up, a mistake on the part of the waiter in preparing the tray and in remembering what he'd put on there. Actually, it's the most important clue in the whole case. It shows that the woman whose body was found in 729 *couldn't* have been the woman who ordered the dinner which was delivered at four-thirty.'

'Well,' Drake said, 'we know what happened, but how the devil are you going to prove it? A jury isn't going to believe Mrs Farrell's story. . . . Or will it?'

'That depends,' Mason said, 'on how much other evidence we can get. And it depends on who killed Rose Calvert.'

'What do you mean?'

'The point that Mrs Farrell completely missed was that Giff was trying to make it appear that Rose's death was a suicide. He entered the room, he found the body, there wasn't any sign of a gun. That was because the murderer had kicked the murder weapon under the bed–unless he threw it there deliberately. Probably he dropped it and then had kicked it under the bed without knowing what he had done. Or perhaps he just kicked it under the bed hoping it wouldn't be found right away, or not giving a damn and just wanting to get rid of it.'

'You mean, you don't think Gifford Farrell is the murderer?'

'The evidence points to the contrary,' Mason said. 'Why would Gifford Farrell have killed Rose and then discharged another gun into the underside of the mattress so there would be an empty shell in that gun and then have left the gun on the floor by the corpse?'

'So as to implicate his wife,' Drake said.

'But don't you see,' Mason pointed out, 'if he'd done that, he'd have taken the other gun? He wouldn't have left it there.'

'Perhaps he didn't know it was there.'

'I'm satisfied he didn't know it was there,' Mason said. 'But *if he had killed* her, he *would* have known it was there, because that was the gun with which she was killed.'

'Oh-oh,' Drake said. 'Now I see your point.'

'Therefore,' Mason said, 'Gifford Farrell was a victim of circumstances. He tried to make the crime appear a suicide. He was carrying that gun with him, probably for his own protection. He discharged it into the mattress and dropped it by the side of the bed.

'If Mrs Farrell hadn't got in such a panic, she would have realized that Gifford was trying to set the stage for suicide. He could very easily have told the authorities that this gun was one he had taken home from the Texas Global, that he had given it to Rose for her own protection, that she had become despondent and had committed suicide. But when Mrs Farrell saw that gun, and saw her husband leaving the room after having heard the shot–which must have been the shot he fired into the underside of the mattress–she became panic-stricken and immediately felt that he was trying to frame the murder on her. So she led with her chin.'

'And then she tried to frame it on Conway?'

'That's right,' Mason said.

'Well, you can mix the case up all to hell,' Drake said, 'but the trouble is, Mason, you've got too much of a reputation for mixing things up. The jury is pretty apt to think all this is a big razzle-dazzle, cooked up by a lawyer to mix things up so his client won't be convicted. If you can't shake this damned hotel clerk in his testimony that Rose Calvert was the one who checked into Room 729 claiming she was the secretary for Gerald Boswell, you're hooked.'

Mason said, 'What I've got to do is to find out what actually happened.'

'When do we eat?' Myrtle Lamar asked.

Mason said, 'Myrtle, you're going to have to feed your own face.'

'What?'

'We'll give you money for the best lunch in town,' Mason said, 'but we're going to be busy.'

She pouted. 'That wasn't the way it was promised. Paul was going to take me to lunch. I want to have lunch with him.'

'I have to be in court,' Drake said.

'No, you don't. You're not trying the case–and I'll tell you one other thing, you hadn't better leave *me* alone, running around here. I know too much. You've got to keep me under surveillance, as you detectives call it.'

Mason laughed, said, 'You win, Myrtle. Paul, you're going to have to take her to lunch.'

'But I want to see what happens in court.'

'Nothing too much is going to be happening in court,' Mason said. 'Not right away. The district attorney is stalling, trying to find some way of accounting for that bullet in the underside of the mattress. He wants to prove that I shot it there and he's just about ready to call Inskip so they can lay a foundation to involve me in the case as an accessory.

'So you can count on the fact that he'll stall things along just as much as he can, and this time I'm inclined to play along with him because I want to find out what happened.

'Someone murdered Rose Calvert. I want to find out who.'

'Well,' Drake said, 'don't ever overlook the fact that it could well have been

Mrs Gifford Farrell. She had the room across the corridor from the girl. She hated the girl's guts. She was seen by a chambermaid coming out of the girl's room. . . . Good Lord! Perry, don't let her pull the wool over your eyes by telling a convincing story which, after all, has for its sole purpose getting herself off the hook.'

'I'm thinking of that,' Mason said.

'And,' Drake went on, 'she's the one who buried the murder weapon down there at the motel. . . . Hang it, Perry! The more you think of it, the more logical the whole thing becomes. She must have been the one who committed the murder.'

'There's just one thing against it,' Mason said.

'What?'

'Circumstantial evidence,' Mason told him.

'Such as what?'

'Why didn't she give Jerry Conway the murder weapon instead of the weapon that Gifford had planted there to make the death appear suicide?'

Drake tugged at the lobe of his ear for a moment, then said, 'Hell's bells, Perry! This is one case I can't figure. Things are coming a little too fast for me. Where do I take Myrtle to lunch?'

'Some place not too far from the courthouse,' Mason said.

'Well, let me out here. This is a darned good restaurant. We'll take a cab and come to court when we're finished. . . . How much of a lunch do you want, Myrtle?'

'Not too much,' she said. 'I'll have two dry Martinis to start, then a shrimp cocktail, and after that a *filet mignon* with potatoes *au gratin*, a little garlic toast, a few vegetables on the side such as asparagus or sweet corn, then some mince pie *à la mode*, and a big cup of black coffee. That will last me until evening.

'Believe me, it's not very often that one of us girls gets an opportunity to look at the left-hand side of the menu without paying a bit of attention to what's printed on the right-hand side.'

Mason glanced at Paul Drake and nodded. 'It may be just as well to keep her out of circulation until the situation clarifies itself.'

Mason stopped the car and let Paul and Myrtle Lamar out.

'That's a scheming little package,' Della Street said when Mason started the car again. 'I hope Paul Drake doesn't get tangled up with her.'

'I hope Paul Drake really turns her inside out,' Mason said.

'What do you mean? She's turned inside out,' Della said.

Mason shook his head, 'For all we know, Della, she could have been the one who committed the murder. Anyone around the hotel could.'

'Including Bob King?' Della Street asked.

'Including Bob King.'

'Well, I'd certainly like to see you wrap it around *his* neck,' she said. 'But somehow, Chief, I'm inclined to agree with Paul. I think that Mrs Farrell is mixed in this thing so deep–'

'That's just the point,' Mason said. 'But then we get back to that business of circumstantial evidence. If she had killed her, she wouldn't have given Jerry Conway the wrong gun.'

'What about the gun that did the fatal shooting?' Della asked. 'What have they found out about it?'

'So far they haven't told us,' Mason said. 'But the grapevine has it that they can't tell a thing about the gun, because it was stolen from a hardware store a year and half ago along with half a dozen other guns.

'Within thirty minutes of the time of the crime, police spotted a car loaded with a bunch of tough-looking kids speeding along. It was about three o'clock in the morning so they took after it. There was quite a chase before they caught the kids. The kids admitted that when they saw the police were taking after them, they threw everything they had taken out of the car windows as they were speeding along. There were half a dozen revolvers, three or four ·22 rifles, a lot of ammunition, and some jackknives. Police recovered most of the stuff, but they didn't find a couple of the guns, and quite a few of the knives. Almost anyone could have picked up this murder weapon the next day.'

'They have the general locality?' Della Street asked.

'That's right.'

'Was it near any place where Mrs Farrell would have been?'

'It was at the other end of town,' Mason said.

'Well, she told him, 'you like circumstantial evidence so much. This is an opportunity to put a jigsaw puzzle together.'

'You can put it together two or three different ways,' Mason said, 'but the pieces don't all fit.

'The trouble with circumstantial evidence isn't with the evidence, but with the reasoning that starts interpreting that evidence. . . . I'm kicking myself over those peas in the dead's girl's stomach. There was the most significant clue in the whole case, and damned if I didn't discount it and think it was simply a waiter's mistake.

'I should have cross-examined that waiter up one side and down the other and made him show that he was absolutely positive those peas couldn't have been on the tray taken to 729. I should have made that the big point in the case.

'However, I knew that the peas *were* in the dead girl's stomach and therefore, like everybody else, thought it must have been a mistake on the part of the waiter, and didn't pay too much attention to it.'

'Well,' Della Street told him,'you've got an assorted set of monkey wrenches now that you can drop into the district attorney's machinery whenever you want to.'

'But this time,' Mason told her, 'I *have* to be right.'

They rode up in the elevator to the courtroom and entered just in time to take their seats at the counsel table before court was reconvened.

Judge DeWitt said, 'The police officer was on the witness stand.'

Elliott, on his feet, said, 'If the Court please, I have a few more questions on direct examination to ask of this witness.'

'Very well,' Judge DeWitt said.

Elliott's questions indicated that he was still sparring for time.

Within ten minutes after court had reconvened, however, the door opened and both Hamilton Burger and Alexander Redfield, the ballistics expert, came tiptoeing into the courtroom.

Redfield took his seat in court, and Hamilton Burger, ponderously tiptoeing forward, reached the counsel table, leaned over and whispered to Elliott.

An expression of beaming good nature was on the district attorney's face.

Elliott listened to Burger's whisper, nodded his head, then said, 'That's all. I have no further questions.'

'No cross-examination.'

Hamilton Burger arose ponderously. 'Call Frederick Inskip to the stand.'

Inskip came forward and was sworn, and Hamilton Burger, walking around the end of the counsel table to examine him where he would appear to best advantage in front of the jurors, gave every indication of being completely satisfied with the turn of events.

'Mr Inskip,' he said, 'what is your occupation? And what was your occupation on the sixteenth and seventeenth of October?'

'A private detective.'

'Were you employed on the sixteenth and seventeenth of October by Paul Drake?'

'Yes, sir.'

'And on what case were you working?'

'The murder at the Redfern Hotel.'

'And did you know who had employed Mr Drake?'

'Perry Mason.'

'How did you know that?'

'I was instructed that Mr Mason, who was the man in charge of the case, would join me.'

'Join you? Where?'

'At the Redfern Hotel.'

'You mean you had checked into the Redfern Hotel?'

'I had, yes, sir.'

'At what time?'

'Well, it was sometime after the murder. I was instructed to go to the hotel and register in Room 728.'

'Why 728? Do you know?'

'I wasn't told.'

'But 728 is right across the hall from 729?'

'Yes, sir. The door of 728 is exactly across the hall from the bedroom door of 729. 729 is a suite, and has two doors.'

'I see,' Hamilton Burger said. 'Now, how did you arrange to get in Room 728?'

Judge DeWitt said, 'Just a moment. Is this pertinent? This took place *after* the murder was committed. It was a conversation, as I take it, between Paul Drake and a man who was in his employ. It was without the presence of the defendant.'

'But,' Hamilton Burger said, 'we propose to show you, Your Honour, in fact, I think we *have* shown that the conversation was the result of the instructions of Mr Perry Mason, who was then acting as attorney for the defendant in this case.'

Judge DeWitt looked down at Mason and said, 'I haven't as yet heard an objection from the defence.'

'We have no objection to make, Your Honour,' Mason said. 'We're quite willing to have any fact in this case that will shed any light on what happened presented to this jury.'

'Very well,' Judge DeWitt said, 'it seeming that there is no objection on the part of the defence, the court will permit this line of testimony.'

'What happened?' Hamilton Burger asked Inskip.

'The phone rang. Paul Drake told me that Mr Mason, the attorney for whom he was working, would be up, that I was to leave the door unlocked so he could come in without knocking.'

'Now, just how did you get Room 728?' Hamilton Burger asked.

'Oh, that was easy. I said I wanted something not too high up and not too low down. They offered me 519 which was vacant. I asked them to see a floor plan of the hotel, and said, "No," and asked them if they had something perhaps a couple of floors higher up. They said they'd had a check-out in 728 and that was available if I wanted it, and I said I'd take it.'

'Now, after receiving that telephone call, what did you do?'

'I left the door unlocked.'

'And then what happened?'

'Well, it was about–I'm sorry to say I didn't notice the exact time, but it was around eleven or eleven-thirty–somewhere along there on the morning of the seventeenth that the door opened abruptly and Mr Mason came in.'

'Now you're referring to sometime around eleven o'clock on the morning of October seventeenth?'

'Yes.'

'And Mr Mason entered the room?'

'Yes.'

'And what happened?'

'Well, we had some conversation. He asked me to identify myself as working for Drake, and then he asked if I'd looked the room over, and I said I had generally. And he asked if I had a flash-light in my bag.'

'And did you have such a flash-light?'

'Yes.'

'And then what happened?'

'Mr Mason looked all around the room carefully with the flash-light, and then he asked me to help him take the sheets and blankets off the bed.'

'You did that?'

'Yes, sir.'

'Then what happened?'

'Then he raised the mattress and found a bullet hole in the underside of the mattress.'

There was an audible, collective gasp from the spectators in the court-room.

Judge DeWitt leaned forward. 'A bullet hole?' he asked.

'Yes, sir.'

'How do you know it was a bullet hole?' Judge DeWitt asked sharply.

'Because working with Mr Mason we got the bullet out of the hole.'

'How did you get it out?' Hamilton Burger asked.

'We cut a wire coat hanger to pieces and made an instrument that would get the bullet out. First we probed and found there was a bullet there, and then we got the bullet out.'

'And what happened to that bullet?'

'I kept it in my possession.'

'Did you mark the bullet so you could identify it?'

'Yes, sir.'

'At whose suggestion?'

'At Mr Mason's suggestion.'

'I show you a bullet and ask you if that was the bullet which you extracted from the mattress?'

The witness looked at the bullet and said, 'It is.'

'Do you know how Mr Mason knew that bullet hole was in the mattress?' Hamilton Burger asked.

'No, sir.'

'But he did suggest to you that there might well be something in the mattress?'

'Yes, sir.'

'And asked you to help him remove the blankets and sheets?'

'Yes, sir.'

'And then he turned up the mattress?'

'Yes, sir.'

'And indicated this bullet hole with the flash-light?'

'Yes, sir.'

Hamilton Burger smiled triumphantly. 'That's all.'

'No questions on cross-examination,' Mason said.

Hamilton Burger seemed somewhat nonplussed by Mason's attitude.

'Call Alexander Redfield,' Burger said.

Alexander Redfield came forward.

'I show you the bullet which has been identified by the witness Inskip,' Hamilton Burger said. 'Do you know what gun discharged that bullet?'

'Yes, sir.'

'What gun?'

'A Smith & Wesson gun, numbered C 48809.'

'A gun which has previously been introduced in evidence here?'

'Yes, sir.'

'The gun which the defendant Conway admitted he had in his possession?'

'Yes, sir.'

'Now then,' Hamilton Burger said, 'there are two bullets in this case, and two guns.'

'Yes, sir.'

'There is a Colt No. 740818?'

'Yes, sir.'

'And a bullet was fired from that gun?'

'Yes, sir.'

'And what bullet was that?'

'That was the fatal bullet.'

'That was the bullet that was given you by the autopsy surgeon as having been the bullet which caused the death of Rose Calvert?'

'Yes, sir.'

'And that bullet was fired from that Colt revolver?'

'Yes, sir.'

'And this bullet which you have now identified is a bullet which was fired from the Smith & Wesson, the one which is received in evidence and which bears the number C 48809. This is the same gun which the evidence shows Mr Conway, the defendant in this case, produced and handed to the authorities as being the gun which he claimed had been pointed at him in Room 729 and which he had taken away from this mysterious woman whom he had described in such detail?'

'Yes, sir.'

'That's all,' Hamilton Burger said.

'No cross-examination,' Mason said.

Judge DeWitt frowned at Mason.

'I'm going to recall Robert King,' Hamilton Burger said.

King came forward and took the witness stand.

'You have already been sworn,' the district attorney said. 'I am going to ask you what the hotel records show in regard to Room 728.'

'It was rented to a Ruth Culver.'

'And what happened to Ruth Culver?'

'She checked out of the hotel at about six-fifty on the evening of October sixteenth.'

'When did she rent the room?'

'Around ten o'clock in the morning of October sixteenth.'

'Who checked her out?'

'I presented her with the bill, which she paid in cash.'

'And then what?'

'It was early enough to have the room made up so we could re-rent it again if we needed to that night.'

'Cross-examine,' Hamilton Burger said.

Mason said, 'You didn't see Ruth Culver when she checked in, did you?'

'No, sir.'

'You weren't on duty at that time?'

'No, sir.'

'So for all you know, the woman who checked out of Room 728 may not have been the same woman who registered in there?'

'I know she was the woman who checked out of 728.'

'How do you know that?'

'Because she paid the bill, and the bellboy went up and brought the baggage down.'

'Quite right. You know some woman checked out of Room 728 but you don't know it was the same woman who checked in, do you?'

'Well, I didn't see her when she checked in. I wasn't on duty.'

'For all you know of your own knowledge,' Mason said, 'the woman who rented 728 could well have been Rose Calvert, whose body was found in Room 729.'

'Oh, Your Honour,' Hamilton Burger said, 'I object to this question. It is argumentative. It is completely incompetent, irrelevant, and immaterial, and it shows the straws at which counsel is clutching.'

'The question *is* argumentative,' Judge DeWitt said.

'If the Court please,' Mason said, 'it is a logical question. The initials of Ruth Culver and Rose Calvert are the same. The baggage which was taken down from 728 had the initials "R.C." and–'

'Your Honour, Your Honour!' Hamilton Burger shouted. 'I object to this statement. I assign the making of it as misconduct. I point out to the Court that the whole specious, fabricated nature of this defence is now coming into court in its true light.

'The defendant in this case admittedly had the Smith & Wesson revolver in his possession from around six-thirty-five on the evening of the sixteenth until it was surrendered to the officers on the morning of the seventeenth.

'The defendant had consulted Perry Mason as his attorney, and presumably had turned the gun over to him. At least he had the opportunity to do so.

'Mr Mason, finding out that there had been a check-out on the seventh floor of the hotel during the evening, had ample opportunity to get to that room to fire a shot in the mattress, then instruct a detective to go to that room and be there so that Mr Mason could make a grandstand of *discovering* the bullet hole in the mattress the next morning.

'This is evidence of unprofessional conduct on the part of the counsel. It makes him an accessory after the fact–'

'Now, just a minute! Just a minute!' Judge DeWitt interrupted, banging his gavel down on the desk. 'We'll have no accusations of this nature at this time, Mr District Attorney. You have objected to the question on the ground that it is argumentative. In the light of Mr Mason's statement, it is now the opinion of the Court that the question is *not* argumentative. Counsel is simply asking the witness what is a self-evident fact, that since the witness doesn't know who checked into Room 728, it could have been anybody. It could have been the young woman who was subsequently found murdered. It could have been anyone.

'Now, the Court suggests that, if you want to show who this person was who checked into Room 728, if it becomes important for any reason, you can produce that person and have her testify, or in the event you can't produce her, and any attempt is made to show that the person who checked into 728 was the person whose body was found in 729, you can produce the register and have a handwriting expert testify as to the differences in handwriting.'

Mason grinned and said, 'And when he does that, Your Honour, the handwriting expert will have to testify that the Ruth Culver who signed the register and checked into 728 was the Rose Calvert whose body was found in 729.'

'Your Honour! Your Honour!' Hamilton Burger shouted. 'This is improper. That is an improper statement. That is misconduct on the part of defence counsel.'

'Well,' Judge DeWitt said, 'let's not have so much excitement about this. After all, the matter is perfectly obvious. Have you checked the registration, Mr District Attorney?'

Hamilton Burger's face purpled. 'No, Your Honour, we haven't because there is no need for so doing. We don't need to check the handwriting of every person who registered in the Redfern Hotel on the morning of the sixteenth in order to negative some perfectly fallacious theory which the defence is trying to advance.'

'Well, if you're not going to anticipate the defence, and call witnesses to refute it in advance,' Judge DeWitt said, 'I fail to see the reason for calling the witness Inskip.'

'We want to show the tactics of defence counsel.'

'Well, go ahead and show them,' Judge DeWitt said, 'but refrain from personalities, and if I were you, Mr Prosecutor, I would put on my own case, and then in the event defence makes any claims, you have an opportunity to call witnesses in rebuttal. It always is a dangerous practice to try and anticipate a defence and negative it in advance, and it is not in accordance with the best practice.

'Proceed with the cross-examination of this witness, Mr Mason.'

'No further cross-examination,' Mason said.

'Call your next witness,' Judge DeWitt said to Hamilton Burger.

'I will call Norton Barclay Calvert, the husband of the dead woman,' Hamilton Burger said. 'Come forward, Mr Calvert, and be sworn.'

There was a moment's delay while the bailiff's voice could be heard outside the courtroom calling Norton Calvert.

A few moments later the door opened and Norton Calvert entered the courtroom and came forward to the witness stand.

He took the oath, settled himself on the witness stand, and Hamilton Burger said, 'Your name is Norton Barclay Calvert, and you are the surviving husband of Rose M. Calvert?'

'Yes, sir.'

'You have identified the body of Rose Calvert? You saw that in the morgue?'

'Yes, sir.'

'When did you first know that your wife was dead?'

Mason said, 'That is objected to, if the Court please, on the ground that it's incompetent, irrelevant, and immaterial. It makes no difference to the issues in this case when he first knew his wife was dead.'

Judge DeWitt nodded his head.

'Just a moment, before the Court rules,' Hamilton Burger said. 'May I be heard?'

'Certainly, Mr Prosecutor.'

'We propose to show by this witness,' Burger said, 'that he was apprised early in the morning of the seventeenth that his wife had been murdered, that this was long before the police knew the identity of the body. We propose to show that he was advised by Mr Perry Mason, who was acting as attorney for the defendant, and that the only way Mr Mason could possibly have known the identity of the murdered woman was by having his client give him that information. And the only way his client could have secured the information was by seeing and recognizing the murdered woman.'

Judge DeWitt looked at Mason. 'That would seem to put something of a different aspect on the situation, Mr Mason.'

'How is he going to prove that the only way I had of knowing the identity of the murdered woman was because of something my client told me?' Mason asked.

'We'll prove it by inference,' Hamilton Burger said.

'I think there is no necessity for having any further discussion on this matter,' Judge DeWitt said. 'I dislike to have offers of proof made in front of the jury. I think the testimony of the witness will speak for itself, but under the circumstances the Court is going to overrule the objection.'

'When did you first know that your wife had been murdered?' Hamilton Burger asked.

'About one o'clock on the morning of the seventeenth.'

'Where were you?'

'At my home in Elsinore.'

'How did you find out your wife was dead?'

'Mr Mason told me she had been murdered.'

'By Mr Mason, you mean Perry Mason, the attorney for the defendant here?'

'Yes, sir.'

'Now, let's not have any misunderstanding about this,' Hamilton Burger said. 'You learned of your wife's death through a statement made by Perry Mason to the effect that she had been murdered, and that statement was made around one o'clock in the morning of October seventeenth in Elsinore, California?'

'Yes, sir.'

'Cross-examine!' Hamilton Burger snapped at Perry Mason.

'Do you remember what time I got to your house?' Mason asked.

'I think it was about twelve-forty-five or so.'

'Do you know when I left?'

'I know that you had left by a quarter past one,' he said. 'You were there about half an hour, I think.'

'Didn't I tell you that I thought your wife had been murdered after I had looked at pictures of your wife?'

'I showed you some pictures, but you seemed pretty positive. Otherwise you wouldn't have gone down to see me at that hour in the morning.'

Hamilton Burger grinned.

Judge DeWitt rebuked the witness. 'Kindly refrain from arguing with counsel. Simply answer questions.'

'Yes, sir, that's what you told me, but you woke me up out of a sound sleep in the middle of the night to tell me.'

'I woke you up?'

'Yes.'

'You had been sleeping?'

'I was sound asleep.'

'You went to bed when?'

'Nine-thirty or ten.'

'Had no trouble getting to sleep?'

'Certainly not.'

'And slept soundly until I came?'

'Yes.'

'Hadn't got up even to take a smoke?'

'No.'

'You know as a heavy smoker that about the first thing a smoker does on awakening is to reach for a cigarette?'

'Certainly.'

'Yet after you let me in, you sat there for five minutes before you had a cigarette, didn't you?'

'I . . . I don't remember that so well. I had been–I can't recall.'

Mason said, 'Didn't I tell you, Mr Calvert, that I got your address from a letter which you had written your wife?'

'I don't remember,' Calvert said. 'I was pretty much broken up, and I don't remember too much about what you said about how you got there, but I remember you came there and told me my wife had been murdered.'

'You had written your wife a letter, hadn't you?'

'Objected to as incompetent, irrelevant, and immaterial and not proper cross-examination,' Hamilton Burger said. 'My interrogation was only as to a conversation with Mr Mason. If Mr Mason wants to make this man his own witness, he can do so.'

'It is entirely proper to show the attitude of the witness and possible bias on the part of the witness,' Judge DeWitt said. 'I don't see what difference it makes.'

'Well,' Mason said, 'in order to come within the technical rules of evidence, I'll reframe the question and ask him if he didn't *tell* me that he had written his wife a letter?'

'I don't remember. I think I did.'

'And,' Mason said, 'isn't it a fact that your wife, Rose Calvert, wrote and told you that she wanted to go to Reno and get a divorce?'

'Yes.'

'That she wanted you to hire counsel to represent you so you could make things easier for her?'

'Yes.'

'And when I rang the doorbell early on the morning of the seventeenth of October and told you that I wanted to talk with you about your wife, that I was an attorney, didn't you tell me that you wouldn't consent to anything, that you wouldn't do anything to make it easier for her to get a divorce?'

'Yes.'

'And didn't you tell me that you had answered the letter she had written and told her something to that effect?'

'I believe I did, yes.'

'And didn't I tell you that that letter was in the mail-box at her apartment?'

'I don't remember.'

'Oh yes, you do,' Mason said.

'The reason you didn't go to the Elsinore police station to find out if your wife had been murdered until considerably later on the morning of the seventeenth was that you suddenly realized that this letter you had mailed your wife would direct suspicion to you. You had told your wife in that letter that you would kill her before you'd let her marry anyone else, didn't you?'

The witness looked at Mason with sullen hostility, then slowly shook his head.

'No, I didn't say anything like that.'

'And,' Mason said, 'the minute I told you that letter was in the mailbox, you knew that that was a clue pointing towards you that you had forgotten, and that you had to go in and get the letter out of the mailbox before you asked the police to find out if your wife had been murdered.'

'That's not true!'

Mason, frowning thoughtfully, turned to survey the courtroom, studying the faces of the spectators.

At that moment the door opened, and Paul Drake and Myrtle Lamar entered the courtroom.

Mason said, 'If the Court please, I notice that Myrtle Lamar has just entered the courtroom. I would like to ask Miss Lamar to come forward and stand by me for a moment. And I would like to ask the witness to arise.'

'What's the reason for all this?' Hamilton Burger asked.

'Myrtle Lamar,' Mason said, 'as one of the elevator operators at the Redfern Hotel, has her own means of making an identification of persons who go up in the elevator. Kindly step forward, Miss Lamar.'

Mason moved over to the swinging gate which divided the bar from the courtroom and said, 'Right this way, please.'

Myrtle Lamar moved through the gate.

'I object,' Hamilton Burger said.

'On what grounds?' Judge DeWitt asked.

'He can't examine two witnesses at once,' Hamilton Burger said.

'He's not trying to,' Judge DeWitt said. 'He is, as I understand it, trying to make an identification.'

'If the Court please,' Mason said, 'I feel that perhaps I do owe Court and counsel an explanation. It seems that Miss Lamar makes it a point of studying the feet of the persons who go up and down in the elevators. I notice that this witness has a peculiar habit of turning his right foot in at a sharp angle. I also notice he is wearing a distinctive shoe, a high-laced shoe with a heavy box-toe cap. I believe these shoes are advertised by one of the well-known mail-order houses as being ideal for service-station attendants in that they will not slip and are resistant to oil and gasoline.'

Mason turned back to the witness. 'Stand up, please.'

Calvert sullenly got to his feet.

'Now, just a minute, just a minute,' Hamilton Burger said, pushing back from his chair and lumbering towards the witness. 'I want to see this.'

Mason said to Calvert, 'You're holding your right foot so the toe is pointed straight ahead. Do you always stand that way?'

'Of course,' Calvert said.

Abruptly Myrtle Lamar started to laugh. 'That's not true,' she said in a loud, clear voice. 'I'd never forget those shoes. When he stands relaxed, his right toe is pointed in. He's deliberately holding it–'

'Order!' Judge DeWitt shouted. 'You will not give any testimony at this time, Miss Lamar. You are being brought up here purely for the purpose of identification. You will now return to your seat in the courtroom. The witness will resume his seat in the witness chair.'

Hamilton Burger said, 'Your Honour, I object. I move all of this statement be stricken as not being the statement of a witness, and–'

'The motion is granted!' Judge DeWitt snapped. 'Mr Mason, can, of course, call Miss Lamar as his witness if he desires, but her statement will be stricken from the evidence.'

'Sit down,' Mason said to Calvert.

Mason stood for a moment, looking at the witness with searching eyes. Then he said in a tone that was not without sympathy, 'You loved your wife, didn't you, Calvert?'

Calvert nodded.

'You felt you couldn't live without her. You wanted her to come back to you.'

The witness was silent.

'And,' Mason said, 'you made up your mind that if you couldn't have her, no one else was going to have her. You were willing to kill her and probably intended to kill yourself at the same time. Then you lost your nerve and didn't go through with the suicide.'

The witness shifted his position uncomfortably. For a swift moment his lips twisted on a choking sob, then he regained control of himself.

Mason said, 'If the Court please, I feel that the circumstances are highly unusual. I would like to have a ten-minute recess so that I can interview certain witnesses.'

'I object to any continuance at this time,' Hamilton Burger said in sputtering protest.

'Is it absolutely necessary to have a recess at this time in order to interview these witnesses, Mr Mason?' Judge DeWitt asked.

'It is, Your Honour. Mrs Farrell was having detectives shadow Rose Calvert's apartment. I can't say for certain what time these detectives went off duty on the night of the sixteenth and the morning of the seventeenth, but I am hoping that one of these detectives can testify that this witness was seen going to the mailbox and taking this incriminating letter he had written out of the mailbox so the police wouldn't find it when they came to search the apartment after the body had been identified.'

'Your Honour, I object to these statements being made in front of the jury,' Hamilton Burger said. 'This is simply a grandstand–'

'Counsel will refrain from personalities,' Judge DeWitt said sharply. 'The

Court has previously stated that it dislikes to have offers of proof made in front of the jury. However, this statement was in response to a question asked by the Court itself, and the question was prompted by the fact that the prosecution objected to the recess. The Court feels that under the peculiar circumstances it is only fair to grant the motion, and Court will take a ten-minute recess.'

Mason hurried through the swinging gate in the bar to Paul Drake. 'Put a shadow on Calvert,' he said.

Drake said, 'Perry, you know those detectives went off duty at around one-thirty on the morning of the seventeenth. There was no one there to see Calvert take that letter, and–'

Mason said in a low voice, 'In poker, Paul, you sometimes shove in a stack of blue chips when you only have a pair of deuces in your hand. Get busy and follow Calvert. *I* think he's going to skip out.'

Calvert, walking doggedly towards the door, was suddenly confronted by Myrtle Lamar. She said, 'You know good and well that I took you up in the elevator on the sixteenth, the day of the murder, and I took you down again. When we got to the seventh floor you asked me–'

Suddenly Calvert shoved her out of the way and started running through the door of the courtroom and pell-mell down the corridor.

'Stop him!' someone screamed. 'Stop that man!'

Two spectators tried to grab Calvert. He engaged in a wild struggle with them. Officers ran up and grabbed the man's arms. His wrists were handcuffed behind his back.

There was pandemonium in the corridor.

16

Mason, Della Street, Paul Drake, Jerry Conway, and Myrtle Lamar sat in the courtroom after the commotion had subsided, after the judge had instructed the jury to bring in a verdict of 'Not Guilty' in the case against Jerry Conway, after Calvert had been taken into custody.

'Where did you get the bright idea of what had happened?' Paul Drake asked Mason.

'That,' Mason said, 'was the simplest part of it, the mathematics of the whole business which had been in the back of my mind but didn't come out until something suddenly clicked.

'The pathologist stated that Rose had died almost two hours to the minute after she had eaten lunch. He thought that lunch had been eaten at four-forty. Actually we know from Mrs Farrell that lunch had been eaten at about twelve-forty. That fixed the time of death at about two-forty. At that particular time Mrs Farrell was out telephoning you, Conway.

'I suddenly remembered that I had told Calvert about locating him from the return address on the letter that was in the mailbox of the apartment house where Rose was living. Yet the police told us no such letter was in the box when they searched the place. Shortly after I told Calvert about the letter, he went all to pieces and insisted that I leave him alone. I felt certain that he would go to the Elsinore police almost immediately. He didn't. He didn't get in touch with them until some time later, just about enough time for him to go and get that letter.

'The rest of it was just plain bluff, based on Myrtle's noticing the guy's shoes.'

'Well,' Jerry Conway said at length, 'I'm going to ask you to appear before that stockholders' meeting, Mason, and tell them the whole story of this murder case. Will you do it?'

Mason nodded.

'I have an idea,' Conway said, 'that *that* will settle Gifford Farrell's hash as far as any attempt to take over is concerned.'

Mason turned to Drake with a grin, and said, 'Well, Paul, having bought Myrtle a good lunch, I think we now owe her a good dinner.'

Myrtle Lamar's eyes instantly became hard and calculating. 'It should be worth more than that,' she said. 'It should be worth a . . . a fur coat!'

Jerry Conway grinned happily, said to Perry Mason, 'Buy the gal a fur coat, Perry, and charge it to me. . . . Put it on your fee as an expense.'

RLE STANLEY GARDNER

The Case of

The Fiery Fingers

FOREWORD

In all the earth there is probably no mental occupation quite as fascinating as that of finding clues and then accounting for them, which is all that detective work really is and about all that astronomy really is.

A detective, for instance, finds the head of an unburnt match broken off and lying by itself on the floor at the scene of a murder. Is it a clue or is it just one more bit of trivia?

Perhaps he will deduce that the murderer was given to the habit of snapping matches into flame with his thumbnail, that this particular match was slightly defective and therefore the head broke off in place of snapping into flame.

Then when the murderer is apprehended the detective will find out that the man simply wanted a small stick with which he could push a key out of the lock in a door, and had broken the head off a match and used the matchstick to fulfil his purpose.

And so it goes. Whenever a man feels that he has an explanation to account for some physical clue he is only too likely to find that his conclusions, while brilliant and logical, are completely incorrect.

But if these clues happen to have been discovered by an officer of the Massachusetts State Police there isn't much possibility of a brilliant but erroneous deduction.

Because such clues are sent to the laboratory of Doctor Joseph T. Walker, scientist, toxicologist and general all-around technical detective, who has an uncanny ability to separate mental wheat from imaginative chaff, the answers given are the right ones.

Let a discarded coat be picked up along one of the Massachusetts highways by a casual pedestrian who happens to notice what seems to be a bloodstain, and watch what happens.

Doctor Walker's piercing eyes make an examination which is different from the ordinary examination because he knows of a dozen things to look for, things that never would occur to the ordinary man.

That little hole, for instance, may seem to be of minor significance until by photographing it in infra-red light he brings out powder stains proving that it is a bullet hole. By using soft X-rays he will find bits of metallic fragments in the garment, and by a spectro-analysis of those fragments will name the manufacturer of the bullet in question.

Or perhaps that peculiar imprint which is visible only under a certain angle of transverse lighting will, when properly photographed, assume the form of a perfect circle indicating that the wearer of the coat may have been struck by a hit-and-run driver. The headlight of the offending automobile left its circular imprint in the garment, whereupon a microscopic examination is quite likely to bring out little slivers of glass, some of which may be distinctive enough to furnish an important clue.

A further microscopic examination of the threads of the garment may disclose a flake-like substance no bigger than the head of a pin, which Doctor Walker will turn on edge, and examine under a powerful microscope. He will then announce that this is a small chip or flake of paint peeled off from an automobile driven by the hit-and-run culprit. The automobile, he will announce, was first painted a robin's-egg blue when it came from the factory, it was next painted a conservative black, then covered with a neutral tan and is now a vivid red.

I have watched Doctor Walker at work in his laboratory. I have peered over his shoulder while he has discovered things that the average man would never even look for, and then has translated those things into clues which, properly evaluated, have on countless occasions led to the apprehension and conviction of a criminal.

I first became acquainted with Doctor Walker at one of Captain Frances G. Lee's seminars on homicide investigation at the Harvard Medical School. I have since had occasion to drop into his laboratory several times. Every time I do so, I find him engaged in some fascinating crime problem where his common sense, his uncanny keenness of mind and his marvellous technical training bring forth logical but unexpected conclusions, just as a magician reaches into an unpromising silk hat and brings forth a very live, very convincing, and very substantial rabbit.

Of course, the rabbit was there all the time, and from the viewpoint of the magician the silk hat was the logical place to look for it.

I know of many cases where Doctor Walker's mind, following physical clues as a bloodhound follows scent, has brought murderers to justice, and I know of some cases where the same mental qualities have been used to prevent innocent men from being unjustly convicted.

Quietly, modestly, unobtrusively, Doctor Walker goes to his work day after day, dedicating his life to the cause of practical justice.

Society needs more men like Doctor Joseph T. Walker. The time and money, spent in the highly technical training such men must have to become thoroughly competent, represents a profitable investment on the part of organised society.

But there is more than mere technical training that makes Joe Walker the man that he is. He has an unswerving loyalty to his ideals, a quiet courage, an inherent faith.

And so I dedicate this book to a competent scientist, a true friend, and a man whose pattern of life is a source of inspiration to those who are familiar with it,

DOCTOR JOSEPH T. WALKER.

Erle Stanley Gardner

I

Perry Mason had just returned to the office after a long day in court.

Della Street, his secretary, pushed a stack of half a dozen letters on his desk and said, 'These are ready for you to sign, and before you go home there's one client in the office whom you should see. I told her I thought you'd see her if she'd wait.'

'How long's she been waiting?' Mason asked, picking up the desk pen and starting to skim through the letters which Della Street had typed out for his signature.

'Over an hour.'

'What's her name?'

'Nellie Conway.'

Mason signed the first letter, Della Street efficiently blotted the signature, picked the letter up, folded it and slipped it in the envelope.

'What does she want?' Mason asked.

'She won't tell me, but she says it's an urgent matter.'

Mason frowned, signed the second letter, and said, 'It's late, Della. I've been in court all day and . . .'

'This girl's in trouble,' Della Street said with quiet insistence.

Mason signed the next letter. 'What does she look like?'

'Thirty-two or thirty-three, slender, dark hair, grey eyes, and the most perfect poker face you have ever seen.'

'No expression?'

'Wooden.'

'How do you know she's in trouble?'

'Just the way she acts. There's a peculiar tension about her and yet her face doesn't show it.'

'Any signs of nervousness?'

'Nothing outward. She drops into a chair, sits in one position without moving her hands or her feet, her face is absolutely expressionless, her eyes move a little bit, but that's all. She doesn't read, she just sits there.'

'But not relaxed?' Mason asked.

'Just like a cat sitting at a gopher hole waiting for the gopher to come out. Not a move that you can see, but you have the feeling of inner tension–waiting.'

'You interest me,' Mason said.

'I thought I would,' Della Street said demurely.

Mason abruptly signed the rest of the letters in the pile of mail without even bothering to glance at them.

'All right, Della, let's get her in. I'll have a look at her.'

Della Street took the mail, nodded, stepped out into the outer office and returned shortly with the client.

'Nellie Conway, Mr Mason,' she said crisply.

Mason motioned the woman to a seat in the soft, comfortable chair which he had installed in the office so that by lulling clients into complete physical relaxation he might relieve their emotional tension and so loosen their tongues.

Nellie Conway disregarded the motion and took one of the less comfortable wooden chairs moving with a gliding silence as though she had trained herself to make no unnecessary sound.

'Good afternoon, Mr Mason. Thank you for seeing me. I've heard a lot about you. I was hoping you'd get in earlier. I'm going to have to hurry because I have to be on duty at six o'clock.'

'You work nights?'

'I'm a nurse.'

'A trained nurse?'

'A practical nurse. I work on cases where the people can't afford hospitalisation or trained nurses. We work longer hours and, of course, we do things a trained nurse won't do, and we get less money.'

Mason nodded.

Nellie Conway turned to fasten steady grey eyes on Della Street.

Mason said, 'Miss Street is my confidential secretary. She will sit through the interview and make notes, if you don't mind. She has to know as much about my business as I do in order to keep things co-ordinated here in the office. Now, what did you want to see me about?'

Nellie Conway folded gloved hands, turned her triangular face towards Perry Mason and, without the faintest flicker of expression in voice or eyes, said, 'Mr Mason, how does one go about preventing a murder from being committed?'

Mason frowned. 'I wouldn't know.'

'I'm serious.'

Mason regarded her with searching eyes, then said, 'All right. This is out of my line. I specialise in defending people who are accused of crime and I try to see that my clients at least get an even break, but if you *really* want to know how to go about preventing a murder I would say there are four ways.'

'What are they?'

Mason held up his hand and checked off the four ways on his fingers. 'One,' he said, 'you remove the victim, or the potential victim, from the danger zone.'

She nodded.

'Two,' Mason said, 'you remove the murderer, or the potential murderer from the place where he can have any contact with the victim.'

Again she nodded.

'Three,' Mason said, 'you remove all weapons of murder, which is pretty difficult to do.'

'So far they've all been difficult,' she said. 'What's the fourth?'

'The fourth,' Mason said, 'is the easy one and the practical one.'

'What is it?'

'You go to the police.'

'I've been to the police.'

'And what happened?'

'They laughed at me.'

'Then why come to me?'

'I don't think you'll laugh.'

Mason said, 'I won't laugh, but I don't like abstractions. My time's valuable. Apparently you're in a hurry. I'm in a hurry. I don't like this business of having a client say, "A wants to murder B." Let's get down to brass tacks.'

'How much are you going to charge me?'

Mason said, 'That depends on how soon you quit beating about the bush.'

'I'm a working woman. I don't make a great deal of money.'

Mason said, 'Therefore it's to your interest to have the charge as low as possible.'

'That's right.'

'So,' Mason said, 'you'd better tell me what this is all about, and talk fast.'

'*Then* how much will you charge me?'

Mason regarded the wooden face across the desk. He glanced amusedly at Della Street. His eyes turned back to his client and softened into a smile. 'One dollar,' he said, 'for advice, if you've told your story within the next four minutes.'

There was not the faintest sign of surprise in her face. She repeated merely, 'One dollar?'

'That's right.'

'Isn't that unusually low?'

Mason winked at Della Street. 'What's your standard of comparison?'

She opened her purse, her gloved hands took out a coin purse. She opened it, selected a folded dollar note, smoothed it out and put it on the desk.

Mason didn't touch it. His eyes kept regarding her with puzzled curiosity.

She closed the coin purse, put it back in her bag, snapped the bag shut, put the bag on her lap, folded her gloved hands on the bag and said, 'I think Mr Bain wants to murder his wife. I'd like to prevent it.'

'Who's Mr Bain?'

'Nathan Bain. He's in the produce business. You may know him.'

'I don't. Who's his wife?'

'Elizabeth Bain.'

'How do you know all this?'

'By using my powers of observation.'

'You're living in the house?'

'Yes.'

'Waiting on someone?'

'Yes. Mrs Bain. Elizabeth Bain.'

'What's the matter with her?'

'She was hurt in an automobile accident.'

'Bad?'

'I'm afraid worse than she realises. There's been an injury to the spine.'

'Can she walk?'

'No, and she isn't ever going to walk again.'

'Go ahead,' Mason said.

'That's all.'

Mason's face showed annoyance. 'No, that isn't all,' he said. 'You think that he wants to murder her. You aren't a mind reader, are you?'

'Sometimes,' was the unexpected answer, delivered in a calm voice.

'And you're getting this from reading his mind?'

'Well, not exactly.'

'There are other things?'

'Yes.'

'What are they?'

She said, 'Nathan Bain wants to marry someone else.'

'How old is he?'

'Thirty-eight.'

'How old's his wife?'

'Thirty-two.'

'How old's the girl he wants to marry?'

'About twenty-five.'

'Does she want to marry him?'

'I don't know.'

'Who is she?'

'Some woman who has an apartment in the city. I don't know exactly where.'

'What's her name?'

'Her first name's Charlotte. I don't know the last name.'

Mason said irritably, 'I'm having to draw it out of you like pulling teeth. How do you know he wants to get married?'

'Because he's in love with this woman.'

'How do you know?'

'They correspond. He met her at a convention. He loves her.'

'All right,' Mason said, 'so what? Lots of healthy men thirty-eight years of age have restless eyes and a roving disposition. It's a dangerous age. They come back home if you leave them alone. Sometimes they don't. There are lots of divorces, but there aren't many murders.'

Nellie Conway opened her purse. 'Mr Bain offered me five hundred dollars if I would give his wife some medicine.'

Mason cocked a quizzical and somewhat sceptical eyebrow. 'You're certain of what you're saying, Miss Conway?'

'Absolutely certain. I have the medicine here.'

'Why did he say he wanted you to give it to his wife?'

'He didn't say. He just said that he thought that this medicine would be good for her. He doesn't like his wife's doctor.'

'Why not?'

'The doctor was an old friend of Elizabeth's.'

'You mean Bain is jealous?'

'I think so.'

'Look,' Mason said irritably, 'all of this doesn't make sense. If Bain wants his wife out of the way he's much rather have her divorce him and marry the doctor than to try and get rid of her by giving her poison. If he wanted to–let's take a look at this "medicine".'

Without a word she handed him a small glass tube which contained four tablets about the size of a standard five-grain aspirin tablet.

'Were you to give these to her all at once?'

'Yes, at bedtime–when she was being quieted for the night.'

'Did he pay you the money?'

'He said he'd pay me the money when I'd given her the medicine.'

'How was he going to know if you gave it to her?'

'I don't know. I guess he trusts me. I wouldn't lie.'

'Not to him?'

'Not to anyone. I don't believe in lying. It weakens your character.'

'Why didn't *he* give her this medicine?'

'He can't go in the room with her.'

'Why not?'

'The doctor has said he couldn't.'

'You mean a doctor tells a husband he can't go in the room where . . .?'

'Elizabeth hates the sight of him. She gets upset, almost hysterical every time she sees his face. We're forbidden even to mention his name.'

'Why does she feel that way?'

'I think she really knows she'll never walk again. Mr Bain was driving the car when the accident happened. She thinks it was avoidable.'

'You mean that he deliberately tried to . . .?'

'Don't put words in my mouth, Mr Mason. I said she thinks the accident was avoidable.'

Mason's facial expression was a combination of exasperation and curiosity.

'I gather you don't like Mr Bain?'

'He's a very strong, fascinating man. I do like him, very much.'

'Does he like you?'

'I'm afraid not.'

'So,' Mason said, 'he comes to you and offers to pay you five hundred dollars to give his wife poison, thereby putting himself entirely in your power, leaving a witness who could testify in case anything did happen to his wife. . . . It doesn't make sense. . . . How do you know it's poison?'

'I just *feel* that it is.'

'You don't know what the medicine is?'

'No.'

'Did he tell you what it was?'

'No, just that it was medicine.'

'Why did he tell you he wanted you to give it to his wife?'

'He said he thought it would make her feel better towards him.'

'This whole thing is screwy,' Mason said.

She said nothing.

'And you went to the police?'

'Yes.'

'To whom did you go?'

'I went to the police station and told them I wanted to see about a murder, and they sent me to a room that had a sign on the door saying "Homicide".'

'And what did you do?' Mason asked curiously.

'I told someone my story and he laughed at me.'

'Do you remember his name?'

'His name was Holcomb, he was a sergeant.'

'Did you show him this bottle?'

'No.'

'Why not?'

'I never got that far.'

'What happened?'

'I told him, just as I've told you, that I thought Mr Bain wanted to murder his wife, and I tried to tell Sergeant Holcomb why, but he laughed at me. He was in a big hurry. He had to go some place and he said . . . well, he said an unkind thing.'

'What did he say?'

'He said I was neurotic, but I'm not.'

'When did Mr Bain give you this medicine?'

'Yesterday.'

'Did you tell him you'd give it to his wife?'

'I made him think that I might.'

'And you've been carrying that little bottle around in your purse ever since?'

'Yes.'

'Taking it out from time to time when you wanted to get at something that was underneath?'

'I suppose so.'

'In other words,' Mason said, 'there aren't any of his fingerprints left on that bottle by this time?'

'I don't suppose so.'

Mason took the bottle, removed the cork, looked down at the contents, then spread out a sheet of paper and dumped all four of the tablets on the table. As far as the eye could determine, they were all identical. Mason picked out one of the tablets, returned the other three to the little tube.

He said, 'Della, get me two plain envelopes, please.'

Della Street opened the drawer of her secretarial desk, took out two envelopes and gave them to Mason.

Mason took the tablet he had taken from the tube, put it in an envelope, sealed the envelope, wrote his name across the flap, then took the tube containing the three tablets, placed it in the second envelope, sealed the flap, wrote his name across that flap and said to Nellie Conway, 'Write your name across the flap so that part of the name is below the sealed flap and part of it is on the flap, just as I've done.'

She took the pen and wrote the name as he had instructed.

'What's Bain's address?' Mason asked.

'Nineteen-twenty-five Monte Carlo Drive.'

'You go on duty at six o'clock?'

'That's right.'

'How late do you work?'

'Until eight in the morning.'

'Then what happens?'

'A day nurse comes on.'

'You have the longer shift?'

'Because the night nurse doesn't have so much to do.'

'Why does she need a night nurse? Doesn't she sleep at night? In other words, couldn't the nurse be within call–'

'Mrs Bain is a little difficult to manage at times.'

'Why?'

'Well, her mind is upset. She's been worrying a lot, and . . . well, the fact she won't let her husband in the room . . . the doctor wants a nurse with her all the time. Expense doesn't mean anything to them.'

'Who has the money?'

'She does.'

'Bain is in the produce business?'

'He makes a living,' she said, 'but Mrs Bain has the money. It's her separate property. She inherited it. She had it when she was married. That's why he married her.'

'Does Mrs Bain know about this other woman?' Mason asked.

'Of course. That's where I first got my information.'

'From Mrs Bain?'

'Yes.'

'How long ago was this accident?'

'Somewhere around a month. She was at the hospital for ten days, then she came home.'

'You've been working there ever since?'

'Yes.'

'Who else is working there?'

'The day nurse.'

'She's been on about as long as you have?'

'Yes.'

'Who else?'

'A housekeeper.'

'What's her name?'

'Imogene Ricker.'

'How long's she been working there?'

'Oh, she's been working there a long time. She's very devoted to Mr Bain.'

'Does Mrs Bain like her?'

'Oh, yes.'

'And she goes into Mrs Bain's room?'

'Certainly. Sometimes she takes spells for us nurses.'

'How old is she?'

'Oh, I don't know. I'd say somewhere in the late thirties. One of those peculiar, shadowy women who seems to be everywhere and nowhere. You never know where she's going to turn up. She gives me the creeps, Mr Mason. You've seen these cartoons of the haunted house with that thin woman sitting there with the dark eyes and the inscrutable expression? Well, she's just like that.'

'The point I'm getting at,' Mason said impatiently, 'is whether Mr Bain trusts her.'

'Oh, I think Mr Bain trusts her implicitly. She's been working for him for years. She worked for his first wife, and after his first wife died, well, then she kept right on as Mr Bain's housekeeper–'

'How long ago did his first wife die?'

'I don't know exactly. He's been married to Elizabeth Bain a little over two years, I think, or right around two years, and I guess he was a widower for three years. Well, that would make his . . . I don't know, somewhere around five or six years. Why?'

Mason said, 'Has it ever impressed you as being exceedingly improbable, young lady, that with a housekeeper in the house whom Mr Bain had known for at least three years, and perhaps considerably longer, he'd pick on you, a total stranger, and out of a clear sky offer you five hundred dollars to poison his wife?'

'Yes,' she said. 'It's occurred to me as being unusual.'

'Unusual,' Mason said, 'is a very, very mild designation. He gets along with the housekeeper all right?'

'Why, of course. They very seldom speak. She's quite taciturn.'

'Any romantic attachment?'

'Heavens, no. She's angular, with deep-set, dark eyes–'

'So there's no reason for Mrs Bain to be jealous of her?'

'Don't be silly, Mr Mason. That housekeeper has no more sex than . . . than an angleworm.'

'So the housekeeper could go into the room at any time and give Mrs Bain medicine?'

'Why, certainly. I told you she helps out with the nursing when we want to get a few minutes off.'

'Then *why* should Mr Bain pick on you?'

'I don't know, Mr Mason. I'm only telling you facts.'

Mason shook his head. 'It's all screwy. I'll get in touch with Sergeant Holcomb at Homicide and get his reaction. You keep the envelope with the medicine in it. I want to keep this one pill. I may get in touch with you later on. There's a telephone out there?'

'Yes.'

'Is it all right to call you there?'

'Oh, yes.'

'What's the number?'

'West 6-9841.'

'Well,' Mason said, 'my advice to you is to keep those pills for evidence, not to commit yourself in talking with Mr Bain, and let me talk with Sergeant Holcomb. If he wants to investigate, he can.'

'He doesn't. He thinks I'm crazy.'

'Your story has certain elements of improbability,' Mason said dryly.

'Could I call you later on tonight?' she asked.

'Not very well.'

'I have a feeling something may happen, Mr Mason, when I go back there. Mr Bain is going to ask me if I gave his wife the medicine and . . . well, if I tell him I didn't, he's going to get angry and suspicious.'

'Then tell him you did.'

'He'll know that I didn't.'

'Why?'

'Because his wife is still alive.'

Mason said, 'I don't get this thing. It's a completely cockeyed story, it doesn't make sense any way you look at it. Yet somehow *you* seem to be completely convinced.'

'Of course I am convinced, Mr Mason.'

Mason said, 'I tell you what I'll do. I'll give you the number of the Drake Detective Agency.'

'What's that?'

'They have offices on this floor,' Mason said. 'They do most of my detective work. I'll arrange to keep in touch with the Drake Detective Agency, and if anything of importance should develop, you can call there. They'll know where to reach me.'

'Thank you, Mr Mason.'

Della Street wrote the number of the Drake Detective Agency on a card, arose from her secretarial desk and moved over to hand the card to Nellie Conway.

'Are they open at night?'

'Yes, they're open twenty-four hours a day,' Della Street said.

'And you'll speak to them about me, so that I–?'

'I'll speak to them about you,' Mason said, and glanced at his wrist watch.

'Thank you very much, Mr Mason.'

She arose from her chair, stopped and regarded the dollar note on the desk. 'Do I get a receipt?'

Suddenly Mason's eyes narrowed. 'I wouldn't try to charge you twice.'

'I'd like a receipt. I'm very methodical in my book-keeping.'

Mason nodded to Della Street. 'Make it for consultation, Della.'

Della Street slipped a printed billhead into her typewriter, moved swift fingers over the keyboard, then handed the typewritten statement to Mason. Mason signed it, handed it across to Nellie Conway and said, 'Here you are, Miss Conway, or is it Mrs Conway?'

'Miss.'

'All right. Here's your receipt. Now we have your dollar and you have the receipt and you will perhaps hear from me again.'

'Thank you, Mr Mason. Good-night to both of you.'

She turned and walked with that strange gliding motion back across the office.

'You can go out this way,' Della Street said, arising swiftly and escorting her out of the exit door that opened into the corridor.

When the door had clicked shut Della Street raised her eyebrows in a silent question at Perry Mason.

The lawyer was sitting at the desk, his face granite hard, his eyes level-lidded with thought.

'Well?' Della Street asked.

Mason said, 'What a set-up! What a plan!'

'How do you mean?'

Mason said, 'It was all right. I was just riding along, half-asleep at the switch, until she asked for the receipt. That did it.'

'I'm afraid I don't get it. I . . . Whatever possessed you to only charge her a dollar, Chief?'

Mason laughed. 'I knew she was sitting there expecting me to say ten dollars or twenty-five dollars, and then going to try to argue me into taking half of whatever figure I set, so I thought I'd trick some expression into her face by surprising her to death. I wish now I'd said a hundred dollars and got her out of here.'

'Why?'

'Because I don't want to have anything to do with her.' Mason said. 'We're in a mess.'

'I don't get it.'

'Look,' Mason said, 'suppose something *does* happen to Mrs Bain. See how the little minx has fixed things? Consider the position she's put us in. She's been to Homicide Squad. She's consulted me. She has my receipted bill to prove it. We all think she's a little screwy. We pass her off as one of these psychopathic screwballs and . . . Get me police headquarters. Let's see if we can get Sergeant Holcomb on the phone.'

'You know he hates the ground you walk on, Chief.'

'I don't feel too overly cordial toward him,' Mason said, 'but I want to try and verify that story, and I want to get myself on record as having tried to get Holcomb to do something. We'll steal a page from Nellie Conway's book and pass the buck.'

'I get you,' Della said, smiling. She moved over to the telephone, looked at her watch and said, 'It's five-thirty. He's probably gone home.'

'We'll try him anyway, and if he isn't there we'll talk to somebody in charge. Perhaps it would be better to get Lieutenant Tragg. Lieutenant Tragg has sense.'

'Tragg likes you. He'd be more apt to listen. . . .'

'I don't care about whether anyone listens,' Mason said, 'I want to get my skirts clean. I don't like the smell of this. I don't like any part of it, and the more I think of it the less I like it.'

Della Street tried for the outer switchboard and said, 'I guess Gertie's gone home, Chief.'

'Get him on my private line,' Mason said.

Della dialled a number, then said, 'I want Homicide Squad, please . . . Homicide Squad? This is Mr Mason's office. Mr Mason would like to talk with Lieutenant Tragg if he's there, or with Sergeant Holcomb if he . . . Will you put him on, please? . . . Yes, Mr Mason is right here . . . Yes, I'll put him on the line.'

She handed the telephone to Mason, saying, 'Sergeant Holcomb.'

Mason put the phone to his ear. 'Hello . . . Hello . . . Holcomb?'

Holcomb's voice was uncordial. 'Hello, Mason, what is it this time? Got a corpse?'

'I don't know,' Mason said. 'Did a woman see you some time today? A Nellie Conway?'

'That nut!' Holcomb said.

'What did she want?'

'Hell, I don't know. She's nuts. She's talking about someone who wants to murder someone, and I asked her how she knew, and she said it was just an intuition or something of that sort, and I told her she was barking up the wrong tree, that she didn't have any evidence.'

'What makes you think she didn't have any evidence?'

'She didn't, did she?'

'I don't think you heard her whole story.'

'Hell, Mason, I haven't time to sit here all day and listen to a lot of psychos . . . Good Lord, I can show you a thousand screwball letters we get down here in the course of a month that–'

Mason said, 'This woman is peculiar. That doesn't mean she–'

'The hell it doesn't!' Holcomb said. 'She's crazy!'

'Well,' Mason said, 'she's been in here and tried to tell me her story. I thought I'd pass it on to you.'

'Thanks,' Holcomb said. 'You've listened to her, you've telephoned me, you've passed the buck. Okay, so what?'

Mason said, 'I just thought I'd tell you it's a situation I don't like.'

Holcomb said, 'There's lots of things we don't like. How do you feel about the income tax?'

'I love it,' Mason said.

'Go to hell,' Sergeant Holcomb told him.

'Now wait a minute,' Mason cautioned. 'This woman tells a peculiar story in a peculiar way. She says the husband of the woman she's nursing–'

'I know,' Holcomb interrupted, 'is in love with some other gal and wants his wife out of the way. So you ask her how she knows, and she says she's intuitive.'

'And the husband wanted her to give his wife some medicine and–'

'Oh, nuts!' Holcomb interrupted. 'I'll tell you what I think. I think this gal is trying to get the husband in bad because she wants to discredit him.'

'That could be.'

'I'll bet it is. Why should the husband give *her* medicine to give his wife?'

'She thinks it's poison.'

'I see, so the husband calls in a nurse who doesn't like him and makes her a witness who can crucify him . . . Now I'll tell you something else. I know something about the background of that case. This guy she's working for is okay. The wife is hysterical, neurotic, and this little tramp of a nurse is . . .'

'Yes?' Mason prompted as Holcomb hesitated.

'Well, I don't think I should tell you *all* I know. She's been to you as a client?'

'Yes.'

Holcomb laughed. 'Well, Mason, I hope she makes you a profitable client–lots of business,' and Holcomb roared with laughter.

'Well,' Mason said, 'I've reported to you.'

'That's right. You've passed the buck. Go to hell and good-bye!'

Sergeant Holcomb, still laughing, banged up the phone.

Mason's face darkened as he dropped the telephone back into its cradle. 'Damn Holcomb,' he said. 'He's getting smart. Now he accuses me of trying to pass the buck.'

'Well, what were you doing?' Della Street asked, a mischievous twinkle in her eye.

Mason grinned. 'Passing the buck. Why else would I call the guy?'

2

Paul Drake, head of the Drake Detective Agency, moved with a shambling gait which to the casual observer seemed slow and tedious, but actually there was a double-jointed suppleness about the man that enabled him to perform a prodigious amount of work and cover a great deal of ground without seeming ever to be in a hurry.

Perry Mason at times likened him to a juggler who would drop a plate and then, when it was hardly more than three inches from the floor, reach down and catch it before it crashed, with a motion so perfectly timed that it seemed to be almost leisurely.

Drake jack-knifed himself into the overstuffed chair, swung his knees up over the arm, clasped his hands behind his head and eyed Mason with a bored indifference that was completely deceptive.

'What's the pitch, Perry?'

'I'm up against just about the goofiest problem I've ever encountered in my whole career.'

'What is it?'

'A woman came in with a proposition that sounded entirely screwy. She wanted to know how much my advice was going to cost her and, just for the hell of it, I told her a dollar.'

'What happened?'

'She paid the dollar.'

'It's better to charge a dollar and get it in cash than to make a charge of a hundred dollars and get beat out of it.' Drake said, grinning. 'What's the trouble with her case?'

'I wish I'd never seen her.'

'Why don't you give her the dollar back and tell her you can't do anything for her?'

'That's just the point, Paul. That's what I *think* she wants me to do.'

'Well, what do you care what *she* wants? Just so you wash your hands and get out of it.'

'There are some things you can't wash your hands of,' Mason said. 'It isn't that easy.'

'Why not?'

'She comes to me with a completely cockeyed story about a wife being in danger, about a husband who's trying to get her to poison the wife–'

'That's easy,' Drake said. 'Advise her to go to the police.'

'She's been to the police, Paul.'

'What did the police do?'

'Laughed at her and kicked her out.'

'That should make a precedent for you. What's the complete story?'

Mason told him.

When he had finished Drake said, 'What do you want me to do, Perry?'

Mason handed Paul Drake the envelope containing the pill he had taken from the bottle Nellie Conway had shown him. 'Let's find out what it is, Paul. It *might* be cyanide of potassium. Then I'd ring up my friend, Sergeant Holcomb, and have him jumping around like a cat on a piece of fly-paper.'

Drake grinned.

'The point is,' Mason went on, 'we have only one tablet. If we use it up in an analysis–'

Drake said, 'It's a cinch, Perry. I have a friend who has access to a crime laboratory where they have one of these new X-ray defractors that uses X-rays and gets a graph from the molecular defraction of a substance. I don't know how it works. All I know is, it does the work. You can take an unknown powder and get a pretty good idea of what's in it in a very short time, and it only takes a microscopic amount of powder to do the job.'

'Okay,' Mason said. 'I want to be sure and keep this tablet so there won't be any possibility of substitution or loss. I've had it in an envelope, sealed, and with my name on it. Now I'll give it to you. You put it in an envelope, seal it and put your name on it, keep it in your possession and–'

'And be prepared to swear that that's the tablet I got from you just as you can swear that's the tablet you got from Nellie Conway?'

'That's right. How much is it going to cost to have this thing given a quick test?' Mason asked.

Drake said, smiling, 'Well, this man is broad-minded. He always takes into consideration the ability of a client to pay. I'll suggest to him that he wouldn't want to charge more than twenty-five per cent of the fee you're getting for the entire case, and that'll probably sound all right to him, and I guess two bits won't be too much for you to pay, eh, Perry?'

Mason made as if to throw a book at the detective and Drake dodged.

'Go on,' Mason told him. 'Get the hell out of here and go to work. How long will it take to tell what's in the pill?'

'I may be able to get it done in an hour.'

'Tell you what we'll do, Paul. Della and I will go out and put on the nosebags, then we'll come back and look in on you and then I'll drive Della home.'

'The way he talks,' Della Street said, 'you'd think a girl *never* had a date.'

'I beg your pardon,' Mason said. 'What do you have on for this evening, Della?'

'Well,' she said demurely, 'now that you bring it up that way, I haven't anything that I can't cancel in favour of a nice thick steak done medium rare, a stuffed, backed Idaho potato with lots of butter, some toasted French bread, a bottle of Tipo Chianti and–'

'Stop it!' Drake said. 'You're driving me nuts. I'm going to have to get by with a hamburger sandwich which I'll hold in one hand while I drink a cup of coffee with the other.'

'Don't let it worry you, Paul,' Mason said, grinning. 'That's just what she *wants*. What she gets may be different. I'll take her to a Chinese place and get her a bowl of white rice. Come on, Della, let's eat.'

Mason switched out the lights in the office and held the door open for Della. 'Another day,' he said.

Della Street held up the dollar note which Nellie Conway had given the lawyer, and said to Paul Drake, '*And* another dollar!'

3

An hour and a half later, Mason and Della Street, leaving the elevator, sauntered into Paul Drake's office, exchanged greetings with a girl at the night switchboard and then walked into Drake's private office.

'I haven't anything yet,' Drake said. 'I'm expecting something any moment.'

'How much of the tablet did you use, Paul?'

'Not much. This guy had a smart idea. He had a hair-like drill and bored a little hole right in the centre so he could get a cross-section right straight through. He had some other stuff he had to find out about on a rush order so that's what's causing the delay. He . . .'

The telephone rang. Drake reached for the receiver and said, 'This will probably be it.'

Drake said, 'Hello . . . Yes, this is Paul Drake . . . All right, go ahead.'

Drake flashed Mason a warning glance, then said, 'Well now, just a minute. Just hold the phone. I'll see if I have his number where he can be reached.'

Drake pushed his hand against the mouthpiece and said, 'This is your girl friend. She's all excited. She wants you right away. She says it's very, very important.'

'Oh-oh!' Mason said. 'This is it!'

'What do I do? Tell her . . .?'

'No,' Mason said. 'Tell her I just came in, that you'll try to find me.'

Drake said into the telephone, 'Well, I don't know where he is right at the moment. I have a number where I can reach him later on. If you could . . . Oh, wait a minute, there's somebody in the other office now. I think I hear Mason's voice . . . Oh, Mason! . . . Was that Mason who just came in? Well, tell him I want him . . . Yes, tell him there's a phone call for him.'

Drake waited a couple of seconds, then said, 'He just this moment came in. Just hold the line. I'll get him on the phone for you.'

Drake nodded to Mason, who took the telephone from the detective and said, 'Hello.'

Nellie Conway's voice, sharp with excitement, reached his ears. 'Oh, Mr Mason, something terrible, absolutely terrible, has happened! I must see you right away.'

'Where?' Mason asked. 'At my office?'

'No, no. I can't leave here. I'm not free to come. Please, can't you come out here right away? It's 1925 Monte Carlo Drive. I . . . oh . . .!'

With that sharp exclamation and with no word of good-bye, she dropped the receiver into place at the other end of the line, severing the connection.

Mason grinned at Paul Drake and said, 'Well, I guess I was right, Paul.'

'What?'

'It's a frame-up of some sort.'

'So what do you do?' Drake asked.

'It isn't what *I* do,' Mason said, 'it's what *we* do. Come on, Della, you're going to drive out with us. We may call you in, in case we want to have someone make a statement.'

'Don't you want me to wait for the call to find out what's in that tablet?' Drake asked.

'The tablet,' Mason said, 'will either be cyanide or arsenic. And in all probability Mrs Bain has just died. Come on, Paul, we're going out and discover a corpse.'

'And then what?'

'Then,' Mason said, 'I'll try to get myself extricated from a very nasty predicament. Nellie Conway will be proclaiming to all and sundry that she told me the whole story while Mrs Bain was still alive. People will think I'm a hell of a lawyer.'

'I don't get it,' Drake said. 'I simply can't see where all this is going to leave your client. It makes her look like . . . just what *is* her position, Perry?'

Mason said, 'All this little byplay leaves Nellie Conway in a position where she can accuse the husband of having administered the poison while she had her back turned, since she had refused to help him. Don't you see, the girl's given herself a perfect alibi. She's gone to the police and tried to get them to prevent a murder that was about to be committed; she's come to me and tried to get me to try to prevent a murder that was about to be committed, and then the murder is committed. My poker-faced client has given herself a beautiful alibi, or at least she thinks she has.'

'Perhaps she has at that,' Drake said.

'By making a goat out of me,' Mason said grimly. 'Come on, let's go.'

4

Della Street whipped Mason's car around corners, swerved in and out of traffic, making fast time, seldom putting on the brake to slow down, seldom pushing down hard on the throttle, managing despite traffic to maintain a steady, even speed.

Paul Drake, in the back seat, shook his head lugubriously. 'Sometimes I'd rather you'd drive, Perry.'

'You kicking again, Paul?' Della Street asked over her shoulder.

'Not kicking, just commenting,' Drake said.

Mason said, 'Paul just isn't accustomed to good driving, Della. He even kicks when *I* drive.'

'Can you imagine *that*?' Della Street exclaimed.

'Just like a taxicab in Paris,' Mason said. 'At first I used to think they went like hell. They don't. They just hit one speed and stay there. The French driver knows that if he puts his foot on the brake it's going to cut down on his gasoline mileage, and the same holds true if he puts his foot on the throttle, so he just goes about thirty miles an hour steady, no matter what's in front of him.'

'And you think I'm doing the same thing?' Della Street asked.

'Heaven forbid!' Drake interposed. 'You're hitting fifty and not giving a damn about anything.'

Della Street slowed. 'Well, I get you there in less time, so you don't suffer so long, Paul. Monte Carlo Drive should be along here somewhere. It's within the next . . .'

'Here it is,' Mason said.

Della Street swung the car to the right, still going fast enough so that the tyres screamed as she whipped around the corner.

Paul Drake made an exaggerated gesture of putting his hands over his eyes.

Della Street slid up to the big two-and-a-half-storey white house, with its lawn, hedge and wide verandas giving it the appearance of a country estate despite the fact that it was within thirty minutes of the centre of town.

'Do you want me to come in with you and bring a book?' she asked.

Mason said, 'No, Drake will be with me. We'll declare ourselves. How is it they say it, Paul?'

'In no uncertain terms,' Drake said.

'That's the stuff,' Mason told him. 'You wait here, Della. Keep the motor running. We may want to go places in a hurry.'

'Regular cops and robbers,' Della Street said, smiling. 'Don't let anybody sell you boys a bill of goods.'

'We'll try not to,' Mason promised, and, with Paul Drake trailing behind him, hurried up the cement walk, ran up the steps to the porch and pressed the bell button by the side of the door.

The porch light clicked on almost as soon as the chimes sounded, and the door swung open.

A short man, who seemed to be bursting from the seams, said, 'Well, it certainly didn't take *you* long to get here.'

Mason said cautiously, 'We didn't violate any speed laws. What seems to be the trouble?'

'Step right this way, please,' the man said.

He turned and led the way across a reception hall into a big living-room.

Mason studied the man's back. The coat was well-tailored but tight. The man's heels pounded the floor with the quick, energetic steps of impatience. Like many short, heavy men he seemed buzzing around in a continual atmosphere of hectic futility, trying to pound time into oblivion by sheer nervous hurry.

'Right in here,' he called over his shoulder. 'Right this way, please.'

He didn't even look back as he pushed his way through curtains and into a sumptuous living-room where everything seemed to have been carefully and systematically planned, a room which radiated the touch of an interior decorator. Each chair was in its proper place so that it balanced the mass and colour design of the room. The curtains had been pulled across the windows, but it was quite evident that the view was on the east, where the huge picture window was in the centre of the room with easy chairs and ottomans on each side.

Nellie Conway was standing near one corner, her eyes widened slightly. Aside from that her face held no trace of expression.

A tall, slender man, whose face had deep lines and who might have been fighting ulcers, was standing behind one of the overstuffed chairs, his forearms resting across the back of the chair, a cigarette dangling from the corner of his mouth. He seemed to be detached from the life in the room, wrapped only in the gloom of selfish dejection.

A woman of uncertain age, tall, gaunt, grim-faced, stood well back in the room. The room seemed to fit her exactly. It could have been her methodical, mathematical mind that had arranged the furniture with such careful precision and kept it so arranged.

She looked at Mason and for a moment her dark, inscrutable eyes locked with his, then she moved silently over to where Nellie Conway was sitting, placed a reassuring hand on her shoulder. 'I think it's going to come out all right, dear,' she said. 'Don't be frightened.' She gave Nellie a little pat, then turned and walked from the room.

'Mr Mason,' Nellie Conway said.

'Eh? How's that?' the fat man asked.

'This is Mr Bain, my employer,' she said.

'Eh? What's that? Who the hell is this?' Bain asked.

Nellie Conway went on talking to Mason without paying the slightest attention to Nathan Bain.

'Mr Bain is my employer,' she explained. 'He has just had the temerity to accuse me of theft. This *gentleman* on the right is a private detective who seems to have been working on my case for some little time without doing me the courtesy of letting me know anything about it, and the police, I believe, are on their way.'

'How's this?' Bain asked, whirling to Perry Mason. 'Aren't you the police?'

The man Nellie Conway had described as a private detective said, dispiritedly, without moving the cigarette from its position, 'Perry Mason, the famous criminal lawyer. That's Paul Drake with him, head of the Drake Detective Agency. Does most of Mason's work. Hello, Drake.'

Drake said, 'I don't think I place you.'

'Jim Hallock.'

'Oh yes. I place you now,' Drake said without cordiality.

'What seems to be the trouble?' Mason asked.

'What the devil are you doing here?' Bain demanded. 'I called the police.'

'Thought I'd drop in and see what the trouble was.'

'Well, where do *you* fit into the picture?'

Mason said, 'Miss Conway asked me to call.'

'Nellie?'

'That's right.'

'You mean Nellie Conway asked *you* to call here?'

'That's right.'

'For Heaven's sake, why?'

'Because,' Nellie Conway said, 'I'm tired of being pushed around. You're trying to frame a crime on me and I don't propose to be framed. Mr Mason is my attorney.'

'Well, I'll be damned!' Bain said, and sat down abruptly in one of the occasional chairs, looking at Mason with gimlet eyes that had been pushed back into his head by the layers of fat that had grown around them.

Jim Hallock shifted his position enough to remove the cigarette and shake ashes from it casually on the expensive carpet. 'She must have phoned Mason when she said she wanted to run upstairs and see how her patient was getting along,' he explained to Bain.

'Mason! Perry Mason, employed by a cheap crook like this!' Bain said. 'I can't believe it. It's preposterous.'

'It's nothing to me,' Hallock said to Bain. 'You're the one who's doing it, but I think I'd qualify that "cheap crook" business. We haven't proved anything yet and . . .'

'The hell we haven't proved anything yet. We've caught the thief. We've caught her red-handed.'

Hallock shrugged his shoulders and said, 'That's what I *thought*.'

'Well, it's so, isn't it?'

Hallock said nothing, merely stood there, leaning over the back of the big, overstuffed reading chair, as though smiling inwardly at some joke which appealed to him very much indeed. 'I guess you've never seen Mason in court,' he said.

'I don't get this,' Bain said.

'I think,' Mason told him, 'that if someone will explain, we may clarify the situation.'

'Are you representing Nellie Conway?' Bain demanded.

'Not yet,' Mason told him.

'Why, yes, you are too, Mr Mason. I paid you a retainer. I have your receipt.'

'That was in another matter,' Mason said dryly. 'What seems to be the trouble here?'

Hallock said to Bain, 'You don't need to talk if you don't want to. The police are coming here. They'll take charge.'

Bain sputtered angrily, 'I'll tell the whole story if I want to. All of a sudden,

I seem to be the one that's on the defensive. *I* haven't anything to hide. My wife is sick, Mr Mason. Nellie is the night nurse. She's not a trained nurse, just a practical nurse. Lately we've been losing jewellery and some cash. Personally, I suspected Nellie right from the first. But before I did anything I consulted Mr Hallock, employed him as a detective. I wanted to get *proof*. I was only too well aware that any false accusation on my part might expose me to a suit for damages. A certain type of individual goes around looking for openings like that.'

'I think that's unfair,' Nellie Conway said.

Bain paid no attention, but went on, 'Hallock had some very practical suggestions. We removed most of the really valuable pieces from my wife's jewel box and substituted imitations. Then we dusted the jewel box with a fluorescent powder so that if anyone touched that box some of the fluorescent powder would adhere to the fingers. Then we took pains to take the jewel box out of my wife's desk and leave it on top of the desk as though we'd overlooked putting it back. We made a complete inventory of the contents of the jewel box, Mr Mason. All of the jewels were imitations but it was such an expensive jewel case no one would ever have thought the jewels were other than genuine.

'This afternoon Hallock and I again made an inventory of the contents of the jewel box. Nothing was missing. Tonight, when the day nurse went off duty, we once more checked the contents of the jewel box. Everything was in its place.

'About half an hour ago, when Nellie came down here to fix some hot malted milk for my wife, she was gone quite a long time. We purposely gave her an opportunity to be alone and undisturbed. Then we entered the room after she'd taken the hot malted milk upstairs, and inventoried the contents of the box. A diamond pendant was missing, so we called Nellie down here, turned off the lights and switched on some ultra-violet light. The results were all that anyone could have asked.

'I don't know how that stuff got on my fingers,' Nellie said.

'Was there fluorescent powder on your fingers?' Mason asked.

Bain said, 'See for yourself,' and, with the self-importance of a showman who is putting on a good act, he marched over to the light switch and jabbed it with his thumb. Instantly the room was plunged in darkness. Then he pushed another switch. There was a buzzing noise and after a second the room was filled with ultra-violet light.

'Show the gentleman your hands, Nellie,' Bain said with sarcasm.

Nellie Conway held up her hands. The finger-tips were flaming with iridescent light that had a peculiar bluish-green tinge and was exceedingly brilliant.

'There you are,' Bain said. 'Try and laugh *that* off.'

He switched the ultra-violet light off and the room lights back on.

Nellie Conway turned pleadingly to Perry Mason. 'Can't you see,' she said, 'this is all a–a part of that thing I was telling you about.'

Nathan Bain said, 'Let's get this straight, please. You're here representing Nellie. Is that right, Mr Mason?'

'She asked me to come.'

'And this gentleman with you is . . .?'

'Mason's detective,' Jim Hallock interposed. 'I warned you, Bain.'

'I see no reason why either of you gentlemen have any right to intrude upon these premises,' Bain said. 'I'm going to ask you to leave.'

Mason said, 'I'm a little dubious about whether Miss Conway is a client, Bain, but I'm not particularly impressed with *your* attitude.'

'You don't have to be impressed with my attitude. This woman is a thief and . . .'

'Just a minute,' Jim Hallock interrupted. 'Let's not jump at conclusions, Mr Bain, if you don't mind. There has been a series of jewel thefts. We're asking the police to investigate. There's certain evidence that Miss Conway will be called on to explain.'

'That's it,' Bain interposed hastily. 'I'm not convicting her before she's tried. I've simply set a trap for her and she's . . . she's got that stuff all over her fingers.'

Hallock smiled sceptically. 'That's better, but it's too late to do any good.'

Bain turned to Nellie Conway. 'I don't see what you think you have to gain, Nellie. After all, I could bring myself to be lenient with you if you would make restitution, and . . .'

He broke off as the door-bell rang, and, saying to Hallock, 'Keep an eye on them, Jim,' he ran to the door, his short legs working like pistons. A moment later he called, 'Well, here are the police. Now we'll see who's running this show.'

The police needed no introductions. Bain, having made a brief explanation in the reception corridor, ushered the two uniformed radio officers into the room, and they immediately made their presence felt.

'Okay,' one of the men said. 'We'll dispense with the attorney and his stooge and see what this girl has to say for herself.'

Mason said to Nellie Conway, 'If that's the way they want it, don't say a word. That fluorescent powder is nice stuff but it doesn't actually *prove* anything. It's used in cases of petty crimes to trap a person and fill him with dismay at the idea of being caught with the evidence clinging to his fingers. A person usually becomes tearfully repentant under such circumstances and confesses.'

'Shut up,' one of the officers said to Mason. 'Bain wants you to go home. It's his house.'

'If it's an attempt to frame an innocent person it won't stand up in front of a jury,' Mason went on, still talking to Nellie Conway. 'Now mind what I'm telling you, the case won't stand up and . . .'

'That's enough,' the officer said, moving belligerently forward.

Mason turned his eyes to the officer. 'I'm advising a client,' he said.

'I want them out,' Mr Bain said. 'They have no business being here.'

'You heard what the man said. Out!'

Mason said, 'Right at the moment I'm trying to advise my client.'

'Well, you can advise her some place else.'

'And,' Mason said, turning back to Nellie Conway, 'don't let them kid you into believing that this is any serious crime. The most they can charge you with is petty larceny.'

'What do you mean, petty larceny?' Bain sputtered. 'Why, my wife's diamond pendant was worth five thousand dollars. It's . . .'

'Sure,' Mason said, 'but you outsmarted yourself. You put cheap imitations in the jewel box. It's the imitation that's missing. How much is that worth?'

'Why . . . I . . . How do you know it isn't the real pendant?'

'Don't get in an argument with him,' one of the officers said. 'Come on,

Mason, on your way. You can advise your client after she's booked at police headquarters.'

'Can you keep quiet?' Mason asked Nellie Conway.

'If you tell me to.'

The officers grabbed Mason and Paul Drake, pushed them out of the door.

'Don't say a word,' Mason cautioned over his shoulder.

'Come on, buddy. Make it snappy,' the officer said.

'Not even about . . . about that other matter?' Nellie Conway called after him.

'Don't talk, period,' Mason shouted back as the officer propelled him out of the front door.

'Well?' Della Street asked, as Drake and Mason approached the car. 'It looked as though you went out on your ear.'

'That made me mad,' Mason said. 'Just for that I *am* going to represent Nellie Conway, and Bain will wish he had never ordered those cops to give us the bum's rush.'

'What happened?' Della asked. 'Who was murdered? The wife?'

'No murder,' Mason said, 'just a case of petty theft, and some smart private detective has been using fluorescent powder. I think I'm going to have to teach that pair a lesson.'

'Specifically what are we going to do?' Della Street asked.

'Specifically,' Mason said, 'we're going to follow that police car. When they take Nellie Conway to jail we're going to bail her out.'

'And then what?'

'And then,' Mason said, 'Paul Drake is going to telephone his chemist friend. We're going to find out just what particular brand of poison Nathan Bain was trying to get Nellie to administer to his sick wife. From that point on there's going to be hell to pay.'

'You mean you'll call the police?'

Mason smiled and said, 'No. I'll represent Nellie Conway in a petty larceny case just for the pleasure it will give me to cross-examine Mr Nathan Bain.'

'Will they bring her right out?' Della Street asked.

'If she follows my advice and refuses to talk, they're pretty sure to bring her right out. If they can get her talking, or trying to explain things, the situation may be a little different.'

Paul Drake said, 'We don't really need to follow that police car, Perry. We could just go on to headquarters and wait for them there.'

'And have her taken to some outlying precinct where we wouldn't know where she was,' Mason said. 'I've had 'em do that before.'

'In murder cases,' Paul Drake said.

'They may do it in *this* case.'

'Nuts. You've never monkeyed with this small stuff, Perry. They may not even charge her.'

'Big oaks grow from tiny acorns,' Mason said cryptically.

'Meaning what?' Drake asked.

'Meaning Nellie planted something,' Mason told him. 'I can feel it sprouting.'

They were silent for a few minutes.

'We can't follow that police car without getting into trouble,' Drake pointed out. 'They'll use their siren and–'

'We'll make a stab at it,' Mason told him. 'Somehow I don't think they'll burn up the road. They may try to get nice and friendly with Nellie on the way to jail so that she'll talk. If she–'

'Here they come now,' Della Street interrupted.

'Move over,' Mason told her. 'Let me get behind that wheel, Della. This may be the kind of driving that Paul *really* likes.'

'Have a heart, Perry,' Drake pleaded.

The officers escorted Nellie Conway down to the radio car. One of the officers walked over to where Mason's car was parked and said, 'No need for you to stick around, Mason. Bain is going to follow us in his car and sign a complaint. He doesn't want to talk with you and we don't want to talk with him. Get smart and go home.'

'I am smart,' Mason said.

'All right. On your way then.'

Mason looked around at the kerb and said, 'I don't see it.'

'Don't see what?'

'The fire-plug.'

'What fire-plug?'

'The way you were ordering me away I thought that I must have parked in front of a fire-plug. However, I don't see it and there seems to be no parking limit in this–'

'Okay, wise guy. See where it gets you,' the officer said, and walked back to his car.

A few moments later a car came rolling out of the driveway and blinked its lights. The officers started their car and drove down the street. Bain's car fell in behind and Mason tagged on behind Bain.

Forty minutes later Nellie Conway was out on a two-thousand-dollar bail bond furnished by Perry Mason.

Then the lawyer walked upstairs and into the office of Homicide to encounter Sergeant Holcomb.

'I think you overlooked a bet on that Conway woman,' Mason said.

'You usually do feel that way.' Sergeant Holcomb seemed to be chortling inwardly.

'I'm warning you that you'd better look into it.'

'I've already looked into it,' Holcomb said, grinning. 'In fact, I happen to know all about it. Bain and I have met, and when he began to suspect Nellie Conway of stealing cash and jewellery, he phoned me for advice.

'I'm the one who told him to get Jim Hallock and use fluorescent powder, and catch her red-handed–and that's just what he did.

'She evidently got wise. Bain had her under suspicion and she decided she'd plant an alibi by accusing him of trying to murder his wife. In that way he wouldn't dare to prosecute her.

'And you, the smart lawyer, walked right into the trap!'

Holcomb threw back his head and laughed. 'For a man who's supposed to have been around, you do the damnedest things. You fell for that little tramp's story. Ha-ha-ha!'

Mason said, 'Don't be too sure. The shoe may be on the *other* foot. When Bain knew she wasn't going to give the poison to his wife, *he* decided to discredit *her*.'

'Oh, nuts,' Sergeant Holcomb said. 'When Nellie knew he was getting on to her, she went and cooked up this story and got some tablets she claimed Bain was trying to get her to administer to his wife. I'd personally be willing to bet even money they're just props to back up her story, and that she grabbed 'em out of the first bottle she found in the bathroom. Nine chances out of ten they're aspirin tablets. That's what they looked like to me.

'Hell, Mason, figure it out. Would Bain be so dumb, even if he wanted his wife to have pills, to give them to a woman he was about to arrest for theft, and put himself in *her* power?'

And Holcomb once more threw back his head and roared with laughter. At length he calmed enough to say, 'Don't let that little minx hypnotise you with a yarn that will arouse your sympathies, Mason. If you're going to be her lawyer, get your fee in advance, and in cash.'

'Thank you so much,' Mason said, and walked out.

Holcomb's booming laughter followed him down the hallway.

Mason rejoined Della Street and drove back to Drake's office.

Paul Drake, who had gone back by taxicab, was waiting for them. He handed Mason a graph some eighteen inches long, consisting of a long period of wavy lines running up into high peaks, down into troughs.

'What's that?' Mason asked.

'That's the way these X-ray defractors do their analysis. Here's the note from the chemist. He says:

'"Dear Paul:

'"The graph is very distinctive. There's no question on earth but what the tablet you gave me consists of acetylsalicylic acid. I'm returning the tablet herewith, with a little hole drilled in the centre."'

'Acetylsalicylic acid!' Della Street exclaimed. 'What's that?'

'That,' Mason said, 'is exactly what Sergeant Holcomb said was in it.'

'Well, what *is* it?' Della Street asked impatiently.

'Acetylsalicylic acid,' Drake said, 'is the chemical name for the active ingredient in good old-fashioned aspirin.'

'Come on,' Mason said. 'Let's go home. We're all washed up–I can't withdraw from that Conway case now. I'll have to defend her. One thing, Paul, slap a subpoena on that housekeeper as a witness for the defence. That'll give Bain something to worry about. This has been the sort of day I *don't* like.'

'Better take this pill along with you, Perry,' Drake observed, grinning. 'It's swell for headaches!'

5

Harry Saybrook, the deputy District Attorney, seemed definitely annoyed that an ordinary petty larceny case had been turned into a jury trial, and his annoyance manifested itself in everything that he said and did.

Perry Mason, on the other hand, was urbane, fair, logical, and smilingly frank to the jury.

Judge Peabody from time to time cocked a quizzical eyebrow in Mason's direction as the noted criminal lawyer sat calmly complacent while James Hallock, private detective, testified that he had been employed by Mr Nathan

Bain, that he had understood generally a whole series of small thefts had been taking place at Nathan Bain's house, and that as a result the witness had secured a neutral coloured powder which would fluoresce to a vivid blue-green colour when exposed to ultra-violet light. He had placed this powder all over a jewel box in which certain articles of jewellery were being kept.

The witness further testified that he had been in the house when the defendant, who was employed as a practical nurse, had come to work on the evening of the tenth. He had, he explained, been introduced to the defendant as a business acquaintance who was selling Mr Bain some mining property.

The witness further testified that in company with Mr Bain he had previously made an inventory of articles contained in the jewel case. The articles, so far as he had seen, were pieces of jewellery. He had made no attempt to ascertain their value. Later on he had been given to understand that they were pieces of costume jewellery. However, at the time of his first examination the witness had contented himself with making a rough pencilled sketch of each article of jewellery and general description of the article.

At the time the defendant had come to work on the evening of the tenth he had examined the jewel case and had found every article which he had inventoried to be intact. Two hours later, at the request of Mr Bain, he had made another inventory of the jewel box and had found that one of the articles, a diamond and pearl pendant, was missing. That thereupon, at the suggestion of Mr Bain, they called the defendant into the living-room; that at a pre-arranged signal the ordinary incandescent bulbs had been switched off and the room had been flooded with powerful ultra-violet light; that under the influence of this light the fingers of the defendant showed as a fiery bluish-green.

Harry Saybrook turned to the jury and nodded, as much as to say, 'So you see, it's as simple as that.'

When Saybrook had assured himself that the jurors had fully realised the damning nature of Hallock's testimony, he turned to Perry Mason with something of a challenge and said, 'You may cross-examine, Mr Mason.'

On the witness stand, Jim Hallock braced himself for the abusive cross-examination which attorneys for accused persons usually heaped upon the head of a private detective.

'Why,' Mason said, apparently with some surprise, 'I have no questions,' and then, turning to the jury, added with the utmost candour, 'I think this man is telling the truth.'

'What?' Saybrook exclaimed in surprise.

'I think he's telling the simple truth,' Mason said. 'What's so surprising about that, Counsellor?'

'Nothing, nothing,' Saybrook blurted. 'I'll call my next witness, Nathan Bain.'

Nathan Bain marched to the witness stand and under Saybrook's question told his story. His wife was sick. It had been necessary to employ a day nurse and a night nurse. The case did not require trained nurses working in eight-hour shifts since there was a housekeeper to lend a hand on occasion, so Bain had hired two practical nurses, a day nurse and a night nurse. The defendant had been the night nurse.

Shortly after the nurses had started work certain things began to disappear around the house, small sums of cash, liquor, items of jewellery. Bain made a point of stating that he couldn't be certain that it was more than a coincidence, so far as the defendant was concerned. But he decided to set a trap. He had taken his wife's jewel case from the desk where it was usually kept, and had purchased articles of costume jewellery which had then been placed in the jewel box. The witness had then consulted James Hallock, the witness who had just testified. At Hallock's suggestion a fluorescent powder had been placed upon the box. The box had then been left on the writing desk as though someone had inadvertently neglected to return it to the interior of the desk.

Then Bain went on to describe the events of the evening of the tenth with particular detail.

Perry Mason yawned.

'Do you wish to cross-examine *this* witness?' Saybrook asked.

Mason hesitated just long enough so that Bain, feeling he was to escape without question, started to arise from the witness chair, then Mason said, 'Just a moment, Mr Bain, I do have one or two questions I want to ask you.'

'Yes, sir,' Mr Bain said.

'When was this fluorescent powder placed upon the jewel case, Mr Bain?'

'On the tenth.'

'At what time?'

'About nine o'clock in the morning.'

'The day nurse then was already on the job?'

'Yes, sir.'

'Who placed the powder on the box?'

'Mr Hallock did.'

'And you stood by and watched him?'

'I did. Yes, sir.'

'And previously you had placed these articles of costume jewellery in the jewel case?'

'Yes, sir.'

'What type of jewel case was that, Mr Bain?'

'It was a casket made in the form of an ancient trunk, covered with leather and studded with silver nails, with leather handles on each side.'

'About what were the dimensions?'

'It was rather a large jewel case. I would say about fifteen inches by ten inches by ten inches.'

'It was the property of your wife?'

'Yes, I'd given it to her for Christmas a year ago.'

'And prior to the time the fluorescent powder was dusted on this jewel case, you had taken an inventory of the contents in company with Mr Hallock?'

'Yes, sir. We did that together.'

'Then the costume jewellery, or the imitation jewellery, was replaced in the casket, and then the casket was dusted with powder. Is that right?'

'That's right. Yes, sir.'

'Now, did you have occasion to investigate that jewel box or casket during the day in order to see if the day nurse had taken something.

'I did. Yes, sir.'

'How many times?'

'Twice.'

'When?'

'About two o'clock in the afternoon and then at six o'clock, shortly before the day nurse went off duty.'

'And then you investigated it again in the evening?'

'Yes, sir.'

'How many times?'

'Twice.'

'When?'

'Immediately after the defendant came on duty so that we knew nothing was missing at that time, and then again about two hours later–which was when we found that one of the articles of jewellery was missing.'

'Who made the examination?'

'Mr Hallock and I.'

'Who opened the jewel case, Mr Bain?'

'I did.'

'Do you mean that you left this jewel case lying around in plain sight with no lock?'

'No, sir, it was locked.'

'And it was kept locked?'

'Yes, sir.'

'Then how could anything have been missing?'

'The thief either had a duplicate key, which was not an impossibility, or the lock was picked, which would not have been difficult.'

'I see. Mr Hallock didn't have a key to the jewel case?'

'No, sir.'

'You had a key?'

'Yes, sir.'

'And your wife had a key?'

'Yes, sir.'

'You weren't using your wife's key then?'

'No, sir.'

'How did you happen to have a key to your wife's jewel box?'

'It was simply a matter of precaution, Mr Mason.'

'I'm afraid I don't understand.'

'Women are always losing things,' Bain said, rather self-righteously, 'so as a matter of precaution against having my wife lose the key to her jewel box, I only gave her one key when I gave her the box. I retained one key in a safe place.'

'Oh, I see,' Mason said, with a swift glance at the five women who were on the jury. 'You felt that the reserve key would be safe in your possession and would guard against your wife's negligence?'

'Yes, sir.'

'That your wife would naturally be inclined to lose her key?'

'Well, I thought she might.'

'As you expressed it, I believe, you have rather a contempt for the ability of woman to keep things?'

'Just a moment, Your Honour,' Saybrook shouted and jumped to his feet. 'The witness didn't say that at all.'

'I certainly understood him to say that,' Mason said. 'Perhaps not in those words, Counsellor, but–'

'If you're going to cross-examine the witness use his own words,' Saybrook said.

Mason smiled and shook his head. 'I know of no rule of law that requires me to do that, Mr Saybrook. I simply ask the witness questions on cross-examination. The witness can correct me if I'm wrong. I certainly understood his testimony to be that he was rather contemptuous of the ability of women to be trusted with responsibilities, and I think the jury will bear me out in that.'

And Mason flashed a quick glance at the jury.

'The witness didn't say any such thing,' Saybrook said.

'Well, now,' Mason said magnanimously, 'I'm going to be the first to apologise if I misunderstood him. It's only a few pages back in the record, Counsellor, and I'm going to ask the court reporter to read back exactly what the witness said.'

Saybrook, suddenly realising that Mason's tactics had been in the nature of a bait which had caused him to make an issue of what otherwise might have been passed over, and was now serving to emphasise it to the jury, said, 'Oh well, there's no use wasting all that time. I'll withdraw the objection. The jurors will remember what the witness said and I know they're not going to let you put words in the witness's mouth or–'

'Not at all, not at all,' Mason said. 'I'm now interested in knowing exactly what the witness did say and I'm going to apologise to him if I've misunderstood what he said.'

'Well, I didn't *mean* that,' Bain interposed uncomfortably.

'You didn't mean what?' Mason asked.

'That women weren't to be trusted with things.'

'I thought that was what you said.'

'I didn't say anything of the sort.'

'Well, now,' Mason said, 'let's have the record read by the court reporter.'

Judge Peabody said, 'All right, gentlemen, if you'll just keep quiet now so the court reporter can search back in his notes, he'll find the testimony in question.'

There was a tense silence in the court-room. Saybrook found outlet for his nervous energy by running his hand through his thick black hair. He didn't like the turn that events were taking.

Bain sat self-righteously erect on the witness stand, waiting to be vindicated.

Mason settled back easily in his chair, waiting with the respectfully attentive attitude of the man who feels that the information which is about to be forthcoming is of the greatest importance.

The court reporter said, 'Here it is. I'll read the question and answer:

"MR MASON: How did you happen to have a key to your wife's jewel box?
ANSWER: It was simply a matter of precaution, Mr Mason.
QUESTION: I'm afraid I don't understand.
ANSWER: Women are always losing things, so as a matter of precaution against having my wife lose the key to her jewel box, I only gave her one key when I gave her the box. I retained one key in a safe place.
QUESTION: Oh, I see. You felt that that reserve key would be safe in your possession and would guard against your wife's negligence?
ANSWER: Yes, sir.
QUESTION: That your wife would naturally be inclined to lose her key?
ANSWER: Well, I thought she might.
QUESTION: As you expressed it, I believe, you have rather a contempt for the ability of women to keep things?"'

Bain squirmed uncomfortably on the witness stand as the court reporter finished reading.

'I thought that's what you said,' Mason observed. 'It was, wasn't it?'

'Well, it wasn't what I meant,' Bain snapped.

'Oh, then you said something you didn't mean?'

'Yes, sir.'

'Under oath?'

'Well, it was a slip of the tongue.'

'What do you mean by a slip of the tongue, Mr Bain? Did you say something that wasn't true?'

'Well, I said something that . . . I said it without thinking.'

'Without thinking of what?'

'Well, I was only trying to say that my wife has a habit of losing things and . . .'

'And you did generalise by stating that that was a trait that women had generally?'

'Oh, Your Honour,' Saybrook said, making his voice weary with exasperation. 'Surely this is a minor matter. Good Lord, we've been over it time and time and time again. The question is already asked and answered in the record *ad nauseam.*'

'I don't think so,' Mason said. 'I think that it's rather important to find out what attitude this witness may have, not only toward women generally, because my client is a woman, but also I'm particularly interested in finding out what's in the back of his mind when he states on cross-examination that he made statements he didn't mean. I'd like to find out how many *other* things in his testimony may have been incorrect.'

'Nothing in his testimony is incorrect,' Saybrook shouted.

'You mean then the witness really does feel that women are not to be trusted with responsibility?' Mason asked.

A few of the scattered spectators in the court-room laughed. Judge Peabody smiled and said, 'Well, Mr Mason, I think you've made your point.'

'But I certainly desire to cross-examine this witness as to just what he means by what he says, Your Honour.'

'Go ahead,' Judge Peabody said.

'Is that the only thing in your testimony that is incorrect?' Mason asked.

'That isn't incorrect.'

'Oh, you meant every word you said then?'

'Yes, I meant it,' Bain shouted.

'I thought you did,' Mason said, smiling. 'Now let's be frank, Mr Bain. After you realised that your statement might offend some of the women on the jury you tried to change it, but actually you meant it. Isn't that a fact?'

'Your Honour, I object,' Saybrook shouted. 'That's not proper cross-examination, and–'

'It goes to show the biased attitude of the witness,' Mason said, 'and is a reflection on his credibility.'

'The objection is overruled. The witness may answer,' Judge Peabody said.

'Isn't that it?' Mason asked.

'All right, if that's the way you want it, have it that way,' Bain snapped angrily.

'Come, come,' Mason said, soothingly. 'It's not the way *I* want it, Mr Bain. I'm simply trying to find out something about your mental processes. Isn't it a fact that you made this statement rather heedlessly without considering its possible effect and . . .?'

'All right, I did. So what?'

'Nothing, nothing,' Mason said, 'I'm simply trying to get your frame of mind, your attitude. You meant what you said and you said what you meant, but when you realised the remark might have been impolite you tried to pass it off as a slip of the tongue. Is that right?'

'That's right.'

'So it really wasn't a slip of the tongue, it was the truth. Is *that* right?'

'That's right.'

'So you were stating an untruth when you said it was a slip of the tongue?'

'Call it a slip of the mind,' Bain snapped.

'Thank you,' Mason said, 'now let's get back to the facts in the case.'

'It's about time,' Saybrook commented, his tone showing extreme weariness.

Mason smiled at him. 'I'm sorry if I've bored you, Counsellor.'

'That will do,' Judge Peabody announced. 'There will be no interchange between counsel. Confine your remarks to the court and your questions to the witness, Mr Mason.'

'Very well, Your Honour,' Mason said cheerfully. 'now you want the jury to understand, Mr Bain, that you yourself opened this jewel casket to look in it shortly after the defendant came on duty that night.'

'I did. Yes, sir.'

'You had your key?'

'Yes, sir.'

'By the way, did you tell your wife that you had an extra key?'

'No, sir. I did not.'

'Indeed,' Mason said. 'Why not?'

'Objected to as incompetent, irrelevant, and immaterial, and not proper cross-examination,' Saybrook said.

'The objection is sustained,' Judge Peabody ruled.

'But,' Mason said, 'you *did* have a key to your wife's jewel casket and you carefully kept that information from her. Isn't that right?'

'That isn't right,' Saybrook shouted. 'Your Honour, Counsel is deliberately distorting the testimony of this witness. He never said any such thing.'

'I'm asking him now,' Mason said. 'He can answer that question yes or no.'

'The objection is overruled,' Judge Peabody said. 'I'll permit an answer to that one question. I think we've gone over the matter several times but nevertheless I will permit the witness to answer this one question.'

Bain hesitated.

'Yes or no?' Mason asked. 'Is it a fact or isn't it?'

'Well, I didn't carefully keep the information from her.'

'You kept it from her?' Mason suggested.

'Yes, I did,' Bain snapped.

'You want the jury to understand that you kept it from her carelessly and negligently, that you simply overlooked mentioning it to her?'

'Well, I . . . I just wanted to have the extra key, then I'd surprise her in case she lost her key and couldn't find it. I . . .'

'But she never did lose her key, did she, Mr Bain?'

'Not that I know of, no.'

'And you feel that you would have known of it if she had lost it?'

'I suppose so.'

'Then,' Mason said, smiling, 'you have to admit that your comments as to your wife's inefficiency in such matters were not well-founded.'

'Objection,' Saybrook shouted. 'That's–'

'Sustained,' Judge Peabody said. 'I think we've gone into this matter far enough, Mr Mason.'

'Very well, Your Honour,' Mason said. 'I have just a couple more questions.'

Mason shifted his position in the swivel chair at the counsel table and, catching the eye of one of the women members of the jury, let his face soften into a half smile.

The woman promptly smiled back.

Mason said, 'Now, let's see, Mr Bain. You opened that jewel case and I understand that when you did Mr Hallock was there with you?'

'Yes, sir.'

'And you pointed out that something was missing?'

'Yes, sir.'

'And Mr Hallock compared the contents of the jewel box with his list?'

'Yes, sir.'

'Now, how was Mr Hallock able to do that without touching the jewel box?'

'I never said he did it without touching the jewel box,' Bain said. 'Don't put words in my mouth!'

'Oh, then he *did* touch the jewel box?'

'I suppose so. He naturally would have. I didn't say he did, and I didn't say he didn't.'

'But your best recollection now is that he did?'

'He may have.'

'Do you know whether he did or not?'

'I assume that he did.'

'So,' Mason said, 'after the fluorescent powder had been placed on the jewel box *you* touched the jewel box and *Mr Hallock* touched the jewel box.'

'Yes.'

'So presumably at that time you and Mr Hallock both had fluorescent powder on your fingers.'

'I assume so. Yes.'

'There were three people in the downstairs part of the house. All three of you had fluorescent powder on your finger-tips. You, Mr Hallock and the defendant. Is that right?'

'Hallock and I had a right to have the fluorescent powder on our finger-tips. The defendant didn't.'

'What do you mean, you had a right to?'

'We had a right to go to the jewel box.'

'Certainly,' Mason said, 'but if you are going to rely on the assumption that the fluorescent powder on a person's finger-tips meant that a piece of imitation jewellery had been stolen, you could say that since Mr Hallock had the fluorescent powder on his finger-tips that he had taken the piece of jewellery.'

'Certainly not.'

'Why not?'

'Because he wouldn't have.'

'How do you know he wouldn't?'

'He was there for the purpose of preventing the theft.'

'Oh, come, come,' Mason said. 'Not for the purpose of preventing the theft. You put the imitation jewellery in there because you felt some was going to be stolen. You left the jewel casket in a place where it was plainly obvious. In other words, you were baiting a trap. You *wanted* some of the jewellery to be stolen, didn't you?'

'Well, I thought we could catch the thief that way.'

'Exactly,' Mason said. 'So, for all you know, Hallock may have gone to the jewel box and taken out that piece of jewellery.'

'He didn't have a key to it.'

'Neither did the defendant, did she?'

'I suppose she must have.'

'Simply because you assume that she took the article of jewellery?'

'Well, she must have got into it in some way.'

'And you had a key?' Mason said.

'I've told you I did a dozen times.'

'And you might have gone to the jewel box and taken out that article of jewellery.'

'I didn't.'

'I'm not suggesting that you did,' Mason said. 'I am simply saying that you might have done so. You had the opportunity.'

'Yes.'

'And,' Mason said, 'you didn't put the fluorescent powder on the *inside* of that jewel box? You put it on the outside?'

'That's right.'

'So that if the defendant had simply moved the jewel case for the purpose of getting at something that was behind it, or if she had inadvertently touched it, she would have had this powder on her fingers.'

'Well, she had it on her fingers.'

'I understand,' Mason said, 'but she could have got that on her fingers simply by touching the outside of the jewel case in an attempt to reach for something back of the jewel case–perhaps to pick up a magazine or–'

'There weren't any magazines around it.'

'Just where was it, by the way?' Mason asked.

'Out on top of the writing desk.'

'Was that where your wife usually left it?'

'No.'

'Where did she usually leave it?'

'It was usually kept inside the writing desk.'

'And the desk was kept locked?'

'I believe my wife kept it locked. Yes, sir.'

'And did *you* have a key to *that* desk?'

The witness hesitated.

'Yes or no?' Mason snapped.

'Yes.'

'Did you give that desk to your wife for Christmas?'

'No, sir.'

'That desk was bought some time ago as part of the household furniture?'

'That's right.'

'Your wife had a key to it?'

'Yes.'

'And you had a duplicate key?'

'Yes.'

'Did your wife know you had that duplicate key?'

'I don't know.'

'You had retained a duplicate key to the desk without telling your wife that you had it?'

'I never said I didn't tell my wife.'

'You said that you didn't know whether she knew that you had a key.'

'Well, I can't remember whether I told her or not.'

'I see,' Mason said, smiling. 'You made it a point to keep a key to your wife's writing desk, and then when you wanted to, shall we say, find some method of discharging the defendant in disgrace, you took the jewel case out of the desk and placed in on top of the desk in an inviting position?'

'Well, I wanted to get the thing cleared up one way or another.'

'That jewel case was rather unusual in appearance, wasn't it?'

'Yes, sir.'

'A woman would naturally want to look at it?'

'Well . . . Nellie Conway wouldn't have any business doing it.'

'A woman who was living in the house, who was there, seeing this rather beautiful jewel case on top of a desk might not have had occasion to look at it?'

'Well, she wouldn't have had occasion to *touch* it.'

'But if she had touched it, just to have felt the leather,' Mason said, 'she would have got this fluorescent powder on her fingers?'

'Yes.'

'Now, when the defendant was arrested, you went to headquarters to sign a complaint?'

'Yes.'

'So the defendant was taken from the house, and you went from the house. Did that leave your wife there all alone?'

'No, sir. I called the housekeeper, Mrs Ricker, and asked her to sit with my wife until I could get back and get a relief nurse.'

'Did you explain to Mrs Ricker the reason it was necessary to call her?'

'Yes.'

'Tell her you had had Miss Conway arrested?'

'Words to that effect.'

'And she was willing to take on this extra work?'

'She certainly was. She was glad we'd caught the thief. She told me she'd been wondering all day why that jewel case had been left out of the desk. She said she'd tried to put it back in the desk twice, but the desk had been locked.'

'Oh, *she'd* tried to put it back?'

'So she said.'

'Then *she* must have picked it up after the fluorescent powder had been put on it?'

'Objected to,' Saybrook snapped, 'argumentative, calling for a conclusion of the witness, not proper cross-examination.'

'Sustained,' the judge said.

Mason smiled at Bain. 'But you didn't examine the housekeeper's hands under ultra-violet light?'

'No.'

'In the name of reason,' Mason said, 'why didn't you put that fluorescent powder on the inside of the jewel box case so that–'

'I don't know,' Bain blurted. 'That was all Hallock's idea. He handled that part of it.'

'But you assisted him, didn't you?'

'I watched him.'

'You were there and saw him do it?'

'Yes.'

'And you were his employer? If you had told him that you wanted the fluorescent powder on the inside he would necessarily have had to follow your instructions.'

'I don't know.'

'But you were paying him?'

'Yes.'

'By the day?'

'Well, I offered him a bonus.'

'Oh,' Mason said, 'you offered him a bonus. What was the bonus for, Mr Bain?'

'Well, I agreed to pay him so much a day and then if he cleared the job up satisfactorily I'd pay him a bonus.'

'You'd pay him a bonus. How interesting. How much of a bonus?'

'A hundred dollars.'

'So,' Mason said, smiling, 'if a piece of relatively inexpensive costume jewellery was missing from that jewel case and there was evidence that would link the defendant with that missing bit of jewellery, Mr Hallock was to get a hundred dollars. Is that right?'

'I don't like the way you express it,' Bain said.

'Well, express it in your own way.'

'It was a bonus for completing the job.'

'The job was to have been completed when Miss Conway was arrested?'

'When we caught the thief, whoever it was.'

'How many people in that house?'

'My wife, Mrs Ricker, Mr Hallock, Nellie Conway and I.'

'You didn't examine Mrs Ricker's hands, notwithstanding you knew she'd handled the jewel box?'

'No. She's been with us for years.'

'And everyone else in that house, except your wife, *did* have fluorescent powder on the fingers?'

'Well . . . yes.'

'Yet you picked Miss Conway as the thief?'

'Yes. It had to be her or nobody.'

'It had to be her?'

'Yes.'

'So your bonus to Mr Hallock was to get this one person arrested and convicted?'

'To get the thief.'

'Have you paid the reward yet?'

'No.'

'Why not?'

'The defendant hasn't been convicted. It was to be paid when the job was finished.'

'I see, then you *do* have a doubt in your own mind as to whether this jury should or would convict the defendant?'

'Objection, argumentative.'

'Sustained.'

Mason smiled and said, 'I have no further questions, Mr Bain. Thank you.'

Saybrook said angrily, 'You didn't tell Hallock that he was to get a hundred dollars in case he got evidence that would convict this defendant, did you? You simply told him that if he could find out who was taking the jewellery you'd give him a hundred dollars.'

'Just a moment, Your Honour,' Mason said, 'that question is viciously leading and suggestive. Counsel is putting words right in the mouth of the witness.'

'Well, this is on redirect examination,' Saybrook said, 'and I'm simply trying to shorten an examination that has been already too prolonged.'

'Come, come,' Mason said, 'let's not assume that just a few minutes spent inquiring into the issues is going to be–'

'Well, the court's time is valuable and Mr Bain's time is valuable, even if yours isn't,' Saybrook said.

'And think of the defendant,' Mason said reproachfully. 'If your attempt to save Mr Bain just two or three minutes of his valuable time is going to obscure the issues, the defendant might be incarcerated in jail for a period of months. She'd have her good name blackened, she–'

'You don't need to go into that,' Saybrook said, 'that's simply to influence the jury.'

'Well,' Mason told him, smilingly, 'your attempt to justify yourself for putting words into Mr Bain's mouth was for the purpose of influencing the court.'

Judge Peabody smiled. 'The vice of a leading question, of course, consists in having asked it. The witness now pretty generally knows what Counsel has in mind. Go ahead, however, Mr Saybrook, and ask a question so that it is a little less leading.'

'Oh, I don't think there's any need of going into all this in any greater detail,' Saybrook said.

'You have any further questions?' Judge Peabody inquired.

'That's all.'

'Any further evidence?'

'That's the People's case, Your Honour.'

Mason smiled at Judge Peabody and said, 'We'd like to move at this time that the court instruct the jury to bring in a verdict of not guilty.'

'The motion is denied.'

'If I may have a ten minute recess, Your Honour,' Mason said, 'I would like to talk with the one person whom I have subpœnaed as a defence witness. Mrs Imogene Ricker.'

'Very well,' Judge Peabody ruled.

In the back of the court-room the housekeeper stood up, gaunt, grim, and defiant. 'I refuse to talk to Mr Mason,' she said.

'This woman has been subpœnaed as a defence witness, Your Honour,' Mason explained. 'She has therefore refused to make any statement to me.'

'I don't have to talk to him,' Imogene Ricker said. 'I came to court and that's all I have to do. I obeyed the subpœna. That doesn't mean I have to talk to him.'

'Very well, then,' Mason said, smiling, 'just come forward, hold up your right hand to be sworn, and get on the witness stand.'

'Do I have to do that?' she asked Judge Peabody.

'If you have been subpœnaed you have to do that,' the Judge said.

She strode past Mason, held up her hand to be sworn, turned and flung herself down in the witness chair. 'All right,' she said grimly, 'go ahead.'

'You're a housekeeper in Mr Bain's employ?' Mason asked.

'I am!' she snapped.

'How long have you been working for him?'

'Six years.'

'On the evening of the tenth did you examine your hands by ultra-violet light to see if they were fluorescent?'

'That's none of your business.'

Mason smiled. 'If your fingers *hadn't* been fluorescent you would have answered the question, wouldn't you?'

'I don't have to tell you that either.'

Mason grinned at the sympathetic jury. 'Thank you. That's all, Mrs Ricker. I just wanted the jurors to see how violently partisan you were.'

'Oh, Your Honour,' Saybrook said, 'that–'

'The witness is excused,' Judge Peabody ruled wearily. 'The jury will pay no attention to comments of Counsel. Who's your next witness, Mr Mason?'

'I don't have anyone,' Mason said. 'I think perhaps the jury have a pretty good concept of the case, Your Honour. An attractive jewel case was deliberately put in a position of prominence where anyone would be inclined to pick it up. We insist that–'

'There's been a ruling on the motion for a directed verdict,' Judge Peabody said. 'Go ahead and put on your defence.'

'I'm certainly not going to put on any defence in the present state of this case,' Mason said. 'It's not incumbent on the defendant to prove herself innocent. It's up to the prosecution to prove her guilty. All they've proven so far is that this defendant, who was in a room where she was required to be under the terms of her employment, touched the outside of an attractive and unusual piece of bric-à-brac. The defence will rest right now and we'll submit the case without argument to the jury.'

'You have already made an argument,' Saybrook said.

'Tut-tut,' Mason told him. 'I was merely explaining to the court why I intended to rest the defendant's case. Do you wish to submit it without argument?'

'I think I should argue it,' Saybrook said.

Mason smiled at him. 'Well, as far as I'm concerned I think this jury understands the issue very clearly. I'm satisfied that they're intelligent citizens and I see no reason for wasting their time. You were very concerned about the value of time a few minutes ago. I'll submit the case without argument. Go ahead and argue if you want to.'

Saybrook thought the matter over, then said sulkily, 'Very well, I'll submit it without argument.'

Mason made a little bow to the Judge.

Judge Peabody said, 'You ladies and gentlemen of the jury have heard the evidence. It is now the duty of the court to instruct you as to certain matters of law.'

Judge Peabody read a stock list of instructions, emphasising the fact that it was incumbent upon the prosecution to prove a defendant guilty beyond all reasonable doubt, and that it was not incumbent upon the defendant to prove himself or herself innocent; that the jurors were the exclusive judges of the fact, although they should take the law as given to them in the instructions of the court.

The jury retired and returned in ten minutes with a verdict of not guilty.

Mason and Nellie Conway walked over to shake hands with the jurors.

The woman juror who had smiled at Mason said, exasperatedly, 'That man Bain! You certainly gave him just what he had coming to him. The idea of his keeping a key to his wife's writing desk. Just a snoop, that's what he is! Poor woman, her lying there sick in bed and having a man like that around the place.'

'I *thought* you were a pretty good judge of character,' Mason said. 'I felt as soon as I looked in your eyes that I didn't need to argue the case.'

'Well, I certainly told them what I thought of *that* man,' she said. 'The only trouble was I didn't have a chance to tell them *all* that I thought, because everyone else felt the same way about it I did.'

She turned to Nellie Conway. 'You poor dear, having to work for a man like that, and now he's gone ahead and had you arrested and sworn to a complaint against you on the ground of theft and blasted your reputation. I certainly think that you should do something about it. I think you should sue him for damages.'

'Thank you very much for the suggestion,' Mason said. 'I was going to advise her something of the sort myself, but I think the fact that the suggestion has come from one of the members of the jury will be something to remember.'

'Well, you can certainly quote me. You have my name and address,' the woman said, and again gave Mason a cordial smile and another handshake.

6

Back in Mason's office, as Mason and Della Street were getting ready to close the office, the telephone rang. Della Street, taking the call, cupped her hand over the mouth-piece and said to Mason, 'Do you want to talk with Nellie?'

'I definitely want to talk with her,' Mason said. 'Long enough to explain to her that she's no longer a client.'

Mason took the telephone and Nellie Conway said in a calm level voice that was as expressionless as her face, 'Mr Mason, I want to thank you for what you did today.'

'That's all right,' Mason said.

'I suppose,' she ventured somewhat diffidently, 'I owe you some more money, Mr Mason? The one dollar I paid you didn't cover all this extra work, did it?'

Mason said, 'Well, of course, if I handled jury cases at a dollar a throw, it would be difficult for me to pay my office rent, my secretarial salaries and my taxicabs back and forth to the Hall of Justice.'

'Oh, Mr Mason, you're being sarcastic now, aren't you?'

'I was just pointing out a few economic facts.'

'Can you tell me just how much I owe you? Would another ten or fifteen dollars be all right?'

Mason said, 'How much money do you have, Nellie?'

'Does that need to enter into it?'

'It might have something to do with it.'

'I'd rather not discuss that, Mr Mason. I'd rather you'd just tell me how much your charges are.'

Mason became serious. 'You called me up to ask me that?'

'Yes.'

Mason was curious now. 'You didn't say anything about any additional compensation after the case was over, Nellie. You just shook hands with me and thanked me. Why have you become so concerned about it now?'

'Well, I . . . I was just thinking that perhaps . . .'

'Look here,' Mason asked, 'has Bain been in touch with you?'

She hesitated, then said, 'Yes.'

'And Bain is offering you some sort of a settlement?'

'Well . . . Mr Bain and I are talking.'

'You mean you're talking with Bain at the present moment? You mean he's with you?'

'I'm with him.'

'Where?'

'At Mr Bain's house.'

'At the Bain house!' Mason repeated incredulously.

'Yes.'

'What in the world are you doing there?'

'Why, getting my things, of course. When the officers took me away they didn't give me any opportunity to pack up my personal things.'

'Let's get this straight,' Mason said. 'Were you *living* there at the Bain house?'

'Why, yes, of course. The day nurse and I shared an apartment over the garage.'

'Well, I'll be damned!'

'Why, what's wrong with that, Mr Mason? Mr Bain has lots of room here, and–'

'But you didn't tell me that.'

'Well, you didn't ask me.'

'Who's taking care of the patient now?' Mason asked.

'Why, the same nurse.'

'I mean as a night nurse. Who's taking your place?'

'They had a temporary nurse for a few days, but she left very abruptly. The housekeeper has been helping out, and, just as a favour, I'll stay on the rest of the night. Mrs Ricker will take a spell with me while I'm packing.'

'You've seen Mrs Bain and talked with her?'

'Why, of course. Elizabeth Bain and I are real friendly. She'd like to have me stay right on at my old job. But I don't think I'll stay . . . I had to tell her all about my arrest, of course, and about the way you questioned–well, the witnesses.'

'By that I take it you mean the way I tore into her husband on cross-examination?'

'Yes.'

'How did she react to that?'

'She thought it was wonderful. She said she wanted to see you. She . . . well, I . . .'

'You mean you can't talk freely?' Mason asked as he hesitated and broke off.

'Oh, yes. That's right. Yes, indeed. Mr Bain is right here.'

'And you're negotiating some sort of a settlement with him?'

'I hope to.'

'Then you'll go back to work for him?'

'I think not. Quite a few of Mrs Bain's relatives are due here some time after midnight. They're flying in from Honolulu. She'll have lots of company. She . . . well, I'll tell you some other time. I wanted to ask you now . . . that is, Mr Bain wanted to know . . . if you'd set a price on your services so–'

Mason said, 'If Nathan Bain is going to pay the fee, you owe me five hundred dollars, and that cleans us up. Do you understand?'

'Well, I should think it would,' she said, rather tartly.

'If Bain doesn't pay the fee, we're quits,' Mason said. 'The one dollar charge is all I'm making.'

'Oh.'

'You understand that?'

'Yes.'

'And,' Mason told her, 'that winds us up, and let's have one thing understood, Nellie.'

'What, Mr Mason?'

'I'm not representing you in connection with any settlement you make with Bain. If you make a settlement with him that's up to you. I think perhaps you should have some lawyer represent you.'

'Then I'd have to pay him, wouldn't I?'

'Most lawyers like to be paid,' Mason told her. 'They have to support themselves, you know.'

'Well,' she said indignantly, 'I don't see why I should take money and pay it over to a lawyer. Mr Bain is willing to be reasonable, and as he's pointed out he couldn't be any more reasonable if a lawyer were there to take fifty per cent out of what I am going to collect.'

'Did he say that?'

'Yes. He pointed out that it would be coming right out of my pocket.'

'All right,' Mason said, 'use your own judgment.'

'I am,' she said, 'and please, Mr Mason, so there won't be any misunderstanding, you're not representing me in the settlement. I'm just trying to find out how much I owe you for your lawyer's fees, but I'm not going to pay five hundred dollars.'

'*You're* not,' Mason said. 'Bain is.'

'But I'm not going to let him pay that much. I think it's too much, Mr Mason.'

'How much do *you* think it should be?'

'Well, I would say not more than fifty dollars. You only did half a day's work.'

Mason said, 'I told you that if you were paying me you only owed me a dollar. If Bain is paying me, the bill would be five hundred dollars.'

'Well, then, I'll get Mr Bain to pay me and . . . well, I'll think it over, Mr Mason. I'll . . . I'll do what's right.'

'I'm satisfied you will,' Mason said. 'And now let's get this straight, Nellie. You and I are finished, the slate is wiped clean. I'm not your lawyer any–'

'I'll say you're not. At any such prices as those! Five hundred dollars for just a little over half a day's work . . . Why, I never heard of such a thing!'

And she slammed the receiver in Mason's ear.

The lawyer rubbed his ear, turned to Della Street. 'That,' he announced, 'is gratitude. I have always said, Della, that the time to fix the amount of a fee is when the client is most anxious to secure the services. Miss Nellie Conway now feels ten or fifteen dollars would be ample compensation, and fifty would be munificent.'

'Come on, Della, let's close up the joint and go home.'

7

When Mason entered his office a few minutes after ten the next morning, Della Street said, 'Congratulations, Chief!'

'A birthday or something?' Mason asked.

'You've missed her by five minutes. Therefore congratulations are in order.'

'Missed who?'

'Your dollar client.'

'Good Lord, don't tell me *she's* been on my trail.'

'Called four times after nine-thirty. I told her I expected you'd be in at ten. She said she'd call at exactly ten o'clock and that was the latest call she could possibly make.'

'What's it all about, Della?'

'Apparently she feels she may need a lawyer.'

'For what?'

'She didn't deem it fit to confide in me.'

'What did you tell her, Della?'

'In a nice way I told her she was poison, smallpox, and had B.O., bad breath, and, in short, that she stank. I told her you were far too busy to be able to handle anything else for her. I suggested that she get in touch with some other lawyer who wouldn't be quite so busy and would be more accessible.'

'Then what?'

'She said no, she didn't have confidence in anyone else. She had to talk with you.'

'Did she call again at ten?'

'Right on the dot. You could have set your watch by it. Just as the second hand on the electric clock got to fifty-nine seconds past nine-fifty-nine the telephone rang and it was Nellie. I told her you weren't here and she said that was a shame because then she couldn't explain things, and she did want to explain things.'

'She'll probably call again,' Mason said.

'I gathered that she wouldn't.'

Mason grinned. 'We've probably lost a chance to make another dollar! What else is new? Anything?'

'There's a woman waiting to see you. A Miss Braxton.'

'What does she want?'

'Now there,' Della Street said, 'you have me. She won't tell me what she wants or what it's about.'

'Tell her I won't see her then,' Mason said. 'Hang it, I waste more time talking with people who want some routine legal chore I wouldn't touch with a ten-foot pole–probably wants me to draw a contract or make a deed or–'

'You should see her,' Della Street said archly.

'Huh?'

Della Street made motions with her hands as though outlining a feminine figure.

'Like that?' Mason asked.

'Wolf bait,' Della Street said. 'I mean she's *really* something.'

'Now,' Mason told her, grinning, 'you *do* have me interested. Keep on.'

'And,' Della Street went on, 'I think she's mad about something. She says that what she wants to see you about is a personal matter and too confidential to mention to anyone. She's been waiting here since nine-fifteen.'

Mason said, 'I love beautiful women who are mad, Della. How old?'

'Twenty-three, on a guess.'

'And neat?'

'Face, figure, clothes, eyes, complexion, even just a trace of the perfume that makes men go nuts. You should see Gertie out at the reception desk. She can't keep her eyes on the switchboard.'

'That does it,' Mason said. 'We're going to see Miss Braxton, but if she doesn't measure up to your build-up I shall resort to stern disciplinary measures.'

'Wait until you see her,' Della Street said. 'You want to take a look at the mail first or–?'

'No, not the mail–the female. Let's go.'

'Prepare yourself,' Della Street said. 'Take a deep breath. Here she comes.'

And Della Street went out to the outer office to escort Miss Braxton into Mason's private office.

Mason saw the young woman enter the office with a swinging confident stride, saw her hesitate, bow coolly, then walk over to stand perfectly calm and collected by Mason's desk.

'This is Mr Mason,' Della Street said. 'Miss Braxton, Mr Mason.'

'How do you do?' Mason said. 'Won't you sit down?'

'Thank you.'

She crossed over to the big, overstuffed client's chair, settled herself, crossed her knees, smoothed her dress, and said to Mason, 'Will you kindly tell me *just* what is happening to my sister?'

'Now, just a moment,' Mason said, noticing the cold steely anger in her eyes. 'I'm not certain that I know your sister and I certainly don't–'

'My sister is Elizabeth Bain. Nathan Bain, her husband, is trying to poison her. Just what has been done about it?'

'Wait a minute,' Mason said. 'You're getting several carts in front of one horse.'

Miss Braxton said, 'I don't think I was ever so mad in my life, Mr Mason. You'll pardon me if I seem to be a little worked up.

'Go right ahead,' Mason told her, 'only don't take it out on me.'

'I didn't come to you for that purpose, Mr Mason. I'm not mad at you.'

'Just why did you come to me?'

'I want to retain you as a lawyer. I think you're the only one who can handle this situation.'

'What situation?'

'What situation?' she exclaimed angrily. 'Good heavens, Mr Mason, do you have the temerity to sit there and ask that question in good faith? Good Lord, my sister has been living in a hell on earth and no one seems to have taken sufficient interest to do anything about it?'

'Are you sure you have your facts right?' Mason asked.

'Mr Mason, let's put it this way. My sister married very much beneath her. The man she married is a cold-blooded, scheming, nasty toad. Do I make myself clear?'

'I gather,' Mason said, 'that you're endeavouring to convey to my mind that you don't like the man.'

'That,' she said, 'is a close approximation of the truth. I hate the ground he walks on.'

'So I gathered.'

She went on, angrily, 'He married my sister entirely for her money. We warned her about it and–well, that's where we made our mistake.'

'Who's "we"?' Mason asked.

'The family. I'm her half-sister. There's a half-brother and–well, we should have kept our noses out of it. But we didn't, and as a result, there was a certain element of stiffness which crept into the family relations. We'd always been very close prior to that time, just as real brother and sisters, and now–well, thank heaven, now it's different. Now we're all back together again.'

'Just what was it you wanted me to do?' Mason asked. 'I have already been retained in connection with one matter involving the Bain household.'

She threw back her head and laughed.

Mason raised his eyebrows.

'You'll pardon me,' she said, 'but I heard Nathan's description of what happened to him on the witness stand. I don't think I ever heard anything that amused me quite as much in all my life. The pompous, vain-glorious, self-centred, egostical toad! And you ripped him up the back and down the front, Mr Mason. You really did a job on him. Oh, how much I would have given to have been there!'

'You learned about all this from him?'

'From him and from Nellie Conway, the nurse.'

'You talked with her?'

'Oh, yes.'

Mason said, 'I was rather surprised that she went back out to the house.'

'I think Nathan was the one who was responsible for that. Nathan was simply frightened stiff, Mr Mason, and I'll say one thing for Nellie Conway, she certainly knew how to keep pouring it on.'

'Just what do you mean?'

'The way she put the hooks into Nathan was really something.'

'Let's see if we can get this straight,' Mason said. 'First, I'd like to find out just what you want me to do and–'

'Why, I thought I'd make myself clear on that. It's not so much what I want you to do as to what my sister wants you to do.'

'Elizabeth Bain?'

'Yes.'

'What does she want?'

'She wants you to represent her.'

'In doing what?'

'In doing lots of things.'

'Go ahead.'

'Well, in the first place, Elizabeth has now seen Nathan in his true colours.

The man tried to kill her. He's been deliberately trying to kill her for some time. Heaven knows what that girl has put up with and heaven knows how many times she's been at the brink of the grave. All of those sicknesses she had, the food poisonings, the things she thought at the time were just stomach upsets, were probably all part of this scheme on Nathan's part to get rid of her.'

Mason's eyes narrowed. 'This has been going on for some time?'

'She's been living a perfect hell, Mr Mason, and the poor girl doesn't know even now that her spinal cord is permanently injured. She thinks that after she has gone through a period of recuperation from the accident, someone is going to be able to operate on her, remove the pressure from the spinal cord and she'll walk again.'

'And she won't?'

Miss Braxton shook her head. Tears came in her eyes. 'She never will.'

'What do you know about the accident?' Mason asked.

Her eyes glittered. 'I know all about it. Nathan says that the brakes gave way on his automobile. He tried his best to stop it. When he found he couldn't he yelled to Elizabeth to jump. A fat chance she had of jumping! Nathan had very carefully engineered the thing so that he was on the inside of the road and Elizabeth was in the seat that looked right out over a yawning chasm. When Nathan yelled to jump he already had his door open. He just jumped out of the car and turned it loose.

'Elizabeth had sufficient presence of mind to reach over and grab the wheel. Then she tried to keep the thing on the road. When she saw that wasn't going to work, and the car was accelerating into terrific speed, she tried to run the car into the bank.'

'The brakes really *were* out of order?'

'There wasn't a brake on the car,' Miss Braxton said. 'But that could have been arranged easily enough. All Nathan had to do was to fix it with a string running up through the floorboard so he could cut through one of the hoses on the hydraulic brakes and put the whole system out of order. And he picked a place to do it where the car would have naturally been expected to plunge over a perpendicular precipice. Fortunately Elizabeth's efforts to keep it on the road managed to get her past the most dangerous place so that when it left the road the car only rolled down the steep slope for a couple of hundred feet. Even so, it was a wonder she wasn't killed.'

'Did anyone examine the car to see whether it had been tampered with?' Mason asked.

'What do *you* think?'

'I'm asking you.'

She said, 'Poor Elizabeth had her spinal cord crushed. She'd received a concussion and was unconscious. They got her to a hospital, and dear old Nathan went right back with a breakdown crew to see what could be done with the car. They managed to get it on a winch and hoist it back up to the highway; then they towed it away–and turned it over to Nathan. And during all the time they were fooling around out there with the winch, Nathan had every opportunity on earth to remove any evidence–'

'In other words, the police weren't called in?'

'The highway patrol made a routine inspection, but that was all. I don't think anyone actually went down to where the car was except Nathan and the garage men who hooked the cable on to the car and winched it back up to the road.'

'Go on,' Mason said.

She said, 'You don't need to be so conservative, Mr Mason. Nellie Conway told me her whole story this morning. I was never so completely flabbergasted in all my life. To think that such conditions could exist. Well, it certainly is time we got here. That's all I can say!'

'Have you talked with Nathan Bain about it?'

'No, I haven't said a word to him. I heard about you from Nellie Conway and I decided you were the attorney my sister wants. She wants to draw up a will that will completely disinherit him and she wants to file a suit for divorce. She hates the ground he walks on; she wants him out of the house.'

'Has Nathan Bain been advised about this?'

'No, Mr Mason. We want you to tell him.'

'Me?'

'That's right. I want you to come out and talk with my sister. She'll tell you what to do, and then I want you to go out and see Mr Bain, tell him he's done and tell him to pack up his things and get out of the house.'

'Who owns the house?' Mason asked.

'My sister. She owns everything.'

'Nathan's business is not profitable?'

'I think it's *quite* profitable,' she said acidly, 'but you'd never find it out from anything he tells you, and you wouldn't find it out from any books he keeps.'

'What do you mean by that?'

'He does business on a cash basis wherever possible. He puts the cash in his pocket and no one knows how much it is or how much he takes. He doesn't believe in paying income tax and he doesn't believe in confiding in anyone. He's one of the most secretive men I know.'

'Don't you think,' Mason asked, 'that it would be a better plan for your sister to call him in and tell him that as far as she's concerned she's all finished, that she wants him to leave, that she intends to file a suit for divorce, and–?'

'No, Mr Mason. I don't think that would be the way to handle it. Elizabeth simply detests the sight of him. She gets almost hysterical every time she thinks of him. Remember that she's not well and she's been taking lots of sedatives which have had an effect on her nervous system. She wants to feel that he is entirely out of her life once and for all, and she doesn't ever want to see him again.'

'All right,' Mason said, 'if that's the way she wants it.'

'You'll do it?'

'I see no reason why not.'

Miss Braxton opened her purse. 'I told Elizabeth I'd come to you and put it right up to you, that if you'd do what she wanted and tell Nathan Bain where he got off, that she could be free of her worries. Elizabeth told me to give you this as a retainer.'

She handed Mason a cheque, dated that day, drawn on the Farmer's and Mechanic's National for an amount of five hundred dollars, payable to 'Perry Mason, attorney for Elizabeth Bain', and signed in a somewhat wobbly handwriting '*Elizabeth Bain*'.

'This is a retainer?' Mason asked.

'That's right.'

'And just what is it Mrs Bain wants me to do?'

'You've started out very nicely showing her husband up. Just keep on doing it. Kick him out of the house and see that things are fixed so he can't ever get a penny of her property.'

Mason said, 'Your half-sister may make you her agent to deliver the cheque. I'll have to have those instructions from her own lips.'

'Of course.'

'When I'm alone with her, so I'll know there hasn't been any . . .'

'Undue influence, Mr Mason?'

'If you want to put it that way, yes.'

'Come on out and talk with her.'

'I will.'

'In the meantime, Mr Mason,' she said, 'I want your opinion about this document–that is, Elizabeth does.'

Miss Braxton opened her purse and took out a sheet of paper on which the date was written in the same wobbling handwriting that was on the cheque, and then the words:

I, Elizabeth Bain, knowing that my husband has tried to kill me on several occasions, having lost all confidence in him, and all affection for him, make this my last will and testament, leaving everything I own share and share alike to my beloved half-sister, Victoria Braxton, and my beloved half-brother, James Braxton, with the understanding that they will take my property

Mason regarded the piece of paper somewhat quizzically, and said, 'Just what is it you want to know about this?'

'Is it good?'

Mason said cautiously, 'That depends.'

'Well, good heavens, you're a lawyer, aren't you?'

'Yes.'

'And you can't say that it's good or that it isn't good?'

Mason smiled and shook his head.

'Why not?'

'Suppose,' Mason countered, 'you tell me something of the circumstances under which this will was made.'

'Well, I don't know as it's so terribly important, Mr Mason. You'll notice that it's dated today. Elizabeth slept very soundly last night. One of the few good nights she's had. I think it was because she knew we were coming.

'Now, Mr Mason, when she wakened about five o'clock this morning, she told me to come and see you, and give you that retainer. She instructed me to have you make a will which would fix it so Nathan Bain couldn't profit by her death. And then she . . . well, I don't know, I suppose perhaps . . . well, in a way she's been reading a lot and . . .'

'What are you getting at?' Mason asked.

'Well, of course, in pictures on the screen and in detective stories and all that, a person who is intending to disinherit someone . . . well, the interval that the lawyer is preparing the new will, you know, is always the most dangerous time. So Elizabeth talked that over with me, and decided that if she'd write it out, in her own handwriting, showing just what she wanted done with her property, that it would be good. Now is that right?'

'That's right,' Mason said, 'up to a certain point.'

'What do you mean by that?'

'In this State, and, mind you, I'm talking now *only* about this State, a will is good if it is made, dated and signed in the handwriting of the testator. It takes those three things, the date, the will and the signature, all in the handwriting of the testator.'

Miss Braxton nodded.

'Now,' Mason went on, 'you'll note that, in the ordinary sense of the word, your sister didn't sign this will.'

'But she wrote her name, Elizabeth Bain, in her own handwriting.'

'She wrote her name,' Mason said, 'in describing herself. In other words, there's a question whether the words "Elizabeth Bain" as they appear in the will were intended as a signature or whether they were intended to be merely descriptive.'

'Well, does it make any difference where the name appears on the will?'

'As a matter of law, it does not,' Mason said, 'provided the courts can establish clearly that the testator intended the writing of the name to be as a signature.'

'Well, that's what Elizabeth intended.'

Mason smiled and shook his head. 'There have been several very interesting cases where the point has been raised. I can't give you the citations offhand, but there are cases where wills such as this have been offered for probate, and the question has always been whether the use of the testator's name was descriptive or whether it was intended as a signature. Now you'll notice one very peculiar thing about this writing.'

'What?'

'There is,' Mason said, 'no final punctuation at the end of it.'

'What do you mean by that?'

'After the word "property",' Mason said, 'there is no full stop.'

'Well, for heaven's sake! Do you mean to say that a little dot one-tenth the size of a pinhead on a piece of paper would–?'

'I mean to say so very definitely,' Mason interrupted. 'There's a case somewhere . . . wait a minute, perhaps I can put my hand on it.'

He walked over to a shelf filled with books, pulled down a book, ran through the pages, then settled himself for a few minutes' intensive study.

Miss Braxton interrupted him to say, 'Well, after all, it isn't that important, Mr Mason. This is just a sort of a . . . well, a stopgap. Elizabeth did it to ease her mind. She thought that if Nathan knew he had already been disinherited it would dissuade him from perhaps trying any last minute final attempt in desperation.'

'You mean that he wouldn't try to kill her?'

'That's right.'

Mason returned to the book, then said, 'From a legal standpoint it's a most interesting question.'

'Well, I've heard of a lot of technicalities,' Miss Braxton said, 'but if you're trying to tell me that a teeny, weeny dot on a piece of paper is going to make any difference as to the validity of a will, I'll say you lawyers are getting altogether too technical.'

'The point is,' Mason said, 'that it goes to the intention of the testator. In other words, when your sister finished with this document, did she consider that it was a complete and final will, or did she start to make a will and was then interrupted by something and never did finish making the will?'

'Oh, I see what you're getting at now.'

'For instance,' Mason said, 'if you're interested in the legal reasoning, here's the Estate of Kinney, reported in 104 Pacific (2d) at page 782, where it was held that the writing of the testator's name only in the beginning of the declaration is a sufficient signing to justify admitting a will to probate, even though there is no affirmative expression adopting the name so placed as the signature of the testator.

'Then in a recent case, Estate of Kaminski, reported in 115 Pacific (2d) at page 21, it was held that the name of the testator at the beginning of an alleged holographic will constitutes a sufficient signature where the instrument appears to be a *complete* testamentary expression of his desires.

'Now, in the Estate of Bauman, 300 Pacific, 62, it was held that in all cases of this sort the entire instrument must be examined to find out whether it was intended to be a complete will. The final expression, the abruptness in closing, and *even the final punctuation* are to be considered for the purpose of determining whether the writer intended to adopt the name as written in the opening clause as a signature or merely as words of description.

'Now you notice that your sister's will has some very peculiar closing words– '*with the understanding that they will take my property*' . . . The testator could very well have been intending to add "subject to the following trust," or "to be used for the purpose of" . . .'

'But she didn't mean that at all,' Miss Braxton interrupted. 'She simply meant that the understanding was that by this will we were to take all of her property so that Nathan Bain wouldn't have any opportunity–'

'I understand that's your contention,' Mason said, 'but you hand me a sheet of paper, you ask me a legal question, and I'm giving you the best answer I can.'

Miss Braxton smiled. 'Well, I guess it won't make two bits' worth of difference, Mr Mason, because you can draw up a formal will and have it executed with witnesses and everything. How soon can you get out there?'

'When would be convenient?'

'The sooner the better. All you need to do is to prepare a will made in conformity with this will and have it all ready for her to sign and–'

'That might not be advisable,' Mason interrupted.

'Why not?'

'I haven't as yet talked with your sister.'

'Well, I'm her agent. She sent me up here to tell you what to do, and gave me this cheque for your retainer.'

Mason nodded and smiled, 'Nathan Bain might contest the will. He might claim there was undue influence on your part.'

'But good heavens, Mr Mason, aren't we crossing a lot of bridges before we come to them? After all, a will wouldn't . . . well, there wouldn't be any occasion for a will unless Elizabeth should die, and now that Jim and I are here she's not going to die; and if you can get Nathan Bain out of the house there won't be one chance in a million that–'

'A lawyer isn't paid to consider *probabilities*,' Mason told her. 'He's paid to consider *possibilities*.'

'But that will mean a delay, won't it, Mr Mason?'

Mason shook his head.

'Why not?'

'I'll take Della Street, my secretary, along with me. She'll take a portable typewriter, and just as soon as your sister tells me she wants the will prepared, my secretary will type it out, call in two witnesses who are completely disinterested, and–'

'What two witnesses?' Miss Braxton interrupted.

'Miss Street can sign as one witness and I'll sign as another.'

'Oh, that'll be fine,' she said, her face beaming. 'That's the way to do it. How soon can you get out there, Mr Mason?'

'Under the circumstances, I can get out there at . . . well, let me see, at two o'clock this afternoon?'

'Could you possibly make it at eleven-thirty this morning, Mr Mason? That will give me time to get home and tell Elizabeth that you're coming out, and give her a chance to get straightened up a bit. After all, a woman wants to look her best, you know, and her hair's a mess! . . . They haven't been giving her the affectionate attention that a sister would give . . . you know, those little personal touches.'

'Eleven-thirty will be all right,' Mason said. 'I'll be there–'

The telephone rang sharply. Della Street picked it up, said, 'Hello . . . Who is it? . . . Vicki Braxton? . . . Just a moment, please.'

She turned to Miss Braxton and said, 'Someone wants to talk with you on this phone and says it's very important.'

'And they asked for "Vicki"?' Miss Braxton asked.

'Yes.'

'Good heavens, I can't understand it. No one in the world knows that I am here, and I'm known as Vicki only to intimates and members of the family. Why, I . . . I can't understand it.'

'Well, suppose you take the phone call,' Della Street said, 'and find out who it is. That is, if you want to.'

From the receiver came a rasping chatter and Della Street said, 'Just a moment.' She placed the receiver to her ear and said, 'What was that again? . . . Oh, yes, I'll tell her.

'It's your brother, Jim,' she said.

Victoria Braxton walked over to the phone, said, 'Hello, Jim. This is Vicki. What is it? . . . What? . . . No! . . . Oh, my God! . . . You're sure? . . . I'll be right over.'

She slammed the phone back on the hook, turned around and said to Perry Mason, 'My God, it's happened! Elizabeth is dying. They've been looking all over trying to find me. Jim, my brother, happened to remember . . . Let me out of here.'

She started towards the door to the outer office, then saw the exit door opening into the corridor, swerved in her course, twisted the knob, jerked the door open, and dashed out.

Mason, looking at Della Street, ran his fingers through thick, wavy hair in a gesture of perplexity.

'This Bain case!' he said.

'I suppose you'd throw me out if I mentioned anything about the bane of your life!'

'I'd draw you and quarter you,' he announced, as Della Street ducked defensively. 'What happened to that holographic will?'

'She grabbed it, put it back in her purse, and took it with her.'

Mason said, 'There's just a chance, Della, that that document might assume the greatest importance.'

'You mean, if Mrs Bain is really dying?'

He nodded. 'The peculiar wording of that last sentence in the holographic will, the absence of any closing punctuation–'

Della Street laughed cynically. 'The next time you see that will, Chief, it will have a very complete period at the end of that sentence. Want to bet?'

Mason pursed his lips. 'No, I don't think I do, Della. I guess you're right. In that event I'd be in a most peculiar position. I'd be bound to respect my client's confidences on the one hand, but, on the other hand, as an attorney at law, who is an officer of the court. . . . Get Paul Drake on the telephone. Tell him I want information about what's going on out there in the Bain household and I want it fast. Tell him I'm not particularly concerned how he gets it. . . . And Nellie Conway's last call was at ten o'clock?'

'Right on the second,' she said.

'And she told you she couldn't call after that?'

'Yes.'

'That,' Mason said, 'makes it *exceedingly* interesting. Also notice that Miss Braxton said no one knew she was here. That would mean her brother must know nothing about Elizabeth Bain's intentions to retain me, and nothing whatever about that rather mysterious holographic will.'

Della nodded. 'Shall we say the plot thickens, Chief?'

'Just like that gravy I tried to make on my last hunting trip, Della. It thickened in lumps. "Thousand Island Gravy", the boys called it.'

8

At 11.55 Paul Drake telephoned.

'Hello, Perry. I'm out here at a service station about two blocks from the Bain house. Elizabeth Bain died about ten minutes ago according to information that was relayed to me by back door scuttlebutt.'

'The cause?' Mason asked.

'Seems to be no doubt that it's arsenic poisoning. They felt she was too ill to be removed to a hospital. They've had a diagnosis of arsenic ever since nine-thirty this morning and have been treating her for it. Symptoms first appeared a little before nine.'

'Any chance that it's suicide?' Mason asked.

Drake said, 'The place is crawling with officers from the Homicide Squad. Your friend Sergeant Holcomb is pretty much in evidence.'

Mason thought things over, then he said, 'Paul, I have a job for you.'

'What?'

'I not only want all the dope on everyone out there at Bain's place, but I want you to canvass the airports. I want to find out what planes left at ten-fifteen this morning. I want that done fast.'

'Okay. I can check that pretty rapidly,' Drake said. 'You can check it yourself by calling the airports–'

Mason said, 'That's only half of it, Paul. When you find what airplanes left, I want you to check descriptions of every woman on those planes. I'm particularly looking for a mousy, poker-faced woman, who will have signed her name on the passenger list with the initials 'N.C.' That is, her first name will begin with an 'N', her last name will begin with a 'C', and I want information so fast that it isn't even going to be funny. How long will it take?'

'Perhaps an hour.'

'Cut that in half,' Mason said. 'Make it fifteen minutes if you can. I'm going to be sitting right here at the telephone. Get going and call me.'

Mason hung up the telephone and began pacing the floor.

'What is it?' Della Street asked.

Mason said, 'Probably around nine this morning, perhaps a little before, Elizabeth Bain was taken violently ill. By nine-thirty they had diagnosed it as arsenic poisoning. About fifteen minutes ago she died.'

'And?' Della Street asked.

'And,' Mason said, 'Nellie Conway was frantically trying to get me all morning, but she had a deadline of ten o'clock. She couldn't call me after that. That was the last minute she'd be able to talk with me.'

'You mean she's on a plane somewhere?'

'She's on a plane,' Mason said, 'and let's hope she had sense enough to sign her name as Nellie Conway. In the event she didn't, her baggage is probably stamped 'N.C.' so she'll use a name that will fit with the initials on the baggage.'

'And if Elizabeth Bain died from arsenic poisoning?' Della Street asked.

'Then,' Mason said, 'in view of the fact that I had certain tablets in my possession which Nellie Conway gave me with the story that Nathan had been bribing her to administer them to Elizabeth Bain, and in further view of the fact I gave those tablets back to Nellie–'

'But those were only aspirin tablets,' Della Street said.

Mason sighed. '*One* of them was an aspirin tablet, Della. Whenever a lawyer begins to regard his work as routine and to think in terms of the average and the usual, he's riding for a fall. People don't pay a lawyer to think of what's probably going to happen. They expect him to think of and anticipate everything that could possibly happen.

'Look up Nathan Bain's telephone number. Ring the house. If Sergeant Holcomb's out there I want to talk with him.'

Della Street said, 'Nellie Conway left us a number, you know. Just a minute, I'll get it. . . .'

She ran through half a dozen cards, said, 'Here it is. West 6–9841.'

'All right,' Mason said, 'get Holcomb.'

Della Street picked up the telephone, said, 'Gertie, ring West 6–9841 and get Sergeant Holcomb on the line. It's important. Rush it.'

Della Street held on to the phone for several seconds, then motioned to Mason and said, 'He's coming on now, Chief.'

Mason took the phone just as he heard a gruff voice saying, 'Hello. This is Holcomb. Who is this?'

'Perry Mason.'

'Oh, yes, Mason. How did you know I was out here?'

'I've been trying to reach you.'

'All right, what is it?'

Mason said, 'You will remember, Sergeant, that Nellie Conway, whom I spoke to you about a few days ago, had claimed that Nathan Bain had asked her to administer certain five-grain pills to his wife. I told you about that.'

'Yeah, go on,' Sergeant Holcomb said.

'And,' Mason said, 'in order to check her story I had one of those pills analysed. It contained aspirin. I thought you should know.'

There was a long period of silence.

'You there?' Mason asked impatiently.

'I'm here,' Sergeant Holcomb said.

'Well?' Mason asked.

'I don't remember the conversation that way,' Sergeant Holcomb said, and hung up.

Mason jiggled the receiver twice, then dropped the telephone into place.

'Did he hang up?' Della Street asked.

Mason nodded, white-faced with anger.

'Go ahead, Chief,' she said. 'Let it go. I've heard all of the words before, and this is once I'd like to hear 'em again.'

He shook his head.

'Why not?'

'Damn it, Della, I can't afford to get mad. I have to think.'

'But, Chief, I was listening to that conversation. I know that you told him that–'

'Your testimony will be somewhat less than conclusive,' Mason said dryly. 'Moreover, you didn't hear what Holcomb said to me by way of reply.'

'What does he *claim* he said?' she asked.

Mason made his lips into a sour grin. 'He hasn't had time to think that up yet. What the hell do you think he hung up for?'

She said, 'I wish you'd let go and cuss him. It's going to sound unladylike if I voice my thoughts on behalf of the firm.'

Mason shook his head. 'A good lawyer must always remember one thing. Never get mad unless someone pays him to do it.'

'Can you imagine that damn cop deliberately lying?' Della Street asked, indignantly.

'I can imagine him doing anything,' Mason said. 'Lieutenant Tragg is tough but he's a square shooter. I should have insisted on getting in touch with Tragg; but the thing sounded like such a complete cock-and-bull story . . . I still don't get it. All I know is that I have a distinct feeling I'm in hot water and it's getting hotter.'

He began pacing the floor. Della Street started to say something, then, changing her mind, stood watching him with worried eyes as he paced back and forth.

At 12.25 the telephone rang.

Della Street picked up the phone and Paul Drake said, 'Hello, Della. I have the information Perry wanted about the airplane passenger.'

Mason jerked himself up sharply. 'That Drake?' he asked.

Della Street nodded.

'Tell him to give you the dope if he has any,' Mason said.

'Shoot,' Della said into the phone.

Drake said, 'A ten-fifteen plane for New Orleans, Della. A woman who answered the description of the party Mason wanted gave her name as Nora Carson.'

Della Street relayed the information to Perry Mason. Mason crossed the office in three swift strides, grabbed the telephone and said, 'Paul, get in touch with whatever agency you correspond with in New Orleans. I want four men working in relays. I want Nora Carson picked up as soon as she leaves the plane. I want to have someone on her every minute of the time, and I don't care what it costs. I want to know where she goes, who she sees, what she does and when. Then wire to the Roosevelt Hotel and reserve a suite for two in *your* name. The registration will be Paul Drake and party.

'Della Street will get us tickets on the first available plane to New Orleans. Tell your men to report to us at the Roosevelt Hotel. Now jump in your car and get up here just as fast as you can because we're leaving on the first available plane and I don't know yet just what the schedules are–'

'There's one at one-fifteen,' Paul Drake said, 'but we can't make that. We–'

'Who the hell says we can't?' Mason asked. 'Drive to the airport. I'll meet you there.'

9

Within two hours of the time Mason and Paul Drake had ensconced themselves in the Roosevelt Hotel in New Orleans, a representative of Paul Drake's affiliated detective agency was in the room making a report.

'We have the party located,' he said. 'She's taken an apartment in the old French Quarter. It was all ready for her. The lease was signed by a man from your city, a fellow by the name of Nathan Bain. Do you know him?'

Mason and Drake exchanged glances.

Mason said, 'Go ahead.'

'This apartment was leased about thirty days ago and Bain took out a six-months' lease on it.'

'What sort of a place?' Mason asked.

'Well, you know how those apartments in the French Quarter are. They're old as the hills, but the place has a certain atmosphere that appeals to tourists and some of the local residents who want high ceilings and low rent. Some of the buildings have been fixed up pretty nice.'

'When Bain negotiated for the lease did he say anything about who was going to occupy the apartment?'

'Simply took a lease on the apartment.'

'How did he pay for the rent?' Mason asked. 'By cheque?'

'No. There's something interesting. He paid by postal money order.'

Mason nodded. 'The girl is living there?'

'That's right. Living there under the name of Nora Carson, and she's dough-heavy.'

'How heavy?' Mason asked.

'I don't know. She has quite a wad of bills in her purse, big bills. Right after she arrived she went to the Bourbon House for dinner and tried to change a hundred-dollar bill. It caused quite a little commotion. She said that was the smallest she had. The manager happened to get a glance at the inside of her purse and saw that it held quite a wad of currency. He thought she was lying and was trying to get rid of a big bill because it might be hot. That made him suspicious. He insisted that she dig up something smaller. She finally left the hundred-dollar bill as security, went out, and was back within twenty minutes with a bunch of small bills.'

Mason digested that information. 'Anything else?' he said.

'Yes. We've followed instructions and kept her spotted all the time.'

'Does she have any idea she's being tailed?'

'Apparently not. She goes about her business just as though it was part of a regular routine. She doesn't seem to pay any attention to people on the sidewalk.'

'All right. What's she doing down here?'

'Well, of course, she's only been here three or four hours, but–'

'What's she done to indicate the purpose of her visit in that time?'

'Nothing.'

'How big a place is this French Quarter apartment house?' Mason asked.

'Not big. Two apartments to a floor, two floors. It's a narrow, three-storeyed place with a praline store on the ground floor, your party and one other woman have the apartments on the second floor, one bachelor and one vacant apartment on the third floor.'

'Who has the other second-floor apartment?' Mason asked.

'A Miss Charlotte Moray. You know how these buildings are in the French Quarter–that is, I'm taking it for granted that you're familiar with it?' The question invited confidences.

'He's familiar with it,' Drake said, shortly.

The New Orleans detective regarded Perry Mason thoughtfully. It was quite evident that he was interested in the identity of Drake's mysterious client, but his curiosity stopped short of actual questions.

'How long has this Moray woman been there?' Mason asked.

'About a week.'

'Know where she comes from or anything about her?'

'Not a thing. We've only been on the job–'

'Yes, I know. Have you a description?'

The detective took a notebook from his pocket. 'Around twenty-four or twenty-five, very dark, good figure, snapping black eyes, dark hair, a lot of personality and pep, wears good clothes and knows how to wear them. We haven't had time to find out much about her. We do know that she gets telegrams every day, sometimes two or three times a day. We don't know where they come from or anything about them, but we do know she gets them.'

'Anything else?' Mason asked.

'That covers it to date. That Moray girl is a nice dish. Five feet four, a hundred and twenty pounds, curves in the right places, lots of fire, and evidently she keeps pretty much to herself. No boy friends, no particular interest in the scenery, seems to be fully familiar with New Orleans, knows where to shop, does some cooking in her apartment, eats out some of the time, very unapproachable, but gracious and smiling to the waitresses, just a woman keeping very much to herself.'

'One more question,' Mason said. 'When did Charlotte Moray rent her apartment?'

'She sub-let it before she came here and was all ready to move in when she got off the plane.'

'Sub-let it? From whom?'

'Why, this man Bain. I thought you understood. He leased the whole second floor, and–'

'Leased the whole second floor!' Mason exclaimed.

'Why, yes. You see, he–'

'Why the hell didn't you say so?'

'You didn't ask. I mean, you seemed to want information only on this

Conway girl. Of course we've been working fast and . . . I'm sorry, sir. I thought you understood.'

'The third floor–does Bain lease that too?'

'No, just the second floor, the two apartments there.'

Mason turned to Paul Drake. 'Pay them off, Paul, and call them off.'

Drake raised his eyebrows.

'We're finished,' Mason said. 'Are these boys pretty good at forgetting things?'

'They should be,' Drake said.

'We are,' the New Orleans detective assured them, his eyes, however, filled with curiosity as he studied Mason.

'All right,' Mason said, 'we don't want any more coverage on the case. Lay the men off and be sure everyone is called off the job.'

'As soon as we're paid off, we're off the job,' the New Orleans detective said. 'We're not anxious to work for nothing.'

Drake pulled a notecase from his pocket, said, 'This is a job where payments are made in cash. Come on in the other room and we'll get straightened up.'

Five minutes later when Drake returned he said, 'I didn't want to seem rude, Perry, but if I hadn't insisted on a private pay-off it would have been suspicious. He would have thought we were pretty closely associated. I wanted him to think you were just an ordinary client.'

Mason nodded. 'How soon will he have his men removed from the job, Paul?'

Drake said. 'Give him fifteen minutes, Perry. I told him to go out and call the thing off. He said he was starting right away. We'll give him fifteen minutes.'

Mason said, 'That'll be fine.'

'But what gets me,' Drake told him, 'is why you're so damn crazy to have this gal covered every minute of the day and night, and after the men have been working on her for four hours, you get in such a lather to have them called off the job. I don't get it.'

'Because we have the information we want,' Mason told him.

'Well, even so, why be in such a rush to get the men off the job?'

Mason lit a cigarette. 'Nellie Conway is going to have a visitor, Paul. Later on, the police may be interested in Nellie Conway. They may find out these detectives were on the job and shake them down to find out what they know. If they don't know who this visitor is, they can't tell.'

'You seem to be pretty sure of your facts,' Drake said.

'I am.'

'Then you probably know who this visitor is going to be–the one you don't want the police to find out about.'

'I do.'

'Who–Nathan Bain?'

'No.'

'Who, then?'

'Perry Mason,' the lawyer told him.

10

After midnight the French Quarter of New Orleans takes on an individuality all its own.

Escorts who have gone to "get the car" drive back down the narrow one-way streets, only to find that their party, instead of waiting on the sidewalk, is lingering over a last drink.

The driver sounds an indignant horn.

In the meantime, his car is blocking the choked one-way street. A car pulls up behind him and the driver sounds a couple of blasts just as a courteous reminder. The driver of the stalled car shows his good faith by blasting his horn in protest.

Two or three other cars fall in behind. Each car, from time to time, emits short, courteous reminders of sound, until, patience exhausted, they all start demanding the driver ahead to move on and clear the street.

At such times the exasperated roar of a dozen blasting horns shatters the night silence to ribbons.

Parties emerging from the noisy interiors of the nightclubs say good-bye to new-found acquaintances. There is an exchange of telephone numbers, and because ears and voices are not as yet oriented to the comparative stillness of the outer air, the information is usually given in a voice audible half a block away.

Then there are the exuberant souls who take advantage of the Quarter's custom of putting garbage cans out on the sidewalk for night collection. These revellers release their animal spirits by kicking the covers of garbage cans along the sidewalks.

Shortly before daylight, when other noises have quieted down, the garbage trucks rumble along, banging and clattering the collection of garbage into the big vans.

All in all, the person who craves quiet in the Quarter should not try to sleep before 6 a.m. Most of them don't.

Mason, threading his way through late revellers and denizens of the Quarter, walked twice around the block in order to make certain there were no shadows watching the entrance to the apartment house. Then he entered a narrow passageway which led to a patio, and climbed an ornamental flight of stairs, whose characteristic wrought-iron banisters led in a sweeping curve to the second floor. Here a hundred and fifty years of foundation settling in the damp soil had caused waving inequalities in a typical floor, which, because of habit, the eye interpreted as being level, with disastrous results to the gait of a sober citizen, but seemingly without undue effect on the inebriated.

The door marked '1.A.' was by the head of the stairs. The door was slightly open. Mason could see the illuminated interior of the apartment.

There was a reclining chair by a table on which were newspapers and magazines; a reading lamp shed brilliance over the scene. In the shadowed area behind the reading lamp, heavy curtains had been partially pulled across french doors opening on a narrow balcony, which in turn stretched out over the sidewalk of the one-way street.

A door at the end of the corridor made a noise. Mason heard the sound of a cautious step, then a half-startled scream.

'How did *you* get here?' Nellie Conway demanded.

Mason said grimly, 'Let's get a few things straightened out, Nellie.'

They entered the apartment. Mason seated himself and indicated a chair for Nellie Conway.

'This isn't going to take long,' he said.

She stood for a moment, dubiously, then fumbled with the catch of the purse which she had been carrying clutched under her arm.

'Honestly, Mr. Mason,' she said, 'you didn't *need* to do this. I intended to send you the money.'

She sat down, opened the purse and took out two one-hundred-dollar notes, hesitated a moment, added another hundred-dollar note and pushed the three hundred dollars across the table to Mason.

Mason regarded the one-hundred-dollar notes thoughtfully. 'Where did you get this?'

'That was part of the settlement.'

'What settlement?'

'The one I made with Nathan Bain.'

'All right,' Mason said, still holding the money in his hand, 'tell me about the settlement.'

'Well, it was like I told you, Mr Mason. Mr Bain was worried and . . .

'Well, of course, when I came to get my things, Mr Bain was a little embarrassed at first. I asked him about the relief nurse he had taking care of his wife, and it seemed she'd quit the job for some reason or other. The housekeeper was helping out. Mr Bain said that he expected his wife's relatives to arrive shortly after midnight.'

'Then what did you do?'

'I went in and talked with Elizabeth . . . Mrs Bain, and helped the housekeeper. We managed to get her really quiet. She had the best sleep she'd had since the accident.'

'Have any conversations with her?'

'Oh, yes. She asked me a lot of questions.'

'What about?'

'About where I'd been and how much she hated to have me leave her, and how she'd missed me while I was gone, and asking me how it had happened that I was leaving.'

'Did you tell her the truth–about being arrested and the trial?'

'Of course, why not?'

'I'm just asking,' Mason said. 'Go on. Did Nathan Bain come in there while you were there? Did he–?'

'Mr Bain never enters his wife's room. It would have a very adverse effect on Elizabeth. The doctor knows that just as Mr Bain knows it. It's lamentable, but it's one of the things that–'

'Never mind that,' Mason said. 'I just wanted to know if he went in.'

'No, he didn't.'

'And did you tell her about how he had tried to bribe you to give her medicine?'

'Oh, no.'

'Why not?'

'That might have been bad for the patient. You shouldn't ever do or say anything to excite your patient.'

Mason studied her thoughtfully. 'All right. Now tell me about where you got this money.'

'That was early in the evening, before I went in to see Mrs Bain. When I first showed up, Mr Bain asked me what I intended to do–you know, about the arrest and all that. That's when I telephoned you.'

'Go ahead,' Mason said.

'Well, I told him that as far as our relations were concerned, that is, Mr Bain's and mine, they would have to be worked out by attorneys, that I didn't care to discuss that phase of the matter with him. I said I had come to get my things, and not to talk.'

'And what did Bain do?'

'Well, then Mr Bain insisted we make some kind of a settlement. He wanted to have things worked out so we could . . . well, as he said, so we could act civilised about the thing.'

'And you made a settlement with him?'

'Well, he explained to me that if an attorney represented me in making a settlement, the lawyer would charge me perhaps fifty per cent of what I received, at least thirty-three and a third per cent. He told me there was no reason why I couldn't have that money just as well as some lawyer. He said that he was willing to acknowledge the fact that he'd made a mistake. He said he'd been betrayed by that private detective who had posed as a smart guy, a sort of know-it-all.'

'What kind of a settlement did you finally make?'

'I don't think that needs to enter into *our* discussions, Mr Mason.'

'What kind of a settlement did you finally make?'

'Well, he said he'd pay me what it would cost him to fight me in court, and in that way the lawyers wouldn't get it all. He said that if I got a lawyer to sue him he'd have to pay a lawyer to fight the case and I'd have to pay a lawyer to bring the case to court, and then they'd suggest a compromise, and he'd pay money to me, half of which would go into the pocket of the lawyer, and his lawyer would then charge–'

'What kind of a settlement did you make?'

'An adequate settlement.'

'What kind of settlement did you make?'

'I felt under the circumstances I had been fairly compensated.'

'How much was it?'

She said, 'Mr Bain asked me not to discuss that matter with anyone and I don't feel free to do so, Mr Mason. I . . . I had enough for your fee. I intended to send you a money order in the morning, the first thing. I really did.'

'How much did he pay you?'

'I am sorry, Mr Mason, I am not at liberty to discuss that. I've paid you your fee and I'd like for you to give me a receipt, please.'

Mason said, 'This money came from Nathan Bain?'

'Of course, where else would I get it?'

'I mean, did he give you a cheque and did you go to a bank and cash the cheque and then–'

'No, no. He gave me the cash in currency.'

'Did you sign anything?'

'I signed a complete release.'

'Had it been drawn up by a lawyer?'

'I don't know.'

'Was it typewritten?'

'Yes.'

'On legal size stationery, or on letter size stationery?'

'On letter size stationery.'

'Do you know whether he'd been to see an attorney?'

'I don't think so. I think he drew it up himself.'

'You took the money?'

'Yes.'

'How did you happen to come here?'

'I've always wanted to come to New Orleans and just relax and see the city. It has always fascinated me. It's a city with such a romantic background, and they say the restaurants here are–'

'How did you happen to come here?'

'Just an impulse, Mr Mason.'

'Did Mr Bain suggest that you come here?'

'Mr Bain? Good heavens, no!'

'How did you happen to get this apartment?'

She lowered her eyes for a moment, then said, 'Really, Mr Mason, I don't think I care to discuss any more of my private affairs. I'm certainly grateful to you but there are some things I can't go into. Please remember that you acted as my lawyer for just one matter. You're not my lawyer now. You defended me, and I've paid you. That winds up all matters between us. I don't want to seem rude, but–'

'Do you know anyone here in New Orleans?'

'Not a soul. No.'

'There was no one you came here to see?'

'No.'

Mason jerked his head towards the door. 'Where were you when I came in?'

'I . . . I'd just dashed downstairs to mail a letter in the mail-box at the next corner.'

'Who was the letter to?'

'To you. I wanted you to know where I was and to tell you I'd send you money for your fee.'

Mason said, 'You had some tablets in a little corked tube.'

'You mean the ones we put in the envelope?'

'Yes. What did you do with those?'

She hesitated a moment, then said, 'I tossed the whole thing in the trash.'

'What do you mean by the whole thing?'

'The envelope, everything.'

'You mean the envelope with our names written across the sealed flap?'

'Yes.'

'You didn't open the envelope?'

'No.'

'Why did you do that?'

'Because, well . . . I don't know. Perhaps I shouldn't have done it, Mr Mason, but after I had made my settlement with Mr Bain and he turned out to be . . . well, he was trying to do the square thing and I thought I'd let bygones be bygones.'

'Did you tell him you were throwing the tablets away?'

'I'd rather not answer that.'

Mason said, 'Let's get a few cards face up on the table for a change. Did you tell him what you had done?'

'Yes. He saw me do it.'

'Saw you throw the envelope in the trash?'

'Yes.'

'What did you tell him?'

'I told him that I wasn't in a position to do what he'd wanted me to, that I'd told you about what had happened when . . . when I talked with you, and that if you'd wanted to, you could have confronted him with that envelope on cross-examination and put him in the position of having tried to see that drugs were given to his wife.'

'What did he say?'

'He said that he had been anticipating such a move and that he was prepared for it.'

'Did he say how he was prepared?'

'No.'

'But he did say he had been anticipating it?'

'He said he thought I might try to pull something like that or that you might.'

'And what did you tell him?'

'I told him that you hadn't needed to do anything like that, and that since he was trying to do the right thing by me, I'd try to do the right thing by him, and I took the envelope with that little bottle in it and tossed it into the waste basket back of the cook stove in the kitchen.'

'Did you tell him you'd do that before he paid you money, or afterward?'

'I . . . I can't remember.'

'Did you tell Nathan Bain you were going to New Orleans?'

'Certainly not. It was none of his business.'

'You got off the plane and moved right into this apartment. You didn't go to a hotel first to get oriented, you just moved right in.'

'Well, what's wrong with that?'

'Apartments aren't that easy to find in New Orleans.'

'Well, what if they aren't? I found this one.'

'You had this one before you ever came to New Orleans.'

'Well, what if I did? I'm not accountable to you for my conduct.'

'How is Mrs Bain getting along?'

'Splendidly. Of course, she'll never walk again, but she's doing fine. She slept like a log, just the realisation that her relatives were there–and they're very nice people, those relatives of hers.

'You met them?'

'Of course. I was helping with the nursing as much as I could. After Mr Bain made his settlement with me, I wanted to do what I could, you know.'

'You didn't have any idea how long she might live when you last saw her?'

'Oh, she'll live for years.'

Mason said, 'Now we'll go back to where we started. How much of a settlement did you get out of Mr Bain?'

'I'm not going to tell you that.'

'You collected money from Mr Bain for my attorney fee?'

'We talked, of course, about the expense I'd been to. That was why he was making a settlement.'

'I told you over the telephone that if Mr Bain was paying my fee, it was going to be five hundred dollars.'

'Well, he wasn't paying your fee. I'm the one who's paying your fee.'

'Nathan Bain was standing right there by the telephone when you talked with me?'

'Yes.'

'And I told you it was going to cost him five hundred dollars for my fee?'

'Something to that effect.'

Mason held out his hand.

She hesitated a long moment, then reluctantly opened her purse again, took out two one-hundred-dollar notes and literally threw them across the table.

Mason folded them, put them in his pocket and walked out.

As soon as he had left the apartment, she slammed the door, and Mason heard the sound of a bolt shooting into place.

Mason walked down the corridor, waited for a moment, then tapped gently on the door of Apartment 1.B.

The floor had sagged enough to leave a half-inch crack under the door. Mason could see a ribbon of light through the crack, could see a moving shadow as some person glided gently into position and stood listening intently.

Mason tapped once more with his finger-tips, a barely audible sound on the panels of the door.

The shadow on the other side of the door moved a few inches. The sound of the bolt being drawn back was almost inaudible. The door opened.

The very attractive woman who was standing on the threshold was clothed only in a filmy *néglìgé*. Light shining through it outlined her figure in sharp silhouette, the gossamer clothing forming a filmy aura about the well-shaped body.

'Oh!' she said, in an exclamation that was a mingling of surprise and dismay, and started to close the door.

Mason stepped forward.

She struggled with the door for a moment, then fell back.

'I'll scream,' she warned.

'It won't get you anything.'

'And this won't get *you* anything!' she retorted angrily.

Mason said, 'Let's make this as painless as possible. I want to talk about the woman who was in here a few minutes ago, the one who has apartment 1.A.'

'I don't know anything about her, except that I saw a young woman moving in there tonight, carrying a couple of suitcases. I haven't met her yet.'

Mason said, 'You'll have to do better than that. Let's talk about Nathan Bain. Does that name mean anything to you?'

'Certainly not.'

'In case you don't know it already,' Mason said, 'Nathan Bain is going to be delayed quite a bit in coming to New Orleans. Now if you want to–'

She elevated a scornful chin. 'Are you trying to intimate something?'

'Merely that Nathan Bain's plans are going to be changed materially.'

'I don't know any Nathan Brame–'

'Bain.' Mason corrected.

'All right, Bain or Brame, or whatever you want to call it. I don't know him and–'

'You've never met him?'

'Of course not. Now, if you don't get out I'm going to start screaming for the police.'

She waited a few seconds, then started towards the window which opened on the patio.

'No telephone?' Mason asked.

'I don't need one. I'll show you how quickly the police–'

Mason waited until she was within inches of the window, then said, 'Elizabeth Bain's death is going to cause Nathan Bain to–'

She whirled. 'What are you saying?'

'I was telling you about Elizabeth Bain's death.'

She straightened, turned and stood looking at him, as stiffly motionless as a statue. '*What* are you saying?'

'I'm trying to give you some information that may be of value.'

She regained her self-possession. 'Who is this Elizabeth Bain?'

'She's the wife of Nathan Bain, or rather she was.'

'Would you mind telling me just who you are?'

'The name is Mason.'

'And are you connected with the police in some way?'

'No. I'm an attorney.'

'And just why do you come here to tell me this, Mr Mason?'

'Because,' he said, 'I wanted to find out whether you already knew about Mrs Bain's death.'

'Mr Mason, you certainly must have me confused with someone else.'

She moved over to the big overstuffed chair, standing with one arm on its back, not bothering to hold the *négligé*.'How did it happen–this death of Mrs Brame?'

'Calling it Brame the first time was a good act,' Mason said. 'The second time is corny. She was poisoned.'

'Oh, good heavens!' she said, and her knees buckled her into the chair. 'Did you say she was . . . was poisoned?'

'Yes.'

'Was it . . . sleeping pills . . . suicide?'

'No.'

'Oh!'

'However,' Mason went on, turning back towards the door, 'since you don't know the Bains, the thing can't be of any possible interest to you.'

'Wait,' she said sharply.

Mason paused.

'Who gave her . . . how did it happen?'

'What do you care? They're strangers to you–remember?'

'I . . . I meant . . . oh, all right, you win. What do you want?'

Mason said, 'You look grown-up. I thought you might be able to act grown-up.'

'What do you want?'

'Information.'

'What information?'

'All you have.'

'Suppose I don't give it?'

'That's your privilege.'

'And you're a lawyer?'

'Yes.'

She said, 'Okay, sit down. I'll buy you a drink.'

Mason sat down. She went to the sideboard, took out a bottle of Scotch, poured two stiff drinks, splashed in soda and said, 'I hope you like Scotch and soda. It's all I have.'

'That'll do fine,' Mason said.

She brought the drink over to him and sat down in the chair, the *négligé* falling away to show glimpses of a figure that would have won a beauty contest anywhere.

'The sooner you begin,' Mason said, 'the sooner it will be over with.'

'All right,' she said. 'I have nothing to hide. The big lug!'

Mason sipped his drink.

She said, 'I met him at a convention six months ago. A producers' convention. He certainly has a good line and he's a good spender.'

'Just what are you looking for?' Mason asked.

She said, 'All right, I'll tell you that, too.'

She took a couple of swallows from her drink, then met his eyes and said, 'I was a green, trusting kid. I found out that men had a good line. I fell for it. It didn't buy me anything. Now I've started to get wise.

'I've worked, and worked hard, ever since I was seventeen years old. I see other women who don't have anything I haven't got, breezing around in expensive automobiles with chauffeurs, all dolled up in furs and with some big sap footing the bills and thinking he's sugar when he's only gravy.'

Mason grinned and said, 'That's better.'

'All right,' she said, 'I met Nathan Bain. I guess at one time he'd been God's gift to women. He can't realise that years and fat do things to a man. He started handing me a line, then when he saw he had to boost the ante he shelled out a little bit here and there.'

'Money?' Mason asked.

'Gems, jewels–nice stuff.'

Mason was thoughtful. 'Did it come by messenger?'

'Don't be silly. He delivered in person,' she said. 'He'd take a nice little diamond something or other from his pocket, hold it on his hand for a while, then slip it around my neck. I'd go nuts with rapture.'

'Nice work if you can get it,' Mason said.

'Don't make any mistake about me, brother. I got it.'

'Then what?'

'Then Nathan rented these apartments down here in New Orleans. I was to take a vacation down here. He'd have the adjoining apartment just for the sake of appearances. He wasn't supposed even to know me. Ostensibly he was down here on business, and he intended to have a business conference or two in his apartment so he could prove what he was here for if he had to.'

'And then what?'

'Then,' she said, 'the damn fool let his wife get hold of my letters. She got them from his office.'

'You wrote him passionate letters?' Mason asked.

'Sure. What did *I* have to lose? I took my pen in hand and drooled all over the paper. After all, I thought the guy had some sense.'

'It bothered you when the wife got the letters?'

'Not a damn bit,' she admitted. 'It bothered him, and then all of a sudden, it bothered me. Up to then I hadn't realised how firmly he was hooked. He was hoping he could find a way to get a divorce with some sort of a property settlement from her, and marry me. Well, I decided to string along on that end of the game for a while.'

'And then what?'

'Then,' she said, 'he got the letters back from his wife. I don't know how he got them but he got them and he sent this girl down to give them to me.'

'You mean the one over in apartment I.A.?'

'Yes. Nora Carson.'

'What do you think of her?'

'All right in a negative sort of a way. She's kept herself under wraps until she doesn't know how to let herself go. She hasn't any voltage. She'd like to play the game my way but she doesn't know how it's done and she'll never find out. She doesn't have anything to show, and nothing to deliver. But she'd like to try. Since she delivered the letters, she's made an excuse to run in here three or four times. The way she looks me over you can see she's wondering what I've got she hasn't–and the pathetic part of it is, she'll never find out.'

'She was sent here just to deliver those letters?'

'Yes. Nathan sent her down here to bring me my purple letters. Wasn't that nice of him? My "good name" is safe now. Think of it. I won't have to be a correspondent after all. I'll be–as though I give a damn–or do I?'

Mason said, 'You're giving me a lot of information. Why?'

'Because I like your looks.'

Mason smiled and shook his head.

'Yes, I do too. You look like a square shooter. You look like a man who knows his way around. You look like a man who will play square with me if I play square with you.'

'And what do you want?'

She said, 'I've put my cards face up on the table.'

'All right, what do you want in return?'

She said, 'If there's a murder, I don't want any part of it. Nathan Bain is a fellow you can have a lot of fun with and he does keep decorating the mahogany, but that isn't going to last. You know that as well as I do. Marriage to him would lead to a career in the kitchen. You have to get what you can out of him and then move on. He likes pastures while they're green and while they're on the other side of the fence. Give him the key to the gate and it would mean nothing.'

'Go on,' Mason said.

She said, 'I have a right guy. He doesn't have quite as much as Nathan Bain, but there's just a chance that I might play it on the up-and-up with him. I've been thinking.'

'And what do you want me to do?'

'Tell me what to do, so I can keep from being smeared in a murder case.'

Mason said, 'Start packing your things. Get out of this apartment within twenty minutes and get out of this city within thirty. You have your letters back. Burn them. The wind is going to blow. Go hunt yourself a cyclone cellar.'

'I thought you were a good egg,' she said. 'Do you know, Mr Mason, I sort of like this other guy. I might . . . hell, you don't suppose I'm falling for another line, do you?'

'I wouldn't know,' Mason said, 'but there's only one way to find out.'

'You're right at that,' she told him.

Mason finished his drink.

She followed him to the door, put her hand on his arm. 'I'll remember you.'

Mason said, 'I'd get out quietly so that girl in the next apartment doesn't know that you're leaving.'

The dark eyes showed sudden bitterness. 'You aren't telling *me* anything,' she said. 'Listen, I've found out that a girl can't trust many men, and she can't trust *any* women.'

'Good luck,' Mason said, and walked down the narrow, winding stairs to the patio and the night noises of St. Peter Street.

11

Back in the Roosevelt Hotel, Mason found Paul Drake with his ear glued to a telephone, getting a long report.

When Drake had finished and hung up, Mason said, 'Paul, I want to get copies of messages from the local files of the Western Union Telegraph Company.'

Drake shook his head. 'It's not only darned near impossible, Perry, but it's illegal.'

Mason said, 'Charlotte Moray, who has the apartment across from the one where Nellie Conway is living, has been receiving telegrams. I think they come from Nathan Bain.'

Drake said, 'I can help you out on the last one of those telegrams, Perry.'

'How come?'

Drake said, 'She may not even have received it as yet. Here it is.' He picked up a sheet of paper on which he had scrawled pencilled handwriting, and read:

Unexpected and entirely unforeseen developments which may cause complications necessitate immediate conference. I am arriving on plane due nine-fifteen a.m. leaving on plane due to depart New Orleans one-thirty-five p.m. which will get me back here before my absence will have been noticed or commented on.

'And,' Drake said, 'the message is signed, "Your Falstaff".'

'And it was sent by?'

'Nathan Bain.'

'How did you get it, Paul?'

Drake said, 'Nathan Bain was quote overcome with grief unquote. He enlisted the aid of a friendly physician who quote administered a sedative unquote, put Bain to bed in a private sanatorium and insisted that he remained undisturbed. A rather bad heart condition, you understand.'

'Go ahead,' Mason said.

'The police apparently fell for it and so did the newspaper reporters, although they grumbled a bit. My man smelled a rat. He found there was an alley exit through a garage. He watched it and sure enough Nathan Bain, showing no evidence whatever of having been given a hypodermic, came boiling out of the back, jumped into a closed car and was whisked away.

'My man followed as best he could, but I think he'd have lost the guy if Bain hadn't been so damn anxious to send this telegram. There was a branch of Western Union office about ten blocks down the street and Bain's car stopped there. Bain ran in and scribbled his message.'

'How did your man get the copy?' Mason asked.

'That's a trick of the trade, Perry.'

'Go on, come through,' Mason told him. 'If there's any way of getting Western Union messages that easy I want to know about it.'

'It was dead easy, Perry.'

'How much did it cost?'

'A dollar and ten cents.'

'How come?'

'Bain grabbed a pencil and wrote this message down on a pad of telegraph blanks that was lying on the counter. My man boldly stepped up as soon as Bain had sent the message, took the same pad of telegraph blanks, tore off a couple of sheets and sent a telegram to his mother telling her he was too busy to write but that he wanted her to know he was thinking of her. The message cost him a dollar and ten cents. Naturally he didn't write it on the sheet of paper that had been immediately under the one on which Bain wrote his message. So it was only necessary for my man to take that sheet of paper, illuminate it with transverse lighting, photograph it and decipher the message which had been indented in the paper underneath by Bain's pencil. Bain writes with a heavy fist.'

Mason grinned. 'Good work, Paul.'

Drake said, 'Here's some stuff you won't like so well. The police searched the trash can back of Bain's kitchen stove. In there they found an envelope that had been sealed, and your name and the name of Nellie Conway had been written across the flap. Then the envelope had been torn open and–'

'Was a phial in there?' Mason asked.

'Apparently not, but an outline on the envelope showed it had contained a little phial or bottle.'

Mason thought that over. 'Can the police tell just when the poison was administered, Paul? She must have taken some food–'

'It wasn't taken in food,' Drake interposed.

'How was it taken?'

'It was taken in the form of three five-grain tablets washed down with a glass of water followed by coffee, and given by Mrs Bain's sister, Victoria Braxton.'

'Are you sure?'

'The police are,' Drake said.

'How do they know?'

'Elizabeth Bain told them. Her half-sister gave her the tablets.'

'What does Victoria Braxton have to say to that?' Mason asked.

'Apparently nothing,' Drake said, 'because the police can't find her.'

'Oh-oh!'

'Your friend Sergeant Holcomb, seems to have taken charge of the affair. For some reason he had a sudden desire to search the Bain house from cellar to garret. He ordered everybody out just as soon as Elizabeth Bain died. He told them to go to hotels and report to the police where they were.'

'So what happened?'

'So they did,' Drake said, grinning. 'Nathan Bain went to his club. He reported to the police that he was there. James Braxton and his wife, Georgiana, went to a down-town hotel, registered and stayed there. Victoria

Braxton went to another hotel, registered and notified the police she was there, and the police seem to be having some difficulty finding out exactly where she is. They want to question her. All they can learn so far is that she's completely broken up over her sister's death, is staying with friends somewhere and isn't in her room."

'What else do you know, Paul?'

Drake said, 'Bain got a new night nurse after Nellie Conway was arrested. Evidently he made passes at her and she walked out in a huff.

'Mrs Ricker, the housekeeper, had been on duty all day, but she said she'd try to see that the patient was comfortable. Then Nellie Conway walked in. Nathan Bain made a settlement of some sort with her, patched up his differences with her and put her to work.

'Mrs Bain had a fine night. She went to sleep early and slept like a log, which was something she hadn't been doing. Sometime after midnight the plane bringing her half-brother, James Braxton, and her half-sister, Victoria Braxton, and Jim Braxton's wife, Georgiana, landed, and all three of them went directly to the house.

'Since Elizabeth Bain was sleeping, they decided they wouldn't disturb her at the moment, but would wait until she wakened.

'She wakened about three a.m. and asked if the folks had come. On being assured they had, she said she wanted to see them. She seemed a little sleepy and groggy, and a lot less nervous and hysterical than she had been. She greeted them warmly and went back to sleep.

'Now get this Perry. Nellie Conway wasn't really working. She'd gone back to get her things. She made some sort of settlement with Nathan Bain and she was just helping out because the housekeeper had been up all day. Nellie had said she'd help out until the folks came and then they could take over with the nursing.'

Mason nodded.

'But,' Drake went on, 'the travellers had been flying from Honolulu and felt a little worn. They decided they'd get a little sleep, and Nellie Conway volunteered to stay on for a while longer.

'After about an hour's sleep, Victoria Braxton came in and told Nellie Conway she was completely rested now and Nellie could leave. The housekeeper had already gone to bed. I'm giving you all of this because I think it's important, Perry.'

'Go ahead.'

'Now, as nearly as we can tell, the doctor, a fellow by the name of Keener, had left three five-grain tablets to be given Mrs Bain when she wakened at any time after six o'clock in the morning, but they weren't to be given to her before six. Those tablets had been left with Nellie Conway who was the nurse in charge.'

'So what happened when Nellie Conway went off duty?'

'She put the tablets on a little saucer, put them on the table and told Victoria Braxton that she was to give them to Elizabeth Bain at any time after six o'clock, but not to wake her up to give them to her, to wait until she wakened naturally.'

'Go on,' Mason said.

'Mrs Bain woke up around five o'clock, I believe, and was awake for a while, talking with her half-sister. Then she went back to sleep, wakened at right around seven o'clock.

'She still felt drowsy and completely relaxed. She didn't want any breakfast, but said she'd like coffee. She had a cup of coffee and took the three pills. Anyway, that's what she told the doctor. And get this, Perry, that coffee and the three pills are all that she took into her stomach from somewhere around eight-thirty the night before. So the arsenic *had* to be in the pills.'

'Or in the coffee,' Mason said.

'You can discount the coffee, because the coffee came out of an urn and several people drank it.'

'Perhaps in the sugar?'

'She didn't take sugar or cream. She took the coffee black.'

'Then what, Paul?'

'The day nurse came on duty at eight o'clock. She found Victoria Braxton on duty. Victoria said she wanted to take a bath, clean up and then she was going up-town for a while. The day nurse took over. Understand, this was a case where they only had two nurses. The night nurse worked from six to eight because she didn't have it quite so hard, and the day nurse worked from eight to six.'

'Go on, Paul.'

'The day nurse found Mrs Bain sleeping, but she was twitching and moaning as though she might be in pain of some sort, but since she was sleeping soundly the nurse didn't disturb her.

'Mrs Bain had been very restless, you know, and it was considered important for her to get sleep whenever possible, so, as it happened, the day nurse didn't do a darned thing about straightening up the room or anything. She just sat down and left everything the way it was so Mrs Bain wouldn't be disturbed. That's important because it means that the evidence was left undisturbed.'

'Go ahead, Paul. Then what?'

'Well, sometime shortly before nine, Mrs Bain wakened and was immediately and violently ill, and she had such typical symptoms of arsenic poisoning that the day nurse, who seems to have been a really competent girl, and who had had training as a nurse, notified the doctor that she suspected arsenic poisoning. The doctor got on the job in a hurry, and by nine-thirty they had a definite diagnosis of arsenic–but in view of Mrs Bain's weakened condition and the fact that she'd been sleeping so heavily and had absorbed so much of the arsenic before her stomach began to reject it, she couldn't pull through. She died sometime shortly after eleven-thirty.

'Victoria Braxton got home about a quarter to eleven. I think at that time Elizabeth Bain knew she was dying. Anyway, Miss Braxton told everyone to get out of the room, said she wanted to be alone for just two minutes with her sister, and since they were a little alarmed about Mrs Bain's nervous condition, the doctor said that Victoria Braxton could see her for just five minutes. No one knows what they talked about.'

'No question that it was arsenic poisoning?'

'Absolutely no question. They are making an autopsy and making an analysis of the vital organs, but the doctor saved some of the stomach contents.'

'How about the time element?' Mason asked. 'Is that all right?'

'That checks, Perry.'

'Do the doctors say so?'

'The doctors aren't saying a damned thing, except to the District Attorney, but I've had my researchers making an investigation.'

'What do you find?'

Once more Drake consulted his notes and said, 'Well, take *Professor Glaister's Medical Jurisprudence and Toxicology*. He says that the symptoms usually appear within an hour. In one case, where the stomach was empty, the symptoms did not appear until after two hours. Then, of course, there have been cases where the symptoms didn't develop for seven to ten hours.'

'And fifteen grains is a fatal dose?' Mason asked.

'Oh, sure. There has been a fatal case recorded where the amount of arsenic was only two grains, according to Professor Glaister.

'Gonzales, Vance and Helpern, in their book entitled *Legal Medicine and Toxicology*, state that three grains of arsenic absorbed into the system will kill a man of average weight. Of course, there have been cases where large doses have been taken without fatal results, but usually the poison was rejected by the stomach before it could get into the system.'

The telephone rang sharply.

Drake answered, said, 'Yes, hello . . . Yes, sure he is . . . Okay, I'll put him on.'

He said, 'Della Street calling you, Perry.'

Mason glanced at his watch. 'Gosh, there must be some major emergency to cause Della to call me at this hour.'

He picked up the telephone, said, 'Hello,' and heard Della Street's voice, sharp with excitement, saying, 'Chief, I don't want to mention names over the telephone, but do you remember the client who consulted you about the will?'

'The one that didn't have the dot at the end?'

'That's right.'

'Yes, I remember her. What about her?'

'She's with me. People are looking for her, lots of people, and she doesn't want to see anyone until she's talked with you. Can she get in touch with you down there if she–?'

'Not very well,' Mason said. 'I'm coming back. Is there something she's trying to conceal?'

'She thinks someone is trying to frame something on her and–'

'All right,' Mason said, 'tell her not to say anything to anyone. Can you keep her out of circulation, Della?'

'I think so.'

'All right. There's a plane leaving here at one-thirty-five in the afternoon. I'll be on it.'

Drake's face showed surprise. 'That's the plane that Bain–'

Mason nodded at Paul Drake, and said into the telephone. 'I'll try and get that plane leaving here at one-thirty-five, Della.'

'Okay.'

'Don't let anything happen until I get there–you know what I mean.'

'I'll try.'

Mason said. 'Okay, Della. I'll be seeing you.'

Mason hung up the telephone, and as soon as he did so the bell started ringing rapidly and insistently.

Drake picked it up, said, 'Hello,' and then waited while the receiver rattled with a voice that was pouring words into it with a rapid insistence.

After a full two minutes, Drake said, 'Thanks. I owe you one for that. We'll remember it.'

He hung up.

'What gives?' Mason asked.

'That was the detective agency we hired to tail Nellie Conway,' Drake said. 'They were just giving me a tip. They have connections down here, you know.'

'Go ahead.'

'Seems the California police became interested in Nellie Conway. They found she'd taken the plane as Nora Carson. They phoned police here. They questioned the taxi drivers who cover the airport. The result is they spotted Nellie Conway in that apartment, and they got on the job just as you were leaving the joint.

'On general principles they tailed you here. Then they picked up Nellie. Where does that leave you?'

Mason looked at his watch. 'Okay, Paul, I want that one-thirty-five plane. I don't want anyone to know that I'm taking it. Get a ticket in your name. Pay for the ticket, then go out to the airport, rent one of the parcel lockers, put the ticket in that locker, deposit twenty-five cents which will pay for twenty-four hours, close the locker, take the key out, and leave it with the girl at the newsstand. Tell her that when I show up and ask for the key to the locker, she's to give it to me without any question. Describe me if you have to.'

'Will you know which locker?' Drake asked.

'Sure,' Mason said, 'the locker number is stamped on the key.'

Drake asked, 'Why don't you get a ticket in your own name? They may have tailed you here, Perry, but you're clean. You can tell–'

Mason shook his head. 'I have five one-hundred-dollar bills in my pocket that may be hot as a stove lid. Here, Paul, put them in an envelope. Address and stamp the envelope and drop it down the mail chute.

'And I don't want to have any ticket for that plane in my pocket because I don't want anyone to know I'm on that plane when it gets in.

'I haven't time to explain, but this is one time I'm skating on thin ice–'

He broke off as knuckles sounded on the door. With a significant glance at Paul Drake, he tossed the folded five one-hundred-dollar notes far back under one of the twin beds, and opened the door.

Two men stood on the threshold.

'Either one of these the guy?' one of the men asked a plain-clothes man who was standing back in the corridor.

'This is the guy right here at the door.'

The detective threw back his coat, showed a badge. 'Come on, you're going places, mister,' he said. 'Somebody important wants to talk with you.'

12

The taxicab drove up to police headquarters. Mason was escorted into an office where the stale, close air gave forth that peculiar smell which clings to a room which is customarily occupied for twenty-four hours a day.

A desk sergeant said, 'We don't like out-of-town guys who bust in here with a muscle racket. What's your name?'

'Suppose I should tell you it's John Doe?'

'Lots of 'em do. We'll book you that way if you want. Then when we throw you in the tank, we'll take all the stuff out of your pockets and maybe find a driving licence or something that will tell *us* who you are. But you'll still be booked as John Doe.'

'What's the charge?'

'We haven't thought one up yet, but I think it's going to be vagrancy. You've been paying unchaperoned calls on single girls at two o'clock in the morning, and–'

'Is that a crime in this city?' Mason asked.

The desk sergeant grinned. 'Could be, particularly if the California officers are interested. It'd be vagrancy. After we saw your driving licence, Mr Doe, we'd know a lot more. Perhaps you'd like to co-operate a little better.'

Mason took his wallet from his pocket, handed a card to the sergeant and said, 'The name's Perry Mason. I'm a lawyer. I came here to interview a witness.'

The desk sergeant whistled in surprise, took Mason's card, stepped out of the office, walked down the corridor and was back within two minutes.

'The Captain wants to see you,' he said.

Officers escorted Mason down the corridor to a door that said 'Captain', opened the door and pushed Mason in.

A big, middle-aged man with sagging pouches under his eyes, a close-clipped greying moustache, sat behind a desk. At a table beside the desk a shorthand stenographer was taking notes. At the other side of the room Nellie Conway sat on the edge of a plain wooden chair, her gloved hands folded in her lap, her face without expression, her eyes staring straight ahead.

She showed no sign of recognition as Mason was pushed into the room.

The police captain looked across at her. 'Is this the man?' he said.

'Yes.'

'This is Perry Mason, the lawyer, you're talking about?'

'Yes.'

The police captain nodded to Mason. 'Sit down.'

Mason remained standing.

The captain said, coldly, 'You're playing hard to get along with. That isn't going to get you anywhere, not in this town. You aren't in California now. Don't try throwing your weight around because in this place you haven't any weight to throw around. Do you want to sit down or do you want to stand up?'

'Thank you,' Mason said, coldly. 'I'll stand up.'

'Want to make any statement?' the captain asked.

'No.'

The captain turned to Nellie Conway. 'All right,' he said, 'you said you did every single thing you did under the advice of counsel. You said the name of the lawyer was Perry Mason. Now this is Perry Mason. Go ahead and keep talking.'

Mason said, 'I'll advise you not to say a word, Nellie. You–'

'Shut up,' the captain said.

'Are you going to keep right on being my lawyer?' Nellie Conway asked, eagerly.

'No.'

'Then I'd better listen to these people,' she said.

The captain grinned.

Mason took a cigarette case from his pocket, lit a cigarette.

'Keep talking,' the captain said to Nellie Conway.

She said, 'Nathan Bain gave me those pills. He offered to pay me five hundred dollars in cash if I would give the pills to his wife. I thought they were poison. I went to see a lawyer.'

'What lawyer?' the captain asked.

'Perry Mason.'

'That's the gentleman here?'

'Yes.'

'What did he say?'

'There were four tablets,' she said. 'He took one of them out of the bottle and put it in an envelope and wrote his name on it. He put the other three tablets back in the bottle, corked the bottle, put it in an envelope, sealed the envelope and had me write my name across the flap of the envelope, and he wrote his name across the flap of the envelope, and he told me to save the envelope because he was going to find out what was in the tablets and was going to communicate with the police.'

'Then what?' the captain asked.

'Then Nathan Bain had me arrested.'

'Then what?'

'Then Mr Mason got me acquitted and told me there wasn't anything in the tablets except aspirin. He intimated that I had been telling him a lie and trying to take him for a ride.'

'Then what?'

'Then I went back to the Bain residence to get my things and Nathan Bain talked with me. He was very much concerned because he was afraid I was going to bring a suit against him for false arrest. He said there was no reason why we couldn't get along. He said we could act civilised about the thing. He said he wanted to make a settlement.'

'What happened?'

'We talked for a while, and then he told me that he'd give me two thousand dollars and an airplane ticket to New Orleans and a key to an apartment where I could stay for two weeks and have a vacation. He told me all I had to do was to sign a release and give the three tablets to his wife.

'I thought those three tablets contained nothing but aspirin because that's what Mr Mason had told me was in them, and I didn't see any reason why I shouldn't. I'd tried to do the best I could for myself under the circumstances. If a girl doesn't look out for herself, it's a cinch no one else is going to.'

'So what did you do?'

'I signed a release Mr Bain had drawn up. I got twenty one-hundred-dollar bills. I was helping that night with nursing his wife. I gave her the three pills about eight-thirty or nine o'clock.'

'Did you tell Mr Bain you had done so?'

'Yes.'

'Did you have any trouble giving them to her?'

'Of course not. I was the nurse. I told her it was the medicine the doctor had left for her.'

'What did she say?'

'She said she'd already had the medicine the doctor had left for her. I told her this was some other medicine, some special medicine that the doctor wanted her to have in addition to the regular medicine.'

'Then what happened?'

'The medicine didn't hurt Mrs Bain a bit. She took it and went right to sleep. I think it really must have been aspirin. It quieted her and she had a nice night. I left about seven o'clock in the morning, about an hour before the day nurse took over. I tried to see Mr Mason to tell him what had happened, but I couldn't get him. He didn't come into his office before ten o'clock. That was the last minute I had to call him. My plane left at ten-fifteen and they called for passengers to get aboard at ten o'clock. I called him right on the dot of ten o'clock. His secretary said he hadn't come in.'

'Did you leave word for him to call you?'

She hesitated. 'No.'

'Did you tell him where you were going?'

Again she hesitated.

'Come on,' the captain said, 'let's get this straight.'

'No,' she said, 'I didn't tell him where I was going.'

'When did you see him again?'

'About half-past two o'clock this morning.'

'What did he do?'

'He came to my apartment.'

'What did he want?'

'He wanted five hundred dollars.'

'Did you pay him that?'

'Yes.'

'Out of the money you received from Nathan Bain?'

'Yes.'

'Did you tell him that's where you got the money?'

'Yes.'

'And he took the five hundred dollars?'

'Yes.'

'Did he give you a receipt for it?'

'No.'

The captain turned to Perry Mason. 'You've heard the statement that has been made in your presence, Mr Mason. Do you wish to deny it?'

Mason said, 'I don't like the way you run things down here. I don't intend to say a damn word.'

The captain said, 'Stick around and try to cut corners down here and you'll like the way we run things a hell of a lot less. The accusation has been made that you told this woman it was all right to give those three pills to Mrs Nathan Bain. Do you deny that?'

Mason said, 'I'm not making any statement. I will say, however, that she is entirely incorrect in that statement.'

'I'm not either, Mr Mason,' Nellie Conway said with some spirit. 'You told me that those tablets contained nothing but aspirin.'

'The tablet that I took out of the bottle contained nothing but aspirin,' Mason said.

'How do you know?' the captain asked.

'That's something I'll discuss at the proper time and in the proper place.'

'All right, these statements have been made in your presence. You have an opportunity to deny them and make an explanation here and now if you want to.'

'I have nothing to say.'

The captain said to Mason. 'That's all. You can go now. Don't try to cut corners here because we don't like smart guys. California may want you. Go back to your hotel and don't try to leave town until we tell you you can. You may be wanted as an accessory on a murder charge–five hundred dollars to give his wife three aspirin pills! You're a hell of a lawyer!'

Mason turned to Nellie Conway. 'Nellie, what time did you give–?'

'I said you could go,' the captain said.

He nodded to the two officers.

They each took one of Mason's arms, spun him around and propelled him out of the door.

The door slammed shut with an ominous bang.

13

The taxi that had taken Mason and the detectives from the hotel was parked in front of police headquarters.

Mason said in a weary voice, 'Take me back to the Roosevelt Hotel.'

'Yes sir. Have a little trouble, sir?'

'Just lost a little sleep, that's all.'

'Oh, well, you can always make that up.'

'I suppose so,' Mason told him, and settled back on the cushions.

At the Roosevelt Hotel, Mason paid the cab driver off, entered the hotel, walked to the desk, asked for the key to the suite, and, swinging the key carelessly, Mason entered the elevator and said, 'Fifth floor.'

Mason got off at the fifth floor and promptly walked back down the stairs as far as the mezzanine.

From the mezzanine he could look down and see the house detective who waited until the elevator had returned to the ground floor, then went over to the desk and put through a phone call. Mason, watching his opportunity, slipped down the stairs, went to the door at the other end of the block, and found a taxicab waiting.

'Drive straight down the street,' he said. 'I'll have to get the address I want.'

'Going to be a nice day,' the cab driver said, 'You're up early.'

'Uh-huh. What time do you quit work?'

'Me? I just went on about twenty minutes ago. I quit at four o'clock this afternoon.'

Mason said, 'That sounds like a nice shift.'

'It is while I have it. I have to switch around.'

'That doesn't sound so good.'

'It isn't.'

'Know the town pretty well?' Mason asked.

'Sure.'

Mason said, 'I've got a day in which I just don't have to do a damn thing. How much would it cost to get this cab by the hour?'

'Well, that depends on whether you want it for shopping and right around town, or–'

Mason took out a fifty-dollar note from his wallet, said, 'I'll tell you what I'll do, driver. I'll give you fifty dollars for the day. Is it a go?'

'What do you mean by all day?'

'Until you quit at four o'clock this afternoon.'

'It's a go!'

Mason said, 'Okay, shut off your radio because the damn thing makes me nervous. Tell your headquarters that you're going to be out of service all day.'

'I'd have to telephone in and get permission, but I'm satisfied it can be done all right.'

Mason said, 'Okay. Tell them that you're going to go to Biloxi.'

'I thought you said you wanted to look around the town.'

'Hell, I don't know what I want to do,' Mason said. 'I used to know a girl in Biloxi.'

'That's a long way to go for a girl,' the cab driver said. 'There are lots of good-looking women nearer than Biloxi.'

'Are there?'

'So they tell me.'

'Well,' Mason said, 'tell them you have a passenger to Biloxi. Ask them if fifty dollars is right for a round trip.'

'Okay. Wait and I'll telephone.'

The cab driver went into an all-night restaurant, telephoned, came back and said, 'I'm sorry. They say I'd have to get seventy-five for all day under circumstances like that. I think it's a stick-up but–'

'What do we care?' Mason said. 'Just so we have fun. Here's a hundred dollars. Now you're paid off for all day and we can go to Biloxi or not, just as we damn please. The extra twenty-five is for you.'

'Say,' the cab driver said, 'you're a real sport.'

'No, I'm not,' Mason said. 'I'm tired of a lot of routine and I want to settle down and enjoy life for a day without having a lot of telephones and a lot of radio. A little later on you can take me to a good place where we can get a nice breakfast and just sit around and enjoy life without being hurried.'

The cab driver said, 'I can find you a place all right. I hate to take all this money on a mileage basis to Biloxi and then let the company get rich just driving around town. If you're going to start to Biloxi we should get go–'

'I've changed my mind,' Mason said. 'I'll–'

'I can phone in and get a better rate for just being around the city.'

'No, let the cab company get rich,' Mason said. 'I'll tell you what you do. Start your meter going and we'll run on the meter. Mileage and waiting time won't amount to as much as the price they gave you, and you can tell them afterwards that your passenger changed his mind.'

'Okay, boss. Anything you say. I can sure use the money but I want to be on the up-and-up. You'd be surprised how strict they get with us and how closely they watch us. Lots of times they plant somebody to see if we'll cut a corner or–'

'There isn't any rule against cruising around with your meter running, is there?' Mason asked.

'Not a bit.'

'Okay, let's go cruise.'

They drove slowly around the city, the driver pointing out places of interest, then, after a while, as Mason started to doze, the driver asked, 'How about that breakfast place now?'

'A good idea,' Mason told him.

'Okay. I know a place that's run by a woman who's a friend of mine. She doesn't run a regular restaurant but she'd be glad to fix up any friend of mine. You'd get a lot better food than you'd get in any of the restaurants.'

'That's what I want,' Mason told him. 'A chance to relax and feel that I don't have a darn thing to do.'

'That's swell. This woman has a couple of daughters that are knockouts.'

'I don't want to be knocked out this early in the morning.'

The cab driver laughed. 'Anyway, you'll like the food, and I mean there's some of the most marvellous Louisiana coffee you ever tasted, made with hot milk. Mister, you're going to have some cooking today that you'll remember as long as you live.'

The cab driver drove toward the outskirts of town, stopped once to telephone ahead, then took Mason to a neat house where a negro admitted them to a spacious dining-room, with the morning sun just beginning to stream in through windows covered with lace curtains which, according to the cab driver, were 'genuine heirlooms.'

An hour and a half later, Mason, once more in the cab, suggested that they drive out to the airport. He said that he liked to watch planes come and go and it would be a good chance to see the town.

The driver felt that Mason might spend his time more profitably, but drove the lawyer out to the airport.

Mason sat in the cab.

The nine-fifteen plane was twenty minutes late.

Nathan Bain hurried from the plane towards a taxi. Two broad-shouldered men fell into step on each side. Bain's face showed startled surprise. The men piloted him across the street to a black sedan. They entered and drove away.

'Don't you want to get out and look around any?' the driver asked.

Mason stretched, yawned, said, 'No, I'd like to find some place where we could walk and stroll around . . . Say, haven't you got a park here?'

'A park!' the cab driver exclaimed. 'We've got several of the best parks in the world! Why, say, we've got parks here with live oaks that are bigger than any tree you ever saw in your life. We've got lawns and walks, and a zoo with all kinds of animals, lakes, canals–'

'That's for me,' Mason said with enthusiasm. 'Let's go down to a park some place where we can get out and lie on the grass and just bask in the sun, and then we can go out and look around the zoo and get some peanuts to feed to the animals, and after that . . . well, after that we'll do just as we damn please.'

The cab driver said, 'If I could only get a fare like you just about once every ten years, it would make up for all the grouchy old crabs that yell because I have to go around a block in order to get headed right on a one-way street. Come on, mister, you've called the turn. Say, do you like to fish? I know where we can get some fishing rods and get some of the best fishing . . .'

'Sounds good,' Mason said. 'Let's go.'

Around eleven o'clock, Mason decided he was hungry. The cab driver found a quaint, isolated place, where Mason had an oyster cocktail, bouillabaisse, oysters Rockefeller, and a firm, white-meated fish that seemed to dissolve on the tongue. An olive-skinned girl with limpid, dark eyes, and exceedingly long lashes, served the meal, and from time to time glanced sidelong under her long lashes at Perry Mason, who was drowsily oblivious of everything except the food.

Shortly before one o'clock, Mason decided he would once more like to go down to the airport and see the planes come in.

This time he got out of the cab and said, 'I'll walk around for a while.'

'About how long?' the cab driver asked.

'Oh, I don't know,' Mason said. 'I just do things on impulse. Come on along, if you want.'

Escorted by the cab driver, Mason moved slowly around the air terminal, then said, 'I think I'll buy a newspaper.'

He walked over to the news-stand while the cab-driver was standing out of earshot, bought a newspaper and said, 'I believe there's a key left here for me.'

The girl looked at him curiously and said, 'Yes, your friend said your bags would be in the locker.'

She handed him a key.

Mason thanked her, gave her a two-dollar tip, walked back to the cab driver and said, 'Go out and wait in the cab, will you? In case I don't show up within half an hour shut your meter off, pocket the rest of the money and report back to duty.'

Mason went to the locker and found that Paul Drake had packed his overnight travelling bag and left it in the locker, together with a letter in a plain envelope.

Mason opened the envelope and found the aeroplane ticket, together with a note which read:

> Della knows you'll be on this plane. Things are moving too fast for me. I'm crawling into a hole and pulling the hole in after me. This is where I check out. I've had police in my hair at intervals all morning and have received intimations that if I don't get out of town I won't stay out of jail. I don't like the way these people play.

The note was unsigned.

Mason picked up the bag, strolled across to the registration desk for outgoing passengers.

'You'll have to hurry,' the attendant told him. They'll be calling the plane in a few minutes.'

He weighed in Mason's bag, checked it, then the lawyer sauntered over to the gate, which opened almost the instant he arrived. He handed his boarding slip to an attendant, climbed aboard the plane, settled down, pulled a pillow out from the receptacle above his chair, and kept his eyes closed until after the plane had taxied down the field. As the plane took off, Mason straightened, looked out of the window and watched Lake Pontchartrain shimmering below. The plane made a half-circle and winged out so that New Orleans, with its buildings, its spacious parks, its busy waterfront, and the famous crescent in the Mississippi River become a panorama. Mason relaxed and dozed fitfully until the plane landed in El Paso.

He noticed two people who boarded the plane, a man about thirty, who had an aura of dreamy-eyed futility about him, and a woman some four or five years his junior, whose nervous alertness indicated that she had taken on many of the responsibilities for her husband as a seeing-eye dog takes over responsibilities for its master.

Mason looked out of the window at the airport. In the twilight he saw that a cold, gusty wind was blowing , yawned, closed his eyes and was dozing by the time the plane taxied down the runway. Half-asleep, he felt the thrust as the powerful engines pushed the big plane into the air, then wakened enough to watch the panorama flowing back beneath him in the gathering dusk, the environs of El Paso, the Rio Grande River, over on the other side the town of Ciudad Juarez.

Someone tapped his shoulder. Mason looked up.

It was the woman who had boarded the plane with the dreamy-eyed individual.

'We'd like to talk with you,' she said.

Mason regarded her thoughtfully, then smiled and shook his head. 'I'm not in the mood for conversation at the moment and . . .'

'Miss Street suggested that we get aboard the plane here.'

'That,' said Mason, 'is different.'

He walked back to the smoking compartment where the man was sitting, waiting.

It was, Mason thought, quite typical that the man should send the woman to make the contact.

'Did Miss Street give you any letter or anything?' Mason asked, feeling his way cautiously.

'No. We talked with her over the telephone. Perhaps we'd better introduce ourselves. I'm Mrs James Braxton and this is James Braxton.'

'You're the other members of the Bain family?'

'That's right. Jim is, or rather was, Elizabeth's half-brother, and I'm his wife. Vicki Braxton is Jim's full sister.'

The woman beamed at him.

'Well, now,' Mason said, adjusting himself comfortably and taking a cigarette case from his pocket, 'that's very interesting. Would you care to smoke?'

They accepted cigarettes and all three took lights from the same match.

'I suppose you know what's happened?' the woman said.

'Just what has happened?' Mason asked.

She said, 'That nurse, that Nellie Conway!'

'What about her?'

'She did give the poison after all. Nathan bribed her to do it.'

Mason raised his eyebrows in silent interrogation, then smoked in silence.

The woman looked at him and said. 'You're not saying a word, Mr. Mason.'

'Your husband isn't saying a word,' Mason said.

She laughed nervously. 'He's a great listener. I'm the talkative one of the family. I go rambling on and on and on.'

Mason nodded.

'We'd like to know what you think of it and what your ideas are concerning the case.'

Mason said, 'Lots of people would like to know that.'

'I'm afraid I don't understand.'

Mason said, 'You tell me that you're Mr and Mrs Jim Braxton. I've never seen you before in my life. For all I know you could be newspaper reporters trying to get an exclusive interview.'

'But, good heavens, Mr Mason, your own secretary told us where we'd find you. We took a plane into El Paso and got in there just half an hour before this plane of yours pulled in. We've certainly been stewing and worrying and we wanted to see you at the earliest possible moment and warn you of what you're up against.'

'Thanks.'

'Mr Mason, you must believe we're who we are. We . . . Jim, don't you have something, some means of identification?'

'Sure,' Jim said, promptly rising to the occasion. 'I have a driving licence.'

'Let's take a look at it,' Mason said.

He studied the licence which the man handed him, then said, 'Perhaps I can clear the matter up by asking a few questions. Where were you up until a few days ago?'

'Honolulu.'

'Who was with you?'

'Just the three of us together. It was a family party. My sister, Vicki, and I have always been very close, and she gets along fine with Georgiana.'

'Got any more means of identification on you?' Mason asked.

'Certainly. I have lodge cards, business cards, club memberships . . .'

'Let's see them,' Mason said.

Mason went through the collection of cards which the man presented, said finally, 'Okay. I guess that does it. Now suppose you tell me the thing Miss Street wanted you to tell me. She didn't have you fly down here just to ask me questions.'

'Well,' the woman said, laughing nervously, 'I was just trying to get acquainted.'

'We're acquainted now. What was it you told Miss Street that caused her to send you down here?'

'It sounds such a horrible thing to say,' she said after a few moments, 'when you blurt it right out this way.'

'But, my dear,' Jim Braxton interposed, 'Mr Mason is our lawyer. You have a right to tell him anything. You're supposed to tell him. Isn't that right, Mr Mason?'

Mason said, 'If you have any information which throws any light on the death of your sister-in-law, I suggest by all means that you tell me what it is.'

She turned to her husband. 'Jim, for the life of me I can't understand you. For the past year whenever I've mentioned that, you've told me I should keep my mouth shut, that I could get in serious trouble, and now you want me to tell the story to a man I've only known for a few minutes.'

'But, dear, the situation is entirely different now. This would be . . .well, the law would protect you in this.'

Mason glanced at his wrist watch. 'We don't have too long to stall around, you know. There may be reporters coming aboard the plane at Tucson.'

'Well,' she said, 'I may as well blurt it right out, Mr Mason. Nathan Bain poisoned his first wife.'

'She was supposed to have eaten something which disagreed with her,' James Braxton said mildly.

'The symptoms were those of arsenic poisoning, 'Mrs Braxton asserted.

'How do you know?' Mason asked.

'Because,' she said, 'I was suspicious of Nathan Bain from the moment he set foot in the house and started making eyes at Elizabeth.'

'Go on,' Mason said.

'Well, that's it, Mr Mason. He's always said he didn't want to talk about it, but one time he told us all about it. It seems she had eaten something which disagreed with her, and the way he described the symptoms . . . well, I just started thinking, that's all.'

'What about the symptoms?'

'All of the typical symptoms of arsenic poisoning. They are not very nice to describe, Mr Mason, but I can assure you she had *all* of the typical symptoms.'

'How do you know what the symptoms are?'

'I made it a point to read up about it.'

'Why?'

'Because I was suspicious of Nathan Bain from the minute I clapped my eyes on him. I felt certain that he'd . . . I think he's a toad.'

Mason said, 'Let's get back to the death of his first wife. That could be one of the most important things in the case.'

Jim Braxton said, 'Your secretary thought so too. She wanted us to get in touch with you and tell you about it.'

'Then tell me about it,' Mason said. 'And tell me how it happened that Nathan Bain got your sister to marry him. I gather that she was rather an attractive young woman.'

'She was.'

'Two and a half years ago Nathan Bain was a lot better looking than he is now.' Jim Braxton interposed. 'And he sure has a smooth line.'

'But he was fat even then,' his wife countered. 'Don't you remember how he was complaining about his clothes being tight? He was always saying he was going to take off weight. First he'd say he was going to take off five pounds in the next six weeks. Then he said ten pounds in the next three months, then twenty pounds in the next six months.

'And all the time he kept putting it on. His clothes were always six months behind his figure. I always felt he was going to burst every time he leaned over. He just wouldn't watch his appetite. He ate everything. All the rich foods–used to boast about his stomach. He'd eat–'

'That isn't telling me about his first wife,' Mason said impatiently, 'and we haven't got all night.'

'Well,' she said, 'his first wife died about three years before he married Elizabeth.'

'Did he profit by her death?' Mason asked.

'I'll say he profited by her death! He picked up about fifty thousand dollars. He used that to gamble in the stock market and get himself established in the produce business. And then when he made some poor investments and found out that the financial shoe was pinching, he deliberately went out and set his cap for someone who had money.

'I tell you, Mr Mason, that was all that he wanted of Elizabeth. He just wanted her money, that was all. I knew that the minute I clapped my eyes on that man. I could just look at him and tell.'

'I've always been good at judging character that way. I can take a look at a person and tell what he's thinking about within the first ten minutes. And what's more, I never have to change my opinion of people. I come to a decision and I don't have to change it.'

'She's good,' Jim Braxton said.

Mrs Braxton tried to look modest and failed.

'Go on,' Mason said.

'Well, that's all there is to it, Mr Mason. There's one thing I'll say about Nathan Bain. He's a marvellous talker. Give him a chance to get started and he can talk the birds right down out of the trees.

'And when he set his cap for Elizabeth he really made a good job of it. He was just the nicest, most considerate man you have ever seen. But as far as I was concerned, I could see the hypocrisy oozing out all over him. It was just like something filled with slime. He didn't fool me for a minute, and he knew it.'

'You told Elizabeth how you felt?'

'I certainly did. I told her exactly how I felt about that man. I warned her against him and . . . well, she wouldn't listen to me.'

'Then what?'

'Well, of course, that made the relationship a little strained because she was completely hypnotised. Nothing would do but she must run right to Nathan and tell him how I felt.'

'Now, wait a minute, dear,' Jim interposed. 'You don't *know* that she went to Nathan and–'

'You mind your own business,' Georgiana interrupted tartly. 'I guess I know what she did and what she didn't do. I could tell the minute she spoke to Nathan. I could just see the change come over him. Before that time he'd been trying to hypnotise me as one of the members of the family, but the minute he knew I was on to him he drew into his shell and got on the defensive.'

'Go ahead,' Mason said. 'Let's get down to something that we can use as evidence if we have to.'

'Well, I'm just telling you, Mr Mason, that after he married Elizabeth for a while he was the most attentive husband. Butter wouldn't melt in his mouth. He was always dancing attendance on her hand and foot. He did let himself go terribly when it came to putting on weight. He started to get real fat. He just ate and ate and ate–'

'Never mind that,' Mason said. 'Let's get back to first principles.'

'Well, as I say, he was very nice for a while, always, however, trying to get Elizabeth to finance this and finance that, and then trying to get her to let him manage her property. But Elizabeth was too smart for that. She was a pretty shrewd business woman and she kept her own property so that she had it entirely in her own hands, and she intended to keep it that way.

'Well, you could just see Nathan change the minute he realised that he had tied himself up for life to a woman who wasn't going to let loose of her property, but was going to keep on handling it herself and regarding it as her own.

'I just knew something was going to happen. I told Jim a dozen times if I told him once. I said to him time afer time, "Jim", I said, "you watch that man, he's going to–" '

'We were talking about his first wife,' Mason interrupted.

'Well, one day when he had been drinking and was unusually talkative, he was telling us about his early life, and then he mentioned his first wife, which was something he very seldom did.'

'What was her name?'

'Marta.'

'And what happened?'

'Well, they had been married about two years or a little better, and they went down into Mexico and she was supposed to have eaten some sea-food, and she became terribly, terribly ill. He decribed what a nightmare it was, driving her back across the border and getting to a point where they could get competent medical attention. By the time he got her home to her family doctor she was in very bad shape. The doctor said it was undoubtedly a case of food poisoning from eating tainted sea-food. Well, she died, and that's all there was to it.'

'How do you know the symptoms were those of arsenic poisoning?'

'I'm telling you the man went into details, Mr Mason. It was positively indecent, but he'd been drinking at the time and he told about all of the trouble he'd had driving this very sick woman miles and miles of wild country. And it was then he mentioned the candy.

'With all Nathan Bain's craving for rich foods, there's one thing he can't touch, chocolate.

'Well, he told me about Marta having taken this box of chocolate creams along in the car, and the minute he said that, the very minute, mind you, I knew what had happened.

'I looked up the symptoms and, sure enough, there they all were. Marta was poisoned by arsenic in that box of candy which she opened and ate right after the sea-food luncheon.'

'Where did she get the candy?' Mason asked.

'Heavens, how should I know? But you can bet one thing, he's the one who put the arsenic in it.'

'He didn't go to a Mexican doctor?'

'No. Marta didn't want one and he didn't think it would be advisable. According to the way Nathan tells the story now, they both felt that she was suffering from food poisoning and that as soon as her system was cleaned out, she'd be all right. So they made a dash to get home.

'If you ask me, the reason he wanted to get her home was because he had a friendly doctor that he used to play golf with, and he knew the doctor would sign a death certificate without asking any embarrassing questions. The doctor accepted their diagnosis of sea-food poisoning, and when she died two days later, he very obligingly filled out the death certificate.'

'Where were they living at the time?' Mason asked.

'San Diego.'

'And what happened to Marta's body? Was she cremated or–'

'That's one thing,' she said. '*He* wanted to have the body cremated, but her mother and father insisted that the girl be buried, so they had their way. She didn't leave any will or anything directing what should be done with her body, so she was buried.'

'Where?'

'In San Diego, in the cemetery there.'

'All right,' Mason said, 'that's fine. I'm glad you've told me that. *Now* we have something to work on.'

'You see,' Jim Braxton said to his wife, 'I told you that was important.'

Mason said, 'Now I want you to get this and get it straight. I don't want either one of you to say a word about this to anyone until I tell you. Do you understand?'

They nodded.

Mason said, 'This thing is terribly important. The facts in this case are all scrambled. Nellie Conway says that Nathan Bain wanted to pay her to give his wife medicine that would make her rest better and get her over being so nervous. She brought that medicine to me. I took one of the tablets and had it analysed. It was aspirin. The thing simply doesn't make sense.

'Now then, Elizabeth Bain is dead. Nathan Bain is going to try to worm out from under. In order to do that he's going to try to involve everyone else. At the proper time I want to hit him with this thing so it will be a bomb-shell. . . . And I don't want any word of this to leak out in advance. Do you understand?'

'Anything you say,' Braxton said.

'Well, that's it,' Mason said, 'and I want you to follow instructions on that to the letter. It may be a lot more important that you realise at the present time.'

'Well, I guess *I* know when to keep my mouth shut,' Mrs Braxton said, 'and as for Jim, he never talks, do you, Jim?'

'No, dear.'

'And you'll follow Mr Mason's instructions, won't you, Jim?'

'Yes, dear.'

'You don't have anything to worry about,' she said to Perry Mason.'

Mason gave a wry grin. 'That,' he announced, 'shows all you know about it.'

14

It was a calm, clear night. Stars were blazing down steadily, but paled into insignificance in the floodlights at the airport.

Mason joined the stream of passengers walking briskly to the exit.

Pursuant to his instructions, Jim and Georgiana Braxton had been among the first to leave the plane. Mason was at the tail end of the procession.

As the lawyer climbed up the ramp to the main floor level of the air terminal, he gave a swift searching glance, looking for Della Street.

She was not there.

Worried, Mason started crossing the big air terminal and suddenly caught sight of Lieutenant Tragg carrying a briefcase and pacing restlessly back and forth, his eye on the big clock.

Mason hurriedly walked towards the exit, carefully keeping his back turned to Lieutenant Tragg. He was just about to push his way through the heavy glass door when Tragg called his name, sharply, peremptorily.

Mason turned with every evidence of surprise.

Tragg was hurrying towards him.

'Hello, Tragg,' Mason said, and waited, obviously impatient to be on his way.

Tragg, tall, intelligent, alert and a dangerous antagonist, gripped Mason's hand. 'How are you, Counsellor?'

'Pretty good. How's everything?'

'I understand you were in New Orleans?'

Mason nodded.

Tragg laughed. 'Police there reported that they told you not to leave New Orleans without permission.'

'The New Orleans police,' Mason said, 'are abrupt, arbitrary, short-tempered and disrespectful.'

Tragg laughed, then asked more seriously, '*Did* you have their permission to leave?'

'I'm not accustomed to asking *any* permission from *any* police officer before I do *anything*,' Mason said.

Tragg grinned good-naturedly. 'Well, let's hope nothing happens to change your habits.'

'I don't think anything will.'

'You always were an optimist.'

'Are you here to meet me?' Mason asked.

Tragg said, 'I have no official interest in you at the moment, Mason. My interest is in an airplane which is scheduled to leave for New Orleans sometime within the next twenty minutes. I'm one of those nervous travellers. I can't sit down and wait until someone calls the plane, but I have to pace the floor and look at the clock as though my eyes would push the minute hand around faster.'

'Going to New Orleans to talk with Nellie Conway?' Mason asked.

'Officially,' Tragg said, 'I'm not supposed to make any statements, but off the record, Mason, there are some rather interesting developments in New Orleans.'

'Of what sort?'

Tragg shook his head.

Mason said, 'You don't need to be so damn secretive. I guess everyone knows Nathan Bain flew to New Orleans and was picked up by police as soon as he got off the plane.'

Tragg tried to keep from showing surprise. 'Is that so?'

Mason raised his eyebrows. 'You didn't know I knew about that, eh?'

'You know lots of things, Mason. Sometimes you amaze me when I find out what you do know, and then again there are times when I'm afraid I never do find out what you know. So I have to try to keep you from finding out what I know.'

'So,' Mason said, 'the fact that Nathan Bain was picked up by the police, that Nellie Conway was picked up by the police and was talking, and that you are impatiently pacing the terminal, waiting for a plane to take off for New Orleans is a pretty good indication that Nathan Bain has made some sort of a statement that is of the greatest importance, or that you expect him to by the time you get there.'

Tragg said, 'You really should get a turban and a crystal ball, Mason. Then you could go into the business of fortune-telling, mind-reading and predicting the future. It's a shame to have these talents wasted on an amateur.'

'Has Bain confessed to the murder?' Mason asked.

'Why don't you look in your crystal ball?' Tragg asked.

'Not giving out any information, Lieutenant?'

Tragg shook his head.

Mason said, 'I'm going to have trouble with your man, Holcomb, Tragg.'

'You've had trouble with him before. It won't be anything new.'

'I mean I'm going to have some real trouble with him. I'm going to put him on a spot.'

'Are you?'

'You're damn right I am.'

'What's he done now?'

'It's what he hasn't done. He's having a very convenient memory in connection with a conversation I had with him, in which I told him all about Nellie Conway.'

Tragg was serious and thoughtful. 'Sergeant Holcomb knows Nathan Bain. They've had quite a few talks together.'

'So?'

'Just a matter of friendship, of course. Holcomb signed up for a class in public speaking that was open to police officers and deputy sheriffs–given under the auspices of one of the service clubs. Nathan Bain was one of the instructors at that class. He made quite an impression on Holcomb.

'Bain is a smooth, convincing talker. He has a good deal of personality when he's on his feet. Holcomb was very much impressed. He made it a point to compliment Bain, and they had quite a talk.

'A couple of months later Bain rang up Holcomb and told him that he was suspicious that a nurse named Nellie Conway, who was taking care of his wife, was stealing jewellery, and asked Holcomb what to do. Holcomb said it was out of his line and offered to refer it to the larceny detail, but after they'd talked for a while Holcomb suggested Bain get a private detective, and recommended James Hallock.

'Now does that answer your question?'

'It explains a lot of facts,' Mason said. 'It doesn't answer my question because I wasn't asking any question. I was making a statement.'

'Well,' Tragg said, 'I thought you'd like to know the low-down on that. Naturally, when you approached Holcomb with a story about the medicine, Holcomb thought you were rigging up an elaborate defence for Nellie Conway, so you could use it later to trap Nathan Bain on cross-examination and get your client released.'

A feminine voice on the public address system announced that passengers for Tragg's plane were being loaded at Gate 15, and Tragg, welcoming the interruption, grinned and said, 'Good luck to you, Counsellor.'

'Thanks, the same to you. Hope you bring back a confession from Nathan Bain and drop it on Holcomb's desk.'

'Any message for the New Orleans police?' Tragg asked.

'Give them my love,' Mason told him.

'They may want you back there.'

Mason said, 'If the New Orleans police want me back there, they can telegraph a fugitive warrant for my arrest, then they can try and find some law I've violated in the State of Louisiana so they can get me extradited. You might explain to them some of the legal facts of life, Lieutenant.'

Tragg grinned, waved his hand and started walking briskly towards the gate.

Mason watched him out of sight, and was just turning, when he heard the patter of quick steps behind him, and Della Street came running up to him.

'Hello, Chief.'

'Hello. Where have you been?'

She laughed. 'You can imagine where I've been. When I saw Lieutenant Tragg waiting around here, I didn't know whether he was looking for you or for me, or just taking a plane. So I retired to the one place where Lieutenant Tragg and his minions would be unable to follow.'

'And then?' Mason asked.

'Then,' she said, 'I kept watch on the situation, decided Tragg was taking a plane to New Orleans, and kept where I could watch him, hoping I would find an opportunity to tip you off, but he would have to be one of those big, restless he-men, and pace back and forth with one eye on the clock as befits a nervous traveller.'

'Where's Victoria Braxton?'

'We're staying at an auto court.'

'Registered all right?'

'Under our own names. That's the way you wanted it, isn't it?'

'That's fine. I'd hate to have it appear she was a fugitive from justice.'

'She isn't.'

'Anyone looking for her?'

'Newspaper people, but as nearly as I can find out, that's all. She's wanted for questioning at the district attorney's office at ten o'clock tomorrow morning.'

'Have they notified her?' Mason asked.

'No, but it's in the press. They did notify her brother, Jim, and Georgiana. I see that they made connections with the plane all right. What did you think of them, Chief?'

'Okay,' Mason said, 'except that once that woman gets started she certainly talks a blue streak.'

'She told you about . . .?'

Mason nodded.

'What are you going to do with it? Do you want it released to the press so we can . . .?'

'No,' Mason said. 'I want that information put in cold storage, to be used at the proper time, in the proper manner, and at the proper place. If Nathan Bain confesses to the murder of his wife, we'll pass the information on to Lieutenant Tragg–although Tragg will probably know all about it before we have a chance to tell him.

'On the other hand, if the police try to give Nathan Bain a coat of whitewash, we'll slap them in the face with it.'

'Why should they try to give Nathan Bain a coat of whitewash?'

'Because,' Mason said, 'our dear friend, Sergeant Holcomb, has been taking lessons in public speaking from Nathan Bain. Isn't that just too ducky?'

'Quite a coincidence, isn't it?'

'It's a coincidence, if you want to look at it in one way.'

'And if you want to look at it in another way, what is it?'

Mason said, 'Suppose you were planning to commit a murder. Suppose you were a member of a service club that was asking for volunteers to coach a class in public speaking that was to be composed of top-flight detectives and peace officers. Suppose you were a smooth, forceful speaker and felt you could make a good impression on people. Wouldn't that be a nice way to make yourself a whole handful of friends who'd be in a position to do you some good, or, to look at it in another way, who'd be in a position to keep anyone from doing you harm?'

Della Street nodded.

'Well,' Mason said, 'Apparently Sergeant Holcomb and Nathan Bain are just like that,' and Mason held up two crossed fingers.

'And that may complicate the situation?' Della Street asked.

'That may raise hell with it. Where's the car, Della?'

'In the parking lot.'

'Okay, I'll get my bag, you get the car, and I'll meet you in front. No newspaper reporters are expecting me back?'

She laughed. 'Apparently not. They've been trying to get in touch with you, but they called the New Orleans police and were assured you wouldn't be leaving Louisiana until the police there had completed their investigations.'

'Well, isn't that something!' Mason said.

'What did you do? Put up bail and then jump it?'

Mason said, 'I walked out. Where did they get that idea that they could tell me not to leave town? The situation would have been different if a crime had been committed in Louisiana. They're trying to investigate a crime that was committed in California. To hell with them!'

'To hell with them is right,' Della Street said, laughing. 'Don't get so worked up about it, Chief. You're fifteen hundred miles from New Orleans now. You get your bag and I'll get the car.'

She flashed him a quick smile and ran towards the parking place. Mason secured his bag from a porter and was standing by the kerb as she drove up. He tossed the bag in the back of the car, slid in the seat beside her and said, 'Let's make sure we aren't wearing a tail, Della.'

'Okay, you keep watch behind and I'll cut around some of the side streets.'

Mason turned so he could watch the road behind him. 'How's Vicki, Della?'

'She bothers me, Chief?'

'Why?'

'I don't know. There's something I can't put my finger on.'

'Anything more about the will?'

Della Street said, 'That will isn't the same now as when you saw it.'

'No?'

'No.'

'What's different about it?'

'At the end of the sentence,' Della Street said, 'there is now a very perfect piece of punctuation, a nice round dot made with ink.'

'How nice.'

'Chief, what could they do in a situation like that?'

'What could who do?'

'Would that be forgery?'

'Any mark that would be put on a document for the purpose of deceiving others and made after the document had been signed, would be an alteration of the document.'

'Even a teeny-weeny dot no bigger than a fly speck?'

'Even a dot half that big, provided it was a significant part of the document and was intended to be such.'

'Well, it's there now.'

'Have you asked her about it?'

'She *said* her sister put it there.'

There was an interval of silence.

Della Street said, 'How are we coming, Chief?'

'No one seems to be taking any undue interest in our driving, Della.'

'How about it? Do we hit the main boulevard?'

'Take one more swing, and then start travelling. I want to hear Vicki Braxton's story about the full stop at the end of the will.'

15

Victoria Braxton, attired in a neatly tailored suit, looking very efficient and business-like, was waiting up for Perry Mason and Della Street in the well-furnished living-room of the de luxe court where Della Street had registered.

Mason lost no time with preliminaries.

'I don't know how much time we have,' he said, 'but it may be a lot shorter than we hope for, so let's hit the high spots.'

'Can you tell me what happened in New Orleans?' she asked.

Mason shook his head, 'It's too long to go into now.'

She said, 'I'd like to know. I'm very much interested in anything Nathan does.'

'So are the police. We'll talk about that after a while if we have time. Right now I want to know certain things.'

'What?'

'Exactly what happened in connection with Mrs Bain's death.'

'Mr Mason, *I* gave her the poison.'

'You're certain?'

'Yes.'

'How did it happen?'

'Nellie Conway put those tablets on the saucer. She said to me, "The first time Elizabeth wakes up after six o'clock in the morning she's to have this medicine. Don't give it to her before six but give it to her just as soon after six as she wakes up." '

'There were three tablets?'

'Yes.'

'Placed on a saucer by the side of the bed?'

'Yes.'

'And then what happened?'

'Well, that's it, Mr Mason. She wakened and I gave her the medicine. It must have been those tablets.'

'To whom have you told this?'

'To Miss Street and to you.'

'Did you tell it to the officers?'

'No, Mr Mason, I didn't, because at the time–well, when the officers were out there making an investigation, we were all excited, and at the time it never occurred to me that by any extreme possibility could *I* have been the one who administered the poison.'

'That's fine.'

'What is?'

'That you didn't tell anyone. Don't tell anyone, don't mention it, don't say anything to the police, don't say anything to anyone.'

'But, Mr Mason, don't you understand, it's only through my testimony that they can really connect Nellie Conway with my sister's death, and Nellie Conway, of course, is the connecting link that leads to Nathan Bain.'

'For the moment,' Mason said, 'we'll let the police worry about their connecting links.'

'Mr Mason, I don't think that's right. I think I should tell them. Those tablets Nellie left in that saucer were poison.'

'Don't tell them.'

'Will you please tell me why?'

'No,' Mason said, 'there isn't time. Now tell me about that will.'

'What about it?'

'All about it. I don't think your brother or your sister-in-law know about it.'

'Does that make any difference?'

'It might.'

'Elizabeth didn't want Georgiana–that's Jim's wife–to know anything about it.'

'Why not?'

'Because it would have made her even more extravagant, just the idea that she'd maybe some day come into some of Elizabeth's money.'

'Is Georgiana that way?'

'Terribly–and she's always jumping at the wildest conclusions from the most trivial data. As it is now, she keeps poor Jim in debt all the time. Heaven knows how much they owe. If she knew about his will–I mean, if she had known about it–the way Elizabeth was injured and all–well, she'd have gone on another spending spree.'

Mason digested that information thoughtfully. 'Did you and Elizabeth discuss that?'

'Yes.'

Mason said, 'That may or may not explain something.'

'What do you mean by that?'

Mason said, 'There are some things about your story I don't like.'

'What?'

'To begin with, when you came to my office you told me that your sister had sent you there, that you were to retain me and I was to draw a will.'

'Well, what's wrong with that?'

'Then, when somebody telephoned and asked for "Vicki", you were surprised. You said only your intimates called you Vicki and no one knew you were there.'

'Oh, you mean my brother and sister?'

'Yes.'

'Well, they didn't know I was there. Only Elizabeth knew where I was, and I knew that Elizabeth wouldn't telephone me. But Jim knew I'd asked Nellie Conway where your office was–and he thought I *might* have gone up there to ask you something about her case or settlement.

'They were, of course, trying frantically to get me. He tried half a dozen places and then he tried your office, just on a blind chance.'

'All right, let's put cards on the table. Why didn't your brother and sister know you were there?'

'For the very reason I've been telling you, Mr Mason. They weren't to know anything about the will. Elizabeth discussed it with me.'

'When?'

'When she woke up about . . . oh, I guess it was about five o'clock in the morning.'

'All right. Tell me what happened.'

'Well, you understand, she woke up first sometime about three o'clock. We all went in there then and talked with her. It wasn't much of a talk. Just greetings and generalities. She kissed us and told us how glad she was to see us.'

'Then what?'

'Then she went right back to sleep. We left Nellie Conway in charge and we all went into the other room to lie down for a while. I slept an hour or an hour and a half, and then I came back and told Nellie I was wide awake and could take over.'

'Then what?'

'That was when she put the tablets on the saucer and told me to give them to Elizabeth whenever she woke up at any time after six a.m.'

'Where had the tablets been before then?'

'In a little box in the pocket of her uniform–anyway, that's where she got them when I first saw them.'

'Why didn't Nellie Conway leave them in the box and simply tell you that–?'

'Apparently she was afraid I'd forget them. She took the saucer out from under the glass that had the water in it, and put the tablets right there in plain sight by the side of the bed.'

'How far from Elizabeth?'

'Why, right by the side of the bed. Not over . . . oh, a couple of feet perhaps.'

'How far from you?'

'I was sitting right near there. They couldn't have been over three or four feet from me.'

'How far from the door of the room?'

'The door of the room was right by the stand. It wasn't over . . . oh, eighteen inches or two feet from the door of the room.'

'I just wanted to get it straight,' Mason said. 'Now what happened after that?'

'Well, Elizabeth was sleeping. She wakened about five o'clock and that was when she started to talk with me. Then was when she made out the will.'

'Then what?'

'I was thinking I'd give her the medicine–I guess it was about twenty minutes to six–but she went back to sleep again. She didn't wake up until around a quarter to seven, and then I gave her the medicine with some coffee.'

'Tell me a little more about what happened when you were talking.'

'She talked to me I guess for half an hour, Mr Mason, telling me about what she'd been going through, about the fact that Nathan had been trying to kill her, that she had been talking with Nellie Conway about you, and that she wanted you to be her lawyer, that she wanted you to go out and tell Nathan Bain that he was all finished, that she intended to file a suit for divorce, and that she wanted to make a will disinheriting Nathan.'

'Did she say anything about her grounds for divorce, about what proof she had?'

'She didn't go into details, but she told me she had documentary proof.'

'Documentary proof?' Mason asked sharply.

'That's right.'

'She was intending to get a divorce because he'd been trying to kill her, wasn't she?'

'I don't know–I presume so.'

'And she had documentary proof?'

'That's what she said. I think it related to infidelity.'

'Where did she keep it?'

'She didn't say.'

'All right,' Mason said, 'go on. What happened?'

'Well, she told me that she wanted to have you come out and prepare a will for her to sign, and she asked me to go and see you. She asked for her cheque-book and told me it was in her purse in a bureau drawer. I brought it to her and she wrote out that cheque for you.'

'Then what?'

'Then we had some discussion about the fact that she was really afraid of Nathan and she felt that before you could draw up a will and have her sign it, something might happen to her.'

'That was rather melodramatic, wasn't it?' Mason asked.

'Not in the light of subsequent events,' Miss Braxton said sharply.

'All right. Go ahead.'

'Well, I told her I didn't think it was necessary. I told her I could go to see you and tell you what she wanted, and that you could probably be out there before noon with a will ready for her to sign. She said that she thought it would be better to execute a will first and have Nathan know that no matter what happened she wasn't going to let him have a cent of her money. She said she'd been thinking it over and had come to that conclusion, and that that was the thing to do.'

'So what did she do?'

'She took a piece of paper and wrote out that will.'

'Let me take another look at that will.'

'But you've seen it, Mr Mason.'

'You have it with you?'

'Yes, of course.'

With obvious reluctance she opened her purse and handed the will to the lawyer.

Mason looked at it carefully, then moved over to study it under the light.

'There's a full stop after the last word now,' he said.

Victoria said nothing.

'When you came to my office,' Mason said, 'there was no stop at the end of the will. I pointed that out to you.'

'I know you did.'

'So then you took a fountain pen and added a stop,' Mason said. 'In order to try and gild the lily you've probably put your neck in a noose. They'll have a spectroscopic analysis made of the ink on that stop. If they have any idea that–'

'You're thinking that they'll show it was made with a different ink and a different fountain pen?' she asked. 'Well, you don't need to worry about that, Mr Mason. That stop was made with Elizabeth's fountain pen and it's the same pen that wrote the will.'

'When did you do it?' Mason asked.

'I didn't do it.'

'Who did?'

'Elizabeth.'

'Do you,' Mason asked, 'know any more funny stories?'

She said, 'I'm going to tell you the truth, Mr Mason. I was very much disturbed about that stop not being at the end of the sentence. After you pointed it out to me, I realised that if anything happened–and then, of course, something did happen; I received word that Elizabeth had been poisoned. I dashed out there in a taxicab just as fast as I could get there, and I went right into the room. Elizabeth was very, very ill. She was suffering excruciating agony, but she was conscious. I told everyone to get out and leave me alone for a few minutes, and then I said, "Elizabeth, Mr Mason says you neglected to put a stop at the end of that will," and I took the fountain pen and handed it to her.'

'Did she reach for it?'

'Well, I . . . she was very sick at the time.'

'Did she reach to take the fountain pen when you handed it to her?'

'I put it into her hand.'

'And then what did you do?'

'I held the will close to her so she could make a dot at the proper place.'

'Did she raise her head from the pillow?'

'No.'

'How did she see where to make the dot then?'

'I guided her hand.'

'I see,' Mason said dryly.

'But she knew what was being done.'

'I like the way you say that,' Mason said. 'In place of saying she knew what she was doing, you say that she knew what was being done.'

'Well, she knew what she was doing, then.'

Mason said, 'You still aren't telling me the truth about that will.'

'What do you mean?'

'I mean that the story you told isn't the right story.'

'Why, Mr Mason, how can you say that?'

'You're talking to a lawyer. Let's cut out the kid stuff and try the truth for a change.'

'I don't know what you mean.'

'That will wasn't finished when you brought it to my office, and you know it.'

'Well, it certainly . . . it certainly is finished now.'

'*Why* did Elizabeth Bain break off in the middle of making that will?'

Victoria Braxton hesitated. Her eyes moved around the room as though seeking some means of escape.

'Go ahead,' Mason said remorselessly.

'If you *must* know,' she blurted, 'Elizabeth was writing the will when Georgiana opened the door and looked in the room to see what she could do–that is, to see if there was any way that she could help.'

'That's better,' Mason said. 'What happened?'

'Elizabeth didn't want Georgiana to know she was making a will, so she whipped the piece of paper down under the bedclothes. Georgiana asked how everything was coming and if we were getting along all right, and I told her yes, to go back and go to sleep.'

'Then what?'

'Then she went back into her room. Elizabeth waited a few moments, lying there with her eyes closed, and then suddenly I realised she'd gone to sleep. So

I took the fountain pen from her fingers, but the will was under the bedclothes and I couldn't find it without waking her up. I decided I'd wait until I gave her the medicine and then get the will. I thought she'd entirely finished with it, because of something she said . . . she's quit writing for a good minute or two before Georgiana opened the door.'

'And when did you get the will?'

'Well, when I gave her the medicine, she took it with water but she wanted some coffee right after that, so I rang the bell and asked the housekeeper for some coffee. At about that time the day nurse came on and she said she'd give her the coffee. I only had time to fish the will out from under the bedclothes. Elizabeth saw what I was doing and smiled and nodded and said, "It's all right, Vicki." So I knew that she felt she'd finished it. Now that's the real honest-to-God truth, Mr Mason.'

'Why didn't you tell me that before?'

'Because I was afraid you might think that . . . well, that you might think the will really hadn't been finished.'

'And no one else was in the room from the time Nellie Conway put those tablets on the saucer?'

'No.'

Mason said, 'We're going to drive you to the airport. I want you to take the first available plane for Honolulu. I want you to send a wire from the plane to the District Attorney that certain business matters in connection with your sister's affairs have made it necessary for you to rush to Honolulu, that you will keep in touch with him, and that he can count on your co-operation, but that there are business affairs of such a serious nature that your attorney advised you to make a personal trip to Honolulu at once.'

'But what affairs?'

'Your sister owned property in Honolulu, didn't she?'

'Yes. Lots of it. We were staying at one of her cottages there. She has a whole string of them.'

Mason said, 'You don't need to tell anyone what the business affairs are.'

'But, good heavens, what will I do when I get there?'

'You won't get there.'

'What do you mean?'

'I mean you'll be called back.'

'Then why go?'

Mason said, 'Because it's a nice way to get you out of circulation. You're not running away, because you've sent the District Attorney a telegram under your own name. You're taking your travel transportation under your own name, and I'm taking the responsibility as your attorney for sending you there.'

'That sounds like such a crazy thing to do,' she said.

'That,' Mason said, 'far from being crazy, is the only sensible thing to do. Now, I'm warning you–do not discuss this case with anyone. Under no circumstances ever tell anyone you gave Elizabeth those tablets. Under no circumstances discuss the case with the police or the District Attorney unless I am there. Do you understand?'

'I still don't see–'

'Will you follow my instructions?'

'Yes.'

'To the letter?'

'Yes.'

Mason turned to Della Street and said, 'Okay, Della. Take her to the airport.'

16

Early the next afternoon, Paul Drake stopped in to see Perry Mason.

Mason made no attempt to disguise his anxiety. 'Paul, what's happening in New Orleans? Has Bain made a statement?'

'The police aren't releasing one single bit of information, Perry. . . . Well, I'll amend that statement. They have released one.'

'What's that?'

'They have a warrant for you.'

'What's the charge?'

'Vagrancy.'

'Anything else?'

'You mean as a charge?'

'Yes.'

'No. Isn't that enough?'

Mason grinned and said, 'They can't extradite me on vagrancy. They know it. They made the charge just as a gesture.'

'They're mad.'

'Let them be mad. But you didn't come here just to tell me that.'

'Lieutenant Tragg has uncovered something.'

'What?'

'Something big.'

'Evidence that Nathan Bain murdered his wife?'

'Apparently,' Drake said, 'evidence that he did not.'

'I'd like to see *that* evidence.'

Drake said, 'I can tell you one thing, Perry. They have some secret evidence in this case, some evidence that they're keeping so closely guarded that no one knows what it is.'

'What sort of evidence?'

'I can't find out.'

'Does it point to Nathan Bain, does it point to the fact she committed suicide, or . . . ?'

'All I know is that it's some super secret evidence.'

'Any chance you can find out?'

Drake said, 'The grand jury is in session today. They're doing something in connection with this case. I have a man up there who has a pipeline into the grand jury. He may be able to give us the low-down.

'I also know that the District Attorney's office is furious because Victoria Braxton didn't show up for questioning.'

'She's on a trip,' Mason said. 'She has business interests in Honolulu that she absolutely has to look after.'

'So you told me,' Drake said dryly.

'She is,' Mason said, 'as far as the business angle is concerned, acting on the advice of her counsel.'

'Well, that makes it fine. Only the D.A. doesn't think so.'

'He wouldn't. Anything else, Paul?'

'The police have been in consultation with Lieutenant Tragg in New Orleans. Something broke there this morning that they consider highly impor–'

The phone rang sharply. Della Street answered, then said, 'It's for you, Paul.'

Drake picked up the phone and said, 'Hello . . . Yes . . . Okay, give it to me. . . . Who else knows about this? . . . Okay, thanks. Good-bye.'

He hung up the telephone, turned to Mason and said, 'There's your answer. The grand jury has just returned a secret indictment against Victoria Braxton, charging her with first-degree murder.'

Mason whistled. 'What's the evidence, Paul?'

'The evidence is secret.'

'It won't be if they put it before the grand jury.'

'Don't worry, Perry, they didn't put anything before the grand jury that they aren't willing to shout from the housetops–that is, officially. They probably whispered something in the ear of the grand jury.'

Mason said, 'I had a hunch something like that might be in the wind.'

He turned to Della Street. 'Della, we'll send a wire to Victoria Braxton, on the plane en route to Honolulu, telling her to come home. I thought we'd have to do that, but I felt it would be a summons from the grand jury rather than an indictment.'

'Telling her what's in the wind?' Della Street asked.

'No. We have to protect Paul Drake's pipeline. We don't dare to let it out that we know what the grand jury did–not yet.'

'What do you want to tell her?' Della Street asked, holding her pencil over the notebook.

Mason thought a moment, then grinned wryly. 'Take this wire,' he said, 'COME HOME AT ONCE ALL IS UNFORGIVEN.'

17

The trial of the People of the State of California versus Victoria Braxton opened with all of that electric tension which underlies a championship prize fight between two men who have heretofore been undefeated.

Hamilton Burger, the big grizzly bear of a District Attorney, savagely triumphant in the assurance that at last he had a perfect case which contained no flaw, was making his preliminary moves with that quiet confidence which comes to a man who knows that he holds the winning cards.

Perry Mason, veteran court-room strategist, worked with cautious skill, taking advantage of each technicality which he felt could be of any possible benefit, feeling his way with caution, realising only too well that the prosecution had prepared a trap for him, and that at any moment the legal ground might fly out from under him.

Inside information was to the effect that the prosecution had carefully saved, as a surprise, evidence that would be completely devastating once it was introduced, and that Perry Mason, despite using every legal trick in the quiver to try and make the prosecution disclose its hand, had finally been forced to enter the court-room without any knowledge of his opponent's case other than the bare out-line which had been utilised to support the indictment of the grand jury.

Betting among insiders was five to one against Mason's client.

Little time was wasted in selecting a jury. Mason had indicated that he wanted only a fair and impartial trial for his client, and Hamilton Burger had quite evidently been willing to accept any twelve individuals who would be guided by the evidence in the case.

Newspaper reporters waited eagerly for Hamilton Burger's opening statement to the jury outlining the case he expected to prove, but veteran lawyers knew that Burger would not even give a hint of the nature of his trump cards this early in the game.

After outlining the fact that he expected to prove Victoria Braxton had poisoned her sister by administering three five-grain tablets of arsenic, knowing that her sister had made a will leaving a full one-half of her property, valued at some half-million dollars, to the defendant, Burger went on to announce:

'I will further state to you, ladies and gentleman of the jury, that in this case the prosecution has no desire to take any technical advantage of the defendant. The prosecution will produce evidence from various witnesses which will make you familiar with the chain of events which led up to the death of Elizabeth Bain.

'This evidence will not follow the usual legal pattern, but will be in the nature of unfolding a story. We will paint for you, ladies and gentlemen, a broad picture with swift, sure strokes of factual evidence. We want you to see the entire background. You will, perhaps, find the evidence in this case somewhat unusual as far as the ordinary cut-and-dried procedure is concerned, but if you will follow it closely you will be led to the inescapable conclusion that the defendant is guilty of first-degree murder, carefully and deliberately planned, executed in a most heartless manner, under such circumstances that it will be necessary for you to return a verdict of guilty by first-degree murder without recommendation, making mandatory the death penalty.'

Hamilton Burger, with vast dignity, walked back to the counsel table, seated himself, and glanced significantly at the judge.

'Does the defence wish to make any opening statement at this time?' Judge Howison asked.

'Not at this time, Your Honour. We prefer to make our opening statement when we present our case,' Mason said.

'Very well. Call your first witness, Mr District Attorney.'

Hamilton Burger settled back in the big counsel chair and turned the preliminary proceedings over to his two deputies, David Gresham, the assistant prosecutor, and Harry Saybrook, the deputy, who, having been ignominiously beaten by Mason in the trial of Nellie Conway, was thirsting for revenge, and so had managed to get himself assigned as an assistant in the present case.

In rapid order, witnesses were called to the stand, proving that Elizabeth Bain had died, that prior to her death she exhibited evidences of arsenic poisoning, that after her death an autopsy had shown sufficient quantities of arsenic in her vital organs to have made it certain that her death was produced solely by arsenic poison.

A certified copy of the probate record showed that a holographic will had been made in the handwriting of Elizabeth Bain, dated the day of her death, and leaving all of her property share and share alike to her half-brother, James Braxton, and her half-sister, Victoria Braxton, the defendant in the present case.

After these preliminaries were over, Hamilton Burger moved in to take personal charge of the case.

'Call Dr Harvey Keener,' he said.

Dr Keener was a slim, professional-looking man with the air of a doctor, even to the well-trimmed Vandyke beard, the cold, analytical eyes, and the dark, plastic-rimmed spectacles.

Taking the witness stand, he speedily qualified himself as a practising physician and surgeon, who had been such on the seventeenth of September last.

'Now, early on the morning of September seventeenth,' Hamilton Burger asked, 'you were called on to treat one of your patients on an emergency call?'

'Yes, sir.'

'At what time were you called, Doctor?'

'At approximately eight-forty-five. I can't give you the exact time, but it was somewhere between eight-forty-five and nine o'clock.'

'And you immediately went to see that patient?'

'I did. Yes, sir.'

'Who was that patient?'

'Elizabeth Bain.'

'Now, doctor, directing your attention specifically to the symptoms which you yourself found at the time you arrived and not those which may have been told to you by the nurse, will you tell us just what you found?'

'I found the typical symptoms of arsenic poisoning, manifested in a gastro-enteric disturbance, an intense thirst, painful cramps, typical vomitus, tenesmus, feeble irregular pulse, a face that was anxious and pinched, the skin cold and clammy. I may say that these are progressive symptoms, and I am referring to them as over a period of time, from approximately the time of my arrival until the time of death, which occurred around eleven-forty that morning.'

'Was the patient conscious?'

'The patient was conscious until approximately eleven o'clock.'

'Did you make any chemical tests to check your diagnosis?'

'I saved substances which were eliminated for more careful analysis, but a quick chemical check indicated the presence of arsenic in the vomitus, and the symptoms were so typical that I was virtually certain of my diagnosis within a few minutes of the time of my arrival.'

'Now then, did you have any conversation with the patient in regard to the manner in which this poison might have been administered?'

'I did.'

'Did she make any statement to you at that time as to who had administered the poison?'

'She did.'

'Will you please state what she said as to the manner of administration of the poison, and by whom?'

'Just a moment, Your Honour,' Mason said, 'I object to this as incompetent, irrelevant and immaterial, and quite plainly hearsay.'

'That is not hearsay,' Hamilton Burger said. 'The patient was even then dying of arsenic poisoning.'

'The point is, Your Honour,' Mason said, 'did she *know* she was dying?'

'Yes,' Judge Howison ruled. 'I think that is a very essential prerequisite to a so-called death-bed declaration, Mr District Attorney.'

'Very well, if Counsel wishes to be technical, I will dispose of that feature of the case.'

'Did the patient know she was dying, Doctor?'

'Objected to as leading and suggestive.'

'The question is leading, Mr Burger.'

'Well, Your Honour,' Burger said, with exasperation, 'Dr Keener is a trained professional man. He has heard the discussion and certainly understands the purpose of the question. However, if Counsel wishes to consume time with technicalities, I will go about it the long way. What was Mrs Bain's mental condition at the time with reference to hope of ultimate recovery, Doctor?'

'Objected to on the ground that no proper foundation has been laid,' Mason said.

'Surely,' Judge Howison said, 'you are not questioning Dr Keener's qualifications now, Mr Mason?'

'Not as a doctor, Your Honour, only as a mind reader,' Mason said. 'The test of a dying declaration, or a death-bed declaration as it is sometimes known, is whether the patient states as part of that declaration that the patient is dying and knows that death is impending, and with the solemnity of the seal of death placed upon the patient's lips, then proceeds to make a statement which can be used as evidence.'

'Your Honour,' Hamilton Burger said irritably, 'I propose to show as part of my case that the defendant was left alone in this room with Elizabeth Bain, that medicine was placed on a saucer to be given to Elizabeth Bain, that the defendant surreptitiously substituted for this medicine three five-grain tablets of arsenic, that when the decedent wakened at approximately six-forty-five, the defendant said to the decedent, "Here is your medicine," and gave her the three tablets or pills which had been substituted for the medicine which had previously been left by Dr Keener.'

'Go ahead and prove it then,' Mason said, 'but prove it by pertinent and relevant evidence.'

'I think in order to show a death-bed declaration, you are going to have to show that the patient knew death was impending,' Judge Howison said.

'That is exactly what I intend to do,' Hamilton Burger said. 'I have asked the doctor the question as to the patient's frame of mind.'

'And that question,' Mason said, 'is to be answered not by the doctor's attempting to read the mind of the patient, but only by what the patient herself may have said.'

'Very well,' Hamilton Burger conceded. 'Limit it to that point, Doctor, to what the patient said.'

'She said she was dying.'

Hamilton Burger smiled triumphantly at Mason.

'Can you give me her exact words?'

'I can,' Dr Keener said. 'I made a note of them at the time, thinking that they might be important. If I may be permitted to consult a memorandum which I made at the time, I will refresh my recollection.'

The doctor's glib patter and his bearing on the witness stand indicated that he was no stranger to the court-room, and knew quite well how to take care of himself.

He produced a leather-backed notebook from his pocket.

'Just a moment,' Mason said, 'I'd like to consult the memorandum, that is, I'd like to look at it before the witness uses it to refresh his recollection.'

'Help yourself,' Hamilton Burger said sarcastically.

Mason walked up to the witness stand and examined the notebook.

'Before the doctor uses this to refresh his recollection,' Mason said, 'I would like to ask a few questions for the purpose of having it properly identified.'

'Very well,' Judge Howison ruled. 'You may ask the questions.'

'Doctor, this entry which appears here is in your own handwriting?'

'Yes, sir.'

'It was made when, Doctor?'

'It was made at approximately the time the statement was made to me by the patient.'

'And by the patient you mean Elizabeth Bain?'

'Yes, sir.'

'It is written in pen and ink?'

'Yes, sir.'

'What pen, what ink.'

'My own fountain pen filled with ink from a bottle which I keep in my office. I can assure you there is nothing sinister about the ink, Mr Mason.'

There was a ripple of merriment which Judge Howison frowned into silence.

'Quite so, Doctor,' Mason said. 'Now, at what time was this statement made?'

'It was made shortly before the patient lost consciousness.'

'Shortly is a relative term, Doctor. Can you define it any better than that?'

'Well, I would say perhaps half an hour.'

'The patient lost consciousness within an hour after this statement was made?'

'Yes, sir. There was a condition of coma.'

Mason said, 'Let me look at this notebook if you will, please, Doctor,' and, without waiting for permission, he turned some of the pages.

'Just a moment,' Hamilton Burger interposed, 'I object to Counsel pawing through Dr Keener's private documents.'

'It's not a private document,' Mason said. 'It's a notebook which he is attempting to identify for the purpose of refreshing his recollection. I have the right to look at the adjoining pages of the notebook and to cross-examine the doctor on it.'

Before Burger could make any answer, Mason, holding the notebook, turned to Dr Keener and said, 'Is it your custom, Doctor, to make entries in this notebook methodically and in consecutive order, or do you simply open the book at random until you come to a vacant page and then make a note?'

'Certainly not. I keep the book in an orderly manner. I fill one page and then turn to the next page.'

'I see,' Mason said. 'Now this entry which you have made here, and which you wish to use at the moment to refresh your recollection as to the words that Elizabeth Bain used in stating that she was dying, are the last words which appear in this notebook?'

'Yes, sir.'

'That has been some little time ago, and I take it that you have treated quite a few patients since then?'

'I have. Yes, sir.'

'Why then did you not make any further entries in this notebook after Elizabeth Bain made this statement to you?'

'Because I read the statement to the police when they appeared at the scene, and the police promptly took that book as evidence, and it has been in their possession ever since.'

'Until when, Doctor?'

'Until this morning, when it was returned to me.'

'By whom?'

'By the District Attorney.'

'I see,' Mason said smiling. 'The idea was that the District Attorney was to ask you if you had jotted down the exact words of the decedent, and you would whip the notebook from your pocket–'

'I object,' Hamilton Burger shouted. 'That's not proper cross-examination.'

'I think it goes to show the bias of the witness, Your Honour.'

'I think it goes more to show the skill of the prosecutor,' Judge Howison said smiling. 'I think you have made your point, Mr Mason. I see no reason for permitting the question to be answered in its present form. The witness has already stated that the notebook was taken by the police and that it was returned to him this morning.'

'And that is the reason there are no entries in the notebook subsequent to the entry by you of the statement made by Elizabeth Bain that she was dying and that she had been poisoned?'

'Yes, sir.'

'*Now*, perhaps you will permit the witness to go ahead with his testimony,' Hamilton Burger said sarcastically.

'Not now,' Mason said smiling. 'I have a few more questions to ask concerning the identification of this written memorandum. This is in your own handwriting, Doctor?'

'Yes, sir.'

'And was made within a few minutes of the time the statement was made?'

'Yes, sir.'

'What do you mean by a few minutes?'

'I would say within four or five minutes at the most.'

'You made notes of that statement because you considered it important?'

'I did.'

'You knew that it would be important to get her exact words?'

'I did.'

'In other words, you have been a witness in court before this, you knew the legal requirement of a death-bed statement, and you knew that in order to get a death-bed statement admitted, it would be necessary to show that the patient knew she was dying?'

'Yes, sir.'

'And you made these notes because you were afraid to trust your own memory?'

'I wouldn't say that. No, sir.'

'Why *did* you make them then?'

'Because I knew some smart lawyer was going to ask me what her exact words were, and I decided I'd be able to tell him.'

Again there was a ripple of merriment.

'I see,' Mason said. 'You knew that you were going to be questioned on this and you wanted to be in a position to cope with counsel on cross-examination?'

'If you want to put it that way, yes, sir.'

'Now, then,' Mason said, 'without saying what her exact words were, did the patient make a statement to you as to who had administered the poison?'

'She did. Yes, sir.'

'And yet you didn't consider that statement particularly important, Doctor?'

'Certainly I did. That was the most important part of the whole thing.'

'Then why didn't you make a note of that in your notebook so that if some smart lawyer started to ask you for the exact words of the dying patient, you would be able to give them?'

'I did make such a notation,' Dr Keener said angrily. 'If you will look back a page you will find the notation giving the exact words of the patient.'

'And when was that notation made?'

'Within a few minutes of the time the patient made the statement.'

'Within five minutes?'

'Within five minutes, yes. Probably less than that.'

'Within four minutes?'

'I would say that is was within one minute.'

'And what about this statement that the patient made that she was dying? What's your best recollection as to when that was written in your notebook?'

'I would say that also was written within one minute.'

'But,' Mason said, smiling, 'the statement from the patient as to who had administered the medicine to her is made on the page preceding her statement that she was dying.'

'Naturally,' Dr Keener said sarcastically. 'You have already questioned me about that. I told you I made my entries in this notebook in chronological order.'

'Oh, then the statement as to who had administered the medicine was made *before* the patient said she knew she was dying?'

'I didn't say that.'

'Well, I'm asking it.'

'Frankly,' Dr Keener said, suddenly aware of the trap into which he had been led, 'I can't remember the exact sequence of these statements.'

'But you do know, do you not, Doctor, that you make your entries in this book in chronological order? You have said so very emphatically on at least two occasions.'

'Well, yes.'

'So that at the time the patient made the statement to you in regard to the administration of medicine, she had not made any statement to you to indicate that she knew she was dying?'

'I can't say that.'

'You don't have to,' Mason said. 'Your notebook says it for you.'

'Well, that's not exactly my recollection.'

'But your recollection is hazy, isn't it, Doctor?'

'No, sir.'

'You had reason to doubt it?'

'What do you mean by that?'

'You were afraid that you couldn't remember exactly what had happened and the exact sequence in which it happened, so you didn't trust your memory but made entries in this notebook so that no smart lawyer could trap you in cross-examination?'

Dr Keener shifted his position uneasily.

'Oh, Your Honour,' Hamilton Burger said, 'I think this cross-examination is being unduly prolonged and I am sure–'

'I don't,' Judge Howison ruled. 'As the court understands the law it is plainly a prerequisite to a death-bed declaration that the person making it knows of impending death and makes a statement to that effect, so that the knowledge which is within the mind of the patient can be communicated to others.'

'Well,' Dr Keener said, 'I can't answer that question any better than I already have.'

'Thank you,' Mason said. 'That's all.'

'All right,' Hamilton Burger said, 'Counsel apparently is finished. Go ahead and state what Elizabeth Bain said, refreshing your recollection from the entry in your notebook, Doctor.'

'I now object to the question,' Mason said, 'on the ground that it is incompetent, irrelevant and immaterial. It appears that the doctor is now testifying to a statement made by the patient at some considerable time interval *after* the statement made by the patient concerning the administration of the medicine, which the District Attorney is trying to get into evidence.'

'The objection is sustained,' Judge Howison said promptly.

Burger's face purpled. 'Your Honour, I–'

'I think the situation is obvious as far as the testimony is concerned at the present time. If you wish to make a further examination of Dr Keener for the purpose of showing the relative times at which these entries were made, those questions will be permitted, but in the present state of the evidence the objection must be sustained.'

'Well, I will withdraw Dr Keener from the stand temporarily and call another witness,' Hamilton Burger said with poor grace. 'I'll get at it in another way.'

'Very well,' Judge Howison said. 'Call your next witness. That's all, Doctor. You may stand aside for the time being.'

'Call Nellie Conway to the stand,' Hamilton Burger said, with the manner of a man getting ready to play his high trumps.

Nellie Conway came forward to the witness stand, was sworn, and, after the usual preliminaries as to her name, address and occupation, was asked by Hamilton Burger, 'You are acquainted with Nathan Bain, the surviving husband of Elizabeth Bain?'

'Yes, sir.'

'And were employed by him as a nurse to nurse Elizabeth Bain?'

'Yes, sir.'

'And on the evening of the sixteenth and the morning of the seventeenth of last September, you were so employed there as a nurse?'

'Yes, sir.'

'Now, did you at any time on the evening of the sixteenth or the morning of the seventeenth, give instructions to the defendant in this case as to medicine that was to be given to Elizabeth Bain?'

'I did. Yes, sir.'

'And those instructions were communicated to the defendant?'

'Yes, sir.'

'And the medicine was left where?'

'The medicine was left in a saucer on a bedside table within some two feet of Elizabeth Bain.'

'What did the medicine consist of?'

'Three five-grain tablets.'

'Who had given you that medicine?'

'Dr Keener had left it with me to be given to Mrs Bain.'

'Where had this medicine been left?'

'It had been given to me personally by Dr Keener.'

'When?'

'About seven o'clock on the evening of the sixteenth when Dr Keener made his evening call.'

'Who was present in the room when you had this conversation with the defendant?'

'Just Elizabeth Bain, who was sleeping, and Victoria Braxton.'

'And what did you tell her?'

'I told her that if Mrs Bain awakened after six o'clock in the morning she was to have this medicine, that it was not to be given to her before six.'

'And that was medicine which you received directly from Dr Keener?'

'Yes, sir.'

'Cross-examine!' Hamilton Burger snapped.

Perry Mason's tone was casual and conversational. 'You don't know what was in the medicine?'

'I know it was three tablets, that's all.'

'It was part of your duties to give Mrs Bain medicine which had been left by the physician?'

'Yes, sir.'

'And you did do that?'

'Yes, sir.'

'You were paid to do that?'

'Yes, sir. Although I wasn't paid for my services the night of the sixteenth and the seventeenth, that is, not specifically.'

'Do you mean you weren't paid by anybody to give any medicine to Mrs Bain on the night of the sixteenth and seventeenth?'

'I know what you're trying to get at,' Hamilton Burger said, 'and you don't need to go at it by indirection, Mr Mason. The prosecution has no objection. The door is open, walk right in.'

And Hamilton Burger smiled smugly.

Nellie Conway said, 'I was paid some money by Nathan Bain on the night of the sixteenth. It was not a payment for services I was to render, it was payment for a settlement that had been made, but I did give Mrs Bain some medicine that Mr Bain wanted me to give her.'

'Medicine?' Mason asked.

'Well, some pills or tablets.'

'How many?'

'Three.'

'What size?'

'Five grain.'

'And they had been given you by Mr Bain to give to his wife?'

'Yes, sir. There had been four originally but I had given one of them to you, and the other three remained in my possession, and when Mr Bain asked me to give them to his wife, I did.'

'At what time?'

'Shortly after Dr Keener had left, I gave Mrs Bain those three pills or tablets.'

'The ones that had been given you by Nathan Bain, her husband?'

'Yes, sir.'

Hamilton Burger sat grinning delightedly.

'Where did you get these tablets that you gave Mrs Bain?'

'From her husband.'

'I mean immediately prior to administering them. Where were they?'

She said, as though she had carefully memorised the words, 'I had taken those tablets to your office. I had told you about the conversation, and you had told me that the medicine was harmless, that it was nothing but aspirin. And you charged me a dollar for advice. You had returned three of those tablets to a small tube-like bottle which was just big enough to hold five-grain pills. That bottle had been sealed in an envelope with your name and my name written on it.

'So when Mr Bain asked me once more to give those pills to his wife, I decided to do so since you had told me they contained only aspirin.'

'Did I tell you that?' Mason asked.

'Yes, and you charged a fee for telling me so. I have the receipt.'

'I told you that the pills you had contained only aspirin?'

'Well, you took one of the pills to be analysed and told me that it contained aspirin.'

'One of the four,' Mason said. 'You don't know what was in the other three.'

'No, only I supposed that if they had been anything harmful you wouldn't have given them back to me so I could give them to Mrs Bain. I went to you for advice and paid you your fee.'

Hamilton Burger chuckled audibly.

Mason said, 'Then am I to understand that on the evening of the sixteenth you opened this envelope and took the three remaining tablets from the small bottle or phial, and gave them to Mrs Bain?'

'I did. Yes, sir.'

'With what effect?'

'No effect, except that she had a better and quieter night than she had had at any time.'

'As far as you know,' Mason said, 'those pills might have contained arsenic or any other poison?'

'All I know is what Mr Bain told me, that the pills were to give his wife a good sleep, and what you told me, that they were aspirin,' she said, with the quick, pert manner of one who is giving a well-rehearsed answer to an anticipated question.

Hamilton Burger was grinning broadly.

'So,' Mason said, 'as far as you know of your own knowledge, you yourself may have given Elizabeth Bain three five-grain pills of arsenic on the evening of the sixteenth at some time shortly after seven o'clock in the evening?'

'I gave her the pills a little after eight o'clock.'

'That's all,' Mason said.

'No further questions,' Hamilton Burger said. 'Now we'll recall Dr Keener to the stand if the Court please.'

'Very well. Return to the stand, Doctor.'

Dr Keener returned to the witness stand.

'Doctor,' Hamilton Burger said, 'I want to ask you, in your opinion as a physician, if three five-grain arsenic tablets had been given to Elizabeth Bain at approximately eight o'clock on the evening of the sixteenth of September, when would the first symptoms of poison have manifested themselves?'

'In my opinion, and because of my knowledge of the patient's condition,' Dr Keener said, 'I would have expected symptoms to have manifested themselves within a period of one to two hours after ingestion, a maximum period of two hours, certainly not later than that.'

'Now then,' Hamilton Burger went on, 'you have heard the testimony of the last witness that you gave her three five-grain tablets to be administered to Elizabeth Bain in the morning.'

'That's right. At any time when she wakened after six in the morning.'

'What were the contents of those pills or tablets, Doctor?'

'They contained soda, acetylsalicylic acid and phenobarbital.'

'There was no arsenic in them?'

'None whatever.'

'Those pills or tablets had been compounded under your direction, Doctor?'

'In accordance with a prescription which I had given. There were certain definite proportions. I may state that the problem at the time was that of administering proper sedatives which would, over a course of time, not upset the stomach, but would control a condition of extreme nervousness which had characterised the patient's reactions to her injuries and to surrounding circumstances.'

'Now then,' Hamilton Burger said triumphantly, 'did you at any time after you gave those three tablets to the nurse, Nellie Conway, on the evening of the sixteenth, see those same three pills again?'

'I did. Yes, sir.'

'When?'

'At about three p.m. on the afternoon of the seventeenth.'

'Those same tablets?'

'Those same tablets. Yes, sir.'

'Now then,' Hamilton Burger said, smiling, 'you may cross-examine, Mr Mason.'

'How do you know they were the same tablets?' Mason asked.

'Because I analysed them.'

'You analysed them personally?'

'It was done under my supervision and in my presence.'

'And what did you find?'

'I found they were the tablets I had prescribed. They contained identical proportions of soda, phenobarbital and acetylsalicylic acid.'

'Where did you find those pills?' Mason asked.

'I found them in a waste-basket that was in the room for the purpose of collecting bandages which had been used, bits of waste cotton and other matter, which had been thrown away while the patient was being treated, things that were used in the treatment, in other words.'

'What time were those pills or tablets found?'

'They were found–'

'Just a minute,' Mason interrupted. 'Before you answer that question, let me ask you one more. Did you find them yourself personally?'

'Yes, sir. That's right, I did. I suggested that a search be made of everything in the room. Frankly, I was looking for–'

'Never mind what you were looking for,' Mason said. 'Just answer the question, Doctor. You know better than to volunteer information. You've been a witness before. I am simply asking whether you personally found them.'

'Yes, sir. I personally went through the contents of this waste-basket and I found one tablet, then I found two more.'

'Then what did you do?'

'They were placed in a receptacle, called to the attention of the police, and certain tests were made.'

'Can you describe the nature of those tests?'

'Just a moment, Your Honour, just a moment,' Hamilton Burger objected. 'That is not proper cross-examination. I have asked the witness on direct examination as to whether he ever saw those same pills or tablets again. Now I have no objection as to this witness testifying on cross-examination as to any tests that were made to determine the *identity* of the tablets, but as to any other matters, I object.'

'But wouldn't the test be for the purpose of determining the identity of the pills?' Judge Howison asked.

'Not necessarily, Your Honour.'

'Well, I feel that the objection is well-taken if the question is deemed to call for tests which were made for any other purpose and with which the witness is familiar. However, I don't see–'

'It will be explained in due time,' Hamilton Burger said, 'but I wish the privilege of putting on my own case in my own way, Your Honour.'

'Very well, the witness will understand that the question is limited as to tests which were made for the purpose of identifying the tablets.'

'Those tests were made by me, by a chemist of the police force, and a consulting chemist from one of the pharmaceutical houses, in the presence of two police officers. The tests disclosed unquestionably that these were the tablets I had prescribed. Those were the same three tablets that I had left to be given to Mrs Bain after she wakened at six o'clock in the morning. There is no question but what a substitution had been made–'

'Just a moment, Doctor,' Mason rebuked sharply. 'You keep trying to go ahead and interject your surmises and arguments into the case. Please confine yourself to answering questions and stopping.'

'Very well,' Dr Keener snapped. 'There is no question but what they were the same tablets.'

'In other words, they had an identical formula as the ones you had prescribed?'

'That's right.'

'And, by the way, Doctor, do you use the term pills and tablets interchangeably?'

'Loosely speaking, the way we have been talking in lay terms, yes. I usually refer to a pill as something that is a ball of medication with a coating on the outside, whereas a tablet is more of a lozenge, a compressed, flat substance. However, in lay language I use the terms interchangeably.'

'But technically what were these?'

'Technically these were tablets. It was a mixture that had been compounded and then compressed into small lozenge-like tablets.'

'How long had you been having trouble with a nervous condition on the part of the patient?'

'Ever since the accident–the injury.'

'And you had used varying methods of sedation?'

'I used hypodermics for a while until the pain had subsided, and then, as I was dealing with a condition of nervousness that threatened to become chronic, I tried to get a treatment that would be a palliative yet without containing sufficient medication to be perhaps habit-forming.'

'So this medication of soda, acetylsalicylic acid and phenobarbital was a part of a continuing treatment?'

'Yes, I had continued it for some time.'

'How long?'

'About one week on this particular formula.'

'And the patient responded?'

'As well as could be expected. I was, of course, finding it necessary to diminish dosage. After all, a patient cannot expect to depend indefinitely upon medication to control nervousness. The patient must co-operate, and there must be an adjustment to circumstances. Therefore, I was continually decreasing the dosage and, of course, the patient was, at the same time, developing a certain tolerance to the medication; therefore results were not entirely satisfactory from a layman's point of view, although as her physician I was keeping a careful watch on the situation and felt that progress was as good as could be expected.'

'The point I am making,' Mason said, 'is that you didn't mix up these pills three at a time. The pills were mixed in quantities.'

'Oh, I see what you're driving at,' Dr Keener said, with a somewhat nasty smile. 'However, I will state that I was very careful never to leave more than three of these pills at any one time, so that these three must necessarily have been the ones that I left that evening on my departure. I had previously given the patient three similar pills or tablets, which I administered personally.'

'Thank you for the benefit of your conclusions, Doctor,' Mason said, 'but all you know is that these three tablets had identical drug content with the ones you had prescribed. You don't know whether they were the three tablets you had left for her that night, or the day before yesterday, or a week ago, do you?'

'I certainly do.'

'How?'

'I know, because they were found in the trash basket, and the trash basket was emptied–'

'How do you know it was emptied?'

'The nurse reported it was emptied. Those were the orders that I had left.'

'You didn't empty it yourself?'

'No.'

'Then you're trying to testify from hearsay evidence, Doctor. You know better than that. I'm asking you of your own knowledge. As far as you're concerned, they might have been tablets that you had left for the patient to take the morning before or the morning before that, or the morning before that.'

'Well, the patient would have told me if she hadn't been given the medicine, and the nurse would have reported–'

'I'm talking of your own knowledge, Doctor. Let's not engage in statements as to the probabilities of a given situation, but as to your own knowledge, is there any way you have of *knowing* that those tablets were the same tablets that you had left that morning, purely from the chemical content?'

'Not from the chemical content, no. However, there were other matters that–'

'I think I've pointed out, Doctor, that we're not going into those other matters at this time,' Hamilton Burger interrupted sharply. 'The questions that you are being asked concern entirely the chemical compounds of the pills or tablets, and the place and time at which they were found.'

'Very well,' Dr Keener said.

'The point I am making,' Mason said, 'is that for perhaps the last four days you had been giving the patient identical medication?'

'For the last five days prior to her death, I had been giving her the same medication. Prior to that time the dosage had been somewhat stronger. I will further state that because I was afraid the patient might develop suicidal tendencies, I was very careful not to leave any surplus of pills or tablets so that the patient could accumulate a lethal dosage. Now does that answer your question, Mr Mason?'

'That answers it very nicely,' Mason said. 'Thank you very much, Doctor.'

Judge Howison glanced at Hamilton Burger. 'It's four-thirty, Mr Burger. Do you have some witness that you can put on who–'

'I'm afraid not, Your Honour. The next witness is going to take some time, but I think we may as well get at it, because I expect his cross-examination will consume a very considerable period.'

'Very well, go ahead.'

'Call Nathan Bain.'

Nathan Bain came forward and was sworn.

It was quite evident from the moment he took the witness stand that this was an entirely different Nathan Bain from the man whom Mason had made to appear at such disadvantage during the trial of Nellie Conway.

Nathan Bain had obviously been carefully prepared, thoroughly coached, and was enough of a public speaker to take full advantage of the situation.

Hamilton Burger stood up and faced the man with a manner which created the impression of a simple dignity and straightforward sincerity.

'Mr Bain,' he said, 'you are the surviving husband of Elizabeth Bain, the decedent?'

'Yes, sir.'

'And under the terms of the will, which has been filed for probate, you are not to inherit any part of her estate?'

'No, sir. Not one penny.'

'You have heard the testimony of Nellie Conway that you gave her certain medication to be administered to your wife?'

'Yes, sir.'

'Will you please tell me, and the jury, very frankly what the circumstances are in connection with that affair, Mr Bain?'

Nathan Bain took a deep breath, turned and faced the jury.

'I had,' he said, 'placed myself in a most unfortunate and lamentable predicament, entirely through my own ill-advised stupidity. I regret that very greatly, but I wish to state the facts–'

'Go ahead and state them,' Mason interrupted. 'I object, Your Honour, to this man making an argument to the jury. Let him answer the question by stating the facts.'

'Go right ahead and state the facts,' Hamilton Burger said, with something of a smirk.

Nathan Bain's manner was that of a man who is baring his chest to his accusers. He said, in a voice that dripped with sorrow and humility, 'For the past few months my relations with my wife had been anything but happy. I gave Nellie Conway four tablets and asked her to adminster those tablets to my wife without the knowledge of her doctor or anyone else.'

'What was the nature of those tablets?' Hamilton Burger asked.

'Those tablets,' Nathan Bain said, 'were four in number. Two of them were five-grain aspirin tablets, two of them were barbiturates.'

Hamilton Burger, veteran jury lawyer and court-room strategist, managed to put into his tone just the right amount of feeling and sympathy, indicating that he disliked to subject Nathan Bain to this ordeal but that the interests of justice made it necessary.

'Please tell the jury the cause of the difference between you and your wife at the time of her death.'

Once more Nathan Bain turned to look the jurors straight in the eyes, then lowered his own eyes, and in a voice of shamefaced humility said, 'I had been untrue to my wife, unfaithful to my marriage vows, and she had learned of my infidelity.'

'Was that the only cause?' Hamilton Burger asked.

'We had been drifting apart,' Nathan Bain admitted, and then, raising his eyes to the jury in a burst of candour, he said, as though baring his very soul, 'If it hadn't been for that I wouldn't have sought affection elsewhere, but . . .'

He broke off, made a little gesture of futility and once more lowered his eyes.

'You will understand that I dislike to go into this as much as you dislike to have me,' Hamilton Burger said, 'but I feel that it is necessary in order to give the jury a complete picture of the situation. *Why* did you want your wife to have this one dose, this heavy dose, of barbiturates?'

Nathan Bain kept his eyes on the floor. 'My wife had intercepted certain letters, certain documentary proof of my infidelity. She was planning to bring a suit for divorce. I didn't want this to happen. I loved her. My other affair was simply one of those flings that a man will take heedlessly, thoughtlessly, when temptation offers, and without proper consideration of the horrible consequences which must inevitably develop. I didn't want my wife to get a divorce.'

'*Why* did you arrange to give her the pills?'

'She wouldn't let me come in the room, yet the door was always unlocked. The nurses were not in there all the time. They came and went. When she was asleep the nurse would step out down to the kitchen to get some hot milk or coffee, or something of that sort. I wanted an opportunity to go into the room and search and find those letters.'

'Couldn't you have done it without drugging her?'

'She was very nervous and very restless after the accident. The poor girl's spine was crushed and I suppose that that injury had a deep-seated effect upon her entire nervous system, but in addition to that there was, of course, the knowledge of her injuries, and I think towards the last she had the feeling that she might never be able to walk again. She slept very fitfully, wakening at the slightest noise. I knew that if she detected me in the room, trying to get those documents, it would be disastrous. Even my presence in the room irritated her, and Dr Keener had warned me not to excite her. He had told me definitely to stay out of the room.'

'How long had that situation been in existence?'

'From the day she returned from the hospital.'

'So what happened on the evening of the sixteenth?'

'On the evening of the sixteenth, this dosage of barbiturates, added to the phenobarbital that Dr Keener had prescribed, put my wife in a deep, restful sleep. She was drugged to a point of insensibility. I waited until both the housekeeper, Imogene Ricker, and the nurse, Nellie Conway, were out of the room. They were down in the kitchen drinking coffee and talking. I felt certain they would be there for some minutes, because my wife was sleeping very soundly that night, and they knew that for some reason she was having a very deep, restful sleep. So I entered the room and after some five minutes' search found the documents and took them back into my possession.'

Nathan Bain looked down at his shoes, took a deep breath and let it out in a sigh. His attitude was that of one who condemns himself most strongly, yet who, after all, recognises that he has been actuated only by human frailties which are a part of every man's make-up. It was a consummate job of acting.

It would have been possible to have heard a pin drop in the court-room.

Hamilton Burger managed to give the impression of one who is respecting another's great sorrow. 'What did you do with these documents after you recovered them, Mr Bain?'

Bain said, 'I arranged to return the letters to the woman who had written them so she could destroy them.'

'And I believe you went to New Orleans immediately after your wife's death?'

Judge Howison looked down at Mason and said, 'Of course, an objection is usually up to opposing counsel, but it seems to me that some of this matter is entirely collateral.'

'I think not,' Hamilton Burger said, with slow, ponderous dignity. '*I* want the jury to get the entire picture here. We want to put all our cards face up and on the table, those that are good and those that are bad. We want the jurors to see the interior of this man's house. We want them to see into his mind, into his soul–'

Mason interrupted dryly, 'One of the reasons I hadn't been objecting, Your Honour, was that I knew Hamilton Burger had this touching speech all prepared and I didn't want to give him his cue.'

There was a slight ripple of merriment. Judge Howison, himself, couldn't help but smile, and Burger frowned as he realised that this emotional release was undermining the effect he was trying to create.

He drew himself up and said with simple, austere dignity, 'If Court and Counsel will bear with me, I think I can convince them of this man's sincerity, of his repentance and of his grief.'

And without waiting, Burger turned to Nathan Bain and said, 'Why did you go to New Orleans, Mr Bain?'

'I went there,' Bain said, 'because the woman who had entered into my life was there, and I wanted to tell her personally that I never wanted to see her again, that the affair had been the result of an unthinking venture and had left me emotionally bankrupt.'

Nathan Bain's words and manner carried conviction. A veteran speaker would have noticed that much of this was due to tricks of delivery, carefully studied, synthetic oratorical accessories, but the average listener heard only a bereaved husband being forced by the exigencies of the situation to make public confession of his wrongdoing, and trying his best to conceal a broken heart beneath a rigid exterior of Spartan self-control.

'Now then,' Hamilton Burger went on, 'you spoke of a settlement that had been made with Nellie Conway, and there has been some talk here of a settlement. Will you describe that and tell us what that actually was?'

'That,' Nathan Bain said, 'was an attempt on my part to adjust what had been a wrong.'

'Tell us about it, please.'

'I was instrumental in having Nellie Conway arrested for theft. I realise now that not only was my action impulsive, but that it was ill-advised. She was represented by Mr Perry Mason, the attorney who is now representing Victoria Braxton, and Mr Mason, I am afraid, caused me to cut rather a sorry spectacle in the court-room. That was because I hadn't fully thought over the various ramifications of the situation. I am afraid I was tempted to act hastily–much too hastily.'

'Just what did you do, specifically?'

' I appealed to the police, and, on their advice, hired a private detective. Things had been missing from the house and I had reason, or thought I did, to suspect Nellie Conway. I took my wife's jewel casket from the desk where it was kept under lock and key, and left it out in plain sight. I filled it with synthetic costume jewellery and made an inventory of the articles. I dusted the outside of the casket with a fluorescent powder.'

'Just describe that to us, if you will, Mr Bain.'

'Well, it was a powder which was furnished me by the private detective whom I employed. I understand it is quite generally used by private detectives for the purpose of catching sneak thieves, particularly in the case of locker burglaries and schoolroom sneak thieves.'

'Can you describe this powder?'

'It is virtually . . . well, it's rather neutral in shade, and when you put it on an object such as this leather-covered jewel case which belonged to my wife, it is practically invisible. It has a quality which makes it adhere to the fingers. It is remarkable in its clinging qualities, yet there is no feeling of stickiness in connection with it.'

'Now you have described that as a fluorescent powder?'

'Yes, sir. When ultra-violet light shines upon that powder it gives forth a very vivid light, that is, it fluoresces.'

'I would, if possible, like to have you tell the jury something more about the case against Nellie Conway. In other words, I want to have it appear why you paid her such a sum of money.'

'Because of the false arrest.'

'You're now satisfied it was a false arrest?'

'After Mr Mason had done with me,' Nathan Bain said, with a wry smile, 'I don't think there was anyone who had any doubt about it, myself included.'

Some of the jurors smiled sympathetically.

'How much did you pay her, by the way?'

'Two thousand dollars for herself, and five hundred dollars for an attorney fee.'

'Now just go ahead and describe the arrest a little more, if you will, please.'

'Well, we dusted the fluorescent powder on this jewel case.'

'And I take it the powder wasn't placed anywhere else?'

'No, sir. Only on the jewel case.'

'And what happened?'

'Well, from time to time, the detective and I would look at the contents of the jewel case to keep an inventory. Nothing was missing until shortly after Nellie Conway came to work, then a diamond pendant was missing. By that I mean a synthetic diamond pendant, a bit of costume jewellery. We made an excuse to switch off the lights and switch on the ultra-violet light, and Nellie Conway's finger-tips blazed into brilliance. That was circumstantial evidence and we jumped at conclusions from it, and naturally jumped at the wrong conclusion, as Mr Mason so ably pointed out.'

'What happened in that case?'

'Nellie Conway was found not guilty in, I believe, record time.'

'By a jury?'

'Yes, sir.'

'Now then,' Hamilton Burger said, 'with reference to those three tablets which were found in the waste-basket, according to Dr Keener's testimony, were you there when the basket was searched?'

'I was. Yes, sir.'

'And what was done with those three tablets?'

'Well, they were examined and placed in a small box and . . . well, when it began to appear that in all human probability the substitution must have been made by the defendant in this case, I suggested to the police officers that when I had told the defendant something about the case against Nellie Conway and how it had been handled, the defendant had wanted to see the jewel case. So I opened the desk, got out the jewel case and let the defendant look at it.'

'Did she handle it?'

'Yes. She took it in her hands.'

'Did anyone else handle it?'

'No, sir. At about that time the defendant's brother, who was upstairs, called to her, and she returned the jewel case to me. I hurriedly placed it on top of the desk and followed her upstairs.'

'Later on, you told the police about this?'

'Yes, sir. I told them that perhaps some of the fluorescent powder which still adhered to the jewel case might . . . well, I suggested to the police officers it might be well to look at those three tablets or pills under ultra-violet light.'

'Did they do so in your presence?'

'Yes, sir.'

'And what happened?'

'There was a very faint, but unmistakable fluorescence.'

There was a startled gasp from the spectators in the court-room, then the buzz of whispering.

It was at that moment that Hamilton Burger, apparently suddenly aware of the time, of which he had previously been unconscious, glanced apprehensively at the clock on the court-room wall, and said, 'Your Honour, I find that I have exceeded the time of adjournment by some ten minutes.'

'So you have,' Judge Howison said, his voice plainly indicating that he himself had been so interested in this dramatic phase of the testimony that he had not noticed the passing of time.

'I'm sorry,' Hamilton Burger said simply.

Judge Howison said, 'It appearing that the examination and cross-examination of this witness will occupy a very considerable period of time, and it now having passed the usual hour for the evening adjournment, the Court will take a recess until tomorrow morning at ten o'clock. During that time the members of the jury are admonished not to discuss the case among themselves or with others, nor permit it to be discussed in their presence. You jurors are not to form or express any opinion as to the guilt or innocence of the defendant until the case is finally submitted to you. The defendant is remanded to custody. The Court will adjourn until tomorrow morning at ten o'clock.'

Judge Howison left the bench and there was instantly a great commotion of voices throughout the court-room.

Mason turned to Victoria Braxton. 'Did you handle that jewel chest?' he asked.

'Yes. I was curious. I asked him about it. He took me downstairs and opened the desk. When we went back upstairs he left it on top of the desk. But while I am the only one who handled it at the time, the others did later.'

'What others?'

'Why, Jim and Georgiana.'

'Did you see them handle it?'

'No, but they went downstairs, and Georgiana asked me when she came back up why Elizabeth's jewel case was out in plain sight–so if they saw it they must have handled it. Georgiana has an insatiable curiosity.'

'And Nathan Bain handled it when he gave it to you, didn't he?'

'Why, yes. I hadn't thought of that.'

'And who put it back in the desk? Did he?'

'The housekeeper, I think.'

'It's the same old story,' Mason said. 'Everyone handled it, yet by building up to this climax just at adjournment, the District Attorney conveys the impression he's proven your guilt.

'That's always the way with these fluorescent powder cases. The thing is so dramatic, the fluorescent finger-tips seem so damning, that everyone loses his mental perspective.

'Now, couldn't Nathan Bain have opened the door of his wife's bedroom, picked up the tablets from the saucer and switched the poison tablets?'

'No . . . I don't think so, not while I was there.'

'They were close to the door?'

'Yes. If he'd opened the door to look in he could have done it, but he didn't. But couldn't he have substituted them while Nellie Conway had them, carrying them around in that box?'

'Don't worry,' Mason interrupted. 'I'm going to cover that phase of the case on cross-examination. What I'm asking now is whether he could have made the substitution *after* Nellie Conway had put the tablets on the saucer and left them with you.'

'No. That would have been impossible.'

'And what time was it that you were handling the jewel case and got that powder on your fingers?'

'Shortly before three in the morning. We got to the airport at one-forty-five, and by the time we arrived at the house it must have been two-thirty.'

'And at about three o'clock you went in to see Elizabeth?'

'Yes.'

'The three of you?'

'Yes.'

'Keep a stiff upper lip.' Mason said, as the deputy sheriff touched her arm.

'Don't worry,' she told him, and followed the officer to the prisoner's exit.

Jim Braxton and his wife, waiting for Mason immediately outside the bar which segregated the space reserved for attorneys and officers of the court from the rest of the court-room, grabbed the lawyer, one by each arm.

It was Georgiana who did the talking.

'That dirty hypocrite,' she said. 'He's sitting there so butter wouldn't melt in his mouth, and the worst of it is, he's getting away with it. That's what I told you about him, Mr Mason, the . . . the toad, the big, fat toad! That's all he is, a toad!'

'Take it easy,' Mason said. 'It's not going to do any good running up a blood pressure over it.'

'He's sitting there just trying to lie his way out of it. He's fixed it up with this Nellie Conway, and between them they're telling a great story for the jury, trying to make it appear that Vicki must have been the one who gave her that poisoned medicine. Mr Mason, you've simply *got* to do something, you can't let him get away with this.'

'I'm going to do the best I can,' Mason said.

'We all know who murdered Elizabeth. It was Nathan Bain, and he and that Conway woman have cooked up a story that will look good in print and will lull the suspicions of the jurors. We know the real Nathan Bain, Mr Mason, and he's not like this at all. He's just a shrewd, selfish, cunning individual–unbelievably cunning–but he does have the knack of standing up and talking to people in a way that makes it seem he's baring his very soul, that he's giving them an insight into his innermost thoughts. Actually the man's innermost thoughts are just as black and impenetrable as . . . as . . . as an ink-well full of ink.'

Mason said, 'I've torn him wide open once. I may be able to do it again, but this time he's been very carefully coached.'

'Humph!' she said. 'The probabilities are he's the one who coached that District Attorney. Between them they're putting on a great show.'

'Aren't they?' Mason said.

'Couldn't you have objected to a lot of that stuff?' Jim interposed timidly.

'Sure,' Mason said, 'but I want it in. The more of this stuff he's putting in, the more latitude it gives me in cross-examination. The more I try to keep out, the more the jurors suspect we're afraid to have them learn all the facts.'

'Georgiana said, 'Don't depend too much on cross-examination. He's been prepared for that. Between him and that District Attorney they've rehearsed that act until they're black in the face. They're both birds of a stripe–I mean a feather. Just a couple of actors putting on a big razzle-dazzle. If you could only know Nathan the way he *really* is, and then see him the way he is on the witness stand, you'd appreciate some of the things I've been telling you.'

'Well,' Mason said, reassuringly, 'perhaps we can find some way of letting the jury see him the way he really is.'

18

Mason, in midnight conference with Paul Drake and Della Street, paced the floor of his office.

'Damn Burger,' Mason said. 'He has some devastating bomb he's going to drop.'

'That fluorescent powder? Could that have been it?' Paul Drake asked.

'No. That doesn't really prove as much as they're trying to make it appear. Anyone in the house could have touched the casket. Nathan Bain saw the defendant touching it, but . . . that damn housekeeper, Paul, what have you been able to find out about her?'

'Just what our reports have shown, Perry. She keeps pretty much to herself, and has no close friends. She apparently was devoted to Bain's first wife and she was devoted to Elizabeth. How she feels towards Nathan is a question.'

'If she felt that Nathan Bain poisoned Elizabeth . . .'

'But she doesn't, Perry. She's positive Vicki Braxton did it. She says Vicki is a pretty smooth article, and she knows about other evidence in the case. She's positive Vicki wheedled Elizabeth into making a will, and then when Elizabeth became suspicious and refused to complete the will, Vicki poisoned her.'

Mason thought that over, then said, 'If she could be *made* to believe that Nathan poisoned Elizabeth, and then that he might have poisoned his first wife, Marta, don't you think she then might tell us something that could help?'

Drake said, 'I don't know. I've had one of my cleverest woman operatives make her casual acquaintance, and get her talking as well as anyone can. Of course, we've asked no questions about Marta's death. The housekeeper says the doctor gave Nellie those three pills. Nellie had them in a little box. She saw them on the kitchen table when she and Nellie had coffee together just before midnight, and knows they were the same pills. She says Hamilton Burger can prove they were, that it had to be Nellie or Vicki who made the switch. The police have positive proof. And, of course, she says Nellie had no motive.'

Mason, pacing the floor, said, 'How do we know she had no motive? That's only what the housekeeper says.'

'We can't find any motive, Perry. Vicki, of course, had the big motive.'

'Nellie had enough motive to give those three sleeping tablets, Paul.'

'Sure–money.'

'Well, why couldn't more money have been the motive for the poison tablets? Those extra three tablets after the confession stuff on the first three would be a masterly touch. Good Lord, Paul, we have every element of proof. Bain gave Nellie money to administer sleeping tablets They both admit it. Then he gave her more money, and someone changed the doctor's three tablets to poison tablets. Nellie and Nathan Bain knew that if he gave her a lot of money it would be traced, so instead of being surreptitious about it, he did it right under our noses.

'He arrested Nellie on a charge where he had no real proof. Nellie had previously contacted me, so he knew I'd rush to her rescue. Then I get her acquitted, and Nathan pays her a lot of dough and puts her back in the room where she has the last three tablets Elizabeth ever took.'

Drake said, 'Gosh, Perry, when you look at it that way it sure seems dead open-and-shut.'

'Sure it does, Paul. It's all this razzle-dazzle stuff that confuses the issues.'

Drake said, 'Just strip the issues down to bare fact like that, Perry, and you may be able to sell the jury on the idea–unless Burger comes up with something new. Even I never realised how damning the bare facts are. It's only when they're all dressed up in this hocus-pocus that they seem to become innocuous. Nellie and Bain could have staged that whole act, the fluorescent powder and everything.

'When you come right down to it, that fluorescent powder on the tablets and on Vicki Braxton's fingers is a terribly damning bit of circumstantial evidence–and yet it was deliberately planted by Bain. By using the case against Nellie as a red herring . . . dammit, Perry, I believe you're right!'

Mason, continuing to pace the floor, said, 'The only thing that I have to be sure of is that Hamilton Burger gets the door wide open.'

'What do you mean?'

'Opens the door so I can start cross-examining Nathan Bain about the death of his first wife, without having Burger be in a position to yell that it's incompetent, irrelevant and immaterial; and that because he didn't touch on anything dealing with her in his direct examination, I can't cross-examine on it.'

'Of course,' Drake said, 'you haven't made a move toward getting the body exhumed.'

'Why should I? I'm going to put that up to the prosecution. I'll dare them to do it.'

'They'd never try to exhume that body in a thousand years. If it *should* turn out she'd died of arsenic poisoning, it would knock the case against Victoria Braxton skyhigh. They know that.'

'That's fine,' Mason told him. 'We'll leave the body in the grave but we'll certainly drag her ghost in front of the jury–if I can only find some way to make it relevant and material. Tell me all you've found out about her, Paul.'

Drake said, 'She came from a rather wealthy family. Her parents were opposed to the marriage. They're Eastern people. This girl, Marta, evidently had a lot of spirit. She fell for Nathan Bain like a ton of bricks. Between you and me, Perry, Nathan Bain, with that ability to impress people and that gift of gab, must have been quite some ladies' man before he started putting on all that weight.'

'Apparently so. Go on, Paul. Tell me more about Marta.'

Well, Marta was independent and high-strung. She had some money of her own, quite a little money. It had come to her from an uncle and was in trust, to be delivered to her when she was twenty-five. Prior to that time she had the income from it.'

'How much money?'

'Something over fifty thousand.'

'Go ahead. What happened?'

'Well, either Nathan Bain convinced her that her parents were persecuting him, or she got the idea in some way. Anyhow, after the marriage there was a very distinct coolness–she tried to be the dutiful daughter all right, but she had thrown in her lot with Nathan Bain and she wanted her parents to understand it. The old folks thought it was simply the fling of a high-strung, impetuous girl, and that she'd get over it and would probably come back home.'

'Tell me some more about the fifty thousand bucks.'

'She was twenty-five on the seventeenth of June. She got the money in her own name. On the first of August of the same year she was dead. Nathan Bain got the money. He was a big shot for a while, and then horse racing and poor investments got him down, and he picked out another girl with money. This time a good wad of money. Elizabeth Bain had at least half a million, and it may run more than that. He thought he was going to get his hands on her money, and she had other ideas, so then Elizabeth Bain died. The trouble is that he made a couple of false passes first and she became suspicious, so she disinherited him with that will. Good Lord, when you summarise the naked facts they make Bain look like a fiend, but when you see him on that witness stand, clothed in grief, humility and repentance, and being so damned human about it all. . . . Hell, Perry, I'll bet there isn't a man on that jury but what's found himself in Bain's shoes at one time or another. I tell you Bain has won them over.

'Perry, I don't want to inquire into your business when it's none of my business, but does it seem to you that there's anything phony about that will?'

'What about it?'

'Well, it was made in the handwriting of the decedent on the morning of the date she died, but the wording sounds a little funny, as though she had been interrupted in the middle of the thing in some way. The housekeeper tells my operative she thinks Vicki was trying to high-pressure Elizabeth into making the will and that Elizabeth balked and refused to complete it and sign it.'

Mason said, 'That's something Nathan Bain's lawyers will have to prove in the Probate Court.'

'I was wondering if you'd noticed the way the will seems to break off in the middle.'

Mason's reply to that was complete silence.

'Well,' Drake said, 'that's the story, Perry. I *could* have people whisper a word or two into the ears of Marta's parents. . . .'

Mason shook his head. 'Then it wouldn't come as any surprise to Hamilton Burger, and he'll keep the door closed so that I can't use it on Bain's cross-examination. No, Paul, I'm going to go to court tomorrow and when Hamilton Burger gets the door opened so I can cross-examine Nathan Bain, I'm going to spring the point. Just as soon as I've done that, I want you to get Marta's parents on the phone, tell them what's happened, and get them to raise hell yelling for an exhumation and autopsy. Remember, Paul, do that the *minute* I spring the point. Have it so you can get to a phone at once.'

'Leave it to me,' Drake said, 'If you play it right you may blast Bain out of that humble, repentant sinner act. And if you can't do it, Perry, that jury's going against you.'

'I know it,' Mason said, grimly. 'You're not telling me anything, Paul.'

19

As court convened the next day, Hamilton Burger's manner gave no doubt but what he was now moving in for the kill.

Once or twice he glanced sidelong at Perry Mason, a glance of sneering triumph.

'Your Honour,' he said, 'Nathan Bain was on the stand, and I'll ask him to resume his place on the witness stand if he will.'

Nathan Bain, moving like an elephant on eggs, marched up to the witness stand, composed himself in the chair, and looked at Hamilton Burger with the expression of a repentant but loyal dog, quite evidently a man who had stripped himself to the bone in the interests of justice, and was willing, if necessary, to make even further sacrifices.

'Mr Bain, directing your attention to events which took place immediately after your wife's death.'

'Yes, sir.'

'Did you assist the officers in making any search of the premises?'

'I did. Yes, sir.'

'Now will you describe the premises, please, generally?'

'Well, the house is a two-and-a-half-storey house. There is a garage at the back, and a patio.'

'Is there shrubbery in the patio?'

'Surrounding the patio, yes. Shrubbery and a hedge.'

'Now in searching this patio did you find anything, or were you present when the officers found anything?'

'Yes, sir.'

'What?'

'A bottle wrapped in paper.'

'Were you present when the officers unwrapped that paper?'

'I was. Yes, sir.'

'And what was in the paper?'

'A bottle containing a label from a Honolulu drugstore, with the word 'arsenic' printed on it.'

Perry Mason heard a commotion back of him.

Victoria Braxton got to her feet, choked, started to say something.

The deputy sheriff, who had her in custody, rushed to her side, and then suddenly wild screams of hysterical laughter penetrated the court-room as Victoria Braxton, laughing, screaming and crying, had hysterics.

'Pardon me,' Hamilton Burger said, with a bow at Perry Mason. 'Your client seems to be emotionally upset. I think, Your Honour, we should have a recess until the defendant is able to proceed with the trial.'

'Recess until eleven o'clock,' Judge Howison said, banging his gavel on the desk. 'Is there a physician in the court-room?'

'Dr Keener is here.'

'He'd better have a look at this defendant,' Judge Howison said, and promptly retired to chambers.

Complete pandemonium broke loose in the court-room, spectators surging forward, deputy sheriffs in attendance grappling with Victoria Braxton, newspaper photographers battling for places to secure photographs from a point of vantage, the jurors, heedless of the admonition of the court, craning their necks to get a glimpse of what was going on.

It was almost forty-five minutes before a white, emotionally-shaken, trembling Victoria Braxton could even talk with Perry Mason in a witness room adjoining the judge's chambers.

'Well?' Mason asked, coldly.

She said, 'Don't start blaming me or I'll blow my top again. I took a chance on disposing of that arsenic, and lost, that's all.'

'Would you mind telling me what it's all about?'

She said, 'It's simple. I bought that arsenic in Honolulu for a cat that had been making life hideous there in the bungalows. The bottle was in my baggage. When I got back to the house and learned that Elizabeth had died from arsenic poisoning, I suddenly remembered having it and thought perhaps the possession of it might be misconstrued. I'd signed the poison register in Honolulu and . . . well, I knew that the police were snooping around and I felt quite certain they'd manage to inspect my baggage, so I stepped to my upstairs bedroom window and threw it out into the shrubbery. Someone must have seen me, otherwise I can't imagine why they'd have searched the premises. Now that's the whole story.'

Mason was silent.

'How bad is it?' she asked.

Mason said, 'Short of some sort of legal miracle, it's bad enough to get you a verdict of first-degree murder at the hands of the jury, probably with the death penalty.'

'That's what I thought,' she said.

Mason got up and started pacing the floor.

'What do we do?' she asked. 'Or is there anything we can do?'

Mason said, 'I could probably get a continuance for a couple of days on the ground that you're emotionally upset. If I did that, it would ruin whatever last faint, glimmering chance we have. If you're telling the truth and can get on the stand and tell it so you convince at least one of the jurors, we can get a hung jury. Our only hope now is to hurry this trial to a conclusion so fast that public opinion doesn't have a chance to crystallise into a feeling of complete hostility. Do you feel that you can go back to the court-room and go through with the thing?'

'I can go through with anything now, I guess. I'm shaking like an autumn leaf, but I'll take it on my chin now.'

Mason said, 'You *might* have told me this before, you know.'

'If I had, you wouldn't have handled my case. I'm grown-up, Mr Mason. I'm a big girl now. I took a gamble and I lost. Don't rub it in. I'm the one who will be executed, not you.'

'Let's go back to court,' Mason said, tersely.

'Will you,' she asked, 'make any explanation of my hysterics to the jury?'

'Sure.'

'When?'

'When I can think up an explanation that won't raise more hell with your case,' Mason said.

There was sudden hope in her eyes. 'Do you think you can do that now–before the bad impression I made has had a chance to sink in?'

'No,' Mason said, 'we can't make any explanation until we can win at least one friend on that jury. Come on, we're going to have to face it.' Turning, he walked back to a court-room which now regarded him with a concentrated stare of sudden hostility.

Judge Howison took the bench and called the court to order. Hamilton Burger, unduly solicitous, inquired of Mason. 'Is your client able to proceed?'

'Quite!' Mason snapped at him.

'Very well,' Hamilton Burger said. 'But I can appreciate the shock she has sustained. The prosecution wishes to be just, but it wants to be humane. If this upset, white-faced, trembling defendant is in as bad shape as she seems, we–'

'She isn't,' Mason interrupted. 'Go on with the case and save your sympathies for your star witness.'

'I can understand and so forgive your short temper,' Burger said with a smirk. 'Mr Nathan Bain, will you resume your position on the stand? Now, Mr Bain, I am going to ask you if you would know that bottle when you saw it again.'

'Yes, sir. My initials are marked on the label as well as those of the officers who were participating in the search.'

'Is this the bottle?'

Hamilton Burger handed him a box with a glass top, containing a small bottle.

'That is it.'

'We ask that this be received in evidence, Your Honour,' Hamilton Burger said.

Mason said shortly, 'Objected to as incompetent, irrelevant and immaterial. No connection whatever has been shown between the bottle and the defendant, and the Court will notice that this bottle contains a white powder. The unmistakable evidence is that if Elizabeth Bain was poisoned she was poisoned with three five-grain tablets.'

'Just a moment,' Hamilton Burger said. 'We can connect this up if the Court please, but it will be necessary to call two witnesses in order to do so. In view of Mr Mason's objection, I will ask that Mr Bain now step aside for just a moment and make way for two witnesses who will be able to dispose of the points raised in the objection.'

'In that case,' Judge Howison said, 'I would suggest that you simply mark the exhibit for identification and then, after you are finished with this witness, you can put the others on.'

That did not suit Burger's strategy and his face showed it. 'Your Honour,' he said, 'one of these witnesses is from Honolulu. It is very important that he get back. If I could call him just briefly.'

'What's he going to testify to?' Mason asked.

Hamilton Burger welcomed the opportunity to turn to Mason. 'That witness,' he said, 'is a clerk in a drug-store on Hotel Street in Honolulu. He is going to identify the defendant as being the woman who entered his drug-store and asked for arsenic in order to poison a cat that had been terrorising the neighbourhood, killing kittens, carrying off birds, and making a general nuisance of himself. He is going to produce a poison register on which will appear the date and the signature of the defendant.'

Mason said casually, 'Why, there's no need to call *him*! We'll stipulate to all that.'

'You'll stipulate to it?'

'Good heavens, yes,' Mason said. 'Of course we'll stipulate to it. It's the truth.'

'Oh, I see,' Burger said slyly. 'In view of the defendant's hysterics–'

'That will do,' Judge Howison said tartly. 'Confine your remarks to the Court, Mr District Attorney. In view of the stipulation of Counsel, the statement of proof just made by the District Attorney will be considered as part of the evidence in this case.'

'And,' Hamilton Burger went on, obviously taken aback, 'he will identify the bottle and the label as being the bottle that was given to the defendant, and will produce samples of typewriting made on the typewriter of the drugstore, which we expect to prove by a handwriting expert will show that this label–'

'No question about it,' Mason said. 'We'll stipulate it. We admit it.'

'And by that stipulation, that, too, will be considered in evidence,' Judge Howison said. 'In view of Mr Mason's stipulation, that disposes of the defendant's objection that the bottle has not been connected with the defendant?'

'Quite right, Your Honour,' Mason said, smiling urbanely. 'I just wanted to make sure the proof was in. That was the sole object of my objection. Now then, I would like to ask at this time if there is any *other* proof connecting this bottle with the defendant? If there is, let's have it all at this time and then we'll stipulate the bottle can be received in evidence.'

Hamilton Burger said, 'There is other evidence.'

'Let's have it.'

'I would prefer to introduce it later.'

'Then,' Mason said, 'I'll renew the objection to the fact that the bottle is incompetent, irrelevant and immaterial. There is no evidence connecting this particular bottle with the defendant.'

'Oh, all right,' Hamilton Burger said. 'The wrapping paper contains a fingerprint of the defendant in the same fluorescent powder that was dusted on that jewel box. It fluoresces under ultra-violet light and it can be seen and identified as a fingerprint of the defendant.'

'You are certain of that?' Mason asked.

'I'm certain of it, and I have a fingerprint expert sitting right here in court who can swear to it.'

'Then I'll stipulate it,' Mason said, cheerfully.

Judge Howison frowned. 'I am not certain that in a case of this gravity I want Counsel to make stipulations as to such an important piece of evidence. I think, Mr District Attorney, I'm going to ask you to put that witness on the stand.'

'Very well,' the District Attorney said. 'If the Court will permit Nathan Bain to step to one side, I'll call Sergeant Holcomb.'

'Very well,' the Court said, 'for this limited purpose of identifying the bottle, we will call Sergeant Holcomb.'

Nathan Bain left the stand. Sergeant Holcomb held up his right hand, was sworn, and took the witness stand.

Nor could he resist a glance of triumph at Perry Mason.

Hamilton Burger said, 'I show you this bottle and ask if you have ever seen it before?'

'Yes, sir.'

'Where?'

'It was found on the seventeenth day of September on the premises of Nathan Bain, in a hedge in the patio.'

'I now hand you a piece of paper and ask you what that paper is?'

'That is the paper that surrounded the bottle, in which the bottle was wrapped.'

'Did you make any test of that paper?'

'I did. Yes, sir.'

'What did you find on it?'

'I found the fingerprint of the middle finger of the right hand of the defendant. That fingerprint, incidentally, bore faint traces of fluorescence. In other words in ultra-violet light it showed the same unmistakable characteristics as the powder which had been placed on the jewel case in the living-room of Nathan Bain.'

'Cross-examine,' Hamilton Burger said.

'That paper was on the *outside* of the bottle?' Mason asked.

'Yes, sir.'

'And the fingerprint was on it?'

'Yes, sir.'

'Any other prints?'

'No prints that were such as could be identified, but there were numerous smudges which were faintly fluorescent. In other words, they had been made with the fingers of a hand that had touched fluorescent powder, but they were mere smudges.'

'And the fluorescence was quite faint?'

'Yes, sir.'

'Now how did that compare with the fluorescence on the tablets which were found in the waste-basket?'

'That on the tablets was much stronger.'

'There were no fluorescent prints, smudges or traces on the bottle, on the label on the bottle, or the inside of the paper in which the bottle had been wrapped, or in fact, on any single thing inside that paper?'

'Well, no.'

'And if the defendant, with enough of that fluorescent powder on her fingers to have left smudges or prints on the paper covering the bottle, had opened the paper to get at the bottle, or had opened the bottle to get at the contents, there would have been such traces of fluorescence, would there not?'

'I am not prepared to say.'

'Why? You're testifying as an expert.'

'Well . . . I don't know when she got the arsenic out of the bottle. That may have been before . . . I don't know, Mr Mason. I can't answer your question. There are too many uncertain factors involved.'

'I thought you couldn't answer it,' Mason said with exaggerated courtesy. 'Thank you very much, Sergeant. That is all.'

'Nathan Bain, will you return to the stand, please,' Hamilton Burger said. 'Now, Your Honour, I renew my offer that this bottle and the wrapping paper be received as People's exhibits.'

'They will be so received. Now let's see, the three tablets have been identified as People's Exhibit A, the bottle will be People's Exhibit B, and the wrapping paper will be People's Exhibit C.'

'Cross-examine the witness, Bain,' Hamilton Burger said sharply.

Mason glanced anxiously at the clock. He had time for only a few questions before the noon adjournment. Any impression he was to make on the jury before adjournment must be done quickly.

'You were estranged from your wife, Mr Bain?'

'Yes. Yes, sir. Unfortunately . . . and as I have been forced to admit, due entirely to my fault.'

It was apparent that any further attempt on the part of Mason to persecute this repentant sinner could only result in further alienating the jury.

Mason said, 'Did you see your wife in her last illness?'

'At the very end, yes, when she was hardly conscious.'

'You have been married once before?'

'Yes.'

'Your first wife died?'

'Yes, sir.'

'You did not see your wife, Elizabeth Bain, during the first part of her illness?'

'No. Due to the matters I have mentioned, she did not wish me to be in the room with her.'

'Were you interested in learning about her symptoms?'

'Certainly I was interested. I paced the floor of my bedroom in an agony of self-torture, Mr Mason. I asked for bulletins from my wife's bedside. I asked the doctor to describe her symptoms. I wanted to make certain that everything that could possibly be done by medical science was being done.'

'You knew that those symptoms as described to you were said to be those of arsenic poisoning?'

'Yes.'

'You were familiar with those symptoms?'

'No.'

'You were not?'

'No.'

'You had never seen them before?'

'Why, certainly not, Mr Mason.'

Mason got to his feet. 'I will ask you, Mr Bain, if at the time of her final and fatal illness your first wife, Marta, didn't exhibit each and every symptom that was exhibited by your wife, Elizabeth Bain?'

'Oh, Your Honour,' Hamilton Burger shouted, 'this is certainly going too far. This is an attempt by innuendo. Why, this is an inhuman, illegal–'

'I don't think so,' Judge Howison said, watching Nathan Bain's face shrewdly. 'The prosecution threw all doors wide open with this witness. I think under the circumstances I am going to give the defence every latitude for cross-examination. The objection is overruled.'

'Answer the question,' Mason said.

'That was different,' Nathan Bain told him, his manner suddenly stripped of all its poise. In his own way he was as badly shocked as Victoria Braxton had been, and he showed it.

'What was different about it?'

'It was a different cause. She died from food poisoning. The doctors said so. The death certificate shows–'

'Was there any autopsy?'

'No. I tell you there was a certificate of death.'

'An autopsy *was* performed on your wife, Elizabeth, was it not?'

'Yes, sir.'

'For the purpose of *proving* that she died of arsenic poisoning?'

'I believe the District Attorney ordered the autopsy.'

'But no autopsy was performed on your wife, Marta?'

'No.' Nathan Bain seemed to have sagged within his clothes.

'You stood to inherit some half a million dollars from your wife, Elizabeth?'

'Apparently not. She seems to have left a will that–'

'You are going to contest that will, are you not?'

'Now, Your Honour,' Hamilton Burger interposed, 'I wish to object to this on the ground that it is calling for something that is far afield–'

'It goes to show the state of mind of this witness,' Mason said. 'He has testified at great length in mealy-mouthed repentance. Let's find out how deep that repentance goes.'

'I think your language in unduly vigorous, Mr Mason,' Judge Howison said, 'but I'm going to permit the witness to answer the question.'

'Answer the question,' Mason said. 'Are you going to contest the will?'

'Yes,' Nathan Bain snapped. 'That will is a complete phony. It is–'

'You expect to keep it from being probated, do you not?'

'I do.'

'And thereby you will inherit some half-million dollars?'

'Possibly,' Bain said, savagely angry.

'Now then,' Mason said, 'tell the jury how much you inherited after your first wife so unfortunately passed away with symptoms so similar to those exhibited by Elizabeth Bain during *her* last illness.'

'Your Honour!' Hamilton Burger shouted. 'This is an insinuation that is not warranted by the evidence. This is not proper cross-examination–'

'I think I will sustain that objection in the form in which the question is asked,' Judge Howison ruled.

'Can you,' Mason said, 'point out to the jury any symptom that your wife, Marta, had that was not a symptom of your wife, Elizabeth Bain, in her last illness?'

Nathan Bain was uncomfortably silent.

'Can you?' Mason asked.

'I wasn't there to see the symptoms of Elizabeth's illness,' Nathan Bain said at length.

'How much money did you inherit from your first wife, roughly speaking?'

'Objected to,' Hamilton Burger said. 'That is–'

'Overruled,' Judge Howison snapped.

'Fifty thousand dollars.'

'How long were you married to her before her death?'

'About two years.'

'How long were you married to Elizabeth Bain before her death?'

'Two years, approximately.'

Judge Howison glanced at the clock. 'I dislike to interrupt Counsel's cross-examination,' he said, 'but this examination has already continued some few minutes past the usual hour for the Court's recess.'

'I understand, Your Honour,' Mason said.

'Court will adjourn until two o'clock this afternoon,' Judge Howison said.

'The defendant is remanded to custody and the jurors will remember the admonition of the Court.'

Nathan Bain took advantage of that moment to dash down from the witness stand while the jurors were still leaving the jury box.

He shouted at Mason in a paroxysm of rage, 'Why you . . . you . . . you dirty, despicable shyster! . . . I could kill you?'

Mason raised his voice. 'No, No! Don't kill *me*, Mr Bain! You wouldn't inherit a dime!'

A newspaper reporter roared with laughter.

Court attendants crowded forward to separate the two men, and the jury filed slowly and thoughtfully from the jury box.

20

Perry Mason, Della Street and Paul Drake sat huddled in conference in the little restaurant across the street from the Hall of Justice. The proprietor, an old friend, had ensconced them in a private dining-room and brought in an extension telephone.

Mason, eating a baked ham sandwich and sipping a glass of milk, said, 'Hang it, Paul, I still can't get a clear picture.'

'Well, the jury have a clear picture,' Drake said. 'Of course, you did a masterful job with Nathan Bain. You may have won over some members of the jury *if* your client can get on the stand and tell a decent story. But you know she can't do it, Perry.'

'Why not?'

'There's too much against her. Her fingerprint on the wrapper, the fact that she hurled that bottle out of the window. She must have hurled it out of the window, and there must have been some witness who saw her. You can't believe that those men would have gone out and started searching the grounds just on the strength of a general investigation. Holcomb hasn't brains enough for that.'

'No,' Mason conceded. 'Some witness saw her throw the bottle out of the window, or saw someone throw it out of the window, that's a cinch.'

'Well, there you are,' Drake said. 'She gets on the stand and tries to tell a story, and then Hamilton Burger jumps up and starts to cross-examine her, and by the time he gets done with her she'll be the greatest poisoner since Lucrezia Borgia.'

Mason nodded glumly.

Drake said, 'I've been watching that court-room, Perry; I've been talking with people who have listened to the evidence, and while you certainly made a magnificent job of stripping the mask off Nathan Bain, nevertheless your client is in a mess. That fit of hysterics put a noose around her neck.'

'I'll say it did,' Mason said wearily. 'This business of getting into court representing a woman and then finding she's been holding out on you is tough on the nerves.'

'Well, what would *you* have done under similar circumstances?' Della Street asked. 'She thought her secret was safe. She knew that if she told you it would prevent you or any other reputable lawyer from taking the case.'

'I suppose so,' Mason agreed glumly, 'but I still don't get the picture. Did you notice Nathan Bain's face when I asked him about the death of his first wife?'

Drake said, 'You surely flabbergasted him.'

'Why?' Mason asked.

'He'd been drilled and rehearsed on how to take your cross-examination; but this was an unexpected blow in a particularly vulnerable place.'

'You agree with me it hit him hard?' Mason asked.

'He damn near fainted,' Paul said.

Mason frowned thoughtfully, then, after a minute or two, asked, 'You phoned Marta's parents?'

'The minute you made the point.'

'How did they take it, Paul?'

'They're catching a plane, demanding the body be exhumed and raising hell generally.'

Mason grinned.

'As I see it,' Drake warned, 'if the body *is* exhumed and if she did die of arsenic poisoning, you may get a hung jury *if* the defendant can tell a convincing story. But if the body is exhumed and she didn't die of arsenic poisoning, Perry, you're a gone goose. You'll have made a martyr out of Nathan and a shyster out of yourself.'

Mason nodded. 'It's not a gamble I like, but it's a gamble I have to take. A lawyer has to throw all his chips out on the table when he gets in a situation like this.'

'If your client could only explain that bottle of arsenic,' Drake said.

'She can. She wanted it for a cat.'

Drake shook his head. 'The jury won't believe her, Perry. Just wait until you hear Burger's argument to the jury.'

'Yes,' Mason said sarcastically, 'I can imagine Hamilton Burger saying, "The murderess thought the wool had been pulled over the eyes of everyone, and then when this damning, this tell-tale piece of evidence, which her Counsel is now trying to minimise, was brought into Court, what did she do?–Ladies and gentlemen of the jury, I don't ask you to accept *my* valuation of this damning bit of evidence. I ask you only to accept the valuation which the defendant herself placed upon it." . . . And so on and so on, ad infinitum.'

'You make it sound damn convincing,' Drake said.

'So will Hamilton Burger,' Mason told him. 'Call your office, Paul. See if there's anything new.'

Drake put through a call to his office and said, 'I'm eating lunch. Anything new in the Bain case? . . . What? . . . Let me have that again. . . . Hold the phone.'

He turned to Mason and said, 'A peculiar development. We've been shadowing Nathan Bain, you know.'

Mason nodded.

'Apparently Bain has no idea he's being tailed. Now I told you that Bain, like all these men who have exploited women by the exercise of irresistible charm, has a fatal weakness himself. As those fellows get older, they almost invariably fall for their own line. Some shrewd, selfish, scheming woman who is younger, is attractive, and on the make, gets them head-over-heels in love with them.'

'Go ahead,' Mason said. 'What's the pitch, Paul?'

'Despite his attitude on the stand, Nathan Bain is absolutely nuts about Charlotte Moray. She's now back here in the Rapidex Apartments.'

'Under what name?' Mason asked.

'Under her own name. She's been living there for months. Nathan Bain went to see her this morning just before he came to court.'

Mason, pacing the floor, gave that matter thoughtful consideration.

'That should give you something to smear him with on further cross-examination,' Drake said.

Again Mason nodded.

'Any instructions?' Drake asked.

Mason said suddenly, 'Paul, I've got an idea.'

'It's about time,' Drake told him.

'Who will be in Nathan Bain's house this afternoon? Anyone?'

Drake said, 'Let's see, Perry. I guess not. Bain and the housekeeper will both be in court and–'

Mason's interruption was sharp. 'Paul, I want you to get a stake-out in some place near-by, where you can instal a recording machine. I want you to get into Bain's house and put a bug in the room that has the telephone.'

Drake's face showed dismay. 'Have a heart, Perry! You can't do that!'

Mason's face was hard as granite. 'Paul, I'm gambling my reputation on this thing, and you're going to gamble right along with me. I want you to get a microphone in that room, a stake-out, and a complete recording device.'

'Good Lord, Perry, he'll find the bug–'

'Put it where he won't find it.'

'But he'll find it eventually, Perry. They'll be dusting or–'

'And by that time,' Mason said, 'they'll trace the wires and only find two loose, dangling ends.'

Drake's face showed a glimmer of hope. 'How long would we have to be on the job, Perry?'

Mason said, 'Put two men on the house. I want to know when Bain comes in. I want to know who else comes in, and when they come in. Within an hour after Bain arrives he's going to get one telephone call. After that you can cut the wires, pick up your equipment and get out.'

'It'll mean my licence if I get caught,' Drake said.

'Then,' Mason told him coldly, 'don't get caught.'

21

At the two o'clock session, Judge Howison addressed the crowded court-room.

'Somewhat against my better judgement,' he said, 'I have permitted the deputy sheriffs to admit spectators for whom there are no seats. These spectators will remain standing at the extreme edges of the court-room, along the walls, so as not to block the aisles. I wish to warn every spectator that his bearing must be compatible with the dignity of the Court. It there are untoward incidents I will clear the court-room.

'Mr Nathan Bain was on the stand being cross-examined. You will resume the witness stand, Mr Bain, and Mr Mason will continue your cross-examination.'

Nathan Bain had lost some of his assurance. Apparently the few questions Mason had asked him prior to the noon adjournment, and his loss of temper, had led him to realise that even the detailed coaching of Hamilton Burger was insufficient armour to protect him against Mason's thrusts.

Mason assumed a conversational tone of voice. 'Mr Bain,' he said, 'going back to your testimony concerning the use of this fluorescent powder. As I understand it, there had been persistent thefts from your house over a period of time?'

'Yes, sir.'

'Coincident with the employment of Nellie Conway?'

'That's right, although I realise now that was merely a coincidence as far as time is concerned.'

'Jewellery had been missing?'

'Yes, sir.'

'And there had been no missing jewellery prior to the time Nellie Conway was employed?'

'No, sir.'

'There had been no complaint from any member of the household as to things that were missing?'

'No, sir.'

'Now, your wife kept her jewellery in a jewel case that was customarily locked in the desk in the living-room?'

'Yes, sir.'

'And Nellie Conway, of course, was employed as a nurse to wait on your wife after the unfortunate accident which had damaged her spinal cord?'

'Yes, sir.'

'And immediately after that accident, and at all times thereafter, your wife developed a feeling of bitterness toward you and would not permit you in the room?'

'My wife was nervous.'

'Answer the question. *Did* your wife develop a bitterness of feeling toward you and would not allow you in the room?'

'Yes, sir.'

'So you had no direct oral communication with your wife from the time of the accident until her death?'

'Unfortunately, that is right.'

'Then you must have known prior to the accident that she had those incriminating papers secreted in her room.'

'I did.'

'How much prior to the accident?'

'I can't remember.'

'Use your best recollection.'

'Well, I . . .'

'Immediately before the accident, isn't that right?'

'Well, it may have been. She told me about those papers on . . . let me see, the . . . the memory of the accident has, of course, obliterated so many things . . . it was such a shock. . . .'

'As a matter of fact, she told you on the very day of the accident that she had the goods on you, that she had the evidence of your infidelity, and she was going to divorce you, didn't she?'

'I . . .'

Mason opened his brief-case and whipped out a letter which had been sent to Victoria Braxton.

'Yes or no, Mr Bain?' he asked sharply, jerking the letter out of the envelope and whipping it open dramatically.

'Yes,' Nathan Bain admitted, shamefacedly.

'Now then,' Mason said, 'you're positive that items of jewellery had been missing from the house over a period of time after Nellie Conway was employed?'

'Yes, but I have repeatedly told you, and I wish to tell you again, that while you are using Nellie Conway's employment as referring to a measure of time, that is *all* it refers to. I am satisfied that Miss Conway had nothing to do with the loss of the jewellery.'

'But it was disappearing?'

'Yes, sir.'

Mason got up and faced him dramatically, standing with his eyes boring into those of the witness, until every person in the court-room felt the tension, then he asked in slow, level tones, 'How–did–you–know?'

'How did I know what?'

'That your wife's jewellery was missing?'

'Why, I know generally what she had and–'

'You weren't communicating with your wife?'

'No.'

'Therefore your wife couldn't have told you?'

'No.'

'The jewel case was kept in the desk?'

'Yes.'

'Your wife couldn't walk?'

'No.'

'How did *you* know the jewellery was missing?'

Bain shifted his position uneasily on the witness stand.

'How did you know?' Mason thundered.

'Well,' Nathan Bain began, 'I . . . I just happened to notice that . . .'

'This desk was your wife's private writing desk, wasn't it?'

'Yes.'

'But you had retained a duplicate key to that desk without her knowledge?'

'I had a key.'

'The jewel case was kept locked?'

'Yes.'

'And you had retained a duplicate key to that jewel box without her knowledge?'

'I explained that all to you once before, Mr Mason.'

'I am not asking for an explanation, I am asking for an answer. Did you or did you not retain a key to that jewel case without your wife's knowledge or consent?'

'Well, in a way, yes.'

'Yes or no.'

'I object to the question on the ground that it has already been asked and answered,' Hamilton Burger said.

'Objection overruled!' Judge Howison snapped.

'Yes or no?' Mason asked.

'Yes,' Nathan Bain said.

'Therefore,' Mason said, 'the only way for you to have known that items of jewellery had been missing *after* your wife's injury was for you to have surreptitiously opened that desk, surreptitiously opened her jewel box, and made a surreptitious inventory of the contents of the jewel box without her knowledge or consent, and without her specific permission. Isn't that right?'

'I was just checking up.'

'Now then,' Mason said, '*what* items of jewellery were missing from your wife's jewel case?'

'A diamond pendant. That is, an imitation–'

'I'm not talking about the items of synthetic jewellery that you placed there, but the items of genuine jewellery.'

'I couldn't say.'

'You didn't have an inventory of the contents?'

'No, sir, not of my wife's jewellery. Not a specific inventory.'

'Then why did you go to the jewel case to make an inspection?'

'Just to check up.'

'But if you didn't know what was in there how could you tell if anything was missing?'

'Well, I . . . I was just looking.'

'And you can't tell us of any single specific item that is missing, or that was missing?'

'No, sir.'

Once more Mason fixed Bain with accusing eyes.

'This girl friend of yours–with whom you had your affair, did you give her presents of jewellery?'

'Sir, do you mean to insinuate–'

'Did you give her presents of jewellery? Answer the question.'

Bain ran his hand across his forehead.

'Yes or no?' Mason thundered.

'Yes.'

'Thank you,' Mason said sarcastically. 'Now, were those presents of jewellery given to her in the boxes in which they came, or did you take them from your pocket and put them on her?'

'I can't remember.'

'Can you remember any store where you bought any one, any single one of the articles of jewellery you gave her?'

'I . . . I mostly bought them at auctions.'

'Do you have any single bill of sale for any one of those articles you now claim you purchased at auctions?'

'No, sir. I destroyed them.'

Mason said, 'I have been advised that the parents of Marta Bain, your first wife, wish to make an application to have the body exhumed. Would you have any objection?'

'Your Honour, Your Honour!' Hamilton Burger shouted. 'I object to that question. It's argumentative. It's not proper cross-examination. It's foreign to the issues in this case. It's incompetent, irrelevant and immaterial and . . .'

'I think I will sustain the objection on the ground that it is argumentative,'

Judge Howison ruled. 'However, I am disposed to allow Counsel for the defence a wide margin of cross-examination, particularly in view of the peculiar nature of the direct examination and the large amount of territory explored by you on direct.'

'Are you willing to have Marta Bain's body exhumed?' Mason asked.

'Same objection.'

'Same ruling.'

Mason said, 'Your Honour, I now ask that this case be adjourned until proceedings can be had for the exhumation of the body of Marta Bain, deceased. I feel that it is vital to the issues in this case to determine whether or not she met her death from arsenic poisoning.'

'Oh, Your Honour,' Hamilton Burger said, his tone showing an exasperation that indicated there was after all a limit to human endurance. 'This is just a very adroit red herring drawn across the trail which is getting too hot to suit Counsel.

'If he had been so concerned about the death of Marta Bain, he could have made application for an adjournment before the case was tried. Now that we have a jury empanelled–'

'Nevertheless,' Judge Howison interrupted, 'the Court is inclined to think there may be something to the motion. I'm not going to rule on it immediately. I will take time to consider the matter and rule on it tomorrow morning. In the meantime, are you prepared to proceed with the trial?'

Perry Mason shook his head. 'Your Honour, the question of whether this motion is granted will effect my entire strategy in the trial. I do not care to go ahead until there has been a definite ruling.'

'Very well.' Judge Howison said, 'I am going to reserve ruling until tomorrow morning at ten o'clock, and in the meantime Court will stand adjourned. The defendant is remanded to the custody of the sheriff, and the jury will remember the admonition of the Court not to converse among themselves or with any other person about the case, or permit it to be discussed in their presence; nor shall the jury reach any opinion as to the guilt or innocence of the defendant until the evidence is all in and the case has been finally submitted to it for decision.

'Court adjourned until ten o'clock tomorrow morning. In the meantime, I'm going to ask Counsel to cite any authorities they may have bearing on the question of the pertinency of an adjournment pending proceedings for the exhumation.

'Court's adjourned.'

22

Paul Drake's tiny cubbyhole of an office was the nerve centre of the operations.

Mason and Della Street sat huddled around Drake's battle-scarred desk. The detective, with four or five telephones in front of him, reported operations from time to time as there were new developments.

'That early adjournment damn near wrecked us,' he said. 'If Nathan Bain had gone straight home he might have caught us. I certainly don't like this, Perry. It's taking last-minute, desperate chan–'

'They're taken now,' Mason interrupted. 'There's no use us worrying about them. Where the deuce do you suppose Nathan Bain is?'

'He left Hamilton Burger's office half an hour ago,' Drake said. 'My shadow hasn't had a chance to report on him yet.'

'If he should go to the Rapidex Apartments we're sunk,' Mason said.

'Why?'

'I'll tell you after a while.'

Drake said, 'You're playing a desperate game. It's too filled with risk for you to let me know what it is. You're afraid that I'll refuse to ride along.'

'No, that isn't it. You'll work better if you don't have your mind occupied with other stuff. Dammit, Paul, why don't you get an office that's big enough to walk around in?'

'Can't afford it.'

'One would never suspect it from the bills you send. Quit worrying, Paul. A lawyer and detective who won't take chances for a client aren't worth their salt. Planting a bug isn't such a heinous offence.'

'It isn't that,' Drake said, 'it's the chances you take getting in so you *can* plant the bug.'

'I know,' Mason sympathised. 'But we can't pick and choose, Paul. We have to get certain information. We can't get it the easy way, so we have to get it the hard way. How did your man get in? With a pass key?'

'Sure.'

'No one knows anything about it? No one saw him?'

'I don't think so. A neighbour *might* have noticed, but my man was carrying a basket of groceries, just as though he were a delivery boy.'

'Where's your stake-out?'

'In a garage that we rented. I'm not too happy about that.'

'Why not?'

'We had to rent it in too much of a hurry. I think the woman who owns the place thinks we're planning to hide stolen cars. I have a hunch she may notify the police.'

Mason looked at his watch. 'Well, we should be out of there within another hour anyway.'

A telephone rang. Drake picked up the receiver, answered the phone, then nodded and said. 'That's a lot better. Keep me posted. I want to know the minute anything happens.'

He hung up the telephone, and turned to Mason. 'All right, Perry, your trap's set, whatever it is. Nathan Bain and the housekeeper arrived at the house five minutes ago. My man tailed them there. This was his first opportunity to get to a telephone and make a report.'

'There's someone else on duty?'

'Sure, sure,' Drake said. 'Don't worry about that. 'That's all part of the routine. We have enough men on the job so we can let you know if anyone goes in or out, and keep you posted on developments.'

Mason turned to Della Street. 'Okay, Della, do your stuff.'

Della pulled a piece of paper from her pocket-book, spread it out on the desk and said, 'I want an outside line, Paul.'

Drake threw a switch. 'All right. That phone's connected. Dial your number.'

Della Street's skilled fingers flew rapidly over the dial of the telephone.

'What's the number?' Drake asked, curiously.

'Nathan Bain,' Mason said tersely.

Della Street sat with the receiver at her ear, waiting for an answer.

'Is it ringing?' Mason asked.

Della Street nodded.

Drake said in a low voice, 'You do the damndest things, Perry. That letter that you pulled out of your brief-case and flashed in front of Nathan Bain, was that really a letter which Elizabeth wrote her sister, or was it–'

'It was a recipe for a fruitcake,' Mason said. Dammit, Paul, you don't suppose they're not going to answer? Wouldn't your men–'

He broke off as Della Street motioned for silence. Placing her mouth close to the telephone, she said in close, clipped, emotionless tones, 'Mr Nathan Bain? . . . Very well, please call him at once upon a matter of the greatest urgency. . . . Hello, is this Mr Nathan Bain? Very well. This is the Receiving Hospital. A patient giving the name of Miss Charlotte Moray, residing at the Rapidex Apartments, has just arrived by ambulance and is being treated for arsenic poisoning. She claims this could only have come from eating chocolate creams which she received through the mail. She has asked us to notify you that she is being given emergency treatment, but suggests that if possible you come to see her at once.'

Della Street waited a half-second, then in the same professional, efficient voice, 'That is right. The name is Charlotte Moray. The address the Rapidex Apartments. Good-bye.'

She hung up.

Drake looked at Mason with wide, incredulous eyes. 'Of all the crazy, damn-fool things to do!'

Mason made an impatient gesture. 'It's the only thing we *can* do, Paul. I have a theory. I have to find out whether it will hold water.'

'But that isn't going to fool him,' Drake said. 'It will simply–'

Mason interrupted to say, 'You keep your men on the job out there, recording any conversations that are heard over the microphone.'

'But good heavens, Perry, you're not going to get anything that way.'

'You can't tell,' Mason told him.

They settled down for a period of anxious waiting.

After ten minutes, Mason said, 'Hang it, Paul, I'll go crazy if I can't start moving around. How much longer do you suppose it will be before we get a report from your men in the stake-out?'

'Whenever they finish recording whatever there is to record. They're making regular routine reports every hour on the hour, but they'll report any developments that aren't routine.'

'This won't be routine,' Mason said. 'It's like putting a camera out in the woods with a thread running to the flash-gun, coming back the next morning and seeing what's on the film. It may be a deer or it may be a skunk. You just have to wait until the film's developed to find out what tripped the shutter. That's the way it is with this stake-out.'

'Perhaps it won't be the shutter that gets tripped,' Drake said. 'It may be a lawyer.'

'It could be,' Mason admitted.

'But, my gosh,' Drake said, 'the first thing he'll do will be to call Charlotte Moray.'

'If he does, it will be interesting to know what he says to her.'

Mason looked at his wrist watch and started drumming with the tips of his fingers on the desk.

Drake started to say something, then, after studying the expression on the lawyer's face, changed his mind and remained silent.

At the end of another five minutes Mason said anxiously, 'How far would your men have to go to get to a telephone, Paul?'

'You mean the men who are watching the front of the Bain house?'

'No, no. The men who are on that stake-out.'

'Not far, Perry. Just to a petrol station on the corner.'

'How far in terms of minutes or seconds?'

'Two minutes at the outside.'

Mason looked at his wrist watch again, then took a pencil from his pocket and nervously started sliding his finger tips up and down the pencil, reversing it with each operation.

'Just what are you expecting, Perry?' Drake asked.

Mason shook his head, said, 'With every minute now I am expecting less and less. We should have heard before this.'

Another five minutes passed.

Mason lit a cigarette, settled back in the chair with a sigh and said, 'Well, Paul, I guess we've lost our gamble.'

'It would help,' Drake said, if I knew what it was we'd bet on, how much we'd bet, and just how much we stand to lose.'

Mason said impatiently, 'Nathan Bain *must* have been in touch with Charlotte Moray and must have known that phone call was a plant.'

'He didn't go out there,' Drake said. 'He and the housekeeper were at the District Attorney's office in conference with Hamilton Burger. When they came out they went directly home.'

'Didn't stop anywhere and telephone?' Mason asked.

'I don't think so,' Drake said. 'I think my man would have reported it if they had. I told him to give me a report on everything they did, and he made that report fifteen or twenty minutes ago.'

Mason wearily got up from his chair. 'Then for some reason they must have called Charlotte Moray from the D.A.'s office. Now we'll have to figure something else. Tell your men at the first opportunity to cut the wires leading to the bug and go home. Clean out their equipment so the police won't find anything if they start following the wires.'

'We'll cut the wires close to the house,' Drake said. 'And we'll do it just as soon as it gets dark.'

'When will you be in touch with your men?'

'Within another twenty minutes. They report on the hour, even if nothing happens.'

'All right,' Mason said, 'I guess that's it. He's probably suspicious.'

The telephone, shattering the silence, caused Della Street to jump nervously.

'This may be it,' Drake said, grabbing the telephone.

Mason stood poised and tense, waiting.

Drake said, 'Hello . . . Yes, go ahead . . . What is it? . . . We'll, do the best you can. Give me a line on it. You'll have to speak louder, I can't hear you. Get up closer to the phone. . . .'

Suddenly Drake's face lightened. He looked up at Mason and nodded, said into the telephone, 'Go ahead, keep feeding it into the line. Give me what you have.'

Finally Drake said, 'Hold the phone a minute. Wait there for instructions. Just hang on.'

Drake pushed the palm of his hand over the mouthpiece of the telephone and said to Mason, 'Bain and his housekeeper had a hell of a fight, standing right there by the telephone. Bain accused her of sending arsenic candy to Charlotte Moray. The housekeeper called him a liar and a bungler, pointed out how clumsy he'd been trying to kill his wife in that automobile accident . . . and then Bain evidently popped her one, and they started throwing mud back and forth. It came in perfectly.'

'Does your man have all of it on wax cylinders?' Mason asked.

'He's got it.'

Mason grinned. 'Tell him to sit out there for a while longer, then report again when it gets dark. Also let us know at once if anything new turns up.'

Mason turned to Della Street, said, 'Get Lieutenant Tragg at Homicide Squad, Della.'

Della started dialling. Drake relayed Mason's instructions into the telephone.

A moment later Della Street nodded to Mason and the lawyer picked up the telephone, said, 'Hello, Lieutenant. This is Perry Mason.'

'What the hell do you want now?' Tragg asked.

'What makes you think I want anything, Tragg?'

'The tone of your voice. It's your polite act.'

Mason laughed. 'How grateful would you be if we gave you the solution of a couple of murders, all wrapped up with pink ribbon in a nice little package?'

'How grateful would I have to be?' Tragg asked cautiously.

Mason said, 'A microphone would have to be police property.'

'You mean that I'd planted it?'

'Yes.'

'How certain are the solutions?'

'The cases are on ice.'

'I guess it could be arranged,' Tragg said, 'but I wouldn't want to be a cat's paw. I'd want to be mighty certain I was playing a sure thing.'

'You would be,' Mason assured him. 'Come on up to Paul Drake's office. By the time you get here we'll have everything ready.'

'Okay, I'll ride along that far,' Tragg told him. 'This guy, Bain doesn't look as good to me as he does to Holcomb and the D.A. . . . But, even so, you're going to have to show me.'

Mason said, 'Come on and be shown.' He hung up the telephone, said to Della Street, 'All right. Get Nathan Bain on the telephone.'

'Nathan Bain!' Drake exclaimed. 'Are you crazy?'

Mason shook his head.

Della Street's fingers were already busy with the manipulation of the dial.

'Hello,' she said. 'Hello . . . Mr Bain? Just a moment, hold the line, please.'

She passed the receiver to Mason.

Mason picked up the telephone, said, 'Good afternoon, Mr Bain. This is Perry Mason calling.'

Bain said, 'I have nothing to say to you, Mr Mason. The District Attorney has promised me he's going to put a stop to your persecution of me. I'll see you in court tomorrow.'

'Perhaps you won't.'

'You're damn right I will!' Bain said angrily. 'And when I do–'

'Just a moment,' Mason interrupted, 'Before you make any definite appointments, Bain, you'd better look around the room and find the microphone. Good-bye.'

Mason hung up the telephone.

Drake came all the way up out of the chair in startled protest. 'Good Lord, Perry, do you know what you're doing? Do you realise–?'

'I think I do,' Mason said grinning. 'Flight, you know, is an evidence of guilt. I think that within about ten minutes your man who's watching the house will report that Nathan Bain has dashed out and driven away in a hurry. I want Lieutenant Tragg to have a strong enough case so Hamilton Burger won't start punching holes in it.'

23

The garage had the dank, musty smell which seems to be spontaneously generated in buildings that are kept too long closed and where sunlight cannot penetrate.

It was cold and draughty. Paul Drake's men, bundled in overcoats, regulated the mechanism which turned the wax cylinders.

Lieutenant Tragg, flanked by Perry Mason and Della Street, leaned over the records, listening.

Paul Drake, nervously apprehensive, was standing slightly to one side, talking with one of his men.

The voices which were played back from the wax cylinder, amplified by a small loudspeaker, were sufficiently clear to be distinctly audible although there was a slight distortion of the tones due to the amplification of the microphone.

At the end of some ten minutes, Tragg straightened as the voices on the end of the record ceased.

'Well, that's it,' Mason said.

'How did you figure out what had happened, Mason?' Tragg asked.

'I was watching Bain's face when I accused him of having murdered his first wife. I saw that the thing hit him like a blow from a sledge-hammer. I thought at the moment it was because he was guilty, but later on I began to think about it and started putting two and two together.

'Of course, if his first wife had been poisoned by eating chocolate creams filled with arsenic, it stood to reason–'

'Wait a minute,' Lieutenant Tragg said, 'why didn't Nathan Bain get some of it if it was in the candy?'

'Because Bain doesn't eat chocolate. That's one thing he's allergic to. That narrows down the field. It had to be either Nathan Bain or the housekeeper.

'So then I started thinking. I wondered what would happen if the housekeeper had fallen in love with him, if she was one of those quiet, repressed, mousy women who would develop into a possessive–'

'Well, she was,' Tragg said, 'there's no question about it, now that I've listened to this conversation. They certainly are a pretty pair, and when they let go at each other hammer and tongs they told plenty.'

'The housekeeper killed the first wife through jealousy. Then when she found she was only one more woman as far as Nathan Bain was concerned, she still kept on in his employ just to be near him. Nathan Bain married money, and when he found he couldn't get hold of that money, he started trying to kill his wife. That guy sure has a way with women, and he sure played the field.

'It's interesting to hear the housekeeper on that record tell him what a clumsy, inefficient murderer he turned out to be, and how she had to step in and do the job, switching the arsenic tablets in place of the medicine the doctor had left when Nellie Conway, leaving the pill-box on the kitchen table, had moved over to the stove to warm up her coffee. That's when Bain popped her–a great pair they turned out to be.'

Tragg suddenly turned to Drake. 'What's the dope, Paul? What's happened over there? You have men watching the place.'

Drake said, 'Nathan Bain left in a hell of a hurry. He threw some stuff in a bag and was on his way. My man tried to tail him but there was absolutely no chance. Bain was hitting fifty miles an hour before he'd got to the end of the block.'

'And the housekeeper hasn't shown?'

'No, she's still there.'

Tragg smoked a thoughtful cigarette. 'I guess it was pretty plain after all,' he said. 'Once you stop to figure it out, if the first wife was murdered and if Bain *didn't* do it, it almost *had* to be the housekeeper. It had to be someone who knew their intimate habits, who was in a position to slip poison into the candy, who knew that Nathan Bain was allergic to chocolate and wouldn't touch it. They're both of them a pretty kettle of fish. So Nathan Bain really did manipulate the accident that crushed his wife's spine, hoping he could kill her. What I don't see, Perry, is why he didn't get the housekeeper to give the sleeping medicine to his wife if they were that intimate.'

'Don't you see,' Mason pointed out, 'that's the one thing that was the dead give away. He was afraid to let the housekeeper know what he was after, because the minute the housekeeper knew what he wanted *she* would have been the one to get those letters from Charlotte Moray. Bain had really fallen for the Moray woman, and he was afraid of what that crazy, insane, jealous housekeeper would have done to Charlotte Moray.'

'I'm not too certain but what we'd better do something ourselves,' Tragg said, 'before she gets any ideas. I think I'll go over and pick this Imogene Ricker up. I'll want those records delivered down at headquarters.'

'You'll have them,' Drake promised.

Tragg looked at Drake thoughtfully and said, 'You took a lot of chances on this thing, Paul.'

Drake's eyes shifted.

'He was acting under my orders,' Mason said.

Tragg cocked a quizzical eyebrow. 'Okay, Perry, you reached in your thumb and pulled out a plum. But one of these days the plum won't be there. You'll just get your thumb burnt and then it's going to be too damn bad.'

'Oh, I don't know,' Mason said. 'I didn't take so many chances on this one. After all, it was almost a mathematical certainty, and the minute it became apparent that Nathan Bain was afraid to trust the housekeeper to get the purple letters written by Charlotte Moray–'

'Okay, you win,' Tragg interrupted. 'You don't have to explain when you've won. Winners never explain. Losers always do. I'm going over to pick up Imogene Ricker. You folks want to tag along behind?'

Mason nodded.

'I'll stay here,' Drake said.

'You get those records down to headquarters,' Tragg said, 'and *be damn certain nothing happens to them.*'

'Are you telling me,' Drake said with feeling.

Tragg got in his police car. 'It's only around the block, Perry, but I want my car there because I'll be taking that Ricker woman to headquarters. Do you want to drive your bus?'

'I think so, Lieutenant. I'll park right behind your car. If she should want to make a statement you can borrow Della Street to take it down in shorthand.'

'I'd have to want that statement pretty damn bad to borrow your secretary,' Tragg said. 'I'm going to keep the Perry Mason angle out of this just as much as possible. The D.A. won't like it.'

'To hell with the D.A.,' Mason told him. 'If you get a confession, call in the newspaper reporters and let the D.A. read about it in the headlines tomorrow.'

'Are you,' Tragg asked, 'telling me how to run my business?'

'Sure,' Mason said, grinning.

'Well, it won't work quite that way,' Tragg admitted. 'I'd get the D.A. on the phone and explain to him what it was all about and tell him he'd better come up to headquarters in a rush, but before he got there, somehow or other the newspaper men would have had a tip. They'd be phoning in the story about the time the D.A. arrived. . . .You give me about two minutes head start,' Tragg went on, suddenly becoming crisply business-like, 'then you can drive up to the house and see what the score is. And you fellows keep those records turned in on that live microphone so that you hear everything. If she wants to get it off her chest, I'll see that she does the talking in the room by the telephone. Okay, let's go.'

Tragg drove away. Mason gave him a two-minute start, then he and Della Street followed.

The police car was in front of the house. There was no sign of Lieutenant Tragg.

One of Paul Drake's men, who was shadowing the house, sauntered over to Mason's car. 'Tragg just went in a few minutes ago,' he said.

'I know,' Mason told him. 'Who let him in? The housekeeper?'

'No. The front door was unlatched. When he didn't get an answer, he opened it and walked in.'

'Oh-oh!' Mason said.

At that moment, the door opened. Lieutenant Tragg beckoned.

The lawyer ran up the steps to the porch.

Tragg said, 'Get you car, pick up Drake's men and get the hell out of here, Perry. I've just telephoned headquarters to send out the squad car.'

'You mean,' Mason asked, 'that she–'

'Evidently he throttled her . . . he was crazy in love with that Moray woman. When he and Imogene got to hurling verbal brick-bats at each other, he started choking her. Perhaps he only intended to make her lose consciousness so he could get away. . . . Anyway, it's a mess now, and I've got to play it my way. Remember, that's been my microphone all along. Round up Paul Drake's men. Tell them to get the hell out of here, and fast.'

'How about Bain?' Mason asked apprehensively. 'That Charlotte Moray woman may be in danger. If he should start for there and–'

'You don't have to *keep* telling me how to run my business,' Lieutenant Tragg said. 'Within sixty seconds a radio car will be staked out in front of the Rapidex Apartments. If Bain shows up they'll collar him. Shake a leg, Mason, get those agency men cleaned out of here.'

Mason nodded, turned, took Della Street's arm, and started running down the porch stairs.

'Well,' Della Street said, as Tragg gently closed the front door, 'perhaps after all it was better that way, Chief. The poor housekeeper must have been about half-crazy. Don't you think it was better?'

'A hell of a lot better,' Mason said grimly. 'I'll chase Paul Drake's men out of here and then you go call up the hotel and get a nice airy room with a good, big bath.'

Della Street raised her eyebrows. 'What cooks?'

'Tell them,' Mason explained, 'that it's for Victoria Braxton, and that she'll be in sometime late this evening.'

RLE STANLEY GARDNER

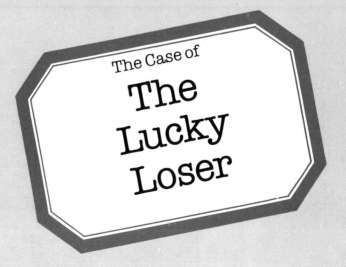

The Case of

The Lucky Loser

FOREWORD

Nearly a year ago my good friend John Ben Shepperd, the Attorney General of the State of Texas, told me, 'The next big development in law enforcement must come from the people rather than from the police.'

General Shepperd wasn't content with merely predicting such a development. He discussed it with several influential businessmen in Texas, and soon these businessmen began to take action.

J. Marion West of Houston, Texas, affectionately known as 'Silver Dollar' West, is an attorney at law, a cattleman, an oil operator, and is widely respected for his knowledge of police science. He spends a large portion of his time assisting local police officers in the Houston area.

I have for some years been associated with Park Street, who is a member of 'The Court of Last Resort', a San Antonio attorney with driving energy, and a boundless enthusiasm for his work. Park Street has as his lifetime ambition a desire to improve the administration of justice.

Jackson B. Love, of Llano, Texas, is an ex-Texas Ranger who has had considerable experience as a peace officer. He owns and operates a large ranch, has exceptionally sound business judgement, is quite an historian, and collects books dealing with the frontier period of the West.

W. R. (Billy Bob) Crim, of Kilgore, Texas, a man with extensive oil interests in Kilgore, Longview and Dallas, is vitally interested in state police work and is an authority on weapons.

Frederick O. Detweiler, president of Chance Vought Aircraft, Incorporated, Dallas, Texas, is representative of the modern executive, with broad interests, a razor-keen mind and a background of knowledge ranging from economics to public relations. He is one of the prominent businessmen of Texas and is known and loved all over the state for his intense interest in better law enforcement.

Dr Merton M. Minter is a prominent physician of San Antonio, a man loved and respected by those who know him. Recently he began to take an active interest in law enforcement. A member of the Board of Regents of the University of Texas, he is particularly interested in the educational aspects of crime prevention and law enforcement.

These people got together with Attorney General John Ben Shepperd and decided to organize the Texas Law Enforcement Foundation, of which my good friend Park Street is Chairman and J. Marion (Jim) West is Vice-Chairman.

When Texas does anything, it does it in a big way, and this Law Enforcement Foundation is no exception.

Col Homer Garrison, Jr, Director of the Texas Department of Public Safety, and as such, head of the famed Texas Rangers, a man who is acclaimed everywhere as one of the outstanding figures in the field of executive law enforcement, is Chairman of the Advisory Council of the Foundation.

I consider myself greatly honoured in that I have been appointed a special adviser of this Foundation.

The Texas Law Enforcement Foundation isn't a 'Crime Commission'. Its primary purpose is to acquaint citizens everywhere with their civic responsibilities in the field of law enforcement. The Foundation wants the average citizen to have a better understanding of the causes of crime, of how crime can be prevented, of the responsibilities of the police officer, the latent dangers of juvenile delinquency, the purpose and problems of penology, and the responsibilities of the organized bar and lawyers generally.

If the average citizen can't learn more about the problems with which the various law enforcement agencies have to contend, the citizen can't play his part in the job of curtailing crime.

As of this writing, organized crime is making an alarming bid for power. Juvenile delinquency is but little understood and is on the increase.

On many fronts we are trying to combat atomic age crime methods with horse-and-buggy thinking.

Efficient law enforcement can't function in a civic vacuum. The police force depends on the training, integrity and loyalty of its members for efficiency, and on public understanding and co-operation for its very life.

It is well known that if the average community had half as much loyalty to its police as the police have to the community we would have far less crime.

Because I consider the work of this law enforcement foundation so important, I have departed from my usual custom of dedicating books to outstanding figures in the field of legal medicine, and I dedicate this book to those citizens of Texas who, at great personal and financial sacrifice, have been responsible for bringing into existence a new concept of law enforcement.

Erle Stanley Gardner

I

Della Street, Perry Mason's confidential secretary, picked up the telephone and said, 'Hello.'

The well-modulated youthful voice of a woman asked, 'How much does Mr Mason charge for a day in court?'

Della Street's voice reflected cautious appraisal of the situation. 'That would depend very much on the type of case, what he was supposed to do and–'

'He won't be supposed to do anything except listen.'

'You mean you wouldn't want him to take part in the trial?'

'No. Just listen to what goes on in the court-room and draw conclusions.'

'Who is this talking, please?'

'Would you like the name that will appear on your books?'

'Certainly.'

'Cash.'

'What?'

'Cash.'

'I think you'd better talk to Mr Mason,' Della Street said. 'I'll try to arrange an appointment.'

'There isn't much time for that. The case in which I am interested starts at ten o'clock this morning.'

'Just a moment, please. Hold the wire,' Della Street said.

She entered Mason's private office.

Perry Mason looked up from the mail he was reading.

Della Street said, 'Chief, you'll have to handle this personally. A youthful sounding woman wants to retain you to sit in court today just to listen to a case. She's on the phone now.'

'What's her name?'

'She say's it's Cash.'

Mason grinned, picked up his telephone. Della Street got on the other line, put through the connection.

'Yes?' Mason said crisply. 'This is Perry Mason.'

The woman's voice was silky. 'There's a criminal case on trial in Department Twenty-Three of the Superior Court entitled People versus Balfour. I would like to know how much it's going to cost me to have you attend court during the day, listen to the proceedings, and then give me your conclusions.'

'And your name?' Mason asked.

'As I told your secretary, the name is Cash–just the way the entry will appear on your books.'

Mason looked at his watch. 'It is now nine twenty-five. I have two appointments this morning and one this afternoon. I would have to cancel those appointments, and I would only do that to handle a matter of the greatest importance.'

'This *is* a matter of the greatest importance.'

'My charges would be predicated upon that fact, upon the necessity of breaking three appointments and–'

'Just what would your charges be?' she asked.

'Five hundred dollars,' Mason snapped.

The voice suddenly lost its silky assurance. 'Oh! . . . I . . . I'm sorry. I had no idea . . . We'll just have to forget it, I guess. I'm sorry.'

Mason, moved by the consternation in the young woman's voice, said, 'More than you expected?'

'Y . . . y . . . yes.'

'How much more?'

'I . . . I . . . I work on a salary and . . . well, I–'

'You see,' Mason explained, 'I have to pay salaries, taxes, office rental, and I have a law library to keep up. And a day of my time–What sort of work do *you* do?'

'I'm a secretary.'

'And you want me just to listen to this case?'

'I did . . . I guess I . . . I mean, my ideas were all out of line.'

'What had you expected to pay?'

'I had hoped you'd say a hundred dollars. I could have gone for a hundred and fifty . . . Well, I'm sorry.'

'Why did you want me to listen? Are you interested in the case?'

'Not directly, no.'

'Do you have a car?'

'No.'

'Any money in the bank?'

'Yes.'

'How much?'

'A little over six hundred.'

'All right,' Mason said. 'You've aroused my curiosity. If you'll pay me a hundred dollars I'll go up and listen.'

'Oh, Mr Mason! . . . Oh . . . thanks! I'll send a messenger right up. You see, you musn't ever know who I am . . . I can't explain. The money will be delivered at once.'

'Exactly what is it you want me to do?' Mason asked.

'Please don't let *anyone* know that you have been retained in this case. I would prefer that you go as a spectator and that you do not sit in the bar reserved for attorneys.'

'Suppose I can't find a seat?' Mason asked.

'I've thought of that,' she said. 'When you enter the court-room, pause to look around. A woman will be seated in the left-hand aisle, fourth row back. She is a red-haired woman about . . . well, she's in her forties. Next to her will be a younger woman with dark chestnut hair, and next to her will be a seat on which will be piled a couple of coats. The younger woman will pick up the coats and you may occupy that seat. Let's hope you aren't recognized. Please *don't* carry a brief case.'

There was a very decisive click at the other end of the line.

Mason turned to Della Street.

'When that messenger comes in with the hundred dollars, Della, be sure that he takes a receipt, and tell him to deliver that receipt to the person who gave him the money. I'm on my way to court.'

2

Perry Mason reached the court-room of Department Twenty-Three as Judge Marvin Spencer Cadwell was entering from his chambers.

The bailiff pounded his gavel. 'Everybody rise,' he shouted.

Mason took advantage of the momentary confusion to slip down the centre aisle to the fourth row of seats.

The bailiff called court to order. Judge Cadwell seated himself. The bailiff banged the gavel. The spectators dropped back to their seats, and Mason unostentatiously stepped across in front of the two women.

The younger woman deftly picked up two coats which were on the adjoining seat. Mason sat down, glancing surreptitiously at the women as he did so.

The women were both looking straight ahead, apparently paying not the slightest attention to him.

Judge Cadwell said, 'People of the State of California versus Theodore Balfour. Is it stipulated by counsel that the jurors are all present and the defendant is in court?'

'So stipulated, Your Honour.'

'Proceed.'

'I believe the witness George Dempster was on the stand,' the prosecutor said.

'That's right,' Judge Cadwell said. 'Mr Dempster, will you please return to the stand.'

George Dempster, a big-boned, slow-moving man in his thirties, took the witness stand.

'Now, you testified yesterday that you found certain pieces of glass near the body on the highway?' the prosecutor asked.

'That is right, yes, sir.'

'And did you have occasion to examine the headlights on the automobile which you located in the Balfour garage?'

'I did, yes, sir.'

'What was the condition of those headlights?'

'The right headlight was broken.'

'When did you make your examination?'

'About seven-fifteen on the morning of the twentieth.'

'Did you ask permission from anyone to make this examination?'

'No, sir, not to examine the car itself.'

'Why not?'

'Well, we wanted to check before we committed ourselves.'

'So what did you do?'

'We went out to the Balfour residence. There was a four-car garage in back. There was no sign of life in the house, but someone was moving around in an apartment over the garage. As we drove in, this person looked out of the window and then came down the stairs. He identified himself as a servant who had one of the apartments over the garage. I told him that we were officers and we wanted to look around in the garage, that we were looking for some evidence of a crime. I asked him if he had any objection. He said certainly not, so we opened the garage door and went in.'

'Now, directing your attention to a certain automobile bearing licence number GMB 665, I will ask you if you found anything unusual about that car?'

'Yes, sir, I did.'

'What did you find?'

'I found a broken right front headlight, a very slight dent on the right side of the front of the car, and I found a few spatters of blood on the bumper.'

'What did you do next?'

'I told the servant we would have to impound the car and that we wanted to question the person who'd been driving it. I asked him who owned it, and he said Mr Guthrie Balfour owned it, but that his nephew, Ted Balfour, had been driving–'

'Move to strike,' the defence attorney snapped. 'Hearsay, incompetent, irrelevant, immaterial. They can't prove who drove the car by hearsay.'

'Motion granted,' Judge Cadwell said. 'The prosecution knows it can't use evidence of that sort.'

'I'm sorry, Your Honour,' the prosecutor said. 'I was about to stipulate that part of the answer could go out. We had not intended to prove who was driving in this way. The witness should understand that.

'Now just tell the Court and the jury what you did after that, Mr Dempster.'

'We got young Mr Balfour up out of bed.'

'Now, when you refer to young Mr Balfour, you are referring to the defendant in this case?'

'That's right. Yes, sir.'

'Did you have a conversation with him?'

'Yes, sir.'

'At what time?'

'Well, by the time we had this conversation it was right around eight o'clock.'

'You got him up out of bed?'

'Somebody awakened him, he put on a bathrobe and came out. We told him who we were and what we wanted, and he said he wouldn't talk with us until he was dressed and had had his coffee.'

'What did you do?'

'Well, we tried to get something out of him. We tried to be nice about it. We didn't want to throw our weight around, but he kept saying he wouldn't talk until he'd had his coffee.'

'Where did this conversation take place?'

'At the Guthrie Balfour residence.'

'And who was present at that conversation?'

'Another police officer who had gone out with me, a Mr Dawson.'

'He is here in court?'

'Yes, sir.'

'Who else was present?'

'The defendant.'

'Anyone else?'

'No, sir.'

'Where did that conversation take place?'

'In the house.'

'I mean specifically where in the house?'

'In a small office, sort of a study that opened off from the defendant's bedroom. The butler or somebody had brought up some coffee, cream and sugar and the morning paper, and we drank coffee–'

'You say "*we* drank coffee"?'

'That's right. The butler brought in three cups and saucers, cream, sugar, and a big electric percolator. We all three had coffee.'

'Now, just what did you say to the defendant and what did he say to you?'

Mortimer Dean Howland, the attorney representing Balfour, was on his feet. 'I object, Your Honour. No proper foundation has been laid.'

Judge Cadwell pursed his lips, looked down at the witness, then at the prosecutor.

'And,' Howland went on, 'I feel I should be entitled to cross-examine this witness before any admission, confession, or declaration by the defendant is received in evidence.'

'We're not laying the foundation for a confession, Your Honour,' the prosecutor said.

'That's precisely my objection,' the defence attorney remarked.

Judge Cadwell gave the matter careful consideration.

Mason took advantage of the opportunity to study the young woman on his right. Having saved a seat for him, she must have known he was to be there. Having known that, the chances were she was the woman who had sent him the retainer.

'What's the case?' Mason asked her in a whisper.

She looked at him coldly, elevated her chin and turned away.

It was the man on Mason's left who tersely said, 'Hit and run, manslaughter.'

Judge Cadwell said, 'I will accept the prosecutor's assurance that no confession is called for by this question and overrule the objection. The witness will answer the question.'

The witness said, 'He said he'd been seeing his uncle and his uncle's wife off on a train, that he'd then gone to a party, where he'd had a few drinks and–'

'Just a moment, Your Honour, just a moment,' the defence attorney interrupted. 'It now appears that the statement by the prosecutor was incorrect, that they *are* attempting to establish a confession or an admission and–'

'I'm going to ask the prosecutor about this,' Judge Cadwell interrupted sternly.

The prosecutor was on his feet. 'Please, Your Honour. If you will listen to the answer, you will understand my position.'

'There is an admission?' Judge Cadwell asked.

'Certainly, Your Honour, but an admission does not rank in the same category with a confession.'

'They are attempting to show that he confessed to being drunk,' the defence attorney said.

'I'll let the witness finish his answer,' Judge Cadwell said. 'Go on.'

'The defendant said that he'd had a few drinks at this party and had become ill. He thought at least one of the drinks had been loaded. He said he passed out and remembered nothing until he came to in his automobile, that–'

'Your Honour, Your Honour!' the defence attorney protested. 'This now has the very definite earmarks of–'

'Sit down,' Judge Cadwell said. 'Let the witness finish his answer. If the answer is as I think it's going to be, I am then going to call on the prosecutor for an explanation. The Court doesn't like this. The Court feels that an attempt has been made to impose on the Court.'

'If you will only hear the answer out,' the prosecutor pleaded.

'That's exactly what I'm going to do.'

'Go ahead,' the prosecutor said to the witness.

The witness continued. 'He said that for a brief instant he came to his senses in his car, that some woman was driving.'

'Some *woman*?' Judge Cadwell exclaimed.

'Yes, Your Honour.'

'Then *he* wasn't driving?'

'That's right, Your Honour,' the prosecutor said. 'I trust the Court will now see the reason for my statement.'

'Very well,' Judge Cadwell said. He turned to the witness. 'Go on. What else did the defendant say?'

'He said that he partially revived for a moment, that he remembered being very sick, that the next thing he remembered he was home and in bed, that he had a terrific thirst, that the hour was four thirty-five in the morning, that he was conscious but very thick-headed.'

'Did you ask him who the woman was who was driving the car?' the prosecutor asked the witness.

'I did.'

'What did he say?'

'He said he couldn't remember, that he couldn't be certain.'

'Which did he say–that he couldn't remember or he couldn't be certain?'

'He said both.'

'What did you ask him?'

'I asked him several questions after that, but I had no more answers. He wanted to know what had happened. I told him that we were investigating a death, a hit-and-run case, and that there was some evidence his car had been involved. So then he said if that was the case he would say nothing more until he had consulted with his attorney.'

'You may cross-examine,' the prosecutor said.

Mortimer Dean Howland, attorney for Balfour, was known for his hammer-and-tongs, browbeating cross-examination.

He lowered his bushy eyebrows, thrust out his jaw, glared for a moment at the witness, said, 'You went out to that house to get a confession from the defendant, didn't you?'

'I did nothing of the sort.'

'You *did* go out to the house?'

'Certainly.'

'And you *did* try to get a confession from the defendant?'

'Yes, in a way.'

'So then you did go out to that house to try and get a confession from the defendant–either by one way or another!'

'I went out to look at the defendant's automobile.'

'*Why* did you decide to go out to look at the defendant's automobile?'

'Because of something I had been told.'

The lawyer hesitated, then, fearing to open that legal door, abruptly changed his tactics. 'When you *first* saw the defendant, you wakened him from a sound sleep, didn't you?'

'*I* didn't. The servant did.'

'You knew that he had been ill?'

'He looked as though he'd had a hard night. That was all I knew until he told me he'd been sick. I thought that he–'

'Never mind what you thought!' Howland shouted.

'I thought that's what you asked for,' the witness said calmly.

There was a ripple of merriment throughout the court-room.

'Just concentrate on my questions!' Howland shouted. 'You could tell that the defendant was not in good health?'

'I could tell that he wasn't fresh as daisy. He looked like a man with a terrific hangover.'

'I didn't ask you that. I asked you if you couldn't tell that he wasn't in good health.'

'He wasn't in good spirits, but he sure looked as though he *had* been in spirits.'

'That will do,' Howland said. 'Don't try to be facetious. A man's liberty is at stake here. Simply answer the questions. You knew that he wasn't his normal self?'

'I don't know what he's like when he's normal.'

'You knew that he had been aroused from sleep?'

'I assumed that he had.'

'You knew that he didn't look well?'

'That's right.'

'How did he look?'

'He looked terrible. He looked like a man with a hangover.'

'You've seen men with hangovers?'

'Lots of them.'

'Have *you* ever had a hangover?'

'Your Honour, I object to that,' the prosecutor said.

Howland said, 'Then I move to strike out the answer of the witness that the defendant had a hangover on the ground that it is a conclusion of the witness, that the answer is merely an opinion, that the witness is not properly qualified to give that opinion.'

'I'll withdraw the objection,' the prosecutor said.

'Have *you* ever had a hangover?'

'No.'

'You have *never* had a hangover?'

'No.'

'You're not a drinking man?'

'I'm not a teetotaller. I take a drink once in a while. I can't remember being intoxicated. I can't ever remember having had a hangover.'

'Then how do you know what a man with a hangover looks like?'

'I have seen men with hangovers.'

'What is a hangover?'

'The aftermath of an intoxicated condition. I may say it's the immediate aftermath of an intoxicated condition when the alcohol has not entirely left the system.'

'You're now talking like a doctor.'

'You asked me for my definition of a hangover.'

'Oh, that's all,' Howland said, making a gesture of throwing up his hands as though tired of arguing, and turned his back on the witness.

The witness started to leave the stand.

'Just a moment,' Howland said suddenly, whirling and levelling an extended forefinger. 'One more question. Did the defendant tell you what time it was that he passed out?'

'He *said* about ten o'clock.'

'Oh, he said about ten o'clock, did he?'

'Yes, sir.'

'You didn't tell us that before.'

'I wasn't asked.'

'You were asked to tell what the defendant told you, weren't you?'

'Yes.'

'Then why did you try to conceal this statement about its being near ten o'clock?'

'I . . . well, I didn't pay much attention to that.'

'Why not?'

'Frankly, I didn't believe it.'

'Did you believe his story about some woman driving his car?'

'No.'

'Yet you paid attention to that part of his statement?'

'Well, yes. That was different.'

'In what way?'

'Well, that was an admission.'

'You mean an admission adverse to the interests of the defendant?'

'Certainly.'

'Oh! So you went there prepared to remember any admissions the defendant might make and to forget anything he might say that was in his favour, is that it?'

'I didn't forget this. I simply didn't mention it because I wasn't asked the specific question which would call for it.'

'What time were you called to investigate the hit-and-run accident?'

'About two o'clock in the morning.'

'The body was lying on the highway?'

'Yes, sir.'

'How long had it been there?'

'I don't know of my own knowledge.'

'Do you know when it was reported to the police?'

'Yes.'

'When?'

'About fifteen minutes before we got there.'

'That was a well-travelled highway?'

'It was a surfaced road. There was some traffic over it.'

'The body couldn't have been there on such a well-travelled road more than ten or fifteen minutes without someone having reported it?'

'I don't know.'

'It's a well-travelled road?'

'Yes.'

'And the defendant was driven home at about ten o'clock?'

'That's what he said.'

'And he was ill?'

'That's what he said.'

'And went to bed?'

'That's what he said.'

The lawyer hesitated. 'And went to sleep?'

'He didn't say that. He said his mind was a blank until he came to around four-thirty in the morning.'

'He didn't say his mind was a blank, did he?'

'He said he couldn't remember.'

'Didn't he say that the next thing he knew he came to in bed?'

'He said the next thing he *remembered* he was in bed, and it was then four thirty-five in the morning.'

'But some of what the defendant told you you didn't remember–everything he said that was in his favour.'

'I told you I did remember it.'

'And neglected to tell us.'

'All right. Have it that way if you want it that way.'

'Oh, that's all,' Howland said. 'In view of your very apparent bias, I don't care to ask you any more questions.'

The witness glared angrily and left the stand.

The prosecutor said, 'No redirect examination. Call Myrtle Anne Haley.'

The redheaded woman who was seated on the aisle two seats over from Perry Mason got up, walked to the witness stand, held up her right hand, and was sworn.

Mason stole a surreptitious glance at the young woman sitting next to him. She held her chin in the air, giving him only her profile to look at. Her expression held the icy disdain that a young woman reserves for someone who is trying to pick her up and is being offensive about it.

3

Myrtle Anne Haley took the oath, gave her name and address to the court reporter, and settled herself in the witness chair with the manner of one who knows her testimony is going to be decisive.

The prosecutor said, 'I call your attention to the road map which has been previously identified and introduced in evidence as People's Exhibit A, Mrs Haley.'

'Yes, sir.'

'Do you understand that map? That is, are you familiar with the territory which it portrays?'

'Yes, sir.'

'I call your attention to a section of Sycamore Road as shown on that map and which lies between Chestnut Street and State Highway. Do you understand that that map delineates such a section of road?'

'Yes, sir.'

'Have you ever driven over that road?'

'Many times.'

'Where do you live?'

'On the other side of State Highway on Sycamore Road.'

'Can you show us on this map? Just make a cross on the map and circle the cross.'

The witness made a cross on the map and enclosed it in a circle.

The prosecutor said, 'I will call your attention to the night of the nineteenth and the morning of the twentieth of September of this year. Did you have occasion to use the highway at that time?'

'On the morning of the twentieth–early in the morning–yes, sir.'

'At what time?'

'Between twelve-thirty and one-thirty.'

'In the morning?'

'Yes, sir.'

'In which direction were you driving?'

'Going west on Sycamore Road. I was approaching Chestnut Street from the east.'

'And did you notice anything unusual at that time?'

'Yes, sir. A car ahead of me which was being driven in a very erratic manner.'

'Can you tell me more about the erratic manner in which the car was being driven?'

'Well, it was weaving about the road, crossing the centre line and going clear over to the left. Then it would go back to the right and at times would run clear off the highway on the right side.'

'Could you identify that car?'

'Yes. I wrote down the licence number.'

'Then what?'

'Then I followed along behind; then at this wide place in the road about four-fifths of the way to State Highway I shot on by.'

'You say you *shot* on by?'

'Well, I went by fast when I had a chance. I didn't want the driver to swerve into me.'

'I move to strike everything about why she passed the car,' Howland said.

'That will go out,' Judge Cadwell said.

'After you got by the car what did you do?'

'I went home and went to bed.'

'I mean immediately after you got by the car. Did you do anything?'

'I looked in the rearview mirror.'

'And what did you see, if anything?'

'I saw the car swerve over to the left, then back to the right, and all of a sudden I saw something black cross in front of the headlights, and then for a moment the right headlight seemed to go out.'

'You say it *seemed* to go out?'

'After that it came on again.'

'And that was on Sycamore Road at a point between Chestnut Street and State Highway?'

'Yes, sir.'

'That is the point at which you saw the light blink off and then on?'

'Yes, sir.'

'At a time when you were looking in your rearview mirror?'

'Yes, sir.'

'And did you know what caused that headlight to seem to go out?'

'I didn't at the time, but I do now.'

'What was it?'

'Objected to as calling for a conclusion of the witness,' Howland said. 'The question is argumentative.'

'The objection is sustained,' Judge Cadwell said. 'The witness can testify to what she saw.'

'But, Your Honour,' the prosecutor said, 'the witness certainly has the right to interpret what she sees.'

Judge Cadwell shook his head. 'The witness will testify to what she saw. The jury will make the interpretation.'

The prosecutor paused for a minute, then said, 'Very well. Cross-examine.'

'You took down the licence number of this automobile?' Howland asked.

'That's right.'

'In a notebook?'

'Yes.'

'Where did you get that notebook?'

'From my purse.'

'You were driving the car?'

'Yes.'

'Was anyone with you?'

'No.'

'You took the notebook from your purse?'

'Yes.'

'And a pencil?'

'Not a pencil. A fountain pen.'

'And marked down the licence number of the automobile?'

'Yes.'

'What was the licence number?'

'GMB 665.'

'You have that notebook with you?'

'Yes, sir.'

'I would like to see it, please.'

The prosecutor smiled at the jury. 'Not the slightest objection,' he said. 'We're very glad to let you inspect it.'

Howland walked up to the witness stand, took the notebook the witness gave him, thumbed through the pages, said, 'This seems to be a notebook in which you keep a lot of data, various and sundry entries.'

'I don't carry anything in memory which I can trust to paper.'

'Now then,' Howland said, 'this number, GMB 665, is the last entry in the book.'

'That's right.'

'That entry was made on September twentieth?'

'About twelve-thirty to one-thirty on the morning of September twentieth,' the witness stated positively.

'Why haven't you made any entries after that?'

'Because, after I read about the accident, I reported to the police, the police took the book, and it was then given back to me with the statement that I should take good care of it because it would be evidence.'

'I see,' Howland said with elaborate politeness. 'And how long did the police have the book?'

'They had the book for . . . I don't know . . . quite a while.'

'And when was it given back to you?'

'Well, after the police had it, the district attorney had it.'

'Oh, the police gave it to the district attorney, did they?'

'I don't know. I know the prosecutor was the one who gave it to me.'

'When?'

'This morning.'

'This *morning*?' Howland said, his voice showing a combination of incredulity and sceptical sarcasm. 'And *why* did the prosecutor give it back to you this morning?'

'So I could have it on the witness stand.'

'Oh, so you would be able to say that you had the notebook with you?'

'I don't know. I suppose that was it.'

'Now then, did you remember the licence number?'

'Certainly I did. Just as I told you. It's GMB 665.'

'When did you last see that licence number?'

'When I handed you the book just a moment ago.'

'And when before that?'

'This morning.'

'At what time this morning.'

'About nine o'clock this morning.'

'And how long did you spend looking at that number at about nine o'clock this morning?'

'I . . . I don't know. I don't know as it makes any difference.'

'Were you looking at it for half an hour?'

'Certainly not.'

'For fifteen minutes?'

'No.'

'For ten minutes?'

'I may have been.'

'In other words, you were memorizing that number this morning, weren't you?'

'Well, what's wrong with that?'

'How do you know that's the same number?'

'Because that's my handwriting, that's the number just as I wrote it down.'

'Could you see the licence number of the car ahead while you were writing this?'

'Certainly.'

'All the time you were writing?'

'Yes.'

'Isn't it a fact that you looked at the licence number, then stopped your car, got out your notebook, and–'

'Certainly not! It's just as I told you. I took out my notebook while I was driving and wrote down the number.'

'You are right-handed?'

'Yes.'

'You had one hand on the wheel?'

'My left hand.'

'And you were writing with your right hand?'

'Yes.'

'Do you have a fountain pen or a ball-point pen?'

'It's a plain fountain pen.'

'The top screws off?'

'Yes.'

'And you unscrewed that with one hand?'

'Certainly.'

'You can do that with one hand?'.

'Of course. You hold the pen . . . that is, the barrel of the pen with the last two fingers, then use the thumb and forefinger to unscrew the cap.'

'Then what did you do?'

'I put the notebook down on my lap, wrote the number, then put the cap back on the pen and put the notebook and fountain pen back in my purse.'

'How far were you from the automobile when you were writing down this number?'

'Not very far.'

'Did you see the number all the time?'

'Yes.'

'Plainly?'

'Yes.'

'Did you write this number in the dark?'

'No.'

'No, apparently not. The number is neatly written. You must have had some light when you wrote it.'

'I did. I switched on the dome light so I could see what I was writing.'

'Now then,' Howland said, 'if you had to memorize that number this morning *after* the prosecutor had given you your notebook, you didn't know what that number was *before* he gave you the notebook, did you?'

'Well . . . you can't expect a person to remember a number all that time.'

'So you didn't know what it was this morning?'

'After I'd seen the book.'

'But not before that?'

'Well . . . no.'

Howland hesitated for a moment. 'After you had written down this number you drove on home?'

'Yes.'

'Did you call the police?'

'Certainly. I told you I did.'

'When?'

'Later.'

'After you had read in the newspaper about this accident?'

'Yes.'

'That is, about the body having been found on this road?'

'Yes.'

'You didn't call the police before that?'

'No.'

'Why did you write down this licence number?'

Her eyes glittered with triumph. 'Because I knew that the person who was driving the automobile was too drunk to have any business being behind the wheel of a car.'

'You knew that when you wrote down the licence number?'

'Yes.'

'Then why did you write it down?'

'So I'd know what it was.'

'So you could testify against the driver?'

'So I could do my duty as a citizen.'

'You mean call the police?'

'Well, I thought it was my duty to make a note of the licence number in case the driver got in any trouble.'

'Oh, so you could testify?'

'So I could tell the police about it, yes.'

'But you didn't tell the police until after you'd read in the paper about a body having been found?'

'That's right.'

'Even after you saw this mysterious blackout of the right headlight you didn't call the police?'

'No.'

'You didn't think there was any reason to call the police?'

'Not until after I'd read in the paper about the body.'

'Then you *didn't* think there had been an accident when you got home, did you?'

'Well, I knew something had happened. I kept wondering what could have caused that blackout of that headlight.'

'You didn't think there had been an accident?'

'I knew something had happened.'

'Did you or did you not think there had been an accident?'

'Yes, I realized there must have been an accident.'

'When did you realize this?'

'Right after I got home.'

'And you had taken this number so you could call the police in the event of an accident?'

'I took the number because I thought it was my duty to take it . . . yes.'

'Then why didn't you call the police?'

'I think this has been asked and answered several times Your Honour,' the prosecutor said. 'I dislike to curtail counsel in his cross-examination, but this certainly has been gone over repeatedly in the same way and in the same manner.'

'I think so,' Judge Cadwell said.

'I submit, Your Honour, that her actions contradict her words, that her reasons contradict her actions.'

'You may have ample opportunity to argue the case to the jury. I believe the fact which you wished to establish by this cross-examination has been established,' Judge Cadwell said.

'That's all,' Howland said, shrugging his shoulders and waving his hand as though brushing the testimony to one side.

'That's all, Mrs Haley,' the prosecutor said.

Mrs Haley swept from the witness stand, marched down the aisle, seated herself on the aisle seat.

She turned to the young woman seated beside Perry Mason. 'Was I all right?' Mrs Haley asked in a whisper.

The young woman nodded.

Judge Cadwell looked at the clock, and adjourned court until two o'clock that afternoon.

4

During the afternoon session the prosecution tied up a few loose ends and put on a series of technical witnesses. By three-thirty the case was ready for argument.

The prosecutor made a brief, concise argument, asked for a conviction, and sat down.

Mortimer Dean Howland, a criminal attorney of the old school, indulged in a barrage of sarcasm directed at the testimony of Myrtle Anne Haley, whom he characterized as 'the psychic driver', 'a woman who could drive without even looking at the road.'

'Notice the driving activities of this woman,' Howland said. 'When she first comes to our notice she is driving without looking at the road because she is getting her fountain pen and her notebook out of her purse. Then she is opening the notebook and making a note of the licence number.

'Look at where she made this notation, ladies and gentlemen of the jury. She didn't open the notebook at random and scribble the licence number on *any* page she happened to come to. She carefully turned to the page which contained the last notebook entry; then she neatly wrote the licence number of the automobile.

'Look at this exhibit,' Howland said, going over and picking up the notebook. 'Look at the manner in which this number is written. Could you have written a licence number so neatly if your eyes had been on the road while you were driving a car? Certainly not! Neither could this paragon of blind driving, this Myrtle Anne Haley. She was writing down this number with her eyes on the page of the notebook, not on the road.

'You'll remember that I asked her on cross-examination if she had sufficient light to write by, and do you remember what she said? She said she turned on the dome light of the automobile, so that she would have plenty of light.

'*Why* did she need plenty of light? Because she was watching what she was writing, not where her car was going.

'If her eyes had been on the road, she wouldn't have needed any light in the interior of the automobile. In fact, that light would have detracted from her ability to look ahead down the road. The reason she needed light, ladies and gentlemen, was because she was driving along, looking down at the page of the notebook as she wrote.

'She was driving at an even faster rate of speed than the car ahead because she admits she *shot* past that car. *But,* ladies and gentlemen, she didn't have her eyes on the road.

'I'm willing to admit that some unfortunate person was struck by an automobile on that stretch of road. Who was more likely to have struck that person? The driver of the car ahead, or some woman who admits to you under oath that she was speeding along that road not looking where she went, with her eyes on the page of a notebook?

'And who was driving this automobile, the licence number of which Myrtle Anne Haley was so careful to write down? The prosecution asked her all about the licence number, but *it never asked her who was driving the car!* It never asked her even if a *man* was driving the car. For all we know, if she had been asked she may have said that a woman was driving the car.'

'Your Honour,' the prosecutor said, 'I dislike to interrupt, but if the prosecution failed to cover that point, we ask to reopen the case at this time and ask additional questions of the witness, Myrtle Anne Haley.'

'Is there any objection?' Judge Cadwell asked.

'Certainly there's an objection, Your Honour. That's an old trick, an attempt to interrupt the argument of counsel for the defence and put on more testimony. It is an attempt to distract the attention of the jury and disrupt the orderly course of trial.'

'The motion is denied,' Judge Cadwell said.

Howland turned to the jury, spread his hands apart and smiled. 'You see, ladies and gentlemen, the sort of thing we have been up against in this case. I don't think I need to argue any more. I feel I can safely leave the matter to your discretion. I know that you will return the only fair verdict, the only just verdict, the only verdict that will enable you to feel that you have conscientiously discharged your sworn duty–a verdict of NOT GUILTY!'

Howland returned to his chair.

The prosecutor made a closing argument, the judge read instructions to the jury, and the jury retired.

Mason arose with the other spectators as court was adjourned, but Mortimer Dean Howland pushed his way to Mason's side. 'Well, well, well, Counsellor. What brings *you* here?'

'Picking up some pointers on how to try a case.'

Howland smiled, but his eyes, gimleted in hard appraisal, burned under bushy eyebrows as they searched Mason's face.

'*You* don't need any pointers, Counsellor. I thought I had glimpsed you in the crowd this morning, and then I was quite certain that you sat through the entire afternoon session. Are you interested in the case?'

'It's an interesting case.'

'I mean are you interested professionally?'

'Oh, of course professionally,' Mason said with expansive indefiniteness. 'I don't know any of the parties. By the way, who was the person who was killed?'

'The body has never been identified,' Howland said. 'Fingerprints were sent to the FBI, but there was no file. The person was evidently a drifter of some sort. The head had been thrown to the highway with a terrific impact. The skull was smashed like an egg-shell. Then both wheels had gone completely over the head. The features were unrecognizable.'

'What about the clothing?'

'Good clothing, but the labels had been carefully removed. We thought, of course, that meant the decedent might have had a criminal record. But, as I say, there were no fingerprints on file.'

'Was this licence number written in the notebook *immediately* under the other entries on the last page?' Mason asked.

'Come take a look,' Howland invited, placing a fraternal hand on Mason's shoulder. 'I'd like to have you take a look at that and tell me what *you* think.'

Howland led the way to the clerk's desk. 'Let's look at that exhibit,' he said, '. . . the notebook.'

The clerk handed him the notebook.

Mason studied the small, neat figures near the bottom of the page.

'You couldn't do that without a light to save your life,' Howland said. 'That woman wasn't watching the road while she was writing down the figures.'

'I take it that you know the right headlight on *her* car wasn't smashed,' Mason said.

'We know lots of things,' Howland observed, winking. 'We also know that it's an easy matter to get a headlight repaired. What's your opinion of the case, Mason? What do you think the jurors will do?'

'They may not do anything.'

Howland's voice was cautious. 'You think it will be a hung jury?'

'It could be.'

Howland lowered his voice to a whisper. 'Confidentially,' he said, 'that's what I was trying for. It's the best I can hope to expect.'

5

Mason sat at his desk, thoughtfully smoking. Della Street had cleaned up her secretarial desk, started for the door, returned for something which she had apparently forgotten, then she opened the drawers in her desk one after another, taking out papers, re-arranging them.

Mason grinned. 'Why don't you just break down and wait, Della?'

'Heavens! Was I that obvious?'

Mason nodded.

She laughed nervously. 'Well, I *will* wait for a few minutes.'

'The phone's plugged in through the switchboard?'

'Yes. Gertie's gone home. She left the main trunk line plugged through to your phone. In case this woman–'

Della Street broke off as the telephone rang.

Mason nodded to Della Street. 'Since you're here, better get on the extension phone with your notebook and take notes.'

Mason said, 'Hello.'

The feminine voice which had discussed the matter of a retainer with him earlier in the day sounded eager. 'Is this Mr Mason?'

'Yes.'

'Did you get up to court today?'

'Certainly.'

'And what did you think?'

'Think of what?'

'Of the case.'

'I think possibly it will be a hung jury.'

'No, no! Of the witness.'

'Which witness?'

'The redheaded woman, of course.'

'You mean Mrs Myrtle Anne Haley?'

'Yes.'

'I can't tell you.'

'You can't tell me?' the voice said, sharp with suspicion. 'Why that's what you went up there for. You–'

'I can't discuss my opinion of Mrs Haley's testimony with a stranger,' Mason interrupted firmly.

'A stranger? Why, I'm your client. I–'

'How do I know you're my client?'

'You should be able to recognize my voice.'

Mason said, 'Voices sound very much alike sometimes. I would dislike very much to have someone claim I had made a libellous statement which wasn't a privileged communication.'

There was silence at the other end of the line, then the woman's voice said, 'Well, how *could* I identify myself?'

'Through a receipt that I gave the messenger who delivered the hundred dollars to me. When you produce that receipt, I'll know that I'm dealing with the person who made the payment.'

'But, Mr Mason, can't you see? I can't afford to have you know who I am. This whole business of using the messenger was to keep you from finding out.'

'Well, I can't give my opinion of testimony unless I'm *certain* my statement is a privileged communication.'

'Is your opinion that bad?'

'I am merely enunciating a principle.'

'I . . . I already have that receipt, Mr Mason. The messenger gave it to me.'

'Then come on up,' Mason said.

There was a long moment of silence.

'I took all these precautions so I wouldn't have to disclose my identity,' the voice complained.

'I am taking all these precautions so as to be certain I'm talking to my client,' Mason said.

'Will you be there?'

'I'll wait ten minutes. Will that be sufficient?'

'Yes.'

'Very well, Come directly to the side door,' Mason said.

'I think you're horrid!' she exclaimed. 'I didn't want it like this.' She slammed the receiver at her end of the telephone.

Mason turned to Della Street, who had been monitoring the conversation. 'I take it, Miss Street, that you have decided you're not in a hurry to get home. You'd like to wait.'

'Try putting me out of the office,' she laughed. 'It would take a team of elephants to drag me out.'

She took the cover off her typewriter, arranged shorthand notebooks, hung up her hat in the coat closet.

Again the telephone rang.

Mason frowned. 'We should have cut out the switchboard as soon as we had our call, Della. Go cut it out now . . . Well, wait a minute. See who's calling.'

Della Street picked up the telephone, said, 'Hello,' then, 'Who's calling, please? . . . Where? . . . Well, just a moment. I think he's gone home for the evening. I don't think he's available. I'll see.'

She cupped her hand over the mouthpiece of the telephone and said, 'A Mr

Guthrie Balfour is calling from Chihuahua City in Mexico. He says it's exceedingly important.'

'Balfour?' Mason said. 'That will be the uncle of young Ted Balfour, the defendant in this case. Looks like we're getting dragged into a vortex of events, Della. Tell long-distance you've located me and have her put her party on.'

Della Street relayed the message into the telephone and a moment later nodded to Mason.

Mason picked up the telephone.

A man's voice at the other end of the line, sounding rather distant and faint, was nevertheless filled with overtones of urgency.

'Is this Perry Mason, the lawyer?'

'That's right,' Mason said.

The voice sharpened with excitement. 'Mr Mason, this is Guthrie Balfour. I have just returned from the Tarahumare Indian country and I must get back to my base camp. I've received disquieting news in the mail here at Chihuahua. It seems my nephew, Theodore Balfour, is accused of a hit-and-run death.

'You must know of me, Mr Mason. I'm quite certain you know of the vast industrial empire of the Balfour Allied Associates. We have investment all over the world–'

'I've heard of you,' Mason interrupted. 'The case involving your nephew was tried today.'

The voice sounded suddenly dispirited and dejected. 'What was the verdict?'

'As far as I know, the jury is still out.'

'It's too late to do anything now?'

'I think perhaps it will be a hung jury. Why do you ask?'

'Mr Mason, this is important! This is important as the devil! My nephew *must not* be convicted of anything.'

'He can probably get probation in case he's convicted,' Mason said. 'There are certain facts about the case that make it very peculiar. There are certain discrepancies–'

'Of course there are discrepancies! Can't you understand? The whole thing is a frame-up. It's brought for a specific purpose. Mr Mason, I can't get away. I'm down here on an archaeological expedition of the greatest importance. I'm encountering certain difficulties, certain hazards, but I'm playing for big stakes. I . . . Look, Mr Mason, I'll tell you what I'll do. I'll put my wife aboard the night plane tonight. She should be able to make connections at El Paso and be in your office the first thing in the morning. What time do you get to your office?'

'Sometime between nine and ten.'

'Please, Mr Mason, give my wife an appointment at nine o'clock in the morning. I'll see that you're amply compensated. I'll see that you–'

'The attorney representing your nephew,' Mason interrupted, 'is Mortimer Dean Howland.'

'Howland!' the voice said. 'That browbeating loud-mouthed bag of wind. He's nothing but a medium-grade criminal attorney, with a booming voice. This case is going to take brains, Mr Mason. This . . . I can't explain. Will you give my wife an appointment for tomorrow morning at nine o'clock?'

'All right,' Mason said. 'I may not be free to do what you want me to do, however.'

'Why?'

'I have some other connections which may bring about a conflict,' Mason said. 'I can't tell you definitely, but . . . well, anyway, I'll talk with your wife.'

'Tomorrow at nine.'

'That's right.'

'Thank you so much.'

Mason hung up. 'Well,' he said to Della Street, 'we seem to be getting deeper and deeper into the frying pan.'

'Right in the hot fat,' Della observed. 'I–' She broke off as a nervous knock sounded on the door of Mason's private office.

Della crossed over and opened the door.

The young woman who had been seated next to Perry Mason in the courtroom entered the office.

'Well, good evening,' Mason said. 'You weren't cordial to me earlier in the day.'

'Of course not!'

'You wouldn't even give me the time of day.'

'I . . . Mr Mason, you . . . you've jockeyed me into a position . . . well, a position in which I didn't want to be placed.'

'That's too bad,' the lawyer said. 'I was afraid *you* were going to put *me* in a position in which *I* didn't want to be placed.'

'Well, you know who I am now.'

'Sit down,' Mason said. 'By the way, just who are you . . . other than Cash?'

'My name is Marilyn Keith, but please don't make any further inquiries.'

'Just what is your relationship to Myrtle Anne Haley?'

'Look here, Mr Mason, you're cross-examining me. That's not what I wanted. I wanted certain information from you. I didn't want you even to know who I am.'

'Why?'

'That's neither here nor there.'

Mason said, 'You're here and it's here. Now what's this all about?'

'I simply *have* to know the real truth–and that gets back to Myrtle Haley's testimony.'

'Do you know the man who was killed?'

'No.'

'Yet,' Mason said, 'you have parted with a hundred dollars of your money, money which, I take it, was withdrawn from a rainy-day fund, to retain me to listen to the case in court so you could ask me how I felt about the testimony of Myrtle Anne Haley?'

'That's right. Only the money came from . . . well, it was to have been my vacation fund.'

'Vacation?'

'Mine comes next month,' she said, 'I let the other girls take theirs during the summer. I had intended to go to Acapulco . . . I will, anyway, but . . . well, naturally I hated to draw against my vacation fund. However, that's all in the past now.'

'You have the receipt?' Mason asked.

She opened her purse, took from it the receipt which Della Street had given the messenger, and handed it to him.

Mason looked the young woman in the eyes. 'I think Myrtle Haley was lying.'

For a moment there was a flicker of expression on her face, then she regained her self-control. 'Lying deliberately?'

Mason nodded. 'Don't repeat my opinion to anyone else. To you this is a privileged communication. If you repeat what I said to anyone, however, you could get into trouble.'

'Can you . . . can you give me any reasons for your conclusions, Mr Mason?'

'She wrote down the licence number of the automobile,' Mason said. 'She wrote it down in her notebook in exactly the place and –'

'Yes, of course. I heard the argument of the defence attorney,' Marilyn interrupted. 'It sounds logical. But on the other hand, suppose Myrtle *did* take her eyes off the road? That would only have been for a minute. She didn't have her eyes off the road *all* the time she was writing. She just glanced down at the notebook to make certain she had the right place and–'

Mason picked up a pencil and a piece of paper.

'Write down the figure six,' he instructed Marilyn Keith.

She wrote as he directed.

'Now,' Mason said, 'get up and walk around the room and write down another six while you're walking.'

She followed his instructions.

'Compare the two figures,' Mason told her.

'I don't see any difference.'

'Bring them over here,' Mason said, 'and I'll show you some difference.'

She started over towards the desk.

'Wait a minute,' Mason said. 'Write another figure six while you're walking over here.'

She did so, handed him the pad of paper with the three sixes on it.

'This is the six that you wrote while you were sitting down,' Mason said. 'You'll notice that the end of the line on the loop of the six comes back and joins the down stroke. Now, look at the two figures that you made while you were walking. In one of them the loop of the six stops approximately a thirty-second of an inch before it comes to the down stroke, and on the second one the end of the loop goes completely through the down stroke and protrudes for probably a thirty-second of an inch on the other side.

'You try to write the figure six when you're riding in an automobile and you'll do one of two things. You'll either stop the end of the loop before you come to the down stroke or you'll go all the way through it. It's only when you're sitting perfectly still that you can bring the end of the six directly to the down stroke and then stop.

'Now, if you'll notice the figure GMB 665 that Myrtle Anne Haley *claims* she wrote while she was in a moving automobile, with one hand on the steering wheel, the other hand holding a fountain pen, writing in a notebook which was balanced on her lap, you'll note that both of the figures are perfect. The loops join the down strokes, so that the loops are perfectly closed. The chances that that could have been done twice in succession by someone who was in a moving automobile, going over the road at a good rate of speed under the circumstances described by Myrtle Anne Haley, are just about one in a million.'

'Why didn't the defence attorney bring that out?' she asked.

'Perhaps it didn't occur to him,' Mason said. 'Perhaps he didn't think he needed to.'

She was silent for several seconds, then asked, 'Is there anything else?'

'Lots of things,' Mason said. 'In addition to a sort of sixth sense which warns a lawyer when a witness is lying, there is the question of distance.

'If Mrs Haley passed that car at the point she says she did, and then looked in the rearview mirror as she says she did, she must have been crossing State Highway when she saw the light go out. She'd hardly have been looking in her rearview mirror while she was crossing State Highway.'

'Yes, I can see that,' the young woman admitted. 'That is, I can see it now that you've pointed it out.'

Mason said, 'Something caused you to become suspicious of Myrtle Haley's testimony in the first place. Do you want to tell me about it?'

She shook her head. 'I can't.'

'Well,' Mason said, 'you asked me for my opinion. You paid me a hundred dollars to sit in court and form that opinion. I have given it to you.'

She thought things over for a moment, then suddenly got up to give him her hand. 'Thank you, Mr Mason. You're . . . you're everything I expected.'

'Don't you think you'd better give me your address now?' Mason said. 'One that we can put on the books?'

'Mr Mason, I can't! If anyone knew about my having been to you, I'd be ruined. Believe me, there are interests involved that are big and powerful and ruthless. I only hope I haven't gone so far as to get you in trouble.'

Mason studied her anxious features. 'Is there any reason as far as you are concerned why I can't interest myself in any phase of the case?'

'Why do you ask that question?'

'I may have been approached by another potential client.'

She thought that over. 'Surely not Myrtle Haley?'

'No,' Mason said. 'I would be disqualified as far as she is concerned.'

'Well, who is it?' she asked.

'I'm not free to tell you that. However, if there is any reason why I shouldn't represent *anyone* who is connected with the case in any way, please tell me.'

She said, 'I would love to know the real truth in this case. If you become connected with it you'll dig out that truth . . . and I don't care who retains you. As far as I'm concerned you are free to go ahead in any way, Mr Mason.' She crossed to the door in one quick movement. 'Good night,' she said, and closed the door behind her.

Mason turned to Della Street. 'Well?' he asked.

'She doesn't lie very well,' Della said.

'Meaning what?'

'She didn't dig into her vacation money just to get your opinion of Myrtle's testimony.'

'Then why *did* she do it?'

'I *think*,' Della Street said, 'she's in love, and I *know* she's frightened.'

6

Perry Mason latchkeyed the door of his private office, hung up his hat.

Della Street, who was there before him asked, 'Have you seen the morning papers?' She indicated the papers on Mason's desk.

He shook his head.

'There was a hung jury in the case of People versus Ted Balfour. They were divided evenly–six for acquittal and six for conviction.'

'So what happened?' Mason asked.

'Apparently, Howland made a deal with the prosecutor. The Court discharged the jury and asked counsel to agree on a new trial date.

'At that time Howland got up, said that he thought the case was costing the state altogether too much money in view of the issues involved. He stated that he would be willing to stipulate the case could be submitted to Judge Cadwell, sitting without a jury, on the same evidence which had been introduced in the jury trial.

'The prosecutor agreed to that. Judge Cadwell promptly announced that under those circumstances he would find the defendant guilty as charged, and Howland thereupon made a motion for suspended sentence. The prosecutor said that under the circumstances and in view of the money that the defendant had saved the state, he would not oppose such a motion, provided the defendant paid a fine. He said he would consent that the matter be heard immediately.

'Judge Cadwell stated that in view of the stipulation by the prosecutor, he would give the defendant a suspended jail sentence and impose a fine of five hundred dollars.'

'Well, that's interesting,' Mason said. 'It certainly disposed of the case of People versus Balfour in a hurry. We haven't heard anything from our client of yesterday, have we, Della?'

'No, but our client of today is waiting in the office.'

'You mean Mrs Balfour?'

'That's right.'

'How does she impress you, Della? Does she show signs of having been up all night?'

Della Street shook her head. 'Fresh as a daisy. Groomed tastefully and expensively. Wearing clothes that didn't come out of a suitcase. She really set out to make an impression on Mr Perry Mason.

'Apparently she chartered a plane out of Chihuahua, flew to El Paso in time to make connections with one of the luxury planes, arrived home, grabbed a little shut-eye and then this morning started making herself very, very presentable.'

'Good-looking?' Mason asked.

'A dish.'

'How old?'

'She's in that deadly dangerous age between twenty-seven and thirty-two. That's about as close as I can place her.'

'Features?' Mason asked.

'She has,' Della Street said, 'large brown expressive eyes, a mouth that smiles to show beautiful pearly teeth–in short, she's a regular millionaire's second wife, an expensive plaything. And even so, Mr Guthrie Balfour must have done a lot of window-shopping before he had this package wrapped up.'

'A thoroughly devoted wife,' Mason said, smiling.'

'Very, very devoted,' Della Street said. 'Not to Mr Guthrie Balfour, but to *Mrs* Guthrie Balfour. There's a woman who's exceedingly loyal to herself.'

'Well, get her in,' Mason said. 'Let's have a look at her. Now, she's a second wife, so really she's no relation to young Ted Balfour.'

'That's right. You'll think I'm catty,' Della Street observed, 'but I'll tell you something, Mr Perry Mason.'

'What?'

'You're going to fall for her like a ton of bricks. She's just the type to impress you.'

'But not you?' Mason asked.

Della Street's answer was to flash him a single glance.

'Well, bring her in,' Mason said, smiling. 'After this build-up, I'm bound to be disappointed.'

'You won't be,' she told him.

Della Street ushered Mrs Guthrie Balfour into Mason's private office.

Mason arose, bowed, said, 'Good morning, Mrs Balfour. I'm afraid you've had rather a hard trip.'

Her smile was radiant. 'Not at all, Mr Mason. In the first place, I was here at home by one-thirty this morning. In the second place, travelling on air-conditioned planes and sitting in sponge rubber reclining seats is the height of luxury compared to the things an archaeologist's wife has to contend with.'

'Do sit down.' Mason said. 'Your husband seemed very much disturbed about the case against his nephew.'

'That's putting it mildly.'

'Well,' Mason said, 'apparently, the young man's attorney worked out a deal with the prosecutor. Did you read the morning paper?'

'Heavens, no! Was there something in there about the case?'

'Yes,' Mason said. 'Perhaps you'd like to read it for yourself.'

He folded the paper and handed it to her.

While she was reading the paper, Mason studied her carefully.

Suddenly Mrs Balfour uttered an exclamation of annoyance, crumpled the paper, threw it to the floor, jumped from the chair, and stamped a high-heeled shoe on the paper. Then abruptly she caught herself.

'Oh, I'm sorry,' she said. 'I didn't realize.'

She stepped carefully off the paper, disentangling her high heels, raising her skirts as she did so, so that she disclosed a neat pair of legs. Then, dropping to her knees, she started smoothing the newspaper out.

'I'm so sorry, Mr Mason,' she said contritely. 'My temper got the best of me . . . that awful temper of mine.'

'Don't bother about the paper,' Mason said, glancing at Della Street. 'There are plenty more down on the news-stand. Please don't give it another thought.'

'No, no . . . I'm sorry. I . . . let me do penance, please, Mr Mason.'

She carefully smoothed out the paper, then arose with supple grace.

'What was there about the article that annoyed you?' Mason asked.

'The fool!' she said. 'The absolute fool! Oh, they should never have let that braggart, that loudmouthed egoist handle the case–not for a minute.'

'Mortimer Dean Howland?' Mason asked.

'Mortimer Dean Howland,' she said, spitting out the words contemptuously. 'Look what he's done.'

'Apparently,' Mason said, 'he's made a pretty good deal. In all probability, Mrs Balfour, while the jury was out, Howland approached the prosecutor, suggested the possibility of a hung jury, and the prosecutor probably didn't care too much about retrying the case. So it was agreed that if there was a hung jury, the case should be submitted to Judge Cadwell on the evidence which had been introduced, which was, of course, equivalent to pleading the defendant guilty, only it saved him the stigma of such a plea.

'The prosecutor, for his side of the bargain, agreed that he would stipulate the judge could pass a suspended sentence and the case would be cleaned up. Of course, the trouble with a stipulation of that sort is that on occasion the judge won't ride along, but takes the bit in his teeth and insists on pronouncing sentence. Judge Cadwell, however, is known for his consideration of the practical problems of the practising attorney. He virtually always rides along with a stipulation of that sort.'

Mrs Balfour followed Mason's explanation with intense interest, her large brown eyes showing the extent of her concentration.

When Mason had finished she said simply, 'There are some things that Ted Balfour doesn't know about. Therefore, his attorney could hardly be expected to know them. But they are vital.'

'What, for instance?' Mason asked

'Addison Balfour,' she explained.

'What about him?' Mason asked.

'He's the wealthiest member of the family, and he's terribly prejudiced.'

'I thought your husband was the wealthy one,' Mason ventured.

'No. Guthrie is pretty well heeled, I guess. I don't know. I've never inquired into his financial status. Under the circumstances, my motives might have been misunderstood,' she said, and laughed, a light, nervous laugh.

'Go on,' Mason said.

'Addison Balfour is dying and knows it. Eighteen months ago the doctors gave him six months to live. Addison is really a remarkable character. He's wealthy, eccentric, strong-minded, obstinate, and completely unpredictable. One thing I do know–if *he* ever learns that Ted Balfour has been convicted of killing a man with an automobile, Addison will disinherit Ted immediately.'

'Ted is mentioned in his will?'

'I have reason to believe so. I think Ted is to receive a large chunk of property, but Addison is very much prejudiced against what he calls the helter-skelter attitude of the younger generation.

'You see, Ted took his military service. He's finished college and is now taking a six-months' breathing spell before he plunges into the business of Balfour Industries.

'Ted had some money which was left him outright by his father. Addison didn't approve of that at all. There is also a fortune left Ted in trust. Ted bought one of these high-powered sports cars that will glide along the highway at one hundred and fifty miles an hour, and Addison had a fit when he learned of that.

'You see, my husband is childless. Addison is childless and Ted represents the only one who can carry on the Balfour name and the Balfour traditions. Therefore, he's an important member of the family.'

'Ted wasn't driving his sports car that night of the accident?' Mason asked.

'No, he was driving one of the big cars.'

'There are several?'

'Yes.'

'The same make?'

'No. My husband is restless. He's restless mentally as well as physically. Most people will buy one make of car. If they like it, they'll have all their cars of that make. Guthrie is completely different. If he buys a Cadillac today, he'll buy a Buick tomorrow, and an Olds the next day. Then he'll get a Lincoln for his next car, and so on down the line. I've only been married to him for two years, but I guess I've driven half a dozen makes of cars in that time.'

'I see,' Mason said. 'Now, just what did you have in mind?'

'In the first place,' she said, 'this man Howland must go. Do you have any idea how it happened that Ted went to him in the first place?'

Mason shook his head.

'You see, my husband and I left for Mexico the day of the accident. This happened the night we left. Ted was very careful that we didn't hear anything about it. We've been back in the wild barranca country. We came to Chihuahua for mail and supplies and there was a letter there from the trustee of Ted's trust fund. Guthrie called you immediately after he'd read that letter. He simply had to return to base camp, and from there he's going out on a dangerous but exciting expedition into very primitive country.'

'You went by train?'

'Yes. My husband doesn't like airplanes. He says they're nothing but buses with wings. He likes to get in an air-conditioned train, get single occupancy of a drawing room, stretch out, relax and do his thinking. He says he does some of his best thinking and nearly all his best sleeping on a train.'

'Well,' Mason said, 'the case has been concluded. There's nothing for me or anyone else to do now.'

'That's not the way my husband feels about it. Despite the court's decision, he'll want you to check on the evidence of the witnesses.'

'What good would that do?'

'You could get the stipulation set aside and get a new trial.'

'That would be difficult.'

'Couldn't you do it if you could prove one of the main witnesses was lying?'

'Perhaps. Do you think one of the main witnesses was lying?'

'I'd want to have you investigate that and tell me.'

'I couldn't do anything as long as Howland was representing Ted.'

'He's finished now.'

'Does he know that?'

'He will.'

Mason said, 'There's one other matter you should know about.'

'What?'

'Without discussing details,' Mason said, 'I was retained to sit in court yesterday and listen to the evidence in the case.'

'By whom?'

'I am not at liberty to disclose that. I'm not certain I know.'

'But for heaven's sake, why should anyone ask you simply to sit in court and listen?'

'That,' Mason said, 'is something I've been asking myself. The point is that I did. Now I don't want to have any misunderstandings about this. I have had one client who asked me to sit in court and listen.'

'And you sat in court and listened?'

'Yes.'

'What did you think of the case?'

'There again,' Mason said, 'is something I have to discuss cautiously. I came to the conclusion that one of the principal witnesses might not be telling the truth.'

'A witness for the prosecution?'

'Yes. The defence put on no case.'

'Well, is that going to disqualify you from doing what we want?'

'Not unless you think it does. It complicates the situation in that Howland will think I deliberately watched the trial in order to steal his client.'

'Do you care what Howland thinks?'

'In a way, yes.'

'But it's not going to be too important?'

'Not *too* important. I would like to have the matter adjusted so that Howland can understand the situation.'

'You leave Howland to me,' she said. 'I'm going to talk with him, and when I get done telling him a few things, he'll know how my husband and I feel.'

'After all,' Mason said, 'Ted is apparently the one who retained him, and Ted is over twenty-one and able to do as he pleases.'

'Well, I am going to talk with Ted, too.'

'Do so,' Mason said. 'Get in touch with me after you have clarified the situation. I don't want to touch it while Howland is in the picture.'

Mrs Balfour whipped out a chequebook. 'You are retained as of right now,' she said.

She took a fountain pen, wrote out a cheque for a thousand dollars, signed it *Guthrie Balfour, per Dorla Balfour*, and handed it to Mason.

'I don't get it,' the lawyer said. 'Here's a case that's all tried and finished and now you come along with a retainer.'

'Your work will lie in convincing Addison that Ted wasn't really involved in that case,' she said. 'And there'll be plenty of work and responsibility, don't think there won't be.

'For one thing, you're going to have to reopen the case. Frankly, Mr Mason, while Addison may blame Ted, he'll be furious at Guthrie for letting any such situation develop. He thinks Guthrie puts in too much time on these expeditions.

'Just wait until you see what you're up against, and you'll understand what I mean.

'And now I must go see Ted, let Howland know he's fired and . . . well, I'm going to let *you* deal with Addison. When you see him, remember *we've* retained you to protect Ted's interests.

'Will you hold some time open for me later on today?' she asked.

Mason nodded.

'You'll hear from me,' she promised and walked out.

When the door had clicked shut, Mason turned to Della Street. 'Well?'

Della Street motioned towards the crumpled newspaper. 'An impulsive woman,' she said.

'A very interesting woman,' Mason said. 'She's using her mind all the time. Did you notice the way she was concentrating when I was explaining what had happened in the case?'

'I noticed the way she was looking at you while you were talking,' Della Street said.

'Her face was the picture of concentration. She is using her head all the time.'

'I also noticed the way she walked out the door,' Della Street said. 'She may have been using her mind when she was looking at you, but she was using her hips when she knew you were looking at her.'

Mason said, 'You were also looking.'

'Oh, she *knew* I'd be looking,' Della Street said, 'but the act was strictly for your benefit.'

7

It was ten-thirty when Mason's unlisted phone rang. Since only Della Street and Paul Drake, head of the Drake Detective Agency, had the number of that telephone, Mason reached across the desk for it. 'I'll answer it,' he said to Della, and then, picking up the receiver, said, 'Hello, Paul.'

Paul Drake's voice came over the wire with the toneless efficiency of an announcer giving statistical reports on an election night.

'You're interested in the Ted Balfour case, Perry,' he said. 'There have been some developments in that case you ought to know about.'

'In the first place, how did you know I am interested?' Mason asked.

'You were in court yesterday following the case.'

'Who told you?'

'I get around,' Drake said. 'Listen. There's something funny in that case. It may have been a complete frame-up.'

'Yes?' Mason asked. 'What makes you think so?'

'The body's been identified,' Drake said.

'And what does that have to do with it?' Mason asked.

'Quite a good deal.'

'Give me the dope. Who is the man?'

'A fellow by the name of Jackson Eagan. At least that's the name he gave when he registered at the Sleepy Hollow Motel. It's also the name he gave when he rented a car from a drive-yourself agency earlier that day.'

'Go on,' Mason said.

'The people who rented the car made a recovery of the car within a day or two. It had been left standing in front of the motel. The management reported it; the car people assumed it was just one of those things that happen every so often when a man signs up for a car, then changes his mind about something and simply goes away without notifying the agency. Since the car people had a deposit of fifty dollars, they simply deducted rental for three days, set the balance in a credit fund, and said nothing about it. Therefore, the police didn't know that Jackson Eagan was missing. The motel people didn't care because Eagan had paid his rent in advance. So if it hadn't been for a fluke, police would never have discovered the identity of the body. The features were pretty well damaged, you remember.'

'What was the fluke?' Mason asked.

'When the body was found there was nothing in the pockets except some odds and ends that offered no chance for an identification, some small coins and one key. The police didn't pay much attention to the key until someone in the police department happened to notice a code number on the key. This man was in the traffic squad and he said the code number was that of a car rental agency. So the police investigated, and sure enough, this key was for the car that had been parked in front of the motel for a couple of days.'

'When did they find out all this?' Mason asked.

'Yesterday morning, while the case was being tried. They didn't get the dope to the prosecutor until after the arguments had started, but police knew about it as early as eight o'clock. The reason it didn't reach the prosecutor was on account of red tape in the D.A.'s office. The guy who handles that stuff decided it wouldn't make any difference in the trial, so he let it ride.'

'That's most interesting,' Mason said. 'It may account for the sudden desire on the part of a lot of people to retain my services.'

'Okay. I thought you'd be interested.' Drake said.

'Keep an ear to the ground, Paul,' Mason said, hung up the telephone and repeated the conversation to Della Street.

'Where does that leave you, Chief?' she asked.

'Where I always am,' Mason said, 'right in the middle. There's something phony about this whole business. That Haley woman was reciting a whole synthetic lie there on the witness stand, and people don't lie like that unless there's a reason.'

'And,' Della Street said, 'young women like Marilyn Keith don't give up their vacation to Acapulco unless there's a reason.'

'Nor women like Mrs Guthrie Balfour literally force retainers on reluctant attorneys,' Mason said. 'Stick around, Della. I think you'll see some action.'

Della Street smiled sweetly at her employer. 'I'm sticking,' she announced simply.

8

By one forty-five Mrs Balfour was back in Mason's office.

'I've seen Ted,' she said.

Mason nodded.

'It's just as I surmised. Ted was given a loaded drink. He passed out. I don't know who had it in for him or why, but I can tell you one thing.'

'What?'

'He wasn't the one who was driving his car,' she asserted. 'A young woman drove him home–a cute trick with dark chestnut hair, a nice figure, good legs, and a very sympathetic shoulder. I think I can find out who she was by checking the list of party guests. It was a party given by Florence Ingle.'

'How do you know about the girl?' Mason asked.

'A friend of mine saw her driving Ted's car, with Ted passed out and leaning on her shoulder. He'd seen her at the parking space getting into Ted's car. She had Ted move over and she took the wheel. If anyone hit a pedestrian with the car Ted had that evening, it was that girl.'

'At what time was this?' Mason asked.

'Sometime between ten and eleven.'

'And after Ted got home what happened?' Mason asked.

'Now as to that,' she said, 'you'll have to find the young woman who was driving and ask her. There were no servants in the house. Remember, Guthrie and I had taken the train. Before that there'd been a farewell party at Florence

Ingle's. I'd told all of our servants to take the night off. There was no one at our house.'

'Ted was in his bedroom the next morning?' Mason asked.

'Apparently he was. He told me he became conscious at four-thirty-five in the morning. Someone had taken him upstairs, undressed him, and put him to bed.'

'Or he undressed himself and put himself to bed,' Mason said.

'He was in no condition to do that.'

'Any idea who this girl was?' Mason asked.

'Not yet. Ted either doesn't know or won't tell. Apparently, she was some trollop from the wrong side of the tracks.'

Mason's frown showed annoyance.

'All right, all right,' she said. 'I'm out of order. I'm not a snob. Remember, Mr Mason, I came from the wrong side of the tracks myself, and I made it, but I'm just telling you it's a long, hard climb. And also remember, Mr Mason, you're working for me.'

'The hell I am,' Mason said. 'You're paying the bill, but I'm working for my client.'

'Now don't get stuffy,' she said, flashing her teeth in a mollifying smile. 'I had Ted write a cheque covering Howland's fees in full and I explained to Mr Howland that as far as Mr Guthrie Balfour and I were concerned, we preferred to have all further legal matters in connection with the case handled by Mr Perry Mason.'

'And what did Howland say then?'

'Howland threw back his head, laughed and said, "If it's a fair question, Mrs Balfour, when did you get back from Mexico?" and I told him that I didn't know whether it was a fair question or not, but there was no secret about it and I got back from Mexico on a plane which arrived half an hour past midnight, and then he laughed again and said that if I had arrived twenty-four hours sooner he felt certain he wouldn't have had the opportunity to represent Ted as long as he did.'

'He was a little put out about it?' Mason asked.

'On the contrary, he was in rare good humour. He said that he had completed his representation of Ted Balfour, that the case was closed, and that if Mr Mason knew as much about the case as he did, Mason would realize the over-all strategy had been brilliant.'

'Did he say in what respect?'

'No, but he gave me a letter for you.'

'Indeed,' Mason said.

She unfolded the letter and extended it across the desk. The letter was addressed to Perry Mason and read:

My dear Counsellor,

I now begin to see a great light. I trust your time in court was well spent, but don't worry. There are no hard feelings. You take on from here and more power to you. I consider myself completely relieved of all responsibilities in the case of the People versus Ted Balfour, and I am satisfied, not only with the compensation I have received, but with the outcome of my strategy. From here on, the Balfour family is all yours. They consider me a little crude and I consider them highly unappreciative in all ways except in so far as financial appreciation is concerned. I can assure you that those matters have been completely taken care of, so consider yourself free to gild the lily or paint the rose in any way you may see fit, remembering only that it's advisable to take the temperature of the water before you start rocking the boat.

With all good wishes,
Mortimer Dean Howland

'A very interesting letter,' Mason said, handing it to Mrs Balfour.

'Isn't it?' she remarked drily after having read it. She returned it to Perry Mason.

'*Now*, what do you want me to do?' Mason asked.

'The first thing I want you to do,' she said, 'is to go and see Addison Balfour. He's in bed. He'll never get out of bed. You'll have to go to him.'

'Will he see me?'

'He'll see you. I've already telephoned for an appointment.'

'When?' Mason asled.

'I telephoned about thirty minutes ago. The hour of the appointment, however, is to be left to you. Mr Addison Balfour will be *very* happy to see the great Perry Mason.'

Mason turned to Della Street. 'Ring up Addison Balfour's secretary,' he said, 'and see if I can have an appointment for three o'clock.'

9

Some two years earlier, when the doctors had told Addison Balfour that he had better 'take it easy for a while,' the manufacturing magnate had moved his private office into his residence.

Later on, when the doctors had told him frankly that he had but six months to live at the outside, Addison Balfour had moved his office into his bedroom.

Despite the sentence of death which had been pronounced upon him, he continued to be the same old irascible, unpredictable fighter. Disease had ravaged his body, but the belligerency of the man's mind remained unimpaired.

Mason gave his name to the servant who answered the door.

'Oh, yes, Mr Mason. You are to go right up. Mr Balfour is expecting you. The stairs to the left, please.'

Mason climbed the wide flight of oak stairs, walked down the second floor towards a sign which said 'Office', and entered through an open door, from behind which came the sound of pounding typewriters.

Two stenographers were busily engaged in hammering keyboards. A telephone operator sat at the back of a room, supervising a switchboard.

At a desk facing the door sat Marilyn Keith.

'Good afternoon,' Mason said calmly and impersonally as though he had never before seen her. 'I am Mr Mason. I have an appointment with Mr Addison Balfour.'

'Just a moment, Mr Mason. I'll tell Mr Balfour you're here.'

She glided from the room through an open doorway and in a moment returned.

'Mr Balfour will see you now, Mr Mason,' she said in the manner of one reciting a prepared speech which had been repeated so many times and under such circumstances that the repetition had made the words almost without meaning. 'You will understand, Mr Mason, that Mr Addison Balfour is not at all well. He is, for the moment, confined to his bed. Mr Balfour dislikes to discuss his illness with anyone. You will, therefore, please try to act as though the situation were entirely normal and you were seeing Mr Balfour in his office. However, you will remember he is ill and try to conclude the interview as soon as possible.

'You may go in now.'

She ushered Mason through the open door, along a vestibule, then swung open a heavy oaken door which moved on well-oiled hinges.

The man who was propped up in bed might have been made of colourless wax. His high cheekbones, the gaunt face, the sunken eyes, all bore the unmistakable stamp of illness. But the set of his jaw, the thin, determined line of his mouth showed the spirit of an indomitable fighter.

Balfour's voice was not strong. 'Come in, Mr Mason,' he said in a monotone, as though he lacked the physical strength to put even the faintest expression in his words. 'Sit down here by the bed. What's all this about Ted getting convicted?'

Mason said, 'The attorney who was representing your nephew appeared to think that the interests of expediency would best be served by making a deal with the district attorney's office.'

'Who the hell wants to serve the interests of expediency?' Balfour asked in his colourless, expressionless voice.

'Apparently your nephew's attorney thought that would be best under the circumstances.'

'What do you think?'

'I don't know.'

'Find out.'

'I intend to.'

'Come back when you find out.'

'Very well,' Mason said, getting up.

'Wait a minute. Don't go yet. *I* want to tell *you* something. Lean closer. Listen. Don't interrupt.'

Mason leaned forward so that his ear was but a few inches from the thin, colourless lips.

'I told Dorla–that's Guthrie's wife–that I'd disinherit Ted if he got in any trouble with that automobile. That was just a bluff.

'Ted's a Balfour. He has the Balfour name. He's going to carry it on. It would be unthinkable to have the Balfour Allied Associates carried on by anyone who wasn't a Balfour. I want Ted to marry. I want him to have children. I want him to leave the business to a man-child who has the name of Balfour and the characteristics of a Balfour. Do you understand?'

Mason nodded.

'But,' Addison went on, 'I want to be sure that Ted knows the duties and responsibilities of a Balfour and of the head of a damn big business.'

Again Mason nodded.

Addison Balfour waited for a few seconds as though mustering his strength.

Addison Balfour breathed deeply, exhaled in a tremulous sigh, took in his breath once more and said, 'Balfours don't compromise, Mr Mason. Balfours fight.'

Mason waited.

'Lots of times you win a case by a compromise,' Balfour said. 'It's a good thing. You may come out better in some isolated matter by compromise than by fighting a thing through to the last bitter ditch.

'That's a damn poor way to go through life.

'Once people know that you'll compromise when the going gets tough, they see to it that the going gets tough. People aren't dumb. Businessmen get to know the calibre of the businessmen they are dealing with. Balfours don't compromise.

'We don't fight unless we're in the right. When we start fighting, we carry the fight through to the end.

'You understand what I mean, Mason?'

Mason nodded.

'We don't want the reputation of being compromisers,' Balfour continued. 'We want the reputation of being implacable fighters. I want Ted to learn that lesson.

'I'd told Guthrie's wife that I'd disinherit Ted if he ever got convicted of any serious accident with that automobile. Scared her to death. She has her eye out for the cash. What do you think of her, Mason?'

'I'm hardly in a position to discuss her,' Mason said.

'Why not?'

'She's somewhat in the position of a client.'

'The hell she is! Ted Balfour is your client. What makes you say she's a client? She didn't retain you, did she?'

'For Ted Balfour.'

'She did that because Guthrie told her to. How was the cheque signed?'

'Your brother's name, Guthrie Balfour, per Dorla Balfour.'

'That's what I thought. She wouldn't give you a thin dime out of her money. Heaven knows how much she's got! She's milked Guthrie for plenty. That's all right. That's Guthrie's business.

'Don't be misled about money, Mason. You can't eat money. You can't wear money. All you can do with money is spend it. That's what it's for.

'Guthrie wanted a good-looker. He had money. He bought one. The trouble is; people aren't merchandise. You can pay for them, but that doesn't mean you've got 'em. Personally, I wouldn't trust that woman as far as I could throw this bed, and that isn't very damn far, Mason. Do you understand me?'

'I understand the point you're making.'

'Remember it!' Balfour said. 'Now, I want young Ted to fight. I don't want him to start out by compromising. When I read the paper this morning I was furious. I was going to send for you myself, but Dorla telephoned my secretary and told her she'd made arrangements to have you step into the picture. What are you going to do, Mason?'

'I don't know.'

'Get in there and fight like hell! Don't worry about money. You have a retainer?'

'A retainer,' Mason said, 'which at first blush seemed more than adequate.'

'How does it seem now?'

'Adequate.'

'Something happened?'

'The case has taken on certain unusual aspects.'

'All right,' Balfour said. 'You're in the saddle. Start riding the horse. Pick up the reins. Don't let anybody tell you what to do. You're not like most of these criminal lawyers. You don't want just to get a client off. You try to dig out the truth. I like that. That's what I want.

'Now remember this: If a Balfour is wrong, he apologizes and makes restitution. If he's right, he fights. Now you start fighting.

'I don't want you to tell Dorla that I'm not going to disinherit Ted. I don't want you to tell Ted. I want Ted to sweat a little blood. Ted's going to have to get in the business pretty quick, and he's going to have to become a Balfour. He isn't a Balfour now. He's just a kid. He's young. He's inexperienced. He hasn't been tempered by fire.

'This experience is going to do him good. It's going to teach him that he has to fight. It's going to teach him that he can't go through life playing around on his dad's money. Scare the hell out of him if you want to, but make him fight.

'Now I'll tell you one other thing, Mason. Don't trust Dorla.'

Mason remained silent.

'Well?' Addison Balfour snapped.

'I heard you,' Mason said.

'All right, I'm telling you. Don't trust Dorla. Dorla's a snob. Ever notice how it happens that people who have real background and breeding are considerate, tolerant, and broad-minded, while people who haven't anything except money that they didn't earn themselves are intolerant? That's Dorla. She's got about the nicest figure I've ever seen on a woman. And I've seen lots of them.

'Don't underestimate her, Mason. She's smart. She's chain lightning! She's got her eye on a big slice of money, and Guthrie hasn't waked up yet. That's all right. Let him sleep. He's paid for a dream. As long as he's enjoying the dream, why grab him by the shoulder and bring him back to the grim realities of existence?

'Guthrie isn't really married to Dorla. He's married to the woman he visualizes beneath Dorla's beautiful exterior. It's not the real woman. It's a dream woman, a sort of man-made spouse that he's conjured up out of his own mind.

'When Guthrie wakes up he'll marry Florence Ingle and really be happy. Right now he's a sleepwalker. He's in a dream. Don't try to wake him up.

'I'm a dying man. I can't bring up Ted. After Ted's family died Guthrie and his wife took over. Then Guthrie's wife died and he bought beauty on the auction block. He thought that was what he wanted.

'He knows I'll raise hell if he neglects Ted's bringing up. Dorla isn't a good influence on Ted. She isn't a good influence on anyone. But she's smart! Damned smart!

'If she has to get out from under, she'll trap you to save her own skin. Don't think she can't do it.

'Guthrie gave you a retainer. Don't bother about sending him bills. Send bills to the Balfour Allied Associates. I'll instruct the treasurer to let you have any amount you need. I know you by reputation well enough to know you won't stick me. You should know me by reputation well enough to know that if you overcharge me it'll be the biggest mistake you ever made in your life. That's all now, Mason. I'm going to sleep. Tell my secretary not to disturb me for thirty minutes, no matter what happens. Don't try to shake hands. I get tired. Close the door when you go out. Good-bye.'

Addison's head dropped back against the pillow. The colourless eyelids fluttered shut over the faded blue eyes.

Mason tiptoed from the room.

Marilyn Keith was waiting for him on the other side of the vestibule door. 'Will you step this way, please, Mr Mason?'

Mason followed her into another office and gave her Balfour's message. Marilyn indicated a telephone and a desk. 'We have strict instructions not to put through any phone messages to anyone who is in conference with Mr Balfour,' she said. 'But Miss Street telephoned and said you must call at once upon a matter of the greatest urgency.'

'Did she leave any other message?' Mason asked.

Marilyn Keith shook her head.

Mason dialled the number of the unlisted telephone in his office.

When he heard Della Street's voice on the line he said, 'Okay, Della, what cooks?'

'Paul's here,' she said. 'He wants to talk with you. Are you where you can talk?'

'Fairly well,' Mason said.

'Alone?'

'No.'

'Better be careful about what comments you make, then,' she said. 'Here's Paul. I'll explain to him that you'll have to be rather guarded.'

A moment later Paul Drake's voice came on the line. 'Hello, Perry.'

'Hi,' Mason said, without mentioning Drake's name.

'Things are happening fast in that Balfour case.'

'What?'

'They secured an order for the exhumation of the corpse.'

'Go ahead.'

'That was done secretly at an early hour this morning.'

'Keep talking.'

'When police checked at the motel, back-tracking the car, they learned something that started them really moving in a hurry. Apparently someone in the motel had heard a shot on the night of the nineteenth. They dug the body up. The coroner opened the skull, something which had never been done before.'

'It hadn't?'

'No. The head had been pretty well smashed up and the coroner evidently didn't go into it.'

'Okay, what happened?'

'When they opened the head,' Paul Drake said, 'they found that it wasn't a hit-and-run accident at all.'

'What do you mean?'

'The man had been killed,' Drake said, 'by a small-calibre, high-powered bullet.'

'They're certain?'

'Hell, yes! The bullet's still in there. The hole was concealed beneath the hair and the coroner missed it the first time. Of course, Perry, they thought they were dealing with a hit-and-run death and that the victim was a drifter who had been walking along the road. The whole thing indicated a ne'er-do-well who happened to get in front of a car being driven by an intoxicated driver.'

'And now?'

'Hells bells!' Paul Drake said. 'Do I have to draw you a diagram! Now it's first-degree murder.'

'Okay,' Mason said. 'Start working.'

'What do you want, Perry?'

'Everything.' Mason said. 'I'll discuss it with you when I see you. In the meantime, get started.'

'What's the limit?' Drake asked.

'There isn't any.'

'Okay. I'm starting.'

Mason hung up and turned to Marilyn Keith. 'Well?' he asked.

'Have you told anyone about me?'

'Not by name.'

'Don't.'

'I'm in the case now.'

'I know.'

'It may be more of a case than it seemed at first.'

'I know.'

'I'm representing Ted.'

'Yes, of course.'

'You know what that means?'

'What?'

'I may have to show who was really driving the car.'

She thought that over for a minute, then raised her chin. 'Go right ahead, Mr Mason. You do anything that will help Ted.'

'This case may have a lot more to it than you think,' Mason told her. 'Do you want to tell me anything?'

'I drove the car,' she said.

'Was that the reason you came to me?'

'No.'

'Why?'

'On account of Ted. Oh, please, Mr Mason, don't let anything happen to him. I don't only mean about the car; I mean–lots of things.'

'Such as what?' Mason asked.

'Ted's being exposed to influences that aren't good.'

'Why aren't they good?'

'I can't tell you all of it,' she said. 'Mr Addison Balfour is a wonderful man, but he's an old man. He's a sick man. He's a grim man. He looks at life as a battle. He was never married. He regrets that fact now, not because he realizes that he missed a lot of love, but only because he has no son to carry on the Balfour business.

'He wants to make Ted a second Addison Balfour. He wants to make him a grim, uncompromising, unyielding fighter.

'Ted's young. His vision, his ideals are younger and clearer than those of Addison Balfour. He sees the beauties of life. He can enjoy a sunset or the soft spring sunlight on green hills. He sees and loves beauty everywhere. It would be a tragic mistake to make him into a grim, fighting machine like Addison Balfour.'

'Any other influences?' Mason asked.

'Yes.'

'What?'

'The influence of beauty,' she said.

'I thought you said you wanted him to appreciate beauty.'

'Real beauty, not the spurious kind.'

'Who's the spurious beauty?' Mason asked.

'Dorla.'

'You mean to say she's married to his uncle and has her eyes on the nephew?'

'She has big eyes,' Marilyn Keith said. 'Oh, Mr Mason, I *do* so hope you can handle this thing in such a way that . . . well, give Ted an opportunity to develop his own individuality in his own way. There'll be lots of time later on for him to become as grim as Addison Balfour, and a lot of time later on for him to become disillusioned about women.

'And if Guthrie Balfour should think that Ted and Dorla . . . Mr Mason, you're a lawyer. You know the world.'

'What you have outlined,' Mason said, 'or rather, what you have hinted at, sounds like quite a combination.'

'That,' she said, 'is a masterpiece of understatement. You haven't met Banner Boles yet.'

'Who's he?'

'He's the trouble shooter for the Balfour interests. He's deadly and clever, and whenever he's called in he starts manipulating facts and twisting things around so you don't know where you're at. Oh, Mr Mason, I'm terribly afraid!'

'For yourself!'

'No, for Ted.'

'You may not be in the clear on this thing,' Mason said, his voice kindly, 'and now that I'm representing Ted, I may have to drag you in.'

'Drag me in if it will help Ted.'

'Does he know you drove him home?'

'He's never intimated it if he does.'

'What happened?'

'He was out in the parking space back of Florence Ingle's place. He wasn't drunk. He was sick. I knew he couldn't drive in that condition. I saw him trying to back the car. He was barely able to sit up.'

'Did you speak to him?'

'I just said, 'Move over,' and I got behind the steering wheel and drove him home.'

'What happened?'

'The last part of that trip he was falling over against me, and I'd have to push his weight away so I could drive the car. He'd fall against the wheel. I guess I was going all over the road there on Sycamore Road, but I didn't hit anyone, Mr Mason. That is, I don't *think* I did. I kept my eyes on the road. I tried to, but he would lurch against me and grab the wheel. I should have stopped, but I wasn't driving fast.'

'You put him to bed?'

'I had a terrible time. I finally got him to stagger up to his room. I took his shoes off. I tried to find a servant, but there didn't seem to be anyone at home.'

'What time was this?'

'A lot earlier than Myrtle Haley said it was.'

Mason was thoughtful. 'How did you get home? If you called a cab we may be able to find the driver and establish the time element by–'

'I didn't call a cab, Mr Mason. I was afraid that might be embarrassing to Ted–a young woman leaving the house alone, the servants all away. I walked to the highway and thumbed a ride. I told the man who picked me up a story of having to walk home.'

Mason looked at her sharply.

'There was no reason why any young woman couldn't have called a cab from that house at ten-thirty or eleven at night.'

'Don't you see?' she pleaded. 'I'm not just any young woman. I'm Addison Balfour's confidential secretary. I know the contents of his will. If he thought I had any interest in Ted . . . or that I had been in Ted's room–Oh, Mr Mason, please have confidence in me and *please* protect my secret!

'I have to go now. I don't want the girls in the office to get suspicious. I'm supposed to be letting you use the phone. The switchboard operator will know how long it's been since you hung up. Good-bye now.'

Mason left Addison Balfour's residence, stopped at the first telephone booth, called Paul Drake, said, 'I can talk now, Paul. Here's your first job. Find out where Ted Balfour is. Get him out of circulation. Keep him out of circulation. Get in touch with me as soon as you have him and–'

'Whoa, whoa,' Drake said. 'Back up. You're not playing tiddlywinks. This is for high stakes, and it's for keeps.'

'What do you mean?' Mason asked.

'Hell!' Drake said. 'The police had Ted in custody within fifteen minutes of the time the autopsy surgeon picked up the telephone and made his first preliminary report about the bullet.'

'Where are they keeping him?' Mason asked.

'That's something no one knows,' Drake said.

'How about the press, Paul?'

'Figure it out for yourself, Perry. Here's the only heir to the Balfour fortune charged with a murder rap which was dressed up to look like a hit-and-run accident. What would you do if you were a city editor?'

'Okay,' Mason said wearily. 'Get your men working. I'm on my way to the office.'

10

Mason hurried to his office and started mapping out a plan of campaign before he had even hung up his hat.

'Paul,' he said to the detective, 'I want to find out everything I can about Jackson Eagan.'

'Who doesn't?' Drake said. 'If they'd been on the job, police would have spotted this as a murder right at the start. I've seen photographs of the body, Perry. You don't smash up a man's head like that in a hit and run. That man had been tied to a car somehow and his face had literally been dragged over the road. His head was then smashed in with a sledge hammer or something. It was done so the authorites would never think to look for a bullet.

'It worked, too. They thought the guy had been hit, his head dashed to the pavement and then his clothes had caught on the front bumper and he'd been dragged for a while.'

'Couldn't it have been that way?' Mason asked.

'Not with the bullet in the guy's brain,' Drake said.

'All right,' Mason told him, 'let's use our heads. The police are concentrating on Ted Balfour. They're trying to get admissions from him.

They're trying to check what he was doing on the night of the nineteenth of September. They'll be putting all sorts of pressure on him to make him disclose the identity of the girl whom he remembers as having driven the car.

'There's just a chance that by using our heads we may have just a few minutes' head start on the police on some of these other angles that they won't think of at the moment.

'Now, these car rental agencies won't rent a car unless they see a driver's licence, and they usually make a note on the contract of the number of the driver's licence. Have operatives cover the car rental agency, take a look at the contract covering the Jackson Eagan car on that date. See if we can get the number of the driver's licence from the contract.

'There's a chance we can beat the police to it in another direction. The police won't be able to get in the Balfour house until they get a search warrant or permission from Ted Balfour. Quite frequently you can tell a lot by going through a man's room. They'll be searching his clothes for bloodstains. They'll be looking for a revolver. They'll be doing all of the usual things within a matter of minutes, if they aren't doing it already.

'Della, get Mrs Guthrie Balfour on the phone for me. Paul, get your men started covering all these other angles.'

Drake nodded, said, 'I'll go down to my office, so I won't be tying up your telephone system, Perry. I'll have men on the job within a matter of seconds.'

'Get going,' Mason said.

In the meantime, Della Street's busy fingers had been whirring the dial of the unlisted telephone which was used in times of emergency to get quick connections. A moment later she nodded to Perry Mason and said, 'I have Mrs Balfour on the line.'

Mason's voice showed relief. 'That's a break,' he said. 'I was afraid she might be out.'

'Mason picked up the telephone, said, 'Hello, Mrs Balfour.'

'Yes, Mr Mason, what is it?'

'There have been some very important and very disturbing developments in the matter which you discussed with me.'

'There have?' she asked, apprehension in her voice.

'That's right.'

'You mean . . . you mean that the matter has been–Why I thought–'

'It doesn't have anything to do with that matter, but a development from it,' Mason said. 'The police are now investigating a murder.'

'A murder!'

'That's right. I don't want to discuss it on the phone.'

'How can I see you?'

Mason said, 'Wait there. Don't go out under any circumstances. I'm coming over as soon as I can get there.'

Mason slammed up the telephone, said to Della Street, 'Come on, Della. Bring a notebook and some pencils. Let's go!'

Mason's long legs striding rapidly down the corridor forced Della Street into a half run in order to keep up. They descended in the elevator, hurried over to Mason's car in the parking lot, and swung into traffic.

'Do you know the way?' Della Street asked.

'Fortunately I do,' Mason said. 'We go out the State Highway. The scene of the accident was only about a mile from the Balfour estate, and maps were introduced in the case yesterday. You see, the prosecution was trying to prove that Ted Balfour would normally have used this route along Sycamore Street to the State Highway, then turned up State Highway until he came to the next intersection, which would have been the best way to the Balfour estate.'

'If there was a murder,' Della Street said, 'how can they prove that Ted Balfour was in on it?'

'That's what they're *trying* to do right now,' Mason said. 'They have a pretty good case of circumstantial evidence, indicating that Balfour's *car* was mixed up in it, but they can't prove Balfour was mixed up in it at least, not from any evidence they had yesterday.'

'So what happens?'

'So,' Mason said, '*we* try to find and appraise evidence before the police think to look for it.'

'Isn't it illegal to tamper with evidence in a case of this sort?'

'We're not going to tamper with evidence,' Mason said. 'We're going to *look* at it. Once the police get hold of it, they'll put it away and we won't be able to find out anything until we get to court. But if we get a look at it first, we'll know generally what we're up against.'

'You think some evidence may be out there?' Della Street asked.

'I don't know,' Mason told her. 'I hope not. Let's look at it this way, Della: the man was shot. The body was mutilated to conceal the gunshot wound and prevent identification. Then it was taken out and placed by the side of the road. They waited for the tipsy driver to come along and then they threw the body out in front of the car.'

'Why do you say "they"?' Della Street asked.

'Because one man wouldn't be juggling a body around like that.'

'Then Ted Balfour may have simply been the means to an end?'

'Exactly.'

'But how did they know that a tipsy driver *would* be coming along that road?'

'That's the point,' Mason said. 'Somebody loaded Balfour's drink. He probably wasn't only intoxicated; he was doped.'

'Then how do you account for his testimony that a girl was driving the car?' Della Street asked.

'That was probably a coincidence. It *may* not be the truth.'

'That was Ted's story,' Della Street said.

'Exactly. Myrtle Anne Haley swore that she was following a car that was weaving all over the road. The prosecutor didn't ask her who was driving the car, whether it was a man or a woman, whether there was one person in the driver's seat, or whether there were two.'

'And all those head injuries,' Della Street asked, 'were simply for the purpose of preventing the corpse from being identified?'

'Probably for the primary purpose of concealing the fact that there was a bullet hole in the head.'

'Would Ted Balfour have been mixed up in anything like that?'

'He could have been. We don't know. We don't know the true situation. Myrtle Haley is lying at least about some things. But that doesn't mean *all* of her testimony is false. I think she wrote down that licence number sometime after she got home. I think she wrote it down in good light and while she was seated at a table. But her testimony may well be true that she was following a car which was weaving all over the road.'

'Then Ted must have been driving it?'

'Don't overlook one other possibility,' Mason said. 'Ted may have been sent home and put to bed in an intoxicated condition, and then someone took the automobile out of the garage, started weaving all over the road as though driving in an intoxicated condition, waited until he was certain some car behind him would spot him and probably get the licence number, then the dead body of Jackson Eagan was thrown in front of the automobile.'

'But why?' Della Street asked.

'That,' Mason said, 'is what we're going to try to find out.'

On two occasions after that Della Street started to say something, but each time, glancing up at the lawyer's face, she saw the expression of extreme concentration which she knew so well, and remained silent.

Mason slowed at the intersection, turned from State Highway, ran for about two hundred yards over a surfaced road, and turned to the right between huge stone pillars marking the driveway entrance in a stucco wall which enclosed the front part of the Balfour estate.

The tyres crunched along the gravelled driveway, and almost as soon as Mason had brought his car to a stop, the front door was thrown open by Mrs Guthrie Balfour.

Mason, followed by Della Street, hurried up the steps.

'What is it?' she asked.

'Have the police been here yet?' Mason asked.

'Heavens, no!'

'They're coming,' Mason said. 'We're fighting minutes. Let's take a look in Ted's room.'

'But why, Mr Mason?'

'Do you know a Jackson Eagan?'

'Jackson Eagan,' she repeated. 'No, I don't believe so.'

'Ever hear of him?' Mason asked.

She shook her head, leading the way up a flight of steps. 'No,' she said over her shoulder, I'm quite certain I haven't heard of any Jackson Eagan. Why?'

'Jackson Eagan,' Mason said, 'is the corpse. He registered at the Sleepy Hollow Motel. He was murdered.'

'How?'

'A bullet in the head.'

'Are they certain?'

'The bullet was still there when the body was exhumed.'

'Oh,' she said shortly.

She fairly flew up the wide oaken staircase, then hurried down a wide corridor and flung open the door of a spacious corner bedroom. 'This is Ted's room,' she said.

Mason regarded the framed pictures on the wall–some of them army pictures, some of them college pictures, a couple of gaudy pin-ups. There were pictures of girls fastened to the sides of the big mirror.

In one corner of the room was a gun cabinet with glass doors. Another locker contained an assortment of golf clubs and two tennis rackets in presses.

Mason tried the door of the gun cabinet. It was locked.

'Got a key to this?' he asked her.

She shook her head. 'I don't know much about this room, Mr Mason. If it's locked, Ted would have the only key.'

Mason studied the lock for a moment, then opened his penknife and started pushing with the point against the latch of a spring lock, biting the point of the knife into the brass, and moving the lock back as far as he could.

'I've got to have something to hold this lock,' he said after a moment.

'How about a nail-file?' Della Street asked, producing a nail-file from her purse.

'That should do it,' Mason said.

He continued prying the latch back with his knife, holding it in position with the point of the nail-file until he could get another purchase on the lock with the knife point. After a few moments the latch clicked back and the door swung open.

Mason hurriedly inspected the small-calibre rifles, paying no attention to the shotguns or the high-powered rifles.

'Well?' she asked, as Mason smelled the barrels.

'None of them seems to have been freshly fired,' Mason said. 'Of course, they could have been cleaned.'

He opened a drawer in the cabinet, disclosing half a dozen revolvers. He pounced on a ·22 automatic, smelled the end of the barrel thoughtfully.

'Well?' Mrs Balfour asked.

Mason said. 'This could be it.'

He replaced the ·22, pushed the drawer shut, closed the glass doors of the cabinet. The spring lock latched into place.

Mason opened the door to the tile bathroom, looked inside, opened the door of the medicine cabinet, opened the door of the closet, and regarded the long array of suits.

'There had been a going-away party in honour of your husband and you the night of September nineteenth?' Mason asked.

She nodded.

'That's when Ted Balfour got–'

'Became indisposed,' she interrupted firmly.

'Became indisposed,' Mason said. 'Do you know what clothes he was wearing that night?'

She shook her head. 'I can't remember.'

'Was it informal or black tie?'

'No, it was informal. You see, my husband was leaving on a train for Mexico.'

'You accompanied him?'

'Yes. He had intended to go alone and have me ride with him only as far as the Pasadena-Alhambra station. But at the last minute he changed his mind and asked me to go all the way. I didn't have a thing to wear. I . . . well, I was a little put out.'

Della Street said, 'Good heavens! I can imagine you would be annoyed, starting out without . . . You mean, you didn't have a *thing*?'

'Not even a toothbrush,' she said. 'I had a compact in my handbag and fortunately I had a very small tube of cream that I use to keep my skin soft when the weather is hot and dry. Aside from that, I just had the clothes I was standing in. Of course, it wasn't too bad. I was able to pick up an outfit at El Paso, and then I got some more clothes at Chihuahua.

'My husband is an ardent enthusiast when it comes to his particular hobby. He had received some information on new discoveries to be made in the Tarahumare country in Mexico. Those Tarahumare Indians are very primitive and they live in a wild country, a region of so-called barrancas, which are like our Grand Canyon, only there are hundreds and hundreds of miles of canyon–'

'What's this?' Mason asked, pouncing on a heavy, square package at the far end of the closet.

'Heavens! I don't know. It looks like some kind of an instrument.'

'It's a tape-recorder,' Mason said, 'and here's something else that apparently goes with it. Does Ted go in for hi-fi?'

She shook her head. 'Not unless it's something new with him. He's not much on music. He goes in more and more for outdoor sports. He wanted to go with my husband on this trip, and Guthrie almost decided to take him, but because of Addison's condition and because my husband felt that Addison wouldn't like having Ted go on the expedition, it was decided Ted should remain here. I now wish to heaven we'd taken him!'

'Ted didn't like the decision?'

'He was very disappointed, Mr Mason.'

'All right,' Mason said. 'Let's be brutally frank. Do you have an alibi for the night of the nineteenth?'

'Heavens, yes, the best in the world. I was on the train with my husband.'

'Well,' Mason said, 'you may be asked–'

He broke off as chimes sounded through the house.

Mason said. 'That may be the police. Are there back stairs?'

She nodded.

Mason said, 'We'll go down the back way. Della, you get my car, drive it around to the garage. I'll get in the car in the garage. Don't tell the officers anything about the stuff I've taken, Mrs Balfour. You'd better go and talk with them yourself.'

Mrs Balfour flashed him a smile. 'We have the utmost confidence in you, Mr Mason. The whole family does.' She glided out of the room.

'Still using her hips,' Della Street said.

'Never mind that,' Mason told her. 'Grab that other package. I'll take this.'

'Chief, are we supposed to do this?'

'It depends on how you look at it.' Mason told her. 'Come on. Let's get down the back stairs. I'll walk over to the garage. Della, you walk around the front of the house very innocently and very leisurely. If there's an officer sitting in the car out in front, flash him a smile. If the car is empty, as I hope will be the case, you can be in a little more of a hurry than you would otherwise. Drive back to the garage, pick me up and we'll get out of here.'

Mason carried the heavy tape-recorder down the back stairs. Della Street carried the smaller package.

They made an exit through the kitchen, down the steps of the service porch. Mason hurried out towards the garage. Della Street swung to the left around the house, her feet crunching gravel as she walked with a quick, brisk step.

'More casually,' Mason cautioned.

She nodded and slowed down.

Mason turned towards the garage, entered and waited until he saw the car, with Della Street at the wheel, come sweeping around the driveway.

'Police?' Mason asked.

She nodded. 'It's a police car. Red spotlight. Inter-communicating system and–'

'Anyone in it?'

'No.'

Mason grinned. 'That's a break.'

He opened the rear door of the car, put the tape-recorder and the other square package on the back floor, slammed the door shut, jumped in beside Della and said, 'Let's go!'

Della Street swung the car in a swift circle, poured gas into the motor as she swept down the curving driveway.

'Okay,' Mason cautioned. 'Take it easier now as we come out on this road. Don't try to make a left turn. We may run into more police cars. Turn right and then make another right turn a mile or so down here. That'll be Chestnut Street and that will bring us to Sycamore Road. We can get back on that.'

Della made a right turn as she left the driveway.

Perry Mason, looking back through the rear window of the car, suddenly whirled his head, settled down in the seat.

'Something?' Della Street asked.

'Two police cars just turning in from the State Highway,' Mason said. 'Apparently we made it in the nick of time.'

11

Back in his office Mason found a jubilant Paul Drake.

'We're ahead of the police all the way, Perry.'

'How come?'

'That car Jackson Eagan rented,' Drake said, 'there was a driver's licence number on the records.'

'What was it?'

'Licence number Z490553,' Drake said.

'Able to trace it?'

'There again we had success. I got in touch with my correspondent in Sacramento. He rushed a man down to the motor vehicle department. That is the number of a driving licence issued to Jackson Eagan, who lives in Chico, a city about two hundred miles north of San Francisco in the Sacramento Valley.'

'You have the address?'

'I have the address,' Drake said. 'I have the guy's physical description from the driver's licence and our correspondent in Chico is checking on Jackson Eagan right now.'

'What's the description?' Mason asked.

Drake read off his notes: 'Male, age 35, height 5′ 10″, weight 175 pounds, hair dark, eyes blue.'

'That helps,' Mason said. 'Now tell me, Paul, what the devil is this?'

Mason removed the cover from the tape-recorder.

'That's a darn good grade of a high-fidelity tape-recorder,' Drake said. 'It has variable speeds. It will work at one and seven-eighths inches a second, or at three and three-quarter inches a second. At one and seven-eighths inches a second it will run for three hours on one side of a spool of long-playing tape.'

'You understand how this particular model works?' Mason asked.

'Perfectly. We use them in our work right along. This is a high-grade model.'

'All right,' Mason said, 'let's see what's recorded on this tape.'

'It's the latest long-playing tape,' Drake said, plugging in the machine. 'You get an hour on one of these spools at three and three-quarter inches to the second, or an hour and a half if you use the long-playing tape. At one and seven-eighths inches per second you get three hours on one side of the tape.'

'What's the reason for the difference in speed?' Mason asked.

'Simply a question of fidelity. You use seven and a half inches for music, three and three-quarter inches for the human voice where you want high fidelity, but you can get a very satisfactory recording at one and seven-eighths.'

'Okay,' Mason said. 'Let's see what's on the tape.'

'I guess the machine's warmed up enough now,' Drake said.

He threw a switch.

The spool of tape began to revolve slowly, the tape being taken up on the other spool, feeding through the listening head on the machine.

'Seems to be nothing,' Drake said after a moment.

'Keep on,' Mason said. 'Let's be certain.'

They sat watching the tape slowly move through the head of the machine for some three or four minutes.

Drake shook his head. 'Nothing on it, Perry.'

Mason regarded the machine in frowning contemplation.

'Of course,' Drake said, 'there might be something on the other side. This is a half-track recording. You record on one side of the tape, then reverse the spools and record on the other half of the tape. That is, the recording track is divided into two segments and–'

'Reverse it,' Mason said. 'Let's see if there's something on the other track.'

Drake stopped the machine, reversed the spool. Again the tape fed through the head of the machine, again there was nothing until suddenly a woman's voice come from the machine said. '. . . fed up with the whole thing myself. You can stand only so much of this gilded–' There followed complete silence.

Drake manipulated the controls on the machine. There was no further sound.

'Well?' Mason asked.

Drake shook his head. 'I don't get it.'

'Let's take a look at this other box,' Mason said. 'What's that?'

Drake opened the box. His eyes suddenly glistened with appreciation. 'This,' he said, 'is *really* something.'

'All right, what is it?'

'A wall snooper,' Drake said.

'What's that, Paul?'

'A very sensitive mike with an electric boosting device. You fasten it to a wall and sounds of conversation in the next room that you can't even hear come in on this mike, are amplified and go on the tape. Then you can plug in earphones, and as the tape goes through a second head, you can hear what's been recorded.

'That's the reason for what we heard on the tape, Perry. The device had been used for a snooping job, then the tape had been fed through the erasing head. They quit erasing on the last few inches of the second half-track and a few words were left.'

Mason thought that over. 'Why would Ted Balfour have been doing a snooping job, Paul?'

'Perhaps a gag,' Drake said. 'Perhaps a girl friend. It could be any one of a hundred things, Perry.'

Mason nodded. 'It could even be that he was checking up on his uncle's new model wife,' he said.

'And the job wound up in murder?' Drake asked.

'Or the job wound up by his having a murder wished on him,' Mason observed.

Knuckles tapped on the exit door of Mason's private office.

'That's my secretary,' Drake said, listening to the rhythm of the code knock.

Della Street opened the door.

'Please give this to Mr Drake,' the secretary said, handing Della a sheet of paper on which there was a typewritten message.

Della Street handed it across to Paul Drake.

'Well, I'll be damned,' Drake said.

'What is it?' Mason asked.

'Telegram from my correspondent in Chico. Listen to this:

'"JACKSON EAGAN WELL-KNOWN TRAVEL WRITER RESIDING THIS CITY. MOVED AWAY. HAD TROUBLE TRACING, BUT FINALLY FOUND RESIDED BRIEFLY AT MERCED THEN WENT TO YUCATAN, WHERE HE DIED TWO YEARS AGO. BODY SHIPPED HOME FOR BURIAL. CLOSED COFFIN. WIRE INSTRUCTIONS."'

Drake ran his fingers through his hair. 'Well, Perry, now we've had everything. Here's a case where the corpse died twice.'

Mason nodded to Della Street. 'Get out blanks for a petition for habeas corpus,' he said. 'We're going to file a habeas corpus for Ted Balfour. I have a hunch that it's up to me to work out a legal gambit which will keep the real facts in this case from ever being brought out.'

'How the hell are you going to do that?' Drake asked.

Mason grinned. 'There's a chance, Paul.'

'One chance in a million,' Drake said.

'Make it one in five,' Mason told him. 'And let's hope it works, Paul, because I have a feeling that the true facts in this case are so loaded with explosive they could touch off a chain reaction.'

12

Judge Cadwell assumed his seat on the bench, glanced down at the court-room and said, 'Now, this is on habeas corpus in the case of Theodore Balfour. A petition was filed, a writ of habeas corpus issued, and this is the hearing on the habeas corpus. I assume that the writ was applied for in connection with the usual practice by which an attorney who is denied the right to communicate with a client applies for a writ of habeas corpus to force the hand of the prosecutor.'

Roger Farris, the deputy district attorney, arose and said, 'That is correct, Your Honour. We have now filed a complaint on the defendant, accusing him of the crime of murder of one Jackson Eagan, who was then and there a human being, the murder committed with premeditation and malice aforethought, making the crime first-degree murder.

'The prosecution has no objection to Mr Perry Mason, as attorney for the defendant, interviewing the defendant at all seasonable and reasonable times.'

'I can take it then,' Judge Cadwell said, glancing down at Perry Mason, 'it may be stipulated that the writ can be vacated and the defendant remanded to the custody of the sheriff.'

'No, Your Honour,' Mason said.

'What?' Judge Cadwell rasped.

'No such stipulation,' Mason said.

'Well, the Court will make that ruling anyway,' Judge Cadwell snapped. 'It would certainly seem that if this man is charged with murder–Now, wait a minute. The Court will not accept the statement of the prosecutor to that effect. You had better be sworn as a witness, Mr Prosecutor, unless the facts appear in the return to the writ on file in this court.'

'They do, Your Honour. The facts are undisputed. Even if they weren't, the Court could take judicial cognizance of its own records.'

'Very well,' Judge Cadwell said.

'May I be heard?' Mason asked.

'I don't see what you have to be heard about, Mr Mason. You surely don't contend that where a petitioner has been formally charged with the crime of first-degree murder and has been duly booked on that crime that he is entitled to be released on habeas corpus, do you?'

'In this case, Your Honour, Yes.'

'What's the idea?' Judge Cadwell asked. 'Are you being facetious with the Court, Mr Mason?'

'No, Your Honour.'

'Well, state your position.'

'The Constitution,' Mason said, 'provides that no man shall be twice put in jeopardy for the same offence. Your Honour quite recently reviewed the evidence in the case of People versus Balfour and found him guilty of involuntary manslaughter.'

'That was committed with an automobile,' Judge Cadwell said. 'As I understand it, this is an entirely difference case.'

'It may be an entirely different case,' Mason said, 'but the prosecution is barred because this man has already been tried and convicted of the crime of killing this same Jackson Eagan.'

'Now just a minute,' Judge Cadwell said as the prosecutor jumped to his feet. 'Let me handle this, Mr Prosecutor.

'Mr Mason, do you contend that because the People mistakenly assumed that this was a hit-and-run case and prosecuted the defendant under such a charge, the People are now barred from prosecuting him for first-degree murder–a murder which, so far as the record in the present case discloses, was perpetrated with a lethal weapon? I take it that is a correct statement, is it not, Mr Prosecutor?'

'It is, Your Honour,' Roger Farris said. 'It is our contention that Jackson Eagan was killed with a bullet which penetrated his brain and caused almost instant death. We may state that the evidence supporting our position is completely overwhelming. The bullet went into the head but did not emerge from the head. The bullet was found in the brain when the body was exhumed and that bullet has been compared by ballistics experts with a weapon found in the bedroom of Theodore Balfour, the defendant. The fatal bullet was discharged from that weapon.

'It was quite apparent what happened. An attempt was made to dispose of the victim by having it appear that the man had died as the result of a hit-and-run accident.

'We are perfectly willing, if Mr Mason wishes, to move to dismiss the former charge of involuntary manslaughter against Mr Balfour so that he can be prosecuted on a charge of first-degree murder.'

'I don't request any such thing.' Mason said. 'The defendant has been tried, convicted, and sentenced for the death of Jackson Eagan.'

'Now just a minute.' Judge Cadwell said. 'The Court is very much concerned with this point raised by Mr Mason. The Court feels that point is without merit. A man who has been tried for involuntary manslaughter committed with a car cannot claim that such a prosecution is a bar to a prosecution for first-degree murder committed with a gun.'

'Why not?' Mason asked.

'Why not!' Judge Cadwell shouted. 'Because it's absurd. It's ridiculous on the face of it.'

'Would the Court like to hear authorities?' Mason asked.

'The Court would very much like to hear authorities,' Judge Cadwell said, 'if you have any that bear upon any such case as this.'

'Very well,' Mason said. 'The general rule is that where a person is indicated for murder, the charge includes manslaughter. In other words, if a man is charged with first-degree murder it is perfectly permissible for a jury to find him guilty of manslaughter.'

'That is elemental,' Judge Cadwell said. You certainly don't need to cite authorities on any such elemental law point, Mr Mason.'

'I don't intend to,' Mason said. 'It therefore follows that if a man is tried for first-degree murder and is acquitted, he cannot subsequently be prosecuted for manslaugher involving the same victim.'

'That also is elemental,' Judge Cadwell said. 'The Court doesn't want to waste its time or the time of counsel listening to any authorities on such elemental points.'

'Then perhaps,' Mason said, 'Your Honour would be interested in the Case of People versus McDaniels, 137 Cal. 192 69 Pacific 1006 92 American State Reports 81 59 L.R.A. 578, in which it was held that while an acquittal for a higher offence is a bar to any prosecution for a lower offence necessarily contained in the charge, the converse is also true, and that conviction for a lower offence necessarily included in the higher is a bar to subsequent prosecution for the higher.

'The Court should also study the Case of People versus Krupa, 64 C.A. 2nd 592 149 Pacific 2nd 416, and the Case of People versus Tenner, 67 California Appelate 2nd 360 154 Pacific 2nd page 9, wherein it was held that while Penal Code Section 1023 in terms applies where the prosecution for the higher offence is first, the same rule applies where the prosecution for the lesser offence comes first.

'It was also held in the Case of People versus Ny Sam Chung, 94. Cal. 304 29 Pacific 642 28 American State Reports 129, that a prosecution for a minor offence is a bar to the same act subsequently charged as a higher crime.'

Judge Cadwell regarded Mason with frowning contemplation for a moment, then turned to the prosecutor. 'Are the people prepared on this point?' he asked.

Roger Farris shook his head. 'Your Honour,' he said, 'I am not prepared upon this point because, frankly, it never occurred to me. If it had occurred to me, I would have instantly dismissed it from my mind as being too utterly absurd to warrant any serious consideration.'

Judge Cadwell nodded. 'The Court feels that the point must be without merit,' he said. 'Even if it has some merit, the Court would much rather commit error in deciding the case according to justice and the equities, rather than permit what might be a deliberate murder to be condoned because of a pure technicality.'

'I would like to suggest to the Court,' Mason said, 'that it would be interesting to know the theory of the prosecution. Is it the theory of the prosecution that if the jury in this case should return a verdict of guilty of manslaughter, and the Court should sentence the defendant to prison, the prosecution could then file another charge of murder against the defendant and secure a second punishment?'

'Certainly not!' Farris snapped.

'If you had prosecuted this man for murder originally,' Mason said, 'and the jury had returned a verdict of not guilty, would it be your position that you could again prosecute him on a charge of involuntary manslaughter?'

'That would depend,' Farris said, suddenly becoming cautious. 'It would depend upon the facts.'

'Exactly,' Mason said, grinning. 'Once the defendant has been placed on trial, jeopardy has attached. Once the defendant has been convicted and sentenced, he has paid the penalty demanded by law. If the prosecution, as a result of poor judgment, poor investigative work, or poor thinking, charges the man with a lesser offence than it subsequently thinks it might be able to prove, the prior case is nevertheless a bar to a prosecution for a higher offence at a later date.'

Judge Cadwell, said, 'The court is going to take a sixty-minute recess. The Court wants to look up some of these authorities. This is a most unusual situation, a most astounding situation. I may state that as soon as I heard the contention of the defendant, I felt that the absurdity of that contention was so great that it amounted to sheer legal frivolity. But now that I think the matter over and appreciate the force of the defendant's contention, it appears that there may well be merit to it.

'Looking at it from a broad standpoint, the defendant was charged with unlawful acts causing the death of Jackson Eagan. To be certain, those acts were of an entirely different nature from the acts now complained of, but they brought about the same result, to wit, the unlawful death of Jackson Eagan.

'The defendant was prosecuted on that charge and he was convicted. Is it possible, Mr Prosecutor, that this whole situation was an elaborate set-up by the defendant in order to escape the penalties of premeditated murder?'

'I don't know, Your Honour,' Farris said. 'I certainly wouldn't want to make a definite charge, but here is a situation where legal ingenuity of a high order seems to have been used to trap the prosecution into a most unusual situation. Looking back on the evidence in that hit-and-run case, it would seem almost a suspicious circumstance that the witness, Myrtle Anne Haley, so promptly and obligingly wrote down the licence number of the car of the defendant, Ted Balfour.

'The situation is all the more significant when one remembers that the witness in question is employed by a subsidiary of the Balfour Allied Associates. Frankly our office was amazed when she came forward as such a willing informant.'

Judge Cadwell pursed his lips, looked down at Perry Mason thoughtfully. 'There *is* some evidence here of legal ingenuity of a high order,' he said. 'However, present counsel did not try that hit-and-run case.'

'But present counsel did sit in court after the case got under way,' Farris pointed out. 'He did not sit in the bar, but sat as a spectator–a very interested spectator.'

Judge Cadwell loooked once more at Perry Mason.

'I object to these innuendoes, Your Honour,' Mason said. 'If the prosecution can prove any such preconceived plan or conspiracy on the part of the defendant to mislead the authorities and bring about a trial for a lesser charge, the situation will be different; but it would have to amount to a fraud on the Court brought about with the connivance of the defendant, and there would have to be *proof* to establish that point.'

'The Court will take a sixty-minute recess,' Judge Cadwell said. 'The Court wants to look into these things. This is a most unusual situation, a very unusual situation. The Court is very reluctant to think that any interpretation of the law could be such that a defence of once in jeopardy could, under circumstances such as these, prevent a prosecution for first-degree murder.'

'And may the Court make an order that I be permitted to communicate with the defendant during the recess?' Mason asked. 'The defendant was arrested and has been held incommunicado so far as any worthwhile communication with counsel, with family or friends is concerned.'

'Very well,' Judge Cadwell ruled. 'The sheriff will take such precautions as he may see fit, but during the recess of the Court Mr Mason will be permitted to communicate with his client as much as he may desire.'

'I can put the defendant in the witness room,' the deputy said, 'and Mr Mason can communicate with him there.'

'Very well,' Judge Cadwell said. 'I don't care how you do it, but it must be a communication under such circumstances that the defendant can disclose any defence he may have to the charge and have an opportunity to receive confidential advice from his attorney. That means that no attempt should be made to audit the conversation in any manner.'

'Court will take a recess for one hour.'

Mason motioned to Ted Balfour. 'Step this way, if you please, Mr Balfour.'

Roger Farris, his face showing his consternation, hurried to the law library in a panic of apprehension.

13

Balfour, a tall, wavy-haired young man who seemed ill at ease, seated himself across the table from Perry Mason. 'Is there any chance you can get me out of this mess without my having to go on the witness stand?'

Mason nodded.

'That would be wonderful, Mr Mason.'

Mason studied the young man. He saw a big-boned flat-waisted individual whose slow-speaking, almost lethargic manner seemed somehow to serve as a most effective mask behind which the real personality was concealed from the public gaze.

Mason said, 'Suppose you tell me the truth about what happened on the night of September nineteenth and the early morning of September twentieth.'

Balfour passed a hand over his forehead. 'Lord, how I wish I knew!' he said.

'Start talking and tell me everything you do know.' Mason said impatiently, 'You're not dealing with the police now. I'm your lawyer and I have to know what we're up against.'

Ted Balfour shifted his position. He cleared his throat, ran an awkward hand through his thick, wavy, dark hair.

'Go on,' Mason snapped. 'Quit stalling for time. Start talking!'

'Well,' Ted Balfour said, 'Uncle Guthrie was going to Mexico. He was going to the Tarahumare country. He's been down there before, sort of scratching the surface, as he expressed it. This time he wanted to get down in some of the barrancas that were so inaccessible that it was reasonable to suppose no other white man had ever been in there.'

'Such country exists?'

'Down in that part of Mexico it does.'

'All right. What happened?'

'Well, Dorla was going to ride as far as Pasadena with him, just to make sure that he got on the train and had his tickets and everything and that there were no last-minute instructions. She was to get off at the Alhambra-Pasadena station, but at the last minute Uncle Guthrie decided he wanted her with him and told her she'd better go along.'

'How long has she been married to your uncle?'

'A little over two years.'

'How long have you been home from the Army?'

'A little over four months.'

'You have seen a good deal of her?'

'Well, naturally, we're all living in the same house.'

'She's friendly?'

'Yes.'

'At any time has she seemed to be overly friendly?'

'What do you mean by that?' Balfour asked, straightening up with a certain show of indignation.

'Figure it out,' Mason told him. 'It's a simple question, and any show of righteous indignation on your part will be a damn good indication to me that there's something wrong.'

Ted Balfour seemed to wilt in the chair.

'Go on,' Mason said, 'answer the question. Was there any indication of over-friendliness?'

Balfour took a deep breath. 'I don't know.'

'What the hell do you mean, you don't know?' Mason blazed. 'Come clean!'

'Uncle Guthrie and Uncle Addison wouldn't like your questions or your manner, if you don't mind my saying so, Mr Mason.'

'To hell with your uncles!' Mason said. 'I'm trying to keep *you* from going to the gas chamber for first-degree murder. As your attorney, I have to know the facts. I want to know what I'm up against.'

'The gas chamber!' Ted Balfour exclaimed.

'Sure. What did you think they did with murderers? Did you think they slapped their wrists or cut off their allowances for a month?'

'But I . . . I didn't do a thing. I don't know anything about this man, Jackson Eagan. I never met him. I surely didn't kill him or anyone else.'

Mason's eyes bored into those of the young man. 'Did Dorla become too friendly?'

Ted Balfour sighed. 'Honest, Mr Mason, I can't answer that question.'

'What do you mean, you can't answer it?'

'Frankly, I don't know.'

'Why don't you know?'

'Well, at times I'd think . . . well . . . it's hard to explain what I mean. She sometimes seems to sort of presume on the relationship, and I'd think she . . . and then again, it would be . . . It's something I just don't know.'

'What did she do?'

'Well, she'd run in and out.'

'Of your room?'

'Yes. It would be different if she were really my aunt. But she's not related at all, and . . . well, there's not any way of really describing what I mean.'

'You never tried to find out? You never made a pass?'

'Heavens, no! I always treated her just as an aunt, but she'd run in and out, and occasionally I'd see her–One night when Uncle Guthrie was away and she thought she heard a noise downstairs, she came to my room to ask me if I'd heard it. It was bright moonlight and she had on a thin, filmy nightgown . . . and she said she was frightened.'

'What did you do?'

'I told her she was nervous and to go back to bed and lock her bedroom door. I said even if someone were downstairs he couldn't bother her if she kept her door bolted and all the stuff was insured.'

'Did your uncle ever get jealous?'

'Of me?'

'Yes.'

'Heavens, no!'

'Is he happy?'

'I've never asked him. He's never confided in me. He's pretty much occupied with his hobby.'

'Look here,' Mason said. 'Was your uncle *ever* jealous of anyone?'

'Not that I know. He kept his feelings pretty much to himself.'

'Did he ever ask you to check on Dorla in any way?'

'Gosh, no! He wouldn't have done that.'

'Suppose he had been jealous. Suppose he thought she was two-timing him?'

'That would be different.'

'All right,' Mason said. 'You have a tape recording machine with a special microphone that's built to flatten up against a wall. Why did you have that and who told you to get it?'

Ted Balfour looked at him blankly.

'Go on,' Mason said. 'Where did you get it?'

'I never got it, Mr Mason. I don't have it.'

'Don't be silly,' Mason told him. 'You have it. It was in your closet. I took it out. Now tell me, how did it get there?'

'Somebody must have put it there. It wasn't mine.'

'You know I'm your lawyer?'

'Yes.'

'And I'm trying to help you?'

'Yes.'

'No matter what you've done, you tell me what it is and I'll do my best to help you. I'll see that you get the best deal you can get, no matter what it is. You understand that?'

'Yes, sir.'

'But you mustn't lie to me.'

'Yes, sir.'

'All right. Have you been lying?'

'No, sir.'

'You've told me the truth?'

'Yes, sir.'

Mason said, 'Let's go back to the night of the nineteenth. Now what happened?'

'My uncle was leaving for Mexico. Dorla was going with him as far as Pasadena. Then Uncle Guthrie changed his mind at the last minute and took Dorla with him. He's funny that way. He has a restless mind. He'll be all enthused about something or some idea, and then he'll change. He'll have a car and like it first rate and then something will happen and he'll trade it in on a new model, usually of a different make.'

'Would he feel that way about women?'

'I guess so, but Aunt Martha died, so he didn't have to trade anything in. I mean, Dorla was a new model. She appealed to him as soon as he saw her.'

'I'll bet she did,' Mason said.

Ted Balfour seemed apologetic. 'I guess that after Aunt Martha died the family sort of expected Uncle Guthrie would marry Florence Ingle. She's a mighty fine woman and they've been friends. But Dorla came along and . . . well, that's the way it was.'

'You don't call her "Aunt Dorla"?'

'No.'

'Why?'

'She doesn't want me to. She says it makes her seem . . . she used a funny word.'

'What was it?'

'De-sexified.'

'So at the last minute and because of something that may have happened on the train, your uncle decided he wouldn't let her stay behind in the same house with you?'

'Oh, it wasn't that! He just decided to take her with him.'

'And she didn't have any clothes with her?'

'No, sir. She purchased things in El Paso.'

'Did you go to the station to see your uncle and Dorla off?'

'Yes, sir.'

'Who else went?'

'Three or four of his intimate friends.'

'How about Marilyn Keith, Addison Balfour's secretary, was she there?'

'She showed up at the last minute with a message Uncle Addison asked her to deliver. She wasn't there to see him off exactly, but to give him the message.'

'Then what happened?'

'Well, there'd been something of a going-away party before.'

'Where was this party held?'

'At Florence Ingle's place.'

'Is she interested in archaeology?'

'I guess so. She's interested in things my uncle is interested in.'

'She knew your uncle for some time before he married Dorla?'

'Oh, yes.'

'And your uncle's close friends felt he might marry this Florence Ingle?'

'That's what I've heard.'

'How does Florence like Dorla?'

'All right, I guess. She's always very sweet to her.'

'Ted, look at me. Look me in the eyes. Now tell me, how does she like Dorla?'

Ted took a deep breath. 'She hates Dorla's guts.'

'That's better. Now, Florence Ingle gave this party?'

'Yes.'

'And you put your uncle and Dorla aboard the train; that is, some of you did?'

'Yes.'

'You left the party to do that?'

'Yes.'

'Where did they take the train?'

'At the Arcade station.'

'And then you went back to the party?'

'Yes.'

'Dorla was to get off the train at the Alhambra-Pasadena station?'

'Yes, sir.'

'And how was she to get back?'

'By taxicab. She was to go back to the house . . . you know, her house.'

'You went back to the Florence Ingle party?'

'Yes.'

'Now, did Marilyn Keith go back there?'

'Yes, she did. Mrs Ingle invited her to come along, and she did.'

'Did you talk with her?'

'Mrs Ingle?'

'No, Marilyn Keith.'

'Some . . . not much. She's a very sweet girl and very intelligent.'

'All this was after dinner?'

'Yes, sir.'

'About what time was it when you got back there?'

'I'd say about . . . oh, I don't know. I guess it was around eight-thirty or nine o'clock when we got back to Florence Ingle's house.'

'And how late did you stay?'

'I remember there was some dancing and a little talk and the party began to break up pretty early.'

'How many people were there?'

'Not too many. Around eighteen or twenty, I guess.'

'And you were not driving your sports car?'

'No, I was driving the big car.'

'Why?'

'Because I was taking Uncle to the train and his baggage was in the car.'

'All right. What happened after you went back to the party?'

'I had two or three drinks, not many. But along about ten o'clock I had a Scotch and soda, and I think that almost immediately after I drank that I knew something was wrong with me.'

'In what way?'

'I began to see double and . . . well, I was sick.'

'What did you do?'

'I wanted to get out in the open air. I went out and sat in the car for a while and then I don't know . . . the next thing I knew I came to in the car. I haven't told anyone else, but Marilyn Keith was driving.'

'Did you talk with her?'

'I asked her what had happened, and she told me to keep quiet and I'd be all right.'

'Then what?'

'I remember being terribly weak. I put my head over on her shoulder and passed out.'

'Then what?'

'The next thing I knew I was in bed. It was four-thirty-five.'

'You looked at your watch?'

'Yes.'

'Where you undressed?'

'Yes.'

'In pyjamas?'

'Yes.'

'Do you remember undressing?'

'No.'

'Did you go out again after Marilyn Keith took you home?'

'Mr Mason, I wish I knew. I haven't told anybody else this, but I just don't know. I must have.'

'Why do you say you must have?'

'Because I had the key to the car.'

'What do you mean?'

'It was in my trousers pocket.'

'Isn't that where you usually keep it?'

'That's where *I* usually keep the key to my car. Whenever I run the car in, I take the key out and put it in my trousers pocket; but I don't think Marilyn Keith would have put it there.'

'You don't leave the cars with keys in them in the garage?'

'No. Everyone in the family has his own key to each of the cars.'

'How well do you know Marilyn Keith?'

'I've seen her a few times in my uncle's office. That's all.'

'Ever been out with her?'

'No.'

'Do you like her?'

'I do now. I'd never noticed her very much before. She's Uncle Addison's secretary. She'd always smile at me and tell me to go right in whenever I went up to visit Uncle Addison. I never noticed her as a woman or thought about her in that way. Then at the party I got talking with her socially and I realized she was really beautiful. Later on, when I got sick . . . I can't describe it, Mr Mason. Something happened. I was leaning on her–I must have been an awful nuisance–and she was so sweet about it, so competent, so considerate. She was sweet.'

'She put you to bed?'

'She took me up to my room.'

'You suddenly realized you liked her?'

'Yes.'

'A little more about Florence Ingle–was she married when your uncle first knew her?'

'Yes.'

'What happened to her husband?'

'He was killed.'

'Where?'

'In a plane crash.'

'A transport plane?'

'No, a private plane. He was doing some kind of prospecting.'

'So Mrs Ingle became a widow, and how long was that before your aunt died?'

'Oh, six months or so, I guess.'

'And after that Florence Ingle resumed her friendship with your uncle?'

'Yes.'

'Then Dorla came along and whisked your uncle right out from under Mrs Ingle's nose?'

'I guess so. I wouldn't want to say.'

'Is there anything else that you think I should know?'

'Just one thing.'

'What?'

'The speedometer on the big car.'

'What about it?'

'There was too much mileage on it.'

'When?'

'The next morning.'

'Why did you notice that?'

'Because I noticed the mileage when we were at the station. The car had to be serviced and I was going to get it serviced. It had turned up an even ten thousand miles as I was driving to the station, and my uncle remarked about it and said that I was to get it serviced. There shouldn't have been over another twenty or twenty-five miles on it at the most.'

'But there was more on it?'

'I'll say there was.'

'How much more?'

'As nearly as I could work it out, about twenty-five miles too much.'

'Did you tell anyone about this?'

'No, sir.'

'Did you tell Howland about it?'

'No, sir.'

'Tell Howland about any of this stuff we've been discussing?'

'No, sir. Howland told me that he didn't want me to tell him anything until he asked me. He said that he liked to fight his cases by picking flaws in the prosecution's case, that if it came to a showdown, where he had to put me on the witness stand, he'd ask me some questions, but he didn't want to know the answers until that became necessary.'

'So you didn't tell him anything?'

'No, sir. I told him I hadn't hit anyone with the car, and that's all.'

'But because you had the key in the pocket of your clothes, and because there was that extra mileage on the car, you think it was taken out again?'

'Yes, sir, because the key was in my *trousers* pocket.'

'But how do you know Marilyn Keith drove you straight home? How do you know that she didn't go out somewhere with you in the car and try to wait until you got sobered up somewhat before she took you home, then decided it was no use and drove you back?'

'I don't know, of course.'

'All right,' Mason said. 'You've given me the information I want. Now sit tight.'

'What's going to happen, Mr Mason? Is the judge going to turn me loose?'

'I don't think so.'

'Mr Mason, do you think I . . . do you think I *could* have killed that man? Could have killed anyone?'

'I don't know,' Mason said. 'Someone got a gun out of your cabinet, killed a man, put in fresh shells, and replaced the gun.'

Ted Balfour said, 'I can't understand it. I . . . I *hope* I didn't go out again.'

'If you had, you certainly wouldn't have taken the gun.'

The young man's silence caught Mason's attention.

'Would you?' he snapped.

'I don't know.'

'What about that gun?' Mason said. 'Did you have it with you?'

'It was in the glove compartment of the car.'

'The hell it was!'

Balfour nodded.

'Now you tell me *why* you had that gun in the glove compartment,' Mason said.

'I was afraid.'

'Of what?'

'I'd been doing some gambling . . . cards. I got in too deep. I was in debt. I'd been threatened. They were going to send a collector. You know what that is, Mr Mason . . . when the boys send a collector. The first time he just beats you up. After that . . . well, you have to pay.'

Mason regarded the young man with eyes that showed sheer exasperation. 'Why the hell didn't you tell me about this before?'

'I was ashamed.'

'Did you tell the police about having the .22 in the car?'

Balfour shook his head.

'About the gambling?'

'No.'

'Did you tell them about the mileage on the speedometer or about having the key to the car in your pocket?'

'No, sir, I didn't.'

'When did you take the gun out of the glove compartment and put it back in the gun cabinet?'

'I don't know. I wish I did. That's another reason I feel certain I must have taken the car out again after Marilyn Keith took me home. Next morning, the gun was in the gun case in the drawer where it belongs. Marilyn certainly wouldn't have taken the gun out of the glove compartment. Even if she had, she wouldn't know where I keep it. It had been put right back in its regular place in the gun cabinet.'

Mason frowned. 'You could be in one hell of a fix on this case.'

'I know.'

'All right,' Mason said. 'Sit tight. Don't talk with anyone. Don't answer any questions the police may ask you. They probably won't try to get any more information out of you. If they do, refer them to me. Tell them I'm your lawyer and that you're not talking.'

'And you don't think the judge will turn me loose on this technicality?'

Mason shook his head. 'He's struggling between his concept of the law and his conscience. He won't turn you loose.'

'Why did you raise the point?'

'To throw a scare into the prosecutor,' Mason said. 'They know now they have a monkey wrench in the machinery which may strip a few gears at any time. You're just going to have to stand up and take it from now on, Ted.'

'I'll stand up and take it, Mr Mason, but I sure would like to know what happened. I–Gosh! I can't believe that . . . well, I just *couldn't* have killed the man, that's all.'

'Sit tight,' Mason said. 'Don't talk with newspaper reporters, don't talk with police, don't talk with anyone unless I'm present. I'll be seeing you.'

Thirty minutes later Judge Cadwell returned to court and proceeded with the habeas corpus hearing.

'Surprisingly enough, this technical point seems to have some merit,' the judge ruled. 'It comes as a shock to the Court to think that a defendant could place himself behind such a barricade of legal technicality.

'However, regardless of the letter of the law, there are two points to be considered: I can't dismiss the possibility that this whole situation has been deliberately engineered so there will be a technical defence to a murder charge. The other point is that I feel a higher court should pass on this matter. If I grant the habeas corpus, the defendant will simply go free. If I hold the defendant for trial by denying the writ, the matter can be taken to a higher court on a plea of once in jeopardy.

'Since a plea of once in jeopardy will presumably be made at the time of the trial of the case, it will be among the issues raised at that trial. This court does not intend to pass on the validity of such a plea of once in jeopardy at this time, except in so far as it applies to this writ of habeas corpus. The Court denies the habeas corpus. The prisoner is remanded to the custody of the sheriff.'

Mason's face was expressionless as he left the courtroom. Paul Drake buttonholed him in the corridor.

'You wanted the dope on that tape recorder,' Drake said. 'I got the serial number, wired the manufacturer, the manufacturer gave me the name of the distributor, the distributor checked his records to the retailer. I finally got what we wanted.'

'Okay,' Mason said. 'Who bought it?'

'A woman by the name of Florence Ingle living out in the Wilshire district. Does that name mean anything to you?'

'It means a lot,' Mason said. 'Where is Mrs Ingle now?'

'I thought you'd ask that question,' Drake said. 'The answer gave us one hell of a job.'

'Where is she?'

'She took a plane. Ostensibly she went on to Miami, then to Atlantic City, but the person who went on to Atlantic City wasn't Mrs Ingle at all. She registered at hotels under the name of Florence Ingle, but it wasn't the same woman.'

'Got a description?' Mason asked.

'Florence Ingle is about thirty-eight, well groomed, small-boned, good figure, rich, a good golfer, brunette, large dark eyes, five feet two, a hundred and seventeen pounds, very gracious, runs to diamond jewellery and is lonely in an aristocratic way. She's rather a tragic figure.

'The woman who impersonated Florence Ingle was something like her, but was heavier and didn't know her way around in the high-class places. She was tight-lipped, self-conscious, overdid everything trying to act the part of a wealthy woman. In the course of time she vanished absolutely and utterly, without leaving a trail. She left a lot of baggage in the hotel, but the bill was paid in full, so the hotel is storing the baggage.'

'Never mind all the build-up,' Mason said. 'Did your men find out where Florence Ingle is now?'

'Yes. It was a hell of a job, Perry. I want you to understand that–'

'I know, I know,' Mason said. 'Where is she?'

'Staying at the Mission Inn at Riverside, California, under the name of Florence Landis, which was her maiden name. She's posing as a wealthy widow from the East.'

'Now,' Mason said, 'we're beginning to get somewhere.'

14

Perry Mason stood at the cigar counter for a few minutes. He lit a cigarette, sauntered across to the outdoor tables by the swimming pool, started towards the entrance of the hotel, thought better of it, stretched, yawned, walked back towards the pool, seated himself in a chair, stretched his long legs out in front of him, and crossed his ankles.

The attractive brunette in the sunsuit who was seated next to him flashed a surreptitious glance from behind her dark glasses at the granite-hard profile. For several seconds she appraised him, then looked away and regarded the swimmers at the pool.

'Would you prefer to talk here or in your room, Mrs Ingle?' Mason asked in a conversational voice, without even turning a glance at her.

She jumped as though the chair had been wired to give her an electric shock, started to get up, then collapsed back in the chair. 'My name,' she said, 'is Florence Landis.'

'That's the name you registered under,' Mason said. 'It was your maiden name. Your real name is Florence Ingle. You're supposed to be on vacation in Atlantic City. Do you want to talk here or in your room?'

'I have nothing to talk about.'

'I think you have,' Mason said. 'I'm Perry Mason.'

'What do you want to know?'

'I'm representing Ted Balfour. I want to know what you know and I want to know *all* you know.'

'I know nothing that would help Ted.'

'Then why the run-around?'

'Because, Mr Mason, what I know would hurt your client. I don't want to do anything to hurt Ted. I'm trying to keep out of the way. Please, *please*, don't press me! If you do, you'll be sorry.'

Mason said, 'I'm sorry, but I have to know what you know.'

'I've warned you, Mr Mason.'

Mason said, 'You can talk to me. You don't have to talk to the prosecution.'

'What makes you think I know anything?'

'When a witness runs away I want to know what she's running away from and why.'

'All right,' she said. 'I'll tell you what it's all about. Ted Balfour killed that man and tried to make it look like an automobile accident.'

'What makes you think so?'

'Because Ted was in a jam. Ted had an allowance and he couldn't afford to exceed it. He got up against it for money and started playing for high stakes, and then he started plunging. He didn't have the money, but his credit was good and . . . well, it's the old story. His cards didn't come in and Ted was left in a terrific predicament.

'If either one of his uncles had known what he was doing, he would have been disinherited–at least Ted thought so. They had him pretty well scared. Personally, I'm convinced that while they might try to frighten the boy, they never would have gone so far as to disinherit him.'

'Go on,' Mason said. 'I take it Ted came to you?'

'Ted came to me.'

'What did he tell you?'

'He told me he had to have twenty thousand dollars. He told me that if he didn't get it, it was going to be just too bad.'

'What made him think so?'

'He had a letter that he showed me.'

'A letter from whom?'

'He knew who had written the letter all right, but it was unsigned.'

'Who had written it?'

'The syndicate.'

'Go on,' Mason said.

'The letter told him that they didn't like welshers. They said that if he didn't get the money, their collector would call.'

'Twenty thousand dollars is a lot of money,' Mason said.

'He never would have got in that deep if they hadn't played him for a sucker. They let him get in deeper than he could pay and then saw that he was dealt with the second-best hands.'

'And then when they had him hooked, they lowered the boom? Is that right?'

'That's right.'

'Did you come through with the twenty thousand?'

'No, I didn't. I wish I had now. I thought Ted had to be taught a lesson. I felt that if he got the money from me, it wouldn't be any time at all until he'd start trying to get the money to pay me back by betting sure things. I felt it was time for Ted to grow up. Oh, Mr Mason, if you only knew how I've regretted that decision!

'Ted was sick over the whole thing. He told me he had a .22 automatic in the glove compartment of his car and he intended to use it. He said that he wasn't going to be waylaid and beaten up and then simply tell the police he didn't have any idea who did it. He said that he was good for the money but that it would take him a while to get it together. There was a trust which had been left him by his parents and he thought he could explain the situation to the trustee, but the trustee was on vacation and he had to have a little more time.'

'All right,' Mason said, 'what happened?'

'The dead man must have been the collector,' she said. 'Don't you see? Ted killed him and then tried to make it look as though the man had been killed in a hit-and-run accident.'

Mason studied her thoughtfully for a moment, then said, 'You told that readily enough.'

'It's the truth.'

'I'm sure it is. I merely said, you told it to me readily enough.'

'I had to. You've trapped me. I don't know how you found me here, but since you found me, I had to tell you what I know, no matter whom it hurts.'

'All right,' Mason said. 'So far, so good. Now tell me the real reason you went to such pains to keep from being questioned.'

'I've told you everything I know.'

'What about the tape recorder?'

'What tape recorder?'

'The one you bought–the wall snooper.'

'I don't know what you're talking about.'

'Come on,' Mason said. 'Come clean!'

'Mr Mason, you can't talk to me like that! You must think I'm someone whom you can push around. Your very manner is insulting. I am a truthful woman, and I am not a woman who is accustomed to being pushed around by–'

Mason reached in the inside pocket of his lightweight business suit, pulled out a folded paper, and dropped it in her lap.

'What's that?' she asked.

'Your copy of a subpoena in the case of People versus Balfour. Here's the original, with the signature of the clerk and the seal of the court. Be there at the time of trial; otherwise be subject to proceedings in contempt of court.'

Mason arose, said, 'I'm sorry I had to do that, but you brought it on yourself, Mrs Ingle. Good-bye now.'

Mason had taken two steps before her voice caught up with him. 'Wait, wait, for heaven's sake, Mr Mason, wait!'

Mason paused, looked back over his shoulder.

'I'll . . . I'll tell you the truth. You can't do this to me, Mr Mason. You can't! You mustn't!'

'Mustn't do what?'

'Mustn't subpoena me in that case.'

'Why?'

'Because if you put me on the stand I . . . it will . . . it will be terrible.'

'Go ahead,' Mason said. 'Keep talking.'

She stood looking at his stern features, her own face white and frightened. 'I don't dare to,' she said. 'I simply don't dare tell anyone.'

'Why not?'

'It's . . . it won't help you, Mr Mason. It will . . . it will be terrible.'

'All right,' Mason said, 'you have your subpoena. Be there in court.'

'But you can't put me on the stand. If I told you what Ted Balfour had asked me to do, if I told about him needing the money and the collector–'

'No one would believe you,' Mason interrupted. 'I've served a subpoena on you. You're trying to get out of circulation. That subpoena is going to smoke you out in the open. The only reason for it is that I want the true story. If you know something that's causing you to take all these precautions, I want to find out what it is.'

She looked at him as though she might be about to faint, then, with difficulty composing herself, she said, 'Come into the bar where we can talk without my making a spectacle of myself.'

'You'll tell me the truth?' Mason asked.

She nodded.

'Let's go,' Mason told her, leading the way to the bar.

'Well?' Mason said after the waiter had gone.

'Mr Mason, I'm protecting someone.'

'I was satisfied you were,' Mason said.

'Someone whom I love.'

'Guthrie Balfour?' Mason asked.

For a moment it appeared she would deny it. Then she tearfully nodded.

'All right,' Mason said. 'Let's have the truth this time.'

'I'm not a good liar, Mr Mason,' she said. 'I never had occasion to do much lying.'

'I know,' Mason said sympathetically.

She had taken off the dark glasses. The eyes that looked at the lawyer were circled with the weariness of sleepless nights and filled with dismay.

'Go on,' Mason said. 'What happened?'

She said, 'Mr Mason, that Dorla Balfour is a scheming, wicked woman who has almost a hypnotic influence over Guthrie Balfour. She's not his type at all. He's wasting himself on her, and yet somehow . . . well, somehow I wonder if she doesn't have some terrific hold on him, something that he can't escape.'

'What makes you think so?' Mason asked.

'She's twisting him around her thumb.'

'Go on.'

'I'll tell you the real story, Mr Mason, the whole story. Please listen and don't interrupt. It's a thoroughly incredible story and I'm not proud of my part in it, but . . . well, it will explain a lot of things.'

'Go ahead,' Mason said.

'Dorla Balfour was and is a little tramp. She was taking Guthrie for everything she could take him for, and believe me, the minute Guthrie Balfour got out of town, she was getting herself in circulation without missing a minute.'

Mason nodded.

'Guthrie had begun to wake up,' she said. 'He wanted a divorce, but he didn't want to get stuck for a lot of alimony. Dorla wouldn't mind a bit if he'd divorce her, but she has her grasping little hand out for a big slice of alimony. She'd go to the best lawyers in the country and she'd make herself just as much of a legal nuisance as is possible. She'd tie up Guthrie's property. She'd get restraining orders. She'd drag him into court on orders to show cause, and she'd . . . well, she'd raise the devil.'

'Meaning that she'd drag your name into it?' Mason asked.

Mrs Ingle lowered her eyes.

'Yes or no?' Mason asked.

'Yes,' she said in a low voice. 'Only there was nothing . . . nothing except sympathy.'

'But you couldn't prove that?' Mason asked.

'She could make nasty insinuations and get notoriety for both of us.'

'Okay,' Mason said, 'now we're doing better. Let's have the story.'

'Well, Guthrie was leaving for Chihuahua City; that is, that's what he told her. Actually, he got on the train at Los Angeles and then left it at the Alhambra-Pasadena station.'

'*He* left it?' Mason asked.

She nodded.

'Why, that's what Dorla was supposed to have done,' Mason said.

'I know,' she said. 'That was all part of the plan he had worked out. When the train stopped at the Pasadena station, he kissed her good-bye and got back aboard the train. The vestibule doors slammed and the train started out, Guthrie sent the porter back on an errand, opened the car door on the other side of the car, and swung to the ground as the train was gathering speed. By the time the train had gone past, Dorla was in a taxicab.'

'And Guthrie?' Mason asked.

'Guthrie jumped in a car he'd rented earlier in the day from a drive-yourself rental agency. He'd parked the car at the station. He followed Dorla.'

'Then, when the train pulled out, neither Guthrie nor Dorla was aboard?'

'That's right.'

'Go ahead. What happened then?'

'Guthrie followed Dorla. Oh, Mr Mason, I'd pleaded with him not to do it. I asked him a dozen times to get some private detective agency on the job. That's their business. But Guthrie had to do this himself. I think he was so utterly fascinated by Dorla that he wouldn't believe anything against her unless he saw it with his own eyes.

'I think he knew the truth, but I think he knew himself well enough to feel she'd be able to talk him out of it unless he saw her himself and had the proof. He wanted proof without any outsiders for witnesses. That's why he asked me to get him that tape recorder. He wanted to record what was happening after she . . . well, you know, after she met the man.'

'Go on,' Mason said. 'What did Dorla do?'

'Drove to the Sleepy Hollow Motel.'

'So then what?'

'She met her boy friend there. They had a passionate reunion.'

'Where was Guthrie?'

'He'd managed to get into the unit that adjoined the one where Dorla's boy friend was staying. He'd put the microphone up to the wall and he had a tape recording of the whole business.'

'You were there with him?'

'Good heavens, no! That would have ruined everything he was trying to do.'

'That's what I thought, but how do you know all this?'

'He phoned me.'

'From Chihuahua?'

'No. Please let me tell it in my own way.'

'Go ahead.'

'After a while Dorla went out. She said she had to go home and let Ted know she was seeking her virtuous couch. She said that she'd pick up a suitcase and be back later in the evening.'

'Then what?'

'That's where Guthrie made the mistake of his life,' she said. 'He thought that he might be able to go into the motel next door, face this man who was registered under the name of Jackson Eagan and put it up to him cold turkey. He thought that this man might get frightened and sign a statement. It was a crazy thing to do.'

'What happened?'

'This man, Eagan, was in a dimly lit motel bedroom. The minute Guthrie walked in Eagan snapped on a powerful flashlight and the beam hit Guthrie right in the face, completely blinding him. Eagan, on the other hand, could see his visitor. He obviously recognized Guthrie, felt certain the irate husband was about to invoke the unwritten law, and threw a chair. He followed it up by hitting the blinded Guthrie with everything he had.

'Guthrie tried to frighten this man by bringing this gun of Ted's that he'd taken from the glove compartment of the car without Ted's knowing it.

'The two men started fighting for the gun. In the struggle the gun went off and Eagan fell to the floor. Guthrie knew from the way he hit the floor he was dead. And all at once Guthrie realized the full implications of the situation. He was afraid someone might have heard the shot and phoned for the police, so he jumped in his car and drove away fast.'

'Then what?'

'Then,' she said, 'Guthrie had this idea. He realized that nobody, except me, knew that he had left the train. He called me from the telephone in his house. He told me everything that had happened. He said that he was going to take the company plane, fly to Phoenix and pick up the train there. He said he'd wire for Dorla to join him at Tucson, and in that way Dorla would have to give him an alibi. He asked me to take a commercial plane to Phoenix and fly his plane back. He said that he would leave a note with the attendant so that I could get the plane, and if I'd do that, well, no one would ever be the wiser.'

'And so?' Mason asked.

'So I did that. I went down to Phoenix the next day. His plane was there and so was the note so that I could get it without any trouble. I flew it back, picked up his rented car where he'd left it at the hangar, and returned it to the rental agency.'

'And Dorla joined him?'

'Dorla must have joined him. Only to hear her tell it, she never got off the train. I know that's a lie because I know from Guthrie what really happened. You can see the whole thing, Mr Mason. He called on her to give him an alibi. He didn't tell her what happened. He didn't need to. When she got her suitcase and returned to the motel, she found her lover boy, Eagan, lying there dead.

'Now, under those circumstances, I know exactly what she'd have done, and it's just what she did. She telephoned for Banner Boles, the ace trouble shooter for Balfour Allied Associates. Boles realized at once that it would be better to have a drunk-driving charge against Ted and try to beat that rap than to have a murder charge against Guthrie. He's unbelievably resourceful and clever.

'So he fixed the whole deal up and Dorla flew to Tucson and picked up the train. Guthrie asked her to swear she'd been on the train all the time. That was right down her alley. Now she has a murder rap on him and she'll bleed him white. There won't be any divorce until she is all ready for it, with a new husband picked out, and she'll strip Balfour of everything he has left when she's ready to cut loose from him.'

'That's all of it?' Mason asked.

'That's all of it,' she said. 'Now you see why I had to get out of circulation. It was all right for a while. It looked like a hit and run. Of course, Ted was mixed up in it, but everyone knew that Ted could get a suspended sentence if he was found guilty.'

'And what did you hear from Guthrie after he went to Mexico?' Mason asked.

'Only this,' she said, fighting to keep her lips straight as she opened her handbag and took out a crumpled wire.

She passed the wire over to Mason. Mason unfolded the yellow paper and read:

'SAY NOTHING OF WHAT HAS HAPPENED. DORLA AND I HAVE REACHED FULL AGREEMENT AND BELIEVE EVERYTHING WILL COME OUT ALL RIGHT IN THE FUTURE.

GUTHRIE'

'That,' Mason said, 'was sent from Chihuahua City?'

She nodded.

'And since that time?'

'Since that time I haven't heard a word. Dorla has been with him, and heaven knows *what* she's done.'

Mason said, 'Would Guthrie Balfour sit back and see Ted convicted of murder?'

'No, of course not, not of murder. He'll come forward if he has to. After all, Mr Mason, it *was* self-defence.'

He'd have a hell of a time proving that now.'

'Well, now you know the facts. What are *you* going to do?'

'There's only one thing I can do,' Mason said.

'What?'

'I'm representing Ted Balfour.'

'You mean you'll blow the whole case wide open?'

'I'll blow the top clean off,' Mason said, 'if I have to.'

She looked at him with angry eyes. 'I played fair with you, Mr Mason.'

'I'm playing fair with my client,' Mason told her. 'That's the only fair play I know.'

'Do you think I'm a complete, utter fool?' she asked. 'You couldn't drag that story out of me on the witness stand no matter *what* you did. I told you so you'd know, so you'd understand what to do. Can't you understand? You're working for the Balfours. They're wealthy. You can have any amount you need as a fee, only fix this thing up so that . . . well, work it out on a basis of legal technicalities so the facts never need to come out.'

Mason got to his feet. 'You already have my answer.'

'What do you mean?' she asked.

'The paper you folded and put in your purse–your subpoena to appear as a witness on behalf of the defendant.'

15

As Perry Mason entered the office, Della Street said, 'We have troubles.'
'What?' Mason asked.
'I don't know. But Addison Balfour telephoned.'
'Personally?'
'Personally.'
'And talked with you?'
'That's right.'
'What did he want?'
'He said that this wasn't the simple case it seemed, that the whole Balfour empire was threatened, that he was going to leave it up to you to work out the best deal possible. He said his right-hand man, Banner Boles, would be in touch with you within a short time, that Boles knew his way around and knew how to handle things.'
'And did he say what the trouble was?'
'No.'
'Or what Banner Boles wanted to see me about?'
'No. It was just to tell you that there was trouble and Boles would be seeing you.'
'Okay,' Mason said, 'I'll see him.'
'How did you come out with Florence Ingle?'
'I had a nice talk with her,' Mason said.
'You don't seem very happy about it.'
'I'm not.'
The phone rang. Della Street answered it, said, 'Yes, just a moment, Mr Boles; I'm quite certain he'll talk with you.' She cupped her hand over the mouthpiece, nodded towards the telephone, and said to Perry Mason, 'This is Banner Boles on the line now.'
Mason picked up the extension phone on his desk, said, 'Yes, hello. This is Perry Mason talking.'
'Banner Boles, Mr Mason,' a hearty voice at the other end of the line said.
'How are you, Mr Boles?'
'Did Addison Balfour telephone you about me?'
'I understand he talked with my office,' Mason said. 'I'm just getting in myself.'
'Well, I want to see you.'
'So I understand. Come on up.'
There was a moment's silence at the other end of the line, then Boles said, 'This is rather a delicate matter, Mr Mason.'
'All right, we'll talk it over.'
'Not in your office, I'm afraid.'
'Why not?' Mason asked.

'I don't go to any man's office with the sort of stuff we're going to talk about.'

'Why not?'

'How do I know it isn't bugged?'

'By me?' Mason asked.

'By anybody.'

'All right,' Mason said. 'Where *do* you want to talk?'

'On neutral grounds,' Boles said laughingly, the good nature of his voice robbing the words of any offence. 'Tell you what I'll do, Mr Mason. I'll come up to your office. As soon as I come in, you leave with me. We'll go downstairs. We'll walk as long as you suggest. Then we'll stop and take the first taxicab that comes by. We'll talk in the taxi.'

'All right,' Mason said. 'Have it your own way.'

He hung up the telephone, said to Della Street, 'One of those things.'

'He's coming in?'

'Coming in,' Mason said. 'And wants to go out where we can talk in privacy.'

'Chief, I'm afraid there's a chance they'll try to frame you if you don't do what they want in this thing. These people are big and they play for keeps.'

'I've had the same thought,' Mason said, pacing the floor.

'You learned something from that Ingle woman, didn't you?'

'Yes.'

'What?'

'Let me think it over a while,' Mason said, and continued pacing the floor. Abruptly he stopped, said to Della Street, 'I want to know everything there is to know about Jackson Eagan.'

'But he's dead.'

'I know he's dead. But I want to know everything about him. All we have is the information from his driver's licence and that telegram from Paul's contact. I want to know what he looked like, where he lived, who his friends were, how it happened he died, where the body's buried, who attended the funeral. I want to know everything.'

'He died in Yucatan, Mexico,' Della said.

Mason said, 'I want Drake to find out who identified the body. I want to find out everything about the guy, and I want a copy of that driving licence of Eagan's. I want to check his thumbprint on the driver's licence with that of the dead man.'

Della Street nodded, went over to the typewriter, typed out a list of the things Mason wanted. The lawyer continued to pace the floor.

Della said, 'I'll take this down the corridor to Paul Drake personally.'

'Have one of the girls take it down,' Mason said. 'I want you waiting here. When Boles comes in I want you to go out and size him up before I have a talk with him.'

'Okay, I'll send one of the girls down right away.' Della Street went to the outer office and was back in a moment, saying, 'I sent Gertie down to Drake's office. Your man, Boles, came in while I was out there in the outer office. I told him I'd tell you he was here.'

'What does he look like?' Mason asked.

'He's rather tall . . . oh, perhaps an inch and a half or two inches under six feet. He's very good-looking, one of those profile guys who holds his chin up high. He has black, wavy hair and very intense blue eyes. He's well dressed and has an air of assurance. You can see he's quite a diplomat.'

'Yes,' Mason said, 'a trouble shooter for the Balfour enterprises would have to be a smart cookie.

'Let's have a look at him, Della. Is he carrying a brief-case?'

She shook her head.

'All right, tell him to come in.'

Della Street went out and escorted Boles to the office. Boles came forward with a cordial smile, gripped Mason's hand in a heavy handshake, said, 'I'm sorry to make a damned nuisance out of myself, Counsellor, but you know how it is. Having the sort of job I do makes things rather difficult at times. Shall we take a walk?'

'Yes,' Mason said. 'We'll go out if you want, but I can assure you it's all right to talk here.'

'No, no, let's take a walk.'

'I see you're not carrying a brief-case.'

Boles threw back his head and laughed. 'You're a smart guy, Mason. I wouldn't pull anything as crude as that on you. I'll admit I have used a concealed tape recorder in a brief-case, but I wouldn't try it with a man of your calibre. Moreover, when I play with men like you, I play fair. I wouldn't want you to try to record my conversation and I'll be damned if I'll try to record yours.'

'Fair enough,' Mason said. He turned to Della Street. 'Della, I'll be back about . . . hang that watch! What time is it, Boles?'

Boles instantly shot out his hand, looked at his wrist-watch, said, 'Ten minutes to three.'

'You're way off,' Mason told him.

'No, I'm not. It's exactly ten minutes to three.'

'Your watch says twelve-thirty,' Mason told him.

Boles laughed. 'You're wrong.'

'Let's take a look,' Mason observed.

'I tell you you're wrong,' Boles said, suddenly losing his smile.

Mason said, 'I either take a look at your wrist-watch, or we don't talk.'

'Oh, all right,' Boles said, unstrapping the wrist-watch, pulling loose two wires and dropping it in his pocket. 'I should have known better than to try it.'

'Any other microphones?' Mason asked. 'How about behind your necktie?'

'Take a look,' Boles invited.

Mason felt behind the necktie, patted the inside pocket of the coat, reached inside, pulled out the small, compact wire recorder, and said, 'Let's take the battery out of this and then I'll feel better.'

'We'll do better than that,' Boles said. '*You* carry the thing in *your* pocket. I'll keep the microphone that's made to look like a wrist-watch.'

'All right,' Mason told him. 'Let's go.'

They walked silently down the corridor to the elevator, rode down the elevator to the street.

'Which way do you want to go?' Boles asked.

'Suit yourself,' Mason told him.

'No, you pick the direction.'

'All right. We'll go up this street here.'

They walked up the street for a couple of blocks. Abruptly Mason stopped. 'All right,' he said, 'Let's catch the first cab that comes along.'

They waited for two or three minutes, then found a cruising cab, climbed inside, and settled back against the cushions.

'Where to?' the driver asked.

'Straight down the street,' Mason told him, 'then turn out of traffic some place. We're closing this window to your compartment because we want to talk.'

'Any particular destination?' the cabdriver asked.

'No. Just drive around until we tell you to turn back.'

'I'm going to keep out of the traffic jams then, if you don't mind.'

'Okay by us,' Mason told him.

The cabdriver pushed the sliding window into place, which shut off the back of the car.

Mason turned to Boles. 'All right,' he said, 'let's have it.'

Boles said, 'I'm the grease in the works of Balfour enterprises. That means I get in lots of tight spots.'

Mason nodded.

'Guthrie Balfour telephoned. He wanted me to fly down and join him in Chihuahua.'

Again Mason nodded.

'Now what I'm going to tell you,' Boles said, 'has to be absolutely confidential. You can't tell anyone anything about it.'

'In talking to me,' Mason said, 'you are talking to a lawyer who is representing a client. I'll make no promises, bind myself to nothing.'

'Remember this,' Boles said ominously. 'You're being paid by the Balfour enterprises.'

'It doesn't make any difference who pays me,' Mason said. 'I'm representing a client.'

Boles regarded him thoughtfully for a moment.

'Does that change the situation?' Mason asked.

'I'm going to tell you certain things,' Boles said. 'If you're smart, you'll play the game my way. If you try to play it any other way, you may get hurt.'

'All right,' Mason said. 'What's the story?'

Boles said, 'You're not to let Mrs Guthrie Balfour know anything about this conversation.'

'She isn't my client,' Mason said, 'but I make no promises.'

'All right,' Boles said, 'here we go. You want to get some dope on Jackson Eagan, don't you?'

'I'm trying to, yes.'

'Here you are,' Boles said, reaching in his pocket. 'Here's Jackson Eagan's driving licence. Here's the carbon copy of the contract that he had with the drive-yourself car agency that rented him the automobile. Here's the receipt for the unit at the Sleepy Hollow Motel. Here's a wallet with some identification cards, some club cards and around two hundred and seventy-five dollars in currency. Here's a key ring containing a bunch of keys. Here's a very valuable wrist watch with a broken crystal. The watch isn't running. It is stopped at one thirty-two.'

Boles took the collection from his pocket, handed it across to Mason.

'What about these?' Mason asked.

'Put them in your pocket,' Boles said.

Mason hesitated a moment, then dropped the assortment into his pocket. 'Where did they come from?' he asked.

'Where do you think?' Boles asked.

Mason flashed a quick glance at the cabdriver, saw the driver was paying no attention to anything except the traffic ahead, then turned to Boles. 'I'm listening.'

'Balfour Allied Associates is a big corporation,' Boles said. 'The stock, however, is held entirely by members of the family. On the other hand, the members of the family have virtually no property except that stock. It's the policy of the Balfour empire to throw everything into the corporation. The members of the family draw substantial salaries. In addition to that, all of their travelling expenses, a good part of their living expenses, and many incidentals are furnished by the company under one excuse or the other, such as entertainment of customers, office rental for homework on Saturdays and Sundays and that sort of stuff.'

'Go ahead,' Mason said.

'You're a lawyer,' Boles went on. 'You can see what a set-up of that kind means. If anything happened and an outsider got a judgement of any sort against one of the Balfours, an execution would be levied on the stock of the individual Balfour. In that way, unless the company made a settlement, there would be a stockholder who was an outsider. No one wants that.'

'To whom are you referring?' Mason asked.

'Dorla Balfour,' Boles said shortly.

'What about her?'

'Addison Balfour is the business brains of the company,' Boles said. 'Guthrie doesn't do very much in connection with the property management. Theodore, who was Ted Balfour's father, was pretty much of a right-hand man for Addison, but Guthrie is a total loss as far as the business is concerned.

'Naturally, when Guthrie remarried and picked up a girl like Dorla, Addison regarded the entire transaction with considerable consternation. He attended the wedding, offered his congratulations, kissed the bride, then very quietly started building up a slush fund in the form of cash which he could use to make a property settlement with Dorla when the time came.'

'Go on,' Mason said.

'However,' Boles said, 'Dorla couldn't even wait to play the game cleverly. She started playing around. I won't go into details. Naturally, Addison while he had hardly dared hope for this, was prepared for it. He told me to keep an eye on her.

'I was ready to get the goods on her which would have taken Guthrie off the hook, when Guthrie somehow or other became suspicious and like a damn fool tried to pick up his own evidence.

'If he'd only come to me, I could have shown him photostats of motel registers where she and this Jackson Eagan had registered together dozens of times.

'However, Guthrie wanted to get the evidence his own way. He was going to be smart–the damn fool!

'Guthrie started out on this trip to Mexico. He told Dorla he wanted her to ride on the train as far as the Pasadena-Alhambra station. That was so she'd know that he was on the train and would get careless.'

'It worked?' Mason asked, his voice carefully masked.

'Admirably. She got off one side of the train: Guthrie opened a vestibule door on the other side of the train, dropped off on the blind side, waited until the train had pulled out, walked over to the car that he had rented, and followed Dorla.

'Dorla was in a hurry. She couldn't wait to get to the Sleepy Hollow Motel, where this steady boy friend, Jackson Eagan, was registered. She went in with him, there was an ardent reunion, and then after a while Dorla came out. She went home to get some things.

'Guthrie had come prepared for all eventualities. But as it happened, fate played into his hands. The motel unit next to the one occupied by Jackson was empty. Guthrie had a tape recorder with a very sensitive microphone that fastens up against the wall. He put the mike up against the wall and settled back to listen.

'That microphone picked up sounds which were inaudible to the ear, but he could plug a pair of earphones in and listen as the tape went over a secondary head, which enabled him to listen to everything that was on the tape.'

Mason nodded again.

'He listened to plenty,' Boles said. 'Then Dorla left in Jackson Eagan's car to get her suitcase.

'Well, that's when Guthrie Balfour did the most foolish thing of all.

'He had all the evidence he needed on the tape recorder. But, like a bungling amateur, he thought he could confront Jackson Eagan, take the part of the outraged husband, and get Eagan to sign some sort of a confession.

'So Guthrie opened the door and went into the dimly lit motel. Eagan aimed a flashlight at his face, recognized him and they started fighting. Guthrie had the .22 automatic he had taken from the glove compartment of Ted's car. There was a struggle. The gun went off and Eagan fell to the floor with a bullet in his head.

'Guthrie got in a panic. He dashed out of the place and ran to the telephone booth that was in front of the office. He called the trouble number. That's where I came in.

'That telephone has right of way over anything. I answered the phone. Guthrie told me he was at the Sleepy Hollow Motel, that he'd had trouble and that it was *very* serious.

'I told him to wait and I'd get out there right away. Guthrie was scared stiff. He could hardly talk on the phone. He seemed to be in pretty much of a daze.

'I got out there in nothing flat. Guthrie was seated in his rented car and was shaking like a leaf. I finally got out of him what had happened.'

'So what did you do?' Mason asked.

'I did the only thing there was to do,' Boles said. 'Guthrie was supposed to be on a train to El Paso, en route to Chihuahua. Nobody knew he'd gotten off that train. I told him to take the company plane, fly to Phoenix, and get aboard the train. I told him that I'd arrange to come down later on and pick up the plane. I told him I'd take care of everything and not to bother.'

'So what did he do?'

'Started off to get the plane, just as I told him.'

'He could fly it himself?'

'Sure, he could fly it himself. He had a key to the hangar. He takes off from a private landing field at the suburban factory. There was absolutely nothing to stand in his way. It was a cinch.'

'What did you do?'

'What do you think I did?' Boles said. 'I took the body out. I tied it on to my car and dragged the face off it. I banged it around so the head was smashed up like an eggshell, took it out and dumped it on the highway, so it would look like a hit and run. Fortunately, the gun was a small-calibre gun, there hadn't been any haemorrhage, and what bleeding had taken place had been on the rug in the motel unit. I took that rug, put it in the car, and subsequently burned it up. I took the rug out of the unit Balfour had been occupying and put it in the unit Eagan had occupied.

'Before I'd got very far with what I was doing, Dorla came back.'

'What did you tell her?'

'I did what any good trouble shooter should have done under the circumstances,' Boles said. 'I told her that I'd been the one who was shadowing her, that I knew all about what she was doing, that I had the dope on her, that I had a tape recording that showed her guilty of infidelity. I told her that I had a written statement from Jackson Eagan, but that after I got the written statement out of him he jumped me and I had to shoot him in self-defence.

'I told Dorla to help me plant the body and make it look like a hit-and-run and then that she was to take the first plane to Tucson, and get aboard the train Guthrie was on. She was to tell Guthrie she was in a jam, that she'd been driving while intoxicated and had hit a man with the family car, that it was up to him to protect her, that he was to swear he'd talked her into staying on the train with him, and that she'd been on the train all the time. He was to take her down to Mexico with him and he was to give her an alibi.

'In that way, I had Dorla mixed into the thing up to her pretty little eyebrows. I had her really believing that Guthrie had been on the train all the time and that *I* was the only one who knew anything about what had been going on.'

'Then she helped you get the car Ted had been driving?' Mason asked.

'Sure. We planted the guy in the right place and then I had Dorla wait until after Ted came home with the car. Fortunately he was pretty pie-eyed. Marilyn Keith took him upstairs and, I guess, put him to bed. Then she came down, and I'll sure hand it to that kid! She was plucky. She didn't even leave a back trail by calling for a taxicab. She walked out to State Highway and took a chance on hitchhiking a ride home. For an attractive girl like that, that was quite some chance. That's a lot of devotion to her job. I'm going to see that that girl gets a real raise in pay as soon as this thing is over.'

'Go on,' Mason said. 'Then what happened?'

'After that, it was all just a matter of cleaning up details,' Boles said. 'Dorla took the car out, smashed into the guy. We left a few clues scattered around. Then she took the car back and parked it. I called the cops next morning and gave them an anonymous tip on the Balfour car.

'Now that's where Dorla double-crossed me. She's a smart little trollop. I had it planned so the evidence would point to *her* as the one who had driven the car and hit the man.

'She played it smart. Before she took the plane to Tucson, she sneaked into Ted's room and planted the car key in Ted's pocket. Ted was dead to the world. The Keith girl had left him with all his clothes on except his shoes. She'd taken those off. Dorla undressed him, put his pyjamas on, and fixed it so he thought he'd gone out a second time and that the accident probably had happened then.

'Now then, Mason that gives you an idea what you're up against.'

'One other question,' Mason said. 'What about the witness, Myrtle Anne Haley?'

'A complete phony,' Boles said. 'I had a body to account for and we wanted to be certain that Dorla was where she could be charged with the hit-and-run–unless she got Guthrie to back her on her fake alibi. That would put Dorla completely in our power. But the time element became confused, Ted talked too much to the investigating officers, and Dorla did too good a job getting Guthrie to back up her phony alibi. So that left Ted holding the bag. I hadn't planned it that way but Ted *shouldn't* have had any trouble beating the case. Then that damn fool, Howland, loused everything up.

'I got this witness, this Myrtle Anne Haley who is working for the Balfour enterprises. I told her what she had to swear to–The dumb cluck got it pretty well mixed up. I've used her before. She's loyal, even if she isn't smart. For a thousand bucks she'll play along with anything.

'I admit I made a mistake with Howland. I didn't pay him by the day. I paid him by the job. So Howland saw an opportunity to wipe it all off the books by making a deal with the prosecution under which Ted would get a suspended sentence.

'Now then, there's the story. I've dumped it in your lap.'

'What do you expect *me* to do with it?' Mason asked.

'You've made a good start already,' Boles said. 'That's one hell of a clever point you made with that once-in-jeopardy business. You go ahead and pull that prior conviction stuff for all it's worth. Never let them get to trial on the merits. Keep hammering home that point of being once in jeopardy. I think it's a hell of a good point. So does a lawyer whom I've consulted. He says you're tops and you've got a point there that will keep them from ever bringing out the evidence they have. He says you're a genius.'

'I may not be able to work it that way,' Mason said coldly.

'What do you mean?'

'Suppose I put in a plea of once in jeopardy and the judge overrules it? Then the district attorney goes to trial.'

'Exactly,' Boles said. 'And at that time you don't take any part in the trial at all. You simply sit back and let them handle it all their own way. You refuse to cross-examine witnesses. You refuse to put on any witnesses of your own. You refuse to argue anything except this plea of once in jeopardy. Then, if the jury returns a verdict of guilty, you're in a position to go before the Supreme Court on that once-in-jeopardy point. You will have aroused the sympathy of the Supreme Court because you didn't put on any evidence and didn't make any defence.'

'Are you,' Mason asked, 'telling me how to conduct the case?'

There was a moment's silence. Boles's blue eyes became hard as steel. 'You're damn right I am. We're paying the bill.'

'You may be paying the bill,' Mason told him, 'but I'm representing a client. Suppose the Supreme Court doesn't set aside the verdict on my once-in-jeopardy theory? Then young Balfour is convicted of murder.'

'A damn sight better to have Ted Balfour convicted of second-degree murder than to have the whole Balfour family rocked by a family scandal and a verdict of first-degree murder. Ted isn't important. Guthrie Balfour is. However, we could easily make out a case of self-defence for Ted where we couldn't for Guthrie.'

Mason said, 'My responsibility is to my client.'

'Look,' Boles said coldly, 'your obligation is to do what I tell you to do. We're paying the freight. I'm master-minding this thing. You try to double-cross me and I'll make you the sickest individual in the state of California, and don't you ever forget I can do it.

'You're supposed to be smart and to know your way around. If you had half of the things to contend with that I've had to take in my stride, you'd realize you didn't know anything. Don't think this is the first killing I've had to square. And some of the things have been pretty damn nasty.'

'All right,' Mason said. 'Now I know your position and you know mine. I'll tell you something to remember: I don't suborn perjury and I don't go for all this crooked business. I rely on the truth. The truth is a better weapon than all these crooked schemes of yours.'

Boles said, 'You're kicking a chance at a hundred-thousand-dollar fee out of the window and you're leaving yourself wide open.'

'To hell with the fee,' Mason said. 'I'm protecting my client. I'll do what I think is for his best interests.'

Boles reached forward and tapped on the window of the cab.

The driver turned around.

'Stop right here. Let me out,' Boles said.

Boles turned to Mason. 'Under the circumstances you can pay for the cab.'

Mason whipped a paper from his pocket and shoved it in Boles's hand as the cab lurched to a stop.

'What's this?' Boles asked.

'A subpoena ordering you to attend court as a witness for the defence,' Mason said.

For a moment Boles's jaw sagged open in incredulous surprise, then he said, 'Why, you dirty son-of-a-bitch!'

Boles slammed the cab door shut with a vigour which rattled the glass.

'Turn around,' Mason instructed the driver. 'Go back to the place where you picked us up.'

16

Perry Mason regarded the letter which Della Street placed on his desk on top of the morning mail.

'You say that came registered mail, special delivery?'

She nodded. 'They don't lose any time, do they?'

Mason read aloud:

'Dear Sir:

'You are hereby notified that, effective immediately, you are relieved of all duties in connection with the defence of Theodore Balfour, Jnr., in the case of People versus Balfour. From now on the defendant will be represented by Mortimer Dean Howland as his attorney. You will please submit any expenses which you have incurred to date, together with the necessary vouchers showing the nature and extent of those expenses. From the date of receipt of this communication, you will incur no more expenses on behalf of the Balfour Allied Associates, and any such bills as you may submit for your personal compensation to date in connection with said case will be predicated upon a per diem basis. Otherwise, those bills will be contested. We will allow you a maximum of two hundred and fifty dollars per day for your time.

'Very truly yours,
'Balfour Allied Associates
'per Addison Balfour.'

'Makes it nice and official, doesn't it?' Mason said.

'What about Ted Balfour? Do you have to withdraw simply because–'

'Not because Addison Balfour says so,' Mason observed. 'But put yourself in Ted's place. Boles goes to him and tells him that I won't co-operate and that the Balfour Allied Associates have lost confidence in me, that they're not putting up any more money for his defence as long as I'm connected with the case in any way, that if Mortimer Dean Howland represents him they will go the limit. What would *you* do under those circumstances?'

'Well, what are you going to do?'

'I'm damned if I know,' Mason said thoughtfully. 'If I go to young Balfour and tell him the truth, Howland will claim that I'm guilty of unprofessional conduct in trying to solicit employment.

'The probabilities are that if I even try to see Balfour, I'll be advised that Balfour has stated I am no longer representing him and therefore I have no visitor's privileges.'

'So what are you going to do?'

'So,' Mason said, 'I'm going to put it up to Ted Balfour. At least, I'm going to try to see him.'

'And what are you going to tell him?'

'I'm going to shoot the works.'

The telephone on Della Street's desk rang. She picked it up, said, 'Just a minute,' turned to Mason and said, 'Your first client is back. Marilyn Keith. Says she has to see you at once on a matter of the greatest urgency.'

'Show her in,' Mason said.

Marilyn Keith had quite evidently been crying, but her chin was high and she didn't try to avoid Mason's probing eyes.

Her quick eyes flashed at the pile of mail on Mason's desk. 'I see you received your notification,' she said.

Mason nodded.

She said, 'Mr Mason, I'm sorry that you had a difference of opinion with Banner Boles. He's . . . well, he's very, very powerful and he's very, very clever.'

Mason merely nodded.

'I know, of course, what it's all about,' she said, indicating the notification on the desk. 'Mr Addison Balfour dictated that to me and had me take it to the main post office, so that you'd get it first thing this morning.'

Mason said, 'Let's be frank, Miss Keith. You're working for the Balfour Allied Associates. A situation has developed where the interests of Ted Balfour may have become adverse to those of your employer. I don't want you to–'

'Oh, forget it!' she blazed. 'Don't be so damn stupid!'

Mason raised his eyebrows.

'For your official information,' she said, 'I am no longer employed by the Balfour Allied Associates.'

'What happened?'

She said, 'I have been accused of betraying my employer, of being disloyal, and of using confidential information which I received in the course of my employment for my personal advantage.'

'Mind telling what happened?' Mason asked, the lines of his face softening somewhat. 'And do sit down. I only have a minute, but I'm anxious to hear what you have to say.'

She said, 'I went up to the jail to call on Ted Balfour.'

'You did!' Mason exclaimed.

She nodded.

'And what did you tell him?'

'I told him that the Balfour Allied Associates were cutting off all their aid as long as he had you for a lawyer, that if he accepted Mortimer Dean Howland as his lawyer and discharged you, the Balfour Allied Associates would put up all of the money that was necessary to fight his case all the way through the courts on the theory that you had raised: to wit, that he had once been placed in jeopardy and therefore couldn't be tried again.

'I also told him that, while I didn't know the details, I knew that the Balfour Allied Associates were prepared to toss him to the wolves in order to save their own skins. I told him that if he insisted on keeping you as his attorney, I was satisfied that you would loyally represent his interests to the best of your ability.'

'And what did he do?'

'Well,' she said, 'he wanted to keep you if there was any way of paying you.'

'He told you that?'

'Yes.'

'So what did you do?'

She opened her purse, said, 'I made out a cheque to you in an amount of five hundred and twenty-five dollars. That's every cent I have in the world, Mr Mason, and I don't know when you're going to get any more. I know that's not the type of fee you get in a murder case. It's just on account.'

Mason took the cheque, studied it for a moment.

'I'll get another job somewhere,' she said bravely, 'and I'll set aside a regular percentage of my cheque. I'll give you a promissory note, Mr Mason, and–'

Mason said, 'You're not likely to get another job with the Balfour Allied Associates making charges that you used confidential information for your own personal gain.'

She fought back tears. 'I'm not foolish enough to try it here,' she said. 'I'm going to some other city and I'm not going to tell them anything about having been with Balfour Allied Associates.'

Mason stood thoughtfully regarding her.

'Will you do it, Mr Mason? Will you, *please*? Oh, will you *please* represent Ted?'

'He wants me to?' Mason asked.

'Very much,' she said. 'It's an uphill battle, but you'll be honest. And you'll have a terrific fight. You have no idea of the ruthless power of Balfour Allied Associates, or the manner in which Banner Boles uses that power.

'Boles was educated as an attorney, although he never practised. He's been a lobbyist and he knows his way around. You give that man unlimited money and all the power of the Balfour Allied Associates back of him, and anything that he can't buy out of his way he'll club out of his way.'

'Do you think Ted will want me after Boles has been to see him?'

'That's why I had to see you now,' she said. 'You go and see Ted. Go and see him right now. Tell him that you're going to stay with him. But please, Mr Mason, please don't tell him that *I* am paying anything. Oh, I know it's pitifully inadequate. But if you only can . . . if you only will . . .'

Mason picked up her cheque, tore it in half, tore the halves into quarters, dropped the pieces in the waste-basket, walked over and put his arm around her shoulder. 'You poor kid,' he said. 'Forget it. I'll go and see Ted Balfour and tell him that I'll stand by him. You save your money for a cushion until you can get another job. You'll need it.'

She looked up at him for a moment, then lost all semblance of maintaining her poise. Her head came forward on the lawyer's shoulder and her body was shaken by sobs.

Della Street tactfully eased out of the room.

17

Judge Cadwell said, 'Gentlemen, the jury has been sworn. The defendant is in court. The jurors are all present.

'I may state that, while I do not consider myself prejudiced so that I am disqualified from trying the issues in this case, I was hoping that it would be assigned to another judge. I have, of course, already become familiar with the legal point raised by the defence in connection with habeas corpus.

'It appears that the facts supporting the plea of once in jeopardy are completely within the knowledge of the Court. There is no dispute as to those facts. There is therefore no issue to go to the jury in connection with a plea of once in jeopardy. It becomes a matter for the Court to pass upon as a matter of law. The Court therefore decides that there is no merit to the plea of once in jeopardy.

'The Court makes this ruling with some hesitancy because it is aware that the point is a close one. However, this Court simply can't conceive that it is the purpose of the law to clothe a defendant with immunity simply because, through a misinterpretation of facts or a paucity of facts, prosecution was originally had upon another theory, or for lesser offence. Yet the Court is forced to admit that the authorities seem to indicate such is the case.

'In view of the undisputed facts in the case the point is one which can be taken to the appellate courts and passed upon by them. Therefore, the real interests of the defendant will in no wise be curtailed by this ruling of the Court. I overrule the plea of once in jeopardy and the prosecution will proceed with its case.'

Roger Farris made a brief opening statement to the jury and then started putting on witnesses.

The autopsy surgeon in the coroner's office testified to having performed an autopsy on a body which had at first been certified out as a hit-and-run case. Afterwards, the body had been exhumed when it appeared that there were certain discrepancies in the evidence. At that time a more detailed examination of the skull had been made, and it was found that death had resulted from a bullet wound. The course and nature of the bullet wound was described and the bullet, which had been recovered from the wound, was introduced in evidence.

Mason offered no questions on cross-examination.

A .22 automatic was produced and identified by manufacturer's number. The sales record showed that the weapon had been sold to the defendant Ted Balfour.

Again there was no cross-examination.

Roger Farris put a witness on the stand who qualified as an expert on firearms and firearms identification. He testified that he had fired test bullets from the automatic and had compared them with the fatal bullet which had been introduced in evidence, and that the markings on the bullet showed beyond doubt that the fatal bullet had been fired from the automatic which had been received in evidence.

Again Mason did not cross-examine.

Judge Cadwell frowned down at Mason. 'Now let me understand the position of counsel,' he said. 'Is it the position of the counsel that, because the Court has overruled the plea of once in jeopardy, counsel intends to take no part in this trial? Because, if such is to be the position of counsel, I feel that the Court should warn counsel that counsel is here for the purpose of representing the interests of the defendant, and that, as an officer of the Court, it is the duty of counsel to see that the defendant is represented.'

'I understand the Court's position,' Mason said. 'I am not cross-examining these witnesses because I have no questions to ask of them. I intend to participate actively in this trial.'

'Very well,' Judge Cadwell said frowning. 'The Court needs only to point out, Mr Mason, the importance of these witnesses. However, the Court will make no comment on the testimony. Proceed with the case.'

'Now then, your Honour,' Roger Farris said, 'it appears that Myrtle Anne Haley, who was a witness for the People at the previous trial of this action when the defendant was indicated for negligent homicide, is at the moment unavailable. We propose to show that we have made every effort to locate her. Being unable to do so, in view of the fact that the parties to this action are the same as the parties in the other action, to wit, the People of the State of California as plaintiff and Theodore Balfour, Jr., as defendant, we wish to read her testimony into the record. I understand there is no objection.'

'Any objection?' Judge Cadwell asked.

Mason smiled. 'Not in the least, Your Honour. I am glad to have this done if counsel will first prove the witness is unavailable. This action on the part of counsel, using the identical evidence used in the other trial shows the solidity of our plea of once in jeopardy.'

'The actions aren't the same,' Farris said. 'The parties are the same, that's all.'

Judge Cadwell stroked his chin. 'Of course,' he said, 'that does tend to give force to the defendant's plea of once in jeopardy. However, the Court has ruled on that, and that ruling will stand. Make your showing, Mr Prosecutor. Counsel will be advised that any objection which counsel wishes to take to any question as contained in the transcript may be made at this time and the Court will then rule on that objection.'

Farris produced an investigator for the district attorney's office who testified that Myrtle Anne Haley had moved from her residence and had left no forwarding address, that he had talked with all of her friends and acquaintances but no one knew where she had gone, that he had made every effort to find her and serve a subpoena on her without avail. She had been employed by a subsidiary of the Balfour Allied Associates and she had left abruptly without even calling for her last pay-cheque. The intimation was strongly that pressure brought to bear by the Balfour Company had caused this prime witness for the prosecution to absent herself.

'Cross-examination?' Judge Cadwell asked Mason.

Mason shook his head. 'No cross-examination.'

'Very well,' Judge Cadwell said, 'I will grant the motion of the prosecution that the testimony of Myrtle Anne Haley may be read in the record, after that testimony is properly authenticated, there being no objection.'

The court reporter was thereupon duly sworn and read the transcript of Myrtle Anne Haley's testimony.

With the manner of a magician bringing a startling trick to a breath-taking conclusion, Roger Farris called out in a ringing voice, 'Will Mr Banner Boles take the stand?'

Banner Boles came forward, held up his hand, was sworn, gave his name, age, residence, and occupation, and settled himself comfortably in the witness stand.

'Are you acquainted with the defendant, Theodore Balfour, Jr.?' Farris asked.

'Yes, sir. Certainly.'

'How long have you known him?'

'For some ten years.'

'What were you doing on the nineteenth of September of this year?'

'I was working for the Balfour Allied Associates.'

'Specifically what duties did you perform that night?'

'Mr Guthrie Balfour was leaving for El Paso. From there he was going to Mexico. It was part of my assignment to see that he got safely aboard the train.'

'Somewhat in the nature of a bodyguard?'

'Well, more in the nature of a general trouble-shooter.'

'You saw him on the train for El Paso?'

'I did.'

'Who else?'

'His wife, Dorla Balfour.'

'She boarded the same train with him?'

'Yes, sir.'

'Where had you been prior to the time you went to the depot?'

'There had been a little social gathering, something in the nature of a going-away party at the home of Mrs Florence Ingle who is a friend of the Balfours.'

'And you had been at that party?'

'I had, yes, sir.'

'And what happened after you escorted Mr and Mrs Guthrie Balfour to the train?'

'I went back to my office.'

'You have an office uptown?'

'Yes, sir.'

'It is not at the Balfour Allied Associates?'

'I have an office there too, but I have an uptown office which is kept open twenty-four hours a day.'

'For what purpose, may I ask?'

'People call me when something comes up and there is any trouble.'

'And were you called on the evening of the nineteenth?'

'No, sir.'

'You were not?'

'No, sir.'

'I thought–Oh, I beg your pardon, it was early in the morning of the twentieth. Were you called then?'

'Yes, sir.'

'Who called you?'

'The defendant.'

'You are referring to the defendant, Theodore Balfour, Jr.?'

'Yes, sir.'

'Do you know where he was calling you from?'

'I only know where he said he was calling me from.'

'And where was that?'

'It was a telephone booth at a service station at the intersection of Sycamore Road and State Highway. The service station was closed but he was calling from the booth.'

'And what did he say?'

'He asked me to join him at once. He said he was in trouble.'

'What did you do?'

'I jumped in my car and got out there as quick as I could.'

'How long did it take?'

'About twenty minutes, I guess.'

'Did you give the defendant any instructions before you left?'

'I told him to wait there until I arrived.'

'Was he there when you arrived?'

'No, sir. He was not.'

'Where was he?'

'Well, I cruised around for a while trying to find–'

'Never mind that. Tell us where you finally found the defendant.'

'I found him at home.'

'That is, at the residence of Mr and Mrs Guthrie Balfour?'

'Yes, sir.'

'That was where he was living?'

'Yes, sir.'

'As a trouble shooter for the Balfour Allied Associates you knew that, did you?'

'Yes, sir.'

'And what did you do?'

'I didn't want to get everybody up. I wanted to find out if the defendant was at home.'

'In your capacity with the organization, do you have keys for the residences of the executives of the Balfour Allied Associates?'

'I have pass keys I can use if there is an emergency.'

'And did you use one of those keys?'

'Yes, sir.'

'Where did you go first?'

'First I looked in the garage to see if the car the defendant had been driving was in the garage.'

'You found that it was in the garage?'

'Yes, sir.'

'What was its condition?'

'Well, I used my flashlight and walked around the car looking for signs of trouble because, from the tone of voice in which the defendant had telephoned me, I thought he had been–'

'Never mind what you *thought*,' Farris interrupted sharply. 'Just tell what you *did*.'

'I looked the car over.'

'What did you find?'

'I found that the right front headlight was smashed, that there was a dent in the right fender, and there were a few flecks of blood on the front bumper near the right-hand side; that is, I assumed the spots were blood. They were red spots which had crusted and looked like blood.'

'So then what did you do?'

'So then I switched off my flashlight, closed the garage door, went to the house, inserted my key in the front door, opened the front door, and walked upstairs.'

'And where did you go?'

'To the room occupied by the defendant.'

'You had been in that room before?'

'Oh, yes.'

'You knew where it was?'

'Yes, sir.'

'And what did you do?'

'I tapped on the door and said, "This is Banner, Ted. Let me in."'

'Did you receive any response?'

'No, sir.'

'What did you do?'

'I went inside the room.'

'And what did you find?'

'I found the defendant very drunk, in what I would call an alcoholic stupor, lying fully clothed on the bed.'

'What about his shoes? Were they on or off?'

'They were on.'

'What time was this?'

'This was about two o'clock in the morning. I had left the service station at one-fifty, and I guess it took me about five minutes to look through the garage and study the automobile.'

'Now, when you say, "the automobile", what automobile do you mean?'

'I mean the automobile photographs of which have been introduced in evidence, the one having licence number GMB 665.'

'Did you have any conversation with the defendant there in his room at that time?'

'Yes, sir.'

'Who else was present?'

'No one.'

'Just the two of you?'

'Yes, sir.'

'What did you do?'

'I had quite a time getting the defendant so he could wake up and talk.'

'What did you do?'

'I took off his coat. I took off his overshirt. I took off his undershirt. I got towels, soaked them in cold water, and put them on his abdomen and on his neck. I sat him up in bed and shook him. I put cold compresses on his eyes and on the back of his neck, and finally he became conscious, or wakened, or whatever you want to call it.'

'He recognized you?'

'Oh, yes.'

'And what was the conversation you had with him at that time as nearly as you can remember?'

'Well, I asked him what he wanted, and he told me he had been in a jam but he had finally figured how to get out of it all by himself.'

'What did he tell you?'

'He told me that he had been gambling at cards pretty heavy, that he had run out of cash and had been using the credit that he had with a certain syndicate, that he had sustained losses and that those losses had piled up and the syndicate had called on him to pay.'

'He told you all this?'

'Yes, sir.'

'How did he speak?'

'His voice was thick. He was quite intoxicated, but I got it out of him a bit at a time.'

'Go ahead. Then what did he tell you?'

'He told me that he had received a couple of telephone calls from the syndicate saying he had to pay up or else. After that he said he had received an anonymous, unsigned letter saying that if he didn't pay up they were going to send their "collector".'

'Did he tell you what he thought the threat meant when they said that they were going to send their collector?'

'Yes, sir.'

'What did he say?'

'He said that that meant someone to beat him up. He said that they got pretty tough with fellows that didn't pay, that the first time they beat them up, and the second time they took them for a one-way ride.'

'Go on,' Farris said, glancing triumphantly at the jurors who were sitting on the edges of their chairs, leaning forward, drinking in Boles's words with rapt attention. 'What else did he say?'

'Well, he said that he had tried to raise twenty thousand dollars, that he didn't dare to go to Addison Balfour, that he had hoped an opportunity would present itself to speak to Guthrie Balfour before he took off for Mexico, but that, in the crush of the party, there had been no opportunity. He knew that he would have to approach the subject very tactfully. Otherwise, he would be rebuffed.

'He stated that he had some money that was in a trust fund which had been left him by his parents, and that he had been trying to reach the trustee in order to get some money from him, but that the trustee was out of town on a vacation, that he was hoping he could stall the matter along until the return of the trustee.'

'Did he say anything else?'

'He said that he had talked to one of his father's friends, a Florence Ingle.'

'That was the woman who had given the party?'

'Yes.'

'Did he say when he had talked with her?'

'He said that night, He said that he had asked her for twenty thousand dollars but that she had been unable or unwilling to give it to him.'

'Then what did he say?'

'He said that he drank more than was good for him, that he was rather intoxicated by somewhere around ten o'clock, that a young woman had driven his car home for him, and had put the car in the garage.'

'Did he tell you the name of the young woman?'

'He *said* that he didn't know the young woman's identity. But I thought he did. However, I didn't–'

'Never mind what you *thought*!' Farris shouted. 'You're familiar with the rules of examination, Mr Boles. Kindly refrain from giving any of your conclusions. Tell us only what the defendant said to you and what you said to the defendant.'

'Yes, sir.'

'Now, what did the defendant say to you about having been brought home?'

'Well, the defendant said he had been brought home by this young woman, that she had taken his shoes off, that he had stretched out on the bed, that he had been pretty drunk and that he had gone to the bathroom and been sick, that after that he felt a little better. He suddenly remembered that the trustee who handled his trust fund sometimes came back early from a vacation, and checked in at a motel on the outskirts of town, that this man was an elderly man with poor eyesight who disliked to drive at night, and that, when he returned from a trip and it was late, he would stay at a motel on the outskirts of town rather than drive in. He said he decided to drive out and see if the trustee had returned.'

'And then what?'

'So he put on his shoes, let himself out of the house, and went to the garage. He said, however, that because of the threats which had been made and because of the late hour, he had opened his gun cabinet and had taken a .22 automatic which he had put in his pocket.'

'Go on. What else did he say?'

'He said that, when he reached the garage, he thought he saw a shadowy figure; that, because he had been drinking, he finally decided it was just his imagination; that he opened the garage door and stepped inside; and that, just as he had his hand on the handle of the car door, someone put his hand on his shoulder from behind and said, "Okay, buddy, I'm the collector."'

'Go on,' Farris said. 'What else?'

'He said he was frozen with terror for the moment and that then the man who had said he was a collector hit him a hard blow on the chest, a blow that slammed him back against the wall of the garage; that the man had then said, "That's a sample! Now get in the car. You and I are going for a little ride. I'm going to teach you not to welsh on bets."'

'Go on,' Farris said. 'What else?'

'And then the defendant told me that almost without thinking and in actual fear of his life he had jerked out the .22 automatic and had fired from the hip; that he was an exceptionally good shot; and that he had shot directly at the man's head. The man staggered back, half-sprawled against the front seat. He was not dead, but was unconscious.

'The defendant said that he knew he had to do something at once; that he lifted this man into the front seat of the automobile; that he closed the car door; that he jumped in the other side, and drove, anxious only to get away from the house for fear that someone might have heard the shot. He said he drove down to the State Highway; that he turned left and stopped at the closed service station on Sycamore; that he called me from the phone booth there and asked me to come at once. He wanted me to tell him what could be done and how he could arrange for medical attention for the man in the car.

'He then told me that after he had hung up and returned to the car, he discovered the man was no longer breathing that he put his hand on his wrist and there was no pulse; that the man had died while he was telephoning.

'He said that changed the situation materially; that he had tried to call me again, but that my assistant who answered the telephone assured him I had already left.'

'Go on,' Farris said, 'what else did he tell you? Did he tell you what he did after that?'

'Yes, sir.'

'What was it?'

'He said that he felt that the problem was simplified because he had only a dead man to deal with. He said that the shock had sobered him up pretty much, that he searched the body and took everything in the line of papers that the man might have – all means of identification; that he took the man's wallet; that he even took his handkerchief, so it would not be possible to trace a laundry mark; that he took his key ring, his pocket-knife, all of his personal belongings.'

'Then what?'

'He said that he ran the car out Sycamore Road and then got out and placed the body on the front bumper; that he drove as fast as he could and then suddenly slammed on the brakes; that the body rolled off the bumper and skidded and rolled for some considerable distance along the highway; that he then deliberately ran over the head, then turned the car around and ran over the head again; that he ran over the head several times, so as to be sure that not only would the features be unrecognizable but that it would prevent the bullet hole from showing.'

'Did he tell you anything about a bullet being in the head?'

'He told me that he thought the bullet had gone clean through the head and was in the garage somewhere.'

'Go on,' Farris said.

'Well, the defendant asked me to take charge of things from there on. I told him that there was nothing much I could do; that he had already done everything; that I felt the best thing to do was to go and find the body and report the matter to the police, stating that he had acted in self-defence and in fear of his life; that this man had assaulted him first.'

'So what was done?'

'I told him to wait there, that I would go and find the body. He described exactly where he had left it.'

'And what happened?'

'I found I was too late. By the time I got there a police car was there and I felt that, under the circumstances, I didn't want to assume the responsibility of notifying the police. I thought that I would wait until I had an opportunity to think the matter over.'

'To discuss the matter with your superiors?' Farris said sharply.

'Well, I wanted time to think it over.'

'You realized that you should have reported this?'

'Yes, sir.'

'And you didn't do so?'

'No, sir.'

'Why?'

'Because I am paid to see that matters are handled smoothly. I didn't want to hash this thing up. I wanted to see one of my friends on the police force and see if I could find some way of making a report that would not be publicized. I knew that if I reported to the police officers who were there with the body, there would be publicity, that the defendant would be picked up and lodged in jail, and I felt that–well, I felt that wasn't the best way for a trouble shooter to handle an affair of this sort.'

'So what did you finally do?'

'I went back and helped Ted Balfour get undressed and into his pyjamas. He wanted some more to drink and I didn't stop him in the least. In fact, I encouraged him to drink, hoping that he might forget about the whole business.'

'And then?'

'And then I took from him the papers he had taken from the body and went home and went to bed.'

'And then?' Farris asked.

'And then I slept late the next morning. When I awakened I learned that police had already interrogated the defendant; that in some way they had learned his automobile had been involved in the matter; and that he was going to be prosecuted for an involuntary homicide with a car.'

'So what did you do?'

'I did nothing.'

Farris, with the manner of a television director who has brought his show to a conclusion right on the exact second, looked up at the clock and said, 'Your Honour, it seems to be the hour for the noon adjournment. While I think I have now concluded my direct examination of this witness, it might be well to have the noon recess at this time, because I would like to go over the testimony in my mind and see if perhaps I have left out a question.'

'Just a minute,' the judge said. 'The court has one question before we adjourn. Mr Boles, you have stated you took those papers from the defendant?'

'Yes, sir.'

'What did you do with them?'

'I held them for a while.'

'Where are they now?'

'To the best of my knowledge, they are in the possession of Mr Perry Mason.'

'What?' Judge Cadwell exclaimed, coming bolt upright on the bench.

'Yes, Your Honour.'

'You gave those papers to Perry Mason?'

'Yes, sir.'

'Has Mr Mason communicated with the district attorney's office in any way concerning those papers?' Judge Cadwell asked Roger Farris.

'No, Your Honour.'

'When did you give Mr Mason those papers?' Judge Cadwell asked.

'I don't have the exact date, I gave them to him after he had become associated, that is, after he had taken over the defence of Ted Balfour. During the first case the attorney representing the defendant was Mortimer Dean Howland.'

'You said nothing to Mr Howland about those papers?'

'No, sir.'

'Did you say anything at any time about having those papers other than to Mr Mason?'

'No, sir.'

'And you gave those papers to Mr Mason?'

'Yes, sir.'

'Mr Mason!' Judge Cadwell said.

'Yes, Your Honour.'

'The Court . . .' Judge Cadwell's voice trailed off into silence. 'The Court is about to take the noon recess,' he said. 'Immediately after the discharge of the jury, I would like to have counsel for both sides approach the bench. The Court will admonish the jury not to form or express any opinion in this case until it is finally submitted to the jury for decision. The jurors will not discuss the case with others or permit it to be discussed in their presence. Court will now take a recess until two o'clock.

'Mr Mason and Mr Farris, will you please come forward?'

Mason and Farris approached the bench, Farris trying to keep his face in a mask of grave, judicial concern as befitted one who is called upon to be present at a time when a brother attorney is subjected to a tongue lash. Judge Cadwell waited until the jurors had filed from the court-room. Then he said, 'Mr Mason, is this true?'

'I doubt it, Your Honour,' Mason said.

'You what?' Judge Cadwell snapped.

'I doubt it.'

'I mean about the papers.'

'Some papers were given to me, yes.'

'By Mr Boles?'

'Yes, Your Honour.'

'And did he tell you those were papers that he had taken from the defendant or that had been given him by the defendant?'

'No, sir.'

'What were those papers?'

'I have them here, Your Honour.'

Mason produced a sealed Manila envelope and handed it to the judge.

Judge Cadwell ripped open the envelope, started looking through the papers.

'Mr Mason,' he said, 'this is a very grave matter.'

'Yes, Your Honour.'

'The papers in this envelope are matters of evidence. They constitute most important bits of evidence in the case.'

'Evidence of what?' Mason asked.

'Evidence corroborating Boles's story, for one thing,' Judge Cadwell snapped.

Mason said, 'If Your Honour please, that's like the man who tells about shooting a deer at three hundred yards and says that the deer fell right by a certain oak tree, that if you don't believe him, he'll point out the oak tree, because it's still standing there and that will substantiate his story.'

'You question Mr Boles's story?'

'Very much,' Mason said.

'But you certainly can't question the fact that this evidence is most important evidence. This is evidence which should have been in the hands of the authorities.'

'Evidence of what, Your Honour?'

'Here is the driving licence of Jackson Eagan.'

'Yes, Your Honour.'

'Do you mean to say that is not important?'

'I fail to see why,' Mason said.

'That would serve as an identification. An attempt has been made by the police to have this corpse identified. So far no identification has been made other than a tentative identification of Jackson Eagan.'

'But Jackson Eagan is dead,' Mason said. 'He died two years before this case ever came up.'

'How do you know he died?' Judge Cadwell said. 'Here is a contract that was signed, apparently by the decedent, a contract for the rental of that automobile. Do you claim these matters are not important, Mr Mason?'

'No, sir.'

'You certainly understand that they are matters of evidence?'

'Yes, Your Honour.'

'As an officer of this Court, as an attorney at law, it is your duty to submit any matter of evidence, any physical matter which you have in your possession to the authorities. To suppress willfully or conceal any evidence of this sort is not only a violation of law but is a violation of your duties as an attorney.'

Mason met the judge's eyes. 'I'll meet that charge, Your Honour, when it is properly made, at the proper time and at the proper place.'

Judge Cadwell's face turned a deep purple. 'You are intimating that I have no right to bring this matter up?'

'I am stating, Your Honour, that I will meet that charge at the proper time and in the proper place.'

'I don't know whether this constitutes a contempt of Court or not,' Judge Cadwell said, 'but it certainly constitutes a breach of your professional duty.'

'That's Your Honour's opinion,' Mason said. 'If you wish to hold me for contempt I'll get a writ of habeas corpus and meet the contempt charge. If you wish to cite me for unprofessional conduct, I will meet that charge at the proper time and in the proper place.

'In the meantime, may I suggest to the Court that a defendant is on trial in this court, that any intimation on the part of the Court that his counsel has been guilty of any breach of ethics might well be held against the defendant by the jury, and that it is the duty of the Court to refrain from expressing any opinion as to the action of counsel in this matter.'

Judge Cadwell took a deep breath. 'Mr Mason,' he said, 'I am going to do everything I can to see that the rights of the defendant are not prejudiced by the conduct of his counsel. However, I can assure you that, as far as this Court is concerned, I feel that you have forfeited the right to the respect of the Court. Quite apparently you, as an attorney, have endeavoured to condone a felony and you have suppressed evidence. As far as the witness Boles is concerned, I assume that he has endeavoured to make atonement by going to the authorities and telling his story, but apparently you have done nothing.'

'I have done nothing,' Mason said, 'except try to protect the rights of my client, and I'm going to try to protect them to the best of my ability.'

'Well, you certainly have a different idea of the professional duties of an attorney than I do,' Judge Cadwell snapped. 'That is all. I'll think the matter over during the noon adjournment. I may decide to take some action when Court has reconvened.'

18

Perry Mason, Della Street, Marilyn Keith, and Paul Drake sat in a booth in the little restaurant where Mason usually ate lunch when he had a case in court.

'Well,' Paul Drake asked, 'just where does that leave us, Perry?'

'Out on the end of a limb,' Mason admitted. 'It's perjury, and it's the damnedest, most clever perjury I've ever encountered.'

'He's clever,' Marilyn Keith said, 'frighteningly so, and he's powerful.'

Mason nodded.'He's had legal training. He's been a lobbyist. He doubtless knows every trick of cross-examination that I do. It's his word against mine and he's manufactured a story that seems to have all sorts of factual corroboration.'

'What about his withholding evidence?' Drake asked.

'Sure,' Mason said. 'He admits it. So what? The district attorney won't do a thing to him. He won't even slap his wrists. He'll tell him he *should* have surrendered the evidence to the district attorney's office, and not to do it again, but that's all.

'The devil of it is,' Mason went on, 'that it puts the defendant in such a hell of a position. It's a clever story. It has aroused a certain amount of sympathy for Ted Balfour on the part of the jurors. If Ted goes on the stand and tells approximately that same story, says that he relied on the advice of the older man, some members of that jury are going to vote for acquittal. They'll finally reach some kind of a compromise verdict.'

'How good is your point about this once-in-jeopardy business?' Drake asked.

'Damn good,' Mason said. 'In the right kind of a case, the Supreme Court is pretty apt to go all the way.'

'Well, it should make a terrific case,' Drake said, 'if we could only get a little more evidence about the collector coming to call.'

Mason said, 'The worst of it is, the story sounds so plausible that I am almost believing it myself.'

'Is there anything you can do?' Marilyn Keith asked him.

'I have one weapon,' Mason said. 'It's a powerful weapon. But sometimes it's hard to wield it because you don't know just where to grab hold of it.'

'What weapon is that?' Della Street asked.

'The truth,' Mason said.

They ate for a while in silence.

'You'll cross-examine him?' Paul Drake asked.

'I'll cross-examine him. It won't do any good.'

'If his story had been true–well, what about it, Perry, what about concealing evidence?'

'As I told Judge Cadwell, I'll cross that bridge when I come to it,' Mason said. 'Right now I'm trying to think of the best way to protect young Balfour.

Of course no matter what anyone says, that driving licence of Jackson Eagan doesn't prove a thing. It shows a thumbprint on the driving licence and it's not the thumbprint of the corpse.' Mason took from his pocket a set of ten fingerprints. 'These are fingerprints of the corpse. This is the thumbprint on the driving licence of Jackson Eagan. You can see that they don't compare at all.'

'Jackson Eagan was buried,' Paul Drake said. 'But no one really identified the body. The body had been shipped from Yucatan, Mexico. The story was that it had been identified down there by the widow.'

'Just what were the circumstances?' Mason asked.

'Eagan was a writer. He was on a trip getting local colour. No one knows exactly how he died. Probably heart failure, or something of that sort. A party of archaeologists stumbled on his body. They notified the authorities. The body was taken in to Merida in Yucatan, and the widow was notified by telegram. She flew down to identify the body and bring it home for the funeral. Naturally under the circumstances, the funeral was held with a closed coffin.'

Mason said thoughtfully, 'Just supposing the widow wanted her freedom and perhaps wanted to collect some insurance. It was quite a temptation for her to swear that the body was that of her husband.'

'Of course we get back to that thumbprint,' Drake said, 'but when you look at the signature on this contract to rent a car, the signatures certainly tally.'

'They certainly seem to be the same signature.' Mason said. 'Paul, how about the application for a driving licence signed by Guthrie Balfour? Did you get that?'

Drake said, 'I wired for a certified copy of Guthrie Balfour's last application for a driving licence. It should be here any minute. I was hoping it would come in this morning. I feel certain that it must arrive in the late morning mail. One of my operatives will bring it up to court as soon as it comes in.'

'I want it as soon as I can get it,' Mason said.

'Do you have any plans for this afternoon's session?' Drake asked.

Mason shook his head, said, 'Something like this catches you flat-footed. I had anticipated that they would try to make things tough for me, but I didn't think I'd have someone get on the stand and commit deliberate perjury like that.

'Paul, the number of that taxicab in which we took the ride was 647. I want to try and find the driver of the cab. I doubt if he'd remember anything that would be of help, but at least we can check. He should remember the occasion, even if he can't identify Boles.'

'I'll have my men round him up,' Drake said.

'Well,' Mason announced, 'I'll just have to go back there and take it on the chin. I've absorbed lots of punishment before and I guess I can take a little more.'

'Of course you have the advantage of knowing what actually happened,' Della Street said. 'Eagan was shot by Guthrie Balfour. He telephoned Florence Ingle and admitted that.'

'Well, why not use that?' Marilyn Keith asked. 'Why not just go ahead on that basis and–?'

Mason smiled and shook his head. 'No can do.'

'Why not?'

'Because Guthrie Balfour told her over the telephone that he had killed this man. He said the killing was accidental, that the gun had gone off in a struggle.'

'Can't you use that?'

'No.'

'Why not?'

'Because that's hearsay. If we had Guthrie Balfour here, we could put him on the stand and question him, and, if he told a different story, we could then put Florence Ingle on the stand and impeach him by having Florence tell what he had said. But the law won't let a witness simply testify to what someone else has said over the telephone.'

'It let Banner Boles testify to what Ted said over the telephone!' Marilyn exclaimed indignantly.

'Sure,' Mason said, 'because Ted's the defendant. You can always show any adverse statement that has been made by a defendant, but, unfortunately for us, Guthrie Balfour isn't a defendant. The technical rules of evidence prevent us getting at what we want.'

'And what does Guthrie Balfour say about it?' Marilyn asked.

'Nobody knows,' Mason said. 'Guthrie headed back to his base camp. How about your men? Any luck, Paul?'

Drake shook his head. 'Guthrie Balfour was in Chihuahua very briefly. He headed back for the Tarahumare country somewhere. He was only in Chihuahua long enough to telephone you and put his wife on a plane to come in and see you. Then he was off again. And my best guess, Perry, is that this expedition of his may have started out as a little archaeological exploration, but it has now developed into a game of hide-and-seek. I don't think he intends to have anybody catch up with him until after this case is all over. Of course, in justice to him, you have to remember that as far as he's concerned it's still only a hit-and-run case. He feels nothing very much can happen to Ted–a fine or a suspended sentence.'

Mason signed the luncheon check, said, 'Well, we may just as well go back and face the music. We may not like the tune but we'll dance to it.'

19

After court had been reconvened at two o'clock, Roger Farris said, 'I have no more questions of this witness. You may cross-examine, Mr Mason.'

Mason said, 'Do you remember an occasion a short time ago when you telephoned me at my office, Mr Boles?'

'Perfectly,' Boles said affably.

'You came up to my office and said you had something to tell me?'

'Yes, sir.'

'And I asked you to talk to me in my office and you said you'd prefer not to do so?'

'Yes, sir, that's quite right.'

'And we went out and rode around in a taxicab together?'

'Yes, sir.'

'You remember that, do you?'

'Certainly, sir. I not only remember it, but I took the precaution of jotting down the number of the taxicab so that the driver could bear me out in case you tried to confuse me on cross-examination or tried to deny that I gave you these papers.'

'You gave them to me while we were in the taxicab?'

'That's right.'

'And what did you tell me when you gave me the papers?'

'The same story that I have told on the witness stand today.'

'At that time, didn't you tell me that Mr Guthrie Balfour had told you that *he* had done the shooting and that the dead man had been someone who was in the Sleepy Hollow Motel?'

Boles looked at Mason with absolute, utter incredulity. 'Do you mean that *I* told you *that*?' he asked.

'Didn't you?' Mason asked.

'Good heavens, no!' Boles said. 'Don't be absurd, Mr Mason. Why in the world should I tell you that? Why, Guthrie Balfour was . . . why, he was on his way to Mexico. I put him on the train personally.'

'What about the company aeroplane? Wasn't that subsequently picked up in Phoenix?'

'Either Phoenix or Tucson, I think,' Boles said. 'But that was at a later date. One of the company employees flew down there on a matter of some importance and then I believe left the plane, as he took a commercial airline on East. I don't know, but I can look up the company records, in case you're interested, Mr Mason. I'm quite satisfied the company records will show that to be the case.'

'I dare say,' Mason said dryly.

There was a moment's pause.

'Did you go out to the Sleepy Hollow Motel on the evening of the nineteenth or the twentieth?' Mason asked.

Boles shook his head, and said, 'I wasn't anywhere near there. No one knew anything about this car at the Sleepy Hollow Motel until I believe the police picked it up, by tracing a key. I don't know about those things. I think the police could tell you, Mr Mason.'

'When did you last see Guthrie Balfour?' Mason asked.

'When he took the train at the Arcade Station.'

'And you haven't seen him since?'

'No, sir.'

'Or heard from him?'

'Yes, sir. I've heard from him.'

'When did you hear from him?'

'I believe that was the day that Mr Balfour was tried the first time before the first jury. I believe that's the date but I'm not certain. Mr Guthrie Balfour had been back in the mountains somewhere. He came in briefly for supplies and learned of the defendant's arrest. He telephoned me and told me that he had just talked with you on the telephone, and that his wife Dorla was flying up to get in touch with you.'

There was an air of complete candour about the witness which carried conviction.

'You recognized his voice?'

'Of course.'

'That's all for the moment,' Mason said. 'I may wish to recall this witness.'

'You may step down,' Judge Cadwell said. 'Call your next witness, Mr Prosecutor.'

'Florence Ingle,' the prosecutor announced.

Florence Ingle came forward, was sworn, gave her name and address.

'You have been subpoenaed as a witness for the defence?' Farris asked.

'Yes, sir.'

'I will ask you whether you saw the defendant on the evening of September nineteenth?'

'I did,' she answered in a low voice.

'What was his condition?'

'When?'

'At the time you last saw him?'

'At the time I last saw him he had quite evidently been drinking.'

'Did he tell you anything at that time about being in debt?'

'Yes, sir. It was a little before that time . . . the evening of September nineteenth.'

'What was the conversation, please? But first let me ask you who was present at that time?'

'Quite a number of people were present at the house, but they were not present when we had the conversation; that is, they were not where they could hear the conversation.'

'Just the two of you were present?'

'Yes, sir.'

'And what did the defendant tell you?'

'He asked if he could borrow twenty thousand dollars. He told me that he was in debt, that he had run up some gambling debts and that the persons with whom he had been dealing telephoned him and threatened to send a collector unless he made immediate payment.'

'Did he say anything about what he thought the collector wanted?'

'Yes, he said those collectors got pretty rough the first time, that sometimes they took people on a one-way ride, but that they beat up anyone who welshed on a bet.'

'And did he tell you what he intended to do if a collector tried to beat him up?'

'He said he was going to defend himself.'

'Did he say how?'

'He said, "With a gun."'

'You may inquire,' Farris said.

'Did you have any talk with Guthrie Balfour, the defendant's uncle, on that day?' Mason asked.

'Objected to as incompetent, irrelevant, and immaterial, not proper cross-examination,' Farris said.

'I would like to have an answer to the question, Your Honour. I think that there is an entire transaction here which should be viewed as a unit.'

'Certainly not as a unit,' Farris said. 'We have no objection to Mr Mason asking this witness about any conversation she may have had with the defendant in this case. We have no objection to Mr Mason asking about any matters which were brought up in connection with the conversation on which the witness was questioned on her direct examination, but we certainly do not intend to permit any evidence as to some conversation she may have had with the uncle of the defendant which was not within the presence of the defendant and which, for all we know, has absolutely nothing to do with the issues involved in this case.

'If there is any such conversation and if it is pertinent, it is part of the defendant's case. This witness is subpoenaed as a witness for the defence. Counsel can examine her as much as he wants to about any conversation with Mr Guthrie Balfour when he calls her as his own witness. At that time we will of course object to any conversation which took place without the presence of the defendant or which has no bearing upon the present case.

'If a person could prove a point by any such procedure as this, there would be no point in swearing a witness. Anyone could get on the stand and tell about some conversation had with some person who was not under oath.'

'I think that's quite right, Mr Mason,' Judge Cadwell said. 'The Court wishes to be perfectly fair and impartial in the matter, but you can't show any evidence of a conversation with some person who is not a party to the proceedings, and you can't frame such a question as part of your cross-examination. The Court will permit you the most searching cross-examination as to this particular conversation the witness has testified to. The objection is sustained.'

'No further questions,' Mason said.

'We will call Mrs Guthrie Balfour to the stand,' Farris said.

While Mrs Balfour was walking forward, Paul Drake stepped up to the bar and caught Mason's eye. He handed Mason a paper and whispered, 'This is a certified photostat copy of Guthrie Balfour's application for a driving licence.'

Mason nodded, spread out the paper, glanced at it, looked at it again, then folded the paper.

Dorla Balfour was making quite an impression on the jury. The trim lines of her figure, the expressive brown eyes, the vivacious yet subdued manner with which she indicated that her natural vitality was being suppressed out of deference to the solemnity of the occasion, made the jurors prepare to like her right from the start.

She gave her name and address to the court reporter, adjusted herself in the witness chair with a pert little wiggle, raised her lashes, looked at the deputy district attorney, then at the jury, then lowered her lashes demurely.

At that moment there was a commotion in the courtroom, and Hamilton Burger , the grizzly bear of a district attorney, came striding purposefully into the courtroom.

It needed only a glance at the smug triumph of his countenance to realize that word of Perry Mason's discomfiture had been relayed to him, and he had entered the case personally in order to be in at the kill.

Too many times he had seen Mason, by the use of startling ingenuity, squeeze his way out of some seemingly impossible situation. Now he had waited until he was certain Mason had shot all the arrows from his quiver before entering court. It was apparent to everyone that Dorla Balfour would be the last witness, and then Mason would be forced to make a decision. Either he would put the defendant on the stand, or he would not. If he put the defendant on the stand and the defendant's story coincided with that of Banner Boles, the defendant might have a good chance of showing self-defence. But in that case, Mason would run the risk of an admission of unprofessional conduct and be branded for withholding evidence Boles had given him. If the defendant's story should differ from Boles' testimony, there was not one chance in a hundred the jury would believe it.

Farris, apparently trying to appear in the best possible light before his chief, said, 'Mrs Balfour, do you remember the evening of the nineteenth of September of this year?'

'Very well,' she said.

'Did you have any conversation with the defendant on that day?'

'I did, yes, sir.'

'When?'

'In the evening.'

'Where?'

'At a party given by Mrs Ingle for my husband.'

'That was in the nature of a going-away party?'

'Yes, sir.'

'Your husband took the train that night?'

'Yes, sir.'

'And did you take the train?'

'Yes, sir, I was to have accompanied my husband as far as the station at Pasadena. However, at the last minute he asked me to go all the way with him.'

'Well, never mind that,' the prosecutor said. 'I'm just trying to fix the time and place of the conversation. Now who was present at this conversation?'

'The one I had with the defendant?'

'Yes.'

'Just the defendant and I were present. That is, there were other people in the group but he took me to one side.'

'And what did he say to you?'

'He told me that he had incurred some gambling debts; that they were debts on which he didn't dare to welsh; that he had been plunging because he had got in pretty deep and he had to make good or he was threatened with personal danger. He said that they told him a collector was coming, that these collectors were sort of a goon squad who would beat him up and–well, that he *had* to have some money.'

'Did he ask you for money?'

'Not me. But he asked me if, while I was on the train, I couldn't intercede for him with my husband and get my husband to let him have twenty thousand dollars.'

'You may inquire,' Farris said.

'And did you intercede with your husband?' Mason asked.

'Not then. I did later on.'

'How much later on.'

'Well, Mr Mason, you understand I was supposed to get off the train at Pasadena, and then Guthrie asked me to go on with him all the way. He said that he felt uneasy, that he felt something perhaps was going to happen. He asked me to accompany him.'

'And you did?' Mason asked.

'Objected to as incompetent, irrelevant, immaterial. Not proper cross-examination in that it has nothing to do with the conversation concerning which this witness has testified. We are perfectly willing to let Mr Mason explore all of the facts in connection with that conversation, but any conversation which subsequently took place between this witness and her husband would be incompetent, irrelevant, and immaterial. It would be hearsay, and we object to it.'

'Sustained,' Judge Cadwell said.

'Didn't you actually get off the train at Pasadena?' Mason asked.

'Objected to as incompetent, irrelevant, and immaterial. Not proper cross-examination.'

'I will permit the question,' Judge Cadwell said. 'I am going to give the defence every opportunity for a searching cross-examination. The question of what this witness may have said to her husband is one thing, but any of the circumstances surrounding the conversation that was had on this occasion may be gone into. Answer the question.'

'Certainly not,' she said.

'Didn't you go to the Sleepy Hollow Motel on that evening?'

'Oh, Your Honour,' Roger Farris protested. 'The vice of this is now perfectly apparent. This is an attempt to befuddle the issues in this case. It is also a dastardly attack on this witness. It makes no difference what she did. She has testified only to her conversation.'

'She testified that she went on the train with her husband,' Judge Cadwell said. 'The Court wishes to give the defence every latitude. I think I will permit an answer to this question.'

'Did you go to the Sleepy Hollow Motel?' Mason asked.

'Certainly not,' she flared at him. 'And you have no right to ask such a question, Mr Mason. You know perfectly good and well that I didn't do any such thing.'

'Do you remember an occasion when your husband telephoned me from Chihuahua?' Mason asked.

'Certainly,' she said.

'You were with him at that time?'

'Yes.'

'And that is when you returned from Chihuahua?'

'Yes.'

'That was the occasion when the defendant was on trial for manslaughter?'

'It was the day after the trial; that is, it was the day of the trial, but after the trial had been concluded.'

'And you did catch a plane from Chihuahua?'

'I chartered a plane from Chihuahua and was taken to El Paso. I caught a plane at El Paso and came here. Yes.'

'And you saw me the next morning?'

'Yes.'

'And you were with your husband when he telephoned?'

'Oh, Your Honour,' Farris said, 'here we go, on and on and on. This is the vice of opening the door on cross-examination. I don't know what counsel is expecting to prove. I do know that we would like to confine the issues in this case to a simple question of fact. I object to this question on the ground that it is not proper cross-examination, that it's incompetent, irrelevant, and immaterial.'

'I am going to permit the answer to this one question,' Judge Cadwell said. 'I think myself this is going far afield, but it may have a bearing on possible bias on the part of the witness.

'The question, Mrs Balfour, is whether you were with your husband at the time he telephoned Mr Mason on that date.'

'I was. Yes, sir.'

'And,' Mason went on, 'were you subsequently with him when he telephoned to Mr Banner Boles?'

'I am not going to object to this question,' Roger Farris said, 'on the sole and specific understanding that it is not to be used to open a door for a long involved line of extraneous questions. I don't think counsel is entitled to go on a fishing expedition.'

'The Court feel that this line of questioning has certainly gone far enough,' Judge Cadwell said. 'The Court wishes to give the defence every opportunity for a cross-examination. Answer the question, Mrs Balfour. Were you with your husband when he telephoned Mr Banner Boles?'

'Yes, sir.'

'Well then,' Mason said, getting to his feet, 'perhaps, Mrs Balfour, you wouldn't mind turning to the jury and explaining to them how it could possibly be that you journeyed on the train to El Paso with a corpse, that you spent some time in Chihuahua with a corpse, that you were with a corpse when he telephoned Mr Banner Boles?'

'What in the world do you mean?' she snapped, before the stupefied Roger Farris could even so much as interpose an objection.

'Simply this,' Mason said, snapping open the paper he was holding. 'The right thumbprint of your husband Guthrie Balfour which is shown on this certified copy of an application for a driver's licence is an exact copy of the right thumbprint of the dead man, as disclosed by the coroner's record. The man who was found with this bullet in his brain, the man who was supposedly the victim of this hit-and-run episode, that man was your husband, Guthrie Balfour. Now perhaps you can explain how it happened that you spent this time with a dead man?'

'It can't be,' she said vehemently. 'I was with my husband. I–'

'Let me see that thumbprint,' Judge Cadwell snapped.

Mason brought up the thumbprint.

'And let me take a look at the exhibit showing the fingerprints of the dead man,' Judge Cadwell said.

For a long moment he compared the two prints.

'Would the prosecution like to look at this evidence?' Judge Cadwell asked.

'No, your Honour,' Hamilton Burger said smiling. 'We are too familiar with counsel's dramatic tricks to be impressed by them.'

'You'd better be impressed by this one,' Judge Cadwell said, 'because unless there's some mistake in the exhibit it is quite apparent that the prints are the same.'

'Then it is quite apparent that there has been some trickery in connection with the exhibits,' Hamilton Burger said.

'Now if the Court please,' Mason went on, 'I am suddenly impressed by certain signatures on the record of the Sleepy Hollow Motel, which I have had photographed. It is evident that one of these signatures, that of Jackson Eagan, is similar to the signature on the driver's licence issued to Jackson Eagan. However, I would like time to have a handwriting expert compare the signature of the man who signed his name "Jackson Eagan" with the handwriting of Banner Boles. I think, if the Court please, I begin to see the pattern of what must have happened on the night of September nineteenth.'

'No just a moment, just a moment,' Hamilton Burger shouted. 'I object to any such statement by counsel. I object to such a motion. I object to the Court permitting any such statement in front of a jury. I charge counsel with misconduct because of that remark, and I ask the Court to admonish the jury to disregard it.'

Judge Cadwell turned to the open-mouthed jurors. 'The jurors will not be influenced by any remarks made by counsel for either side,' he said. 'The Court, however, of its own motion, is going to take an adjournment for an hour, during which time certain records will be examined. I am particularly anxious to have a qualified fingerprint expert examine this unquestioned similarity between a thumbprint of Guthrie Balfour on this application for a driving licence, and the right thumbprint of the dead man who is the decedent in this case. Court will take a one-hour recess, during which time the jurors are not to converse with anyone about this case, not to discuss it among yourselves, and not to form or express any opinion. Court will take a recess.'

Judge Cadwell banged down his gavel, rose from the bench, and said, 'I'd like to see counsel for both sides in chambers.'

20

In Judge Cadwell's chambers an irate Hamilton Burger said, 'What I want to find out first is why Perry Mason withheld and concealed this evidence.'

'Well, what *I* want to find out,' Judge Cadwell said, 'is Mr Mason's theory of what happened in this case.'

'With all due respect to Your Honour,' Hamilton Burger said, 'I think Mr Mason's explanation should come first. I don't think he is entitled to appear here in good standing until he has purged himself of this charge.'

'With all due respect to your opinion,' Judge Cadwell snapped, 'this is a first-degree murder case. Mr Mason seems to have a theory which accounts for this startling fingerprint evidence. I want to hear that theory.'

Mason grinned at the discomfited district attorney and said, 'I think it's quite simple, Your Honour. The rented car which was found at the Sleepy Hollow Motel was a car which had apparently been rented by Jackson Eagan, despite the fact that the records show that Jackson Eagan has been dead for some two years.

'That car actually was rented by Banner Boles. Obviously Boles must have been in Mexico when the body of Jackson Eagan was discovered. He took charge of Eagan's papers. He knew that Eagan would have no further use for his driving licence. He noticed that the physical description fitted his own physical description. Occasionally, when he was working on a job where he didn't want to use his own name, or when he wanted to go on a philandering expedition, he knew that by renting a car and using the Eagan name, with the Eagan driving licence as a means of identification, there was no way his real identity could be traced.

'I could have proved that Guthrie Balfour got off the train to follow his wife if the rules of evidence had permitted me to show a conversation Guthrie Balfour had with Florence Ingle. I couldn't show that in court, but I can tell Your Honour that that's what happened.

'Dorla Balfour was having an affair with none other than Banner Boles of Balfour Allied Associates.'

'Oh, bosh!' Hamilton Burger snapped.

Judge Cadwell frowned. 'We'll let Mr Mason finish, Mr Burger. Then you may have your turn.'

Mason said, 'Florence Ingle had a conversation over the telephone with Guthrie Balfour. He was ready to divorce Dorla, he wanted to get evidence on her, so he wouldn't have to pay excessive alimony. She got off the train, as planned, at Pasadena and Guthrie Balfour got off the train as he had planned it all along, getting off on the other side of the train. He hurried to a car which he had rented earlier in the day and left there at the station so he could jump in it and drive off. He followed his wife to the place of rendezvous. He secured an adjoining cabin, set up a very sensitive microphone which recorded everything that took place in the adjoining cabin on tape. Then Dorla went home to get her suitcase and planned to return to spend the night.

'The tape recorder recorded all of the words that were spoken in the other cabin, but because of the extreme sensitivity of the microphone there was a certain distortion and Guthrie Balfour still didn't know the identity of the man who was dating his wife. After Dorla left, he determined to enter the cabin, act the part of the outraged husband, and get a statement.

'He entered the cabin. The lights were low. Banner Boles who occupied that Cabin, was waiting for Dorla to return. To his surprise and consternation, he saw the husband, who was not only the man whose home he had invaded, but who was one of the men he worked for.

'He knew that Guthrie Balfour hadn't as yet recognized him, and he didn't dare to give Balfour the chance. He dazzled Balfour by directing the beam of a powerful flashlight in the man's eyes. Then, having blinded Balfour, he threw a chair and launched an attack, hoping that he could knock Balfour out and make his escape from the cabin before his identity could be discovered.

'Balfour drew his gun, and in the struggle the gun went off. That was when Banner Boles, acting with the rare presence of mind which has made him such a skilful trouble-shooter, sank face down on the floor, pretended to be mortally wounded, then lay still.

'In a panic, Guthrie Balfour ran out, jumped into his rented car and drove home. He didn't know what to do. He knew that his shot was going to result in a scandal. He wanted to avoid that at all costs. Then it occurred to him that no one really knew he had got off the train, except the man whom he had every reason to believe was lying dead in the Sleepy Hollow Motel.

'In the meantime, Banner Boles got to his feet, ran to the telephone booth, and put through a call to Dorla at her home telling her exactly what had happened.'

'You know this for a fact?' Judge Cadwell asked.

'I know most of the facts. I am making one or two factual deductions from the things I know.'

'Using a crystal ball,' Hamilton Burger sneered.

'So,' Mason went on, 'Guthrie Balfour planned to take the company plane to Phoenix, board the train there, and pretend that nothing had happened. He rang up Florence Ingle and asked her to go to Phoenix on a commercial plane and fly the company plane back. He felt that he could trust Florence Ingle. She was the only one in whom he confided. However, he overlooked the fact that Dorla Balfour was at home, that she had been warned that her perfidy had been discovered, that her house of cards was about to come tumbling down. She concealed herself. As soon as she heard his voice, she tiptoed to a point of vantage where she could hear what he was saying. While she was listening to that phone conversation she suddenly knew a way by which she could extricate herself from her predicament.

'So Dorla waited until her husband had hung up, then rushed to him in apparent surprise and said, "Why, Guthrie, I thought you were on the train. What happened?"

'Balfour had probably placed Ted's gun on the stand by the telephone. Dorla, still acting the part of the surprised but faithful wife, with her left arm around her husband, picked up the gun and probably said, "Why, dear, what's this?"

'Then she took the gun and shot him in the head without warning.

'Then she telephoned Banner Boles at whatever place he had told her he'd be waiting, and asked him to come at once. So he grabbed a cab and joined Dorla. Then he took charge. Between them they got the idea of banging the body around so that the features would be unrecognizable, making it appear to be a hit-and-run accident and framing Ted with the whole thing, knowing that in case that didn't work they could use Florence Ingle to make it appear Guthrie Balfour was the murderer and that he had resorted to flight.

'So Boles returned the car that he had rented in the name of Jackson Eagan and left it there at the motel. He hoped the hit-and-run theory would work and the corpse would remain unidentified, but if things didn't work another anonymous tip to the police would bring Jackson Eagan into the picture. Boles wanted to have a complete supply of red herrings available in case his scheme encountered difficulties anywhere.

'Thereafter, as things worked out, it was relatively simple. Banner Boles returned to the Florence Ingle party. He managed to drug a drink so that Ted Balfour hardly knew what he was doing. Boles intended to take charge of Ted at that point, but Marilyn Keith saw Ted in an apparently intoxicated condition, so she drove him home and put him to bed.

'However, after she had gone home, the conspirators got the car Ted had been driving, took it out and ran over Guthrie Balfour's body, smashed up the headlight, left enough clues so that the police would be certain to investigate, and then, in order to be certain, arranged that there would be a witness, a Myrtle Anne Haley, who would tie in the accident directly with Ted Balfour. They arranged to have an anonymous tip send the police out to look at Ted's car.

'It only remained for the conspirators to take the company plane, fly it to Phoenix and get aboard the train, using the railroad ticket which they had taken from Balfour's body. Since Dorla had overheard her husband's conversation with Florence Ingle, she knew that Florence Ingle would go to Phoenix and bring the plane back, feeling certain that she was helping Guthrie Balfour in his deception.

'Of course, the planning in this was part of the master-minding of Banner Boles. That's been his job for years–to think fast in situations where another man would be panic-stricken, to mix up the evidence so that it would be interpreted about any way he wanted to have it interpreted. This was probably one of the high lights of his career.

'He crossed the border, taking out a tourist card as Guthrie Balfour. He was very careful not to telephone anyone who could detect the deception. For instance, he never telephoned Florence Ingle to thank her for what she had done or to tell her that everything had worked out according to schedule. He didn't dare to do that because she would have recognized that the voice was not that of Guthrie Balfour. On the other hand, since *I* didn't know Guthrie Balfour and had never talked with him, Boles was able to ring me up, disguise his voice slightly, tell me that he was Guthrie Balfour and that he was sending his wife to see me.'

'That's all very interesting,' Judge Cadwell said, 'How are you going to prove it?'

'*I'm* not going to prove it,' Mason said, 'but I think that the police can prove it if they will go out to the unit in the Sleepy Hollow Motel which was occupied by Banner Boles when he registered under the name of Jackson Eagan, and I think they'll find there's a small bullet hole in the floor which has hitherto been unnoticed. I think that if the police dig in there, they'll find another bullet discharged from that gun belonging to Ted Balfour.'

'Very, very interesting,' Judge Cadwell said. 'I take it, Mr District Attorney, that you will put the necessary machinery in motion to see that this case is investigated at once.'

'If Mr Mason is entirely finished,' Hamilton Burger said angrily, 'I'll now ask the Court to remember that I'm to have my innings. I want to ask Mr Mason how it happened he was in possesion of this evidence which he was concealing from the police.'

'I wasn't concealing it from the police,' Mason said. 'I was waiting for an opportunity to present it in such a manner that a murderer could be apprehended.

'For your information, when we were in that taxicab Banner Boles confessed the whole thing to me, except, of course, that he didn't admit that he was the Beau Brummell who had been making love to Dorla Balfour. He offered me a fee of more than a hundred thousand dollars to see that the facts didn't come out in court. Under the circumstances, I was entitled to hold the evidence until the moment when a disclosure would bring the real criminal to justice. I wasn't concealing any evidence. I was waiting to produce it at the right time.

'However, Banner Boles got to the stand, committed perjury, and forced my hand. I had to surrender the evidence before I was ready.'

'Your word against Banner Boles,' Hamilton Burger said.

'Exactly,' Mason told him, smiling. 'My word against that of a perjurer and accessory to murder.'

'How are you going to prove that?' Hamilton Burger snapped. 'You've come up here with a cockeyed theory, but how are you going to prove it?'

'*You* can prove it if you get busy and recover that extra bullet,' Mason said. 'And you can prove it if you ask him how it happened that, under oath, he swore to a conversation with a man whose fingerprints show that he had been dead for some time before the conversation took place. You can also prove it by getting in touch with the Mexican government and finding the tourist card that was issued to Guthrie Balfour. You'll find that that was in the handwriting of Banner Boles and you'll find that when Banner Boles left Mexico, he surrendered that tourist card properly countersigned.'

Judge Cadwell smiled at the district attorney. 'I think, Mr District Attorney,' he said, 'most of the logic, as well as *all* of the equities, are in favour of Perry Mason's position.'

21

Perry Mason, Della Street, Marilyn Keith, Paul Drake and Ted Balfour gathered for a brief, jubilant session in the witness room adjacent to Judge Cadwell's court-room.

'Remember now,' Mason cautioned Ted Balfour, 'at the moment you are jubilant because you have been released. But your uncle has been murdered. You had an affection for him. You're going to be interviewed by the press. You're going to be photographed, and you're going through quite an ordeal.'

Balfour nodded.

'And then,' Mason said, 'you're going to have to get in touch with your Uncle Addison Balfour and explain to him what happened, and you're going to have to see that Marilyn Keith is reinstated.'

'You leave that to me,' Balfour said. 'I'm going to have a talk with him within thirty minutes of the time I leave this court-house.'

A knock sounded on the door. Mason frowned. 'I'd hoped the newspaper reporters wouldn't find us here. I didn't want to face them until we were ready. Well, we'll have to take it now. I don't want them to think we're hiding.'

Mason flung the door open.

However, it wasn't a newspaper reporter who stood on the threshold, but the bailiff of Judge Cadwell's court who had arranged, in the first place, to have the witness room made available for the conference.

'I don't like to disturb you, Mr Mason,' he said, 'but it's a most important telephone call.'

'Just a moment,' Mason told the others. 'You wait here. I'll be right back.'

'There's a phone in this next room,' the bailiff said.

'Better come along, Paul,' Mason said. 'This may be something you'll have to work on. You, too. Della.'

Della Street and Paul Drake hurried out to stand by Mason's shoulder as Mason picked up the receiver.

'Hello,' Mason said.

A thin, reedy voice came over the line. 'Mr Mason, I guess you recognize my voice. I'm Addison Balfour. Please don't interrupt. I haven't much strength.

'I'm sorry that I was deceived about you. I shouldn't have listened to others. I should have known that a man doesn't build up the reputation you have built up unless he has what it takes.

'I'm all broken up about Guthrie but there's no help for that now. We all have to go sometime.

'You have done a remarkable piece of work. You have, incidentally, saved the Balfour Allied Associates from a great scandal, as well as a great financial loss.'

'You know what went on in court?' Mason asked.

'Certainly I know,' Addison Balfour snapped. 'I also know what went on in the judge's chambers. I may be sick, but I'm not mentally incapacitated. I've had reports coming in every half-hour. Don't think I'm a damn fool because I acted like one when I let Banner Boles talk me into firing you, so he could try to get Mortimer Dean Howland to take over Ted's defence.

'You send your bill to the Balfour Allied Associates for a hundred and fifty thousand dollars for legal services, and you tell that secretary of mine to get the hell back here on the job. I'm going to make a very substantial cash settlement with her to compensate her for the defamation of character connected with her temporary discharge. As for my nephew, you can tell him to stop worrying about his gambling debt now. I think he's learned his lesson.

'And if you want to cheer up a dying old man, you people will get out here as soon as you can and tell me that I'm forgiven. That's all. Good-bye.'

Addison Balfour hung up the phone at the other end of the line.

Mason turned to find the anxious faces of both Paul Drake and Della Street.

'Who was it?' Della Street asked.

'Addison Balfour,' Mason told her. 'He's anxious to make amends. He wants us there as soon as possible.'

'Well, then we'd better get out there as soon as possible,' Paul Drake said. 'In fact, it would be a swell thing from a standpoint of public relations if the newspaper reporters had to interview us *after* we got out there.'

'We won't be able to leave the building undetected,' Mason said. 'We can tell the reporters that we're going out there, but we're going to be interviewed within a few minutes, Paul.'

Mason pushed open the door to the witness room, then suddenly stepped back and gently closed the door.

'We'll wait a minute or two before we go in,' he said, grinning. 'I think the two people in there are discussing something that's damned important–to them.'

ERLE STANLEY GARDNER

The Case of

The Calendar Girl

I

George Ansley slowed his car, looking for Meridith Borden's driveway.

A cold, steady drizzle soaked up the illumination from his headlights. The windshield wipers beat a mechanical protest against the moisture which clung to the windshield with oily tenacity. The warm interior of the car caused a fogging of the glass, which Ansley wiped off from time to time with his handkerchief.

Meridith Borden's estate was separated from the highway by a high brick wall, surmounted with jagged fragments of broken glass embedded in cement.

Abruptly the wall flared inward in a sweeping curve, and the gravel driveway showed white in Ansley's headlights. The heavy iron gates were open. Ansley swung the wheel and followed the curving driveway for perhaps a quarter of a mile until he came to the stately, old-fashioned mansion, relic of an age of solid respectability.

For a moment Ansley sat in the automobile after he had shut off the motor and the headlights. It was hard to bring himself to do what he had to do, but try as he might, he could think of no other alternative.

He left the car, climbed the stone steps to the porch and pressed a button which jangled musical chimes in the deep interior of the house.

A moment later the porch was suffused with brilliance, and Ansley felt he was undergoing thorough, careful scrutiny. Then the door was opened by Meridith Borden himself.

'Ansley?' Borden asked.

'That's right,' Ansley said, shaking hands. 'I'm sorry to disturb you at night. I wouldn't have telephoned unless it had been a matter of considerable importance–at least to me.'

'That's all right, quite all right,' Borden said. 'Come on in. I'm here alone this evening. Servants all off. . . . Come on in. Tell me what's the trouble.'

Ansley followed Borden into a room which had been fixed up into a combination den and office. Borden indicated a comfortable chair, crossed over to a portable bar, said, 'How about a drink?'

'I could use one,' Ansley admitted. 'Scotch and soda, please.'

Borden filled glasses. He handed one to Ansley, clinked the ice in his drink, and stood by the bar, looking down at Ansley from a position of advantage.

He was tall, thick-chested, alert, virile and arrogant. There was a contemptuous attitude underlying the veneer of rough and ready cordiality which he assumed. It showed in his eyes, in his face and, at times, in his manner.

Ansley said, 'I'm going broke.'

'Too bad,' Borden commented, without the slightest trace of sympathy. 'How come?'

'I have the contract on this new school job out on 94th Street,' Ansley said.

'Bid too cheap?' Borden inquired.

'My bid was all right.'

'Labour troubles?'

'No. Inspector troubles.'

'How come?'

'They're riding me all the time. They're making me tear out and replace work as fast as I put it in.'

'What's the matter? Aren't you following specifications?'

'Of course I'm following specifications, but it isn't a question of specifications. It's a question of underlying hostility, of pouncing on every little technicality to make me do work over, to hamper me, to hold up the job, to delay the work.'

Borden made clucking noises of sympathy. His eyes, hard and appraising, remained fixed on Ansley.

'I protested to the inspector,' Ansley said. 'He told me, "Why don't you get smart and see Meridith Borden?"'

'I don't think I like that,' Borden said.

Ansley paid no attention to the comment. 'A friend of mine told me, "You damn fool. Go see Borden." And . . . well, here I am.'

'What do you want me to do?'

'Call off your dogs.'

'They're not *my* dogs.'

'I didn't mean it that way.'

There was a moment of silence.

'How much are you going to make on the job?' Borden asked.

'If they'll let me alone and let me follow specifications according to any reasonable interpretation, I'll have a fifty-thousand-dollar profit.'

'Too bad you're having trouble,' Borden said. 'I'd want a set of the specifications and a statement by you as to the type of trouble you've been having. If I decide you are being unjustly treated, I'll threaten a full-scale investigation. I don't think you'll have any more trouble. I'd need money, of course.'

'Of course,' Ansley said dryly.

'And,' Borden went on, 'after we start working together you won't have *any* trouble with the inspectors. Just make your stuff so it's good construction, so that it'll stand up, and that's all you need to worry about. Don't measure the placement of your structural steel with too much accuracy. Make your mix contain just enough concrete to do the job, and don't worry about having absolutely uniform percentages.'

'That isn't what I wanted,' Ansley said. 'I only wanted to have a reasonable break.'

'You'll get it,' Borden promised. 'Mail me a retainer of two thousand dollars tomorrow, pay five thousand from the next two progress payments you get, and give me five per cent of the final payment. Then we'll talk things over on the next job. I understand you're planning to bid on the overhead crossing on Telephone Avenue?'

'I've thought about it. I'd like to get cleaned up on this job and get my money out of it first.'

'Okay. See me about that overhead crossing before you put in your bid. We'll talk it over. I can help you. A good public relations man who knows the ropes can do a lot on jobs of this kind.'

'I'm satisfied he can,' Ansley said bitterly.

'I wish you'd seen me before you took that school job,' Borden went on. 'There might have been more in it for both of us. You didn't have any public relations expert to represent your interests in connexion with the bidding?'

'No. Why should I need a public relations expert just to submit a bid?'

Borden shrugged his shoulders. The gesture was eloquent.

Ansley finished his drink. 'I'm sorry that I had to bother you at this hour of the night, but the inspector found two places in the wall where he claimed the steel was incorrectly spaced. It didn't amount to more than a quarter of an inch, but he demanded I conform to specifications. I can't tear out the whole wall, and to try to cut and patch now would be prohibitive.'

Borden said, 'See that inspector tomorrow and tell him to take another measurement. I think the steel's all right. The rods may have been bent a little off centre. Quit worrying about it. Tomorrow's a new day.'

Ansley put down the drink, got up, hesitated, then said, 'Well, I guess I'll be getting on.'

'I'm glad you dropped in, Ansley,' Borden said, 'and I'll take care of you to the best of my ability. I feel quite certain you won't have any more trouble with the inspectors. They don't like adverse publicity any better than anyone else, and, after all, I'm a public relations expert.'

Borden laughed and moved to accompany Ansley to the door.

'I can find my way out all right,' Ansley said.

'No, no, I'll see you to the door. I'm all alone here tonight. Sorry.'

He escorted Ansley to the door, said good night, and Ansley went down the steps into the cold rain.

He knew that his trouble with the inspectors was over, but he knew that the trouble with his self-respect had just begun.

They had told him at the start that it was foolish to try to build anything without getting in touch with Meridith Borden. Ansley had thought he could get by, by being scrupulously fair and conforming to the specifications. He was rapidly finding out how small a part fairness and specifications played in the kind of job he was getting into now.

Ansley sent his car crunching along the gravel driveway. His anger at himself and the conditions which had forced him to go to Meridith Borden made him resentful. He knew that he was driving too fast, knew that it wasn't going to do him any good to try to hurry away from Meridith Borden's palatial estate on the outskirts of the city, knew that it wasn't going to do him any good to try to get away from himself. He had lost something important in that interview; a part of him that he couldn't afford to lose, but he had yielded to the inexorable pressure of economic necessity.

Ansley swung the wheel around the last curve in the driveway and slowed for the main highway as he saw the iron gates.

It was at that moment that he saw the headlights on the road swinging towards him.

Apparently the driver of the oncoming car intended to turn in at the gate, and was cutting the corner before realizing a car was coming. The smooth, black surface of the road was slippery with an oily coating from the first rain in weeks.

For a brief moment headlights blazed into Ansley's windshield, then the other car swirled through the gate into a sickening, skidding turn. The rear fender of the car brushed against the bumper of Ansley's car.

In vain Ansley tried to bring his car to a stop. He felt the jar of impact, saw the careening car tilt upward, swerve from the driveway. He heard a crash, dimly saw the hedge sway under the impact, heard another jarring sound and then silence.

Ansley braked his car to a stop just outside the gates. Without bothering to shut off the motor or dim the headlights, he scrambled out from behind the wheel, leaving the front left-hand door swinging wide open. He ran back through the soggy gravel to the gap in the hedge.

He could see the other car only as a dim, dark bulk. The motor was no longer running, the lights were off. He had the impression that the car was lying over on its side, but he couldn't be certain. The machine had crashed through the hedge, but there remained enough broken twigs and jagged branches to make progress extremely difficult and hazardous.

'Is everyone all right?' Ansley asked, standing midway through the tangle of the jagged hedge.

There was no answer, only a dead silence.

Ansley's eyes were gradually becoming accustomed to the darkness. He plunged forward, pushing his way through the water-soaked leaves.

A projecting snag caught the leg of Ansley's trousers, tripped him, threw him forward. He heard ripping cloth, felt a sharp pain along his shin. Then, as he threw out his hands to protect himself, his right hand was snagged by the sharp projection of a broken branch. The ground was sloping sharply, and Ansley found himself with his head lower than his feet. It was with difficulty that he got to his knees, and then once more to a standing position.

The car was directly in front of him now, only some twenty feet away. By this time he could see plainly that the car was resting on the right-hand side of the top.

'Hello,' Ansley called. 'Is everybody all right?'

Again there was no answer.

'Is anybody hurt?' Ansley asked.

The night silence was broken only by the gurgling noises of liquids draining from the car. There was the harsh odour of raw gasoline.

Ansley knew he didn't dare to strike a match. He remembered then, belatedly, that he kept a small flashlight in the glove compartment of his car. He ran back, floundering through the hedge, opened the glove compartment of his car and returned with the flashlight.

This light, carried for emergencies, had been in the glove compartment for a long time. The battery was all but dead. The bulb furnished a fitful reddish glow which Ansley knew wouldn't last long. In order to save the battery, he switched out the light and again floundered through the broken hedge in the dark. He approached the car, saw that one of the doors was swinging partially open. He thrust his arm inside the car and turned on the flashlight.

There was no one inside.

Ansley moved around the front of the car, holding the flashlight in front of him. What should have been a beam of bright light was now only a small cone of faint illumination. It was, however, sufficient to show the girl's feet and ankles, feet which were eloquently motionless.

Ansley hurried around so that he could see the rest of the form which lay huddled there on the wet grass.

She had evidently been thrown to the ground and had skidded forward. The legs were smooth, shapely and well rounded. The momentum of the young woman's slide had left her legs exposed to the thighs, her skirts rumpled into a twisted ball. Ansley raised the flashlight, saw one arm twisted up and over the face, and then the light failed completely.

Instinctively, and without thinking, Ansley threw the useless flashlight from him, bent over the young woman's body and in the darkness groped for her wrist.

He found a pulse, a faint but regular heartbeat.

Ansley straightened, and starting groping his way across to the gravel driveway, only to find that the hedge barred his progress. He moved along parallel with the hedge, raised his voice and shouted, 'Help!' at the top of his lungs.

The soggy darkness swallowed up the cry, and Ansley, annoyed at the thick hedge which kept him from the open gravel driveway, lowered his shoulder and prepared to crash through the intertwined branches.

It was then he heard the faint, moaning call from behind him.

Ansley paused and listened. This time he heard a tremulous cry of 'Help! Help!'

Once more Ansley turned and groped his way back through the darkness to the overturned car.

The young woman was sitting up now, a vague figure in the darkness. Ansley could see the blurred white oval of her face, her two hands and the lighter outline of flesh above her stockings.

'Are you hurt?' Ansley asked.

By way of answer she instinctively pulled down her skirt.

'Where am I?' she asked.

'Are you hurt?'

'I don't know.'

'Let's find out,' Ansley said, dropping down beside her. 'Any broken bones?'

'Who . . . who are you?'

'I was driving the car that you . . . ran into.'

'Oh.'

'Tell me, are you all right? Try moving your arms, your legs.'

'I've moved my arms,' she said. 'My . . . my legs. . . . Yes, I'm all right. Help me up, will you, please?'

She extended a hand and Ansley took it. After two abortive attempts, she managed to get to her feet. She stood, wobbling for a moment, then swayed against him.

Ansley supported her with an arm around her waist, a hand under her armpit on the other side. 'Take it easy,' he said.

'Where . . . where am I?'

'You were just turning in at the driveway of the Meridith Borden estate when you apparently lost control of your car,' Ansley said, choosing his words carefully, not wishing to accuse the shaken young woman of having hit him, but carefully avoiding any admission that his car had hit hers.

'Oh, yes,' she said, 'I remember now. . . . There was something in the road ahead, a dead cat or something. I didn't know what it was. I swerved the car slightly and then all of a sudden I was dizzy, going around and around. I saw headlights and then there was a crash. I felt myself going over, and the next thing I knew, I was sitting here in the grass. I'm . . . I'm all right now. My head is clearing rapidly.'

'Were you alone?' Ansley asked.

'Yes.'

'Do you have anything in the car?'

'Nothing except my handbag. I'll get that. Do you have a flashlight?'

'No. I had one that was just about completely run-down. I was able to get a few minutes' light from the thing before the battery ran down completely.'

'Do you have a match?'

'Don't strike a match,' Ansley warned. 'There's gasoline draining out of the motor somewhere, or out of the gas tank.'

'I can find it,' she said. 'At least I hope I can.'

'Can I get it for you? Can I–'

'No,' she said, 'I'll get it.'

She stooped, crawled through the open door, and once more Ansley saw the rounded flesh above her stocking tops as she struggled back, getting out through the door feet first.

'Get it?' Ansley asked.

'I got it,' she said. 'Heavens! I'll bet I was a spectacle *that* time.'

Ansley said, 'It's dark. Thank heavens you're not hurt. The first thing for us to do is to get you where you want to go, and then we'll send a tow car out and notify Borden.'

'I'll take care of that,' she said hastily. 'Don't bother about it. And don't worry about the accident. It wasn't your fault. I think it was just one of those unavoidable things. Your car isn't damaged, is it?'

'I didn't look,' Ansley said, 'but I don't think so. The way it felt you just grazed my bumper.'

'Let's go take a look,' she said.

'Do you have anything in there besides your handbag?'

'That's all. There's a raincoat in there somewhere, but that can wait until the tow car shows up.'

'Can I get it for you?'

'No, I know about where it is.'

'It's dark,' Ansley said.

She said, 'Yes, but I think I can find it.'

She wiggled her way into the car again, came out pulling a coat after her and said, 'Okay, let's go.'

'Now, we're supposed to do something about this, I think,' Ansley said, as he led the way through the hedge. 'I think we're supposed to make a report or something.'

'Oh, sure, we're supposed to check one another's driving licences and all that. We'll have time to talk that over while you're driving me into town. You *are* headed towards the city, aren't you?'

'Yes.'

'Well, that's fine.'

'I'll take you anywhere you want to go,' Ansley said.

'Do you know the Ancordia Apartments?'

'No, I'm not familiar with them.'

'Well, turn off–I'll show you. Just go on in on the freeway.'

'All right,' Ansley said. 'I'll take a look at my car, but I'm quite certain there's no damage done.'

Ansley looked at his car, found a dented fender and a scrape of paint on the bumper.

'No damage to my car,' he said.

'Do I just hop in?' she asked.

Ansley laughed and held the door open. 'Hop in,' he invited.

Ansley had a chance to size the young woman up as the light in the interior of the car disclosed reddish hair, even, regular features, dark brownish eyes, a firm chin and a good figure.

'We may as well get acquainted,' she said, laughing. 'I'm Beatrice Cornell. I live in the Ancordia Apartments. My friends call me Bee for short.'

'George Ansley,' he told her. 'A struggling contractor trying to get by.'

'And,' she observed, taking out a notebook, 'I suppose, in order to comply with the amenities of the situation, I've got to have the licence number of your automobile.'

'JYJ 113,' he told her.

'Mine is CVX 266. I'm all covered by insurance and I suppose you are.'

He nodded.

'Then we can forget the legal aspects of the situation and discuss the personal. Can you tell me exactly what happened?'

'Not very well,' he said. 'I was just coming out of the driveway. You were coming along the road, and I thought you were turning in at the driveway.'

She shook her head. 'I was trying to avoid this thing in the road, a clod of earth, a dead cat or something. The car swung out all right around the obstruction, whatever it was, and then when I started to straighten, I couldn't. I saw your headlights right ahead of me. Then they pin-wheeled off to one side, then I was rolling over, and that's the last I remember. . . . Can you go on from there?'

'I got out of my car and ran through the hedge to see if there had been any damage,' Ansley said, 'and you were out like a light. Evidently you'd hit the ground feet first and skidded along on the damp grass.'

'You had a flashlight?'

'I had a worn-out flashlight. The batteries didn't last long.'

She glanced at him archly. 'And a good thing, too–from my point of view,' she said.

'Unfortunately, I couldn't see much,' he told her.

She laughed. 'Oh, well, legs are standard equipment anyway, and, thanks to the wet grass, I didn't lose any skin, although I feel a little muddy in places.'

Ansley took out his wallet, handed it to her, and said, 'My driving licence is in the cellophane compartment there. Copy the number and the address.'

'Oh, that isn't at all necessary,' she said. 'After all, that's a formality reserved for strangers who intend to sue each other. I hope we'll be friends.'

'Believe me,' Ansley said, 'I can't tell you how relieved I am that you're not hurt.'

'I'm all right. No doubt I'll be a little sore tomorrow.'

'You're sure that's all it is?'

'Sure.'

'You must have had something of a concussion,' Ansley said. 'You certainly were out cold.'

'Probably hit the back of my head on the ground,' she said, ' but it's been hit before. I've done some ski-ing and swimming and what with one thing and another I've had my share of knocks.'

'Rather an active career,' Ansley said.

She laughed. 'I'm an active woman. I like action. . . . You said the property belonged to Meridith Borden?'

'Yes.'

'He's a politician, isn't he?'

'Public relations is the way he describes himself.'

'That's just another way of saying lobbyist, isn't it?' I've read comments about him. Some people seem to think he's a man with a cloven hoof.'

'I guess any person in politics has his share of enemies,' Ansley said noncommittally.

'Do you know him?'

'I've met him.'

'You were coming from there?'

'That's right.'

'Oh, all right,' she said, laughing. 'I didn't want to pry into your private affairs. I was just making conversation.'

'I didn't mean to be secretive,' he said.

'Perhaps you didn't mean to be, but you are. I think you're naturally secretive. Do you know, George, I'm getting just a little headache. If you don't mind, I'm going to settle back and close my eyes.'

'Now, look here,' Ansley said, 'you're going to a doctor. You've had a concussion, and–'

'Don't be silly!' she protested. 'I don't need a doctor. If I do, there's a doctor who lives in the same apartment house. I'll get him to give me a sedative. Now, don't be a silly boy, just go ahead and drive me to the Ancordia and forget it.

'You turn on Lincoln Avenue and go to 81st Street, and then turn right and–'

'Oh, I know where it is now,' Ansley said. 'I'll take you there.'

She settled back against the cushions, closed her eyes.

After some five minutes Ansley eased the car to a stop in front of the Ancordia Apartments.

His passenger opened her eyes, seemed dazed for a moment, sighed sleepily, leaned over against him. Her chin came up as her head cradled against the side of his arm. Her lips were half-parted, her eyes were dreamy as she raised and lowered the lids.

'Well, here we are,' Ansley said.

'Here–Who . . .?'

'Look here,' Ansley said, bending over to look into her face, 'are you quite all right?'

Her eyes opened then. For a moment they were fastened on his with a provocative smile. Her lips remained parted. Her chin tilted just a little more.

Ansley bent forward and kissed her.

She sighed tremulously; her warm lips clung to his, then suddenly, as though wakening from a dream, she stiffened, pushed him back and, for a moment, seemed indignant.

'I was asleep,' she said. 'I–'

'I'm sorry,' Ansley said.

Abruptly she laughed. 'Don't be. I guess I led with my chin. . . . I was half asleep thinking of one of my boy friends.'

'I couldn't resist the temptation,' Ansley said contritely. 'I–'

'Don't apologize. Men aren't supposed to resist temptation. That's in the feminine department. Am I going to see you again?'

'I'll take you to your apartment,' Ansley said.

'Indeed you won't,' she told him. 'I'm quite all right.'

'No, no, I want to see you up.'

'Well, as far as the street door,' she compromised. 'After all, you're going to have to leave your car double-parked.'

Ansley hurried around the car to help her out, but she had the door open before he arrived. She gave him her hand, slid out from the seat, paused, said, 'I'll bet I'm mud from head to toe.'

She moved her skirt up along the nylon stocking with a gesture that seemed entirely natural and uninhibited, then suddenly laughed, let her skirt drop, and said, 'I guess I'd better make that inspection in the privacy of my apartment.'

She ran lightly up the steps to the apartment, fumbled in her handbag, said, 'Oh, dear, I left my key at the office again. I'll have to get one of my friends to let me in.'

She pushed on the button and a moment later a buzzer announced the latch was being released on the street door.

She opened the door for an inch or two, held it open with her foot, turned to Ansley and said, 'I'm going to let you kiss me again, George. Either my dreams deceived me or you're an expert. I'm fully awake now.'

Ansley swept her into his arms.

His kiss was long. Her response was practiced.

'I'm fully awake now, myself,' Ansley said, looking at her hungrily.

She smiled at him. 'Mustn't try to make too much progress the first night, George. I hope to see you again. Give me a ring. Bye now.'

She slipped through the door.

Ansley stood for a moment watching the slowly closing door, hearing the click of the latch as the door closed.

He turned, retraced his steps to his automobile and sat for a moment behind the wheel, his forehead puckered in thought.

2

Perry Mason and Della Street, enjoying a leisurely dinner, had sat through the floor show, had danced twice and were finishing up on brandy and Benedictine when Della Street looked up with a slight frown of annoyance at the young man who was approaching their table with a businesslike directness which indicated he had some definite objective in mind.

'Mr Mason,' the man said, 'my name is George Ansley. I was finishing a cocktail here earlier this evening just as you came in. I know you by sight. I dislike to intrude in this way, but . . . well, I'm in need of some legal advice. It's a minor matter, something you can tell me offhand. Here's my card. If you'll just answer a question and then send me a bill, I'll . . . well, I'll certainly appreciate the favour.'

Mason said, 'I'm sorry, but I'm–' Suddenly, at the look in Ansley's eyes, he changed his mind. 'Sit down, have a drink and tell us about it. This is Miss Street, my confidential secretary. For your information, Ansley, I do mostly trial work and I only take the cases that interest me. Somehow or other that has led me to gravitate towards the defence of persons accused of murder, and, unless you want to go out and commit a murder, I'm afraid you're not going to interest me.'

'I know, I know,' Ansley said. 'This is just a minor matter, but it may be important to me.'

'Well, what is it?' Mason asked.

'I was driving my car. I left here to keep a business appointment. The roads were wet, and a car driven by a young woman skidded into me and overturned.'

'Much damage?' Mason asked.

'Virtually no damage to my car, but the other car was, I'm afraid, pretty completely wrecked. The car was in a skid when it hit me, and it went off the road, through a hedge and rolled over.'

'Anybody hurt?'

'No, and–That's what bothers me.'

'Go ahead,' Mason said.

'A young woman was driving the car. She seems to be a delightful personality and she . . . well, I guess she liked me and somehow I–To tell you the truth, I don't know how I feel about her, Mr Mason. When I was with her I felt that I liked her, and she certainly was attractive.'

'Go on,' Mason said.

'After I had left, I began to realize that there was something terribly peculiar about the whole episode. She sort of led me along and . . . I kissed her a couple of times and I didn't think of too much else. I . . . well, here's the point, Mr Mason. She was unconscious for a while, and then she came to. She seems to be feeling quite all right, but I've heard a lot about these cases of concussion. I suppose I should notify my insurance company. I'll take care of that all right, but what about the police? That's the thing that bothers me. Should I report the accident to the police?'

'The young woman was unconscious?' Mason asked.

'That's right.'

'And the car was damaged?'

'Yes.'

'What kind was it?'

'It was a good-looking Cadillac, a late model.'

'Get the licence number?'

'Yes. It was CVX 266.'

'Notify the police,' Mason said. 'Where did the accident happen?'

'That's just it, Mr Mason. I . . . I don't want to notify the police unless I absolutely must.'

'Why?' Mason asked.

'Well,' Ansley said, 'that's something of a story and–Look here, Mr Mason, I know you're a busy man, I know you work under quite a strain, I know you're trying to relax here tonight, and I feel like a heel, but the man who handles my legal business is out of town at the moment and I don't know anyone else. I saw you here and . . . well, this may be very, very important to me. I need the best in the line of legal advice.'

'Why is it important?' Mason asked. 'And why don't you want to report it to the Highway Patrol?'

'Because I'm a contractor. I'm contracting on some city jobs and they've put the bite on me.'

'Who has?'

Ansley shrugged his shoulders and said, 'How do I know? All I know is that the inspectors are making life impossible for me. I've been told to tear out a whole section of wall because a couple of pieces of structural steel were less than an inch out of place. I have inspectors hanging around the job looking things over with a microscope. . . . Well, I knew the answer. I put off doing what had to be done as long as I could, but now it's a question of whether I make a profit on the job or whether the thing wipes me out. This is one of my first big jobs. I've stretched my credit to the limit, and everything I have is riding along on that job.'

'I still don't get what you're trying to tell me,' Mason said.

'I was given the tip that the remedy for my troubles was to see Meridith Borden. I went out and saw him. The accident occurred just as I was leaving his grounds. The other car has rolled over and is on his grounds. I don't want to make a report to the Highway Patrol which will show I was leaving Meridith Borden's house. If it should get written up in the newspaper and–Well, you can see the position I'm in.'

'Forget it,' Mason said, 'but notify your insurance carrier. And, of course, you've got to take a chance that the girl wasn't hurt. She seemed all right?'

'She seemed all right,' Ansley said, 'and yet there's something that isn't all right.'

Mason glanced across at Della Street's disapproving face. 'Now you've got me interested,' he said. 'Tell me about it. Do you know the girl's name?'

'Oh, yes, of course. I got her name.'

'What is it?'

'Beatrice Cornell. She lives at the Ancordia Apartments.'

'See her driving licence?' Mason asked.

'No.'

'Why not?'

'Well, that's one of the things that I got to thinking about later. She acted so peculiarly about the entire accident. The–Well, it was a funny thing, but I know she lied about one thing. She was deliberately turning her car into the driveway to Borden's house when she lost control of it, and it went into a skid. But she tried to tell me she didn't know Borden and was simply driving along the highway when she swerved to avoid a cat or something on the road, and–'

'Tell me about it,' Mason said. 'Start at the beginning and tell me the whole thing.'

Della Street sighed, produced a shorthand notebook from her handbag, pushed the half-emptied glass of brandy and Benedictine to one side and started taking notes.

Ansley told the entire story.

Mason's forehead creased in a frown. 'You say this girl was unconscious?'

'Yes. There was a steady pulse, but it was thin and weak.'

'Then you started for the house and she screamed and you ran back?'

'Yes.'

'And the minute you ran back she seemed to be in full possession of her faculties?'

'Yes.'

'You saw this young woman when she was lying there unconscious with her legs and thighs exposed. Your flashlight was working then?'

'Yes.'

'What did she look like?'

'Well, of course, I had only a very general impression while she was lying there on the ground. Later on in the car I had a chance to see more of her.

'She was nice-looking, rather young–oh, say twenty-four or five and her hair was sort of a reddish brown. I think her eyes were dark brown. She had even, regular teeth, which flashed when she smiled, and she seemed to smile easily.'

'Now,' Mason said, 'let's concentrate on her shoes. Can you remember anything about her shoes?'

'Her shoes? Why?'

'I'm just asking,' Mason said.

'Why, yes, they were sort of a brown. They were sort of dark with open toes.'

Mason said, 'All right. *She* told *you* she didn't want a doctor. *I'm* going to let her tell *me*. I'm going to ring her up and tell her I'm your attorney, that I want to send a doctor around to look at her and make certain she's all right.'

'She'll refuse,' Ansley said.

'Then we'll have made the offer,' Mason told him. 'Up to this time, it's your word against hers. Now *I'll* call up as your attorney, and she'll refuse to see a doctor and that will be that.'

Mason nodded to Della Street. 'Look up Beatrice Cornell, Della. See if she has a phone listed. If she doesn't we'll have to get her through the Ancordia Apartments.'

Della Street nodded, pushed back her chair and went to the telephone booth.

A moment later she beckoned Perry Mason, and, when the lawyer crossed over to the booth, Della said, 'May I speak with Miss Beatrice Cornell, please? Yes. . . . This is Miss Street. I'm the secretary for Mr Perry Mason, the attorney. He wants to talk with you. . . . Yes, Perry Mason. . . . No, I'm not fooling. Will you hold the line a moment, please . . . ? Yes. . . . My name is Street. S-t-r-e-e-t. I'm speaking for Mr Mason. He's right here. Will you hold the line, please?'

Mason stepped into the booth.

'Miss Cornell?' he asked into the telephone.

'Yes.'

'I'm Perry Mason, the lawyer.'

'Say, just what sort of a gag *is* this?' the voice on the line demanded. 'I thought I'd heard them all, but this is a new one.'

'And why does it have to be a gag?' Mason asked.

The voice over the telephone was pleasing to the ear, but an element of humorous scepticism was quite apparent. 'My friends,' she said, 'know of my admiration for Mr Mason. I make no secret of it and I suppose this is someone's idea of a gag. But go right ahead. I'll ride along with it. Let's suppose that you're Mr Perry Mason, the attorney, and I'm the Queen of Sheba. Where do we go from here?'

'As it happens,' Mason said, 'I'm calling you on behalf of a client.'

The voice suddenly lost its humorous scepticism and took on a note of genuine curiosity. 'The name of the client?'

'George Ansley,' Mason said. 'Does the name mean anything to you?'

'Should it?'

'Yes.'

'It doesn't.'

'He is the one who took you home a short time ago.'

'Took me home?'

'From the automobile accident.'

'What automobile accident are you talking about, Mr Mason?'

'The accident in which your car was overturned. You have a Cadillac, I believe, the licence CVX 266?'

She laughed. 'I am a working girl, Mr Mason. I haven't had a car for several years. All I have is an interest or an equity or whatever you want to call it in the public buses. I have been here in my apartment all evening, reading, as it happens, a mystery story, and hardly anticipating that I was going to be called in connexion with one.'

'And you live at the Ancordia Apartments?'

'That's right.'

'Miss Cornell, this may be a matter of some importance. Would you mind giving me a physical description of yourself?'

'Why should I?' she asked.

'Because, as I told you, it may be a matter of some importance. I think perhaps someone has been using your name.'

She hesitated a moment, then said, 'I'll give you the description that appears on my driving licence, acting on the assumption that perhaps this *is* Mr Perry Mason. I am thirty-three years of age, I am brunette, my eyes are dark, I am five feet, four inches in height, I weigh 122 pounds, and I'm trying to take off five of those pounds. Now, is there anything else I can tell you?'

'Thank you,' Mason said, 'you have been of the greatest help. I am afraid someone has been using your name. Do you know anyone who might have used your name?'

'No.'

'Someone perhaps who lives in the same apartment house?'

'I know of no one, Mr Mason. . . . Tell me, is this on the level? Is this really on the up-and-up?'

'It is,' Mason said. 'A young woman was in an automobile accident earlier this evening. Mr Ansley offered to drive her home. She gave him the name of Beatrice Cornell, the address of the Ancordia Apartments. This man drove her to that address. She thanked him and went in.'

'Can you describe her?'

Mason, suddenly cautious, said, 'I haven't as yet checked on her physical description with my client, but I might be able to call you back later on. Say perhaps tomorrow sometime.'

'I wish you would,' she said. 'I'm very curious, and if this is really *the* Perry Mason with whom I'm talking, please accept my apologies for my initial scepticism. May I say that this was due to the fact that all my friends know I am a fan of yours. I have followed your legal adventures with considerable interest and enjoy reading about your cases in the newspapers.'

'Thanks a lot,' Mason told her. 'I'm honoured.'

'*I'm* the one that's honoured,' she said.

'You'll probably hear from me later,' Mason told her. 'Good night.'

Mason hung up the phone, frowned at Della Street, said, 'Ring up Paul Drake at the Drake Detective Agency, Della. Ask him to get busy at once on a car having the licence plates of CVX 266. I want to find out about it fast. I'll go back and rejoin Ansley.'

'Well?' Ansley asked as Mason returned to the table.

Mason smiled. 'She says she wasn't in any automobile accident, that she's been home all evening, that she doesn't know what it's all about. The description, according to her driving licence, is age, thirty-three, brunette, dark eyes, height, five-feet-four, weight, 122 pounds.'

Ansley frowned. 'I don't think the woman in the car could have been more than thirty. I'd say maybe twenty-eight. That weight is a little heavy, and I'm quite certain the hair was reddish brown. I . . . well, I just don't know.'

'What about the height?'

'That's another thing. I think she was more than five feet, four inches. Of course, I don't remember all the details. She jumped in the car and then I–'

'But she was standing alongside of you,' Mason said. 'What happened when you said good night?'

'I kissed her.'

'All right,' Mason said, 'get a visual recall of that event. How was she when you kissed her? Did she tilt her chin up, or was her face more nearly on a level with yours? How tall are you?'

'Five-feet-eleven.'

'All right. Did you bend over when you kissed her?'

'Slightly.'

'You think five-feet-four is about the right height?'

'I . . . I'd say she was taller. I saw her legs, and they seemed to be . . . well, they were long legs.'

'Slender or chunky?'

'Well formed. I . . . I suppose I should be ashamed of myself, but when the flashlight gave its last flicker of light and showed her lying there, I realized how beautiful a woman's legs can be. I thought there were lots *of* them–the legs I mean.'

'You would, under the circumstances,' Mason said. 'You were standing at her feet and looking up. The legs would look longer under those circumstances. Your best way to estimate her height is how she stood when she was close to you and you were kissing her good night. Was she wearing shoes with fairly high heels?'

'Let me think,' Ansley said, frowning.

'Oh-oh!' Mason said. 'Here's Della with something important.'

Della Street came hurrying towards the table from the phone booth.

'What?' Mason asked as he saw the expression on her face.

'Paul Drake took a short cut on getting the ownership of that automobile,' she said. 'I told him you were in a hurry so he decided to work through a friend in police headquarters.'

'And what happened?' Mason asked.

'CVX 266,' she said, 'is the licence number of a Cadillac sedan that was stolen about two hours ago. The police have broadcast a description, hoping they could pick up the car. It seems it belongs to someone rather important and was stolen from the place where it had been parked at some social function. Quite naturally, when Paul Drake telephoned in and asked for the registration report on a Cadillac, CVX 266, and the man at Headquarters found out that the car was hot and police were trying to locate it, you can imagine what happened.'

'In other words, Drake finds himself in a spot,' Mason said.

'Exactly,' she said.

'What did he do?'

'He told the police that he *thought* the car had been involved in an accident of some sort, that a client of his had telephoned in asking him to check the ownership, that he expected the client to call back again in a short time, and at that time Drake would tell the client to report to the police at once.'

'The police are satisfied with that?' Mason asked.

'They're not satisfied,' she said. 'They're accepting it temporarily because they have to. Drake told me he's had trouble enough with the police because of things he's had to do for you in the past, and he doesn't want any more.'

Ansley said, 'Good heavens! I don't want to have it known that I was out there at Borden's. Can't we–?'

Mason said to Della Street, 'Call Paul Drake, tell him he can tell the police that the client he's working for is Perry Mason, that Mason is going to call in after a while, and Drake will tell Mason to report to police everything he knows about the car. That will put Paul Drake in the clear.'

'Where will that leave you?' Della Street asked.

'I'll be all right,' Mason said. 'I'll report to the police where the car is, but *I* won't tell them the name of *my* client. I'll simply state that I happen to know the car tried to turn into the driveway and was going at too fast a speed and rolled over.'

'That wasn't what happened,' Ansley reminded Mason. 'She was dodging something in the road.'

'That's what she told you,' Mason said. 'Now let's think a little more about that woman who was driving the car. We were talking about shoes. What sort of heels?'

Ansley said thoughtfully, 'You suggested she must have been wearing high heels. She wasn't. The shoes were–Say, wait a minute. She must have–She *couldn't* have changed shoes!'

Mason's eyes were level-lidded. 'Go on,' he said.

'Why, I remember now. I saw one of the shoes when she was lying unconscious. When she got out of the automobile, they weren't the same kind of shoes.'

'What do you mean?'

'When she was lying there I saw . . . let's see, I guess it was the right shoe. It was open at the end. You know, open over the end of the toe. But when she got out of the car, her shoes were solid over the toe. She couldn't have had one shoe on one foot and another on another foot, and yet she couldn't have changed shoes. She–'

Mason pushed back his chair from the table. 'Come on,' he said, 'we're going out and take a look at that car.'

'At the car?'

'Sure,' Mason said. 'There were *two* women.'

'What!'

'One woman was lying there unconscious,' Mason went on. 'You saw her, then you started running towards the house and yelling for help. The other girl didn't want that. She must have dragged the unconscious girl to one side, taken her place, assumed the same position of the other girl, then called out for help. When you came back, she gave you just enough of a glimpse so that you would see she was lying in the same position the other person had been. Then she scrambled to her feet, said she was all right, told you she'd been driving the car by herself and asked you to take her home. . . . You said you didn't see her driving licence, didn't you?'

'That's right. I remember she laughingly said something about the fact that it was only when people were formal that they were supposed to show their driving licences and all that, but that we were getting along informally.'

'And she let you kiss her in order to show that it *was* informal. I take it, it was an informal kiss?'

'Well,' Ansley admitted, 'it distracted my attention from such things as her driving licence.'

'Come on,' Mason told him. 'Let's go. I want to see how deep you're into this thing before I start cutting any corners.

'Della, ring up Paul Drake. Tell him he can tell the police I am the one who made the inquiry, but have him tell the police that he doesn't know where I can be reached. That will be technically true.

'I'll be getting the car while you're phoning, and we'll run out there and take a look at the situation.'

'Then what?' Ansley asked anxiously.

'If that other young woman isn't hurt too badly,' Mason said, 'you may be able to keep from reporting the accident. If, as I rather suspect may be the case, we find another woman rather badly injured, we're going to have to do some tall explaining, and you're going to have to answer a lot of questions.'

3

The drizzle which had been intermittent during the late afternoon and early evening had settled into a cold, steady rain by the time Mason's headlights picked up the entrance to Meridith Borden's grounds.

'Here you are,' Ansley said. 'It happened right here. Right inside the gate there. If you'll stop right here, you can see the gap in the hedge.'

Mason braked his car to a stop, opened the glove compartment and took out a flashlight.

'Now, we're not going to get caught prowling in the grounds,' Mason said. 'The first thing is to find out whether my suspicions are correct. If they are, we'll take a quick look for this other young woman who was a passenger in the automobile. If we don't spot her right away, we'll go to Borden's house and then you'll have to notify the police. Do you know much about Meridith Borden?'

'Only his reputation and what little I know from talking with him,' Ansley said.

Mason said, 'He's supposed to have lots of enemies. This wall topped by broken glass and barbed wire is rather eloquent in itself. I understand that at a certain hour electrically controlled gates are swung shut. Moreover, savage watchdogs can be released to patrol the grounds in case of any alarm. Now, let's stay together, carry on an organized search in an orderly manner and get out of here. First let's take a look at the car. You can show us that.'

'The car's right over here, Mr Mason, through this gap in the hedge.'

Mason said to Della Street, 'Perhaps you'd better stay in the car, Della. This is going to be wet and muddy and–'

She shook her head emphatically. 'You'll need witnesses if you find anything, and if it's a woman, you'll want me along.'

She slid across the seat and out of the car.

Ansley led the way through the gate towards the overturned automobile. Mason directed the beam of his flashlight on the pathway, pausing to help Della Street through the tangled, wet, broken branches of the hedge.

'We'll give the place one quick going over,' Mason said, 'and then we'll know what to do. Where was this young woman lying, Ansley?'

'Right over here on the other side of the car–around this way.'

Mason played the beam of the flashlight along the ground.

Abruptly Della Street said, 'Someone with heels did a lot of walking around here, Chief.'

'Yes,' Mason said, 'and you can see over here where she was dragging something. She braced herself. Look at those heel marks. She was digging in with her heels.'

'Then there *were* two women,' Ansley said.

'It looks like it,' Mason commented, the beam of his flashlight playing around on the ground.

'She couldn't have dragged the other woman very far,' Della Street said. 'Not in the brief time she had.'

Mason sent the beam of the flashlight in questing semi-circles over the wet grass.

'Well,' Mason said at length, 'it's pretty certain that this other woman either recovered consciousness and walked off, or else someone came for her and carried her off. In the brief interval that elapsed from the time you left the automobile and started for the house, Ansley, and then returned to find the young woman struggling to a sitting position, a body could hardly have been dragged more than a few yards. Unless, of course, there were three people in the automobile, and one person continued to drag the body over the wet grass while the other one spread herself out to decoy you back.'

'Do you think that could have happened?'

'It could have,' Mason said, 'but I doubt it. In the first place, there are lots of heel tracks in the wet soil there around the automobile, but we don't find any others after that.'

'Miss Street isn't making any heel tracks where she's walking,' Ansley pointed out.

'Because she's not dragging anything,' Mason said. 'If she were trying to drag a body, she'd leave tracks.'

'So what do I do now?' Ansley asked.

'We'll take a look inside of the automobile, then we'll take one more quick look in the immediate vicinity. If we don't find someone lying here unconscious or wandering around in a dazed condition, we get in the car and you go home and forget it.'

Mason turned his flashlight on the interior of the car. 'There doesn't seem to be anything there,' he said, 'and I don't want to leave fingerprints on it, making a detailed search.'

He moved the beam of the flashlight around the interior of the car.

'What about the car being stolen?' Ansley asked.

'I'll let Paul Drake tell the police that a client of mine saw a car skid off the road and overturn, then he happened to remember the licence number of the car, that it was driven by a young woman who gave the name of Beatrice Cornell, that she said she was unhurt, that he picked her up and took her to her home at the Ancordia Apartments. I'll state that I was consulted simply because my client wanted to know whether it was necessary to report the accident to the police. That will be the truth, perhaps not all the truth, but it covers the essential facts. I'll make it appear a routine matter, and the police may let it drop at that.'

'Suppose they don't?'

'Then,' Mason said, 'I'll protect you as much as I can as long as I can.'

'That suits me,' Ansley said. 'Let's go. This place gives me the whillies. I feel shut in.'

'Yes,' Mason agreed. 'Wandering around these grounds at night with a flashlight without permission puts us in a questionable position. We–'

He broke off as an electric gong sounded a strident warning.

'What's that?' Ansley asked apprehensively.

'I don't know,' Mason said. 'It may be we've set off an alarm. Come on, let's get out of here.'

'Which direction is your car?' Ansley asked.

'This way,' Mason said. 'Now, let's keep together. Della, hang on to my coat. Ansley, keep at my right hand.'

A peculiar whirring sound came from the darkness ahead. As they came through the hedge, they heard the clang of metal. The flashlight disclosed that the heavy iron gates had shut. A lock clicked.

'Now what?' Ansley asked in dismay. 'We'll have to go to the house to have the gates opened for us.'

Mason went to the gates, studied the lock.

Ansley reached for the gates.

'Don't touch them,' Mason warned. 'There may be a–'

The warning came too late. Ansley pulled at the gates. Almost instantly a siren screamed from some place in the yard. Big floodlights came on, dispersing the shadows in a blaze of light.

Suddenly they heard the barking of a dog.

'Come on,' Mason said, breaking into a run and dashing through the break in the hedge. The others followed his lead.

The brick wall loomed ahead of them.

The barking dog had now been joined by another dog, and the frenzy of barking was drawing unmistakably closer.

'All right,' Mason said, 'there's only one way out of this fix. Della, we're boosting you up the wall. Help me put her up, Ansley, then I can give you a boost to the top of the wall. Then you can help me up. Here, take off your coat.'

Mason whipped off his own coat and threw it up over the broken glass at the top of the wall. Ansley, after a moment, followed suit.

'Come on,' Mason said, picking Della Street up in his arms. Then, cupping his hand under her foot, said, 'Put a hand on my head, reach up to the top of the wall. Be sure to grab the coat. Straighten your knees. Keep your legs rigid. Up you go.'

Mason boosted Della Street up to the wall. 'Watch your hands,' he warned. 'Keep the coats between you and the glass and barbed wire.

'All right, Ansley, you try it. Della, give him a hand. Ansley, put your foot here on my leg. Now get your hip up on my shoulder. Hold your legs rigid as soon as I get hold of your feet and ankles. Then after I've raised you, you can–We're going to have to hurry.'

Ansley scrambled up, extended a hand to Della Street.

'Careful now,' Mason warned. 'Don't pull Della off. Let me give you a shove.'

The lawyer pushed Ansley up, then caught his shoes and said, 'Straighten your legs now. That's it! Get hold–All right, quick! You're going to have to grab me–both of you.'

Della Street, crouched on the wall, reach down a hand. Ansley did likewise. Mason caught the two hands and jumped. They slowly straightened, pulling the lawyer up to where he could get his feet on the wall. Mason had no sooner reached the top of the wall than a dark object came streaking out of the dazzling light to hurl itself against the wall, leaping almost to the top.

'Doberman Pinscher,' Mason said, 'and he's trained for this sort of stuff. Come on, let's get down on the other side. We lower Della first, Ansley. Then you and I make a jump for it.'

The dog was jumping up against the wall, snapping his teeth in an ecstasy of rage, coming within a matter of inches of the feet of the trio as they stood on the wall.

Della Street backed over the edge of the wall. Mason and Ansley lowered her.

'Go ahead, jump,' Mason said to Ansley. 'It isn't over six feet.'

Ansley placed a hand on the folded coats, vaulted to the ground. Mason followed.

'What about your coats?' Della Street asked.

Mason said, 'I'll lift you on my shoulders. Try to salvage the coats. You won't be able to keep from tearing them when you pull them loose, but try not to leave enough for evidence. We'll have to hurry! Those confounded lights will make us the most conspicuous objects on the highway.'

Mason picked up Della Street. 'All right,' he said, 'straighten your knees, Della. Don't get panicky and don't scratch your hands.'

'I can help hold her,' Ansley said, 'if–'

'No. You get the coats as she hands them down,' Mason said. 'This is all right. I can hold her.'

Della Street worked at the garments. 'They're pretty badly tangled on the barbed wire,' she said.

'Tear them loose,' Mason said, 'a car's coming.'

The dog continued its frenzied barking from the other side of the wall. Della Street glanced down the highway at the headlights which were coming through the rainswept darkness, tugged at the coats, got them loose, tossed them to Ansley, then said, 'Okay, Chief, I'll slide down.'

A moment later she was on the ground.

Mason said, 'Get your coat on quick, Ansley. Let's be walking along here and try to look inconspicuous.'

The twin headlights became two dazzling eyes. The car swerved, slowed for a moment, then hissed on past, throwing out a stream of moisture which splashed drops on the trio as they stood motionless.

'Let's go,' Mason said, 'before another car comes.'

The lawyer fished the flashlight from his hip pocket, illuminated the way along the shoulder of the road, disclosing a muddy path at the base of the masonry wall.

Della Street took the lead, running lightly. Ansley came behind her, and

Mason, holding the flashlight, brought up the rear.

The path followed the wall until it came to the driveway.

Mason said, 'Let's have a look at these gates.'

'Do we have to do anything more? Can't we just go on?' Ansley asked.

Mason said, 'Suppose that other woman who was in the car *didn't* get out of the grounds, but is wandering around the grounds. Think what the dogs will do to her.'

'Good heavens!' Della Street said.

Mason said, 'In all probability she got out of the grounds, or else she got to the house. However, there's always the probability. Let's–Here's a button.'

Mason's flashlight disclosed a call button set in solid cement in the masonry. Over the button was a bronze plaque bearing the words, PRESS THIS BUTTON THEN OPEN THE DOOR ON THE LEFT. PICK UP THE TELEPHONE AND STATE YOUR BUSINESS.

Mason jabbed his thumb against the button, opened the door of a metallic box embedded in the cement, picked up a telephone, and held it to his ear.

Seconds elapsed during which he pressed the button repeatedly and listened at the telephone.

Ansley, plainly nervous, said, 'Well, we've done all we can.'

'You and Della get in the car,' Mason instructed. 'Get out of the rain. I'll give this another try.'

Mason again pressed the button in a series of signals and held the receiver to his ear.

There was a faint buzzing noise on the line, but nothing else.

Ansley hurried to the car. Della Street stood in the rain at the lawyer's side. 'Isn't there any other way of reaching the house? Couldn't we–?'

A feminine voice came over the telephone. 'Hello, yes, what is it, please?' she asked.

Mason said, 'There's been an accident. A car is wrecked in your driveway. A young woman may be wandering around the grounds.'

'Who are you?' the voice asked.

'We just happened to be passing by,' Mason said.

'I'll see what I can do. I don't think Mr Borden wants to be disturbed, but–'

An abrupt click at the other end of the line indicated she had hung up.

Mason jabbed the button repeatedly.

After a few moments, he said to Della Street, 'Take this, will you, Della? Keep jabbing away. Something caused the woman to hang up. She may be calling Borden. I'll get things straightened out in the car.'

Della Street put the receiver to her ear, continued to press the button.

Suddenly she said, 'Yes, hello.'

There was a moment's pause. She looked at Mason, nodded, and said, 'Mr Borden, this is an emergency. We're the party at the gate who reported the auto accident. There's a possibility that a young woman may have been dazed and thrown out of the car, and may still be wandering around the grounds.'

There was silence for a few moments, broken only by the squawking noises coming from the receiver in the telephone.

Then, as the receiver ceased making noise, Della Street said with dignity, 'I see no reason to give you my name. I'm simply a passer-by.'

She hung up.

Mason raised his eyebrows.

'That was Borden himself,' she said. 'He told me that someone had set off a burglar alarm by tampering with the gates. He said that the burglar alarm automatically releases watchdogs and turns on the floodlights. He's going to call the dogs back into their kennels and switch off the floodlights. He insisted someone had tried to open the gates from the inside. We'd probably better get out of here. I think he'll send someone to investigate.'

Mason grabbed Della Street's arm and hurried over to the car.

'Well?' Ansley asked.

'We've done our duty,' Mason said. 'We've warned them that someone may be inside the grounds. There's nothing more we can do. Let's get out of here. There'll be someone at the gates any second now.'

'I'm a mess,' Ansley said. 'My coat has a tear in it and I'm soaking wet.'

Della Street laughed nervously. 'Who *isn't* a mess?'

Mason eased the car into gear. 'I've got to make up some excuse that will get Paul Drake off the hook as far as that stolen-car report is concerned.'

He turned to Ansley. 'I'm going to take you back to where you left your car. Get in it and drive home. Don't send your clothes to the cleaners. Take them off, hang them in a closet and forget about them. Say nothing to anyone about what happened. I'll take care of the rest.

'In due course I'll send you a bill for my services.'

Mason drove back to the night club. 'Okay, Ansley, pick up your car. Go home. Keep quiet. Notify me if anything happens. I think you're in the clear.'

Ansley got out in the drizzle. 'I'm sure glad I put it in your hands,' he said. 'You don't think I have to tell the police about the accident?'

'You have to report an accident in which someone was injured,' Mason said. 'You don't *know* anyone was injured. Moreover, the accident took place on a private driveway, not on a public road.'

'Then I don't need to report it?'

'I didn't say that,' Mason told him. 'I'm simply suggesting that you leave all of that to me.'

'That I'll gladly do. Exactly what am I supposed to do now?'

'Get in your car and go home.'

Ansley shook hands with Mason and went across to the place where he had parked his car.

Mason said, 'All right, Della, I'm driving you home where you can get into some dry clothes, then I'm going up to talk with Paul Drake.'

'And what about you?'

'I'll change a little later on.'

'Now look, Chief, you're not going to go wandering around in those wet clothes. Paul Drake isn't in such a jam that it can't wait, and I'm going up with you.'

'Oh no, you're not.'

'Oh yes, I am. I'm going to see that you get into some dry clothes before you start running around. You can drive by my apartment. It'll only take me a minute to change. Then we'll stop at your place on the way to see Paul Drake.'

'All right,' Mason said after an interval. 'Remember what I told Ansley. Don't send any torn clothes to the cleaners. You didn't leave any part of your wearing apparel on the barbed wire, did you?'

'Not of my wearing apparel,' she said, 'but I'm afraid I left a little skin.'

'Where?' Mason asked. 'Where were you scratched?'

She laughed. 'Where it won't show. Don't worry.'

'You'd better get some antiseptic on the places where you're scratched,' Mason told her.

'It's all right. I'll take care of it.'

Mason drove to Della's apartment.

'Come on up and have a drink,' she invited, 'while I change. It will at least warm you up a bit.'

They went to Della Street's apartment. She opened the door, said, 'The liquor is in the closet over the icebox. While I change, get out some water, sugar and nutmeg and you can mix a couple of those hot buttered rums you make so well. I'm so cold the marrow of my bones feels chilly.'

'You get into a hot bath,' Mason told her. 'I'll go see Drake and–'

'No, I'm going to stay with you and see that you get into some dry clothes. Otherwise you'll put off changing until after you've seen Drake. And, for your information, Chief, there's a very nasty, jagged tear in the back of your coat.'

'That confounded wall,' Mason said. 'It certainly was armed to the teeth with barbed wire and broken glass.'

'I'll only be a minute,' she told him.

'At least take a hot shower,' Mason said.

She laughed. 'Just get that water hot and use plenty of Bacardi, Chief.'

'In yours,' he said, 'not in mine. When I'm driving I'm sober.'

She hurried into the bedroom. Mason went to the kitchenette, fixed a hot buttered rum for Della Street, a hot, black coffee for himself. Ten minutes later they were on the road to Mason's apartment, where the lawyer hurriedly changed into dry clothes. Then he and Della Street went to Paul Drake's office, which was on the same floor of the building where Mason had his offices.

Paul Drake, tall, quizzical and quiet, looked up in annoyance. 'It took you two long enough to get here,' he said. 'The police have given me a bad time. They don't like it.'

Mason said, 'Go ahead. Get the call through.'

Drake sighed with relief, put the call through to the stolen-car department, said, 'This is Paul Drake. My client who wanted to know about that car, Number CVX 266, just came in. I'll put him on the line. Here he is now.'

Mason took the phone from Drake, said, 'Hello. Perry Mason talking. . . . That's right, Perry Mason, the lawyer.'

'Now, what's the idea of the lawyer?' the voice at the other end of the line complained. 'We're trying to trace a stolen car and we keep getting a run-around.'

'No run-around at all,' Mason said. 'I had a client who called me in connexion with an automobile, CVX 266. The car had gone out of control, skidded into a private driveway and turned over. He had picked up the young woman who was driving the car and wanted to know whether he should report the accident to the police.'

'Anyone injured?'

'Apparently not.'

'That's a stolen car.'

'So I understand–now.'

'Well, where is it?'

'It's lying in the grounds of Meridith Borden, a public relations expert. He has a country estate about twelve miles out of town, and–'

'I know the place. You mean the one with the wall around it?'

'That's the one.'

'And the car's there?'

'That's right.'

'Well, it sure took us long enough to get the information,' the officer said irritably. 'Why didn't you let us know so we could pick up the car?'

'I didn't know it was that important,' Mason said. 'I just thought it would be a good idea to trace the registration.'

'All right. Who's this client of yours?'

'That,' Mason said, 'is a confidential matter. I can't divulge the name of a client without the client's permission. I can, however, tell you where to recover the automobile, and I have done so.'

'Now look here,' the officer said, 'we're trying to find out about a stolen car, and–'

'And I've told you where the car is,' Mason said. 'I have no other information I am at liberty to give. You're interested in a car. I'm interested in a client.'

Mason hung up the phone.

He grinned at Della Street, said, 'Go on home, Paul. If anyone tries to get tough with you, put the blame on my shoulders. I'm going to leave the car parked down here in the parking lot, and Della and I are going down to the Purple Swan, have about three of their hot buttered rums and go home in a taxi. I won't drive when I've been drinking, and I need a drink.

'Get out of here. If you stick around you *may* get–'

Paul Drake lunged for his hat.

'Save the rest of it,' he said. 'I'm half-way down in the elevator right now.'

4

Perry Mason latchkeyed the door of his private office, tossed his hat on the shelf of the hat closet, grinned at Della Street and said, 'Hi, Della. How did you recover from last night–okay?'

'Okay,' she told him.

'No sniffles?'

'No sniffles, no sneezes, no sinuses.'

'Good girl.'

'Paul Drake telephoned a few minutes ago and said he wanted to have you call just as soon as you came in.'

'Give him a ring,' Mason said. 'The police have probably been giving him a bad time again.'

Della Street picked up the telephone, said to the switchboard operator, 'Tell Paul Drake Mr Mason is in now.'

Mason lit a cigarette, regarded the pile of mail on his desk with some distaste, pushed it to one side, said, 'We haven't heard anything from Ansley this morning, have we?'

'Not a word.'

Drake's code knock sounded on the office door.

'Well,' Della said, 'I guess Paul Drake decided to come down in person.'

'That means he wants something,' Mason said, grinning. 'Open the door, Della, and let's see what it is.'

Della Street opened the door, and Paul Drake, his face an unsmiling mask of grave concern, entered the office, said, 'Hi, everybody. What the hell were you two doing last night?'

'Now that,' Mason said, 'has all the earmarks of being an impertinent question.'

'I trust you weren't out at Meridith Borden's,' Drake said.

'We reported that a car had swerved into Borden's driveway and overturned,' Mason said. 'Isn't that enough to satisfy the police?'

'You mean you haven't heard?' Drake asked.

'Heard what?'

'It was announced on the radio on the newscast at eight-thirty.'

'What was?' Mason asked.

'Meridith Borden, noted public relations expert, was found dead in the palatial residence on his country estate at seven o'clock this morning by his housekeeper. He was lying on the floor in his photographic room and had been shot through the heart, apparently with a revolver.'

'Police find any weapon?'

'No weapon, no indication of suicide. On the other hand, no indication of a struggle. However, shortly after eleven o'clock last night a burglar alarm was turned in from the Borden estate, at least from the grounds. Police found indications that some unauthorized persons had been in the grounds and had probably managed to get over the wall.'

'Was the burglar alarm connected with police headquarters anywhere?' Mason asked.

'No. A passing motorist heard the siren of the alarm and saw the floodlights go on. Everything was normal at midnight when a sheriff's patrol car made a regular run by the place, so someone must have turned off the lights and reset the alarm.

'The estate is protected by a masonry wall covered with broken glass and barbed wire on top. There are huge iron gates protecting the driveway, and there's an electric timing system by which those gates are automatically closed at eleven o'clock each night. A bell or gong gives a warning sound one minute before the gates close. Then the gates clang shut, and after that the only way anyone can get in is by telephoning from the outer gate.'

Mason gave Drake's statement thoughtful consideration.

'What do the police say about it?' Mason asked at length.

'They're not saying anything just yet. They found some tracks in the damp soil around that automobile you reported, indicating that people had been milling around it, evidently looking for something.'

'Indeed,' Mason said.

'Someone had climbed over the wall,' Drake went on. 'Some garments had evidently been thrown over the top of the wall covering the broken glass and barbed wire, and then people had climbed over. Police are inclined to think there were three people, and that one of them was a woman.'

'How come?' Mason asked.

'Tracks of a woman's heels on both sides of the wall,' Drake said, 'and the way the police have it worked out, it would have taken a minimum of three people to have scaled the wall. Two people could hardly have done it. A man could have boosted a woman up to the top of the wall, but she couldn't have pulled him up by herself. However, she could have given an assist to another man who was also being helped up from the ground.'

'All very interesting,' Mason said.

'I thought you might find it *quite* interesting,' Drake observed. 'Under the circumstances, the police are naturally taking quite an interest in the stolen car which was found overturned on the grounds.'

'When did they find the car, by the way?' Mason asked.

'Not until this morning. Police telephoned Borden last night to see if any such car was in the grounds, but there was no answer on Borden's telephone. They sent a squad car out, and, since the gates were closed and the place locked up for the night, they decided to let it wait until morning.'

'Any indication as to the identity of the people who were in Borden's grounds last night, Paul?'

'Not yet, Perry. At least, if the police have any evidence, they're not releasing it. Doubtless you'll receive a visit from members of the Homicide Squad this morning. They'll want to ask you more about the client who reported the stolen car careening off the highway.'

'Well,' Mason said, 'that starts the day off with a bang, Paul. I was afraid I was going to be up against a routine morning of answering mail. Thanks for telling me.'

'You want me to do anything?' Paul Drake asked.

'Just keep quiet,' Mason said.

'I mean along investigative lines.'

Mason stretched back in his chair and yawned. 'I had met Meridith Borden a couple of times, and, of course, I'm sorry to learn of his tragic demise. But the mere fact that a client reported seeing a car swerve and go out of control into the Borden driveway doesn't give me any interest in the Borden murder.'

Drake's face showed unmistakable relief. 'Well, thank heavens for that! I was afraid you'd become mixed up in something that could prove embarrassing. There's no chance you, Della and your mysterious client were climbing over Borden's wall last night, is there?'

Mason threw back his head and laughed. 'You do a lot of worrying, Paul. What put that idea into your head?'

'The curve of the driveway,' Drake said dryly, 'is such that a person following a car along the highway might have seen the car swerve into the Borden driveway, but couldn't possibly have seen the car crash through the hedge and then roll over–not without stopping the car, backing up and then walking along the driveway to investigate. There's evidence that quite a number of people were leaving tracks around the Borden driveway. Or, let me put it this way, there's evidence that some people left a lot of tracks. There must have been quite a bit of nocturnal activity, probably prior to eleven o'clock, when the gates were automatically closed by this timing device.'

'I see,' Mason said thoughtfully.

'And,' Drake went on, 'in view of the fact that the police are now investigating a murder which may have taken place between nine and eleven o'clock last night, it might be very embarrassing for you to withhold information or to make some statement which you might have to amend at a later date.'

'Thanks for the tip, Paul.'

'Not at all,' Drake said. 'You're sure you don't want me to do anything–any investigative work?'

'Not now,' Mason said.

'Okay. Keep your nose clean,' Drake told him, and, heaving his long length from the overstuffed chair, started for the door, paused, looked speculatively at Mason and said, 'You know, the police are pretty thorough, Perry. There are times when you think they do dumb things, but once they start after something, they sure as hell keep after it.'

'Well?' Mason asked.

'You and Della went out to dinner,' Drake said. 'I saw you when you left the office building. You were wearing a brown, double-breasted business suit. Della Street had on a dark-blue tailored suit with white trim. When you came into my office to report that an automobile had skidded into Borden's driveway, you were wearing different clothes.'

'Do you *always* notice things like that?' Della Street asked.

'It's my business,' Paul said. 'The point is, Perry, that the police, as I have said, aren't dumb. The fact that they haven't called on you this morning *may* be because they're digging out some facts to work with. They may have found some bits of clothing or some threads stuck to the barbed wires or the broken glass on the Borden wall. It would be just like the police to check on where you had dinner last night, to ask some of the waiters who know you how you were dressed, and then call on you this morning and ask if you'd have any objection to producing the clothes you were wearing last night.'

'Why should I have any objection?' Mason asked.

'There might be some significant tears in the cloth.'

'And if there were?'

'They might match threads that police found adhering to the barbed wire and the broken glass on top of the wall at Borden's place.'

'And if they did?'

'You'd have some explaining to do.'

'And if I explained?'

Drake shrugged his shoulders. 'It's up to you, Perry. I'm not telling you how to practise law. I'm telling you what the score is.'

'Thanks,' Mason said. 'I'll let you know if I want anything.'

'Okay,' Drake told him. 'Be seeing you.'

As soon as Drake had closed the door, Mason nodded to Della Street. 'Get Ansley on the phone.'

Della Street hurried to the phone book, looked up his number, said, 'Shall I have Gertie at the switchboard dial him, or–'

Mason shook his head. 'Try him on our unlisted line, Della. Perhaps it's just as well not to let Gertie know anything about this.'

Della Street's nimble fingers dialled the number. After a moment, she said, 'Mr Ansley, please.'

She cupped her hand over the mouthpiece, said to Perry Mason, 'His secretary wants to know who's calling.'

'Tell her,' Mason said.

Della Street removed her hand, said into the telephone, 'It's Mr Perry Mason, the attorney, and it's quite important.'

There was a moment's silence, then she said, 'I see. Will you please tell him when he comes in to get in touch with Mr Mason, that Mr Mason would like to have him call at his earliest convenience. And please tell him that it's a matter of some importance.'

She hung up the phone, turned to Mason. 'Ansley isn't in. He phoned his office that he wouldn't be in this morning and might not be in all day.'

'Didn't leave a number where he could be reached?'

Della Street shook her head. 'His secretary said he's undoubtedly out on the job somewhere. There are no phones on those construction projects, and Ansley moves around quite a bit from the jobs to the supply houses. She said that she'd have him call as soon as he came in.'

'All right,' Mason said, 'I guess that determines our pattern for the day, Della.'

'What does?' she asked.

'We're out of the office and may not be in all day. I've got to talk with Ansley before I talk with the police.'

'How much time do we have before they develop a clue which will lead them here?' Della Street asked.

'That's hard to tell,' Mason said. 'Remember that my car was parked in front of Borden's wall for a while last night. Someone may have noticed the licence number. Remember that we told the police the stolen car was in Borden's grounds and that a client had seen it swerve off the road and roll over, a story which is completely impossible because a motorist couldn't have seen the car after it swerved off the road, and couldn't have known that it rolled over. Put all of these things together in connexion with a murder case, and you can gamble that our friends from the Homicide Squad are working on other clues pointing to me, otherwise they would have been here before this.'

'And the other clues are?'

'Probably threads torn from our garments. Did you notice Ansley's coat?'

'I know there was a section torn from the lining,' she said. 'I–Gosh, Chief, I could have been more careful. As it was, I was in a hurry and–well, those barbs seemed to be sticking in every place and I–'

'Sure,' Mason said, 'you were simply trying to get the clothes free and get away from there as quickly as possible. You had no reason to realize the importance of not leaving threads or bits of cloth. . . . I take it you have some shopping you'd like to do today and perhaps you'd like to spend the afternoon at a beauty parlour, or drop in at a matinee?'

'And in case I'm questioned, what do I say about where I spent the day and how I spent the day?'

'You are entitled to a day off,' Mason said. 'You've been working overtime.'

'When?' she asked.

'That's a good point,' Mason told her. 'Don't try to cover up. In case you're questioned, say you did quite a bit of work last night.'

'And then what?'

'If they ask you anything else, state that you don't answer questions concerning business matters unless I give you permission.'

'Chief, shouldn't I stay with you today?'

Mason shook his head.

'Why not?'

'I don't want to seem to be avoiding the police. If we're together, we would have to be working. If we were working, it would have to be on some case. And if we were working on some case, we might be picked up and questioned before we're ready to be questioned. If, however, you're taking a day off, you can keep yourself out of circulation where the police wouldn't be picking you up.'

'And how about you?'

'Well, I'll have to take care of myself,' Mason said, grinning. 'I think perhaps I can do it.'

'If word gets around that they want to question you, they'll be able to pick you up. You're too well known to circulate around the city without leaving a trail.'

'I know it,' Mason said, 'but I don't think they'll announce that they want to question me. That is, they won't give the information to the radio or the Press–not just yet.'

'Suppose Ansley calls in while we're gone?'

'I don't think he will,' Mason said. 'He won't unless the police pick him up. Tell Gertie at the telephone that you're taking a day off, that I'm going to be in and out during the day, that if Ansley should telephone, she's to explain to him that I have to see him and that he's to leave a phone number where he can be contacted.'

Mason walked over to pick up his hat.

'Be seeing you, Della,' he said.

Her eyes were anxious as she watched him out of the door.

Mason got his car from the parking lot, drove some twenty blocks until he was away from the immediate vicinity of his office, found a parking place, went to a drugstore and consulted the telephone directory. He found the number of Beatrice Cornell in the Ancordia Apartments and dialled it.

A woman's voice, sounding calm and impersonal, said, 'Yes, hello.'

'Minerva?' Mason asked eagerly.

'What number were you calling, please?'

'I want Minerva.'

'There's no one named Minerva here.'

'Sorry,' Mason said, dropped the receiver into its cradle, returned to his car and made time to the Ancordia Apartments.

He found the name of Beatrice Cornell listed as being in Apartment 108.

Mason pressed the buzzer and almost instantly the electric door release sounded.

The lawyer opened the door, walked through a somewhat gloomy lobby, down a corridor, found Apartment 108 and tapped gently on the door.

The door was opened by a woman who said, with crisp, businesslike efficiency, "I'm Miss Cornell–Why, it's Perry Mason!'

Mason bowed. 'I called you last night, but I've never met you, have I?'

'Heavens, no! You've never met me. I'm one of your fans. I've followed your cases with the greatest interest. Your picture is very familiar to me. . . . I suppose you want to see me about what happened last night–your phone call. Come in and sit down,' she invited.

Mason entered the sitting-room of a double apartment, noticed a large, executive desk on which were three telephones. There was a smaller, secretarial desk with a typewriter, a stenographic chair and a considerable amount of typed material.

She caught the surprise in his face and laughed. 'I run a sort of catchall service, Mr Mason. I answer telephones for a whole select list of confidential clients who want to leave night numbers where messages can be taken, yet want a little more personalized service than the average telephone-answering service. For instance, I have several doctors who telephone me when they're out on the evening calls. I keep track of exactly where they are, and, in case of any emergency, know where they can be located in the shortest possible time. I also have a mail service for clients, do a little secretarial work, run a model service, and, all in all, manage to make a living out of odds and ends. In fact, I'm building up a pretty good business.'

'Isn't it rather confining?' Mason asked, accepting the chair she indicated.

'Sure, but it's a good living.'

'How long have you been doing this?' Mason asked.

'Seven years, and I've built up a very nice business. Before that I was a photographic model. After a while I began to realize that every tick of the clock was undermining my stock in trade. First, I began to put on a little weight here and there, and then I had to start dieting, and . . . well, after a while I saw the light and got out of the business. Now I have a list of models I book for photographers who want professionals.

'But you didn't come here to talk about me, Mr Mason. I suppose you want to know about last night, and what you're trying to find out is whether I was involved in an automobile accident.'

'And I'd like to find out about your models,' Mason said.

'That's simple. I used some of my old connexions and friendships to build up a model-booking service. I have half a dozen photographic models who let me handle their bookings.'

Mason said, 'Thanks for your cordiality and co-operation. I hate to be a nasty, suspicious, sceptical audience, but you're talking to an attorney in a matter which may be of some importance.

'A young woman was involved in an automobile accident last night. She was unconscious for a while. She gave your name and this address. My client took her to this apartment house and delivered her here.'

'I see,' she said thoughtfully. 'And you want some assurance that I wasn't the woman?'

He nodded.

'How serious was the automobile accident?'

'One of the cars overturned.'

'You say this young woman was injured?'

'She was thrown out and apparently skidded for a ways. She was lying unconscious. Later on, she came to.'

'There were bruises?' she asked.

'Probably. On the legs and hips.'

'Well, Mr Mason,' she said, 'I was here last night. I answered telephones fifty times. I'm here every night. I feel certain I have no information that would help you.'

'Do you know Meridith Borden?' Mason asked.

Her eyes narrowed. 'Yes. Why?'

'He's dead.'

'What!'

'He's dead. The police think he was murdered some time last night.'

'Good heavens!' she exclaimed.

'And,' Mason said, 'the automobile accident that I refer to is one that took place in the grounds of Meridith Borden's country estate. You remember it was rainy last night. A car skidded off the road, went through the gates, crashed through the hedge, then turned over.'

'Does the registration of the car mean anything?' she asked.

'The car was stolen,' Mason said.

She was thoughtful for a few moments, then she said, 'Well, I may as well tell you, Mr Mason. Meridith Borden is–I mean, was . . . a client of mine.'

'In what way?'

'He was an amateur photographer. He played around with pin-up art. Sometimes he got models through me.'

'Recently?'

'No, not recently. I think that lately he'd made a private deal with some amateur model who wasn't adverse to serving cheesecake either for thrills or for cash.'

Mason said, 'I'm trying to find out who it was who used your name. She was someone who probably knew Borden and she must have known you. She was taller than you, younger than you. She had dark, chestnut hair with brown eyes. She's someone who knows you personally. She came to this apartment house about–'

'About ten o'clock?' Beatrice Cornell interrupted.

'Probably,' Mason said.

'I remember that my bell rang,' she said, 'and I pressed the buzzer releasing the door catch on the outer door. But no one came to my apartment. I didn't think too much of it at the time. Quite frequently you get wrong calls, and–'

'Do you always press the button opening the door without knowing who it is?' Mason asked.

'Oh, sure,' she said. 'I suppose I should find out, but after all, I'm in business, Mr Mason. I have two dozen different irons in the fire, and clients drop in to see me, to pick up personal messages or leave instructions, and some of these models–'

'Let's concentrate on the models,' Mason interrupted. 'Do you have a model of that description?'

'I have some models,' she said. 'I . . . I don't like to betray the interests of my clients.'

Mason said, 'I'll try a different approach. I am an amateur photographer. I'm looking for a model. I don't want one of the slender, long-legged models, I want one with curves. A good figure but well curved. Could you put me in touch with one of your models?'

'I have some sample photographs,' she said. 'I could show you those.'

'Please,' Mason said.

She smiled and said, 'This is strictly business. These girls will want twenty dollars an hour. They'll want pay from the time they leave their apartment until they return. You'll have to furnish the transportation. You'll have to furnish any special costumes you may want. You'll have to see that they're fed. They have stock costumes, Bikini bathing suits. Some of them want chaperons. Some of them will take a chance if they know you. Some of them will take a chance, period.'

'Do I get photographs and addresses?' Mason asked.

'You do not,' she said. 'You get photographs with numbers on them. My addresses are my stock in trade. I get a commission on any booking. Most of the specimen photographs are in Bikini bathing suits.'

'That's fine,' Mason said. 'Let's take a look.'

She said, 'Just a minute,' and went through the door to an adjoining room. Mason heard the sound of the drawer in a filing case opening and closing.

A moment later she was back with a dozen eight-by-ten glossy photographs of good-looking girls in attractive poses. Each photograph had a number pasted to it.

Mason regarded the photographs thoughtfully, eliminated several, said, 'I'd like studio appointments with numbers six, eight and nine.'

'It'll cost you twenty dollars an hour.'

Mason nodded.

She opened an address book.

Abruptly Mason said, 'Wait a minute, Miss Cornell. I have a better idea. Ring up every one of your models on the list, ask if they're free today and ask if they can pose for a series of bathing beauty pin-up pictures. And, of course, please understand that I want to pay for your time, whatever it's worth.'

'All right,' she said. 'Sit down and make yourself comfortable. I'll get busy on the phone.'

Beatrice Cornell struck pay dirt on the third telephone call. She said, 'Just a minute, dearie, I'll . . . well, I'll call you back.'

She hung up the telephone, turned to Perry Mason.

'That's Dawn Manning,' she said, 'an attractive girl with a beautiful torso, pretty well upholstered, an awfully good scout. She says she's out of business for four or five days on account of some rather unsightly bruises. She says she was badly shaken up last night in a minor automobile accident.'

'That's my girl,' Mason said.

'What do you want to do?'

'Could you get her to come out here?'

'She said she can't pose.'

'Tell her,' Mason said, 'that I've seen her photographs, I like her looks, that we can probably cover up the bruises so they won't show. Ask her if she'll come out here and meet me. Tell her she gets paid from the time she leaves her apartment. Tell her to jump in a taxi and come out.'

Beatrice Cornell frowned. 'She's going to feel that I've double-crossed her.'

'You haven't double-crossed her at all,' Mason said. 'You're booking photographic models. I've heard of your services. You don't need to mention that I'm an attorney. I'm simply Mr Mason, a photographer. Ask her to come out here for an interview. Tell her you have the money.'

Beatrice Cornell hesitated, said, 'Well, I guess it's all right.'

Mason took his wallet from his pocket, took out a twenty and a ten. 'There's thirty dollars,' he said. 'Twenty dollars for an hour of her time, and the balance will cover taxi fares and incidental expenses.'

'What are you going to do?' she asked. 'Are you going to tell this girl who you are and what you want?'

'That depends,' Mason said.

'You're going to be a photographer?'

Mason nodded.

'Then you'd better get yourself a camera.'

'Is there a photographic store near here?'

'One about four blocks from here. I'm in close touch with him. Want me to telephone?'

'No,' Mason said, 'I'd prefer you didn't.' I'll walk in and get an outfit. I'll have a chance to get back here by the time your girl arrives?'

'Probably. It might be a little better for you to let me talk with her first, and–'

'That's fine,' Mason said. 'I'll be back in half an hour.'

5

Thirty minutes later Mason returned to Beatrice Cornell's apartment. He was armed with a twin-lens camera, a Strobolite, a leather carrying case and a dozen rolls of film, both colour and black and white.

Dawn Manning was there ahead of him.

Beatrice Cornell performed the introductions.

Dawn Manning's slate-grey eyes appraised the evident newness of Mason's photographic equipment.

'You're an amateur, Mr Mason?'

He nodded.

'Rather a new amateur, I would say.'

Again Mason nodded.

'What is it you want, Mr Mason?'

'I want some shots,' Mason said, 'of a model. I'd like to try some . . . well, some . . . well, some–'

'Pin-ups?'

Mason nodded.

She pulled the tight-fitting sweater even more closely to the contours of her body. 'I have nice breasts,' she said, 'and my legs are good. You understand about my rates?'

'He understands,' Beatrice Cornell said.

Dawn met Mason's eyes frankly. 'If you're looking for a woman,' she said, 'go get someone else. If you're looking for photographs, that's different. We don't have trouble with the professionals or the experienced photographers who are accustomed to hiring models. We do have lots of trouble with amateurs, and I don't want trouble.'

'Mr Mason is all right,' Beatrice Cornell interposed quickly. 'I told you that, Dawn.'

'I know you told me that, but . . . well, I just don't want to have any misunderstanding, that's all.'

Mason said, 'I am willing to pay your rates and I assure you, you won't have to fight me off.'

'All right,' Dawn Manning said crisply, after a moment's hesitation, 'but it'll be a few days before you're able to take shots showing my legs.'

'You were in an automobile accident?' Mason asked.

She nodded, said, 'I got out lucky at that.'

Mason took a cigarette case from his pocket. 'Is it all right if I smoke?' he asked.

'Certainly,' Beatrice Cornell said.

Dawn Manning took one of Mason's cigarettes.

Mason held a match. Dawn Manning inhaled deeply, held the smoke in her lungs for a moment, then exhaled.

She settled back in the chair, started to cross her legs, then suddenly winced.

'How bad is it?' Mason asked.

'Frankly,' she said, 'I didn't look at myself in the mirror this morning. I was sleeping late. When Beatrice called, I jumped up, piled into some clothes and came on over.'

'Without breakfast?'

She laughed. 'I have to watch my weight. Breakfast and I are strangers. Let's take a look and see how things are coming.'

She got up from the chair, and, as freely and naturally as though she had been making an impersonal appraisal of a piece of statuary, raised her skirts almost waist-high and examined her left hip. 'That's where it's the most tender.'

Beatrice Cornell said, 'Gosh, Dawn, that would take a *lot* of retouching. It's bad now and by tomorrow it'll be worse.'

Dawn Manning kept twisting around trying to look at herself, said, 'I feel like a puppy chasing its tail. Let me take a look in that full-length mirror, Beatrice.'

She crossed over to stand in front of a door which contained a panel mirror, and shook her head dolefully as she surveyed herself. 'It's worse than it was last night when I went to bed. I'm afraid I'm not going to be available for a few days, Mr Mason. Will this wait, or do you want another model? I'm sorry. Under the circumstances, I'll only charge you taxi fare.'

Mason said, 'I think we could arrange things with the proper lighting. . . . Could we go to your apartment? I'd like to have a couple of hours of your time.'

Dawn Manning's face flushed. 'You certainly can not,' she said, 'and I'm going to be frank with you, Mr Mason. I don't work with amateurs without a chaperon. If you're married, bring your wife along. If you aren't married, I'll arrange a chaperon. It's going to cost you three dollars an hour extra.'

'All right,' Mason told her. 'We're chaperoned here. Let's talk here.'

'About what? About photographs?'

Mason shook his head. 'I may as well confess. I was interested in the bruises.'

'In the *bruises*?'

'I wanted to see the nature and extent of your bruises.'

'Say, what is this, anyway? What kind of a goof are you?'

'I'm a lawyer.'

'Oh-oh,' Beatrice Cornell interposed.

'All right, so you're a lawyer,' Dawn Manning said indignantly. 'You've got me out of bed and up here under false pretences. You–'

'Not under false pretences, exactly,' Mason interrupted. 'I told you I was willing to pay for your time. Miss Cornell has the money.'

Dawn Manning's face softened somewhat.

'What is it you want, Mr Mason? Let's put the cards on the table and see how our hands stack up.'

Mason said, 'I was interested in your bruises because I am interested in the automobile accident which took place last night.'

'Are you intending to sue somebody?'

'Not necessarily. I would like to have you tell me about it. And, since we're taking up Miss Cornell's time without payment, I suggest that we go some place where we can talk and let her get ahead with her work, or that I make arrangements to compensate *her* for *her* time.'

'And you don't want pictures?' Dawn Manning asked.

'Yes, I want pictures.'

'It's all right if you want to talk here,' Beatrice Cornell said. 'I get a commission on this job, you know, and I–'

'You'll do better than that,' Mason told her. 'You'll get twenty dollars an hour for *your* time, as well as the commission.'

Mason arose, opened his billfold once more, took out forty dollars and said, 'I'll probably use up two hours of your time, first and last, and here's another twenty for Miss Manning.'

'Well now, look, that's not necessary, Mr Mason. I–'

'You have a living to make, the same as anyone else,' Mason told her.

'What do you want from me?' Dawn Manning asked.

'First I'd like to know all about the automobile accident,' Mason said.

'Well, there wasn't much to it. I went to a studio party last night. A photographer friend of mine was showing some of his pictures and he invited a group of us in for cocktails followed by a buffet dinner. Ordinarily I wouldn't have gone, but he had some pictures of which he was quite proud. I'd been the model and I hadn't seen the proofs. I was interested and he was terrifically proud of his work.

'Quite frequently, at a time like that, a model picks up new business and new contacts, and it's nice to be out with your own kind. Most people who learn you're a photographic model and are willing to pose in Bikini bathing suits or without them, under proper circumstances, get the idea you're cheap and that everything you have is for sale.

'However, when you're out with a crowd that knows the ropes and understands each other, you can have a good time and . . . well, it's a nice, free-and-easy professional atmosphere. Everyone respects the work the other one is doing. We like good photography and we like good photographers. They need models to stay in business, and we need photographers to keep us going.'

'All right,' Mason said, 'you went to this party.'

'And,' she said, 'because I wanted to go home early, I went alone. I didn't have an escort and took a taxi. I had some drinks, I had a buffet dinner, I saw the pictures, and they were darned good pictures. He'd used a green filter, which is about as kind to the human skin as anything you can get for black-and-white photography, and the pictures came out nice. As I said, I wanted to get home early, so I broke away before things got to a point where the drinks began to take effect. I was looking for a taxicab when this woman pulled up to the kerb in a nice Cadillac and said, "You were up at the studio party. I saw you there. It's a rainy night. You'll have a hard time getting a cab. Want a ride?'

'I didn't place her, but she *could* have been there. There must have been fifty people in the place altogether at cocktail-time. I think only ten or twelve were invited to stay for dinner.'

'So you got in with this woman?'

'I got in with this woman and she started driving towards town.'

'Did you get her name?'

'I didn't. I'm coming to that. She chatted with me as though we were old friends. She knew my name, where I lived and all that.

'She told me it was a rainy night, that I'd have trouble getting a cab, and that was the reason she'd asked me to ride with her. She said that she had to make one brief stop on the road home.'

'This cocktail party was here in town?'

Dawn Manning shook her head. 'Out in Mesa Vista,' she said. 'This whole story is a little weird. Mr Mason. To understand it you'll have to know a little about my background. I'll have to tell you some of my personal history.'

'Go ahead,' Mason told her, his eyes narrowing slightly, 'you're doing fine.'

'I've been married,' she went on, 'Dawn Manning is my maiden name. I took it after we split up. My ex-husband is Frank Ferney. He's associated with Meridith Borden. He's a chiseller. When we split up, I couldn't go to Reno to get a divorce. Frank agreed to go. He wrote me he'd filed papers, and I made an appearance so as to save problems of serving summons. I thought everything had been taken care of.

'I don't know how much you know about Meridith Borden. He makes his living out of selling political influence. I did some posing for him. I met a local politician, the politician fell for me, and Borden wanted to use me just as he'd use some party girl to get his politician to the point where–well, where Borden could get something on him.

'I hate these man-and-wife feuds where people are intimate for years and then suddenly start hating each other. My ex-husband wasn't what I thought he was, but I had tried to keep friendly with him.

'This Borden deal was too much. I told them both off. I told the amorous politician he'd better do his playing around home, and I walked out on the lot of them.

'Well, last night we drove along the road, and this woman said she wanted to turn in to see a friend very briefly. Then she mentioned casually that someone had told her that my husband and I had planned a divorce but that he had not gone through with it. About that time she started to swing into Meridith Borden's driveway. I sensed a trap and grabbed at the wheel to keep her from turning in. We met another car coming out of the driveway. I guess I shouldn't have grabbed at the wheel, but I wasn't going to let them trap me. Anyway, we went into a skid.'

'Go on,' Mason said, 'what happened?'

'We went completely around. I know the other car hit us because I felt the bump, or perhaps I should say we hit the other car. Then I have a recollection of crashing through a hedge and the next I knew I was lying on the damp grass on my left hip with my skirts clean up around my neck as though I had skidded or been dragged some little distance. I was lying in a cold drizzle and I was wet and chilled.

'I moved around a bit, trying to find where I was and thinking what had happened, and finally recollection came back to me all at once. I tested myself to see if I had any broken bones. Apparently, all that I had was a bruised and skinned fanny. I was lying up against the stone wall that surrounds Borden's place. The car I had been riding in was on its side. I looked around for the other woman. She was nowhere around. I was cold, wet and shaken up. I found my way to the driveway, walked through the gates to the highway. After a while a motorist stopped. I hitch-hiked to town.'

'Do you know this motorist?'

'No, I don't. I didn't get his name and I didn't want his name. He had an idea he could furnish me board and lodging for the night and was rather insistent. I didn't tell him anything about myself or my background. I let him think I was walking home from a ride during which I'd had an argument with my boy friend.

'As Beatrice can tell you, in this business we get so we can handle ourselves with most men, turn them down and still leave them feeling good. But this particular specimen was a little hard to handle. However, I put up with things until I got to where I could get a bus. Then I slapped his face good, got out, and removed the dollar bill I always keep fastened to the top of my stocking. I took a bus to the corner nearest my apartment and then had to ring the manager to get a duplicate key. I'd lost my handbag and everything in it–cigarettes, lipstick, keys, driving licence, the works.'

'Did you look for your handbag?'

'I felt around in the car and on the ground. I couldn't find it. Evidently this woman took it with her.'

'What time was this?' Mason asked. 'Can you fix the time?'

'I can fix the time of the accident very accurately.'

'What time was it?'

'Three minutes past nine.'

'How do you know?'

'My watch stopped when I hit the ground, or when I hit the side of the car or something. In any event, the watch stopped and hasn't been running since.'

'Do you know what time it was when you left the grounds?'

'I can approximate that.'

'What time?'

'I would say about twenty-five minutes before ten. I arrived home at perhaps fifteen minutes past ten, I think. Why? Does it make any great difference?'

'It may make quite a difference,' Mason said.

'Would you mind telling me why, Mr Mason?'

'Unfortunately, I'm a one-way street as far as information is concerned at the moment. I can receive but I can't give. There's one other thing I want. I want the best possible description you can give of the woman who picked you up and gave you a ride in that car.'

'Mr Mason, you're putting me through quite a catechism here.'

'I'm paying for your time,' Mason reminded her.

'So you are,' she said, laughing. 'Well, this woman was somewhere in the late twenties, or say, on a guess, around thirty. She was about my height . . . well, from 116 to 120, somewhere in there. She had reddish hair, the dark, mahogany type of red that–'

'Comes out of a bottle?' Mason asked.

'Come in a hair rinse of some sort. I have an idea she might have been a natural brunette.'

'What can you remember about her eyes?'

'I remember her eyes quite well because she had a peculiar habit of looking at me, and when she did, it gave me rather an uneasy feeling. Her eyes were dark and . . . it's hard to describe, but there's a sort of a reddish, dark eye that doesn't seem to have any pupil at all. I suppose if you looked carefully enough you could find a pupil, but the colour of the eyes is dark and sort of reddish, and you just don't see any pupil.'

'You remember that?'

She nodded.

'Anything else?'

'She wore rings on both hands, I remember that. Diamonds. Fairly good-sized stones, too.'

'How was she dressed?'

'Well, as I remember it, she didn't have any hat on and her coat was a beige colour, rather good-looking. She had a light wool dress in a soft green that went well with her colouring.'

'You hadn't seen this woman before?'

'You mean to know her?'

'Yes.'

'No. I'm quite certain I haven't.'

Mason glanced at Beatrice Cornell.

Beatrice Cornell slowly shook her head. 'There's something vaguely familiar about the description, Mr Mason, but I don't place it–at least at the moment.'

'All right,' Mason said. 'I guess that covers the situation at the moment. I'd like some pictures.'

'Bruises and all?' Dawn Manning asked, laughing.

'Bruises and all–particularly the bruises.'

'Okay. We'll throw in the all,' Dawn Manning said. 'Beatrice can show you how to work that Strobolite.

'Pull the shades, Beatrice, and we'll get to work.'

6

The cafeteria was a small, cosy place that featured home cooking.

Perry Mason, moving his tray along the smoothly polished metal guide, selected stuffed bell peppers, diced carrots, fried eggplant, pineapple-cottage-cheese salad and a pot of coffee. He moved over to a table for two by the window and settled himself for a leisurely lunch.

A shadow formed back of Mason's shoulder. A man's voice said, 'Is this seat taken?'

Mason said somewhat irritably, 'No, it's not taken, but there are half a dozen empty tables over there.'

'Mind if I sit down?'

Mason looked up in annoyance to encounter the eyes of Lt Tragg of the Metropolitan Homicide Department.

'Well, well, Tragg,' Mason said, getting up and shaking hands as Tragg put his tray down on the table. 'I didn't know *you* ate here.'

'First time I've eaten here,' Tragg said. 'They tell me the food's pretty good.'

'It's wonderful home cooking. How did you happen to find the place?'

'*Modus operandi*,' Tragg said.

'I don't get you.'

'So many people don't,' Tragg said, putting a cup of consommé, some pineapple-cottage-cheese salad and a glass of buttermilk on the table.

Mason laughed. 'You won't sample the cooking here by eating that combination, Tragg. The stuffed bell peppers are wonderful.'

'I know, I know,' Tragg said. 'I eat to keep my waistline down within reason. About the only pleasure I get out of being around good cooking is to have the aroma in my nostrils.'

'Well,' Mason said, as Tragg seated himself, 'tell us about the *modus operandi*, Lieutenant.'

'I don't know whether you remember the last time you disappeared or not,' Tragg said. 'It was in connexion with a case where you didn't want to be interviewed. And after you finally showed up and got into circulation, you may remember that I asked you where you had been and what the idea was in running away.'

'I remember it perfectly,' Mason said, 'and I told you that I hadn't run away.'

'That's right,' Tragg said. 'You told me you had been out interviewing some witnesses and that quite frequently when you did that, you didn't go back to the office but had lunch at a delightful little cafeteria where they featured home cooking.'

'Did I tell you that?' Mason asked.

'You did,' Tragg said, 'and I asked you about the cafeteria. So then I went back to the office, took out my card marked "Perry Mason, Attorney at Law" and on the back of it under *modus operandi* made a note, "When Perry Mason is hiding out, he's pretty apt to eat at the Family Kitchen Cafeteria."

'For your information, Mr Mason, that's what we call *modus operandi*. It's something we use in catching crooks. Unfortunately, the police can't stand the strain of being brilliant and dashingly clever, so they have to make up for it by being efficient.

'You'd be surprised what we can do with that *modus operandi* filing system of ours and compiling a lot of notes. It may be that a man has certain peculiar eating habits. He may call for a certain brand of wine with his meals. He may like to have a sundae made by putting maple syrup on ice cream. All of those little things that the brilliant, flashy geniuses don't have to bother with, the plodding police have to note and remember.

'Now, take in your own case. You're brilliant to the point of being a genius, but the little old *modus operandi* led me to you when we were looking for you, when you didn't want to be found.'

'What makes you think I didn't want to be found?' Mason asked.

Tragg smiled and said, 'Oh, I presume you were out interviewing witnesses again.'

'That's exactly what I was doing,' Mason said.

'Are you finished?'

'With the witnesses?'

'Yes.'

'No.'

'Well,' Tragg said, 'that's fine. Perhaps I can be of some help.'

'And then again perhaps you couldn't,' Mason said.

'All right, we'll look at it the other way,' Tragg said. 'Perhaps *you* could be of some help to *me*.'

'Are you seeking to retain my services?'

Tragg sipped the buttermilk, poked at the cottage-cheese salad with his fork and said, 'Damn, but that stuffed bell pepper smells good!'

'Go on,' Mason said, 'go on and get yourself a stuffed bell pepper. It will make the world look brighter.'

Tragg pushed back his chair, picked up his check, said, 'You've made a sale, Perry.'

Tragg returned carrying a tray on which were two stuffed bell peppers, a piece of apple pie, a slab of cheese and a small jar of cream.

He seated himself at the table, said, 'Now, don't talk to me until I get these under my belt and get to feeling good-natured once more.'

Mason grinned at him, and the two ate in silence.

After he had finished, Tragg pushed his plate back, took a cigar from his pocket, cut off the end with a penknife, said, 'I feel human once more. Now let's get down to brass tacks.'

'What kind of brass tacks?' Mason asked.

'Arrange them any way you want,' Tragg said. 'If you put the heads down, the points are going to be up and that's going to be tough–on you.'

'What do you want to know?'

Tragg said, 'Meridith Borden was murdered. You were out there. You climbed over a wall and set off a burglar alarm. Then, like a damn fool, you didn't report to the police. Instead, you make yourself "unavailable", and Hamilton Burger, our illustrious district attorney, wants to have a subpoena issued and drag you in before the Grand Jury, accompanying his action with a fanfare of trumpets.'

'Let him drag,' Mason said.

Tragg shook his head. 'In your case, no, Perry.'

'Why?'

'Because you're mixed up in too many murder cases where you're out on the firing line. You aren't content to sit in your office the way other people do and let the evidence come to you. You go out after it.'

'I like to get it in its original and unadulterated form,' Mason told him.

'I know how you feel, but the point is you have to look at these things from the standpoint of other people. Why didn't you come to us and tell us about the murder?'

'I didn't know about it.'

'Says you.'

'Says me.'

'What were you doing out there?'

'If I told you,' Mason said, 'you'd think I was lying.'

Tragg puffed contentedly at his cigar. 'Not me. I might think you'd play hocus-pocus with the district attorney, I might think you'd juggle guns if you had a chance, or switch evidence. You have the damnedest quixotic idea of protecting a client, but you don't lie.'

Mason said, 'I was peacefully eating dinner, minding my own business. A man came to me and told me he'd been involved in an automobile accident. He had reason to believe someone might have been injured. I went out to the scene of the accident with him, and, while I was there inside the grounds, the iron gates clanged shut. Apparently, they were actuated by some sort of a time mechanism. It was exactly eleven o'clock.'

'That's right,' Tragg said. 'There's an automatic timing device that closes the gates at eleven o'clock.'

'So we were trapped,' Mason said. 'Moreover, a nice, unfriendly Doberman Pinscher started trying to tear out the seat of my trousers.'

Tragg's eyes narrowed. 'When?'

'While we were trapped inside. We worked our way along the wall to the gate; the gate was locked tight. There were spikes on top of the gate, and we couldn't climb over it. Somehow we triggered the alarm. Dogs started barking and coming towards us. We got over the wall.'

'Who's we?'

'A couple of people were with me.'

'Della Street was one,' Tragg said.

Mason said nothing.

'The other fellow probably was a contractor by the name of George Ansley,' Tragg observed.

Again Mason was silent.

'And you didn't know Borden had been killed?'

'Not until this morning.'

'All right,' Tragg said. 'You've been out hunting witnesses. What witnesses?'

'Frankly, I was trying to find the driver of the automobile that had turned over in the Borden grounds.'

'You had Paul Drake looking for that last night. The car was stolen.'

'So I understand.'

'You're not offering me much information.'

'I'm answering questions.'

'Why don't you talk and *then* let me ask the questions?'

'I prefer it this way.'

Tragg said impatiently, 'You're playing hard to get, Mason. You're letting me drag everything out of you. The idea is that you aren't trying to tell me what you know, but are trying to find out how much or how little I know so you can govern yourself accordingly.'

'From my standpoint,' Mason asked, 'what would *you* do?'

'In this case,' Tragg said, 'I'd start talking.'

'Why?'

'Because,' Tragg told him, 'whether you're aware of it or not, I'm giving you a break. When I get done talking with you, I'm going to move over to that telephone, call Homicide and tell them that there's no need to get a subpoena for Perry Mason, that I've had a very nice, friendly chat with him and he's given me his story.'

Mason's face showed slight surprise. 'You'd do that for me?' he asked.

'I'd do that for you,' Tragg said.

'This isn't a gag?'

'It's not a gag. What the hell do you think I'm here for?'

'Sure,' Mason said, 'you're here, but you've got a couple of plain-clothes men scattered around. And, by the time the D.A. releases the story to the newspapers, it will be to the effect that Perry Mason was run to earth by clever detective work on the part of Lt Tragg of the Homicide Squad.'

'I'm handing it to you straight,' Tragg said. 'I looked at your *modus operandi* card, I got the name of this cafeteria, I felt there was a chance you'd be here, I came out entirely on my own. No one knows where I am. I simply said I was going out to lunch. As far as I know, there isn't a plain-clothes man within a mile.'

Mason studied Tragg's face for a moment, then said, 'If you have any information that will give you the identity of my client, you'll have to rely on that. I'm not going to admit the identity of my client right at the moment. I'll tell you the rest of it.

'Della Street and I were having dinner. It was a little after ten o'clock. This man came up to us, he told us that an hour earlier a car had swung past him and overturned in the grounds of Meridith Borden, that the licence number was CVX 266, that it had apparently been driven by a young woman who was injured.

'He had a flashlight. As it turned out, the batteries were on their last legs. He got out and walked around the front of the overturned car. He found a woman who had evidently been thrown out and had skidded along on the wet grass. He was looking at lots of legs. She was still alive but unconscious. He didn't dare to move her because he knew that might not be the thing to do. He started towards the house and then heard a call for help behind him. He turned and groped his way back through the darkness. Apparently, the woman had regained consciousness. He helped her to her feet, she said there were no bones broken, she was bruised, that was all, and suggested he drive her home.

'He drove her home. That is, he drove her to the address she gave.

'After I questioned him about it, and he began to think things over, there were things that made me suspicious there might have been *two* young women in the car, that when my client started towards the house the other passenger, who may or may not have been the driver of the car, had pulled the unconscious woman along the wet grass into a position of concealment against the wall, and then had taken her place and started calling for help.'

'Why?' Tragg asked.

'Apparently so my client wouldn't go up to the house.'

Tragg took the cigar out of his mouth, inspected the end with thoughtful concentration, then returned the cigar, puffed on it a few times, slowly nodded his head, and said, 'That might check. What did you do this morning?'

Mason said, 'I tried to find out who the young woman was.'

'What did you find out?'

'I went to the address where my client had left her.'

'What was the address?'

Mason thought for a moment, then said, 'The Ancordia Apartments. The woman had given him the name of Beatrice Cornell. There was a Beatrice Cornell registered. She's some kind of a talent agent and has a telephone-answering service. A lot of people know about her and she has a lot of clients. She says she wasn't out of the apartment yesterday evening, and I'm inclined to believe her.'

'Go ahead,' Tragg said.

Mason said, 'I came to the conclusion that this young woman had given the name of Beatrice Cornell, that she had gone to the apartment house where she knew Beatrice Cornell lived, had rung Beatrice Cornell's doorbell so as to be admitted, had kissed my client good night, then–'

'That cordial already?' Tragg interrupted.

'Be your age, Lieutenant,' Mason said.

Tragg grinned. 'That's the trouble, I am. Go ahead.'

'She went in the apartment house, seated herself in the lobby, waited until my client had driven away, then called a cab and left the place.'

'So what did you do?'

'I got Beatrice Cornell to show me her list of pin-up models–girls who rent themselves out at twenty dollars an hour to art photographers.'

'In the nude?' Tragg asked.

'I would so assume,' Mason said. 'Not from the models, but from some of the calendars I've seen. However, it's legal and artistic. They're nude but not naked, if you get what I mean.'

'It's always been a fine distinction as far as I'm personally concerned,' Tragg said, 'but I know the law makes it. Go on, what happened?'

'I found a young woman who seemed to answer the description.'

'How?'

'By a process of elimination.'

'Such as what?'

Mason grinned and said, 'Looking for a girl with a bruised hip.'

'Well, that's logic,' Tragg said. 'You make a pretty damned good detective for a lawyer. What happened?'

'I got this young woman to come out to Beatrice Cornell's apartment. I paid her for two hours' time and her taxi fare. I asked her questions and she told her story.'

'Which was?'

'That she had been at a party, that she had gone alone and was planning to return via taxicab, that when she went to the kerb to pick up a cab, the party who was driving this Cadillac with the licence number CVX 266 pulled in to the kerb, seemed to know her by name, and acted as though they had met. This woman offered the girl, Dawn Manning, a ride home. She accepted it.

'The woman driving the car said she wanted to stop just for a moment to leave something with a man she knew, and started to turn into Borden's driveway. Another car was coming out–'

'Your client's?' Tragg asked sharply.

Mason said doggedly, 'I'm giving you Dawn Manning's story. She said a car was coming out; that she had known Meridith Borden and didn't like his style; that her ex-husband was associated with Borden; that apparently they had wanted to use her in some sort of a badger game to trap a politician; for that reason her husband had delayed finishing up the divorce action. Dawn Manning wouldn't go for it, so naturally she didn't want to be taken into the Borden place; she pulled at the wheel; the Cadillac went into a spin, skidded, grazed the bumper of the other car, crashed through the hedge and that was all she remembered.

'She became conscious, perhaps thirty minutes later, tried to orientate herself, found the overturned car, made her way out to the highway, and–'

'Gates open at that time?' Tragg asked.

'Gates open at that time,' Mason said. 'She hitch-hiked home. That's her story.'

'You think it's true?'

'It checks with my theory.'

'All right. What about this woman who was driving the car, the one your client took to the Ancordia Apartments?'

'I feel that woman must have known Beatrice Cornell more or less intimately.'

'Why?'

'She knew her name, she knew her address, and, in some way, she knew some of the models that Beatrice Cornell had listed. It must have been because of that knowledge that she knew Dawn Manning.'

Tragg thoughtfully puffed at his cigar.

'What have you done about locating this other woman–provided Dawn Manning is telling the truth?'

'Dawn Manning has to be telling the truth,' Mason said. 'She doesn't fit the description given by my client of the young woman he drove home–at least I don't think she does.'

'And what have you done about locating the other woman?'

'Nothing yet. I'm thinking.'

'All right, let's quit thinking and act.'

'What do you mean, let's?'

'You and me,' Tragg said.

Mason thought that over for a moment.

'You know,' Tragg said, studying Mason over the tip of his cigar, 'you're acting as though you had some choice in the matter.'

'Perhaps I do,' Mason said.

'Maybe you don't,' Tragg told him. 'We're taking over now. What you apparently don't realize is the fact that I'm giving you an opportunity to come along as a passenger and take a look at the scenery.'

'Okay,' Mason told him, 'let's go.'

Tragg pushed back his chair, walked over to the telephone booth, dialled a number, talked for three or four minutes, then came back to join Perry Mason.

'All right,' he said, 'you're clean.'

'Thanks,' Mason said.

'What's more,' Tragg said, 'we're not going to be trying to pick up Della Street. We *are* going to talk with George Ansley.'

'How does Ansley's name enter into the picture?' Mason asked.

Tragg grinned. 'When he put his coat over the barbed wire on that wall, part of the lining tore out. It was the part that had a tailor's label in it. You couldn't have asked for anything better. All we had to do was read the guy's name and address, then match the torn lining with the lining that the tailor knew had been put into his coat.'

'Simple,' Mason said.

'All police work is simple when you come down to it. It's just dogged perseverance.'

'Want to go see Beatrice Cornell?' Mason asked.

'Why?'

'Because she must have a clue somewhere in her list of clients. This woman, whoever it was, must know Beatrice Cornell pretty well and is probably a client.'

'Could be,' Tragg said. 'We're trying the simple ways first.'

'What's that?'

'Combing all the taxi companies,' Tragg said. 'After all, we've got the location, the Ancordia Apartments. We've got the time, probably a little before ten. The guy got in touch with you a few minutes past ten, and you went out there and did some running around before the gates closed. What time do you suppose you got there?'

'I would say that we must have arrived around ten minutes before eleven. We were there about that long before the gates closed, and, as I remember it, the gong sounded and the gates closed right at eleven o'clock.'

'Right,' Tragg said. 'Okay, we've got the time. Police are searching taxi calls. There's a phone booth in the lobby of the Ancordia Apartments. It's almost a cinch this babe went inside, waited just long enough to see Ansley drive off, then stuck a dime in the telephone and called a cab.

'What do you say we go on down to my car? I've got a radio on it and I'll get in touch with Communications. They'll have the information for me by the time we're ready to go.'

Mason said thoughtfully, 'There's a lot of advantage being a police officer.'

'And a hell of a disadvantage,' Tragg said. 'Come on, let's go.'

7

The loudspeaker on Lt Tragg's car crackled.

'Calling Car XX-Special. Calling Car XX-Special.'

Tragg picked up the mouthpiece, said, 'Car XX-Special, Lt Tragg.'

The voice replied, 'Go to telephone booth and call Communications. Repeat, telephone booth, call Communications. Information party desired now available.'

'Will call,' Tragg said, and dropped the transmitter back on the hook. He grinned at Mason and said, 'That means they've located something. They don't want it put out on the general communications system. They–'

Tragg glanced swiftly behind him and swung the car into a service station where a telephone booth was located at the back of the lot.

'Sit here and hold the fort, Perry,' he said. 'If a call comes in for XX-Special, just pick up the receiver and state that Lt Tragg is calling Communications on a telephone circuit and any message can be sent to him there.'

Tragg hurried into the phone booth, and Mason could see him talking, then taking notes.

Tragg hung up the phone, returned to the car, grinned at Mason, 'All right, we have our party.'

'You're sure it's the one we want?' Mason asked.

'Hell, no!' Tragg said. 'The way we work we're not sure of anything. We just run down leads, that's all. We run down a hundred leads and finally get the one we want. Sometimes the one we want is the second one we run down, sometimes it's the one hundredth. Sometimes we run down a hundred leads and don't get anything. This looks pretty live. A woman about thirty years old, height, five-feet-four, weight, 115 to 120, called for a taxi to go to the Ancordia Apartments last night. She gave the name of Miss Harper. We chased down the number of the cab, found that he took her to the Dormain Apartments in Mesa Vista, and that's where we're going now.'

'About a chance in a hundred?' Mason asked.

'Make it one in ten,' Tragg said. 'But I have an idea it'll pay off. Remember the police system is to cover leads. We ring doorbells. We cover a hundred different leads to find the one we want, but we have a hundred people we can put on the job if we have to. And don't ever discount the efficiency of that system, Mason. It pays off. We may look pretty damned stupid when we're running down one of the leads that takes us up a blind alley, but sooner or later we'll get on the right trail.'

Tragg piloted the car through the city traffic with a deft sureness that marks the professional driver.

'You're out in traffic a lot,' Mason said. 'Have any accidents?'

'Hell, no!' Tragg told him. 'The taxpayers don't like to have their cars smashed up.'

'How do you avoid them?'

'By avoiding them.'

'How?'

'You keep alert. You watch the other guy. Accidents are caused by people being discourteous, paying too little attention to what they're doing, and not watching the other guy.

'When I've got a car, I know damn well *I'm* not going to hit somebody. It's the other man who's going to hit me; therefore, the other man is the guy I watch. This is a cinch. But remember that we get leads we have to run down on bad nights, holidays, rush-hour traffic. . . . And the really bad hours are around one to four o'clock in the morning. The man who's had a few drinks and knows he'd had a few drinks is pretty apt to be driving cautiously. In fact, the traffic boys pick up a lot of those fellows because they're driving too slowly and too cautiously.

'The boy that's really dangerous is the guy who's been whooping it up until two or three o'clock in the morning, and then when he starts home, he's so drunk he doesn't realize he's drunk. About that time he gets a feeling of great superiority and feels that if he can only go through an intersection fast enough, nobody can get half-way across the intersection before he's *all* the way through it. It sounds like swell reasoning when you're drunk, at least that's what they tell me.'

Tragg chuckled a few times, drove to Mesa Vista, then drove steadily along one of the main streets, turned to the left, then to the right and slowed his car.

'You know where every apartment house in the country is located?' Mason asked.'

'Damned near,' Tragg said. 'I've been on this job a long time. You'd better come up with me.'

Tragg picked up the transmitter, said, 'Car XX-Special, out of contact for a short time and parked at the location of the last lead I received on the telephone. Will report in when I get back in circulation.'

The voice on the loudspeaker said, 'Car XX-Special, out until report.'

'Come on,' Tragg said to Mason.

The Dormain Apartments had a rather pretentious front and a swinging door to the lobby. A clerk looked up as Mason and Lt Tragg entered the lobby, looked down, then suddenly did a double take.

Tragg walked over to the desk. 'You have a Harper here?' he asked.

'We have two Harpers. Which one did you want?'

'A woman,' Tragg said. 'Around thirty; height, five-feet-four; weight, maybe 120 pounds.'

'That would be Loretta Nann Harper. I'll give her a ring.'

Tragg slid a leather folder on the desk, opened it to show a gold, numbered badge. 'Police officers,' he said. 'Don't ring, we'll go on up. What's the number?'

'It's 409. I trust there's nothing–'

'Just want to interview a witness,' Tragg said. 'Forget about it.'

He nodded to Mason and they went to the elevator.

'I repeat,' Mason said, 'being a police officer has its advantages.'

'Yeah,' Tragg said. 'You ought to follow me around for a while and then you'd change your tune. Think of when you get on the witness stand and some smart lawyer is walking all over you, asking you how the guy was dressed, what colour socks he had on, whether he wore a tiepin, how many buttons on his vest, and every time you say you don't know, the guy sneers at you and says, "You're a police officer, aren't you? You're on the public payrolls. As an officer you're supposed to have a special aptitude for noticing details, aren't you?"'

Mason grinned. 'Well, you *may* have something there.'

'May have is right,' Tragg said. 'The guy just throws questions at you and sneers at you and tosses you insults, and the jurors just sit there and grin, getting a great kick out of seeing some lawyer make a monkey out of a dumb cop.'

The elevator, which had been on an upper floor, slid to a stop. Tragg and Mason got in. Tragg pushed the fourth-floor button and they were silent until the cage slid smoothly to a stop.

Tragg oriented himself on the numbers, walked down the corridor, knocked on the door of 409.

There was no answer.

Tragg knocked again.

There was a gentle swishing sound of motion from the other side of the door. The door opened a few inches and was held in position by a chain.

The young woman on the inside bent over slightly so that her body could not be seen, only the eyes, nose and forehead.

'Who is it, please?'

Tragg once more displayed his badge. 'Lt Tragg, Homicide,' he said. 'We'd just like to talk with you a minute.'

'I . . . I'm dressing.'

'Are you decent?'

'Well, yes.'

'Okay, let us in.'

She hesitated a moment, then released the catch of the safety chain and opened the door. 'I meant . . . that is . . . I'm getting ready to dress to go out. I've just had lunch and–'

'Then you haven't been out yet,' Tragg said.

'Not yet.'

Mason followed Tragg into the apartment. It consisted of a luxuriously furnished sitting-room. Through an open bedroom door, sunlight streaming into the room through a fire escape made a barred pattern on an unmade bed. Another partially opened door gave a glimpse of a bathroom, and there was a powder-room on the other side of the sitting-room.

A swinging door opened into a kitchen, and the aroma of coffee came to their nostrils.

Tragg said, 'Nice place you have here.'

'I like it.'

'Live here alone?'

'If it's any of your business, yes.'

'Lots of room.'

'I hate to be cramped.'

Tragg said, 'We're trying to find a young woman who was at the Ancordia Apartments last night, say around nine-forty-five to ten o'clock. We thought perhaps you could help us.'

'What makes you think that?'

'Can you?'

'I don't know.'

'Were you there?'

'I . . .'

'Well?' Tragg said as she hesitated.

'Is it particularly important, one way or another?'

'Uh-huh.'

'May I ask why?'

Tragg said, 'I'd prefer to have you answer my questions first, ma'am. Why did you give the name of Beatrice Cornell when George Ansley let you out in front of the apartment house?'

'Does he say I did that?'

'Did you?' Tragg asked.

'Really, Mister–Lieutenant–I'd like to find out why you're asking these questions.'

'To get information,' Tragg said. 'We're investigating a crime. Now, you can answer these questions very simply, and then I'll be in a position to ask you about the automobile accident.'

'What accident?'

'The accident where you were pitched out of the car at Meridith Borden's place, the accident where you grabbed the other young woman by the ankles and dragged her away from the car, then slid down on to the ground and started calling for help.'

Loretta Harper bit her lip, frowned, said, 'Sit down, Lt Tragg. And this is . . .?'

'Mr Mason,' the lawyer said, bowing.

'I . . . I hope you can keep my name out of this, Lieutenant.'

'Well, you'd better tell us about it. How did it happen you were driving a stolen car?'

'*I* was driving a stolen car!' she exclaimed with such vehement emphasis on the *I* that Tragg cocked a quizzical eyebrow.

'Weren't you?' he asked.

'Heavens, no! Dawn Manning was driving the car, and she was driving like a crazy person.'

'How did it happen you were with her?'

'She forced me to get into the car.'

'How?'

'With a gun.'

'That's kidnapping.'

'Of course, it is. I was so mad at her I could have killed her.'

'Well, go ahead,' Tragg said. 'What happened?'

'She accused me of playing around with her ex-husband.'

'Were you?' Tragg asked.

'She had absolutely no right to say the things she did. She and Frank are divorced and she doesn't have any control over him. She certainly doesn't let anyone have any control over her, I can tell you that much. She does exactly as she likes, and–'

'Who's Frank?' Lt Tragg asked.

'Frank Ferney, her ex-husband.'

'And her name?'

'Dawn Manning is her *professional* name.'

'What profession?'

'You should ask *me*! You're an officer.'

'And how did you happen to get into this stolen car?'

'You're *certain* it was stolen?'

'That's right. A Cadillac, licence number CVX 266. It was stolen last night.'

'I'll bet she did that so no one could trace her.'

'Well, suppose you tell us about it,' Tragg said.

'I had a little dinner party last night, a foursome, people who were very intimate friends–a married couple.

'We ran out of cigarettes and ice cubes. I went out to get them and a few other supplies. My friends were watching television.

'It was some time after eight o'clock, eight-forty-five perhaps. I had stopped to wait for a traffic signal. When the signal changed, I started to walk across, and this car swung right in front of me, blocking the way. It came to a stop. The right-hand door swung open and Dawn Manning said, "Get in."'

'You know her?' Tragg asked.

'I've never met her, but I know her by sight.'

'She knows you?'

'Apparently.'

'What did she say?'

'She said, "Get in, Loretta, I want to talk with you."'

'What did you do?'

'I hesitated and she said again, "I can't stay here all night, I'm blocking traffic. Get in."'

'Then what happened?'

'There was something in her voice that alarmed me. I started to pull back and then I saw the gun she was pointing at me. She was holding it right on a level with the seat. She said, with deadly earnestness, "I said get in, and I meant it. You and I are going to have a talk."'

'So what did you do?'

'I got in. I thought perhaps that would be the best thing to do. I felt certain she was going to shoot if I refused to get in the car.'

'Then what?'

'She started to drive like mad. She was half-hysterical, pouring out a whole mess of things.'

'Such as what?'

'That Frank–that's Frank Ferney, her ex-husband–had told her over a year ago that he'd gone to Reno and secured a divorce. Dawn said she had acted on the assumption she was free to remarry. Then she'd decided to check up on it, and an attorney had told her no such divorce had ever been granted, that Frank had admitted he'd never gone ahead to finish the divorce and wouldn't do so unless he received a piece of money. He said some rich amateur photographer was giving Dawn a tumble.

'She was so mad about it I thought perhaps she'd shoot Frank and me, too. She said I'd been playing around with Frank and she was going to make us both sign a statement.'

'Did she say what would happen otherwise?'

'No, she didn't say, but she had that gun.'

'Go on,' Tragg said. 'Take it from there.'

'She was like a crazy woman. I think she was half-hysterical and jealous and upset and frightened. She drove the car like mad and when we came to Borden's place she started to turn in, and, just as she did, saw apparently for the first time a car that was coming out. She slammed on the brakes on wet road just as she was making a turn. The tyres skidded all over the road. We just barely hit the bumper of the other car and crashed through the hedge. I guess we turned completely around. It felt like it to me.

'The car crashed through the hedge and turned over. The doors on the front of the car flew open, or perhaps she opened the door on the driver's side. I know I had opened the door on my side and I was thrown out. I skidded across the grass for a ways and sat up feeling pretty bruised and dazed. And then I saw the glow of a light of some kind and saw this man bending over a figure by the car.

'I had a glimpse in the weak light that was given by the flashlight of Dawn Manning lying there unconscious where she'd been thrown from the car and had skidded on the wet grass.'

'Go on,' Tragg said. 'What happened?'

'Well, then this man seemed to be having trouble with the flashlight. It went out and he threw it into the darkness. I heard it from where I was crouching, dazed and shaken and wondering just what had happened, and whether she still had the gun.'

'Go on,' Tragg said.

'Well, I . . . I don't feel very proud of this, Lieutenant, but it seemed to be the best thing at the moment, and . . . well, at a time like that you just have to think of yourself and for yourself.'

'Go on, go on, what did you *do*? Never mind the explanations or the alibis.'

'Well, I saw this young man running over towards the driveway to the house and I knew he was going to ask for help and all of that, and I just didn't want to be mixed up in that sort of a mess. In fact, I can't afford to have my name dragged into court or get a lot of newspaper notoriety.

'I grabbed Dawn Manning by the ankles and started pulling. The grass was wet from the rain, and she slid along just as easily as though I had been dragging a big sled. I got her out of the way and put myself in the same position she'd been occupying. I pulled my skirts way up as though I'd skidded. Then I called out for help, and . . . well, this young man came back and I let him get a good look at my legs and then help me up. I got my handbag, and in the dark wondered if I could have made a mistake and had Dawn's handbag instead of mine. So I stalled around, drove into the car for the second time after my raincoat, found a second handbag, concealed it in the folds of the coat and got out.

'I told him that I had been driving the car. I didn't want to have any trouble about it. I let him drive me into the city. I told him it was my car and kidded him along so he didn't ask to see my driving licence. I was desperately trying to think of some name I could give him, and then I remembered someone had told me about a telephone service given by Beatrice Cornell over at the Ancordia Apartments, so I just gave him her name. I knew it would be on the mailbox in case he wanted to check on it, and . . . well, I let him drive me there and let him think he was driving me home.

'He told me his name was Ansley and he was very, very nice. I let him kiss me good night, then I rang the bell of Beatrice Cornell's apartment. She buzzed the lock on the door, I went in, sat in the lobby until Mr Ansley drove off, then I telephoned for a taxicab and came back here to this apartment.'

'Then what?'

'That's all.'

'Why did she drive to Meridith Borden's place?'

'That's where her husband works. Frank is associated in some capacity with Meridith Borden. She thought he was there. He wasn't. Actually, he was the fourth guest at my dinner party. He's my boy friend.'

'And you left her there in the grounds?' Tragg asked.

'Yes.'

'Unconscious?'

'Yes . . . I didn't know what else to do. I had to look out for myself.'

Lt Tragg frowned thoughtfully, fished a cigar from his pocket. 'Mind if I smoke?' he asked.

'I'd love it,' Loretta Harper said.

The officer regarded her with quizzical appraisal. 'Either you,' he said, 'or this Manning woman is lying. I suppose you know that.'

'I can readily imagine it,' she said. 'Any woman who will take chances on threatening another woman with a gun and pulling a kidnap stunt like that would naturally be expected to lie about it, wouldn't she?'

'And you've got her handbag?'

'Yes. I took both handbags only because I wanted to be absolutely certain I didn't leave mine behind. I couldn't afford to be mixed up in the thing–and I'll be frank with you, Lt Tragg, Frank and I are . . . well, he's my boy friend.'

'I'll want her handbag. Did you look in it?'

'Only just to be certain it was hers.'

Tragg scraped a match into flame and puffed the end of his cigar into a glowing red circle. 'Okay,' he said, 'let's see it.'

She opened a drawer, took out a handbag and handed it to Lt Tragg, who started to open it and look inside, then changed his mind.

Mason said, 'I'd like to fix the time element, Miss Harper. Can you tell me exactly when Dawn Manning picked you up?'

'Not the exact minute. I would say it was somewhere between eight-forty and–oh, say a few minutes before nine, right around there sometime.'

'And when you had the accident?'

'It must have been nine o'clock or a few minutes after that.'

'Then Ansley got out of his car and came running over to where Dawn Manning was lying?'

'That's right.'

'And from that point on you were in his company until . . . well, suppose you tell us. Until about what time?'

'I would say I was with him there in the grounds until right around nine-twenty, and then he drove me to the Ancordia Apartments.'

'Do you think there's any chance you're mistaken about the time–about any of the times?'

'No. That is, my times are approximate only.'

'But you've fixed them as best you can?'

'Yes.'

Tragg's eyes narrowed. 'You know, Mason,' he said, 'you're trying to cross-examine this witness. You're getting her story sewed up as much as possible.'

'I'm assuming she's telling the truth,' Mason said.

'In that event, somebody else isn't.'

'I have to make allowances for that also, Lieutenant.'

Tragg said to Loretta Harper, 'I suppose you know that you violated the Motor Vehicle Act in not reporting an accident where a person was injured.'

'I don't think I did,' she said. 'I wasn't driving the car.'

'And,' Tragg went on, 'since an assault with a deadly weapon was made on you and you didn't report that to the police, you concealed a felony.'

'I don't care to prosecute for private reasons. And I don't think the law compels me to go into court and file a complaint on which I wouldn't prosecute.'

Tragg twisted the cigar around in his mouth. 'Well,' he said, 'you're going to have to take a ride up to the D.A.'s office and talk things over a bit. Mason, this is where you came in.'

Mason grinned. 'You mean this is where I go out.'

'The same thing,' Tragg said.

Mason shook hands with him. 'Thanks, Lieutenant.'

'Don't mention it,' Tragg said. And then added with a grin, '*I'm* sure *I* won't!'

8

Mason called Beatrice Cornell's number.

'Perry Mason talking,' he said when he heard her voice on the line. 'How well do you know Dawn Manning?'

'Not too well.'

'Would she lie?'

'About what?'

'About a murder.'

'You mean if she were involved?'

'That's right.'

'Sure, she'd lie,' Beatrice Cornell said. 'Who wouldn't?'

'How is she otherwise?'

'Nice.'

'What do you mean by nice?'

'I mean nice.'

'Boy friends?'

'What the hell, she's normal.'

'Do you keep records of your calls there?'

'Yes.'

'What time was it when someone rang your doorbell and then didn't go on in?'

'I can't tell you that. I don't keep records of things like that, but I think it was about ten.'

'Do you remember when I called you and asked you about an automobile accident and you said you hadn't been in one?'

'Of course.'

'Would you have a record of the time of that call?'

'Sure,' she said. 'I record all telephone conversations.'

'And the time?'

'And the time,' she said. 'I have a tape recorder and whenever the phone rings, and before I answer it, I pick up a time clock stamp and stamp that on the piece of paper. Then I mark down the figure which shows on the footage indicator of the tape recorder, switch on the tape recorder and then answer the telephone.'

'And what about this particular call that I placed?'

'I simply marked that personal.'

'But the conversation would be saved?'

'Yes.'

'On the tape recorder?'

'That's right.'

'And the time?'

She said, 'While I've been talking with you, Mr Mason, I've been pawing through papers looking for the time sheet. Give me just a minute more and I think I can find it.'

Mason grinned. 'How about *this* conversation? Is it being recorded?'

'It's being recorded,' she said. 'I–Here we are. It was ten-twenty-three when you called, Mr Mason.'

'Thanks a lot,' Mason told her. 'Try and keep that record straight, will you, so you'll know the time?'

'It's all straight,' she said, 'and this conversation is recorded. I can always refer back to it and tell you the time I gave you.'

'That's fine,' Mason told her. 'Thanks a lot.'

He hung up and called his office.

'Hello, Gertie,' Mason said when the receptionist and switchboard operator answered the phone. 'Della isn't around, is she?'

'No,' she said. 'You told her to take the day off because she'd been working late last night.'

'That's right, I did. She hasn't shown up?'

'No.'

'Anyone looking for me?' Mason asked.

'Lots of people.'

'Anyone in the office now?'

'Yes.'

'Waiting?'

'That's right.'

'Anyone who looks official?'

'I don't think so.'

'Can you tell me who it is?'

'He says his name is Ansley, George Ansley. You left a message for him.'

Mason's voice showed excitement. 'Put him in my private office, Gertie,' he said. 'Lock the door of the private office and don't let anyone in there. Tell him to wait. I'm coming right up.'

Leaving his car parked in the parking lot at the Family Kitchen Cafeteria, Mason took a cab direct to his office, went up in the elevator, hurried down the corridor, unlocked the door of his private office and found George Ansley seated in the big, overstuffed chair reading a newspaper.

'Hello, Mr Mason,' Ansley said. 'Gosh, I'm glad you showed up. What's new?'

'*You* should ask *me*!' Mason told him.

Ansley raised his eyebrows. 'What's the matter?'

'Have you been out of circulation all day?' Mason asked.

'Not all day. I checked in about two o'clock this afternoon and . . . well, I saw the paper.'

'That was the first you'd known about it?' Mason asked.

Ansley nodded.

'Now, look here,' Mason told him, 'I want to know *exactly* what happened at your interview with Borden, everything that was said by either party, and I want to know whether you went back to Borden's place after you left me.'

Ansley straightened in the chair. '*I* go back to Borden's place?'

Mason nodded.

'Good heavens! You don't mean that anyone would think I could have gone back there, and–?'

'Why not?' Mason asked. 'The building and contract construction inspectors start picking on you. You get the tip to go and see Meridith Borden. Borden is a crooked politician. He's smart enough so he doesn't hold office himself, but acts as go-between.

'It was to Borden's financial advantage to have you come and see him. Surely you aren't so naïve that the possibility hadn't occurred to you that Borden was responsible for all your troubles–putting you in such a position that you'd have to come to him.'

'Of course he was responsible,' Ansley said. 'That's the way he worked.'

'You didn't have a gun, did you?' Mason asked.

'No.'

'Where's your car?' Mason asked.

'In the parking lot down here.'

'Okay,' Mason said, 'let's go take a look. Let's look in your glove compartment.'

'For what?'

'Evidence.'

'Of what?'

'Anything,' Mason said. 'I'm just checking.'

The lawyer opened the door and led the way down the corridor. They descended in the elevator, went to the parking lot, and Ansley pulled out a key container. He fitted the key in the lock of the glove compartment, turned the key, then frowned and said, 'Wait a minute, that's the wrong way.'

'You're locking it now,' Mason said.

'It won't turn the other way.'

'Then it probably was unlocked all the time.'

Ansley turned the key and said sheepishly, 'I guess it was.'

Ansley opened the glove compartment. 'I usually keep it locked. I must have unlocked it the other night and left it unlocked.'

'Let's take a look,' Mason said.

'My God!' Ansley exclaimed. 'There's a gun in there!'

Ansley reached in to take out the weapon. Mason jerked his arm away.

'Close the glove compartment,' Mason said.

'But there's . . . there's a gun there, a blued-steel revolver.'

'Close the glove compartment,' Mason said.

A voice behind them said, 'Mind if I look?'

Mason whirled to see Lt Tragg standing behind him.

Tragg pushed Mason to one side, showed Ansley a leather container with a gold badge. 'Lt Tragg of Homicide,' he said.

Lt Tragg reached inside the glove compartment and took out the gun.

'Yours?' he asked Ansley.

'Definitely not. I've never seen it before.'

Tragg said, 'I guess we'd better sort of take this gun along and check it. You know, Borden was killed with a ·38 Colt.'

'You don't mean he was killed with *this* gun,' Ansley said.

'Oh, sure, sure, not with *your* gun. But just the same, we'd better take it along. The ballistics department will want to play around with it, and then they'll give you a clean bill of health. You won't have anything to worry about. You'll come with me.'

'I tell you it isn't *my* gun.'

'Oh sure, I know. It just parked itself in your car because it didn't have any place to go. Let's go take a ride and see what Ballistics has to say about the gun.'

'Mason coming with us?' Ansley asked.

'No,' Tragg said, grinning. 'Mason has had a busy day and he's been away from his office. He has a lot of stuff to take care of up there. We won't need to bother Mr Mason. There isn't anything you have on your mind, no reason why you *should* have a lawyer with you, is there?'

'No, certainly not.'

'That's what I thought,' Tragg said. 'Now, if you don't mind, we'll just take this gun and go on up to Headquarters. Probably you'd better drive up in your car. The boys may want to check the car a little bit, find out when you last saw Meridith Borden, and so on. You know how those things are. . . . Okay, Perry, we'll see you later. I'm sorry to have to inconvenience your client, but you know how those things are.'

'I certainly do,' Mason said dryly, as Tragg took Ansley's arm and virtually pushed him into the automobile.

9

The clerk of Judge Erwood's court indicated the spectators could be seated. The judge called the case, 'People versus Ansley.'

'Ready for the defendant,' Mason said.

'Ready for the prosecution,' Sam Drew, one of Hamilton Burger's chief trial deputies, said.

'Proceed with the case,' Judge Erwood said.

Sam Drew got to his feet. 'May the Court please, I think at the start it would be well to have the situation definitely understood. This is a preliminary hearing. The prosecution frankly admits that it doesn't have any intention of putting on enough evidence at this time to convict the defendant of first-degree murder. But it certainly does intend to put on enough evidence to show that first-degree murder has been committed and that there are reasonable grounds to believe the defendant committed that murder.

'As we understand it, that's the sole function of a preliminary hearing.'

'That is correct,' Judge Erwood said. 'This is a preliminary hearing. The Court has noted that some attorneys seem to have an erroneous idea of the issues at a preliminary hearing. We're not trying the defendant now, and, above all, we're not trying to find out if the evidence introduced by the prosecution proves him guilty beyond all reasonable doubt.

'All the prosecution is *trying* to do here, and all the prosecution *needs* to try to do here, is to prove that a crime has been committed and that there is reasonable ground to believe the defendant is guilty thereof.

'The Court is going to restrict the issues in this case, and the Court is not going to permit any dramatics. Is that understood, gentlemen?'

'Quite, Your Honour,' Mason said, with great cheerfulness.

'Exactly,' Sam Drew said.

'Who's your first witness?'

Drew called a surveyor who gave a sketch of the Borden estate and showed its location. He also introduced a map of the city and the suburbs and the location of the Golden Owl Night Club.

'The Court will take judicial recognizance of the location of the various cities in the county,' Judge Erwood said. 'Let's not take up the time of the Court with anything except the essential facts. Do you wish to cross-examine this witness, Mr Mason?'

'No, Your Honour.'

'Very well, the witness is excused. Call your next witness,' Judge Erwood said.

Drew's next witness was Marianna Fremont, who stated that she had been Meridith Borden's housekeeper for some years. Monday was her day off because quite frequently Meridith Borden did entertaining on Sunday. On Tuesday morning, when she drove up in her car, she had found the gates locked, indicating that Meridith Borden was not up as yet. That was not particularly unusual. The housekeeper had a key, she inserted the key in the electric connexion, pressed the button, and the motors rolled the gates back wide open. The housekeeper had driven in and parked her car in its accustomed place in the back yard.

'Then what did you do?' Drew asked.

'Then I went to the house and opened the door and went in.'

'Did you see anything unusual?'

'Not at that time, no, sir.'

'What did you do?'

'I cooked Mr Borden's breakfast and then went to his room to call him. Sometimes he would come out for breakfast in a robe, sometimes he had me bring breakfast to him.'

'And did you notice anything unusual then?'

'Yes.'

'What?'

'There was no sign of him in his bedroom.'

'What did you do, if anything?'

'I looked to see if he had left me a note. Sometimes when he was called out overnight he'd leave a note telling me when to expect him.'

'Those notes were left in a regular place?'

'Yes.'

'Did you find any note that morning?'

'No, sir.'

'Very well,' Drew said. 'Tell us what happened after that.'

'Well, I started looking the place over after I found that Mr Borden hadn't slept in his bed that night.'

'Now, just a minute, that's a conclusion,' Drew said. 'And, while this hearing isn't like a trial before a jury, I think we'd better keep the record in shape. When you said his bed hadn't been slept in, what do you mean?'

'Well, his bed was made fresh.'

'Go on.'

'Well, then I started looking around and went into the studio.'

'Now, what's the studio?'

'That's the room where he did his photography.'

'Can you describe it?'

'Well, it's just a room. It's up a short flight of stairs, and it's arranged with a big skylight on the north, a big, long slanting window so he could get the right kind of illumination. There's ground glass in the windows. And then there are a lot of electrical outlets so he could turn floodlights on and use spotlights.'

'Mr Borden used this room?'

'Oh, yes, he used it lots. He was a photographer and liked to photograph things, particularly people.'

'And when you went into that room, what did you find?'

'I found Mr Borden sprawled out on the floor with a bullet hole–'

'Tut-tut. Now, *you* don't *know* it was a bullet hole,' Drew interrupted. 'You saw something which directed your attention to his chest?'

'Yes. There'd been a lot of bleeding coming from a hole in the chest.'

'Mr Borden was dead?'

'Oh, yes, he was stiff as a board.'

'So what did you do?'

'I called the police.'

'That's all,' Drew said.

'Do you wish to cross-examine?' Judge Erwood asked Mason.

'This photographic studio,' Mason said, 'can you describe it a little better? Was there anything in it other than what you have mentioned?'

'Oh, yes. A darkroom opens off it. There's a stand with a portrait camera on wheels so you can move it forward and back. And there are a lot of curtains. You know, great big, roller-shade things like curtains that have painted scenery for a background. You know the type of thing photographers use, like beach scenery and mountain scenery and all that.'

'Can you tell us just how Mr Borden was lying?'

'Well, he was on his back with–It's hard to describe. He was all stiff and awkward.'

'We have a photograph taken by the police photographer,' Drew said.

'I'll stipulate it may go in evidence,' Mason said, 'and that will eliminate the necessity of asking any more questions of this witness.'

Drew produced an eight-by-ten photograph, handed one copy to Mason, one copy to Judge Erwood and one copy to the clerk of the court.

'This photograph will be received in evidence,' Judge Erwood said. 'Call your next witness.'

'Officer Gordon C. Gibbs,' Drew said.

Gibbs came forward and was sworn.

'You're a police officer connected with the Metropolitan Police Force?'

'Yes, sir.'

'On last Tuesday, did you have occasion to enter the apartment leased by the defendant?'

'I did, yes, sir.'

'Did you have a search warrant?'

'Yes, sir.'

'What were you looking for?'

'Bloody clothing, a murder weapon, anything that would indicate the defendant had been involved in a crime of violence.'

'Did you find any of the things you were looking for?'

'Yes, sir.'

'What did you find?'

'I found a suit of clothes with rusty brown spots all over them. I took these clothes to the police laboratory and they found the spots were–'

'Just a moment!' Drew snapped out the interruption as Mason was getting to his feet. 'The laboratory expert will testify as to what he found. Now, did you do anything in the way of identifying this suit of clothes?'

'I did, sir.'

'What?'

'I took it to the cleaner whose mark was on the clothes and asked him if he was familiar with the suit and how often he'd seen it and who had sent it in when it had been cleaned. I suppose I can't testify to his answers.'

'That's right, you can't,' Drew said.

Ansley leaned forward and whispered to Mason. 'That was a suit I'd worn when I had one of my nosebleeds. I have them at intervals. This was a windy day, and I had to walk from the job to where I'd parked my car.'

Mason turned his attention to the police witness.

'Cross-examine,' Drew said.

'You don't know of your own knowledge that these were bloodstains, do you?' Mason asked.

'No, sir.'

'You don't know of your own knowledge that it was the defendant's suit?'

'No, sir.'

'You don't know of your own knowledge that these stains weren't the result of the defendant's having a bloody nose, do you?'

'No, sir.'

'All you know is you found a suit of clothes?'

'Yes, sir.'

'You tried to check the cleaning marks on that suit of clothes and you delivered it to the police laboratory, is that right?'

'Yes, sir.'

'And that's really *all* you know about that suit of clothes?'

'I know the appearance of the stains on it.'

'Certainly,' Mason said. 'You *thought* they were significant stains, otherwise you wouldn't have bothered with it.'

'That's right.'

'You don't know how long those stains had been on that suit, do you?'

'I know what the cleaner told me as to when he had last cleaned the suit, and–'

'You're an officer,' Mason said. 'You know you're supposed to testify as to your own knowledge, and not to what someone told you. Now, I'll repeat, you don't know how long those stains had been on that suit, do you?'

'No, sir.'

'Thank you,' Mason said. 'That's all.'

'I'll call Lt Tragg to the stand,' Drew said.

Lt Tragg came forward, testified as to his name and occupation.

'Do you know the defendant in this case?'

'Yes, sir.'

'When did you first meet him?'

'On Tuesday, the ninth.'

'Where did you meet him?'

'In a parking lot.'

'Who was with you at that time?'

'No one.'

'Who was with the defendant at that time?'

'Mr Perry Mason, who is acting as his attorney.'

'Did you have any conversation with the defendant?'

'Yes, sir.'

'Can you state the general subject of that conversation? I won't bother you for the exact words at this time.'

'We don't want the witness testifying to his conclusions as to the conversation,' Mason said.

'I'm not asking for that. I'm only asking if he can remember generally the subject of the conversation.'

'Yes, sir.'

'What was it?'

'I asked him about a gun in the glove compartment of his car.'

'Now, what did you do at that time?'

'I took a gun from the automobile.'

'Where was it?'

'In the glove compartment.'

'Can you describe that revolver?'

'Yes, sir. It was a Colt ·38-calibre of the type known as a police model.'

'Did you have occasion to notice the number?'

'I did.'

'What was it?'

'613096.'

'What did you do with that gun?'

'I turned it over to the ballistics department.'

'Now, Lieutenant,' Drew said, 'you didn't turn it over to a department, you turned it over to some person in that department.'

'That's right, to Alexander Redfield.'

'He's the police expert on ballistics?'

'Yes, sir.'

'Then what happened?'

'I told the defendant I wanted him to go to Headquarters with me.'

'Did he make any objection?'

'No, sir.'

'He went to Headquarters?'

'Yes, sir.'

'And, while he was there, did he make any statement to you?'

'He did, yes, sir.'

'What did he say?'

'He made a statement about what he had done the night before, and about the time he had seen Meridith Borden. I asked him if he had any objection to writing down what he had said and giving us a signed account of what had happened. He said he didn't, so I gave him pencil and paper and he wrote out a document.'

'Do you have that document with you?'

'I do, yes, sir.'

'That was entirely written, dated and signed by the defendant and is in his handwriting?'

'Yes, sir.'

'Did anyone tell him what to put in there?'

'No, sir, only to write down what had happened.'

'Did anyone offer him any promises, threats or inducements?'

'No, sir.'

'Was he subjected to any physical or mental pressure whatever in order to get him to make this statement?'

'No, sir.'

'He did it of his own free will and accord?'

'Yes, sir.'

'And you have the statement here with you?'

'Yes, sir.'

'If the Court please,' Drew said, 'I will offer this gun in evidence and also this statement.'

'Very well,' Judge Erwood said.

'Those are all the questions I have of this witness at this time. I may wish to recall him later,' Drew said.

'Quite all right,' Mason said. 'I know the witness will be available. We waive cross-examination.'

'You waive it?' Drew asked incredulously.

'Certainly,' Mason said. 'I have no questions, none whatever.'

'Call your next witness,' Judge Erwood said.

Sam Drew said, 'Call Harvey Dennison to the stand, please.'

Harvey Dennison came forward and was sworn. He testified that he was an owner and proprietor of a general hardware store known as the Valley View Hardware Company, that he had been with the company for a period of more than three years, that he had examined the Colt revolver, Number 613096, that his records showed that this revolver had been purchased from the wholesaler, placed in stock, but that it had not been sold. He said that some three years ago it had been called to his attention that the gun was missing from the showcase, that this theft had turned up in connexion with an inventory which was being taken, and the only possible conclusion was that the gun had been stolen, that there had been two occasions at about that time when the store had been entered by someone who had picked the lock on the back door, that certain things had been missing, but the fact that the gun was missing was not discovered until some time after the burglaries.

'Any cross-examination?' Sam Drew asked of Mason.

'No cross-examination,' Mason said.

'Call Alexander Redfield,' Drew said.

Redfield came forward, was sworn and qualified himself as a ballistics expert and an expert on firearms and firearm identification.

'I show you a Colt ·38 which has previously been introduced in evidence and is marked People's Exhibit 13. This weapon bears the manufacturer's serial number of 613096. Have you seen that weapon before?'

'I have.'

'Have you fired a test bullet from it?'

'I have.'

'Describe briefly what you mean by a test bullet.'

'Each individual barrel has certain defects, irregularities or individualities; little scratches, projections, et cetera, which leave a mark on any bullet which is fired through that gun.'

'Are you referring now to the lands and grooves?'

'Oh, no, those are entirely different. Those leave what is known as class characteristics on a bullet. I am referring now to the striations which are known as the individual characteristics of a bullet.'

'And by firing a test bullet through a gun, you collect evidence of these defects and irregularities?'

'We do. They cause bullet striations, numerous tiny scratches which are spaced at irregular distances, yet which are always uniform in any bullet fired from any given barrel.'

'You mean that it is possible to identify a bullet which has been fired from any particular barrel?'

'That's right, if you have the gun, the fatal bullet and a test bullet.'

'And how do you get these so-called test bullets?'

'We fire the gun into a long box in which there are materials such as cotton waste, pieces of paper, cotton, or things of that sort, to retard the bullet without defacing it.'

'You fired a test bullet through this gun you are now holding?'

'I did.'

'And did you subsequently have occasion to compare that bullet with another bullet?'

'I did.'

'Where did you get that bullet?'

'From the coroner.'

'When?'

'Tuesday afternoon, the ninth.'

'And what can you say, with reference to the two bullets?'

'The bullet given me by the coroner agreed in such a large number of details with test bullets fired from this gun that I have no hesitancy in declaring that the so-called fatal bullet was fired from this gun.'

'Do you have the bullet which was given you by the coroner?'

'I do.'

'And one of the test bullets?'

'I do.'

'Will you produce them, please?'

The witness took two small, plastic vials from his pocket, said, 'This is the bullet given me by the coroner which, in my photographs, I refer to as the fatal bullet, and the bullet in this container is what I refer to as the test bullet.'

'You made photographs showing a comparison of those bullets?'

'I did. I made photographs in which the test bullet was partially superimposed upon the fatal bullet so that it was possible to follow the striations of the bullets as they continued on the overlapping image.'

'The striations matched?'

'Yes, sir.'

'Do you have photographs here?'

'I do, yes, sir.'

'I will ask that these be received in evidence,' Drew said.

'No objection,' Mason announced cheerfully.

'Any cross-examination?' Drew asked Mason.

'None, Your Honour. I have the greatest confidence in Mr Redfield's integrity and ability.'

'That's all,' Drew said.

The coroner was then called to testify that, under his supervision and direction, an autopsy had been performed upon the body of Meridith Borden, that a bullet had been found embedded in the torso of Borden, that this bullet had been carefully removed by the autopsy surgeon, placed in a plastic vial with a screw top, sealed in the vial, and the vial had been turned over by him to Alexander Redfield, the ballistics expert.

'That's all,' Drew said.

'No questions on cross-examination,' Mason announced.

Judge Erwood settled back in his chair with something akin to relief. Sam Drew, on the other hand, acted like a man who is walking over a mined area and momentarily expects an explosion to blow him into kingdom come. His case was proceeding all too regularly, all too swiftly and according to blueprint specifications. Everyone who was familiar with Perry Mason's court-room strategy knew he never permitted cases to proceed in such a manner–not for long.

Drew called the autopsy surgeon to the stand and questioned him concerning the findings at the autopsy. The surgeon read from notes stating that he had recovered a ·38-calibre bullet which he had placed in a plastic container and turned over to the coroner, who, in his presence, had turned it over to Alexander Redfield; that the bullet which the coroner turned over to Redfield was the same bullet which he had recovered from the body of Meridith Borden, that the bullet had entered the left chest at a point slightly to the left of the median line and had ranged slightly downward, that he had recovered the bullet in the skin of the back, that the bullet had torn one corner of the heart completely out, and that in his opinion, death had been due to this bullet wound and had been virtually instantaneous.

'In addition to your other qualifications,' Drew asked, 'have you had experience in blood classifications and serology?'

'Yes, sir.'

'I show you a suit of clothes on which there are certain spots, and ask you if you have examined those spots.'

'I have, yes, sir.'

'What are they?'

'Blood.'

'Can you tell what kind of blood?'

'Yes, sir.'

'What kind?'

'Human blood.'

'Can you further classify this human blood as to type?'

'Not on all of the spots. Some of them are too minute to permit a classification. But I have been able to classify the larger spots.'

'What classification?'

'The group that is known as AB.'

'Is this the relatively common group?'

'No, sir. It is a very rare blood grouping.'

'Can you estimate the percentage of people who have this grouping?'

'I would say not to exceed twelve per cent.'

'What type was the blood of the decedent, Meridith Borden?'

'The same type as the blood which appears on this suit, type AB.'

'Cross-examine,' Drew said.

'Could you tell how old those stains were?' Mason asked.

'Not exactly.'

'They had dried and changed colour?'

'That is right.'

'What is the type of the defendant's blood?' Mason asked.

'I don't know.'

'You don't?'

'No. Probably it is type O. That is the most common type. Around fifty per cent of the people have that type.'

'But for all you know the defendant's blood may be type AB?'

'That is right. Once we show his suit is spotted with human blood, it's up to him to show that it's his–at least that's the way I look at it.'

'That's all,' Mason said.

He turned to Ansley and whispered, 'What's your blood type?'

'I don't know,' Ansley said. 'I only know that I was wearing that suit when I had the nosebleed.'

'No further questions on cross-examination,' Mason said as the witness remained on the witness stand.

'That's all,' the judge said. 'Call your next witness, Mr Prosecutor.'

'Call Beeman Nelson,' Drew said.

Nelson was sworn, gave his occupation as operator of a cleaning establishment, identified the cleaning mark on the bloodstained suit, stated that he had cleaned and pressed the suit on at least five different occasions, that the suit on each occasion had been received from and delivered to George Ansley, the defendant; that the last date he had cleaned, pressed and delivered the suit to Ansley was about ten days before the murder. At that time the suit had been in good condition and there were no blood spots on it.

'Any questions?' Drew asked Perry Mason.

'None whatever,' Mason said.

Judge Erwood indicated impatience, glancing at the clock, quite evidently prepared to make an order binding the defendant over to the higher court for trial.

Drew, noticing the signs of judicial impatience, said, 'If the Court please, I have just one or two more witnesses. I feel that I can conclude this case within a short time.'

'Go ahead,' Judge Erwood said. 'Call your witnesses.'

'Call Jasper Horn,' Drew said.

Jasper Horn, a tall, raw-boned, slow-moving individual, came forward, held up a big, calloused hand and was sworn.

'Your name is Jasper Horn?'

'Yes, sir.'

'What's your occupation, Mr Horn?'

'I'm a foreman.'

'Are you acquainted with the defendant, George Ansley?'

'I am, yes, sir.'

'Do you work for him, or have you worked for him?'

'That's right. I'm foreman on a job he's doing, building a school out in the west side.'

'I'm going to direct your attention to last Monday morning and ask you if you had any conversation with George Ansley.'

'Sure, I had lots of conversations with him. He was out on the job and we were looking around.'

'Was there anything particularly unusual or annoying–I'll withdraw that. Let me ask you this. Had there been any complaints about the buildings not being up to specifications?'

'Lots of them.'

'Was there any particular matter which you were discussing with Mr Ansley last Monday morning about the problems of inspection?'

'Yes, sir.'

'What was it?'

'Well, some of the steel supports in one of the walls had warped a little bit out of line. The distance between centres was not quite uniform, and one or two of them were slightly off.'

'Had you previously had some conversation with the inspector about that?'

'I had.'

'And what did the inspector tell you?'

'He told me that stuff would have to be fixed up or the wall would have to come out.'

'You argued with him?'

'I'll say I argued with him.'

'And then, later on, you reported this conversation to Ansley?'

'Sure. I told him about it.'

'And did you make any suggestion to Ansley at that time?'

'Yes, sir.'

'What was it?'

'I told him that if he was smart, he'd go and see Meridith Borden and his troubles would be over.'

'And what did Mr Ansley say at that time?'

'He told me that he'd take a gun and shoot Borden through the heart before he'd knuckle under to a guy like that and pay tribute. He said that if Borden was making all these troubles for him hoping he'd get a shakedown, Borden was out of luck. He said killing was too good for people like that.'

There was a slight murmur in the court-room.

'Your witness,' Drew said.

Mason straightened in his chair. 'That conversation was Monday?'

'Yes, sir.'

'Had you had previous conversations about defective construction with inspectors?'

'I'll say I had. . . . Nothing else but, if you ask me.'

'The inspectors had been rather critical?'

'Mr Mason,' the witness said vehemently, 'the inspectors had been tough, mighty tough. They'd crawled all over the job looking for the most microscopic details they could dig up. They'd throw those things at us, make us tear stuff out and replace it. They were crawling all over the place, getting in my hair, hampering construction, driving us all nuts.'

'Up until Monday of last week?'

'That's right.'

'Including Monday?'

'Including Monday.'

'Now, directing your attention to Tuesday morning, did you have any conversation with the inspectors?'

'Just a minute,' Sam Drew said, 'that's incompetent, irrelevant, immaterial and not proper cross-examination. I didn't ask the witness anything about Tuesday morning.'

'I think I'm entitled to examine the witness as to all of his conversations with the inspectors,' Mason said. 'After all, he's testifying as to conclusions. He's testifying that the inspectors were unreasonable, that they were tough, and so I've got a right to show *all* of the experiences this man has had with inspectors, what he means by saying they were unreasonable, what he means by saying they were tough. There must be some standard of normal that he is referring to in his own mind.'

'I think I'll allow the question,' Judge Erwood said.

'Tuesday morning,' the witness said, 'there was a great big difference. The inspector on the job came to me and told me he was satisfied there had been a substantial compliance with the specifications on the steelwork on the wall. He said he'd watched our work, that he felt it was very good and that he was satisfied we were doing a good job. He said that from now on he was going to leave me pretty much on my own to complete it.'

'That was Tuesday morning?' Mason asked.

'Yes, sir.'

'Thank you,' Mason said. 'That's all.'

'No further questions,' Drew said.

'You're excused,' Judge Erwood told the witness.

'I'm going to call Frank Ferney,' Drew said.

Ferney came forward and was sworn. 'You were in the employ of Meridith Borden in his lifetime?'

'Yes, sir.'

'In what capacity?'

'Oh, sort of a general assistant. I did whatever needed to be done.'

'You took messages for him?'

'That's right.'

'Ran errands?'

'That's right. I did anything and everything that was required. I helped him when he'd entertain, I kept liquor glasses full, tried to keep the guests happy. I did anything that needed to be done.'

'Directing your attention to last Monday. Do you have a day off?'

'No, sir. I don't work that way. I'm around most of the time but when I wanted to take off, I just told him I was going.'

'And what about last Monday night?'

'I told him I wouldn't be there Monday evening until late. I said I wanted to have an evening with my girl friend.'

'And what time did you actually leave last Monday evening?'

'Six o'clock.'

'Are you acquainted with Marianna Fremont, the housekeeper?'

'Certainly.'

'Does she do the cooking?'

'When she's there she cooks the meals.'

'Mondays are her days off?'

'That's right.'

'Who cooks on Mondays?'

'Well, she did the cooking when we didn't have company. Usually he had another cook come in when we were entertaining, or sometimes a caterer brought in a meal if he was entertaining quite a few people.

'When Mr Borden and I were there alone, I'd scramble up some eggs and cook some bacon for breakfast. We'd usually have a salad for lunch, and sometimes I'd cook up some stuff Monday night. We sort of camped out on the cook's day off unless we were entertaining. If we were, he'd get a caterer or another cook.'

'Was any meal cooked last Monday night?'

'He told me he was going to open up some canned sauerkraut and have some weenies. I was going out for dinner.'

'What time did he usually eat on Monday evening, if you know?'

'I object, if the Court please,' Mason said. 'If the testimony has any bearing, it is incumbent to show what actually happened on this particular night. I object to this specific question as being incompetent, irrelevant and immaterial.'

Drew said, 'It is very important, if the Court please, to get this point established because, while the time of death can only be fixed as between eight-thirty and eleven-thirty from the temperature of the body, the development of the *rigor mortis* and post-mortem lividity, the time could be fixed much more accurately if we knew when the last meal was ingested.'

Judge Erwood turned to Ferney. 'And that is something that you don't know–except by referring to general custom?'

'That's right, Your Honour. Monday night he had the house to himself. He could have gone out there at five minutes after six, after I left, and eaten, or he could have waited until eight-thirty and eaten, or he could have waited until after Ansley had finished with his appointment. I know when we usually ate on Monday night. That's the only way I can fix the time.'

'I see,' Judge Erwood said thoughtfully. 'I think I'll sustain the defendant's objection–as the evidence now stands.'

'I think that covers all our questions. You may cross-examine,' Drew said to Perry Mason.

'There is a wall surrounding the entire estate?' Mason asked.

'That's right.'

'And electric gates?'

'That's right. They're controlled by electricity.'

'Is there any other means of ingress and egress except through those gates?'

'There's a back entrance.'

'And where is that?'

'That's in back of the garage.'

'Of what does it consist?'

'It's a heavy, solid iron gate which is kept locked at all times.'

'You have a key to it?'

'Of course.'

'The housekeeper has a key to it?'

'Yes, sir.'

'And, of course, Mr Borden had a key to it?'

'Right.'

'Are there any other keys?'

'Not that I know of.'

'Is that gate wide enough for an automobile to enter?'

'No, sir, just wide enough for a person to go through. It's a heavy, solid iron door. All the traffic comes in through the main gates. There's a rubber tube embedded in the ground under a movable apron there at the gate, and whenever a car drives in, it rings a bell in the house so that Mr Borden knows someone's coming in.'

'I see,' Mason said thoughtfully. 'How did the gates close?'

'You could close them by pressing a button in the house, or the gates closed automatically with a timing device which was set for eleven o'clock, although that time could be changed.'

'How did the gates open?'

'They had to be opened by pressing a button in the house, or by manipulating a locked switch out on the driveway. If you used the switch in the driveway, the gates would open long enough for a car to go through, and then they'd automatically close again.'

'Was there some way of opening the gates from the outside?'

'Sure. There's a switch with a key. You use the key to unlock the switch, press a button and the gates open long enough for a car to drive through, then they automatically close again.'

'You had keys to all those switches?'

'Sure.'

'And the housekeeper?'

'That's right. She had keys, too.'

'There's a telephone there at the gate?'

'That's right.'

'And with what is that telephone connected?'

'That's a private line that goes right through to the house where there are two telephones that ring whenever the button is pressed.'

'Where are those telephones located?'

'One of them is in Mr Borden's study, the other is in the place where I stay, my room.'

'And where is your room?'

'Down in the basement.'

'Why the two telephones?'

'Because when the gate bell rings, I pick up the receiver and ask who is there and all about it. Mr Borden would be listening in on his extension. If it was someone Borden wanted to see, he'd then cut in and say, "This is Mr Borden himself. I'll open the gates for you and you can drive in." But if after a while I didn't hear Borden saying anything like that, I'd just tell the guy that I was sorry, the gates were closed for the night, that Borden couldn't be disturbed, and hang up.'

The telephone at the gate connected then with just those two instruments?'

'That's right.'

'Mr Borden spent most of his time in this study?'

'Practically all of it.'

'What about the photographic studio?'

'He was up there some of the time, mostly at night.'

'Did you ever help him in there?'

'Not him. When he went to the studio, he was to be left alone. You didn't disturb him in that studio.'

'He kept the door locked?'

'It had a spring lock on it.'

'Sometimes he worked with models?'

Drew said, 'If the Court please, this is not proper cross-examination. It calls for matters which are entirely extraneous, and unquestionably represents simply a fishing expedition on the part of counsel.'

'The Court is inclined to agree with that statement,' Judge Erwood said. 'The objection is sustained.'

'That's all,' Mason said.

'No further questions,' Drew said.

Drew looked at the clock. 'If the Court please, it is approaching the hour of the noon adjournment. I feel that we have presented this case expeditiously. That is our entire case. We feel we have proved the elements necessary to bind the defendant over.'

Judge Erwood said, 'I think you have more than established them. You could have quit half an hour ago and still have been entitled to an order binding the defendant over. It is, therefore, the order of this Court that the defendant be bound over to–'

'May the Court please,' Mason said, getting to his feet.

Judge Erwood frowned his annoyance. 'Yes, what is it, Counsellor?'

Mason said, 'The defence has the right to put on testimony.'

'Certainly,' Judge Erwood said. 'I am not trying to foreclose you from putting on a defence, if you desire, although I may state that in hearings of this sort it is rather unusual for the defence to put on a case. Very frankly, Mr Mason, since there is no jury present, I feel free to state that I don't know what defence you could possibly put on which would keep the Court from binding the defendant over. You might or might not have something that would raise a reasonable doubt in the mind of a jury, but as far as this Court is concerned, the evidence is simply overwhelming that a murder was committed and that there is probably cause to believe that the defendant committed the crime.'

'Except for one thing, if the Court please,' Mason said. 'There is one point which is very much in doubt.'

'I don't see it,' Judge Erwood said somewhat testily.

'The time element,' Mason said. 'If my client committed the murder, he must have done so before nine o'clock.'

'The evidence doesn't so show.'

'Well, the evidence can be made to so show,' Mason said, 'and we propose to show that Meridith Borden was alive and well a long time after nine o'clock.'

Judge Erwood stroked his chin. 'Well,' he said at length, 'that, of course, would be a perfect defence *if* you could establish it, Mr Mason.'

'We propose to establish it.'

'How long will you take?'

'At least all afternoon,' Mason said.

Judge Erwood said, 'I have rather a full calendar and I had anticipated this was a routine matter that would perhaps consume an hour, certainly not more than the entire morning.'

'I am sorry, Your Honour, I'm quite certain that I didn't give the Court any impression that such would be the case.'

'No, *you* didn't,' Judge Erwood admitted. 'I guess perhaps it was due somewhat to a misunderstanding. These matters usually are disposed of rather promptly. However, I have no desire to foreclose the defendant from putting on a case. I will state this, Mr Mason, proof of an alibi will have to be very, very clear and very, very convincing in order to keep the Court from binding the defendant over.

'You are a veteran trial attorney and are, of course, aware of the disadvantages to a defendant of putting on a defence at a preliminary examination. Now then, in the face of that statement of the Court, do you wish to proceed?'

'I do.'

'Very well,' Judge Erwood said. 'I will make one more statement, which is that I have noticed in the Press that in certain cases where you have appeared in a preliminary examination there have been dramatic developments, developments which in my opinion have not been justified.

'I mean no personal criticism by this. It is simply my opinion that Courts have been far too lenient with counsel in permitting a certain type of evidence to be brought into the preliminary hearing. I do not intend to foreclose any of the rights of the defendant, but, on the other hand, I certainly do not intend to open the door to a lot of extraneous matter.'

'Very well, Your Honour,' Mason said, 'I wish to address my proof to the Court on the theory that if the defendant killed Meridith Borden, the crime must have been committed before nine o'clock in the evening. I think I can show conclusively that the crime was *not* committed prior to nine o'clock.'

'Very well,' Judge Erwood said. 'The Court will take a recess and–'

'Just a moment. If I may have the indulgence of the Court,' Mason interrupted, 'I dislike to interrupt, but there is one matter that may be of great importance to the defendant.'

'What is that?'

'The body of Meridith Borden was found in his photographic studio. The inference would therefore be that after his interview with the defendant, Borden went to his photographic studio to take photographs, and that therefore someone must have been with him. Borden would hardly be taking photographs of himself.'

Judge Erwood frowned. 'That reasoning, Mr Mason, is predicated entirely upon your belief in whatever story the defendant may have told you. If you proposed to base your alibi on evidence of this kind, you are wasting your time.

'For all the Court knows, Meridith Borden could have been talking with the defendant, George Ansley, in the photographic studio. Borden might have been taking George Ansley's picture.

'I am assuming that the defendant is prepared to testify that his interview took place in the study, but this Court would pay absolutely no attention to such testimony. A jury might or might not believe the defendant. As far as this Court is concerned, on a preliminary examination where it appears that a murder has been committed with the murder weapon found in the defendant's possession, the Court is certainly not going to take the defendant's unsupported word as proof that he was not in the room where the murder was committed.'

'I understand that, Your Honour,' Mason said, 'and I am not asking the Court to take his word. I would, however, like to ask the deputy district attorney if it isn't true that there was evidence in the studio that certain photographs had been taken that evening. If so, I wish to have those photographs produced in evidence.'

Drew said testily, 'We don't have to disclose all our evidence to the defence.'

'But were there no exposed plates?' Mason asked. 'Nothing, perhaps, in the camera?'

'There were exposed plates,' Drew said, 'and there was an exposed plate in the camera; but there is no indication as to *when* the plate was exposed.'

'If the Court please,' Mason said, 'I feel that some of this can be connected up. If those exposed films have not been developed, I feel that they should be developed so that we can see what is on them.'

'Have those films been developed?' Judge Erwood asked Sam Drew.

'They have, Your Honour.'

'I take it,' Judge Erwood said, 'that if there were photographs of the defendant, those films or prints made from those films would have been introduced in evidence.'

'That is quite correct,' Drew said testily. 'The decedent, at the time of his death, was carrying on a camera contest with some of his cronies. They were having a somewhat good-natured contest to see who could get the best calendar-girl photograph. It is our opinion that the films which were in the camera had been photographed either during the day or during the preceding day. We don't feel that there was any significance attached to Mr Borden's presence in the photographic studio, except that he probably went there to get these films out of the camera and develop the exposed films which he had. He probably was rather anxious to get started on his work in this contest.'

Mason said, 'I'd like to suggest to the prosecution that those films be brought into court this afternoon, or at least prints from those films.'

'I see no reason for that whatever,' Drew said. 'This is not a trial before a jury. The prosecution doesn't need to disclose any more than enough evidence to show that a crime has been committed and that there is reasonable ground to believe that the defendant committed that crime.'

'That's right,' Judge Erwood said. 'But where the defence wishes to put on testimony, it *does* have the right to subpoena witnesses. The defence could subpoena the persons who have these films. I think you had better produce them, Mr Drew, it will save time.'

'But they have no bearing on the case, no bearing whatever,' Drew said.

'Then you can object to their introduction in evidence. But the defendant, in a preliminary hearing, certainly has the right to subpoena witnesses on his own behalf and to introduce evidence in his own behalf.'

Drew yielded with poor grace. 'Very well,' he said, 'I'll bring the pictures into court.'

Judge Erwood said, 'Court will take a recess until two o'clock this afternoon.'

Mason hurried over to Paul Drake. 'All right, Paul,' he said, 'give the signal. Have your men serve subpoenas on Loretta Harper, Dawn Manning, Beatrice Cornell and Frank Ferney.'

Drake turned, signalled to one of his men who was in the court-room by holding up his hand with the thumb down and four fingers extended.

'Okay,' he said to Mason. 'That's all taken care of, Perry, but I don't see what you're going to do except tip your hand. This judge is going to bind Ansley over, come hell or high water.'

'He isn't going to bind him over until I've found out a lot more about the prosecution's case,' Mason said. 'I'm going to get just as much evidence before the Court as I can.'

'But,' Drake protested, 'they'll object on the ground that it's immaterial, and the judge will sustain them.'

'Not after I get done, he won't,' Mason said. 'Either Loretta Harper or Dawn Manning is lying, one or the other. Dawn Manning makes a beautiful picture of sweet innocence, but the cold logic of the situation points to the fact that she probably was turned loose in the grounds at about nine o'clock, and there's no real proof that she didn't go to the house and remain there until after the murder was committed.'

'Go to it,' Drake said, 'I still say it won't do you any good. Sam Drew is one of the happiest men in the whole legal profession right now. He's been able to put on a *prima facie* case, the judge is with him, and he feels you don't stand a ghost of a chance of changing the judge's mind.'

Mason grinned. 'The presiding judge assigned Judge Erwood to sit on this hearing with the understanding that he would see the case was handled according to the usual cut-and-dried routine. Burger protested I'd been given too much leeway in the past.'

'Think you can beat a situation like that?' Drake asked dubiously.

Mason pursed his lips thoughtfully. 'I can sure as hell try.'

10

When Court reconvened at two o'clock, Paul Drake had a whispered word of warning for Perry Mason.

'Watch Sam Drew,' he said. 'He's so tickled he can hardly contain himself. Something has happened during the recess that has given him a big kick. The gossip is that he's passed the word down the line, and Hamilton Burger, the district attorney, is coming in to watch you fall flat on your face.'

'Any idea what it's all about?' Mason asked.

'I can't find out,' Drake said, 'but the whole camp is just bursting with suppressed excitement, and–'

He broke off as Judge Erwood entered the court-room from his chambers. Everybody stood and waited for the stroke of the gavel which signalled they were to be seated.

'People versus Ansley,' Judge Erwood said. 'Are you ready to proceed, Mr Mason?'

'Yes, Your Honour.'

'Very well, Mr Mason, proceed with your case.'

Mason said, 'As my first witness I will call my secretary, Miss Della Street, to the stand.'

Judge Erwood frowned, started to say something, then changed his mind.

Della Street went to the stand, held up her right hand and was sworn.

At that moment the court-room door opened, and Hamilton Burger, the district attorney, made a personal appearance, quite obviously enjoying the whispered comments as he came lumbering down the aisle, pushed his way through the swinging mahogany gate in the bar and seated himself beside Drew.

Burger made no attempt to conceal the broad grin on his face.

Mason felt his way cautiously through the examination.

'Your name is Della Street and you are now and for some time have been in my employ as my confidential secretary?'

'Yes, sir.'

'You are acquainted with the defendant?'

'Yes, sir.'

'When did you first see the defendant?'

'On the evening of Monday, the eighth.'

'Where did you see him?'

'At the Golden Owl Night Club.'

'What was the time?'

'The time was approximately two or three minutes past ten o'clock.'

'And what happened?'

'Mr Ansley approached the table where we were sitting and asked you to–'

Mason held up his hand.

'We object to anything the defendant may have said at that time, as a self-serving declaration, as hearsay and as incompetent, irrelevant and immaterial,' Drew said.

'There is no need for the objection,' Mason said. 'I don't want the witness to relate the conversation. I will just ask you, Miss Street, as to what was done.'

'Well, the defendant asked you to do certain things, and after some conversation we left the Golden Owl Night Club.'

'At what time?'

'At exactly ten-thirty-two.'

'Now, when you say "*we*", who do you mean?'

'You, Mr Ansley and myself.'

'And where did we go?'

'We went to Meridith Borden's place.'

'Were the gates open or closed?'

'The gates were open.'

'What did we do?'

'We parked the car just outside the gates.'

'Then what?'

'We looked around for some ten or fifteen minutes, I would judge.'

'And then what happened?'

'Then a gong sounded and the gates closed.'

'Then what happened?'

'Then Mr Ansley went to the gates, tried to open them and apparently set off a burglar alarm. . . .'

'Objected to as a conclusion of the witness. Move to strike,' Drew said.

'Stipulated it may go out,' Mason said. 'Just what happened?'

'A bell sounded, floodlights came on, on the grounds, and we could hear the barking of dogs.'

'Then what?'

'Then we climbed over the wall and a dog came charging at us. Just as you got up on the wall, the dog was snapping at your heels and leaping up at the wall.'

'Then what?'

'Then we descended the wall on the other side.'

'Do you know what time it was then?'

'It was just after eleven.'

'Then what happened?'

'We went to the front gate.'

'And what happened there?'

'You looked around and discovered a telephone.'

'And what happened?'

'You talked into the telephone.'

'Now, just a moment, just a moment,' Drew objected. 'This is incompetent, irrelevant and immaterial. It is a conclusion of the witness.'

'It's no conclusion of the witness,' Mason said. 'It would be a conclusion if I asked her to whom I was talking, but she is testifying only to a physical fact, that I talked into the telephone. I talked into the telephone and she can testify to that fact.'

'Go ahead,' Judge Erwood said to Della Street. 'The objection is overruled. Any motion to strike is denied. Don't tell us what Mr Mason said or to whom he talked, just what happened.'

'Yes, Your Honour. Then Mr Mason hung up, and–Would I be permitted to state what he told me?'

Judge Erwood shook his head and said, 'Not if the prosecution objects.'

'We object,' Drew said.

'Very well. That would be hearsay, just go ahead and state what was done if it is at all pertinent.'

'I think it is quite pertinent,' Mason said. 'We are now coming to the part that I feel is very important.'

'Very well,' Judge Erwood said. 'What happened, Miss Street?'

'Then, after Mr Mason hung up the telephone, I picked up the telephone and kept pressing the button at regular intervals.'

'And what happened?'

'Mr Borden answered the phone.'

'Just a minute, just a minute,' Drew said. 'We move to strike that out as the conclusion of the witness. No proper foundation laid.'

Judge Erwood turned to Della Street, his face showing considerable interest. 'You state that Mr Borden answered?'

'Yes, sir.'

'Did you know him in his lifetime?'

'No, Your Honour.'

'Then how did you know it was Mr Borden?'

'He said it was Mr Borden.'

'In other words, there was a voice over the telephone announcing that it was Mr Borden talking?'

'Yes, Your Honour.'

Judge Erwood shook his head. 'The objection is sustained. The motion to strike is granted. That is a conclusion of the witness. You may, however, state as nearly as you can recall the conversation which took place over the telephone.'

'We object to it, if the Court please,' Drew said, 'with all due respect to the Court's question. Unless it can be shown definitely that it was Meridith Borden on the other end of the line, we object.'

Judge Erwood shook his head. 'Counsel has already laid the foundation by showing that the telephone at the gate is connected directly with the house. Now then, Miss Street has testified she pressed the button on the telephone and she had a conversation with someone. She is entitled to relate that conversation. Then it can be shown that the person at the other end of the line was Mr Borden, either by direct or by circumstantial evidence. The Court may state that the foundation as far as circumstantial evidence is concerned, is pretty well laid at this moment. It appears that Mr Borden was alone in the house, according to the prosecution's own testimony. According to the testimony of this witness, some man answered the telephone. I have stricken out the statement that the man said he was Mr Borden, as a means of proving the identity of the person at the other end of the line, but I will permit the witness to state what the conversation was.'

Della Street said, 'I believe the man's voice asked who was calling. I said that we were passers-by, that we wanted to speak with Mr Borden. The voice said that it was Mr Borden speaking, that he didn't want to be disturbed, and I told him that this was a matter of an emergency, that we had reason to believe there was a young woman who had been in an auto accident and who might be wandering around the grounds somewhere.

'Then the man's voice stated that someone had been tampering with the gates; that this had triggered a burglar alarm and released watchdogs; that he would turn off the lights and call the dogs back to the kennels; that the dogs were not going to hurt anyone; that they were trained to hold a person motionless and bark until someone could arrive; that they weren't going to kill anyone. Then the voice asked me who I was, and I refused to give my name, saying I was merely a passer-by.'

'Then what?' Mason asked.

'I hung up the telephone and told you–That is,' Della Street amended with a smile at the prosecution's table, 'I know I'm not permitted to state what I told you.'

'Now, what time was this?' Mason asked.

'It was possibly ten minutes after eleven, perhaps fifteen minutes after eleven, when I had this conversation.'

'Then what did we do?'

'We drove Mr Ansley back to the Golden Owl Night Club where he picked up his car.'

'We were with Mr Ansley until what time?'

'Until right around eleven-thirty, perhaps eleven-thirty-five.'

'And we left him where?'

'At the Golden Owl Night Club.'

'Then you, yourself and of your own knowledge, can vouch for the whereabouts of the defendant in this case from a time which you estimate to be two or three minutes after ten until eleven-thirty on the evening of the murder?'

'That is right,' Della Street said.

Mason turned to Drew.

'You may cross-examine,' he said.

Drew, grinning broadly, said, 'We have no questions of this witness.'

'No cross-examination?' Judge Erwood asked in surprise.

Drew shook his head.

'The Court may point out to you, Mr Drew, that unless the testimony of this witness is questioned in some way, there is a very strong presumption that she was actually talking with Mr Borden.'

'We understand, Your Honour,' Drew said. 'But we don't intend to try to establish our rebuttal by cross-examination.'

'Very well,' Judge Erwood snapped.

'That's all,' Mason said. 'That's our case, Your Honour.'

Judge Erwood looked at the table where Hamilton Burger and Sam Drew were engaged in smiling conversation. 'It would seem, Mr Prosecutor,' the judge said, 'that we now have a very material difference in the situation. We have the testimony of a disinterested witness, one whose integrity impresses the Court, that some male person was in the Borden house a few minutes after eleven o'clock, that this male person answered a telephone, that according to the testimony of the prosecution's own witnesses, the only person left in the Borden house at that time was Meridith Borden.'

'If the Court please,' Hamilton Burger said, smiling indulgently, 'we would like to put on some rebuttal evidence before the Court, which will clarify the situation.'

'Very well, go ahead, call your witness.'

'We recall Frank Ferney,' Hamilton Burger said.

Frank Ferney returned to the witness stand.

'You've already been sworn,' Hamilton Burger said. 'There's no need for you to be sworn again. Have you heard the testimony of Miss Street who was just on the stand?'

'Yes, sir.'

'Do you know anything about the conversation that she has related?'

'Yes, sir.'

'What do you know about it?'

'I was the person at the other end of the line.'

Hamilton Burger grinned triumphantly. 'You were the person who said you were Meridith Borden?'

'Yes, sir.'

Hamilton Burger bowed with exaggerated courtesy to Perry Mason. 'You may cross-examine,' he said, and sat down.

Mason arose to face the witness. 'You told us,' he said, 'that you left the Borden house at six o'clock; that you took a night out and had dinner with your girl friend.'

'That's right. But I came back. I have my living quarters there and I sleep there.'

'What time did you get back?'

'Actually it was about–oh, I would say around ten minutes to eleven.'

'And how did you get there?' Mason asked.

The witness grinned. Hamilton Burger grinned. Sam Drew grinned.

'I drove back in an automobile,' he said.

'Alone?' Mason asked sharply.

'No, sir.'

'Who was with you?'

'A woman.'

'Who was this woman?'

'Dr Margaret Callison.'

'And who is Dr Callison?'

'A veterinary.'

'How did you enter the premises?'

'We drove up to the locked back gate. Dr Callison parked her car, and I took a dog out of her car. The dog was on leash. I opened the door, took the dog to the kennel, unlocked the kennel door and put the dog inside. That was at approximately ten minutes to eleven, perhaps five minutes to eleven, by the time I got the dog in there.

'I then asked Dr Callison if she wanted a drink, and she said she'd run in and have a drink. She wanted to see Mr Borden and tell him something about the dog.'

'So what did you do?'

'I escorted her to the back door of the house, opened the door with my key and we went in.'

'Then what?'

'I went to Mr Borden's study and he wasn't there. I assumed that . . . well, I guess I'm not permitted to say what I assume.'

'Go right ahead,' Mason said. 'I don't hear any objection from the prosecution and I certainly have none. I want to know *exactly* what happened. I'm not afraid of the facts in this case.'

'Well, I assumed that he was up in the studio doing some photographic work, perhaps some development, and I suggested to Dr Callison that we wait a few minutes and see if he came down. I poured a couple of drinks, and about that time the burglar alarm sounded, the lights came on and the kennel doors opened automatically.

'I heard the dogs run to the wall and bark, and then I could tell by the way one of the dogs was barking and jumping that whoever had set off the burglar alarm had gone over the wall. I returned to Dr Callison and suggested we finish our drinks in a hurry and go see what had happened and what had turned on the burglar alarm.

'Then I went out and whistled the dogs back to the kennel.

'While I was still outside, I heard the telephone ring. I hurried back and found that Dr Callison had answered the telephone. She told me that some man had asked for Mr Borden, and she had told him Mr Borden didn't want to be disturbed.'

'Then what?' Mason asked.

'Then, after a short time, the phone continued a long series of jangling rings.'

'So what happened?' Mason asked.

'I answered the telephone. I thought probably it was the police calling about the burglar alarm.'

'And what happened?' Mason asked.

'A young woman was on the other end of the telephone. I recognize her voice now as that of Miss Street. She has given a very accurate statement of the conversation which took place over the telephone. That is, I said I was Borden and told her the dogs wouldn't hurt anyone; that I would turn off the light and put the dogs back in the kennels. Actually, I had already put the dogs back.'

Mason regarded the witness with thoughtful eyes.

Over at the prosecution table, Hamilton Burger and Sam Drew were grinning expansively at the spectacle of Mason bringing out the prosecution's case on cross-examination. Having resorted to the time-honoured trick of asking Ferney only a few devastating questions on direct examination and then terminating their questioning with no explanation, they had virtually forced Mason to crucify himself.

'Is it your custom to state over the telephone that you are Meridith Borden?' Mason asked.

'Sure,' the witness said. 'At times, when Borden didn't want to be disturbed and someone insisted on talking with him, I'd say that I was Borden and tell whoever I was talking with that I couldn't be disturbed.'

'Did you do that often?'

'Not often, but I have done it. Usually Mr Borden was listening on the telephone, and if he wanted to see the person, he'd cut in on the conversation. If he didn't, I'd say that he wasn't there, or that he couldn't come to the phone.'

Mason moved slowly forward.

'Will you describe Dr Callison?' he asked.

'Why, she's a woman veterinary who has a wonderful way with dogs.'

'How old?'

'I'm sure I wouldn't guess at a woman's age, but she's relatively young.'

'Around your age?'

'I would say she was around thirty-two or three.'

'Heavy?'

'No. Very well formed.'

'Surely you weren't entertaining her in your bedroom?' Mason asked, making his voice sound highly sceptical.

Ferney came up out of the witness chair angrily. 'That's a lie!' he shouted.

Burger was on his feet, waving his hands. 'Your Honour, Your Honour, this is uncalled for, this is completely outside of the scope of legitimate cross-examination. It is a gratuitous insult to an estimable woman. It–'

Judge Erwood pounded his gavel. 'Yes, Mr Mason,' he said, 'it would seem that this is certainly not called for under the circumstances.'

Mason looked at the judge with an expression of wide-eyed innocence. 'Why, Your Honour,' he said, 'it's the *only* inference to be drawn from the evidence. The witness has stated that there was a telephone in his bedroom where he slept, which was in the basement, that there was another phone in Meridith Borden's study, that when the phone rang the witness would answer, that Borden would listen in.'

'But not this time,' Ferney interrupted angrily. 'This time *I* was answering the telephone from Borden's study.'

'Oh,' Mason said. 'Pardon me, I didn't understand you. Then you took Dr Callison into Borden's study, did you?'

'Yes, of course. I wouldn't have taken her down to my bedroom.'

'Well,' Mason said, 'I beg the Court's pardon. I certainly misunderstood the witness. I thought it was quite plain from what he had said that he always answered the telephone from his bedroom.'

Judge Erwood looked down at Ferney speculatively. 'You certainly did give that impression in your testimony, Mr Ferney,' he said.

'Well, I didn't mean to give it. That is, that's . . . well, that's where I usually answered the phone from. But this time, because Dr Callison was there, it was different.'

'Where were you talking from?' Mason asked.

'From the study.'

'Meridith Borden's study?'

'Yes.'

'Let's see if we can get this straight about Dr Callison. She is a veterinary?'

'That's right.'

'And she had been treating one of the dogs?'

'Yes.'

'And you were to call and get the dog?'

'Yes.'

'What time?'

'Around nine o'clock.'

'But you didn't call at nine o'clock?'

'No, sir.'

'When did you call?'

'It was around ten-thirty.'

'Why didn't you call at nine o'clock?'

'I overslept.'

'You overslept?' Mason asked, his voice showing his surprise.

'All right, if you want to know,' Frank Ferney said, 'I was drunk. I went up to a party at the home of my fiancée and passed out.'

'And who is your fiancée?'

'Loretta Harper.'

Mason's brows levelled down over his eyes. 'Have you been married?'

'Yes.'

'Have you ever been divorced?'

'Your Honour,' Sam Drew said, 'this is incompetent, irrelevant and immaterial. It is not proper cross-examination.'

'On the contrary,' Judge Erwood said, 'this is a matter in which the Court is very much interested. The testimony of this witness indicates a most peculiar set of circumstances, and, since he is apparently being relied upon to refute the defence witness, the Court wants to get at the bottom of it. Just answer the question.'

'Yes, I'm married. I haven't been divorced.'

'What is your wife's name?'

'She's a model. She goes under the professional name of Dawn Manning.'

'All right,' Mason said. 'Now, let's get this straight. On this Monday night, the night of the murder, the eighth of this month, you went up to Loretta Harper's apartment. Where is that?'

'That's about a mile and a half south of Borden's place, in the town of Mesa Vista.'

'What time did you go there?'

'I went there right after I had left Borden's place.'

'You didn't have dinner at Borden's place?'

'No, Miss Harper had cooked dinner for two friends and myself. There was a foursome.'

'And you became drunk?'

'Well, I'll change that, I didn't mean it that way. We had some cocktails before dinner and we were giving some toasts. I guess I got a little too much. I was mixing cocktails in the kitchen. There were some cocktails left in the shaker that no one wanted, and I didn't want to pour them down the sink. I very foolishly drank them, and then there was some wine with the meal and I began to get a little dizzy. I wasn't drunk, I was just feeling the liquor a little bit, and I began to get sleepy.'

'So what happened?'

'I rested my head on my hand, and . . . well, I guess I went sound asleep there at the table. I was terribly embarrassed. They put me in the bedroom and I stretched out on the bed.'

'With your clothes on?'

'I believe they took my shoes off, and took my coat off and hung it on the back of the chair. . . . Well, the next thing I knew, Loretta woke me up and it was then about twenty minutes past ten. Loretta had just come in and she told a story about being held up, and–'

'Never mind what anyone said,' Hamilton Burger interrupted ponderously. 'Just describe what happened. Since Mr Mason is so concerned with getting at this time element, we'll let him get *all* the facts.'

'Well, I asked how long I'd been asleep and then I looked at my watch and suddenly remembered that I was supposed to have gone down to Dr Callison's place to pick up this dog. I asked one of the guests to call Dr Callison and say I'd be right down. And, believe me, I sprinted for my car.'

'Which you'd left parked in front?'

'That's right. Where else would I leave it?'

Judge Erwood said, 'The witness will confine himself to answering questions. There is no occasion for repartee. Counsel is simply trying to get the picture clear in his own mind, and the Court confesses that the Court wants it clarified as much as possible. Go on, Mr Mason.'

'And then?' Mason asked. 'What did you do then?'

'I made time getting out to Dr Callison's kennel. She was very nice about it. I explained to her that I'd had a little something to drink, so she took her station wagon and drove me up to Borden's house.'

'What gate?'

'The back gate.'

'You had a key to that?'

'Yes, that's close to the kennels.'

'And what did you do?'

'We put the dog in the kennel, and . . . well, that was it.'

Mason eyed the witness thoughtfully. 'Why didn't Dr Callison turn around and drive back in her station wagon?'

'She wanted to come in to talk with Mr Borden.'

'So you entered the house at about what time?'

'A few minutes before eleven, perhaps quarter to eleven.'

'And you tried to locate Mr Borden, didn't you?'

The witness fidgeted.

'Go ahead,' Mason said. 'You tried to locate Mr Borden?'

'Well, I went in the study and he wasn't there.'

'So what did you do?'

'I told Dr Callison to sit down and I'd find him, and . . . well, I did the honours.'

'What do you mean by that?'

'I bought her a drink.'

'What do you mean by buying her a drink?'

'I got some liquor from the compartment back of the bar and gave her a drink.'

'Did you customarily "do the honours" for guests when Mr Borden was not there?'

'Well, not customarily, but Dr Callison is . . . well, sort of a privileged individual, sort of a special personage.'

'I see,' Mason said. 'Then what happened?'

'I looked around for Mr Borden.'

'Did you call his name?'

'Yes.'

'Did he answer?'

'No.'

'And then what happened?'

'I can't remember a lot of details, but the burglar alarm went off, and the lights came on, and I heard the dogs barking.'

'Then what?'

'Well, then I ran out and tried to find out what all the commotion was about. I whistled the dogs to me and put them in the kennels. When I came back, Dr Callison was on the telephone talking with someone. I presume it was someone at the gate.'

'Never mind your presumption,' Drew interrupted.

'The Court will draw its own conclusions and presumptions, Mr Prosecutor,' Judge Erwood remarked testily. 'The witness will continue.'

'Well, then the phone kept ringing and ringing and ringing, so I answered, and . . . well, then I told them I was Borden.'

Mason turned to the prosecutor. 'I will ask the prosecution if the exposed films which were in the film holders and in the camera have been developed and printed. I believe the prosecution offered to produce prints of those.'

'Do you have those prints, Mr District Attorney?' Judge Erwood asked. 'The Court will be interested in viewing them.'

Hamilton Burger said, 'I am quite certain, if the Court please, that they have no significance as far as this case is concerned. The prosecution and the police are quite satisfied that these films had been taken at a much earlier date.'

'The question,' Judge Erwood said somewhat testily, 'is whether you have them.'

'Yes, Your Honour, we have them.'

'Will you produce them, please, and give them to the Court? And I think you should show a copy to counsel for the defence.'

'We are going to object to having these pictures received in evidence,' Hamilton Burger said. 'We are willing to *show* them to the Court if the Court requires, but they are not proper evidence, they have no bearing on the case. We feel quite certain they were taken some days earlier.'

'Why don't you want them in evidence?' Judge Erwood asked curiously.

'When the Court sees the nature of the pictures, the Court will understand,' Hamilton Burger said. 'The decedent was an amateur photographer. Evidently he was engaged in some sort of friendly rivalry or contest with some other amateur photographers, and an attempt was being made to create some amateur art calendars. There is nothing actually illegal or indecent about these pictures, but they are, nevertheless, very beautiful pictures of a very beautiful woman. The Court will understand the manner in which evidence of this sort could be seized upon by the public press.'

Hamilton Burger passed a series of five-by-seven prints to the Judge, then grudgingly extended a duplicate series to Perry Mason.

Mason regarded the pictures with thoughtful appraisal.

The photographs showed Dawn Manning posing in the nude against a dark background. She was turned so that her left side was towards the camera. The poses were artistic, with the left arm stretched in front of her, her right leg extended behind with the toes just touching the floor. She was leaning slightly forward. Apparently the attempt on the part of the photographer had been to capture the semblance of motion. The posing was remarkably similar to that of metallic ornaments which at one time graced the radiator caps of automobiles.

Judge Erwood raised his eyebrows over the pictures, spent some time examining them. Slowly he nodded. 'These pictures are very artistic,' he said. 'I am going to permit them to be introduced in evidence if the defence asks to have them introduced.'

'I ask they be received in evidence,' Mason said.

'They prove nothing,' Hamilton Burger objected.

'They may or may not prove anything,' the judge ruled, 'but they may be received in evidence.'

'Just one more question of this witness, if the Court please,' Mason said, turning to Ferney. 'Have you seen those pictures?'

'No, sir.'

'You'd better take a look at them,' Judge Erwood said.

Ferney looked at the photographs which Mason extended to him. 'That's Dawn!' he exclaimed. 'That's my wife.'

It was Mason's turn to bow to Hamilton Burger and hand him a hot potato. 'That's all,' he said. 'I have no further questions of this witness.'

Burger and Drew held a heated, whispered conference, trying to decide whether to let the witness go from the stand or to ask further questions.

Drew finally obtained seemingly reluctant consent from Hamilton Burger, and got to his feet.

'Mr Ferney,' Drew said, 'just to get the essential issues on this case straight, you were the one who talked on the telephone shortly after eleven o'clock?'

'Yes, sir.'

'You were the one who said you were Meridith Borden?'

'Yes, sir.'

'As far as you know of your own knowledge, Meridith Borden was not alive at that time. You can't say whether he was or whether he was not?'

'That is right.'

'You called his name?'

'Yes, sir.'

'And he didn't answer?'

'That's right.'

'And Dr Margaret Callison was the woman who answered the telephone when it rang around eleven?'

'Yes, sir.'

'Thank you,' Sam Drew said. 'That's all.'

Mason said, 'I have no further questions of this witness, but at this time, if the Court please, I desire to recall Harvey Dennison to the stand for further cross-examination.'

'The manager of the Valley View Hardware Company?' Hamilton Burger asked.

'That's right.'

'Any objection?' Judge Erwood asked.

Hamilton Burger smiled. 'No objection, Your Honour. Counsel can cross-examine Mr Dennison as much as he wants to, any time he wants to.'

Harvey Dennison returned to the stand.

Mason said, 'Mr Dennison, are you acquainted with a young woman by the name of Dawn Manning?'

'I am.'

'Was she ever in your employ?'

'She was.'

'When?'

'About three years ago she worked for us for . . . oh, about six months, I guess.'

'Was Dawn Manning in your employ at the time the Colt revolver Number 613096 was found to be missing from stock?' Mason asked.

'Just a moment, just a moment, Your Honour,' Hamilton Burger said. 'That is not proper cross-examination, that's making an accusation by innuendo, that's completely incompetent, irrelevant and immaterial.'

Judge Erwood shook his head. 'The objection is overruled. Answer the question.'

'She was in our employ,' Dennison said.

'Dawn Manning was her maiden name?'

'It was.'

'Do you know when she was married?'

'I can't give you the exact date, but she was in our employ until she married. She left our employ when she married.'

'Do you know the name of the man she married?'

'I don't remember that.'

'Thank you,' Mason said. 'That's all.'

'Now, just a minute, just a minute,' Hamilton Burger said, angrily. 'An accusation has been made that Dawn Manning stole this gun. Do you have any evidence whatever that would lead you to believe she took the gun, Mr Dennison?'

'None whatever,' Dennison said. And then added firmly, 'My opinion of Dawn Manning is that she is a very estimable–'

'Your opinion is uncalled for,' Judge Erwood interrupted. 'Just confine yourself to answering questions.'

'Did you ever have any occasion to doubt her honesty?' Hamilton Burger asked.

'None whatever.'

'That's all!' Burger snapped angrily.

Mason smiled.

'Any redirect?' Judge Erwood asked.

Mason, still smiling, said, 'You have no occasion to doubt the honesty of Dawn Manning, but she was working for you at a time when the gun disappeared. Now, I will ask you this Mr Dennison: Did George Ansley, the defendant, ever work for you?'

'Your Honour!' Hamilton Burger shouted. 'That is improper, this is misconduct, that is not proper cross-examination.'

Judge Erwood smiled in spite of himself. 'The question, as such, is, I believe, proper. The witness may answer it yes or no.'

'No,' Harvey Dennison said, 'George Ansley never worked for us.'

'As far as you know, was he ever in your store?'

'No.'

'That's all,' Mason said.

'No further questions,' Hamilton Burger said, so choked up with anger that he could hardly talk.

Judge Erwood, still smiling slightly, said, 'That's all, Mr Dennison. You're excused. You may leave the stand.'

Drew and Hamilton Burger conferred in whispers, then Drew got to his feet.

'It would seem, Your Honour, that despite the desperate attempts of the defence to drag another person into this case, the defendant has no alibi, and, under the circumstances, there can be none. It would seem quite apparent that Meridith Borden was lying dead in the studio, that he was killed by a weapon which was subsequently recovered from the possession of the defendant, that the defendant had threatened to kill Borden, that the defendant had the motive and the opportunity to carry out his threats. In view of the fact that this is a preliminary examination, I fail to see what more evidence needs to be supplied in order to entitle the prosecution to an order binding the defendant over.'

Judge Erwood hesitated a moment, then slowly nodded.

'Just a moment,' Mason said. 'I don't think the case is ready for argument at this time. The prosecution was putting on rebuttal evidence.'

'Well, that's all of it. That's all there is. That's our case,' Drew said.

'In that case,' Mason announced urbanely, 'I wish to put on some further evidence of my own in surrebuttal. I want to call Loretta Harper to the stand.'

'Loretta Harper will come forward and be sworn,' Judge Erwood said.

Loretta Harper came forward with her chin up, her lips clamped in a line of firm determination. She took the oath and settled herself on the witness stand.

Mason said, 'Your name is Loretta Harper.'

'That's right.'

'Where do you reside?'

'At Mesa Vista.'

'That is how far from Meridith Borden's place?'

'About a mile and a half.'

'You are acquainted with the defendant, George Ansley?'

'Until I saw him at the Borden place, I don't think I'd ever met him in my life.'

'Are you acquainted with Frank Ferney?'

'I am.'

'Do you know his wife, who goes under the professional name of Dawn Manning?'

'I do.'

'Do you have occasion to remember the night of Monday, the eighth of this month?'

'I do, indeed.'

'Will you tell us exactly what happened on that evening?'

'Objected to,' Hamilton Burger said, 'as incompetent, irrelevant and immaterial. What happened to *this* witness on the night of the murder has absolutely no bearing on the limited issues of the case at this time.'

Judge Erwood frowned thoughtfully, then turned to Mason. 'Can you narrow your question?' Erwood asked.

'With reference to what took place at the home of Meridith Borden,' Mason added.

'With that addition,' Judge Erwood said, 'the objection is overruled.'

'I do, indeed. I know exactly what happened.'

'Will you please tell us,' Mason said, 'exactly what happened, commencing at the time you had occasion to be in or about the grounds of Meridith Borden's estate.'

'I was driven through the gates,' she said, 'by Dawn Manning. Dawn lost control of the car. She was trying to drive with one hand and holding a gun with the other, and–'

'Just a minute, just a minute,' Hamilton Burger interrupted. 'If the Court please, we are now getting into something that is entirely extraneous. The answer shows plainer than any objection I could make the vice of permitting counsel to put a witness on the stand and ask a blanket question covering activities which are in no way connected with the issues before the Court.'

Judge Erwood said, '*I* will ask the witness a question. What time was this, Miss Harper?'

'You mean when we entered the grounds?'

'Yes.'

'It was, I would say, right around nine o'clock.'

'The objection is overruled,' Judge Erwood said. 'The witness will be permitted to tell her story. Counsel for both sides will note that we are now dealing with events which happened on the premises where the murder took place, at a time when the expert medical testimony indicates the murder could have taken place. Under those circumstances, the defence is entitled to call any witness and ask any question that will shed light on what happened. This is a court of justice, not a gym wherein counsel may practice legal calisthenics. Proceed, Miss Harper.'

'Well, Dawn Manning was driving with one hand. The other hand was holding a gun. The roads were wet, she lost control of the car and started to skid. Just at that time another car, driven by George Ansley, the defendant in this case, was coming out of the Borden place.'

'And then what happened?' Mason asked.

'This car being driven by Dawn Manning ticked the front of the Ansley car and we shot through the hedge and the car turned over.'

'Go on,' Mason said.

'I was thrown clear of the car when it turned over. I hit with something of a jar, but it wasn't bad enough to hurt me at all. It was sort of a skid . . . that is, I slid along on the wet grass. There was a lawn. It had been raining and the grass was long and wet.'

'Go on,' Mason said. 'What happened?'

Judge Erwood was leaning forward on the bench, his hand cupped behind his ear so that he would not miss a word.

Over at the prosecution's table, Sam Drew and Hamilton Burger were engaged in a whispered conference. It was quite evident that they were far from happy.

'Well,' Loretta Harper went on, 'the first thought that flashed through my mind–'

Mason held up his hand.

'We're not interested in your thoughts,' Judge Erwood said. 'We wanted to know what you did.'

'Well, I got up and stood there for a moment, and then I saw Mr Ansley coming with a flashlight. The flashlight, however, was giving just a faint illumination, a reddish glow, not enough to do much good.'

'When you say it was Mr Ansley coming,' Mason said, 'you are referring to the defendant in this case?'

'Yes, sir.'

'And what did Mr Ansley do?'

Mr Ansley walked around the car, and then I saw Dawn Manning lying there where she had skidded after being thrown from the car. She was unconscious.'

'Then what happened?'

'Mr Ansley started to lean over to look at her and then the light went out and it was impossible to see anything. He threw the flashlight away.'

'Did you see him throw it?'

'Well, I saw his hand go back. I could dimly make that out. It was pretty dark, but I saw that, and then I saw the flash of reflected light from a nickel-plated flashlight as he threw it away, and I heard it thud when it hit the ground.'

'Go on,' Mason said. 'Then what happened?'

'Mr Ansley started towards the house. I knew that he was going to–'

'Never mind what you thought,' Mason said. 'We're only interested in what you did.'

'Well, I grabbed Dawn Manning by the heels and pulled her along the wet grass for a distance of . . . oh, I don't know, fifteen or twenty feet, almost up against the wall.'

'And then what?'

'Then, I . . . well, I arranged my clothes just the way hers had been so it would look as though I had skidded along the grass, and put myself in the position she had been occupying, and shouted for help.'

'Then what?'

'I waited a few seconds and shouted "Help" again.'

'Then what?'

'Then I heard steps coming towards me. Mr Ansley was coming back. That was what I wanted.'

'Go on,' Mason said. 'What did you do?'

'I waited until he was near enough so he could see the way I was lying, and then I straightened up and pulled my skirt down a little and asked him to help me up.'

'What did he do?'

'He gave me his hand and I got to my feet. He wanted to know if I was hurt and I told him no, and he said he would drive me home.'

'And where was Dawn Manning all this time?' Mason asked.

'Dawn Manning,' she said with acid venom, 'had recovered consciousness, had regained possession of the gun and had gone–'

'Just a minute, just a minute,' Hamilton Burger interrupted. 'We submit, if the Court please, that the witness is testifying as to things about which she knows nothing of her own knowledge.'

'Did you *see* Dawn Manning regain the gun?' Judge Erwood asked.

'No, sir. I only know what she must have done. It was exactly what happened. She wasn't lying there when I got to my feet. She had recovered consciousness, and–'

'Now, just a minute, just a minute,' Judge Erwood interrupted. 'I want you to understand, Miss Harper, that you can only testify as to things you know of your own knowledge, not as to conclusions. Now, did you see Dawn Manning recover consciousness and get to her feet?'

'No, I didn't *see* her, but by the time I got to my feet and after I had talked for a few minutes with Mr Ansley and got him to agree to take me home, I had to walk around the front of the car, and I could look into the darkness and see that Dawn Manning was no longer where I had left her. She had recovered consciousness and moved.'

'Did you see her move?'

'No, but I know she wasn't there where I had left her.'

'Then that's all you can testify to,' Judge Erwood said. 'Proceed with your questioning, Mr Mason.'

'Did the defendant take you home?' Mason asked.

'No.'

Judge Erwood looked at her with a frown. 'I thought you said that he took you home.'

'He thought he took me home, but he didn't.'

'What do you mean by that?' Judge Erwood asked impatiently.

'I asked him to take me home and he said he would. He asked me where I lived and I told him the Ancordia Apartments, and he took me there.'

'Then he took you home!' Judge Erwood snapped.

'No, sir, he did not.'

The judge's face flushed.

'I think the witness means,' Mason hastened to explain, 'that she didn't live at the Ancordia Apartments.'

'Then why did he take her there?' Judge Erwood asked.

'Because that's where she *told* him she lived.'

Judge Erwood looked again at the witness. 'You mean that you lied to him?'

'Yes, Your Honour.'

'Why?' Judge Erwood asked.

'If the Court please,' Hamilton Burger said, 'with all due respect to the Court's question, I submit that we're getting into a lot of things here which are extraneous.'

'Yes, I suppose so,' Judge Erwood said. 'After all, this is direct examination. You have the right to cross-examine. The situation seems confused to the Court. However, when we analyse the testimony of this witness, it would appear that all we have shown is that another person was perhaps at the scene of the crime–'

Judge Erwood stroked his chin thoughtfully, then turned to the witness. 'You're certain that Mrs Ferney, or Dawn Manning, as you call her, had moved before you left the grounds?'

'Absolutely certain, Your Honour, and I am certain she had gone on to Meridith Borden's house.'

'Now, why do you say that?'

'She was photographed there,' Loretta Harper said.

'That's a conclusion of the witness,' Judge Erwood said. 'It may go out of the record. There's no need for you to make the motion, Mr District Attorney. The Court will strike that of his own motion.'

Mason moved forward, presented the photographs of Dawn Manning to the witness. 'Do you recognize these photographs?' he asked.

'Yes!' she snapped.

'Who is the person shown in the photographs?'

'Dawn Manning.'

'State to the Court whether that is the same person you have referred to as the one who turned into Meridith Borden's estate at about nine o'clock on the night of the eighth of this month.'

'That is the one.'

Mason turned to the prosecution's table. 'Cross-examine,' he said.

Again there was a whispered conference.

At length, Hamilton Burger arose ponderously. 'You don't know that Dawn Manning, as you call her, ever went near that house, do you, Miss Harper?'

'Of course I know it.'

'Of your own knowledge?'

'Well, I know it as well as I know anything. Her photographs were there.'

'Don't argue with me!' Hamilton Burger said, pointing his finger at the witness. 'You only surmise it from these photographs, isn't that right?'

'No!' she snapped.

'No?' Hamilton Burger asked in surprise.

'That's right!' she snapped at him. 'I said no!'

'You mean you have some other means of knowledge?'

'Yes.'

Hamilton Burger, recognizing that he had got himself out on a limb, hesitated as to whether to ask the next logical question or to try to cover by avoiding the subject.

It was Judge Erwood who, having taken a keen personal interest in the proceedings, solved the dilemma. 'If you have some other means of information,' he said, 'indicating Dawn Manning went to the house, and you have not disclosed that, it would be advisable for you to tell us how you know she was in the house.'

'Frank Ferney knocked on the door of the studio,' Loretta Harper said. 'A woman said, "Go away", and Frank recognized her voice as the voice of his wife.'

'How do you know that?' Hamilton Burger shouted at the witness.

'Frank told me so himself.'

'I move that this statement of the witness be stricken from the record, that all of this evidence about Dawn Manning having gone to the house be stricken as a conclusion of the witness and as being founded on hearsay,' Hamilton Burger said.

'The motion is granted,' Judge Erwood ruled, but there was a speculative frown on his face.

'I have no further questions,' Hamilton Burger said.

'No redirect,' Mason said.

The witness started to leave the stand. 'Just a moment,' Judge Erwood said. 'This is a most peculiar situation. The Court is, of course, keenly aware that under the law, evidence is restricted so that extraneous evidence and hearsay evidence is not permitted in Court. But here we have a most unusual situation. The Court is going to ask a few questions to try to clarify the matter somewhat.'

The judge turned to the witness. 'Miss Harper, you stated that Dawn Manning was driving the car.'

'Yes, sir, Your Honour.'

'With one hand?'

'Yes, sir.'

'And the other hand was holding a gun?'

'Yes, sir.'

'Where was that gun pointed?'

'At me.'

'How did it happen that you were riding in the car with Dawn Manning?'

'She forced me to get in at the point of a gun.'

'Then she had a gun with her all of the time?'

'Yes, Your Honour.'

'Of course, you have no means of knowing whether this was the gun which, according to the testimony of the ballistics expert, was the weapon from which the fatal bullet was fired.'

Loretta Harper said, 'It *looked* like the same gun. She stole the car, and she could just as easily have stolen the gun. Frank Ferney has been trying to protect her. Make *him* tell what happened.'

Judge Erwood said hastily, 'Well now, of course, we are getting into a lot of extraneous matters. That last remark is legally irrelevant. However, what appears to have been a rather simple case now becomes more complicated. Do you have any more questions, Mr Prosecutor?'

'None,' Burger said.

'Mr Mason?'

'None,' Mason said.

'The witness is excused.'

Mason said, 'I now desire to recall Mr Ferney for further cross-examination.'

'That is objected to, if the Court please,' Hamilton Burger said. 'The prosecution has concluded its case, the defence had ample opportunity to cross-examine Mr Ferney, and covered his testimony thoroughly.'

'The Court feels that it understands the question Mr Mason wants to ask of Mr Ferney,' Judge Erwood said. 'And, since the order of proof in motions of this sort are addressed to the sound discretion of the Court, the Court will grant the motion. In fact, the Court will state that if Mr Mason had not made this motion, the Court of its own motion would have asked Mr Ferney to return to the stand.

'The motion is granted, Mr Mason. Mr Ferney, return to the stand.'

Ferney came forward and took the witness stand.

'Go ahead, Mr Mason, resume your cross-examination.'

Mason said, 'Directing your attention to the time when you have testified that you were looking for Meridith Borden after you and Dr Callison had entered the house, did you go up the stairs to the room used as a photographic studio?'

'I did.'

'Was the door open or closed?'

'It was closed.'

'Did you knock on that door?'

'Yes.'

'What happened?'

'A woman's voice called out, "Go away."'

'Why didn't you tell us about this before?'

'Because I wasn't asked.'

'Weren't you asked if you tried to locate Borden and had been unable to do so, if you had called his name and had received no answer?'

'I called his name. I received no answer. I told the truth.'

'But now you say there was a woman in the studio.'

'Sure. Lots of times women were there. This is the first time anyone asked me about her.'

'And she said, "Go away"?'

'Yes.'

'Now then,' Mason said, 'I ask you if you know of your own knowledge who the woman was who was on the other side of that closed door?'

Ferney hesitated, then said in a low voice, 'I feel that I do.'

'Who was it?'

'It was my wife, Dawn.'

'You mean the woman who has been variously described as Dawn Manning and as Mrs Frank Ferney?'

'That is correct.'

'She was your wife?'

'Yes, sir.'

'That is all,' Mason said.

'I have no questions,' Hamilton Burger said.

'Now just a moment,' Judge Erwood said. 'The Court dislikes to be placed in the position of carrying on the examination of witnesses, but certainly there is a situation here which is most unusual. Mr Ferney?'

'Yes, Your Honour.'

'When you gave your testimony before, why didn't you state that you heard the voice of a woman on the other side of that door in the studio?'

'No one asked me.'

'You made no attempt to open the door?'

'No, sir.'

'Was it locked?'

'I don't know.'

'Isn't it unusual that a person should hear the voice of his wife on the other side of the door and simply turn away without making any attempt to open the door?'

'No, Your Honour. That door had to be kept closed. One never knew whether the darkroom was in use, or whether the studio was being used for photographic purposes. I was working for Meridith Borden. If I had opened the door at that time, he would have fired me on the spot.

'I also wish to point out to the Court that my wife and I have separated, and the fact that we have not been formally divorced was entirely due to my fault.'

'In what way was it your fault?' Judge Erwood asked.

'I went to Reno and established a residence. I was supposed to get the divorce. The case was ready to be disposed of, but I got in an argument with my lawyer. I felt he was trying to hold me up. I simply sat tight and decided to outwait him.'

Judge Erwood looked at Ferney with a puzzled expression. 'I feel this matter should be clarified,' he said, shifting his glance to the district attorney.

'We have no further questions,' Burger said doggedly.

Judge Erwood's face showed annoyance. He turned to Perry Mason.

Mason bowed to the Court. 'With the Court's permission,' he said, and arose to walk towards the witness stand, facing the discomfited witness. 'Let's get our own time schedule on the night of the murder straight,' he said. 'You say you left Borden's house a little after six o'clock?'

'Yes.'

'And you went where?'

'To the apartment of Loretta Harper, my fiancée.'

'Did your fiancée, as you call her, know that you were not divorced?'

'Not at that time. She thought I was divorced.'

'You lied to her?'

Ferney flushed, and for a moment started to make some hot rejoinder, then caught himself.

'You lied to her?' Mason repeated.

'All right,' Ferney said defiantly, 'I lied to her.'

'Who was present when you arrived at the apartment of Miss Harper?'

'Just Loretta Harper.'

'Later on, other people came in?'

'Yes.'

'How much later?'

'About fifteen or twenty minutes later.'

'Who were these people?'

'Mr and Mrs Jason Kendell.'

'And how long did they remain?'

'They remained until . . . well, until quite late, until Loretta–I mean Miss Harper–got back from having been kidnapped.'

'Now, when you say kidnapped, what do you mean?'

'If the Court please,' Hamilton Burger said, 'I feel that this witness can't possibly know what transpired with Miss Harper–'

'I'm not asking him what transpired,' Mason said. 'I'm asking him to simply define what he meant by the use of the term kidnapped.'

'The witness is presumed to understand the ordinary meaning of the words he uses,' Judge Erwood said. 'The objection is sustained.'

'All right,' Mason said to the witness, 'you went to this apartment. What floor is it on?'

'The fourth.'

'You had some drinks?'

'Yes.'

'And you had dinner?'

'Yes.'

'And then you became a little dizzy?'

'Quite dizzy.'

'You were intoxicated?'

'I was intoxicated, yes.'

'And then what happened?'

'I went to sleep at the table.'

'What do you know after that? How much do you remember?'

'I have a vague recollection of being placed on the bed.'

'Who did that?'

'Jason and Millicent–that is, Mr and Mrs Kendell, assisted by Miss Harper. I remember they took my shoes off and that's the last I remember until I woke up because I heard a lot of excitement–that is, excited voices, and looked at my watch.'

'Were you intoxicated at the time?'

'No, I'd slept it off. I had a thick feeling in my head.'

'And, at that time, Miss Harper was back in the apartment?'

'That's right.'

'So then you called this veterinary, Dr Callison?'

'I didn't wait to call her. I asked one of the others to call and say that I was on my way, and I made a dash for my automobile. I drove to the kennels.'

'That's all,' Mason said.

Loretta Harper jumped up from her seat in the courtroom. 'Tell them the truth, Frank,' she shouted. 'Quit trying to protect her! Mr Mason, ask him what he told Dr Callison! He–'

'That will do!' Judge Erwood said, banging his gavel. 'Miss Harper, come forward.'

Loretta Harper came forward, her face flushed with indignation.

'Don't you know that you're not supposed to rise in court and shout comments of that sort?' Judge Erwood asked.

'I can't help it, Your Honour. He's still concealing things, still trying to stick up for her. He heard–'

'Now, just a minute,' Judge Erwood said. 'This situation is getting entirely out of hand. I am not interested in any further comments from you, Miss Harper. If you know anything about the case of your own knowledge, that's one thing, but this Court certainly doesn't care to have interpolations from spectators. Now, the Court is going to hold you in contempt of this Court for interrupting the proceedings in this case and comporting yourself in a manner which you knew was improper. The Court will determine the extent of the punishment later. But in the meantime, you're to consider yourself held in contempt of Court and you are technically in custody. Do you understand that?'

'Yes, sir.'

'Call me Your Honour.'

'Yes, Your Honour.'

'Very well. Be seated now and keep quiet.'

Judge Erwood turned angrily to Frank Ferney. 'Mr Ferney,' he said, 'you're under oath. You are called here to tell the truth, the whole truth and nothing but the truth. Now, you've certainly placed yourself in a most unfavourable light, not only by your testimony but by the manner in which you've given that testimony. The Court is thoroughly out of patience with you. Now, is there anything else that you know, anything at all that you know of your own knowledge that would shed any light on this matter?'

Ferney lowered his eyes.

'Yes or no?' Judge Erwood asked.

'Yes,' Ferney said.

'All right, what is it?' Judge Erwood snapped.

Ferney said, 'As we were leaving, driving away from the place, I thought I heard . . . well, I could have been mistaken about that. I–'

'What did you think you heard?' Judge Erwood asked.

'I thought I heard a shot.'

'A shot!'

'Yes.'

Judge Erwood glowered at the witness.

'Did you mention this to Dr Callison?' Mason asked.

'We object,' Burger snapped.

'Sustained.'

'You were riding in the car with Dr Callison?' Mason asked.

'Yes.'

'You rode back to the kennels with her?'

'Yes.'

'What time did you reach there?'

'Around eleven-thirty or perhaps a little after.'

'And you then picked up your own car there?'

'Yes.'

'And returned to your room at the Borden place?'

The witness fidgeted. 'No. I didn't stay there that night.'

'That's all,' Mason announced.

'Any further direct examination?' Judge Erwood asked Hamilton Burger.

'No, Your Honour.'

'The witness is excused,' Judge Erwood said, 'but don't leave the courtroom. The Court feels that your conduct has been reprehensible. You have endeavoured to conceal facts from the Court.'

Mason said, 'If the Court please, there *is* one further question I would like to ask, a question by way of impeachment.'

'Go ahead,' Judge Erwood said.

Mason said, 'Unfortunately, Your Honour, I can't lay a foundation by giving the exact time and the exact place or the exact persons present, but I can ask a general impeaching question. Isn't it a fact, Mr Ferney, that at some time after the night of Monday, the eighth of this month, you told Loretta Harper that you knew your wife had murdered Meridith Borden and that you were going to try to protect her if you could?'

'Just a moment, just a moment!' Hamilton Burger shouted, getting to his feet. 'That question is improper, it's improper cross-examination, it's objected to.'

'What's improper about it as cross-examination?' Judge Erwood snapped.

Hamilton Burger, caught off balance, hesitated.

Sam Drew jumped to his feet. 'If the Court please, no proper foundation has been laid. A question of that sort should specify the exact time and the persons present. Moreover, the opinion of this witness is of absolutely no value.'

Judge Erwood said, 'Counsel has stated that he doesn't know the time; that he doesn't know who was present. He has, however, asked the witness specifically if he didn't have a certain conversation with Loretta Harper. The object of that question is not to prove the fact, but to prove the motivation of the witness, his animosity towards any of the parties, his reason for concealing testimony. I'm going to let him answer the question.'

The judge turned to Ferney. 'Answer the question.'

Ferney twisted and squirmed on the chair. 'Well, I . . . I may have said–'

'Yes or no?' Judge Erwood snapped. 'Did you make such a statement?'

'Well, yes, I did. I told her that.'

'That's all,' Mason said.

'That's all,' Hamilton Burger said, his manner showing his extreme annoyance.

Judge Erwood said, 'The witness is excused.'

Mason said, 'If the Court please, I would like to have a subpoena issued for Dr Margaret Callison, and I would ask the Court to grant the defence a continuance until such a subpoena can be served.'

'Any objection on the part of the prosecution?' Judge Erwood asked.

'Yes, Your Honour,' Sam Drew said. 'In the first place, counsel has had ample opportunity to prepare his case. In the second place, the case in chief has all been submitted. The prosecution has rested its case, the defence has rested its case, the prosecution has called rebuttal witnesses, the issues are limited at this time.'

Judge Erwood looked down at Mason, said, 'The Court is going to take a ten-minute recess, Mr Mason, and, at the end of that recess, the Court will rule on your motion.'

Mason pushed his way through the crowd of spectators to catch Paul Drake's arm. 'Get a subpoena, Paul. Serve it on Dr Callison. Get her here. Rush!'

'You don't think he's going to give you a continuance so you can get her here?' Drake asked.

'I don't know,' Mason said. 'I *think* he's giving me an opportunity to get her here without granting the continuance. I don't know. Judge Erwood, of course, was planning to shut me off and show me that this was only a preliminary hearing, and I couldn't pull any of my legal pyrotechnics here. Now he's interested, and–Get started, Paul. Get going.'

'On my way,' Drake said.

'Bring her back with you,' Mason told him, 'and rush it.'

Drake nodded and pushed his way out of the court-room.

Mason turned back to where Della Street was standing.

'Well?' she asked.

Mason said, 'I'm darned if I know, Della. There's something here that is very peculiar.'

'I think it's plain as can be,' she said. 'Frank Ferney is trying to protect his wife, or, rather, was trying to protect her, and that made Loretta Harper furious.'

Mason said, 'There's something back of all this. Della, what would you do if you were a crooked politician, if you adopted the position that you were only a public relations expert, that you wouldn't think of acting as intermediary in the taking of bribes, that you would act only in a consulting capacity–and then you took in large sums of money which, in turn, you passed out as bribes?'

Della Street made a little grimace. 'I'd probably kill myself about the second night. I don't think I could sleep in the same bed with myself.'

'But suppose you got to the point where you were putting up with yourself and making a very good living out of what you were doing?'

'What are you getting at?' she asked.

Mason said, 'Borden undoubtedly took some steps to protect himself. He knew that when Ansley called on him, Ansley felt he was passing out bribe money. Borden had to accept that money and he had to use it as bribe money. But, in order to keep his skirts clean, he had to adopt the position that he was acting legitimately as a public relations counsellor.'

'Under those circumstances, if I were Borden, I would keep a tape recording of every conversation which took place and be able to produce those tape recordings if I ever got in a jam.'

'Well?' she asked.

'No one has said anything about a tape recording of the Ansley conversation.'

'Would you want one?' she asked. 'Would it help your client?'

'There's one way,' Mason said, 'in which it would help my client a lot.'

'What? I'm afraid I don't understand.'

'If Ansley went there to kill him,' Mason said, 'he wouldn't first employ him as a public relations counsellor, and *then* kill him.'

'But he might have become angered after having the conversation.'

'He might have,' Mason said, grinning, 'but there's one very significant matter which I think our friends on the prosecution have overlooked. . . .

Where's Lt Tragg? Is he around?'

'Yes, he's sitting in court taking in all the testimony.'

'Fine,' Mason said, grinning. 'Tragg will tell the truth.'

11

When Judge Erwood returned to the bench, Hamilton Burger arose to renew his objection.

'If the Court please,' he said, 'if the defence had wanted to call Dr Callison as a witness, they should have had her under subpoena.

'I think it is quite apparent to this Court that what the defence is doing is merely going on a general fishing expedition, trying to call as many witnesses as possible, trying to find out what they know about the case, trying to get them on the record so that the defence counsellor will have a record from which to impeach their testimony when they get into the superior court.

'I know that Courts don't approve of these tactics generally, and I think this Court will agree with me that there has been a tendency in the past to transform some preliminary hearings into spectacular trials which go far outside the issues that should have been determined at a preliminary examination.'

'You are continuing to resist the motion for a continuance so that Dr Callison can be subpoenaed?' Judge Erwood asked.

'Exactly, Your Honour. And may I point out further that the case has now reached the point of rebuttal and surrebuttal. If counsel wishes a continuance in order to serve this subpoena, counsel should make a formal motion, supported by an affidavit stating exactly what it is he expects Dr Callison to state once she is sworn as a witness. Quite obviously, counsel can't do that, because counsel is simply engaged in exploring the possibilities of the situation by calling every witness he feels may ultimately be called as a witness for the prosecution in the higher court.'

Mason, smiling urbanely, said, 'Well, if the Court please, we can debate that point a little later. Right at the moment, I have another witness I wish to recall for further cross-examination.'

Burger's face darkened. 'There you are, Your Honour. Counsel is simply stalling. He undoubtedly has sent out to have Dr Callison subpoenaed, and now he'll recall witness after witness for cross-examination, simply stalling around until Dr Callison can get here.'

'What witness do you wish to recall for further cross-examination?' Judge Erwood asked.

'Lt Tragg, Your Honour.'

'This motion is addressed to the sound discretion of the Court. You have heard the charge made by the district attorney that the purpose of this motion is simply to gain time by a long, drawn-out cross-examination, Mr Mason.'

'Yes, Your Honour.'

'Are you prepared to deny that charge?'

Mason grinned and said, 'Not in its entirety, Your Honour. I hope to have

Dr Callison here by the time I have finished with Lt Tragg's cross-examination. But I will further state to the Court that I am not asking to recall the witness for further cross-examination simply to gain time. I have a definite purpose in mind.'

'What is that purpose?' Judge Erwood asked.

'I think, if the Court please,' Mason said, 'the purpose will become readily apparent as soon as I start questioning the witness. Naturally, I do not want to give my hand away by showing the prosecution my trump cards.'

Judge Erwood frowned thoughtfully, then said, 'Lt Tragg will come forward for further cross-examination. The Court will state that this cross-examination must be brief and to the point, and the Court will not permit what is generally referred to as a fishing expedition on the part of counsel.

'Lt Tragg, come forward, please.'

Lt Tragg resumed the witness stand.

'Proceed, Mr Mason,' Judge Erwood said. And, from the manner in which he was leaning forward, it was quite evident that the judge intended to enforce his ruling that there be no attempt on the part of Mason to stall for time by a long, drawn-out cross-examination.

Mason said, 'You have described what you found at the scene of the murder, Lt Tragg, and you have described what you found in the studio where the body was found?'

'Yes, sir.'

'I will now ask you, Lt Tragg, if it isn't a fact that when you examined the study or office of Meridith Borden, you found something which had considerable significance in your own mind, but which has been suppressed at this examination.'

Tragg frowned.

'Your Honour, I resent that,' Hamilton Burger said. 'I think that constitutes misconduct. Nothing has been suppressed.'

'You're willing to state that?' Mason asked Hamilton Burger.

'Certainly, sir!'

Mason grinned at Lt Tragg's evident discomfiture. 'Let's hear what the witness has to say in answer to the question,' he said.

Judge Erwood started to make some impatient rejoinder, then, turning to look at Tragg's face, suddenly checked himself and leaned towards the witness.

Tragg said uncomfortably, 'I'm not certain that I know what you mean by the word suppressed.'

'Let me ask it this way,' Mason said. 'Isn't it a fact that something was found which you felt had evidentiary value and that you were instructed to say nothing about it while you were being examined in court?'

'Your Honour, I object,' Hamilton Burger shouted. 'This is not proper cross-examination, it is not proper surrebuttal, no proper foundation has been laid, the witness hasn't been asked who is supposed to have instructed him to say nothing, and the article hasn't been described.'

Mason, now sure of his ground, smiled and said, 'I will supplement that with another question, if the Court please.'

'You withdraw your prior question?'

'Yes, Your Honour.'

'Very well, go ahead.'

'Isn't it a fact, Lt Tragg, that when you searched the study of the decedent, Meridith Borden, you found a concealed microphone leading to a recording device of some sort, and isn't it a fact that on that recording device you found a recording of the conversation between Meridith Borden and George Ansley? And isn't it a fact that Hamilton Burger suggested to you that you should make no mention of that recording in the preliminary examination?'

'Your Honour,' Hamilton Burger said, 'we object on the ground that there are several questions here, that this is not proper cross-examination, not proper surrebuttal, and–'

Judge Erwood interrupted. 'Ask your questions one at a time, Mr Mason.'

Mason said, 'When you were examining the premises, you looked through the study of Meridith Borden, Lt Tragg?'

'Yes, sir.'

'Did you find a concealed microphone in there?'

'Yes, sir.'

'Did that microphone lead to, or was it connected with, a recording device of some sort?'

'Yes, sir.'

'Did you find a record on that recording device?'

'Yes, sir.'

'Did that record contain a recording of the complete conversation between George Ansley and Meridith Borden?'

'I don't know.'

'It contained, or purported to contain, a recording of that conversation?'

'Well, *a* recording of *a* conversation.'

'And isn't it a fact that Hamilton Burger told you that you were not to mention this recording at the preliminary hearing?'

'Now, just a moment, Your Honour,' Hamilton Burger said. 'Before the witness answers that question, I want to interpose an objection that it is argumentative, that it is incompetent, irrelevant and immaterial, that it is not proper cross-examination, that it is not proper surrebuttal, and that it calls for hearsay testimony.'

'As the question is now asked,' Judge Erwood said, 'it may call for hearsay evidence. However, in view of the prosecution's indignant denial that anything had been suppressed, it would seem that this objection is somewhat technical. However, the Court will sustain the objection on the ground that it is hearsay. That objection, Mr Mason, is to the question *in its present form*.'

'I understand, Your Honour,' Mason said, noticing the emphasis which Judge Erwood placed on the last words. 'I will ask the question this way: Lt Tragg, why did you not mention this recorded conversation when you gave your testimony here in court?'

'Objected to as incompetent, irrelevant and immaterial, and not proper cross-examination,' Hamilton Burger said.

'In the present form of the question, the objection is overruled.'

'Well, I wasn't asked about it.'

'You were asked about certain things you found in the room in question?'

'Yes, sir.'

'And you described the things you had found?'

'Yes, sir.'

'Now, in your own mind, Lieutenant, was there an intention to avoid mentioning this tape recording unless you were specifically asked about it?'

'That is objected to, Your Honour,' Hamilton Burger said. 'It is argumentative, it is not proper cross-examination.'

'The objection is overruled!' Judge Erwood snapped. 'As the question is now asked, it is eminently proper because it tends to show bias on the part of a witness. Questions are always pertinent for the purpose of showing bias. Answer the question, Lt Tragg.'

'Well, I made up my mind I would avoid saying anything about it unless the specific question was asked.'

'And did you reach that decision in your own mind, Lieutenant, purely because of instructions which had been given you by the district attorney?'

'I object,' Hamilton Burger said. 'If the Court please–'

Judge Erwood shook his head. 'Your objection is overruled, Mr Burger. The question now goes entirely to the state of mind of the witness. If it appears that the witness reached a decision not to mention certain things because he had been asked by the prosecutor not to mention them, that shows bias on the part of the witness which not only can properly be disclosed by direct questions, but the Court may state that it is a matter of considerable interest to the Court. Answer the question, Lieutenant.'

Lt Tragg hesitated a moment, then said, 'Yes, I was instructed to say nothing about it unless I was asked.'

Mason, following up his advantage, said, 'The only reason that caused you to determine to say nothing about that recording unless you were specifically asked about it was an admonition which had been given you by the district attorney. Is that right?'

'Same objection,' Hamilton Burger said.

'Overruled,' Judge Erwood snapped. 'Answer the question.'

'That's right.'

'Now then,' Mason said, 'I feel that in the interests of justice, we should have the recording of that interview played to the Court.'

'If counsel wants to put it on as part of his case,' Hamilton Burger said, 'let him get the recording, bring it in and offer it, and then we will make an objection on the ground that it is completely incompetent, that this Court is not bound by two unidentified voices on a tape recording.'

'Where is that recording now?' Mason asked Lt Tragg.

'I turned it over to the district attorney.'

Mason said, 'I ask that the district attorney be ordered to produce that recording, and that it be played to the Court. I think that this conversation between the defendant and Meridith Borden may be of great importance. The charge is that the defendant killed Meridith Borden. Quite obviously, one doesn't have a conversation with a dead man.'

Hamilton Burger, on his feet, said angrily, 'There's no reason why he can't have a conversation with a man and then shoot him. That tape recording shows that he had every reason to murder Meridith Borden.'

'Then it should be a part of your case,' Mason said.

'I'm the sole judge of what is a part of my case,' Hamilton Burger said. 'All I need to do at this time is to show that a murder was committed and then produce evidence which will convince this Court that there is reasonable grounds to believe the defendant committed that murder.'

'I think that is correct,' Judge Erwood said. 'However, the situation is now somewhat different. The defence counsel is calling upon the prosecution to produce that tape recording as a part of the *defendant's* case. The Court is going to grant that motion. That is, that the tape, or whatever the recording was on, will be played to the Court. The Court admits that this case is taking a peculiar turn and the Court is interested in finding out what actually happened.'

'All of Mr Mason's cases take peculiar turns,' Hamilton Burger said angrily.

'That will do, Mr Prosecutor. If you have that tape recording in your possession, produce it.'

'It will take a few minutes to get it here and set up so we can play it.'

'How long?'

'At least half an hour.'

'Then the Court will take a recess for half an hour.'

Drew tugged at Hamilton Burger's coat-tails, and, as the district attorney bent over, Drew whispered vehemently.

'Just a moment, just a moment,' Hamilton Burger said suddenly. I'll try to have everything set up and get it here within ten minutes.'

Judge Erwood looked at Burger thoughtfully. 'You said it would take half an hour, Mr Prosecutor.'

'I find, on consulting with my associate, that the tape recorder is immediately available and we can get the tape here, I think, within ten minutes.'

'Is that what your associate whispered to you?' Mason asked. 'Or did he whisper to you that a half-hour delay would enable me to get Dr Callison here?'

Hamilton Burger turned angrily. 'You mind your business and I'll mind–'

Judge Erwood's gavel banged on the desk. 'That will do, gentlemen,' he said. 'We will have no further exchange of personalities between counsel. However, Mr Prosecutor, the Court was not born yesterday. You said that it would take half an hour to get the recording here, and the Court made an order that the Court would recess for thirty minutes. The Court sees no reason to change that order. The recess will be for thirty minutes.'

And Judge Erwood got up from the bench and stalked angrily into chambers.

12

Five minutes before Court reconvened, Paul Drake came hurrying into the court-room, accompanied by a trim-looking woman.

Mason beckoned them over to the defence counsel table where he was seated in conversation with George Ansley.

'This is Dr Margaret Callison, the veterinary,' Paul Drake said, 'and this is Perry Mason, the lawyer for Ansley.'

'How do you do, Mr Mason,' she said, giving him her hand and a warm smile. 'I've read about you for a long time. I hardly expected to meet you. I told Mr Drake that I don't believe I know a thing that has any bearing on what happened.'

'Perhaps if you'll tell me exactly what happened,' Mason said, 'we can correlate your story with other facts in the case, and perhaps find something which will be of value. I have subpoenaed you as a witness and I want you to stand by, but I may not have to put you on the stand. Tell me what happened.'

She said, 'I had one of the Borden dogs for treatment. Mr Borden liked to have the dogs there at night. They would be brought in early in the morning, as a rule. I would treat them during the day and he would come for them at night.'

'And on this particular Monday?' Mason asked.

'I had one of the dogs which had been delivered at eight o'clock in the morning. I treated the dog, and Mr Ferney was to come for it at nine o'clock that night.

'When he didn't come, I waited around for his call, feeling that he had probably been detained. Actually, that call didn't come until right around ten twenty-five, and then it wasn't Mr Ferney who called. It was a man who said he was calling for Mr Ferney, that Mr Ferney had been unavoidably detained. He asked me if I could have the dog ready, despite the lateness of the hour. The man said Mr Ferney was on his way.'

'You agreed?'

'Yes, I told him I would have the dog in my station wagon; that it would take me about five minutes to get the dog and load it.'

'You did that?'

'That's right.'

'And when did Frank Ferney arrive?'

'Just after I had the dog loaded in my station wagon. He parked his car in front of my place, and I drove the station wagon to Borden's place.'

'How far are you from the Borden place?'

'Only a little over two miles.'

'Then what happened?' Mason asked.

'Well, we went up to the gate. Mr Ferney opened the gate with a key, and took the dog from me.

'I told him that I wanted to talk with Mr Borden about the dog's condition. I thought an operation might be advisable. There are a couple of glands which have a tendency to become calcified, and the dog was no longer a young dog. I suggested to Mr Ferney that it would be well to discuss the matter with Mr Borden, and he said that I should come on in with him, and I probably would have a chance to talk to Mr Borden.'

'Then what?'

'Well, we entered the house, and Ferney said Mr Borden wasn't in his study, he thought he was up in the studio; he'd go to look for him, and–'

The clerk pounded with his gavel. 'Everybody stand up, please.'

Mason whispered hastily to Dr Callison as Judge Erwood entered the court, 'When you left, did Ferney go with you?'

'Yes.'

'Was he alone or out of your sight any time there in the building?'

'Not in the building. The burglar alarm came on, and he went out to call the dogs back and turn out the lights. That was when I answered the phone and said I didn't think Mr Borden wished to be disturbed. I felt someone had been tampering with the gates, some idle curiosity seeker. I knew I shouldn't intrude on Mr Borden wherever he was.'

'But was Ferney out of your sight while he was *inside* the house?'

'Only when he went up the short flight of stairs to knock on the door of the studio.'

'Did you hear him knock?'

'Yes.'

'Did you hear any voices?'

'No.'

'Could he have entered the room?'

'Heavens, no! There wasn't time. I heard him knock and then he came right back down. I'll tell you this, Mr Mason, when he came down those stairs, he looked as if someone had jolted him back on his heels. He told me Borden was in the studio and didn't want to be disturbed. He said–'

The bailiff shouted, 'Silence in the court! You may be seated,' as Judge Erwood seated himself on the bench and glanced at the district attorney.

'The tape recording is ready, Mr District Attorney?'

'Yes, Your Honour. I again desire to object to it on the ground that it is inadmissible, that it is not the best evidence, that it is not properly authenticated, that it is completely incompetent, irrelevant and immaterial at this time, and is no part of rebuttal or surrebuttal.'

'The tape recording is the actual recording that was found in the Borden residence?'

'Yes, Your Honour.'

'Then the objections are overruled. We will hear the recording.'

With poor grace, Hamilton Burger turned on the tape recording. For some ten minutes the recording played the voices of George Ansley and Meridith Borden.

Then the voice of Ansley coming through the loudspeaker, said, 'Well, I guess I'll be getting on.'

Borden's voice said, 'I'm glad you dropped in, Ansley, and I'll take care of you to the best of my ability. I feel quite certain you won't have any more trouble with the inspectors. They don't like adverse publicity any better than anyone else, and, after all, I'm a public relations expert.'

Borden's laugh was ironic.

'I can find my way out all right,' Ansley's voice said.

'No, no, I'll see you to the door. I'm all alone here tonight. Sorry.'

The tape recorder ran on for some ten seconds, then a peculiar thudding sound registered on the tape. After that, abruptly the noises ceased, although the spools of the tape recorder continued to revolve.

Hamilton Burger moved over and shut off the tape recorder, started rewinding the spools.

'That's it, Your Honour,' he said.

Judge Erwood was frowning thoughtfully. 'The series of crackling noises which come from the tape recorder after the voices had ceased are caused by what, Mr District Attorney?'

'The fact that the tape recorder was continuing to run with a live microphone.'

'And that muffled sound?'

'That was the sound of the shot that killed Meridith Borden,' Hamilton Burger said. And then added with apparent heat, 'We feel, if the Court please, that this is forcing us unnecessarily to show our hand. We had intended to produce this evidence in the superior court when the defendant was held for trial.'

'Well, the defence has a right to produce it,' Judge Erwood said. 'I believe it is being produced on order of the Court in response to a demand by the defendant and as a part of the defendant's case.'

'Well, the defendant has heard it now,' Hamilton Burger said with ill grace.

'And, doubtless, when he finally gets on the witness stand to tell his story in front of a jury, he will have thought up the proper answers, or they will have been thought up for him.'

'There is no occasion for that comment, Mr District Attorney,' Judge Erwood said. 'The defence in any case is entitled to present evidence to a Court.'

'In this case,' Hamilton Burger said, still angry and still insistent, 'they're presenting the prosecution's case.'

'We won't argue the matter!' Judge Erwood snapped. 'Are there any further witnesses, Mr Mason?'

'Yes, Your Honour,' Mason said, 'I desire to have Mr Ferney recalled to the stand for further cross-examination.'

'We object,' Hamilton Burger said. 'The defence in this case has done nothing but recall witnesses for cross-examination. The law does not contemplate that a defendant can cross-examine a witness piecemeal. The defendant is supposed to conduct his cross-examination and be finished with it.'

'Anything further, Mr Prosecutor?' Judge Erwood asked.

'No, Your Honour, that covers my position.'

'Objection is overruled. The examination of witnesses is within the province of the Court. Mr Ferney, you will return to the witness stand.'

Ferney, obviously ill at ease, returned to the witness stand.

'Directing your attention to the night of the eighth of this month, at a time when you were at the Borden residence with Dr Callison present, the time being shortly after eleven o'clock in the evening, did you state to Dr Callison that you had climbed the stairs to the studio where Mr Borden carried on his photographic work, and that Mr Borden had told you he didn't want to be disturbed, or words to that effect?'

'That's objected to as hearsay and not proper cross-examination,' Hamilton Burger said.

'Overruled!' Judge Erwood snapped. 'It's an impeaching question. The Court is going to hear the conversation.'

'But it certainly can't be binding on the prosecution anything that this witness *said*, Your Honour.'

'It may not be binding on the prosecution, but it shows the attitude and the bias of the witness. The Court is going to permit the question. Go ahead and answer, Mr Ferney.'

'Well,' Ferney said, 'I went up the stairs to the studio. I knocked on the door–'

'That's not the question,' Judge Erwood interrupted. 'The question is what you told Dr Callison.'

'Well, I told her that Mr Borden was up in the studio taking pictures and that he didn't want to be disturbed.'

'Did you say he *told* you he didn't want to be disturbed?' Mason asked.

Ferney looked over to where Dr Callison was seated in the court-room. 'I don't remember exactly what words I used.'

'After you left the house with Dr Callison in her station wagon, did you ask her if she had heard a shot?'

'I think what I said was a noise like a shot.'

'You asked her that?'

'I may have.'

'That's all,' Mason said.

'I have no further questions,' Hamilton Burger said.

'That rests our case, Your Honour,' Mason said.

'I have no further evidence, Your Honour,' Hamilton Burger said. 'I now move the Court to bind the defendant over to the superior court. Regardless of what the record may show as to contradictions, the fact remains that the defendant had the fatal weapon in his possession, the defendant had threatened the decedent, and, furthermore, it is apparent that the defendant fired the shot which killed the decedent within a few seconds after the termination of the interview, and apparently while the decedent was showing the defendant to the door. The sound of that shot is quite apparent on the tape recorder.'

Judge Erwood frowned at the district attorney. 'Is it your contention that Mr Borden was showing him to the front door through the photographic studio?'

'Not necessarily, Your Honour.'

'Then how did it happen that his body was found in the photographic studio?'

'It could have been taken there, Your Honour.'

Judge Erwood turned to Perry Mason. 'The Court will hear from you, Mr Mason.'

Mason said urbanely, 'What happened, Your Honour, was that when Meridith Borden escorted George Ansley to the door, he slammed the front door. And it was that muffled slamming of the front door which made the sound on the tape recorder. The proof that Meridith Borden was alive after George Ansley left the house is that he returned and *immediately* shut off the tape recorder. It is quite apparent on the tape itself that the tape recorder was shut off.'

'Do you question that, Mr District Attorney?' Judge Erwood asked the prosecutor.

Burger said, 'It's quite apparent that the tape was shut off shortly after the sound of the shot, but it was the murderer, George Ansley, who shut off the tape recorder.'

Judge Erwood looked at Mason. Mason smiled and shook his head.

'George Ansley didn't know where the tape recorder was,' he said. 'He didn't know the interview was being recorded. The testimony is that it was a *concealed* microphone. The tape recorder was in another room. It was necessary for the tape recorder to be shut off by someone who knew that it was on and who knew exactly where the tape recorder was located. Ansley didn't have that knowledge and couldn't have done it.

'There is, if the Court please, one other most persuasive circumstance. The Court will notice that the inspectors on the job the next day were more than courteous. Now, that means just one thing. It means that Meridith Borden had been in communication with the inspectors. Since we have now heard a complete tape recording of the interview with George Ansley, we know that at no time during that interview did Meridith Borden go to the telephone, ring up an inspector and say, in effect, "It's all right. George Ansley has called on me and is going to kick through. You can take off the pressure."

'Or, since Meridith Borden is dead and cannot refute any charge against him, perhaps I should express it this way: He didn't go to the telephone and say to the inspector, "George Ansley has just called on me and has retained me as a public relations expert. I feel that your inspection on this construction job has been far more rigorous than is required by the contract, and represents some personal animosity on your part, or an attempt to get some kind of a bribe or kick-back. Therefore, unless the situation is changed immediately, I am going to take steps to see that publicity is given the type of inspection to which Mr Ansley has been subjected."'

For a moment Judge Erwood's angry face relaxed into something of a smile. 'A very tactful expression of a purely hypothetical conversation, Mr Mason.'

'Out of deference to the fact that Borden is now deceased and is not in a position to defend himself,' Mason said.

Judge Erwood looked down at the prosecutor. 'I think, Mr Prosecutor,' he said, 'that by the time you think over the entire evidence in this case, you will realize that you are proceeding against the wrong defendant, and that the very greatest favour the Court could do you at this time would be to dismiss the case against this defendant.

'You are here asking for an order that this defendant, George Ansley, be bound over for trial, and the Court feels that if such an order should be made, it would put you in a position where at a later date you would either have to dismiss the case against George Ansley, or, if you went to trial before a jury, you would have a verdict of acquittal at the hands of the jury.

'The Court realizes thoroughly that it is not incumbent upon the prosecution to put on all of its evidence in a preliminary examination, that in general the purpose of the examination is simply to show that a crime had been committed and that there is reasonable cause to believe the defendant has committed that crime. However, there is another duty which devolves upon the prosecutor, and that is to conduct his office in the interests of justice and to see that the innocent are released and not subjected to the annoyance and expense of trial, and that the guilty are prosecuted.

'The Court feels that, with the facts in this case brought into evidence as they now are, there is every indication that the defendant is being prosecuted for a crime that he did not commit, for a crime that he could not have committed.

'It is not incumbent on this Court to suggest to the prosecutor how the office of the district attorney should be conducted. But the Court does suggest that in this case further action should be taken and against an entirely different defendant.

'As far as this instant proceeding is concerned, the case against George Ansley is dismissed. The defendant is discharged from custody, and Court is adjourned.'

Judge Erwood arose and strode from the court-room.

There was a demonstration among the spectators. Newspaper reporters dashed for the nearest telephones and Mason turned to shake hands with George Ansley.

Photographers exploded flashbulbs as Hamilton Burger, glowering at the group around Mason, pushed his angry way through the spectators, strode out of the court-room and down the corridor.

13

It was well after nine-thirty in the morning when Mason unlocked the door of his private office, grinned at Della Street and said, 'The newspapers didn't do very well by our friend Hamilton Burger.'

Della Street laughed. 'As a matter of good public relations, he should have at least hung around the court-room and talked with some of the reporters. Pushing the reporters to one side and striding down the corridor didn't do him any good.'

'So I see in the Press,' Mason said. 'Well, here we are, starting all over again. What's new–anything?'

'You have another client,' Della Street said.

'What kind of a case?' Mason asked.

'Murder.'

'Indeed!' Who's been murdered now?'

'Meridith Borden.'

Mason raised his eyebrows.

'Dawn Manning telephoned,' Della Street said. 'She is in *durance vile*. She said that she had been permitted to telephone for an attorney, and that she wanted you to represent her.'

'Where is she?'

'Up in the women's section of Detention,' Della Street said.

Mason walked over and picked up his hat.

'You're going?'

'Sure, I'm going.'

'Chief, can you take her case after–'

'After what?' Mason asked.

'After virtually accusing her of murder in court yesterday.'

'Did I accuse her of murder?'

'You did–at least by innuendo. And so did Judge Erwood.'

Mason said, 'All the time I was discussing the matter, I was thinking what an embarrassing situation Hamilton Burger was going to find himself in if he charged Dawn Manning with the crime.'

'What do you mean? There's virtually a perfect case against her. You can see what she did. She was thrown out of that car, she retained the gun, she found herself in the Borden grounds, she went to keep an appointment with Meridith Borden. The evidence is all there. She can't possibly deny her presence in view of the new testimony of the undeveloped photographs in the camera. She's got to admit that she was there with him, and once she admits that, she has to admit she's lied. . . . Oh, Chief, don't get mixed up in *her* case.'

'Why not?'

'Well, for one thing,' Della Street said, 'suppose Hamilton Burger should manipulate things so that the preliminary hearing comes up in front of Judge

Erwood. You know how Judge Erwood feels; his temper, his ideas about the administration of justice; and the way he feels about the duties of attorneys as officers of the court. He'd *really* be laying for you this time.'

'It's a challenge,' Mason said, 'and Dawn Manning is a very beautiful woman.'

Della Street said, 'Chief, let me make a prediction. If the grapevine from the jail shows that you went up to see her, Hamilton Burger will manipulate things so that the preliminary hearing will come up before Judge Erwood. I'll bet you ten to one on it.'

Mason thought that over and said, 'No takers, Della. I think you're right. I think that's exactly what he'll do. It's what I would do if I were in Hamilton Burger's position.'

'Well,' Della Street said, 'Judge Erwood will–He'll . . . he'll throw everything at you, including the kitchen sink.'

'I'm good at dodging,' Mason said. 'If anybody wants me for the next hour, I'll be up talking with Dawn Manning, and I rather think we'll take her case, Della.'

14

Mason sat in the visitors' room and looked across through the thick, glass panel at Dawn Manning.

The heavy sheet of plate glass kept them separated, but a microphone on each side enabled them to hear each other.

She surveyed him with cool, slate-grey eyes and said, 'Well, you certainly sold *me* down the river!'

'*I* did?' Mason asked.

'You don't need to apologize,' she said. 'When you represent a client, you go all out for that client. You were representing George Ansley then, and you could get him off by tossing me to the wolves. The question is, how good a job you and that wonderful husband of mine have done in framing me.'

'Did you call me up here to berate me for what happened?' Mason asked.

'I did not. I want you to be my lawyer.'

'Well?' Mason asked.

'And I haven't a lot to pay on a fee. But I do feel that you owe me some consideration.'

Mason said, 'The fee won't be the most important thing. The most important thing is whether you told me the truth when you talked with me.'

'I told you the truth. Well, anyway, most of it.'

'You knew that Frank hadn't secured a divorce?'

'I had just found out.'

'You knew that Loretta was his girl friend?'

'I knew that he was playing around with a Loretta Harper, but I didn't know her from Eve. I didn't know her when I saw her.'

'But you had modelled for Meridith Borden?'

'Of course. I told you about that. I had, however, never modelled for him in the nude, and I don't know where those pictures came from. I wasn't in the house that night. I didn't like Meridith Borden. He . . . well, I told you he wanted to use me as bait for some sort of a badger game, or to get the goods on some official. I don't go for that sort of thing. I walked out.'

'Was there a scene?'

'There was one hell of a scene. I slapped his dirty face.'

'Can the district attorney prove that?'

'Of course he can. Meridith Borden tried to–Well, there was a scene.'

'Others were present?'

'Yes.'

'Did you threaten to kill him?'

'I said I'd shoot him like a dog. . . . Oh, I suppose I'm in one hell of a position!'

'*Did* you kill him?'

'No. I told you the truth. I walked out of the grounds as soon as I knew where I was.'

'Then how did it happen he took your pictures in the nude?'

'He didn't.'

'The camera says he did, and cameras don't lie.'

'I can't explain those pictures, Mr Mason, but I wasn't there.'

'You do pose in the nude?'

'For photographers I know and for what are known as "art" nudes, yes. I've posed thousands of times for calendar pictures, both in colour and in black and white.'

'Did you have a gun?' Mason asked.

'I *never* had a gun.'

'Never carried one?'

'No, of course not.'

Mason said, 'You get into situations at times where you probably need some protection.'

'What do you mean by that?'

'You're out with photographers in the wilds, being photographed in skimpy bathing suits, and–'

'And you don't try to conceal a ·38-calibre revolver in the folds of a Bikini bathing suit, Mr Mason,' she interrupted. 'A model learns to take care of herself. You do it one way or another, but you don't carry guns.'

Mason said, 'Okay, Dawn, I'm your attorney.'

15

Judge Erwood looked down at the jammed court-room, said acidly, 'The People of the State of California versus Dawn Ferney, also known as Dawn Manning. This is the time fixed for the preliminary hearing.'

'We're ready, Your Honour,' Hamilton Burger said.

Judge Erwood said, 'Does the Court understand that Mr Mason is representing this defendant?'

'That is quite right, Your Honour,' Mason said.

Judge Erwood said, 'The last time you were in this court, Mr Mason, you were presenting evidence which pointed the finger of suspicion very strongly at this defendant.'

'That evidence will now be presented by the district attorney,' Mason said, smiling, 'and I will be permitted to cross-examine the witnesses.'

Judge Erwood hesitated a moment, as though casting about in his mind for some ground on which he could administer a rebuke, then he said, 'Proceed, Mr District Attorney.'

Hamilton Burger delegated the preliminaries to his associate counsel, Sam Drew, who once more introduced evidence as to the location of the premises, the finding of the body, the location and identification of the fatal bullet, and firing the test bullets through the gun which had been recovered from Ansley's car, and the identification of the fatal bullet with the test bullet. Now the pictures of Dawn Manning which had been found in Borden's studio were introduced by the prosecution as a telling point in its case.

'My next witness will be Harvey Dennison,' Hamilton Burger said.

Harvey Dennison came forward, was sworn and once again told the story of the missing gun.

'Any cross-examination?' Judge Erwood asked Mason.

'Yes, Your Honour.'

Mason arose and stood by the edge of the counsel table, looking at Harvey Dennison with steady eyes. 'Mr Dennison, I take it you have consulted the records of the store in order to get the information on which your testimony is based?'

'Yes, sir.'

'The defendant was working for you during the period when the gun was found to be missing?'

'Yes, sir.'

'You can't tell the date when the gun was taken?'

'No, sir.'

'As I understand your testimony, your records show that the gun was ordered and received from the wholesaler on a certain date, that, at a later date, perhaps some months later, you took an inventory and found that the gun was not in your stock.'

'That's right.'

'How many employees did you have in your store?'

'You mean as salesclerks?'

'No, I mean your total employees.'

'Well, counting bookkeepers, stock clerks, salespersons, we had–let me see, about twelve, I think.'

'Including the owners?'

'No, sir.'

'How many owners are there?'

'Three.'

'So there was a total of fifteen persons who could have taken that gun?'

'Well . . . yes, sir, I guess so.'

'And, during the time between the date the gun was received by you and the date when it was found to be missing when an inventory was taken, there were two burglaries of the store, were there not?'

'Yes, sir.'

'And what was taken in those burglaries?'

'Objected to as incompetent, irrelevant and immaterial, and not proper cross-examination,' Burger snapped.

Judge Erwood said, 'I think you should limit your question somewhat, Mr Mason.'

'Very well, I will. I'll withdraw that question and ask Mr Dennison if it isn't true that sporting goods were taken when the store was burglarized on each occasion.'

'Same objection,' Hamilton Burger said.

'Overruled,' Judge Erwood snapped.

'Yes, sir,' Dennison admitted. 'As nearly as we could tell, all that was taken on those occasions was hunting and fishing material, and some cash.'

'What do you mean by hunting and fishing material?'

'Ammunition, rifles, shotguns, fishing rods, reels.'

'On both occasions the material taken consisted solely of sporting goods?'

'And money.'

'Both times?'

'Yes.'

'No further questions,' Mason said.

'Just a moment,' Hamilton Burger said. 'I have one or two on redirect. If that gun had been taken on the occasion of either of those burglaries, you would have found that it was missing at that time, isn't that correct?'

'Objected to as argumentative, leading and suggestive, and calling for a conclusion of the witness,' Mason said.

'Sustained,' Judge Erwood said.

'Well, you took an inventory after each of these burglaries, didn't you?'

'Yes, sir.'

'Now then, I am going to ask you if you found that this gun was missing immediately after either one of the burglaries?'

'No, sir.'

'That's all,' Hamilton Burger said.

Mason smiled.

'Did either of those inventories disclose this gun as being present?'

'No, sir, it did not. As I have said, something happened to our records on this gun. I don't understand it exactly, but all I can state is that the gun was *not* sold over the counter.'

'That's all,' Mason said, smiling.

'And during the time of this shortage, the defendant was in your employ?' Hamilton Burger asked.

'That's right.'

'No further questions,' Hamilton Burger said.

'And fourteen other people were also in your employ?' Mason asked.

'Well, yes.'

'No further questions,' Mason said.

'That's all,' Hamilton Burger announced. 'Mr Dennison will be excused. I will now call Frank Ferney. I may state to the Court that in some respects Mr Ferney is an unwilling witness. He has, I believe, tried to protect this defendant wherever possible, and–'

Mason arose.

Hamilton Burger said, 'And I may have to ask leading questions.in order to get at the truth. I think this witness has perhaps–'

'Just a moment,' Judge Erwood said. 'Do you wish to object, Mr Mason?'

'Yes, Your Honour. I feel that it is incumbent on the district attorney to ask questions, and then, if it appears the witness is hostile, he can ask leading questions. But I see no reason for the prosecution to make a speech at this time, a speech which is quite evidently intended to arouse sympathy for this witness.'

'The Court feels Mr Mason is correct, Mr Burger. Just go ahead and ask your questions.'

'Very well,' Hamilton Burger said. 'Your name is Frank Ferney?'

'That is right.'

'You were employed by Meridith Borden at the time of his death?'

'That's right.'

'Now, directing your attention to the night when Mr Borden was murdered, the night of the eighth, were you at Meridith Borden's house on that night?'

'Yes, sir.'

'At about what time?'

'Just a moment,' Mason said, 'if the Court please, at this point I wish to object to this question and ask that this witness be instructed not to answer any questions as to anything that happened on the night of the eighth.'

Judge Erwood showed surprise. 'On what ground?' he asked.

'On the ground that the witness is married to the defendant, and the relationship of husband and wife exists, and that a husband cannot be examined for or against his wife without the consent of the wife.'

'Just a minute,' Hamilton Burger said, 'I'll clear that up. *Are* you married to the defendant, Mr Ferney?'

'No, sir.'

'You are *not* her husband?'

'No, sir.'

Hamilton Burger grinned at Perry Mason.

'May I ask a question on that, Your Honour?' Mason asked.

'Very well, on that particular point only,' Judge Erwood said.

'You married the defendant at one time?'

'Yes, sir.'

'When?'

'Some three years ago.'

'You have been living separate and apart for some period of time?'

'Yes, sir.'

'How long?'

'About eighteen months.'

'And you have now divorced this defendant?'

'Yes, sir.'

'When was that divorce decree granted?'

'Yesterday.'

'Where?'

'In Reno, Nevada.'

'I take it you flew to Reno, Nevada, obtained your decree and flew back here in order to be a witness?'

'Yes, sir.'

'You had previously filed this suit for divorce, the issues had been joined, but you hadn't gone through with the divorce?'

'That's right.'

'You *were* married to the defendant on the night of the eighth when the murder was committed?'

'Yes, sir.'

'That's all, Your Honour,' Mason said.

'But you aren't married to her *now*,' Hamilton Burger said. 'There is no longer any relationship of husband and wife.'

'That's right,' Ferney said.

'If the Court please,' Hamilton Burger said, 'I am prepared to argue this point. People versus Godines 17 Cal App 2nd 721, and the case of People versus Loper 159 California 6 112 Pacific 720, both hold that a divorced spouse is not prohibited from testifying even to anything that happened during the period the marriage was in force.'

Mason said, 'Doesn't the case of People versus Mullings 83 California 138 23 Pacific 229, and Kansas City Life Insurance Company versus Jones 21 Fed Sup 159 hold that a divorced wife cannot testify as to confidential communications between herself and the accused while they were married?'

'Who's asking about any confidential communications?' Hamilton Burger shouted. 'I'm asking about facts.'

'Aren't you going to ask him if he didn't knock on the door of Borden's studio and hear his wife's voice say, "Go away"?' Mason inquired.

'Certainly,' Burger snapped.

'There you are,' Mason said. 'That's a privileged communication between husband and wife. This witness can't testify to that, both under the provisions of Subdivision 1 of Section 1881 of our Code of Civil Procedure, as well as Section 1332 of the Penal Code.'

Hamilton Burger's eyes widened in astonishment. 'That's not what the law had in mind in regard to privileged communications between husband and wife. The defendant merely spoke to this witness without knowing she was addressing her husband.'

'How do you know what she knew?' Mason asked.

Burger, so angry he was all but sputtering, said, 'Your Honour, if the Court should enforce any such rule, it would mean that the defendant in this case would be allowed to get by with murder. And I mean literally to get by with murder. She has committed the crime of murder. A witness is now on the stand who knows facts that force us to the conclusion that this defendant committed the crime. They are no longer husband and wife, they have been living separate and apart for over a year, there is no relationship between them which the law should encourage. The reason for the rule has ceased, and so the rule itself should cease.'

'Whatever a wife may have said to her husband is a confidential and therefore a privileged communication,' Mason said. 'If this defendant was in that room and asked her husband to go away, she was appealing to him as his spouse. She was his wife at that time.'

'Poppycock!' Hamilton Burger exploded. 'She had no idea who it was at the door. She only knew someone had knocked and she didn't want the door opened while she was standing there in the nude.'

'Not at all,' Mason said. 'If the witness could have recognized his wife's voice, she could have recognized his.'

'But she didn't mean it as a *confidential* communication,' Burger said.

Mason smiled. 'If you're going to testify as to what my client *thought*, Mr District Attorney, you'll have to get on the stand, and then you'll have to qualify as a mind reader. You'll probably need your crystal ball to hold in your hands while you're testifying.'

Judge Erwood, fighting back a smile, said, 'Let's not have any more personalities, gentlemen. In the face of the objection on the part of the defence, Mr District Attorney, this Court is going to sustain the objection to anything it is claimed a wife said to her husband while the marriage was in existence, particularly at a time when she was in a room where a corpse was subsequently found.'

'But, if the Court please,' Hamilton Burger protested, 'that simply tears the middle right out of our case. We don't have a leg to stand on unless we can rely on the testimony of this witness.'

'Just a moment,' Judge Erwood said. 'Let me point out to you, Mr District Attorney, that in this court you are not building up a case to prove the defendant guilty beyond all reasonable doubt. You only need to establish a *prima facie* case. That is, that the murder has been committed (a fact which you have now established), and that there is reasonable ground to believe the defendant committed that crime. You have proven she had an opportunity to possess herself of the murder weapon. Now, all you need to do is to prove the presence of the defendant on the premises at the time the crime could have been committed. That's all you need to establish in *this* court.

'You can then take this question of evidence to the superior court, where it can be properly ruled upon and after the ruling can be properly reviewed.'

Hamilton Burger thought that over.

'I take it,' Mason said, 'that the Court is not intimating in advance what its decision will be.'

Judge Erwood frowned at Mason. 'The Court is not precluding the defence from putting on any evidence it may desire, if that is what you mean. If that evidence indicates that the defendant should be released, the defendant will be released.

'However, the Court *is* stating that if the evidence in this case, when it is all in, tends to prove that this defendant probably had possession of the weapon with which the murder was committed, at the time of the murder, that the murder was committed at a time *when* the defendant was on the grounds *where* the murder was committed, the Court will consider that as sufficient evidence to make an order binding the defendant over.'

'Very well,' Hamilton Burger said, his face brightening somewhat. 'We'll withdraw you from the stand, Mr Ferney, and call Loretta Harper.'

Loretta Harper was sworn and testified that she had been giving a party in her apartment, that Jason and Millicent Kendell, two very old friends, were there in the apartment, that she had left shortly before nine o'clock to run across the street and get some cigarettes, that a Cadillac had slowed down opposite her while she was in the crosswalk, that the defendant had been in the car, that the defendant had accused her of 'playing around' with the defendant's husband and keeping the defendant's husband from getting a divorce. The defendant had ordered Loretta into the automobile with her at the point of a gun.

Loretta went on to testify about being taken out to Meridith Borden's place along the wet roads, about the defendant driving with one hand, about the car skidding and overturning. She admitted that she substituted herself for the defendant in order to try to keep her name from getting in the papers, that she had then told George Ansley that her name was Beatrice Cornell in order to keep herself from becoming 'involved', and had had him drive her to the Ancordia Apartments, from which she had taken a taxicab back to her own apartment where she had suddenly realized her fiancé, Frank Ferney, had failed to keep an appointment with Dr Callison and had aroused him from a deep sleep and started him hurrying to Dr Callison's veterinary hospital.

'You may cross-examine,' Hamilton Burger said.

'You occupy an apartment in the Dormain Apartments?' Mason asked.

'Yes.'

'What is the number of that apartment?'

'409.'

'It is your recollection that the defendant was holding a gun in her hand at the time of the accident?'

'Yes.'

'Did you see that gun after the accident?'

'I did not.'

'Did you look at her hands after the accident to see whether she was still holding the gun?'

'I did not, but I don't think the gun was in her hands. I think it had been thrown out somewhere and was doubtless lying on the grass.'

'No further questions,' Mason said.

Hamilton Burger thought for a moment, then said, 'If the Court please, that's our case.'

'Well,' Judge Erwood said, 'it's not a particularly robust case, but the Court can well understand that it is only a technicality which keeps it from being a *very* robust case. This is, of course, the second time the facts in this case have been called to the Court's attention. Does the defence wish to make any showing, Mr Mason?'

'It does, Your Honour.'

'Very well, put on whatever evidence you have,' Judge Erwood said in a tone which plainly indicated that evidence would do no good.

'My first witness is Beatrice Cornell,' Mason said.

Beatrice Cornell took the stand, testified to her name, address and occupation.

'Was the defendant, Dawn Manning, listed with you as one of the models you had available to be sent out on photographic work?'

'She was.'

'And that was on the eighth of this month?'

'Yes.'

'On the ninth of this month did someone ask you to have Dawn Manning go out on a job?'

'Yes.'

'And did you have occasion to see Dawn Manning's body, particularly the area around her left hip, on that date?'

'I did.'

'Can you describe the condition of that hip?'

'From the hipbone down along the thigh, she was scraped. Part of the scraping was simply a mild scrape which had left a bruise and a discoloration, but there were two or three places where the skin had been taken completely away.'

'Leaving unsightly bruises?' Mason asked.

'Yes.'

'Do you know whether she was photographed on the morning of the ninth?'

'She was.'

'I show you a colour photograph and ask you what that picture is.'

'It is a picture showing Dawn Manning, taken on the ninth. It shows the condition of her left thigh and the left hip.'

'Cross-examine,' Mason said to Hamilton Burger.

The district attorney smiled. 'In other words, Miss Cornell, everything that you have noticed substantiates the story told by the prosecution's witness, Loretta Harper, that the defendant had been in an accident the night before?'

'Yes.'

'Thank you,' Hamilton Burger said, bowing and smiling. 'That's all.' And then he couldn't resist turning to Mason and bowing and smiling and saying, 'And thank *you*, Mr Mason.'

'Not at all,' Mason told him. 'My next witness will be Morley Edmond.'

Morley Edmond was called to the stand, qualified himself as an expert photographer, a member of several photographic societies, a veteran of several salon exhibitions, winner of numerous photographic awards, contributor to various photographic magazines.

'I now show you certain pictures of the defendant which have heretofore been introduced in evidence, and ask you if you are familiar with those pictures.'

'I am.'

'You've seen them before?'

'I've studied them carefully.'

'I will ask you if you are familiar with the studio camera which was in the photographic studio of Meridith Borden.'

'I am.'

'Can you tell us whether or not these pictures were taken with that camera?'

'I can.'

'Were they?'

'Just a minute, just a minute,' Hamilton Burger said. 'Don't answer that question until I have an opportunity to interpose an objection. Your Honour, this is something I have never encountered before in all of my experience. This question calls for an opinion and a conclusion of a witness in a matter where the physical evidence speaks for itself. Of course the pictures were taken with that camera. They were found in the camera.'

'What is your specific objection?' Judge Erwood asked.

'That the question calls for the opinion of the witness, that no proper foundation has been laid, and that it is a case where the issue on which the witness is expected to testify cannot be covered by expert testimony.'

Judge Erwood looked at Perry Mason.

Mason merely smiled and said, 'We propose to *prove* to the Court that the pictures of the defendant were planted in that camera, that they couldn't have been taken with that camera.'

'But how in the world can you prove whether a picture was taken with a certain camera?' Judge Erwood asked.

'That,' Mason said, 'is what I am trying to illustrate to the Court.'

'I'll permit the question,' Judge Erwood said, leaning forward curiously. 'However, the Court would want to have some very, very good reasons from this expert, otherwise a motion to strike the testimony would be entertained.'

'We'll give the Court reasons,' Mason said. 'Just answer the question, Mr

Edmond. Were those pictures, in your opinion, taken with the Meridith Borden camera?'

'They were not.'

'And on what reasons do you base your opinion?'

'The size of the image.'

'Explain what you mean by that.'

'The size of the image on a photographic plate,' Edmond said, 'is determined by the focal length of the lens and the distance of the subject from the camera.

'If the lens has a very short focal length, with reference to the area that is to be covered, the lens usually gives a wider field of coverage on the photographic plate, but the size of the object is smaller. If the focal length of the lens is very large, with reference to the area of the plate, the image shown is shown in larger size but with a very small field.

'In order to get a proper plate coverage, it is generally conceded that the standard focal length of the lens should be the diagonal of the plate to be covered. However, in portrait work it is generally considered that a focal-length lens of one and a half or two times the diagonal will result in more pleasing proportions.

'A rather simple illustration of what I mean has doubtless been noticed by Your Honour in television photography. When the television camera is focused, for instance, on the second baseman, a long focal-length lens is used in order to build up the image. At that time, if the Court has perhaps noticed, the centre fielder seems to be within only a few feet of the second baseman. In other words, the perspective is distorted so that it no longer bears the ordinary relationship which the eye has accepted as standard in photographic reproductions.

'To some extent, this principle makes for a better portrait of a face, and, therefore, the longer focal-length lens is used in portrait photography.'

'But what does all this have to do with whether the picture of the defendant was taken with Meridith Borden's camera?' Judge Erwood asked.

'Simply this, Your Honour: The full-length picture of the defendant shown on the photographic films occupies but little more than one-half of the perpendicular distance. With the longer focal-length lens used by Meridith Borden in his camera, and taking into consideration the dimensions of his studio, it is a physical impossibility to take a full-length which will occupy only one-half of the perpendicular distance of the film. Even if the camera is placed at one corner of the studio and the model at the other corner so that we have the maximum distance permitted within the room, the image on a five-by-seven plate or cut film would be materially larger than that shown on the developed plates.

'Therefore, I have been forced to the inescapable conclusion that these pictures of the defendant were taken with some other camera and then, before those pictures were developed, the film holders were placed in the Meridith Borden studio, and one of the film holders bearing an exposed film was placed inside the camera itself.

'However, for the physical reasons stated, none of these pictures could have been taken with the Borden camera.'

'Cross-examine,' Mason said.

Hamilton Burger's voice was sharp with sarcasm. 'You think because you found a certain focal-length lens in the Borden camera, the photographs of the defendant couldn't have been taken with that camera and that lens.'

'I know that they couldn't have been.'

'Despite the fact that all the physical evidence shows that they must have been taken with that camera?'

'That is right.'

'In other words, you're like the man who went to the zoo, saw a giraffe and said, "There isn't any such animal".'

There was laughter in the court-room.

'That question is facetious, Mr District Attorney,' Judge Erwood said.

'I think not, Your Honour. I think it is perfectly permissible.'

'I have made no objection,' Mason said.

'I'm not like that man at all,' the witness said. 'I know photography and I now what can be done and what can't be done. I have made test exposures using a duplicate of the Borden camera, and at various distances. I used a model having exactly the same measurements as the defendant as far as height is concerned. Those pictures were taken on five-by-seven films with a lens that had the same focal length as that in the Borden camera. I have compared the image sizes. I can produce those films, if necessary.'

'No further questions,' Hamilton Burger said. '*I'm* going to rely on the physical evidence in this case, and I think His Honour will also.'

'Call James Goodwin to the stand,' Mason said.

James Goodwin testified that he was an architect, that he had designed the apartment house known as the Dormain Apartments, that he had his various plans showing the apartment house, and he identified and introduced in evidence a floor plan of the fourth floor.

Hamilton Burger gave a contemptuous glance at the floor plan and said, 'No questions,' when Mason turned the witness over for cross-examination.

'That's all of our evidence, Your Honour,' Mason said.

'Do you have any rebuttal?' Judge Erwood asked Hamilton Burger.

'None, Your Honour. It certainly appears that there is reasonable ground to believe the defendant committed the crime. The testimony of Loretta Harper standing alone is sufficient to warrant an order binding the defendant over.'

'May I be heard in argument?' Mason asked.

'I don't think it is necessary, Mr Mason, nor do I think it would do any good. However, I'll not preclude you from arguing the case.'

'Thank you, Your Honour.'

'The prosecution has the right to open the argument,' Judge Erwood said.

Hamilton Burger, smiling, said, 'We waive our opening argument.'

'Proceed, Mr Mason,' Judge Erwood said.

'If the Court please,' Mason said, 'I claim that this case is a frame-up. Those pictures of the defendant were not taken in Meridith Borden's photographic studio. We have the evidence of the camera expert that the photographs could not have been taken with Meridith Borden's camera. And now, if the Court please, I will call the Court's attention to one other item of physical evidence. The Court will note that according to the testimony of Loretta Harper, the defendant had been thrown from the car and had skidded along on her hip. Thereafter, the witness had dragged the defendant a still further distance on her hip.

'The Court will notice that the next day the hip of the defendant was so bruised and scraped that she could not pose as a model for any so-called cheesecake shots.

'Now then, if the Court will carefully examine the photographs which purport to have been taken with the camera in Meridith Borden's studio at a time *after* the accident, the Court will find irrefutable evidence that these pictures were taken at some time prior to the night of the murder and then planted in the Borden camera.

'Bear in mind that this defendant is a professional model. She poses almost daily for amateur photographers who are interested in various types of photography, particularly the so-called cheesecake pictures.

'It would have been readily possible for any accomplice to have paid this defendant her posing rate, have taken these pictures and then have held them for as long a period of time as desired until finally turning them over to the murderer of Meridith Borden to be planted in the camera of the victim.

'If the Court will carefully study the left hip of the defendant, as shown in the Borden photographs, the Court will see that there are absolutely no grass stains, no mud stains, no scrapes, no blemishes of any sort. It would have been a physical impossibility for the defendant to have been photographed immediately after that accident without some of these defects showing.

'For the benefit of the Court, I wish to call the Court's attention to this picture of the defendant which was taken the day after the accident, and which shows the extent of the scrapes and bruises on the defendant's left hip.

'The Court will notice that the defendant worked at the Valley View Hardware Company until her marriage. In other words, it is reasonable to suppose that Frank Ferney was courting her during the time she was engaged as a clerk in that store.

'Someone stole the murder weapon from the store. That thief was a man. If the defendant had been dishonest enough to steal a weapon for her own protection, she would have taken one of the small automatics of a type that could be placed in her handbag. This weapon is a man's weapon. It was stolen by a man. It is reasonable to suppose that Frank Ferney was in and out of the store many times, and, enjoying the confidence of the defendant, that he was permitted behind the counter.

'Turning to the so-called time schedule, or alibi of Frank Ferney, I ask the Court to notice the plans which have been introduced by James Goodwin showing the fourth floor of the apartment house where Loretta Harper has her apartment.

'It is to be remembered that Frank Ferney was supposed to have passed out and to have been placed in this bedroom to sleep it off. The Court will notice that the fire escape runs right past this bedroom in 409. It was a simple matter for Ferney to slip out of the window, go down the fire escape, go to Meridith Borden's house, commit the murder and return in time to be aroused from his apparent sleep when Loretta Harper came in to tell the spectacular story of her kidnapping.

'I think it is a fair inference that there was a deliberate attempt on the part of Loretta Harper and Frank Ferney to kill Meridith Borden and to do it under such circumstances that the crime would be blamed on this defendant.

'The evidence of that frame-up not only exists in the extrinsic evidence in this case, but, if the Court will carefully study the pictures which were taken of this defendant, and which were in Meridith Borden's camera, the court will realize that those pictures simply couldn't have been taken on the night of the murder.'

Mason sat down.

Judge Erwood frowned, said, 'Let me look at those pictures.'

He started comparing the Borden pictures with the photograph Mason had taken of the hip of Dawn Manning.

Hamilton Burger jumped to his feet. 'That's all very simple, Your Honour. Just a little retouching would have fixed up those pictures.'

'But these pictures haven't been retouched,' Judge Erwood said. 'The films are here in Court.'

Hamilton Burger slowly sat down.

Abruptly Judge Erwood reached his decision. 'I think some more investigative work needs to be done in this case,' he said. 'I am going to dismiss the case and discharge the defendant from custody. The Court is satisfied there is something peculiar here, and the Court feels that there should be a much more careful check of the evidence.

'The defendant is discharged, the case is dismissed, and Court is adjourned.'

16

Perry Mason, Della Street, Paul Drake, George Ansley and Dawn Manning sat in the lawyer's private office.

'Well,' Dawn Manning said, 'I have to hand it to you, Mr Mason. I certainly thought you had tossed me to the wolves.'

'I did,' Mason admitted, 'but then I came along with another car and picked you up before the wolves got there.'

'Just what do you think happened?' Della Street asked.

Mason said, 'I think that Meridith Borden had caught Frank Ferney in some theft or embezzlement. I believe Borden handled large sums of money in the form of cash which were passed out here and there as bribes and which were received by various people. Borden didn't care to have cheques made so they could be traced on his bank account. He didn't give cheques.

'It is reasonable to suppose that with that much cash around, Frank Ferney had managed to embezzle some. The probabilities are he was about to be discovered, or perhaps he had been discovered and Borden had decided to report the case to the police.

'An elaborate plan was worked out by which Dawn Manning would have been brought on the grounds immediately after nine o'clock and then left there. She would have been escorted to the photographic studio by Loretta Harper. In the meantime, Frank Ferney would apparently have been nowhere around. Loretta Harper, who was driving a stolen car so that the car and the driver couldn't be traced from the licence plates, would have asked Dawn to excuse her for a moment, telling Dawn to go ahead and run up to the studio. Then Loretta would have vanished. She would have been back at her apartment in time to corroborate Frank Ferney's alibi.

'However, everything depended upon split-second timing. It was necessary to kill Meridith Borden precisely at a certain minute, so that Ferney could get back to the apartment house, climb up the fire escape and get into bed. The understanding was that he was to be aroused in order to keep his appointment with Dr Callison.

'Ferney carried out his end of the bargain right on schedule. George Ansley's visit had been unexpected. As soon as Ansley left and Borden had telephoned the inspectors, Ferney lured Meridith Borden up into the studio and killed him. Then he waited impatiently for the arrival of the car with Dawn Manning.

'For reasons that we know, that car didn't arrive.

'That called on Ferney to do some quick thinking. For one thing, he decided he'd have to change the time of the murder to a time when Loretta Harper would also have an alibi. Dr Callison was going to be his alibi.

'It wasn't until the next day, after it was seen how far their original plan had gone awry, that it was decided to plant the murder gun in the glove compartment of George Ansley's automobile and blame the murder on him. For a while they thought they could get away with it. Then, when it appeared that I was knocking holes in their case against Ansley, Loretta Harper, who was the shrewder of the pair, signalled Frank Ferney to go back to their original plan and blame the crime on Dawn Manning.'

The telephone rang.

Della Street picked up the receiver, said, 'It's for you, Paul.'

Drake took the phone, listened for several moments, then said, 'Thanks, let me know if there are any more details.' He hung up and turned to Mason.

'Well,' he said, 'your hunch was right. Ferney has just broken down and confessed. The details are just about the way you figured them. Ferney knew that he was trapped, so now he's trying to blame Loretta as the originator of the scheme. The D.A. found a witness who saw a man going down the fire escape from the fourth floor of the Dormain Apartments. If the police had been on the job, they'd have had the information long ago, because the witness telephoned in to the police station to report a prowler. The Mesa Vista police went out, looked the place over and then did nothing more about it.'

'Well,' Dawn Manning said, 'I've heard of people getting out of trouble by the skin of their eyeteeth. I never thought it would apply to me.'

There was a twinkle in Della Street's eye. 'Not your eyeteeth,' she said demurely.

RLE STANLEY GARDNER

The Case of

The Deadly Toy

I

With the politeness that characterized everything he did, Mervin Selkirk said to Norda Allison, 'Excuse me, please.'

Then he leaned forward and slapped the child's face–hard.

'Little gentlemen,' he said to his seven-year-old son, 'don't interrupt when people are talking.'

Then Mervin Selkirk settled back in his chair, lit a cigarette, turned to Norda Allison and said, 'As you were saying . . .?'

But Norda couldn't go on. She was looking at the hurt eyes of the child, and realized suddenly that that wasn't the first time his father had slapped him like that.

Humiliated, fighting back bitter tears in order to be 'a little man', the boy turned away, paused in the doorway to say, 'Excuse me, please,' then left the room.

'That's his mother's influence,' Mervin Selkirk explained. 'She believes in discipline from a theoretical standpoint, but she can't be bothered putting it into practical execution. Whenever Robert returns from visiting with her in Los Angeles, it's a job getting him back on the beam.'

Suddenly in that instant Norda saw Mervin Selkirk in his true character. The indolent, smiling politeness, the affable courtesy of his manner, was a mask. Beneath the partially contemptuous, partially amused but always polite manner with which he regarded the world, was a sadistic streak, an inherent selfishness which covered itself with a veneer of extreme politeness.

Abruptly Norda was on her feet, stunned not only by her discovery, but by the clarity with which her new realization of Mervin's character came into mental focus.

'I'm afraid I'm bushed, Mervin,' she said. 'I'm going to have to leave you now. I've been fighting a beastly headache, and I'm going home to see if some aspirin and a little rest won't help.'

He jumped up to stand beside her. His left hand reached out and caught her wrist in a tight grip.

'Your headache was rather sudden, Norda.'

'Yes.'

'Is there anything I can do?'

'No.'

He hesitated then, just as he had hesitated for a moment before slapping the child. She felt him gathering forces for an onslaught.

Then it came with no preliminary.

'So you can't take it.'

'Can't take what?'

'Disciplining a child. You're a softie.'

'I'm not a softie, but there are ways of disciplining children,' she said.

'Robert is sensitive; he's intelligent and he's proud. You could have waited until I had left and explained to him that it wasn't gentlemanly to interrupt, then he'd have accepted the correction.

'You didn't do that. You humiliated him in front of me. You undermined his self-respect, and–'

'That will do,' Mervin Selkirk said coldly. 'I don't need a lecture on parental discipline from an unmarried woman.'

'I think,' Norda said quietly, 'I'm just beginning to really know you.'

'You don't know me yet,' he told her, his eyes threatening and hard. 'I want you, and what I want I get. Don't think you can walk out on me. I've noticed lately that you've been talking quite a bit about that Benedict chap who works in the office with you. Perhaps you don't realize how frequently you're quoting him. It's Nate this and Nate that.–Remember this, Norda, you've announced your engagement to me. I won't let any woman humiliate me. You've promised to marry me and you're going through with it.'

For a moment his fingers were like steel on her wrists, his eyes were deadly. And then, almost instantly, the mask came back. He said contritely: 'But I shouldn't bother you with these things when you're not feeling well. Come, dear, I'll take you home . . . . I'm really sorry about Robert. That is, I'm sorry if I hurt you. But, you see, I happen to know Robert quite well, and I think I know *exactly* how he should be handled.'

That night, after giving the matter a lot of thought, Norda wrote a formal letter breaking her engagement to Mervin Selkirk.

Three nights later she went out with Nathan Benedict for the first time. They went to the restaurant which Nate knew was Norda's favourite. There was no incident. Two nights later Mervin called to ask if he might talk with her. 'It won't do any good,' she told him. 'Anyway, I'm going out tonight.'

'With Nate?' he asked. 'I understand you let him take you to *our* restaurant.'

'It's none of your business,' she snapped and slammed the phone back into its cradle.

Later on when the phone rang repeatedly she didn't answer it.

Nate came for her promptly at eight.

He was tall, slender in build, with wavy, dark-brown hair and expressive eyes. They went once more to the same restaurant.

There was some delay at the table reservation. It was suggested they wait in the cocktail lounge.

Norda didn't see Mervin Selkirk until it was too late, nor could she swear afterwards that he had actually thrust out his foot so that Nathan Benedict stumbled.

There were plenty of witnesses to what happened after that.

Mervin Selkirk got to his feet, said: 'Watch who you're pushing,' and hit Benedict flush on the jaw.

As Benedict went down with a broken jaw, two of Mervin's friends, who were seated at the table, jumped up to grab his arms. 'Take it easy, Merv,' one of them said.

There was a commotion, with waiters swarming around them, and eventually the police. Norda had been certain she had seen a glint of metal as Mervin Selkirk's right hand had flashed across in that carefully timed, perfectly executed smash.

The surgeon who wired Benedict's broken jaw was confident the injuries had been caused by brass knuckles. However, police had searched Selkirk at

Norda's insistence and had found no brass knuckles; nor were there any on the friend who was with Selkirk and who volunteered to let the police search him. The second friend who had been with Selkirk had disappeared before the police came. He had had an engagement, Selkirk explained, and he didn't want to be detained by a lot of formalities. He would, however, be available if anybody tried to make anything of it.

Selkirk's story was quite simple. He had been sitting with his friends. His back was to the door. Benedict, in passing, had not only stepped on his foot, but had kicked back at his shin. He had got to his feet. Benedict had doubled his fist. Mervin Selkirk admitted he had beat Benedict to the punch.

'What else was there to do?' he asked.

A week after that, Norda Allison began to get the letters. They were mailed from Los Angeles, sent air mail to San Francisco. They were in plain stamped envelopes. Each envelope contained newspaper clippings; sometimes one, sometimes two or three. All of the clippings dealt with stories of those tragedies which are so common in the press: The divorced husband who couldn't live without his wife, who had followed her as she walked from the bus and shot her on the street. The jilted suitor who had gone on a drinking spree, had then invaded the apartment where his former fiancée lived and fired five shots into her body. The drink-crazed man who had walked into the office where his former girl friend was working, had said: 'I can't live without you. If I can't have you, no one else will.' Despite her screams and pleading, he had shot her through the head, then turned the gun on himself.

Norda, naturally, had seen such stories in the press, but since they hadn't concerned her, she had read them casually. Now she was startled to find how many such cases could be assembled when one diligently clipped stories from the papers of half a dozen large cities.

She went to a lawyer. The lawyer called in the postal authorities. The postal authorities went to work and the letters continued to come.

It was impossible to get any proof. The person mailing the letters evidently wore gloves. There was never so much as the smudge of a fingerprint which could be developed in iodine vapour. The envelopes were mailed in drop boxes in various parts of Los Angeles. Norda Allison's name and address had been set in type on a small but efficient printing machine, such as those frequently given children for Christmas.

At the suggestion of Norda's lawyer, Lorraine Selkirk Jennings, Mervin's divorced wife, who was now living in Los Angeles with her second husband, was consulted. She remembered having given Robert a very expensive printing press for Christmas the year before. Robert had taken it to San Francisco when he went to visit his father. It was still there. Mervin Selkirk had, it seemed, enjoyed the press even more than his son.

This information gave Norda's lawyer ground for jubilation. 'Now we'll get him,' he gloated. Norda made an affidavit. Her attorney handled it from there. Police served a search warrant on Mervin Selkirk.

The printing press was located without difficulty. From the condition of the rollers, it was evident it hadn't been used for some time. Moreover, the experts gave it as their opinion that the envelopes had most certainly not been addressed on that press. The type was of a different sort.

Mervin Selkirk was excessively polite to the officers. He was only too glad to let them search the place. He was surprised to find Miss Allison had been having trouble. They had been engaged. He was quite fond of her. The engagement had been broken over a minor matter. Miss Allison was working altogether too hard and had been under great nervous tension. She had not been like herself for some weeks before the engagement was broken. If there was anything Mervin could do, he wanted it understood he was willing to help at any time. He would be only too glad to render any financial assistance in tracking down the persons who were annoying Miss Allison. The police were welcome to drop in at any time. As far as he was concerned, they didn't need any search warrant. His door would always be open to the authorities. And would they please convey to Miss Allison his sincere sympathy. He admitted he had tried to call her himself a couple of times, but she had hung up as soon as she recognized his voice.

It wasn't until Lorraine Selkirk Jennings called long distance that Norda's frayed nerves began to give way.

'Was it the printing press?' she asked Norda.

'No,' Norda said. 'The press was there all right but it hadn't been used for some time.'

'That's just like him,' Lorraine said. 'I know exactly how his mind works. He saw Robert's press. He then went out and got one similar to it, but with different type. He probably printed about two hundred envelopes in advance, then he took the press out on his yacht and dropped it overboard. He knew you'd suspect him; that you'd find out about Robert's press and get a search warrant–that's his way of showing you how diabolically clever he is. I'm surprised you went with him as long as you did without recognizing the sort of man he is beneath his mask.'

Norda resented Lorraine's tone. 'At least I found out in time to avoid marrying him.'

Lorraine laughed. 'You were smarter than I was,' she admitted. 'But you'll remember I dropped you a note telling you not to be fooled.'

'I thought it was the result of jealousy,' Norda said somewhat ruefully.

'Heavens, I'm happily married again,' Lorraine said. 'I was trying to save you from what I'd gone through with him. . . . If I could only get sole custody of Robert, I wouldn't want anything more.'

Norda said apologetically: 'Of course, Mervin told me stories about you. I was in love with him–or thought I was–and it was only natural for me to believe him, since I'd never met you.'

'I understand,' Lorraine agreed sympathetically. 'Let's not underestimate either the man's cleverness or his ruthless determination, my dear. He'll stop at nothing and neither will his family.

'I tried to stick it out for Robert's sake, but I could take only so much. I left him when Robert was four and returned to Los Angeles, since it was my home.

'The family is even more powerful here than in San Francisco. They retained a battery of clever lawyers, hired detectives, and they threw mud all over me. Some of it stuck. Three witnesses perjured themselves about Robert and about me. Mervin managed to get part-time custody of Robert. He doesn't really care about Robert. He only wanted Robert so he could hurt me. I'm happily married now to a normal man, who's normally inconsiderate, who grumbles when things don't go to suit him and puts the blame on me for some of his own mistakes. I can't begin to tell you what an unspeakable relief it is.

'I'm terribly glad you broke the engagement, but don't underestimate Mervin. He simply can't stand being humiliated and he'll hound you until finally he gets you where you lose the will to resist.'

'Will he . . . I mean, is he . . . dangerous?' Norda asked.

'Of course he's dangerous,' Lorraine said. 'Perhaps not in the way you think, but he's scheming, cunning, completely selfish and cruel. He had detectives shadowing every move I made. . . . Of course you're not vulnerable that way, but be careful.'

Norda thanked her and hung up. She remembered the torrid charges Mervin had hurled against Lorraine at the time of the divorce. She remembered something of the testimony in the sensational trial, and Lorraine's tearful protests of innocence. At the time, Norda had not even met Mervin Selkirk and reading the newspapers she had considered Lorraine's charges of a frameup the last ditch defence of an erring wife who had been detected in indiscretion . . . after all, where there had been so much smoke there must have been some fire.

Now Norda wasn't so certain.

It was at this time that Norda made a discovery about law enforcement.

The officers were nice about it; were, in fact, exceedingly sympathetic. But they pointed out that they had their hands full trying to apprehend persons who had broken the law. They didn't have enough men to furnish 'protection' on a day-to-day basis.

To be sure, if they had definite evidence that a crime was about to be committed, they would assign men on what was technically known as 'stake-out'. That was the most they could do.

They knew hardly a day passed without some jealous estranged husband, some jilted suitor taking a gun and committing murder. The police would like to prevent those murders, but, as they pointed out, for every murder that was actually committed there were hundreds, perhaps thousands, of threats by neurotic individuals who were simply trying to 'throw a scare' into the recipient of their affections and so frighten her into reconciliation.

It was, the police pointed out, something like the women who threaten to commit suicide by taking sleeping pills if their lovers don't return. Many women actually had carried out such threats and had committed suicide. Many thousands of others did not.

The police told Norda that it took evidence to convict a person of crime. It took far more than mere guesswork. There had to be evidence which was legally admissible in a court of law, and, moreover, such evidence had to prove tne guilt of the accused beyond all reasonable doubt.

The police suggested that Norda Allison pay no attention to the clippings she was receiving in the mail. After all, they pointed out, the situation had existed now for some time and if Mervin Selkirk had really intended to resort to violence, he would have done so quite a bit earlier.

Norda reminded them of Nathan Benedict's broken jaw, but the police shrugged that aside. After all, the evidence in that case was in sharp conflict. Even Nathan Benedict admitted that he had 'stumbled' over Selkirk's foot. He had felt that Selkirk had deliberately tripped him; but the cocktail lounge was crowded, the light was poor, Benedict had been looking towards the bar and not down on the floor, and he could only surmise what must have happened. Since Selkirk was abundantly able to respond in damages, Benedict's recourse was a civil action for violent and unprovoked assault.

It was at this point that Lorraine Selkirk Jennings again telephoned Norda Allison.

'Norda,' she said excitedly, 'I have news for you. I can't tell it to you over the phone. It's something we can do that I feel certain will be of a lot of help. You can help me and I can help you. Can't you possibly come down? If you could catch a plane after office hours, my husband and I could meet you, and you could get back on the first plane in the morning. Or you could come Friday, have the week-end for a talk and get back without being all tired out.'

Lorraine sounded full of enthusiasm, but refused to give Norda even a hint of what she had in mind. So Norda agreed to fly down on Friday night, stay over Saturday and come back Sunday.

The next day she received two tickets in the mail, a flight down on United, a return flight on Western. There was a note from Lorraine:

My husband and I will meet the flight. Wear gloves, keep the left-hand glove on and carry your right-hand glove in your left hand. I don't drive any more. An accident I had left an indelible imprint but Barton is a wonderfully clever driver. We'll both meet you.

We got a ticket back on another airliner just in case anyone should be having you followed. Please take all precautions after you leave the office. Get a cab, be certain you're not being followed, then go to one of the hotels and switch to another cab before going to the airport. We'll meet you.

Norda read the letter with amusement. She saw no reason to pay out all that money in cab fares. She confided in Nate and it was Nate who picked her up in his car an hour and a half before the plane was scheduled to leave, made a series of complicated manoeuvres to be certain he was not being followed, and then drove her to the airport.

2

Coming up the runway at the Los Angeles Airport, at ten o'clock that night, Norda Allison looked anxiously at the little group of people who were surveying incoming passengers. She wore one glove on her left hand, carrying the right-hand glove conspicuously in her left hand.

Suddenly there was a flurry of motion and Lorraine was hugging her.

'Oh, Norda,' she said, 'I'm so glad–so glad you could make it! This is Barton Jennings, my husband–why, you're beautiful! No wonder Mervin is crazy about you!'

Norda shook hands with Barton Jennings, a stocky, quiet, substantial individual, and listened to Lorraine carry on a conversational marathon while they walked to the baggage claiming counter.

'You're going to stay with us,' Lorraine said. 'We have a nice spare room and we can put you up without any trouble. Barton is going over and get the car, then he'll drive around to pick us up and by that time your baggage will be ready. Let me have your baggage check, dear. I have a porter here who knows me.'

'What's it all about?' Norda asked.

'Norda, it's one of the greatest things you've ever seen. We're going to come out on top. I have the nicest attorney. His name is A. Dawling Crawford. Did you ever hear of him?'

Norda shook her head, said: 'I've heard of Perry Mason down here in this part of the state. I was told to get in touch with him if–'

'Oh, Perry Mason is for murder cases,' Lorraine interrupted, 'but Art

Crawford–that's his name, Arthur, but he always signs it A. Dawling Crawford for some reason–is an all-round lawyer. He handles criminal cases and everything else. Norda, I'm so excited! We're going to get sole custody of Robert. I'm going to want you to testify, and–'

'Want *me* to testify!' Norda exclaimed.

Lorraine handed Norda's baggage check to a porter, said: 'Why, yes of *course*, Norda. You understand the situation and I know that you are fond of Robert.'

'But wait a minute,' Norda protested, 'I thought from what you said over the telephone this was something that was going to benefit *me*. All I want to do is to get Mervin Selkirk out of my hair. I want to get away from him. I want him to forget me. I want to quit receiving those newspaper clippings. I certainly don't want to get involved with him again.'

'But that's just the point,' Lorraine explained. 'Mr Crawford tells me that if you appear in court and testify on our behalf, then it's almost certain that Mervin will make some threats against you and *then* we can go to the judge and state that those threats were made because you are a witness in the case. Then the judge will make an order restraining him. Then it will be contempt of court if he does anything further.'

'Listen,' Norda said patiently, 'he's done everything short of attempting murder and I'm not at all satisfied but what he'll do that next. It isn't going to be much satisfaction for me to be a corpse and to know that Mervin Selkirk is held for contempt of court. I don't care how good an attorney you have, you have to have *proof* before you can do anything. And that's just what we can't get at the present time–proof.'

'But we have proof,' Lorraine said. 'We have a witness to whom Mervin said he didn't really have any love for Robert, that he only wanted part-time custody of him to teach me a lesson.'

'That's fine,' Norda said coldly, 'for you. It doesn't help me with *my* problem.'

'But you aren't going to let me down,' Lorraine wailed.

'I don't know,' Norda said, 'but I do know I'm not going to get mixed up in any of Mervin Selkirk's affairs until I know exactly where I stand. I'm going to see an attorney of my own.'

'This is Friday night,' Lorraine said. 'You can't see anyone over the week-end. Mr Crawford has made arrangements to be at his office tomorrow shortly before noon so he can take your affidavit.'

Norda stood by the incoming baggage platform, thoughtfully silent.

'You aren't going to let us down. You can't,' Lorraine went on. 'It isn't only for me, it's for Robert. You've seen him. You know what this means to Robert. You're anxious to get away from the Selkirk family, but think of poor Robert.

'I've been trying for the last two years to get Robert's exclusive custody. Every time the matter comes up, Mervin goes into court and blandly testifies to absolute falsehoods. I am cast in the role of a woman who is trying to strike at my former husband, and Mervin is poised, suave and quite sure of himself. The last time this thing came up I told of how frightened Robert was of his father and Mervin gravely told the judge that I was solely responsible for Robert's attitude, that I had carefully and deliberately poisoned Robert's mind. Then Mervin produced witnesses who swore Mervin was the personification of fatherly love when Robert was with him.

'The judge was impressed. He made an order that Robert was to spend two months out of every year with Mervin and that I was to be particularly careful not to discuss Mervin with the boy. Then the judge continued the case for seven months.

'The seven months are up a week from Monday. Now, with this new testimony, and with your testimony, we can show Mervin up for just the sort of a man he really is. Then I can get the sole custody of Robert, and–'

'I'm not so sure you can,' Norda interrupted. 'Remember I only saw him slap Robert's face once.'

'But you *saw* it!' Lorraine insisted. 'You saw the way he did it; the hardness of the slap. You saw him reach out in that deadly, self-contained way of his and slap a little child half across the room.'

'It wasn't half across the room.'

'Well, it was a hard slap.'

'Yes,' Norda conceded, 'it was a hard slap.'

'Administered in front of company and only because he had interrupted you with some childish request.'

Norda remained dubious, feeling somehow that she had been tricked. 'After all, Lorraine, I was almost one of the family. Robert called me "Aunt Norda" and he couldn't have been expected to be as formally polite with me as with a stranger!'

'Of course,' Lorraine agreed. 'That's what makes the cruelty of it all the more flagrant.'

Norda turned to Barton Jennings, but he forestalled the question. 'Don't look at me,' he laughed. 'I'm just the guy who drives the car. Lorraine's troubles with her former spouse are out of bounds for me. If he comes around me, I'll bounce a hammer off his head. I don't want any part of him, but I'm trying desperately to keep out of Lorraine's private affairs. I'll furnish whatever financial help is needed. . . . Of course, I'm crazy about Robert.'

'Who isn't?' Norda laughed. 'By the way, where is he? I had hoped you'd bring him.'

'He's leaving early in the morning for a four-day camping trip,' Lorraine explained. 'It's a great event for him because he can sleep out and take his dog with him. Frankly, we didn't tell him you were coming. You have no idea how much he cares for you. If he'd known you were coming I know he'd have preferred to stay and visit with you . . . and then there would have been speculation as to why you were here and all that.

'We don't want Robert to know anything about all this. We think it's better that way. There'll be time for a visit with you on some more propitious occasion. You must come and spend a week with us after all of this is ironed out.'

Norda was silent, thinking of Robert, knowing how fond he was of her, wondering what would have happened if she hadn't broken the engagement but had gone ahead and married Robert's father. . . . Then it suddenly dawned upon her that had she done so, Mervin would have undoubtedly have used her affection for Robert and the child's regard for her as a lever to get at least half-time custody of Robert.

With a sudden shock she wondered if Lorraine had ever considered this possibility.

As soon as she had that thought, she felt certain Lorraine had at least explored the possibilities. It wouldn't be like her not to have thought of that. Any woman would have. And Mervin had admitted a reluctant admiration for

Lorraine's foresight and mental agility. 'There's one thing about my former wife,' he had told Norda, 'she never overlooks a bet. She is constantly chattering and has a baby-face, but she's as cold-bloodedly accurate as an adding machine and she lies awake nights thinking of the things that will happen if such and such takes place.'

Norda's thoughts were interrupted by Lorraine, who had been studying her face. 'At least, Norda, you'll come out to spend the night with us and then talk with our lawyer tomorrow morning. I know you'll see things in a different way after that.'

At that point Norda would have much preferred to have gone to a hotel, but Lorraine was so insistent that she permitted herself to be driven to the Jenning's home in Beverly Hills.

She asked where Robert was sleeping and was told he was in a tent in the patio. Of late he had become quite an out-of-door character, watching television shows featuring the famous plainsmen of the west. He had finally insisted on moving from his bedroom and sleeping outside.

Lorraine said they usually had a baby-sitter for him when they were out. Tonight, however, both of their favourite baby-sitters were tied up and couldn't come. So they had waited until Robert was asleep in his tent in the patio, and then had driven to the airport.

They had known he would be quite safe because Rover would be on guard. Rover was the Great Dane Lorraine had insisted on keeping when she had made her property settlement with Mervin. Norda had heard Robert talk about the dog, and then she herself had been 'introduced' to the animal once when Robert was visiting Mervin.

The dog was a huge creature with great dignity and expressive eyes. He had taken to Norda and to her delight had remembered her when he had next seen her, waving his tail and showing his pleasure when she stroked his forehead.

Barton Jennings went to the back door to look out in the patio. He reported everything was all right, that Rover was asleep where he could keep one eye on the house, one on Robert's tent.

Norda asked about going out to speak to the dog, but Barton said he'd probably get excited, make a noise and waken Robert.

Once Robert knew Norda was there, Lorraine said, he'd be certain to refuse to go on the camping trip and that wouldn't be fair to the other boys, or to Robert himself.

There was something in her voice that gave Norda a vague sense of disquiet. Robert and Norda had been great pals. She felt she had won Robert's complete confidence. Was it possible there was an element of jealousy on the part of Lorraine?

She dismissed the thought as soon as it occurred to her, pleaded fatigue from a long day, and was shown to her bedroom, a second-floor front room on the north-west side of the house.

3

Perry Mason latch-keyed the door of his private office to find his secretary, Della Street, waiting for him.

Mason made a little grimace of distaste. 'Saturday morning,' he said, 'and I have to drag you out to work.'

'The price of success,' Della Street told him smilingly.

'Well, you're good-natured about it, anyway.'

Della Street made a sweeping gesture, which included the office, the desk with its pile of correspondence, the open law books which Mason was to use in the brief he was about to dictate, 'It's my life and it's yours. We may as well face it.'

'But it's work,' Mason said, watching her face. 'There are times when it must be sheer drudgery for you.'

'It's more fascinating than any type of play,' she said. 'Are you ready?'

She opened her notebook and held a pen poised over the page.

Mason sighed and settled into his chair.

The private unlisted telephone rang.

There were only three people in the world who had the number of that telephone. Perry Mason himself, Della Street, his confidential secretary, and Paul Drake, head of the Drake Detective Agency, which had offices on the same floor with Perry Mason.

'How does Paul know we're here?' Mason asked.

'He saw me coming up in the elevator,' Della Street said. 'He told me he had something he might bother us with. I warned him that you wouldn't interrupt dictation this morning for anything short of murder.'

Mason picked up the telephone. 'Hello, Paul. What's the trouble?'

Drake's voice came over the wire. 'Despite the fact Della told me you are working on an important brief this morning and don't want to be disturbed, Perry, I thought I should call you. There's a young woman in my office who insists she *must* see you. She's really worked up, almost hysterical, and ....'

Mason frowned. 'I can't see anyone this morning, Paul. Perhaps this afternoon . . . how did she happen to come to you?'

'The telephone directory,' Drake explained. 'Your office number is listed for day-time calls and then my number is given for night calls and on Saturdays. She called the office and sounded so worked up that I decided I'd talk with her. I hadn't intended to pass her on to you, but I think you may want to talk with her, Perry.'

'What's her name?'

'Norda Allison.'

'What's it about?'

'It's quite a story. You'll like her. She's good-looking, clean-cut, fresh and unspoiled. And this trouble of hers has engulfed her. She feels she should go to the police, she thinks she's probably in danger, and yet she doesn't know just what to do.'

Mason hesitated a moment, then said: 'All right, Paul, send her down. Tell her to knock on the door of the private office and I'll let her in.'

'A young woman, I take it,' Della Street said. 'I gather Paul Drake told you she was very good-looking.'

Mason raised his eyebrows in surprise. 'How did you know that? Could you hear what he said?'

Della Street laughed. 'You impressionable men! She's sold Paul Drake and now she's selling you.'

'It'll only be a short time,' Mason promised. 'We'll give her fifteen or twenty minutes to tell her story, and then we'll get on with the brief.'

Della Street smiled knowingly, made it a point to close her shorthand notebook, put the cap back on her pen.

'I see,' she said demurely.

A timid knock sounded at the door of Mason's private office.

Della Street crossed over and opened the door.

'Good morning,' she said to Norda Allison. 'I'm Della Street, Mr Mason's secretary, and this is Mr Mason. What's your name, please?'

Norda Allison stood in the doorway, seemingly in something of a daze. 'I'm Norda Allison,' she said, 'from San Francisco. I . . . oh, I'm so sorry to bother you this morning. Mr Drake told me you were working behind closed doors on a most important matter, but . . . well, I'd always heard that if anyone got into trouble–that is real serious trouble–Mr Mason was the man to see, and . . . .'

Her voice trailed away into silence.

Della Street, giving the visitor the benefit of a swift and professional appraisal, indicated her approval. 'Come in, Miss Allison. Mr Mason is very busy, but if you can tell your story just as succinctly as possible, perhaps he can help you. Please try and be brief.'

'But give us *all* the facts,' Mason warned.

Norda Allison seated herself, said: 'Are you acquainted with the Selkirk family?'

'*The* Selkirks?' Mason asked. 'Horace Livermore Selkirk?'

She nodded.

'He owns about half the city down here,' Mason said dryly. 'What about him?'

'I was engaged to his son, Mervin.'

Mason frowned. 'Mervin is in San Francisco, isn't he?'

She nodded. 'I'm from San Francisco.'

'All right, go ahead,' Mason said, 'tell us what happened.'

She said: Mervin has been married before. His wife, Lorraine, is now married to Barton Jennings. There was one child of the first marriage, Robert. I am very fond of him and I was, of course, fond of Mervin.'

Mason nodded.

Swiftly, Norda told Mason of her experiences with Mervin Selkirk, of her trip to Los Angeles, of spending the night at the Jenning's house.

'I take it something happened at the house last night that upset you?' Mason asked.

She nodded. 'I was nervous. I went to bed and took a sleeping pill. The doctor told me this campaign of sending me newspaper clippings was doing me more harm than I realized. He gave me some quieting pills to take at night when I felt on edge.

'Last night, after I found out what Lorraine really wanted, I was terribly upset. When that first pill didn't quiet my nerves, I got up and took another. That really did the trick.'

Mason watched her shrewdly. 'Something happened during the night?' he asked.

She nodded. 'It was this morning. However, I did think I heard–a shot in the night.'

'A shot?' Mason asked.

She nodded. 'At least I thought it was a shot. I started to get up, and then I heard a boy crying. I guess that must have been Robert, but that second sleeping pill really laid me out. I kept thinking I *should* get up, but put off doing do, and then I guess I just went back to sleep.'

'All right,' Mason said. 'What happened when you finally wakened?'

'It was this morning, really early–I guess it must have been before six o'clock. I got up and there was no one around the house. I dressed and walked downstairs and opened the front door. I walked back to the patio. Robert's tent was there, the flaps of the tent were open. There was a camp cot inside with a sleeping bag, but the tent was empty. Robert had left for his camping trip. The dog went with him.'

'What happened?' Mason asked. 'Please tell me what upset you.'

'I saw an envelope on the grass under the cot in the tent,' she said. 'It was an envelope exactly the same as the ones I had been receiving. My name was printed on it. Robert had started a letter to me.'

She opened her purse, handed Mason a sheet of paper which had words pencilled on it in a childish scrawl:

Dear Aunt Norda:

I found this inveloape in the basment. It has your name on it. I will rite you and put it in. I want you to come see me. I am going to camp with Rover. I have a gun. We are all well. I love you.

Robert

Mason's eyes narrowed. 'Go on. What did you do after you found this envelope?'

Her lips tightened. 'The stamp was uncancelled. My name and address were printed on it. It was exactly the same as the envelopes I had been receiving. Robert's letter said he had found it in the basement. I tiptoed to the back door. There was a flight of stairs from the porch leading down to a rumpus-room. Back of the rumpus-room was a store-room . . . well, it was there I found it.'

'Found what?'

'The printing press.'

'Do you mean the printing press that had been used to print the envelopes that you had been receiving in the mail?

She nodded. 'My name and my San Francisco address were still set in type on the press. The press was really a good grade of printing press, not just a toy. It had a round steel plate on top and there was printer's ink on this plate. Every time the handle was depressed, the rubber rollers would move over this inked table and the table would make a part of a revolution. Then the rollers would go down over the type and back out of the way, and the envelope or paper would be pushed up against the type.'

'You examined the press?' Mason asked.

'Of course I looked at it. As I said, I'd been trying to find a printing press of that sort. After I'd complained to the postal authorities and . . . and it turned out Robert's mother had given the child a press of that sort to play with and it was still in San Francisco . . . Of course, I went ahead and made the natural assumption that the envelopes had been printed on that press. That's typical of the way Mervin loves to play with people.'

'Go on,' Mason said. 'Tell me about the press you found this morning.'

'Well, this press had been freshly used. The ink was still sticky on it.'

'How do you know?'

She looked at the tip of her middle finger. 'I touched it and fresh ink came off on my finger.'

'Then what?' Mason asked.

'Then,' she said, 'I looked a little further and there was a box with a lot of freshly printed envelopes, the same kind of stamped envelopes that had been used in forwarding those threatening clippings to me. Don't you see? It's Lorraine Jennings who is back of all this. She has been trying to poison my mind against Mervin so I would co-operate in giving testimony when she tried to get full custody of Robert.'

'Now wait a minute,' Mason said. 'You're all mixed up. First you're talking about Mervin's diabolical ingenuity in having a printing press that would throw the authorities off the trail, and now you're making it appear that the whole thing was Lorraine Jennings's idea.'

Norda thought that over for a moment, then said: 'I guess I am confused, but . . . but whether I'm confused or not, I'm right. Now I suppose you'll say that sounds just like a woman–I don't care if you do–there are *other* things.'

'All right,' Mason said. 'What are they?'

She said: 'I know that a shot was fired during the night. I heard it.'

'You might have heard a truck backfire.'

'I heard a shot,' she said, 'and after that there was a sound of a boy crying. It must have been Robert. A woman was trying to comfort him. When I . . . well, when I went to the tent and looked around, I found an empty cartridge case, the kind that is ejected from a ·22 automatic, lying there on the grass.'

'What did you do with it?'

'I picked it up.'

'Where is it now?'

'I have it here.'

She opened her purse, took out the empty ·22 cartridge case and handed it to Mason.

The lawyer looked it over, smelled it, then placed the empty cartridge case upright on the desk. 'Did you take anything else?' he asked.

'Yes.'

'What?'

'Some of the envelopes that had been printed with my name on them. I took two of them out of the box.'

She took two folded stamped envelopes from her purse and handed them to Mason.

Mason studied the printed address. 'Well,' he said 'that's your name printed on there, and the address I assume is accurate?'

She nodded.

'And you think those are the same envelopes that ...'

'I'm sure of it, Mr Mason. I have here one of the envelopes which came through the mail with one of the newspaper clippings.'

She handed him another envelope.

Mason compared the envelopes for a moment, then shook out the newspaper clipping which had been contained in the envelope. It had headlines, JILTED SUITOR KILLS WOMAN. The clipping had a New York dateline and told of a jilted suitor who had waited until his ex-fiancée, who had become engaged to another man, had left the place where she was working. It was the lunch hour. He had accosted the woman on a crowded sidewalk. Frightened, the woman had turned to flee. The man had drawn a revolver, fired four shots into her, then as she lay dying on the sidewalk in front of a crowd of horror-stricken spectators, he had turned the gun on himself and blown his brains out.

Mason took a magnifying glass and compared the printing on the envelope that had been mailed, with the printing on the stamped, addressed envelope that Norda Allison had handed him.

'They seem to be the same, all right,' Mason said thoughtfully. 'What did you do after you made this discovery, Miss Allison?'

She said: 'I suppose I was a coward. I should have gone in and confronted them with the evidence but I was so disgusted at their double-crossing and . . . and I was a little frightened . . . I guess in a way I lost my head.'

'What did you *do*?'

'I didn't go through the house. I walked back out into the patio, around through the gate, into the front door which I had left unlocked, tiptoed up to the room where I had been sleeping, packed my suitcase and came downstairs. There was a telephone in the hall and I called a taxicab.'

'You didn't encounter anyone in the house?'

'No one. I think they were all sleeping.'

'What did you do after you took the taxicab?'

'I went to the Millbrae Hotel, registered, got a room, had breakfast and–well, at first I intended just to catch the first plane back to San Francisco. Then I kept thinking that . . . I can't explain the apprehension that I have, Mr Mason, the feeling that something is impending that . . . I think they're intending to say I . . . I did something . . . I have that feeling.'

'All right,' Mason said. 'There may or may not be any reason for it but there's only one thing for you to do.'

'What's that?' she asked.

'Strike first,' Mason told her. 'When you're worried and apprehensive, assume the offensive. No one knows that you found this printing press or the envelopes?'

She shook her head. 'I'm certain they don't. They were either asleep or else they had both gone with Robert to start him on his trip. There were no noises at all in the house. They told me to sleep as late as I could, that they'd call me in time to see the lawyer.'

Mason thought the situation over.

'Well anyway there's the printing press and the stamped, addressed envelopes,' he said. 'That's one clue we can accept as a tangible fact–that is, if you're being completely truthful with me.'

'I am. What are you going to do?'

'Call the postal inspectors. In the meantime we'll see that nothing happens to that printing press,' Mason said. '*Then* we're going to let Lorraine Jennings explain how those threatening letters came to you in the mail.'

'I thought that's what I should do,' she said. 'But it seemed so . . . so abrupt.

I thought perhaps I should ask them for an explanation. I thought perhaps you could call them and–'

'And by that time the evidence would be destroyed,' Mason said. 'No, we'll go out there and pick up that evidence right now, and *then* Mrs Jennings can explain how she happened to be sending you those letters.'

'Do I have to go along to show the officers where it is?'

'You have to go,' Mason told her, 'and I'm going with you. We'll get there before the officers.'

Suddenly her eyes filled with tears. 'Oh, thank you, thank you!' she exclaimed. 'Thank you so much, Mr Mason, you're . . . you're wonderful.'

4

Mason eased his car to a stop in front of the house Norda indicated.

'Well,' Mason said, 'they're undoubtedly up by now. I saw someone moving by the window.'

He opened the car door, went around and assisted Norda Allison and Della Street from the car. The trio walked up the wide cement walk to the porch and Mason rang the bell.

Lorraine Jennings opened the door.

'Well, for heaven's sake!' she exclaimed. 'What in the world *happened* to you, Norda? We thought you were sleeping and didn't want to disturb you, and then finally I went up to your room and tapped gently on the door. When there was no answer, I eased the door open and you were gone. What's more, your suitcase, your personal things . . . what in the *world* happened? And . . . who are these people?'

'Permit me,' Mason said. 'My name is Perry Mason. I'm an attorney at law. This is Miss Della Street, my confidential secretary.'

Lorraine Jennings' jaw fell open. For a moment she was speechless. Then she called over her shoulder: 'Barton!'

A man's voice answered: 'What is it, dear?'

'Come here,' she said, 'quick . . . no, no, not quick! I forgot about your arthritis.'

She turned quickly to Norda. 'Barton's arthritis bothered him again last night. It's his knee and when the weather's going to change it stiffens up. He's walking with a cane this morning, and...'

They heard the sound of the cane, of steps, and Barton Jennings stood in the doorway.

'Barton,' she said, 'Norda has shown up with Perry Mason, the attorney, and this is Miss Della Street, his secretary.'

Barton's face showed a flash of surprise, then he bowed gravely to Della Street, shook hands with Perry Mason, said: 'Well, Lorraine, what's holding us up? Invite them in. Have you folks had breakfast?'

Lorraine hesitated, then stood to one side. 'Yes,' she said, 'do come in. What about breakfast, Norda?'

'I've had breakfast,' Norda said shortly.

'And so have we,' Mason said. 'I want to talk to you about a rather serious matter. I am at the moment representing Miss Allison, and something happened early this morning which disturbed her greatly. I would like to discuss it, but I want you to understand that I am an attorney and that I'm representing Miss Allison. If you care to have any attorney of your own here, I would suggest you get in touch with him, or you can refer me to your attorney. But there are certain things which should be explained.'

'Well, for heaven's sake!' Lorraine Jennings said. 'I never heard of any such thing in my life! What in the world *are* you talking about? Norda, what *is* this?'

Norda said: 'It's something I found, Lorraine. It proves exactly what you were trying to do . . . what–'

'Just a minute,' Mason said. 'Let me handle this, if you will, please, Miss Allison. And I suggest we all go inside.'

'Well, *I'd* certainly like to know what happened,' Lorraine said, leading the way into a living-room. 'I knew Norda was a little worried about seeing my lawyer, but there was no reason for her getting a lawyer of her own. If she didn't want to co-operate with me, all she had to do was to say so. But since she has you here, Mr Mason, I can explain exactly what I plan to do.

'Please do sit down and let's try and get this situation unscrambled. I've never been so absolutely bewildered in my life. I went up to Norda's room and found she'd left. . . . As I told you, Barton's bad knee started bothering him in the night and he took codeine. And I took some too because by that time he had me wide awake, what with his twisting and turning, putting on hot compresses. I didn't even hear him when he got up to take Robert and the dog out to the place where the boys were to meet at five o'clock this morning, and . . . well, I guess we owe you an apology, Norda. After Barton returned we slept pretty late. We're usually up and have breakfast a lot earlier. What in the world possessed you to leave, and *when* did you leave? If you were hungry, why didn't you just go out in the kitchen and look in the icebox? We had fruit juice, eggs–'

'Never mind that,' Norda said. 'Something happened which upset me.'

'I think,' Barton Jennings said to Mason, '*you'd* better start talking, Mr Mason.'

'Would you care to be represented by counsel?' Mason asked.

'Heavens no!' Jennings said impatiently. 'We've tried to accommodate Norda Allison. My wife wanted to do her a favour. We know something of what she's been going through–that is, at least Lorraine does. Now, if you have anything to say, please go ahead and say it.'

Mason said: 'Did you know Miss Allison had been getting offensive matter in stamped envelopes which had been addressed by a small, hand printing press? The letters contained clippings of–'

'Of course we did,' Lorraine interrupted. 'That's one of the reasons I had Norda come down here. Mervin Selkirk was bombarding her with those clippings, trying to frighten her–the poor child, I know exactly what she went through. Mervin can be the most–'

Barton Jennings interrupted his wife to say: 'Just a moment, Lorraine. Let's let Mr Mason tell us what *he* has in mind.'

Mason said: 'I believe you know Miss Allison's address on those envelopes had been printed on a small hand press, Mrs Jennings?'

'Of course I did. I'm the one who suggested to Norda that she check on a small printing press I had given my son Robert. As I understand it, the postal authorities got hold of that press and checked it, but the envelopes couldn't have been printed on that press–the type wasn't the same.'

Mason nodded gravely and said: 'Miss Allison was restless this morning. She got up early, walked out in the patio and then went into a rumpus-room. There's a storage-room down below. She took the stairs down to the storage-room.'

'The old basement,' Lorraine interposed.

'I suppose I had no right to,' Norda apologized. 'However, something happened which led me to think . . . I mean...'

'Norda, *please*,' Lorraine interrupted. 'You're our house guest. I don't suppose it's particularly usual for a house guest to get up early in the morning and go exploring, but you were our guest and I told you to make yourself at home. If you wanted to look around, it was *quite* all right. What in the world are you leading up to?'

'Simply,' Mason said, 'that in the basement Miss Allison found the printing press on which she believes those envelopes had been printed. She found some of the envelopes with the address on them, and her name and address were all set up in type in the printing press. Moreover, the press showed evidence of having been recently used. There was, I believe, printer's ink glistening on the steel table over which the rollers operate.'

Barton Jennings motioned his wife to silence. 'Just a minute, Mr Mason. You say that Norda claims she found that in *this* house?'

Mason nodded.

'Well,' Barton said, 'that's very easily solved. First, we'll go take a look at that printing press and then we'll try and determine where it came from.'

'I want to warn you,' Mason said, 'that that printing press is evidence. I suggest that no one touch it. Miss Allison will show you where it is, but as soon as we have done that, I intend to call the authorities.'

'*You* intend to?' Barton Jennings said. 'What about us? We want to get at the bottom of this thing just as much as you do.'

Lorraine Jennings arose, looked at Norda, and for the first time there was angry exasperation on her face. 'Norda,' she said, 'if you found anything, why didn't you come to us? Are you absolutely certain you found what you said you did?'

'Of course I am!' Norda snapped. 'I found a whole package of envelopes waiting to be used. I know now where those clippings came from. You pretended to–'

'Just a moment, just a moment,' Mason interrupted. 'I think Mr Jennings and I understand the situation. It's going to be advisable for all of us to withhold comments until after we've appraised the evidence and called the officers. Now let's go take a look at that press. Will you lead the way, Miss Allison?'

'I suppose there's a shorter way,' Norda said. 'I went around the back, and...'

'Just go right through the kitchen,' Lorraine said.

'Follow me,' Barton Jennings said, stepping quickly forward, then grimacing with pain. 'I guess you'd better do the honours, Lorraine. I forgot about the knee for the moment.'

'This way,' Lorraine said, and stalked across the living-room, through the dining-room. She flung open the door of the kitchen, crossed it and stood on the stairs leading to the rumpus-room.

'Now where, Norda?' she asked.

'Down the stairs,' Norda said, 'then into the basement store-room. It's just under the big shelf to the left of the stairs.'

'It's going to be a little crowded for all of us to get down there,' Jennings pointed out. 'Why don't you and Mr Mason go down, Lorraine. Norda can stand at the head of the stairs and direct you.'

'Very well,' Lorraine said, gathering up her skirt and wrapping it around her legs so it wouldn't drag on the stairs. She descended to the basement storage-room. 'Now where, Norda?' she called over her shoulder.

'Right to the left of a big box. You can see the handle of the printing press,' Norda said.

'I don't see any handle of any printing press,' Lorraine Jennings retorted.

Mason said: 'Just a moment, please.'

He moved over around Lorraine Jennings and peered under the shelf. 'Is it behind these boxes, Miss Allison?' he asked.

'It's just back under a shelf and behind . . . Here, I'll come down and show you.'

Norda ran quickly down the stairs, pushed Lorraine to one side, held her skirt, stooped, then paused open-mouthed. 'But it's no longer here!' she exclaimed.

'Let's move these boxes,' Mason said, 'You said that there was a box containing a package of envelopes?'

'Stamped envelopes that had been addressed and were all ready for mailing to me,' Norda said.

Lorraine whipped her skirt into her lap, bent down and started pulling out boxes. 'Well,' she said, 'here's some old recipes. I've been intending to put them into a scrapbook. Here's some letters from Mother. I suppose they might as well be thrown away. Here's . . . for heaven's sake, Barton, here's a whole box of those reprint books. I thought you were going to give them to the hospital.'

'I was,' Barton said from the head of the stairs, 'but I hadn't finished reading them. Let's not bother with that now, Lorraine. Get the boxes cleaned out and let's see what's under the shelf.'

'But,' Norda protested, 'there's no need to start moving everything out. It was there and now it's gone.'

'*Well!*' Lorraine exclaimed, getting to her feet and shaking out her skirt. Her tone showed extreme scepticism.

'I suggest you look around, Lorraine,' Barton Jennings said, 'and I'd like to have Mr Mason look around. Let's be absolutely certain that there's no foundation for this charge before we have any further discussion.'

Mason prowled around through the basement storage-room, moving boxes.

'Well,' he said, 'it would certainly appear the press is no longer in the exact place where Miss Allison saw it, at any rate.'

'*No longer*,' Lorraine repeated after him furiously. 'I never heard such a story in my life! I–'

'Just a moment, dear,' Barton Jennings cautioned from the top of the stairs. 'Let's all go back to the library and sit down.'

Lorraine said coldly: 'I'm afraid, Norda, that you've probably been influenced by some bad dream, to put the most courteous interpretation on it. Perhaps you took too many drugs. You said you'd been having to take pills to get to sleep.'

'Well, I like that!' Norda exclaimed. 'You found out that I'd been down in that basement store-room this morning and found that printing press. So you've been very clever in getting rid of it. I suppose you've been smart enough so it can never be traced.'

'I think,' Barton Jennings said, 'that it's going to be a lot better for all concerned if neither party makes any accusations. What do you think, Mr Mason?'

'I think you're right,' Mason said, noticing Della Street seated at a table in the rumpus-room, her pen flying over the page of her shorthand notebook as she took down the conversation. 'Let's go into the living-room and see if we can discuss this matter quietly and intelligently.'

'As far as I'm concerned, there's nothing to discuss,' Lorraine Jennings said. 'We invited Norda Allison to be our house guest. We tried to help her. As nearly as I can see, she has abused our hospitality. She told me she was going to take sleeping pills last night. I presume she had some drug-induced nightmare, and now she's trying to hold *us* responsible–'

'I didn't dream up those two envelopes I took out of the box,' Norda Allison flared, 'and which are now in Perry Mason's office.' She started to mention the note she had received from Robert but then decided to leave Robert out of it. Regardless of what it might cost her, she had a feeling it might be better in the long run if neither Robert's mother nor Barton Jennings knew that it had been Robert who had first made the discovery.

'Now, just a minute,' Mason said. 'Let's keep our heads, please. We are faced with a peculiar situation. Let me ask you, Mr and Mrs Jennings, do you have any objection to calling in the authorities for an investigation?'

'I certainly do!' Lorraine said. 'Not until we have some tangible evidence to go on, I'm not calling in anyone. If your client wants to proceed with this absurd charge against us, Mr Mason–well, you're a lawyer and you can tell her what the consequences will be.'

Mason smiled. 'I can appreciate your position, Mrs Jennings, but under the circumstances my client is not going to be frightened. She isn't making any accusations against *you*. She is simply stating that she found an important piece of evidence in your house this morning, and, as it happens, she had the foresight to take two of the envelopes with her. I am going to have an expert examine those envelopes to see if they are the same as the envelopes she has been getting through the mail. If they are, we are going to report the entire matter to the postal authorities.'

Barton Jennings said: 'I think that's the wise thing to do, Mr Mason. I can assure you that this is all news to us.'

'It isn't news at all!' Lorraine flared. 'She's been sending herself those notices, Barton, and now for some reason that happens to be her personal and selfish interests, she's taken advantage of our hospitality. She brought two of those envelopes down here with her in her purse, got up in the morning before anyone was up, sneaked out, went to a lawyer with those envelopes, and–'

'I repeat,' Barton Jennings interrupted, 'that neither party should make any accusations at this time. If it's all right with you, Mr Mason, we'll disregard any statements and accusations which have been made by your client on the ground that she is naturally somewhat nervous and upset. And it will be agreed that your client will disregard any statements made by my wife, who is also quite naturally nervous and upset.'

'I think that is probably the best way of disposing of the entire matter at this time,' Mason said. 'We now offer to make such an agreement with you.'

'We accept that offer,' Barton Jennings said.

'And now,' Lorraine Jennings said to Norda, 'if you'll kindly leave my house, Miss Allison, we will chalk off our attempts to befriend you as another unfortunate experience in misjudging human nature.'

Mason turned to Norda Allison. 'Come on, Miss Allison,' he said, 'let's go.'

5

Inspector Hardley Chester listened carefully to Norda Allison's recital of facts, then turned to Perry Mason.

'There's nothing out there now?' he asked.

'No sign of the printing press, no sign of the envelopes,' Mason said.

Inspector Chester ran his hand up over the top of his head, down back of his ears and stroked the back of his neck with his finger-tips. 'We can't very well go out there and accuse anyone of anything on the strength of evidence like that, Mr Mason.'

'I don't expect you to,' Mason said.

'What do you expect me to do?'

'I expect you to do your duty,' Mason told him.

Inspector Chester raised his eyebrows. 'It's been a while since I've heard that one.'

'You're hearing it now.'

'What's my duty?'

'I don't know what it is,' Mason said. 'I'm not telling you what it is. My client made a discovery. She discovered some evidence in a case that has been bothering the postal authorities. I told her it was her duty to report what she had found. She's reported it.'

'Thereby putting me in something of a spot,' Chester said.

'That,' Mason told him, 'is something we can't control. We've told you what we found. We had a duty to do that. That duty has now been discharged.'

Inspector Chester turned to Norda Allison. 'You are quite certain this was a printing press?'

'Of course it was a printing press.'

'You saw it plainly?'

'I saw it, I felt it, I touched it.'

'And you think it had been used?'

'Of course it had been used.'

'Recently?'

'It had been used for printing my name and address on those envelopes. If you don't believe me, how do you account for the fact that I have two of the stamped envelopes which bear uncancelled stamps with my name and address printed on them and that they're identical with the envelopes which were sent me through the mail?'

'I'm not saying I don't believe you. I'm asking questions. Do you have any evidence which would indicate the press had been used recently?'

'The ink was still moist on it. That is, still sticky.'

'How do you know?'

'I touched the tip of my finger to it and then pulled the finger away. The ink was sticky and my finger-tip was black.'

'How did you clean it?'

'I opened my purse, took some cleansing tissue from a little package I carried and scrubbed my finger off.'

'What did you do with the tissue?'

'It's still in the purse, I guess. I didn't want to just throw it down on the floor. I *must* have put it back in my purse, intending to throw it away as soon as I had an opportunity.'

She opened her purse, fumbled around inside, then triumphantly produced a crumpled piece of cleansing tissue. There were black smears on the paper and Inspector Chester took possession of it.

'Well,' he said, 'I'm going out and ask Mr and Mrs Jennings if they care to make a statement. I'm going to ask them if they object if I take a look around–not that that will do any good because I understand you've already convinced yourselves the press isn't there.'

'The press certainly isn't where it was when I saw it,' Norda Allison said firmly.

Inspector Chester got to his feet. 'Well, I'll go look around.'

'Will you let us know if you find anything?' Mason asked.

The inspector smiled and shook his head. 'I report to my superiors.'

'But Miss Allison is an interested party,' Mason said.

'All the more reason why I shouldn't report to her,' Chester said, shaking hands with Mason and bowing to Norda Allison. 'Thanks for the information. I'll check on it.'

'Now what?' Norda Allison asked when Inspector Chester had left.

'Now,' Mason said, 'we do a little checking of our own.' He turned to Della Street. 'Please ring the Drake Detective Agency and ask Paul Drake to come in.'

Della nodded, went to the outer office and a moment later returned to say: 'Drake said to tell you he's coming right away.'

Mason said, by way of explanation to Norda Allison: 'You talked with him. He's a very competent detective.'

'I know. He's nice. That's how I got in touch with you. I –'

She broke off as Paul Drake's code knock sounded on the corridor door of Mason's private office.

Della Street opened the door. Paul Drake, tall, informal, loose-jointed, said: 'Hi, Della,' flashed Norda Allison a keen glance of professional appraisal, said: 'How is everything, Miss Allison?' and then turned to Mason.

'Sit down, Paul,' Mason invited.

Drake sat crosswise in the big overstuffed chair; one of the rounded arms propping up his back, his long legs draped over the other arm.

'Shoot.'

'You're familiar with Norda Allison's story?'

'Up to the time she came in to see you this morning. What's happened since then?'

Mason told him.

'What do you want me to do?' Drake asked.

'Get on the job,' Mason said. 'Get out there and see whether the postal authorities are going to let Mr and Mrs Jennings give them a routine run-around, whether they're taking Norda Allison's story seriously and if they're making a search of the place.

'Visit around with the neighbours. Pretend you're getting magazine subscriptions or selling books or something of the sort at first. See if you can get some of the women gossiping.'

'They'll throw a magazine salesman or a book salesman out on his ear so fast that–'

'All right,' Mason said. 'Tell them you're going to give away a free vacuum-cleaner to families who represent the highest intellectual strata. Tell them it's sort of a house-to-house quiz show; that you're asking questions and you give a rating and that the person having the highest rating in the block gets a free vacuum-cleaner or a set of dishes or something. Then ask questions to test their powers of observation. After a few routine questions you can start asking about the people next door.'

Paul Drake shook his head. '*You* might be able to work a stunt like that, Perry. I couldn't. Each man has to shoot his own particular brand of ammunition–is there any reason I shouldn't tell them I'm a detective?'

Mason thought that over for a moment, then said: 'No, but they'll freeze up on you as soon as they think you're a detective, won't they?'

'If I try to pump them they will,' Drake said. 'But let me get talking to the average housewife and tell her I'm a detective and right away she wants to know what I'm doing out there. Then I act mysterious and tell her it's something in the neighbourhood. Then she invites me in, gives me a cup of tea or coffee, I get friendly with her, let it slip that it's the people next door I'm interested in, and then become very embarrassed at having let the information slip out. I make her promise she won't tell, and, as consideration for that promise, she insists that I tell her what it's all about and I start sparring, trying to keep from telling her and *she's* cross-examining *me*. I get in a few questions here and there. The first thing anyone knows she's told me all she knows, all she surmises, and has given me all the neighbourhood gossip.'

'Be careful you don't tell them anything that might serve as a basis for a suit for defamation of character,' Mason warned.

Drake grinned. 'I've been using this technique for ten years, Perry. Once a woman opens up with the neighbourhood gossip she'll never repeat anything I say because I'll have her so badly involved she won't dare to peep.'

'And then if she denies it?' Mason asked.

'Then,' Drake said, 'I have a little recording device which looks like a hearing aid. I pretend I'm hard of hearing and wear this counterfeit hearing aid. Of course, tactics like that don't work *all* the time, but they work most of the time.'

'Okay,' Mason said. 'Use your own technique. I want a couple of tails.'

'One to each?' Drake asked.

'One to each,' Mason told him.

Drake heaved himself up out of the chair. 'On my way.'

Mason smiled across at Norda Allison. 'Well, that's the best *I* can do,' he said. 'Now I'll try getting back to that brief. Where are you staying?'

'The Millbrae Hotel.'

'We'll call you if we learn anything,' Mason told her. 'In the meantime, don't talk to anyone. If anyone calls on you or tries to pump you for information, say that I'm your attorney and am answering all questions.'

Norda Allison gave him a grateful hand. 'I don't know how I can thank you enough, Mr Mason.'

'You don't have to,' Mason said. 'I hope we can get the thing straightened out. We'll do the best we can.'

6

It was three-thirty in the afternoon when Paul Drake called in on Mason's unlisted telephone.

Mason, who had been dictating steadily since one-thirty, regarded the ringing telephone with annoyance. He picked up the receiver, said: 'Hello, Paul, what is it?'

Drake's voice over the wire said: 'I have an idea you better get out here, Perry.'

'Where's here?'

'Next door to the Jennings' house.'

'What's it all about?' Mason asked.

Drake, speaking guardedly, said: 'I'm visiting with a Mr and Mrs Jonathan Gales. The address is 6283 Penrace Street. They have some information that I'd like to have you check. I think you'd like to get their story.'

Mason said irritably: 'Now listen, Paul, I'm terribly busy at the moment. I got Della to give up her weekend in order to get this dictation out and we're right in the middle of a very important matter.

'If you've uncovered any information there, write out a statement and get them to sign it. Get–'

'Then you're going to be out,' Drake interrupted. 'How soon can you get here, Perry?'

Mason thought that over, said into the phone: 'I take it you're where you can't talk freely, Paul.'

'That's right.'

'How about leaving the house and going to a telephone booth where you can tell me what it's all about?'

'That might not be advisable.'

'You have some information that's important?'

'Yes.'

'About that printing press or something?'

'About the bloodstains,' Drake said.

'About the what?'

'The bloodstains,' Drake said. 'You see, Perry, the postal authorities started an investigation and then after they found this gun under the pillow of the bed where Norda Allison had been sleeping, they called in the local police. She's been taken to Headquarters for questioning. For some reason the authorities are hot on her trail.

'Now, Jonathan Gales knows something about the bloodstains that I think you should know. There's some evidence, here that you'd better get hold of before the police–'

'I'll be right out,' Mason interrupted.

'Don't come in your car,' Drake warned. 'Get a taxi-cab, let it go as soon as you get to the house. I have an agency car out here that is rather inconspicuous. I'll drive you back when you're ready to leave.'

'I'll be right out,' Mason promised.

He dropped the telephone into the cradle, said to Della Street: 'That's the worst of this damned office work. It gets your mind all cluttered up with stuff–I should have known the minute Drake telephoned and asked me to come out that it was important, but I had my mind so geared to trivia that I forced his hand and made him tell me what it was he considered so important. Now, the witnesses may decide to clam up.'

'What was it?' she asked.

'I'll tell you in the taxi,' Mason said. 'Come on, let's go. The address is 6283 Penrace Street. Apparently that's next door to where the Jennings live. Grab a shorthand book and we'll take a cab. Hurry!'

They raced down the corridor to the elevator, found a cab waiting at the cab-stand at the corner, climbed in and Mason gave the address.

'Now tell me what it's all about,' Della Street said.

'Bloodstains,' Mason told her.

'I heard you say that over the telephone. What's the significance of the bloodstains?'

'Apparently,' Mason said, 'the police have been called in. They found a gun under the pillow where Norda Allison had been sleeping. You remember she told about having found an ejected empty cartridge case in front of the tent where Robert was sleeping out in the patio. Now, apparently, bloodstains enter into the picture, and from the way Paul Drake talked, I have an idea the police don't know anything about those stains *as yet*.'

'Well,' Della Street said, '*we* seem to be getting into something.'

'We seem to already have got into it,' Mason told her, 'up to our necks.'

Mason lapsed into frowning concentration. Della Street, glancing at him from time to time, knowing the lawyer's habits of thought, refrained from interruption.

The cab pulled in front of the address on Penrace Street.

'Want me to wait?' the driver asked.

Mason shook his head, handed him a five-dollar bill, said: 'Keep the change.'

The cabby thanked him.

Mason glanced briefly at the police car which was parked next door at the Jennings' house, walked rapidly up the cement walk to a front porch and extended his thumb towards the bell button.

The front door was opened by Paul Drake while Mason's thumb was still a good three inches from the bell button.

'Come on in,' Drake said. 'I was waiting at the door hoping against hope you wouldn't drive up until after Lieutenant Tragg had left.'

'That's Tragg over in the other house?' Mason asked.

Drake nodded, said: 'Come on in and meet the folks.'

Drake led the way into a cosy living-room which had an air of comfortable simplicity.

There were deep chairs, comfortable in appearance, books, a large table, a television set, floor lamps conveniently arranged by the chairs, newspapers and magazines on the table. Through the archway could be seen a dining-room with a big sideboard, a glass-enclosed cupboard for dishes. The house itself was modern, but the furniture gave the impression of being comfortably old-fashioned without qualifying for the label of 'antique'.

A somewhat elderly couple arose as Paul Drake escorted Mason and Della Street into the living-room.

'This is Mr and Mrs Gales,' Paul Drake said by way of introduction. 'They have quite a story; at least Mr Gales has.'

Gales, a tall, bleached individual with a drooping moustache, bushy white eyebrows and grey eyes, extended a bony hand to Perry Mason. 'Well, well,' he said, 'I'm certainly pleased to meet *you*! I've read a lot about you, but never thought I'd be seeing you–Martha and I don't get out much any more and we spend a lot of time reading. I guess Martha has followed every one of your cases.'

Mrs Gales reached out to take Della Street's hand. 'And I've seen photographs of Miss Street,' she said. 'I'm really a fan of yours, my dear, as well as of Mr Mason. Now, do sit down and if we can do anything that will be of any help, we're only too glad to do it.

'How about making a cup of tea? I could . . .'

Drake glanced at his wrist-watch, then looked significantly through the windows over towards the Jennings' house. He said: 'We may be interrupted at any minute, Mrs Gales. If you don't mind, I'd like to have you tell your story just as briefly as possible–what you have to say about Robert.'

'Well, do sit down,' she said, 'let's be comfortable. Heavens to Betsy, I certainly feel shoddy having people like you here and not being able to offer a cup of tea. I've got some nice cookies I baked yesterday–'

'About the gun,' Drake said. 'Tell Mr Mason about Robert and the gun.'

'Well, there's not much to tell. Robert is a mighty nice, very well-behaved boy. But he's just crazy about guns. He's always watching those Western television shows–"pistol pictures", Jonathan calls them.

'They have a baby-sitter over there who takes care of him when Mr and Mrs Jennings go out, and I've noticed that when the baby-sitter is there Robert has a *real* gun to play with.'

'A real gun?' Mason asked.

'An automatic,' Jonathan Gales supplemented. 'Looks like a Colt Woodsman model. I think it's a .22 calibre.'

'He only has that when the baby-sitter is there?' Mason asked.

'Well, now, that's the only time I've *seen* him with it,' Mrs Gales said, 'but if you ask me, a seven-year-old boy has got no business playing around with a real pistol . . . personally, I think it's bad enough when they start pulling these imitation six-shooters out of holsters, pointing them at people and saying: "Bang! Bang! You're dead!" Good heavens! When I was a girl, if my brother had even pointed a cap pistol at anybody, my dad would have warmed him up good and proper.

'Nowadays, boys go around with these toy pistols and think nothing of pointing them at somebody and saying: "Boom! You're dead!" You can see what it's doing. Pick up the paper almost any day and you see where some child ten, twelve or fifteen years old killed off a parent because he was mad at not being allowed to go to a movie. I don't know what the world's coming to when–'

'Do you know who this baby-sitter is?' Paul Drake interposed.

'No, I don't. They have a couple of them. This one I'm talking about has only been working there about six weeks. The Jennings aren't much for being neighbourly, and . . . Well, this is a peculiar neighbourhood. People seem to live pretty much to themselves.

'Time was when people used to swap a little gossip and borrow things back and forth, but now there's a car in the garage and whenever they have a minute they get up and scoot off someplace. Then when they're home they're watching television or something. Seems like times are changing right under our eyes.'

'This baby-sitter,' Mason prompted, 'an older or a younger woman?'

'The one who lets him have the gun is an older woman–oh, I'd say somewhere in the forties.' She laughed. 'Of course, that's not old at all, you understand. It's just that she's older than the other one, and, of course, older than some of the baby-sitters they have these days; girls going to high school who come and sit with kids for an evening. I don't know what would happen if there was any sort of an emergency. I don't know what one of those girls could do.'

'Well, as far as that's concerned, what could a woman of forty-five do?' Jonathan Gales commented. 'Suppose some man walked in and–'

'We have to hurry along,' Drake interrupted, his voice apologetic. 'I would like to have Mr Mason hear your story just the way you told it to me. We'll have time only for high lights. You've seen the child playing with this automatic?'

Mrs Gales nodded emphatically.

'How about you?' Drake asked, turning to Jonathan Gales.

'I've seen him two or three times,' Jonathan Gales said. 'The very first time I saw it, I said to Martha: "It looks to me like that kid's got a real gun over there," and Martha said: "No, it can't be. That's just some kind of a wooden gun. They're making imitations these days that look so much like the real thing they scare a body to death."

'Well, I took a good, long second look at it and I said: "Martha, I'm betting that's a real gun," and sure enough, it was.'

'Did you ever have it in your hands?' Mason asked.

'No, but I did think enough about it to get my binoculars and take a look at it–Martha and I do a little bird-watching out in the back yard and we've got a mighty good pair of binoculars, coated lenses and all. They're sharp as a tack.'

'All right,' Drake said, hurrying things along. 'The child at times plays with a real gun. You've noticed that only when this one baby-sitter was there.'

They both nodded.

'Now, about the bloodstains,' Drake said.

'Well, that's the thing I can't understand,' Gales said. 'This morning Barton Jennings was up before daylight. He went some place. Then, later on, he had a hose and he was out there washing off the sidewalk and pretending he was watering the lawn. It wasn't five-thirty.

'Now, of course, that's not unusually early for people that are accustomed to getting up early, but over there in the Jennings' house they like to sleep late–you take on a Saturday or a Sunday when they aren't going anywhere they'll stay in bed until nine–ten o'clock in the morning. You'll see Robert up playing around by himself out there in the patio.'

'Not that we're the nosy kind,' Martha Gales interposed, 'but we do our bird-watching, a lot of it, in the morning. That's when birds are moving around and both Jonathan and I are early risers. There's a hedge between the properties, but you can see through it if someone is moving around. If anybody over there is sitting still-like, it isn't easy to see him. But if a body's moving around over in the patio in the Jennings' house you can see sort of a shadowy outline through the leaves in the hedge.'

'Jenning was watering the lawn?' Mason prompted.

'Well, it wasn't so much watering the lawn,' Gales said, 'as hosing it off. He was *pretending* to water the lawn, but he was holding the hose almost straight down and walking it along the lawn, using too much force to just be watering the grass. He was putting the full stream of water along a narrow strip–oh, maybe two or three feet wide–walking right along with it. Then he came to the sidewalk and he hosed off the sidewalk and in a couple of places I saw him put the nozzle right down within eighteen inches of the cement, just like he was trying to wash something away.

'Well, I didn't think too much of it until I went out to get my paper. The delivery boy had tossed the paper and usually he tosses it right up on the porch. This morning it didn't seem to be on the porch and I went out looking for it and I found it in the gutter. Evidently it had slipped out of the delivery boy's hand. It looks like there had been blood in the water that ran down the gutter.'

'You have the paper?' Drake asked.

Gales handed the newspaper to Mason. 'Now, it was rolled up this way,' he explained, rolling up the front page, 'and then there was a rubber elastic band around it. You can see the water had quite a reddish tinge to it.'

'But what makes you think it's blood?' Mason asked.

'I'm coming to that,' Gales said. 'When I went out looking for the paper, Jennings was just finishing up watering along the sidewalk. I said to him: "Good morning" and told him it looked like it was going to be a nice day, just sort of neighbourly-like, and he seemed right startled to see me out there. And, before he thought, he said sharply: "What are *you* looking for?" Well, I told him I was looking for my newspaper; that it wasn't on the porch or on the front lawn and sometimes when the boy threw it out of the car it would hit against the side of the car door and drop down in the gutter. So then I looked down in the gutter and said: "Here it is; right here in the gutter."

'I picked it up and Jennings said: "Gosh, I hope I didn't get it wet. I was watering the lawn." Well, I looked at it and saw it was wet all right, but I said: "Oh, well, it'll dry right out. It isn't very wet; just the corner. You're up early this morning, aren't you?"

'Well, he said he'd had to take Robert and the dog out someplace to meet with some other boys that were going out on a camping trip, and then I saw his eyes rest on the paper I was holding. Something in the expression of his eyes caused me to look down, and I could see there was this reddish stain on the paper. Well, I didn't say a word, but I brought the paper in and dried it out, and Martha and I had our cup of coffee. We both like a cup of coffee first thing in the morning and then we read the newspaper. Sometimes we don't actually get around to breakfast for an hour or two. We sit out in the yard and watch birds and maybe sip coffee, and–'

'There was a bloodstain,' Drake said.

'That's right. I'm coming to that. I got to thinking about the reddish colour on the paper, and along about ten or eleven o'clock I could see there was a lot of unusual activity over there at the Jennings' house, with people coming and going, so I got to wondering about the way he'd been washing off that sidewalk with the hose. You see, he quit doing that the minute I got out there. He acted just as if he'd been a kid that had been caught in some kind of mischief. Well, I went out to look around. Out there in the gutter, just alongside the kerb above where the paper had been lying, there was a red blotch of blood that hadn't been washed away yet. I'm pretty sure it was blood, and out a little ways from the kerb you could see two spots of blood–looked like somebody had been bleeding and had left the place, walking along the lawn instead of along the walk and then stood for a moment at the gutter, getting a car door open, then had stepped into the car and driven away.

'Now, you probably think I'm . . . well, maybe you'll think I'm a little mite too nosy or something, but I just got to wondering about that blood. I said to Martha, I said: "Martha, suppose that seven-year-old kid was playing with a gun? Suppose they let him have it and took the shells out of it whenever he was playing with it, but suppose this time they didn't get *all* the shells out. Suppose there happened to be a shell left in the barrel and suppose he'd shot somebody?'

'Anything that makes you think he did?' Mason asked.

Gales hesitated for a moment, then slowly shook his head. 'Nothing in particular–nothing I can put my finger on.'

'Don't be so cautious, Jonathan,' Martha Gales prompted. 'Why don't you go ahead and tell them what you told *me*?'

'Because I can't prove anything and I may be getting in pretty deep.'

'Go ahead,' Drake said impatiently, 'let's have it.'

'Well, of course, it's only just a surmise, but Robert was going out on some kind of a Scout trip or something this morning–now why in the world would anyone get up to take a kid out on a Scout trip at four o'clock in the morning–and *I* thought I heard a shot sometime last night.'

Mason and Drake exchanged glances.

'They took Robert out at four o'clock in the morning?' Mason asked.

Gales nodded. 'Must have been around there. It was before daylight.'

'If you couldn't see, how did you know it was Robert?'

'I heard them talking. I didn't look at the time, but it must have been right around four o'clock.'

'And it was after Robert left that you saw Jennings washing off the sidewalk?'

'That's right.'

'His arthritis is bothering him this morning, I believe,' Mason said.

'Yes, he had his cane with him this morning.'

Drake, looking out of the window, said: 'Oh-oh, here comes Lieutenant Tragg.'

Mason said to Jonathan Gales: 'All right, tell me about the baby-sitter. What do you know about her? Does she drive her own car?'

'That's right.'

'What make is it?.

'I can't tell you the make. It's an older type of car–a sedan.'

'She's in her forties?'

'I would say so.'

'Heavy-set?'

'Well, not fat, just . . . well, rather broad across the beam.'

'How long has she been baby-sitting for them?'

'Well, I guess maybe six–eight weeks or so. Robert is only there for part time.

You know, he's a child by another marriage–Selkirk, his name is, and–'

The doorbell sounded.

Martha Gales said: 'I'll get it.'

'Never mind Robert,' Mason said. 'I know all about him. I'm interested in this baby-sitter. Do they say anything about her, or . . .'

'No, we don't visit much back and forth. I–'

'You don't think she's some relative, or . . .?'

'No, I think they got her through an agency. I think they said–'

Lt Tragg's voice said: 'How do you do, madam. I'm Lieutenant Tragg of the homicide department. I'm making an investigation and I'd like to ask you a few questions. Do you mind if I come in?'

Tragg didn't wait for an answer but pushed his way into the interior of the house, then jerked back in surprise as he saw Mason, Della Street and Paul Drake.

'Well, well, well,' he said, 'what brings all of *you* here?'

'What brings *you* here?' Mason countered.

Tragg hesitated a moment, then said: 'Well, you'll read it in the papers so I guess there's no harm in telling you. Mervin Selkirk was found dead in his automobile in the parking lot of the San Sebastian Country Club shortly after one o'clock this afternoon. He'd been dead for some time. There'd been an extensive haemorrhage from a chest wound. The doors of the car were closed and the windows were all up. The fatal bullet was of .22 calibre and there's reason to believe it was fired from a Colt automatic.'

Lt Tragg looked to the horrified faces of Martha and Jonathan Gales. 'You folks know anything about Mervin Selkirk?' he asked. 'Ever meet him? Know him when you see him? Did you see him here last night?'

They shook their heads.

'We don't know him,' Gales said.

'Anything unusual take place next door during the night?' Tragg asked. 'The boy, Robert, was Mervin Selkirk's son, you know.'

Martha Gales shook her head.

Jonathan Gales said: 'Not that we know of. The only thing I know about is the bloodstains.'

Lt Tragg snapped to attention as though he had received an unexpected jolt of an electric current. 'Bloodstains! Where?'

'Next door and on the sidewalk. I was telling Mr Mason, his secretary and Mr Drake here about what we saw–'

Tragg said: 'Hold it, hold it! Okay, Mason, I guess you've beaten me to it, but from now on we'll follow standard procedure. We'll excuse you. This is a police investigation of a murder.'

As Mason hesitated, Tragg added: 'We can, of course, just take these people up to the district attorney's office and interrogate them there, but it will be more convenient for all of us if we do it here. And,' he added with a wry smile, 'if you're as fast as you usually are, you already have all the information you need.'

Mason shook hands with Mr and Mrs Gales. 'Thanks for your co-operation,' he said. 'You'll find Lieutenant Tragg likes to adopt a hard-boiled exterior. He barks and he growls, but he really doesn't bite.'

'On your way,' Tragg said gruffly.

Mason led the way to the door.

'I'll drive you folks to the office,' Drake said, as he held open the door of his car.

'No, you won't,' Mason said. 'There isn't time for that. Drive us to the nearest taxi stand, then get out to the San Sebastian Country Club, find out everything you can dig up out there. I also want you to locate the Selkirk boy. I want to interview him. You'd better telephone your office, and, while you're about it, tell them to find out who the Jennings' baby-sitter is.'

'That's like looking for a needle in a haystack,' Drake protested.

'No, it isn't, Paul,' Mason said. 'We don't give a damn about the haystack, so that will help. Burn up the haystack and wash away the ashes. That will leave the needle where you can find it. It's the needle we're interested, in, not the haystack. Now, get busy.'

7

Mason followed Della Street into the elevator, said: 'Well, I guess the day is all shot to pieces now.'

Della laughed. 'And how you enjoy it! You hate routine work and whenever any excuse comes up that enables you to break away from office work and dictation you're as pleased as a seven-year-old kid who has just learned that the schoolhouse has burned down.'

Mason grinned at Della Street's comment. The assistant janitor who operated one of the elevators on Saturday afternoons said: 'I think you've someone waiting to see you, Mr Mason.' He brought the cage to a stop, still holding the door closed.

Mason frowned.

'He came up about half an hour ago. I told him you weren't in and he'd have to sign the register to get in on Saturday afternoon, unless he was going to one of the offices that were regularly open on a twenty-four-hour basis, such as the Drake Detective Agency.'

'What did he say?' Mason asked.

'He looked me right in the eye and said he was really intending to go to the Drake Detective Agency; that he'd simply asked about you on the off-chance you might be in your office. I think he was lying.'

'Okay,' Mason said. 'We can turn him down fast.'

'And hard,' Della Street amended.

The janitor slid the doors open. Mason and Della Street stepped out into the corridor.

A man who had been standing just beside the door of the Drake Detective Agency said: 'Are you Mr Mason?'

Mason regarded him without cordiality. 'I'm Mr Mason,' he said. 'It's Saturday. My secretary has sacrificed her week-end in order to help me get out some emergency work and I'm not seeing clients.'

The man, who seemed to be having some difficulty with his speech, said: 'This is an emergency, Mr Mason. It has to do with Miss Norda Allison. It's very important.'

Mason regarded the man sharply. 'All right,' he said, 'I'll let you come in. You'll have to be brief.'

The three of them walked in silence down the echoing corridor of the building, turned at the door of Mason's private office. Mason unlatched the door, held it open for Della Street and his visitor, then followed them in, seated himself behind the desk, said: 'All right, let's have it.'

'I'm Nathan Benedict,' the man said. 'I have known Miss Allison for some time. I knew about her . . . her attachment for Mervin Selkirk–Selkirk broke my jaw.'

'Oh, yes,' Mason said. 'And what are you doing down here, Mr Benedict?'

Benedict started to say something, then seemed momentarily unable to speak. When he had recovered himself, he said: 'You're going to have to make allowances, Mr Mason. My jaw gives me a little trouble yet–not so much the bones as the muscles.'

Mason nodded.

'I came down here to protect Norda Allison,' Benedict said. 'I think a great deal of her. This Selkirk is a dangerous man, Mr Mason; an absolutely dangerous man. I know from experience.'

Mason sat silently contemplating his visitor while Della Street took rapid notes in her shorthand book.

'Selkirk deliberately attacked me,' Benedict went on. 'He thrust his foot out as I walked across the floor, then jumped up, yelled, "Who are you pushing?" and pulled his fist, with the brass knuckles already in place, out of his pocket. He hit me a terrific blow, then stepped back and slipped the brass knuckles to one of his acquaintances.'

'Any idea who those friends of his were?' Mason asked.

'One of them remained and gave his name to the police. The other seemed to fade out of the picture. I think it was the other one who took the brass knuckles away with him.'

'You don't know his name?'

Benedict shook his head.

'All right,' Mason said, 'in view of developments I think we can find who that man was, and it's vitally important to find out something about him.

'Della.'

Della Street looked up from her notebook.

'As soon as Mr Benedict leaves,' Mason said, 'contact Paul Drake. Tell him we want the complete low-down on that altercation in the bar in which Mr Benedict was injured; we want the names of the people who were with Selkirk, and we want to interview them before the police do. I want to find out something about those brass knuckles.

'All right, Benedict, go ahead. What's the rest of it?'

'Well, that's all there is,' Benedict said. 'I knew Norda Allison was coming down here to see Lorraine Jennings, who was Selkirk's first wife. I have an idea they're trying to get Norda mixed up in a fight over the custody of the child. If she gets mixed up in that, I *know* she'll be in danger.'

'How did you happen to come to me?' Mason asked.

'I rang up the Jennings' residence a while ago. Jennings answered the phone. I told him it was important that I speak with Norda. I was told she wasn't there. Jennings seemed rather frigidly formal about it, too. I suppose he doesn't understand my motives.

'He told me that if I wanted to know anything about Norda Allison I would have to get in touch with you; that you were the only one who could give me any information.'

'And what made you think I would be at my office this afternoon?'

'Jennings said he thought you were here, or would be here later.'

'I see,' Mason said thoughtfully. 'And Jennings didn't seem to be cordial?'

'He was very cool over the telephone. Of course, I can't blame him. I suppose Norda will be angry, too.'

'When did you arrive here in this city?' Mason asked.

'Last night, about ten-thirty.'

'How did you know Miss Allison was here?'

'I drove her to the airport.'

'And then?'

'I saw her on the plane, then went and purchased a ticket and took the next plane.'

'And then?'

'I rented a car at the airport.'

'And then?'

Benedict cleared his throat. 'I drove out to the Jennings' place to keep watch.'

Mason glanced over at Della Street's busy pen. 'What happened–if anything?'

'I was watching the house. Foolishly, I was smoking. A prowl car drove past. The officers saw the glowing tip of the cigarette. They went on by. An hour later they came cruising by again and asked me what I was waiting for. They made me show them my driving licence and told me to get out of the neighbourhood and go to bed.

'I felt terribly humiliated, but I went to a motel. About eight-thirty I rang the Jennings' residence and asked for Norda. I was told she was still asleep. I left word for her to call and left my number.'

'Then what?' Mason asked.

'Then I waited and waited. When she hadn't called by mid-afternoon I was afraid she was angry. I felt I'd messed things up some way. I called again an hour or so ago and that was when Jennings said I'd have to see you.'

'I see,' Mason said thoughtfully. 'Just how did you propose to protect Miss Allison, Mr Benedict?'

'I don't know, but I intend to protect her.'

Mason said: 'You're not particularly robust physically and in dealing with Mervin Selkirk you would have been dealing with a cold-blooded, ruthless individual who would stop at nothing. You have already had one contact from which you emerged second best.'

Benedict nodded, tight-lipped.

'Yet you say you intend to protect Norda Allison?'

'Yes.'

'How?'

'Well, if you must know,' Benedict said, 'in my position I sometimes have occasion to carry large sums of money. I have a permit to carry a weapon, and–'

'Let's see it,' Mason said.

Benedict frowned and hesitated.

'Come on,' Mason said, 'let's see it.'

Benedict reached inside of his coat and pulled a revolver from a shoulder holster. He placed it on the table.

'A .38-calibre, lightweight Colt revolver,' Mason said. He picked it up, swung open the cylinder, inspected the shells and then added: 'It is now fully loaded.'

Mason smelled the barrel. 'Either it has not been fired recently or it has been cleaned after it was fired.'

'May I ask what causes your detailed scrutiny?' Benedict inquired. 'You're acting rather strangely, Mr Mason.'

Mason said: 'For your information, Mervin Selkirk was shot and fatally wounded. He died in his automobile out at the San Sebastian Country Club. As yet, I don't know the exact time of death. You say you have a permit to carry this gun?'

Benedict said with widened eyes: 'You mean Mervin Selkirk is dead?'

'He's dead,' Mason said. 'Murdered. You say you have a permit to carry this gun. Let's see it.'

As one in a daze, Benedict extracted a wallet from his pocket, took out a sheet of paper which had been folded and bore evidences of having been carried for some period of time.

Mason studied the permit, then looked at the number of the gun.

'Well,' he said, 'they check. I would suggest that you board the first plane, go back to San Francisco, go about your regular routine business and forget you were ever down here.'

'But Norda. Where's Norda?' Benedict asked.

'As nearly as I can find out,' Mason said, 'she is either at police headquarters or at the district attorney's office. She's probably being questioned, but she *may* have been booked on suspicion of murder.'

'Norda!' Benedict exclaimed. 'Murder!'

'That's right.'

'But I can't understand! I can't . . . it simply isn't possible.'

'What isn't possible?'

'That Norda killed him.'

'I didn't say she killed him,' Mason said. 'I said she might have been booked on suspicion of murder. Now, I'm not in a position to advise you. I'm representing her. Speaking not as an attorney but just as a person who would like to be your friend, I suggest that having learned there's nothing you can do to protect Norda from Mervin Selkirk, you return to San Francisco.'

Benedict shook his head. 'I'm sorry, Mr Mason, but I can't do that. I'm going to have to stay here now to see if there is anything I can do.

'Mr Mason, I . . . I'm employed on a salary, but I have made some rather fortunate investments. I am a bachelor, I have saved my money, and if . . . well, I'll be perfectly frank with you, Mr Mason. In all, I have nearly forty thousand dollars in the bank. I would be prepared to assist Norda financially if that is necessary.'

'We'll find out about that after a while,' Mason said, 'but you can assist her financially from San Francisco as well as from down here.'

'No,' Benedict said. 'I intend to remain here.'

'You remain here,' Mason said angrily, 'and not only will the police pick you up and shake you down but if they crowd my client, I'll lower the boom on you myself. It's not my duty to help the police solve murders. It's my duty to protect my clients. But right now you're about the best murder suspect I could dig up, if I had to provide a good red herring.'

Benedict thought that over for a moment, then his face lit up. 'Mr Mason, that's exactly the thing to do! If anyone intimates Norda killed him, you can use me as a red herring. In that way I can help . . . will Norda be able to have visitors? I mean can I talk with her?'

'Not for a while,' Mason said, 'not if they charge her with murder.'

'But *you* can see her as her attorney?'

'Yes.'

'Tell her I'm here,' Benedict said. 'Tell her what I told you about having funds available to help her financially.'

'You stick around here,' Mason said, 'and keep packing that gun, and I won't need to tell her anything about you. She'll pick up the newspaper and read *all* about you. You'll have your photograph published with headlines to the effect that police questioned Mervin Selkirk's broken-jawed rival and found him carrying what may have been the murder weapon.'

'That certainly makes it sound sensational,' Benedict said.

'Well, what did you expect?'

'If,' Benedict said with dignity, 'the police are no more efficient in locating me than they were in locating the brass knuckles which Mervin Selkirk used in breaking my jaw, they'll *never* know I'm here.'

Mason said: 'In the one instance you were dealing with a bar-room altercation over a woman. Now you're dealing with murder. You'll find there's a difference. Now let me ask you one other thing. Do you by any chance own any other weapon, say, for instance, a ·22 automatic?'

'Why yes, I do, but I only carry that on fishing trips, as a protection against snakes and to kill grouse for camp meat.'

'Where is that gun now?'

'At my apartment in San Francisco.'

'You're certain?'

Benedict hesitated.

'Well?' Mason prompted.

'No,' Benedict said. 'I can't *swear* to it. I looked for it yesterday afternoon; I wanted to bring it with me. I couldn't find it. I suppose I put it . . . well, I didn't make any search. I just looked in the drawer where I usually keep both guns. The ·38 was there, the ·22 wasn't.'

Benedict's eyes searched Mason's face. 'I'm afraid you're attaching too much emphasis to a fact which has no real significance, Mr Mason. The gun's around my apartment somewhere. I'm a bachelor and not much of a housekeeper. Things get scattered around me. I . . . come to think of it, I may have left it rolled up in the sleeping bag I used on a fishing trip two months ago. I love to fish.'

Mason studied the man.

'I want to know more about this charge against Norda,' Benedict said. 'I don't see how anyone on earth could possibly suspect that . . .'

He broke off as knuckles pounded authoritatively on the exit door leading from Mason's private office to the corridor.

After a moment the knock was repeated.

Mason pushed back his chair, walked over to the door, called out: 'Who is it?'

'Lieutenant Tragg,' came the voice from the other side. 'Open up. We're looking for Nathan Benedict. He's supposed to be in your office.'

Mason opened the door. 'Hello, Tragg. Meet Nathan Benedict,' he said.

Lt Tragg said: 'How are you, Benedict? When did you get in?'

'You mean here in the office?'

'Here in the city.'

'By plane last night.'

'What time?'

'I arrived about ten-thirty.'

'Where?'

'At the International Airport.'

'Where did you go from there?'

'I rented a car and drove out to Barton Jennings' house. I wanted to see Norda Allison. She'd evidently retired. I sat there for a while, then went to a motel.'

'What motel?' Tragg asked.

'The Restwell.'

'Then what?'

'This morning I tried to call Norda Allison. I left my number.'

Tragg eyed him narrowly.

Mason said: 'For your information, Lieutenant, since I am not representing Mr Benedict and the information which he gave me was volunteered and not on a confidential basis, he came down here to protect Norda Allison from Mervin Selkirk. He knew that he was unable to resist Selkirk on a physical basis, so he carried along a ·38-calibre Colt lightweight revolver for which he seems to have a permit which is perfectly in order.'

'Well, what do you know about that!' Tragg said. 'Where's the gun?'

Benedict reached inside of his coat.

'Bring it out slow,' Lt Tragg warned, stepping forward. 'Put it down on the desk with the butt towards me and the end of the barrel pointed towards you.'

Benedict placed the gun on the desk.

Lt Tragg picked it up, snapped open the cylinder, looked at the shells, smelled the barrel, snapped the cylinder shut, put the gun in his pocket.

'All right, Benedict,' he said, 'you and I are going to have a nice little talk, and since Mr Mason isn't your attorney and since he has a lot of work to do, we'll just move on and let Mr Mason get back to his work.'

'But I don't *have* to go with you,' Benedict said, drawing himself up.

Lt Tragg's mouth clamped into a thin, firm line. 'That's what *you* think,' he said. 'Come on.'

At the door Tragg turned and said over his shoulder to Mason: 'I was prepared for Benedict here to offer himself as a sheep for the slaughter, but hardly prepared to have you drive him into the killing pen for us quite so soon.'

Mason sighed wearily. 'I try to co-operate and that's all the thanks I get.'

Tragg said thoughtfully: 'When you co-operate you do it so willingly, so damned eagerly. And this guy might even go so far as to put on an act just to take the heat off his girl friend–with a little coaching from you, of course.'

Mason said angrily: 'You might also ask him if he happens to own a ·22 Colt automatic.'

'If you think we won't, you're crazy,' Tragg said, 'but we might not believe all his answers. The D.A. gets suspicious of the Greeks when they bring gifts–of red herring!

'Come on, Benedict, you're worth looking into, even if we are going to listen to any admissions you may make with sceptical ears.'

Tragg took Benedict firmly by the elbow and escorted him out into the corridor.

The automatic door check slowly closed the door and clicked it shut.

Mason and Della Street exchanged glances.

'Well,' Della Street said, 'shall we go on with our dictation?'

Mason made an expression of distaste, looked at his wrist-watch and said: 'For your information, Miss Street, we are not going on with any dictation. This man, Benedict, has turned out to be a confusing element which raises the devil with my desire to concentrate on dictation. In order to show you my sincerity in determining not to work on any more details, I hereby invite you out for a cocktail and a nice steak dinner.'

'And afterward?' she asked.

'And afterward,' Mason said, 'we might look around some of the nightspots and do a little dancing, if that appeals to you.'

'And the brief?' she asked.

'Under the circumstances,' Mason said, 'I'll go into court Monday morning, explain the emergency which arose over the week-end and get a week's extension.'

'Under those circumstances,' Della Street said, 'my duty is perfectly obvious. Shall we stop by Paul Drake's office and tell him to look up the San Francisco brass knuckles affair?'

Mason shook his head. 'No,' he said, 'there's no use now. Tragg will shake Benedict down at police headquarters. Newspaper reporters will eagerly pounce on him as a sensational development in the Selkirk murder. Tragg will let them take pictures. They'll call the San Francisco newspapers. The San Francisco papers will start ace reporters trying to cover the local angle of the case, and tomorrow morning's paper will have the names of the men who were with Selkirk in the cocktail lounge. By that time, police will have interviewed both of the men and probably exerted considerable pressure to find out about the brass knuckles.

'There's no use paying out our client's money to get information we can read in the newspaper.'

'But is there any chance Paul Drake's men could get to these men first, and–'

Mason smiled and shook his head. 'Don't underestimate the San Francisco newspaper reporters, Della–and while you're about it, don't underestimate the San Francisco police.

'Come on, let's go get those cocktails.'

'Plural?' Della Street asked.

'Two,' Mason said, 'and then dinner.'

8

Della Street, looking up from her plate, said: 'Oh-oh, I think we're going to have company, Chief.'

Mason, who particularly detested having persons who recognized him in restaurants and night clubs come barging up with excuses to get acquainted or to present some legal problem, tightened his lips.

'Right behind you,' Della Street said, 'walking very purposefully towards you. He chatted with the waiter for a minute and . . . oh-oh, here comes Fred, the manager.'

'Good for Fred,' Mason said.

'Fred's intercepted him,' Della Street said. 'Relax, he'll be on his way out in a moment.'

Della Street cut off another piece of her steak, raised the bite half-way to her lips, then paused, frowning.

'What now?' Mason asked.

'He evidently has some influence,' Della Street said. 'Fred's coming over.'

A moment later the manager bent over Mason's chair. 'Mr Mason, I know how you dislike to be disturbed. I dislike very much to do this, but–'

'Don't do it then,' Mason snapped.

'It's not that simple,' Fred said apologetically. 'Mr Selkirk, Horace Livermore Selkirk, the banker, insists that he's going to talk with you. I headed him off. Then he suggested that I come and ask your permission but . . . well, you know how it is. We appreciate your patronage enormously, Mr Mason, and we try to respect your desire for privacy but we're hardly in a position to give Horace Selkirk the old heave ho.'

Mason hesitated for a moment. 'I see your problem, Fred,' he said. 'All right. Tell Mr Selkirk that I'll make an exception in his case.'

'Thanks a million, Mr Mason!' the manager exclaimed in relief. 'Gosh, Mr Mason, you don't know what a load you've taken off my shoulders. I was afraid I was going to have to go back and . . . well, I have a loan with Mr Selkirk's bank. He put me in a very embarrassing position.'

'Does he know you have the loan?' Mason asked, grinning.

'He didn't,' Fred said, grinning, 'but he will very shortly after I go back to him.'

Mason laughed outright. 'Go ahead, Fred, spread it on as thick as you want. I'll see him but I don't think the interview will be very satisfactory to him.'

'That's not in my department,' the manager said. 'Emily Post's book on etiquette says that when you owe a bank twenty thousand dollars it's not considered exactly proper to ask two waiters to escort the president of that bank to the door.'

The manager moved back to Selkirk, and Della Street, watching what was going on with keen interest, said: 'I'll bet Fred *is* spreading it on thick–well, here they come.'

Fred led Selkirk over to the table. 'Mr Mason,' he said, 'I wish to present Horace Livermore Selkirk, the president of the bank with which I do business. I certainly will appreciate anything you can do for Mr Selkirk as a personal favour and I do want to tell you, Mr Mason, how very deeply I appreciate your granting me the personal favour of giving Mr Selkirk an interview. I know your unfailing policy in regard to privacy.'

Mason shook hands with Horace Selkirk, said: 'This is Miss Street, my secretary, Mr Selkirk. Would you care to be seated?'

The manager deferentially held a chair and Selkirk dropped into it.

'A drink?' Mason asked.

'No, thanks.'

'You've dined?'

'Yes, thank you.'

'Anything we can do for you?' the manager asked.

'Nothing,' Selkirk said crisply.

The manager bowed and withdrew. Mason studied the banker, a man who had bushy white eyebrows, slate-grey eyes, a profuse mane of iron-grey hair, and a mouth which indicated he was accustomed to getting his own way.

'I take it,' Mason said, 'you wish to consult me on a matter of some importance.'

'That's right. My own time is exceedingly valuable, Mr Mason. I can assure you that I wouldn't waste it on a trivial matter even if I wanted to waste yours.'

'May I ask how you happened to locate me here?' Mason said curiously.

'I get information the same way you do, Mr Mason.'

Mason raised his eyebrows.

'I feel that information is the most important ammunition a man can have to fire at an adversary in a business deal. Therefore I try to have accurate authentic information and try to get it fast. There are specialists in the field of getting information just as there are specialists in the field of law and in the field of banking. I have the best detective agency I can get and when I put it to work I get results.'

Mason studied the other man thoughtfully. 'Am I to assume that detectives have been shadowing me during the day so that you could put your finger on me at any time you wanted me?'

'Not during the day. However, when you entered my affairs, I entered yours. You can be assured that when I wanted you, I knew where to find you and that whenever I want to know where to find you in the future I will be able to do so with the briefest delay possible.'

'All right,' Mason told him. 'What do you want? Why go to all that trouble?'

'Because you're representing Norda Allison,' Selkirk said. 'She's going to be charged with the murder of my son. I can assure you, Mr Mason, that I intend to see that my son's murder is avenged. I don't care what I have to do, to what lengths I have to go, or how much it costs. I am going to avenge my son's death.'

'Surely,' Mason said, 'you didn't come here simply to tell me that.'

'I wanted to warn you. You are reputed to be a very resourceful and adroit attorney. You have the reputation of skating right along the thin edge of legal ethics in order to serve your clients. Frequently your ethics have been questioned but you have always managed to come up with the right answer and extricate yourself from the difficulty.'

Mason said nothing.

'In those cases in the past, however,' Selkirk went on, 'you haven't been up against a determined, resourceful antagonist who is perhaps equally intelligent, equally adroit, and if you come right down to it, equally unscrupulous.'

Mason said, 'You'll pardon me, Mr Selkirk, but I've had a busy day. I want to relax and enjoy my dinner and I'm not interested in having you come to my table in order to make threats.'

'Whether you're interested or not, I'm here.'

'All right,' Mason told him. 'You've stated your position. Now I'll state mine. I don't propose to have you sit at my table and keep making threats.'

'I think I'm in control of the situation,' Selkirk said. 'I have a mortgage on this restaurant. There's no one here who's going to throw me out.'

'Take another look,' Mason said.

'Where?'

'At me. I'll throw you out.'

Selkirk looked him over. 'Give me a year, Mr Mason, and I can bring about your financial ruin in this city regardless of your ability.'

'Give me forty-five seconds,' Mason said, pushing back his chair, 'and I'll bring about your physical ruin if you don't get the hell out of here.'

Selkirk held up a restraining hand. 'Calm down, Mason,' he said. 'You're enough of a fighter to realize you can't put up your best fight when you're angry. A prize fighter never gets mad; if he does, he loses the fight. A good lawyer puts on quite a show about being mad, but if he's a topflight attorney, he is cool as a cucumber all the time he's registering indignation.

'Now then, I may have over-emphasized my initial point. I wanted to have you understand that I have a considerable amount of power. I can be a powerful enemy, but, on the other hand, I can be an equally powerful friend.'

'A bribe?' Mason asked coldly.

'Don't be silly,' Selkirk said. 'I know you wouldn't take a bribe. I'm not offering to befriend you. You don't want my friendship–now. You can't turn down the friendship for your client–a friendship and assistance I am prepared to offer.'

'Under what conditions?'

'My son,' Horace Selkirk said, 'was a Selkirk. Therefore he had the benefit of such protection as the family could give him. I have from time to time used my influence on behalf of that boy. I have had to extricate him from rather serious situations. I know that he was not perfect. He had a nasty habit of being unfailingly polite while engaged in sadistic skirmishes.

'I'm not that way. I never skirmish. I either get along on a peaceful basis of live-and-let-live or I go to war. When I go to war I make a major campaign out of it. I destroy my enemy absolutely, ruthlessly and completely. I don't believe in half-way measures.

'I mention this, however, because I want you to know that the things my son did never met with my entire approval.

'My son was infatuated with Norda Allison. He quite probably would have ruined her mental health before he'd have let her marry someone else. I am not contending that my son was always in the right.

'However, we now come to the main reason for my visit. That is my grandson, Robert Selkirk.'

Mason's face, which had been ominously unsmiling, suddenly showed interest. 'Go on,' he said.

'The story the child's mother, Lorraine Jennings, and her husband, Barton Jennings, told the police was that Robert was going on a three-day camping trip. They had to take him and his dog to a place where he could join the group. They said they left him at the appointed place early this morning.

'For your private information, Mr Mason, that is a complete fabrication. Robert did not join any group early this morning. There was no occasion for him to do so. The group was not scheduled to depart until ten-thirty. Actually it got away at eleven-twenty-two. Robert was not with the group.'

'Where is he then?' Mason asked.

'Evidently he has been spirited away somewhere and is being held in concealment.'

'Why?' Mason asked.

'I *thought* you might be interested in finding out why,' Selkirk said.

'Go ahead,' Mason said.

'It might develop into a story which would be of some interest to you as the legal representative of Norda Allison. It might result in her acquittal. You see, since my son is dead, Robert's mother, Lorraine Jennings, is now the person who would legally be entitled to his sole custody. I don't intend to let Lorraine bring up my grandson. I never did think it was a good idea.

'I want the legal custody of Robert. Lorraine doesn't like me. She doesn't want me to have much to do with Robert. She says she doesn't intend to have any child of hers brought up to be a financial robot. As it happens, Mr Mason, while I have always tried to control my feelings, I am very, very fond of my grandson. There is where you can help me.'

'How?' Mason asked.

'By proving Lorraine Jennings guilty of my son's murder,' Horace Selkirk said, pushing back his chair. 'In that way you can acquit your client and at the same time make it possible for me to achieve my own goal. And if you need help in order to do it, you may call on me for anything you need. In the meantime, I'll be doing a few things on my own. Thank you, Mr Mason, and good night.'

He bowed formally and withdrew without shaking hands.

'Whew!' Della Street said. 'There's a man who gives me the creeps.'

Mason watched the banker's retreating figure. 'There's a man,' he said thoughtfully, 'who can be very, very damned dangerous.'

'And very, very damned disagreeable,' Della Street said. 'He's ruined a mighty good dinner.'

Mason said thoughtfully: 'He may do more than that. He may be going to ruin a mighty good case.'

'Or save it,' Della said.

'Or save it,' Mason agreed dubiously and without even the faintest enthusiasm. 'When a man like that starts messing around with the evidence, you can't tell *what* will happen.'

9

'Well,' Della Street said, as Mason signed the check at the restaurant, 'what happens next? There was some talk about dancing, you'll remember.'

Mason nodded, said: 'First we're going to give Paul Drake a buzz and let him know where we are.'

Della Street blew a kiss at the ceiling.

'Meaning?' Mason asked.

'Good-bye dancing,' Della said.

'Probably not,' Mason said. 'There's nothing much we can do tonight. Paul is holding the fort, but it's too soon for him to have any real results. We'll call him just to keep him in good spirits. Give him a ring, Della, and ask him if there's anything particularly important.'

Della Street went to the phone booth, dialled Paul Drake's number, and was back within less than a minute.

'He says we're to come up there right away,' she said. 'It's important–now don't you ever say anything about a woman's intuition again, Mr Perry Mason.'

'Did he say what it was?'

'Lots of things,' she said. 'Among other things he has the name of the baby-sitter.'

'Oh-oh,' Mason said. 'That's a break. How did he get that?'

'He wouldn't say. Says he's sitting on four telephone lines, all of them going like mad; that we're not to gum up his circuits by telephone calls, but that we'd better get up there.'

Mason grinned. 'Everybody seems to be ordering us around tonight, Della.'

'Just restaurant managers, bankers and detectives, so far,' she pointed out.

They drove to the office building, put his car in its accustomed parking space, took the elevator up to Drake's office.

The night switchboard operator, looking back over her shoulder, nodded to Mason and gestured down the corridor towards Drake's private office.

There were four lights glowing simultaneously on the switchboard.

Mason grinned at Della and said: 'I guess the guy's busy. Come on, Della.'

He opened the gate at the end of the enclosure which served as a reception-room and Mason and Della Street walked down the long corridor past half a dozen different doors to enter Paul Drake's private office.

Drake looked up as they entered, nodded, said into the telephone: 'Okay, stay with it. Now I want everything you can get on that . . . okay, call in just as soon as you get a chance.'

Drake took a big bite from a hamburger sandwich, mumbled while he was chewing: 'Sit down. I'm going to eat while I have a chance. These phones are driving me crazy.'

He poured coffee into a big mug, put in cream and sugar, gulped a swallow of the coffee, said: 'I can never get to eat a hamburger before it gets soggy.'

'You wanted to see us?' Mason said.

'You've eaten?' Drake asked.

Mason nodded.

'I know,' Drake said. 'A thick filet mignon or a New York cut, French fried onions, imported red wine, baked potatoes with sour cream, coffee and apple-pie à la mode–don't tell me, it's torture.'

'Go ahead,' Mason said, 'torture yourself.'

Drake regarded the soggy hamburger with distaste, started to take a bite but stopped as the telephone jangled.

Drake unerringly picked the one of the four telephones on which the call was coming in, held it to his ear, said: 'Drake talking . . . okay . . . go on, give it to me.'

Drake listened carefully, asked: 'How do they know?' He listened some more, then said: 'Okay, keep an ear to the ground. Hang around Headquarters. Keep in touch with the boys in the press-room. They'll be looking for a late story.'

Drake hung up the phone, picked up the remnants of the hamburger sandwich, looked at it for a moment, then with a gesture of disgust threw it into the waste-basket.

'What gives?' Mason asked.

'I ruined my appetite for that stuff talking about your nice meal,' Drake said. 'We have the name of the baby-sitter, Perry.'

'Who?'

'She's a professional. Works through an agency. It's called the Nite-Out agency. That's spelled N-i-t-e–O-u-t. It specializes in baby-sitters. Her name is Hannah Bass. I have a complete description with make of car, licence number and everything here on a card for you.'

Drake slid over a neatly typewritten card.

'How the devil did you get that?' Mason asked.

'Leg work,' Paul Drake said wearily. 'One time the Jennings' phone was out of order. They wanted a baby-sitter. They went over to one of the neighbours, asked to use the phone, had forgotten the number of the agency. The phone book wasn't handy. They called Information and asked for the number of the Nite-Out Agency, and the woman who lived there in the house happened to remember the name Nite-Out because it struck her as such a nice name for a baby-sitting agency.'

'Then you called up and asked for the name of the woman who did baby-sitting for Jennings?' Della Street asked.

Drake shook his head. 'You can't be that crude in this game. You might get slapped down. Moreover, they might tip off someone whom you didn't want tipped off.

'I played it the long way round. I had my man camp there with the neighbours and keep talking, asking them to try and remember any other conversation. They remembered that the baby-sitter had been mentioned by name. They remembered the first name was Hannah because it was the name of their aunt, and they had been wondering whether their aunt might not have been making a little money on the side by baby-sitting, so they perked their ears up. But it turned out the last name didn't mean anything to them so they forgot it. They thought the name was Fish. But then that didn't sound right. Then the man thought it might have been Trout. And then the woman remembered it was Bass. They'd taken one of those memory courses where they use association of ideas to help in recalling things. They could both of them remember Fish, but it was just luck they remembered Bass.'

'That's the name all right?'

'That's the name all right,' Drake said. 'I telephoned the Nite-Out Agency and asked them if they had a Hannah Bass working for them and if they could recommend her credit. They said they didn't know anything about her financial affairs, but she was one of their baby-sitters; that she was very well liked; that they had never had any complaints; that they had investigated her character before taking her on as one of their sitters, and that she was thoroughly reliable and they had no hesitancy in recommending her for jobs. They felt under the circumstances her credit should be all right.'

Again the telephone rang. Drake picked up one of the instruments, said: 'Yeah? Hello. This is Paul Drake.

'The hell . . . you're sure . . .? Okay. Keep me posted on anything new. Good-bye.'

Drake hung up the telephone, turned to Perry Mason and said: 'That's a hell of a note. Someone had messed up the gun they found under the pillow where your client had been sleeping.'

'What do you mean?' Mason asked.

'Someone ran a rat-tail file up and down the barrel until the thing is all scratched and cut. Test bullets fired through it are valueless.'

'Then how can they tell it's the murder gun?' Mason asked.

Drake grinned. 'That's the hell of it; they can't. You can imagine how Hamilton Burger, the district attorney, feels. He's biting his finger-nails back to the knuckles.'

Mason was thoughtful. 'If that gun was found under Norda Allison's pillow it was planted there. She left that house early in the morning and went to a hotel. Do you think she'd have gone away and left a gun under her pillow?'

'Save it for the jury,' Drake said, 'don't try it on a detective with a bad stomach.'

'What's the physical history of the gun?' Mason asked.

'It was purchased by Barton Jennings. He doesn't have a permit. He used it on a camping trip up in Idaho. He was hunting and said he wanted to take along a .22 to get some game.'

'How does he explain its being under Norda Allison's pillow?'

'*He* doesn't explain. *He* doesn't have to.'

'It was his gun,' Mason said. 'It should have been in his possession. It's up to him to explain. Where did he keep it?'

'In a bureau drawer in the room where they put Norda Allison for the night.'

'And very conveniently left the gun in the drawer for her to find?'

'That's their story.'

'That's a hell of a story,' Mason said.'Anything else, Paul?'

'Yeah. I've got the names of the people who were with Mervin Selkirk up in San Francisco. That is, a newspaper reporter up there got them.'

'Go on,' Mason said.

'Well, Mervin Selkirk hit this fellow with brass knuckles. They've now established that as a fact. Some inoffensive bird named Benedict was the target. Selkirk had the brass knuckles and he was laying for Benedict. He socked the guy then slipped the brass knuckles to this other chap who pretended he didn't want to have his name involved as a witness and got the hell out of there.'

'You got the story?' Mason asked,

'I've got the story. So have the police. So have the newspapers.'

'How did you get it?'

'I got it after the reporters dug out the facts. My San Francisco correspondent knew I was working on the case. I was trying to get some angles up there and they called me as soon as it broke.'

'What's the name of the fellow who went out with the brass knuckles?' Mason asked.

'Nick Fallon,' Drake said. 'His full name is Arturas Francisco Fallon, but Nick is his nickname. He's the guy who furnished the brass knuckles. Selkirk knew he had them; said he wanted to borrow them; had them in his pocket; stuck his foot out when Benedict walked by. Then when Benedict stumbled, he began cussing him and as Benedict straightened up to show a little indignation, Selkirk cracked him on the jaw, then slipped the knuckles back to Fallon–Fallon knew what he was supposed to do right quick. He got out there fast.'

Mason digested that information, turned to Della Street, said: 'Okay, Della, let's go.'

'Dancing?' she asked.

Mason shook his head. 'Come on,' he said.

'Where will you be?' Drake asked.

'We'll be in touch with you, Paul. Keep on the job. Get all the information you can. What have they done with Norda Allison?'

'They're booking her for suspicion of murder.'

'Find out anything about Robert Selkirk, the seven-year-old son of Mervin by his former marriage?'

'Not yet,' Drake said. 'He's supposed to be on some kind of a camping trip. He and his dog went out with a Scout group of some sort. They're on a two- or three-day camping trip.'

'I have a tip he's not with that group,' Mason said.

'Then I've sure sent a man on a wild-goose chase,' Drake told him. 'He's rented a jeep and is going in over mountain roads. I told him to find out if Robert was with the group, then get to the nearest phone and let me know.'

'When will you be hearing from him?'

'Probably within an hour.'

'We'll call you back,' Mason said. 'Come on, Della.'

They rode down in the elevator.

'How,' Mason asked, 'would you like to pose as my wife?'

Her eyes were without expression. 'How long?' she asked tonelessly.

'An hour or two.'

'What for?'

'We're going to borrow a baby.'

'Oh, *are* we?'

'And then phone for a baby-sitter,' Mason said. 'Now anybody in your apartment house who would co-operate?'

Della Street thought things over for a moment, then said: 'Well . . . there's a grass widow on the lower floor . . . the baby'd be asleep.'

'That's fine,' Mason said. 'We'll see if we can fix it up.'

She laughed enigmatically, said: 'I thought for a moment your intentions were . . . skip it.'

Mason drove her to her apartment house, opened the door of the car. She jumped out on the other side. 'Let's go.'

They went up to Della's apartment. Della excused herself and a moment later came back with a woman of about her own age.

'This is Mrs Colton, Mr Mason. I've asked her if we could borrow her baby and . . . well, she wanted to look you over.'

'We need a baby-sitter,' Mason said, 'and I want it to look convincing. You can stay out in the hall if you want.'

'Oh, I don't think that's necessary,' she said, laughing. 'I just want to size up the situation. It's such an unusual request.'

'She's asleep now,' Della Street explained, 'but we can move her bed in here or we could put her in my bed.'

'It's going to look rather crowded for a couple and a baby,' Mason pointed out.

'You ought to see my apartment if you think this one would look crowded,' Mrs Colton said.

Della Street looked at Mason and raised her eyebrows. Mason nodded.

'Well, thanks a lot, Alice,' Della said. 'If you don't mind we'll bring her in.'

'Need help?' Mason asked.

'With the crib, yes,' Mrs Colton said. 'I think we'd better bring her up in the crib. In that way we won't waken her–I hope.'

Mason went to Mrs Colton's apartment. The woman, Della Street and Mason carried the crib with the sleeping child to Della Street's apartment.

Mason seated himself, thumbed through the pages of the telephone book, got the number of the Nite-Out agency and entered it in his notebook.

'You'd better call me if she wakens,' Alice Colton said. 'She knows you, Della, but if she should waken and find herself in a strange apartment, she . . .

well, I'd like to be there.'

'Don't worry,' Della said. 'We'll call you. We just want to use her for a short time for . . . look, Alice why don't you stay right here with us?'

'Would it be all right if I did?'

'Sure it would,' Della said. 'Only just be careful to appear as a friend of ours and not as her mother. For the purposes of this masquerade I want to be the mother of the baby.'

She turned towards Perry Mason and elevated her eyebrows.

Mason nodded, picked up the telephone, dialled the number of the agency.

'Hello,' he said, when a voice answered. 'We find ourselves confronted with an emergency. We need a baby-sitter right away and it may be she will have to stay here all night. I'm not certain.

'Now we're willing to pay forty dollars for the right person, if she'll be willing to stay all night.'

The voice of the woman at the agency was reassuring. 'That will be *quite* satisfactory. I'm certain we can get you a reliable sitter for that price.'

'Well now,' Mason told her, 'there's a problem. My wife is very nervous and we simply won't feel satisfied if we leave the child with someone who is a total stranger.'

'Do you know any of our sitters?' the voice asked.

'Not personally,' Mason said, 'but you have a Hannah Bass. Some people who have used your agency recommend her very highly. Would it be possible for you to get her?'

'I'll see,' the voice said. 'If you'll give me your telephone number, I'll find out and call you back.'

Mason gave her the number and hung up.

Alice Colton watched them with puzzled eyes.

'It's all right, Alice,' Della Street said.

A few moments later Della Street's telephone rang. Mason answered it.

'This is the Nite-Out Agency,' the feminine voice said. 'We've contacted Hannah Bass and it's quite all right with her. She wants to know, however, if it is definitely assured that it will be an all-night job and that you are willing to pay forty dollars.'

'That's right,' Mason said. 'If anything happens and the emergency doesn't materialize, she'll get the forty dollars anyway and cab fare home.'

'She has her own car. Will you give me your name and address?'

'The apartment,' Mason said, 'is in my wife's name. I'm a buyer for a large concern and I don't want to be disturbed on week-ends by a lot of salesmen who are trying to interest me in bargains. The name is Della Street. You have the telephone number and if you have a pencil, I'll give you the address.'

Mason gave her the address of Della Street's apartment house and the feminine voice said: 'Mrs Bass will be there within thirty minutes.'

'Thank you,' Mason said.

'Is it a job where she can get some sleep, or will she have to sit up?' the feminine voice inquired.

'She'll have to sit up and watch the baby,' Mason said. 'I'm sorry but that's the way it is.'

'That's quite all right. She's prepared to do that. She'll stay until eight in the morning, or nine if necessary.'

'Have her come right along, if you will, please,' Mason said.

He hung up the telephone.

Alice Colton looked around the apartment, said, 'The feminine influence predominates pretty much, Della. Mr Mason doesn't seem to be . . . well, he doesn't seem to *live* here.'

Mason said: 'I guess you have a point there. If you folks will pardon me.'

He took off his coat, untied his necktie, opened the shirt at the neck, kicked off his shoes, settled back in his stocking feet, picked up the paper and turned to the sporting section.

'How's that?' he asked.

'Better,' Alice Colton said, smiling. 'You know, you two . . . well, when you look like that you . . . you seem to sort of fit in.'

'Thanks,' Mason said as Della Street blushed slightly.

Alice Colton continued to regard them with speculative curiosity.

'Now when Mrs Bass comes in,' Mason said to Alice Colton, 'we're going to have to have a story for her. It's this: Della and I are married. You're Della's sister. Your mother is very ill and we're trying to get a plane to Denver.

'My sister is coming in tomorrow to relieve the baby-sitter and take care of the child until we return. We're awaiting confirmation on plane tickets.

'Della, you'd better load up a couple of suitcases and bring them out here and you, Mrs Colton, had better get a suitcase and have it ready.

'And while you're about it, Mrs Colton, I'd appreciate it if you'd ring up Western Union and send a telegram to Della Street at this address saying: Mother passed away an hour ago. No need to make this trip. Will advise you concerning funeral arrangements. Florence.'

'You want that sent?'

'I want it sent,' Mason said. 'Go to your apartment and get a suitcase, throw some books in it or anything you want and come back here, but telephone that message just before you leave your apartment. You'll have to charge it to your phone. Della will fix up the financial arrangements.'

'This is a real thrill,' Mrs Colton said, laughing nervously. 'I feel all cloak-and-daggerish.'

'This is routine,' Della Street said, laughing.

'After Mrs Bass comes,' Mason instructed Mrs Colton, 'you're to be the tragic one. Della and I will take it more or less as a matter of course. Della will be philosophical about her mother. After all, she's been sick and the end was not unexpected. You will be quiet and moody and perhaps sob a bit in a quiet, unobtrusive way–you will, however, listen very carefully to everything that is said and remember what is said because you may have to testify.'

'In court?' Alice Colton asked in consternation.

'Sure,' Mason said, making his voice sound casual. 'There's nothing to it. Just get up on the witness stand and tell what you heard. Della Street will be right along with you. Just be sure you're telling the truth and there's nothing to worry about.'

Alice Colton laughed nervously. 'Good heavens,' she said, 'I'll never sleep tonight, not a wink. I'll get the suitcase and send the telegram.'

She was back in some ten minutes carrying a suitcase, in the meantime Della Street had placed two suitcases near the door.

A few minutes later the street bell rang and Hannah Bass announced herself.

'Come on up,' Della Street said. 'My husband is just dressing but he's decent. We're awaiting a wire from Denver and a confirmation of plane reservations. If you can come right up, we'll explain your duties.'

A few moments later chimes sounded and Della Street opened the door.

Hannah Bass was in the middle forties, a matronly appearing, muscular woman whose body appeared thick rather than fat. Her eyes were small, restless and glittering.

Della Street came towards her, said: 'I'm Mrs Street and this is my husband. This is my sister. We're waiting for a confirmation of reservations.'

Mason, who had been adjusting his tie in front of the mirror, smiled and said: 'Do sit down, Mrs Bass. The baby is in the bedroom. I'm quite certain you won't have any trouble. My sister will be here by morning. You see, my mother-in-law is quite ill.'

Hannah Bass shook hands with the others, sat down on the edge of the davenport, grey restless eyes surveying the apartment, taking in every detail. 'How old's the baby?' she asked.

'My daughter is sixteen months old,' Della Street said. 'You won't have any trouble, I'm certain.'

'Sometimes when a baby wakes up with a stranger,' Mrs Bass said, 'she gets panic-stricken and . . .'

'Not Darlene,' Della Street interrupted, 'I can guarantee she won't give you any trouble. She's a lamb. Just tell her that Mommie asked you to wait until Aunt Helen could come. Tell her that Aunt Helen will be here in the morning.'

'You don't think you should wake her up now and tell her that you have to go?'

'Oh, we've already told her,' Della Street said. 'We told her that Mommie was going to have to go away and that a friend of Mommie's would stay with her until Aunt Helen came. She'll wake about seven in the morning, and I'm certain you won't have any trouble. Helen will be here by seven-thirty or eight.'

Hannah Bass seemed a little dubious. 'Sometimes they get frightened,' she said.

'I know,' Della Street said, 'but this is an emergency.'

'After all,' Mason said reassuringly, 'we *may* not have to go. If we can't get confirmation of our reservations on this plane, we just can't make it and that's all there is to it.'

Hannah Bass looked at him coldly. 'I understood it was a forty-dollar job,' she said.

'It is,' Mason told her. 'You get the same amount of money whether we go or whether we don't. Just sit back and relax.'

Alice Colton wiped her eyes with a handkerchief.

Della Street said: 'It's all right, Alice. Everything's going to be for the best.'

'The agency tells me that you asked especially for me.'

Della Street looked inquiringly at Perry Mason.

Mason said: 'That's right, Mrs Bass. You see, I'd heard about you through the Jennings. They speak very highly of you.'

'The Jennings?' she asked.

'Lorraine and Barton Jennings,' Mason explained. 'They have a boy, Robert Selkirk. Her child by another marriage.'

'Oh yes,' she said. 'Bobby is quite a boy. He has a certain dignity that is exceptional in a child.'

'Crazy about guns, isn't he?' Mason said.

'Well, he's like any normal boy–what can you expect with all these "pistol pictures" on television. He loves to watch galloping horses and, after all, those shows put on some pretty spirited gun battles.'

'They do for a fact,' Mason agreed. And then added, 'I suppose Robert has the special pearl-handled imitation six-shooters with the holsters tied down in the most approved Western style.'

Hannah Bass became suddenly uneasy. 'He likes guns,' she said, and clamped her lips together.

Mason eyed her thoughtfully. 'That,' he said, 'is the only thing which causes us some uneasiness, Mrs Bass.'

'What is?' she asked, instantly on the defensive.

'Giving Robert a real gun to play with.'

'Who says I gave him a real gun?'

Mason let his face show surprise. 'Didn't you?'

'Who said so?'

'Why I understood that you did. Barton Jennings has this ·22 automatic, you know, and Robert plays with it.'

There was a long interval of silence. Hannah Bass had little suspicious grey eyes and they glittered as they probed Mason's face.

The lawyer met her gaze with searching candour. 'Don't you let him play with Barton's gun?' he asked.

'What difference does it make?' Hannah Bass asked.

'I just wondered,' Mason said.

'I don't talk about my other clients when I'm baby-sitting,' Hannah Bass announced with finality.

Mason said deprecatingly: 'We were only discussing your recommendations and the reason we sent for you, Mrs Bass.'

'I didn't know anybody knew about it,' she said suddenly. 'It was just a secret between Robert and me.'

Mason's smile was enigmatic.

The street bell rang. Della Street went to the telephone, said: 'Yes . . . oh, hurry up with it, will you? I'll open the door for you.'

She pressed a buzzer and said to Perry Mason: 'A Western Union telegram.'

Mason showed excitement. 'He's on the way up?'

Della nodded.

Alice Colton said: 'Oh, Della,' and suddenly flung herself into Della Street's arms.

Hannah Bass's glittering eyes kept moving around the apartment, taking in every detail. 'I want to look at the baby,' she said suddenly.

Della Street glanced at Mason.

Mason partially opened the door of the bedroom.

Della Street continued to comfort Alice Colton.

Hannah Bass got up and strode to the bedroom door, looked inside at the sleeping child, then stepped inside the bedroom and looked around.

The buzzer sounded on the door of Della Street's apartment.

Della Street disengaged herself from Alice and went to the door. She accepted the telegram, signed for it and tore the envelope open.

For a moment she stood there with the telegram in her hand saying nothing.

'Oh, Della, it isn't . . . it isn't . . .?'

Della Street nodded, said: 'Mother has passed away.'

There was a long moment of silence, then Alice Colton began to sob audibly.

'Well, after all,' Della Street said, 'it's for the best. Mother was bedridden and she had nothing to look forward to. The doctors said there was virtually no hope.'

Hannah Bass stood in the door of the bedroom for a moment. Then she marched over to where Della Street was holding the telegram, said: 'Say, what kind of a plant *is* this, anyway?'

'What do you mean?' Della Street asked.

'You know what I mean,' Hannah said, snatching at Della Street's left hand. 'Where's your wedding ring?'

'At the jewellers, being repaired,' Della Street said coldly. 'That is, if it's any of *your* business.'

'It's lots of my business,' Hannah Bass said. 'You're not married. That's not your baby. This isn't your husband. I've seen his face somewhere before–in newspapers and magazines somewhere–what are you trying to do?'

Della Street said: 'My mother has just passed away. Here's the telegram.'

She extended the telegram, holding her thumb over the top part of the telegram so that Hannah Bass could see the message, but not the place where the telegram had originated.

'Well, we won't argue about it,' the woman said. 'This was a forty-dollar job. Give me my forty dollars and I'll be on my way.'

Della Street looked at Perry Mason.

Mason smiled and shook his head.

'Now don't pull that line with me,' Hannah Bass said belligerently.

'What line?' Mason asked.

'Trying to talk me out of the forty dollars.'

'No one's trying to talk you out of the forty dollars, Mrs Bass,' Mason told her. 'What you wanted, you know, was an all-night job; you wanted to be guaranteed it would be an all-night job. It is.'

'I wanted the forty dollars, not necessarily an all-night job.'

'You'll get the forty dollars,' Mason told her, 'and you'll sit right there all night to earn it.'

Hannah Bass looked at him sharply. 'You're the lawyer,' she said. 'You're the man who does all that spectacular stuff in court. You're Perry Mason!'

'That's right,' Mason said. 'Now, then, just sit down there and tell me how it happened that you would let Robert Selkirk play with a real gun whenever you were baby-sitting with him.'

'So *that's* what you're after!' Hannah Bass said.

'That's what I'm after,' Mason told her.

Hannah Bass slowly seated herself. 'So this was all a plant.'

'It was all a plant, if that will make you feel any better,' Mason told her.

'I don't have to answer your questions. I can get up and walk out through that door. You don't have any authority to question me.'

'That's entirely correct,' Mason said. 'You were hired to sit here until eight o'clock in the morning. You're to get forty dollars for it. If you walk out through that door, you don't get forty dollars and you'll still have to answer the same questions; but this time before a grand jury.'

'What difference does it make?' Hannah Bass asked.

'For your information, so there won't be any misunderstanding, Mervin Selkirk was murdered. Norda Allison has been accused of that murder. She's my client.

'I don't know what happened. I'm trying to find out. I'm not making any accusations, at least not yet, but apparently when you were baby-sitting you let Robert have a ·22 automatic revolver, probably a Colt Woodsman model.'

'You can't prove it,' Hannah Bass said.

'I think I can,' Mason told her. 'If you have anything to conceal, if you are implicated in any way in the murder of Mervin Selkirk, you had better get out of here and retain a lawyer to represent you. If you have nothing to conceal, there is no reason why you can't talk to me.'

'You got me here under false pretences,' she said.

'I asked you to come here,' Mason told her. 'I wanted to talk with you where I wouldn't be interrupted by the police.'

'What do you mean, the police?'

'*You* should know what I mean. The police are employed by the taxpayers to look into matters of this sort. In case you haven't met Lieutenant Tragg of the homicide department, you have a delightful experience in store. Tragg is very thorough, very shrewd, very fair and very determined.

'Sooner or later you're going to have to tell your story–officially. You can tell it to me now unofficially. If there's anything about it that sounds fishy, I'll point it out to you.'

'Why should any of it sound fishy?' she asked.

'I don't know,' Mason said. 'All I know is that your extreme reluctance to talk may be an indication of guilty knowledge. You'd better consult a lawyer, if that's the case.

'And remember this, Mrs Bass, some day you're going to be on the witness stand and I'm going to cross-examine you and if you don't tell me your story now, I'm going to ask you why you were afraid to tell it.'

'Who says I'm afraid to tell it?'

'I say so.'

'Well I'm not.'

'Then why won't you tell it?'

'I didn't say I wouldn't tell it.'

'Make up your mind.'

The room was silent for several seconds, then Hannah Bass said: 'There wasn't anything wrong with it, it was just yielding to a childish whim. Robert is an unusual boy. He loves Western pictures. He wants to grow up and be a marshal or a cowpuncher or something of that sort. He's crazy about firearms. I've never seen anything like it.'

'How did it happen that you started letting him have the ·22?' Mason asked.

'It was one time when I was baby-sitting with him. I had to stay there for two days while Mr and Mrs Jennings were away. They left Robert with me.'

'You occupied the spare bedroom on the second floor?'

'Yes.'

'At the front of the house?'

'Yes.'

'Go on,' Mason said.

'Well, I opened a drawer in the bureau in order to put some of my things away and found this gun.'

'What sort of a gun?'

'A Colt Woodsman.'

'You know something about guns?'

'I was married to a man who ran shooting galleries. He was one of the best ·22 revolver shots in the country. He taught me how to handle guns.'

'And how to shoot?' Mason asked.

'I became a very good shot,' she admitted.

'All right what happened?'

'Robert came walking into the room while I was looking this gun over. He was completely fascinated with it. He wanted to hold it for a while.'

'What did you do?'

'I took out the magazine clip and saw that it was fully loaded. I snapped back the recoil-operated mechanism and found there was no shell in the barrel. So I let Robert handle the gun.'

'And then what happened?'

'He was completely fascinated. He had seen me work the mechanism. He wanted to know how to handle the gun and all about it.

'So then I took the shells out of the magazine, put the magazine in place and let him play with the empty gun for a while. Then I put it back in the drawer. I don't think Robert talked about anything else all day. I was afraid his parents wouldn't like what I had done, although for my part I think the best way to teach boys about firearms is to teach them at an early age and teach them to handle them safely. However, all parents don't have the same idea.'

'So what did you do?' Mason asked.

'I made Robert promise that he wouldn't tell his folks anything about that gun.'

'And after that?' Mason asked.

'Well,' she said, somewhat reluctantly, 'after that Robert had sort of a hold on me. When his parents would be gone he'd insist on having me unload the gun and let him keep it in his hand. At first I made him stay in the house, but after a while–well, I let him take it outdoors and play with it.

'For the life of me I don't see that there was anything wrong with what I did, but there were times when I felt as though I should go to Mrs Jennings and discuss the matter with her.

'The trouble was I had already let Robert play with the weapon. I don't think I have ever seen a child as completely fascinated with any toy as Robert was with just holding that automatic in his hands.'

'Did he ever pull the trigger?' Mason asked.

'Of course he did. However, I made him promise that he'd never, never pull the trigger when the gun was pointed at anyone. I showed him the safety, showed him how to put it on and keep it on, and it was part of his agreement with me that he was always to have this safety in place while he was handling the gun.'

'You were there with him at night?' Mason asked.

'Sometimes. I've stayed as much as a couple of days at a time.'

'And Robert has played with the gun each time?'

'Yes.'

'And at night has he ever slept with the gun under his pillow?'

'Once, yes.'

'How did that happen?'

'He's a rather nervous, high-strung child despite the fact that he keeps his emotions under such excellent control. He liked to camp out in that tent on the patio and he told me it would give him a feeling of assurance if he had the gun with him. He said there were noises in the night and he wanted some protection, was the way he expressed it.'

'And you let him take the gun?'

'Just that once. That was when I found he had a shell for it. That's when I began to get frightened of the whole business. I told him he was just a little boy seven years old, that he couldn't have any gun for protection until he got to be a big man.'

'Now then, when Lorraine Jennings and Barton Jennings went down on Friday night to meet Norda Allison at the airport, did you take care of Robert?'

She shook her head.

'Who did?'

'I think they left him there alone with the dog. Rover wouldn't let anyone get near Robert. I think his folks put Robert to bed and then just quietly went down to meet the plane.'

'Would they leave him alone like that?'

'Sometimes. The dog was always there. Sometimes they'd leave after he'd gone to sleep. I don't like the idea of that. I think that whenever you are planning on leaving a child alone, you should tell him. I think if a child wakes up at night and finds he's alone, when he expects his parents to be there, it gives him an emotional shock.'

'Did they ever say anything to you at any time about the gun, or did you ever say anything to them? In other words, do you think that they knew you were letting him take the gun?'

'I never said anything to them and they never said anything to me. Robert promised me that he wouldn't tell them and I'm satisfied he wouldn't. Robert is a child, but he's a man of his word.'

'But you do know Robert wanted the gun when he was sleeping out in the patio?'

'Yes.'

'If Robert had wakened and wanted something in the house and found his mother and his stepfather were away, do you think it is possible that he could have gone to that bedroom and taken the gun out of the drawer?'

A look of sudden alarm came on her face.

'Do you?' Mason asked.

'Good heavens, *did* he do that?' she asked in a half whisper.

'I'm asking you if it's possible.'

'It's very possible,' she said.

Mason smiled and said: 'I think that does it, Mrs Bass. Here's your forty dollars for the baby-sitting.'

'Good heavens,' she said, 'if he had done that, if . . . Mr Mason, do you think that child could possibly have . . . good heavens, no! It's preposterous! He wouldn't have done anything like that!'

Mason said: 'Those are the words you use to reassure yourself, Mrs Bass, but if there had been a mirror in front of your face, you would have seen from your dismayed expression exactly how possible you thought that would have been.'

Mason handed her four ten-dollar bills.

Hannah Bass blinked for a moment, then abruptly got up and without a word walked out into the corridor, pulling the door shut behind her.

Mason smiled reassuringly at Alice Colton. 'You may take the child back now, Mrs Colton, and thanks a lot. We certainly appreciate your co-operation. You may have aided the cause of justice.'

10

It was ten o'clock on Sunday morning when Mason's unlisted telephone rung.

Mason picked up the receiver. 'This is Perry.'

Paul Drake's voice, sharp with urgency, came over the telephone. 'I have something, Perry, that you'd better look into. I'm afraid my man pulled a boner, but there was nothing to tip him off.'

'What do you mean by that?'

'I had tails put on the Jennings' house the way you wanted. Barton Jennings went out this morning, visited an apartment house and then came back. My man tailed him both ways, but he's a little uneasy about it.'

'Why?' Mason asked.

'Call it an investigator's sixth sense, if you want,' Drake said, 'but my man feels that Barton Jennings went out there on a specific errand and managed to accomplish that errand right under the nose of the operative.'

'Where's your man now?'

'Up here.'

'You're at the office?'

'Yes.'

'Hold him there,' Mason said. 'I'm coming up.'

Mason telephoned the garage man in the apartment house to have his car ready for action. He took the elevator to the garage, jumped in his car, drove to the all but deserted parking lot in front of the office building, left his car and went to Drake's office.

Drake's operative was a small man whose silver-grey eyes were thoughtfully watching beneath bushy white eyebrows. He was small in stature, somewhere in his late fifties, and as keenly incisive as a sharp razor. He had, nevertheless, cultivated a habit of blending into the background as successfully as a chameleon.

Mason had a vague impression that this man's name was Smith. He had met him on half a dozen different cases but had never heard him referred to by any other name than 'Smithy'.

Paul Drake, tilted back in his chair with his heels up on the desk, smoking a contemplative cigarette, waved a greeting to Mason.

Smithy shook hands.

Mason sat down.

'You tell him Smithy,' Drake said.

The operative said: 'At eight o'clock this morning Barton Jennings left his house carrying a suitcase. He was moving with some difficulty. His leg was bothering him. He had a cane in one hand, the suitcase in the other. He got in his automobile and drove very slowly and casually down to a gas station. He had the car filled up with gas, the windshield washed, the tyres checked, then he drove around the block and started back towards home.

'Just something about the way the fellow was driving the car made me feel he had something in mind that he intended to do, if he was certain he wasn't wearing a tail. So I hung way, way back, just taking a chance.

'Then I saw him swing over to the side of the road a bit. I've had guys pull that trick with me before, so I turned down a side street, went for half a block and made a U-turn.

'Sure enough, Jennings did just what I thought he was going to do. He made a complete U-turn and came tearing back down the street going fast. I was where I could get a brief glimpse of the manœuvre, so I came dawdling out of the side street at slow speed and crossed the intersection just ahead of him. That gave him a chance to pass me and it never occurred to him I was following him. After about eight or ten blocks at high speed he slowed down and then drove directly to this apartment house.

'He parked the car, took the suitcase, went in, and was there for about half an hour; then he came out and drove to his house. After he left the apartment house, he didn't take any precautions to see that he was free of a tail. He had all the assurance of a man who had accomplished a mission and wasn't worrying about anything any more. He had the same suitcase with him that he'd taken in.'

'He went home?' Mason asked.

'He went home, put his car in the garage, went in the house, and after a while came out and sat on the porch, ostensibly reading the Sunday papers, but actually looking around to see if anybody was keeping him under surveillance.

'When a subject does that, it's a lot better to get off the job and have somebody else come on, so I beat it to a phone, telephoned Paul for a relief and told him I had something to report.'

'You have any idea what apartment the guy went to?' Mason asked.

'No.'

'What apartment house was it?'

'The Cretonic. It's a small apartment house out on Wimberly. I don't think there are over fifteen or twenty apartments in the place altogether. It's a walk-up, two-story affair, moderately priced apartments–the kind that would appeal to persons in the low white-collar brackets.'

'Let's go,' Mason said.

'I thought you'd want to take a look,' Smithy said. 'Two cars?'

'One,' Mason said. 'We'll go in mine. You sit here on the job, Paul, and we may telephone for some help. Come on, Smithy, let's go.'

Smithy and the lawyer took the elevator down to Mason's car, drove out to the Cretonic apartments. Mason got out and looked the place over.

'Jennings needed a key,' Mason said, 'to get in or else he pressed the bell of some apartment and they buzzed the door open.'

Smithy nodded.

'You don't have any idea which?'

'No, Mr Mason, I don't. I just wasn't close enough to see what he was doing, and I didn't dare to get close enough. I can tell you one thing though, he was stopped over here at the side of the building. I could see his left elbow hanging pretty well down.'

'Well, that's, a clue,' Mason said. 'Let's look at the lower cards.'

Mason took his notebook, jotted down some names, said: 'There's half a dozen, but that's still too many.'

'I'll tell you what, Mr Mason,' Smithy said, 'if you'll stand right here in the doorway and look down at the names on the directory and let your left arm stick out a little bit the way it would if you were leaning over and punching a button with your right thumb, I might be able to do a better job. I'll go back to the place where I had my car parked and in that way we may be able to narrow it down a little bit.'

'Go head,' Mason told him.

He waited until the detective was in the right position and then Mason stooped down and made a pretence of jabbing each one of the lower call buttons with his thumb.

When he had finished, Smithy came moving up and said: 'I think it's the lowest one on the left-hand side, Mr Mason. Your elbow looked just about right.'

Mason examined the card. It was oblong, but evidently from an engraved calling card, and said simply, *Miss Grace Hallum.*

'We'll give it a try,' Mason said.

'Any idea what you're going to tell her?'

'I'm not going to tell her anything,' Mason said. 'She's going to tell us.'

He pressed the button.

There was no answer.

Mason pressed the button two or three times more, then pressed the button marked *Manager*.

A moment later the outer lock buzzed open and Mason entered the small lobby. A door opened behind a counter in the corner of the lobby and an intelligent looking well-kept woman in her early fifties stepped out to smile at the lawyer and the detective.

'Something for you gentlemen?' she asked.

'Vacancies?' Mason asked.

She smiled and shook her head.

'I understand that Grace Hallum's apartment was to be vacant,' Mason said. 'I tried to ring her but she doesn't answer. Do you know anything about her?'

'Oh yes,' the manager said. 'She's going to be gone for some time. She made arrangements with me to feed her canary.'

'When did she leave?' Mason asked.

The manager looked at him curiously. 'Are you a detective?' she asked.

Mason grinned and jerked his thumb at Smithy. 'He is.'

'Oh–what's the trouble?'

'No trouble,' Mason said, 'we're just trying to get a line on her.'

The manager's lips clamped together. 'Well, I'm sorry. There's nothing I can tell you except that she's gone.'

Mason played a hunch. 'Did she have the boy with her?'

'She had the boy with her.'

'Suitcases?'

'One doesn't go for an indefinite stay without suitcases.'

'Taxicab?' Mason asked.

'I don't know. I didn't ask.'

'Does she own a car?'

'I don't think so.'

Mason tried to be as charming as possible. 'It wouldn't hurt you to be a little more communicative.'

'I'm not so certain about that. I don't discuss tenants' affairs.'

'Oh well,' Mason said, 'it isn't particularly important. We're just checking, that's all. How long has she had the boy, do you know?'

'I'm sure I couldn't tell you.'

'Well, thanks a lot,' Mason said. 'Good-bye.'

He gave her his best smile and led the way out of the apartment house.

'I don't get it,' Smithy said.

'What?'

'Your technique,' Smithy told him. 'I'd have flashed my credentials and suggested she might get into trouble if she tried to withhold information.'

'I have a better idea,'Mason told him, studying the directory. 'Let's see, Grace Hallum was in 208. Let's look at 206 and 210–who's in 206?'

Smithy consulted the directory.

'Miss M. Adrian,' he said.

'Give her a ring,' Mason instructed.

Smithy pressed his thumb against the button.

In a few moments the door was buzzed open.

Mason and the detective again entered the apartment house. The manager had now returned into her apartment and the door behind the little counter was closed.

The two men climbed the steps to the second floor.

Mason tapped on the door of 206.

The door opened the scant two or three inches allowed by a heavy brass safety chain. A woman with a long, thin nose surveyed the two men suspiciously. 'What is it?' she asked.

Mason studied the blinking eyes, the nose, the thin lips, the prominent chin, said: 'Show her your credentials, Smithy.'

Smithy took a worn billfold from his pocket, extended it so the woman could look it over.

'Detectives!' she said.

'Smithy is a detective,' Mason said. 'I'm a lawyer. We want to talk with you.'

'What's *your* name?'

Mason gave her his card.

Her face showed surprise. She looked from the card to Mason's face and then said: 'Good heavens, you *are*!' Why *you're* Perry Mason.'

'That's right.'

The chain snapped off the catch. 'Well, come in,' she said. 'I'm honoured. Of course, I haven't been preparing for visitors and Sunday is usually my morning to straighten up the apartment. I usually go out to a movie on Saturday night and . . . well, sit down and tell me what this is all about.'

'It's about your neighbour next door,' Mason said.

Miss Adrian, a woman in her late fifties, small boned, spry as a bird, paused in mid-stride. 'Well now, I just *knew* there was something wrong there,' she said.

Mason nodded. 'That's why we came to see you.'

'But I didn't tell anybody. I've kept my own counsel. Now, how in the world did you know that I'd seen anything?'

'We have ways of finding out things like that,' Mason said. 'Would you mind telling us about it?'

'What do you want to know?'

'When did the boy come here?'

'Yesterday morning,' she said. 'Yesterday morning at exactly four-thirty-five.'

'Do you know who brought him?'

'His father, I suppose.'

'And what do you know about Grace Hallum?'

'She's divorced–lives on alimony. She works as a baby-sitter part of the time for extra money and calls herself Miss Grace Hallum rather than Mrs Hallum. She used to be a model and she never lets a body forget it.'

'Does she work for the Nite-Out Agency?'

'I believe that's right, yes.'

'Well, then,' Mason said, smiling casually, 'you didn't think there was anything unusual about it, simply someone bringing a boy to stay with her.'

'Nothing unusual about it!' Miss Adrian exclaimed. 'Well, I *like* that!'

'There was something unusual then?'

'I'll say there was. At that hour in the morning with my wall bed down, my head right up against that partition and . . . I'll say one thing about the apartment house, the only way you can have any complete privacy is to talk in sign language.'

'You heard what was said?'

'I heard enough of it.'

'Such as what?'

'Well, Grace Hallum was a little shocked at the idea of being called at that hour in the morning but the man was a regular client of hers so she opened the door and let him in. Well, you know, she was terribly coy about not being dressed and all that.'

'How old is she?'

'Twenty-seven, but she *says* it's twenty-four,' Miss Adrian snapped, 'and she has looks. She is very, very well aware of those looks and she had just as soon other people would be aware of them too, if you know what I mean. She's a blue-eyed, tall blonde and she's always posing. She wears dresses that show her hips, if you know what I mean.'

'We know what you mean,' Mason said affably. 'Just what was the conversation?'

'This man wanted her to keep the boy until he gave her further instructions. He asked her to get some suit-cases ready because she might have to travel and . . . that's about all there was to it yesterday morning.'

'And then what happened after that?'

'Well, the man came up *this* morning and I've never heard such a conversation in my life.'

'What do you mean?'

'The man was talking with the boy about some sort of a shooting. He kept saying: "Now remember, *you* didn't shoot anyone. You had a bad dream," and I heard the boy say, "I did too shoot the pistol," and the man laughed and said, "So what of it?" and then said, "You *thought* you shot the pistol, you dreamed you did, but the pistol really wasn't fired at all!" '

'Then what?'

'Then the boy said: "No, I fired the pistol. The rest of it may have been a dream, but I know I fired the pistol." '

'Go on,' Mason said. 'What happened after that?'

'Well, the man talked with the boy awhile and said he was going to send him on a long trip with Miss Hallum and to be sure and be a good boy and do everything Miss Hallum told him to.'

'Did Miss Hallum seem surprised?'

'Not her–now I can tell you this much, there's been a lot of goings on in that apartment, suitcases banging around, people coming with this and that. She was packing and talking with the boy and the boy was doing quite a bit of crying. He seemed to be terribly upset about something.'

'Go on,' Mason said.

'Well, that's about all I know except that another woman came and called on her last night. I gathered she was the woman who runs the Nite-Out Agency. They had quite a conversation. A lot of it was in whispers. Apparently the boy was asleep and they were trying to keep him from knowing anything about it.'

'What happened this morning?' Mason asked.

'Well, this man came again with some clothes for the boy. Right after the man left she went to the phone and called a taxicab. I heard her say she wanted to go to the airport.'

'The cab came?'

'That's right.'

'And she left?'

'Yes, she and the boy.'

'How long ago?'

'Well, it must have been–oh, I guess an hour and a half ago.'

'Did you have any idea where they were going?' Mason asked.

'The man said something about Mexico.'

Mason got up and gave his hand to Miss Adrian. 'Thank you very much for your co-operation,' he said. 'We're just checking.'

'Well, for heaven's sake, I'll certainly say you're checking, coming around to see a body on a Sunday morning. Can you tell me what it's all about?'

'I'm sorry,' Mason said. 'We just wanted to make sure that the boy had left.'

'Yes, he left all right, but can you tell me why all this mystery?'

Mason smiled and shook his head. 'I'm terribly sorry, Miss Adrian, I hate to be a one-way street on these things, but you know how it is.'

She sniffed: 'Well, I can't say as I do. It seems to me that if *I* give *you* information, *you* should give *me* information.'

'I may be back after a while,' Mason said. 'It may be a few hours or it may be a few days, but I'll talk with you some more and by that time I may be able to give you a little more information.'

'Well, I'd certainly like to know what it's all about,' she said. 'It's not that I'm curious, you understand. I like to lead my own life and let other people lead theirs, but what's all this about a boy crying because he thinks he's fired a gun that his daddy didn't want him to, and all of that?'

'Oh, children do have nightmares,' Mason said.

'Yes,' she snapped. 'Nightmares of shooting people and then they're brought to a baby-sitter at half past four on a Saturday morning and then a lawyer and a detective come and ask questions. Don't think I'm foolish, Mr Mason. I wasn't born yesterday.'

Mason shook hands with her, held her hand for a long moment in his, patted the back of it with his left hand and said: 'Now don't go making a mountain out of a mole-hill, Miss Adrian, and please don't say anything to anybody else, at least for a while. I'd like to have the information all to myself for a day or so.'

'And then you'll tell me what it's all about?'

Mason lowered his voice and said: 'Look, if you'll be co-operative, I think I can promise you that you'll have an opportunity to get on the witness-stand and–'

'The witness-stand!' she almost screamed in dismay.

'That's right,' Mason said, 'you'll pose for newspaper photographs and your testimony may make quite a commotion. But that will only happen if you're very, very careful not to say anything to anyone prior to the time of trial.'

'Good heavens, I don't *want* to get on the witness-stand.'

'Why not?'

'Standing up in front of all those people and telling how old I am.'

Mason shook his head: 'You won't have to tell how old you are, just say that you're over thirty. . . .' He paused to lean forward and look at her intently. 'You *are* over thirty, aren't you?'

Miss Adrian was suddenly coy.

'Well,' she said, 'it's all right if someone doesn't ask me how *much* over thirty I am . . . it's longer than I like to think of.'

'That's all right,' Mason said, 'the judge will protect you. You won't have to tell anything about your age. Now, we've got to move on, Miss Adrian, but if you'll just try to think over the events of the last day or so–just so someone doesn't get you mixed up on cross-examination.'

'Cross-examination?'

'Of course,' Mason said casually, 'all witnesses have to be cross-examined, but that's nothing.'

'Well, I'd always heard it was quite an ordeal.'

'Not if you're telling the truth.'

'I'm telling the truth.'

'And not if you remember *all* the details and don't get confused.'

'Well, I remember all the details, but I don't know whether I'm going to get confused standing up there in front of a whole crowd of people like that.'

Mason smiled affably. 'Just start planning on what you're going to wear, Miss Adrian. I'm sure you'll want to look your best. Sometimes the flashlight photographs they use in newspapers aren't the most flattering photographs a person can have but . . . you'll be all right.'

'Well, I'm glad you gave me some notice in advance,' she said, going over to the mirror, patting her hair and smoothing the wave around back of the ears. 'I'll tell the world some of those newspapers *are* terrible!'

'Good-bye,' Mason said. 'Remember now, not a word of this to anyone.'

Mason let himself and the detective out in the corridor.

'Pay dirt,' Smithy said under his breath.

'Pay dirt,' Mason agreed. 'Now we've got to phone Paul and get some operatives out at the airport in a rush.'

11

From the nearest phone Mason called Paul Drake.

'Rush some men out to the airport, Paul. Look for Robert Selkirk, a boy of seven years of age, aristocratic in bearing. He's accompanied by a woman named Grace Hallum, blonde, blue eyes, twenty-seven years old, with a good figure. She worked for a while as a model, married, collected some alimony and is living now partially on alimony and partially by supplementing her income by baby-sitting. They'll probably have a couple of hours' start on you and will have been on a plane for someplace outside of the jurisdiction of the local courts. Try Mexico City first, then try everything you can get. Cover all passenger lists, see if you can locate a woman, any woman, travelling with a seven-year-old boy.'

'There'll be hundreds of them,' Drake said.

'Not with a departure time of the last two hours. My best guess is that reservations were first made over the telephone, then Barton Jennings took some cash and some of the kid's clothes in a suitcase up to Grace Hallum's apartment. He transferred the clothes there, came out with the empty suitcase.

'A taxicab went to the Cretonic Apartments and picked them up. See if you can locate the cab driver, find out what airline they were travelling on. Get busy.'

'Okay,' Drake promised. 'You coming up here?'

'We're on our way,' Mason told him.

The lawyer hung up the phone and he and Smithy drove back to the parking place at the office.

'I could tell by the way he was carrying that suitcase when he came out that there was something wrong,' Smith said. 'That's what it was, all right; the suitcase was empty when he came out.'

Mason nodded.

They entered the elevator.

'Your secretary just came in,' the operator told Mason.

'Stop at Paul's office?' Mason asked.

'I don't think so. I think she went on down the corridor to your office.'

'I'll pick her up,' Mason said.

They stopped at Drake's office. 'Go on in,' Mason told Smith, 'and tell Paul about what happened. I'll see if Della Street has anything on her mind and then come back.'

Mason walked down to his office, latchkeyed the door, found Della Street standing in front of the mirror.

'Hello,' she said. 'I just got here.'

'How come?' Mason asked.

'I rang the unlisted phone in your apartment, no answer. I rang Paul and he said you were out on a hot lead. I thought I'd come up and see if you needed anything.'

'Good girl,' Mason told her. 'We're working on something hot.'

'What is it?'

'Robert Selkirk. The way things look now, his mother and his stepfather left him alone while they went to the airport to meet Norda Allison. Robert was sleeping in a tent in the patio. It's beginning to look as though Robert got frightened, sneaked into the house, took possession of that ·22 Colt Woodsman, then went back to bed in his tent in the patio. Sometime in the night he was aroused by someone prowling around. That just could have been Mervin Selkirk who was engaged in planting that printing press in the Jenning's store-room.

'Evidently the dog they keep knew Mervin Selkirk well enough so he let Selkirk prowl around the place as a friend. Whoever it was, it was someone the dog knew.

'Robert got frightened and took a shot in the dark. That shot probably hit the boy's father. He left a blood trail all the way to his automobile, drove to the country club and died before he could get out of the car.

'Barton Jennings was supposed to take Robert to this camping expedition where the boys were going with their dogs. So he was able to ditch the dog somewhere, probably at a boarding kennel, and take Robert up to another baby-sitter the boy knew. He did all that before five o'clock in the morning.'

'Good heavens,' Della Street said, 'you mean the boy killed his own father?'

'It was an accident,' Mason said. 'Now then, Barton Jennings is giving the boy a good brain-washing. He's making Robert think it was all a nightmare, some hideous dream that he had in which he dreamed that he had pulled the trigger on the gun.

'In order to keep the boy from being called as a witness, they're trying to spirit him out of the country. By the time anyone can get the boy back as a witness, the kid will be convinced he may have had a nightmare but that he didn't actually pull the trigger on the gun.'

Della Street watched Mason for a moment with thoughtful eyes. 'So what do you do?' she asked.

Mason said: 'I block the attempt. I get hold of the boy before his brain has been washed, and . . .' suddenly his voice trailed off into silence.

'Exactly,' Della Street said. 'What's it going to do to a seven-year-old boy if he believes that he has killed his father?'

Mason started pacing the floor. 'Hang it, Della,' he said, 'my duty is to my client. I can't sit back and let a client take a murder rap simply to spare the feelings of a seven-year-old boy. . . . And yet I can't have that seven-year-old boy dragged up in front of the authorities.'

'As far as that's concerned, how are we going to prove our contention once we get him picked up?' Della Street asked.

Mason paced the floor saying nothing.

'Can't you,' she asked, 'use the knowledge you have so you can drop a monkey wrench in the prosecutor's machinery and get Norda Allison acquitted without dragging the boy into it?'

'I'm darned if I know,' Mason admitted, and then added, grinning, 'of course, you *would* look at it from a woman's viewpoint and want to protect the child regardless of anything else.'

'It's the right viewpoint,' Della Street said.

'Come on,' Mason said, changing the subject, 'let's go down to Paul Drake's office and see what *he's* discovered.'

He held the door open and the two of them walked down the echoing corridor of the deserted building to enter the offices of the Drake Detective Agency. Mason waved a greeting to the girl who was busy at the switchboard, held the gate open for Della Street and they walked down to Drake's office.

Drake was just hanging up one of his telephones as Mason and Della Street entered the office. Smithy was sitting in a corner of the office, scribbling in a notebook.

Drake said: 'Well, we've traced your taxicab, Perry, we were lucky. One of my operatives picked up the trip on the dispatcher's records and managed to interview the driver. He was particularly impressed with the little boy. It happens he has a kid of his own and the youngster made quite an impression.

'Here's what happened: On the trip out to the airport the woman was telling the boy about going to Mexico City, all about Mexico and something about the history of Mexico City. She told him he'd see the famous Calendar Stone in the museum and quite a few things of that sort. The boy seemed to have something on his mind and she kept up quite a steady stream of conversation.

'They were going to take an American Airlines plane to Dallas and then Dallas to Mexico City. He took them to the American Airlines.

'Now here's a peculiar thing. They never got on that plane.'

'What plane?'

'The one on which they had reservations. Reservations had been made over the telephone for Mrs Hallum and son. The reservations were confirmed all the way to Mexico City. They were told they would have to pick up their tickets thirty minutes before plane time and they promised to be there. They never showed up.

'The airlines felt certain there had been some unexpected delay in transportation to the airport and actually didn't sell out the reservations until the last minute. Then about five minutes before time of departure they had a couple of stand-bys and they put the stand-bys aboard the plane and wired Dallas to cancel the two tickets on the Mexico City flight unless other information was received.'

'Then what happened to the woman and the child?' Mason asked. 'Was it just an elaborate plant to throw us off the trail?'

'It could have been,' Drake said, but somehow I'm not so certain.'

'Wasn't it unusual for the woman to be talking so much about Mexico City in the taxicab?' Della Street asked. 'Wouldn't that indicate it was a plant?'

'It *might*,' Drake said, but the taxi driver felt certain it was on the up and up. Those taxi drivers get to handle a lot of people and become pretty darn good judges of human nature.'

Mason nodded.

'Well,' Drake asked, 'what do we do?'

'Cover all the other airline offices,' Mason said, 'and see if the pair switched to another airline, and–'

'That's being done,' Drake said, 'but it's quite a job. I thought you'd want to know about the taxi driver right away.'

Mason nodded.

One of the telephones on Drake's desk rang sharply. Drake picked up the receiver said: 'Paul Drake talking,' then frowned in thoughtful concentration as the receiver made a series of squawking noises which were audible throughout the room.

'Okay,' he said, 'that's a lead. Stay with it. Have you got a description of that man?'

Again Drake listened and then said: 'See what you can do.'

He hung up the phone turned to Mason and Della Street and said: 'Well, part of the mystery is clearing up.

'One of my operatives scouting for leads around the place found that a porter remembered the woman and the boy. He took their baggage to the weighing-in scales at the American Airlines desk. The woman and the boy went up to the ticket counter, then two men came up and talked with the woman–one man did most of the talking. He had an air of authority. Then they took the two suitcases off the weighing scales, and the two men, the woman and the boy walked out towards the kerb.

'The porter didn't know what happened after that. He was hanging around because he expected a tip for handling the baggage and no one offered to tip him. Naturally he remembered the transaction.'

'The devil!' Mason exclaimed.

'Police?' Smith asked.

'Could be,' Drake said. 'They acted with that unmistakable air of authority. The porter said he didn't think they looked like police.'

'They don't any more,' Mason commented thoughtfully. 'Good police detectives look like bankers or sales executives.'

Drake said: 'Incidentally, Perry, I heard from the operative I sent up to the camp, where Robert and his dog were supposed to be.'

'They weren't there?' Mason asked.

'Robert wasn't there. He never did show up at the starting point. My man had a wild-goose chase: took a trip by automobile, then transferred to saddle horse, rode five miles over mountain trails, got bitten by a dog, turned around and rode the five miles back. He says the only two places he isn't sore is on the top of his head and the soles of his feet. He said that was some gathering of kids and dogs, mongrels, pure breds and general canines of all sizes. They'd started out with the dogs on leash, but after a while they just turned 'em loose. The guy in charge said they'd only had a couple of dog fights and then everything had worked out beautifully. The dogs seemed to enter into the spirit of the thing.

'The man in charge said Robert and his dog had been booked for the trip but hadn't shown up. There were seven kids in all.'

Mason was thoughtful for a while, then said: 'Keep a watch on Jennings, Paul. See what you can find out.'

'Something in particular?' Drake asked.

'If they started for Mexico City,' Mason said, 'he undoubtedly arranged for some sort of a code signal, either by way of telephone or telegram, to let him know that they were safely outside the jurisdiction of the court. When he doesn't hear from them, he'll begin to get alarmed.

'In the meantime, if the police have moved in, they'll be trying to find out just what it is Robert Selkirk did and just what it is he knows. I'm going to apply for a writ of habeas corpus for Norda Allison tomorrow morning.

'If the police have Robert, there's no use trying to do anything more about him, but I sure would like to know whether they have him, and if so, what story they got. Any chance of finding out?'

Drake shook his head. 'Not if they don't want you to know, Perry. They'll have Robert and the woman buried somewhere. They *may* tell Barton Jennings what had happened so he won't be too nervous.'

'Suppose they do? Then what?' Mason asked.

'That'll mean they're all working hand in glove,' Drake said.

'And if they don't?'

Drake grinned. 'That'll mean Robert has told his story to the police and the police don't like it. Then they won't be so certain Norda Allison is guilty.'

'Keep your operatives on Barton Jennings,' Mason said, 'and if he begins to get a little restive and nervous, we'll know that it's time to rush a preliminary hearing for my client.'

Again the phone rang, again Drake picked up the receiver, said: 'Hello,' listened in frowning concentration, asked a couple of questions, hung up the telephone and turned to Perry Mason. 'This,' he said, 'is completely cockeyed.'

'What is?'

'The printing press on which envelopes had been addressed to Norda

Allison was found where it had been concealed out in some brush at the San Sebastian Country Club. It was on a lower level of the hill on which the club-house is situated. It's about twenty yards from a service road which winds up to the back of the club-house through some thick brush. In an airline it's about two hundred yards from the place where the body of Mervin Selkirk was found, but it's out of sight of that location.

'And,' Drake went on before Mason could make any reply, 'in the middle of the inked circular steel disc on top of the printing press was found a very nice imprint of the right middle finger of Norda Allison.'

'Well,' Mason said, '*that* opens up a lot of interesting possibilities.'

'Keep talking,' Drake said.

Mason was thoughtful for a moment, then said: 'If Norda Allison's story is true, she must have made that fingerprint on the printing press sometime early yesterday morning.'

'And Mervin Selkirk was killed sometime around two or three o'clock, according to the best estimate the police can get at the moment,' Drake said.

'Then the printing press must have been taken out to the Country Club *after* Selkirk's death,' Mason said. 'This may give us an opportunity to drag Barton Jennings right into the middle of it.'

Paul Drake said dryly: 'You're overlooking one thing, Perry.'

'What's that?'

'You're assuming your client is telling the truth about *when* that fingerprint got placed on the printing press.'

'I always assume my clients are telling the truth.'

'Yes, I know,' Drake retorted, 'but figure it out, Perry. Suppose she found the printing press in his car, took it out, drove down the service road and hid it in the brush.'

Mason thought the thing over. 'I think it's quite apparent now that someone is trying to frame my client.'

'Famous last words,' Drake said ironically. 'Incidentally, Mervin Selkirk kept a room at the San Sebastian Country Club. He's been a member for several years. Two weeks ago he arranged for a room there. They have a couple of dozen they rent out, mostly on week-ends. Mervin Selkirk said he wanted his by the month.'

Mason thought over Paul Drake's statement, then abruptly turned to Della Street. 'Come on, Della. We're going to see Horace Livermore Selkirk and suggest that *he* file habeas corpus proceedings to force the authorities to surrender his grandson, Robert Selkirk.'

'You're going to tell him what you know?' Della Street asked.

'Not only that, but I'm going to tell him what I *surmise*,' Mason said, grinning.

12

Horace Livermore Selkirk's house was spread out on the top of a sunny knoll.

The lower part of the knoll was parched and browned by the California dry-season sunlight, but the upper part which contained the house, the grounds and a small golf-course, was dark with shade, green with grass, cool with the scent of growing vegetation. The house was of stainless steel, glass and aluminium.

The driveway wound up the slope until it came to the meshed wire fence which stretched a ten-foot barrier, topped with barbed wire. A caretaker's cottage was just outside the electrically operated gate and Mason's car came to a stop where the road narrowed in front of the gate.

The caretaker, a man in his early fifties with a deputy sheriff's star pinned to his shirt, a belt with holstered gun and shells, came to the door and surveyed Mason and Della Street appraisingly.

'Perry Mason,' the lawyer said, 'and this is my secretary. We want to see Mr Selkirk.'

'What about?' the man asked.

'Mr Selkirk will know when you mention the name.'

'We don't disturb him unless we know what it's about.'

Mason fixed the guard with cold eyes. 'It's about a matter in which he is very much interested,' he said. 'I am Perry Mason and I wouldn't have driven out here unless the matter was of considerable importance.'

'Why didn't you telephone for an appointment?'

'Because I didn't choose to,' Mason said. 'I'm going to put some cards on the table and the manner in which Mr Selkirk receives my information will depend on how many cards I put down.'

The man hesitated, said, 'Just a minute,' stepped inside the house and picked up a telephone.

He spoke briefly, then a moment later hung up the telephone and pressed a button.

The huge steel gates moved silently back on their heavy roller bearings. The caretaker motioned Mason on and the lawyer sent his car through the gates up along the scenic driveway to the parking place in front of the house.

Horace Selkirk came strolling out from the rear portion of a huge patio to meet his guests. The patio contained a swimming-pool, a barbecue grate, a picnic table and luxurious lounging furniture.

The patio had been ingeniously designed so that it could be opened to the sun or completely roofed over and glassed in, if desired. Wet splotches on the cement indicated the pool had been in recent use. Two inflated inner tubes floated on the water. A toy boat had drifted to one side of the pool. A floating rubber horse nodded solemnly in the pool, actuated by a faint breeze. High-ball glasses were on the table, one partially filled. Ice cubes in the glasses had melted down to about half size.

'How do you do?' Selkirk said, somewhat coldly. 'This is rather an unexpected visit.'

Mason said: 'So it is.'

'Usually,' Selkirk said, 'those desiring to consult with me telephone and ask for an appointment.'

'So I would assume,' Mason said.

Selkirk's eyes were frosty. 'It is a procedure I like to encourage.'

'Doubtless,' Mason said. 'However, since you seem so well versed as to *my* movements, I thought perhaps it would be unnecessary.'

'I am not telepathic,' Selkirk said.

'You said that you relied on the services of private detectives.'

'I do.'

'If *I* were having *you* shadowed,' Mason told him, 'I would know when you were coming to call on me.'

'You think I'm having you shadowed?' Selkirk asked.

'Someone is,' Mason said. 'It was rather neatly done. I appreciate the technique.'

'What do you mean?'

'The manner in which the shadowing was done. A casual appearance from time to time of two different cars which would pass me, then turn a corner, appear once more behind me and then again pass me. And at times in the city I would notice that I was being shadowed by a car which must have been running on a course parallel to my own, some two blocks distant. That is, I believe, electronic shadowing which is made possible by means of a small device fastened somewhere to the underside of my car, which emanates a certain radionic signal that can be picked up and located by the shadowing car–I'll have to have my car looked over by a mechanic, I suppose.'

Selkirk suddenly threw back his head and laughed. 'It won't do you any good, Mason. By the time you found one device, my men would have something else pinned on.'

'And,' Mason said, 'I assume my car has been bugged so my conversations can be duly recorded?'

'No, no, not that,' Selkirk protested. 'We'd get into difficulties with that and besides, I would want you and your very estimable secretary to be able to discuss business matters in private without feeling that I was eavesdropping. But do come in.

'It's a little warm today, but not really warm enough for the full air conditioning. I have a shaded corner out here in the patio where it's really delightful, just shirt-sleeve weather, and if Miss Street has no objection you might as well slip off your coat and be comfortable.'

'Thanks,' Mason said, removing his coat.

Selkirk led the way to a shaded corner where a breeze blowing up the hill was somehow funnelled through steel latticework to cool a deeply shaded L-shaped nook. Light filtered in through heavy plate-glass windows which had been tinted a dark green.

'I took the liberty of having a couple of mint juleps prepared for you,' Selkirk said. 'I was drinking one and I thought you and Miss Street would care to join me.'

He indicated a table on which was a tray and two frosted glasses decorated with sprigs of mint.

'Perfect hospitality,' Mason said, as Della Street seated herself and picked up one of the glasses. 'Next time you might telephone your guard that we're coming so that the gates can be opened.'

Selkirk shook his head. 'I trust my detectives, but not quite that far. I like to have visitors inspected before they arrive.'

Selkirk tilted his glass towards his visitors. 'Regards,' he said.

Mason sipped the drink.

Selkirk raised his eyebrows inquiringly.

'Excellent,' Mason said.

'Thank you. Now what was the object of your visit?'

'Your grandson,' Mason said.

Selkirk's body became instantly motionless; his face was a frozen mask. The man seemed to be holding his breath, yet without displaying even a flicker of changing expression. 'What about Robert?'

'His mother,' Mason said, 'seems to have arranged for him to be taken to Mexico City by a baby-sitter named Grace Hallum.'

'Mexico City?'

'Yes.'

'Why?'

'Apparently because some time Friday night Robert fired a Colt ·22 Woodsman in the general direction of a prowler–or someone who was moving around outside his tent, perhaps with the idea of taking Robert away while his mother and Barton Jennings were at the airport greeting Norda Allison.'

'Do you know this or do you surmise it?' Selkirk asked.

'I know it.'

'How do you know it?'

'That is something else,' Mason said. 'I thought you would be interested in the information.'

'They're in Mexico City?'

'No. I said that Robert's mother had arranged for him to be taken to Mexico City. I don't think they made it.'

'What *do* you think happened?' Selkirk asked, still holding his glass motionless half-way to his lips, his body tense, leaning slightly forward, his eyes cold, hard and watchful.

'I think,' Mason said, 'that the police decided that the matter had gone far enough. Before the child was whisked out of their jurisdiction, detectives moved in and took Robert and his escort to Headquarters for questioning.'

'Detectives?'

'I think so,' Mason said. 'A porter remembered two men with that indefinable air of authority which sometimes characterizes police officers. They removed the baggage from the scales at the checking-in counter of American Airlines. Robert and Miss Hallum accompanied these two men.'

Selkirk digested the information for a moment, then settled back in his chair, raised the mint julep glass and took a long sip of the cooling contents.

'Why did you come to me?' he asked after a moment.

Mason said: 'It is possible that your grandson is being subjected to suggestion and repetitious assertion of certain things which he is told must have happened while he was asleep. There is also, of course, the possibility that your son was planning to take Robert outside the jurisdiction of the California courts before new guardianship or custody proceedings could be instituted, and that Robert, hearing a prowler, pointed and discharged Barton Jennings' ·22-calibre automatic.

'In any event, there is persuasive evidence that the shot fired from the tent where Robert was sleeping found a human target.'

'What sort of persuasive evidence?' Selkirk asked.

'A blood trail which led from the vicinity of the tent to the kerb where a car was parked. The blood trail was removed, at least in part, by a stream of water played on the grass and the sidewalk through a hose early yesterday morning.'

'Barton Jennings?'

Mason nodded.

Selkirk toyed with his glass for several seconds, his eyes hard with concentration, his face a mask.

'Just what do you expect me to do, Mason?'

'There are two things which can be done. You can do one. I can do the other.'

'What would you suggest that *I* do?'

'As the child's grandfather, you might insist that the police detention is violating the law. You might allege that Grace Hallum was contributing to the delinquency of a minor in trying to lead your grandson to believe that he had fired the shot which had resulted in his father's death. You might file a writ of habeas corpus stating that Grace Hallum, an entirely unauthorized person, has the child in custody. This would force Lorraine Jennings, the child's mother, either to yield the point or to come out in the open and state that *she* had ordered the child removed from the jurisdiction of the court.'

Selkirk thought the matter over for a moment, then said: 'Just sit here and cool yourselves with these drinks. If you want a refill, just press that button. I'm going to telephone my legal department. Excuse me for a moment please.'

Selkirk took another swallow of his mint julep, put down the partially empty glass and walked around the corner of the L-shaped alcove. Presently they heard the sound of a heavy glass partition sliding on roller bearings.

Della Street started to say something. Mason motioned her to silence, said conversationally: 'Nice place Selkirk has here.'

'It must cost him a fortune to keep it up.'

'He has a fortune.'

'Why should he be having your car shadowed?'

'I wouldn't know,' Mason said. 'We weren't shadowed earlier in the day. However, that's entirely up to Selkirk. If he wants to spend his money on detectives, finding out where I go, it will at least be a bonanza for the detectives and will keep some of Selkirk's money in circulation.'

Mason closed his eye in a broad wink to Della Street, then stretched, yawned and said sleepily: 'I've been losing too much sleep lately. I guess there's nothing I can do from now on except . . . I guess we can afford to slow down until Norda Allison's preliminary hearing comes up . . . ho . . . ho . . . hummmm! This place certainly is relaxing. It's making me sleepy.'

Once again Mason closed his eye in a broad wink.

'That mint julep hits the spot,' Della Street said. 'It also has a relaxing effect.'

Mason said sleepily: 'It does for a fact–well, Della drink it up because as soon as Selkirk returns we're going to get away from here. We'll check with Paul Drake to see if there's anything new, then call it a day and I'll see you at the office in the morning.'

'Aren't you going to finish your drink?' Della asked.

'I'm driving,' Mason said. 'The drink was so tempting I had to taste it, but I'm limiting myself to a couple of swallows. I have an aversion to drinking and driving.'

'One drink isn't going to affect your driving,' Della Street said.

'It isn't that so much,' Mason told her, 'as the fact that I dislike to lose lawsuits. Suppose someone runs into me at an intersection. He may have gone through a red light, may have been going too fast and have defective brakes, but an officer comes up to investigate, smells liquor on *my* breath and I tell him that I've had one mint julep. You know how a jury would react to that. They'd say: "Yeh, the guy *admits* to having one. That means he must have had a dozen." '

'Under those circumstances,' Della Street said, 'you can have the sole responsibility. *I'm* going to finish this drink. It's the most wonderful mint julep I've had in a long time.'

'Thank you,' Selkirk's voice said, as he came unexpectedly around the corner of the alcove. 'I've telephoned my legal department, Mason, and they'll get on the job immediately.'

'That's fine,' Mason told him, getting to his feet. 'Your relaxing atmosphere has made me drowsy.'

'Care for a swim and a little relaxation by the pool?' Selkirk asked. 'I have plenty of suits and dressing-rooms.'

'No, thank you,' Mason told him. 'I'm a working man and have to be on my way.'

'I hope you and Miss Street come back again,' Selkirk said, and then his voice suddenly taking on an authoritative note said: 'And it will be better if you telephone.'

'Thank you for the invitation,' Mason told him.

They shook hands. Selkirk escorted them past the pool, to the parking space.

Della Street jumped in the car, slid under the steering-wheel and over to the far side of the seat. Mason got in behind the steering-wheel.

'Just drive right on through the other end of the parking place and around the circle,' Selkirk said. 'The gate will be open for you as you go out.'

Mason nodded, swept the car into motion.

It was a neighbourhood of rolling hills and vistas of country estates. Glistening white houses and hillside sub-divisions met their eyes as they swung down the long driveway to the highway.

Mason made the boulevard stop, then put his car into motion, swung over to the stream of fast-moving traffic and stepped on the throttle.

'You're very anxious to get where you're going, all of a sudden,' Della Street said.

'Yes,' Mason told her, 'I have decided there's no use working too hard. Let's get where we can relax. I know a cocktail bar about a mile down the road. We can pull in there and–'

'But I thought you wouldn't have a drink when you were driving.'

'I won't be driving for a while,' Mason said. 'We'll get in there where it's cool and dark and comfortable and forget about the case. There's nothing more I can do now until the matter comes up for the preliminary examination . . . not unless Paul Drake's men uncover some new information.'

Della Street started to say something, then checked herself.

Mason drove silently until he came to a small hotel, said: 'There's a parking lot here. We'll leave the car and go relax for a while. It will do us good.'

He swung into the parking lot and led Della Street into the hotel.

'What in the world *are* you doing, Chief?' she asked.

'I don't know whether the car is bugged or not,' Mason said. 'But we do know one thing. They have it rigged up so they can follow us by using electronics. Quick, Della, right through the cocktail bar and . . . there's a taxi stand right outside and . . . thank heavens there's a taxi there.'

Mason signalled a cab driver, caught Della Street's elbow in his hand, hurried her across to the taxicab, jumped in beside her, slammed the door shut and said to the driver: 'Straight on down the street. I want to catch a party who just left here.'

The driver put the cab into motion.

Mason, looking through the rear window, said: 'Turn to the left at the first street and then turn to the left once more.'

The cab driver obediently followed instructions.

Della Street said in a low voice: 'What's the idea, Chief?'

Mason said: 'Horace Livermore Selkirk has Grace Hallum and Robert up there in the house with him.'

'You're certain?' Della Street asked.

'Pretty certain,' Mason said. 'There was a toy boat in the swimming-pool when we went in. When we came out it was no longer there. Horace Selkirk could well have been one of the men with the aura of authority who stopped the trip to Mexico City.'

Mason said to the cab driver: 'Turn to the left once more and then to the right. I'll tell you where to go.'

'But, Chief,' Della Street protested, 'we can't go back up there in a taxicab and even expect . . . Why, he won't let us inside the gates.'

'That's true,' Mason told her. 'But I think he's afraid now that I'm suspicious and my best guess is he's going to get rid of the boy–after all, he's in a very vulnerable position.'

'He is if he gets caught,' Della Street said. 'But . . . I'm afraid I don't get it.'

'Well,' Mason told her, 'our car is hotter than a fire-cracker. He's got it bugged up so his private detectives can follow it. We put it in the parking place there at that hotel and cocktail lounge, and you can bet that his detectives followed right behind us. We went into the cocktail lounge and they probably watched where we were going, then went to telephone a report to Horace Selkirk.

'We fooled them by going right on through and jumping in a cab. There's a good chance they didn't even see us take the cab. If they did, they didn't have a chance to follow us because there's no one on our tail now, and they certainly don't have these cabs bugged so they can be followed by electronics–it is, of course, taking a chance, but it's a chance worth taking. If we hit anything, we hit the jackpot. If we lose out, we're out the price of one taxi trip and we can go back and sit in the cocktail lounge for an hour or so, and then lead Horace Livermore Selkirk's spies back to the office.'

'They'll tell him we took a taxi ride?' Della Street asked.

Mason shook his head. 'They won't be certain just *what* we did. Therefore, they'll simply state, "Subjects parked their car, entered the hotel, went into the cocktail lounge and emerged two hours later to get in their car and drive to the office.'

'Later on, if it should appear that the point was important, they would say:

"Why, yes, we missed them for half an hour or so, but we assumed they were around the hotel somewhere because their car was there so we didn't consider the matter worth while reporting." On a shadow job of that kind, you can't stand right at the subject's elbow all the time.

'Turn off up here at the right,' Mason said to the cab driver after some ten minutes.

'That road doesn't go anywhere,' the cab driver said, 'except up to some private property. There's a gate–'

'I know,' Mason told him, 'but I'm expecting a person to meet me . . . slow down . . . slow down, cabbie. Get over to the side of the road and take it easy.'

Mason nudged Della Street as a cab came down the road headed towards them. The cab passed them and they got a glimpse of a woman and a boy in the back seat.

Mason turned to the cab driver: 'I think that's the couple we want, but I can't be certain of it until I get a closer look. Turn around and follow that cab. Let's see if we can get a closer look and find out where they're going.'

'Say, what is this?' the cab driver asked.

'It's all right,' Mason told him, 'you're driving a cab.'

'That's *all* I'm doing. I'm not mixing in any rough stuff,' the driver said.

'Neither am I,' Mason assured him. 'Just keep that cab in sight. I want to find out where it goes. If you're really interested, I'm getting evidence in a divorce case. Here's twenty bucks. Any time you don't like the job, quit it, but when you get finished, if you make a *good* job of it, you get another twenty on top of this. Now are you satisfied?'

'I'm satisfied,' the driver said, and accelerated the car.

'Not too fast,' Mason warned. 'I don't want them to get nervous,

'They're looking straight ahead,' the driver said, 'but the cabbie up front will spot me. A good cab driver keeps his eye on the rear-view mirror from time to time.'

'Fix it so he doesn't notice you,' Mason said. 'Don't drive at a regular distance behind him. Where there's not much chance he's going to turn off, drop way behind, then close the gap when you get into traffic.'

The driver handled the car skilfully, keeping some distance behind the car in front until traffic thickened, then moving up and, from time to time, changing lanes so that the relative position of the two cars varied.

The cab ahead eventually came to a stop at a relatively small hotel. The woman and the child got out. The cab driver lifted out suitcases.

'Around the block and stop,' Mason told the driver, handing him another twenty-dollar bill.

As soon as the cab rounded the corner, Mason had the door open. Della Street jumped out and the two hurried around the corner and into the hotel.

The well-tailored blonde had just finished registering as Mason and Della Street approached the desk.

The clerk smacked his palm down on a call bell, said: 'Front! . . . take Mrs Halton to 619.'

Mason approached the desk. 'Do you have a J. C. Endicott in the house?' he asked the clerk.

The clerk frowned at him impatiently and motioned towards the room phone. 'Ask the operator,' he said.

Mason went to the room phone, picked up the receiver, said to the operator: 'Do you have a Mr J. C. Endicott in the house?'

'From where?' the operator asked.

'New York,' Mason said.

There was a moment of silence; then she said: 'I'm sorry. He doesn't seem to be registered.'

'Thank you. That's all right,' Mason said.

The lawyer hung up the telephone and walked across to where Della Street was waiting within earshot of the clerk.

'He's in,' Mason told her. 'He says for us to come right up. Boy, it's sure going to seem good to see good old Jim and hear all about that hunting trip.'

He led Della Street to the elevators, said, 'Seventh floor, please,' and then after the cage came to a stop, led Della Street to the stair door. They opened the door, walked down one flight to the sixth floor.

The bellboy who had taken the woman and the boy up to 619 was just getting aboard the elevator on the way down when Mason and Della Street entered the sixth floor hallway. They walked down to 619 and Mason tapped on the door.

'Say it's the maid with soap and towels,' Mason said to Della Street in a whisper.

After a moment of silence, a woman's voice on the other side of the door said: 'Who is it, please?'

'Maid, with soap and towels,' Della Street said in a bored voice.

The door was unlocked and opened.

Della Street walked in, followed by Perry Mason.

They found themselves in a two-bedroom suite with a central parlour and two bedrooms.

Mason kicked the door shut and turned the bolt.

The tall blonde moved back, her eyes wide with alarm.

'Sit down, Mrs Hallum,' Mason said. 'You're not going to get hurt if you tell the truth. Why didn't you go to Mexico City the way you were supposed to?'

'I . . . I . . . Who are you? What do you want? And–'

'I want to know why you didn't go to Mexico City,' Mason said.

She bit her lip. 'I suppose you're representing Mrs Jennings. I . . . well . . . I've been wondering if what I did was right, but . . .'

'Go ahead,' Mason said.

'I don't know as I should tell it to you.'

'Want to talk with the police?' Mason asked, moving towards the telephone.

'No. Heavens, no! That's the one thing we must avoid at *all* costs.'

'All right,' Mason told her. 'Talk to me.'

He turned to Della Street who had taken a shorthand notebook from her purse. 'Sit over at that table,' he said. 'Take down what she says. All right, Mrs Hallum, let's have it.'

She walked through to the connecting room, said: 'Robert, you stay in there for a little while. Just sit down and wait until I come for you.'

'Yes, ma'am,' Robert said politely.

Mrs Hallum came back and closed the door.

'Just what is it you want to know?' she asked.

Mason said: 'You were supposed to take Robert to Mexico City. You didn't do it. Why?'

'Because his grandfather told me I'd be arrested if I did.'

'And what did you do?'

'I accompanied him to his house up on the hill, then a short time ago he told me I had to leave, that I was to go to this hotel, that rooms had been arranged for me.'

'And why were you to take Robert to Mexico City?' Mason asked.

'Because,' she said, 'Robert . . .'

'Go on,' Mason said.

'Robert may have killed his father,' she said.

'And they want to keep Robert from finding that out?'

'They want to protect Robert until there can be a more complete investigation. Robert knows he shot somebody. It's a horrible thought for a child to have in his mind. He hasn't been told that his father is dead.'

'What do *you* think?' Mason asked.

'I don't know,' she said. 'Barton Jennings, that's the man who married Robert's mother, keeps telling Robert that he mustn't worry, that it was just a dream. He can't quite convince Robert that it was.'

'How did Robert happen to have the gun?' Mason asked.

'His mother had a baby-sitter who let him play with the gun. She would always unload it before she gave it to him. The boy had a habit of looking at Western pictures and Western shows. He feels a gun is a symbol of protection, of security, of manhood. He's nervous and sensitive and–well, he's resourceful.'

'Go on,' Mason said.

'It wasn't long before Robert wanted a loaded gun. Without this baby-sitter, a Mrs Hannah Bass, knowing anything about it, he got hold of a ·22-calibre cartridge. He'd amuse himself by putting that shell in the magazine, then working the recoil mechanism by hand.

'About a week ago Mr Jennings, the boy's stepfather, found Robert had been playing with the gun. At first he was angry, but then he got over it.

'Friday night they both drove to the airport. Robert knew they were going and hadn't been able to get a baby-sitter. They told him they'd only be gone for an hour.

'Robert asked for the gun and Mr Jennings let him put it under his pillow in the tent in the patio. Robert loaded the gun with the ·22 cartridge and put it under his pillow.

'I've never seen a boy with such an obsession about guns.'

'All right,' Mason said. 'What happened Friday night?'

'Robert must have had a nightmare. He says he heard steps coming towards his tent, then he saw the form of a big man looming in the doorway. He says he groped for the gun–and it went off. He really wasn't conscious of pulling the trigger, but there was the roar of an explosion, then he heard somebody running away. Robert says he fired the gun. I'm not certain but what someone else, standing just outside the tent, fired a shot. That's my own idea for what it's worth. Mr Jennings says Robert should be led to believe it was all a bad dream. Robert knows better.

'Of course, Robert was only half-conscious at the time. He knows he was holding the gun. He thinks he fired it. Probably he could be made to think it was a dream. Mr Jennings thinks it can be managed.'

'What did Robert do after the shot?'

'He ran into the house and wakened his mother. She told him Barton Jennings was asleep and had been suffering pain for his arthritis. She told Robert his step-father had taken medicine to deaden the pain, had gone to sleep and mustn't be wakened. She told Robert that it was simply an accident;

that accidents happen to everyone; that if Robert had heard somebody running away it meant that he had only frightened someone and hadn't hurt the man. Robert was reassured. After a while he was persuaded to go back to the tent.

'Mrs Jennings took the empty gun and started to take it back upstairs to put it where it belonged, then remembered a guest, Norda Allison was in the room. So she left the gun on the stand in the front hall at the foot of the stairs and went back to bed.'

'Where was her husband?' Mason asked.

'Asleep in another downstairs bedroom. When he has his attacks of arthritis, he takes codeine and sleeps in a separate room.'

'How did he find out about it?' the lawyer asked.

'Mrs Jennings was worried. She slept for an hour or two and then wakened and couldn't go back to sleep. She heard her husband moving around in his room. This was about daylight. She went to him and told him what had happened. He became very much alarmed. He went out to look around and evidently found something which caused him great concern. He told Mrs Jennings to take the gun from the place where she had left it on the hall-stand and as soon as Norda Allison got up to return it to the drawer where they kept it. Then Mr Jennings took Robert and brought him to me. I kept Robert all day yesterday and reassured him as best I could. Mr Jennings said I should do a job of brain-washing.

'Then this morning Mr Jennings brought some of Robert's clothes to me and said I was to leave at once and take Robert to Mexico City. He said we had reservations at the Hotel Reforma. He gave me money for the fare, told me that we had reservations on a plane and everything was all cared for. We were to leave this morning.

'So we went down to the airport and Mr Horace Selkirk, the boy's grandfather, showed up. I had never met him, but he identified himself to me and told me that under no circumstances was Robert to leave the jurisdiction of the court. He said we were to come with him and that he would take the responsibility. He said he would send for Barton Jennings and get the thing straightened out.

'He had a man with him and they put us in an automobile and took us up to Horace Selkirk's big house. Robert was happy there but I was worried because Mr Jennings didn't show up to tell me that I had done the right thing.

'I took Robert in swimming and he had a wonderful time in the pool. He's visited there several times and always has had the time of his life. His grandfather keeps toys and things for him and Robert loves it.

'Well, almost as soon as we had finished dressing after our swim Mr Selkirk came rushing into the rooms he had assigned us in the west wing of the house. He was very excited and said we were to pack up at once, get ready to leave and were to come here and wait here until he gave us further orders.'

'What about Barton Jennings?' Mason asked. 'Did he ever find out you weren't going to Mexico City?'

'No. Mr Horace Selkirk had us write postal cards which he said would be flown to Mexico City and then mailed to Mr and Mrs Jennings. He told us that police were questioning the Jennings and that it was absolutely essential that we remain concealed so no one would know where we were. We had an understanding with Mr Jennings that we would send postal cards that would simply be signed G.R. That stood for Grace and Robert.'

'And you wrote some of those cards?'

'Yes.'

'How many?'

'There must have been a dozen or so. Horace Selkirk almost threw them at us. He said he'd have them sent to Mexico City and mailed at intervals so no one would become suspicious. He had me scrawling post cards until I became dizzy.'

Mason studied her carefully for a moment, then said: 'All right, now tell me the rest of it.'

'What do you mean?'

'There's something else. How much did Selkirk promise you, or how much did he give you?'

She lowered her eyes.

Mason stood silent, his eyes steady, waiting.

At length she sighed, raised her eyes. 'He gave me a thousand in cash and promised me five thousand more if I followed instructions.'

Mason thought things over for a moment, then said: 'Ever hear about the kidnapping law?'

'What do you mean?' she flared. 'He's the boy's grandfather!'

'And as such has no more to say about his custody than anyone you'd meet on the street,' Mason said. 'Right at the moment the child's mother is the only one who has any say about where he's to be kept. She told you to take him to Mexico City.'

'It was her husband who told me.'

'But he was speaking for her. You were given custody of the boy to take him to Mexico City. If you take him anywhere else it's kidnapping.'

'Mr Selkirk said he'd fix it up with the Jennings.'

'And did he do so?'

'He said he would.'

'Then why promise you money?'

She was silent for several seconds. Then abruptly she said: 'I knew I was doing something wrong. Okay, you win. I'm going to Mexico City.'

'That's better,' Mason told her. 'I'm going down and get a taxicab. Give me your suitcases. This is Miss Street, my secretary. We'll take the suitcases down and handle things so no one will know you checked out. You wait exactly twenty minutes, then take Robert, go down in the elevator, ask if there's a drugstore near here, walk out of the hotel and turn to the right. Miss Street and I will be waiting in a taxicab on the corner. You've made a wise decision. We must keep Robert away from all these emotional stresses. Now you go to Mexico where you can take Robert's mind off what has happened. It's particularly important you stay where Horace Selkirk won't know where you are.'

'But how can we do that?' Grace Hallum asked. 'He'll be furious. He'll find us.'

Mason said: 'No he won't. You'll be at the one place where he'd never expect you to be. The Hotel Reforma in Mexico City.'

Grace Hallum said: 'The suitcases are all packed. We haven't unpacked. We just got here.'

Mason nodded to Della Street, said: 'If you don't mind, we'll take the suitcases to another floor. We don't want it to appear that *you're* checking out.'

'But what about the bill on these two rooms?'

'The reservations were made by Horace Livermore Selkirk,' Mason said. 'Let him pay the bill.'

'How long will it be before anyone finds out we're not here?'

Mason grinned. 'It *could* be a long time.'

'And then?' she asked.

'Then,' Mason said, 'when Horace Livermore Selkirk finally put two and two together, he may quit being so damned patronizing.'

13

Back in the cocktail lounge at the hotel where they had engaged the cab Mason said to Della: 'I think those are our shadows over there.'

'Where?'

'The man and the woman in the corner. There have been surreptitious glances in our direction, and the man's not as interested in her as he should be in an attractive woman companion who is being plied with liquor.'

'Why plied?' Della Street asked.

'It makes them pliable,' Mason said.

She laughed. 'Ever try it?'

'What we need,' Mason told her, 'is a red herring. Go to the phone booth, call Paul Drake and tell him we want a woman operative who is about twenty-seven, blonde, rather tall, with a good figure, and a seven-year-old boy, well-dressed, quiet and dark.'

'Why do we want them?' she asked.

'Because,' Mason said, 'we're going to give Horace Selkirk's detectives something to think about.'

'And what do they do?' Della Street asked.

Mason said: 'They move into the hotel where Horace Selkirk got the two connecting rooms for Grace Hallum and Robert Selkirk. Drake can fix them up with a pass-key and they can move right into the hotel as though they owned the place. Tell Paul not to ever let them charge anything, but to pay cash for everything. The woman isn't *ever* to sign the name of Grace Hallum. She's simply to pay cash for everything.'

'But won't the clerk know the difference? That is, won't he–'

'We'll wait until the night clerk comes on duty,' Mason said, 'then this operative and the boy will go into the hotel, take the key to 619 and 621, move in there and stay there.

'The woman is to keep the key to the room in her purse, never to go near the desk, never to say to anyone that she is Grace Hallum.'

Della Street thought the matter over, then said: 'You don't suppose they've got the line tapped here, do you?'

'I doubt it,' Mason said. 'It's a chance we'll have to take. Just go to the phone and call Paul Drake. I'll keep an eye on the couple over there and see what they do.'

Ten minutes later when Della Street was back, Mason said: 'They were certainly interested in your telephone call, Della, but they didn't dare appear too curious. They're wondering what kept us out of circulation for so long–how did Paul Drake react?'

'The same way you'd expect,' she said. 'He agreed to do it, but he's not happy about it.'

'Why isn't he happy?'

'Says he's violating the law.'

'What law?'

'What law!' Della Street asked. 'Good heavens, here's a woman who moves into some other woman's room in a hotel, and–'

'What do you mean?' Mason asked. 'She isn't moving into any other woman's room. Grace Hallum has left the hotel.'

'But she didn't pay her bill.'

'The bill was already paid,' Mason said. 'Horace Selkirk arranged for that, and even if she *had* left the hotel without paying the bill, she would have been the one who defrauded the hotel-keeper. Drake's operative isn't defrauding anybody.'

'But she's moving into a room in a hotel.'

'Exactly,' Mason said. 'She's prepared to pay for the accommodations. The hotel keeps its rooms for rental to the public.'

'But she didn't register.'

'Is there any law that says she has to?'

'I think there is.'

'Grace Hallum didn't register. She simply went and picked up the key. That means somebody had registered into those rooms and left instructions with the clerk that the key was to be delivered when a woman with a child asked for it.'

'Well,' she said, 'Paul Drake wasn't happy.'

'I didn't expect him to be happy,' Mason said. 'When you hire a detective you pay his price for services rendered. If he follows instructions, you can guarantee to keep him out of jail, but you can't guarantee to make him happy.'

14

Judge Homer F. Kent looked down at the people assembled in the court-room and said: 'This is the time fixed for the preliminary hearing in the case of the People versus Norda Allison.'

'Ready for the People,' Manley Marshall, a trial deputy from the district attorney's office, said.

'Ready for the defendant,' Perry Mason responded.

'Very well. Proceed,' Judge Kent said.

Marshall, following a generally recognized pattern with the crisp efficiency of a man who knows both his case and his law, and is determined to see that no loop-hole is left open, called the caretaker at the San Sebastian Country Club.

The caretaker testified to noticing a car parked early on the morning of the eighteenth. He had thought nothing of it as occasionally golfers came early for a round of golf. Later on, at about eleven-thirty, one of the golfers had told him that there was someone out in one of the parked cars who apparently had been drinking and was sound asleep.

The caretaker looked, saw the figure slumped over the wheel, did nothing about it for another hour. Then he had taken another look, had seen blood on the floor of the car and had notified the police.

'Cross-examine,' Marshall said to Mason.

'Did you,' Mason asked, 'look inside the car?'

'I looked inside the car,' the witness said.

'Did you open the door?'

'I did not open the door. I looked in through the glass window in the door.'

'Through the glass window in the door?'

'Yes.'

'Then the glass window in the door was rolled up?'

'I . . . I believe it was, yes.'

'The glass in all the windows was rolled up?'

'I think so.'

'That's all,' Mason said.

Marshall called the deputy coroner who testified to being called to the scene, a photographer who introduced photographs, an autopsy surgeon who testified that death had been caused by a ·22-calibre bullet. The bullet had entered on the left side of the chest, just in front of the left arm. It had ranged slightly backward and had lodged in the chest and had not gone all the way through the body. The autopsy surgeon had recovered the bullet and had turned it over to Alexander Redfield, the ballistics expert. Death, in the opinion of the physician, had not been instantaneous. There had been a period of consciousness and a period of haemorrhage. That period was, in his opinion, somewhat indefinite. It might have been an interval of ten or fifteen minutes after the shot had been fired and before death took place; it might have been only a minute or two.

'Cross-examine,' Marshall said to Perry Mason.

'With reference to this indeterminate interval,' Mason said, 'it is then possible that the decedent had sustained the fatal wound at some other place and had driven the car to the place where the body was found?'

'It is possible but not probable.'

'It could have been done?'

'I have said that it was possible.'

'Would you say that the interval between the time the fatal wound was sustained and death could not have been more than ten minutes?'

'It could have been as much as ten minutes.'

'Could it have been more?'

'I don't think so.'

'Could it have been eleven minutes?'

'Well, yes. When I say ten minutes I am not referring to an interval which I time with a stop watch.'

'Well, you know how long ten minutes is, don't you?' Mason asked.

'Yes.'

'Now you say it could have been eleven minutes.'

'It could have been.'

'Twelve?'

'Possible.'

'Thirteen?'

'Well, yes.'

'Fourteen?'

'I can't fix the time exactly, Mr Mason.'

'Fifteen?'

'I'm not going to say that it couldn't have been fifteen minutes.'

'Twenty?'

'I doubt very much if it was twenty minutes.'

'It could have been.'

'It could have been.'

'The decedent could have been driving the car during that time?'

'During at least a part of that time. There was considerable haemorrhage and he was losing blood and losing strength.'

'Thank you,' Mason said. 'That's all.'

The doctor left the stand, and Marshall called Sgt Holcomb to the stand.

Sgt Holcomb testified that he was connected with the homicide squad of the police department; that he had gone to the San Sebastian Country Club, had examined the body and the car.

'Did you make any examination of the surrounding terrain?' Marshall asked.

'I did.'

'Did you find anything which you considered significant?'

'I did.'

'Please tell us what it was that you found.'

Sgt Holcomb glanced triumphantly at Perry Mason. 'Concealed in the brush, within a hundred yards of the place where the automobile was parked, and just a few yards off a service road which skirts the hill on a lower level, I found a printing press.'

'What sort of a printing press?' Marshall asked.

'A portable printing press of a very good quality which was capable of doing good work. It weighed in the vicinity of eighty-five pounds, I would say.'

'What else can you tell us about that printing press, Sergeant?'

'A name and address had been set in type in that press. The name was the name of the defendant in this case and the address was her address in San Francisco.'

'Did you find anything else significant about that printing press?'

'I did.'

'What?'

'There was the imprint of a fingerprint in the ink on the steel table over which the rollers ran when the press was operated.'

'That was a circular table?'

'It was.'

'And it revolved with each impulse of the press; that is, each time the press was used the round steel table revolved?'

'It did.'

'And there was black ink on this round steel plate?'

'There was.'

'Can you describe that ink?'

'It is a very thick, sticky ink such as is used in printing presses of that type. When the rollers move over the steel table the ink clings to the rollers; that is, a small coating of ink clings to the rollers, and then as the rollers go down over the type, the type *is* inked just enough to make a legible print on the paper.'

'That ink was thick enough and sticky enough to hold a fingerprint?'

'It held it very well, yes, sir.'

'And were you able to identify the fingerprint which was on that table?'

'Yes, sir, absolutely.'

'Whose print was it?'

'It was the print of the middle finger of the defendant in this case.'

'Now then, Sergeant Holcomb, you described the operation of the press. Do I understand that whenever this press was put in operation the rollers moved over this steel table?'

'Yes, sir.'

'And the table itself revolved?'

'Well, it didn't make a complete revolution, but it moved a few degrees of arc.'

'Then, as I understand it, if the press had been actuated after that print had been made, the print would have been obliterated by the joint action of the rubber rollers, of which I believe there are two, and the rotation of the steel table?'

'That is correct.'

'Did you find anything else in your search of the premises, Sergeant Holcomb?'

'I did.'

'What?'

'I found an empty cartridge case.'

'What sort of a cartridge case?'

'A ·22-calibre cartridge case.'

'Do you have that with you?'

'I do.'

Sgt Holcomb produced an envelope from his pocket, opened it, took out a small glass bottle which contained an empty ·22-calibre cartridge case.

'This you found where?'

'At a point about twenty feet, as nearly as we could tell, twenty feet and two inches from the steering-wheel of the automobile in which the body of Mervin Selkirk was found.'

'What was the nature of the terrain at that point?'

'At that particular point the terrain was grassy. There was a practice putting green bordering the side of the parking space on the north. This cartridge case was in the grass. On the south side of the parking space there was native brush on the slope of the hill.'

'That's all,' Marshall said. 'You may inquire, Mr Mason.'

Mason's smile was affable. 'How long had this cartridge case been there in the grass before you picked it up, Sergeant?'

'If it had held the murder bullet, it couldn't have been there more than twelve hours.'

'*If* it had held the murder bullet?'

'Yes.'

'Had it held that bullet?'

'I think it had.'

'Do you *know* it had?'

'Well we can prove it by inference.'

'Do you *know* it had?'

'No.'

'Do you *know* how long the cartridge case had been there before you picked it up?'

'No, of course not. I wasn't there when the cartridge was fired. If I had been–'

'Could it have been there *two* days, Sergeant?'

'I suppose so.'

'Ten days?'

'I suppose so.'

'What was the nature of the terrain where you found the printing press?' Mason asked.

'It was on the sloping hill. The terrain there was covered with native brush.'

'Where was the printing press, with relation to the brush; in deep brush or relatively in the open?'

'In the brush.'

'Was it sitting up or was it on an angle, as would have been the case if it had been thrown into the brush?'

'It was sitting straight up.'

'As though it had been carefully placed there?'

'I can't say as to that. It was sitting straight up.'

'And the fingerprint of the defendant was not smudged in any way?'

'No, sir, it was a perfect print.'

'Did you find any other prints on the press?'

'Well, I didn't process the press myself. The fingerprint expert did.'

'In your presence?'

'Yes, in my presence and the presence of Lieutenant Tragg.'

'Also of Homicide?'

'Yes.'

'Were any other prints of the defendant found?'

'None that I know of.'

'Would it have been possible for a woman of the build of the defendant to have picked up an eighty-five pound printing press of this sort and transported it into the brush without leaving fingerprints on it?'

'Certainly. She could have used gloves.'

'Did you see any indication that the brush had been trampled, that some person had gone in there carrying a heavy object?'

'Yes, there were places where the brush had been broken.'

'Could you get any footprints?'

'No.'

'Now, Sergeant, you're an expert crime investigator.'

'I consider myself such.'

'In transporting an object awkward to carry, such as a printing press of that sort, the transportation of that heavy, unwieldy object would have been attended with some difficulty?'

'I would say so.'

'And do you consider that the press was placed there at night?'

'I don't know.'

'It is a possibility?'

'Yes.'

'It is a probability?'

'Yes.'

'Moving in the dark that way through a brushy terrain, there was quite a possibility the person would have stumbled?'

'Perhaps, if the press had been transported in the dark, but we don't know that it happened in the dark.'

'It is a reasonable surmise?'

'I wouldn't say so.'

'Pardon me, I have misunderstood you.'

'I said that it was a reasonable surmise that the press had been transported at night, but that didn't mean in the dark.'

'Why not?'

'The person could have used a flashlight.'

'I see,' Mason said. 'Holding an eighty-five pound printing press in one hand and a flashlight in the other?'

'Well, I didn't say that.'

'Where would such a person have held the flashlight–in his teeth?'

'*She* could have held it in *her* mouth,' Sgt Holcomb said.

'I see,' Mason said. 'You are assuming that the defendant transported the press to this place of concealment.'

'Yes.'

'She did that, in your opinion, in order to conceal the press?'

'Naturally.'

'She carried this eighty-five pound press in her hands and a flashlight in her teeth?'

'So I would assume.'

'There would have been ink on the rollers?'

'Yes.'

'And ink on the edges of the steel table?'

'To some extent, yes.'

'And isn't it a fact that in picking up the press, the edges of the steel table would have pressed against the forearms of the person picking it up?'

'They might.'

'And that would have left ink on the garments of the defendant, if *she* had been carrying it?'

'She might have been wearing short sleeves.'

'At night?'

'Yes.'

'And it would have been difficult to have transported that press through the brush at night without stumbling and falling?'

'I don't know.'

'You didn't make a test to determine that?'

'Well, not exactly.'

'You were the one who found the press?'

'I was,' Sgt Holcomb said, beaming with pride.

'And when you found it, were there other persons present?'

'Yes, sir.'

'Who?'

'Two technicians and Lieutenant Tragg.'

'And did you call to them to come and see what you had found?'

'Yes.'

'And they came over to where you were standing in the brush?'

'Yes.'

'And did any of them stumble?'

'Lieutenant Tragg caught his foot and fell flat.'

'Did any of the others stumble?'

'The fingerprint man almost fell.'

'Neither of these people were carrying anything?'

'No.'

'And it was daylight?'

'Yes.'

'Now, if the defendant had been trying to conceal the printing press, Sergeant, why would she have concealed it so near the scene of the crime?'

'You'd better ask her,' Sgt Holcomb said. 'She's your client.'

'That will do,' Judge Kent said sharply. 'There will be no repartee between the witness and counsel. Answer the question.'

'I think, if the Court please,' Marshall said, 'the question is argumentative and not proper cross-examination.'

'It certainly is argumentative,' Judge Kent said. 'I was wondering if there would be an objection on that ground. The objection is sustained.'

'Assuming,' Mason said, 'that some person, either the defendant or someone else, murdered Mervin Selkirk at the place where his car was parked, it is obvious that the murderer must have made an escape, presumably by automobile. Did you check the vicinity for the tyre tracks of another automobile, Segeant?'

'Certainly,' Sgt Holcomb said sneeringly. 'We don't overlook the obvious.'

'And did you find any such tracks?'

'We did not. The parking place was hard-topped and there were no other significant tyre tracks that we could find.'

'Did I understand you to say you didn't overlook the obvious?' Mason asked.

'That is quite correct,' Sgt Holcomb said.

'Then how did it happen that you overlooked the obvious fact that if a person had wanted to conceal the printing press, the murderer would have taken it away in the escape car rather than leave it in the brush within a hundred yards of the decedent's body where it was certain to be discovered?'

'That question is objected to as argumentative,' Marshall said.

Judge Kent smiled faintly.

'The question was asked because of the statement of the witness that the police didn't overlook the obvious,' Mason observed.

This time Judge Kent's smile broadened. 'That was a statement which the witness shouldn't have volunteered,' he said. 'And while it is a temptation to overrule the objection because of the manner in which the assertion was volunteered, the Court will sustain the objection to this present question on the ground that it is argumentative.'

Judge Kent looked at Perry Mason, inclined his head slightly and said: 'However, the parties will note that counsel has made his point.'

'Thank you. Your Honour,' Mason said. 'That is all.'

Marshall called Lt Tragg to the stand.

'Lieutenant Tragg, did you make any search of the room which had been occupied by the defendant on the night of the seventeenth and eighteenth; that is, Friday and Saturday nights?'

'I did, yes, sir.'

'What did you find, if anything?'

'Under the pillow of the bed I found a ·22-calibre Colt automatic of the type known as a Colt Woodsman, number 21323-S.'

'Do you have that weapon with you?' Marshall asked.

'I do.'

'Will you produce it, please?'

Lt Tragg opened a brief-case which he had taken in with him, and produced the weapon.

'Were there any fingerprints on this weapon?' Marshall asked.

'None that we were able to use; that is, none that were legible.'

'Does the fact that there were no fingerprints on the weapon indicate to you that the fingerprints had been removed?'

'No, sir.'

'Why not?'

'Because it is rather unusual to find fingerprints on a weapon of this type. The surface is usually somewhat oily and it is the exception rather than the rule to find any fingerprints. There is, however, one place where fingerprints are *sometimes* found. That is on the magazine clip. The clip is usually grasped between the thumb and forefinger and then pushed into place with the ball of the thumb. The magazine clip is not as oily as a rule as the rest of the gun, and sometimes we do find prints on the magazine.'

'Did you find any prints on the magazine of this weapon?'

'None that we could use.'

'Now, can you tell us exactly where you found this weapon?'

'Yes, sir. I found it under the pillow of the bed in the front room of the house occupied by Barton and Lorraine Jennings.'

'Do you know that this was a room occupied by the defendant?'

'Not to my own knowledge, no, sir. I know only that.it was a room in the front of the house, and I know that the defendant had at one time been in that room.'

'How do you know that?'

'Her fingerprints were in various parts of the room, on door-knobs, by a mirror, on a table top and in other places.'

'Did you photograph the exact position of the gun after the pillows had been removed?'

'I did.'

'Do you have that photograph with you, or a copy of it?'

'I do.'

'May I see it, please.'

Tragg produced a photograph from the brief-case. Marshall stepped to the witness stand to take it from the witness, showed it to Perry Mason and said: 'I would like to introduce this photograph in evidence.'

The photograph showed the head of a bed, a rumpled sheet, two pillows and an automatic lying on the rumpled sheet.

'No objections,' Mason said. 'It may be received in evidence.'

'Cross-examine the witness,' Marshall said.

'I take it, Lieutenant Tragg,' Mason said, 'that the pillows which are shown in the photograph had been moved prior to the time the photograph was taken?'

'Yes, sir.'

'But the gun was in exactly the same position that it was when you found it?'

'Yes, sir.'

'Then, in removing the pillows, the gun was not disturbed?'

'No, sir.'

'In removing these pillows then, you were looking for a weapon, were you not?'

'We hoped to find a weapon, yes.'

'Was that gun loaded or unloaded when it was found?' Mason asked.

'It was unloaded. It had been unloaded.'

'How do you know it had been unloaded?'

'Because of the things that had been done to the barrel.'

'There was no shell in the firing chamber?'

'No.'

'None in the magazine?'

'No.'

'Were there shells in the bedroom where the defendant had left her fingerprints?'

'Yes. There was a partially filled box of ·22 shells.'

'Did you find any fingerprints on that box of shells?'

'None that we could positively identify.'

'That's all,' Mason asked.

'If the Court please,' Marshall said, 'Lieutenant Tragg can, of course, corroborate the finding of the empty cartridge cases and the finding of the printing press, but I didn't ask him about those matters because this is merely a preliminary hearing and since Sergeant Holcomb has already given his testimony I see no reason in cluttering up the record. I will state, however, to counsel that if he desires to cross-examine Lieutenant Tragg upon these matters we have no objection.'

'I have only one question on cross-examination in regard to that phase of the case,' Mason said.

He turned to Lt Tragg. 'Do you think it would be possible to pick up the printing press in question without getting some smears of ink on your clothing?'

'It would be possible,' Lt Tragg said.

'But it would require some care in order to avoid doing so?'

'It would.'

'Who carried the printing press out from its place of concealment to the car which eventually transported it to police headquarters?'

'I did.'

'Did you get ink on your clothing?'

'Unfortunately, I did.'

'You have heard Sergeant Holcomb's testimony about your falling through the brush?'

'Yes, sir.'

'Did you fall?'

'I fell.'

'Did you fall going out with the printing press?'

'No, sir, I used great care.'

'But it was daylight?'

'It was daylight.'

'In your opinion, Lieutenant Tragg, as an officer, was the printing press placed in a position of concealment where it was reasonably safe from detection?'

Marshall started to get to his feet and object, then changed his mind and sat back in his chair, quite evidently feeling Tragg could take care of himself.

'It wouldn't be safe from the detection in the sort of examination which is usually made in a homicide case.'

'In other words, you don't join with Sergeant Holcomb in considering that his discovery of the printing press represented an epochal achievement in the chronicles of crime detection?'

There was a ripple of laughter in the court-room and this time Marshall, on his feet, angrily objected.

'The objection is sustained,' Judge Kent said, but again there was a ghost of a twinkle in his eyes.

'No further questions,' Mason said.

'We ask that the ·22 Colt automatic, number 21323-S be received in evidence,' Marshall said.

'No objection,' Mason said.

'Call Alexander Redfield,' Marshall said.

Redfield, the ballistics and firearms expert, came forward, was sworn and qualified himself as an expert.

Having been the victim of some of Mason's ingenious cross-examination several times in the past, the expert was exceedingly careful in answering questions.

'I show you a Colt Woodsman automatic, number 21323-S, which has been received in evidence,' Marshall said, 'and ask you if you have conducted a series of experiments with that weapon and if you have examined it.'

'I have.'

'I show you a ·22-calibre bullet which has been received in evidence and which the testimony shows was the so-called fatal bullet taken from the body of Mervin Selkirk, and ask you if you have examined that bullet.'

'I have.'

'Did that bullet come from this gun?' Marshall asked.

'I don't know.'

'You don't know?'

'No, sir. I know that it was fired from a weapon made by the Colt Manufacturing Company similar to this weapon, but I can't say that it came from this particular weapon.'

'Why not?' Can't you usually tell whether a given bullet comes from a given weapon?'

'Usually you can tell.'

'How?'

'There are certain characteristics which are known as class characteristics,' Redfield said. 'Those relate to the pitch of the lands in the barrel, the dimension of the lands and grooves, the direction in which they turn, the angle of turn which gives a twist or rotation to the bullet, and from those class characteristics we can generally tell the make of the weapon from which the bullet was fired.

'In addition to these general or class characteristics there are characteristics which are known as individual characteristics. Those are little striations which are found on a bullet, and are caused by individualized markings in the barrel itself. By comparing these markings, we are able to tell whether the striations on a fatal bullet coincide with those on a test bullet fired through a weapon, and from that we are able to determine whether a bullet was fired from a certain weapon.'

'But you are unable to make that determination in the present case?'

'Yes.'

'Why?'

'Because the barrel of the gun number 21323-S has been tampered with.'

'What do you mean by being tampered with?'

'That's the best way I can explain it. It is as though someone had taken a small circular file of the type known as a rat-tail file, and scratched and filed the interior of the barrel so that the characteristics were entirely altered; that is, the individual characteristics.'

'In your opinion, that was done?'

'In my opinion, the barrel was tampered with, yes, sir.'

'Do you know when?'

'After the last bullet had been fired through that barrel.'

'How do you know that?'

'Because of bits of metallic dust, or scrapings, which remained inside the barrel of the gun and the peculiar appearance of certain blemishes in the barrel which would have been altered in appearance by the firing of a bullet.'

'Now then, I call your attention to the empty cartridge case introduced in evidence and found near the place where Mervin Selkirk's body was found. I ask you if you are able to tell whether that empty cartridge case had been fired in the gun in question.'

'Yes. That cartridge was exploded or fired in the weapon which has been introduced in evidence.'

'And how are you able to determine that?'

'By a microscopic examination of the imprint of the firing pin in the rim of the shell, and a microscopic examination of the ejector marks on the cartridge case.'

'You may cross-examine,' Marshall said to Mason.

'Did you check the ownership or registration of this weapon, number 21323-S?' Mason asked Redfield.

'I did. Yes, sir.'

'And who is the registered owner of that weapon?'

'Mr Barton Jennings.'

'You found the weapon in his house?'

'Yes.'

'And you found the weapon was owned by him?'

'Yes, sir.'

'Now, let me see if I understand your testimony,' Mason said. 'If the defendant in this case had killed Mervin Selkirk, she would have gone to a house owned by Barton Jennings, she would have found some way of possessing herself of a weapon belonging to Barton Jennings, she would then have left the house and gone to the San Sebastian Country Club; she would have fired a single shell which resulted in a fatal wound, bringing death to Mervin Selkirk, and then, regardless of whether she carried an eighty-five pound printing press out into the brush in the dark without stumbling, tearing her clothes, or getting ink all over her garments, she would have returned to her room in the Jenning's house, would have taken a rat-tail file and spent some time working on the barrel of the gun so that the bullet could not be identified, and then would have conveniently left that gun under the pillow of the bed in which she had been sleeping so that you could find it there without any difficulty. Now my question is this, is there anything in your testimony that is inconsistent with such facts?'

'Your Honour, I object,' Marshall said. 'The question is argumentative. It assumes facts not in evidence. It is not proper cross-examination.'

'The objection is overruled,' Judge Kent said after some deliberation. 'The question is skilfully framed. Counsel is asking the witness if certain things must have happened, whether his testimony indicates any evidence in contradiction of these facts. He is aking that question for the purpose of trying to clarify or modify the opinion testimony of an expert witness. I will permit the question only because this witness is an expert and for that one limited purpose.'

Redfield said reluctantly: 'I have no way of knowing the sequence of the events or who altered the barrel of the gun. It is quite possible that the defendant could have left the gun under the pillow and that thereafter some other person could have altered the barrel by mutilating it with a rat-tail file.'

'Exactly,' Mason said, smiling. 'Now we're coming to the point which I wish to bring out, Mr Redfield. You state that you have no way of knowing who altered the barrel.'

'That is correct.'

'You assume that someone else could have done it.'

'Yes, sir.'

'That alteration of the barrel required the use of a long, thin, circular file of the type known as a rat-tail file?'

'Yes, sir.'

'Do you know if any such implement was found in the possession of the defendant?'

'No, sir.'

'It is not the type of implement that a woman would customarily carry in her purse?'

'Objected to as argumentative and calling for a conclusion of the witness,' Marshall said. 'The witness is an expert on firearms, not on woman's purses.'

'Sustained,' Judge Kent ruled.

'But you have stated that it is quite possible that some other person, such as Barton Jennings for instance, took this weapon from under the pillow and mutilated the barrel with a rat-tail file and then replaced it?'

'Yes, sir.'

'Now isn't it equally plausible to assume,' Mason said, 'that the barrel of the weapon was mutilated and then it was placed under the pillow of the bed in which the defendant had slept, and that that was the first time the weapon had ever been in that bed.'

'That, of course, is an assumption which *can* be drawn,' Redfield said.

'A weapon of this sort placed upon a sheet leaves a certain imprint?'

'It may.'

'I call your attention to the photograph which has been introduced in evidence showing the weapon in place where it was found, and ask you if you can find any place on that sheet as shown in the photograph where it appears that the weapon could have previously reposed.'

The witness studied the photograph. 'No, sir, I cannot.'

'It would have been virtually impossible to have picked the weapon up, mutilated the barrel and then restored it to the exact position from which it had been taken?'

'It would not have been impossible . . . well, that depends on what you mean by the *exact* position.'

'I mean the exact position.'

'Well, if you are talking about a thousandth of an inch, it would have been virtually impossible. But it *could* have been carefully placed so that it was in *virtually* the same position from which it had been taken.'

Mason stepped forward and said: 'I now hand you an empty cartridge case and ask you to compare that with the cartridge case which has previously been introduced in evidence and to examine the mark of the firing pin and the marks made by the automatic ejector and ask you if it appears to you that both cartridges were fired from the weapon in question.'

Redfield took the empty cartridge case which Mason handed him, took a magnifying-glass from his pocket, studied it carefully, said: 'I can't tell you, Mr Mason, with such examination as I can make at this time. I can state that it has the external appearances of having been fored from this weapon, but in order to make certain I would have to make a very careful check of the impression left by the firing-pin in the rim of the cartridge case.'

'How long would that take?'

'Perhaps a couple of hours.'

'I suggest that you do it,' Mason said. 'I also suggest that you take care to mark this cartridge case so that it can be identified again without confusion.'

'Now just a moment,' Marshall said. 'I don't know what counsel is getting at, but this is the same old run-around. As far as this case is concerned, it doesn't make any difference where this empty cartridge case came from. It doesn't have any bearing on the case. It is incompetent, irrelevant and immaterial.

'It is, however, a well-known fact that in cases of this sort counsel has a habit of cross-examining experts by juggling bullets, by introducing other weapons and generally confusing the issues.'

'Do you mean that I substitute evidence?' Mason asked angrily.

' I mean that you juggle evidence.'

'That will do,' Judge Kent ruled. 'There will be no repartee between counsel. The Court will do the talking. The objection is overruled. The question will stand and the expert will be asked to make tests on the cartridge case presented to him by Mr Perry Mason as counsel for the defence.

'And since the matter has come up, the Court will take this opportunity of stating that this is a perfectly legitimate question, regardless of where the cartridge case came from. This is an attempt to cross-examine the witness by testing his qualifications as an expert. If the witness has stated that one cartridge case came from a given weapon, it is certainly within the province of the defence to give him another cartridge case and ask him if that cartridge case also came from that same weapon.

'The Court is inclined to agree with Mr Mason that in a case involving the life or liberty of a citizen, counsel representing the defendant should have the greatest latitude in cross-examination and that it is not the purpose or intent of the law to have the cross-examination confined to a conventional type of attack. If counsel has the ingenuity and the wit to bring in a collateral line of attack, which is still pertinent but somewhat unconventional, counsel should be accorded that privilege.

'The Court may further state that the Court has heard criticism of Perry Mason's somewhat unorthodox methods of cross-examination before. That criticism is usually voiced by prosecutors.

'As far as this Court is concerned, the primary function of cross-examination is to test the recollection, the skill and the accuracy of witness. Any method, regardless of how unconventional or dramatic that method may be, which tends to bring about the desired object is going to be perfectly permissible in this court. It is far better to resort to the unorthodox and the dramatic than it is to have an innocent defendant convicted of crime.

'Since there is no jury present and this is a proceeding addressed to the sound discretion of the Court, the Court is also going to state that the Court itself is very anxious to have this question cleared up. Why in the name of sense should any person use a weapon in order to commit a murder, then return that weapon to a position where it is certain to be found and connected with the defendant, but first go to all the bother of mutilating the barrel so that the weapon cannot be identified?'

'May I answer that question?' Marshall asked Judge Kent.

'I'd be glad to have you *try* to do so,' Judge Kent said.

'The answer is simply this,' Marshall said. 'The defendant perhaps did not deliberately intend to commit premeditated murder. She went to meet Mervin Selkirk, she possessed herself of a weapon. We don't know what happened at that meeting; that is for the defendant to tell us if she chooses to take the stand. But she did press the trigger of that gun and released the bullet which killed Mervin Selkirk. Then she returned to the room where she had been sleeping and, because she didn't know that the identity of the weapon could be checked by microscopic comparison of the impression made by the firing-pin on the rim of the cartridge, she thought she would cover the back trail by mutilating the barrel of the weapon so that the weapon which fired the fatal bullet could never be identified.'

'And then left the weapon under her pillow?' Judge Kent asked.

'Yes, Your Honour, we know she must have done that. The evidence shows she did.'

Judge Kent shook his head indicating utter disbelief.

'The reason she did that,' Marshall went on, 'as we shall presently show, is that the weapon had been left on a table in the front hall. Under ordinary circumstances the weapon would have been returned to the bureau drawer in the front bedroom, which was the place it was usually kept. However, that night the defendant was occupying the bedroom. So the gun was left in plain sight on the hall table.

'The defendant left her bedroom and tiptoed down the stairs. It is a fair inference that Mervin Selkirk either had an appointment with her or had found some way of communicating with her. She went downstairs, saw the gun, decided to take it with her, and fired one shot from it.

'Then when she returned to the house she had the gun with her. She went back to her room to decide what to do. She was worried for fear the fatal gun could be identified by ballistics experts so she roughed up the barrel.'

'And then conveniently left it under her pillow?' Judge Kent asked sceptically.

'Yes, Your Honour, she was afraid she had left fingerprints on the gun and thought it would be better to say she had taken if from the hall table to her room. She didn't realize a ballistics expert could tell the barrel had been tampered with or that this tampering had been done after the last shell had been fired in the gun.'

Judge Kent thought that over, then said dryly: 'I take it that you have further evidence which you intend to introduce and which you hope and believe will support this position.'

'We do.'

'Very well,' Judge Kent said, 'the Court will keep an open mind. At the present time the Court is very frank to state that it considers the theory far-fetched.'

'The Court will bear in mind the imprint of the defendant's finger on the printing press which was found at the scene of the crime,' Marshall said somewhat irritably.

'The Court will keep all of the evidence in mind,' Judge Kent said, 'and the Court will listen to you when you are ready to argue that evidence. I take it you are not ready to close your case and start the argument now?'

'No, Your Honour.'

'Go ahead then and put on your other evidence,' Judge Kent said. 'In the meantime, the witness Redfield will be asked by the Court to check this cartridge case handed him by Mr Mason.

'I take it, Mr Mason, that you have some particular reason for making this suggestion, and that this particular cartridge case is of importance to your theory of the case?'

'It is, Your Honour.'

'Very well. The witness Redfield will make that check and return to court with his report this afternoon,' Judge Kent said.

Marshall said: 'We'll call Miss Frances Delano to the stand.'

Frances Delano, wearing the uniform of an airline hostess, came forward, was sworn and seated herself on the witness chair.

Judge Kent looked at the trim young woman approvingly.

Marshall said: 'What is your occupation, Miss Delano?'

'I am employed as a stewardess on the United Airlines.'

'Where is your run?'

'Between San Francisco and Los Angeles, and Los Angeles and San Francisco.'

'On the night of the seventeenth were you a stewardess on a plane flying between San Francisco and Los Angeles?'

'I was.'

'What was your schedule?'

'We left San Francisco at eight-fifteen.'

'I ask you to look at the defendant and ask you to tell us if you have ever seen her before.'

'Yes, I have seen her. She was a passenger on my plane.'

'There's no question about that,' Perry Mason said. 'That's stipulated, Your Honour. There's no need to call a witness to prove that.'

'I am getting at something else,' Marshall said.

He turned to the witness. 'Now, Miss Delano, will you explain to us what happens with tickets which are purchased?'

'They're on a form,' she said, 'a folder. There are carbon copies made and at various control points the ticket part is torn off. There is a final carbon copy on the cover which is left in the possession of the passenger.'

'I now show you a document and ask you if you can tell us what that is.'

'May I see it?' Mason asked.

'Certainly,' Marshall said.

He handed Mason a bloodstained, folded bit of heavy paper, then after Mason had inspected it, showed it to the witness.

The witness said: 'That is the passenger's portion of a ticket. That is what the passenger retains on a one-way ticket.'

'And this ticket has the name "Miss N. Allison" on it?'

'That is correct.'

'And what does that indicate?'

'That the ticket was issued to a Miss N. Allison.'

'That is her signature?'

'No, that name was probably written by the person issuing the ticket. It is not necessarily the signature of the passenger, but this is retained by the passenger as an identification coupon and there's a memo so that in case of making out expense accounts or deductions for income tax purposes this is a voucher for the passenger.'

'Cross-examine,' Marshall said.

'No questions,' Mason said.

'I would like to call Harry Nelson,' Marshall said.

As Nelson was coming to the witness-stand, Mason turned to Norda Allison. 'That ticket has bloodstains on it,' he whispered. 'It must have been found on the body of Mervin Selkirk. Did you see him that night?'

'Absolutely not.'

'How did he get possession of your ticket?'

'That,' she said, 'is more that I can tell you.'

'Where was that ticket?' Mason asked, still whispering.

'In my purse.'

Mason frowned. 'If you're either lying or mistaken, you're going to get a jolt,' he warned, then turned to face the witness-stand.

Nelson was sworn, testified that he was a deputy coroner, that as such he had searched the clothes on the body of Mervin Selkirk when the body had been delivered at the morgue, that the aeroplane ticket identification cover which had been identified by the previous witness was in the inside right-hand pocket of the coat worn by Mervin Selkirk at the time the body was delivered to the morgue.

'Cross-examine,' Marshall said.

'No questions,' Mason said.

The bailiff approached Judge Kent on the bench and held a whispered conversation with him.

Mason took advantage of the opportunity to turn to Norda Allison.

'Was your purse ever out of your possession that night?'

'Not that I remember.'

Mason frowned. 'You're going to have to account for that ticket,' he whispered, 'and you're going to have to tell a convincing story. Judge Kent has been with us all the way. He's ready to dismiss the case on the evidence so far introduced. He's not impressed by that gun having been found under your pillow. But this is something different.'

Judge Kent looked up and said: 'Gentlemen, I am going to ask the deputy district attorney and Mr Mason to attend a conference in my chambers. A matter has come up in connection with this case which should be discussed in private. I can assure both counsel that the circumstances are very unusual. The Court will take its usual noon recess at this point and court is adjourned until two o'clock this afternoon. Will counsel please meet with me in my chambers?'

A policewoman approached to take Norda Allison into custody.

'You do some thinking about that ticket,' Mason said. 'There's something peculiar here, some explanation that . . . wait a minute! You had a suitcase with you?'

'Yes.'

'That was checked?'

'Yes.'

'Now then,' Mason said, 'the aeroplane companies sometimes staple the baggage check to the inside of the ticket stub. Was that done in your case?'

'Why . . . I guess so, yes.'

'And when you arrived in Los Angeles, Lorraine Jennings and her husband met you?'

'Yes.'

'Then,' Mason said, 'you would have surrendered your baggage check to Barton Jennings for him to get your suitcase.'

'Not Barton Jennings,' she said. 'I think it was Lorraine. As I remember it, Barton went to get the car and Lorraine asked me for my baggage check. I think I tore it off the baggage check and gave it to her and she . . . now wait a minute. She *may* have had the entire ticket stub.'

'You think it over,' Mason said. 'That ticket stub got into the possession of Mervin Selkirk in some way. You're going to have to get on the stand and tell your story and you're going to have to tell exactly what happened.'

'I . . . I just can't remember, Mr Mason. It's my impression that I pulled the baggage check loose and left the stub of the ticket in my purse. I . . . I'm almost certain that's what happened.'

'Now look,' Mason said in an angry whisper, 'don't be *almost* certain. If you just say you can't remember anything about it, I can probably convince Judge Kent that you handed the ticket stub to Barton Jennings so that he could claim your suitcase, and then we'll leave it up to Barton Jennings to explain what happened to the ticket; whether he dropped it, threw it away or put it in his pocket. But when you–'

'No,' she said, with conviction. 'The more I think of it, the more I'm *certain* that I tore the stub off and handed it to Lorraine Jennings. Her husband went to get the car while Lorraine took care of the suitcase. I know she was standing there with it when Barton Jennings drove up in the car. A porter took my suitcase to the car and Jennings gave him a tip. I had put the ticket cover back in my purse.'

'Well,' Mason said, 'think it over during the noon recess. I've got to go and see what Judge Kent wants. It's something rather important, otherwise he wouldn't have called a conference.'

15

Mason pushed open the door of Judge Kent's chambers and entered.

Manley Marshall was standing by the window. Judge Kent was seated at his big desk and seated to the right of the desk was Horace Livermore Selkirk.

Judge Kent said: 'Come in, Mr Mason. Sit down. You too, Mr Marshall. A matter has been called to my attention which I think merits an off-record discussion.'

Mason seated himself and after a moment Manley Marshall also seated himself.

Judge Kent looked at his watch. 'I have telephoned the district attorney Hamilton Burger, and asked him to attend this conference in person if he will. He should be here. He . . .'

The office door was pushed open and Hamilton Burger, somewhat short of breath, entered the judge's chambers. 'How do you do, Judge Kent,' he said.

'How do you do, Mr Burger. Are you acquainted with Horace Livermore Selkirk?'

Selkirk got up and extended his hand. 'Glad to meet you, Mr Burger,' he said.

'I have never met Mr Selkirk personally,' Burger said, beaming as he shook hands. 'I have seen him at meetings and have heard him make a talk at a banquet, but have never met him personally. How do you do, Mr Selkirk. It's indeed a very great pleasure.'

'Sit down, gentlemen,' Judge Kent said. 'Mr Selkirk has a communication of some importance in connection with a case which is pending before this Court. I felt, under the circumstances, the communication should be made in private, and I think that you gentlemen will agree with me it is not a matter for the press.'

Burger nodded briefly to Perry Mason, seated himself, said: 'Very well.'

Horace Selkirk cleared his throat. 'I am, of course, the father of Mervin Selkirk, the victim of the shooting in this case. I am the grandfather of Robert Selkirk, the seven-year-old son of Mervin Selkirk. Under the circumstances, Robert is the last of the Selkirk line. Mervin was my only child and Robert is his only child.'

There was a moment of impressive silence.

'Under the circumstances,' Horace Selkirk went on, 'Robert is my sole heir.

'Robert's mother, who has been divorced and is now married to Barton Jennings, is in my opinion a shrewd, unscrupulous, scheming character. She knows that in all probability I will die before Robert attains his majority. She is not at all unaware of the fact that as Robert's legal guardian she would be entitled to certain perquisites and certain advantages, and, moreover, would be in a position to play upon Robert's sympathies and his natural affection for a mother so that she would eventually derive certain material advantages no matter how I tried to safeguard my estate–I can, of course, keep her from getting her fingers in most of my fortune, but Robert is impressionable and there is a bond of natural respect and affection.'

Judge Kent frowned. 'Does that have any bearing on the present case, Mr Selkirk?' he asked. 'I sympathize, of course, with your position. I know that you have lost a son under very tragic circumstances. I know that you must have undergone great emotional strain. But it would seem to me that the facts you have mentioned are somewhat extraneous.'

'They are not extraneous,' Horace Selkirk said coldly. 'My grandson, Robert, killed his father, Mervin Selkirk.'

'What?' Hamilton Burger all but shouted, half getting up from his chair.

Judge Kent leaned forward attentively, frowning at Horace Selkirk.

'I know what I am talking about,' Horace Selkirk said, 'and Perry Mason also understands the situation. And Mr Perry Mason intends to make a last-minute grandstand to save his client by showing what actually happened. I feel that in the interests of justice Mr Mason should not be permitted to drag my grandson into the case and thereby place an irreparable stigma upon the boy's name.'

'You say that Robert killed his father?' Judge Kent asked.

'Robert Selkirk was the instrumentality chosen by Lorraine Jennings to get rid of my son,' Horace Selkirk said coldly. 'Under a property settlement which had been made with my son at the time of the divorce, she received certain properties, and in the event of Mervin's death she not only received additional properties in her own name but Robert would inherit certain very valuable properties and she would naturally be the guardian of his person and estate, and as such entitled to compensation.'

'I think,' Hamilton Burger said, glancing suspiciously at Perry Mason, 'we had better hear a little more about what you have in mind, Mr Selkirk. And may I caution you not to be deceived by any elaborate scheme which may have been thought up by Perry Mason in order to extricate his client from a charge of first-degree murder. We have evidence in this case that points the finger directly at Norda Allison.'

'Doubtless you do,' Horace Selkirk said, 'but that evidence has been carefully fabricated and you are the one who has been deceived, not me.'

'You have some proof of your statements?' Judge Kent asked Selkirk.

'I have ample proof,' Selkirk said.

'Perhaps you had better tell us what it is.'

'I dislike to keep harping on this,' Selkirk said, 'but my son's ex-wife, Lorraine Jennings, is a very scheming, clever woman. She is, in my opinion, a fiend incarnate. She deliberately framed the seven-year-old Robert to be the innocent instrumentality of her hatred. I am not a demonstrative man, but I love my grandson very deeply.

'The child has been allowed to take an undue interest in firearms. He has been trained to watch television programmes of the kind that are known as "pistol pictures". Then Lorraine permitted him to take the Colt Woodsman which has been introduced in evidence in this case and play with it, assuring him always that it was unloaded, but letting him point it and shoot it at people.'

'You're certain of that?' Judge Kent interrupted incredulously.

'Evidence is available to that effect,' Horace Selkirk said. 'Neighbours who have watched proceedings at the Jennings' house have seen the child pointing the pistol at people and pulling the trigger.'

Judge Kent frowned.

'Then,' Horace Selkirk went on, 'after the boy had been properly conditioned to shoot this gun, believing it was always empty and unloaded, Lorraine Jennings let him have the weapon when it actually was loaded. Then she decoyed the child's father into going to the tent where the boy was sleeping, telling the father that he should surprise the boy. The thing happened which she hoped would happen. The boy heard the noise of the father entering the tent. He was wakened from a sound sleep. It was night. He had the gun with him, he raised it and pulled the trigger. The bullet entered my son's chest.

'My son staggered to his automobile in front of the house, leaving a bloody trail along the grass. He got in the car and drove away, trying to find help. He knew that a doctor, whom he felt could be trusted to treat his wound and say nothing, quite frequently played poker on Friday nights at the San Sebastian Country Club. He drove up there, not realizing the seriousness of his wound. He parked the car, but before he was able to leave the car he became unconscious. Death ensued some time after he became unconscious.

'I can produce proof of what I am talking about and I have reason to believe that Mr Mason also has that proof. I am here to prevent the exploitation of my grandson.'

'In what way?' Judge Kent asked.

'Perry Mason has been interrogating the neighbours,' Selkirk said. 'He has talked with some of them personally. He has talked with others by means of the private detective agency which handles his work in cases of this sort. He knows that a shot was fired from inside the tent where Robert was sleeping. He knows that shot inflicted a serious injury upon someone, that the person left a blood trail along the grass and that Barton Jennings arose early in the morning to eliminate this blood trail with a hose.

'Mr Mason knows that my grandson was given the ·22 Woodsman to play with, that the boy knew how to work the mechanism of the gun so as to pull back the barrel in a way that would cock it; then he would point the gun and pull the trigger. Mr Mason has made careful inquiry and has all of this data at his finger-tips.

'At the proper time, probably after court convenes this afternoon, he plans to ask Barton Jennings on cross-examination if it isn't a fact that the boy was permitted to play with this gun. He then intends to show that the boy had the gun on this fateful Friday night; that there was a trail of blood leading along the grass to the kerb. Then Mr Mason intends to ask the Court for an order bringing my grandson into court so that he can be interrogated.

'I wish to spare my grandson this frightful ordeal. It is true he is a bright little chap. It is true that he senses that something awful may have happened. He is not certain that he actually shot anyone, but he knows that he pulled the trigger of the gun and that the gun was loaded. He knows that it was pointed at some person who was about to enter his tent.

'Barton Jennings tried to convince my grandson that all this was a horrible dream, a nightmare. I don't think he was able to convince the boy, but the boy certainly has no inkling at the present time that he actually killed his father. Nor does he have any idea that the killing of his father was part of a cold-blooded, deliberate plan hatched in the mind of the boy's mother.

'Mr Mason is representing Norda Allison. As an attorney it is, I presume, his duty to do everything in his power to see that she is acquitted. However,

Mr Mason is well known for his flair for the dramatic. He is looking for an opportunity to cross-examine Barton Jennings on the stand in such a way that the facts will be brought out in the most dramatic manner possible.

'When Mason has finished cross-examining Barton Jennings, Barton Jennings will be reduced to a hopeless wreck. The case will be so dramatized that Perry Mason will once more emerge as the invincible champion of the court-room, and my grandson will have been stigmatized for life.'

Horace Selkirk paused to survey Mason coldly.

Hamilton Burger, the district attorney, took a cigar from his pocket, clipped off the end and lit the cigar.

Judge Kent looked speculatively at Hamilton Burger's face. Then he looked at Mason, then back to Horace Selkirk.

'You are making rather sweeping charges, Mr Selkirk,' he said.

'I know what I'm talking about.'

'You have proof?'

'Yes.'

'What?'

Selkirk said: 'I can produce my grandson, Robert, here in chambers within thirty minutes, I ask only that you, Judge Kent, take this young man into a private conference, where you–as a judge who is accustomed to handling problems with juveniles–can talk with him in a confidential manner. I suggest that you get his story. When you have that story, you will realize the truth of what I am saying.'

Judge Kent frowned. 'This procedure is, of course, highly irregular,' he said. 'As the judge in this case I am supposed to keep myself completely aloof from any outside influence.'

'I grant you that,' Selkirk said, 'but as a citizen–a citizen who is not without some influence in the community, I may state–I feel that your primary function is to administer justice. I feel that it is getting to be inhuman to allow Mr Perry Mason to appear again in public as a master of legal legerdemain at the cost of wrecking the life of a seven-year-old boy. After all, Judge Kent, you are charged with looking after the rights of juveniles who, because of their tender age, must be, in a measure, wards of the state.'

Again Judge Kent looked at Hamilton Burger.

Hamilton Burger removed the cigar from his mouth, blew out a wisp of pale blue smoke. His expression indicated that he was savouring the aroma of the cigar.

Manley Marshall sat there perfectly still, trying to look utterly non-committal.

Judge Kent seemed somewhat irritated at Burger's attitude. 'Do you,' he asked, 'know anything about this, Mr Burger?'

Burger studied the tip of the cigar for a moment, holding the cigar between the thick first and second fingers of his powerful right hand. Then he said thoughtfully: 'I'm not prepared to say that I know *nothing* about it. I am prepared to state that we consider this entire procedure irregular, that we wish to try our case in the court-room, and particularly that I don't intend to disclose our evidence in this case in front of counsel for the defence. I simply don't intend to give him that advantage.'

Judge Kent turned to Mason. 'You have heard what Mr Selkirk has said, Mr Mason.'

'I have heard what he has said.'

'May I ask if there is some element of truth in it?'

'Since you ask, I can tell you that there is *some* element of truth in it. I'd like to ask Mr Selkirk a question.'

Mason turned to Horace Selkirk. 'You are, I believe, attached to your grandson, Mr Selkirk?'

Selkirk's face softened for a moment, then became hard. 'That boy,' he said, 'is the only Selkirk who can carry on a proud name and the proud traditions of a proud family. I am proud of those traditions. I love him and I don't intend to see his life ruined.'

'And,' Mason said, 'you would like to have his sole custody and guardianship?'

'That is beside the point.'

'I don't think so,' Mason said. 'I would like to have you answer that question.'

'You have no right to sit here and cross-examine me,' Selkirk flared. 'You know that I called the turn on you. You know exactly what you plan to do in connection with this case. You know the type of dramatic disclosure you intend to make when court reconvenes this afternoon. You know how you intend to cross-examine Barton Jennings. You know that you have been out getting information about the blood trail and about the gun.'

'Do *you* know anything about a blood trail?' Judge Kent asked Hamilton Burger abruptly.

'Frankly, Your Honour, we do,' Hamilton Burger said. 'And, equally frankly, we don't think either Perry Mason or Mr Selkirk knows *all* of the facts in this case. We are quite content to try this case in the court-room, which is where it should be tried.'

Judge Kent drummed on the desk with his fingers, then looked at Perry Mason. 'Is it true that Robert Selkirk was permitted to play with a weapon, Mr Mason?'

'I think it is,' Mason said.

'The same weapon that has been introduced in evidence in this case as the murder gun?'

'I believe so, Your Honour. But that doesn't necessarily indicate it as the murder gun.'

'I think it is the murder weapon,' Hamilton Burger said. 'I think we've established that point by the imprint of the firing-pin.'

'I am not prepared to admit it,' Mason said.

'Have you evidence concerning a blood trail, Mr Mason?' Judge Kent asked.

'One of the neighbours has told me about it,' Mason said.

'A *blood* trail, Mr Mason?'

'That is my understanding,' Mason said.

Judge Kent glanced across to Hamilton Burger. 'I think the Court is entitled to find out more about this, Mr District Attorney.'

'Perhaps the Court is,' Hamilton Burger said, 'but counsel for the defence isn't.'

'Just what do you mean by that?'

'I mean that there is no chance on earth that Robert Selkirk killed his father. The death of Mervin Selkirk was at the hands of Norda Allison. We are prepared to prove that.'

'I take it you have a surprise witness?'

'A surprise witness, and we intend to keep this witness as a surprise witness.'

Judge Kent thought for a moment, then turned to Horace Selkirk. 'You have talked with your grandson?'

'Naturally.'

'And you are sincere in your belief that your seven-year-old grandson, Robert, killed his father?'

'I feel absolutely certain of it.'

'All right,' Judge Kent said. 'You get your grandson here without letting him know what it's all about. I'm going to talk with him during the noon recess. The procedure may be irregular, but I certainly am not going to let this case get to a point where it is made to appear in court that a seven-year-old boy inadvertently killed his father until I know more about the facts in the case.

'It may be that before I finish I will ask counsel to make certain stipulations, but in the meantime I am going to talk with this boy. How long will it take to get him here?'

'Fifteen minutes,' Horace Selkirk said. 'That is, if I may use your phone.'

'Use the phone,' Judge Kent snapped.

Selkirk crossed over to the phone, picked it up and asked for an outside line. Then he dialled a number.

Manley Marshall leaned over to whisper to Hamilton Burger, but Burger, holding up his left hand, gestured his assistant to silence.

The big district attorney puffed contentedly on his cigar.

Selkirk spoke into the telephone. 'This is Horace Selkirk,' he said. 'How about the woman and the boy whom you were shadowing. Are they in the next room? All right,' Selkirk said, 'Bring them up to the courthouse, to the chambers of Judge Homer F. Kent. Bring them up right away . . . I said bring them . . . All right, if they don't want to come we'll send an officer, but I don't want to waste that time. I want them here in fifteen minutes. Tell them that the judge has sent for them.'

'Now, just a minute,' Judge Kent said. 'I didn't issue any such peremptory summons. I–'

'It's all right, Judge,' Horace Selkirk said. 'They'll be here. This woman is in my employ and she is supposed to do what I tell her to. I am the one who issues instructions.'

Judge Kent looked at his watch. 'Do you think they'll be here in fifteen minutes?'

'They certainly should be.'

'That's cutting it rather thin,' Judge Kent said. 'I'm going to terminate this conference at this time. I am going to go to the lunch counter here in the building and get a quick sandwich. I will be back here in exactly twenty minutes–well, let us say twenty-five minutes. I will expect you gentlemen to meet me here, and when young Robert Selkirk comes in, I am going to suggest that I handle the interrogation of the young man. I don't want any interruptions. I don't want any suggestions from anyone. I am going to ask a few questions and, as you can readily understand, I don't intend to have the young man understand the object of those questions. I want to find out what actually happened and what he knows.'

'You will understand,' Selkirk said, 'that I have so conditioned his mind that he actually knows only that he fired the gun. He doesn't know the person who ultimately received the bullet from that gun.'

'I'll talk with him myself,' Judge Kent said. 'And since we are working on a very close time schedule, I will suggest that we terminate this conference at once and that we meet here in exactly twenty-five minutes. Is that satisfactory, gentlemen?'

Burger nodded.

'Quite satisfactory,' Horace Selkirk said.

'I'll be here,' Mason observed.

16

At exactly twenty-five minutes after Judge Kent had adjourned the meeting, the parties regrouped in the judge's chambers.

Judge Kent, who had evidently given the matter a great deal of serious thought during the intermission, regarded Horace Selkirk thoughtfully. 'You are prepared to go ahead, Mr Selkirk?' he asked.

'I am.'

'My bailiff tells me that the woman and the boy whom you summoned are waiting in the witness-room. They asked that word be sent to you.'

'Very well.'

'Do you wish to go and get them?'

'You can have the bailiff bring them in,' Selkirk said. 'I believe you have said you wanted to be the one to examine the boy, and I don't want you to feel that I have been talking with him or telling him what to say.'

'Very well,' Judge Kent said. 'The couple will be brought in. I am going to ask that you gentlemen remain quiet and let me ask the questions. I don't want any prompting, any suggestions or any instructions. Regardless of what the facts may show, this is a serious situation and a particularly serious situation in the life of a young man.'

Judge Kent plugged in the intercommunicating speaker and said to his bailiff: 'You may bring the woman and the boy in now.'

There was a moment of tense, strained silence, then the door opened. A tall blonde woman and a seven-year-old boy entered the room; the boy looked a little dazed, the woman completely self-possessed.

'Come in,' Judge Kent invited, 'and sit down. Now, as I understand it, you're–'

Horace Selkirk's chair crashed over backwards as he jumped to his feet. '*Those* aren't the ones!' he shouted.

Judge Kent looked at him with annoyance. 'It was understood that I–'

'Those aren't the ones! That isn't Robert! That isn't the woman! That–who the hell are *you*?' Selkirk shouted at the woman.

'That will do,' Judge Kent rebuked. 'We'll have no profanity here and no browbeating of this woman. May I ask who are you, madam?'

'I'm a detective,' she said to Judge Kent. 'I'm employed by the Drake Detective Agency. I have been instructed to occupy rooms 619 and 621 at the Anandale Hotel. I have done so.'

'Who gave you those instructions!' Horace Selkirk shouted.

'Paul Drake.'

There was a tense silence which was broken by Hamilton Burger's chuckle.

'This is no laughing matter, Mr District Attorney,' Judge Kent rebuked.

'I beg your pardon,' Burger said, in a voice which showed no regret. 'It is amusing to me to see someone else experiencing annoyance at the unconventional tactics of a certain well-known defence attorney.'

'What became of Grace Hallum and Robert Selkirk who were in those rooms?' Horace Selkirk demanded.

'I'm sure I don't know,' the woman said calmly. 'I am a licensed detective. I act within the law. I followed the instructions of Paul Drake. I was told to go to the Anandale Hotel, to take my seven-year-old son with me and to remain there until I received further instructions.

'A short time ago I was advised that Judge Homer F. Kent had instructed me to leave the hotel and come here to the chambers. I promptly called Paul Drake for instructions and was advised by him to go to Judge Kent's chambers, take my son with me and give him my true name.'

Horace Selkirk, his face livid, turned to Perry Mason. 'This is once you can't get away with it!' he shouted. 'I don't know what you've done with my grandson and the woman who has his custody, but this time you've really violated the law. You're guilty of kidnapping, at least technically.'

Hamilton Burger surveyed Selkirk with speculative eyes. 'Do you wish to charge Mason with kidnapping?' he asked. 'If you do, and are willing to sign a complaint, we'll see that one is issued.'

Horace Selkirk said with cold fury: 'You're damn right I'll sign a complaint.'

Judge Kent said dryly: 'I once more want to caution you against profanity in these chambers, Mr Selkirk, particularly in the presence of a child–now it is rapidly becoming apparent that this is a situation which should never have developed in this case. I feel that an attempt has been made to prejudice me by appealing to my sympathies and my desires to save a seven-year-old boy from an emotional shock. This inquiry has now gone far afield and if we are not careful I am going to be disqualified from continuing with this case.'

Hamilton Burger got to his feet. 'I think that is a point which could well have been made earlier in the case. I'm going to ask this woman and the boy to come with me. My office wants to ask some questions about what happened here, and if Mr Selkirk wishes to take the responsibility of signing a complaint charging Mr Perry Mason with kidnapping, I can assure him that the personal element in the situation will make no difference to my office. We will proceed without fear or favour.'

Burger nodded to Selkirk and started for the door. 'You come with me,' he said to the woman detective.

Mason got to his feet, bowed to Judge Kent. 'I'm sorry these matters had to interfere with your lunch hour,' he said.

Judge Kent regarded Perry Mason with puzzled eyes. There was a faint hint of admiration back of his bewilderment.

17

Court reconvened promptly at two o'clock.

Hamilton Burger now sat in the prosecutor's chair alongside Manley Marshall.

'If the Court please,' Hamilton Burger said, 'I am going to call a witness who will eliminate any doubt in this matter. Call Millicent Bailey.'

A woman in her late twenties came walking down the aisle. She was slender-waisted but well curved, and the rhythm of her walk showed that she was fully concious of those curves. There was an almost defiant air about her as she entered the railed enclosure, held up her hand and took the oath.

She seated herself on the witness-stand.

Hamilton Burger himself conducted the examination.

'Your name is Millicent Bailey?'

'Yes, sir.'

'Miss or Mrs?'

'Mrs.'

'Are you living with your husband?'

'I am not. I'm divorced.'

'I am going to call your attention to the night of the seventeenth and the eighteenth of this month. Do you remember the occasion?'

'You mean the night of the seventeenth and the early morning of the eighteenth?'

'That's right.'

'Yes, I remember them.'

'May I ask what you were doing?'

'I was out with a boy friend.'

'Do you wish to give us the name of that boy friend?'

'I do not. He is a respectable married man, but his home life is not happy. He is contemplating leaving his wife and filing an action for divorce, but I don't want anything that I may say to jeopardize his interests, and so I am not going to give his name.'

'I feel certain,' Hamilton Burger said, 'that under the circumstances counsel will not press you for his name, and I know that I will not. I think as men of the world we'll appreciate the situation.'

And Hamilton Burger bowed with elaborate courtesy to Perry Mason.

'I will not agree to restrict my cross-examination in the least,' Mason said. 'I will ask any questions that I feel are necessary to protect the interests of my client.'

'Quite naturally,' Hamilton Burger said, 'but *I* feel that since it will soon develop that the identity of this man has absolutely nothing to do with the testimony of this witness, you will realize the expediency of refraining from bringing out the man's name.'

Hamilton Burger turned back to the witness. 'Now, Mrs Bailey, I am going to ask you to describe generally what happened on the night of the seventeenth.'

'I got off work at eight o'clock. I went to my apartment and bathed and changed my clothes. My boy friend had said that he would call for me at ten o'clock.

'At ten o'clock he was there. We had a drink in my apartment and then we went to a night club where we danced until–well, it was somewhere around one o'clock.'

'Then what happened?'

'Then we left the night club and took a drive.'

'And where did you go on this drive?' Hamilton Burger asked.

'To the San Sebastian Country Club.'

'Just where at the country club?' Burger asked.

'To the wide parking place where cars are parked; that is, a place which is reserved for the cars of members.'

'What time was this?' Hamilton Burger asked.

'I can't tell you the time. It was perhaps one-thirty.'

'That would be one-thirty in the morning of the eighteenth?'

'Yes.'

'Just why did you go there?'

'We wanted to . . . to talk.'

'Can you describe this parking place where you went?'

'Yes. There is a road which winds up the hill to the country club, then there is a very wide parking space where members can leave their cars. It is a big, flat space with lines ruled in it in white.'

'When you drove up were there any other cars there?'

'Yes.'

'I wish you would tell us exactly what happened after you arrived at the parking place,' Hamilton Burger said.

'Well, there was a car there.'

'Can you describe the car?'

'I didn't pay too much attention to it. It was a big car, one of those expensive cars.'

'Were the lights on or off?'

'You mean on that car?'

'Yes.'

'The lights were off.'

'What was the car doing?'

'It was just sitting there.'

'Did you see anybody in it?'

'No. I assumed the car had been left–'

'Never mind what you assumed,' Hamilton Burger interrupted. 'I am asking you only what you saw and what you heard.'

'Yes, sir.'

'What did you do?'

'My friend and I wanted to talk where we would be private. We . . . I mean, he, drove on past this car that was parked and went down to the far end of the parking lot. There are some trees there; some big live oaks, and there are perhaps half a dozen parking places that are right under these trees.'

'And what did you do?'

'My friend parked his car there.'

'Was the area lighted?'

'No, sir. There is a light, sort of a floodlight over the lawn in front of the entrance to the club-house that's on all night. There's a certain light from that which illuminates the parking place, but the parking place itself isn't really lighted up. It's fairly dark there.'

'And *quite* dark under the trees?'

'Yes.'

'Now, did your companion park the car so that it was facing into the trees?'

'No, sir, he did not. He turned the car around so that when we wanted to start out he only needed to step on the starter and pull right out.'

'So you could see through the windshield and see the parking space?'

'Yes.'

'And the road leading into the parking space?'

'Yes.'

'And the car which was already parked there in the space?'

'Yes.'

'Then what happened?'

'Well, we sat and talked.'

'For how long?'

'For some time. We were trying to get things settled. I wasn't going to break up any home. I told him–'

'Now never mind what you talked about,' Hamilton Burger said. 'I am not going to interrogate you as to that point. I am simply trying to get the time element.'

'Yes, sir.'

'Do you know how long you were there?'

'Some little time.'

'An hour?'

'I guess all of an hour.'

'And what happened?'

'Well, we talked, and–'

'I'm not interested in that,' Hamilton Burger said. 'I want to find out . . . I'll get at it another way. What time did you leave there?'

'It was about . . . I guess about, well, perhaps half past three in the morning; perhaps three o'clock, I don't know. I didn't look at my watch.'

'Now, did anything happen just prior to the time you left?'

'Yes.'

'What?'

'Another car came up the roadway to the parking place.'

'That's what I'm trying to get at,' Burger said. 'Now, can you describe that car?'

'Yes, sir. It was an Oldsmobile and it had white side-wall tyres.'

'Do you know the licence number?'

'I do?'

'What was the licence number?'

'JYJ 113.'

'What did that car do?'

'It parked just behind this car that had been there all the time.'

'Do you mean it went into a parking space alongside this parked car?'

'No, sir. It came to a stop right behind it. It wasn't in any parking place. It was right behind the car.'

'And what happened?'

'Well, a woman got out of the car.'

'You saw this woman?'

'Yes.'

'Were the lights on?'

'In what car?'

'In the car that had just driven up.'

'Yes, the lights were left on.'

'You say that a woman got out?'

'Yes, sir.'

'Do you know whether she was alone in the car?'

'There was no other person in the car.'

'How could you tell?'

'When she got out, she left the door open and a light came on in the inside of the car–you know, the way a light automatically comes on when the door is left standing open.'

'And what did this woman do?'

'She walked over to the parked car.'

'Now then,' Hamilton Burger said, 'I'm going to show you a photograph of a car parked in the parking place at the San Sebastian Country Club and ask you if you recognize that car from the photograph.'

'I do.'

'What is it?'

'That is the car that was parked that night.'

'You mean the evening of the seventeenth and the early morning hours of the eighteenth?'

'Yes.'

'The car which you have referred to as the car which was parked when you drove up?'

'Yes.'

'The car which was there all the time you were parked under the trees there?'

'Yes.'

'The car which was in front of the car that was driven by the woman?'

'Yes.'

'Very well. Now, referring to the car which came driving up there, what did you do? What did you see?'

'I saw this woman get out of the car.'

'And what, if anything, did she do?'

'She walked across to the parked car.'

'And then what?'

'She paused by the door of that car. She took something from her purse.'

'Could you tell what she took from her purse?'

'I think it was a gun.'

'Did you see a gun?'

'I saw the light reflect from something metallic.'

'And then what?'

'I don't know what happened after that. We got out of there, fast.'

'Her car was still there when you drove out?'

'Yes.'

'She was standing there?'

'Yes.'

'Do you know whether she had seen your car; or that is, the car in which you were riding before you started the motor and turned on the lights?'

'I don't think she had. If she did, she hadn't paid any attention to it. It was when we drove out that she jerked back to look at us and I think she screamed; at least her mouth was wide open and I think she was screaming.'

'Did you see her face?'

'I saw her face.'

'Plainly?'

'Plainly.'

'Would you recognize that woman if you had seen her again?'

'I would.'

'Do you see that woman here in the court at this time?'

'I do.'

'Can you point her out?'

The witness arose from the stand, levelled a pointing finger at Norda Allison and said: 'That's the woman, the one sitting right there.'

'The one sitting over here next to Mr Perry Mason?'

'That's the one.'

'Would you please step down from the witness-stand and put your hand on her shoulder.'

The witness marched down, placed her hand on Norda Allison's shoulder, turned and walked back to the witness-stand.

Hamilton Burger smiled. 'You may cross-examine,' he said to Perry Mason.

Mason arose to face the witness. 'When you entered the parking lot,' he said, 'were you sitting on the side nearest the parked car?'

'Yes.'

'Then the car was parked on the right-hand side of the parking lot as you drove in?'

'Yes.'

'Then as you drove out, the car would have been to your left?'

'Yes.'

'Then you must have looked across the driver of the car; that is, the driver of the car in which you were riding, to see the two cars as you left?'

'What do you mean, the driver of the car?'

'Exactly what I said,' Mason replied. 'The driver of the car in which you were riding.'

'I was driving the car.'

'When you went out?'

'Yes.'

'Where was your companion?' Mason asked.

'Crouched down on the floor in the back of the car,' she announced defiantly.

There was a slight ripple of mirth in the court-room which Judge Kent frowned into silence.

'Perhaps you can explain exactly what happened a little more clearly,' Mason said.

'I've told you my boy friend was married. When we saw this car in there, the first thing we thought of was that it was one of those things–you know, a private-detective raiding party with a camera and flashbulbs. We thought his wife had framed him so as to get the kind of a settlement she wanted.'

'Do you mean that she had framed him or caught him?'

'Well, caught him.'

'That's what you both thought?'

'Sure,' she said. 'What else would you expect? This car comes driving up there around three o'clock in the morning, coming like sixty.'

'Now, when you say one of those things,' Mason asked, 'do I gather that this is something usual in your life, that you have been previously photographed by some raiding party led by an irate wife?'

The witness was silent for a moment.

'We object, if the Court please,' Hamilton Burger said. 'That's not the proper cross-examination. The question is asked only for the purpose of degrading the witness. It is prejudicial misconduct on the part of counsel.'

Judge Kent said: 'There was that in the answer of the witness which seemed to invite the question. However, under the circumstances, I think it makes little difference in this case. The situation speaks for itself. The Court will sustain the objection.'

'Were you sitting at the steering-wheel when this other car came up the driveway?' Mason asked.

'No, I was not.'

'Did you get behind the steering-wheel at your own suggestion?'

'My boy friend suggested I had better drive it out.'

'I take it then that he didn't see the woman who got out of the car?'

'He didn't see anything. He was down on the floor just as flat as he could get, and I took that car out of there just as fast as I could snake it out.'

'But you did notice the licence number of the car which drove up?'

'Sure.'

'Why?'

'I thought . . . well, he said, "My God, that's my wife" and . . . well, I looked the car over, looked at the licence plate and it was an easy licence plate to remember and I told him that it wasn't his wife's car.'

'You know his wife's car?'

'Yes, I've seen it.'

'When you and your boy friend drove into the San Sebastian Country Club parking place you turned the car around so that it was headed out?'

'Yes.'

'And why was that?'

'So we could make a quick getaway if we had to without having anyone get the licence number of the car. If the car had been left headed into the trees, then we'd have had to back and turn.'

'And the idea was that if you saw headlights coming you'd get out of there fast.'

'Yes.'

'But when you saw headlights coming you didn't get out of there immediately. You waited until after the other car had come to a stop and a woman had got out.'

'Well . . . yes.'

'And you got in the driving seat and the man who was with you remained in the rear.'

'I didn't say he remained in the rear.'

'Well, you did say he was on the floor in the rear.'

'Yes.'

'And that is right, is it?'

'Yes.'

'Now when you identified the defendant you pointed a finger and said that the woman you had seen was the defendant at whom you were pointing.'

'That's right. That was the truth.'

'And then you got up and went down and put a hand on her shoulder.'

'Yes, sir.'

'Now, that identification had been carefully rehearsed, hadn't it?'

'What do you mean?'

'You had been talking with the deputy district attorney, Manley Marshall, about how you were to make that identification and he told you, "Now, when I ask you if you can see that woman in the court-room you are to point at the defendant. Just point right straight at her and say, 'that's the woman, sitting right there.' " Didn't he say that?'

'Well, he told me to point at her.'

'And did he tell you to put some feeling in your voice?'

'No, sir. He did not.'

'Did he tell you that he was going to ask you to get up and walk down and put your hand on her shoulder?'

'No, sir.'

'Didn't anyone tell you to put some feeling in your voice and be dramatic and say, "That's the woman sitting right there," or words to that effect?'

'Well . . . that wasn't what you asked me.'

'What do you mean?'

'You asked me if Mr Marshall had said that.'

'Oh, it was someone else that told you that?'

'Well, someone else told me to put some feeling in my voice when I said it, to make it dramatic, was the way he expressed it.'

'And who was that?'

'Mr Hamilton Burger, the district attorney.'

'And when was that?'

'Just before I went on the witness-stand.'

'And did you repeat the words after Mr Burger, "That's the woman, sitting right there"?'

'Well, I . . . he told me that's what I was to say, and I said it.'

'And he told you to put more feeling in it, didn't he?'

'Yes.'

'So then you tried it again, with more feeling.'

'Yes.'

'Once or twice?'

'Two or three times. I . . . well, it's hard to be dramatic when you're not accustomed to acting. I guess you're inclined to say things in just an ordinary tone of voice, but Mr Burger told me this was the dramatic highlight of the trial and that I had to be dramatic about it.'

Mason smiled. 'That,' he said, 'is all.'

'No questions,' Hamilton Burger said, his face flushed an angry red.

The witness left the stand.

'I will now call Barton Jennings to the stand,' Hamilton Burger said.

Barton Jennings, still using his cane, came forward, took the oath, and settled back in the witness stand, his stiff leg out in front of him. His hands clasped the head of the cane.

Hamilton Burger examined the witness and brought out the story from the time he had met Norda Allison at the airport to the time they had gone home. He got the witness to tell about Norda Allison and Perry Mason coming to the house, of Norda Allison's claim that she had seen the printing press in the store-room. He had Barton Jennings identify the gun, and the witness testified that it was usually kept in the drawer of a dresser in the guest bedroom which was occupied that night by Norda Allison.

'Cross-examine,' Hamilton Burger said to Mason.

Mason arose to stand in front of the witness. 'I'm going to ask a few questions, Mr Jennings,' he said. 'The answers to some of these questions may prove to be embarrassing, but I want to clear up certain matters. Now, your wife had been married before?'

'That is right.'

'She had been married to Mervin Selkirk, the decedent?'

'Yes, sir.'

'And there was a child, the issue of said marriage, Robert Selkirk?'

'Yes, sir.'

'Robert lived with you and your wife from time to time?'

'Yes, sir.'

'You are attached to him? That is, I mean, you are both attached to him?'

'Yes, sir. He is a very fine boy.'

'And do you know where he is now?'

'Objected to,' Hamilton Burger said. 'Not proper cross-examination and incompetent and irrelevant and immaterial. The whereabouts of this young man have no bearing on the present case. I see no reason for turning loose a lot of newspaper reporters to embarrass this young man.'

Judge Kent thought for a moment, then said: 'At the present time I am going to sustain the objection.'

'Robert Selkirk was staying with you the night of the seventeenth and the morning of the eighteenth?'

'Yes, sir.'

'You drove him away early on the morning of the eighteenth?'

'I took him away. Yes, sir.'

'Why?'

'He was going to a gathering of young people.'

'But he didn't go.'

'No.'

'Why?'

'The dramatic events of the day made it inadvisable for him to go.'

'But you didn't know that Mervin Selkirk was dead until quite a bit later than that, did you?'

'Later than what?'

'Later than when you took Robert away from your house.'

'No, sir, I didn't.'

'The young people were to rendezvous at about eleven o'clock?'

'I thought they were supposed to be there at seven o'clock. I now understand they didn't leave until eleven. I misunderstood the time over the telephone. I asked the man who was arranging the party what time the boys were to leave and I understood him to say that they would leave at seven o'clock, but to be there an hour before that. Later on I realized he had said eleven o'clock but I had misunderstood him.'

'What time was it when you took Robert away?'

'It was . . . quite early. I don't know. I didn't look at my watch.'

'And where did you take him?'

'There again,' Hamilton Burger said, 'I object. I have carefully refrained from asking this witness questions about Robert Selkirk, and counsel has no right to cross-examine him on that subject. The question is not proper cross-examination. It is incompetent, irrelevant and immaterial.'

'I think I will permit this question,' Judge Kent said. 'You may answer. Where did you take Robert?'

'To a friend.'

'A friend of his or a friend of yours?' Mason asked.

'Both.'

'Now why did you take him away that early in the morning?' Mason asked.

'Because I didn't want him to be disturbed.'

'Why?'

'Because–well, frankly, Mr Mason, an action was to be brought and the object of that action was to get the sole custody of Robert; that is, my wife wanted to have his sole custody. Miss Allison, the defendant in this case, was going to testify as a witness; at least we hoped she would. I didn't want Robert to know anything about what was being planned until after the plans had been made. I didn't want him to hear the discussion.'

'So you got up early in the morning and took him away?'

'Yes, sir.'

'And that's your best explanation?'

'Yes, sir.'

'Did you know when you took Robert away that he claimed he had discharged a gun during the night?'

'Objected to,' Hamilton Burger said, 'as incompetent, irrelevant and immaterial, as calling for hearsay testimony, and as not proper cross-examination.'

'In the present form of the question I will sustain the objection,' Judge Kent said.

'Did you take him away,' Mason said, 'because he had claimed during the night that he had fired a shot?'

'Same objection,' Hamilton Burger said.

Judge Kent shook his head. 'The question in its present form is permissible.'

'All right,' Barton Jennings said defiantly. 'That may have entered into it.'

'When did you first know that he claimed he had fired a shot during the night?'

'Objected to, not proper cross-examination, incompetent, irrelevant and immaterial,' Burger said.

Judge Kent stroked the angle of his jaw, ran his hand around the back of his neck, rubbed the palm back and forth a few times and looked at Mason. 'Aside from the technical rules of evidence, Mr Mason,' he said, 'you must realize that the Court and counsel have certain responsibilities. Your questions and the answers of the witness will doubtless be given some prominence in the press, and the Court feels that the examination of the witness along these lines should be restricted to the legal issues, regardless of the technical rules of evidence.'

Mason, on his feet, waited deferentially for Judge Kent to finish speaking. Then he said: 'I am fully aware of that, if the Court please. But I am representing a client who is charged with murder. I am going to protect her interests. I can assure the Court that I am not merely asking questions for the purpose of clouding the issues. I have a very definite objective which the Court will see within a short time.'

'Very well,' Judge Kent said. 'I am going to overrule the objection. The witness may answer the question.'

Hamilton Burger said: 'If we go into any part of this, Your Honour, I want to go into *all* of it.'

Judge Kent hesitated, then said: 'I think the evidence is pertinent. Defence counsel has a duty to perform. I am going to let the witness answer the question.'

Barton Jennings: 'I guess it was about midnight, something like that, that Robert came crying into the house. I understand he told his mother that he had had a bad dream and he had fired a shot.'

'Did he say he had had a bad dream?'

'Well, from what he told her I know I felt it was a bad dream.'

'He thought someone had been in the tent?'

'He said he thought someone had been in the tent, groping along the bed. He had been awake at the time and it seems that this gun had been under his pillow.'

Judge Kent said to the witness: 'Robert told this to his mother?'

'That's right,' Jennings said. 'I had had one of my spells with my knee and had taken codeine. I was asleep.'

Judge Kent looked over at Hamilton Burger. 'This would seem to be hearsay, Mr Prosecutor.'

Hamilton Burger said angrily: 'I'm not going to object. That's what counsel was hoping for. He hoped he could get headlines in the press and then have me shut him off. That's what I meant when I said that if we went into this we were going into it *all* the way. Robert told his mother about shooting the gun that night. The next morning he told this witness the same story.'

Judge Kent said: 'In the one instance it is part of the *res gestae*. In the other it is hearsay.'

'We have no objection,' Hamilton Burger said. 'Having gone this far, it is only fair to the boy himself to go the rest of the way.'

Judge Kent frowned.

'What gun was under Robert's pillow?' Mason asked.

'The gun that has been introduced in evidence, the Colt Woodsman, the ·22 automatic.'

'And he had pulled the trigger?'

'He had a dream. He dreamt he was pretending to be asleep. He heard someone prowling around the outside of the tent, or thought he did, and then he dreamt that this person entered the tent and at the height of the nightmare he thought that he had discharged the weapon.'

'You say that was a nightmare?'

'Yes, sir.'

'How do you know it was a nightmare?'

'Because the weapon was unloaded. It was empty when it was given to Robert.'

'Who gave it to him?'

'I did, but I desire to explain that answer.'

'Go ahead,' Judge Kent said, 'explain it.'

'I had found out very shortly before that date that one of the baby-sitters who had been employed to sit with Robert had been letting him use or play with this empty gun. Robert had some imitation weapons, as most boys do. He liked to play cowboy, city marshal, and things of that sort. He had, however, discovered there was a genuine weapon in the house and had been determined to play with that. One time when the baby-sitter was having a great deal of trouble with him, in order to quiet him and keep him from having a nervous tantrum, she let him play with this weapon.

'I hadn't found that out until shortly before the seventeenth.'

'How did you find it out?'

'I usually left the gun loaded and in the bureau drawer of the front room. At intervals I would clean and oil it. On or shortly before the sixteenth I took the gun out to oil it. It was unloaded and there were no shells in the magazine clip. This bothered me. I asked my wife about it and then I asked Robert about it. It was then that I found out about Robert having had the gun.'

'And how did you happen to let Robert take the weapon on the night of the seventeenth and eighteenth?'

'We had to go to the airport to meet the defendant in the case. We didn't expect to be gone but a very short time. My wife is too nervous to drive but she wanted to be the one to greet the defendant at the airport, so I drove her there. Robert was asleep in a tent out in the patio, or that is, he was *going* to sleep in a tent out in the patio. I had asked some neighbours to come in and stay with him for the hour and a half it would take us to make the round trip and pick up the defendant.'

'And what happened?'

'At the last minute it was impossible for the neighbours to come in. They had some unexpected company. I telephoned the agency which usually supplies us with baby-sitters and it was impossible for either of our regular baby-sitters to come that night. They were both engaged. Robert doesn't like to be with a strange baby-sitter. I explained the situation to him. I told him he would be perfectly safe out there in his tent in the patio, and he said that it would be quite all right to leave him provided he could have this unloaded gun under his pillow. It gave him a sense of security.

'In view of the fact that I had found out that he had been playing with the weapon, I made certain the gun was unloaded and let him have it.'

'You yourself made certain that the gun was unloaded?'

'I did, yes, sir.'

'Now then,' Mason said, 'when did you next see the gun?'

'Robert brought it in to his mother after the nightmare.'

'And did she try to quiet him?'

'She did.'

'Did he return to bed?'

'Yes. After he had become fully awakened, he realized that he had probably had a nightmare and he wanted to go back into the tent and go to sleep. As he expressed it, he wanted to be a "real scout".'

'And he did that?'

'Yes.'

'And the weapon?'

'My wife put it in the hall-stand. I wakened an hour or so after Robert had gone back to the tent. My wife told me what had happened.'

'Where was the gun?'

'On the hall table. My wife placed it there intending to take it to its regular place in the bedroom after Miss Allison had left the room. Miss Allison was sleeping there that night.'

'Was the gun unloaded at *that* time?'

'Of course it was unloaded.'

'Did you at any time tamper with the barrel? Did you run a rat-tail file or any other instrument through the barrel?'

'No, sir.'

'Or an emery cloth?'

'No, sir.'

'Did you tamper with the barrel in any way?'

'No, sir.'

'Did it occur to you that Robert might have loaded and fired the gun, that Robert's shot must have hit something and that the bullet could have been shown to have been fired from that gun, and therefore you roughed up the barrel so as to protect Robert?'

The witness shifted his position, then said: 'No, sir.'

'Because if you had,' Mason pointed out, 'in view of the testimony of the ballistics expert that the barrel had been tampered with *after* the last bullet had gone through the barrel, it would prove that this defendant couldn't have fired the fatal shot–at least with that gun. Do you understand that, Mr Jennings?'

'Yes, sir.'

'And you are positive you yourself didn't rough up the barrel to protect Robert?'

'I did not.'

'Did you load the weapon?'

'I didn't load it. When I gave the gun to Robert I unloaded it.'

'How about the barrel? Do you know whether there was a shell in the barrel?'

'I told you, Mr Mason, that I unloaded the gun. I was very careful to unload it.'

'You mean by that, that you worked the mechanism so as to be sure there was no shell in the gun?'

'Yes, sir.'

'Then how did it happen Robert was able to fire the gun?'

'The answer is obvious. He only dreamt he fired it.'

'And where was the gun the next time you saw it?'

'Under the pillow of the bed which had been occupied by the defendant.'

'You were up rather early the morning of the eighteenth?'

'Yes, sir. I thought I had to take Robert away from the house earlier than was necessary. I have explained the reason for that.'

'Now about washing away the blood that was on the front lawn,' Mason said. 'What can you tell us about that?'

'That is objected to,' Hamilton Burger said, 'as incompetent, irrelevant, and immaterial. It is not proper cross-examination. I didn't ask this witness a thing about his activities in regard to a blood trail or anything that was on the lawn.'

'The Court will overrule the objection,' Judge Kent said. 'This is a very interesting development in the case and the Court wants to go into it. The Court is trying to do substantial justice here and the Court doesn't care about technicalities, particularly at this time and on a matter of this sort. Answer the question, Mr Jennings.'

'There was no blood trail,' Jennings said.

'Didn't you get up early and hose the lawn?'

'I got up early. I took Robert to a friend. I came back and no one seemed to be up in the house so I took a hose and watered the lawn.'

'Didn't you actually hold the hose down on the lawn, washing it?'

'I may have directed a stream a short distance in front of me.'

'And weren't you washing away a trail of blood?'

'Very definitely not.'

'You weren't trying to do that?'

'No, sir.'

'Did you notice any reddish tinge to the water which floated across the sidewalk and under the gutter while you were watering the lawn?'

'No, sir.'

'Notice any red stains of blood in the gutter?'

'No, sir.'

'Or at the kerb?'

'No, sir.'

'Are you prepared to state there were no such stains?'

'I am prepared to state that I didn't notice them.'

'I notice that you are using a cane,' Mason said.

'Yes, sir. I have trouble with my right knee. At times it becomes very stiff.'

'I take it you have consulted a physician?'

'Certainly.'

'Can you give me the name of any physician you consulted recently?'

'I haven't been to a physician recently–not about this.'

'If the Court please,' Hamilton Burger said, 'I think this examination is getting far, far afield. I see no possible connection between this physical infirmity and the issues in this case.'

'I do,' Mason said. 'I'd like to have the question answered.'

'What is the connection, Mr Mason?' Judge Kent asked.

'The connection is simply this,' Mason said. 'Barton Jennings went to the tent where Robert was sleeping. He listened in the doorway of the tent. Robert was feigning sleep. This witness thought Robert was fully asleep. He tiptoed into the tent, intending to get the weapon out from under Robert's pillow. He didn't speak as he entered the tent. Robert was frightened, and in his terror, pointed the gun and pulled the trigger. There was one shell in the barrel. That shell penetrated Barton Jenning's leg. Barton Jennings hurried out of the tent and across the lawn to the kerb. He left a trail of blood. Somewhere out on the kerb, or perhaps in a car, he managed to bandage his leg and stop up the flow of blood. He has, I believe, been afraid to go to a doctor for fear that the doctor would be forced to report the gunshot wound. I have every reason to believe that the ·22 bullet is still in his leg, embedded either in the knee or in the fleshy part of the leg. I believe that if that bullet is extracted and the ballistics experts check the striations, it will be readily apparent that that bullet was fired from the same weapon which killed Mervin Selkirk. That is the reason for my entire line of examination.'

'Your Honour! Your Honour!' Hamilton Burger shouted, jumping to his feet, gesticulating angrily. 'This is the plainest kind of grandstand! This is the same old rigmarole, the same four-flushing tactics which counsel has employed in so many cases. This is a story which is made up out of whole cloth, something that has absolutely no support anywhere in the evidence.'

'If you're so certain of that,' Mason said, 'let the witness pull up his trouser leg and let's look at that knee of his. Let's let the Court see the nature of the injury.'

Barton Jennings, on the stand, said quietly: 'Take a look if you want to.'

He pulled up his trousers leg.

Judge Kent leaned forward. 'There's no sign of a bullet wound or any other wound in that leg, Mr Mason. The knee is swollen but there is no sign of a wound.'

Hamilton Burger threw back his head and laughed. Spectators echoed the district attorney's laughter.

Judge Kent, angered, shouted: 'Order! Order or I'll clear the court-room.'

He turned to Perry Mason, who seemed as calmly serene as if nothing had happened. 'Is that all, Mr Mason?'

'No, Your Honour,' Mason said.

He turned to the witness. 'I believe you own a very large dog,' Mason said. 'A Great Dane.'

'Yes, sir.'

'That Dane was on the premises on the night of the seventeenth?'

'He was.'

'What is his name?'

'Rover.'

'Was he on the premises on the morning of the eighteenth?'

'No, sir, he was not.'

'What happened to him?'

Barton Jennings shifted his position on the witness-stand. 'I have rather inquisitive neighbours. I wanted it to appear that I had taken Robert to this expedition on which he was to depart, and that he had taken Rover with him. They knew the boys were supposed to take their dogs with them.

'Since, however, I was actually taking Robert to the apartment of this friend, I made other arrangements for the dog.'

'What other arrangements?' Mason asked.

'I don't think I need to answer that question,' Jennings said.

'If the Court please,' Hamilton Burger said, 'this is all going very far afield. I have asked this witness certain particular questions. Counsel has taken him down a long, weary, winding path on cross-examination; a path filled with detours and irrelevant excursions. Surely, what this witness did with his dog is not proper cross-examination and is not part of the issues in this case. I have been very patient in letting *everything* about this mysterious shot which had been fired at night be introduced in evidence, because I thought defence counsel was going to claim the bullet had lodged in the knee of this witness. I wanted counsel to expose the folly of his own position.

'I was also aware, Your Honour, that it might be claimed the firing of that shot and evidence concerning it might be considered part of the *res gestae*.

'Evidence about this dog is, however, an entirely different matter. No one can claim that what a witness does with his dog is part of the *res gestae*.'

'I think I will sustain that objection,' Judge Kent said.

'Did you,' Mason asked Jennings, 'notice a pool of blood by the kerb on the morning of the eighteenth?'

'I have told you I did not.'

Mason said: 'I show you a morning newspaper which indicates that it has been stained with a reddish liquid.'

'Yes, sir.'

'Now then,' Mason said, 'I will state to the Court and counsel that I expect to prove this liquid is a mixture of water and blood, and I now expect to be able to show by a precipitin test that this is dog blood. Now I am going to ask you if it isn't a fact that Robert actually did fire that weapon on the night of the seventeenth or the early morning of the eighteenth, if the bullet didn't hit your dog, Rover, and if Rover didn't lose large quantities of blood. I am going to ask you if you hadn't left your car parked at the kerb and if you didn't take the bleeding Rover to your car, wrap him in a blanket so the blood wouldn't get on the car, and drive him hurriedly to a veterinarian.'

Jennings again shifted his position. 'I am not going to answer that question.'

'The same objection,' Hamilton Burger hastily interposed. 'This is getting at the same matter in a slightly different form of questioning. The Court has already ruled on it.'

'Well, the Court is going to reverse its ruling,' Judge Kent said. 'The question as it is now framed by counsel certainly indicates a situation which should be inquired into and which may well be pertinent to the issues in this case. The witness will answer the question.'

Jennings gave every evidence of uneasiness. 'I found my dog had been hurt,' he said. 'I took him to a veterinarian.'

'What veterinarian?'

'I don't think I have to tell that.'

'What veterinarian?' Mason asked.

'Dr Canfield,' Jennings said sullenly.

'At what time did you take him there?'

'About one o'clock in the morning, I guess.'

'Now,' Mason said, 'let us assume for the sake of this question that young Robert woke up from a sound sleep, that he was startled, that he thought someone was about to attack him, that he had this weapon under his pillow and that the weapon, in some manner, had become loaded. He raised the weapon and pulled the trigger. He could very well have shot this dog, Rover, couldn't he?'

'I suppose he could have. I don't know. I found Rover bleeding. He evidently had been injured. I didn't know whether he'd been struck by an automobile or what had happened, so I took him to a veterinarian.'

'And did the veterinarian work on the dog?'

'Yes, sir.'

'Did the vererinarian tell you what was wrong with the dog?'

'I don't know. I didn't wait to find out. I left the dog, told the veterinarian to do whatever was required and then returned home.'

'Have you seen the dog since?'

Again Jennings hesitated, then said: 'Yes, the dog is recovering.'

'From a bullet wound?'

'I have not asked.'

'Have you been informed?'

'I told the veterinarian I didn't care about the details, all I wanted was for the dog to get well.'

'If the Court please,' Mason said, 'an X-ray can determine if a bullet is somewhere in the dog's body. If the bullet was fired from the same gun which killed Mervin Selkirk, the bullets will have the same characteristics. It can, therefore, be determined that the bullet which killed Mervin Selkirk was fired from the Jennings gun, despite the fact that the barrel has been mutilated so that it is impossible to get the characteristics of that barrel with a test bullet.'

Jennings moistened his lips with the tip of his tongue. Hamilton Burger started to say something, then changed his mind.

'Now then,' Mason went on, 'Robert subsequently told you that a man had been entering the tent where he was sleeping?'

'Yes.'

'That was supposed to have happened before you had taken the dog to the veterinarian?'

'Yes.'

'And that dog was a trained watchdog?'

'Yes.'

'He would have guarded Robert with his life?'

'Yes.'

'But the dog made no noise?'

'No. That's how I knew it was just a dream that Robert had,' Barton Jennings said triumphantly.

'Yes,' Mason said, 'it could have been a dream, or it could have been that the man who was entering the tent was one that the dog trusted. Suppose Mervin Selkirk had gone to the tent to kidnap Robert, or suppose you yourself had decided you wanted that gun, Mr Jennings. Suppose you went to the tent and listened. You heard Robert apparently sleeping peacefully so you tiptoed your way into the tent without speaking, hoping to reach under his pillow and get the gun, and then suddenly there was the roar of an explosion. You heard the bullet hit the body of the dog, the dog ran from the tent and you ran after him. You saw that the dog was bleeding quite badly. You had left your car with the licence number JYJ 113 parked at the kerb. You hurriedly wrapped a blanket around the dog and rushed him to the veterinarian. Then you returned to the house, parked your car in front of the house and entered to have your wife tell you about the story Robert had told of firing the gun.'

'It didn't happen that way. I was asleep. I didn't hear about Robert's dream until much later.'

'Tut-tut,' Mason said. 'A neighbour remembers hearing the sound of a shot. You admit that you took the dog to Dr Canfield, the veterinarian. We will check Dr Canfield's records and I think we will find that those records show you arrived at his place with the wounded dog prior to one o'clock in the morning.'

'Well, what if I did?'

'Then you couldn't have been asleep while Robert was relating his dream,' Mason said.

'All right,' Barton Jennings said, 'I wasn't asleep. I had taken the dog to the veterinarian just as you suggest.

'You were wakened by the shot?'

Jennings hesitated, then said: 'Yes, I was wakened by the shot.'

'And dressed?'

'Yes.'

'And then went out to the tent to see what had caused the shot?'

'No, I went to the wounded dog.'

'And where was the wounded dog?'

'Lying by the car.'

Mason smiled and shook his head. 'You're wrong, Jennings. The wounded dog wouldn't have gone to the car unless you had taken him to the car. The wounded dog would have gone to the house, looking for help. The fact that the dog went directly to the car and that there was a trail of blood on the lawn leading to the car indicates that you were with the dog at the time he was shot.'

'That question is argumentative, if the Court please,' Hamilton Burger said.

'It may be argumentative, but its logic is so forceful that the Court will take judicial cognizance of it,' Judge Kent said.

He leaned forward. 'Mr Jennings.'

'Yes, Your Honour.'

'Look at me.'

The witness turned to look at the Court.

'You have already contradicted yourself upon two or three vital points. Those contradictions when a person is under oath constitute perjury, and perjury is punishable by imprisonment. Now I want to know what happened. Did you take the dog to the car after the dog was shot?'

Jennings hesitated, looked down at his feet, looked at Hamilton Burger, then hastily avoided his eyes, turned to Perry Mason, found no comfort there, and remained silent with his eyes downcast.

'Did you?' Judge Kent asked.

'Yes,' Barton Jennings said after a moment.

'In other words,' Mason said, 'you went out to the tent to get that gun from under Robert's pillow, didn't you?'

'Well . . . all right, I did.'

'You listened at the tent and heard Robert breathing regularly and thought he was sleeping?'

'Yes.'

'You didn't realize until afterwards that Robert, not recognizing you and utterly terrified, was feigning sleep, but had the gun in his hand.'

'I guess so, yes.'

'So you entered the tent with the dog either at your heels or just in front of you. You reached out towards the pillow and it was then that Robert shot.'

'All right.'

'As you heard the bullet hit the dog, you turned and raced out of the tent and saw that the dog was injured. You remembered that your automobile was parked there at the kerb and you raced towards the automobile with the dog following you.

'While you were getting the door of the automobile open, the dog stood there, and there was a pool of blood at the kerb where he stood. Then you wrapped the dog in a blanket, got him in the automobile and hurried to the veterinarian. You left the dog and then returned as fast as you could to your home. You found your wife had comforted Robert and had put him back to bed. Your wife had told Robert that you were sleeping in the bedroom, but actually she knew better.'

Jennings was silent.

'Is that what happened?' Mason asked.

'Yes,' Jennings said, 'that's what happened.'

'So then,' Mason said, 'you took the gun which your wife had taken from Robert. What did you do with it?'

'My wife had put it on the hall-stand. I picked it up and looked at it, then left it on the hall-stand and went back to bed.'

'And when you put it back on the hall-stand, you must have loaded the magazine and put the clip of ammunition back in the gun.'

'I guess I must have. I guess that's right.'

'And then you went to bed?'

'Yes.'

'And you believe that some time during the night the defendant got up, left her bedroom, went down to the hall-stand, got the gun, went out to your car with licence plate bearing the number JYJ 113 which you had left parked at the kerb, drove out to the San Sebastian Country Club and killed Mervin Selkirk.'

'She must have. There's no other explanation. The evidence shows she did.'

'How did she know that Mervin Selkirk was to be at the San Sebastian Country Club?'

'I don't know.'

'How did she know that your car was left at the kerb with the key in it?'

'She saw me park the car there.'

'And leave the key in it?'

'I don't know, I may have–No, wait a minute, I left the key in it when I returned from the veterinarian's office. I was excited.'

'And who used a rat-tail file to roughen up the barrel of the gun so that the ballistics experts could not tell what gun had fired the fatal bullet?'

'I presume she did.'

'Why?'

'So that the gun couldn't be traced to her.'

'Then having done that, she deliberately left the gun under the pillow of the bed where she had been sleeping?'

'She probably did that inadvertently.'

Mason smiled and shook his head. 'The gun was registered in *your name*, Mr Jennings. *You* were the one who would be more interested than anyone in making it impossible for the fatal bullet to be traced.'

Jennings said nothing.

'And you now think that you must have loaded the gun after your wife put it on the hall-stand?'

'Yes, I must have.'

'Then where did you get the shells? You surely didn't go to the defendant's room?'

Jennings rubbed his cheek with a nervous hand. 'I guess I was mistaken. I couldn't have loaded the gun.'

'Then if the defendant fired the gun, she must have descended the stairs, found the gun, inspected it, found it was unloaded, then climbed the stairs to her room, found the box of shells, loaded the gun and then gone to the country club to kill Mervin Selkirk?'

'I . . . I guess that's right.'

'How would she have known there was ammunition in the room?'

'She must have found it.'

'How would she have known the gun was on the hall table?'

'She must have seen it when she started out.'

'How would she have known it was unloaded?'

'She must have inspected it.'

'And then climbed the stairs to her room to get shells?'

'Of course. Why don't you ask *her*?'

'I'm asking you.'

'I don't know what she did.'

'Now, when your dog was shot at perhaps twelve-thirty to one o'clock on the morning of the eighteenth, the barrel of the gun hadn't been tampered with, had it?'

'No.'

'Then if the bullet is still in the dog, that bullet can be recovered by a surgical operation and the individual characteristics of the barrel of your gun can be determined just the same as though a test bullet had been fired from it. In other words, the bullet which was fired into the dog would then become a test bullet.'

'I guess so.'

'And how do you know that the barrel of the gun hadn't been tampered with at the time the dog was shot?'

'I . . . I don't know.'

'Yes, you do,' Mason said. 'You know because you were the one who tampered with the barrel. You were the one who used the rat-tail file. You were the one who knew that Mervin Selkirk was to be at the San Sebastian Country Club and you went out there to kill him.'

'I didn't do any such thing,' Barton Jennings said, 'and you can't prove it.'

'Then,' Mason asked smilingly, 'why did you go out to Robert's tent at twelve-thirty-five on the morning of the eighteenth to get the gun which was under Robert's pillow?'

'Because I didn't think it was a good thing for the boy to sleep there with a gun.'

'Then why didn't you get the gun before you had gone to bed?'

'I didn't think of it.'

'You knew he had the gun?'

'Well, yes.'

'But you didn't think of it until after you went to bed?'

'Well, it wasn't until after I went to bed that I . . . well, that's right, I got up and dressed and went out to get the gun.'

'Did you waken your wife when you dressed?'

'No, she was sound asleep.'

'But she wakened when she heard the shot?'

'I don't think so. She wakened when Robert came running into the house, telling the story of his nightmare.'

'Of what you have characterized as his nightmare,' Mason said. 'Actually, Robert told exactly what had happened; that he had wakened to find a man groping his way towards his bed, that he had instinctively thrown up the gun and pulled the trigger.'

Barton Jennings was silent.

'I think,' Mason said, 'I have no further questions of this witness.'

'I have no questions on redirect examination,' Hamilton Burger said. 'I may state to the Court that while this cross-examination has revealed many unexpected developments, the fact remains that the positive identification of the defendant speaks for itself.'

'I'm not certain it does,' Judge Kent said.

' I would like to ask a few more questions of Millicent Bailey on cross-examination,' Mason said.

'Very well. Mrs Bailey, you may return to the witness-stand,' Judge Kent ruled.

'Your Honour, I object,' Hamilton Burger said. 'This is a piecemeal cross-examination and–'

'And it is entirely within the control of the Court,' Judge Kent ruled. 'Recent developments have made the testimony of this witness appear in an entirely different light. Return to the stand, Mrs Bailey. Mr Mason, you may proceed with your cross-examination.'

Mason said: 'Mrs Bailey, you state that you saw the defendant at around three or three-thirty on the morning of the eighteenth?'

'Yes sir.'

'When did you next see her?'

'On the morning of the nineteenth, at about ten o'clock.'

'Where did you see her?'

'I picked her out of a line-up at police headquarters.'

'How many other people were in that line-up?'

'There were five women in all.'

'And you picked the defendant as being the one you had seen?'

'Yes.'

'Now that was the next time you had seen the defendant?'

'Yes.'

'You hadn't seen her after that time when you saw her in the morning at about three or three-thirty, or somewhere in there?'

'Well, I . . . I had had a glimpse of her.'

'Oh, you had had a glimpse of her. Where was that?'

'At police headquarters.'

'And where did you see her at police headquarters?'

'I saw her when she was being escorted into the show-up box.'

'Was anyone with her at that time?'

'A police officer.'

'Were there any other people in the show-up box?'

'Not at that time, no.'

'The defendant was put in there by herself?'

'Yes.'

'And you had a good look at her?'

'Yes.'

'And then afterwards four other women were brought into the show-up box?'

'Yes.'

'And then the officers asked you to pick out the one that you had seen out there at the San Sebastian Country Club?'

'Yes.'

'And you unerringly picked the defendant?'

'Yes.'

Mason said: 'I am going to ask Mrs Barton Jennings to please stand.'

There was silence in the court-room.

'Please stand, Mrs Jennings,' Mason said.

Lorraine Jennings made no move to get to her feet.

'Stand up, Mrs Jennings,' Judge Kent ordered.

Reluctantly Lorraine Jennings stood.

'Will you come forward, please?' Mason asked.

'Come forward,' Judge Kent ruled.

'Now then,' Mason said to Mrs Bailey, 'is there any chance that this is the person whom you saw getting out of the car and approaching the car that was parked at the San Sebastian Country Club?'

The witness studied Mrs Jennings for a long moment, then said: 'I . . . I don't think so.'

'But it could have been?'

'Well, she's got very much the same build and complexion as the defendant, but . . . no, I don't think so.'

'That's all, Mrs Jennings,' Mason said.

Lorraine Jennings turned abruptly and walked so rapidly she was almost running.

'Wait! Wait!' the witness said.

'Wait, Mrs Jennings,' Mason said.

Mrs Jennings paid no attention.

'Now that she walks rapidly,' the witness said excitedly, 'I know that it was this woman. There's a peculiar way she has when she walks; that hurrying walk, that was just the way she walked when we saw her.'

Mason smiled and said to Hamilton Burger: 'That Mr District Attorney, concluded my cross-examination. Do you have any redirect examination?'

Hamilton Burger slowly got to his feet. 'If the Court please,' he said wearily, 'I suggest that this matter should be adjourned until tomorrow morning at ten o'clock. There are some things which I feel should be investigated.'

'I think so, too,' Judge Kent said dryly. 'The case is adjourned until tomorrow morning at ten o'clock, and in the meantime this defendant is released on her own recognizance.'

18

Mason and Della Street were in the lawyer's private office when Drake's code knock sounded on the door.

'Let Paul in,' Mason said wearily.

Della Street opened the door.

Drake, grinning broadly, said: 'Well, you did it, Perry.'

'What happened?' Mason asked.

'Complete confessions,' Drake said. 'Also, you have a suit against Horace Livermore Selkirk. He filed a complaint charging you with kidnapping, then it turned out you had sent the boy to the place where his mother told him to go, and Hamilton Burger's face is red over that.'

'But what about the case itself? What about the murder?' Mason asked.

'Mervin Selkirk was a cold-blooded, highly efficient individual. I guess he took after his dad as far as his efficiency and ruthlessness were concerned,' Drake said. 'When Lorraine left him and married Barton Jennings, Selkirk quietly proceeded to get all the information he could on Barton Jennings. It was plenty. He found that Jennings was treasurer and manager of the Savings and Loan Corporation. Selkirk deliberately schemed to get Jennings to invest in some so-called sure things, and before Jennings knew it, he was hopelessly involved. Then Mervin Selkirk began to put on the pressure. He owned Barton Jennings, body and soul.

'Lorraine had no idea there was any contact between the two men, but her husband was reporting regularly to her ex-husband.

'When Lorraine got together with Norda Allison and wanted to get sole custody of Robert, Selkirk cracked the whip. He had previously forced Barton Jennings to get a printing press and print the envelopes which had been used to mail the threatening letters to Norda Allison. That press had been at Jenning's office, concealed in a closet, until the day before the murder. At that time Jennings's secretary had announced she was planning to clean out the closet and get rid of a lot of junk that had been accumulating over the years.

'So, while Lorrain Jennings was away that afternoon, Barton Jennings had taken the printing press and the envelopes to a temporary place of concealment in his basement. He had previously reported to Selkirk that Norda was going to join his wife in Los Angeles and that a move was to be made to get sole custody of Robert for Lorraine.

'Mervin Selkirk ordered Barton to listen in on their plans and then sneak out of the house to meet him at the San Sebastian Country Club at one-thirty in the morning. He gave Barton an ultimatum. Either Barton was to fix things so that Lorraine gave up all claim to Robert, or Selkirk was going to expose Barton Jennings, have him sent to prison, and use that to defeat the application for custody of the child.

'That evening, on the way back from the airport, was when Jennings made up his mind to kill Selkirk, but the only gun that he could put his hands on was under Robert's pillow. He went out to get the gun. Robert was panic-stricken and fired the gun. The bullet hit the dog.

'Jennings took the dog to the veterinarian, came back, found his wife had quieted Robert, and then confessed everything to his wife. He went out for a showdown with Mervin Selkirk. In the course of that showdown he shot Selkirk, probably just a few minutes before Millicent Bailey and her boy friend drove up. Then Jennings returned to the house. His wife was waiting up for him. He told her what had happened. Then he went down to his workshop to rough up the barrel of the gun.

'While he was doing that, Lorraine decided to frame the crime on Norda Allison. She still had Norda Allison's aeroplane ticket. She got in the car, went out to the place where the death car was parked and dipped Norda Allison's ticket into the pool of blood on the floor of the car, then put it in the side pocket of Selkirk's coat. She didn't realize that Millicent Bailey and her boy friend were doing a little necking and that they had seen her drive up. When Millicent drove out, Lorraine was in a panic. But she still went ahead with her plan to frame the crime on Norda Allison because that was the only thing left for her to do.

'When Barton Jennings had roughed up the barrel of the gun with a rat-tail file, Lorraine placed it under Norda's pillow after Norda had left. In their anxiety to make the case look good they overdid it.

'However, the police played right into their hands. Having come to the conclusion that Norda Allison was guilty, they virtually forced Millicent Bailey's identification.

'After they had planted the gun under the pillow, Barton Jennings suddenly remembered the printing press down in the spare room, the one he had used in printing the envelopes which he sent to Mervin Selkirk in San Francisco.

'He had no way of knowing Norda had found this press. The only sleep Jennings and his wife got that night was after Jennings had moved Robert, washed the dog's blood from the grass, and while they were waiting for Norda to get up. They were so tired they slept soundly for a couple of hours and didn't hear Norda in the basement.

'By that time Jennings felt it could be made to appear Mervin Selkirk had had the printing press in his car and that Selkirk had been printing the envelopes, just as Norda had suspected all along.

'So Jennings loaded the printing press in the trunk of his car and drove out to the country club to scout around. Selkirk's body hadn't been found as yet, but since it was broad daylight Jennings didn't dare park in the parking place. He did, however, explore the service road and find a place where his car was out of sight, both from the country club headquarters, as well as from the parking lot.

'He got rid of the press and returned home. By that time Lorraine had learned of Norda's departure. They realized, of course, she must have discovered something, so they became more determined than ever to frame the murder on her. They sat there, waiting for the explosion to take place. They were, however, frightened to death when Norda showed up with you. They had no way of knowing she'd found the printing press. That must have been a real jolt.'

'He's confessed?' Mason asked.

'They've both confessed,' Drake said.

'What about Norda Allison?' Mason asked.

'You don't need to ask that one,' Drake said. 'She was released on her own recognizance, you'll remember, and she and this Nathan Benedict did quite a bit of dining and dancing at The Purple Swan Night Club. They drove away in Benedict's rented car and somehow my operative, who was trying to tag along, got lost in the shuffle. That was about one-thirty. Norda Allison showed up in front of her hotel at three-forty-five this morning. She seemed to be walking on air. Nathan Benedict, who drove her to the hotel, escorted her in, and my man didn't have any trouble following him after that. He went directly to his hotel and went to bed.'

'I see,' Mason said dryly.

'So that's the case,' Drake commented.

'Well, I'm sorry,' Mason said. 'I'm sorry for Robert . . . although, when you come right down to it, a jury isn't going to be too rough on Barton Jennings for killing a man who was blackmailing him. They'll make it manslaughter. I don't know but what a proper presentation of the case might get Lorraine Jennings out of it scot-free without a prison sentence. After all, a court will consider Mervin Selkirk's character if she applies for probation and . . .'

The phone rang.

Della Street picked up the instrument, said to the receptionist: 'Hello, what is it, Gertie?'

'Just a minute,' she said.

Della Street turned to Perry Mason. 'Lorraine Jennings is calling you. Gertie says she's absolutely frantic. She wants to know if you'll go to the detention ward to see her.'

Mason hesitated for a long five seconds, then slowly nodded. 'Tell her that I'll be down to see her,' he said. And then added: 'For Robert's sake. I guess I owe them both that much, and I can use my claim against the grandfather for filing a false charge to make him go along. He really loves Robert, and I guess we can make him quit being such a cold-blooded greedy grandfather and get him to co-operate with Lorraine in doing whatever is best for Robert.

'Tell her I'll be down to see her, Della.'

RLE STANLEY GARDNER

The Case of

The Mischievous Doll

FOREWORD

As a rule the experts in legal medicine come from the medical profession. Many of them are both doctors of medicine and lawyers.

Others, however, have specialized in the law and then because of interest in the medical aspects of the legal profession become medicolegal specialists.

The point is that the area where law and medicine overlap is a field of vital importance to the public, and yet, one which is little understood by the public.

My friend, W.R.Rule, Major, U.S.A.F., M.S.C., started out in the field of law, then specialized in the field of legal medicine, particularly as it applies to the military.

Having studied law in this country as well as in England, Major Rule is currently the Legal Counsel for the Armed Forces Institute of Pathology, and has occupied that position since early 1959.

From time to time in connection with his official activities I have corresponded with him and have been impressed by the man's zeal, his clear-cut understanding of the importance of legal medicine, his high sense of duty, and his feeling that there has been too much separation of law, medicine and law enforcement, and that these sciences should be more closely connected and better understood.

Despite the fact that relatively few people realize it, the Armed Forces have developed nearly as perfect a system for the administration of justice as human minds can devise; and because this is true, they are taking a keen and ever-increasing interest in the field of legal medicine, particularly in co-ordinating forensic pathology with their investigations.

There are several outstanding individuals in this field, and from time to time, with their permission, I intend to dedicate books to them, calling to the attention of the public the work these men are doing and the importance of that work.

Because Major W. R. Rule has such a clear concept of the importance of legal medicine in the administration of justice and has done so much to improve the administration of justice in and through the military, I dedicate this book to my friend,

W.R.RULE, Major, U.S.A.F., M.S.C., Legal Counsel, A.F.I.P.

Erle Stanley Gardner

I

Della Street, Perry Mason's confidential secretary, entering Mason's private office, approached the big desk where the lawyer was seated and said, 'A law office is the *darnedest* place.'

'It certainly is,' Mason said. 'Now may I ask what brings forth this observation?'

'A certain Miss Dorrie Ambler.'

'And I take it Miss Ambler is in the outer office, asking for an appointment?'

'She says she has to see you *right* away.'

'How old?'

'Twenty-three or -four, but she's been around.'

'Description?'

'Auburn hair, hazel eyes, five feet three; around a hundred and twelve; figure, thirty-four, twenty-four, thirty-four.'

'And now,' Mason said, 'we come to the comment of yours–a law office is the *darnedest* place. What brought that up?'

'You could guess for a long time,' she said, 'but you would never guess what Miss Ambler wants–that is, at least what she says she wants.'

'I'll bite,' Mason said. 'What does she want?'

'She wants to show you her operation,' Della Street said.

'Her *what?*'

'Her operation.'

'A malpractice suit, Della?'

'Apparently not. She seems to feel that there is going to be some question as to her identity and she wants to prove to you who she is, or rather, who she is not. She wishes to do this by showing you the scar of an appendectomy.'

'What is this,' Mason asked, 'a gag? Or is she laying the foundation for some sort of a shakedown? I certainly am not going to permit any young woman to walk in here and–'

'She wants witnesses present,' Della Street said.

Mason grinned. 'Now *this* would be right down Paul Drake's alley. . . . I take it her figure is one that he would appreciate.'

'Leave it to Paul,' she said. 'He has a keen eye. . . . Shall I call him?'

'Let's talk with our client first,' Mason said. 'I am anxious to see the mysterious Miss Ambler.'

'Before I bring her in,' Della Street said, 'there is one other thing you should know.'

Mason said, 'Della, I get very, very suspicious when you start breaking things to me in easy stages. Now, suppose you tell me the whole story *now*.'

'Well,' Della Street said, 'your prospective client is carrying a gun in her purse.'

'How do you know?' Mason asked.

'I don't actually know,' Della Street said. 'I am quoting Gertie.'

'Gertie,' Mason said, grinning, 'sits there at the switchboard, sizes up clients as they come in, and works her imagination overtime. And she has a very high-powered imagination.'

'Conceded,' Della Street said, 'but Miss Ambler put her purse on that plastic-covered seat in the outer office and, as she leaned forward to get a magazine, touched the purse with her elbow–that plastic is as slippery as a cake of wet soap. The purse dropped to the floor and when it hit it made a heavy thud.

'Gertie says that Miss Ambler jumped about a foot, and then looked around guiltily to see if anyone had heard the sound of the heavy object striking the floor.'

'Did Gertie let on?' Mason asked.

'Not Gertie,' Della Street said. 'You know how Gertie is. She has eyes all over her body but she keeps a poker face and you never know just what she's seen. However, Gertie has an imagination that can take a button, sew a vest on it and then not only give you a description of the pattern of the vest, but tell you exactly what's in the pockets–and the stuff that's in the pockets is always connected with some romantic drama of Gertie's own particular type of thinking.'

'And in this case?' Mason asked.

'Oh, in this case,' Della Street said, 'Dorrie Ambler is an innocent young girl who came to the big city. She has been betrayed by a big, bad monster of a wolf who is now leaving the girl in a strange city to fend for herself. And Dorrie had decided to confront him with his perfidy and a gun. He will have the horrible alternative of making an honest woman out of her or being the *pièce de résistance* at Forest Lawn.'

Mason shook his head. 'Gertie should be able to do better than that,' he said.

'Oh, but Gertie has. She has already created the man in the case and clothed him with a whole series of ideas that are very typically Gertie. The man in the case, in case you're interested, is the son of a very wealthy manufacturer. The father has picked out a woman that he wants the boy to marry. The boy is really in love with Dorrie Ambler, but he doesn't want to disobey his father, and the father, of course, is going to disinherit the boy in the event he marries Dorrie. The boy is a nice enough kid, but rather weak.'

'And what about Dorrie?' Mason asked.

'Oh, Dorrie, according to Gertie's scenario, is a very determined young woman who has a mind of her own and isn't going to let the father dominate her life or ruin her happiness.'

'Hardly the type of innocent young woman who would permit herself to be seduced by a young man who has no particular force of character,' Mason said.

'You'll have to argue with Gertie about that,' Della Street told him. 'Gertie's got the whole script all finished in her mind and no one's going to change it. When Gertie gets an idea in her head, it's there.

'You could pound dynamite in her ear, set off the charge and blow most of her head away, but the idea would still remain intact.'

'Well,' Mason said, 'I guess under the circumstances, Della, we'll have to see Dorrie Ambler and find out how Gertie's romantic mind has magnified the molehill into the mountain.'

'Don't sell Dorrie short,' Della Street warned. 'She's a mighty interesting individual. She looks like a quiet, retiring young woman but she knows her way around and she wasn't born yesterday.'

Mason nodded. 'Let's have a look at her, Della.'

Della slipped through the door to the outer office and a few moments later returned with Dorrie Ambler in tow.

'So nice of you to see me, Mr Mason,' Dorrie Ambler said in a rapid-fire voice.

'You are concerned about a problem of personal identification?' Mason asked.

'Yes.'

'And you wanted to have me take steps to . . . well, let us say, to be sure you are you?'

'Yes.'

'Why are you so anxious to establish your individual identification?' Mason asked.

'Because I think an attempt is going to be made to confuse me with someone else.'

'Under those circumstances,' Mason said, glancing at Della Street, 'the very best thing to do would be to take your fingerprints.'

'Oh, but *that* wouldn't do at all!'

'Why not?'

'It would make me–well, make a criminal out of me.'

Mason shook his head. 'You can have your fingerprints taken and send them to the FBI to be put in their non-criminal file. Actually every citizen should do it. It establishes an absolute means of identification.'

'How long does it take?'

'To have the fingerprints taken and sent on? Only a very short time.'

'I'm afraid I don't have that much time, Mr Mason. I want you to–well, I want to establish my identity with *you*. I want you to look me over, to. . .' She lowered her eyes, '. . . to see the scar of an operation.'

Mason changed a quizzical glance with Della Street.

'Perhaps,' Mason said, 'you'd better tell me just what you have in mind, Miss Ambler.'

'Well,' she said demurely, 'you'd know me if you saw me again, wouldn't you?'

'I think so,' Mason said.

'And your secretary, Miss Street?'

'Yes,' Della Street said. 'I'd know you.'

'But,' she said, 'people want to be absolutely certain in a situation of this sort and–Well, when the question of identification comes up they look for scars and . . . well, I have a scar.'

'And you want to show it to us.'

'Yes.'

'I believe my secretary told me that you'd like to have some other witness present.'

'Yes, as I understand it, a lawyer can't be a witness for his client.'

'He shouldn't be,' Mason said.

'Then perhaps we can get someone who could be a witness.'

'There's Paul Drake,' Mason said, again glancing at Della Street. 'He's head of the Drake Detective Agency. He has offices on this floor and does most of my work.'

'I would have preferred a woman,' she said. 'It's–rather intimate.'

'Of course,' Mason said, 'you could retire to one of the other rooms and Della Street could make an inspection.'

'No, no,' she said hastily. 'I want *you* to see, personally.'

Mason glanced at Della Street again and said, 'I'll send a message to Paul Drake. We'll see if we can get him to step in for a few minutes.'

The lawyer pulled a pad of paper to him and wrote:

Paul: Della will tell you what this is all about, but I want you to have one or more operatives shadow this young woman when she leaves my office. Keep on her trail until I tell you to stop.–Della, try to get an opportunity to look in her purse and see if she really does have a gun.

Mason tore off the sheet from his pad, handed it to Della Street and said, 'Take this down to Paul Drake, will you please, Della?'

Della Street, keeping the formal atmosphere which would be compatible with the transmission of a message by paper rather than by word of mouth, said, 'Yes, Mr Mason,' and opened the exit door.

Dorrie Ambler crossed good-looking legs. 'I suppose you think I'm being very mysterious, Mr Mason.'

'Well, let's put it this way,' the lawyer said. 'you're a little out of the ordinary.'

'I . . . I just have a suspicion that someone is trying to set me up as a–What is it you call a person who is made the victim of a frame-up?'

'A fall guy,' Mason said, 'or a Patsy.'

'Since I am not a *guy*,' she said, smiling, 'I prefer the word Patsy. I don't want to be a Patsy, Mr Mason.'

'I'm sure you don't,' Mason told her. 'And, by the same token, *I* don't want to be placed in a position which might prove embarrassing to *me*. . . . I take it you gave your name and address to my secretary?'

'Oh, yes, to the receptionist. The young woman at the switchboard.'

'That's Gertie,' Mason said.

'I gave her the information. I reside at the Parkhurst Apartment, Apartment 907.'

'Married, single, divorced?'

'Single.'

'Well,' Mason said, 'you must have people there who can vouch for your identity–the manager of the apartment, for instance.'

She nodded.

'How long have you lived there?'

'Oh . . . let me see. . . . Some six months, I guess.'

'You have a driving license?' Mason asked.

'Certainly.'

'May I see it, please?'

She opened her handbag, holding it in such a way that Mason could not see down into the interior, then took out a purse and from that extracted a driving license.

Mason studied the name, the residence, the description, said, 'This was issued five months ago.'

'That's right, that was my birthday,' she said, and smiled. 'You know how old I am now, Mr Mason.'

The lawyer nodded. 'This being a California license, there is a thumbprint on it.'

'I know.'

'So your objection to having your fingerprints taken was at least partially overcome by–'

'Don't misunderstand me, Mr Mason,' she said. 'I have no objection to having my fingerprints taken. It's simply that the idea of having them taken and sent to the FBI . . .' She shuddered.

'We can make a perfect identification from this thumbprint,' Mason said.

'Oh,' she said, and looked at her thumb. 'Are *you* a fingerprint expert, Mr Mason?'

'No,' Mason said, 'but Paul Drake is, and I know a little something about comparing prints.'

'I see.'

'Do you have any other scars?' Mason asked. 'Any other operations?'

She smiled. 'Just the appendectomy. It's so recent I'm conscious of it all the time.'

Drake's code knock sounded on the outer door, and Mason crossed the room to admit Della Street and Paul Drake.

'This is Paul Drake, the detective, Miss Ambler,' Mason said.

Drake bowed.

She smiled, said, 'How are you, Mr Drake.'

Mason said, 'We have a peculiar situation here, Paul. This young woman wants to have a witness who can establish her identity. She wants you to take a good look at her and she even wants to go so far as to show the scar of a recent operation for the removal of her appendix.'

'I see,' Drake said gravely.

'And,' Mason went on, 'I have explained to her that since it now appears she has a California driving license with her thumbprint on it, that's all that will be necessary. It will only be necessary to compare her thumbprint with the print on the driving license.'

'Well now,' Drake said, 'a thumbprint is, of course, identification, but on the other hand if she wants to–'

'I do,' she interposed. 'I don't like fingerprints. That is, I don't like the idea of being fingerprinted. However, if you would like to compare my thumbprint with the print on the license, here's my thumb. But I *don't* want to make fingerprints. I just don't like the idea of getting ink all over my fingers and feeling like a criminal. . . . Can you compare the thumb itself with the print and tell?'

Drake gravely took a small magnifying glass from his pocket, moved over to sit beside her.

'Permit me,' he said as she produced the driving license. He gently took her hand in his, held the thumb under the magnifying glass, then looked at the print on the driver's license.

'I have to make a transposition this way,' he said, 'and it's a little difficult. It would simplify things if you'd . . .'

'No ink,' she said, laughing nervously.

'It just means I'll be a little longer,' Drake said.

Della Street winked at Perry Mason.

Drake moved his glass back and forth from the thumb to the print on the driver's license, then looked up at Perry Mason and nodded. 'All right,' he said, 'check. You're Dorrie Ambler. But, of course,' he added hastily, 'we'll check on the appendicitis operation.'

She got to her feet abruptly, moved over to a corner of the room.

'I'll get away from the windows,' she said.

She slipped off her jacket, raised her blouse to show a small strip of bare skin, then became suddenly self-conscious and pulled it back down.

'Actually,' Mason said, 'the thumbprint is enough.'

'No, no,' she said, 'I want you to . . .' She broke off, laughing nervously. 'After all,' she said, 'I suppose a lawyer is like a doctor and I think nothing of being examined by my doctor. Well, here goes.'

She pulled a zipper at the side of her skirt, slipped her waistband down and pulled up her blouse.

She stood there for a second or two, letting them view smooth, velvety skin, its beauty marred by an angry red line, then suddenly shook her head, pulled the skirt into position and pulled up the zipper.

'Heavens,' she said, 'I don't know why, but I just feel horribly undressed.'

'Well, we've seen it,' Drake said, 'and in a few months the color will leave that scar and you'll hardly know it's there.'

'You can identify me?' she asked.

'Well,' Drake said, smiling, 'with that thumb and that appendectomy scar I think I can make a pretty good identification if I have to.'

'That,' she said, 'is all I want.'

While she had been fumbling with her clothes, Della Street had swiftly opened Dorrie Ambler's handbag, looked inside, snapped the bag shut and then catching Mason's eye, nodded to him.

'All right, Paul,' Mason said significantly, 'I guess that's all. You're a witness. You can make the identification.'

'Perhaps it would help,' Drake said, 'if I knew what this was all about.'

'It would help,' Dorrie Ambler said, 'if *I* knew what it was all about. All I know is that either I have a double or I'm being groomed as a double for someone else and I'm–I'm afraid.'

'How are you being groomed?' Mason asked.

'I've been given these clothes to wear,' she said, flouncing the skirt up in such a way that it showed a neat pair of legs well up the thighs. 'I've even been given the stockings, the shoes, skirt, jacket, blouse, underwear, everything, and told to wear them, and I'm following certain instructions.'

Mason said, 'Are there any cleaning marks on those clothes?'

'I haven't looked.

'It might be a good plan to look,' Mason said, 'but it probably would take a fluorescent light.'

She said, 'I–I'm doing something on my own, Mr Mason, and I'll be back later on.'

'Just what do you contemplate doing?' Mason asked.

She shook her head. 'You wouldn't approve,' she said, 'and therefore you wouldn't let me do it, but I'm going to force the issue out into the open.'

Abruptly she picked up her handbag, looked at her watch, turned to Mason and said, 'I presume your secretary handles the collections.'

Mason said to Della Street, 'Make a ten-dollar charge, Della, and give Miss Ambler a receipt.'

Della said, 'This way please,' and led the client out of the office.

Mason and Drake exchanged glances.

'You've got a man on the job?' Mason asked.

'Jerry Nelson,' Drake said. 'He's one of the best in the business. It just happened he was in my office making a report on another assignment when

Della came in with your note. I also have a second man in a car at the curb. . . . Boy, that's a dish!'

Mason nodded.

'What do you suppose is eating her?' Drake asked.

'I don't know,' Mason said. 'We'll find out. Probably someone is grooming her for a double in a divorce action. Let me know as soon as your men have a definite report.'

'She'll just go back to her apartment now,' Drake said.

Mason shook his head. 'I have a peculiar idea, Paul, she's going someplace with a very definite plan of action, and she has a gun in her purse.'

'The deuce she does!' Drake exclaimed.

Mason nodded. 'Gertie spotted it when she was in the outer office, and Della confirmed it by taking a peek in her purse while you were studying feminine anatomy.'

'Well,' Drake said, 'next time you have a client who wants to do a strip tease, be sure to call on me.'

Della Street entered the office.

'She's gone?' Mason asked.

Della Street nodded.

'What about the gun?'

'I didn't have time to do more than just give it a quick look, but there aren't any bullets in it.'

'You mean it's empty?' Mason asked.

'No. The shells are in the gun. You can see them by looking down the cylinder, but there aren't any bullets in the shells, just caps of blue paper at the end of the cartridge.'

'Blank cartridges!' Mason excalimed.

'I guess that's what they are,' Della Street said. 'It's a small pistol. It looks like a twenty-two caliber.'

Drake gave a low whistle.

'She gave you ten dollars and you gave her a receipt?' Mason asked Della Street.

'For services rendered,' Della Street said. 'Then she *wanted* to give me a hundred dollars as a retainer on future services. I told her I wasn't authorized to accept that, that she'd have to talk with you; so she said never mind, she'd let it go, and hurried out of the office saying she had a time schedule that she had to meet.'

'Well,' Mason said thoughtfully, 'let's hope that schedule doesn't include a murder.'

'We're having her shadowed,' Paul Drake said. 'She won't lose my men. They'll know where she goes and what she does.'

'Of course,' Mason said thoughtfully, 'she can't commit a murder with blank cartridges, but something tells me your report from Jerry Nelson and his assistant is going to be somewhat out of the ordinary. Let me know as soon as you hear from your men, Paul.'

2

It was shortly after one-thirty that afternoon when Paul Drake gave his code knock on the door of Mason's private office.

Mason nodded to Della Street. 'Let Paul in, Della. He'll have some news.'

Della Street opened the door.

Paul Drake said, 'Hi, Beautiful,' and ushered a chunky, competent-looking man into the office.

'This is Jerry Nelson, one of my operatives,' he said. 'Jerry, this is Della Street, Mr Mason's confidential secretary, and Perry Mason. Now I want you to tell these people what happened just as you told it to me.'

Drake turned to Mason and said apologetically, 'I got this over the telephone. It sounded so cockeyed I told Jerry to dash in and report personally. Now then, I'm turning him over to you all. Go ahead, Jerry.'

Mason smiled and said, 'Sit down, Nelson, and let's have the story.'

Nelson said, 'I know you people are going to think I'm a little screwy but I'm going to tell you exactly what happened.

'Paul Drake told me there was a woman in your office that you wanted shadowed; that I was to pick her up in the elevator; that another operative would be waiting with a car in front of the entrance; that there would be a vacant taxicab waiting just in case anything went wrong. I gathered it was an important job of tailing so I wanted to be on my toes. Drake said we weren't to let her out of our sight no matter what happened.'

Mason nodded.

'Okay,' Nelson said. 'this young woman left the office. She was above five feet three, somewhere in her early twenties, had chestnut hair, hazel eyes. She wore a green and brown plaid suit and a green blouse–'

'Now, wait a minute,' Mason said, 'we know all about her appearance.'

'I know, I know,' Drake interrupted, 'but get this thing straight, Perry. We want to be sure of our facts.'

'All right, go ahead,' Mason said.

'Well, anyway,' Nelson said, 'I got aboard the elevator with this young woman. My partner was waiting out in front.

'She wanted a cab. The cab that we were holding at the curb had its flag down and she tried to get that. The driver pointed to his flag and she started to argue with him but just then another Yellow came along and she flagged it down.

'I was still playing it cautious because we didn't know what was going to happen. The only orders we had were to see that she didn't get out of our sight, and to spare no expense–so I jumped in the cab that we had waiting at the curb, and my buddy pulled out in his car and both of us followed the cab which had been taken by the girl.

'What's more, we had the number on the cab ahead and a twenty-dollar bill got my cabdriver to radio in to the dispatcher and ask him where the cab was going as soon as he got a report.

'The report came in in about two minutes. The cabdriver said he was headed for the airport.

'So both of us tagged along behind and sure enough she went right to the airport without any attempt to shake off any shadows or even paying the slightest attention to what was happening behind her.

'Those cabdrivers get pretty sharp in watching traffic and I felt the cabdriver might be keeping an eye out behind, so I had my cab drop back and the other operative moved in close behind. Then after a while the other operative dropped back and my cab moved up. Between us we kept her in sight all the way.'

'All the way where?' Mason asked.

'To the airport.'

'Then what?'

'Then she just stuck around.'

'How long?'

'Over an hour,' the operative said. 'She was waiting for something and I guess I was maybe dumb that I didn't pick up what it was, but because I thought she might be trying something shifty I kept my eye on *her* and didn't try to look around too much at the scenery.'

'What are you getting at?' Mason said.

'Well, I'd better tell you just the way it happened. You see, when two operatives are working on a case that way, one of them has to be in charge, and because of seniority I was the one to call the shots on this deal. I probably should have had my colleague keeping a look around the place but, as I say, I thought this babe might be trying something shifty so we were keeping our eyes on her.'

'What happened?' Mason asked.

'All of a sudden she jumped up, ran over to the newsstand, shouted, "This isn't a stick-up," pulled a revolver out of her handbag and fired three shots.

'It was so darned sudden and so completely, utterly senseless that it caught me flat-footed.'

'Now, wait a minute,' Mason said. 'You said that she said, "This *isn't* a stick-up"?'

'That's right. I was within ten feet of her and I heard her distinctly.'

'Go on,' Mason said. 'What happened? Did you grab her?'

'Not me. I was like everyone else. People stood there just frozen in their tracks. It was one of the darnedest sights I ever saw, just as though you had been watching a motion picture and all of a sudden the thing stopped and the picture froze on the screen.

'One minute everybody was hurrying around, bustling here and there; people sitting waiting for planes, people buying tickets, people moving back and forth; and then *wham!* Everything stopped and people just stood in their tracks.'

'And what about the young woman?'

'The young woman didn't stand in *her* tracks,' Nelson said. 'She brandished the gun, whirled, and made for the ladies' rest room.

'Now, as far as I'm concerned there's a brand-new crime angle. You have a lot of guards around an airport, and police on duty, but there was no police*woman* immediately available.

'So here's a babe with a gun, barricaded in the women's rest room, and who's going after her?'

'You?' Mason asked, his eyes twinkling.

'Not me,' Nelson said. 'Facing a crazy woman with a gun is one thing, and facing irate women who have been disturbed in a rest room is another, and when you add the two together you've got too many risks for any mere man. I just stood around where I could watch the door of the rest room.'

'And what happened?'

'Well, a couple of cops came running up and held a conference and seemed to be as perplexed about the situation as I was. Then they evidently decided to go through with it and started for the rest room. About that time the door opened and this babe came walking out, just as cool as you please.'

'With a gun?'

'I'm telling you,' Nelson said, 'she came out just as cool as a cucumber–just like any normal woman who had been powdering her nose and was emerging to take a look at the bulletin board and see just when her plane was scheduled to depart.'

'What happened?' Mason asked.

'Well, the officers hadn't seen her when she fired the gun so they didn't recognize her when she came out. She walked right past them and it wasn't until one of the bystanders yelled, "There she is!" that one of the officers turned.

'By that time three or four of the bystanders were pointing their fingers and yelling, "That's her! Grab her!" and then everybody started to run.'

'Then what happened?'

'You've never seen anything like it,' Nelson said. 'This woman stood there with the most utterly bewildered expression on her face, looking around to see what it was all about.

'One of the officers came up and grabbed her and for a moment she was startled, then she was indignant and demanded to know what it was all about. Then a crowd gathered and a lot of people started talking all at once.'

'What about the gun?' Mason asked.

'The gun had been left in the rest room. A woman came out and handed the officer the gun. It had slid across the floor and scared this woman to death. The officers asked our woman if she'd mind if they looked in her handbag and she told them to go ahead. Naturally they couldn't search *her* but they did look in her handbag. Then one of the officers opened the gun and looked at it and seemed more puzzled than ever. He said something to his companion, and the other fellow looked at the gun.

'Now, I don't think anyone there heard what the officers said except me. I was right up at the officer's elbow and I heard him say, "They're blanks."'

'How many shots were fired?' Mason asked.

'Three.'

'Then what?' Mason asked.

'All of a sudden this woman smiled at the officer, said, "All right, let's get it over with. I just wanted a little excitement. I wanted to see what would happen."'

'And she admitted firing the shots?'

'She admitted firing the shots,' Nelson said. 'Well, that was all there was to it. The officers took her into custody. They gave her an opportunity to go to Headquarters in a private police car. We tried to tag along, but you know the way officers handle things when they are arresting a woman.'

'What do you mean?' Mason asked.

'They play it safe,' Nelson said. 'A woman is always in a position to claim that officers made advances and all that sort of stuff, so whenever they arrest a woman they use their radio telephone to telephone Headquarters, giving the time and location, and stating that they are on their way with a woman prisoner. Then the dispatcher notes the time and the place and then as soon as the officers get to the place where they're booking the prisoner they check in on time and place.

'The idea is to show that considering the distance traversed, there was absolutely no time for amorous dalliance. So when they have a woman prisoner they're taking in, they really cover the ground.

'They didn't use the red light and siren but they were driving just too damned fast for us to keep up. I got my colleague and we tried our best. We followed the car for . . . oh, I guess three or four miles, and then they pulled through a signal just as it was changing and we lost them.'

'So what did you do?' Mason asked.

'So I telephoned to Drake and told him generally what had happened, and Drake told me to come on in and report to him in person.'

Mason looked at Drake.

'That's it,' Drake said. 'That's what happened.'

Mason looked at his watch. 'Well,' he said, 'under those circumstances I assume that our client will be asking for an attorney and we'll be hearing from her within the next few minutes.'

Drake said, 'Evidently she had this thing all planned, Perry, and she was just coming to you to get you retained in advance. I thought you should know.'

'I certainly should,' Mason said.

Drake said to Nelson, 'Well, Jerry, I guess that covers the situation. We've done all the damage we can do.'

'The point is, Mr Mason,' Nelson said, 'if anything happens I'm in an embarrassing position.'

'What do you mean?'

'The officers took my name and address. I had to give them one of my cards. My associate saw what was happening and managed to duck out of the way, but I was standing right there and one of the bystanders said to the officer, "This man was standing right by me and he saw the whole thing," so the officer turned to me and said, "What's your name?" and I didn't dare to stall around any because I knew that they'd get me sooner or later and if they found I was a private detective and had been a little reluctant about giving them the information they wanted, they'd have put two and two together and figured right away I was on a case. So I just acted as any ordinary citizen would and gave the officer my name and address.'

'Did he check it in any way?'

'Yes. He asked to see my driver's license.'

'So he has your name and address.'

'Right.'

'And if you were called as a witness you'd have to testify to the things that you've told me here.'

'That's right.'

'Well,' Mason said, 'if you're called as a witness you'll have to tell the truth. But I want you to remember that she said that it was *not* a stick-up.'

'That's the one thing I can't understand,' Nelson said. 'She walked over toward the newsstand, opened her purse, caught the eye of the girl behind the counter at the newsstand, jerked out the gun, said, "This *isn't* a stick-up" and then bang! bang! bang! Then she turned and dashed into the women's room.'

'But you can swear if you have to that she said it was *not* a stick-up.'

'Very definitely. But I guess I'm about the only one that heard it because she said *isn't* and I'll just bet about half of the people–in fact, I guess all of the people–who were around, would swear that she said, "This *is* a stick-up."'

'Well, that *isn't* might be rather important,' Mason said, 'in view of the fact that there were only blank cartridges in the gun. . . . You heard one of the officers say that they were blanks?'

'That's right.'

'Okay,' Mason said, 'I guess that's all there is to it.'

Nelson got up and shook hands. 'I'm mighty glad to meet you, Mr Mason. I'm sorry that I may be a witness against you–that is, against your side of the case.'

'What do you mean, against?' Mason asked. 'You may be one of the best witnesses I have.'

Drake, holding the door open for Nelson, said, 'You get more goofy cases, Perry, than anyone else in the business.'

'Or more goofy clients,' Mason said.

In the doorway Jerry Nelson paused and shook his head. 'That's the thing I can't understand,' he said. 'That woman, when she came out, was the most perfectly poised woman you have ever seen in your life. She acted just completely natural. You wouldn't have thought she even knew what a gun was, let alone having just caused a commotion with one.'

'You can't always tell about women,' Drake said.

Mason grinned. 'You can't *ever* tell about women, Paul.'

3

An atmosphere of tense expectancy hung over Perry Mason's office until a few minutes before five o'clock when Perry Mason said, 'Well, Della, I guess our client has decided she doesn't need an attorney–and I'm hanged if I know why.'

'Do you suppose they've been interrogating her and won't let her get to a phone to put through a call?'

'I don't know,' Mason said. 'I can think of a lot of explanations but none of them is logical. However, I'm not going to worry about it. Let's close up shop, go home and call it a day. We should have closed the office at four-thirty–Wait a minute, Della, it's almost five. Let's tune in on the five o'clock newscast and see if there is some mention made of what happened. It'll be worth something to find out whether I'm going to have to try to defend a client on a charge of shooting up an airport with blank cartridges.'

'About the only defense to that would be not guilty by reason of insanity,' Della Street said.

Mason grinned.

Della Street brought out the portable radio, tuned it in to the station and promptly at five o'clock twisted the knob, turning up the volume.

There were comments on the international situation, on the stock market, and then the announcer said, 'The local airport was thrown into a near panic today when an attractive young woman brandished a revolver, shouted "This is a stick-up!' and then proceeded to fire three shots before retreating into the women's rest room.

'While police were organizing to storm the citadel, the woman in question casually emerged. Upon being identified by spectators and taken into custody by the police, the woman at first professed her innocence, then finally smilingly admitted that she had done the act as a prank. Frankly skeptical, police soon determined two facts which lent strong support to the woman's statement. One fact was that the revolver was loaded only with blank cartridges and apparently the three shells which had been fired were blanks. The other fact was that an inspection of the woman's driving license identified her as Minerva Minden, who has been designated in the past by at least one newspaper as the madcap heiress of Montrose.

'Miss Minden has from time to time paid visits to Police Headquarters; once for deliberately smashing dishes in a restaurant in order to get the attention of a waiter; once for reckless driving and resisting an officer; once for driving while intoxicated; in addition to which she has received several citations for speeding.

'The young heiress seemed to regard the entire matter as something in the nature of a lark, but Municipal Judge Carl Baldwin took a different view. When the defendant was brought before him to fix bail on charges of disturbing the peace and of discharging firearms in a public place, Judge Baldwin promptly proceeded to fix bail at two thousand dollars upon each count.

'A somewhat chastened Miss Minden said she would plead guilty to the charges, put up cash bail and left the courtroom. She is to appear tomorrow morning at nine-thirty for a hearing on her application for probation and for receiving sentence.'

The broadcaster then went on to discuss the weather, the barometric pressure and the temperature of the ocean water.

'Well,' Della Street said, as she switched off the radio, 'would you say our Miss Ambler is a double of Minerva Minden, the madcap heiress?'

Mason's eyes narrowed. 'The crime,' he said, 'was evidently premeditated, and the driving license and the thumbprint were most certainly those of Dorrie Ambler–so now the scar of the appendectomy *may* assume considerable importance.'

'But how?' Della Street asked. 'What could be the explanation?'

Mason said, 'I can't think of one, Della, but somehow I'm willing to bet . . .'

The lawyer broke off as timid knuckles sounded against the door from his private office to the corridor.

Mason glanced at his watch. 'Fifteen minutes past five. Don't open *that* door, Della. Go out through the door from the reception room and tell whoever it is that the office is closed for the day, that I'm not available; to telephone tomorrow morning at nine o'clock and ask you for an appointment.'

Della Street nodded, slipped out of Mason's private office into the reception room.

A moment later she was back. 'Guess who?' she asked.

'Who?' Mason asked.

'Dorrie Ambler.'

'Did she see you?'

Della shook her head. 'I just opened the door from the reception room into the corridor and started to step out when I saw her. I thought perhaps you'd want to talk with her even if it is after hours.'

Mason grinned, stepped to the door and opened it just as the young woman was dejectedly turning away.

'Miss Ambler,' Mason said.

She jumped and whirled.

'The office is closed,' Mason said, 'and I was on the point of leaving for the night, but if it's a matter of some importance I'll see you briefly.'

'It's a matter of great importance,' she said.

'Come in,' Mason invited, holding the door open.

Della Street smiled and nodded.

'Sit down,' Mason invited. And then when she had complied said, 'So you're really Minerva Minden, sometimes referred to as the madcap heiress of Montrose.'

She met his eyes with a steady frank gaze. 'I am *not!*" she said.

Mason shook his head, his manner that of a parent reproving a mendacious child who persists in an incredible falsehood. 'I'm afraid your denial isn't going to carry much weight, but this is your party. You wanted to see me upon a matter of some importance and it's only fair to remind you that you're paying for my time. Moreover, one of the factors in fixing my charges is the financial ability of the client to pay. Now, you just go ahead and take all the time you want. Tell me any fairy story you want me to hear and remember that it's costing you money, lots of money.'

'You don't understand,' she said.

'I'm afraid I do,' Mason told her. 'Now I'm going to tell you something else. When you were here in the office I knew that you had a gun in your purse. I hired a detective to shadow you. You were shadowed up to the airport, and a detective was standing within a few feet of you when you staged that demonstration.

'Now then, Miss Minden, I'd like to know just what your game is, what you have in mind and how you expect me to fit into the picture.

'For your further information, I don't like to have clients lie to me, and I feel that after I have heard your story there is every possibility that I will not care to have you continue as a client.'

She was watching him with wide eyes. 'You've had me shadowed?'

Mason nodded.

'You knew there was a gun in my purse?'

Again the lawyer nodded.

She said, 'Thank God!'

Mason's face showed his surprise.

'Look,' she said, 'I'm *not* Minerva Minden. I'm Dorrie Ambler, and the thing I did this afternoon at the airport was for the purpose of forcing Minerva Minden to tell what was really going on, but she was too smart for me. She outwitted me.'

Mason's eyes showed dawning interest. 'Go ahead,' he said.

She said, 'It all started four days ago when I answered an ad for a young woman, either trained or untrained, who could do special work. The ad specified that applicants must be between twenty-two and twenty-six years of age, that they must be exactly five feet three inches tall, weighing not less than a hundred and ten pounds nor more than a hundred and fifteen pounds, and offered a salary of a thousand dollars a month.'

Della Street flashed a glance at Perry Mason. 'I saw that ad,' she said. 'It only ran for one day.'

'Go ahead,' Mason said to Dorrie Ambler.

'Someone mailed me a copy of the ad and I applied for that job,' she said, 'and so did scads of other people–and there was something phony about it.'

'Keep talking,' Mason said, his eyes now showing keen interest.

'Well, to begin with, we were asked to go to a suite in a hotel in order to make application. A very efficient young woman sat at a desk in a room in that suite, on which had been pasted a sign, PERSONNEL MANAGER.

'Opening out of this suite were two rooms. One of them had a label, RED ROOM. The other had a label, BLACK ROOM. The young woman at the desk would give each applicant a ticket. The red tickets went to the red room, the black tickets went to the black room.'

'Then what?' Mason asked.

'As far as the red room is concerned I don't know for sure, but I did talk with one girl who was given a ticket to the red room. She went in there and sat down and she said there were about twenty young women who came in and sat down in that room. They waited for about fifteen minutes and then a woman came to them and told them that there was no need for them to wait any longer; the situation was no longer open.'

'All right,' Mason said, 'you were given a ticket to the black room. What happened there?'

'Apparently only about one applicant out of fifteen or twenty got a black ticket. I was one of them. I went in there and sat down and one other girl came in while I was there.

'After I'd been there for ten or fifteen minutes, a door opened and a man said, "Step this way, please."

'I went into still another room in the suite–heavens, that suite in the hotel must have cost a small fortune.'

'Who was the man?' Mason asked.

'He said he was a vice president in charge of personnel, but the way he acted *I* think he was a lawyer.'

'What makes you think so?'

'The way he threw questions at me.'

'What sort of questions?'

'He had me sit down and asked me a lot about my background, all about my parents, where I'd been employed, and so forth. Then he asked me to stand up and walk around. He was watching me like a hawk.'

'Passes?' Mason asked.

'I don't think that was what he had in mind,' she said, 'but he certainly was looking me over.'

'And then?'

'Then he asked me how my memory was and if I could give quick answers to questions and a lot of things like that, and then said, "What were you doing on the evening of the sixth of September?"

'Well, that hadn't been *too* long ago, and after thinking a minute I told him that I had been in my apartment. I hadn't had a date that night although it had been a Saturday, and he asked me who was with me and I told him no one. He wanted to know if I'd been there the entire evening and I told him I had. Then he asked me if I'd had any visitors at all during the evening, or had had any phone calls, and a lot of personal questions of that sort, and then asked me for my telephone number and told me that I was being seriously considered for the job.'

'Did he tell you what kind of a job it was?'

'He said it was going to be a rather peculiar job, that I was going to have to undergo intensive training in order to hold down the position but that I would be paid during the period of training. He said that the pay was at the rate of a thousand dollars a month, that the position would be highly confidential, and that I would be photographed from time to time in various types of clothing.'

'Did he say what type?' Mason asked.

'No, he didn't. Of course I became suspicious right away and told him there was no use wasting each other's time, did he mean I'd be posing in the nude, and he said definitely not, that it was perfectly legitimate and aboveboard, but that I'd be photographed from time to time in various types of clothing; that the people I was to work for didn't want posed photographs. They wanted pictures of young women on the street, that I wasn't to be alarmed if someone pointed a camera at me and took pictures of me on the street, that that would be done often enough so that I would lose all self-consciousness.'

'And then what?'

'Well, then I went home and after I'd been there about two hours the telephone rang and he told me I'd been selected for the position.'

'You were unemployed at the time?' Mason asked.

'As it happened, I was. I'd been foolish enough to think I could support myself by selling encyclopedias on a door-to-door basis.'

'Couldn't you?' Mason asked.

'I suppose I could,' she said, 'if I'd absolutely *had* to. But I just didn't have the stamina for it.'

'What do you mean?'

'You ring doorbells,' she said. 'Someone comes to the door. You only get invited in about once out of five times if you're *really* good. If you're not, you're apt not to get invited in at all.'

'If you do, what happens?'

'Then you get in and make your sales pitch and answer questions and arrange for a follow-up.'

'A follow-up?' Mason asked.

'Yes, you call during the daytime and the woman doesn't like to take on that much of an obligation without consulting her husband. So if you've really made a good pitch you're invited to come back in the evening when he's home.'

'And you didn't like it?' Mason asked.

'I liked it all right but it was just too darned exhausting. In order to stay with a job of that sort you have to develop a shell. You become as thoroughly professional as a–as a professional politician.'

'So you quit?' Mason asked.

'Well, I didn't exactly quit but I made up my mind that I'd only work mornings. Afternoons are rather nonproductive anyway because so many times you find women who are planning on going to a club meeting or have got their housework caught up and want to do something else during the afternoon. They are either not going to give you the time to let you talk with them or they're impatient when they do talk with you.'

'I see,' Mason said. 'Go ahead.'

'All right,' she said. 'I went back to my apartment. It was a day when I was resting. I didn't feel too full of pep anyway and I was taking life easy when the phone rang and I was told that I'd been selected and asked to come back to the hotel.'

'Then what?'

'Then I went to the hotel and everything had changed. There was no longer the woman at the desk, but this man was sitting in the parlor of the suite and he told me to sit down and he'd tell me something about the duties of the job.

'He gave me the plaid suit I was wearing this morning, the blouse, the stockings, even the underthings. He told me that this was to be my first assignment, that he wanted me to put on these clothes and wear them until I got accustomed to them, that I was to get them so they looked as though they were a part of my personality, and I was not to be at all self-conscious. He suggested that I could step in to the bedroom and try the clothes on.'

'Did you?' Mason asked.

'I did after some hesitancy,' she said, 'and believe me, I saw that both doors into that bedroom were locked. I just had a feeling that I had got into something that was a little too much for me.'

'All right,' Mason said, 'go on. What happened? Did he make passes?'

'No, I had the deal sized up a hundred per cent wrong. The man was a perfect gentleman. I put on the clothes and came out. He looked me over, nodded approvingly and then gave me a hat and told me I was to wear that hat. He told me that my duties would be very light for the first few days, that I was to sleep late in the next morning, that I was to get up and have had breakfast by ten-thirty; that I was to go to the intersection of Hollywood and Vine and cross the street fifty times. At the end of that time I was free to go home.'

'Crossing the street from what direction?' Mason asked.

'He said it didn't make any difference. Just walk back and forth across the street, being careful to obey the signals, and that I was to remember not to pay any attention to anybody who might be there with a camera.'

'Was somebody there?' Mason asked.

'Yes, a man was there with a camera. He took pictures mostly of me but occasionally he would take a picture of someone else.'

'And you walked back and forth?' Mason asked.

'That's right.'

'The clothes fit you?'

'As though they'd been made for me. They were the ones I wore this morning.'

'Now then,' Mason said, 'this is an important point. Were these clothes new or had they been worn?'

'They were new. They hadn't been sent to the cleaner as nearly as I could tell. They had, however, evidently been made specially. There were even some bits of the basting threads left in the seams.'

'Did you,' Mason asked, 'ever see any of the pictures?'

'No, just the man with the camera.'

'All right, go on. What happened?'

'I was told to telephone a certain unlisted number for instructions. I telephoned the number and was told that everything was okay. I had done all that I needed to do for the day and I could have the rest of the time off.'

'Then what?' Mason asked.

She said, 'I did a little detective work on my own.'

'Such as what?'

'I called the unlisted number, disguised my voice and asked for Mac. The man said I had the wrong number and asked what number I was calling and I gave him the number. It was, of course, the correct number. He said I had made a mistake and had the wrong number. I told him that I didn't, and I knew the number Mac had given me. So then he started getting a little mysterious and I think a little concerned. He said, 'Look, this is a detective agency, Billings and Compton. We don't have any Mac working for us," and I said, "A detective agency, huh?" And slammed up the phone.'

'So then what?'

'Then,' she said, 'I looked up the address of Billings and Compton Detective Agency and decided to go up there and ask for a showdown. I didn't know just what I was getting into.'

'And what happened?' Mason asked.

'I never went in,' she said. 'I–Well, something happened and I thought I saw the picture.'

'What was it that happened?'

'I drove my car up there. There's a parking lot right next door to the building. I put my car in the parking lot and was just getting out when I saw my double.'

'Your what?'

'My double.'

'Now,' Mason said, 'I'm beginning to get the picture. Just what did your double look like?'

'She looked *exactly* like me. She was dressed exactly the same way, and there was more than a superficial resemblance. It was really startling. She was my height, my build, my complexion, and of course since we were wearing identical clothes–well, I had to stop and do a double take. I thought I was looking at myself in the mirror.'

'And what was your double doing?'

'Standing in line, waiting for her car to be brought to her.'

'And what did you do?'

'I kept on doing detective work. I stopped my car and continued to sit in it and when the man gave me a parking ticket I just kept on sitting there until I saw her car being delivered and I got the license number of her car, WBL 873.'

'So then you looked up the registration?' Mason asked.

'That's right.'

'And the registration was Minerva Minden?'

'Right.'

'And then?' Mason asked.

'Well, then I reported for work the next day and I was told to go to another locality. This time it was Sunset and La Brea and I was to cross the street fifty times.'

'You did that?'

'Yes.'

'And the photographer was there?'

'Part of the time the photographer was there, part of the time he drove by in an automobile. Once I'm certain that he had a motion-picture camera in the automobile when he stopped and parked the car and took motion pictures of me.'

'And then what?'

'Then I called the unlisted number again and was told that my work was done for the day, that I could relax, have cocktails and dinner and that there would be no more calls on my time.'

'So what did you do?'

She said, 'I came to the conclusion that I was being groomed for something and that I was going to be what you called a Patsy.'

'Perhaps Minerva Minden wants an alibi for something,' Mason said,

'I've thought of all that,' she said. 'We're not twins but there certainly is a startling resemblance. But wait until you hear what happened the next day.'

'Okay, what did happen?'

'So,' she said, 'the next day I was told to go to Hollywood Boulevard and Western, that I was to cross the street, walk one block along Hollywood Boulevard, wait ten minutes, walk back, cross Western, then cross Hollywood Boulevard and go up the other side of the street; wait ten minutes, then come back down and retrace my steps. I was to keep that up at ten-minute intervals for two hours.'

'You did it?' Mason asked.

'I only did part of it.'

'What part?'

'About the third time–I think it *was* the third time I was making the trip up Hollywood Boulevard I passed a store and a little girl cried out, "Momma, there she is now!"'

'Then what happened?'

'A woman ran to the door and took a look at me and then suddenly dashed out of the store and started following me.'

'What did you do?'

'I walked up Hollywood Boulevard just as I had been instructed, and the photographer was there at the corner and took a picture of me, and I think of the woman following me. Then suddenly I got frightened. I jumped in my car which I'd left parked on the side street and drove away as fast as I could.'

'That was when?'

'That was yesterday.'

'And then what?'

'Then I made it a point to look up Minerva Minden, and the more I saw of the thing the more I was satisfied that I was being groomed as a double for some sinister purpose. So I made up my mind that I'd just bring matters to a head.'

'By shooting up the airport?'

'I decided I'd do something so darned spectacular that the whole business would be brought out into the open.'

'So what did you do?'

'I rang up the number for instructions. They told me I didn't need to do anything today. I learned that Miss Minden was taking a plane for New York. I checked her reservation. So I got all prepared and went to the airport.

'She was wearing the same clothes that I was and–well, I got the pistol, loaded it with blank cartridges, had you inspect my appendicitis operation scar so there could be no question–Oh, it's terribly mixed up, Mr Mason, but it was the best way I could think of, of–'

'Never mind all that,' Mason said. 'Tell me what happened.'

'Well, I went down to the airport. I waited until Minerva showed up and went into the women's room, then I jumped up, grabbed the gun, yelled "This *isn't* a stick-up" and shot into the air. Then I dashed into the women's room. There are several stalls in there for showers where a person can put in a coin, get a shower, towels and all of that. Those stalls insure complete privacy. So I ran into the rest room, skidded the gun along the floor, put the coin in the slot and went into the shower.

'I felt sure that Minerva would walk into the trap, and of course she did.'

'You mean she came out of the rest room and was identified?'

'She came out of the rest room and was promptly identified. People came crowding around her and the cops started questioning her and of course that gave her a pretty good background of what happened.'

'And at that time you thought she'd say that she hadn't done it at all, that it was someone else and the officers would look in the rest room and find you.'

'Well, I wasn't certain that it would go *that* far. I thought that I would have an opportunity to get out of the rest room in the excitement before the officers came in and searched, but what I was totally unprepared for was to have her realize what had happened and with diabolical coolness say that *she* had been the one who had fired the shots.'

Mason looked at his client steadily.

'She *was* the one who fired the shots, wasn't she, Dorrie? And you're working some part of a carefully rehearsed scheme?'

'On my honor, Mr Mason, I was the one who fired those shots. Minerva was the one who tried to take the blame–and I can tell you how you can prove it in case you absolutely have to. I was afraid that if I said "This is a stick-up," that even if the gun had blank cartridges in it I might be guilty of some sort of felony, of trying to get money by brandishing a firearm or something, so I played it safe by shouting at the top of my voice, "This *isn't* a stick-up."

'Now, I know that most of the witnesses heard what they thought they should have heard, and claim the person brandishing the gun said this *is* a stick-up. But if you should ever have to cross-examine them and should ask them if it wasn't a fact that the woman said this *isn't* a stick-up, I'll bet you they would admit that that's what they really heard–but you know how it is. No one wants to come forward and be the first to say the woman said this *isn't* a stick-up. It would make them sound sort of foolish and–well, that's the way it is. No one would want to be the first, but once someone tells the real truth the others will fall in line.'

'Just what did you have in mind?' Mason asked. 'What do you want *me* to do now?'

She said, 'I want you to protect my interests. I would like to find out what it is that happened on the sixth of September that would have caused someone to go to all this trouble.'

'You feel that you were built up as a fall guy, a substitute, a Patsy.'

She said, 'I'm quite satisfied that I have been built up as a double and am going to be called on to take the blame for something I didn't do. And if you had detectives follow me to the airport, you *know* I was the one who fired those shots and then the woman who came out–this Minerva Minden, did some quick thinking and decided to take the blame rather than let it be known I was her double.'

'Would you mind letting me see your driving license again?' Mason asked.

'Certainly not.'

She opened her purse, took out her driving license and handed it to Mason.

Mason checked the license, then said, 'Let me have your thumb. I'm going to make a comparison.'

'Good heavens, but you're suspicious!'

'I'm a lawyer,' Mason said. 'I hate to have anything slipped over on me.'

She immediately extended her thumb.

Mason said, 'I know your aversion to fingerprints so I'll try making a check from the thumb itself.'

He took a magnifying glass from his desk, studied the thumb and the print on the driving license.

'Satisfied?' she asked.

Mason nodded.

'Now I'll show you the scar.'

'That won't be necessary,' Mason said, 'I'm convinced.'

'Very well,' she said. 'Now will you try and find out what it is I'm being framed for? In other words, what sort of racket I'm mixed up in?'

Mason nodded.

'Now look,' she told him, 'this is going to take some money. I don't have very much but–'

'Suppose we skip that for the moment,' Mason said. 'I'll give the case a once-over and then get in touch with you.'

'I'm so . . . so frightened,' she said.

'I don't think you need to be,' Mason told her.

'But I'm fighting someone who has unlimited money, someone who is ruthless and unbelievably clever, Mr Mason. I'm afraid that even with your help I–Well, I'm afraid they may pin something on me.'

Mason said, 'Call that unlisted number right now and ask the person who answers what your duties are for tomorrow.'

Mason caught Della Street's eye. 'You can call him from this phone,' he said, 'and I want to listen in and see what the man says.'

She hesitated a moment.

'Any objections?' Mason asked.

'I'm not supposed to call until later on.'

'Well, let's try it now,' Mason said. 'Let's see if there's an answer. Miss Street will fix the telephone connection so you're connected with an outside line and you can go right ahead and dial the number.'

Della Street smiled, picked up the telephone, pressed the button and a moment later when a light flashed on the phone, handed the instrument to Dorrie Ambler.

'Go right ahead,' Mason said. 'Dial the number.'

Dorrie seated herself at Della Street's desk and dialed the number, When she had finished dialing, Mason picked up the telephone to listen.

A man's voice said, 'Yes? Hello.'

'Who is this?' Dorrie Ambler asked.

'Who are you calling?'

Dorrie Ambler gave the number.

'All right, what do you want?'

'This is Miss Ambler–Dorrie. I wanted to know what instructions there were for tomorrow.'

'Tomorrow,' the man's voice said, 'you simply sit tight. Do nothing. Take it easy. Go to a beauty shop. Have a good time.'

'I do nothing?'

'Nothing.'

'And my salary?'

'Goes on just the same,' the man said, and hung up.

Dorrie Ambler looked over at Mason as though for instructions and slowly dropped the telephone receiver into its cradle.

'All right,' Mason said cheerfully, looking at his watch, 'we've got to close up the office and go home, Miss Ambler, and I guess the best thing for you to do is the same.'

'Suppose something should happen–there should be some developments. Where can I reach you?'

'I don't have a night number where you can reach me,' Mason said, 'but if you want to call the Drake Detective Agency which is on this floor and leave a message for me, they'll see that I get it within an hour or so at the latest. . . . You feel something may be going to happen?'

'I don't know. I just have that feeling of dread, of apprehension, of something hanging over my head. Minerva Minden knows what happened, of course, and she's apt to do almost anything. You see, she'll know I've found out she's the one I'm doubling for.'

Mason said, 'We'll try to find out what it's all about, and don't worry.'

'I feel better now that the situation is in your hands–but I do have a definite feeling that I'm being jockeyed into position for a very devastating experience.'

'Well, we can't do very much until we know more of the facts,' Mason said.

'And remember, Mr Mason, I want to pay you. I can get some money. I can raise some. Would five hundred dollars be enough?'

'When can you raise five hundred dollars?' Mason asked.

'I think I could have it by tomorrow afternoon.'

'You're going to borrow it?'

'Yes.'

'Who from?'

'A friend.'

'A boy friend?'

She hesitated a moment, then slowly nodded.

'And does he know anything about all of this?' Mason asked.

'No. He knows that I have a rather peculiar job. He's been asking questions but I've been sort of–well, giving indefinite answers. I think any young woman who has training in the business world should learn to keep her mouth tightly closed about the things she observes on the job. I think she should keep them entirely removed from her social life.'

'That's very commendable,' Mason said. 'You go on home and I'll try and find out something more about all this and then get in touch with you.'

'Thank you *so* much,' Dorrie Amber said, and then acting on a sudden impulse, gave him her hand. 'Thank you again, Mr Mason. You've taken a tremendous load off my shoulders. Good night. Good night, Miss Street.'

She slipped out of the door into the corridor.

'Well?' Della Street asked.

'Now,' Mason said, 'we find out what happened at Western and Hollywood Boulevard on September sixth. Unless I'm very much mistaken, Minerva Minden was driving while intoxicated and became involved in a hit-and-run, and now she wants to confuse the witnesses so they'll make a wrong identification.

'Telephone the traffic department at Headquarters, Della, and see what they have on file for hit-and-run on the sixth.'

Della Street busied herself on the phone, made shorthand notes, thanked the person at the other end of the line, hung up and turned to Perry Mason.

'On the night of the sixth,' she said, 'a pedestrian, Horace Emmett, was struck in the crosswalk at Hollywood Boulevard and Western Avenue. He is suffering from a broken hip. The car which struck him was driven by a young woman. It was a light-colored Cadillac. The woman stopped, sized up the situation, got out of the car, then changed her mind, jumped into the car and drove away. She apparently was intoxicated.'

Mason grinned. 'Okay, Della. We close up the place and I'll buy you a dinner. Tomorrow we'll see about Minerva Minden. By tomorrow night we'll have a very nice cash settlement for our client, Dorrie Ambler, and a very, very handsome cash settlement for Horace Emmett.

'And we'll let Paul have his man, Jerry Nelson, cover Minerva Minden's hearing tomorrow and see what the judge does to her–and better tell Paul to get all the dope on that Horace Emmett accident.'

4

At ten o'clock the next morning Paul Drake's code knock sounded on the door of Mason's private office.

Mason nodded to Della Street, who opened the door for the detective.

'Hi, Beautiful,' Paul said. 'It does you good to get out and dance. Your eyes look like the depths of a deep pool in the moonlight.'

Della Street smiled, said, 'And it does you good to sit in an office and drink cold coffee and eat soggy hamburgers. Your mind is filled with matters of romance.'

Drake made a wry face. 'I can taste that cold coffee yet.'

He turned to Perry Mason. 'I sent Jerry Nelson down to the hearing on the report for probation and the fixing of sentence in Minerva Minden's case, Perry. I gave him your number and told him to report to me here. I felt that you'd want to know just as soon as I heard from him.'

Mason nodded.

'I held him up a little while,' Drake said, 'because it wasn't certain that Minerva Minden was going to be in court personally. She might have appeared through an attorney.'

'She's there?' Mason asked.

'In person, with all her charm,' Drake said. 'She is adept at showing just enough leg to win the judge over to her side and stop just short of indecent exposure. That's quite a gal.'

Drake looked at his watch. 'We should be hearing from Nelson any minute now.'

'Wasn't there some litigation over the Minden inheritance?' Della asked.

Drake grinned. 'There was some and there could have been a hell of a lot more. Old Harper Minden left a whale of a fortune and not a single heir in the world that anybody could find until finally some enterprising investigator dug up Minerva.

'Minerva at the time was slinging hash and was something of a problem. She was supposed to be wild in those days. Now that she's got a whole flock of money, she's a quote madcap unquote.'

'But Harper Minden wasn't her grandfather, was he?' Mason asked.

'Hell, no. He was related to her through some sort of a collateral relationship, and actually the bulk of the estate is still tied up. Minerva has received a partial distribution of five or six million, but–'

'Before taxes?' Mason asked.

'Proviso in the will that the estate was to pay all taxes,' Drake said, 'and boy, it was quite a bite. But old Harper sure had it piled up. He had so much money he didn't know how much he had. He had gold mines, oil wells, real estate, the works.'

The telephone rang.

'That's probably Jerry now,' Drake said.

Della answered the phone, nodded to Paul and held out the receiver.

Drake said, 'You have an attachment you can put this on a loud-speaker, haven't you, Della?'

She nodded, pressed a button, and put a conference microphone in the middle of Mason's desk.

'All the voices will come in,' she said.

Drake, sitting some ten feet from the microphone, said, 'Hello, Jerry. Can you hear me?'

'Sure I can hear you,' Nelson said, his voice, amplified through a loud-speaker, filling Mason's office.

'You seen this gal yet?' Drake asked.

'Have I seen her?' Jerry said. 'I'm still gasping for breath.'

'That much of a knockout?'

'Not only that much of a knockout, but that much of a resemblance.'

'She's really a dead ringer?'

'Well, not exactly a dead ringer but it would easily be possible to get them mixed. Now look, Paul, is there any chance those girls are related? I mean close related. Does anybody know whether Minerva Minden had a sister?'

'She wasn't supposed to have,' Drake said.

'Well, as I remember it,' Nelson said, 'the thing was mixed up in some kind of litigation. Minerva Minden was able to prove her relationship so she got several million dollars, but the family tree has never been completely uncovered. There was some talk about Minerva's mother having a sister who might have had a child before she died.'

'You feel pretty certain the two women are related?' Drake asked.

'I'd bet my last cent they're relatives,' Nelson said. 'I've never seen anything so completely confusing in my life. The two women look alike, they're built the same way, they have the same mannerisms. Their voices are different and the hair and general coloring is a little different but there's one hell of a resemblance. I don't know what you fellows are working on. I suppose it ties in with that inheritance. There's still twenty or thirty million dollars to be distributed. All I want to say is that you've struck pay dirt.'

'Okay,' Drake said, glancing at Mason, 'keep that angle under your hat. Where are you now?'

'Up at court.'

'And what's happening?'

'Oh, the usual thing. The judge is looking over his glasses at Minerva and giving her a lecture. He's imposed a five-hundred-dollar fine on each of the two charges, making a total of a thousand dollars, and he's busy now explaining to her that it was touch and go with him whether to give her a jail sentence as well; that he finally decided against it because he feels that in her case it wouldn't do any good. He's read the report of the probation officer, he's heard the application for probation, and despite the vehement requests of the defense attorney, he is going to deny probation and let the fines stand. He feels that it would be unfair to give this defendant probation.'

'Okay,' Drake said, 'keep on the job and study her as much as possible.'

'Boy, I've studied her!' Nelson said.

'Okay,' Drake told him, 'come on up then. Has she noticed you staring?'

'Hell, it's a crowded courtroom,' Nelson said. 'Everybody's staring.'

'Well, come on up,' Drake said.

'Okay. 'Bye now.'

'Good-by.'

Della Street pressed the button that turned off the telephone. 'What do you know,' Drake said, looking at Mason.

'Apparently not half enough,' Mason said thoughtfully.

'What's the story behind all this, Perry?' Paul asked.

'Apparently,' Mason said, 'Minerva Minden wanted a ringer to take a rap for her.'

'The hit-and-run?' Drake asked.

Mason nodded thoughtfully.

'So what happened?'

'So,' Mason said, 'you may have noticed an ad in the paper a while ago offering a salary of a thousand dollars a month to a woman who had certain physical qualifications as to age, height, complexion and weight, and could qualify for the job.'

'I didn't notice it,' Drake said.

'Apparently a lot of people did,' Mason told him, 'and the women were given an intensive screening. They wanted someone who could wear Minerva Minden's clothes, or clothes that would duplicate hers, and spend some time walking back and forth past the scene of the accident where at least one of the witnesses lived and where an identification would be made.'

'Of the wrong woman?'

'Of the wrong woman,' Mason said. 'That would let Minerva off the hook. If they subsequently found out it was the wrong woman, the witnesses would have all made at least one demonstrable mistaken identification. That would weaken the prosecution's case tremendously.

'If, on the other hand, the charge stood up against the ringer, then Minerva was in the clear.'

'And they got that good a ringer?' Drake asked incredulously.

Mason nodded. 'One of those coincidences, Paul. Apparently some detective agency was looking for a girl of just the right size, build and complexion who could wear Minerva's clothes and could walk back and forth in front of at least one of the witnesses until there was an identification. Then presumably the other witnesses would be called in and they'd all identify the wrong person.'

Drake grinned. 'Now, wouldn't it be poetic justice, Perry, if this babe put an ad in the paper in order to get herself out of a jam and in so doing had to split up an inheritance of fifty-odd million dollars–and where does that leave us?'

'Sitting right out on the end of some kind of a golden limb,' Mason said. 'We–'

The telephone rang.

Della Street picked up the instrument, said, 'Hello,' cupped her hand over the mouthpiece and said to Perry Mason, 'Dorrie Ambler.'

Mason made a motion. 'Put her on loud-speaker, Della.'

A moment later Della Street nodded, and Mason said, 'Hello, Miss Ambler.'

'Oh, Mr Mason!' she said, her voice excited. 'I know I have no business asking this but *could* you come to my apartment?'

'Why don't you come here?' Mason asked.

'I can't.'

'Why not?'

'I'm being watched. I'm being pinned down here.'

'Where's here?'

'At the Parkhurst Apartments. Apartment 907.'

'What's pinning you down there?'

'There are men–a man out in the corridor, ducking in and out of the broom closet. . . . From the window of my apartment I can see my car where I parked it, and there's another man keeping watch on that car.'

'All right,' Mason said, 'that means the police have got you located and you're going to be picked up on a hit-and-run charge.'

'A hit-and-run charge?' she asked.

'That's right. That's what happened on the sixth of September.'

'And you mean that was the thing they've been getting ready to frame me for?' she asked indignantly. 'I'm supposed to be offered as a sacrifice for that terribly rich woman who–'

'Take it easy, take it easy,' Mason said. 'This is a telephone and we don't know who may be listening.

'Now look, Miss Ambler, a matter has come up of very, very great importance. I have to see you and I would like to see you right away.'

'But I can't leave. I'm not going to. I'm just absolutely frightened to death.'

'Those people are police officers,' Mason said. 'They aren't going to hurt you, but they're going to stick around until they're absolutely sure that you're up and dressed and then they're going to come barging in to your apartment and ask you questions about the driving of the automobile and the accident on the sixth of September.'

'Well, what do I tell them?'

'Tell them nothing at the moment,' Mason said. 'We haven't got all our proof together but we're getting it. Tell them you were home on the sixth of September and don't tell them anything else.

'In the meantime we've got to get on the job. Now, where's your car?'

'Downstairs.'

'You said you could see it?'

'Yes.'

'Where is it?'

'At the curb.'

'Isn't there a garage connected with that building?'

'Yes, there are private garages but something happened to the lock on my garage door and my key won't work. However, I don't use the garage much anyway. It hasn't been too well ventilated and there's a mildew smell in there that I don't want to get in my car. Lots of the tenants leave their cars out.'

'All right,' Mason said. 'I have something to discuss with you, Miss Ambler. . . . Tell me something, is your father living?'

'No.'

'Your mother living?'

'No.'

'But you know all about your family?'

'Why are you asking this, Mr Mason?'

'It's something that has just come up and it may be important.'

'Actually, Mr Mason, I don't know a thing about my family. I was–Well, I was put out for adoption. I think I'm–All right, I may as well tell you, you're my attorney. I'm an illegitimate child.'

Mason and Paul Drake exchanged glances.

'How do you know you are?' Mason asked.

'Because I was put out for adoption by my mother and–Well, I've never looked into it. I guess it was just one of those things. I've wondered sometimes who my people really were.'

'You've never taken any steps to find out?' Mason asked.

'No. What steps *could* I take?'

'You stay right where you are,' Mason said. 'I'm coming up. I want to talk to you. I'll have Mr Drake with me–the detective, you know.'

'Oh. . . . Could you come right away, Mr Mason?'

'I'm coming right now,' Mason said.

'I'll be waiting.'

'Wait right there,' Mason said. 'No matter what happens, don't leave.'

Mason nodded to Della Street, who punched the button which shut off the phone.

'Come on, Paul,' Mason said. He turned to Della Street. 'Just as soon as Jerry Nelson comes in, tell him to follow us out there. You have the address. I want Jerry to take another look at this girl and compare her with the other one. It may be we've stumbled onto a red-hot lead.'

'A red-hot lead in a fifty-million-dollar jackpot,' Drake said. 'Boy, wouldn't *that* be a juicy jackpot to hit.'

5

Drake parked his car in front of the Parkhurst Apartments. Paul Drake and the lawyer cautiously emerged.

'See anyone watching the building or spotting a car, Paul?' Mason asked.

'Not yet,' Drake said, his trained eyes moving swiftly from side to side. 'Do you know what kind of a car she drives, Perry?'

'No, I don't,' Mason said. 'She's been a working girl. Probably it'll be a medium-priced model four or five years old.'

'Lot of those here,' Drake said. 'Probably second cars that the wife uses in going shopping while the head of the house takes the good car to work.'

'Rather charitable for a bachelor this morning, aren't you?' Mason asked.

'Romantic as hell,' Drake said, his eyes still restlessly searching. 'It must have been something in that bicarbonate of soda I had last night. It *couldn't* have been anything in the hamburger. . . . Okay, Perry, the place is clean down here. Not even anyone in a parked car.'

'Okay, let's go up,' Mason said.

'Better lay our plans,' Drake said. 'Suppose this guy in the corridor tries to duck out of sight when we go up there.'

'We go pull him out of hiding and see what makes him tick,' Mason said.

'If he's a police officer you'll have trouble.'

'If he isn't, he'll have trouble,' Mason said grimly. 'In any event he'll have some explanations to make. Come on, Paul, let's go.'

They went up in the elevator, got out at the ninth floor and Mason said to Paul, 'You take the left, I'll take the right, Paul. Cover the entire corridor.'

The two men walked down the corridor to the end, then turned, retraced their steps and met again in front of the elevator.

'Anything at your end?' Drake asked.

Mason shook his head.

'Mine's clear.'

'All right, let's go talk with her. . . . Now remember, Paul, any of this business about the estate is entirely extracurricular. At this time, we aren't going to bring that up. We'll look the situation over. So far I'm retained only for one specific purpose.'

'And what is that?' Drake asked.

Mason grinned. 'Just to keep her from being a fall guy for something she didn't do. Okay, Paul, here we go.'

They advanced to the door of 907.

Mason pressed his fingers against the mother-of-pearl button, and chimes sounded on the inside of the apartment.

There was complete silence from the interior.

Mason said, 'She certainly should be here,' He pressed the button again, listened to the chimes, then knocked on the door.

Drake said, 'I can hear something inside, Perry, a dragging sound.'

Mason pressed his ear to the door.

'Sounds like something being moved across the floor,' he said, and banged peremptorily on the door.

From inside the apartment something fell with a thud that jarred the floor, then a woman screamed and the scream was interrupted as though someone had pressed a hand across her lips.

Mason flung himself against the door. The latch clicked, and the door opened a scant three inches to the end of a brass chain safety lock.

From the interior of the apartment a door banged shut.

'Let's go,' Mason said, and slammed his shoulder against the door.

Wood creaked in protest, the chain snapped taut but the door still held.

'Come on,' Mason shouted at Drake, 'all together–both of us now. Let's *GO!*'

The two men hit the door simultaneously. The screws pulled from the safety lock, and the door slammed wide open, banged against a doorstop, then shivered on its hinges.

Mason and Drake stood for a split second in the doorway looking at the scene of confusion which met their eyes.

The apartment consisted of a living room, a bedroom, bath and kitchen. The door to the bedroom stood open so that it was possible to see the drawers which had been pulled from the bureau, the chest of drawers, and the contents dumped helter-skelter over the floor.

In the living room a man lay sprawled on his back, motionless, in a grotesque sprawl, his mouth sagged open.

Sounds came from behind the closed door which evidently led to the kitchen.

Mason pushed past Paul Drake, ran to hurl himself against the kitchen door.

The door gave an inch or two, then closed itself as Mason backed away for another lunge at the door.

'Come on, Paul,' the lawyer shouted, 'get this door open!'

Both men flung their weight against the door. Again the door opened an inch or two and again closed.

'Somebody's braced against the door on the other side,' Drake said. 'Watch out! They may start shooting through the panels.'

'Never mind,' Mason said, 'there's a woman in danger on the other side of that door. Smash it down.'

Drake grabbed him and pulled him to one side. 'Don't be a fool, Perry. I've seen too many of these things. We've trapped a killer in the kitchen. Telephone for the police. Use your head, and above all don't stand in front of those panels. When the killer knows he's trapped, there'll be a fusillade of bullets coming through there.'

Mason stood contemplating the door, said, 'All right, Paul. Telephone the police. I'll take a look at this man and see how long he's been dead.'

The lawyer moved a step or two, then suddenly and unexpectedly hurled himself again at the kitchen door.

Once more the door yielded slightly, then pushed back shut.

Mason said, 'Wait a minute, Paul. There's no one holding this door shut. It's a chair or something propped against it and cushioned on some rubber so it–Come on, give me a hand.'

'Just a minute,' Drake said. 'I've got the police.'

The detective gave the address and number of the apartment, announced a dead man was on the floor, that the murderer or murderers were in the kitchen; that evidently they had a young woman who rented the apartment held as a hostage.

Drake hung up the phone.

Mason picked up a chair, swung it around in a circle and crashed it against the panels of the kitchen door.

The door panels splintered. Mason kicked some of the splinters away with his heel, looked inside the kitchen and said, 'A big kitchen table against the door and mattresses jammed between the wall and the table.'

'They're in the kitchen, I tell you,' Drake said. 'Get away–the police will be here within a matter of seconds.'

Mason swung the chair again, crashed another panel in the door, ripped out the panel with his bare hands, looked through the wrecked door into the kitchen, then suddenly turned and sprinted for the corridor.

'What's the matter?' Drake asked.

'There's a back door,' Mason said. 'It's open.'

The lawyer reached the corridor, rounded a turn, went down an L in the corridor, came to an open door and entered the kitchen. Drake was a few steps behind him.

'Well,' Drake said, 'we certainly fell for that one. It felt just as though someone was holding that door. You can see what happened. They took two mattresses, put one between the table and the door, the other between the table and the electric stove. It would give just an inch or two but not enough to get the door open. It felt as if someone was holding it from the inside.'

Drake ran back to the telephone, again called police, said, 'Get your dispatcher to alert the cars coming in on that murder and kidnaping charge that at least one man and a woman–the woman probably being a hostage–have just made their escape from the apartment house. They may have reached the street but they can't have gone far. The radio car should be on the alert.'

Drake hung up the phone, then went over to where Mason was kneeling by the motionless figure on the floor.

'This guy's still alive,' the lawyer said.

Drake felt for the man's pulse. 'Faint and thready,' he said, 'but it's there. Guess we'd better phone for an ambulance. Oh-oh, look here.'

The detective indicated a small red stain on the front of the man's shirt.

He opened the shirt, pulled down the undershirt and disclosed a small punture in the skin.

'What the deuce?' Drake asked.

'The hole made by a twenty-two caliber bullet,' Mason said. 'Let's be careful not to touch anything, Paul. . . . Get on that phone and tell the police that this man is still alive. Let's see if we can get an ambulance to rush him to the hospital.'

Again Drake went to the phone and put through the call. Then the lawyer and the detective stood for a few moments in the doorway.

'Where did those mattresses come from?' Drake asked.

'Apparently off the twin beds in the bedroom,' Mason said, 'they were taken to the kitchen. Evidently the idea was they would barricade themselves and shoot it out, and they found they could close off the kitchen door and give themselves a chance to slip out into the corridor and down the stairs.'

'You think there were two?'

'There were two mattresses,' Mason said. 'Evidently from the way the bedclothes are arranged, someone simply took hold of the ends of the mattresses and dragged them across the room. There probably wasn't time to make two trips, so there must have been at least two people or perhaps three people, because one of them must have been holding the girl–and that accounts for the scream we heard which was stifled.'

'They had to work fast from the time we first rang the chimes,' Drake said. 'Of course we could hear the sound of people moving. It must have been–'

'It was probably all of fifteen seconds,' Mason said. 'A lot could have been done in fifteen seconds. If that girl had only screamed earlier, we'd have been smashing our way in instead of standing there at the door like a couple of nitwits.'

'And the girl?' Drake asked.

'My client, Dorrie Ambler,' Mason said.

'You wouldn't think they could have gone far,' Drake protested. 'They–'

A voice from the doorway said, 'What's going on here?'

Mason turned to the uniformed officer. 'Evidently there's been a shooting, a kidnaping and burglary. We trapped the people in the kitchen but they barricaded the kitchen door and got out through the service door.'

The officer moved over to the man on the floor, said, 'Looks to me as though he'll be another D.O.A.'

'We have an ambulance coming,' Mason said.

'So I've been advised. You have any description of the people who were in on this caper?'

Mason shook his head, said, 'I notified the police to have the dispatcher–'

'I know, I know,' the officer said. 'We've got four radio cars converging on the district and they're stopping everyone coming out of the apartment house. But it's probably too late to do anything.

'Here's the ambulance now,' he said, as they heard the sound of the siren.

The officer said, 'Okay, you fellows have done everything you can here. Now let's get back out in the corridor where we don't leave any more fingerprints than necessary. Let's try and keep all the evidence from being obliterated.'

Mason and Drake waited in the corridor until stretcher-bearers had taken the man from the room, until police had arrived, and then finally Lt Tragg of Homicide.

'Well, well, well!' Tragg said. 'This is an unusual experience. Usually you're on the other side of the fence, Perry. I understand now you've asked for police co-operation.'

'I sure did,' Mason told him. 'I could now use a little of that police efficiency which has proven so embarrassing in times past.'

'What can you tell us about the case?' Tragg asked.

'Nothing very much, I'm afraid,' Mason said. 'The occupant of this apartment consulted me in connection with a matter that I'm not at liberty to disclose at the moment, but she had reason to believe her personal safety might be jeopardized when she called me this morning.'

'What time?'

'About twenty minutes past ten.'

'How do you fix the time?'

'By other matters and by recollection.'

'What other matters?'

'A court hearing in which I was interested, and which I was having covered.'

'Playing it just a little bit cozy, aren't you, Perry?' Tragg asked.

'I'm trying to do what's best for my client,' Mason said. 'I'm aware of the fact that communications made to the police quite frequently result in newspaper publicity and I'm not at all certain that my client would care to have any publicity concerning those matters. However, she did telephone me this morning and told me that she would like to have me come here at once, that she felt her apartment was being placed under surveillance by people who might have plans for her which she didn't like.'

'And you and Paul Drake here constituted yourselves a bodyguard and came storming out to the scene,' Tragg said. 'Why didn't you telephone the police?'

'I don't think she wanted the police notified.'

'What makes you think so?'

'She could have called them very easily and very handily if she had.'

Tragg said, 'There's a garage which goes with this building and we're going down and take a look in it. I think you and Drake had better come along with us. I don't like to leave you out of my sight.'

'What about the stuff in there?' Mason asked, indicating the apartment.

'All that can wait,' Tragg said. 'Things are being guarded and whatever clues are there will be preserved, but I want to take a look at the garage and see what we find.'

'You won't find anything,' Mason said.

'What makes you think so?'

'Well, I feel that you *probably* won't find anything.'

'You think the young woman was kidnaped in her car?'

'I don't know.'

'But you do think she was kidnaped.'

'I certainly think she was abducted against her will.'

'Well, let's take a look,' Tragg said. 'I have some news for you, Perry.'

'What?'

'The apartments in this building have private garages that are rented with the apartments. Our boys looked in the private garage that goes with this apartment and guess what they found?'

'Not the body of Miss Ambler?' Mason said.

'No, no, no,' Tragg said hastily. 'I didn't want to alarm you, Perry. I was trying to break it to you gently, however. We found something we've been looking for for a few days now.'

'What?'

'We've been looking for a hit-and-run automobile, a light-colored Cadillac, license number WHW 694 that had been stolen from San Francisco on the fifth of September and was involved in a hit-and-run accident here on the sixth of September.'

'You mean that car was in the garage?'

'That's right. Stolen automobile, slight dent in the fender, broken left headlight lens–a perfect match for a jagged bit of broken headlight that was picked up at the scene of the accident. I'd like to have you take a look.'

'Then she was right,' Mason said.

'Who was right?'

'My client.'

'In what?'

'I don't think I can give you all the details at the moment, Tragg, but I may say that the presence of this automobile ties in with the reason she came to see me in the first place.'

'Very, very nice,' Tragg said. 'Now, if you want to help your client and help the police find her before something very serious happens to her, you can tell me a little bit more about just what it was she was worried about.'

'All right, I'll tell you this much,' Mason said. 'She had the distinct feeling that an attempt was going to be made to tie her in with that–Well, she felt it would be with *something* that happened on the sixth of September. She didn't know for sure what it was.'

'And you took it on yourself to find out?'

'I did a little investigating.'

'And learned about the hit-and-run?'

'Yes.'

'And you knew the car that was involved in the hit-and-run was in this garage?'

'I certainly did not,' Mason said, 'and for your information I haven't been an accessory after the fact on any hit-and-run. I haven't been covering up any crime, and that car was put in the garage a few minutes ago as a part of this thing we're investigating.'

An officer came up in the elevator, handed Tragg a folded piece of paper.

Tragg opened it, read the message, folded the paper again, put it in his pocket, glanced at Perry Mason and said, 'Well, you can see what it feels like to be on the other side now, Perry.'

'What do you mean?'

'The man who was removed in the ambulance was dead on arrival, so now we have a homicide.'

'Let's hope we don't have two of them,' Mason said.

Tragg led the way to the elevator, down to the basement floor, out into a parking place in the rear where there were rows of numbered garages.

'This way,' Tragg said, leading the way across the parking place to the garage which bore the figure 907 above it.

Tragg took a key from his pocket, unlocked a padlock, said, 'Now, I'm going to have to ask you to keep your hands in your pockets, not to touch a thing. I just want you to take a look, that's all.'

Mason pushed his hands in his pockets. After a moment Drake followed suit.

Tragg switched on a light.

'There's the car,' he said.

Mason looked at the big light-coloured automobile.

'What about it?' he asked.

Tragg said, 'Take a look at the right-hand fender, Perry. Stand over this way a little bit–a little farther–right here. See it? See that spider's web and the flies in it? That spider web goes from the emblem on the car to the edge of the little tool bench in the garage, and notice the flies that are in it. That spider web has been there for some time.'

Tragg, watching Mason's face, said, 'I've been in this business, Perry, long enough to know that you can't trust a woman when she's telling a story, particularly if she's had an opportunity to rehearse that story.

'If Dorrie Ambler is your client, she may or may not have been abducted. There was a murdered man on the floor of her apartment. She may or may not have been responsible for that, but there's an automobile in her garage and she sure as hell is responsible for that automobile. That's a stolen automobile in the first place, and in the second place it was involved in a hit-and-run.

'Now then, Perry, I'm going to ask you just how much do you know about Dorrie Ambler?'

Mason was thoughtfully silent for a moment, then said, 'Not too much.'

'Everything based on what she's told you?'

'Everything based on what she's told me,' Mason said.

'All right,' Tragg said. 'I'm not going to tell anybody that I showed you that spider web. We're going to have it sprayed and photographed. It'll be a big point in the district attorney's case whenever the case comes up.

'I've shown you that on my own responsibility. I want to make a trade with you. That's information that's vital to your client. I think you have some information that's vital to me.'

Tragg ushered Mason and the detective from the garage, locked the door behind them.

'How about it, Perry?' he asked.

Mason said, 'Tragg, I'd like to co-operate with you but I'm going to have to think things over a bit and I'm going to have to do some checking on certain information.'

'And after you've checked on it you'll give us everything you can?'

'Everything I feel that I can conscientiously give you and which will be to the advantage of my client, I will.'

'All right,' Tragg said, 'if that's the best you can do, that's what we'll have to take.'

'And,' Mason said, 'I'd like to ask one thing of you.'

'What?'

'As soon as you get in touch with my client, will you let me know?'

'When we get in touch with your client, Mason, we'll be questioning her in regard to a murder and a hit-and-run and we'll tell her she has an opportunity to consult counsel if she desires, but we're going to do everything in the world to make her talk. You know that.'

'Yes,' Mason said, 'I know that.'

6

Mason turned to Drake as soon as Tragg was out of earshot and said, 'Get your office, Paul. I want Minerva Minden. I want to talk with her before the police do.'

'Okay,' Drake said, 'we'd better go down the street a ways before we do any telephoning.'

Mason said, 'She may still be at the courthouse.'

'Could be,' Drake said, 'but I have an idea her lawyer whisked her out of circulation just as rapidly as possible.

'You know and I know that a thousand-dollar fine means no more to Minerva Minden than the nickel she dropped into the parking meter. The tongue-lashing given her by the judge was just so much sound as far as Minny Minden was concerned. That girl has been in enough scrapes to learn how to roll with the punch. She listened demurely to the judge's lecture, paid the thousand dollars with due humility and then looked for some place where she could open a bottle of champagne and celebrate her victory.

'Judges don't like to have persons who have been sentenced by them start celebrating. Attorneys know that, and the attorney is thinking not only about this case but about Minny's next one and about the next one before that same judge, so my best guess is he's told her to get out of circulation, stay away from the public, see no one and refuse to come to the telephone.'

'That,' Mason said, 'makes sense. That's what I'd do under the circumstances if she were my client, Paul. However, let's go phone your office and see what the reports are.'

They drove half a dozen blocks before Mason found a gasoline station with a telephone booth which seemed sufficiently removed from the scene of operations.

Drake put through the call, came back and said, 'Everything checks, Perry.

She was whisked away from the courthouse by her attorney. She went into the telephone booth to make some jubilee calls, but he caught up with her after the first two and dragged her out of there. He put her in his car and personally drove her to Montrose. Presumably they're both there now.'

'Who's her attorney?' Mason asked.

'Herbert Knox,' Drake said, 'of Gambit, Knox & Belam.'

'Old Herb Knox, huh?' Mason said. 'He's a smooth article. Tell me, did he act as her attorney when she received her inheritance?'

'I don't know,' Drake said, 'but I don't think so. As I remember it she's done a little shopping around with attorneys.'

'Well, she couldn't have had a better one than Herbert Knox for this particular job,' Mason said. 'He's smooth and suave and a wily veteran of the courtroom.'

'All right, what do we do now?' Drake said.

Mason thought for a moment, then said, 'We get busy on the telephone. Let's call Minerva at her place in Montrose and see what we can get.'

'It'll be an unlisted number,' Drake said.

Mason shook his head. 'They'll have two or three telephones, Paul. Two of them will be unlisted but there'll be one telephone that's listed. That will be answered by a secretary or a business manager but we can at least use it to get a message through to her.'

'Will getting a message through do any good?' Drake asked.

'I think it will,' Mason said. 'Think I can convey a message which will make her sit up and take notice.'

Drake, who had been looking through the telephone book, said, 'Okay, here's the number. You were right. There's a listed telephone.'

Mason put through the call and heard a well-modulated feminine voice saying, 'May I help you? This is the Minden residence.'

'This is Perry Mason, the attorney,' Mason said. 'I want to talk with Miss Minden.'

'I'm afraid that's impossible, Mr Mason, but I might be able to take a message.'

'Tell her,' Mason said, 'that I know who fired the shots at the airport and that I want to talk with her about it.'

'I'll convey that message to her. And where can I communicate with you, Mr Mason?'

'I'll hang on the line.'

'I'm sorry, that's not possible. I can't reach her that soon.'

'Why not? Isn't she there?' Mason asked.

'I'll call you later at your office. Thank you,' the feminine voice said, and the connection clicked.

Mason said, Paul, there's just a chance we can get out to her place at Montrose before Herbert Knox leaves. If I can talk with her, I may be able to clear up certain things and we may be able to get some information that will save Dorrie Ambler's life. I don't want to tell the police all that I know but I have a feeling that–Come on, Paul, let's go.'

'On our way,' Drake said, 'but I'll bet you old Herb Knox won't let you get within a mile of his client.'

'Don't bet too much,' Mason said. 'You may lose.'

They made good time over the freeways which at this time of the day were free of congestion and handling a stream of swiftly moving traffic which was a trickle compared to the masses of cars that would crowd through during the afternoon rush hour.

The Montrose estate of Minerva Minden was an imposing edifice on a hill, and Mason, driving up the sweeping graveled driveway through the beautifully landscaped grounds, swung his car into a parking place which contained an even dozen automobiles.

'Looks like there might be a lot of other people with the same idea,' Drake said.

'Probably some of them are reporters, some are employees,' Mason said. 'You don't know what kind of a car Herbert Knox drives, do you, Paul?'

'No.'

'I have an idea one of these cars may be his. I hope so.'

The men parked their car, went up the stairs to the broad porch. Mason rang the bell.

A burly individual who looked more like a bodyguard than a butler opened the door and stood silent.

'I would like to see Minerva Minden's confidential secretary or business manager,' Mason said. 'I am Perry Mason and I'm calling in connection with an emergency.'

The man said, 'Wait there,' turned to a telephone in the wall and relayed a message into a mouthpiece so constructed that it was impossible for bystanders to hear what was being said.

After a moment, he said, 'Who's the gentleman with you?'

'Paul Drake, a private detective.'

Again the man turned to the phone, then after a moment hung up and said, 'This way, please.'

Mason and Drake entered a reception hallway, and followed the butler into a room which had at one time evidently been a library. Now it was fixed up as a sort of intermediate waiting room with a table, rugs, indirect lighting, deep leather-cushioned chairs and an atmosphere which combined that of a luxurious room in an expensive residence with that of an office where people waited.

'Be seated, please,' the butler said, and left the room.

A moment later a tall, keen-eyed woman in her late forties or early fifties entered the room and strode directly across to Mason. 'How do you do, Mr Mason,' she said. 'I am Henrietta Hull, Miss Minden's confidential secretary and manager; and this, I presume, is Mr Paul Drake, the detective.'

She moved easily to a chair, regarded the men with keen, appraising eyes for a moment, then said, 'You wished to see me, Mr Mason?'

'Actually,' Mason said, 'I want to see Minerva Minden.'

'Many people do,' Henrietta Hull said.

Mason smiled. 'Is it Miss Hull or Mrs Hull?'

'It's Henrietta Hull,' the woman said, smiling, 'but if you *need* any other handle, it's Mrs.'

'Would it be possible for us to see Miss Minden?'

'It would be utterly impossible, Mr Mason. Nothing, absolutely nothing, that you could say would gain you an audience. In fact I may go a little further and state that when Miss Minden's attorney learned that you were seeking an interview, he gave Miss Minden particular instructions that under no circumstances was she to talk with you.'

'I'll talk with him if I have to,' Mason said.

Henrietta Hull shook her head. 'That would do no good, Mr Mason. Mr Knox is not Miss Minden's regular attorney.'

'Who is?' Mason asked.

'There isn't any,' Henrietta Hull said. 'Miss Minden retains counsel as she needs them. She tries to get the very best in the field. For a matter of this sort Herbert Knox was considered the best available attorney.'

'May I ask why?' Mason asked.

Her eyes softened somewhat. 'You're asking because you feel professionally slighted?' she asked.

'No,' Mason said, 'I was just wondering. You seemed so positive. I gathered that you keep some sort of list of attorneys.'

'We do, Mr Mason,' she said, 'and you might be interested to know that you head the list of attorneys available in murder cases or serious felonies. There are other attorneys who are selected for their ability in connection with automobile cases and traffic violations. Mr Knox was selected in this case because of various qualifications, not the least of which is that he is frequently a golfing partner of the judge before whom the case was tried.'

'And how,' Mason asked, 'did you know the particular judge who would be assigned to the case?'

She smiled and said, 'After all, Mr Mason, you had a matter you wanted to take up with Miss Minden.'

'All right,' Mason said, 'I'll put my cards on the table. Miss Minden has hired a double.'

'Indeed?' Henrietta Hull said, her eyebrows raising. 'You're making a positive statement, Mr Mason?'

'I'm making a positive statement.'

'All right,' Henrietta Hull said. 'Your statement is that she hired a double. Now what?'

Mason said, 'The disturbance at the airport was shrewdly engineered to bring out the fact that Miss Minden had a double, but Miss Minden did some very fast and some very shrewd thinking and decided it would be better for her to take the responsibility of firing the shots than to expose the fact that she had hired a double.'

'This is rather a startling statement, Mr Mason. I trust you have evidence to back up your statement.'

'I am making a statement,' Mason said. 'I would like to have you convey it to Minerva Minden. I would also like to have you tell her that I can be rather a ruthless antagonist, that I don't know *all* the ramifications of the game she is playing but that I rather suspect the ad by which this double was chosen–or rather the ad which served as bait to bring this double into the position that had been selected for her–was shrewdly designed as the elaborate bait in a deadly trap.

'I don't know whether Minerva Minden knew that this double of hers was going to be placed in a position of danger or not, but a situation has now developed where that young woman is in very great danger. I have been invited to tell the police what I know. I don't want to release a story which may result in a lot of newspaper notoriety for Miss Minden.'

Henrietta Hull smiled and said, 'Miss Minden is not a stranger to newspaper notoriety.'

'You mean she enjoys it?' Mason asked sharply.

'I mean that she is not a stranger to it.'

'All right,' Mason said. 'I think I've told you enough so that you can appreciate my position and the fact it is imperative I have an immediate interview with Miss Minden.'

'An immediate interview is out of the question,' Henrietta Hull said. 'But, as I told you over the telephone, Mr Mason, I will be glad to convey a message and to call you at your office.'

'When?' Mason asked.

'As soon as necessary arrangements have been made, or perhaps I should say as soon as necessary precautions have been taken.'

'All right,' Mason said. 'I just want to point out to you that traffic violations are one thing, firing blank cartridges is another thing. But kidnaping is a felony that carries very serious penalties, and murder is punishable by death.'

'Thank you, Mr Mason,' Henrietta Hull said. 'Of course you're an attorney, but as a business woman I am familiar with certain phases of the law.'

She arose abruptly, signifying that the interview was terminated. She gave Mason her hand and the benefit of a long, steady appraisal. Then she turned to Paul Drake. 'I'm very pleased to have met you, Mr Drake. I may also advise you that your agency is at the top of the list which we maintain in cases where a highly ethical agency is required.'

Drake smiled. 'Meaning that you have a list of un-ethical agencies?'

'We have very complete lists,' she said enigmatically. Then again turned to Mason. 'And don't forget, Mr Mason, that your name is absolute tops in cases carrying a serious penalty.'

'Such as murder?' Mason asked.

'Such as murder,' Henrietta Hull said, and then after a moment added, 'and such as kidnaping or abduction.'

7

Mason fitted his latchkey to the door of his private office, entered and was confronted by Della Street, who said, 'Why secretaries get gray. . . . Do you realize, Mr Perry Mason, that you have two appointments I've had to stall off and if it hadn't been for the noon hour intervening you'd have had more. I told them that you were out at a luncheon club making a speech.'

'You're getting to be a pretty good extemporaneous prevaricator,' Mason said.

She smiled. 'Freely translated that means I'm a graceful, gifted, talented offhand liar. . . . You see what you've done to my morals, Mr Perry Mason.'

'The constant dripping of water,' Mason said, 'can wear away the toughest stone.'

'We were talking about morals, I believe. I suppose there was some major emergency.'

'There was a very great major emergency.'

'Have you had lunch?'

'No.'

'You have some appointments that I've been stalling off. I told them you'd see them right after lunch and then told them that you were delayed getting back from lunch.'

'They're in the outer office?'

'Yes.'

'What else?' Mason asked.

'I believe you are acquainted with a very firm and dignified young woman named Henrietta Hull who is the secretary to Minerva Minden?'

'She isn't young,' Mason said. 'She has a sense of humor. She puts up a good front of being firm. What about her?'

'She called up, said that she was to leave a message for you, that she was sorry that there was no possibility of your seeing Miss Minden; that you might care to know, however, that Dorrie Ambler had been followed by a detective agency employed by Miss Minden ever since Miss Ambler had attempted to blackmail Miss Minden into making a property settlement on her.'

'What else?' Mason asked.

'That was all,' she said. 'She told me that perhaps you should have that information.'

'I'll be damned,' Mason said.

'And,' Della Street went on, 'Jerry Nelson, Drake's operative, said he missed you at the place he was told to report. He said Drake was out so he came down here to tell me that there's a difference in coloring between Dorrie Ambler and Minerva Minden but aside from that the resemblance is startling. He said it might be very easy for an eyewitness to confuse one with the other.'

'But there was a discernible difference?'

'Oh, yes. He felt *he* could tell one from the other.'

'By what means? Just what is the difference?'

'Well, he couldn't put his finger on it. He said that it's something–He thinks the hair may be a little different and something about the complexion, but he says there's a resemblance that–Well, the only way that he could describe it was to say it was startling.'

Mason's unlisted phone rang.

'That's Paul Drake,' Mason said, and picked up the receiver.

Paul Drake's voice came over the line. 'I'm sorry to bring you bad news, Perry.'

'What?'

'We were followed out to Minerva Minden's.'

'How do you know?'

'I found out when I was parking the car.'

'How do you mean?'

'They have a plug they can slip on the end of the exhaust pipe. It releases drops of fluorescent liquid at regular intervals. By wearing a certain type of spectacles with lenses that are tinted so it can make these drops visible, they can follow a car even if they're ten or fifteen minutes behind it.'

'And you know your car was fixed?'

'It was fixed all right.'

'But you don't know that they followed us.'

'I don't *know* they followed us,' Drake said, 'but knowing Tragg as I do, I know he wasn't wasting the taxpayers' equipment just for the sake of the exercise.'

'Thanks, Paul,' Mason said. 'I have an office full of irate clients and I've got to get down to a little routine work, but you get busy and see what you can find out.'

'We're already busy,' Drake said. 'I've got tentacles stretching out in every direction, trying to cover everything I can.'

'What about the kidnaping, Paul?'

'I don't know. The police are playing it awfully close to their chest. Of course, under the circumstances you can realize that they wouldn't take us into their confidence, and it's probably good business not to tell the newspapers too much about it, but they're certainly playing it cozy.'

'All right,' Mason said, 'you get busy, Paul, and find out everything you can. Try particularly to find out something about the background of Dorrie Ambler.'

'You don't think you should tell the police what you know?'

'I'm hanged if I know, Paul,' Mason said. 'I think probably I will, but I want to think it over a bit. I'll get rid of a few pressing appointments and then be in touch with you.'

'Okay,' Drake said, 'I'll be on the job.'

Mason said to Della Street, 'I guess I'll copy Paul Drake's diet, Della. Get me a couple of sandwiches from the restaurant around the corner and put some coffee on. I'll start seeing these clients who have been waiting.'

'Don't you want to wait and eat afterwards?' Della Street asked.

'Frankly I do,' Mason said, 'but some of those clients are a little angry. They feel they've been cooling their heels in my outer office while I've been out to lunch, enjoying myself.

'The psychological effect of having a hamburger sandwich in one hand and a lawbook in the other is remarkably soothing to the irate client. I'll tell them I had such an important matter come up I had to break my luncheon engagement.'

'In other words,' Della Street said, 'these sandwiches are to be props.'

'Props with a use,' Mason said. 'Send in the first client, Della, and go get the sandwiches as soon as he comes in.'

She glided out into the outer office and a moment later Mason's first client came stalking into the room.

Mason said, 'I'm sorry I had to keep you waiting. I was out on a major emergency. I'm going to impose on your good nature by grabbing a sandwich while we talk. I'm famished.

'Della, hand me that file with the memorandum on this case and get a couple of hamburgers, if you will.'

'Right away,' Della Street promised, handing him the filing jacket.

As Mason opened the folder the expression on the client's face softened.

Mason hurried through the interview and four more, nibbling at sandwiches and drinking coffee.

He was interviewing his last client when the telephone rang three short bells signaling that the switchboard operator was holding an important call.

Della Street picked up the telephone, said, 'Yes, Gertie,' then turned to Mason. 'Lieutenant Tragg,' she said.

'In the office?' Mason asked.

'No, on the line.'

Mason picked up the telephone, said, 'Yes, Lieutenant, this is Mason.'

Tragg said, 'I've given you some breaks today, Mason. I'm going to give you some more.'

'Yes,' Mason said dryly. 'I hope the substance you put on the exhaust of my automobile doesn't interfere with the operating efficiency.'

'Oh, not at all, not at all,' Tragg said.

'I presume my car was followed,' Mason observed.

'Oh, of course,' Tragg said casually. 'You wouldn't expect us to have you right in our hands, so to speak, and then let you slip through our fingers. We know all about your trip out to Miss Minden's at Montrose.'

'I presume,' Mason said, 'you're going to extend some more favors and I'll find that they were simply bait for a very elaborate trap.'

'Oh, but such beautiful bait,' Tragg said. 'This is something that you absolutely can't resist, Perry.'

'What is it?' Mason asked.

Tragg said, 'I felt that you couldn't make time enough to get here so I'm sending an officer. He should be in your office within a matter of seconds. If you and Della Street will come up here–just walk right into my office in case I shouldn't be there. If I'm not in, I won't keep you waiting very long. I'll really do you a favor.'

'Bait?' Mason asked.

'Beautiful bait,' Tragg said, and hung up.

Again the phone rang, a series of short, sharp rings. Della Street picked it up, said, 'Yes, Gertie?' Then turned to Mason. 'A uniformed officer is in the outer office. He has a police car down in front with the motor running and instructions to get both of us to Headquarters just as fast as possible.'

Mason's client jumped up. 'Well, I think we've covered most of the points, Counselor. Thank you. I'll get in touch with you.'

Mason said, 'Sorry,' pushed his chair, cupped his hand over Della Street's elbow, said, 'Come on, Della, Let's go.'

'You think it's that important?' Della Street asked.

Mason said, 'At this stage of the case I welcome any new developments, either pro or con. . . . Remember, Della, no talking in the police car. Those officers sometimes have big ears.'

Della Street nodded.

They hurried out to the outer office. The waiting officer said, 'I'm under instructions to get you to Headquarters just as fast as possible without using red light or siren, but hogging traffic all the way.'

'All right,' Mason told him, 'let's hog traffic.'

They hurried to the elevator. The officer escorted them to a curb where another officer was sitting behind the wheel of a police automobile, the motor running.

Perry Mason held the rear door open for Della Street, assisted her in, jumped in beside her and almost immediately the car whipped out into traffic.

'Good heavens,' Della Street said under her breath as they went through the first intersection.

'It's their business,' Mason told her reassuringly. 'They drive in traffic all the time and they're in a hurry.'

'I'll say they're in a hurry,' Della Street said.

The car wove its way through traffic, crowded signals; twice the driver turned on the red light. Once he gave a light tap on the button of the siren. Aside from that they used no official prerogatives except the skill born of long practice and a deft, daring technique.

There had been no need for Mason's admonition about conversation. The occupants of the automobile had been far too busy to engage in any small talk. As the car glided in to the reserved parking place at Police Headquarters, the driver said, 'Just take that elevator to the third floor. Tragg's office.'

'I know,' Mason said.

The elevator operator was waiting for them. As they entered, the door was slammed shut and they were taken directly to the third floor without intermediate stops.

Mason exchanged a meaningful glance with Della Street.

As the operator came to a stop they left the elevator, crossed the corridor and opened the door to Tragg's office.

A uniformed officer sitting at the desk jerked his thumb toward the inner office. 'Go right on in,' he said.

'Tragg there?' Mason asked.

'He said for you to go in,' the officer said.

Mason crossed over to the door, held it open for Della Street, then followed her into the room and came to an abrupt stop.

'Good heavens, Miss Ambler,' he said, 'you certainly had me worried. Can you tell me what happened to–'

Della Street tugged at Mason's coat.

The young woman who sat in the chair on the far side of Lt Tragg's desk swept Mason with cool, appraising eyes, then said in a deep, throaty voice, 'Mr Mason, I presume, and I suppose this young woman with you is your secretary I've heard so much about?'

Mason bowed. 'Miss Della Street.'

'I'm Minerva Minden,' she said. 'You've been trying to see me and I didn't want to see you. I didn't know that you had enough pull with the police department to arrange an interview under circumstances of this sort.'

'I didn't either,' Mason said.

'However,' she said, 'the results seem to speak for themselves.'

Mason said, 'Actually, Miss Minden, I didn't have any idea that *you* would be here. Lieutenant Tragg called me and asked me to come to his office. He said that if he wasn't in we were to go to the private office and wait. I assume that he intends to interview us together.'

'I would assume so,' she said, in the same low, throaty voice.

'All right,' Mason said, turning to Della Street, 'is this the woman who was in our office, Della?'

Della Street shook her head. 'There are some things that only a woman would notice,' she said, 'but it's not the same one.'

'All right,' Mason said, turning to Minerva Minden, 'but there's a startling resemblance.'

'I am quite familiar with the resemblance,' she said. 'In case you're interested, Mr Mason, it has been used to try and blackmail me.'

'What do you mean?'

'I mean that Dorrie Ambler feels that she is related to the relative from whom I received a large inheritance. She has been importuning me to make her a very substantial cash settlement and when I told her I wouldn't do anything of the sort, she threatened to put me in such a position that I'd find myself on the defensive and would be only too glad to–as she put it–pay through the nose in order to get out.'

'You've seen her?' Mason asked.

'I haven't met her personally but I've talked with her on the telephone and I have–Well, frankly, I've had detectives on her trail.'

'For how long?'

'I don't think I care to answer that question, Mr Mason.'

'All right,' Mason said, 'that's not the story I heard.'

'I'm satisfied it isn't,' she said. 'I'm satisfied that Dorrie Ambler, who apparently is a remarkably intelligent and ingenious young woman, and who is being master-minded by a very clever manager, has arranged a series of circumstances so that she would have a very convincing background against which to reassert her claims.

'I may tell you, Mr Mason, that that stunt she pulled following me to the airport, of getting clothes that were the exact duplicates of the clothes I had, of waiting until I had gone to the rest room, then firing a revolver loaded with blank cartridges and dashing into the rest room, jumping into the shower compartment and closing the door, was a remarkably ingenious bit of work.

'If I hadn't kept my head I would have found myself in quite a sorry situation.'

'Just how?' Mason asked.

'Well, naturally,' Minerva Minden said, 'being in a cubicle behind a closed door I wasn't entirely conversant with what had happened. However, when I went out and was immediately identified by bystanders as the woman who had caused the commotion, I did some mightly quick thinking and realized what must have happened.'

'And so?' Mason asked.

'So,' she said, 'I took it in my stride. Instead of insisting that there was a mistake and getting the officers to have a policewoman search the rest room, and have Dorrie Ambler claim, when she was brought out, that *I* was the one who had fired shots, thus giving the newspapers a field day; and instead of giving Dorrie Ambler the chance to insist in public that our rather striking resemblance was due to common ancestors, I simply accepted the responsibility and permitted myself to be taken to the station. There I was booked on charges of disturbing the peace and discharging a firearm within the city limits and in a public place.'

'You're lucky that's all of the charges that were made against you,' Mason said.

'Yes,' she said. 'Dorrie was considerate there. I misunderstood the witnesses for a moment, or rather I think they all misunderstood Dorrie. She evidently said "This is *not* a stick-up," but when the witnesses identified me, two of them said that I had brandished a gun and said "This *is* a stick-up" and I didn't deny it until afterwards, when I had my hearing in court this morning. By that time my attorney had unearthed witnesses who had heard what was said and remembered it accurately. I think that was one of the big facts in my favor.'

Mason said, 'I'm going to put it right up to you fairly and frankly: Did you put an ad in the paper asking for a young woman who–'

'Oh, bosh and nonsense, Mr Mason,' she said. 'Don't be a sap. Dorrie Ambler put that ad in the paper herself. Then she went out and got a detective agency to front the case. She would give them instructions over the telephone at an unlisted number and had everything all arranged so that quite naturally she would be the one who was selected for the job. It was an elaborate job of window-dressing.'

'And the detective agency will then defeat it all by showing that she was the person who was back of it all?'

'The detective agency is not in a position to do any such thing,' she said. 'I've tried to uncover it without any success. The detective agency simply knows that they were hired on a cash basis to screen applicants; that they were given photographs and told that whenever any woman bore a really striking resemblance to those photographs she was to be tentatively hired.'

'And the photographs were of you?' Mason asked.

'The photographs were *not* of me,' she said, 'although they might well have been. Actually, and that is where Dorrie Ambler made a fatal mistake, she couldn't get photographs of me so she had to use some of herself. While I have had many news photographs taken, she wanted portrait photos of front and side views and she had to have them in a hurry.

'It would have attracted attention if a woman who looked so much like me had either solicited photographs of me or tried to get someone else to procure them. It was much more simple to go to a photographer and have the shots taken that she wanted.'

'All of this must have taken a certain amount of money,' Mason said.

'Of course it took a certain amount of money,' she said. 'I don't know who's financing her, but I have an idea it's some very crooked, very clever Las Vegas businessman.

'And furthermore, I don't think Dorrie Ambler entered the picture under her own power, so to speak. I think that this confidence man or promoter got to nosing around and found her in Nevada and got her to come here and take this apartment, to settle down here just as if she were an average young woman planning on living here. Then instead of coming out and trying to make a claim against the money I had inherited and putting herself in a position where *she'd* be carrying the burden of proof, they were smart enough to think up a whole series of situations in which I would be the one that was on the defensive and it would suit the convenience of the newspapers to play up the startling resemblance. That would get her case against me off to a flying start.'

'The hit-and-run?' Mason asked.

'I'm not prepared to say about the hit-and-run,' Minerva said. 'That may have been accidental. But she *was* teamed up with crooks. You know that because the car was stolen.'

'It was her idea,' Mason said dryly, 'that perhaps *you'd* been the one to hit this man in the hit-and-run accident and had used her as a cover-up.'

Minerva Minden laughed. 'Now, isn't that a likely story,' she said. 'Don't tell me that *you* fell for that one, Mr Mason.

'The pay-off, of course, is that the accident took place in a stolen car. I am not the possessor of a completely untarnished reputation, Mr Mason. My driving record is fairly well studded with citations and I would dislike to have to acknowledge another traffic accident. However, I think you will agree that the idea that I would be driving a stolen car is just a little farfetched.

'And,' Minerva Minden went on, 'the man who was found fatally wounded in Dorrie Ambler's apartment was the detective who had assisted her in putting her swindle across, a member of the firm of Billings and Compton. The dead man was Marvin Billings. His death will seal his lips so he can't testify against her. I make no accusations, but you must admit his death is quite fortunate.

'I'm not any plaster saint. I've been in lots of scrapes in my time and to be perfectly frank with you I expect to be in a lot more before I retire from active life. I want life, I want adventure, I want action, and I intend to get all three.

'I'm given to the unconventional in every sense of the word and in all of its various forms, but I am not given to stealing, I am not given to murder, and I don't have to use stolen cars to take me where I'm going.'

Mason said, 'Have you ever been operated on for appendicitis, Miss Minden?'

'Appendicitis? No, why?'

'This is very unconventional,' the lawyer said, 'but it happens to be important. Would you mind turning your back to me and letting Miss Street look to see if there's a scar on your abdomen?'

The girl laughed. 'Why must I be so modest? Good heavens, you'd see that much of me in a Bikini. If you think it's important, take a look.'

She got up, faced them, pulled up her blouse, loosened her skirt, slipped it far down and stretched out the skin over the place where a scar would have been.

'Satisfied?' she asked. 'Feel the skin if you want to.'

Before Mason could answer, the door from the outer office burst open explosively, and Lt Tragg hurried into the room.

'Well, well, well,' he said, 'what is this–a strip tease?'

Minerva Minden said, 'Mr Mason wanted to check to see if I had had an operation for appendicitis.'

'I see,' Tragg said. 'Now that we're all here I'll ask your pardon for having kept you waiting. I want to ask a few questions.'

'What questions do *you* want to ask?' Minerva Minden inquired, adjusting her clothing.

'In *your* case,' Lt Tragg said, 'quite frankly, Miss Minden, I wanted to ask questions about a murder and you may be the prime suspect. I feel I should warn you.'

'If you want to interrogate me about a murder case,' she said, 'and there's any possibility that I am going to be a suspect, I will have to ask you to interrogate my attorney and get your facts from him.'

'And your attorney?' Tragg asked.

Minerva Minden turned to Perry Mason with a slow smile. 'My attorney,' she said, 'is Mr Perry Mason. I believe you were told by my secretary and manager, Henrietta Hull, Mr Mason, that you were at the top of the list as potential counsel in the event of any serious charge being made against me.'

Tragg turned to Mason. 'You're representing her, Mason?'

'I am not,' Mason said vehemently. 'I'm representing Dorrie Ambler, and there's a very distinct conflict of interest. I couldn't represent Minerva Minden even if I wanted to.'

'Now, that's not a very chivalrous attitude, Mr Mason,' Minerva Minden said. 'What's more, it's not a very good business attitude. I am perfectly willing to let you represent Miss Ambler in any way that you want to in connection with any claims to an inheritance, but I am quite certain Lieutenant Tragg will assure you that in case any murder charges are to be pressed against me–'

'I didn't say they *were*,' Tragg said. 'I said that I wanted to interrogate you in connection with a murder and that you *may* be a suspect.'

'Whose murder?'

'The murder of Marvin Billings,' Lt Tragg said. 'His partner says Billings was working for you at the time of his death, that he was going to interview

Miss Dorrie Ambler at your request.'

'And so I killed him–to keep him from following instructions?'

'I don't know,' Tragg said. 'I only wanted to question you.'

'You'll have to see my lawyer,' she said. 'I'm not going to talk with you until I've talked with him.'

Tragg asked, 'Do you know Marvin Billings, the man who was found in a dying condition on the floor of Miss Ambler's apartment?'

'The apartment is one that I know nothing about,' she said firmly. 'And I have never met Marvin Billings.'

'The landlady identified your picture as being the one who lived in the apartment under the name of Dorrie Ambler, and she picked you out of a line-up.'

Minerva Minden said casually, 'Well, before she identifies me as Dorrie Ambler, you'd better have Dorrie Ambler in the line-up and *then* see who she identifies.'

'I know, I know,' Lt Tragg said. 'We're investigating, that's all. We're just trying to get the situation unscrambled.'

'Well, if you ask me,' Minerva Minden said, 'this girl is a complete phony, a fraud, an adventuress who has been trying to lay a foundation to present a claim against my uncle's estate.

'If she were on the square, she'd have come right out in so many words and made her claim. She'd have gone to the probate court and said she was a relative of Harper Minden and therefore was entitled to a share of the estate.'

'Evidently,' Tragg said, 'she knew nothing about her rights as a potential heiress.'

'Phooey!' Miss Minden said. 'She's already tried to shake me down for a settlement. That's what started this whole thing. Then she got plastered, clobbered a pedestrian and suddenly decided she'd kill two birds with one stone, getting me involved in a lot of publicity and–I'm not going to sit here and argue. I'm going to get up and walk out of here. If you want me for anything in the future, you can come out with a warrant for my arrest, and not ask for *me* to please come to Headquarters to help clarify things–and then run Perry Mason in on me.

'Now then, is this interview going to be kept confidential or not?'

'I'm afraid,' Lt Tragg said, 'that in matters which are subject to police investigation, we are not in a position to withhold facts from the public.'

'And I presume,' Mason said, 'that you wanted to get a spontaneous identification from Miss Street and from me and for that reason you carefully arranged this so that we would walk in on Miss Minden and you would be in a position to hear our remarks.'

'He wasn't in the room at the time,' Minerva Minden said.

Mason smiled. 'I'm afraid you underestimate the police intelligence, Miss Minden. I take it, Lieutenant, that the room is bugged.'

'Sure, it's bugged,' Tragg said. 'And you're quite right. I wanted to see your reaction when you first entered the room. Now, I take it there is a very strong resemblance between these two women, Dorrie Ambler and Minerva Minden.'

'I don't think that I care to add anything to my comments at this time,' Mason said. 'I somewhat resent being dragged down here to make an identification for you.'

'Oh, you weren't dragged,' Tragg said. 'You came of your own volition and you got something that you wanted very much–an opportunity to talk with Minerva Minden.'

'In other words you baited the trap with something that you thought I would fall for,' Mason said.

'Of course, of course.' Tragg beamed. 'We wouldn't bait a mouse trap with catnip and we wouldn't bait a cat trap with cheese.'

'*I* feel that *I* have been betrayed all the way along the line and that the police have abused their power,' Minerva Minden said. She turned to Perry Mason. 'I wish you *would* agree to represent me, Mr Mason–not on anything in connection with the estate, just this.'

Mason shook his head. 'I'm afraid there would be a conflict of interests.'

'Are you going to represent Dorre Ambler in a claim against the estate?'

'I don't know. I haven't talked with her about that.'

Lt Tragg said, 'Of course, Perry, I can begin to put two and two together now and I'd like very, very much to have you tell us the conversation you had with Miss Ambler. I think it might give us some clues–And what about the appendicitis scar?'

'I'm sorry,' Mason said firmly, 'I don't feel that I'm in a position to make any disclosures.'

'All right,' Tragg said, smiling, 'school's dismissed, Police cars are waiting to return you to your respective destinations.'

Minerva Minden stalked toward the door, suddenly whirled, came over to Perry Mason and extended her hand. 'I like you,' she said.

'Thank you,' Mason said.

'You won't reconsider about being my attorney?'

'No.'

Minerva smiled at Della Street, turned her back on Tragg and left the room.

'That was rather rough,' Mason said to Tragg.

'It was, for a fact,' Tragg said, 'but I had to find out for sure about the extent of the resemblance.'

'You're now satisfied that there's a strong resemblance?' Mason asked.

'I'm satisfied it's a striking resemblance,' Tragg said. 'I notice Della Street was watching her like a hawk. What did you think, Della?'

'Her hair isn't quite the same colour,' Della Street said. 'She doesn't have the same make-up, the tinting of the nails is different and–oh, there are quite a few little things that a woman would notice, but I can tell you the physical resemblance is really startling. The voices are the big difference. Dorrie Ambler talks rapidly and in a high-pitched voice.'

'Well, thanks a lot,' Tragg said. 'I had to do it that way, Perry, because you wouldn't co-operate otherwise. The car will take you back to your office.'

8

Mason and Della dropped in at Paul Drake's office on the way back from Police Headquarters.

'Got a crying towel handy, Paul?' Mason asked.

'I always keep one in the upper right-hand drawer,' Drake said.

'Get it out,' Mason told him, 'because you've lost a lucrative job.'

'How come?'

'The police have moved in. I think the FBI may move in. They're considering the possibility of a kidnaping but the local police are still about two-thirds sold on the idea that Dorrie Ambler killed the detective who was trying to shake her down and then slipped out.'

Drake said, 'That sounds logical enough.'

'Or she could have been defending herself when they tried to abduct her,' Mason said.

'And killed a blackmailing detective?' Drake asked.

'Stranger things *have* happened,' Mason pointed out.

'Name one,' Drake said.

Mason grinned. He said, 'For your information, I've now talked with Minerva Minden.'

'She finally consented to see you?' Drake asked.

'Lieutenant Tragg arranged a trap,' Mason said. 'He sent for me to come up to his office on a very urgent matter. He insisted that Della Street come along. He had us shown into his office. Minerva was sitting there. I think Tragg wanted to see just how close the resemblance was between Minerva and Dorrie Ambler.'

'How close was it?' Drake asked.

'So darned close that it had *me* fooled,' Mason said. 'Della Street saw the difference.'

'I saw a difference in the little things that a woman would notice,' Della Street said. 'The coloring, mostly.'

'The voices are quite different,' Mason said, 'but in my opinion the resemblance simply can't be coincidental. I think when we find Dorrie Ambler we'll find another heir to the Harper Minden fortune.'

'And then there'll be a knock-down, drag-out fight between Minerva Minden and Dorrie Ambler?'

'That would be my guess,' Mason said. 'You'll remember that Minerva Minden's mother had a sister who died, presumably without leaving any issue. She lived with her married sister for a while. On the strength of the resemblance alone I'd be willing to gamble that Minerva's father may have slept in more than one bed. The resemblance between Dorrie and Minerva is too striking to be coincidental.'

'You think Dorrie Ambler was kidnaped Drake asked.

'I keep trying to convince myself she wasn't,' Mason said. 'And so far I haven't made much headway.'

'I'm thinking about the time element,' Drake said. 'They'd have had a deuce of a time getting her out of the apartment house and down the stairs. They couldn't have used the elevator because that would have brought them back into our line of vision, or rather where we might have seen them. They couldn't afford to take that chance.'

'I've been thinking about that, too,' Mason said. 'I'm wondering if perhaps they didn't keep her right there in the building.'

'You mean they had another apartment?' Drake asked.

Mason nodded, thought for a moment, then said, 'Check that phase of it, Paul. Try and find who has the apartments rented on the floor below and the floor above. There's a chance they spirited her into another apartment.'

'How about the shadowing jobs?'

'Call them off,' Mason said. 'The cops wouldn't like it, and shadows can't do any good now.'

'Okay, Perry, I'll take a crack at that angle of another apartment.'

'And now,' Della Street said, 'let's hope we can get the office routine back to some semblance of order, Mr Perry Mason. You have had a lot of cancelled appointments and quite probably some irate clients.'

'And,' Mason said, 'I know I have a stack of important mail that's unanswered and I suppose you're going to bring that up.'

'It will be on your desk within five minutes,' she said.

Mason made a gesture of helplessness, turned to Paul Drake. 'Okay, Paul, back to the salt mines.'

9

As Perry Mason entered the office the next morning, Della Street said, 'Good morning, Chief. I presume you've seen the papers.'

'Actually I haven't,' Mason said.

'Well, *you* certainly made the front page.'

'The Ambler case?' Mason asked.

'According to the newspapers it's the Minden case. You can't expect a newspaper to waste headlines on an unknown when there's a voluptuous young heiress in the picture.'

'And she's in the picture?' Mason asked.

'Oh, definitely. Cheesecake and all.'

'She considered the occasion one for cheesecake?' Mason asked.

'Probably not, but the newspapers have a file on her, and she's posed for lots of cheesecake pictures. She has pretty legs–or hadn't you noticed?'

'I'd noticed,' Mason confessed, picking up the newspaper which Della Street handed to him, and standing at the corner of his desk, glancing at the headlines. He made a step toward his swivel chair, then remained standing, fascinated by what he was reading.

The telephone rang.

Della Street said, 'Yes, Gertie.' Then, 'Just a minute. I'm sure he'll want to talk.'

'Lieutenant Tragg,' she said.

Mason put down the paper, moved over and picked up the telephone. 'Hello, Lieutenant,' Mason said. 'I guess that your office was not only bugged but the bug must have been connected to one of the broadcasting studios.'

'That's what I wanted to talk with you about,' Tragg said. 'I had to make a report, and the news got out from the report, not from me.'

'You mean the release came from your superiors?'

'I'm not in a position to amplify that statement,' Tragg said. 'I'll say the publicity came from the report and not from me.'

'I see,' Mason said.

'That is,' Tragg amended, 'the initial publicity. But after it appeared that the papers had the story, your client filled in the details.'

'My client?' Mason asked.

'Minerva Minden.'

'I've tried to tell you she's *not* my client. My client is Dorrie Ambler, who was abducted from the Parkhurst Apartments. . . . What have you found out about her, Lieutenant?'

'Precisely nothing, as far as I'm concerned,' Tragg said. 'I understand informally that the FBI is working on the case, although they haven't entered it officially as yet. You know how they are. Their purpose in life is to collect information, not to give it out.'

'That would seem to be a logical attitude,' Mason said. 'I'm a little surprised at Minerva Minden. I thought perhaps she would prefer to have the story kept under wraps, but it's all here in the paper, all the details and ramifications, including the fact that this may reopen the entire question of her inheritance.'

'You'd think she wouldn't want that broadcast,' Tragg said, 'but she's not particularly averse to newspaper notoriety.'

'I've noticed,' Mason said.

'Well, I just wanted to call you up and explain.'

'Thanks for calling,' Mason told him. 'I'm tremendously concerned about Dorrie Ambler.'

'I think you have a right to be,' Tragg told him. 'We're doing everything we can, I know that. No matter whether it's an abduction or a murder and flight, we want to find her.'

'Will you let me know as soon as anything turns up?' Mason asked.

Tragg's voice was cautious. 'Well, I'll either let you know or see that *she* has an opportunity to do so.'

'Thanks,' Mason said. 'And thanks again for calling.'

'Okay,' Tragg told him. 'I just wanted you to know.'

The lawyer cradled the telephone, returned to the newspaper.

'Well,' he said at length, 'it's certainly all in here–not only what she told them but some pretty shrewd surmises.'

'What effect will that have,' Della asked, 'on the matter Dorrie Ambler wanted to have you work on?'

'She wanted to be sure she wasn't a Patsy,' Mason said. 'She wanted to have it appear that . . .'

'Yes?' Della Street prompted, as the lawyer suddenly stopped midsentence.

'You know,' Mason said, 'I keep trying to tell myself that it needn't have been an abduction–that this thing could have all been planned.'

'Including the murder?'

'Not including the murder,' Mason said. 'We don't know what caused that murder, but we have a premise to start with. Our client was rather an intelligent young woman, and rather daring. She was quite willing to resort to unconventional methods in order to get one thing.'

'And that one thing?' Della Street asked.

'Newspaper publicity,' Mason said. 'She wanted to have the story of the look-alikes blazoned in the press. She *said* she wanted it because she didn't want to be set up as a Patsy in some crime that she hadn't committed.'

Della Street nodded.

'Now of course,' Mason said, 'that *may* not have been the real reason. The real reason may have been that she wanted to publicize her resemblance to Minerva Minden and then let the newspaper reporters get the bright idea they were related and have her case all built up in the newspapers.'

'And that would have helped her case in court?' Della asked.

'Not only would it have been of help to her case in court,' Mason said, 'but it would put her in a prime position to make a compromise with Minerva Minden.'

Della Street nodded.

'But,' Mason said, 'thanks to the quick thinking on the part of Minerva Minden, the scheme for newspaper publicity in connection with the airport episode fizzled out. So, under those circumstances, what would an alert young woman do?'

'Try to think of some other scheme for getting her name in the papers,' Della Street said.

Mason tapped the paper on the desk with the back of his hand.

'Well, I'll be darned,' Della Street said. 'You think she arranged the whole business? The abduction, the–'

'There are certainly some things that indicate it,' Mason said. 'I keep hoping that's the solution. It would have been difficult if not impossible for a man or two men to have taken an unwilling woman out of that apartment house. The police were on the scene within a matter of minutes. The way the elevator was placed they didn't dare use the elevator. They would have had to use the stairs. Unless they had another apartment, they could hardly have taken her from the building.'

Della's eyes were sympathetic. 'You keep trying to convince yourself it was all part of a scheme,' she said, 'and I find myself trying to help you–even when I don't believe it.'

Mason said, 'It's quite a problem getting a woman to leave the house against her will.'

'They could have held a gun on her, or a knife at her back,' Della Street said.

'They could have,' Mason said, 'but remember that just about the time they reached the street the police cars were converging on the place.'

'Would they have noticed her at that stage of the game?' Della Street asked.

'You're darned right they would,' Mason said. 'They are trained in that sort of thing. You'd be astounded to see what these officers can pick out of thin air. They've trained themselves to be alert. They have a sixth sense. They notice anything that is just a little bit out of the ordinary. At times it seems they're telepathic.

'If three people were walking down the sidewalk or into the parking lot–two men with an unwilling woman between them–they'd have noticed it.'

'You think there were two men?'

'I think the mattresses were dragged from the bedroom into the kitchen after Paul Drake and I rang the doorbell,' Mason said. 'I don't think one person would have had the time to take two trips. I think there were two mattresses and therefore two persons dragging mattresses.

'Moreover, the problem of getting the girl out of the apartment house would have been almost insurmountable for one person. Remember that he had not only to get her out of the apartment house but he had to get her into a car and make a getaway. I keep thinking things will work out all right, that Dorrie knew what she was doing and that it was all part of a plan–all except the murder. The murder fouled things all up. That forced a change in plans–but Dorrie's all right–somewhere.'

Knuckles tapped a code signal on the door of the private office and at Mason's nod Della Street opened the door to let Paul Drake in.

'What's new, Paul?' Mason asked.

'Quite a write-up in the papers,' Drake said.

'Wasn't it?'

'The only thing it lacked was to have your picture alongside the cheesecake. The photograph they used of you was very somber and dignified.'

'They pulled it out of the newspaper's morgue,' Mason said. 'They had to use what was available. . . . What's new, Paul?'

Drake said, 'It's possible, Perry, that your hunch about the apartment in the building could be an explanation.'

Mason face etched into hard lines. 'How come, Paul?'

'The day before the abduction a man who gave his name as William Camas inquired about vacancies. He was told there was one on the eighth floor, apartment 805. He looked at it and said he wanted his wife to look at it, that he thought it would be all right. He put up a hundred dollars for what he termed an option for three days, with the understanding that at the end of three days he'd either sign a lease or forfeit the hundred dollars.'

'And moved in?' Mason asked.

'Well, nobody knows for certain. The manager gave him the key to the apartment.'

'And what's the condition of the apartment now? What does it indicate?' Mason asked. 'Any fingerprints? Any–'

'Don't be silly,' Drake said. 'You thought of it and the police thought of it. The police started asking questions, found out about Camas and got a passkey to the apartment–and that's all anyone knows. The street comes to a dead end at that point. If the police found out anything, they're not passing out the information.'

'But they did check the apartment?'

'With a fine-toothed comb,' Drake said.

'And do you know if they talked with Camas?'

'No one knows if they talked with Camas.'

'You couldn't find him?'

'Not a trace,' Drake said. 'He gave a Seattle address. I've got my man checking it. My best guess is the address is phony.'

The telephone rang. Della Street picked up the receiver, said, 'Hello,' then motioned to Drake. 'For you, Paul.'

Drake picked up the telephone, said, 'Drake speaking,' listened for a few minutes, said, 'You're sure? . . . Okay, keep digging.'

Drake hung up, turned to Perry Mason and said, 'That's right. The address was a phony.'

Mason said, 'Hang it, Paul, that scuttles my last hope. I was banking on the theory they couldn't have got her out of that apartment against her will.'

'I know,' Drake said sympathetically. 'I know how you feel, but facts are facts. I have to give you the facts. That's my job.'

'Damn it,' Mason said, 'we've got to do something, Paul. Wherever she is, she's counting on us for help.'

'Take it easy, Perry. A whole army of law enforcement people are working on the case. There's nothing more we could do except get in their way.'

'You're sure they're working on it?'

'Hell, yes. My man in Seattle found the Camas address was a phony. He was third in line. The Seattle police had been working on it, the Seattle FBI had been working on it.'

Mason said, 'That girl is in danger.'

'Not now she isn't,' Drake said. 'I don't want to be heartless about it, but if anything's going to happen to her it's happened already. If she's dead, she's dead. If she isn't dead, it's because she's being held for some particular purpose, ransom or blackmail or something of that sort. There's just nothing you can do, Perry, except wait it out.'

Mason sighed. 'I have always been accustomed to controlling events, within reason. I hate like hell to find myself in a position where events are controlling me.'

'Well, they are now,' Drake said. 'There's nothing we can do.except wait. I'm going back to the office, Perry, and I'll keep in touch.'

'What about your men?' Mason asked. 'Would it help to put more men out?'

'I'm calling them in,' Drake said. 'My men would simply run up an excessive bill for you to pay and they would get in the way of the law enforcement agencies that are working on the case. Let's just give them a free hand.'

Mason was silent for several seconds, then said, 'Okay, Paul.'

Drake glanced at Della Street, then left the office.

Mason started dictating.

Halfway through the second letter the lawyer gave up, started pacing the office. 'I can't do it, Della. I can't get my mind off–See if you can get Lieutenant Tragg on the phone.'

She nodded sympathetically, went to the telephone and a few moments later nodded to Mason. 'He's on the line, Chief.'

Mason said, 'Hello, Lieutenant. Perry Mason talking, and I'm worried about what's happening in the case of Dorrie Ambler. I'm just not satisfied with the way things are going.'

'Who is?' Tragg countered.

'Have you found out anything?'

'We've found out a lot,' Tragg said, 'and we're trying to evaluate it, Perry.'

'Can you tell me what it is?'

'Not all of it, no.'

'What about this Apartment 805?'

'What do you know about that?'

'I'm asking you what you know.'

'And I'm not in a position to tell you everything I know. . . . Look here, Perry. You aren't trying to slip a fast one over on us, are you?'

'What do you mean by that?'

'This isn't some elaborate scheme that you've thought up to serve as a smoke screen?'

'A smoke screen for what?' Mason asked.

'That's what I'd like to know,' Tragg said.

'You're barking up the wrong tree, running off on a false scent, chasing a red herring and–Well, damn it, that's what I was afraid of, that you'd think this was some scheme or other I'd hatched up and would go at the whole business halfheartedly. I tell you, that girl is in danger.'

'You're worried over the fact you didn't protect her from that danger?' Tragg asked.

'Yes.'

'All right, I can help you put your mind at rest on that point,' Tragg said. 'Your client wasn't a victim but an accomplice. She went from Apartment 907 down the stairs to Apartment 805. She remained there until after the heat was off. Then she left there willingly and under her own power.'

'What gives you that idea?'

'An eyewitness.'

Mason was silent for some seconds.

'Well?' Tragg asked.

Mason said, 'Frankly, Lieutenant, you've relieved me a lot.'

'In what way?'

'I have been aware of the possibility that this might be some part of an elaborate scheme.'

'Not one that you thought up?'

'No, one that was intended to fool me as well as the police.'

'Well, frankly, Perry, that's a theory that is being given more and more consideration by the investigators. And of course that leaves us with an unexplained murder on our hands. As you are probably aware, we don't like unexplained murders.

'Now, there's a very good possibility this whole deal was hatched up simply in order to account for the presence of a corpse in the apartment of your client. If it should turn out that's the case, we wouldn't like it.'

'And I wouldn't like it,' Mason said.

'All right,' Tragg told him, 'I'll put it right up to you, Perry. Is there some reason for you to believe–any good, legitimate reason–that your client may have been laying the foundation for a play of this sort?'

Mason said, 'I'll be fair with you, Tragg. There is just enough reason so that I have given the subject some consideration.

'If that girl has been abducted and is in danger, I can't just sit back and wait. If, on the other hand, this is part of an elaborate scheme to account for a murder, I'm not only going to wash my hands of her but I'd do anything I could to help solve the case and find out exactly what did happen. Of course I'd have to protect the confidence of my client because she was my client for a while.'

'I understand,' Tragg said, 'but she wasn't your client as far as any murder case was concerned.'

'That's right. She wasn't–and I'll tell you something else. She isn't going to be.'

'Well,' Tragg said, 'I'll tell you this much. I think you can wash your hands of the case. When she left that apartment, she simply went downstairs and into

Apartment 805. We know that later on that evening a woman who has an apartment on the sixth floor saw your client riding down in the elevator. The woman noticed her because despite the fact it was night Dorrie was wearing dark glasses and didn't want to be recognized. This woman had the idea Dorrie was going to some surreptitious trysting place and–My own private opinion, Mason, is that the witness may be just a little frustrated and a little envious.

'Anyway, she saw Miss Ambler in the elevator. She knows Dorrie Ambler and has chatted with her. Dorrie was fond of this woman's dog, and the dog was fond of Dorrie. It's a strange dog. He isn't vicious but he wants to be left alone. He growls if people move to pet him.

'Now, this woman witness saw that Dorrie Ambler for some reason didn't want to be recognized. Dorrie moved to the front of the elevator and kept her back to the woman and the dog, but the dog wanted her to pet him; he muzzled her leg and wagged his tail. Well, after a minute Dorrie put her hand down and the dog licked her fingers. Then the elevator came to a stop and Dorrie hurried out.'

'The woman was walking her dog, and the dog stopped when they got to the strip of lawn just outside the door, but the woman saw a man waiting in a car at the curb and Dorrie almost ran to the car, jumped in and was whisked away.'

'Fingerprints?' Mason said.

'None,' Tragg said. 'That's a strange thing. Both Apartments 907 and 805 have evidently been scrubbed clean as a whistle. There isn't a print in them except the prints of Marvin Billings. He left his prints all over Apartment 907.'

'Did he have keys?' Mason asked.

'I shouldn't tell you this,' Tragg said, 'but I know how you feel. There wasn't a single thing in Billings' pockets. No keys, no coins, no cigarettes, no pencil, nothing. He'd been stripped clean as a whistle.'

Mason smiled, 'Well, Lieutenant,' he said, 'you make me feel a lot better, even if it looks as if I have been victimized. You've lifted a great big load off my shoulders.'

'All right, Perry,' Tragg said. 'I just want to warn you of one thing, that if this is a scheme that *you're* in on, you're going to get hurt. We don't like to have citizens arrange synthetic abductions and we don't like murder. And I can probably tell you without violating any confidence that Hamilton Burger, our district attorney, is firmly convinced that this is a hocus-pocus that has been thought up by you to confuse the issues so that when your client is finally apprehended he'll have a hard time convincing her of murder–and knowing Hamilton Burger as we both do, we know that this has made him all the more determined to expose the scheme and convict the plotters–*all* of them.'

'I can readily understand that,' Mason said. 'Thanks for the tip, Lieutenant. I'll keep my nose clean.'

'And your eyes open,' Tragg warned.

'I will for a fact,' Mason said as he hung up.

The lawyer turned to Della Street. 'Well, Della, I guess we can get on with the mail now. I guess our erstwhile client was a pretty clever little girl and quite a schemer. . . . You listened in on Tragg's conversation?'

Della Street nodded, said suddenly and savagely, 'I hope they catch her and convict her.'

Then after a moment she added, 'But if Dorrie Ambler had only played it straight and let you represent her claim to the estate, she could have shared in several million dollars. Now she's got herself into a murder case.'

Mason said, 'That's something *I* don't have to worry about. After she's arrested, she can get a copybook, sit down and write "honesty is the best policy" five hundred times.'

'It'll be too late then,' Della Street pointed out.

Mason arose and started pacing the floor. 'If it weren't for two things,' he said at length, 'I'd question the accuracy of Tragg's conclusions.'

Della Street, knowing the lawyer wanted an excuse to think out loud, said, 'What things, Chief?'

'First,' Mason said, 'we know that our client has been scheming up bizarre situations to attract publicity. We *know* she wanted to do something to make the newspapers publicize the resemblance between her and Minerva Minden.'

'And the second thing?' Della asked.

'The dog,' Mason said. 'Dogs don't make mistakes. Therefore our client was alive, well, and navigating under her own power long after the supposed abduction.

'I guess, Della, we're going to have to accept the fact that Miss Dorrie Ambler decided to use me as a pawn in one of her elaborate schemes and then something happened that knocked her little schemes into a cocked hat.'

'What?' Della Street asked.

'Murder,' Mason said. 'Billings was a detective with an unsavory reputation. Those on the inside who knew the game, knew he'd blackmail a client if the opportunity presented itself.'

'And so?' Della asked.

'So,' Mason said, 'realizing now Dorrie was merely trying to inveigle me into her scheme, knowing that she overreached herself, that she was perfectly free to call me long after her supposed abduction and didn't do so, I can wash my hands of her. I'm certainly glad you didn't walk into the trap of accepting that retainer, Della. As matters now stand, we did one piece of work for her and owe her nothing. . . . Now, thanks to a little dog, I can quit everything. Let's get back to that pile of mail.'

10

Della Street, entering from the outer office, paused in front of Perry Mason's desk. When the lawyer looked up she said, 'I hate to do this to you, Chief.'

'What?' Mason asked.

'It's been ten days since Dorrie Ambler disappeared,' Della Street said, 'and you've managed to forget about it and get yourself back to a working schedule.'

'Well?' Mason asked.

'Now,' she said, 'Henrietta Hull is in the outer office, waiting–impatiently.'

'What does she want to see me about?'

'The police have picked up Minerva Minden. Henrietta Hull says she's not certain of the charge against her but she was told they were going to question her in connection with that murder.'

Mason shook his head. 'I'm representing Dorrie . . .'

Della Street raised inquiring eyebrows as Mason's voice trailed off into silence.

For some ten or fifteen seconds the lawyer was silent, then abruptly he said, 'Bring her in, Della. I want to talk with her.'

Della Street nodded, left the office and a few moments later returned with Henrietta Hull striding along in her wake.

'Mrs Hull,' Della Street announced.

'We've met,' Henrietta Hull said, marching across to Mason's desk, giving him a firm grip with a bony hand, then seating herself in the client's chair.

'I told you, Mr Mason, that you were at the top of our list on felony cases.'

'And?' Mason asked, prompting her as she hesitated.

'Minerva has been taken into custody.'

'Arrested?'

'I don't think so. They picked her up at three o'clock this morning to take her in for questioning. She hasn't returned and she hasn't telephoned.'

'What do you want me to do?'

'Accept a retainer of twenty thousand dollars, go ahead and represent her.'

'She is being questioned in connection with the murder of that man who was found in Apartment 907–Marvin Billings?'

'I don't know. All I know is that they told her they wanted her to answer some questions in connection with a murder, that it was quite important.'

'She rebelled at going with them at that hour in the morning?'

Henrietta Hull said, 'As a matter of fact, she didn't. They evidently had been waiting for her. She was just getting in.'

'Unescorted?' Mason asked.

'Unescorted.'

'You were up at the time?'

'No. She left me a note explaining things. They let her do that. She said she would telephone. If I didn't hear from her by nine o'clock this morning, I was to go to you and give you a check for twenty thousand dollars as a retainer.'

'You can write checks on her account?'

'Certainly. I'm her manager.'

Henrietta Hull calmly opened her purse, took out a tinted oblong piece of paper, glanced at Della Street and said, 'I presume your secretary takes the fees.'

'That's the check?' Mason asked.

'Twenty thousand dollars,' she said.

'I have tried to explain to you,' Mason said, 'that I have represented Dorrie Ambler and I'm afraid there is going to be a conflict of interest.'

'You were only retained by Dorrie Ambler to keep her from being a Patsy, a fall guy, to use what is, I believe, the proper slang,' Henrietta Hull said. 'You gave her the advice she wanted and she left your office.

'For your information, Mr Mason, Dorrie Ambler is a fraud and a cheat. She lied to you all the way through. You don't owe her anything. The young woman was an opportunist blackmailer. You definitely do not want to be tied up with her.'

Abruptly Paul Drake's code knock sounded on the door of the private office.

Mason said. 'Excuse me a moment,' crossed the office, opened the door a crack and said, 'I'm busy, Paul. Can it wait?'

Drake said, 'It *can't* wait.'

Mason hesitated a moment.

'Come in,' he said. 'You've met Mrs Hull.'

Drake entered the office, said, 'Oh . . . hello. I don't want to interrupt, Mrs

Hull. However, it's necessary that I give Mr Mason some information–at once.'

Henrietta Hull said, 'How do you do, Mr Drake. I was going to drop in to see you as soon as I had finished with Mr Mason, or perhaps I should say, as soon as he had finished with me. I explained to you that I kept a list of people to whom I should turn in the event of serious trouble.

'Mr Mason heads the list of attorneys in connection with felony cases, and your agency heads the list as an investigating agency, particularly in cases where Mr Mason acts as counsel.

'I have just given Mr Mason a check as a retainer and I have here in my purse a check made out to you for twenty-five hundred dollars as retainer.'

'Now, just a minute,' Mason interrupted. 'Miss Minden was picked up this morning for questioning. That's about all you know about it. It was questioning in connection with a murder. She hasn't communicated with you and apparently you haven't communicated with the police or the prosecutor in order to find out what has happened, yet you have made out checks totaling twenty-two thousand, five hundred dollars and are seeking to retain counsel for her and a detective agency to investigate facts.'

'That's right.'

'You say that you are following instructions given to you in a note by Miss Minden?'

'Yes.'

'Do you have that note with you?'

'Actually I have.'

'I think I'd like to see it,' Mason said.

She hesitated a moment, then said, 'Can I be assured that the contents will be confidential if I show it to you, Mr Mason?'

Mason shook his head.

Drake said, 'I want to talk with you alone, Perry.'

'About this case?' Mason asked.

'Yes.'

'I think you'd better talk right here,' Mason said. 'I think we'd better have this out in a joint session, so to speak.'

'All right,' Drake said. 'Dorrie Ambler is dead. She was murdered. Her body has been uncovered, and police have what they consider an airtight case against Minerva Minden.'

Mason pushed back his chair, got to his feet, stood in frowning concentration for a moment, then walked around the corner of his desk over to the window, turned his back to the interior of the office, looked down at the street for a few minutes, turned around, said to Henrietta Hull, 'If what Paul Drake says is true, Mrs Hull, your employer is in a most serious predicament; exceedingly serious.'

'I understand that.'

'Did you know Miss Ambler was dead?'

'I knew the police said . . . that they had discovered her body–yes.'

'Let me ask you this; Is Minerva guilty?'

'She is *not* guilty,' Henrietta Hull said with firm conviction.

'How do you know she isn't guilty? Simply because of what you know of her?'

'No. Because of what I know of the case. Dorrie teamed up with a couple of crooks. They killed her. Now they want to blame that murder on Minerva.

Miss Ambler tried to pull a fast one. Her scheme boomeranged. Minerva is not guilty of anything. Does all this make a difference about your taking Minerva's case?'

'It makes a difference,' Mason said. 'Technically no matter how guilty a person may be he is not convicted until final judgment has been passed. He is entitled to have an attorney at every stage of the proceedings; not necessarily in order to prove him innocent but to see that all his legal rights are protected.'

'And Minerva would have that right as a citizen?'

'She would have that right as a citizen.'

'She wants you as her attorney.'

Drake cleared his throat, caught Mason's eye, imperceptibly shook his head.

'Why not, Paul? Come out with it,' Mason said. 'Let's not be beating around the bush or equivocating.'

'All right,' Drake said. 'Police have got an airtight case against her.'

'You said that before.'

'Her accomplice has confessed,' Drake said.

'Who was it?' Mason asked.

'The man she hired to accompany her to Dorrie Ambler's apartment and abduct her.'

'He says Minerva was with him at that time?' Mason asked.

'I understand that he does.'

'Do you know the details, Paul?'

'Only generalities. This fellow's name is Jasper. He says that Minerva told him that she had inherited a fortune, that Dorrie Ambler stood in the way of her keeping exclusive control of the estate, that she wanted Dorrie Ambler out of the way, that she would arrange a background which would give them absolute protection but she wanted Jasper to help her at the proper time.

'Jasper, incidentally, has a long criminal record. Billings tried to blackmail Minerva, not Dorrie Ambler. He wound up with a fatal bullet in his chest.'

'And they've arrested Minerva Minden for the murder of Dorrie Ambler?'

Drake shook his head. 'They're going to prosecute her for the murder of Marvin Billings. Then, in case she should get an acquittal or a verdict that didn't carry the death penalty, they're going to prosecute her for the murder of Dorrie Ambler. The Ambler murder depends on circumstantial evidence. They've got the deadwood evidence, several admissions and an eyewitness in the Marvin Billings murder. Minerva can never beat *that* rap.'

Mason reached a sudden decision. He said, 'I'll represent her on the murder of Marvin Billings. If that's the murder she's being charged with, I'll be her attorney in that case. I won't promise to represent her if she is being charged with the murder of Dorrie Ambler. I'd have to think that one over.'

'Fair enough,' Henrietta Hull said. 'Consider yourself retained, Mr Mason.'

'Just a minute,' Mason said. 'If you haven't communicated with her, how do you know that the case on which she's being prosecuted is the Billings murder and not the Dorrie Ambler murder?'

Henrietta Hull hesitated for just the bat of an eyelash, then said, 'Frankly, I don't, Mr Mason. But if it should turn out to be the other way around, you could always give back the retainer and withdraw from the case. It would be all right with us.'

Mason said, 'Let me take a look at that note that Minerva left you.'

Henrietta Hull opened her purse, took out a folded piece of paper and handed it to Mason.

The note read: 'Henny–Going to headquarters. If I'm not in by nine do the necessary.'

'There are no specific instructions in this letter,' Mason said. 'Certainly not to retain me or to call on the Drake Detective Agency.'

'I think you're mistaken, Mr Mason.' She said, 'and I quote, "*Do the necessary*".'

'Does that mean that you and Minerva had discussed this matter in advance?'

'It means,' she said, 'that Minerva trusted my discretion to do the necessary and I am doing it.'

'Now look,' Drake said, 'I'm not going to hang any crepe, but there have been two deliberate cold-blooded murders here. One of them was carefully planned in advance. The other *may* have been done in the heat of passion. But they've now got an open-and-shut case against Minerva Minden. You know it and I know it. They have eyewitnesses. They wouldn't have dared touch her with a ten-foot pole if they didn't have the deadwood.'

Mason, who had been frowning thoughtfully, said, 'Give Mrs Hull a receipt for twenty thousand dollars as a retainer fee, Della.'

II

Perry Mason, seated in the consulting room in the jail building, looked across at Minerva Minden and said, 'Minerva, before you say a word to me, I want to tell you that Henrietta Hull called me this morning. She gave me a check for twenty thousand dollars as a retainer to represent you. I told her that I would defend you on the charge of murdering Marvin Billings; that I couldn't as yet tell whether I would defend you on the charge of murdering Dorrie Ambler.'

'As I understand it,' she said, 'the Billings murder is the one on which I am being held.'

'Has a formal complaint been signed?'

'I believe they're intending to have an indictment by the grand jury and for some reason they want to have the trial itself take place just as soon as possible–and that suits me.'

'Ordinarily,' Mason said, 'we spar for time in a criminal case and try to see what develops.'

'This isn't an ordinary case,' she said.

'I'm satisfied it isn't,' Mason told her. 'I'm beginning to have a glimmering of what *I* think happened.'

She shook her head and said, 'I don't think you know enough of the facts to reach any conclusion.'

'Perhaps I don't,' Mason said. 'I am going to ask you one question. Did you murder Marvin Billings?'

'No.'

'At the moment that's all I want to know,' Mason said.

'All right,' she told him. 'Now I have a confession to make to you. I–'

'Is this to confess a crime?' Mason interposed.

'Yes, but it's–'

Mason held up his hand. 'I don't want to hear *any* confession.'

'This isn't what you think it is. It doesn't relate to–'

'How do *you* know what *I'm* thinking?' Mason interrupted.

She said, 'Because this is something that would never have occurred to you. It's about another matter entirely. It doesn't have to do with this murder, it has to do with–'

Mason said, 'Hold it, Minerva. I want to explain my position to you. You've told me that you're innocent of the murder on which you're going to be tried. If you have lied to me, that is your hard luck, because it's going to put me in a position where I'll be acting on a false assumption.

'Now then, any confession which you may want to make is entirely different.

'Any communication made by a client to an attorney is a privileged communication, but if you tell me that you have committed some particular crime, particularly if it's a different crime from the one you're charged with, the situation becomes different. I am your attorney but I am also a citizen. I can advise you in connection with your legal rights, but if I know that you have committed a serious crime and then try to advise you what to do to avoid being apprehended for that crime, I put myself in the position of being an accessory.

'I don't want to get put in that position.'

She thought that over for a few seconds, then said, 'I see.'

'Now,' Mason went on, 'you must realize that they have a lot against you–some perfectly devastating evidence that clinches the case in their hands. Otherwise they would never have dared to proceed in this manner. They would have gone to your home and very courteously asked you questions. Then they would have checked on your answers, asked you more questions and eventually would have instituted proceedings only after they had convinced themselves of your guilt.

'The manner in which they're acting at the present time indicates that they have some deadly bit of evidence which they are counting on to bring about a conviction, and which probably is going to take you by surprise–or at least they think it's going to take you by surprise.'

'From their questions,' she said, 'I gathered that this man, Dunleavey Jasper, has told them quite a story.'

'Involving you?'

'Yes.'

'What dealings have you had with Dunleavey Jasper?'

'None.'

'Have you ever seen him?'

'I think I have.'

'When?'

'Two detectives brought a man into the office when I was being interrogated by the prosecutor. The man looked at me, looked at the prosecutor, nodded, and then they took him out.'

Mason thought that over for a few seconds, suddenly got up, said, 'All right, Miss Minden, I'm going to represent you, But I just want to point out that some of the things you have been doing are not going to be conducive to securing acquittal.

'You've more or less deliberately played up to the press in their characterization of you as the madcap heiress of Montrose.

'In addition to the things which you have done, and which have been documented, there's a lot of whispering about nude swimming parties and things of that sort.'

'All right,' she said, 'what of it? It's my body, I like it and it's beautiful. I'm not dumb enough to think that it isn't.

'People go to nudist camps and everybody takes those camps for granted and leaves nudists alone, but if a person is reasonably broadminded and objects to the–'

'You don't need to argue with *me*,' Mason said, smiling, 'but I'm simply telling you that many a person has violated the moral code and then been unfortunate enough to be charged with murder. Jurors of a certain type love to throw the book at someone who has violated their particular moral code.

'Many an unfortunate individual has been convicted of murder on evidence that proved he or she was guilty of adultery.'

'All right,' she said, 'in the eyes of many people I'm a scarlet woman. Is that going to keep you from taking my case?'

'No.'

'Is it going to interfere with my chances of an acquittal?'

'Yes.'

'Thanks, Mr Mason,' she said. 'I wondered if you'd be frank or whether you'd engage in a lot of double talk. You don't need to tell me anything about the hatchet-faced frustrated biddies who love to sit in judgment on their fellow women.'

'What I was trying to point out,' Mason said, 'was that when a young woman tries to emancipate herself from the conventions and goes out of her way to build up a reputation for being a madcap heiress, it sometimes proves embarrassing.'

'If she gets charged with murder,' Minerva said.

'And you're charged with murder,' Mason pointed out.

'Thank you for the lecture,' she said. 'I'll try and be a good girl after I get out. At least I'll keep my name out of the papers.'

Mason said, 'Apparently you have no realization of what's going to happen. You're good copy. The fact that you're charged with murder is going to sell papers, and when something happens that sells papers it gets played up big.'

'I take it you mean really big,' she said.

'I mean really big,' Mason told her. 'That brings up the picture I want to present to the public–a rather demure but highly active young woman who is big-hearted, acts on impulse, and is sometimes misunderstood; but at heart you're rather demure.'

'That's the face you want to present to the public?'

'Yes.'

'To hell with it,' she said, shaking her head. 'I'm not going to try to change my personality just to beat a murder rap. That's up to you, Mr Perry Mason. I'm not demure and I'm not going to put on that mask for public consumption in the press.'

Mason sighed as he picked up his brief case and started for the door. 'I was afraid you'd have that attitude,' he said.

'I've got it,' she told him. 'And now you know.'

12

Judge Everson Flint glanced at the deputy district attorney who was seated with Hamilton Burger at the prosecutor's counsel table. 'The peremptory is with the People.'

'We pass the peremptory,' the deputy announced.

Judge Flint looked at the defense table. 'The peremptory is with the defense, Mr Mason.'

Mason stood up and made a gesture of acceptance, a gesture which somehow managed to be as eloquent as a thousand words. 'The defense,' he said, 'is *completely* satisfied with the jury.'

'Very well,' Judge Flint said, 'the jury will be sworn.'

The deputy district attorney sneeringly mimicked Mason's gesture of moving the left hand outward. 'There's no need to make a speech about it,' he said.

Mason's smile in the direction of the prosecutor's table was deliberately irritating. 'Why try then?'

Judge Flint said, 'Let's try and get along without personalities, gentlemen. The jury will now be sworn to try the case.'

After the jury had been sworn, Colton Parma, the deputy, as a nod from Hamilton Burger, the district attorney, made the opening statement.

'This is going to be a very brief opening statement, if it please the Court, and you, ladies and gentlemen of the jury,' he said. 'We propose to show that the defendant in this case inherited a fortune from Harper Minden. But she had reason to believe that there were other relatives of Harper Minden who were entitled to share in the estate; specifically, a young woman named Dorrie Ambler, who was the daughter of the defendant's mother's sister.

'The sister had died unmarried and it was presumed she had left no issue. However, we will introduce evidence showing that the defendant, by her own statement, had unearthed evidence that Dorrie Ambler was actually the daughter of her mother's sister, born out of wedlock, and that she and the defendant *had the same father*.

'We are not going to try to confuse the issues in the case by going into the intricacies of the law. We are simply setting forth the facts as I have explained them to you in order to show the state of mind of the defendant.

'The defendant was at the Montrose Country Club attending a dance on the night of September sixth. Liquor was served, and the defendant had had several drinks. She had an altercation with her escort, decided to leave him, and left the country club in a fit of anger.

'We expect to show that the defendant is spoiled, impulsive, and somewhat arrogant at times. She found an automobile in the parking place that had the keys in it and the motor running. It was a Cadillac automobile with license number WHW 694 and it had been stolen from an owner in San Francisco, although the defendant had no means of knowing that at the time. The defendant jumped in this stolen car and drove away, apparently intending to go home.

'At the intersection of Western Avenue and Hollywood Boulevard she went through a stop signal, struck a pedestrian, hesitated a moment, jumped out of the car, started to go to the injured pedestrian, then changed her mind, jumped back in the car and drove rapidly away.

'Now, I wish to impress upon you, ladies and gentlemen of the jury, that any evidence which will be introduced tending to connect the defendant with hit-and-run, or with any other violation of the law, is introduced solely for the purpose of showing the background of the present case *and the motivation of the defendant*.

'We will show that the defendant concocted a brilliant scheme for absolving herself of liability. She hired a firm of private detectives and placed an ad in the newspaper offering employment to a young woman who had a certain particular physical description.

'She instructed the persons who were screening the applicants for that job to get someone who was as near a physical double as possible.

'Dorrie Ambler answered that ad. As soon as the person in charge of screening the applicants saw her, it was realized that Dorrie Ambler bore a startling resemblance to the defendant; a resemblance so striking that it aroused the defendant's suspicion that Dorrie Ambler must be related to her and in short must be the illegitimate daughter of her mother's sister.

'We propose to introduce evidence showing that the scheme hatched by the defendant was to have Dorrie Ambler walk by the witnesses who had seen the defendant at the time of the hit-and-run accident. She hoped that Dorrie Ambler would be identified by those witnesses.

'Once they had made a mistaken identification, the defendant felt that *she* herself would be immune from subsequent prosecution.

'However, when she saw the manner in which Dorrie Ambler resembled her, the defendant realized that she had set in chain a sequence of events which she couldn't control. She knew that the newspapers would seize upon that resemblance and would soon find out that the two girls were actually closely related.

'It was at this point that the defendant entered into a conspiracy with one Dunleavey Jasper, who had tracked her down, and as a result of that conspiracy–'

'Now, just a minute,' Mason said. 'We dislike interrupting the prosecution's opening statement, but the prosecution is now bringing in evidence of other crimes with the purpose of prejudicing the jury. We assign the remarks as misconduct and ask the Court to admonish the prosecutor and at the same time to instruct the jury to ignore those remarks.'

'We know exactly what we are doing,' Parma said to Judge Flint. 'We will stand on the record. We are entitled to introduce evidence of *any* crimes as motivation for the murder with which this defendant is being charged.'

Judge Flint said to the jury, 'It is the law that a defendant being tried for one crime cannot be presumed guilty because of evidence of other crimes, except where such evidence is for the purpose of showing motivation. In view of the assurance of the prosecutor that that is the case here, I warn you that you are not to pay any attention to any evidence of any other crimes alleged to have been committed by this defendant, or to any evidence indicating the commission of such crimes, except for the purpose of showing motivation for the murder of the decedent, Marvin Billings.

'Proceed, Mr Deputy, and please be careful to limit your remarks.'

'We know exactly what we are doing, Your Honour,' Parma said. 'Our remarks are limited and will be limited. The evidence of other crimes is solely for the purpose of showing motivation.'

'Very well, proceed,' Judge Flint said.

'I am virtually finished, Your Honor.' Parma turned to the jury. 'We expect to show that Dunleavey Jasper traced the stolen car to the possession of the defendant, that the defendant learned Dunleavey Jasper had a criminal record and that the car was stolen; that she thereupon conspired with Dunleavey Jasper to abduct Dorrie Ambler so that she could be removed as a possible applicant for a share of the Minden estate, and to discredit Miss Ambler by making it seem Dorrie Ambler had been the hit-and-run driver.

'We expect to show that in the course of carrying out this conspiracy the private detective, Marvin Billings, found out what was happening. I think it is a reasonable inference which you can draw from the evidence that Billings tried to blackmail the defendant.

'Had it not been that Marvin Billings felt that the remarkable resemblance between these women was due to a common ancestry, had he not felt he could work with Dorrie Ambler to get a share of the Harper Minden estate, this case would never have been brought to trial because then there would have been no murder.

'We hold no brief for the dead man. The evidence will show you he was in effect playing both ends against the middle. But no matter how cunning he may have been, no matter how low he may have been, the law protects him. His life was a human life. His killing was murder.

'So Marvin Billings went to the apartment of Dorrie Ambler, and his arrival was at the moment when Miss Ambler was being spirited down to another apartment on the floor below.

'Billings sounded the chimes. After a moment's hesitation, the defendant opened the door, trusting to her resemblance to Dorrie Ambler to carry off the scene.

'At first Billings was deceived, but when he kept talking to the defendant he soon realized the impersonation. That was when he tried blackmail, and that was when the defendant shot him with a twenty-two revolver.

'Shortly after the shooting of Billings, the chimes on the apartment door sounded again.

'We expect to show you that the persons then at the door were none other than Perry Mason, the attorney for the defense, and Paul Drake, a private detective.

'The conspirators had to get out of the back door of the apartment. Acting upon the asumption that their callers did not know of this back door, they hurriedly dragged mattresses from the twin beds in the bedroom across the living room into the kitchenette, and by using a kitchen table and the mattresses, barricaded the door.

'When Mason and Paul Drake entered the apartment, which they did after a few minutes, they found Marvin Billings unconscious and in a dying condition. They found the kitchen door barricaded in such a way that they thought for a while it was being held against their efforts to open it by someone in the kitchen.

'We expect to show that the unfortunate Dorrie Ambler, having been taken to Apartment 805, was given a hypodermic injection of morphia against her will and–'

'Now, just a moment,' Mason said. 'Again we are going to interrupt the deputy district attorney and object to any evidence of what may have happened to Dorrie Ambler.'

'It goes to show motive,' Parma said.

'It can't show motive for the murder of Marvin Billings,' Mason said, 'because what the deputy prosecutor is talking about now is something that occurred after the shooting of Marvin Billings.'

'I think that is right,' Judge Flint ruled.

'Very well, if I am going to be limited in my proof . . . I'll pass this matter on my opening statement, ladies and gentlemen, but we expect to introduce proof and we will have a ruling on the matter as the witnesses come on the stand.

'I am going to weary you with details. I have told you the general nature of the case so you can understand the evidence you will hear. You will hear the confession of one of the members of this conspiracy and you will hear evidence of admissions made by the defendant herself.

'We are going to ask a verdict of first-degree murder at your hands. However, as far as this trial is concerned, it is only necessary for you to determine just one thing.'

Parma held up his left index finger high above his head. 'Just one thing, ladies and gentlemen,' he said, shaking the outstretched finger. 'That is, whether or not the evidence in this case proves the defendant guilty of the crime of murder, the killing of Marvin Billings.

'We shall ask a verdict of guilty at your hands, a verdict of first-degree murder.'

Parma turned and walked back to his seat at the prosecutor's table.

'Do you wish to make an opening statement, Mr Mason?'

'No,' Mason said, 'except that I wish the Court to admonish the jury that the statement of the prosecutor was inaccurate as a matter of law.'

'In what respect?' Judge Flint asked.

Mason arose and extended his left hand above his head, extending the left forefinger. 'It isn't a matter, Your Honor, of proving just one thing: whether the evidence shows the defendant guilty. It is a matter of proving two things.'

And Mason slowly raised his right hand and extended the right index finger. 'It is a question of proving the defendant guilty beyond all reasonable doubt. I think the Court should so advise the jury.'

'Well, I think the jury understands that in any criminal case the evidence must prove the defendant guilty beyond all reasonable doubt.'

'Otherwise the defendant is entitled to a verdict of acquittal.'

'The Court will cover that matter in its instructions,' Judge Flint said.

Mason slowly lowered his hands with the extended forefingers and seated himself.

Judge Flint repressed a smile at the skillful manner in which Perry Mason, waiving his opening statement, had nevertheless scored a telling point on the prosecution.

'Call your first witness,' Judge Flint said to the prosecutor.

'I will call Emily Dickson.'

Mrs Dickson, a rather attractive woman in her early forties, took the oath and seated herself on the witness stand after giving her name and address.

'What was your occupation on the sixth of September?' Parma asked.

'I was the manager of the Parkhurst Apartments.'

'You were residing there in the apartments?'

'I was.'

'Did you know Dorrie Ambler in her lifetime?'

'Just a minute,' Mason said. 'If the Court please, I ask that the jury be admonished to disregard that question. I ask that the prosecutor be cited for misconduct. I object to any statement intimating that Dorrie Ambler is dead. It assumes a fact not in evidence.'

'I didn't say she was dead,' Parma said. 'I merely asked the witness if she knew Dorrie Ambler during her lifetime. That's a perfectly permissible question. I can always ask that about anybody. I could ask her if she knew you during your lifetime.'

'The inference is that the person inquired about is no longer alive,' Mason said, 'and I feel the question was deliberately slanted so as to convey that impression.'

'I think so too,' Judge Flint said. 'Now, gentlemen, let's not have any misunderstanding about this. I am willing to permit the prosecution to introduce the evidence of any other crime, provided that evidence is necessarily pertinent to the present question before the jury, for the purpose of showing motive or method or a general pattern within the provisions of the rule with which I am quite sure you are all familiar.

'I have ruled that there is not going to be any evidence introduced of any crime committed *after* the alleged crime in this case was completed.'

'I'll withdraw the question,' Parma said with poor grace.

Judge Flint said, 'I advise the jury to disregard the question and any insinuation contained in the question or any thoughts which may have been placed in your minds because of the nature of the question. I am going to state further to the prosecutor that I will declare a mistrial in the event there are any further attempts to circumvent the ruling of the Court.'

'I wasn't trying to circumvent the ruling of the Court,' Parma said.

'Well,' Judge Flint observed dryly, 'you're too much of a veteran not to know the effect of your question. Now I suggest that you proceed, and be *very* careful.'

'Very well,' Parma said, turning to the witness. 'Did you know Dorrie Ambler prior to the sixth of September?'

'Yes.'

'For how long had you known her prior to September sixth?'

'Approximately–oh, I guess five or six months.'

'Miss Ambler had an apartment in the Parkhurst Apartments?'

'She did.'

'Where was it?'

'Apartment 907.'

'Now I'm going to ask you if you also rented Apartment 805 prior to the twelfth day of September, and if so, do you know the name of the tenant?'

'I do now. His name is Dunleavey Jasper, but at the time he told me he was William Camas.'

'*When* did you rent him Apartment 805?'

'On the eleventh of September.'

'Of this year?'

'Yes.'

'I have some further questions to ask of this witness upon another phase of the matter,' Parma said, 'but I will put the witness on the stand at a later date.'

'Very well,' Judge Flint said, turning to Mason. 'Cross-examine.'

'Can you describe Dorrie Ambler?' Mason asked.

'Yes. She was about twenty-five or six.'

'Eyes?'

'Hazel.'

'Hair?'

'Auburn.'

'General appearance?'

'She was almost the exact image of the defendant in this case, the woman sitting there at your left.'

'Oh, you notice the resemblance, do you?' Mason asked.

'I notice a very distinct resemblance–a startling resemblance.'

'Did you ever comment on it?'

'I certainly did.'

'Would it be possible to confuse the defendant with Dorrie Ambler and vice versa?'

'It would be very possible.'

'When did you first see the defendant?'

'When she was placed in a show-up box.'

'And at that time you identified her as Dorrie Ambler, didn't you?' Mason asked.

'Objection,' Parma said. 'Incompetent, irrelevant and immaterial. Not proper cross-examination.'

'Overruled,' Judge Flint snapped.

'Well, I had been told that I was going to be called on to pick out Minvera Minden and I told them–'

'Never mind what *you* told *them*,' Mason said. 'What did *they* tell *you?*'

'That they wanted me to pick out Minerva Minden.'

'And did you tell them you had never seen Minerva Minden before?'

'Yes.'

'But they still wanted you to identify a woman you had never seen?'

'They wanted me to see if she resembled Dorrie Ambler.'

'And you saw her in the show-up box?'

'Yes.'

'And noted her resemblance?'

'Yes.'

'How close a resemblance?'

'A very striking resemblance.'

'I'm going to repeat,' Mason said. 'Did you identify the defendant as Dorrie Ambler?'

'Objection, Your Honor,' Parma said.

'Overruled,' Judge Flint snapped.

'Yes, I did. I told them that was Dorrie Ambler that they had in the show-up box and then they convinced me–'

'Never mind what they convinced you about,' Mason said. 'I'm just trying to find out what happened. Did you identify the woman in the show-up box as being Dorrie Ambler?'

'At first I did. Yes.'

'Oh, you made two identifications?'

'Well, they told me that–Well, if I'm not allowed to say what they told me I–Well, first I identified her as Dorrie Ambler and then I identified her as Minerva Minden.'

'Despite the fact you had never seen Minerva Minden?'

'I had seen her picture.'

'Where?'

'In the newspapers. That was how it happened that the police called on me in the first place.'

'How did they know you had seen her picture in the papers?'

'I rang them up and told them that the picture in the paper of Minerva Minden was actually the picture of Dorrie Ambler who had rented the apartment from me.'

'So then the police came to talk with you?'

'Yes.'

'When did Dorrie Ambler rent the apartment from you?'

'In May.'

'And how do you know it wasn't the defendant, Minerva Minden, who rented the apartment from you?'

'Because I didn't know her at that time. I had never seen her at that time.'

'But you admitted that you couldn't tell her from Dorrie Ambler.'

'Oh, but I could, Mr Mason. After I realized the resemblance and studied the defendant, as I told you, I made a second identification. I said after looking more closely, that the woman I had identified as Dorrie Ambler was someone who looked very much like her, but it wasn't Miss Ambler.'

'At that time you were certain Miss Minden, the defendant, was *not* the person who had rented the apartment?'

'Absolutely certain.'

'Because of things the police had told you?'

'No. There were other means, other reasons. I convinced myself.'

'Thank you,' Mason said. 'No further cross-examination.'

Parma said, 'You may step down, Mrs Dickson.

'Now then, I am going to call Lieutenant Tragg to the stand very briefly, simply for a matter of identification.'

'Very well, Lieutenant Tragg to the stand,' Judge Flint ordered.

Tragg came forward, was sworn, testified that he had gone to Apartment 907 at the Parkhurst Apartments in response to a call, that he had found there a man in a dying condition; that the man was subsequently identified as Marvin Billings, a private detective.

'Now, what happened to Mr Billings?'

'He died.'

'When?'

'He died on the way to the Receiving Hospital. He was dead on arrival. He had been shot in the chest and that wound proved fatal. That was on the twelfth day of September.'

'And how soon did he leave the apartment after you first saw him? That is, when did the ambulance take him away?'

'Within a matter of ten minutes–well, fifteen minutes at the outside.'

'Thank you,' Parma said. 'You may cross-examine.'

'No questions,' Mason said.

'Call Delbert Compton,' Parma said.

Compton, a competent-appearing, heavy-set individual in his early fifties, eased himself into position in the witness chair and surveyed the courtroom with steely, watchful eyes.

'Your name is Delbert Compton, you reside in this city and are now and for some years last past have been the junior partner and manager of the Billings & Compton Detective Agency.'

'Yes, sir.'

'You handle most of the office work, and your partner, Marvin Billings, was in charge of the outside operations?'

'Yes, sir.'

'If the Court please,' Hamilton Burger said, getting to his feet, 'I think my associate is a little hesitant about pointing out that this man is a hostile witness. I would like to have the Court rule that he is a hostile witness and give us permission to ask leading questions.'

'He has shown no hostility so far,' Judge Flint said. 'When the matter reaches that point, in case it does reach that point, you may then renew your motion. For the present the Court will take it under advisement. Go ahead, Mr Parma.'

'Were you carrying on your business in this city on the sixth of September?'

'Yes, sir.'

'During the month of September were you employed by the defendant in this case?'

'Well . . . I suppose so . . . yes.'

'Who employed you?'

'The defendant's representative, Henrietta Hull. I believe Mrs Hull is her manager.'

'And what was the purpose of the employment?'

'I was instructed to put an ad in the paper, an ad asking for unattached women of a certain description.'

'Did you put such an ad in the paper?'

'I did.'

'The compensation was rather high?'

'A thousand dollars a month.'

'Then what did you do?'

'I had one of my female operatives rent a suite in a hotel and interview applicants.'

'And what instructions did you give your female operatives?'

'Objected to,' Mason said, 'as incompetent, irrelevant and immaterial, hearsay, a conversation taking place outside of the hearing of the defendant.'

'Sustained,' Judge Flint said.

'All right, I'll put it this way,' Parma said. 'What instructions were you told by Henrietta Hull to give your operative?'

'She didn't tell me.'

'She didn't tell you what to do?' Parma asked.

'I didn't say that. I said she didn't tell me what instructions to give my operative.'

Parma looked at Judge Flint somewhat helplessly.

'All right,' Judge Flint said, 'take your ruling. Ask leading questions.'

'I'll put it this way,' Parma said. 'Didn't Henrietta Hull, acting on behalf of the defendant in this case, advise you in general terms to arrange an elaborate setup for interviewing applicants, but that their qualifications had nothing whatsoever to do with their ultimate selection, that you were to wait until a young woman came in who resembled a photograph which she gave you. That you were to hire the person who had closest resemblance to that photo.'

The witness hesitated for a long time.

'Answer the question,' Judge Flint said.

'Well . . . yes.'

'Didn't you hire a young woman named Dorrie Ambler, and didn't she telephone you each day at an unlisted number in order to get instructions as to what she was to do?'

'Yes.'

'And didn't you report to Henrietta Hull that you had been able to hire not only an applicant who looked like the young woman in the photograph, but had hired the person shown in the photograph?'

'Yes.'

'And didn't Henrietta Hull say that was impossible and didn't you tell her to see for herself, that you'd have this woman walk across a certain intersection at a fixed time and that Henrietta Hull could make surreptitious observations so as to convince herself?'

'Yes.'

'And didn't Henrietta Hull then tell you to start looking up this young woman's background?'

'Yes.'

'And didn't you, in pursuance of instructions given by Henrietta Hull, get this woman to walk back and forth, up and down Hollywood Boulevard in the vicinity of the Western Avenue intersection to see if a witness, Mrs Ella Granby, wouldn't identify her as the person driving the car involved in a hit-and-run accident on September sixth?'

'Well, no, not exactly.'

'What do you mean, not exactly?'

'I didn't tell her all that.'

'But you did tell her to walk up and down Hollywood Boulevard near the intersection of Western?'

'Well . . . yes.'

'And to report to you anything that happened?'

'Yes.'

'And did she report that a woman had made an identification?'

'Yes.'

'And didn't you then advise her that she could take the next day off and didn't need to do anything?'

'I can't remember my detailed instructions but something of that sort probably happened.'

'And all of that was under instructions from Henrietta Hull?'

'Yes.'

'You were reporting to Henrietta Hull regularly?'

'Yes.'

'Cross-examine,' Parma snapped.

Mason said, 'How did you know Henrietta Hull was the representative of the defendant?'

'She told me so.'

'In a conversation?'

'Yes.'

'In person or over the telephone?'

'Over the telephone.'

'Then you have never seen Henrietta Hull. Is that correct?'

'That is correct. I talked with her over the telephone.'

'You received compensation for your work?'

'Yes.'

'Did you bill the defendant for that?'

'No, I did not.'

'Why?'

'I was paid in advance.'

'Who paid you?'

'I received the money from Henrietta Hull.'

'In the form of a check?'

'In the form of cash.'

'But if you have never met Henrietta Hull, she couldn't have given you the cash.'

'She sent it to me.'

'How?'

'By messenger.'

'How much?'

'Thirty-five hundred dollars.'

'Did you see Dorrie Ambler personally?'

'Yes.'

'And you have seen the defendant?'

'More recently, yes. I am, of course, looking at her now.'

'Was there a striking physical resemblance between Dorrie Ambler and the defendant?'

'A very striking resemblance.'

Mason held his eyes on the witness. 'For all you know, Mr Compton,' he said, 'you were hired, not by the defendant, *but by Dorrie Ambler*.'

'*What?*'' the witness asked, startled.

'Dorrie Ambler,' Mason said, 'wanted to establish a claim to the Harper Minden estate. She wanted a certain amount of money or notoriety in order to launch her campaign. She needed newspaper publicity. So she rang you up and told you she was Henrietta Hull and–'

'Just a minute, just a minute,' Parma shouted, jumping to his feet. 'All this assumes facts not in evidence. It consists of a statement by counsel and I object to it on–'

'I withdraw the question,' Mason said, smiling, 'and ask it this way. Mr Compton, *if* Dorrie Ambler had wanted to attract attention to her remarkable similarity to the defendant in this case, and *if* she had called you up, told you she was Henrietta Hull and had asked you to put that ad in the paper and to hire Dorrie Ambler when she showed up to apply for the job, was there anything in the facts of the case as you know them as covered by your testimony which would have negatived such an assumption?'

'Objected to,' Parma said, 'as being argumentative and calling for a conclusion of the witness, as being not proper cross-examination and assuming facts not in evidence.'

'Sustained,' Judge Flint said.

Mason, having made his point so that the jurors could get it, smiled at the witness. 'You don't know that the person you were talking with on the telephone was Henrietta Hull, do you?'

'No, sir.'

'Did you ever at any time during the employment call Henrietta Hull?'

'No, sir. She called me.'

'Why didn't you call her?'

'Because she told me not to. She said she would call me.'

'So you were *never* to call her at the house or her place of business?'

'Those were the instructions.'

'Given to you by someone who, for all you know, could have been Dorrie Ambler or any other woman?'

'Objected to as argumentative and not proper cross-examination,' Parma said.

'Overruled,' Judge Flint said.

'It was only a voice over the telephone,' Compton said.

'And from time to time this same voice would call you and give you instructions as to what you were to do?'

'Yes.'

'And tell you what instructions you were to give to Dorrie Ambler?'

'Yes.'

'You never met the defendant prior to her arrest?'

'No.'

'You didn't ever have any conversation with her on the telephone?'

'No.'

'You never called the defendant to find out if she had authorized Henrietta Hull to make you any such proposition, and you never called Henrietta Hull?'

'That's right.'

'No further questions,' Mason said.

Hamilton Burger rose to his feet. 'If the Court please,' he said, 'this next witness will undoubtedly be controversial. I am going to call him somewhat out of order. I am going to state to the Court that I make no apologies for what we have done in granting this witness a certain immunity from prosecution. We–'

'Just a minute,' Mason interrupted, getting to his feet, 'I submit that this is an improper statement in front of the jury. This is not the time to argue the case, this is not the time to apologize for giving some criminal immunity in order to further the interests of the prosecutor.'

'Just a minute, just a minute, gentlemen,' Judge Flint interrupted. 'I don't want any personalities from either side, and there is no need for any argument. Mr Burger, if you have another witness, call him.'

'Very well,' Burger said, turning and smiling at the jury, knowing that he had registered with them the thought that he wished to convey. 'Call Dunleavey Jasper.'

Dunleavey Jasper was a rather slender young man in his early thirties who managed to convey the impression of slinking as he walked forward, held up his hand, was sworn, and took the witness stand.

'Now, your name is Dunleavey Jasper,' Hamilton Burger said. 'Where do you reside, Mr Jasper?'

'In the county jail.'

'You are being held there?'

'Yes.'

'You are charged with crime?'

'Yes.'

'Do you know the defendant?'

'Yes, sir.'

'When did you first meet the defendant?'

'It was around the eleventh of September.'

'Did you know Dorrie Ambler in her lifetime?'

'Now, just a minute,' Judge Flint said. 'I've already ruled on this matter. The words, "in her lifetime," are extraneous. The jurors are instructed to ignore that part of the question. Now, the question is, Mr Jasper, whether you knew Dorrie Ambler.'

'Yes, sir.'

'How did you get acquainted with Dorrie Ambler?'

'It's rather a long story.'

'Just go ahead and answer the question and never mind how long it takes. Keep your answer responsive to the question but tell how you happened to meet her.'

'She stole my getaway car.'

There was a startled gasp from many of the spectators in the courtroom. The jurors suddenly sat forward in their chairs.

'Will you repeat that, please?' Hamilton Burger said.

'She stole my getaway car.'

'What was your getaway car?'

'It was a Cadillac automobile, license number WHW 694.'

'This was *your* getaway car?'

'My partner and I were going to use it for a getaway. We didn't have title to the car.'

'Where had you picked up the car?'

'We had stolen it in San Francisco.'

'Who was this partner you refer to?'

'A man named Barlowe Dalton.'

'And you say this was a getaway car.'

'Yes, sir.'

'Where was it when it was taken from you?'

'It was at the Montrose Country Club.'

'And why do you call it a getaway car?'

'Because my partner and I had intended to get in the women's cloakroom, go through the cloaks there, get some fur coats, purses, anything of value we could find, and make a getaway.'

'And what happened?'

'A woman stole our car.'

'Can you explain that?'

'This woman was at the dance. She was intoxicated. She had a fight with her escort and walked out on him, jumped in our getaway car which was standing there with the motor running and drove away.'

'And what did you do after that?'

'Well, there was one thing we had to do. We *had* to find that car.'

'Why?'

'Because we had left something over ten thousand dollars in currency in the glove compartment.'

'And where did this currency come from?'

'We had held up this branch bank in Santa Maria and had taken about eighteen thousand bucks. Ten thousand was wrapped up and was in the glove compartment. The rest of the money we had divided and had on us, about three–four thousand dollars apiece.'

'This was stolen money?'

'That's right.'

'And how about the money that was in the glove compartment? What were the denominations?'

'That was all in one-hundred-dollar bills. The other money we had was in smaller bills, twenties, tens, a few fifties; but there was ten thousand in hundred-dollar bills, and we thought that money might be hot.'

'What do you mean, hot?'

'That perhaps the bank had the serial numbers on it. We had decided to hold it for a while.'

'Go ahead.'

'Well, we had to find the car, so we made inquiries through some of our underworld connections and learned that the car had been involved in a hit and run accident. And then we had a tip that the car was stashed in the garage of Dorrie Ambler, so we found the car but the money was gone. So then we started shadowing Dorrie Ambler.'

'And did you shadow her?' Burger asked.

'Yes. We had some difficulty picking up her trail but we finally did so and shadowed her for several hours.'

'Where did she go and when?' Burger asked.

'Objected to as incompetent, irrelevant and immaterial,' Mason said.

'We'll connect it up, Your Honor,' Burger said.

'Overruled.'

'She went to the office of Perry Mason,' the witness said.

'And then?' Burger asked, as the jurors leaned forward in tense interest.

'And from there to the airport where she waited until the defendant went into the women's room. At that time she jumped up, approached the newsstand, said, "This *isn't* a stick-up," fired a gun three times and ran into the women's room.'

'Then what happened?' Burger asked.

'Shortly after that the defendant emerged from the room and was arrested. At first she had us fooled, but there was a difference in voices. So after the police took the defendant away we waited, and sure enough Dorrie Ambler emerged from the rest room. At this time she was wearing a coat which covered her clothes, and dark glasses.'

'What did you do then?' Burger asked.

'Followed Dorrie Ambler back to her apartment. By that time we had learned the other woman, the one the police had arrested, was Minerva Minden, an heiress; so we decided we might be on the track of something big.'

'And what did you do then?'

'We waited until the defendant had been released on bail and then we contacted her.'

'By her, you mean the defendant?'

'Right.'

'Both you and Barlowe Dalton contacted her?'

'Yes, sir.'

'Where did you meet her?'

'At a cocktail lounge that she suggested.'

'And what happened there?'

'We had a conversation in which we tried to pin something on her–something that would give us an opening for a shakedown, but she was too smart for us.'

'What do you mean by that?'

'She suggested that we had better go to the police if we thought something was wrong.'

'And then what happened? Go right ahead.'

'Well, naturally we couldn't afford to have the police nosing around, and what with one thing and another she found out we were a couple of pretty hot torpedoes. The next thing I knew *she* was propositioning *us*.'

'What do you mean by propositioning?'

'She suggested that she wanted to have Dorrie Ambler kidnaped. She offered to pay twenty-five thousand dollars if we'd do the job.'

'Did she say why?'

'Yes.'

'What did she say?'

'She said Dorrie Ambler had seen her pictures in the papers and had decided to cash in on the resemblance by claiming she was the daughter of her mother's sister and that they had the same father, that Dorrie's father was also her father.

'She said Dorrie was clever and that she was trying to bring about some situation where she would be mistaken for the defendant, that some man was backing Dorrie with a lot of money and was trying to make such a spectacular case of it that it would cost her a lot of money to buy Dorrie off.

'So then we told the defendant Dorrie had grabbed off ten grand that belonged to us and that we'd decided to get it back–that she couldn't do that to us, and one thing led to another and finally the defendant asked us if we could get Dorrie–well, out of the picture.'

'And what did you and your partner say to that?' Burger asked.

'Well, we said we could if the price was right. Well, she offered us twenty grand and we laughed at her and then she finally came up to fifty grand with five grand additional to cover initial expenses and as a guarantee of good faith on her part.'

'Go on,' Hamilton Burger said to the witness. 'What happened after that?'

'We started making plans.'

'Immediately?'

'Yes, sir, that's right–at the time of that same conversation.'

'Now, when you say *we* started making plans, whom do you mean?'

'Well, there was the defendant, Minerva Minden, my partner, Barlowe Dalton, and me.'

'And what did you do?'

'Well, she gave us the five grand and told us we'd better get busy.'

'And what did you do?'

'We went to the Parkhurst Apartments; that is, I did, and cased the joint.'

'Now, what do you mean by casing the joint?'

'Well, we looked the place over and made plans for handling things.'

'And what did you decide on? What did you actually do?'

'The first thing we did was to get in touch with the manager to see if some apartment on the eighth or ninth floors was vacant. We wanted a close-in place for a base of operations.'

'What did you find?'

'I found an apartment on the eighth floor was vacant, 805; that was right close to the stairs and almost directly under Apartment 907 where this Dorrie Ambler had her residence.'

'You rented that apartment?'

'Yes, sir. I told the manager that I wanted an apartment, that I thought that 805 would be right but that I wanted my wife to look at it, that my wife was coming down from San Francisco, that she'd been up with her father who'd been very sick, and she wouldn't be in for a day or so. I suggested that I pay a hundred dollars for a three-day option on the place and that my wife would look at it and if she liked it, then I'd sign up a lease on it and pay the first and last months' rent.'

'What name did you give?'

'The name of William Camas.'

'And you were given a key to the apartment on that basis?'

'Yes, sir.'

'Then what did you do?'

'Well, it was all fixed up with the defendant that right after the court hearing on her case, which was coming up the next day, she'd rush out to the apartment house and we'd put our plan in operation and get rid of Dorrie Ambler.'

'Now you say, "get rid of her." Do you mean–Well, what *do* you mean?'

'Well, it eventually turned out we were supposed to get rid of her, but at first the talk was only about kidnaping.'

'All right, what happened?'

'Well, you see the defendant was going to come down to join us immediately after her court hearing was finished.'

'Did she say *why* she'd picked that particular time?'

'Yes, she said that would be the time when she would be free of shadows and reporters and all that stuff. She said that her attorney would get her out of the court and down in his car and drive her for half a dozen blocks to a place where she had her car parked, that the attorney would give instructions to her to go into hiding and stay in hiding, probably to go home; that she'd come and join us. She said that in case anything should go wrong with our scheme that she could go to the door and impersonate Dorrie Ambler and explain any noise or commotion or anything of that sort. In that way we wouldn't stand any risk.'

'All right, what happened?'

'Well, we had a chance to nab Dorrie Ambler while she was in the kitchen. We knocked on the back door and said we had a delivery, and she opened the door and we grabbed her right then.'

'What did you do?'

'We put a gag in her mouth, put a gun in her back and hustled her down the back stairs and into Apartment 805. Then we doped her with a shot of morphine and put her out.'

'Then what?'

'Shortly after that the defendant showed up. *She* wanted us to get out fast. She said Dorrie Ambler had been consulting Perry Mason and we didn't have much time, that Mason wasn't the sort to let grass grow under his feet. But we reminded her about the ten grand. We really took that apartment to pieces, looking for it.'

'Did you find it?'

'No. . . . That is, I don't think we did.'

'What do you mean by that?'

'Well, my partner, Barlowe Dalton, acted just a little bit strange. I got to thinking afterwards perhaps he might have found it and just stuck it in his pocket and pretended that he hadn't found it. In that way he'd have had the whole thing for himself instead of making a split.'

'You don't know that he found it?'

'No, sir. All I know is that I *didn't* find it.'

'Very well. Then what happened?'

'Then I told the defendant we'd better arrange for a getaway in case something went wrong.'

'What did you do?'

'I started barricading the kitchen door; that is, the door between the kitchen and the living room so we could open it ourselves but hold off anyone that came in the front door–and that was when the doorbell rang and this man was there.'

'What man?'

'This detective, this man that was killed, Marvin Billings.'

'All right, go on. Tell us what happened.'

'Well, I'm getting just a little ahead of my story. The defendant also frisked the apartment looking for something. She didn't tell me what, but she had found a twenty-two-caliber revolver.'

'The defendant had this?'

'That's right. She said she was going to show Dorrie Ambler a thing or two about the difference between lead bullets and blank cartridges.'

'And then?'

'Well, then is when we come to this thing that I was telling you about. The doorbell rang, and this Marvin Billings was there, and the defendant went to the door and tried to shoo him away.'

'What happened?'

'He just pushed his way right into the place and of course right away he saw that it was a wreck, that we'd been searching it, and he wanted to know what was going on. And the defendant, pretending to be Dorrie Ambler, said that somebody had evidently been in looking for something and that was when Billings tried to put the bite on her.'

'Now, what do you mean by that?'

'Well, he wanted to shake her down.'

'Where were you?'

'I was in the bedroom.'

'Did he see you?'

'No, he couldn't see me. I was behind the door.'

'What happened?'

'He told the defendant that he knew what she'd been up to. He thought he was talking to Dorrie–'

'Never mind telling us what you think he thought,' Hamilton Burger interrupted with ponderous dignity, creating the impression that he wanted to be thoroughly fair and impartial. 'All you can testify is what *you* saw and heard in the presence of the defendant.'

'Well, he told her he knew what she'd been up to, that she was an impostor and that she needed a better manager than she had; that he was declaring himself in and that he wanted part of the gravy, and he said something about not being born yesterday, and–Well, that's when she said–'

'Now, when you say "she," to whom do you refer?'

'Minerva Minden, the defendant.'

'All right, what did she say?'

'She said, "You may not have been born yesterday but you're not going to live until tomorrow," and I heard the sound of a shot and then the sound of a body crashing to the floor.'

'What did you do?'

'I ran out and said, "You've shot him!" And she said, "Of course I've shot him. The blackmailing bastard would have had us all tied up in knots if I hadn't shot him. But they'll never pin it on me. It's in Dorrie Ambler's apartment and she'll get the blame for it."'

'And then what?'

'Well, then I bent over him and said the guy wasn't even dead, and she said, "Well, we'll soon fix that," and raised the gun and then lowered it and a smile came over her face. She said, "No, better yet, let him recover consciousness long enough to tell his story. He thinks Dorrie Ambler shot him. That will account for Dorrie's disappearance. Everyone will think she shot this guy and then took it on the lam."'

'The defendant said that?'

'That's right. And from that time on she was just tickled to death with herself. She was feeling as though she'd really done a job.'

'And what happened?'

'Well, almost immediately after that the chimes rang, and I grabbed the other mattress and rushed it into the kitchen and we arranged a table against the door and the mattresses so that it barricaded the kitchen door. Then we waited a minute to see what would happen. That's when the defendant got in a panic and wanted to run down the stairs. I slapped her and she started to scream. I had to grab her and put a hand over her mouth.'

'Why?' Hamilton Burger asked.

'Because with someone at the door we couldn't get to the elevator. Our escape was cut off that way. We'd have to go down the stairs. I didn't want them to come around to the back door and catch us there, so I wanted to be sure they were all the way in the apartment before we sneaked out the back door. That tension of waiting was too much for the defendant's nerves.'

'What did you do?'

'I left the back door open.'

'Where was your partner, Barlow Dalton, at that time?'

'He was down in 805 riding herd on Dorrie Ambler.'

'Go on, what happened?'

'Well, the people at the door turned out to be Perry Mason and this detective, Paul Drake. I waited until they smashed their way into the apartment and had got into the living room, and then the defendant and I slipped out the back door, went down the stairs and holed up in Apartment 805 with Barlowe Dalton and Dorrie Ambler. Dorrie Ambler had been doped and was unconscious by that time.'

'Go on,' Hamilton Burger said. 'What happened after that?'

'Well, we holed up there. Cops were all over the place and we just sat tight and believe me, I was scared stiff. I told the defendant that if the cops started checking and found us there, it was the gas chamber for all of us, that she'd had no business killing that guy!'

'What did she say?'

'She'd got her nerve back by that time. She laughed and called me chicken and brought out some cards and suggested we play poker.'

'And then what happened?'

'Well, we hung around there until quite late and then the defendant said she'd put on Dorrie Ambler's clothes and go out and see if the coast was clear; that we could watch out the window and if the coast was all clear she'd blink her lights a couple of times on her parked automobile at the curb and that would show us that no cops were around, and we could take Dorrie out.'

'Was Dorrie conscious by that time?'

'She was conscious but groggy. We persuaded her that she wasn't going to get hurt if she did exactly what we told her.'

'So what happened?'

'Well, the defendant went out. She left us a gun–a thirty-eight.'

'Did you have any talk with her about what happened after that?'

'Yes, she told me about it the next day.'

'What did she say?'

'She said that just as luck would have it, she got in the elevator with some woman and a dog, who was already in the elevator, evidently coming down from one of the upper floors. She said that the woman acted like she knew her but that she turned her back and stood up in front of the elevator door, wondering if the woman was going to speak to her. She said the dog must have known Dorrie Ambler because he got Dorrie Ambler's smell from her clothes and came and pushed his nose against her skirt and leg and wagged his tail. She said it really gave her a bad time.'

'And what did she do, of your own knowledge? That is, what do you know?'

'Well, I was looking out of the window of the apartment, and she drove her car around to the designated place and blinked the lights so we knew the coast was clear, so then we took Dorrie Ambler down.'

'And what happened with Miss Ambler?'

'I don't know of my own knowledge, only what Barlowe Dalton told me.'

'You didn't stay with Barlowe Dalton?'

'No, it was understood that he'd take care of Dorrie and that I'd go over the apartment with an oil rag, covering every place where fingerprints might have been left. . . . Incidentally, we'd done that in Dorrie Ambler's apartment as we were searching it. We all wore gloves, and I was going over things with a rag, scrubbing out fingerprints.'

'Now then,' Hamilton Burger said, 'I'm going to ask you a question which you can answer yes or no. Did Barlowe Dalton tell you what he had done with Dorrie Ambler?'

'Yes.'

'Did you subsequently communicate with the police to tell them what Barlowe Dalton had told you? Mind you now, I am not asking for hearsay. I am not asking what Barlowe Dalton told you. I am asking you simply what you did.'

'Yes. I communicated with the police.'

'With whom?'

'With Lieutenant Tragg.'

'And what did you tell him? Now, don't say what you actually told him, simply describe what you told him with reference to what Barlowe Dalton had told you.'

'I told him what Barlowe Dalton had told me.'

'Where is Barlowe Dalton now?'

'He is dead.'

'When did he die and how did he die?'

'He died on the twentieth.'

'How did he die?'

'He was killed by a policeman in a holdup.'

Hamilton Burger turned to Perry Mason and bowed. 'You may cross-examine,' he said.

Minerva Minden grabbed Mason's coat sleeve, pulled herself close to his ear. 'That's a pack of lies,' she said, 'absolute, vicious lies. I never saw this man in my life.'

Mason nodded, got to his feet and approached the witness.

'How do you know that Barlowe Dalton is dead?' he asked.

'I saw him killed.'

'Where were you?'

'I was standing near him.'

'And were you armed at the time?'

'Objected to as not proper cross-examination,' Hamilton Burger said. 'Incompetent, irrelevant and immaterial.'

'Overruled,' Judge Flint snapped.

'Were you armed at the time?' Mason asked.

'Yes.'

'What did you do with the gun?'

'I dropped it to the floor.'

'And the police recovered it?'

'Yes.'

'Where was your partner when he was shot?'

'At the Acme Supermarket.'

'At what time?'

'About two o'clock in the morning.'

'And what were you doing there?'

'Objected to as not proper cross-examination, incompetent, irrelevant and immaterial, calling for matters not covered under direct examination,' Hamilton Burger said.

'Overruled,' Judge Flint snapped.

'My partner and I were holding up the place.'

'Your partner was killed and you were arrested?'

'Yes.'

'And you were taken to jail?'

'Yes.'

'And how long after you were taken to jail was it that you told the police all you knew about the defendant and Dorrie Ambler?'

'Not very long. You see, my conscience had been bothering me about that murder and about what had happened to Dorrie Ambler. I couldn't get that off my mind.'

'How long after the time that you were arrested did you finally tell the police the complete story?'

'It was–well, it was a couple of days.'

'You had been caught red-handed in connection with the perpetration of a burglary.'

'Yes, sir.'

'You knew that?'

'Yes, sir.'

'Have you previously been convicted of a felony?'

'Yes, sir.'

'How many times?'

'Three times.'

'Of what felony?'

'Armed robbery, grand larceny, burglary.'

'You knew that you'd go up for life as an habitual criminal?'

'Just a minute,' Hamilton Burger interrupted. 'That is objected to as incompetent, irrelevant and immaterial, not proper cross-examination.'

'I am simply trying to show the bias and motivation of the witness,' Mason said. 'I am going to connect it up with my next questions.'

'I think I see the line of your questioning,' Judge Flint said. 'The objection is overruled.'

'Yes.'

'You knew kidnaping was punishable by death?'

'Under certain circumstances, yes.'

'You knew that you had conspired with the defendant to commit a murder?'

'Yes.'

'As well as a kidnaping?'

'Yes.'

'You knew that you were an accessory after the fact in the murder of Marvin Billings?'

'Well–all right, I suppose I was.'

'And you were in quite a predicament when the authorities were questioning you.'

'Yes, I was.'

'And didn't you finally offer to give them a confession on a crime they were very anxious to solve, if they would give you immunity from prosecution on all of these other charges?'

'Well . . . not exactly.'

'What do you mean by that?'

'I mean that they told me that I had better come clean and throw myself on their mercy and–Well, they were the ones who said they had the deadwood on me and it would mean that I got life as an habitual criminal and they'd see that I served every minute of it, unless I co-operated and helped them clear up a bunch of unsolved crimes.'

'So then the conversation took another turn, didn't it?' Mason said. 'You started talking about what would happen to you if you were able to help the officers clear up a murder that they wanted to make a record on.'

'Well, something like that.'

'You told Lieutenant Tragg that you could clear up some matters for the police if you received immunity for your part in the crime, and if you received immunity for the holdup of the supermarket. Isn't that right?'

'Well, I believe I brought the matter up, yes.'

'In other words, you told Lieutenant Tragg you were willing to make a trade.'

'Not in those words.'

'But that was what it amounted to.'

'Well, yes.'

'And you wanted to be guaranteed immunity before you told your story to the district attorney.'

'Well, that was good business.'

'That's the point I'm getting at,' Mason said. 'This conscience of yours didn't take over all at once. You decided to do a little bargaining before letting your conscience take over.'

'Well, I wasn't going to tell the police what I knew unless I got immunity. I wasn't going to put my head in a noose just to accommodate them.'

'And *did* you get immunity?'

'I got the promise of immunity.'

'A flat promise of immunity?'

'In a way, yes.'

'Now, just a minute,' Mason said. 'Let's refresh your recollection. Wasn't it a conditional promise of immunity? Didn't the district attorney say to you in effect that he couldn't give you immunity until he had first heard your story? That if your story resulted in proving a murder and bringing the murderer to justice, that then you would be given immunity provided your testimony was of material help?'

'Well, something like that.'

'That was what you were angling for.'

'Yes.'

'And that's what you got.'

'Yes.'

'So,' Mason said, leveling his finger at the witness, 'as you sit there on the witness stand, you are charged with a crime which, with your prior record, will probably mean a sentence to life imprisonment, and you have made a bargain with the district attorney that if you can concoct a story which you can tell on this witness stand, which will convince this jury so that they will convict the defendant of first-degree murder, you can walk out of this courtroom scot free and resume your life of crime; but if, on the other hand, your story isn't good enough to convince the jury, then you don't get immunity.'

'Now, just a minute, just a minute,' Hamilton Burger shouted, getting to his feet. 'That question is improper, it calls for a conclusion of the witness, it's argumentative–'

'I think I will sustain the objection,' Judge Flint said. 'Counsel can ask the question in another way.'

'The district attorney told you that if your story resulted in clearing up a murder you might be given immunity?'

'Yes.'

'And that he couldn't guarantee you immunity until he had heard your story on the witness stand.'

'Not exactly.'

'But the understanding was, as he pointed out, that you had to come through with your testimony on the witness stand before you got immunity.'

'Well, I had to complete my testimony, yes.'

'And it had to result in *clearing up a murder*.'

'Yes.'

'And bringing the murderer to justice.'

'Yes.'

'In other words, obtaining a conviction,' Mason said.

'Well, nobody said that in so many words.'

'I'm saying it in so many words. Look in your own mind. That's the thought that's in the back of your mind right now, isn't it? You want to get this defendant convicted of murder so you can go free of the crimes you committed.'

'I want to get square with myself. I want to tell the truth.'

Mason made a gesture of disgust. 'The truth!' he exploded. 'You had no intention of telling your story to the police until you were apprehended in the commission of a crime. Isn't that right?'

'Well, I had thought about it.'

'You'd thought about it to this extent,' Mason said. 'You'd thought about it to the extent of believing that you had an ace trump which you could play when you got into trouble. That you were going to go out and hit the jackpot. You were going on a crime binge; and that in the event you were caught, you would then make a deal with the prosecutor to clean up a murder case in return for immunity.'

'I didn't have any such idea.'

'How many other crimes had you committed during the period between the Dorrie Ambler episode and your attempt to rob the supermarket?'

'I . . . I . . . not any.'

'Wait a minute, wait a minute,' Mason said. 'Didn't your bargain with the police include the fact that you were going to clean up certain other holdups and clear the record on them?'

'Well, yes.'

'In other words, you were going to confess to all those crimes.'

'Yes.'

'And be given immunity.'

'Yes.'

'Did you or did you not commit those crimes that you were going to confess to?'

'If the Court please,' Hamilton Burger said, 'this cross-examination is entirely improper. The questions are purely for the purpose of degrading the witness in the eyes of the jury and they have no other reason.'

'The objection is overruled,' Judge Flint said.

'Had you or had you not committed all those crimes that you were going to confess to?' Mason asked. 'Crimes that you did confess to.'

'I hadn't committed *all* of them, no.'

'You had committed *some* of them?'

'Yes.'

'And on the other crimes,' Mason said, 'you were going to tell a lie in order to clear up the records so that the police department could wipe them off the books, with the understanding that you would be given immunity for all those crimes and wouldn't be prosecuted.'

'Well, it wasn't exactly like that,' the witness said. 'They wouldn't buy a pig in a poke. I had to make good first.'

'Make good in what way?'

'With my testimony.'

'Exactly,' Mason said. 'If your testimony wasn't strong enough to result in a conviction for this defendant, the deal was off. Isn't that right?'

'I . . . I didn't say it that way.'

'You may think you haven't,' Mason said, turning on his heel and walking back to his chair. 'That's all the cross-examination I have of this witness at this time.'

Hamilton Burger, his face flushed and angry, said, 'I'll recall Lieutenant

Tragg to the stand.'

'You have already been sworn, Lieutenant Tragg,' Judge Flint said. 'Just take the stand.

Tragg nodded, settled himself in the witness chair.

'Lieutenant Tragg,' Burger said, 'I will ask you if, following a conversation with Dunleavey Jasper, you made a trip to the vicinity of Gray's Well by automobile?'

'I did.'

'And what did you look for?'

'I looked for any place where the automobile road ran within a few feet of a sloping sand dune so constituted that one man could drag a body down the slope of the sand dune.'

'I object, if the Court please,' Mason said, 'to the last part of the witness' statement as a conclusion of the witness, not responsive to the question and having no bearing on the facts of the case as we have those facts at present.'

'The objection is sustained. The last part of the answer will go out,' Judge Flint said.

'And what did you find?' Hamilton Burger asked, smiling slightly at the knowledge he had got his point across to the jury.

'After three or four false leads, we found a sand hill where there were faint indications that something had disturbed the surface of the sand, and by following those indications to the bottom of the sand hill and digging we found the badly decomposed body of a woman.'

'Were you able to identify that body?'

'Objected to as incompetent, irrelevant and immaterial,' Mason said.

'The objection is overruled. The evidence, ladies and gentlemen of the jury, is being admitted purely for the purpose of corroborating the testimony of the previous witness and not with the idea that any less evidence would be required in the case at bar because there might be evidence indicating the possible commission of another crime. Nor are you to permit yourselves to consider any subsequent crime, even for the purpose of proving motivation, but only for the purpose of corroborating the testimony of the previous witness. You are to consider this evidence only for that limited purpose. Continue, Mr Prosecutor.'

'I will ask you this, Lieutenant Tragg. Was there anything anywhere on the body that gave you any clue as to its identity?'

'There was.'

'Will you describe it, please?'

'The tips of the fingers were badly decomposed. The weather had been intensely hot. The body had been buried in a rather shallow sand grave. Putrefaction and an advanced stage of decomposition made it difficult to make a positive identification. However, by a process of pickling the fingers in a formaldehyde solution and hardening them, we were able to get a fairly good set of fingerprints sufficient to give certain aspects of identification.'

'Now then, Lieutenant Tragg. I will ask you if you made prints of the thumbs of this body.'

'We did. We printed all the fingers as best we could.'

'I am at the moment particularly interested in the thumbs. I am going to ask you if you found any other physical evidence on the body.'

'We did.'

'What did you find?'

'We found a purse, and in that purse we found a receipt for rent of Apartment 907 at the Parkhurst Apartments. That receipt was made out in the name of Dorrie Ambler. We also found a key to Apartment 907. We found some other receipts made to Dorrie Ambler.'

'Did you find a driving license made to Dorrie Ambler?'

'Not there.'

'Please pay attention to my question, Lieutenant. I didn't ask you that question. I asked you if you found a driving license made out to Dorrie Ambler.'

'We did.'

'Where did you find that?'

'That driving license was in the possession of the defendant at the time of her arrest. It was tucked down in a concealed pocket in her purse.'

'And did that driving license contain the thumbprint of the applicant?'

'It contained a photostat of it.'

'And did you subsequently attempt to compare the thumbprint of the cadaver you discovered with the thumbprint on the driving license of Dorrie Ambler?'

'I did.'

'With what result?'

'Objected to as calling for a conclusion of the witness,' Mason said. 'It is incompetent, irrelevant and immaterial. It is not the best evidence. The jury are entitled to have the thumbprints presented to them for comparison, and Lieutenant Tragg can, if he wished, point out points of similarity in the prints. But he cannot testify to his conclusion.'

'I think I will sustain the objection,' Judge Flint said.

'Very well. It will prolong the case,' Hamilton Burger said.

'In a case of this magnitude the time element is not particularly essential, Mr Prosecutor,' Judge Flint rebuked.

Hamilton Burger bowed gravely.

He introduced a photographic enlargement of the thumbprint of Dorrie Ambler, taken from her application for a driving license. Then he introduced a photograph of the thumbprint of the woman whose body Lieutenant Tragg had found.

'Now then, Lieutenant Tragg,' Hamilton Burger said, 'by pointing to these two enlarged photographs which are on easels standing where the jurors can see them, can you point out any similarities?'

'I can. I have listed the points of similarity.'

'How many do you find?'

'I find six.'

'Will you point them out to the jury, please? Take this pointer and point to them on the easels.'

Lt Tragg pointed out the various points of similarity.

'And these are all?' Hamilton Burger asked.

'No, sir. They are not all. They are the only ones that I can be sufficiently positive of to make a complete identification. You will realize that due to the process of putrefaction and decomposition it was exceedingly difficult to get a good legible fingerprint from the body of the deceased. We did the best we could, that's all.'

'Were you able to form an opinion as to the age and sex of the decedent?'

'Oh, yes. The body was that of a female, apparently in the early twenties.'

'And you took specimens of hair from the body?'

'We did. And those were compared with the hair color of Dorrie Ambler as mentioned in the application for driving license.'

'Did you find anything else at or near the body of this woman?' Hamilton Burger asked.

'We found a thirty-eight-caliber revolver with one discharged shell and five loaded shells. It was a Smith and Wesson with a two-inch barrel, Number C-4 8809.'

'Did you subsequently make tests with that gun in the ballistics department?'

'I did.'

'You fired test bullets through it?'

'Yes, sir.'

'And did you make a comparison with any other bullet?'

'Yes, sir.'

'What bullet?'

'A bullet that had been recovered from the skull of the body I found there in the sand hills.'

'And what did you find?'

'The bullets showed identical striations. The bullets had been fired from the same gun; that is, the fatal bullet matched absolutely with the test bullets.'

'Do you have photographs showing the result of the experiments?'

'I do.'

'Will you present them, please?'

Lt Tragg presented photographs of the fatal bullet and the test bullet.

'What is this line of demarcation in the middle?'

'That is a line of demarcation made in a comparison microscope. The bullet above that line is the fatal bullet; the bullet below is the test bullet.'

'And those bullets are rotated on this comparison microscope until you reach a point where the lines of identity coincide? Where the striations are continuations of each other?'

'Yes, sir.'

'And when that happens, what does it indicate, Lieutenant?'

'That the bullets were both fired from the same gun.'

'And that is the case here?'

'Yes, sir.'

'You may cross-examine,' Hamilton Burger said abruptly.

Mason approached the witness. 'Lieutenant Tragg, was the body you discovered that of Dorrie Ambler? Please answer that question yes or no.'

Lt Tragg hesitated. 'I think it–'

'I don't want to know what you *think*,' Mason interrupted. 'I want to know what you *know*. Was the body that of Dorrie Ambler or not?'

'I don't know,' Tragg said.

'You didn't get enough points of similarity from the fingerprint to establish identification?'

'I will state this,' Lt Tragg said, 'we got enough points of identification to show a very strong probability.'

'But you can't establish it by definite proof as to identification?'

'Well . . .'

'Be frank, Lieutenant,' Mason interrupted. 'It takes a minimum of twelve points of identity to establish positive identification, does it not?'

'Well, no, it does not,' Tragg said. 'We have had rather a large number of cases where we were able to make identification from fewer points of identity.'

'How many?'

'Well, in some instances, nine or ten points are sufficient where the circumstances are such that we can negative the possibility of accidental duplication.'

'But those circumstances didn't exist in this case?'

'No.'

'You don't consider that six points of similarity are sufficient to prove identity.'

'Not by themselves. There are, of course, other matters. When you consider the probabilities of six points of similarity in the fingerprints where it was impossible to obtain a completely legible impression; when you consider rental receipts in the name of Dorrie Ambler; when you consider the key to the apartment being found in the purse of the decedent; when you consider the age, the sex, the size, the coloration of the hair, and group all those together, we can determine a very strong mathematical probability.'

'Exactly,' Mason said. 'You have a strong mathematical probability of identity. Yet you can't testify that the body was that of Dorrie Ambler.'

'I can't swear to it positively, no, sir.'

'Now, you talk about the mathematical probabilities of sex, among other things,' Mason said. 'Sex alone would be of poor probative value, would it not?'

'Well, yes.'

'Now, the similarity of six points of identification would not prove the fingerprints were identical?'

'No, I have explained that. However, I can list the probabilities in this way. The identity of the six points of similarity would give us, I would say, about one chance in fifty that the body was not that of Dorrie Ambler. The presence of the key to the apartment makes another mathematical factor. There are hundreds of apartment houses in Los Angeles. In the apartment house in question there are ten floors. Each has thirty apartments, and the fact that the key to Apartment 907 was found would then be one in three hundred, and multiplying one in three hundred by fifty we have a factor of one in fifteen thousand, and–'

'Now just a minute,' Mason interrupted. 'You are not qualifying as an expert mathematician, Lieutenant Tragg?'

'Well, I'm an expert in the field of criminal investigation and I can make the ordinary mathematical computations.'

'Exactly,' Mason said, 'and you can twist them so that you can come up with a perfectly astronomical figure when it suits your purpose.

'We could, for instance, go at it this way. You could say that there are only two sexes; therefore the fact that the decedent was a female gives us a one out of two chance; that there are only one-tenth of adult females within the age bracket you were able to determine; that therefore you have a factor of twenty to one that this was the person in question; that of the persons in that age group only approximately one in twenty have that coloration of hair so you can multiply and get a factor of four hundred to one; and–'

'Now, that's not fair,' Lt Tragg interrupted. 'That's distorting the facts.'

'But it's following the same line of reasoning that you use in trying to establish a mathematical law of probabilities,' Mason said. 'I'm going to put it to you just this way. You can't state beyond a reasonable doubt that the body was that of Dorrie Ambler, can you?'

'No.'

'That's all,' Mason said.

'Now I wish to call one more witness, perhaps out of order,' Hamilton Burger said. 'I wish to call Rosy Chester.'

Rosy Chester, a red-haired, rather voluptuous woman with a hard, cynical mouth and alert eyes, came forward and was sworn.

'Where is your residence?' Hamilton Burger asked.

'At the present time in the county jail.'

'Are you acquainted with the defendant?'

'I am.'

'When did you first meet the defendant?'

'We were cell mates for a night.'

'On that occasion did you have any discussion with this defendant about Dorrie Ambler?'

'Yes.'

'What, if anything, did the defendant say about her?'

'The defendant said that Dorrie Ambler would never be seen again.'

'Was there any further conversation?' Burger asked.

'I asked her if she wasn't worried that Dorrie Ambler could collect a share of the estate, and she laughed and said Dorrie Ambler would never show up to claim any share of any estate.'

'Do you know whether this was before or after the body had been discovered?'

'I think the body had been discovered, but the defendant didn't know about it. It hadn't been announced publicly.'

'Cross-examine,' Hamilton Burger said.

'Are you awaiting trial on some charge?' Mason asked.

'Yes.'

'What?'

'Possession of marijuana.'

'As soon as you had this conversation with the defendant you communicated with the prosecutor?'

'Shortly afterwards.'

'How did you reach him?'

'He reached me.'

'Oh,' Mason said, 'then you were told that you were going to be put in the same cell with the defendant and to try to get her to talk?'

'Something like that.'

'And you did try to get her to talk?'

'Well–Of course when you're together in a cell that way you don't have much to talk about and–'

'Did you or did you not try to get her to talk?'

'Well . . . yes.'

'And tried to lead her into making some incriminating statement?'

'I tried to get her to talk.'

'Under instructions from the district attorney?' Mason asked.

'Yes.'

'And why did you take it on yourself to act as a source of information for the district attorney?'

'He asked me to.'

'And what did he tell you he would do if you were successful?'

'He didn't tell me anything.'

'He didn't make you any promises?'

'Absolutely not.'

'Now then,' Mason said, 'what did he say about the fact that he couldn't make you any promises?'

'Oh,' she said, 'he told me that if he made any promises to me that that would impair the weight of my testimony so that I'd just have to trust his sense of gratitude.'

Mason smiled and turned to the jury. 'That,' he said, 'is all.'

Hamilton Burger flushed, said, 'That's all.'

Judge Flint said, 'Court will now take a recess until tomorrow morning at nine-thirty a.m. During that time the defendant will be remanded to custody, and the jurors will not discuss the case among themselves or permit it to be discussed in their presence or form or express any opinion as to the guilt or innocence of the defendant.'

Judge Flint arose and left the bench.

Minerva Minden clutched Mason's arm.

'Mr Mason,' she said, 'I have a confession to make.'

'No, you haven't,' Mason told her.

'I do, I do. You *must* know something, you simply *must*. Otherwise I'll . . . I'll be convicted of a murder I didn't do.'

Mason's eyes met hers. 'I'm going to tell you something that I very seldom tell a client,' he said. 'Shut up. Don't talk to me. Don't tell me anything. I don't want to know anything about the facts of the case.'

'But, Mr Mason, if you don't know, they'll–Can't you see, the evidence against me is overwhelming? They'll convict me of a murder that –'

'Shut up,' Mason said. 'Don't talk to me and I don't want to talk to you.'

Mason got to his feet and motioned to the policewoman.

Mason said as a parting shot to his client, 'Don't discuss this case with *anybody*. I don't want you to answer *any* questions. I want you to sit absolutely tight. Say nothing, not a word.'

13

Back in his office Mason paced the floor while Della Street watched him with anxious eyes.

'Can you tell me what's worrying you, Chief?' she asked.

Mason said, 'It's a tricky situation, Della. I've got to handle it in just the right way. If I do *exactly* the right thing and say *exactly* the right thing at *exactly* the right time, that's one thing. If I misplay my cards, it's another.'

Abruptly Mason stopped in his pacing. 'Della,' he said, 'get Paul Drake on the line, tell him I want to know every circumstance connected with the holdup of the bank at Santa Maria.'

'Is that pertinent?' Della Street asked.

'That's pertinent,' Mason said. 'Tell Paul I want a complete report listing every circumstance, every bit of evidence. Nothing is too minute, nothing is to be discarded.

'Have him charter a plane, fly an operative up there. Get busy. Work with witnesses.'

'You want the report by morning?' Della Street asked,

'I want the operative who makes the investigation to be back here by morning,' Mason said. 'I want him in the courtroom where I can talk with him. Tell Paul to spare no expense, to charter a plane.

'Also tell Paul I want a complete report of all unsolved stick-ups betweeen San Francisco and Los Angeles on the fifth, sixth and seventh of September. he can start collecting those by long distance telephone.

'Have him call police chiefs at the various cities. I want everything I can get.'

'But, look here,' Della Street said, 'you can't get around Jasper's testimony about the gun, the conversation and the place where the body was found unless you–'

'All that testimony isn't going to hurt the defendant,' Mason said.

'What!' she exclaimed.

'The murder of Dorrie Ambler doesn't mean anything in *this* case,' Mason said, 'unless the jury believes Minerva *told them* to murder her. If I can open up a doubt on that one point, then I can blast Jasper's testimony. The death of Dorrie Ambler doesn't mean a thing unless Minerva Minden *told* them to kill her.

'Even if Minerva Minden had an argument with Dorrie Ambler and killed her in the heat of passion, it wouldn't have anything to do with *this* case unless it corroborated Jasper's testimony, and if he is lying about being told to murder Dorrie Ambler, then he could be lying about the murder of Billings.'

Della Street shook her head. 'You could never get a jury to believe that. They'd convict Minerva anyway.'

'If I play this right,' Mason said, 'the judge is going to have to instruct the jury to return a verdict of not guilty.'

'He'd never dare to do that on a technicality,' Della Street said.

'Want to bet?' Mason asked.

14

Hamilton Burger was on his feet as soon as court had convened the next morning and Judge Flint had taken the bench.

'If the Court please,' he said, 'in the case of the People of the State of California versus Minerva Minden I have one more piece of evidence to put in. I have here a certified copy of the firearms register showing the purchase by Minerva Minden of a thirty-eight-caliber Smith and Wesson revolver, Number C-48809.

'This is a sales record kept in accordance with law and is, I believe, prima-facie evidence of the matters therein contained. I offer this in evidence.'

'We have no objection,' Mason said. 'The matter may go in.'

Paul Drake, accompanied by Jerry Nelson, hurriedly entered the courtroom, caught Mason's eye.

The lawyer said, 'May I have the indulgence of the Court for a moment, please?' and as Judge Flint nodded, Mason moved over to join the detectives.

Drake said in a low voice, 'Nelson has all that's known on that Santa Maria bank job, Perry. There were three persons on it, two in the bank, one driving the getaway car. Witnesses got a partial license number and description. It's the same car as the hit-and-run car and–'

'The driver,' Mason interrupted. 'Was it a woman?'

'Drake's face showed surprise. 'How did you know? Yes, it was a woman.'

'Any other jobs?' Mason asked.

'Yes, a liquor store stick-up in Bakersfield. It's probably the same gang again–a light-colored Cadillac and a woman getaway driver.'

'Thanks,' Mason said. 'That's all I need.'

He turned to face Judge Flint. 'If the Court please, before the prosecutor calls his next witness I have a question or two in regard to fingerprints which I would like to ask of Lieutenant Tragg on cross-examination. I notice that he is here in court and I ask the Court to be permitted to resume my cross-examination of this witness.'

'Is there any objection?' Judge Flint asked.

'There is, if the Court please,' Hamilton Burger said. 'I think defense counsel should cross-examine his witnesses and complete his cross-examination. It is a habit of counsel to conduct piecemeal cross-examinations and–'

'The sequence of proof and all matters of procedure in connection with the examination of a witness are in the exclusive control of the Court,' Judge Flint said. 'The Court in this case is particularly anxious to see that the defendant is not foreclosed in any manner from presenting her defense.

'The Court has decided to permit the motion. Lieutenant Tragg will return to the stand for further cross-examination.'

As Tragg stepped forward Mason nodded to Della Street, who opened a leather case, took out a folding tripod, placed it in front of the witness, put a small projector on the tripod, ran an electrical connection to a socket and put up a screen.

'This is to be a demonstration?' Judge Flint asked.

'I simply want to project a fingerprint so that I can get it to an exact size,' Mason said, 'and question Lieutenant Tragg concerning points of similarity.'

'Very well, proceed.'

Mason turned on the projector, experimented for a moment with a spot of light on the screen, then said, 'Now, Lieutenant, I am going to take a print of the thumb of the defendant on this specially prepared glass slide.'

Mason went over, extended his hand and Minerva Minden put out her thumb. Mason pressed the thumb against the slide for a moment, then said apologetically to the Court, 'I may have to repeat this experiment, if the Court please, because I am not an expert in taking fingerprints.'

He went to the projector, put in the slide, focused it for a moment, said, 'I am afraid I have smudged this one.'

He took another slide from his pocket, again went to the defendant, again received a thumbprint, then returned to the projector and focused the lens on the screen.

'Ah, yes,' Mason said, 'we're getting it now. I think this thumbprint is clear enough. You can see that, can you, Lieutenant?'

'Very well,' Lt Tragg said.

'All right, I'll arrange it so the three prints are as nearly the same size as possible; that is, the print on the left, which is the thumbprint of Dorrie Ambler; the print on the right of that which is the print of the thumb of the dead woman; and over on the right of that again, this print which I am projecting.'

'Now, just a minute,' Hamilton Burger said, getting to his feet. 'This is simply a projection, an evanescent bit of evidence which we can't identify. The other prints are enlarged photographs which can be introduced in evidence.'

'Well,' Mason said, 'you can have this slide introduced in evidence, put in an envelope and marked an appropriate exhibit.'

'Very well,' Hamilton Burger said, 'if that's the best we can do. I should prefer a photograph.'

'It depends somewhat on the point counsel is trying to make,' Judge Flint said.

Mason said, 'I am trying to test the qualifications of this witness, and to show the fallacy of an identification made from only six points of similarity.'

'Very well,' Judge Flint said, 'proceed with your questioning, and when you have finished, this slide can be put in an envelope, marked for identification and then introduced as an exhibit if either side desires.'

'Now then, Lieutenant,' Mason said, 'these prints are all about the same size. Now, I am going to call your attention to this projected print and ask you if you can find points of similarity between that and the print of the dead girl.'

'There should be some points of similarity,' Lt Tragg said, 'and there might be several, depending upon certain similarities of design.'

'Well, just approach the exhibits and indicate with a pointer any points of similarity you can find.'

'Well, here's one to start with,' Lt Tragg said. 'They have almost identical whorl patterns in the center.'

'All right, proceed.'

'Now, here's a junction . . .'

'Go right ahead, Lieutenant.'

Tragg looked at the fingerprints thoughtfully, then said, 'I'll just trace out these points of similarity, if I may, because once the projection is removed from the paper, there will be nothing to indicate what points of similarity I was referring to.'

'That's quite all right. Go right ahead,' Mason said. 'There's a sheet of white paper on which I am projecting this fingerprint and you may make tracings of any of the points of similarity which you discover.'

Lt Tragg took a pen from his pocket, traced lines, studied the print, made more tracings and finally after some five minutes backed away from the print.

'Any more points of similarity?' Mason asked.

'No,' Tragg said, 'I see none at the moment.'

'Now, how many points of similarity have you discovered, Lieutenant?'

'Six,' Lt Tragg said.

'The exact number that you had discovered with the print of Dorrie Ambler,' Mason said. 'I think, Lieutenant, that is rather a graphic and dramatic demonstration of the fact that an absolute identification cannot be made from six points of similarity. You have now established that this defendant is the dead woman you discovered.'

Lt Tragg studied the two fingerprints with frowning concentration for a moment, then returned to the witness stand.

'I have no further questions,' Mason said.

'No redirect examination on this point,' Hamilton Burger said. 'The witness said earlier that six points of similarity did *not* necessarily prove identity.'

'That's all. You may leave the stand,' Judge Flint said.

Mason switched out the light in the projector, removed the slide and said, 'Now, I believe the Court instructed that this slide was to be placed in an envelope and marked for identification.'

Mason put the slide in an envelope and handed it to the clerk.

Hamilton Burger thoughtfully studied the tracings of lines which had been made by Lt Tragg on the white paper underneath the projected fingerprints. He beckoned to Lt Tragg, and Tragg, on his way from the witness stand, paused to confer in whispers with the prosecutor.

Now that the projection had been removed, the six points which Lt Tragg had traced on the white paper showed out with startling clarity.

Suddenly Hamilton Burger pushed Lt Tragg back, jumped to his feet, said, 'Just a moment, Lieutenant. Return to the stand. Now, Your Honor, I do have some questions on redirect and I want to get this envelope from the clerk. I want that projection to be put on the white paper screen once more.'

'I'll be only too glad to accommodate the prosecutor,' Mason said.

'You keep your hands off that envelope,' Hamilton Burger shouted. 'I want someone to take that envelope, that very identical envelope right there, which you have just had marked for identification. I don't want any hocus-pocus here.'

'I think that insinuation is uncalled for, Mr Prosecutor,' Judge Flint said in an acrid rebuke.

'You just wait a moment,' Hamilton Burger said, his voice so excited that it was hard for him to control it. 'Just wait a moment and see if it's an unjustified criticism. Look at that paper screen with the marks on it and then look at the photograph of the fingerprints of Dorrie Ambler.

'Not only did Lieutenant Tragg find six points of similarity between the projected print and the print of the dead woman, *but they're exactly the same points of similarity as shown on the Dorrie Ambler fingerprint*.'

'I'm afraid I don't understand,' Judge Flint said.

'Well, I understand,' Hamilton Burger said. 'That print that was projected on the screen wasn't the fingerprint of the defendant at all. Perry Mason took her thumbprint, pretended that it had been smeared, went back to take another print and that gave him an opportunity to juggle slides. The fingerprint he projected on the screen wasn't the fingerprint of the defendant at all but was a fingerprint of Dorrie Ambler which he had managed to have made into a slide by some photographic process which would duplicate the appearance of a freshly made fingerprint.'

'Are you making this as a charge, Mr Burger?'

'I'm making it as an accusation and I demand that Mr Mason be searched. I want that other slide taken from his pocket before he has a chance to destroy it. This is a fraud upon the Court, it is an attempt to conceal evidence, it is a criminal conspiracy and unprofessional conduct.'

'Now, just a minute,' Judge Flint said. 'We're going to go at this in an orderly manner. Mr Clerk, you will put that slide back in the projector. Mr Mason, you will stand right here, please, and the Court is going to ask you to take the other slide from your pocket, the one that you said was smeared, and hand it to the Court.'

Mason put his hand in his pocket, handed a slide to the Court.

'Now then, Judge Flint said, 'let's have that slide which was marked for identification put back on the screen.'

Hamilton Burger, intensely excited, said, 'I want it just the same size as it was. It can be matched by the markings made by Lieutenant Tragg on the screen.'

'We'll have it the same size,' Judge Flint said. 'There's no reason to shout, Mr Burger. I can hear you perfectly.'

The clerk focused the projector.

'Move that projector back just a little,' Hamilton Burger said, 'just an inch or so. Get the marks so they coincide with the tracings made by Lieutenant Tragg . . . there we are.'

Hamilton Burger turned to Lt Tragg.

'Now, Lieutenant,' he said, 'forget all about the print of the dead woman. Look at the projected print and the photographic print of Dorrie Ambler and tell me how many points of similarity you find in *those* prints!'

'Lt Tragg said, 'I will take a pointer and–'

'Here, take this red crayon,' Hamilton Burger said. 'Mark the points of similarity with the red crayon. Let's see how many points of similarity you find between the projected print and that of Dorrie Ambler.'

Lt Tragg went to the exhibits, started tracing ridges with red crayon. After some few minutes he said, 'I have already found more than eighteen points of similarity, if the Court please. Twelve points of similarity are sufficient to make an absolute identification.'

'And that means?' Judge Flint asked.

'It means that the projected print is not the print of the defendant at all but is the print of Dorrie Ambler.'

'You're absolutely certain of that?' Judge Flint asked.

'Absolutely certain.'

Judge Flint turned to Perry Mason. 'Mr Mason,' he said, 'you stand charged before this Court with a very grave offense, an offense which could well lead to disciplinary action or disbarment proceedings. It would certainly lead to a charge of contempt of Court. I am going to ask you to plead guilty on the charge of contempt of Court right here and right now.

'In view of the fact that this matter came up while the jury was present, I am going to have it determined while the jury is present. Now then, Mr Mason, I am going to ask you how it happened that in pretending to take an imprint of the defendant's thumb you substituted a slide with the imprint of Dorrie Ambler.'

Mason said, 'I am sorry, Your Honor, I have no explanation.'

'In that event,' Judge Flint said, 'the Court is going to–'

'May I make one statement?'

'Very well,' Judge Flint snapped. 'Make a statement.'

'I simply suggest,' Mason said, 'that in order to avoid any confusion, the witness, Lieutenant Tragg, take a fingerprint of the defendant's thumb. Then we will project that on the screen and Lieutenant Tragg can see how many points of similarity he finds between that and the print of the dead woman. In that way there can be no question of confusion. I have here an acetate slide coated with a substance which will show the fingerprint characteristics.'

Judge Flint hesitated.

'I would like very much to have that done,' Hamilton Burger said.

'Very well. You may proceed,' Judge Flint said.

Mason handed a slide to Lt Tragg who inspected it carefully, took a magnifying glass from his pocket, looked at it, then approached the defendant, took her thumbprint, returned to the projector, removed the slide which was in the projector and inserted the slide of the thumbprint he had just taken.

'Now then,' Mason said, 'perhaps the Lieutenant will be good enough to tell us how many points of similarity there are between *that* fingerprint, the fingerprint of the dead woman and the fingerprint of Dorrie Ambler.'

Lt Tragg adjusted the focus just right, then approached the projected print.

Suddenly he stopped.

'They coincide,' he said.

'What coincides?' Hamilton Burger snapped at him.

'The points of similarity which I have traced on the paper in red and in green coincide with the pattern now projected on the screen.'

Hamilton Burger said, 'Well–They can't.'

'But they do,' Mason said. 'It's quite evident. The Court can see for itself, and the jurors can see the same thing.'

'Now, just a moment!' Hamilton Burger shouted. 'Here's some more hocus-pocus. I insist that we have this phase of the matter disposed of in the absence of the jury.'

'We've had the rest of it in the presence of the jury,' Judge Flint said. 'I think we'll clear up this entire situation in the presence of the jury. . . . Now Lieutenant, exactly what is the meaning of this?'

'I don't know,' Lt Tragg said.

'I suggest,' Mason said, 'that it means the projected fingerprint which I put on the screen *was* the fingerprint of the defendant and that the prosecutor's charge that I had juggled slides, the prosecutor's charge that I had substituted fingerprints and all of his remarks concerning misconduct, were unjustified, were accusations made in the presence of the jury and constituted misconduct on the part of the prosecutor.'

'Now, let's get this straight,' Judge Flint said. 'Lieutenant, look up here. Now, Lieutenant, is it true that there are eighteen points of similarity between the fingerprint of the defendant and the fingerprint of Dorrie Ambler?'

'Yes, Your Honor.'

'How could that happen, Lieutenant? You have just testified under oath that twelve points of similarity would show an absolute identification; yet you have here eighteen points of similarity between the prints of two different people.'

'I'm afraid,' Lt Tragg said, 'that there's something here I don't understand. I have now noticed more points of similarity. I could go on and probably get many other points of similarity.'

'And what does that mean?' Judge Flint asked.

'It means,' Perry Mason said drying, 'that either the science of fingerprinting is breaking down or that this defendant and Dorrie Ambler are one and the same person, in which event there never was any Dorrie Ambler and the testimony of the witness, Dunleavey Jasper, that he saw the two women together and noticed their similarity is absolute perjury.

'The Court will notice that other witnesses have testified to the similarity of appearance of Dorrie Ambler on the one hand and the defendant on the other, but no witness had been produced who had seen them together, and no witness could be produced who had seen them together because there was only one person. Therefore the testimony of Dunleavey Jasper that he saw them together is–'

Judge Flint shouted, 'Bailiff, apprehend that man! Keep him from leaving the courtroom.'

Dunleavey Jasper, halfway through the swinging door was grabbed by the bailiff. He turned and engaged in a frantic struggle.

The courtroom was in an uproar.

Judge Flint shouted, 'The spectators will be seated! The jurors will be seated! Court will take a fifteen-minute recess.'

15

As court was reconvened amidst the breathless hush of excitement, Mason got to his feet. 'If the Court please,' he said, 'it appearing that there never was any such person as Dorrie Ambler, and in view of the fact that the prosecutor now knows a confession of perjury has been obtained from Dunleavey Jasper, I move the Court to instruct the jury to return a verdict of not guilty and discharge the defendant from custody.'

'Does the prosecutor have any statement?' Judge Flint asked.

Hamilton Burger dejectedly got to his feet.

'I don't understand it, Your Honor,' he said, 'and I think that the patience of the Court has been imposed upon by reason of the fact that the defense did not disclose this matter to the Court at an earlier date but chose to present it in this dramatic manner. However, that is a matter for the Court to take up with Counsel for the defense. As far as the present motion is concerned, I will verify the fact that Dunleavey Jasper has made a confession.'

'I think,' Judge Flint said, 'that it would clarify matters if the general substance of that confession were a part of the record. Would you care to make a statement, Mr Prosecutor?'

'It seems,' Burger said, 'that Dunleavey Jasper, Barlowe Dalton, and a young woman named Flossie Hendon, stole this Cadillac car and started south.

'These people had committed various crimes before they stole the Cadillac. Afterwards they committed other crimes, among them the holdup of the branch bank at Santa Maria where they secured some eighteen thousand dollars. They divided eight thousand dollars of this money into three equal lots, and the balance of ten thousand dollars was wrapped in paper, held in place with rubber bands, and placed in the glove compartment of the stolen automobile.

'They went to the Montrose Country Club intending to steal valuable furs from the cloakroom, to hold up the cashier, for the large sum of money which they thought would be in the safe that evening. They left their getaway car with Flossie Hendon at the wheel, and she was supposed to be there with the motor running, ready to help them escape as soon as they had completed their crime.

'However, Flossie Hendon succumbed to the feminine urge to look in at the gowns of the dancers who were in the country club. She left the wheel of the car for only a few moments but that was long enough.

'Minerva Minden had apparently forfeited her driving license for drunk driving some months earlier. So that she wouldn't be deprived of the privilege of driving a car, she had established a dual identity, taking the name of Dorrie Ambler and renting the apartment in the Parkhurst Apartments, staying there on occasion and building up a bona fide identity so in case the validity of this second driving license should ever be questioned she could have proof of her identity.

'Since the attendant at the parking lot saw she was under the influence of liquor and asked to see her driving license, she showed him the only one she had–the one made out to Dorrie Ambler.

'Later on, she had an argument with her escort, ran blindly out of the club seeking a taxicab. She saw the stolen Cadillac with the motor running, jumped in and took off, driving to her apartment.

'We can only surmise what happened. Presumably she became involved in a hit-and-run accident, put the car in the garage at the Parkhurst Apartments and from there on the situation seems to have been deliberately obscured in order to keep the police from involving her in another accident involving drunken driving, which would have resulted in the revocation of her probation and the imposition of a long jail sentence.

'Quite naturally the three criminals wished to recover the stolen automobile since there was ten thousand dollars in the glove compartment. They traced the automobile to Dorrie Ambler, through the parking lot attendant, eventually traced Dorrie Ambler to the Parkhurst Apartments, and went there to search the apartment after having rented Apartment 805 as a base. While they were there in Apartment 907, Marvin Billings caught them red-handed. Barlowe Dalton shot him with the twenty-two-caliber revolver they had found in the apartment where they had also found the thirty-eight revolver.

'It was at that time that Perry Mason and Paul Drake came to the door of the apartment.

'Subsequently, after having made their escape by barricading the door to the kitchen and going down the service stairs to Apartment 805, which they had rented for the purpose of giving them a base of operations, the two men read in the paper about Perry Mason's connection with the case and the similarity of identities, and came to the conclusion that either Dorrie Ambler or Minerva Minden had found their stolen ten thousand dollars.

'At about that time Flossie Hendon, a young delinquent who had gone with the two hoodlums on their career of crime for kicks, as she expressed it, was quite concerned about the murder of Marvin Billings. Murder was more than she had bargained for.

'So Jasper says his partner, Barlowe Dalton, was the one who took her for a ride, killed her with the thirty-eight they had stolen from the apartment in the Parkhurst Apartments. Of course now that Dalton is dead, Jasper glibly puts all the murders on his shoulders.

'Later on, when Jasper was apprehended in a burglary where Barlowe Dalton had been killed, Jasper conceived the idea of getting immunity for himself by means of confessing to the kidnaping of Dorrie Ambler and involving Minerva Minden.

'Flossie Hendon had been murdered to keep her from talking. Apparently the body which was discovered, the badly decomposed body, was that of

Flossie Hendon, and Jasper shrewdly counted on advanced putrefaction to make positive identification impossible.

'In the meantime the defendant, going to the apartment she had rented under the name of Dorrie Ambler, learned of the murder and left the building in a state of some excitement. It was at that time she was seen by the witness.'

Hamilton Burger paused, then said, 'If the Court please, I dislike to make this confession, but there are times when we who are prosecutors have to rely upon the evidence as it comes to us and have to use our judgment.

'We felt that Dunleavey Jasper was telling the truth. We were willing to give him immunity on a relatively minor crime in order to convict a murderess. The fact that things didn't work out that way, the fact that we were victimized, is one of the hazards of law enforcement.

'I have made this statement so that the record may be cleared. We are going to proceed against Dunleavey Jasper for the crimes he has admitted, and I think we will proceed against him for murder, both the murder of Marvin Billings and the murder of Flossie Hendon.'

Hamilton Burger, with what dignity he could muster, turned and stalked from the courtroom, leaving to his associates the unpleasant task of remaining through the final stages of the case.

Judge Flint said, 'The jurors will be instructed to return a verdict of not guilty in this case of the People of the State of California versus Minerva Minden.'

16

Mason, Della Street and Paul Drake sat in the lawyer's office.

'When,' Della Street asked, 'did you realize there weren't two women?'

'When Minny Minden showed us there was no scar on her abdomen,' Mason said.

Della Street glanced at Paul Drake. 'I don't get it,' she said.

Mason said, 'When I asked Minerva if she had the scar of an appendicitis operation, she promptly exhibited the precise spot where such a scar would have been.

'Now, if she hadn't read up on the location of such a scar, how would she have known the exact location to have exhibited? If you've had such an operation, you know where the scar is. If you haven't you don't know, not unless you're a doctor, a nurse, or have read up on it.'

'Now I get it,' Della Street said, 'but what was the scar she showed us when she first came to the office?'

'Tinted transparent tape and collodion,' Mason said. 'Remember her modesty? She backed into a corner away from the windows, bared herself for a moment, then overcome by modesty covered herself again. She didn't give any of us a really good look. Tinted tape and collodion can make an almost perfect surgical scar from a distance.'

'But why in the world didn't you call the attention of the Court to what you had learned earlier in the trial?' Drake asked.

'Because if I had,' Mason said, 'Minerva Minden would have been convicted of the murder of Marvin Billings.

'After all, Dunleavey Jasper only needed to state that regardless of the lies he had told us as to the first part of what had happened, that actually Minerva Minden had killed Marvin Billings.

'Remember also that Flossie Hendon was killed with Minerva's gun.

'I had to manipulate things just right so that the ending came in such a dramatic manner that Jasper would cave in all the way.'

'But now the district attorney will prosecute Minerva on a hit-and-run charge,' Drake said, 'so I don't see that you've gained a thing.'

'He won't prosecute her,' Mason said.

'What makes you think he won't?'

'Because,' Mason said, grinning, 'she is going to make a voluntary appearance before the judge who had placed her on probation for her previous violations of the vehicle code. She is going to confess to her part in the hit-and-run accident and take her medicine.'

'What will that medicine be?' Della Street asked. 'Surely she's been punished enough because of this ordeal she's been through.'

'That,' Mason said, 'is something we don't need to concern ourselves with. It's up to the judge. He may extend probation on this charge or he may revoke her probation and send her to jail. My own guess is he will find that the consequences of this last escapade of hers have resulted in subduing the madcap heiress of Montrose into a very penitent, humble young woman who now realizes she can't pit her personality, her wealth and her nylons against the majesty of the law.'

'You mean he will give her probation?' Della Street asked.

'I think it's quite possible,' Mason said. 'He will, of course, revoke her driving license for a long period and order her to make a generous settlement on the victim of the hit-and-run. Remember, she tried to confess to me on several occasions but I headed her off. I had to.'

'Why?' Drake asked.

'Because,' Mason said, 'I am an officer of the court. I didn't want her to confess to the hit-and-run crime until I had secured her release on this murder charge. I didn't want to have any official confirmation from her own lips of what I suspected to be the case until the murder charge had been disposed of.'

'But why did she take these elaborate precautions to fool us?' Della Street asked. 'Why all the business of the blank cartridges at the airport?'

'Because,' Mason said, 'she had found the ten thousand dollars in the glove compartment, had learned the car was a stolen one operated by crooks, and so she had to have Dorrie Ambler vanish into thin air in order to get the crooks off her own neck. Therefore, she put the ad in the paper, answered it herself, victimized the firm of detectives, and then called me *from the courthouse* as soon as the court hearing was over, saying she was at her apartment and that men were keeping her under surveillance and would we please come at once. Then Minerva hung up the telephone.

'You'll remember Drake's detective said she went to the phone booth right after the hearing. That's when she intended to have Dorrie disappear, leaving me very much concerned over the disappearance.

'It was a nice scheme. It *might* have worked the way she planned it. As it happened, however, at the time she was telephoning me, the crooks who had stolen the car and who had used the apartment on the lower floor as a base of operations were in the apartment searching for ten thousand dollars. The detective caught them there and was shot by Dunleavey Jasper.'

'Wouldn't it have been something,' Della Street asked, 'if you hadn't been able to bring things to such a dramatic conclusion that Dunleavey Jasper lost his head and confessed to what really happened? Good heavens, Minerva Minden *might* have been convicted of her own murder!'

She thought for a moment, then asked, 'How could Jasper have known all those facts, Chief?'

Mason grinned. 'He didn't get the facts until later. Tragg's interview with us in the room that was bugged, and the subsequent story in the newspapers, gave him his chance to put one over on the police and Hamilton Burger. Jasper is smart. He desperately wanted immunity for his crimes–and of course he'd found Minerva's thirty-eight-caliber gun in the apartment at the Parkhurst. You can also bet that the police questioning gave him enough leads so he could build a pretty convincing story. Naturally the police were anxious to have all the details explained, and Jasper, having rented Apartment 805 studied the tenant of 907, knew a lot of details he could use to make his story convincing. Because Hamilton Burger was so anxious to get something on me and to convict my client, he was an eager victim.

'Minerva Minden tells me she was out in the parking lot. The attendant thought she had been drinking and asked to see her driving license. She showed him the only license she had–the one in the name of Dorrie Ambler. The parking lot attendant remembered the name, Ambler, and told Dunleavey Jasper he thought that was the name of the woman who had stolen his car. But Jasper, of course, didn't dare tell this to the police because it would ruin the story he was putting across, so he said on the stand he had located the car through underworld connections.'

The phone rang. Della Street answered it, said, 'Henrietta Hull wishes to know how much your fee is going to be.'

Mason grinned. 'Tell her it's one hundred and fifty thousand dollars and to make the check payable to the Children's Hospital. After all, I don't think Minerva should get off *too* easy.'

RLE STANLEY GARDNER

The Case of

The Amorous Aunt

FOREWORD

The arch-enemy of the murderer is autopsy.

In crimes of emotion the autopsy can determine facts that no subsequent fabrication, however clever, can confute.

In cold-blooded crimes committed by an intellectual and scheming murderer who has greed or revenge as his goal, the medical examiner, following clues which would never be apparent to a less thoroughly trained individual, can establish the truth.

It is for this reason that I have, in these Perry Mason books, tried to interest the reader in the vital importance of legal medicine.

Legal medicine is, of course, international in scope. In Mexico City, for instance, the number of official autopsies performed is approximately equal to those performed in New York City.

My friend Dr Manuel Merino Alcántara is Sub-Director of the Mexican Forensic Institute, Professor of Legal Medicine at the National University of Mexico Medical School, and editor of *El Medico*, the Mexican medical journal, similar in scope to the American Medical Association's *Journal* in this country. He is diligently working to bring about international co-operation and understanding in the field of legal medicine, and has sent me a great deal of statistical information.

And so I dedicate this book to Mexico's outstanding authority in forensic medicine,

DR MANUEL MERINO ALCÁNTARA

Erle Stanley Gardner

I

Della Street, Perry Mason's confidential secretary, said, 'A couple of lovebirds have strayed into the office without an appointment. They insist it's a matter of life and death.'

'Everything is,' Mason said. 'If you start with the idea of perpetuating life, you must accept the inevitable corollary of death–but I presume these people aren't interested in my philosophical ideas.'

'These people,' Della Street announced, 'are interested in each other, in the singing of the birds, the blue of the sky, the moonlight on water, the sound of the night wind in the trees.'

Mason laughed. 'It's infectious. You are getting positively romantic, poetic, and show evidence of having been exposed to a highly contagious disease. . . . Now, what the devil would two lovebirds want with the services of a lawyer who specializes in murder cases?'

Della Street smiled enigmatically. 'I told them that I thought you'd see them, despite the fact they have no appointment.'

'In other words,' the lawyer said, 'your own curiosity having been aroused, you decided to arouse mine. Did they tell you what they wanted to see me about?'

'A widowed aunt,' Della Street said, 'and a Bluebeard.'

Mason made an elaborate show of rubbing his hands together.

'Sold!' he exclaimed.

'Now?' Della Street asked.

'Immediately,' Mason said. 'When's the next appointment, Della?'

'Fifteen minutes, but you can keep him waiting for a few minutes. He's the witness in that Dowling affair, the one that Paul Drake located.

Mason frowned. 'I don't want to take any chances on having *him* leave the office. Let me know the minute he comes in, Della, and send in the lovebirds. What are their names?'

Della Street consulted a memo.

'George Latty and Linda Calhoun. They're from some little town in Massachusetts. It's their first trip to California.'

'Bring them in,' Mason said.

Della Street went to the reception room, to return in a matter of seconds with the young couple.

Mason sized them up as he rose and smiled a greeting.

The man was twenty-three or twenty-four; tall, rather handsome, with two-inch sideburns and wavy black hair that had been carefully groomed.

The young woman was certainly not more than twenty-two, with round blue eyes which she held wide open in such a way as to give her face an expression of almost cherubic innocence.

As they stood surveying Mason, the girl's hand unconsciously groped for and found the hand of her escort, and they stood there hand in hand, the girl smiling, the man self-conscious.

'You're George Latty,' Mason said to the man.

He nodded.

'And you're Miss Linda Calhoun.'

The girl nodded.

'Sit down, please,' Mason said, 'and tell me what seems to be the trouble.'

They seated themselves, and Linda Calhoun looked at George Latty as though signalling him to break the ice. Latty, however, sat looking straight ahead.

'Well?' Mason asked.

'You tell him, George,' the girl said.

Latty leaned forward and put his hands on the lawyer's desk. 'It's her aunt,' he said.

'And what about the aunt?' Mason asked.

'She's going to get murdered.'

'Have you any idea who is going to commit the murder?' Mason asked.

'Certainly,' Latty said. 'His name is Montrose Dewitt.'

'And what,' Mason asked, 'do you know about Montrose Dewitt, aside from the fact that he's a potential murderer?'

It was Linda Calhoun who answered the question.

'Nothing,' she said. 'That's why we're here.'

'Now, you folks are from Massachusetts, I believe?'

'That's right,' Latty said.

'You've known each other for some time?'

'Yes.'

'If it's not a personal question, may I ask if you're engaged?'

'Yes, we are.'

Mason said, 'Forgive me if I seem to be impertinent, but if we're going to get into a case of this sort where there may be some name calling, I want to be sure of my facts, has the date been set for the wedding?'

'No,' she said. 'George is studying law and I'm . . .' She flushed. 'I'm helping him through law school.'

'I see,' Mason said. 'You're employed?'

'Yes.'

Mason raised his eyebrows in silent interrogation.

'I'm a secretary in a law firm,' she said. 'I applied for and received a month's leave of absence and came out here. Before I left, I asked the senior partner for the name of the best attorney in this part of the country and he said that I should consult you if it came to a knock-down, drag-out fight.'

'And it has come to a knock-down, drag-out fight?' Mason asked.

'It's going to.'

Mason looked at Latty. 'Now,' he said, 'as I take it, you young people came on here together. May I ask if you drove, came by plane or–'

'I drove,' she said. 'That is, I came with Aunt Lorraine, and George came out by plane when I telephoned him.'

'And when was that?'

'Last night. He just got in this morning and we had a council of war and decided to come to you.'

'All right,' Mason said, 'that gives us the preliminaries. Now tell me about Aunt Lorraine. What's her last name?'

'Elmore. E-l-m-o-r-e.'

'Miss or Mrs?'

'Mrs. She's a widow. And she's . . . well, she's at the foolish age.'

'And exactly what age is considered the foolish age?'

'She'll be forty-eight on her next birthday.'

'And what has she done that indicates her foolishness?'

'She's gone overboard,' Latty said.

Mason raised his eyebrows.

'In love,' the young woman explained.

Mason smiled. 'I take it that people around twenty-one and twenty-two who are in love are perfectly normal, but they're supposed to have a corner on the emotion and anyone above that age who falls in love is indulging in foolishness?'

Linda flushed.

'Well, at that age,' Latty said, 'well . . . sure.'

Mason laughed, 'You two have all the arrogance of youth. Perhaps the best thing one can say for youth is that it's not incurable. Your aunt's husband died, Miss Calhoun?'

'Yes.'

'How long ago?'

'About five years ago. And please don't laugh at us, Mr Mason. This is serious.'

Mason said, 'I would say your aunt had every right in the world to fall in love.'

'But it's the way she did it,' Linda protested.

Latty said, 'Some adventurer is going to strip her of all her money.'

Mason's eyes narrowed. 'Are you the only relative?' he asked Linda.

'Yes.'

'And presumably you were the sole beneficiary under her will?'

The girl flushed again.

Mason waited for her answer.

'Yes, I suppose so.'

'Is she wealthy?'

'She has . . . well, rather a comfortable nest egg.'

'And within the last few weeks,' Latty said, 'her entire attitude has changed. She used to be very affectionate with Linda and now her affections have been alienated by this cad. Yesterday there was a fight and Lorraine walked out on Linda and told her to go back to Massachusetts and quit messing up her life.'

Mason said, 'And just what is your interest in the matter, Mr Latty?'

'Well, I . . . I'm–'

'You're in love with Linda and expect to marry her?'

'Yes.'

'And perhaps you had been rather counting on Aunt Lorraine's nest egg coming in at some time in the future?'

'Absolutely not!' he said. 'I resent that.'

'I was asking you,' Mason said, 'because if we take any action other people will ask you that question, and perhaps in a sneering tone of voice. I thought I'd prepare you, that's all.'

Latty said, 'Let them make that accusation to my face and I'll flatten them.'

Mason said, 'You'll do a lot better to keep your temper, young man. Now, Miss Calhoun, I'd like to hear the facts of the case. Can you begin at the beginning and tell me when this first came up?'

She said, 'Aunt Lorraine has been lonely. I know that, and I sympathize with her. I'm the only one she has and I've done what I could.'

'Doesn't she have friends?' Mason asked.

'Well, yes, but not . . . well, not what you'd call intimate friends.'

'But you've been in touch with her?'

'I've given her every minute of my time that I could, Mr Mason, but–Well, I'm a working girl. I have to keep up my apartment and I have a job to do. I know that Aunt Lorraine would like to have seen more of me and–'

'And you put in a good deal of your time seeing something of George Latty?' Mason asked.

'Yes.'

'And your aunt, perhaps, resented that?'

'I think she resented him.'

'All right. Now, what happened with this Montrose Dewitt?'

'She met him by correspondence.'

'One of those lonely heart things?' Mason aked.

'Heavens, no! She isn't *that* foolish. It was some kind of a deal where Aunt Lorraine wrote to a magazine expressing an opinion on one of the articles that the magazine had published, and the magazine published the letter with her name and not her street address but the city where she lived.

'Mr Dewitt sent her a letter just addressed to her at that city, and the post office located her address and delivered the letter, and that started a correspondence.'

'And then?' Mason asked.

'Then Aunt Lorraine became very much smitten. She wouldn't admit it, of course, not even to herself, but I could see it.

'She sent him her picture and, incidentally, it was a picture that was taken some ten years ago.'

'Did he send her his picture?'

'No. He told her that he wore a patch over one eye and was very self-conscious about it.'

'And then?' Mason asked.

'Then he called her long distance and after that he would call her quite frequently, two or three times a week.

'So of course Aunt Lorraine insisted she was going to take a vacation; a long motor trip. Well, that didn't fool me any, and I knew what she had in mind, but there was nothing anyone could do about it. You couldn't stop her at that time. Things had gone too far, and the man had her completely hypnotized.'

'So you decided to go with her.'

'Yes.'

'And you came out here with her and then what happened?'

'We checked in at a hotel and she said she was going to lie down for a while. I went out to do some shopping. When I came back she was gone. There was a note on the dresser for me, saying she might not be back until late.

'When she came in I accused her of having gone out to see Montrose Dewitt and she became angry and said she didn't care to be chaperoned, nor did she care to have me treat her as though she were in her second childhood.'

'Her feelings were quite understandable,' Mason said.

'I know,' Linda Calhoun said, 'but there are other things, other disturbing factors.'

'Such as what?'

'I found out that she had taken the blood tests necessary to obtain a marriage license, that she had been converting a great deal of property to cash. She had been selling some of her stocks and bonds, and she came out here with something like thirty-five thousand dollars in cash.'

'No traveler's checks?'

'Just cold, hard cash, Mr Mason. A roll of bills that would–I believe the expression they customarily use is, choke a horse.'

'And what caused her to do that?'

'Your guess is as good as mine,' she said, 'but I don't think there's any question but that it was an action prompted by instructions she had received from Montrose Dewitt over the telephone.'

'This Dewitt seems to be rather a vague and shadowy character,' Mason said. 'What has she told you about his background?'

'Nothing. Absolutely nothing. She has been very mysterious about it.'

'So you had an argument last night?'

'No, that was yesterday. The night she went out was night before last. Then yesterday she told me she was going to be gone all day and I could be free to do whatever I wanted to, and then I started talking to her and I guess that was the first time I let her know that I knew anything about the money.'

'And?' Mason asked.

'And she became absolutely furious. She told me that she had thought I cared for her for herself but that now she was convinced that I cared for her only for what I thought I could get out of her . . . that–Well, she said some things about George that I simply couldn't take.'

'Such as what?' Mason asked.

'I don't like to repeat them.'

'Does George know?'

'I know,' George said. 'That is, I know generally.'

'He doesn't know *all*,' Linda Calhoun said.

'She said that he was a sponge and a heel?' Mason asked.

'That was the start of it,' she said. 'She went on from there and amplified. She said that if it came to a question of talking about boy friends, at least *her* boy friend was self-supporting and was a *man*, and had some ability to take care of himself in the world without hiding behind a woman's skirts. She–

'Oh, Mr Mason, I'm not going to tell you *all* of it. You can use your imagination and–'

'So your aunt told you to go back home?'

'She made it a very humiliating experience. She carefully counted out the money for the airplane fare, pointed out that it was first-class fare on a jet plane and told me to take the plane.'

'What did you do?'

'I threw the money on the floor, and last night I telephoned George. Then I wired him the money for plane fare.'

'Out of your savings?' Mason asked.

'Out of my savings.'

'And that's the situation to date?'

'That's all of the situation to date.'

Mason said, 'Look here, your aunt is a mature woman. If she wants–'

'I know what you're going to say,' Linda interrupted, 'and I'm not going to interfere with whatever she wants to do. But I do want to find out something about this Montrose Dewitt. I want to protect her from him and from herself.'

'That,' Mason said, 'is going to cost you money . . . more from your savings.'

'How much more?'

'A really good private detective agency would want around fifty dollars a day and expenses.'

'How many days would it take?'

'Heavens knows,' Mason said. 'A detective might get all the information he needed in a few hours. He might get it in a day. He might have to work for a week or a month.'

'I can't afford to have him for a month,' she said, 'but I could–Well, I thought that I could pay two hundred dollars–but of course there'd be *your* fee.'

'You don't need me,' Mason said. 'There's nothing connected with the case that has any legal angles. You don't contend that your aunt is unable to manage her own affairs, that she's mentally unsound?'

'Certainly not. She's simply at a dangerous age and she's in love.'

Mason smiled and said, 'Whenever a person falls in love it's automatically a dangerous age. Now, do I understand you want to engage a private detective?'

'Yes. And if you could see that we didn't go wrong–Well, I understand there are some private detectives who–Well, some are better than others.'

'And you want the best. Is that it?'

'Yes.'

Mason nodded to Della Street. 'Ring the Drake Detective Agency and ask Paul Drake to step in, if you will please, Della.'

Mason turned to his visitors. 'Paul Drake,' he said, 'has his offices on this floor. The Drake Detective Agency does all my business and has for years, and you'll find Paul Drake exceedingly competent and completely honest.'

A few moments later when Drake's code knock sounded on the door, Della Street let him in and Mason performed the introductions.

Paul Drake, tall, loose-jointed, surveyed the young couple with shrewd eyes, and seated himself.

Mason said, 'I'll make it short, Paul. Linda Calhoun and George Latty are engaged. Linda has an aunt, Lorraine Elmore, forty-seven, a widow. Mrs Elmore engaged in correspondence with a man by the name of Montrose Dewitt and seems to have fallen pretty much under his influence. She has had blood tests taken, apparently to get a marriage license. Linda and her aunt came out here on a vacation. Her aunt is carrying perhaps as much as thirty-five thousand in cash. She and Linda had a fight. Mrs Elmore told Linda to go home. Instead of that, Linda wired money to George Latty and had him fly out to join her. They want to save her aunt from herself. Their home is Massachusetts.

'Particularly, they want to find out all the background on Montrose Dewitt. What will it cost?'

'I don't know,' Drake said. 'My rates are fifty dollars a day.' He turned to Linda Calhoun. 'You have his address?'

'Yes. He lives in the Bella Vista Apartments in Van Nuys.'

'Photograph?'

'No.'

Drake said, 'I don't want to take any of your money unless it's a matter of sufficient importance to let me feel I'm not robbing you.'

'Do you consider murder a matter of importance, Mr Drake?'

The detective smiled. 'Yes,' he said.

'That's what I'm worried about,' Linda Calhoun said. 'I want to prevent a murder.'

Drake said, 'I gather you've been reading some of the so-called true crime magazines.'

'I have,' she stated, 'and I'm proud of it! I think every law-abiding citizen should realize the crime hazards of civilized life. One of the big troubles with the administration of justice is that the average citizen doesn't have any idea of the menace of crime.'

'You have a point there,' Drake agreed, studying her thoughtfully.

'Don't you think it's a suspicious circumstance that Aunt Lorraine is carrying over thirty thousand dollars in cash with her?'

'I think that is more apt to indicate foolishness or falling in love.'

'Falling in love with a complete stranger,' Linda pointed out.

'All right,' Drake said smiling. 'You win. Do you want me to go to work on this Montrose Dewitt?'

'I wish you would. At least for . . . well, shall we say, two days?'

'Two days it is,' Drake said.

She turned to Mason. 'Do you think I should notify the police?'

'Heavens, no!' Mason exclaimed. 'That way you really would stir up a hornet's nest. But I do think it's a good idea to have Paul Drake give the situation a once-over. . . . And now, if you'll pardon me, I have an important appointment.'

'How much do we owe you, Mr Mason?'

Mason grinned. 'Nothing, as yet. But keep in touch with me and I'll keep in touch with Paul Drake. He'll report to you.'

Drake said, 'You two had better come down to my office and give me all the data you have. I'll want some background on your aunt and I want everything you know about Montrose Dewitt.'

2

Shortly before noon Della Street, answering the telephone, turned to Mason and said, 'There's another development in the Case of the Amorous Aunt.'

Mason raised his eyebrows in silent interrogation.

'A man named Howland Brent would like to see you at once upon a matter of the greatest importance connected with the affairs of Lorraine Elmore.'

'How did he happen to come to me?' Mason asked.

'Apparently Linda Calhoun told him you were representing her.'

Mason frowned. 'I told her she didn't need an attorney. I did this so she could take what money she had to spend and hire the Drake Detective Agency.'

'Well?' Della Street asked. 'Do we refer him to Paul Drake or . . .'

Mason looked at his watch. 'I have about fifteen minutes before I have to leave for my luncheon appointment, Della. Go take a look at him. If it's routine, refer him to Paul Drake. If it impresses you as being something worth while, come back and let me know and I'll give him fifteen minutes.'

Della Street nodded, slipped through the door to the outer office, was gone about five minutes, then returned and said, 'I think you'd better see him, Chief.'

'How come?' Mason asked.

'He's flown out here from Boston. He's Lorraine Elmore's financial manager. He has charge of all of her investments and he's worried.'

'How worried?'

'Plenty. He flew out here.'

Mason frowned. 'Everyone else regards this situation as being more serious than I do. What does he look like, Della?'

Della Street said slowly, 'Let's see. He's somewhere in his late forties, a tall, cadaverous individual with narrow shoulders, a thin waist, high cheekbones, sunken cheeks, a little mustache and one of those little hats that Easterners wear with about an inch and a half brim. He's wearing a tweed suit, rather heavy-soiled walking shoes, and carries a cane.'

'In short,' Mason said, grinning, 'he looks like you expected him to look.'

Della Street smiled. 'And we'll see him?'

'By all means,' Mason said. 'We'll see him.'

Della Street left the office to return in a few moments with Howland Brent.

'This is Mr Mason, Mr Brent,' she said.

Brent dropped the crook of his cane over his left arm, strode across to Mason's desk, extended a bony hand.

'Ah, Mr Mason,' he said.

'Sit down,' Mason invited. 'I only have a moment. My secretary tells me you're interested in a matter concerning Lorraine Elmore?'

'Perhaps I should introduce myself in greater detail,' Brent said. 'I will, however, explain the circumstances as succinctly as possible.'

Mason caught Della Street's eye. 'Go ahead.'

'Very well. I am a financial consultant and manager. I have several clients who give me complete carte blanche in connection with their financial affairs. I invest their monies and reinvest. Beyond a checking account which they carry in their own names, I relieve them of all financial details. From time to time I make reports, of course.

'As my clients need money, they call on me for whatever amount they need. Every thirty days I mail them a complete statement showing their investments, and, of course, the client has the final power of disposition. If the client wishes me to sell certain securities, I sell. If the client wishes to buy, I buy.

'However, Mr Mason, I point with pride to my record. I have, over a period of years, made substantial capital gain increases for my clients. I have a very select clientele–one which is also very limited because in matters of this sort I do not believe in the delegation of authority. I reach my own decisions, although those decisions are of course based upon detailed analyses of the securities market and these analyses are, of course, prepared by experts.'

Mason nodded.

'I cannot violate the confidence of a client, Mr Mason, except in a matter that would be tantamount to life or death. I feel that this matter is of such a nature.'

'After talking with Linda Calhoun, I take it,' Mason said.

'Yes, after talking with Linda Calhoun; although I may point out, Mr Mason, that my talk with Linda Calhoun was the result of suspicion on my part and that the suspicion was not engendered by my talk with her. In fact, the reverse is the case.'

Mason nodded.

'Because my relation with my clients is so highly confidential and so very intimate, I have powers of attorney from the various people I represent; and from time to time I can, if necessary, secure any information which I need from their financial depositaries.

'In this particular case there are blanket instructions that if the checking account falls below a certain amount, the bank is to notify me and I make a sufficient deposit to keep the minimal balance. A situation of this sort seldom arises, but there have been times when my client was travelling when it has been necessary for me to deposit funds.

'I may say without divulging any confidence that Mrs Elmore's financial sense is very good but her mathematical sense is somewhat deficient. She frequently makes expenditures without keeping accurate account of the aggregate amount.'

Mason nodded.

'So, when Mrs Elmore advised me that she was driving to the West Coast on a vacation, I simply made a routine notation. I may say, however, that she had shortly before the trip asked me to deposit a very substantial amount of cash in her checking account. While I cannot divulge the exact amount, I will state that I considered it somewhat excessive and pointed out that commercial accounts were barren as far as income-producing returns were concerned and that there would be an inevitable loss of interest. However, I was instructed not to bother myself about that but simply to see that sufficient securities were sold so that the fund could be placed in the checking account.

'You follow me, Mr Mason?'

'One might say I'm a paragraph ahead of you,' Mason said. 'I take it Mrs Elmore gave some checks which resulted in the bank's balance falling below the minimum amount; the bank notified you; you were astounded; you used your power of attorney to check with the bank and found out Mrs Elmore had withdrawn a huge sum in the form of cash.'

Brent's expression showed surprise. 'That is a remarkable deduction, Mr Mason.'

'It is accurate?'

'It is accurate.'

'And why do you come to me?'

'I came out here to consult Mrs Elmore. I arrived at the airport about two hours ago. I called at the hotel where she was stopping. I found that she had left, that her niece, Miss Calhoun, was there; and, while I did not of course confide in Miss Calhoun, I let her know that I was there upon a matter of some urgency and Miss Calhoun confided in me.'

'About Montrose Dewitt?'

'Exactly.'

'And why did you come to me?' Mason asked.

'I wanted you to have certain information which I felt I could disclose–information which you have deduced so that I do not now have to make a disclosure, and this, of course, is exceedingly gratifying to me because I do like to preserve the confidences of my clients.

'However, Mr Mason, I wish to impress upon you that the situation is, in my opinion, serious and that it should not be discounted. I would like to have you report to me everything that you find out about my client and about Mr Dewitt.'

Mason shook his head.

'No?' Brent asked.

'No,' Mason said.

'You mean it is impossible?'

'I mean it is inadvisable,' Mason said. 'In the first place, I do not actually have a lawyer-client relationship with anyone. I have recommended a reputable detective agency. Your present contact is with Linda Calhoun, and I would suggest that you can best secure the information you want by keeping in touch with her.'

Brent arose from his chair, said, 'I see,' thought for a moment and added, 'I appreciate your position, Mr Mason. You cannot give me information. However, you have the information which I wanted to be certain was in your hands. Thank you, and good morning.'

'Good morning,' Mason said.

Brent strode in a dignified manner toward the door through which he had entered the office.

Mason said, 'You may go out through the exit door here, if you prefer, Mr Brent.'

Brent turned, surveyed the office, unhooked the cane from his left arm, put it in his right hand and made a dignified exit through the door into the corridor.

Just as he stepped into the corridor, he turned, said, 'Thank you, Mr Mason–and Miss Street,' put the narrow-rimmed hat on his head and then released the door, letting it gently close behind him.

Mason looked at Della Street and grinned.

She looked at her watch. 'You have just sufficient time to make your luncheon appointment,' she said.

Mason shook his head. 'I'll wait thirty seconds,' he said. 'Riding down in the same elevator with Howland Brent might lead to an elevator conversation, and I deplore elevator conversations.'

3

It was nearly three that afternoon when Drake's code knock sounded on the hall door of Mason's private office.

Mason nodded to Della Street and she opened the door.

'Thanks, Beautiful,' Drake said.

'What's new, Paul?' Mason asked. 'Getting anywhere with the Bluebeard?'

Drake looked serious. 'There's just a chance, Perry–just a ten-to-one chance–that these people may have something.'

'How come?'

'Dewitt had a bank account, something like fifteen thousand dollars. He drew a check which cleaned it out, told the manager of the apartment house where he has an apartment that he might be gone for a month or six weeks, paid two months' rent in advance. He sold his car for cash and took off in an automobile with a rather good-looking woman. They seemed to be very palsy-walsy. The back of the car was loaded with baggage, and the car had a

Massachusetts license plate.'

'You didn't get the number?'

'Not the number, just the state.'

'What did you find about his background?'

'He's been living in this apartment house, the Bella Vista, out in Van Nuys, for about fourteen months. He's rather a dashing type, wears a black eye patch, but has never explained to anyone how he lost the sight of that eye.

'No one seems to know exactly what he does, but it's some kind of a manufacturer's agency deal. He comes and goes on selling trips, keeps pretty much to himself, and apparently has never had a girl friend.

'The manager of the apartment sort of worried about that. There are two types of tenants that bother her: those that have too many girl friends and those that don't have any.

'Of course she's suppose to be running a respectable place, and when one of her single tenants has a crush on someone of the opposite sex the manager pretends not to notice, but she notices all right and knows pretty much what's going on.

'When a lone tenant–a bachelor in particular–doesn't have any girl friends, she sizes up the situation with a jaundiced eye because it's abnormal and–Well, you get the picture.'

'I get it,' Mason said. 'You don't know where they went, do you, Paul?'

'Not yet, but I'll find out. I have men working on that angle.'

'You say this woman was good-looking, Paul?' Mason asked.

'I gather that she wasn't any chicken,' Paul said, 'but she was snaky. You can figure it out. Here's a widow who has been lonely for several years. She's too young to be put on the shelf. She meets a man who is interested in her as a woman and starts blossoming out and all of a sudden she's tripping the light fantastic in the romantic environment of a second springtime.'

Mason frowningly digested Drake's information.

'So,' Drake said, 'I just dropped in to tell you that there *may* be something to Linda's suspicions.'

'Not Linda's,' Mason corrected, smiling. 'George's.'

'You think he's the one at the back of it?'

Mason said, 'I'll put it this way. I think he triggered the crisis.'

'Well,' Drake said, 'I hated to take Linda's money, but I realized she was going to get some other agency if I didn't get on the job, and I thought I could perhaps clean it up fast, getting some character references on Dewitt and perhaps letting him know he was being investigated.

'You know how it is with a con man, Perry. The minute he thinks that his potential sucker is investigating him he drops that sucker like a hot potato. The one thing those con people can't stand in an investigation.'

Mason nodded.

'So,' Drake went on, 'I had one of my men get into Dewitt's apartment. He was in there for three hours dusting the place for fingerprints, and there wasn't a single fingerprint in the whole apartment.'

Mason frowned. 'Not a single latent?'

'Not a one.'

'But there'd have to be,' Mason said. 'Good heavens . . .'

'Exactly,' Drake said as Mason stopped. 'It was deliberate. Someone had taken a chamois skin or a treated dust rag and had gone over every place where there would have been a fingerprint; the medicine cabinet in the bathroom; the kitchen faucets; the ice box; the jars inside the ice box–every single place where you'd expect to find a fingerprint had been wiped absolutely clean.'

Mason's eyes narrowed.

'So,' Drake said, 'we then traced the car Dewitt had sold. It's five years old, in pretty good mechanical shape. He got eight hundred and fifty dollars cash from a dealer.

'My man got on the good side of the dealer, got permission to dust the car for fingerprints, telling him that he was looking for the fingerprints of a passenger to whom Dewitt had given a ride.

'There wasn't a single fingerprint in the car.'

'Not even on the back of the rearview mirror?' Mason asked.

'Not anywhere on the car; not a single fingerprint. It had been gone over clean. My man made judicious inquiries and found that Dewitt had been wearing gloves when he drove in and sold the car.

'So I got busy on another angle,' Drake said. 'I traced the history of the car. It had been sold by a used car dealer to Dewitt when he had moved into Van Nuys a little over a year ago.'

'What was the idea checking the car?' Mason asked.

'Because there wasn't anything else to check,' Drake said, 'and I wanted to do a job. I wanted to find out, if I could, something about the guy's background, and I was running down every lead I could get.

'Now, here's a peculiar thing, Perry. Dewitt is away quite a good deal of the time. He's supposed to be traveling on the road. He is supposed to be a manufacturer's agent, but he bought this car thirteen months ago. The used car dealer had his records on the car although it was a job digging up those records. It happens that he keeps careful records on everything because of his guarantee on used cars. The car had gone a little over thirty thousand miles when it was sold to Dewitt, and the car now has thirty-one thousand, eight hundred and seventy-six miles.'

Mason frowned.

'In other words,' Drake said, 'the car has been driven a little over eighteen hundred miles in thirteen months. Now, try and figure that one out.'

Mason's eyebrows leveled in frowning concentration. 'And yet he's supposed to do a lot of traveling, Paul?'

'Supposed to do a lot of traveling.'

'It doesn't add up,' Mason said. 'Are you sure about the mileage?'

'Just as sure as anyone can be.'

'Perhaps the speedometer has been set back, or perhaps a new speedometer was put on.'

'In the case of a new speedometer,' Drake said, 'the mileage would have gone back to zero. In case it had been set back, the question is why, and by whom?'

Mason said, 'By Dewitt, in order to make the car look like a better buy when he returned it in.'

'It could have been, all right,' Drake said. 'But I've had a mechanic check the speedometer. There's no sign that it had ever been tampered with, and the mechanic said if it had been tampered with recently, he'd have found evidence.'

'I suppose you've traced all the marriage records?' Mason asked.

'Sure. There was a marriage license for a Montrose Dewitt and Belle Freeman taken out a little over two years ago, but the marriage never seems to have taken place.

'I got Miss Freeman's address and telephone number, but my men haven't been able to locate her. No one answers the phone. However, I passed that information on to Linda Calhoun. She said she'd keep trying to get Belle Freeman on the phone.

'Of course, just a marriage license doesn't mean anything. That is, you can't pin a bigamy charge on a person simply on the strength of a marriage license. But my men are working on it and they'll contact her before very long, and Linda will probably reach her. Right at the moment this Freeman girl appears to be our best lead.'

Mason reached a sudden decision. 'All right, Paul,' he said. 'Put more men on the job. Get Dewitt located by finding that car with the Massachusetts license number. It shouldn't be too difficult. Put as many men on it as you need and send the bill to me.

'You can bill Linda Calhoun for two days' work at fifty dollars a day, and don't let her know anything about my contributions to the cause.

'I feel I dismissed this matter too lightly and that I may thereby be responsible for any of Aunt Lorraine's future misfortunes. I felt that if it cost Linda a couple of hundred dollars to find out that her aunt was still relatively young and full of romance, it would be a good lesson for her. She'd leave her aunt alone in the future and eventually the affection which had existed between them would be restored. However, I guess we'd better get busy.'

'Of course,' Drake said, 'it *may* be just coincidence, but it is a perfect setup for–'

'Coincidence be damned!' Mason interrupted. 'In this business we can't afford to overlook the obvious. We can't afford to overlook anything.

'Get busy, Paul, and try to find out where they are. Put out enough men to cover the motels and–'

'Whoa, back up!' Drake said. 'You leave that end of the business to me, Perry. You're going at this thing like an amateur. It would cost a fortune to put out men to cover all the motels and try to trace a big, shiny car with a Massachusetts license number.'

'Well, how else *would* you get them?' Mason asked.

Drake grinned. 'You have to figure human nature.'

The detective turned to Della Street. 'What would *you* do if you were in her shoes, Della?'

'Put off my departure long enough to spend some time at a beauty parlor,' Della said promptly.

Drake grinned. 'There you are, Perry. In a deal of this kind we always try to locate the beauty shop the woman went to. That usually isn't too difficult, and a beauty shop is frequently a gold mine of information. A woman all keyed up with a new romance, bursting with the desire to confide in someone, spending two or three hours in a beauty shop, is certainly going to let the cat out of the bag somehow, somewhere.

'You'd be surprised at what these girls in the beauty shops hear, and you'd also be surprised at how shrewd they are at putting two and two together.'

'Okay,' Mason said, 'cover the beauty shops.'

'The one we want is already being covered,' Drake said. 'It wasn't too difficult to find where she went. I'm waiting for a report which should come in at any minute.'

Mason pushed back his swivel chair, got up and started pacing the floor. 'What annoys me. Paul, is that I underestimated the potential dangers of the situation. When you come right down to it, I was just a little irritated at George

Latty. The guy isn't working his way through law school. He's letting Linda put him through law school, and when she phoned him she'd had a fight with her aunt, instead of telling her, "Well, Linda, it's your aunt and your business," he jumps on a plane and spends Linda's money coming out to hold her hand.'

'*She* was holding *his* hand,' Della Street said, smiling.

The telephone rang.

'That's the unlisted, direct line,' Della Street said. 'It's probably for you, Paul. Your office has the number.'

Drake scooped up the telephone, said, 'Hello . . . yes. . . . Yes, this is Paul. What is it?'

Drake listened for a few minutes, said, 'Okay, good work. All right, I'll check into it. I'll probably be calling you back. Where are you now?–Okay, stay there until I give you a ring. I'll call you–win, lose or draw.'

Drake hung up the phone, said, 'Mrs Elmore talked to the hairdresser. She got started and couldn't stop. She was simply bursting with excitement. They're driving to Yuma to get married. Then they're going to spend their honeymoon at Grand Canyon.'

Mason looked at his watch. 'You say he withdrew all his balance from the bank, Paul?'

'That's right.'

'And paid two months' rent in advance?'

'Yes.'

'By check?'

'I don't know. The manager of the apartment house said the rent was paid.'

'You talked with her?'

'Yes. I talked with her shortly before noon.'

'Friendly?'

'Yes.'

Mason gestured toward the phone. 'Get her on the line, Paul. Let's see if it was a check. If it was, let's see if its good. He may have overlooked a bet there.'

Drake put through the call to Van Nuys, talked a few minutes, then cupped his hand over the phone, turned to Mason. 'She presented the check at the bank an hour ago; the check was turned down, account closed, no funds.'

Mason reached a sudden decision.

'Go out there and grab that check, Paul. Get her to let you represent her for collection–'

'She doesn't want to prosecute,' Drake interrupted, still holding his palm over the mouthpiece. 'She says it's an oversight and he'll make it good.'

Mason said, 'Damn it, Paul, don't be a sap. Go out there. Get that check. Buy it if you have to. Meet us at the airport. We'll have a chartered plane ready.'

He turned to Della Street. 'Ring up our plane charter service, Della. Get a twin-motored plane that will take us to Yuma.'

Paul Drake said into the phone, 'I want to talk with you, Mrs Ostrander. Will you wait for me, please? I'll be right out.'

Della Street reached for the phone as Paul Drake put it down.

'At the airport, Paul,' Mason repeated, as the detective headed for the door. 'Step on it.'

4

The checkerboarded fields of the Imperial Valley were refreshingly green with irrigated crops. Then the highline canal stretched like a huge snake below the plane and immediately the desert took over.

It was as abrupt as that.

Below the highline canal irrigation had turned the desert into a rich, fertile area. On the other side of the canal there was nothing but sand and a long straight ribbon of paved highway.

Mason, looking down on the highway and at the cars that were a mere succession of moving dots, said, 'Somewhere down there our quarry is speeding along toward Yuma.'

Della Street, her eyes thoughtful, said, 'What a situation it is. A woman, at a time of life when affection could mean so much to her, thinking that she has found a perfect mate, hypnotized by her own loyalty, looking through the windshield with starry eyes; while the man driving the car is debating in his mind the details of murder–just when it shall take place so that he can be assured of a safe getaway.'

Paul Drake, up in the copilot's seat, looked back and said, 'Don't feel too sorry for that woman, Della. Women like her keep fellows like Dewitt in business. She should have done some checking.'

'I suppose so,' Della said, 'but somehow you just can't blame her.'

'Well,' Mason said, 'we're probably a good two hours ahead of them. We'll land at Yuma and take a good long look at Dewitt when he comes driving up to the border.'

'What will he do?' Della Street asked.

'He'll answer a lot of questions,' Mason said, holding the oblong of tinted paper in his hands. 'A check payable to Millicent Ostrander for one hundred and fifty dollars with no funds. He'll have a chance to do quite a bit of explaining.'

'Remember,' Drake cautioned, 'that Mrs Ostrander is friendly. She doesn't want to prosecute or make any trouble.'

'But she did authorize you to collect on the check?'

'Yes, she did that.'

The billowing waves of the sand dunes cast long shadows in the late afternoon as the plane started losing altitude. The Colorado River, once a twisting serpent of water, now merely a succession of lakes imprisoned behind dams, became a mere trickle under the bridge as the plane crossed into Arizona. They came to a landing at the airport just as the sun was setting.

A man, waiting for them at the gate, gave a sign to Paul Drake.

Drake said, 'One of the affiliated agencies over here, Perry. We work together.'

The man shook hands and introduced himself.

'Everything okay?' Drake asked.

'Okay,' the man said. 'We put a man on watch at the border checking station. Only two cars with Massachusetts licenses have been through since then, and neither of them was the one you wanted.'

'I'm satisfied we're well ahead of them,' Mason said.

Mason turned to the pilot. 'You'd better get your plane taken care of and then keep in touch with this detective agency by telephone. We'll let you know when we want to go back. You're licensed to fly at night?'

The man nodded. 'Take you back any time.'

They got in the car, and the Arizona operative drove them to the Arizona State Line checking station where all cars coming into Arizona were briefly checked for agricultural products which might be contaminated.

Here another operative came forward to meet them, introduced himself and assured them that the car they wanted had not crossed the border.

The group settled down for a long wait.

'No need for you to stay here, Della,' Mason said. 'You can go up to town and look around. There are some excellent Western and curio shops up here. You can get Indian goods, stamped leather and souvenirs. They'll be open until–'

She interrupted him with a shake of her head. 'I'm going to wait right here,' she said. 'I think, when it comes to the showdown, Aunt Lorraine would rather have a woman in the party. You men are pretty grim and purposeful. You don't any of you impress me as having a good shoulder to cry on.'

'How about the man at the checking station?' Mason asked the Arizona detective.

'Oh, he's all right, he's accustomed to it; besides there is nothing he can do. We can wait here if we want to, but he's a good scout. I know him; he'll co-operate.'

A steady stream of cars poured across the interstate bridge, down the highway, stopped briefly at the checking station. Paul Drake, with binoculars, sized up each of the oncoming cars, looking quickly at the license numbers.

After an hour, a car with a Massachusetts license came along, and in a flash Drake, Mason and the Arizona detective went into action.

The men stood in the background while the agent at the Arizona checking station asked a few pertinent questions, then returned to the car.

'False alarm,' Drake said, stretching and yawning. 'How are you folks making out?'

'Fine,' Della Street said.

Drake grinned. 'This is the part of the job they don't tell you about in the movies, but it's the part that takes up most of the time, leg work and waiting.'

Again they settled down in the car.

Big, summer flying beetles started buzzing in a cloud around the glaring lights of the checking station.

'Do you suppose there's a chance they may not cross tonight?' Mason asked Paul Drake.

Drake shrugged his shoulders.

'Aunt Lorraine from Massachusetts,' Della Street said, 'would be almost certain to observe the proprieties.'

Mason settled down in the seat, said, 'Sometimes they fool you.'

'Surprising how fast you get dehydrated in this climate,' Drake said. 'You don't know you're perspiring because the perspiration evaporates just as soon as it comes to the surface of the skin but you can lose a gallon of water pretty fast. I could go for one of those root beer floats across the street.'

'Go ahead,' Mason said. 'I'll keep watch and–'

'Hold everything,' Drake said suddenly. 'We've got a customer.'

'Isn't that a California license?' Mason asked.

'It's a California license,' Drake told him, the binoculars at his eyes, 'and it's a rented car being driven by none other than the boy friend, George Keswick Latty.'

'Well, what do you know?' Mason said.

Drake said, 'Let me talk with him, Perry, and then if the situation seems to call for it, I'll give you the high sign and you come on over.'

'What do you suppose *he's* doing *here*?' Della Street asked.

'I don't know,' Drake said, putting the binoculars down on the car seat, 'but we're certainly going to find out.'

The detective strode across to the car with the California license as the border men flagged it to a stop.

Mason, watching Latty's face, saw the look of amazement which came over the young man's features. Then, after a few moments' conversation, Drake signaled.

The lawyer flung the door of the car open.

'Don't slam it,' Della Street warned. 'I'm coming.'

Mason turned back in time to catch the closing door and get a flash of her legs as she slid across the seat and jumped to the ground.

Her hand clamped on his arm. 'I wouldn't miss this for anything,' she said.

Latty, talking earnestly with Paul Drake, shifted his eyes over toward the couple approaching him, then his jaw sagged.

'For heaven's sake,' he exclaimed, as Mason and Della Street walked up to the car.

'What's the matter?' Mason asked.

'I . . . I didn't have any idea–You people amaze me.'

'What's amazing about it?' Mason asked.

'The idea of you being here. I . . . I thought . . . well, I thought you were at least two hundred and fifty miles away.'

'No, we're here,' Mason said. 'Probably you'd better drive over and park your car by ours so we can talk without blocking the station.

They walked alongside Latty's car while he moved it slowly over to the place where the car of the Arizona detective was parked.

Della Street, walking along beside the car, said in a low voice to Mason, 'Look at his face. He's thinking desperately.'

'I know,' Mason said. 'We had to give him this much time.'

Latty brought the car to a stop.

'Come on,' Mason said, opening the door on the driver's side. 'Get out and let's see what this is all about.'

'I don't understand just what you're doing here,' Latty said to Mason.

'And I don't understand just what *you're* doing here,' Mason said.

Latty laughed. 'Well, it's sort of mutual surprise, a–'

Mason said, 'Latty, quit stalling. Let's have it right on the line and let's have it now.'

'Who's stalling?' Latty asked.

'You're trying to,' Mason said, 'and the more you stall the more suspicious your actions become. Where's Linda?'

'Back in Los Angeles.'

'Where did you get this car?'

'I rented it.'

'Did she give you the money?'

'No.'

'Where did you get the money?'

'That's none of your business.'

'I think it is. Where did you get the money?'

'All right, if you want to know, I had a little nest egg saved up.'

'Saved from what?' Mason asked.

'All right,' he flared, 'from my allowance, if you want to put it that way.'

'Did Linda know about that nest egg?'

'No.'

'All right, you rented a car. At ten cents a mile that's going to run into money. You must have had a nice little nest egg saved up. Now, what are you doing here? Are you and Dewitt working together?'

The surprise on Latty's face was obvious. 'Working together?' he echoed. 'Working with that con artist? Certainly not. I'm trying to prevent a murder, that's what *I'm* doing here.'

'And why did you come here?'

'Because I followed Aunt Lorraine's car to within fifteen miles of here. That's what I'm doing here, and as far as the money is concerned, I hadn't any idea it was going to be this big a trip. I thought I could rent a car and shadow them just to sort of find out what was going on–and then they started driving out of town and I fell in behind them and–Well, it turned out to be quite a trip. I don't know whether they're starting back for Massachusetts or–'

'They're coming across the state line to get married,' Mason said. 'Arizona will honor premarital health certificates on California forms. They can get married immediately.'

'Oh,' Latty said, 'I see.'

'You didn't know that?' Mason asked.

Latty shook his head.

'All right, you followed them to within fifteen miles of here. Then what happened?'

'I lost them.'

'What do you mean, you lost them?'

'As soon as it got dark, I was in a bad spot. I could tag along while it was daylight and they didn't know I was following them. Sometimes I'd drop way behind. Sometimes I'd get up closer.

'They stopped for gas back there at Brawley, and I went on a block down the street, pulled in and tried to get my tank filled, but the attendant was busy with another car and the driver of that car wanted every little thing done. By the time the attendant got to my car, they had gone on past so I just paid for the gas that was actually in my car, about two and a half gallons, then took off after them.

'I didn't know what to do. My gas tank was almost empty. I'm just about out of money and–Well, it looked to me as if they were starting back for Massachusetts. I was going to stop here in Yuma and telephone Linda for instructions and ask her to come ana pick up the car and wire me enough money for plane fare home.'

'But you lost them?' Mason asked.

'They knew I was following them after I had to turn the headlights on. This man, Dewitt, didn't use the rearview mirror much. He just kept on going, and I don't think he had any idea he was being followed until after it got dark and them I made the mistake of trying to keep too close behind him so he wouldn't get away.

'First he slowed down for me to pass and there was nothing else for me to do; I had to pass. Then I pulled into a gas station as though I were going to get gas, and he went on by me and then I got on his trail again, but he spotted me right away that time and pulled off to the side and slowed down for me to pass.

'So I went on ahead trying to pretend that I wasn't the least bit interested in him and went on about five miles down the road and came to another service station. I pulled in there and waited for him to pass and–Well, he didn't pass, that's all.'

'So then what?'

'So then I went back along the road looking for them, but I saw that wasn't any good because the headlights of approaching cars would blind me and–Well, frankly, I don't know whether they passed me or not. I don't think they did, but after half a dozen cars had passed me, I saw that wasn't any good so I turned around and decided to come on to Yuma and telephone.'

Mason said, 'You've *really* messed things up! We knew they were coming here to get married and we were waiting to intercept them and give this man Dewitt a shakedown. Now we've lost our lead, thanks to your bungling. Shadowing is a job for a professional. When an amateur tries to play detective, he simply messes things all up.'

'I'm sorry,' Latty said.

The lawyer turned to Paul Drake. 'What's your best guess, Paul?'

Drake shrugged his shoulders. 'They could have done any one of a dozen things. The probabilities are they simply doubled back to Holtville, Brawley or perhaps Calexico. They'll spend the night there, come on over here tomorrow and get married–or they may go back to have dinner and then come over here to Arizona. You can't tell.'

'I must telephone Linda,' George Latty said. 'She'll be frantic.'

'What do you want to tell her?'

'I want to tell her what happened.'

'And you want to get back?' Mason asked.

'I've *got* to get back and–Well, I haven't enough money. I want her to wire me funds and that's going to take a while. I . . . I'm sorry, I guess I just botched things all up.'

'You got a good look at Dewitt?' Mason asked.

'I saw him, yes, several times.'

'You watched his apartment?'

'No, I was simply shadowing Lorraine Elmore's car.'

Mason glanced significantly at Paul Drake.

'All right, Latty,' he said, 'you've done enough interfering.'

The lawyer reached in his pocket, pulled out a billfold, said, 'Here's twenty dollars. Go in to Yuma. Drive through the city and on to the Bisnaga Motel. Register there under your own name. Since you're here, we *may* be able to use you. Have a snack and wait for my call. We have reservations and will be there later on, but we may call you at any time. You're willing to help?'

'I'll say I am. I'll do anything you want.'

'All right,' Mason told him, 'you've loused it up this far. Now try to follow instructions and *don't* mess things up any more.'

Latty said, 'I don't want to make suggestions but shouldn't you start looking for them–tonight?'

'I'm trying to protect her life, not her virtue,' Mason said shortly. 'If they know they're being followed, that may make them a little cautious.'

'Or it may make *him* desperate,' Latty said.

'You should have thought of that before you left Los Angeles,' Mason snapped. 'Now get on to that motel and wait for our call.'

Latty flushed. 'You're treating me like a child, Mason. I want you to understand that it was my judgment, my influence, my advice and my initiative which got Linda to come to you in the first place.'

'All right,' Mason said, 'I'm not going to argue with you about that because I don't know anything about it and it doesn't make any difference. All I want you to do is to take that initiative of yours, that perspicacity, that decision, and park them at the Bisnaga Motel until we can get this thing worked out. You've heard the old story about too many cooks spoiling the broth. If the broth isn't already spoiled, we'll take over.'

Mason moved away from the car, followed by Della Street.

Paul Drake jerked his thumb down the road. 'That-a-way,' he said.

Latty flushed angrily, said, 'All right. Just remember that you've now taken the *sole* responsibility.'

He stepped on the throttle, and the car leaped ahead with the tires squealing a high-pitched protest.

'So what do we do now?' Drake asked.

Mason said, 'We go and get some dinner. We leave the Arizona operatives here. The minute they pick up that car, they notify us.'

'Suppose they double back, leave the car in Holtville, Brawley or El Centro and rent a car and come on here and get married in that?'

'Then we're licked,' Mason said. 'Even if we stayed here that would lick us, because we don't know Dewitt and we don't know Lorraine Elmore. The Massachusetts car license was our only sure lead. We can, of course, tell the operatives to check on any car that's driven by a man with a patch over one eye.

'However, now that they've been alerted, they can get around us in a variety of ways. For instance, they could simply park their car at El Centro and get on the first bus going to Yuma.

'Instruct the Arizona detectives to cover as best they can. If they spot the car with the Massachusetts license number and the two people in it, or if they pick up the trail of a man with a patch over one eye, let them get in touch with us. When they do, I want to handle it myself. I want to be exceedingly careful that we don't give this man a foundation for a damage suit.'

Drake said, 'Okay, I'll instruct the men. That idea of a dinner sounds good to me.'

Drake talked with the Arizona detectives, then said, 'We'll have to get a cab to go to town, Perry, and leave the detectives on duty here.'

Mason nodded.

Drake phoned for a cab and gave the driver the name of the restaurant the detectives had recommended.

When they entered the place Drake said to the cashier, 'My name is Paul Drake; this gentleman is Perry Mason. We are expecting a telephone call. Will you remember the names and if the call comes in, let us know?'

'I'll be glad to,' the cashier said. 'What is it, Drake and Mason?'

'That's right, Paul Drake, Perry Mason.'

'All right, I'll see that you're called to the phone if anything comes in. Take that table over there in the corner, if you please. There's a phone jack on the wall there and we can have the call transferred right to your table.'

As they seated themselves at the table, Paul Drake said, 'I'm so hungry I can taste it, but if I order a steak it will take fifteen or twenty minutes to get it and I suppose that call will come just as we're getting ready to eat.'

'Let it come,' Mason said. 'We'll simply have the Arizona detectives follow the parties. If they go to a motel, that's one thing. If they go to a justice of the peace to try to get a marriage fixed up, that will be something else.'

Mason said to the waitress who came to the table, 'You'd better bring three lobster cocktails that we can nibble on while we are waiting; plenty of green olives and celery. We want three of your best steaks, all medium rare, lots of coffee and we're in a hurry. We'll have our salad with the meal.'

The waitress nodded and withdrew.

'Well,' Drake said after the waitress had left, 'this is going to be a surprise to my stomach *if* I get it. My hunch is that phone will ring just as the steaks are being brought in. It will be a rush emergency and we'll scramble out of here with the steaks left on the table.'

'She's bring the lobster cocktails now,' Mason said, 'so we'll at least have that much to go on.'

They ate their lobster cocktails in silence, nibbled on olives and celery and then Drake, looking toward the kitchen door, said, 'Here she comes with the steaks. Come on, telephone!'

The waitress put the covered dishes down on a serving table, picked up the first one with a napkin, placed it in front of Della Street and, with a flourish, removed the silver cover. The appetizing aroma of steak and baked potato filled the air.

The cashier, coming up behind Paul Drake, said, 'It's a call for you, Mr Drake. Here's the phone.'

Drake groaned, picked up the telephone, said, 'Yes, yes, hello. Paul Drake talking . . .'

'Just a moment,' the cashier said. 'I have to plug it in; there you are.'

'Hello!' Drake said. 'Hello, this is Drake . . . yeah . . .'

Della Street said, 'Pardon me, folks,' and grabbing her knife and fork, cut into her steak. 'I'm going to see that this isn't a *total* loss.'

The waitress put the platter down in front of Mason, removed the cover. 'How about him?' she asked. 'Want to wait until he's finished telephoning?'

'No,' Mason said, 'emphatically not. Serve him now.'

Drake pushed the phone a little to one side, nodded to the waitress, said into the telephone, 'You're not sure . . .? Nothing else new . . . no sign of our people? . . . We'll be out of here within twenty minutes or so.'

He cradled the receiver, pushed the phone to one side, grabbed knife and fork and attacked the steak.

'Well?' Mason asked.

Drake didn't answer him until he had a mouthful of the savory meat, then he mumbled, 'Nothing important. It can wait.'

'How long?' Mason asked.

'Until I've finished this steak,' Drake said, 'and if anybody watched my table manners and sees me wolfing the food, they can stare and be damned.'

'We're not standing on ceremony, Paul,' Della said.

Drake kept feeding steak and potato into his mouth.

'What sort of dressing on your salad?' the waitress asked.

'Thousand Island,' Della Street said.

Mason held up two fingers. 'Make it two.'

'Three,' Paul Drake mumbled.

At length Drake looked at his watch, swallowed, took a gulp of water, said, 'Well, this certainly is a surprise. I never expected to get this far. That call, Perry, was from one of the Arizona operatives at the checking station and he says he saw a car going out, headed back to California, that he thinks it was the same car we checked coming in–that is, the one George Latty was driving. He wanted to know if he should send someone after Latty or just concentrate on the job there. I told him to stay there until we called.'

Mason's eyes narrowed. 'He wasn't certain?'

'No, it was just a glimpse and something of a hunch.'

'No sign of the Massachusetts car?'

'No sign of the Massachusetts car.

'They've made a hurried check of two buses which came through without spotting anyone with a patch over his eye, but they can't really cover those buses and keep a check on the people coming through in cars and, of course, they're concentrating mostly on the cars.'

Mason pushed back his chair, leaving the last half of his steak unfinished, walked to the cashier's desk, said, 'Could you get the Bisnaga Motel on the line and put the call on the phone there at our table?'

'Certainly, Mr Mason. I'll be glad to.'

Mason went back to his steak and a moment later when he had a signal from the cashier, picked up the phone. 'Bisnaga Motel?' he asked.

'That's right,' a man's voice said.

'I wonder if you have a George Latty there?' Mason said. 'He would have registered within the last hour.'

'How do you spell it?'

'L-a-t-t-y.'

'Just a minute. Let's see. . . . No, no Latty.'

'You're not holding any reservation for a Latty?'

'Just a minute, I'll check that. . . . Nope, no Latty. Not staying here and not any reservation.'

'Thank you,' Mason said. 'I'm sorry I bothered you. I'm rather anxious to get in touch with him.'

'That's what we're here for,' the man said. 'Glad to be of any assistance. Sorry I couldn't locate him for you.'

Mason pushed back the telephone. His face was grim.

'No dice?' Drake asked.

'No dice.'

'What does that mean, Perry?'

'Your guess is as good as mine,' Mason said. 'I'm sorry I gave the guy that twenty bucks.'

'He probably called Linda,' Drake said, 'and she wanted her hand held. I think that has to be the solution.'

Mason said, 'Probably. He certainly is a card, talking about his allowance and the money he "saved." If he doesn't start learning to stand on his two feet, he'll make a hell of a lawyer.'

'Assuming he can pass the bar examination,' Della Street said.

Mason finished his steak.

A few minutes later they left the restaurant and took a taxi back to the checking station.

'No luck?' Drake asked the Arizona operatives.

'No luck. How long do you want us to stay with it?'

Drake looked questioningly at Perry Mason.

'How long are you good for?' Perry Mason asked.

'All night if you want.'

'All right,' Mason told him, 'we're going to the Bisnaga Motel. They have phones in the rooms. Call either Paul Drake or me the minute you hit pay dirt–and you'd better get another automobile out here so that one of you can follow the subjects and the other one can dash down to the motel to get us. Give us a ring first. We'll sleep with most of our clothes on and be ready to go at a moment's notice.'

'You want us to stay on all night?'

'All night,' Mason said, 'unless we call it off sooner. They can get married at night here?'

'If they've got money and want to spend it, they can get spliced any time, day or night.'

'They'll have money,' Mason said, 'and they'll want to spend it.'

'I don't get it,' one of the operatives said. 'These people aren't minors.'

'They're very mature,' Mason said, 'but I believe there are some statutes in this state providing that an applicant for a marriage license can be put under oath.'

'I believe so,' the detective said.

'I want to have the prospective bridegroom put under oath and asked about prior marriages,' Mason said, 'and I'll probably suggest a few additional questions to the clerk who is issuing the license–with a twenty-dollar tip on the side to see he remembers what I'm asking.'

'All right,' the operative said, 'we'll back your play. We just want to know how far you wanted to go.'

'All the way,' Mason said.

They returned to Yuma in the waiting taxi, rented a car and drove to the Bisnaga Motel. Mason called Linda Calhoun on long distance.

'Mr Mason!' she exclaimed. 'Where are you now?'

'Right now we're at Yuma, Arizona,' Mason said, 'We are checking on incoming cars to see if your aunt is going to marry Dewitt here.'

'Mr Mason, *how* did you get there?'

'By airplane.'

'That must have been terribly expensive. I wasn't prepared to–'

'Your end of this,' Mason interrupted, 'is going to run to one hundred dollars and no more. That's going to pay for two days' detective work. The rest of it is on me.'

'But why on you?'

'Just a contribution to the better administration of justice,' Mason said. 'Don't worry about it, Linda. You haven't heard anything more from your aunt?'

'No, but I have met Belle Freeman, the girl Dewitt promised to marry. She's here at the apartment with me now.'

'Can she hear what you're saying?' Mason asked.

'Oh, yes.'

'Well, don't talk any more than you have to. I can ask questions; you can answer yes or no if it–'

'Oh, she's all right,' Linda interrupted. 'She was in love with him two years ago but she's over it now. She knows him for what he is. He got her to turn over her savings to him. He said he had a sure-fire investment that would show a profit. He just took her money and skipped out. She wants to get her money back.'

'How much?'

'Three thousand dollars.'

'That's fine!' Mason said. 'We can get her to confront Dewitt with her claim, and that may make your Aunt Lorraine wake up. Is there any chance there is merely a similarity of names?'

'No. This is the man all right. He had lost an eye in some sort of a gun-running expedition and he always wore a black eye patch and posed as a daring soldier of fortune. It attracted women like flies to a honey jar.'

Mason said, 'You've told her why you're interested?'

'Yes. She's very sympathetic. She'll do just what we say. She wants to help. She's in love with another man now.'

'Did you know that George Latty had tried to follow your aunt's car?' Mason asked.

'George? Heavens, no. I've wondered where he was. I've been ringing and ringing and ringing and–'

'You mean that you haven't heard from him?'

'No.'

'Well,' Mason said, 'he was trying to do a little detective work. He'll probably call you. You keep in touch with the phone; we'll call you later. Now, if you want us, we're at the Bisnaga Motel in Yuma.'

'Who is us?'

'Paul Drake, my secretary, Della Street, and I.'

'Good heavens, Mr Mason, all of that expense–'

'I told you not to worry about the expense,' Mason told her. 'Call me if you hear anything.'

The lawyer hung up, reported the conversation, then said, 'Things are looking up. I'm going to take my shoes off and that's about all. I think we're coming to a show-down.'

'I'll be ready on two minutes' notice,' Drake said.

Della Street said, 'You give me five minutes, Perry, and I'll be on deck.'

Mason said, 'Look, Della, there's no need for *you* to–'

'I wouldn't miss it for worlds, Perry. All I really need is five minutes, but I must have those five minutes.'

'You'll have it,' Mason promised.

'Can you give them that much of a time margin–Montrose Dewitt, I mean?'

'I think so,' Mason said. 'They'll want to get freshened up before the ceremony.'

They retired to their rooms. Mason took off his shoes, propped himself up on the bed with the pillows behind his head, smoked a cigarette, started to doze; then, after an hour, was awakened by the strident ringing of the telephone.

'Yes,' Mason said, grabbing the instrument.

'Mr Mason?'

'Yes.'

'There's a long distance call for you from Los Angeles. Want it?'

'Put the party on,' Mason said.

A moment later he heard Linda Calhoun's voice. 'Oh, Mr Mason, I'm so glad I got you, I . . . I've heard from Aunt Lorraine.'

'Where is she?' Mason asked.

'She's at Calexico. Do you know where that is?'

'Yes,' Mason said, 'that's the town on the border. It's Calexico on one side and Mexicali on the other. Now, you're in your apartment?'

'Yes.'

'Alone?'

'No, Belle Freeman is here. She got all excited after I talked with you earlier. We've been sitting up, drinking coffee and getting acquainted. She's fine company.'

'I see,' Mason said. 'I was trying to get the picture. She's friendly?'

'Oh, *very!*'

'All right, now, why did your aunt call you? To tell you she was married?'

'Oh, no. She just wanted to tell me that everything was forgiven, and that she desperately wanted my friendship.'

'That,' Mason said grimly, 'means that they're married. They went across to Mexico and had some sort of a marriage ceremony.'

'Oh, Mr Mason, I hope not! Aunt Lorraine sounded more like herself than she has in a long time. She told me that she regretted very much the scene that she had with me. She told me that she was a little nervous and upset but that things were different now and . . . she said she would be seeing me tomorrow afternoon.'

'In the afternoon?'

'Yes.'

'Did she say where?'

'Why, no. I suppose here at the hotel.'

'Did she tell you where she's staying?'

'The Palm Court Motel.'

'Did she say anything about Dewitt?'

'No, and I didn't ask her but . . . the way she talked, the sound of her voice and everything, I'm satisfied she's–Well, if she *had* been married I'm quite certain she would have told me.'

'I'm not so certain,' Mason said. 'The way she called you, her apology and all, sounds to me as if she had been married. Have you heard anything from George?'

'Yes,' she said shortly.

'What was it?' Mason asked.

'He asked me to transfer twenty dollars to him by telegraph and waive identification.'

'Where was he?'

'El Centro.'

'Did he wire or phone?'

'He telephoned collect.'

'You sent him the money?' Mason asked.

'I'm going to, but I have to go out to do it and I wanted to talk with you and let you know what was happening before I went out.'

'Okay,' Mason said, 'he's your boy friend and it's your money.'

She laughed. 'I'm afraid you don't approve of George, Mr Mason, and I'm quite sure Aunt Lorraine doesn't.'

'I'll repeat,' Mason said. 'He's *your* boy friend and it's *your* money. Did he call you before or after your conversation with your aunt?'

'Just afterwards.'

'And you told him where your aunt was?'

'Of course. He asked me if I knew anything, so naturally I told him about her call. I don't approve of George taking off like that. He's going to have some explaining to do. I was worried about him. I'd been calling his room all afternoon.'

Mason said, 'I feel your aunt is either married now or that she intends to be married early in the morning and then take a plane back to see you.'

'I . . . I hadn't thought of it in that way,' she said, 'but now that I come to think it over–Is there anything we can do, Mr Mason?'

'I don't know,' Mason said. 'I'll think it over.'

'It would be such a tragedy for her to throw herself away on him,' she said.

'I know how you feel,' Mason told her. 'You'll hear from me tomorrow.'

'Thank you so much. . . . Good night.'

'Good night,' the lawyer said, and hung up.

Mason walked over to the connecting door leading to Paul Drake's room, tapped gently, then opened the door and listened for a moment to the detective's rhythmic, gentle snoring.

'Wake up, Paul,' Mason said. 'We have some information and we're going to have to act on it.'

Drake sat up in bed, rubbing his eyes, yawning prodigiously.

'Huh?' he asked.

Mason said, 'Lorraine Elmore and, presumably, Montrose Dewitt are at the Palm Court Motel in Calexico.'

Drake digested that information.

'Now then,' Mason said, 'there's something a little strange about the whole picture. Aunt Lorraine called Linda Calhoun just a few minutes ago, told her that she wanted to be friends, that she was going to see Linda at the hotel tomorrow afternoon.'

'Are they married?' Drake asked.

'I'm afraid they are,' Mason said, 'although it could be they've decided to wait over in Calexico until morning, then come across here and get married, then return to Los Angeles, but I don't think so.

'Remember that they know they were being followed, thanks to George Latty's clumsiness.'

'So what do we do?' Drake asked.

'You stay here,' Mason said, 'and keep in touch with the Arizona detective agency. I'm going to take the rented car and go to Calexico. I'm going to get them out of bed and call for a showdown with Dewitt.'

'Do you have enough on him to do that?' Drake asked.

'I think I have enough on him now, what with Belle Freeman and this bad check, so that we have a basis on which we can start asking questions.

'The thing I'm afraid of is that the telephone conversation may have been a ruse to throw Linda off the trail. They may have told her they were staying at the Palm Court Motel simply as a blind, and they may be on their way right now to Yuma.

'Now, if they should cross the border, you're just going to have to get on their trail and be very, very careful. Don't make any accusations. Simply identify yourself and say that you want to know what he meant by leaving his landlady a check that bounced. He'll probably dig right down into his pocket and make that good with cash.

'Then you can ask him if he is the same Montrose Dewitt who took out a marriage license with Belle Freeman, and if he says he is, then ask him if it is true that he still has some three thousand dollars of her money for investment, and whether the investment was ever made and if so, where.

'Be very careful you don't make any direct accusations, Paul–anything that would lay the foundation for a suit for slander or defamation of character.'

Drake, fully awake now, said, 'All right, Perry, I'll handle it. I'll put the guy on the defensive–and of course you want me to do it in front of the woman.'

'I didn't *say* that,' Mason said, grinning.

'I just read your mind,' Drake said. 'What about Della?'

'She's going to have to go with me,' Mason said, 'because I think I'm the one that will make the contact and I want to have notes of the conversation.'

The lawyer crossed over to the other door of the suite and tapped on Della Street's door. 'You've got five minutes, Della,' he said.

Her voice, drugged with sleep, said, 'Okay, Chief, I'll be there.'

5

As the lights of Calexico appeared, Mason said to Della Street, 'You'll have to wake up now, Della. We're here.'

She struggled up to an erect position, shook her head, smiled sleepily, said, 'I'm afraid I wasn't much company.'

'There was no reason for both of us to stay awake,' Mason told her.

'What do we do now?' she asked.

'You get your shorthand book and pen all ready to take notes; we go to the Palm Court Motel and get Aunt Lorraine and Montrose Dewitt out of bed.'

'The same bed?' Della Street asked.

'That,' Mason said, 'remains to be seen.'

'And then what do we do?'

'Then we ask questions,' Mason told her.

'And suppose he doesn't answer them?'

'We keep on asking.'

'Would he have the right to throw you out bodily?'

'He'd have that right,' Mason said.

'Would you let him do it?'

'No.'

'In other words, this may warm up to quite a little scrap.'

'It might,' Mason admitted, 'but remember this: Aunt Lorraine is in love with the guy. Everything we do is for the purpose of showing him up in his true colors. If he wants to get nasty, we handle things in such a way that it's very evident he's the one who is in the wrong. My job is to make our every action seem reasonable, our every request courteous, and if he wants to be mean about it, we put him in such a position that everything he does seems to be unreasonable and discourteous.'

'Do you know where the Palm Court Motel is?' Della Street asked.

'We'll find it,' Mason said. 'It's not such a big city that we can't just drive around and locate it.'

'And over there is Mexico?' Della Street asked.

'That's right, right across that border–just through the gate. Everything on the other side of the high wire fence is Mexico.'

'They could get married over there?'

'Presumably.'

'You think they've done so?'

'I don't know,' Mason said. 'The case is a little peculiar, but the main thing is to try and get the scales to drop from Aunt Lorraine's eyes.'

'And that's going to hurt,' Della Street warned.

'It's better for her to be hurt than killed.'

'You think she's in that much danger?'

'We wouldn't be here if I didn't.'

The lawyer turned at the intersection, said, 'I think the motels are up on this street, as I remember it–they'll probably all be dark now. They–Wait a minute, what's that sign down there, Della?'

'That's it!' Della Street said. 'It's an illuminated sign: "The Palm Court."'

'That's fine,' Mason said. 'They'll have vacancies, otherwise they wouldn't have left their sign on. And if they have vacancies, the manager won't be too mad when we get him or her out of bed; in fact, we may as well get some units here ourselves and make it all one big family party.'

The lawyer drove the rented car to a stop in front of the building marked OFFICE, got out of the car and pressed the bell button.

It was more than a minute before a matronly woman in her late forties, belting a robe around her, opened the door.

She sized Mason and Della Street up.

'A cabin?' she asked.

'Two cabins,' Mason said.

'Two?'

'Two.'

'Now, look,' she said, 'one cabin we rent without any questions. We don't ask to see your marriage license, but when you get two cabins–well, we want to be sure everything's all right.'

'Everything's all right,' Mason said, 'otherwise we wouldn't want two cabins. This young woman is my secretary. I'm an attorney here on business.'

'Oh, I see. That's all right. Will you just register here, please?'

'By the way,' Mason said, 'I'm expecting some people here. What unit do the Dewitt's have?'

'The Dewitts?'

'Yes.'

'Mr and Mrs–Oh, you mean Montrose Dewitt! Well, that's strange, they have two units, too. There's a Montrose Dewitt in Fourteen, and a Mrs Elmore in Sixteen. They came together.'

'I see,' Mason said, filling out the cards. 'Did they say how long they intended to be here?'

'Just overnight.'

'That's fine,' Mason said. 'How much is it?'

'That'll be twelve dollars for the two.'

Mason gave her the twelve dollars. She handed him the keys.

'Just park your car in front of the cabins; everything will be all right. Thank heavens those are my last two vacancies. I can shut off the signs and go to sleep.'

The lawyer parked the car, carried Della Street's overnight bag to the unit allotted her, said, 'Meet me in front of my unit in five minutes, Della.'

The lawyer took his own bag from the car, turned on the lights in his cabin, inspected the accomodations, then waited until Della Street came out of her door.

'All ready?'

'Ready.'

'Here we go,' Mason said. 'We'll try Aunt Lorraine first because we want her to hear everything that's said. She's in sixteen.'

The lawyer tapped gently on the door of Unit 16.

When there was no answer after the second knock, Della Street whispered, 'They're probably both in Fourteen–that's going to prove embarrassing.'

'Not to us,' Mason said.

He crossed over to Unit 14 and tapped on the door.

'I don't like to do this,' Della Street said. 'It's trapping her in a most embarrassing position.'

Mason said, 'She put herself in that position, we didn't. After all, as I told George Latty, we're not trying to protect her morals, we're trying to save her life.'

Again the lawyer tapped on the door.

When there was no answer, he looked at Della Street and frowned. 'You'll notice, Della, there's no car in the parking spaces in front of these cabins and no car anywhere on the lot that has a Massachusetts license plate.'

'Oh-oh,' Della Street said. 'Does *that* mean they're out getting married?'

'Presumably,' Mason said. 'I was afraid of this. They knew they were being followed so they doubled back here, Aunt Lorraine placed a telephone call that was intended to lull Linda into a sense of security and get her to call off her shadows. Then they made a break for Yuma. They're probably there by this time, and Paul Drake is probably in it up to his necktie.'

'So what do we do?'

'We call Paul Drake. After all, there's not much we can do now by doubling back, because the action will be all over before we could get there.'

'Where do we place the call?'

Mason nodded toward a phone booth at the corner. 'See if you can get Paul Drake at the Bisnaga Motel,' he said. 'Use our credit card, Della.'

Della Street went into the phone booth, placed the call, then after a few moments said, 'Hello, Paul. Perry wants to talk to you.'

Mason stepped into the phone booth, said, 'Hello, Paul. I hardly expected to find you there.'

'Why not?' Drake asked, his voice thick with sleep. 'You told me to stay here.'

'But our quarry has left Calexico,' Mason said. 'I thought they'd have reached Yuma by this time.'

'I haven't heard a word.'

'They *might* have slipped through,' Mason said.

'Not past those operatives,' Drake said. 'Not in a car with a Massachusetts license.'

'Well,' Mason said, 'that means they've crossed the border down into Mexico. They're probably married by this time. I'm not familiar with the

Mexican marriage laws, but it's a cinch they are by this time. Sorry I bothered you, Paul, but I had to check.

'We're at the Palm Court Motel. That's where Dewitt and Aunt Lorraine are registered, but I doubt if they'll ever come back here. I'm in Unit Nine and Della is in Unit Seven. There are telephones in the rooms. If anything happens, call us.'

'Okay,' Drake said. 'And if I don't hear anything more, then what do I do?'

'You can have the pilot bring the plane down to Calexico first thing in the morning,' Mason said. 'We're probably all washed up as far as this phase of the case is concerned. When we see Aunt Lorraine, she'll be Mrs Montrose Dewitt.'

Mason hung up, said to Della Street, 'There's no use waiting up, Della. I'll sit up for a while on the off chance they're coming back. If they're not here by that time, they won't–'

'You'll do no such thing,' she interrupted. 'I've had a couple of hours sleep–you haven't had any. You go to bed and . . .'

He shook his head. 'I want to think about the situation a bit, Della. I wouldn't go to bed until I'd got it clarified in my mind, no matter what happens. You roll in and I'll see you in the morning. I'll give you a ring.'

'I'd like to take over for you, Chief. I can–'

'No, you go to sleep, Della. I want to think this thing over for a while. See you in the morning. 'Night, now.'

Mason turned out the lights, drew up a chair by the door of his unit and sat there smoking, watching the yard, giving the problem the benefit of frowning concentration.

When the Massachusetts car hadn't shown up by three-thirty, Mason closed the door, undressed, rolled into bed and was almost instantly asleep.

It was six-thirty in the morning when Della Street tapped on Mason's door. 'You up?' she asked softly.

Mason opened the door. 'Just finished shaving,' he said. 'How long have you been up?'

'Just got up. Our lovebirds have flown the nest.'

'Apparently so,' Mason said. 'I looked out of the window as soon as I woke up. They–Well, *what* do you know!'

'What?' Della Street asked.

Mason nodded in the direction of the rear cabins. 'Take a look,' he said. 'The man just opening the car door. Turn slowly.'

'Why, it's George Latty!' Della Street exclaimed, looking over her shoulder.

'It certainly is,' Mason said. 'Let's see what *he* has to say for himself.'

Latty was just opening the glove compartment of his car when Mason said, 'Good morning, Latty.'

Latty whirled, an expression of startled incredulity on his face. 'You!' he exclaimed. 'What are *you* doing here?'

'All right, I'll begin all over again the way we did in Arizona,' Mason said. 'What are *you* doing here?'

'I . . . I had to sleep somewhere.'

'You knew Aunt Lorraine was here?' Mason asked.

'Hush,' he said. 'Not so loud. . . . Come in. They've got the adjoining cabin.'

'And they're there?' Mason asked.

'Why, of course.'

Mason beckoned to Della Street.

They entered Latty's cabin.

'How long have you been here?' Mason asked.

'I don't know. I didn't look at the time.'

'The records will show the time.'

'All right, I got here a little before midnight, I guess.'

'And you've been in your cabin all this time?'

'I went out to . . . well, to look around a bit and I wanted to see Mexico. I–'

'How long have you been out?'

'Quite a while. I just got–I don't know.'

'You're a poor liar,' Mason said. 'Now tell me what you've been doing.'

'That is none of your business.'

'Now look,' Mason said, 'apparently you've been trying to play detective again. You've loused this thing up once and now you've loused it up again. Suppose you give me a couple of straightforward answers for a change. When you arrived here, was the car with a Massachusetts license on it parked in front of those cabins?'

'Why, yes. . . . Now, wait a minute–Well, specifically, I don't remember seeing the car.'

'You knew that Dewitt and Aunt Lorraine were here?'

'Yes.'

'That's why you came here?'

'Well . . .'

Mason said, 'I haven't time to do any sparring with you, Latty. You telephoned Linda from El Centro. You got some money transferred to you. You found out, from talking with her, that Aunt Lorraine and Dewitt were here. So then what did you do?'

'I came down here and got the unit that was next to them. They're right in that next unit, and for your information the walls are pretty thin. They can hear everything we're saying.'

'If they're there,' Mason said.

'They're there.'

'Not now, they aren't.'

'They were.'

'When?'

'When I got in. . . . Well, sometime after I got in I heard them talking.'

Mason said, 'I have neither the time nor the inclination to try to squeeze the truth out of you drop by drop. Quit stalling and answer my questions. Why didn't you stay in Yuma as I told you to?'

'Because I . . . I didn't want to. And I'm not going to answer any of your questions. I don't like the tone of your voice. Once and for all, Mr Mason, *I'm* hiring *you*. *You're* not telling *me* what to do.'

'All right, we'll get it straight,' Mason told him. 'You're not hiring me. You're not hiring anybody. As far as I'm concerned, you're excess baggage. You're a barnacle, a sponge, a parasite. You're a green adolescent trying to act like a man, and you don't know how.

'For your information, I'm washing my hands of this whole business as long as you have anything to do with it. I'm finished. I'm going to call Linda and tell her exactly how I feel.'

Mason nodded to Della, turned and walked out.

From the phone booth the lawyer called Paul Drake. 'Anything new at your end, Paul?'

'Nothing.'

'All right, get the plane,' Mason said. 'Come to the airport here. Pick me up, then I'll turn in the rented car and we'll go back to Los Angeles. We're washing our hands of the case.'

'What's happened?' Drake asked.

'Too damned much boy friend,' Mason said, 'plus the fact that the fat's all in the fire now. I don't know what's happened and I haven't time to try to get the truth out of him. You come on over and we'll go back to Los Angeles.'

Mason got Linda Calhoun on the phone, said, 'I'm just reporting progress, Linda. The birds have flown the coop.'

'What happened?'

'Your boy friend, George, tried to do some more detective work and apparently loused things up.'

'What did he do? He's in El Centro; that is, he *was* in El Centro. He's on his way home now.'

'No, he isn't,' Mason said. 'He's right here at the Palm Court Motel. He came down late at night, managed to get the unit that was next to that occupied by Montrose Dewitt and evidently did a little eavesdropping because he told me that the walls were so thin it was possible to hear ordinary conversation in the adjoining units if one listened carefully.'

'Well, of *all* things!' Linda exclaimed.

'I don't know what happened,' Mason said, 'but apparently the units are vacant at this time and–'

'There were two units?' she interrupted.

'That's right–Units Fourteen and Sixteen. And George rented Twelve. Apparently they went out somewhere. George may have tried to follow them and bungled the job, or else they spotted George and decided to move. George is being uncommunicative with me, and I just haven't time to waste finding out just what did happen. I have the feeling he's been up to something and is covering up.

'I have a plane and will be back in Los Angeles within a couple of hours. We've lost all contact with your aunt, and it isn't going to be worth my time or your money trying to re-establish a contact where we have absolutely nothing to go on.

'Your aunt promised that she'd see you this afternoon. Right now that's the best thing we have to work on. I'll be there when she gets in touch with you. Let's hope Dewitt is with her.'

'But what about George?' she asked.

'That's your problem,' Mason said. 'However, I'd like to ask you if you sent him enough money for a round-trip plane ticket?'

'No, just one way.'

'Well, you'd better get him started back,' Mason said. 'I want him out of my hair, and if you'll take a suggestion from me you'll give him bus fare back instead of paying his first-class fare on a jet plane. Let him realize that a man who tries to be a big shot on someone else's money is–'

The lawyer was interrupted by the sound of a piercing scream which penetrated through the closed glass door of the telephone booth.

'What was that?' Linda asked. 'It sounded as if someone screamed and–'

The scream was repeated, this time nearer to the phone booth.

Mason opened the door.

A woman carrying a mop in one hand, a pail of water in the other, was running down the parking place toward the road, screaming at the top of her voice.

As Mason stood watching she dropped the pail, and as the pail rolled, clattering across the hard-surfaced parking place, hot soapy water left a steaming trail.

The running woman continued to carry the mop for four more strides, then flung it from her as though it had been contaminated. She ran to the sidewalk, turning right screaming, 'Misses Chester! Misses Chester! Murder!'

Then the closing of a door muffled the sound.

Mason took one quick step back to the telephone. 'Hold the line, Linda,' he said. 'Don't let anybody break the connection. Hang on, I'm going to take a look. That woman came out of the door of Fourteen and it's still open.'

The lawyer left the glass door of the phone booth open and, with Della Street at his side, sprinted across the parking surface to the partially opened door of Unit 14.

The lawyer looked inside.

The bed was still made, the throw in place, although pillows had been pulled out and propped up against the headboard.

Sprawled on the floor was the fully clothed figure of a man lying partially on his back. A black patch covered one eye. The face had the unmistakable color of death.

'Good heavens,' Della Street said, 'what's in the other apartment?'

Mason looked back over his shoulder, said, 'We'll damned soon find out,' and took the passkey which the maid had left in the door of Unit 14, turned to the door of Unit 16 and unlocked the door.

Della Street, looking back toward the sidewalk as Mason fitted the key in the lock, said, 'You'd better hurry. Here comes the maid and the manager.'

Mason unlocked the door, flung it open unceremoniously.

There were several articles of rather expensive luggage which had been opened. The contents were strewn about the room. For the most part these were articles of feminine wearing apparel.

Here again the bed had not been slept in.

'Who are you?' the woman approaching demanded of Perry Mason.

'Perry Mason,' the lawyer said, 'and this is my secretary. We heard the maid saying there'd been a murder.'

'Not in here, not in here,' the maid said. 'It's the other one–Fourteen.'

'Oh, pardon me,' Mason said.

'Are you an officer?' the manager asked.

Mason smiled. 'I'm a lawyer,' he said, stepping back.

The manager looked in the door of Unit 14, then stepped inside the room.

'Well, well,' Mason said as though seeing the corpse for the first time, 'apparently there's a dead man–however, I see no indication of murder.'

The door of Unit 12 opened, and George Latty, his shirt removed, his face covered with lather, a razor in one hand, stood in the doorway, attired in trousers and undershirt. 'What's all the commotion about?' he asked.

Mason ignored the question to say to the manager, 'It would seem to be a natural death, but you'd better call the authorities.'

The manager backed out of the room, pushing Mason back from the door as she did so. She slammed the door shut, walked over to Unit 16 and pulled that door shut.

A door from one of the other units opened. A man attired in pajamas and robe said, 'What's all the screaming about?'

'Something frightened the maid,' the manager said, smiling.

George Latty said to Mason, 'What's this all about, Mason?'

Mason turned to look at him. 'What's what all about?'

'All the screaming.'

'Oh, you heard the screaming?'

'Of course I heard the screaming. It sounded like the whistle of a locomotive.'

'And ran right out, just the way you were?'

'Of course.'

Mason said, 'Was your face lathered before or after you heard the scream?'

'Before, why?'

'Then you must have waited some time before opening the door.'

'I . . . I wasn't very presentable.'

'You mean you changed clothes?' Mason asked.

'No, I was the way I am now but I . . . I hesitated.'

'So I see,' Mason said and, turning his back on him, strode rapidly back to the phone booth.

The lawyer picked up the telephone, said, 'Are you still on, Linda?'

'Heavens, yes. I've had a fight to hold the line. What is it? What's happened?'

'Apparently,' Mason said, 'Montrose Dewitt is dead. Your aunt is missing. Someone has apparently gone through all the baggage in both units very hastily and, since George Latty has been in the adjoining unit to that occupied by Dewitt, there will undoubtedly be complications.'

'Good heavens, you don't mean there's been a fight? George wouldn't . . .'

'I'm quite satisfied that George wouldn't,' Mason said as she hesitated, 'but the main problem before the house is what's happened to your aunt–Wait a minute. Does your aunt have reddish hair?'

'Yes.'

'I *think*,' Mason said, 'the woman who has just hurried past me and is approaching the door of Unit Sixteen is–I'll call you later. Good-bye.'

The lawyer slammed up the phone, sprinted across the parking place.

George Latty had retired behind the door of Unit 12 and closed the door. The manager and the maid were back in the office, presumably telephoning the police.

The woman tried the door of Unit 16, frantically rattled the door, then was starting for 14 when Mason put his hand on her arm.

'Lorraine Elmore?' the lawyer asked.

She whirled to face him with wide, panic-stricken eyes.

'Yes, who are you?'

'I'm an attorney,' Mason said, 'and I think you'd better talk with me before you talk with anyone else.'

'But I have to get in my room and I have to locate my . . . my friend.'

'You don't have a key?'

'No.'

'Where is it?'

'It was . . . taken.'

Mason said, 'Please, Mrs Elmore, come with me. For your information, I am acquainted with your niece, Linda Calhoun.'

'With Linda–you?'

'Yes,' Mason said, exerting gentle pressure on her arm as he led her across the parking area, 'and this is Miss Della Street, my confidential secretary. If you'll just come with us for a few moments, Mrs Elmore, we may be able to help you, and I think perhaps you're going to need help.'

6

As Mason nodded to Della Street, she seated Lorraine Elmore in the overstuffed chair, and Della Street drew up a straight-back chair to take a seat beside her.

Mason stood for a moment, then sat on the edge of the bed. 'Can you tell me about it, Mrs Elmore?'

'You're a friend of Linda's?'

'Yes. She has been in touch with me in connection with another matter. I think she'd be interested in–'

'If you're a friend of Linda's, that's all I need to know. They've murdered Montrose.'

'Who has?' Mason asked.

'Enemies,' she said vaguely.

'Whose enemies?'

'His,' she said and started to cry.

Della Street patted her shoulder. 'If you can just let us know what happened, Mrs Elmore, before giving way to emotion . . .'

'Just give us the bare facts,' Mason said.

Lorraine Elmore choked back tears, said, 'Oh, we were going to be so happy.'

'Never mind,' Della Street said. 'Please try and tell Mr Mason exactly what happened.'

She said, 'It was terrible. We were just trying to live our own lives, to start out by ourselves in search of our own happiness, to begin all over again and–'

'Can you just please tell me what happened,' Mason asked, 'just the events, Mrs Elmore.'

'We were followed,' she said, 'and Montrose became deathly afraid. He said there were people who . . . who had it in for him and . . .' Again she started to cry.

Mason said, 'All right, Mrs Elmore, I'm going to have to question you. Please answer my questions briefly and to the point. Where's your car?'

'Out there,' she said, with a vague motion of the wrist.

'Where?'

'On a dirt road.'

'Where?'

'Miles from here.'

'How far?'

'I don't know.'

'How long did you drive before you abandoned your car?'

'It happened about . . . about twenty minutes, I guess, after we left here.'

'What time did you leave here?'

'I don't know, perhaps around midnight.'

'Why?'

'That same car that had been following us was parked in the parking space. Montrose recognized it.'

'Did he know who was driving it?'

'No.'

'But it had been following you?'

'Yes.'

'You're sure?'

'Of course. The man had stopped in a gasoline station to let us go by and then tried to pick us up again and we slowed down and let him drive past us.'

'You didn't recognize the driver?'

'Why should I recognize him? I'm from Massachusetts. This is California. Anyway, I was on the right side. He passed on the left.'

'I see,' Mason said. 'So you and Montrose got in your car. Where were you going?'

'He wanted to talk. We wanted to make plans and we thought we were being spied upon, so we went out to park where we could talk without being interrupted and without anyone overhearing us.'

'Where?'

'We went out on the pavement and then turned off on a dirt road.'

'Do you know which way you went on the pavement?'

'The way we had come in.'

'Toward Yuma?'

'Yes, I guess so. It was in that direction.'

'And then what happened?'

'Well, we came to a dirt road that led off to the side and we turned off on it and parked.'

'How far did you go on it before you parked?'

'I don't know, just a little ways–just far enough to get away from the highway.'

'You walked back?' Mason asked.

'That was after . . . afterwards.'

'After what?'

'After the man made Montrose get out of the car.'

'All right,' Mason said. 'You were parked. You were sitting there talking and what happened?'

'This car drove up behind us. It didn't have any lights. We didn't notice it until it was right on top of us, and then Montrose opened the door and started to get out and this man was standing there with a handkerchief over his face. You couldn't see a thing–that is, what he looked like–just a thin white handkerchief hanging down from his hatband over his face, and he said, "Get out," and pushed the gun out right in front of Montrose.'

'You saw the gun?'

'Yes, yes! It was moonlight, and I saw the moonlight glinting from the blue steel on the gun.'

'Then can you tell me what happened?' Mason asked. 'And please hurry as much as you can–it's important.'

'The man told me to stay there, and he and Monty walked back and all of a sudden Monty tried to get the gun from him, and he clubbed Monty, and Monty fell down, and then the man just stood over him and clubbed him, and clubbed him, and clubbed him–Oh, it was terrible, terrible, terrible! I just–!'

'Now hold it,' Mason said. 'You're getting hysterical. What happened? Never mind your emotions, we have to know.'

'Well, the man left Monty there sprawled out by the side of the road. He was dead. I know he was dead. Such a horrible clubbing! You could hear the sound of the blows and–'

'All right, the man came back to the car. Then what?'

'He got in beside me, searched around the inside of the car and through the glove compartment. Then he grabbed my handbag and told me to drive the car straight ahead.'

'Now, that was in the direction that was away from the highway?'

'Yes.'

'You were on a dirt road?'

'Yes.'

'And the man sat behind you?'

'No, he went back to his car and got in it and drove right behind me.'

'With lights on?'

'No, he still had his lights off.'

'And the handkerchief over his face?'

'Yes.'

'Then what happened?'

'I kept on driving until he blew on the horn and turned on the lights, and then I stopped and he got out of the car and said, 'Now, Sister, drive straight on, just as far as you can go.'

'Then what?'

'Then he got in his car and started backing up.'

'And what did you do?'

'Just what he told me to, only it was what I wanted to do anyway because I wanted to get away from him. I saw him start backing his car and turning around and, believe me, I put my car into gear and stepped on the throttle and just started flying down that road.'

'And what happened?'

'All of a sudden there was sand all over the road, and I started skidding, and I guess I lost my head. I raced the wheels and just dug a hole and the motor stalled.'

'Then what?'

'I tried and tried to get the car out but I couldn't. The wheels just kept digging deeper and deeper in that sand.'

'So what did you do?'

'I waited awhile and then I started walking back.'

'And you walked back the way you had come in?'

'Yes.'

'Now,' Mason said, 'this is important. Did you recognize the place where the man had stopped you when you came to it?'

'No, I just kept on walking. I just followed the road. I kept thinking I would see Monty lying there . . . his body . . . but the man had loaded the body in the car and taken it away with him.'

'You didn't hear any shot being fired?' Mason asked.

'No.'

'And what happened to you?'

'I walked and walked until I got tired and then I just had to rest. I had sand and gravel in my shoes and I guess somewhere I got lost. I got off on a side road somewhere and I wandered around in sand hills and . . . finally I came to the highway and after what seemed like hours a man gave me a ride.'

'Let's see your feet,' Mason said.

She held up her foot.

'I took off my stockings,' she explained. 'They got all snagged and worn and I just walked in my shoes.'

Mason slipped off the shoe, looked at the rawness of the blistered feet, said, 'You saw this man beating Montrose Dewitt?'

'Heavens, yes! I saw him and I heard him. Oh, it was terrible! He clubbed and clubbed and after Monty was down and lying still he just clubbed him and kicked him and–'

'But no shot?' Mason asked.

'No, I didn't hear any shot.'

Mason said, 'I want you to sit right there, Mrs Elmore, and rest. My secretary and I have to put through a phone call.'

'I . . . I'll use the bathroom,' she said and got up out of the chair, started to take a step and would have fallen if Mason hadn't held her.

'Oh, my feet!' she said. 'My poor feet.'

'Take it easy,' Mason told her.

She hobbled to the bathroom, closed the door.

Mason said to Della Street, 'Della, she's lying.'

'How do you mean?'

'I saw the body,' Mason said. 'There isn't a mark on the face, nothing to indicate the man had been clubbed. I don't know how he died, but if she tells that story . . . we just can't let her tell it.'

'How can we stop it?'

Mason said, 'Look, Della, this is the time when we need someone who knows the ropes. There's a lawyer here that I've worked with named Duncan Crowder. You go to the outside telephone, get him on the line, and tell him to come here at once. Tell him I want him to work with me on a case. Tell him to drop anything he's doing and get here fast.'

Della Street nodded, said, 'Suppose he isn't in?'

'If he isn't in we're sunk,' Mason said, 'because I don't know any other lawyer I can trust. Crowder is a seasoned campaigner.'

The lawyer moved over to the window, moved the drapes back, looked out.

There were several cars parked in front of Unit 14, and a dozen or so people were gathered in a little group near the door.

When Della Street came back, Lorraine Elmore was still in the bathroom.

'Get him?' Mason asked.

'I got him and he's on his way down. He wanted to take time to explain something to me, but I told him there wasn't time for anything, to just get down here; that you wanted him and wanted him right away.'

'Good girl,' Mason said. 'Now . . .'

He broke off as the bathroom door opened and Lorraine Elmore, looking wan and drawn, started limping toward the chair.

Della hurried to her side.

'Wouldn't you like to lie down a little while?' she asked.

'Yes,' Mrs Elmore said. 'I took some pills last night and then . . . I guess . . . I must have dozed–Oh, I want to forget! Can you get me some medicine to quiet me?'

Della Street escorted her to the bed, stretched her out, said, 'Now just lie there and I'll soak a towel with cold water and put it over your eyes.'

Mrs Elmore smiled gratefully and said, 'I . . . I have to tell the police. It–'

'There's time for that later,' Mason said. 'Take care of her, Della.'

The lawyer hurried outside and into the phone booth. He rushed through a call to Linda Calhoun.

When she answered, Mason said, 'Linda, this is Perry Mason. Now I want you to listen and get this–'

'Mr Mason, whatever in the world has happened? What's happening to Aunt Lorraine? What's–'

'Shut up,' Mason said, 'and listen. Listen carefully. Montrose Dewitt is dead. Your aunt has been through a harrowing experience. According to her story he was clubbed to death before her eyes. But your aunt is hysterical and upset. There are certain things that don't fit into the picture. The story she tells is simply–Well, frankly, it isn't convincing.'

'Aunt Lorraine wouldn't lie,' Linda said.

'Are you sure?'

'Well, I . . . I'm reasonably sure.'

'Not even if someone told her to?'

'If . . . if she's in love and–'

Mason said, 'There's something about this I don't understand. Now, is it all right with you if I represent your aunt? She needs a lawyer and she needs one now.'

'Why, of *course* it's all right! That's what I wanted you to do all along, Mr Mason. I wanted you to–'

'Now, wait a minute,' Mason said. 'This is where the catch comes in. If I'm representing your aunt, I'm not representing you and I'm not representing George.'

'But I want you to represent my aunt and–Well, what does George have to do with it?'

'I don't know,' Mason said. 'George may or may not know something. If I'm representing your aunt, she's my client. Now, do you want me to represent her or not?'

'Yes, yes, please, Mr Mason.'

'All right,' Mason said, 'stick by the telephone. I'll report to you as soon as there's anything to report.'

'Shouldn't I come down there? Shouldn't I–'

'I think you should,' Mason said. 'You'll probably have to charter a plane unless you have someone who can drive you down.'

A man standing outside the telephone booth tapped on the glass door, called in, 'I'm a reporter, Buddy. I've got to rush a story in to my paper. How's for giving me a break?'

'Okay,' Mason said, and then into the telephone, 'I'll call you later.'

He hung up and opened the door of the phone booth. The reporter hurried past him and started dialing a number.

Mason went back to his room, opened the door gently to see Della Street sitting on the edge of the bed, holding a wet towel over Lorraine Elmore's forehead and eyes.

Della Street raised her finger to her lips, motioning for silence.

Mason quietly moved over to the window, looked out on the parking place and the people who were standing in groups.

A knock sounded at the door.

Lorraine Elmore started to raise herself up on the bed.

'Now, just keep quiet,' Della Street said. 'It's all right.'

Mason went to the door, said, 'Who is it?'

A man's voice said, 'It's Duncan Crowder, Mr Mason.'

The lawyer opened the door, a welcoming smile on his face, then suddenly stiffened. The young man who stood on the threshold was fully as tall as Mason. He had dark, wavy hair; steady slate-colored eyes; even, regular features, and a reassuring smile.

Mason said, '*You're* not the man I sent for.'

The visitor said, 'I tried to explain to your secretary that my father is in the hospital. I'm taking over as best I can. She didn't give me a chance to tell her anything, but said to get down here at once and then hung up.'

'I see,' Mason said thoughtfully. 'I'm sorry to hear about your father. You have a partnership?'

'That's right–Crowder and Crowder. I'm Duncan Crowder, Junior.'

Mason said to Della Street, 'Is your unit open, Della?'

She nodded.

'We'll talk there,' Mason said, and stepping outside appraised the young man.

'I'm sorry,' Crowder said, as Mason gently closed the door. 'I gathered it was a matter of great urgency. There was no opportunity for making explanations over the phone so I thought I'd come and explain personally.'

'How long have you been practicing?' Mason asked.

'About two years, Mr Mason. I've heard my father speak of you many times and I feel that I know you. I've followed your cases in the papers–as who hasn't?'

'All right,' Mason said, leading the way to the unit which had been occupied by Della Street and opening the door. 'Come on in and sit down. You're going to learn something about the practice of law that isn't contained in the books.'

'You want me to work with you?' he asked.

Mason nodded.

'What is it?' Crowder asked.

Mason took out a billfold and said, 'Here, I'm giving you a dollar. You're retained. There'll be a further fee forthcoming. I don't know how much it's going to be. I don't know how much my fee is going to be. But now you've been properly retained so there's a professional relationship.'

Crowder gravely took the dollar, pocketed it and said, 'Go ahead.'

Mason said, 'There's a dead man in Unit Fourteen. There's a possibility he's been murdered. I don't know.

'What I do know is this: Lorraine Elmore, who is our client, is in there in a state of hysteria. We've managed to get her quiet now. She thinks she witnessed the murder.'

'In the motel?' Crowder asked.

'*Not* in the motel,' Mason said. 'That's the trouble with her story. It is a weird, somewhat improbable story and when you tie it in with the physical facts it's completely contradictory to the evidence. I don't want her to tell that story and yet, if she doesn't tell it, she's going to be in as bad a position as if she did tell it.

'Therefore, there's only one thing to do.'

Crowder looked Mason in the eyes, thought for a long moment, then said, 'You mean we want a good doctor.'

Mason said, 'Young man, you have a remarkable legal mind. I guess you're a chip off the old block.

'There are two reasons why I need a local attorney on the job. In the first place I need a doctor, and in the second place I want someone who can get in touch with a coroner, the newspaper reporters and the local people and get the facts of the case before our client has to do any talking.'

Crowder said, 'How about this phone–is it connected?'

'It goes through a switchboard of some sort in the office,' Mason said, 'and your call will be monitored. There's a phone booth outside.'

Crowder nodded, stepped to the door, then came back and shook his head. 'They're lined up three deep in front of that phone booth,' he said.

'Okay,' Mason told him, 'we'll use this phone. Be careful what you say.'

Crowder picked up the phone and after a moment said, 'May I have an outside line, please? . . . Oh, I see, if you have to dial the numbers, I want–I don't remember his number and I don't have a phone book here, but it's Dr Kettle. . . . Would you ring him, please.'

There was a period of silence, then Crowder said, 'Horace, this is Duncan Crowder, Junior. I'm down here at the Palm Court Motel in Unit Seven. Now, that's near the street as you turn into the parking place on the right-hand side. I want you to get down here right away. Yes, *right* away. . . . Sure it's an emergency–no, not surgical, but I want you here just as fast as you can get here. . . . Okay.'

Crowder hung up and said, 'He'll be here right away. Incidentally, Dr Kettle does a lot of autopsy work for the coroner.'

'I see,' Mason said. 'I take it that he's friendly to you?'

'Very friendly. He's a client and Dad's personal physician.'

'Yours?' Mason asked, grinning.

Crowder matched his grin. 'I haven't needed one yet.'

Mason said, 'The dead man is Montrose Dewitt. Our client is Lorraine Elmore. She's a widow from Massachusetts. There's every indication that Dewitt was a crook–one of the type who preys on women–and there *may* be a more sinister angle to it.'

'Murder of his victims?' Crowder asked.

Mason nodded.

'And what happened to him?'

'He's dead,' Mason said. 'He was found lying on the floor of Unit Fourteen. Our client was in Sixteen. There's also every indication that both Units Fourteen and Sixteen were subjected to a very hasty search. Whoever did the searching apparently had more time in Unit Fourteen. The suitcase is open and some things have been taken out, but there's no indication of disorder.

'In Unit Sixteen, however, the one that was occupied by Lorraine Elmore, the search was apparently more hurried, and feminine wearing apparel has been pulled out of the suitcases and scattered all over the place. Our client may have been carrying a large sum of money in cash.

'I became interested in the case because of a niece of Mrs Elmore's–a girl named Linda Calhoun–who wanted me to protect her aunt from possible murder.'

'And marriage?' Crowder asked.

Mason said, 'The more I see of you, Crowder, the more I think you and I are going to get along.

'Now, Linda Calhoun has a boy friend, George Latty, who is here at the motel and has been here since sometime last night. Incidentally he has Unit Twelve, which is immediately adjacent to that occupied by Montrose Dewitt, and he told me that the walls of the units were so thin it was possible to hear conversation in an adjoining unit.

'The numbers are odd on this side and even on the other side, so if Latty heard conversation through the walls it must have been either conversation from Unit Fourteen, or from Unit Ten on the other side.'

'He didn't say?' Crowder asked.

'He didn't say and he isn't going to say,' Mason said. 'What he did say slipped out inadvertently. I think he's going to clam up.'

'Any chance he knows anything about it?' Crowder asked.

'Lots of chance.'

'What sort is he?'

'He's studying law,' Mason said. 'He looks as if he spends quite a bit of time looking at himself in a mirror after he's watched some of the current crop of heroes on T.V.

'Linda works,' Mason went on, 'and evidently makes a fair salary. From that salary she's putting up money for George Latty's education. Now, here's the part that to my mind is indicative of his character: Latty told me that he had a small amount of money saved from his–and I quote–allowance–unquote and that Linda knew nothing about this amount, which evidently represented a surreptitious saving.'

'I see,' Crowder said. And then after a moment asked, 'Sideburns?'

Mason indicated a spot halfway down his cheek. 'To here.'

'In what respect does our client's story differ from the physical facts?' Crowder asked.

'In quite a few respects,' Mason said. 'She insists the man was beaten and then clubbed to death out in the desert. Her car is out there somewhere and heavens knows what evidence will have been left in her car. I have a detective due here almost any minute and a chartered airplane. Her description about where she left the car is a little indefinite because she doesn't know the country, but I thought after the doctor gets on the job we could do a little flying and–'

There was a knock at the door.

Mason crossed over to open the door.

The man who stood on the threshold was in his fifties, a small-boned, energetic, poker-faced individual, whose keen eyes surveyed Perry Mason.

'Crowder here?' he asked.

'You're Dr Kettle?'

'That's right.'

'I'm Perry Mason.'

Crowder stepped forward and said, 'Hello, Doctor. Come in.'

Dr Kettle said, 'So you're Perry Mason, the great attorney.'

Mason grinned, 'I see I must have had a good press agent.'

'You have,' Dr Kettle said. 'What is it you people want?'

Crowder said, 'Do you mind, Mr Mason?'

'Not at all,' Mason said. 'Go ahead.'

'We have a client in the adjoining unit,' Crowder said, 'who needs medical treatment. I'd better describe her symptoms.'

Dr Kettle shook his head. 'You'd better let me make my own diagnosis.'

Crowder said, '*I'd* better describe the symptoms.'

'Can she talk?' Kettle asked.

'Yes.'

'Then *I'll* get the symptoms.'

Crowder said, '*I'd* better describe the symptoms.'

Suddenly Dr Kettle grinned. 'I guess I'm a little dense this morning. Go ahead, describe the symptoms.'

'This woman,' Crowder said, 'may or may not have been a witness to a murder. She has gone through a very harrowing experience. She is somewhere in her forties and has become emotionally upset and hysterical.

'Of course, later on it will be necessary for her to tell her story to the police, but at the moment it would be, at least in my opinion as a layman, medically unwise for her to do so.'

'Why?' Dr Kettle asked in a single whiplash question.

'Because she is emotionally upset and hysterical and her recollection may be at variance with some of the physical facts. It would, therefore, be exceedingly unfair to this witness for her to be interrogated while she was in her present emotional state.'

'I'll take a look at her,' Dr Kettle said, 'but from your description of the symptoms, Duncan, I feel quite sure she's in a state of acute hysteria and it will be necessary to have absolute quiet. I'm going to give her heavy sedation, transfer her to a hospital, put special nurses on the job, see that there are no visitors, and keep her completely quiet for at least twenty-four hours. At the expiration of that time, when she is completely out from under sedation, I'll determine whether it will be advisable for her to make any further statement.'

Mason said, 'I think, now, Doctor, it's time for you to see the patient.'

'I'm quite certain it is,' Dr Kettle said.

'You'll transfer her in an ambulance?' Mason asked.

Dr Kettle shook his head. 'Ambulances attract attention. I'll get her out to my car and take her to the hospital personally; that is, if she can walk.'

'I think she can,' Mason said. 'It will be rather painful.'

'Why?'

'She had a long walk in the desert.'

'I see.'

Mason opened the door of the unit. Dr Kettle stepped out, looked to the right and left, then walked over toward the adjoining unit.

Mason opened the door, said, 'This is my secretary, Della Street, Dr Kettle. . . . Now, Mrs Elmore, I have a doctor here who is going to see if he can help you a little bit, and take a look at those feet of yours. We don't want to have any chances of infection.'

Mason said to Della Street, 'I think, Della, that it would be better to leave the doctor alone with his patient.'

Dr Kettle, opening his bag, took out a bundle of gauze, unwrapped a hypodermic syringe and said, 'Do you feel nervous, Mrs Elmore?'

Lorraine Elmore pulled the cool bandage from her flushed forehead, tried to struggle to a sitting position.

'Just take it easy,' Dr Kettle said. 'I understand you've had a harrowing experience.'

Lorraine Elmore nodded, tried to talk, then started to sob.

Dr Kettle tilted a bottle. The odor of alcohol filled the room. 'Just let me have your left arm, if you will, please, Mrs Elmore.'

Mason said, 'Just one question, Mrs Elmore, before Dr Kettle gives you a shot to steady your nerves. You had a large sum of money with you?'

She gave a convulsive start. 'Heavens, yes! I'd forgotten all about it. Monty had a lot of cash with him, too.'

'Where is it?' Mason asked.

'I–We–It's under the seat of the overstuffed chair in his cabin. We decided it would be best to hide the money before we went out in the car.'

'You talked it over?' Mason asked.

'Yes. We decided we'd leave the money and–Ouch!'

'That's all,' Dr Kettle said, withdrawing the hypodermic needle.

'Will you take care of the money?' Mrs Elmore asked.

'We'll do the best we can,' Mason promised.

Dr Kettle motioned toward the door.

Mason, Della Street and Duncan Crowder moved silently out of the unit.

'I'm sorry,' Duncan Crowder said to Della Street, 'you didn't give me a chance to explain about my father being in the hospital and the fact that I'm carrying on the business as best I can.'

'It's my fault,' Della Street said. 'We were faced with a real emergency here, and I simply didn't dare take the time to listen. Mr Mason said to get Duncan Crowder and get him here at once, and when I asked you if you were Duncan Crowder and you said you were, and then went on to say "but", I'm afraid I interrupted rather sharply.'

'You did,' Crowder said, grinning.

Mason said, 'Crowder, we have a job to do.'

'The money?' Crowder asked.

Mason nodded.

Crowder looked across at the group of curious people milling around the unit which had been occupied by Montrose Dewitt. 'If it's all the same to you, Mr Mason,' he said, 'I'd suggest you wait here. Your photograph has been published a good many times. People are going to recognize you and start talking.

'Let me go over there and work around the edges of the crowd. I know the coroner and I know the chief of police. I can probably get a look but I couldn't remove anything.'

'Go ahead,' Mason said. He took Della Street's arm and they stood in the doorway of the cabin Della Street had occupied, watching Duncan Crowder as he moved around in the group exchanging greetings here and there; then they saw him speak to one of the men and step inside, with the calm assurance of a person entering his own home.

Crowder was in there for a good five minutes, then he emerged with crisp, businesslike efficiency. This time he did not pause to talk with the people gathered outside the cabin but strode directly down to where Mason and Della Street were waiting.

'Find it?' Mason asked.

'Nothing,' Crowder said.

'You looked under the cushions of the big chair?'

Crowder nodded.

'Any indication that the cushion had been removed from the big chair?'

Crowder shook his head. 'No indication that would be any good either way. You can pull the cushion out of the chair and put it back without disturbing anything. However, there's one point that *may* be significant.'

'What's that?'

'Quite a bit of small change in the space between the cushion and the chair,'

Crowder said, 'where it *could* have fallen out of the side trousers' pocket of some man who sat there with one leg crossed over the other–the change would have dribbled out. Or it could have been planted there by someone who wanted it to appear the cushions had been undisturbed.'

Crowder went on, 'Personally I'd give her the benefit of the doubt, but–Well, *what* do you know!'

Mason followed the direction of Crowder's gaze.

'Look at that guy,' Crowder said. 'They talk about our broad-brimmed hats being conspicuous in Boston. Look at that little capsule perched on that guy's head. It reminds me of when my mother used to make apple pies. She'd pinch the crust off the end of the plate and then trim off that little–'

Mason interrupted him. 'Crowder,' he said, 'get across there quick! That's Howland Brent from Boston. He's Lorraine Elmore's business manager. He must have been occupying one of these units. Find out when he got in here, and under what name he registered–Good Lord, does *this* complicate the situation!'

'On my way,' Crowder said. 'Keep back in the doorway out of sight, if you will, please, Mr Mason.'

Crowder moved over to the office of the motel, was back in a few minutes, stating, 'That's the name, all right; Howland Brent, from Boston, Massachusetts; apparently driving a rented car because it has a California License plate. Registered in shortly before you did last night. He has Unit Eleven. That's next to you.'

Mason's eyes were level-lidded with concentration.

'You're beginning to attract attention,' Crowder warned. 'You somehow stand out in a crowd, and Miss Street is *far* from unattractive. I have noticed a few wolf-like glances from the local citizens at the other end of the court.'

'I've noticed them myself,' Della Street said laughing, 'even when I pretended not to.'

'I think we'd better leave,' Mason said. 'I think Mrs Elmore is in safe hands.'

'She won't make any statement for at least twenty-four hours,' Crowder promised. 'Not with Dr Kettle on the job. At least, nothing that will be passed on. Anything she says will be a confidential communication to her physician.'

'Or a nurse,' Mason said,

'Or a nurse,' Crowder amended.

'I think we'd better leave,' Mason said, 'although I *am* waiting for Paul Drake.'

'Who's he?'

'The detective I have working on the case. He should be here at any minute.'

Crowder said, 'All right, we're safe for twenty-four hours. What are you going to do at the end of that time?'

'I wish I knew,' Mason said.

Crowder said, 'I think you'd better get in your car, drive out to the street, and you can watch for the detective from there.'

'Wait a minute,' Della Street said, 'here's a cab coming now.'

'That's Paul,' Mason said, reaching an instant decision. 'You get in the rented car, Della, and Mr Crowder can ride with you. I'll get in the cab with Paul.'

Mason hurried out to the sidewalk as the cab slowed and started to turn.

Paul Drake was reaching in his pocket.

Mason said, 'Keep the cab, Paul. I'm joining you.'

The lawyer jerked the door open, jumped in and said to the cabdriver, 'Back to the airport, if you will, please.'

The cabdriver backed the cab into a turn, said, 'Hey, what's happened here? The court is full of people.'

'A fight or something I guess,' Mason said, 'or maybe someone ran into one of the parked cars. How quick can you get us to the airport?'

'Right fast,' the cabdriver said. 'Hey, is that car behind following us?'

'It's following us,' Mason said. 'Those are people who are with us.'

'I see.'

Drake raised his eyebrows at Mason.

The lawyer warned him to silence with a glance. 'Is the plane all ready to go, Paul?'

'All gassed up and ready,' Drake said.

'That's fine,' Mason told him. 'This is going to be a busy day, Paul.'

'So I gather,' Drake said.

7

As the cars came to a stop at the airfield, Mason approached the pilot.

'You're all ready to go?' he asked.

'Yes.'

'Plenty of gas?'

'That's right.'

Mason turned to Crowder, said, 'Your office has rather a wide acquaintance here in the Imperial Valley?'

'Down at the south end of it,' Crowder said.

'And,' Mason said, 'doubtless some of your clients have property for sale?'

'I'm quite sure they do.'

'Know anyone in particular that has property out east of here that would be interested in selling, or wants to sell?'

'Yes, I think I do,' Crowder said.

'Could you point out that property from the air?'

'I could try.'

'I'm interested in property down here in the valley,' Mason explained. 'I think it might be a good investment. I'd like to find out something about the topography of the country and just where the sand hills are located. I understand there are some to the east and a little to the north of here. Before I return to Los Angeles it might be a good idea for us to fly over the country.'

'I'll go with you,' Crowder said. 'Later on I'll get some specific pieces of property lined up, together with prices. Right at the moment I can only give you general information.'

'General information is all I need,' Mason told him. 'I think the best thing to do would be to go east of here and follow all of the roads which turn north. That's the section generally that I'm interested in, and I'd like to get an idea of the topography of the country.

'If you'll accompany me and answer any questions I may have, we'll bring you back to the airport.'

'I'll be glad to go,' Crowder said.

'We're going to have to do some low flying,' Mason told the pilot, 'and then we may have to take off for Los Angeles without stopping to refuel.'

'It's all right,' the pilot said. 'I can take you anywhere you want to go, within reason.'

They climbed into the plane and fastened seat belts. The pilot warmed the motors up, taxied down the field and took off.

'Where to?' he asked.

Mason turned to Duncan Crowder.

'Go east about twelve miles,' Crowder said. 'Fly over Calexico for a fix, then follow the paved road out toward Yuma.'

The pilot nodded. The plane banked into a turn.

As they flew over the motel at Calexico, Mason studied the situation, noticed that a machine of the type used by undertakers for picking up bodies was backed up to the door of Unit 14.

The plane made a circle. 'Okay?' the pilot asked.

'Okay,' Crowder said, and pointed to the east.

They flew for a few minutes out over the gleaming strip of highway.

'From here on,' Mason said, 'explore every road leading to the north.'

'For how far?'

'Until you come to the end of it. It's only a few miles up to the other highway from El Centro and Holtville. We want to check the area in between.'

'Can you tell me what you're looking for?' the pilot asked.

'Just property,' Mason said.

The pilot brought the plane down to within a thousand feet of the ground, explored one side of the road, then circled back to the highway, started to explore another and said, 'That *may* be what you *should* be looking for, up ahead.'

Mason, in the copilot's seat, said, 'I don't see anything.'

The plane swept on, zoomed over the stalled car, climbed into a banking turn and came back.

'Apparently stuck in the sand,' the pilot said. 'That's the way it looks.'

'Okay,' Mason said, 'fly north a couple of miles, then go back to the field. Stay with the plane when you get there. Have plenty of gas and be ready to take off the minute we show up.'

'Okay,' the pilot said, and climbed to a higher altitude as they started back for the field.

Mason turned to Crowder. 'You can find that road all right?'

Crowder nodded.

'Is that near the property your client owns?' Mason asked Crowder.

'Right on it,' Crowder said, turning toward Mason and closing one eye.

'I'd like to look at it from the ground,' Mason said.

'I'll drive you out there,' Crowder promised,

'Well, *that* didn't take long,' the pilot said.

The plane was circling back over the field within a few minutes and settled down to a landing. The pilot taxied up to the rented car, turned the plane and stopped.

The passengers disembarked and approached the car.

When they were out of earshot of the pilot, Mason said to Crowder, 'You'd better drive. You know the country. You know this road all right?'

'I know it,' Crowder said. 'It's up beyond the irrigated lands. It's a road that runs across to the Holtville Highway. There's a hard-packed desert gravel for a way, and then sand for a spell.'

'What do you mean, "hard-packed desert gravel"?' Mason asked.

Crowder said, 'We have winds down here–at times very violent winds. After thousands of years they've blown everything that's movable in the line of sand away from the surface. What's left is a hard-packed surface of sand-worn gravel. Then when these winds slow down a bit, they start depositing sand. For that reason you'll find a lot of contrast down here; soil that's pure silt, sand hills and then hard-packed soil with little rocks that are polished smooth by sand and coated by the sunlight. I guess there's a chemical or something that gives the rocks kind of a dark, shiny surface on the part that's exposed to the sunlight.'

'Hard to track in soil of that sort?' Mason asked.

'You can follow an automobile track, if it's fresh–if that's what you mean.'

'That wasn't exactly what I meant,' Mason said, 'but we'll take a look. Get there as soon as possible. We're fighting time.'

Crowder nodded, pressed the foot throttle and eased the car into speed.

'Now, I'm not certain about the ethics of this situation,' Crowder said. 'I'm leaving that entirely up to you.'

'What do you mean, "ethics"?'

'I take it,' Crowder said, 'we're going to discover evidence.'

'Evidence of what?' Mason asked.

'I don't know,' Crowder said.

'Neither do I,' Mason told him. 'We're inspecting physical facts.'

'But what do we do with those facts? Do we–Well, suppose those facts should become evidence–at a later date?'

'That's exactly what I have in mind,' Mason said. 'We try to keep the date as much later as possible *if* the facts indicate that our client was emotionally disturbed.'

'But if they're pertinent, what do we do?'

'If we *know* they're pertinent,' Mason said, 'we call the attention of the authorities to the facts.'

'And you think they may be pertinent?'

'I'm afraid,' Mason said, 'they may be pertinent. However, as far as ethics are concerned, don't overlook the fact that a lawyer is ethically bound to protect his client. That's the first and foremost of all rules of legal ethics.

'The people who formulate the canons of legal ethics take it for granted that an attorney will be protecting his client, so they lay down rules of professional conduct for the purpose of seeing the lawyer doesn't go too far. But the number one canon of ethics which should dominate all the others is that an attorney should be loyal to his client and should protect his client.

'Now then, we have a client who is hysterical. She is emotionally disturbed. She has told me a story which I can't repeat to the authorities because it's something she has told me as a professional confidence.

'If I can't tell it to the authorities in words without violating legal ethics, I can't very well tell the same story by actions.'

'What do you mean?'

'If,' Mason said, 'the authorities knew that we took off in an automobile and came out here, the authorities would naturally assume that there was some reason for it and that our client had told us something that led us to take such an action.'

'I see,' Crowder said.

'Therefore,' Mason said, 'I see no reason for letting the authorities know that we drove out here looking for a car.'

'I am beginning to understand,' Crowder said, 'why you were interested in looking over some property and the elaborate disinterest with which you regarded that car.'

Mason said, 'I think our pilot is fully trustworthy, but there's no use subjecting him to a practical test.'

'And that's why you're anxious to have him get back to Los Angeles?' Crowder asked.

Mason grinned and said, 'If he's not around here and doesn't hear about any murder case, he won't be doing any talking.'

'Check,' Crowder said.

Thereafter they were silent until Crowder made a left-hand turn.

'Is this the road?' Mason asked.

Crowder nodded.

'Let's take it slow and look for tracks.'

'There's only a little traffic,' Crowder said. 'A few hunters come up in here. This road skirts some of those drifting sand hills I was telling you about. For some reason there's an eddy in the wind here, and as the wind, carrying sand, loses velocity, the sand spills out so to speak and starts forming drifting sand hills.'

'This ground is hard packed,' Mason said, 'almost as if there were some kind of a cement binder.'

'I think perhaps there is,' Crowder said. 'You can see those smooth pebbles all along here. They glisten in the sunlight.'

The car sped along the road, then slowed as it went through a patch of sand, then speeded up again over another hard flat with pebbles reflecting the sunlight.

'There's the car up ahead,' Crowder said. 'Massachusetts license.'

'I think we stop here,' Mason said. 'No, wait a minute. Go as far as you can without getting stuck.'

'I can go pretty far,' Crowder said, 'because I was raised in this country. I know how to drive it. If you start fighting the sand, you get stuck. If you just ease the wheels into motion and don't start churning the sand, you don't have any trouble. And if you do get into trouble, you can let some air out of your tires and–'

'That's it,' Mason said. 'Let's stop the car and let some air out of the tires. I don't want to leave any more tracks than necessary.'

'All right,' Crowder said, 'we'll let a little air out of the tires and you'll be surprised what a difference it makes.'

They stopped the car. Crowder took a match and depressed the valve stems, letting air out of the tires.

'We'll have to go pretty slow going back until we get to a service station,' he said.

'That's all right,' Mason told him.

'You want to tow that car out?' Crowder asked. 'We could do it.'

'We haven't a tow rope,' Mason said.

'We can find some barbed wire around here somewhere,' Crowder said.

'Wrap it around several times and it makes a pretty good tow chain.'

'I don't think we want to move the car,' Mason said, 'but there's no reason why we can't drive up until we find the road blocked by the car.'

Crowder drove the car up to within five or six feet of the stalled automobile.

'You can see what happened,' he said. 'The driver tried to pour on the power . . . apparently trying to reverse . . . just churned up the sand and dug the car down into it.'

Mason nodded, said to Crowder, 'You and I are going to get out. Paul, you and Della sit inside. I don't want to leave any more tracks than necessary.'

'There are tracks around here now,' Crowder said. 'Looks as though people had walked around here, and someone got out of the car on the left-hand side and didn't even bother to close the door. A light comes on automatically when that door is opened. In the course of time that will run down the battery. Think we should close the door?'

'I don't think so,' Mason said. 'We'd probably better leave things pretty much as we find them.'

They approached the car, looked inside.

'Looking for blood or something?' Crowder asked.

'Something,' Mason said.

He put a handkerchief over his hand, opened the rear door, looked inside, then suddenly straightened.

'What's that?' Crowder asked.

'That,' Mason said, 'is a green capsule lying on the driver's seat. From the size and appearance it may well be a barbiturate–one of the hypnotics.'

'Sometimes used as a so-called "truth serum" I understand,' Crowder said.

'Injected hypodermically for a truth serum,' Mason said, 'so they can control the dosage–Now, what do you suppose *that's* doing here?'

'Think we should take it with us to find out what it is?' Crowder asked.

'We leave the capsule right where it is,' Mason said, 'but we take the keys out of the ignition and open the trunk.'

The lawyer reached through the open door, extracted the keys from the ignition, selected the trunk key, walked back to the rear of the car, opened the trunk and looked inside.

'Nothing,' Crowder said. 'Is that what you expected?'

'I'm not expecting,' Mason told him. 'I'm looking and thinking.'

Mason closed the trunk, put the ignition keys back in the lock, nodded to Crowder, and they returned to the rented automobile.

'That's all?' Crowder asked.

'That's all.'

'What did you find?' Drake asked.

'Nothing that we could detect by a hurried superficial examination,' Mason said, 'but there was a green capsule on the driver's seat just to the right of where the driver would be sitting. The capsule could have been spilled from a woman's purse.'

'And that's all you found?' Drake asked.

'That's all.'

'And,' Drake said, 'you seem relieved.'

'Well,' Mason told him, 'in a situation of this sort you never know what you might find in the car.'

'You mean another corpse?' Drake asked.

Mason said, 'I mean that you never know *what* you may find.'

Crowder skillfully backed the car, then made a Y-turn in the soft sand, depressing the throttle just the right amount to put power in the wheels without letting them slip or start churning up the sand.

They rode in silence back to the paved road.

They followed the pavement to the first service station, where Crowder had the tires inflated. While the attendant was putting in air, Mason went to the telephone booth and phoned the office of the sheriff.

When a voice answered saying, 'Sheriff's office,' Mason said, 'I am an attorney from Los Angeles. I've been interested in some real estate in the valley and while making a flight in a chartered plane to look over the topography, I saw an automobile which apparently had been stuck in the sand and abandoned.

'This automobile is out on a road stretching from the Calexico-Yuma Highway north toward the Holtville-Yuma Highway. The turnoff is about fifteen miles east of Calexico. I would suggest you investigate.

'There was no sign of life, no one making any distress signals, so we didn't pay too much attention to it, but later on when I was making a more detailed inspection of the property and was out in the vicinity, we drove up to the car. It seems to be a car with a Massachusetts license number; it was stuck in the sand and abandoned. I thought you'd like to know about it.'

'Thank you. We'll make a note of it,' the officer said.

Mason hung up the phone, walked over to Duncan Crowder and said, 'I'm leaving you on the job here. Paul Drake will stay here and help out. I've reported finding the car to the sheriff's office. You'll remember that we were looking at some property one of your clients had for sale.'

'I'll remember,' Duncan promised. 'Anything else?'

'Nothing else,' Mason said.

'Back to the airport?' Crowder asked.

Mason nodded, said, 'I've given you a fee. Here's some money for expenses.'

The lawyer opened his billfold, took out two one-hundred-dollar bills.

'Okay,' Crowder said, 'you have my telephone number. Keep in touch.'

'And,' Mason said, 'you report to me on developments. Linda Calhoun will be showing up and making inquiries about her aunt. Linda is very friendly with George Latty. Anything Linda knows, she'll probably tell Latty. Anything Latty knows, he's damned apt to tell anyone.

'Paul, you keep this rented car, hang around here in Calexico, keep in touch with Crowder, and keep an ear to the ground–see what you can find out. Also put a shadow on Howland Brent. If he gets suspicious, tell the operative to drop him.'

'What do I say in case I'm questioned–officially?' Drake asked.

Mason smiled and said, 'You are making all of your reports to me, and I am, of course, co-operating with the authorities.'

'Yes, I understand your co-operation,' Drake said, running his forefinger in a cutting motion around his throat.

'Why, Paul,' Mason told him, 'I'm surprised! We're co-operating with the authorities. We've told them everything we've found.'

'But you didn't tell them why you were looking for it.'

'Certainly I did,' Mason said. 'I told them that I was interested in buying some real property here. I am. It's a very fine investment. In fact, I wouldn't be too surprised if I didn't actually take an option on some piece of property for thirty days or so.'

'I see,' Drake said dryly.

'And of course,' Mason said, 'now that you mention it, the fact that that car has a Massachusetts license *is* something of a coincidence, Paul.'

When they were back at the airport Mason turned to Crowder and shook hands. 'Stay on the job, Duncan,' he said. 'Telephone me just as soon as there are any developments. Paul Drake will keep in touch with you and he'll also keep in touch with me.'

Crowder said, 'I think I understand what you want, Mr Mason.'

'I'm quite satisfied you do,' Mason said, grinning. 'And I trust you are equally conversant with what I *don't* want.'

'That, of course,' Crowder said, 'is a little more difficult but I think I have a general idea. I know that you're a very busy man and don't have time to fill me in on a lot of details. It's unfortunate as far as the authorities are concerned that you're in such a hurry to get back to your office in Los Angeles that we don't have time to sit down and talk things over.'

'Indeed it is,' Mason told him. 'You'll have to use your judgement.'

'I'll do my best,' Crowder promised.

Mason took Della Street's arm, escorted her to the plane and helped her in. The pilot revved up the motors, and Duncan and Paul Drake waved good-by as the plane taxied down the field.

'Now there,' Della Street said, 'is a young attorney who should be going places.'

Mason grinned. 'He has what you can only describe as a good legal mind.'

8

As Mason and Della Street entered the office, Gertie, the receptionist and switchboard operator, said, 'Oh, Mr Mason, Paul Drake is calling from Calexico. He wanted to get in touch with you just as soon as you came in. He said he would wait at the telephone. He expected you would be here about this time.'

'All right,' Mason said, 'put the call through, Gertie, and see if we can get him.'

Mason and Della Street went on into Mason's private office. Della Street started opening the mail with secretarial efficiency and was only halfway through the pile when the phone rang.

Mason nodded to Della Street to pick up her extension and heard Drake's voice on the line saying, 'Hello, Perry.'

'Okay,' Mason said, 'I'm on.'

'This whole thing is a tempest in a teapot,' Drake said. 'The guy died a natural death.'

'You're sure, Paul?'

'The coroner is. The guy just died a natural death–probably heart failure. There isn't any murder at all. Downright accommodating of him, I'd call it.'

'You've advised Crowder?' Mason asked.

'Yes.'

'Have you heard anything from Linda Calhoun?'

'Yes, she's down here. She must have arrived just about as you were taking off. She was at the motel when I got there.'

'Did you tell her anything about Crowder?'

'Yes, I had Crowder with me and introduced him, and he told her that he was working with you and took her to his office.'

'What about George Latty?'

'He's disappeared somewhere. He checked out of the motel. I guess he's headed back for Los Angeles.'

'And what about the abandoned car?'

'As nearly as I can tell,' Drake said, 'no one's doing anything about the car. They took your report and filed it. I don't think anyone's worried about it.'

'What about Howland Brent, Paul?'

'He's moving heaven and earth trying to get Dr Kettle to wake Lorraine up so he can talk with her. Dr Kettle refuses. So Brent got in a rented car and took off. I have a man following him. He's probably headed back to Los Angeles.'

Mason reached a quick decision. 'All right, Paul, if it's a natural death there's no reason for the authorities to keep those motel units sealed up. Get busy and rent them before someone beats you to it. Tell the manager you're representing Lorraine Elmore and pay the rent in advance. Say she's lost the key. Get another key. Get in there and go over the place inch by inch.

'The coroner will want to remove the things from Dewitt's cabin. As soon as that has been done, you move in. Get a reservation on the place. Tell the manager I'm coming down to join you. Don't give her my name. Rent both units in your name.'

'Okay,' Drake said. 'Can do.'

'One other thing,' Mason said, 'rent that unit Latty moved out of. That will give us three in a row. Now, go through those units with a fine-toothed comb.'

'What for, Perry? There hasn't been any murder and–'

'There's been a theft of over thirty-five thousand dollars,' Mason interrupted. 'We probably can't find where the money is, but we sure as hell can find out where it isn't.'

'Okay,' Drake promised. 'I'll get busy.'

'Right away,' Mason said.

'*Right* away,' Drake said, and hung up.

Mason and Della Street hung up simultaneously.

'Well?' Della Street asked.

Mason shook his head.

'Do we let it rest there if the authorities will?' she asked.

'Why not?'

'You have the story of a woman who says she saw him murdered.'

'And,' Mason said, the body doesn't have a mark on it. There isn't any sign of violence and he died a natural death.'

'Do *you* think he died a natural death?' she asked.

'I don't question the opinion of the authorities,' Mason said. 'See if you can get Duncan Crowder on the phone, Della.'

Della Street relayed the call through to Gertie at the switchboard and a moment later nodded to Perry Mason. He's coming on.'

Mason picked up the phone and heard Duncan Crowder say, 'Hello.'

'Perry Mason, Duncan,' the lawyer said. 'How's everything coming at your end?'

'Everything's fine. The man died a natural death. I presume your detective told you?'

'That's right,' Mason said. 'What else do you know?'

'Not very much. Linda Calhoun is here in the office with me. We've been visiting and . . . well, sort of getting acquainted. Has George Latty been in touch with you?'

'No.'

'He's apparently headed back to Los Angeles and will try to get in touch with you.'

Mason said, 'While you're talking with Linda, you might point out to her that all the physical evidence in this case indicates that her aunt has been emotionally upset. Now, I don't know what would cause this disturbance, but I would assume that it could be the use of barbiturates over a long period of time.

'She probably went to Montrose Dewitt's unit and tapped on the door and, when he didn't answer, opened the door to look in and saw him lying there on the floor dead. That was a very great emotional shock and she dashed into her unit, started tearing things to pieces, then jumped in her car and took a ride out in the desert.

'Now, I'm not a doctor but I assume that if a woman had taken a heavy dose of sedatives and then had experienced a shock like that and had started driving a car out into the desert with the subconscious realization in the back of her mind that a friend of whom she was very fond was dead, it might well be possible for her to have imagined this whole idea of a murder scene.'

'I guess anything is possible,' Crowder said. 'We don't know very much about the workings of the human mind.'

'It's a situation you might suggest to Dr Kettle,' Mason said.

'Now, wait a minute,' Crowder told him. 'Kettle will co-operate with us every way he can, but he wouldn't falsify a fact for anyone.'

'This isn't a fact,' Mason said. 'It's a theory. You might point out to him that the indication is that Lorraine Elmore took a very heavy dose of barbiturates in order to sleep. She might have heard some noise–perhaps Dewitt called her name from the adjoining motel unit when he felt a heart attack coming on. She hurried to his side and he expired in her arms. That could have triggered a whole set of ideas.'

'I get it,' Crowder said. 'I got it the first time, but I'm just pointing out to you, Mr Mason, that Dr Kettle won't go for it unless it's medically sound.'

'Mason said, '*I* think it's medically sound. You might talk with Linda along those lines.'

'I'll talk with her,' Crowder said. 'She seems very intelligent.'

'I'm satisfied you both are,' Mason told him, and hung up.

The lawyer had no sooner replaced the phone than Della Street's phone rang and she picked up the instrument, said, 'Yes, Gertie,' then said, 'Just a minute.'

She turned to Mason and said, 'Belle Freeman is in the office. She'd like to see you.'

'Belle Freeman?' Mason asked. 'That's the one that knew Dewitt and took out the marriage license with him?'

Della Street nodded.

'I think we want to see her,' Mason said, 'but this case certainly is taking some puzzling turns. Go get her and bring her in, Della. Let's see what she has to say.'

Della nodded, went to the reception room and returned with a woman in her mid-thirties, a woman who had the figure of a woman in her twenties. Her blue eyes sparkled, her step was full of bounce.

'Mr Mason,' she said, 'I *know* this is an imposition, but I talked with Linda Calhoun last night and somehow I feel that I know you and I think perhaps you can help me.'

'Well, now wait a minute,' Mason said. 'In the first place I'm glad you came in. I had been thinking about getting in touch with you; however, *I* can't help *you*. This is case in which I already have a client. I wouldn't want to even consider representing anyone whose interests might be in conflict. . . .'

'But they're not in conflict,' she said. 'All I want is my money back, and I have a boy friend in El Centro who will help.'

'Well, that might–it just might–be in conflict,' Mason said. 'But with the understanding that anything you tell me is not in confidence and that I can't represent you as long as there is any possibility of conflict, I'd certainly be glad to talk with you, because you have some information that I want.'

'What, Mr Mason?'

'I would like to know a great deal about Montrose Dewitt.'

'The man's a heel, a fourflusher, a phony from way back.'

'I can understand all that,' Mason said. 'I'm not talking about his character. I'm talking about his background.'

'I don't know too much about his background, but I know everything about his character, and I hope you can send him to jail. That's what I came to see you about. I wanted–'

'You can't send him to jail,' Mason interrupted.

'You can't?' she asked, her face showing her evident disappointment. 'Now that you've found him why can't–'

Mason shook his head. 'He's dead.'

'What?'

'He's dead. He died last night in Calexico.'

'How–Why–How did it happen?'

'Apparently he just died in his sleep,' Mason said.

She started to say something, then caught herself.

Mason raised his eyebrows.

'I'm sorry,' she said. 'I make it a rule never to speak ill of the dead. I didn't know.'

'Well, that isn't going to keep you from telling me something that would give me a clue as to his past.'

She said, 'I'm not going to be able to help you there very much, Mr Mason. The man had the most mysterious personality and background–he simply vanished.'

'He defrauded you out of some money?'

'All of my savings.'

'How much?'

'It was more than the figure I've admitted. There was an inheritance and he got away with everything.'

'You went to the police?'

'No, I didn't, Mr Mason. I–There were reasons. I couldn't afford publicity. I suppose this is all an old story to you, but I was a babe in the woods. I walked in like a sheep to the slaughter. He told me we were going to pool our assets and that he was going to raise some more money from his friends. He had a sure-fire opportunity to make millions and all it needed was a little capital.'

'A convincing talker?' Mason asked.

'He convinced me.'

'By talk?'

'Well, he had what you would call a skillful approach. He knew how to flatter a woman and make her feel important and . . . well, I fell for it.'

'How did you meet him?'

'Through correspondence. I wrote a letter of protest to a newspaper. The newspaper published it. It didn't publish my address, of course, but he found out my address–that wouldn't have been too difficult. I was a registered voter. He wrote me a letter telling me how smart I was, how well I had expressed my ideas, how much they meant to him and how refreshing it was to encounter a person of such intelligence and perspicacity in the readers' column of the paper.

'Well, of course I fell for it. His address was on the upper left-hand corner of the envelope, and I wrote him a brief note thanking him, and he wrote me enclosing a newspaper clipping that he thought would be interesting to me, and the first thing I knew we were meeting, having dinner dates, and then . . . well, then he just went ahead with a whirlwind campaign.'

'But what did he tell you about himself?' Mason asked. 'What did he say he was doing?'

'He wasn't doing anything. He had just returned from Mexico. He had been engaged in some activities there which he said were classified and he couldn't talk about them, but he had had many adventures. He was the dashing soldier-of-fortune type.'

'How long did he say he'd been in Mexico?'

'He said he'd been there for more than a year–but you know there's something funny, Mr Mason. The man couldn't speak Spanish.'

'No?'

'I don't think he knew more than a dozen words of Spanish. He told all about his adventures, and then I introduced him to a friend who could speak Spanish and mentioned something about Montrose having been in Mexico, and the friend started speaking Spanish to him.'

'What happened?'

'Montrose stopped the man, said that he had never bothered to learn Spanish because he felt that it put him at a disadvantage; that it was always better to have an interpreter and work through the interpreter.'

'And you were taken in by that explanation?'

'At the time, yes. I'd have been taken in by anything he did.'

'And then, after the man got your money, what happened?'

'We were to be married, but he just never showed up, that's all. He simply vanished.'

'No word from him, no explanation?'

'Nothing,' she said, her lips tightening. 'If you could ever realize the way I felt when it began to dawn on me. . . . First there was that awful period of anxiety, feeling that he'd been hurt in an automobile accident, or something; then an attempt to trace him, and gradually the sickening realization that I'd been played for a fool.'

'And you did nothing about it?'

'I tried to find him.'

'How?'

'I hired a private detective until I realized that was throwing good money after bad.'

'And the detective couldn't find him?'

She shook her head. 'Not a trace.'

'The detective made reports?'

'Oh, yes, he made copious reports telling me what he'd done. He referred to Montrose as the subject, and the reports were skillfully designed to show me that I was getting a run for my money. That's all I was getting, a run for my money.'

Mason said, 'By any chance do you have those reports? Did you save them?'

'I have them here,' she said. 'I came prepared to do everything I could to help Linda and . . . well, I wanted to do something to get even with Montrose Dewitt.'

She opened her purse, took out an envelope and handed it to Mason.

'May I keep these reports for a while?' Mason asked.

'Keep them forever, if you want,' she said. 'I don't know why I was saving them. They're just a memory of a headache.'

Mason said, 'The man must have had some hide-out where he could vanish–probably some other city where he carried on his activities. Perhaps he worked several cities at the same time. It's unusual for a man to keep the same name and then to vanish completely.'

'That's what I thought,' she said, 'but I felt that I was throwing good money after bad and, as a friend pointed out to me, there wasn't very much I could do if I did catch up with him except–Well, I didn't want to try to prosecute him for obtaining money under false pretenses, or anything of that sort.

'In fact, Mr Mason, I don't know that there were any false pretenses. I simply trustingly turned over my money to him to invest. We were going to be partners in life and all that sort of stuff–and I went completely overboard.

'I guess with your experience and legal background you can just about put the whole story together. I was a fool.'

'You'd been married?' Mason asked.

She shook her head. 'I was a bachelor girl. I had been very much in love, and the man I loved had been killed. I was true to his memory for quite a while. Then things began to happen. I drifted into an attachment and that didn't pan out, and the first thing I knew I was no longer a young woman and I tried to pretend I didn't care. I was a bachelor girl. I was going to live my own life beholden to no one. Women aren't made to do that, Mr Mason. They want someone to work for, someone to love, someone to cherish and, if you come right down to it, someone to obey.

'Then along came Montrose Dewitt with this dashing devil-may-care air of his and I was just like putty.'

'Did he have an automobile?' Mason asked.

'Yes, it's all in those reports. The detective traced the ownership of the automobile and all of that.

'You'll find that there's no record of Montrose Dewitt ever paying income taxes, ever having a social security number, but he did have a driving license.'

'And you were living here in Los Angeles at the time?'

'No, Mr Mason, I was living in Ventura, working there. And Montrose Dewitt had an apartment in Hollywood. The job I had was . . . well, if there had been any scandal connected with my name–Well, I just had to grit my teeth and start all over again. I just couldn't afford the publicity, and I can't very well afford it now. That's one of the reasons I came up here to see you, Mr Mason. I would dislike very much to have Linda Calhoun say anything that would involve me.

'I tried to reach her this morning but couldn't get her and I knew you were representing her, so I thought I'd come to you and give you what help I could and ask you to protect me as much as possible–I mean from publicity.'

'Thanks a lot,' Mason told her. 'If you'll let me study those reports I may be able to learn something from them, and I certainly appreciate the fact that you have told me this much.'

She gave him her hand, said, 'I've tried to make it a closed chapter in my life but it keeps cropping up. I feel better now that I've told you the whole story and given you those reports. I was hoping they might be of some help.'

'I'll study them,' Mason promised as Della Street escorted Belle Freeman to the exit door.

'Well?' Mason asked, when the door closed.

Della Street shook her head. 'The man certainly seemed to have a way with women.'

'And,' Mason said, 'what the police refer to as a *modus operandi*. He'd make his initial contact through the mails. That means he must have written quite a few letters to different people. He couldn't have picked live prospects every time just by taking the names of persons who had written letters that were published. There must have been times when the women who wrote those letters were married, or didn't have any money, or did have boy friends who wouldn't have meekly surrendered their women to some character who had a dashing manner, a black eye patch, and a mysterious background.'

'That's right,' Della Street said.

'In other words,' Mason said, 'the man must have written dozens of letters. When he'd get a reply he'd start checking. If he found the party had some money, then he would follow up.'

'Will that help us?' she asked.

'It may give us a little help on his background,' Mason said. 'It probably won't help otherwise because we already knew how he worked. I was merely pointing out the problems which he faced as a confidence man. The thing that is puzzling is the manner in which he could completely disappear.

'You would have thought that a man who was engaging in a confidence game wouldn't have had the temerity to use such a distinctive means of identification as the black eye patch.'

'That probably made him distinctive and more dashing and more attractive,' Della Street said.

'But a thousand times more conspicuous,' Mason said, 'and . . .'

Suddenly he stopped.

'What?' she asked.

Mason snapped his fingers and said, 'Of course! I should have thought of it before.'

'What?'

'He wore the eye patch because he wanted to be conspicuous. He only put on his eye patch when he was going to make a swindle. Then when he disappeared he simply took off the eye patch and substituted a glass eye. Then he could fade into the background and blend with thousands of other individuals.

'No one would ever think of looking for him except as the man with the black eye patch.'

'*That* certainly sounds logical,' Della Street said.

Mason, suddenly excited, said, 'Let's get hold of Paul Drake, Della. I want him to get a colored sketch of Montrose Dewitt's remaining eye. Then we'll get in touch with people who manufacture glass eyes. There aren't many of them–it's quite a specialty–'

Mason was interrupted by the telephone ringing a succession of short bells, a signal always used by Gertie at the switchboard when there was some emergency, or when she was excited.

Della Street picked up the telephone, said, 'Yes,' then said to Mason, 'It's Paul Drake on the line. He's excited.'

Mason picked up the telephone, said, 'Hello, Paul. What is it?'

'There's hell to pay down here,' Drake said.

'How come?'

'Montrose Dewitt left a pint whiskey flask in his suitcase,' Drake said. 'One of the boys from the coroner's office took a nip, just to have a drink on the dead man. It was pretty good whiskey and he felt it shouldn't be wasted.'

'What happened?' Mason asked.

'The guy's in the care of a physician right now,' Drake said. 'The whiskey was loaded to the gills with some powerful drug, probably one of the barbiturates.

'That puts an entirely different aspect on the whole case and makes it look like murder after all. They're going to analyze the contents of Dewitt's stomach and send the vital organs to a laboratory to be tested for barbiturates. I thought I'd let you know.'

'Does Crowder know?' Mason asked.

'He knows.'

'Linda?'

'I understand Crowder is getting in touch with her.'

'All right,' Mason said, 'here's what I want you to do, Paul. Get the coroner to let you make a colored sketch of the man's single eye. Get an artist with some colored crayons and make a sketch of the coloring of that eye. I want all of those little islands of coloring that you find in the eye, the most accurate chart you can make.'

'Then what?' Drake asked.

'Then,' Mason said, 'I want you to get back here as fast as you can and start covering people who make glass eyes. I want to see if we can find whoever it was who made the glass eye for Montrose Dewitt.'

'But he didn't have a glass eye, Perry. He wore the patch all the time and–'

'And then when he disappeared,' Mason interrupted, 'he simply put the patch in the bottom of a bureau drawer, put the glass eye in and very probably assumed another identity.

'You'll remember the significant fact that while he was supposed to be a travelling man his automobile showed only a very low mileage. Put all that stuff together, Paul and it means that Montrose Dewitt had another identity somewhere pretty near Los Angeles.

'Now, if that happened, two men are missing and there's only one corpse. I want you to get busy and check on all missing persons. I want you to check on that glass eye. You had better get back here and start putting men to work.'

'Well,' Drake said thoughtfully, 'that's sure an angle, Perry. I'll be seeing you.'

'Has the sheriff done anything about that car yet?'

'That report you made,' Drake said, 'is probably buried in the files.'

'Okay,' Mason told him, 'we've got some time yet before Lorraine Elmore comes out from under her sedation. We probably don't have that much time before the police start checking on her car and then appreciate the significance of the report I made.

'We've got to be well ahead of them by that time, because this development of the drugged whiskey means that someone is going to be charged with murder and it may well be our client.'

'Oh-oh,' Drake said, and then after a moment added, 'I see your point, Perry. I'll get up there right away.'

9

It was mid-afternoon when Paul Drake's code knock sounded on the door of Mason's private office.

Della Street opened the door and said, 'You got back in a hurry, Paul.'

'I was told to. I caught a plane out of Imperial via Palm Springs.'

'Anything new, Paul?' Mason asked.

'Quite a bit of it,' Drake said, 'but I can't unscramble it.'

'What is it?'

'Well, in the first place, Perry, I'm afraid I started something when I got the coroner to let me make a color sketch of the dead man's eye.'

'What happened?'

'There was an artist down there who really had a lot of talent and she was perfectly willing to make a color sketch of a dead eye.

'However, it's a small community, and the coroner thought that was a story that was good enough for the newspapers. He's going to run for office so he wanted newspaper support, and he let the cat out of the bag.'

'What else?'

'Well, that's about the story, Perry. I got in an hour ago, passed the color sketch on to one of my best operatives and started him covering the persons who make glass eyes to order.

'That's quite a profession, Perry. It's an art to make a really good artificial eye with all the natural coloring.'

Mason nodded.

The phone rang.

Della Street picked up the instrument, said, 'Hello,' then nodded to Paul Drake. 'For you, Paul.'

Drake went over to the instrument, said, 'Hello,' then after listening for a moment said, 'All right, what's the address?'

The detective made a notation on a pad of paper, said, 'He's sure?'

'That's right.'

'And what's the name? Hale? H-a-l-e. Okay, what's the first name? Spell it. W-e-s-t-o-n. Okay, that's all you can do at that end. We'll check on it.'

Cradling the phone and turning to Mason, Drake said, 'Well, we seem to be getting somewhere, Perry. My operative located a Selwig Hedrick, who is one of the top experts in the business, and he recognized the eye immediately; said that he had made it for a man named Weston Hale. The address is the Roxley Apartments.'

Mason said, 'It's a good even-money bet that Weston Hale will turn up missing tonight and no one will be sure where he is or what happened to him.'

'In other words, Weston Hale and Montrose Dewitt are one and the same?' Drake asked.

Mason nodded.

The telephone rang and Della Street picked up the instrument, said, 'Hello,' then gestured to Mason. 'Duncan Crowder calling from Calexico,' she said.

Mason picked up his telephone, said, 'Hello . . . yes, this is Perry Mason . . . hello, Duncan, what's new?'

Crowder said, 'I hate to bring you bad news, Mr Mason, but I guess that's what it is.'

'What is it?'

'For some reason the authorities suddenly woke up to the significance of the report you made on the car out in the middle of the desert with the Massachusetts license. They sent a tow car out, snaked the car out of the sand, and have brought it in for investigation. There was a capsule of Somniferal on the front seat, and in the cabin that was occupied by Lorraine Elmore they found a bottle which had contained Somniferal capsules. The bottle was a large one with a capacity for a hundred capsules and is so labeled.'

'Prescription?' Mason asked.

'Yes. It was a prescription. It seems our client has been emotionally disturbed. A doctor has been prescribing for her. She told him she was taking a long trip and wanted enough sleeping medicine to last her. He gave her the prescription.

'The sheriff talked with him on the phone. He said Mrs Elmore's trouble was such that if she started worrying about not having enough sleeping medicine along it would have been the worst thing possible. He said she only takes a capsule when she becomes disturbed, that she averages about eight to twelve capsules a month but if she felt she didn't have enough to last her she'd become so upset her nervous trouble would be greatly exaggerated.

'Naturally they're now very anxious to get Mrs Elmore's story, and particularly they want to know how the Somniferal from her bottle got into Montrose Dewitt's stomach.'

'They can't prove it's the *same* Somniferal,' Mason said.

'Perhaps not, but they're certainly acting on that assumption. Dr Kettle is standing firm. His client is under sedation and he says any statement that she might make at the present time would reasonably be expected to be inaccurate, and perhaps the facts might be all mixed up with imaginative memories from the dream world. He's expressed it rather strongly and quite vividly.'

Mason thought for a moment, then said, 'All right, Duncan, let Dr Kettle emphasize the fact that any statement she might make is very apt to be inaccurate, colored by imaginative facts from a world of fantasy, and completely unreliable; but if they want to accept the responsibility of a statement being made under those circumstances he'll let them talk with the patient as soon as she wakes up.'

Crowder said, 'They'll grab that offer. They're tremendously anxious right now to find out what this is all about, how the car got out there, what the connection is between Dewitt and Mrs Elmore, and when she saw him last and all that. Should Dr Kettle waken her now?'

'No. Wait until she wakes up. Tip Dr Kettle off to play it up strong, that any statement she may make will be very apt to be inaccurate, and then when she wakes up let her make that statement.'

'You know what they'll do then,' Crowder said. 'They'll take her into custody and later on when she is in full possession of her faculties they'll play the tape recording of that statement back to her and ask her how much is true and how much of it isn't true.'

'And by that time,' Mason said, 'we will have advised her to say nothing to anyone.

'Keep in touch with the situation. The minute she makes a statement you notify me. Then I express great indignation over the telephone that any such advantage should be taken of a client. I state that under the circumstances I am advising her not to make any more statements under any circumstances, except in the presence of both of her attorneys.'

'And she dries up like a clam?'

'Like a clam,' Mason said.

'Think she'll do it?'

'She will if you talk with her in the right way.'

'What's the right way?' Crowder asked.

'Scare the pants off her,' Mason said.

'Okay,' Crowder told him, 'will do.'

'We're working on a new angle up here,' Mason said. 'Play that one down there in just exactly that way and get her to clam up immediately after she's told that story.'

'That's the way it'll be done,' Crowder said, and hung up.

10

'We check on Weston Hale?' Drake asked after Mason had returned the receiver to its cradle.

Mason nodded. 'This is one case where we're keeping just one jump ahead of the police, Paul, instead of being two jumps behind. It's a wonderful sensation.'

Drake said, 'I'm thinking of what the sensation is going to be when they do catch up with us.'

'We're not violating any law,' Mason said. 'We're not concealing any evidence. We're simply checking. Anyone has a right to do that.'

'I know, I know,' Drake said, 'but I'm worried about it just the same.'

'Anyway,' Mason pointed out, 'there won't be any Weston Hale. We'll find that he's disappeared.'

'Do you want me along?' Della Street asked.

Mason thought for a moment, then said, 'No, Della. You stay here and tend the store. We're just running down a blind alley, but in order to prove our point we have to determine that it is a blind alley. Come on, Paul, let's go.'

The Roxley Apartments proved to be a six-story apartment house of the better class. The directory showed that Weston Hale's apartment was 522.

'We may as well go up,' Mason said, 'and knock on the door. Then we'll hunt up the manager and see what we can find out.'

They went up in the elevator, walked down to the apartment and pressed the mother-of-pearl button.

Chimes sounded on the inside, then lapsed into silence.

'Do it about three times,' Mason said. 'We just want to make sure there's no answer.'

Drake nodded, pressed the button again.

Almost instantly the door opened. A man with a robe around him, his eyes swollen, his nose red, said in a voice so thick it was hard to understand, 'Whaddyuh wand?'

'Are you Mr Hale?' Mason asked.

The man shook his head. 'Hale ain't here. Whaddyuh wand with Hale?'

'We wanted to talk with him,' Mason said. 'Does he live here?'

'Hale and I share the apardmend. I gotta cold–gettin' the flu, I think. You guys gonna get the flu if you stick around. Come back later.'

'Where is Mr Hale?' Mason asked.

'On the job–working.'

'Where?'

'Investors' Mortgage & Refinancing Company.'

'Where's it located?'

'West Bemont Street. Whaddyuh wand with him? Who are you?'

'Mr Hale has a glass eye?' Mason asked.

'A what?'

'A glass eye.'

'News to me,' the man said. 'Always looked all right to me. Whaddyuh wand? Who are you?'

'What's *your* name?' Mason asked.

'Ronley Andover. Now look, I've got a fever and I've been in bed for a coupla days, fighting this thing. I'm standing in a draft right now. Why don't you guys go home before you get the flu?'

'We'll come in,' Mason said. 'We'll only be a minute.'

'If you're coming in you're going to talk to me in bed. I've got a fever and I'm supposed to stay in bed and keep covered up, drink lots of fruit juices, a little whiskey, and take a lot of aspirin. Now, if you fellows want to take a chance on the flu, come on in.'

Drake looked dubious but Mason said, 'We'll take a chance.'

They entered the apartment.

'This is a double apartment?' Mason asked.

'That's right. Hale's room is over there. He has his own bath. My bedroom is over there. I have my own bath. We use this as a sitting room and there's a kitchen in back. Now, I can't tell you fellows anything about Hale except he's on the job. Go see him there. I'm going to bed. I feel lousy.'

The man went into the bedroom, jumped into bed with the robe still around him, shivered slightly, produced an inhaler, took a long sniff, sneezed, and regarded them with watery eyes.

Mason said, 'We're trying to find out all we can about Weston Hale. It's very important.'

'What's important about it?' Andover asked.

Mason hurried on without answering the question. 'I'm an attorney and this man is a detective.'

'Police or private?'

'Private.'

'What do you want?'

'We want to find out about Hale.'

'Why not go ask him?'

'We will as soon as we leave here.'

'Go ahead and leave, then. No one's holding you.'

'We are going to go and see Hale,' Mason said, 'but first we'd like to find out if he is the specific person in whom we are interested. May we look in his room?'

'Sure, why not? . . . No, now, wait a minute–Hell, no! I don't feel right or I wouldn't have said yes in the first place–Of course you can't look in his room. That's his. I don't know what he's got in there. I'm not going to let a couple of strangers go prowling around in there.'

'Could you come to the door with us–just open the door and let us just look inside without touching anything?'

'What are you looking for?'

'We want to try and get a line on him.'

'Why?'

'We have a matter of considerable importance to take up with him,' Mason said.

'You can't take it up with him by looking in his room,' Andover said. 'I don't think he'd like it that way. I wouldn't like it that way, and I'm not gonna get out of bed. I feel like hell and if you guys get the bug I've got, you're gonna wish to hell you'd never heard of Weston Hale.'

'How long has he been sharing the apartment with you?' Mason asked.

'I don't know. Four or five months. I had another fellow here. He got transferred. . . . I'd rather have somebody sharing the apartmend with me and have a big apartmend than be cooped up in one of these little singles. . . . What's all the urgency about Weston Hale?'

'We're just trying to reach him,' Mason said. 'Tell me, did you ever know him to wear a black patch over his bad eye?'

'I tell you, I didn't know he had a bad eye. The guy seems to see all right.'

Mason asked, 'Does he have a portable typewriter?'

'He sure does.'

'Doing some writing?'

'Lots of it. He keeps pounding that typewriter, when he's home, into the small hours. He's a worker, that guy.'

Mason said, 'We think a friend of his, Montrose Dewitt, is in trouble and we'd like to talk to Hale about him. Did you ever hear him mention Montrose Dewitt?'

The man on the bed rolled his head from side to side in a gesture of negation.

'Never heard him mention Montrose Dewitt?'

'No, I told you.'

Mason said, 'We'll come back when you're feeling better, Andover.'

'What's all the excitement about? What about Dewitt?'

Mason said, 'We think he was murdered in Calexico sometime last night.'

'Murdered!'

'That's right.'

'Well, whaddyuh know?' Andover said.

'Under those circumstances, may we look in Hale's room?' Mason inquired.

'Under *those* circumstances, you can just get the hell out of here until you come back with a police officer.'

Andover turned over in bed, coughed, pulled the blanket up over him and said, 'Now I'm warning you, don't go prowling around on the way out. Just beat it.'

'We thank you for you're co-operation, Mr Andover,' Mason said. 'I'm sorry you're not feeling well and I'm sorry you don't appreciate our position.'

'Well, you guys just quit worrying about that,' Andover said. 'It doesn't make any difference whether *I* appreciate *your* position, I sure as hell appreciate mine and nobody's going in there until somebody shows up who has the authority to go in there.'

Mason nodded to Drake, said, 'Well, thanks a lot, Andover.'

'Don't mention it,' Andover said sarcastically.

Mason and Drake left the bedroom, paused momentarily in the sitting room. Drake looked toward the door on the other side. Mason shook his head, opened the door into the corridor. 'Good-bye, Andover,' he called.

There was no answer from the bedroom.

'He wrote letters,' Mason said. 'There must have been a lot of replies. The man must have had a lot of nibbles before he'd be ready to sink his hook in the fish he wanted. It might help a lot if we could find some of those letters.'

'That wouldn't give any indication of who killed him,' Drake said.

Mason's eyes were level-lidded with concentration. 'It would show what a heel he was and how he made his living. Lots of times in a murder case, Paul, it pays to show that the corpse was a rat and that whoever killed him was a public benefactor.'

'So now we go see Hale?'

'Now we go see what excuse Hale had made for not being available. Hale's dead.'

11

Henrey T. Jasper, president of the Investors' Mortgage & Refinancing Company, said, 'This is really an honour, Mr Mason. I've heard a lot about you, and I'm familiar with some of your more spectacular cases.

'And this is Paul Drake of the Drake Detective Agency?

'I assume, gentlemen, that you would not be calling upon me at this late hour in the afternoon unless it was on a matter of some major importance.'

'I don't know,' Mason said. 'Frankly, I am puzzled and we're trying to get information.'

'And perhaps I can assist you?'

'I think you can. What can you tell us about Weston Hale?'

'Not very much,' Jasper said, smiling, 'because there's not very much to tell. Hale is one of those quiet,retiring personalities who revels in detail. He is one of our most trusted employees, has been with us for a period of some seven years, and is invaluable to the business.'

'Would it be possible for us to talk with him?' Mason asked.

'Why, certainly,' Jasper said.

'Now?'

'Come, come, gentlemen. It's after our closing hours. I was working here on a matter of some importance and of course some of the clerical staff are here but . . . well, I assume Mr Hale has gone home. Just a moment, I'll find out.'

Jasper pressed a button on his desk and a few moments later a rather tired-looking woman in her early forties opened the door and said, 'Yes, Mr Jasper?'

'Is Hale here?'

'No, sir.'

'He's gone home?'

'He wasn't here today.'

'Oh, he wasn't?'

She shook her head. 'He was going to make some appraisals up in Santa Barbara. You remember you asked him about a survey of the physical assets supporting the bond issue in that subdivision?'

'Oh, that's right,' Jasper said. 'I *did* want him to go over that. We discussed it a few days ago and he said he'd go up there just as soon as he could get some things cleaned up here.'

'Do you know where we could reach him?' Mason asked Jasper.

Jasper in turn relayed the inquiry on to the woman standing in the doorway by raising his eyebrows.

She shook her head. 'Just in Santa Barbara. He probably is staying at a motel. I think he drove up.'

'May I ask why you're interested, Mr Mason?' Jasper inquired.

'It's a question of identity,' Mason said. 'Could you tell me, does Mr Hale have an artificial eye?'

Jasper smiled and shook his head. 'No, he has both eyes and . . .' Suddenly he broke off at something he saw on the face of the woman in the doorway. 'What is it, Miss Selma?' he asked.

'I've sometimes wondered,' she said. 'Have you ever noticed, Mr Jasper, whenever Mr Hale looks at anything he turns his head. You never see him turning his eyes. He will sit in a conversation with two or more people, will listen to one, then gravely turn his head to face the other when he wants to hear what that person has to say.

'I've noticed it for some time. At first I thought he was deaf and was resorting to lip reading but more recently I've been puzzled. I've been wondering why he did it. The explanation of an artificial eye had never occurred to me, but now that the thought has been suggested I think perhaps that may be the explanation.'

'Is he married?' Mason asked.

Jasper was the one who answered the question. 'No, he is not. I think the man virtually lives for his work. He spends many of his evenings here. Hale has a great mind for detail and he makes it a point to keep a check on the background of most of the companies issuing securities in which we are interested from a standpoint of investment.'

Mason glanced at Paul Drake. 'I guess that covers it,' he said. 'I would like very much to get in touch with Mr Hale. If he should phone in, will you ask him to please give me a ring?'

'Oh, he'll be in tomorrow,' Jasper said. 'that is, I assume he will, unless something in that Santa Barbara situation is more complicated than would appear on the surface.'

'That's an unusual situation?' Mason asked.

'Well, in a way, yes. We have invested some money in securities issued by a corporation engaged in subdivision work. The securities represent improvement bonds and recently there has been some question–You'll have to pardon me, I'm afraid, Mr Mason. I don't think I care to go into it at this time, particularly in advance of a report from Hale.'

'Hale is fully qualified to check into a matter of that sort?' Mason asked.

Jasper smiled and said, 'Hale is the greatest little ferret you ever saw. He'll nose into a situation, worm his way through masses of detail and has an uncanny instinct for getting to the heart of the matter. . . . That's all, Miss Selma, thank you. I just wanted to see if Mr Hale was in the office.'

She smiled and withdrew.

'Well,' Mason said, 'I guess that pretty much covers the situation.'

'I'll be glad to have Mr Hale get in touch with you,' Jasper said. And then added with a note of curiosity in his voice, 'I assume that the fact you came here personally, Mr Mason, means that you want to see him about something that is rather out of the ordinary.'

'Yes, I think perhaps it is,' Mason said. 'By the way, did Hale have any brothers–a twin brother, perhaps?'

'Not that I know of. I have never heard him mention any relatives. He–Did you say, *did* he have, Mr Mason?'

Mason nodded.

'You're using the past tense?'

Mason said. 'There is a possibility that a man who died in a motel at Calexico last night might have been related to Hale.'

'Oh,' Jasper said. 'He doesn't have any relatives, at least in this part of the country. I'm quite certain of that, and if there'd been a brother I–But you used the past tense in regard to Mr Hale himself.'

'That's right,' Mason said. 'In the event the corpse isn't Hale's twin brother there's a very good possibility the corpse is that of Weston Hale.'

'What!' Jasper exclaimed incredulously.

'I'm simply mentioning possibilities,' Mason said. 'I'm not prepared to make any statement to that effect, and my visit here is purely in the nature of a search for information.'

'Why . . . why–You must have *some* grounds for your assumption, Mr Mason.'

'I wish I did have,' Mason said. 'At the present time I'm simply following a trail. Do you know if Hale is related in any way to a Montrose Dewitt?'

'Dewitt . . . Dewitt,' Jasper said. 'The name has a familiar ring somehow, but I can't seem to place it specifically.'

'Well, no matter,' Mason said. 'The situation will doubtless be cleared up after I've had a chance to talk with Mr Hale tomorrow. Thank you very much, Mr Jasper.'

Drake and Mason shook hands with Jasper and left the office, leaving the president of the company standing by his desk, a look of perplexity on his face.

'Well,' Mason said, as they left the building, 'it looks very much as though we're headed in the right direction.'

'In the right direction, but how far are we going?' Drake asked.

'To the end of the trail,' Mason said.

Drake was pessimistic. 'It looks as if it might be a blind alley,' he said.

Mason might not have heard him. His face was a mask of concentration. He drove to his office building without speaking more than a dozen words.

As they left the elevator and Drake opened the door of his office, Mason paused for a moment in the doorway. 'I want to keep in touch with you, Paul, and–'

Drake's switchboard operator said, 'Oh, Mr Mason, I have a message for you.'

Mason moved on into the office.

'Miss Street telephoned on the unlisted phone,' the operator said, 'and asked that you call her before you go down the hall to your office.'

Mason raised his eyebrows. 'No idea what it is?'

'No,' she said. 'Something important.'

'All right,' Mason said, 'get her on the line. What phone can I take?'

'That one on the desk,' she said.

Drake said, 'The probabilities are, Perry, that there's an official delegation waiting for you in your office and Della wants to tip you off.'

Mason shook his head. 'If the police were in the office, Paul, they wouldn't give Della a chance to get to the telephone to tip me off.'

The switchboard operator put through the call and nodded to Mason.

Mason said, 'Hello, Della.'

Della, her voice low, said, 'You have company, Chief. I thought you might like to know before you reach the office.'

'Who?' Mason asked.

'One of them,' she said, 'is your friend, George Latty.'

'And the other?' Mason asked.

'The other is Baldwin L. Marshall, the district attorney of Imperial County.'

'That,' Mason said, 'is a strange combination. Do they seem antagonistic or otherwise?'

'It's a little hard to state,' Della said, 'but I think it's otherwise. Latty has a chip on his shoulder, but I would gather he had reached some sort of an understanding with the district attorney and that's the reason I thought you should be tipped off.'

'What sort of a fellow is the district attorney?' Mason asked.

'In his middle thirties, very alert; reddish hair, blue eyes and a quick, nervous manner. He's very aggressive.'

'How tall?'

'Around five feet eleven; rather slender; nervous and tense and . . . well, dangerous, if you know what I mean.'

'I know what you mean,' Mason said. 'I'll come to the office in a few minutes. . . . I take it that the district attorney of Imperial County is just a little hostile?'

'Well,' Della Street said, 'he's being very, very official.'

Mason said, 'Latty has told him something–the question is what, and how much? All right, Della. Don't let on that I've been tipped off. I'll be there in a minute or two. Where are these people?'

'I put them in the law library. I didn't want to leave them in the reception room.'

'And where are you talking from?'

'From the phone behind Gertie's desk at the switchboard.'

'All right,' Mason said, 'go into the private office, leave the door to the law library open–'

'It's already open,' she said. 'They left it open.'

'All right, that's fine. I'll come in from the hall door. As soon as I open the door you can start with the act.'

'What sort of an act?'

'Just ad lib,' Mason said. 'Follow my lead.'

Mason hung up the telephone, turned to Paul Drake, narrowed his eyes thoughtfully and said, 'Now, just what could George Latty have told the district attorney of Imperial County that would turn the heat on me?'

'Well,' Drake said dryly, 'he *could* have told him the truth.'

Mason smiled. 'The question is, how much of the truth?'

'How much truth could you stand?' Drake asked.

Mason grinned by way of answer, said, 'Well, I guess I'll go down and see what it's all about, Paul.'

'Want me along?' Drake asked.

Mason shook his head. 'Just keep on the job, Paul. Keep operatives on Howland Brent, and just for good measure you'd better put a tail on George Latty when he leaves the office. That young man is getting just a little too ubiquitous to suit me.'

Mason left the detective's office, walked down the corridor to his own office, fitted his latchkey to the door marked PERRY MASON–*Private* and opened the door.

Della Street was standing by the lawyer's desk sorting mail.

'Hello, Della,' Mason said. 'It's time to go home. What's new, anything?'

Della Street said, 'You have a couple of visitors, Mr Mason. Mr Baldwin Marshall and Mr George Latty.'

'Latty, huh?' Mason said. 'That guy certainly gets around. What's he want, and who's Marshall?'

'Mr Marshall is the district attorney of Imperial County and they're right here in the law library,' Della Street said, gesturing toward the open door.

'Well, I'll be glad to see them,' Mason said. 'Bring them in here, Della.'

Mason was moving over to his desk as the two figures came from the law library, Baldwin Marshall in the lead, stalking determinedly, Latty hanging behind, as though just a little afraid.

Mason said, moving toward Marshall, 'I presume you're Baldwin Marshall–district attorney of Imperial County–right?'

'Right,' Marshall said, extending his hand. 'I believe you know Latty.'

'Heavens, yes,' Mason said. 'I run into him every time I turn around. What is the reason for *this* visit?'

'You're representing Lorraine Elmore?'

Mason nodded.

'Montrose Dewitt was murdered in Calexico,' Marshall said, 'and we want to question Mrs Elmore. We–'

'Murdered?' Mason interrupted.

'I think so,' Marshall said. 'Of course, I'll be frank with you, Mr Mason. We're working largely on circumstantial evidence at the moment but there are some things about the case that I'm free to confess I can't understand. Mrs Elmore seems to have played a rather peculiar part. . . . In fact, there seems to be a distinct conflict between some of her statements and the facts as we understand them.'

'To whom did she make the statements?' Mason asked.

'To you,' Marshall said.

Mason raised his eyebrows.

Marshall said, 'I've heard a lot about you, Mr Mason. You're supposed to be a dangerous antagonist who will rip me to pieces. You've a background of years of experience and you're a genius in the art of forensic strategy.

'I'm a cow county district attorney. It may be I'm no match for you, but I'll tell you one thing, I'm not going to be afraid of you and I'm not going to be bluffed.'

'That's most commendable,' Mason said. 'Now perhaps you can tell me what this is all about.'

'Mr Latty here,' Marshall went on, 'has some things on his conscience.'

Mason regarded Latty curiously. 'And came to you?'

'No,' Marshall said, 'I went to him. Latty tried to conceal what he knew for a while, but I sensed he was holding something back and . . . well, frankly, I put a little pressure on him, just as I'm going to put a little pressure on you.'

'On me?' Mason asked.

'Exactly,' Marshall said. 'I have told you that I don't have your experience, I don't have your metropolitan background. Now I'm going to tell you something else; I have the law on my side. What's more, I have a majority of the voters in Imperial County back of me. If it comes right down to a fight, you can win the argument but by God you'll lose the case, because I'll throw the book at you just as quick as I would at anyone. Your reputation isn't frightening me a damned bit.'

'I wouldn't want it to,' Mason said. And then turning to Latty, said, 'Just what is it that you were holding back, George?'

'Now, just a minute,' Marshall said, '*I'm* going to do the talking here. You'll probably be cross-examining Latty on the witness stand, so I'm going to tell you some of the things I know, and then I'm going to tell you some of the things I want, and Latty is going to keep quiet.'

Marshall turned to Latty. 'You understand that?'

Latty nodded.

Marshall said, 'Mrs Elmore told you quite a story about having driven her car out on a side road. Someone forced Montrose Dewitt out of the car, marched him down the road a few feet, then clubbed him to death; then came back and told Mrs Elmore to drive her car on ahead until she was stuck in the sand.'

'She told me this?' Mason asked.

'Yes.'

'And may I ask the source of your information?'

'You can ask,' Marshall said, smiling, 'and you won't get any answer. I'm asking you for a verification. Did she tell you this? Yes or no?'

Mason said, 'Sit down. Make yourselves comfortable. Evidently this is going to be more than just a brief interview and–'

'It's all right, I don't mind standing,' Marshall said, 'and it's not going to be a long interview as far as I'm concerned. I want to know whether she made that statement to you.'

Mason said gravely, 'I am representing Mrs Elmore. She's my client.'

'So I understand.'

'Therefore,' Mason went on, 'any statement she might have made to me is completely confidential. I couldn't repeat it.'

'You certainly can tell me whether Mrs Elmore was the victim of a holdup and an assault,' Marshall said.

'I'm afraid I can't even tell you that,' Mason said.

'Why not?'

'So far anything and everything I know about the case is information derived from sources I consider confidential.'

'Now then, I'm going further than that,' Marshall said. 'You were in Calexico this morning. You had a chartered airplane. You got the pilot to fly low over some roads out to the east of Calexico until you located an automobile that was stalled in the sand. Then you had the pilot go back to the airport.'

'And may I ask the source of that information?' Mason asked.

'I'm not going to be the one who answers *all* the questions,' Marshall said.

Mason smiled. 'I thought perhaps you would want to establish a precedent.'

'I will, in this instance,' Marshall said, 'because I checked at the airport, found out the number of the plane you had, contacted the pilot and interviewed him.'

'You seem to have been rather active,' Mason said.

'I try to run down leads while they're hot,' Marshall told him.

'A very commendable trait,' Mason said. 'I think you're going to prove a most dangerous antagonist.'

'Do we have to be antagonists?' Marshall asked.

'That's up to you,' Mason said. 'Unless you charge my client with some crime, there's certainly no reason for us to assume adversary positions.'

'I don't want to charge her with any crime unless she's guilty.'

'Most commendable.'

'But unless I can get some satisfactory answers to some of my questions, I will at least have to hold her as a material witness.'

Mason smiled and said affably, 'That will give her an opportunity to put up bond and I'm quite certain she has sufficient resources to put up any reasonable bond which a court may require.'

'In that event I might have to go further and hold her for investigation.'

'In which event,' Mason said, 'I would have to file *habeas corpus* and force you to either charge her or turn her loose.'

'In which event, we'd charge her,' Marshall said shortly.

'In that event, we would of course occupy the position of adversaries,' Mason said, smiling.

'All right, I'll go further,' Marshall said. 'I have reason to believe that after you located that stalled automobile from the air, you left the plane at the airport, hurriedly took off in an automobile and drove out to the place where that car was parked. That car had a Massachusetts license plate and was the property of Lorraine Elmore, your client.

'You looked around at the scene, and I have reason to believe you took some evidence that you didn't want the authorities to find, and you may have left other evidence–or perhaps I'll put it this way, you may have left other objects which you *hoped* the authorities would consider evidence.'

'Wouldn't that be unethical?' Mason asked.

'I think so.'

'Yet you think I did it?'

'I'll put it this way: there's evidence indicating that you may have done so.'

Mason was silent.

'Did you?' Marshall pressed.

Mason said, 'No.'

'You mean you didn't go out to that car?' Marshall asked. 'You mean you didn't get out and look it over?'

'I didn't say that,' Mason said.

'You said no.'

'And I meant no. You asked me if I'd looked the car over, if I'd left objects which I hoped would be taken as evidence, if I had withdrawn other objects and I told you no.'

'All right,' Marshall said, 'I'll split my questions up. Did you go out to the place where that car was stuck in the sand?'

'No comment,' Mason said.

'Did you take anything out of that car?'

'No comment.'

'Did you put anything in it?'

'No comment.'

'All right,' Marshall said, 'that's all I wanted to know. I just wanted to know if you'd co-operate. You won't. Now then, I'm going to tell you something, Mr Mason. I was prepared to give you every consideration. I was prepared to give your client every consideration. You have refused to co-operate with me so I'm under no obligation to co-operate with you.

'Up here in Los Angeles you seem to have the courts pretty well under the spell of your reputation. That reputation seems to dazzle the authorities. Down in my county, you're just another Los Angeles lawyer butting into a community where he's a stranger. I can throw the book at you and if I have to, I will.'

'Go ahead and throw,' Mason said. 'I used to be good at catching and dodging. I'd dislike very much to lose my agility.'

'I'll see that you have plenty of practice,' Marshall promised, turning on his heel. 'Come on, George.'

'Wait a minute,' Mason said. 'Did you really expect me to answer all those questions, Marshall?'

'I asked them in my official capacity.'

'That's not my question. Did you expect me to answer them?'

'No.'

'Then why come up here to ask them?'

'Off the record,' Marshall said, 'I wanted to have the press in Imperial County tell the citizens of Imperial County that I had asked you those questions and that you had refused to answer.'

'Like that, eh?' Mason asked.

'Like that,' Marshall said, and escorted Latty out of the office.

Della Street looked at Mason with apprehensive eyes.

'Get Crowder,' Mason said.

Della Street put through the call, then nodded to Mason when she had him on the line.

Mason picked up the telephone, said, 'Duncan, this is Perry Mason. I've just had an official visit from your district attorney. There's been a leak.'

'What sort of a leak?'

'A big one. Now, I want to know where it came from.'

'Can you tell me more about it?'

'Any chance of your phone being tapped?' Mason asked.

'Hell, yes,' Crowder said. 'There's a good chance my phone is tapped and there's a good chance your phone is. The authorities pay lip service to the laws about wire tapping, but from what my friends who are skilled in electronics tell me, there are thousands of wire taps in existence. You and I could be among them.'

'All right,' Mason said, 'I'll start asking questions. Has Dr Kettle talked to anyone?'

'About what?'

'About anything his patient might have told him.'

'I'll answer that one right off the bat,' Crowder said. 'The answer is no. Kettle, you can trust. He wouldn't talk to anyone.'

'How about you? Have you talked to anyone?'

'Hell, no.'

'I mean, even in confidence.'

'No, I tell you.'

Mason said, 'This morning I had a Unit Nine there at the Motel. Della Street had Seven. Howland Brent had Eleven, which adjoined me on the other side.

'I understand the walls are thin in that motel. I want to find out how thin. Go back there and rent Units Nine and Eleven and see what you can find out about voices carrying through the walls.

'Okay,' Crowder said, 'when do you want that done?'

'Now. I want to know if Brent could have heard everything we said in there.'

'And when do I report?'

'Just as soon as you have the information. I'll wait here at the office.'

'Okay,' Crowder said, 'I should be able to move in right away. Those units won't have been rented–unless, of course, Brent held onto his unit.'

'If he did, get Units Seven and Nine and make a test,' Mason told him.

'I don't think you have the same conditions,' Crowder said. 'Seven and Nine are in separate buildings. On the other hand, Nine and Eleven are in one building and there's just a door between them–a thin door. In case of necessity, that can be opened into a double cabin. The units are all designed that way, units of two in one building.'

'Oh-oh,' Mason said, 'now I'm beginning to get the picture. Go take a look and give me a ring, will you, Duncan?'

'I'll take a look,' Duncan said. 'I'll take someone with me and we'll see how voices register. Do you want me to take a tape recorder and make a formal test?'

'No,' Mason said, 'this isn't for evidence. This is just for my own information.'

'Okay, stick around. I'll call you back,' Crowder said.

Mason hung up.

Della Street said, 'What can he do?'

'Crowder?'

'Marshall.'

'He can talk,' Mason said. 'He's talked. He can threaten. He's threatened. He can have our client arrested or he can serve a subpoena on her to appear before the Grand Jury. He said a mouthful when he said he had the law behind him. He can do anything the law will let him do, and he can make a stab at doing some of the things the law won't let him do. . . . Now, what the hell do you suppose Latty told him that started all this? What do you suppose Latty has on *his* conscience?'

'Heaven knows,' Della Street said.

'Well,' Mason said, 'Drake will have an operative pick up his trail and shadow him from the time he leaves here. We may find out a little more about him.

'You'd better put some coffee in that percolator, Della and we'll kill a little time while we're waiting for Duncan Crowder to report.'

'I have an idea it won't be long,' Della Street said.

Mason grinned, nodded.

Della Street made coffee, brought out a package of cream-filled cookies.

Mason settled down with a sigh, munching on cookies, sipping coffee.

'This,' he announced, 'has been a fine, large day.'

'And it was a fine, large night last night,' Della Street said. 'We got darned little sleep.'

Mason nodded, yawned. 'That's the way things go in the law business.'

He finished his coffee, put the cup and saucer on the edge of his desk, settled back in the chair, closed his eyes and was almost instantly asleep.

Della let him sleep until Crowder's call came through from Calexico. Then she roused him. 'Duncan Crowder on the line, Chief.'

Mason picked up the telephone on his desk and motioned to Della Street to listen on her extension.

'Okay, Duncan,' Mason said, 'what did you find out?'

'I found out lots of things,' Crowder said. 'That place has been condemned down there. They either have to repair and change the construction or tear the place down. They're fighting it. Some of the units are more modern but some of those units where they can make either a double or two singles out of one unit have walls that are like paper.

'Between Nine and Eleven there's just one thin door. By putting your ear up to the door you can hear ordinary conversation in the adjoining unit, if things are quiet. You can hear plain enough to get most of the words.'

'I guess that's it,' Mason said. 'What about between Twelve and Fourteen?'

'The same situation exists there,' Crowder told him. 'Of course I didn't try Twelve and Fourteen, but I did take a look at the construction and know that it's another one of those units that can be rented either double or single, and I assume the same situation applies there.'

'Okay, Duncan,' Mason said, 'we're in a fight down there. As soon as you can get to Dr Kettle, relay a message to Lorraine Elmore. Tell her that she is not to answer any questions. She's not to make any statement to anyone under any circumstances.'

'How soon do you want her to get that message?' Crowder asked.

'Before your district attorney can get back to his office,' Mason said, 'and preferably before he can telephone the sheriff.'

'Will do,' Crowder said cheerfully, and hung up.

12

At nine o'clock the next morning, Perry Mason used his latchkey to open the door of his private office, grinned at Della Street and said, 'The dawn of a new day.'

'I'll say,' she said.

'What's new, Della?'

'Duncan Crowder called about five minutes ago. He wants you to call back.'

'All right, get him on the line,' Mason said. 'What have we heard from Paul Drake?'

'Paul wants to make a personal report. He's had a lot of men working and has some information that he says is puzzling.'

'Anything else?'

'Linda Calhoun called. She wants to know where her boy friend is.'

'Where's she?'

'Calexico.'

'The plot thickens,' Mason said. 'Let's try Crowder.'

A few moments later when he had Crowder on the line, Mason said, 'This is Perry Mason, Duncan. What's new down at your end?'

'Quite a bit,' Crowder said. 'My esteemed contemporary, Baldwin L. Marshall, seems to be out to make a record for himself.'

'How come?'

'He's making quite an issue of local boy going up against the big-city slicker–kind of a David and Goliath thing.'

'Where's he doing all this?'

'In the newspapers.'

'Quotes?'

'Not direct quotes, but reports of the activities of our fearless prosecutor and statements from the quote, authorities, unquote. The *Sentinel*, down here, has been pretty much in his corner during the campaign and now they're really going to town.'

'That's a local paper?'

'El Centro, the county seat.'

'What's the line of attack?'

'The Imperial Valley David going up against the Los Angeles Goliath, making something of a partisan issue out of it. By the time we try to impanel a jury we'll find that it's the home team against the big, bad city slickers, and of course the jury, residing in this community, will be just a little partisan.'

'Interesting,' Mason said. 'I guess this man, Marshall, is dangerous.'

'He's dangerous; also he's ambitious.'

'What else?' Mason asked.

'Well, it seems the main suspect at the moment is Lorraine Elmore. Marshall doesn't exactly say that Lorraine Elmore is a dope fiend but he has admitted to reporters that she was addicted to a very powerful sleeping medicine; that when she left Boston she managed to get her doctor to give her a prescription that should have lasted her for more than three months.

'For your information, the authorities are trying to trace this medicine. Apparently Lorraine Elmore took seven capsules during the interval between leaving Boston and arriving at Calexico. She took one capsule the night of the murder. One capsule was found on the front seat of the automobile. Approximately ninety capsules are not accounted for.

'The liquor which was found in the whiskey flask in the suitcase of Montrose Dewitt was simply saturated with this hypnotic.

'The authorities believe that Lorraine Elmore, who is under the care of a physician in a local hospital with no visitors permitted, was whisked away at the suggestion of none other than Perry Mason. Baldwin Marshall, our fighting district attorney, is said to have in his possession evidence indicating that as soon as astute defense counsel learned that the story told by Lorraine Elmore was in direct contradiction to the physical facts in the case, steps were taken to prevent the authorities from interrogating her.'

'Well, that's interesting,' Mason said. 'It looks as though the case is going to be tried in the newspapers.'

'Oh, perish the thought!' Crowder said. 'Marshall deplores all this newspaper publicity. He says, however, that he feels the people are entitled to know what is being done in connection with the investigation of a mysterious death which begins to look more and more like deliberate murder.'

'The newspaper doesn't say anything about any large sum of money Lorraine Elmore was supposed to have had?'

'No. The newspaper states that Marshall has announced to his intimate friends that he has had enough of being given the run-around; that these tactics may work in the large metropolitan areas but they are not going to work in a law-abiding, rural community; that at ten o'clock this morning he is going to call on Mrs Elmore for a statement. If her private physician still insists that she is unable to give a statement at that time, he is going to ask the court to appoint a physician to examine her, and he intends to serve a forthwith subpoena on her, ordering her to appear before the Grand Jury.'

'You've passed the word on to Mrs Elmore that she isn't to talk?'

'I've told her not to give them so much as the time of day.'

'Can we count on her?'

'I don't know, but I've impressed upon Linda Calhoun that she isn't to talk no matter what the circumstances. Linda Calhoun is a mighty sensible girl, Perry. She has her feet on the ground and her head on her shoulders.'

'All right,' Mason said. 'Don't let Dr Kettle get his neck stuck out too far. We're going to have to shift our position. Mrs Elmore is not going to make any statement now on the advice of counsel.'

'That means Marshall will take her into custody and charge her with murder.'

'He's going to do it anyway,' Mason said. 'Now, here's one thing I want you to do, Crowder. If we're going to try this case in the newspapers, we'll do a little something ourselves.'

'Okay, what do you want?'

'Ring up that doctor in Boston,' Mason said. 'Have an interview with him. You can point the direction of that interview. When you get done, you can make a statement to the press as the *local* attorney.

'Now, I want to accomplish several things by that statement. I want to let the people know that there's a local attorney, that isn't simply the rural David against the big-city Goliath; that you are to take an important part in the case.'

'I figured you'd want that,' Crowder said. 'What else? What do I do with the Boston doctor?'

'You point out to the doctor that Mrs Elmore is at a period in life when romance is not dead; that she has been living in a small community under the watchful eyes of a neighbourhood which is inclined to pity her as a relatively young and attractive widow; that there are no eligible men in the community; no social life; that as a result, she has suffered from frustration and we understand he deemed it advisable to quiet her nerves with tranquilizers during the daytime and sedatives at night.

'When she left on the trip she was inclined to worry that she couldn't replenish her supply of sedatives, and he gave her a big supply, knowing that she did not have suicidal tendencies and knowing that her temperament was such that if she started worrying about not having sedatives when she needed them it would completely upset her nervous system.

'The large quantity of sedatives he supplied was simply a psychological factor in connection with her treatment. He is familiar with her character and reputation. She is a woman of the highest integrity and there was no risk at all in prescribing a large quantity of sleeping capsules.'

'You think he'll say that?' Crowder asked.

'Sure, he'll say it,' Mason said. 'He damned well has to say it. Otherwise he'd be put on the pan for giving a patient a prescription for such a large amount of powerful hypnotics. You can point out to him that *his* reputation is going to be put on the line and that before the press smears him, you think that it would be a good idea for the press to learn the true facts.'

'And then tell him what the true facts are?' Crowder asked.

'Sure,' Mason said. 'Can you think of any more logical explanation?'

'I wouldn't even try,' Crowder said modestly.

Mason laughed. 'All right, Duncan, go to it. If they want to try the case in the newspapers, we'll give the newspapers a little something on which to base publicity that will favour the defendant, a poor, bewildered, frustrated widow, whose life was just opening up into a new vista of hope and promise when it was ruthlessly shattered again by the cruel hand of death. No wonder she's prostrated. The wonder is that she's retaining any vestige of sanity.'

'I get it,' Crowder said. 'You want it spread on thick.'

'Thick,' Mason said.

'Okay,' Crowder said, 'can do,' and hung up.

Mason grinned at Della Street. 'If the D.A. wants to play rough, we'll play rough,' he said. 'That newspaper publicity is something two can play at.'

'Well,' Della Street said, 'we seem to have the fat in the fire.'

'We have a whole fire full of fat,' Mason said. 'Let's see what Paul Drake has to say for himself.'

Della Street gave Paul Drake a ring, and within less than a minute the detective's code knock sounded on the door to Mason's private office.

Mason nodded to Della Street, who opened the door and let Paul in.

'Hi, Beautiful,' Paul said. 'What gives with you folks this lovely morning?'

'Gives, is right,' Mason said. 'We're having it thrust upon us.'

'The D.A.'s tough?' Drake asked.

'He's–Well, let's say he's brash,' Mason said. 'He's playing the angle of local patriotism. He represents Imperial County, I represent the city slickers. We're going to do battle in front of a jury of Imperial County farmers and businessmen.'

'But you have local counsel down there.'

'He's brushing local counsel under the rug,' Mason said. 'The battle is between the bright, conscientious young D.A., filled with rural virtue, and the sophisticated city slicker who will resort to every trick in the book. Moreover, our client is a dope fiend, who is to be pitied, but that can't condone murder.'

'How interesting,' Drake said.

'The hell of it is,' Mason said, 'that I don't see how they can make a case out against Lorraine Elmore. When she tells her story, it is one thing; but she hasn't told her story.'

'But they know what it is?'

'They seem to know what it is,' Mason said, 'thanks to the thin walls at the Palm Court Motel in Calexico. But I still don't get what they're trying to do. The case doesn't add up.

'The district attorney should be adopting a cautious attitude of saying, "It's too early yet for us to tell exactly what happened but we want to question Lorrain Elmore, and the fact that she has an attorney who apparently wishes to keep her from being questioned is a suspicious circumstance."

'If he'd adopt that gambit he'd put some pressure on me and would build up suspense as to what Mrs Elmore's story was. Instead of that, he's apparently acting on the assumption he has a case against her and is laying the foundation for a favorable jury by feeding out information to the newspapers.'

'Well, you can't blame him for that,' Drake said. 'He wants to win his case.'

Mason's eyes glittered. 'And I want to win mine, Paul. . . . But what about the various and sundry people you've been shadowing. Anything on them?'

Drake said, 'Hold your hat, Perry. You're going to have a surprise.'

'What?'

'Well, let's put it this way: two surprises.'

'Start dishing them out, Paul.'

'We'll start with Howland Brent. Now, there's a nice, conservative tweed-suited, pie-plate-hatted Boston investment counselor who suddenly goes hog-wild in Las Vegas, Nevada '

'Las Vegas!' Mason exclaimed.

'That's right. He drove a rented car to Palm Springs then took a plane to Las Vegas, and really went to town.'

'What do you mean, went to town? You mean he plunged?'

'Plunged all over the lot,' Drake said, 'and apparently made a killing.

'The hell he did!'

'That's right.'

Mason said, 'You never can tell about these conservative Easterners, Paul. They all of them have a streak in them of wanting to be Wild West. I'll bet if someone would give that fellow a twin-holstered rapid-draw gun belt with a couple of guns in it, he'd stand up in front of a mirror, practice a fast draw and take fiendish delight in the process. How much did he win?'

'You can't tell,' Drake said, 'but he did a peculiar thing. He got hotter than a firecracker. He had chips going all over the board in a big-time roulette game. People just gathered around to watch him. Boy, did he plunge!'

'And then what happened?'

'As nearly as we can tell the guy won about thirty-five thousand bucks.'

Mason whistled.

'He certainly was a plunger. And then, all of a sudden something happened and he got cold as a cucumber.'

'You mean he started to lose?'

'He started to lose,' Drake said, 'and he quit cold. He just walked away from the table and from then on he turned his back on every gambling device in Las Vegas. He wouldn't even put a nickel in a slot machine.'

'Where is he now?'

'According to last information, he's sleeping late in Las Vegas. I have a couple of men tailing him and they're giving him a round-the-clock treatment. As soon as he gets up and gets in circulation, they'll phone the office.'

'Good work, Paul,' Mason said. 'What's the other surprise?'

'Your friend, George Keswick Latty.'

'What about him?'

'He's the fair-haired boy child of the district attorney of Imperial County,' Drake said.

'How come?'

'After the district attorney left your office he seemed to have an idea that you might try to have them followed. He used routine precautions to throw a shadow off the trail, stuff that he's probably read about in magazines featuring detective stories, stuff that would have been effective ten years ago; but we were using an electronic shadowing device.'

'How come?'

'A cinch,' Drake said. 'We checked the parking lot, found three cars that had licenses from Imperial Valley, looked at the registration certificates, found the one that was registered to Baldwin Marshall, put an electronic bug on it and had two men waiting in cars.'

'And what did Marshall do?'

'Oh, he made figure-eights around the blocks, he went through traffic signals just as they were changing, he kept looking behind him, and finally became very smug and self-satisfied and then took Latty to–guess where?'

'Las Vegas?' Mason asked.

Drake shook his head. 'Tijuana. In a chartered plane.'

'Tijuana!' Mason exclaimed.

'That's right. Over the Mexican line. Any subpoenas you may try to serve on him will be valueless even if you find him. The guy is out of the jurisdiction of our courts and is in another country.'

'Well, I'll be darned,' Mason said.

'He puts this boy up at the best hotel in Tijuana,' Drake said, 'and explains to the clerk that the County of Imperial will pay for his room and board.'

'And then?'

'Then Baldwin Marshall, feeling very much pleased with himself, flies back here in the chartered plane, picks up his car at the airport, drives to El Centro and starts dishing out interviews to his closest friends, who promptly relay the information to the public press.'

'How interesting,' Mason said.

'Now then, I have more news for you,' Drake said. 'Your friend has been subsidized.'

'What do you mean?'

'I mean that the district attorney not only agreed to pay his room and board, but gave him a slug of money.'

'You're sure?'

'The guy was broke, and now he's buying things,' Drake said. 'He has the attitude of the rich American tourist. He was probably instructed to act the part, and it's a part that suits George Latty to the ground. The guy's reveling in it.'

Mason's eyes narrowed. 'Paul,' he said, 'I don't care how many men it takes, put them on Latty's trail. Every time he buys something, find out how much it was. In other words, I want to find out every nickel that fellow spends.

'Then when the D.A. puts him on the stand, I'll teach Baldwin Marshall something about the practice of law that he may have forgotten. It's one thing to put a witness up in a hotel where he won't be disturbed. It's quite another thing to hand a witness a bunch of cash for so-called expenses, particularly when the witness, who has been completely flat broke, goes out and becomes a heavy spender. In one case it's defraying expenses. In the other it's bribery.

'I wonder if George has let Linda know where he is.'

'My best guess is that he hasn't.' Drake said. 'From the elaborate precautions that were taken by Marshall, I have an idea that Latty is completely incommunicado.'

The telephone rang.

Della Street picked up the instrument, said to Mason, 'Duncan Crowder calling from Calexico.'

Mason nodded. 'Stay on the line, Della,' he said, and picked up his own instrument. 'Hello, Duncan,' he said.

Crowder said, 'Got some news for you, Perry. What do you know about an ice pick?'

'An ice pick?' Mason asked.

'That's right. A murder weapon.'

'Murder? I thought the guy died from an overdose of barbiturates.'

'That's what everybody thought up to a short time ago,' Crowder said, 'but it seems the D.A. has been holding an ace up his sleeve. Evidently Dewitt was put to sleep with a dose of drugged whiskey, then somebody took an ice pick and stuck it in his head right above the hairline and then, with fiendish deliberation and wanting to make sure he was dead, stabbed him a couple of times in the heart.

'However, there wasn't any hemorrhage from the heart stabs, indicating that the man was already dead at the time those stabs were administered. The wounds on the body were so small that they could have been overlooked if it hadn't been for the fact that Marshall wanted a complete autopsy. He wired Los Angeles and had one of the best forensic pathologists come down to assist in the autopsy.'

'Well,' Mason said, 'that changes the complexion of the case quite a bit.'

'I'll tell you some more about the complexion of the case,' Crowder said. 'They found the murder weapon in Lorraine Elmore's car.'

'What!' Mason exclaimed.

'That's right, hidden under the floor covering in the baggage compartment, and moreover, the ice pick has been identified as one that came from Unit Sixteen of the Palm Court Motel–that's the unit that Lorraine Elmore occupied.'

'How can they make that identification of an ice pick?' Mason asked.

'The units each have a bottle opener and an ice pick,' Crowder said. 'The numbers are stamped in the wood, small numbers that you wouldn't see unless you happened to be looking for them, but the landlady wanted to be sure that each ice pick was in its proper unit and so she numbered them–no particular reason except she had a numbering outfit and decided to stamp the numbers on the wood. She did the same thing on the bottle openers.'

'So that's what's been in the background,' Mason said.

'That's what's in the background, and Marshall is yelling for an immediate hearing. He wants Lorraine Elmore in court. Now, I can probably get Dr Kettle to insist that there should be a sufficient delay to–'

'Hold everything,' Mason interrupted. 'Don't try for any delay. Let Marshall go right ahead.

'I want you to be rather inept and give the impression of being sort of dazed at the whole business. Let Marshall sweep along in a grand triumphant march and get the case into preliminary hearing just as soon as he wants.'

'The defendant is entitled to a continuance,' Crowder said.

'I know,' Mason said, 'but you're not exactly certain of your rights. You sort of flounder around. It's going to put you in a bad light down there but I'll make it up to you later on.'

'You've got a plan?' Crowder asked.

'Hell, no,' Mason said, 'I haven't got a plan, but I've caught Baldwin

Marshall sucking eggs. I've caught him bribing a witness.'

'Bribing a witness!' Crowder exclaimed.

'It'll be that before I get done with it,' Mason said, his eyes glinting. 'You just let Marshall go ahead and set a date. The only thing is that you have to get in touch with me to find out just what my calendar is, and that will cause a little stalling around.

'I don't want the preliminary to take place until at least twenty-four hours have elapsed, but I don't want to go in and ask for a continuance on the ground of defense witnessess or constitutional rights.'

'You want to let him try to deprive her of her constitutional rights?' Crowder asked. 'That won't work if she's represented in court by counsel, will it?'

'She'll be represented in court by counsel, all right,' Mason said, 'and we're not going to rely on technical defenses about her constitutional rights, but I just want our friend, Baldwin Marshall, to give all the newspaper interviews and all of the tub-thumping possible and then I'm going to lower the boom on him by proving he's bribed a witness.'

'That would be something,' Crowder said.

'In fact,' Mason said, 'I think I'll let *you* bring out that evidence. That should give you a nice fat part in the play and keep the contest more on a local level.'

'You interest me a lot,' Crowder said. 'By the way, Linda Calhoun is worried sick about Latty. What did you do to him?'

'I didn't do anything to him,' Mason said.

'She thinks you did. She thinks you beat his ears back, put him on a bus and sent him back to Boston.'

'I did nothing of the sort,' Mason said.

'Well, where is he?'

'Hasn't he communicated with Linda?'

'No.'

'That's funny,' Mason said.

'It sure is,' Crowder said, 'because he should have been putting the bite on her.'

'He certainly should have,' Mason said. 'The guy was broke and Linda wired him twenty dollars at El Centro. I gave him twenty dollars at Yuma, and he had gasoline to buy and then he had to pay for his room at the motel. Well, we'll probably be hearing from him pretty quick.'

Mason turned to Drake and closed his eye in a wink.

'Okay. Anything else?' Crowder asked.

'That's it,' Mason said. 'We're starting for El Centro within an hour. Hold the fort until we get there.'

13

Linda Calhoun and Duncan Crowder met Mason, Della Street and Paul Drake at the airport as the plane landed.

'Welcome back to Imperial County,' Crowder said. 'I've been dodging reporters. Knowing that the preliminary hearing is coming up tomorrow, they rather anticipated that you'd be here today and they want interviews.'

'Why not?' Mason said.

'You mean you're willing to be interviewed?'

'Certainly.'

'I didn't know. I thought I'd put it up to you first. This man, Marshall, is full of tricks. Some of them are rather clever.'

'So I understand,' Mason said.

Linda Calhoun said, 'Mr Mason, I want you to find out what's happened to George Latty.'

'Something has happened to him?' Mason asked.

'I don't know. I think so.'

'You haven't heard from him?'

'I've heard from him. Just a brief message, but I don't know where he is now.'

'What was the message?' Mason asked.

'He called up the hotel when I was out and asked if he could leave a message. The operator told him that he could. He said to tell me that circumstances which he couldn't explain at the present time necessitated that he keep out of the picture for a while; that he was all right, that I wasn't to worry, but that he couldn't communicate with me, and that he was going to have to trust to my loyalty.'

'I see,' Mason said.

'Do you suppose he's all right?' she asked.

'That,' Mason said, 'depends on what you mean by all right. Do you mean, is he sober, is he leading a moral, upright life, is he loyal to you, or do you mean is he safe?'

'At the moment I mean is he safe?'

Mason said, 'I would gather from the message that he is safe.'

'But where in the world is he?'

Mason said, 'I can't tell you that, Linda, and I want to point out once more that I'm representing your aunt. I'm doing it at your request, but she's my client. Her interests come first.'

'But what does that have to do with George?'

'I can't even tell you that,' Mason said. 'It may have a lot, it may not have anything to do with him, but there are some things on which I can't afford to take any chances.'

She said, 'I have a peculiar feeling that you and Duncan are keeping things from me, Mr Mason.'

Mason glanced at the young attorney as he heard Linda Calhoun use his first name so easily and naturally.

Crowder, interpreting his glance, grinned and said, 'Linda and I are on a first-name basis, Perry.'

'So I see,' Mason said.

Linda flushed slightly, turned to Paul Drake. 'You're investigating the facts in this case, Mr Drake. Don't *you* have any idea where George is, or what has happened?'

Drake grinned. 'A detective gets lots of ideas, Miss Calhoun, but many times they don't pay off.'

Della Street took Linda's arm. 'I'm satisfied there's nothing to worry about, Linda,' she said.

'But I can't understand it. George is–Well, he doesn't have a great deal of initiative in financial affairs and he has no money. He came out here to be with me and–Well, it's simply that this is not like him, that's all.'

Mason said, 'I think the police have probably interrogated him as to what he knows.'

'And just what *does* he know, Mr Mason?'

'That,' Mason said, 'is hard to tell. He was of course there in the motel and he said that the walls were paper-thin. An inspection of the unit he was occupying shows that it was one side of a double unit and the other side was occupied by Montrose Dewitt. Under those circumstances he might very well have heard something.'

'No doubt he did,' she said, 'but why didn't he tell me, and what does that have to do with his disappearance?'

'I can't tell you,' Mason said.

'Do you know?'

Mason said, 'Let's put it this way, Miss Calhoun. We'll go to Duncan's office. You can call up the district attorney and ask him point-blank if he knows anything about George or any reason why George shouldn't communicate with you.'

'Would he tell me?'

'Is there any reason why he shouldn't tell you?'

'Not that I know of.'

'Well, let's go do that,' Mason said, giving Crowder a quick glance. 'You can talk on one phone, and Duncan and I will listen in on extensions and we'll see if the district attorney knows anything about this.'

'Once you get to my office,' Crowder said, 'you're going to have a problem with newspaper reporters.'

'We'll cross that bridge when we come to it,' Mason said. 'Right now I'd like to hear what Marshall has to say in response to Linda Calhoun's question.'

They drove to Crowder's office, where Linda put through the call to Baldwin Marshall, the district attorney.

Perry Mason and Duncan Crowder listened in on extensions.

'This is Linda Calhoun, Mr Marshall,' Linda said, as soon as she had the district attorney on the line.

'Oh, yes, Miss Calhoun,' Marshall said, his voice combining a synthetic cordiality with cold caution.

'I'm trying to find out what has happened to George Latty,' she said. 'I thought perhaps you could help me.'

'What makes you think anything has happened to him?'

'I haven't heard from him.'

'Not at all?'

'Just one brief, cryptic message telling me not to worry about him, that he'd have to trust to my loyalty.'

'But he told you not to worry.'

'Yes.'

'Are you worrying?'

'Yes.'

'He must have sent you that message for *some* reason,' Marshall said.

'I'm quite certain he did.'

'And he went to some trouble to tell you that you weren't to worry.'

'Yes.'

'And here you are, worrying.'

'But I want to know where he is.'

'I'm afraid I can't help you there.'

'Well, let me ask you a direct question. Do you know where he is?'

There was a moment's hesitation, then Marshall said, 'No, Miss Calhoun, I'll be frank with you. I don't know where he is.'

'But you think that he's all right?' Linda persisted.

'I think if he told you not to worry that I wouldn't worry. I'd have that much confidence in him, and in the integrity of his friendship, regardless of what any other persons might say.

'Now, let me ask you a question, Miss Calhoun. Did you make this call of your own volition?'

'Why, yes, certainly.'

'I mean, did anyone suggest to you that you should call me and ask that question?'

She hesitated.

'Did your attorney, Perry Mason, suggest that you should call me and ask me where Latty is?'

'Why . . . I . . . I was worried and–'

'Yes, thank you very much,' Marshall said. 'I was quite satisfied Perry Mason was behind your inquiry, and let me ask you another question. Is Perry Mason perhaps listening on the line?'

Linda Calhoun gasped.

'Right here,' Mason said. 'Good morning, Marshall.'

'I thought perhaps you had inspired this call,' Marshall said. 'If I have any inquiries of you, Mason, I'll ask them man to man and not try to hide behind the skirts of some woman.'

'I'm not hiding behind the skirts of some woman,' Mason said. 'I'm simply checking on your statements. I don't want her to talk with you unless I hear what's being said.'

'Well, you know what's been said now,' Marshall said.

'I heard you very distinctly,' Mason said. 'I heard you state that you didn't know where Latty is.'

'I've told Miss Calhoun, and I'm telling you, that I don't know where George Latty is,' Marshall said, and slammed up the telephone.

'Now I *am* worried,' Linda said.

'I'm sorry I can't help you,' Mason said. 'You're going to have to adjust yourself to the situation.'

'But what's the situation?'

'That,' Mason said, 'remains to be determined. I'm satisfied that Latty is not in any physical danger–at least I feel quite certain he isn't.'

Crowder's secretary said, 'Two reporters are in the office insisting that they have an opportunity to interview Mr Mason.'

'Let them come on in,' Mason said.

Crowder nodded and the secretary opened the door.

Two reporters and a newspaper photographer entered the office. One of the reporters said, 'Mr Mason, I'm going to ask you a question straight from the shoulder. Were you talking with Baldwin Marshall on the phone just now?'

Mason said, 'I was talking with Baldwin Marshall on the phone.'

'May I ask the reason for the conversation?'

'Miss Calhoun is somewhat concerned about the absence of her fiancé, George Latty. She thought that perhaps Marshall might know where he was.

She rang him up and asked him, and I listened in on the line.'

'Then you weren't talking with Marshall, you were simply listening.'

'I was talking with Marshall.'

'Would you mind giving me the gist of your conversation?'

Mason hesitated.

'Were you offering to plead Lorraine Elmore guilty of manslaughter if he'd reduce the charge?'

'Heavens, no,' Mason said. 'What gave you that idea?'

'There's a rumor to that effect.'

'Inspired, perhaps, by the district attorney?' Mason asked.

'I don't know where it came from. All I know is that there's a rumor. We've heard it and lots of people have heard it.'

'For your information,' Mason said, his eyes suddenly hard, 'there was nothing of that sort in the conversation and there is nothing of that sort in our minds–absolutely no intention of making any such absurd offer.

'I can also tell you that I did talk personally with Marshall after Miss Calhoun had finished her conversation. I can further state that Marshall assured Miss Calhoun and assured me that he did not know the whereabouts of George Latty.'

'Why's Latty so important?' the reporter asked.

'That is something I'm not prepared to discuss at the moment,' Mason said.

'Why not?'

'I don't have the necessary information.'

'Let me ask you this. The preliminary hearing is scheduled to start tomorrow at ten o'clock. Are you going to ask for a continuance?'

'It's always difficult to look into the future,' Mason said, smiling. 'But, as you can see, Mr Crowder is here; I'm here, and thanks to the efforts of Baldwin Marshall and the sheriff, Lorraine Elmore, the defendant, is going to be available.'

'Does that mean you're going to be ready to proceed with the preliminary?'

'It could,' Mason said. 'However, I'd like very much to talk with George Latty before we went ahead.'

'Why? Is he a witness?'

'Not for us.'

'Is he for the prosecution?'

'I can't tell about the prosecution.'

One of the reporters said, 'Look, you're certain that Baldwin Marshall told you he didn't know where Latty is?'

'That's right.'

'But why should Latty disappear?'

'I'm sure I couldn't say.'

The other reporter said, 'The word is being passed around that you're either going to offer to plead guilty to a lesser crime tomorrow, or that you won't put up any defense and will consent to having the defendant bound over for trial.'

'Where do those rumors originate?' Mason asked.

'Well,' the reporter said, 'one of them originated right in the office of Baldwin Marshall. He stated positively and absolutely that he was not going to accept any offer to let Lorraine Elmore plead guilty to manslaughter and take that plea.'

'Did he say any overtures had been made along those lines?'

'He said that he was not going to consider the proposition.'

'Ask him,' Mason said, his eyes glinting, 'if anyone has made him any such a proposition, and if he says that anyone representing the defendant has, you can state that Mr Mason would, under those circumstances, call him a liar.'

The reporters started scribbling gleefully.

'If,' Mason went on, 'the district attorney has conveyed any impression that anybody connected with the defense has offered to plead Lorraine Elmore guilty to manslaughter in order to secure a dismissal of the murder charge thereby, Mr Marshall has stated facts that were not so.'

'Well, wait a minute,' one of the reporters said, 'actually all he said was that he would not consider the proposition. He didn't say that one had been made.'

'All right,' Mason said, 'under those circumstances you can state that we will not consider any proposition which may be made by the D.A. for Mrs Elmore to plead guilty to simple assault. We want a complete vindication.'

The reporter broke out laughing. 'May I quote you on that?'

'You may quote both of us,' Mason said. 'Don't forget that Duncan Crowder is in this case.'

'We won't forget,' the reporter assured him, 'and we'll be covering the case tomorrow.'

Mason grinned. 'So will we,' he said.

The reporters left the office.

When the reporters had left, Drake made a significant gesture to Perry Mason, and Mason followed him into a private office.

'That district attorney is lying,' Drake said.

'About Latty?'

'About Latty. Latty is staying across the line in Mexicali right now. He's registered at a hotel under the name of George L. Carson. He called the district attorney's office not over an hour ago and had a long talk with Marshall.'

'What else is he doing?' Mason asked.

'He's living it up,' Drake said. 'He got just a little plastered last night. He had a dinner of roast venison, tortillas, frijoles and champagne. He had a side dish of two quail but he bogged down before he finished and only ate one of the quail. He finished the champagne, however, and was feeling no pain as he wended his way back to the hotel. He's planning on being available tomorrow at the preliminary hearing, but he isn't coming over until the district attorney sends for him. He's going to be a surprise witness and he evidently has some evidence that Marshall feels is going to be a bombshell for the defense.'

Mason said, 'Marshall is quite a chap, isn't he, Paul?'

'Are you going to call him a liar in court?'

Mason raised his eyes. 'What did he lie about?'

'Why, he said right out, didn't he, that he had no idea where Latty was?'

'He assured Linda that he couldn't tell her where Latty was–that he didn't know.'

'Well?' Drake asked.

Mason said, 'Linda wasn't smart enough to ask him if he knew where Latty had been half an hour ago, or an hour ago, or at any time during the morning. She simply asked him if he knew where Latty was, and he said he didn't. His exact words were, "No, Miss Calhoun, I'll be frank with you. I don't know where he is." '

'Why didn't you nail him on that?' Drake said. 'If he's taking advantage of that kind of a technicality, why didn't you come right out and ask him if he knew where Latty had been earlier in the day?'

Mason said, 'If I'd done that, I'd have let him off the hook.'

'What do you mean, off the hook?'

'He's hooked,' Mason said, smiling. 'He's been so smart he's outwitted himself.'

'How come?'

'I'm going to bring the matter up in open court tomorrow. I'm going to assure the court that we had the solemn statement of the district attorney that he didn't know anything about where Latty was. That will bring the district attorney to his feet, stating that he told us no such thing, that he said he didn't know where Latty was at the moment we were telephoning; that Linda had asked him, "Do you know where George Latty *is*?"'

'Well?' Drake asked.

'And by the time he gets done,' Mason said, 'or by the time I get done with him, he's going to look like a shyster, a crook and a liar. Whereas, if I had asked him if he knew where Latty had been earlier in the day, he'd have told me to go to hell and hung up and if I'd tried to take the matter up in open court, then *I* would have been the one that wasn't reporting the entire conversation.

'Tomorrow I'm going to be dignified, injured and perhaps just a little dazed by the rapidity of developments. We'll let Marshall do the explaining.'

'Are you going to be an injured martyr or are you going to get mad?' Drake asked.

'It depends on which way will do my client the most good,' Mason told him.

'My best hunch is you should get mad,' Drake said.

'We'll think it over,' Mason said.

'Won't you get mad anyway?' Drake asked.

'A good lawyer can always get mad if somebody pays him for it, but after you've been paid a few times for getting good and mad, you hate like the deuce to get mad on your own when nobody's paying you for it.'

Drake grinned. 'You lawyers,' he said.

'You detectives,' Mason told him. 'Keep your men on the tail of George Latty.'

'We've got men looking down his shirt collar right now,' Drake said.

14

Judge Horatio D. Manly took his place on the bench, regarded the packed courtroom, said, 'This is the time heretofore fixed for the preliminary hearing in the case of the People of the State of California versus Lorraine Elmore.'

'Ready for the People,' Marshall said.

'Ready for the defense,' Mason said, placing a reassuring hand on the shoulder of Lorraine Elmore.

Judge Manly cleared his throat. 'Before this case starts, I want to state that there has been a lot of newspaper publicity about the case, about the facts, and about the people involved. I want to caution the spectators that this is not a show, this is not a debate, this is not entertainment. This is a court of justice. The spectators will comport themselves accordingly; otherwise the Court will take steps to insure proper decorum.'

Mason stood up. 'May I be heard?' he asked.

'Mr Mason,' Judge Manly said.

'It happens,' Mason said, 'that the defense is very anxious to get in touch with one George Latty. We have reason to believe that the prosecution is either keeping Mr Latty concealed, or knows where Mr Latty is, despite the fact the district attorney has given his verbal assurance that he does not know where Latty is.'

'Just a minute, just a minute,' Marshall said, getting to his feet, 'I resent that.'

'Are my facts incorrect?' Mason asked.

'Your facts are incorrect.'

Mason said, 'I was a party to a telephone conversation yesterday, Your Honor, at which time the district attorney assured Linda Calhoun, the niece of the defendant, that he did not have any idea where George Latty was. I would like to have that statement repeated in open court.'

'Now, that's simply not so,' Marshall said. 'I did not make any such statement.'

'You didn't?' Mason asked in surprise.

'I did not. Miss Calhoun asked me specifically, "Do you know where Mr Latty is?" and I told her I didn't know. I had no way of knowing. I was talking with her on the telephone. I didn't know what he was doing at the moment, or where he was at that particular moment.'

'Oh, *at the moment!*' Mason said. 'But you didn't *say* that to her. You said that you didn't have the faintest idea where he was, or words to that effect.'

'I think that counsel is deliberately misquoting me, Your Honor,' Marshall said.

'Well, so there may be no misunderstanding at the moment,' Mason said, 'do you know where Latty is now, or do you know where he was an hour ago, half an hour ago, or twenty-four hours ago; or can you tell me how Linda Calhoun can get in touch with Mr Latty? Linda Calhoun and George Latty are engaged to be married, Your Honor.'

'I don't have to answer your questions. I don't have to submit to your cross-examination,' Marshall said. 'I'm running the district attorney's office, not a matrimonial agency. If Latty wants to get in touch with Linda Calhoun, he certainly can do so.'

'Unless he has been instructed not to,' Mason said. 'And, so there can be no misunderstanding, I will ask counsel if he did or did not instruct Latty not to get in touch with Linda Calhoun.'

'I certainly did not do any such thing,' Marshall said. 'In fact, I specifically instructed Latty *to* get in touch with Linda Calhoun.'

Mason raised his eyebrows. 'And tell Miss Calhoun where he was?'

'I didn't say that,' Marshall said.

'Well then, perhaps I should express myself differently,' Mason said, 'and ask you if you didn't instruct Mr Latty specifically *not* to tell Linda Calhoun where he was.'

'I don't have to answer your questions. I don't intend to be cross-examined by you,' Marshall said.

'In short,' Mason said, 'I think the Court can see the technicalities, the equivocation, the dodging, the subterfuges, the evasions, which have characterized the prosecutor's office in connection with our attempts to locate

George Latty. I wish the Court would instruct the district attorney to disclose Mr Latty's present whereabouts to the defense.'

Mason sat down.

'Do you know where Latty is?' Judge Manly asked Marshall.

'If the Court please, that isn't a fair question,' Marshall said. 'Let the defense attorney state that he wants to use Latty as a defense witness, and then there would be some reason for the inquiry. We don't have to disclose our knowledge to defense counsel simply to facilitate some budding romance between a relative of the defendant and an important witness for the prosecution.'

Judge Manly glanced at Mason.

Mason rose with dignity and said, 'If the Court please, we don't know whether Latty will be a witness for the defense or not. We haven't had an opportunity to question him since certain matters came to our attention. It might well be that we will desire to use him to establish some points in connection with the defense of this case.'

'If the Court please,' Marshall said, 'they haven't the faintest intention of putting on any defense. This entire furor over the whereabouts of George Latty is simply for the purpose of embarrassing the prosecution.'

'Well,' Judge Manly said, 'I'll get back to my question: Do you know where Latty is?'

'Certainly, we know where he is,' Marshall said. 'He's a witness for the prosecution and we're keeping him where he won't be tampered with.'

'May I ask what the prosecution means by being tampered with?' Mason asked.

'Being influenced so that his testimony will be changed,' Marshall said. 'Because of his romantic entanglement with the niece of the defendant, this witness would be in a position where shrewd and inscrupulous counsel could get him to change his testimony.'

Mason said, 'Do you mean that this witness is so vacillating that he might change his recollection of what he knew or what he saw by being exposed to contact with a relative of the defendant?'

'You know what I mean!' Marshall shouted. 'I mean that *you* could bring pressure to bear so that you'd have this young man all mixed up.'

'If,' Mason said, smiling, 'the district attorney now admits that his appraisal of his own witness is that the witness can't stand interrogation by anyone other than the prosecution without changing his testimony, I'm quite willing to accept that statement.'

'That isn't what I said! That isn't what I meant and you know it!' Marshall shouted, his face dark with anger.

Judge Manly said, 'Gentlemen, gentlemen, that's enough. The remarks of counsel in the future will be addressed to the Court. Now, the Court will ask you, Mr Prosecutor, since it now appears you know where George Latty is, is there any reason why his whereabouts can't be disclosed to the young woman to whom he is engaged, or why defense counsel can't serve a subpoena on him?'

Marshall said, 'He's in the office of the district attorney, waiting to be called as a witness for the prosecution in this case–as a most important witness, I may say.'

'Then,' Mason said, 'I take it, Your Honor, that Miss Calhoun can be assured that the failure of her fiancé to get in touch with her and disclose his whereabouts was due to the fact that the witness was acting under orders of the prosecution.'

'Miss Calhoun isn't a party to this action. She doesn't have to be assured of anything,' Marshall said.

Judge Manly said, 'Do I understand that you expect to produce George Latty in this courtroom, Mr Prosecutor?'

'He will be here within an hour,' Marshall said.

'Very well,' Judge Manly said, 'I think that answers the questions. Regardless of what has been done in connection with concealing or not concealing the whereabouts of this witness, or the reason for it, the witness will be present in court and counsel will have an opportunity to question the witness as to where he has been and why he failed to communicate with–'

'But I consider those questions would be entirely improper, Your Honour,' Marshall interrupted. 'Latty is only a witness. He's not a party to a controversy.'

Mason said, 'Counsel may *always* examine the bias of a witness, and any witness who is so completely biased, so completely under the control of the prosecution that he is willing to forgo communicating with his fiancé in order to further the interests of the prosecution's case, can certainly not be considered a fair and impartial witness. The defense should have a right to inquire into his motivation.'

'I would certainly think so,' Judge Manly said.

Marshall said, 'Your Honor, we would like to argue the point later on when the question comes up.'

'Yes. There's no need for a discussion at this time,' Judge Manly said. 'I'll rule on the matter when the witness is called to the stand.'

'I take it, the prosecution promises to call him,' Mason said.

'The prosecution doesn't have to disclose its witnesses to the defense.'

'You have already assured the Court that you would call Latty as a witness within the hour.'

'I expect to call him,' Marshall said.

Mason smiled and bowed graciously to the Court. 'If the prosecution had only made that statement earlier, it would have saved a lot of time and perhaps some recriminations.'

Marshall thoroughly angry said, 'I don't like being forced to disclose my case to the defense in advance.'

'Well, you've disclosed it now,' Judge Manly said. 'Call your first witness.'

Marshall seemed ready, for the moment, to argue the matter with the Court but finally, and after frantic whispering on the part of his deputy who sat beside him at the counsel table, said, 'I will call the county surveyor as my first witness.'

The county surveyor introduced a diagram of the Calexico motel, a map of the roads out of Calexico, and located on the map the place where Lorraine Elmore's automobile had been found.

There was no cross-examination.

The sheriff, called as a witness, testified to finding the automobile stuck in the sand and to the presence of a capsule on the front seat.

'Do you know what that capsule contained?' Marshall asked.

'I do now, yes.'

'And do you have that capsule with you?'

'I have.'

'Will you produce it, please?'

The sheriff produced a small bottle from his pocket. Within that bottle was the green capsule.

'And what does this capsule contain?' Marshall asked.

Crowder glanced at Mason. 'Want to object?' he whispered.

Mason shook his head.

'The capsule,' the sheriff said, 'contains Somniferal.'

'And do you know what that is?'

'Yes, sir.'

'What is it?'

'It is one of the newer forms of hypnotics. It is quite powerful and has the peculiar property of taking effect very quickly and lasting for a long time. For the most part, the hypnotics which take rather quick effect are soon dissipated, whereas the hypnotics that last for a long time are slower acting. This relatively new drug, Somniferal, which is, by the way, a trade name, is both quick in its action and long lasting.'

'Did the defendant tell you anything about this capsule?' Marshall asked.

'She refused to make any statement concerning it, saying she was doing so on the advice of counsel.'

'Did you,' Marshall asked, 'ever find the container from which this capsule was taken?'

'Yes,' the sheriff snapped. 'In the defendant's handbag.'

Crowder watched Mason anxiously, then seeing that the lawyer was making no move to object, leaned closer and whispered, 'That's a conclusion. He *can't* know what container the capsule came from.'

Mason smiled, placed his lips close to Crowder's ear. 'Don't object to those things,' he said. 'That's the mark of an amateur. Let the evidence go in and then get the guy all flustered on cross-examination. Remember now, when you cross-examine him, bear down on the point of *how* he knew it was this container. Get him to show that he's relying on hearsay evidence. Ask him if he didn't know that was improper. Ask him if he didn't discuss this phase of his testimony with the district attorney–if the district attorney didn't tell him in effect, "I'm going to ask you this question and you answer it fast before the defense can object. It's hearsay but we'll try and get it in anyway." Show his bias.'

'Wait a minute, wait a minute,' Crowder whispered, 'when *I* cross-examine him?'

'Sure, you,' Mason said. 'You want to get your hand in, in this case, don't you?'

'My gosh, I'd love it,' Crowder said, 'but I didn't know that you were going to let me take part in the examination of witnesses.'

'Don't you want to?'

'Heavens, Yes. I–There's a young lady in the courtroom that I'd–Well, frankly, I'd like to have an opportunity to impress her.'

'You'll have the opportunity,' Mason said.

Judge Manly, noticing the colloquy between counsel, said, 'The question asked the sheriff was whether he had ever discovered the container from which this capsule had been taken and he said that he had; that it came from a bottle which was found in the handbag of the defendant in the Calexico motel.'

'Were those capsules dispensed on a prescription?' Marshall asked.

'They were.'

'Did you talk with the physician who dispensed the prescription?'

'Yes.'

'Where was he located?'

'In Boston, Massachusetts?'

'He is not here as a witness?'

'No.'

'But nevertheless he did explain to you why he had issued a prescription for an unusually large number of these capsules?'

'Yes.'

'I have no further questions at this time. You may cross-examine,' Marshall said, bowing to Mason as though by giving him an opportunity for cross-examination he was generously conferring upon defense counsel a very great privilege, all in the interests of fair play.

Mason jerked his head toward Crowder. 'Go ahead, Duncan,' he said.

Crowder said, 'You have stated, Sheriff, that this capsule contained Somniferal?'

'That's right.'

'And how do you know it contained Somniferal? Was it analyzed?'

'I had the prescription.'

'What prescription?'

'The prescription under which the capsule was purchased.'

'And where did you get the prescription?'

'From the doctor who issued it.'

'Did you have the original prescription?'

'Certainly not. The drugstore has that.'

'Oh, then you *didn't* have the prescription.'

'Not the original.'

'And you didn't have the capsule analyzed?'

'Certainly not. The capsule is intact.'

'Then how do you know it is a capsule from this prescription?'

'Because the label is on the bottle.'

'And the bottle was found where?'

'In the unit of the motel occupied by the defendant.'

'And how do you know the capsule came from that bottle, Sheriff?'

'Because it's the same kind of a capsule that was in the bottle.'

'How do you know it is?'

'Well, it has the same color, the same physical appearance.'

'Then you know that the capsule came from the bottle, because the bottle was reported to have contained Somniferal, and you know the capsule contained Somniferal because you deduce it came from the bottle. Or, to put it the other way, because you assume the capsule contained Somniferal, then it must have come from the bottle which you assume contained Somniferal because someone told you over the long distance telephone line that it contained Somniferal.'

'That's not a fair way of putting it,' the sheriff said.

'All right,' Crowder said, 'put it in what you consider a fair way then.'

'Well, I talked with the doctor who issued the prescription and he told me what was in the prescription. I checked . . .'

'Yes, yes,' Crowder said, 'keep right on, Sheriff. You checked what?'

'Well, I checked the contents of the bottle with the prescription the doctor told me over the telephone he had issued to the defendant.'

'Then you didn't go to the trouble of telephoning the drugstore that had filled the prescription, giving them the number on the bottle and getting *their* version of the contents?'

'No. I didn't think that was necessary.'

'Do you know generally that hearsay evidence is inadmissible?'

'Certainly.'

'Didn't you realize all this was hearsay evidence?'

'Well, it was the only way we could get the evidence. We couldn't have these people come on from Boston, just to testify to something that was perfectly obvious.'

'And how do you know this capsule came from the bottle?'

'Because it's the same size, shape and color.'

'Is there anything about the size or shape that would differentiate it from any other three-grain capsule?'

'The color is distinctive.'

'And the color is green?'

'Yes.'

'And did the doctor tell you that Somniferal was put up in capsules and the color was green?'

'No, he didn't.'

'Who did?'

The sheriff squirmed uncomfortably. 'A druggist in El Centro.'

'And is that druggist here to testify?'

'Not that I know of.'

Crowder said, 'If the Court please, I move to strike out all the testimony of the sheriff relating to the nature and contents of the capsule, and the contents of the prescription bottle, upon the ground that it now appears the entire evidence was based upon hearsay and conclusions.'

'Oh, Your Honor,' Marshall said, 'here we go, with a lot of petty, technical objections dreamt up by my young erudite friend. By the time he's practised law a little longer he'll learn that on the nonessentials we grant professional courtesies and a certain amount of give and take.'

'We haven't seen any giving yet, Your Honor,' Crowder said. 'It's all taking. No one knows what's in that capsule. The prosecution has assumed it's Somniferal because they have assumed it came from that bottle, and they have assumed the bottle contained Somniferal, because a doctor in Boston said it did, but there isn't any proof as yet that the capsule ever came from that bottle.'

'Your motion is granted,' Judge Manly said. 'The testimony is stricken in regard to the drug in this capsule.'

'But, Your Honor,' Marshall said angrily, 'this goes to the very gist of the case. We want to show that the deceased was given a drink of drugged whiskey; that the whiskey was drugged with Somniferal. We want to show that the defendant had that drug in her possession.'

'Show it by competent evidence and we have no objection,' Crowder said, 'but we're not going to have the entire case against this defendant built upon a structure of hearsay testimony and pure assumptions on the part of the authorities.'

'The Court has ruled on the matter,' Judge Manly said.

'But, Your Honor, this is just a preliminary examination,' Marshall protested.

'And the same rules of evidence apply as in any court of law,' Crowder snapped.

'I think that is technically correct,' Judge Manly said. Then added in a more kindly voice to the district attorney, 'Perhaps you can connect it up later.'

'Not without having a witness fly out here all the way from Boston,' Marshall said.

'The defense will be only too glad to consent to a continuance so the witness can be brought out here,' Crowder said affably. 'We would like very much to cross-examine the doctor in question, to find out how he knows what was in the bottle and how he was able to identify the bottle on the telephone. I think it will appear that the doctor only issued a prescription and had nothing to do with filling it. Only the druggist could tell what's in the capsules.'

'Well, we'll have the druggist fly out here too, if that's what you want,' Marshall said.

Crowder smiled. 'All *I* want is to have the prosecution introduce competent evidence and not rely on hearsay evidence.'

'The Court has ruled,' Judge Manly said. 'You'd better call your next witness and try to connect it up later on, Mr District Attorney.'

'Very well,' Marshall snapped with poor grace, conscious of the fact that the newspaper reporters were scribbling copious notes. 'I'll call Hartwell Alvin, chief of police in Calexico.'

'Very well,' Judge Manly said. 'Come forward and take the stand, Chief Alvin.'

Alvin, a tall, cadaverous individual in his fifties with expressionless eyes which seemed to hide behind an opaque film, came forward, held up his hand, was sworn, and took his seat on the witness stand. His manner was calmly detached.

'Your name is Hartwell Alvin and you are now and have been for the last several years chief of police of Calexico in Imperial County, California?'

'That's right,' Alvin said.

'Directing your attention to the morning of the fourth of this month, did you have occasion to go to the Palm Court Motel in Calexico at an early hour in the morning?'

'I did.'

'Now, since counsel wants to object to all hearsay testimony, I won't ask you what it was that caused you to go there, because anything you learned over the telephone would be hearsay. But just tell us what you found at the time you arrived.'

'I found a dead man in Unit Fourteen.'

'Did you know this man?'

'No.'

'Was he subsequently identified?'

'Yes.'

'Was he identified as being a certain Montrose Dewitt of Los Angeles?'

'That's right.'

'What time did you arrive at the unit?'

'Shortly after seven.'

'In the morning?'

'That's right.'

'What else did you find?'

'I found the body of this man lying on the floor of Unit Fourteen. I found that things were disturbed in the room as is shown in photographs which I had taken. That is, some of the drawers were open and a suitcase and bag were open.

I found a state of much greater confusion in Unit Sixteen. Drawers had been pulled open, things spread out on the floor, baggage was open, and clothing and other objects had been strewn all over the floor.'

'You took photographs of these units?'

'I did. That is, I caused them to be taken.'

'And you have prints of these photographs?'

'I have.'

'Will you hand them to me, please, and tell me as you hand them to me, what each one represents.'

There was a period of some minutes during which the witness handed the prosecutor photograph after photograph, and explained what was shown in each photograph, the position from which it was taken, and in which unit it was.

'Did you consult the register of the motel?' Marshall asked.

'Yes. Unit Sixteen had been rented to a person using the name of Lorraine Elmore, and Unit Fourteen to a person registered under the name of Montrose Dewitt.'

'Were you with the sheriff when an automobile, registered in the name of Lorraine Elmore, was found in the desert?'

'I was.'

'Did you look around in the vicinity of that automobile?'

'I did.'

'Did you take photographs?'

'That was later. I caused the photographs to be taken.'

'Do you have those photographs with you?'

'I have prints, yes, sir.'

Again, Alvin introduced half a dozen prints showing the car stuck in the sand.

'Did you find anything in the car?'

'I did.'

'What?'

'In the baggage compartment underneath the floor covering I found an ice pick.'

'Do you have that with you?'

'I do.'

'Produce it, please.'

The witness produced the ice pick, which Marshall asked to have marked for identification.

'I show you the figure sixteen on this ice pick and ask you if that figure was stamped in the handle of the ice pick when you found it?'

'It was.'

'Did you find anything else?'

'I saw the sheriff pick up a greenish capsule on the front seat of the automobile.'

'Were you present when the sheriff found a bottle with a prescription number?'

'I was.'

'Where was that found?'

'In Unit Sixteen, in a small handbag.'

'You may cross-examine,' Marshall said.

Mason whispered to Duncan Crowder, 'Take him on, Duncan. There's not very much you can do with him. Don't generalize. Pounce on the one point that you can emphasize and then let him go.'

Mason sat back and watched the young man with keen interest.

Duncan Crowder rose, smiled at the chief of police, said, 'As I understand your testimony, and as I observe from these photographs, Unit Sixteen had been pretty much taken to pieces.'

'That's right.'

'Someone had disturbed the baggage, the contents of the drawers in the dresser.'

'That's right.'

'Did you look for fingerprints?'

'We tried to develop latents, yes.'

'And did you develop any latents?'

'We did.'

'Why didn't you mention those in your testimony when you were being examined by the prosecutor?'

'He didn't ask me.'

'Why didn't he ask you?'

Marshall was on his feet. 'Your Honor, I object to this as improper cross-examination and assign it as an improper question. This witness can't read the mind of the district attorney.'

'Sustained,' Judge Manly said.

Crowder smiled. 'I'll reframe the question and put it this way. Did you discuss the case with the prosecutor?'

'Certainly.'

'Before you went on the stand?'

'Yes, of course.'

'And you went over with him what your testimony was going to be?'

'Yes.'

'And did the prosecutor, at the time of that conference, state to you that he didn't want you to say anything about the latent fingerprints you had discovered unless you were specifically asked, and tell you that he wasn't going to ask you about the fingerprints on direct examination?'

'That's objected to, if the Court please,' Marshall blurted angrily. 'That conversation, or any conversation this witness may have had with the prosecutor, has no bearing whatever on the case. I am not on trial here.'

Crowder said, 'But if it should be made apparent that the witness deliberately shaped his testimony and deliberately withheld certain facts from his direct examination at the request of the prosecutor, that would show bias on the part of the witness, Your Honor, and would be perfectly proper on cross-examination.'

'I think that is correct,' Judge Manly said. 'The objection is overruled.'

'Answer the question,' Crowder said.

Marshall apparently debated whether to argue the point further. He stood for an uncertain moment or two, then reluctantly sat down.

The witness said, 'He told me not to say anything about the fingerprints unless I was asked.'

'Did he say why?'

'He said that it was simply going to confuse the issue.'

'All right, *I'll* ask you about the fingerprints. What did you find?'

'There were fingerprints of Lorraine Elmore, the defendant. There were fingerprints of Montrose Dewitt.'

'In both cabins?'

'In both cabins.'

'Go on. What other latents?'

'There were fingerprints that had been made by the maid who makes up the rooms, and there were several latent fingerprints which couldn't be identified.'

'They were sufficiently clear so an identification could he made?'

'If we can find the person whose hand made those fingerprints, the latents are clear enough so a match can be made.'

'You have photographs of those latent fingerprints?'

'I have.'

'Produce them, please.'

'If the Court please,' Marshall said, 'the witness can be asked about what he found on cross-examination, but the defense has no right to introduce photographs of what was found as part of cross-examination. If the defense wants those fingerprints in evidence, they can call this witness as a defense witness and put them in.'

'Oh, I think not,' Judge Manly said. 'This witness was asked what he found; he photographed the interior or had photographs taken and those were introduced in evidence. Now, if photographs were deliberately withheld at the request of the district attorney and that is brought out on cross-examination, counsel has a right to have those photographs of the fingerprints introduced.'

'I object, if the Court please, to the statement that they were deliberately withheld on the advice of the district attorney.'

'You may object it,' Judge Manly said, 'but it's part of the evidence. I'm simply commenting on the evidence.'

The witness produced the fingerprints, and Crowder had them introduced in evidence.

'Now then,' Crowder said, pleasantly, 'the indication in those units was that some person had very hurriedly searched the baggage and the drawers as though looking for something. Is that right?'

'That's right.'

'But that same condition could have existed if a person had been planting some evidence such as this prescription bottle in the baggage somewhere. Isn't that right?'

'Well, not exactly. If a person had been planting something, it would have been planted in one place and all of the other baggage wouldn't have been disturbed.'

'Well, then, I'll put it this way,' Crowder said. 'If some person had searched the baggage in order to make sure that some object *wasn't* in the baggage and then, having found that the object was not in the baggage, had planted another similar object so that investigators would be sure to find it, the condition of things in the units would have been just about as you found them.'

'That's right,' the witness conceded. 'When you find things disturbed that way, you can't tell whether anything was taken or whether a person was just looking for something, and unless you have an inventory of what was in the room in the first place, you can't tell what's missing and you can't tell what's been added.'

'Thank you very much indeed for an impartial statement of the situation, chief,' Crowder said with a little bow. 'I appreciate your frankness and we have no further questions.'

'There's no need for defense counsel to a make a speech,' Marshall said.

'Oh, he was simply thanking the witness,' Judge Manly observed, a twinkle in his eye.

'Well, he has no right to do that.'

'Perhaps not,' Judge Manly said, 'but there's no jury present and it isn't going to hurt anyone, and while we're on the subject the Court also wants to thank the witness for being commendably frank. You're excused Chief Alvin.'

Alvin left the stand.

'Call Ronley Andover,' Marshall said.

Mason turned to raise a quizzical eyebrow at Paul Drake, who, in turn, shrugged his shoulders, indicating that he had had no previous knowledge that Andover was to be a witness.

Andover was sworn, took the stand, gave his name and address.

Marshall said, 'Did you see a body at the office of the coroner? A body that was listed on the coroner's records as that of Montrose Dewitt?'

'I did.'

'Did you know that individual in his lifetime?'

'I did.'

'And what was the name under which you knew him?'

'That of Weston Hale.'

'Did you share an apartment together?'

'We did.'

'Do you know whether this individual had a relatively large amount of cash on his person when he left Los Angeles?'

'Yes, sir.'

'How much was the amount?'

'Fifteen thousand dollars.'

'You may cross-examine,' Marshall snapped.

Mason nudged Crowder and said, 'I'll take him, Duncan.'

Mason got to his feet. 'How do you know that he had fifteen thousand dollars, Mr Andover?'

'Because I gave it to him.'

'And where did you get it?'

'I cashed a check which Weston Hale made to me in an amount of fifteen thousand dollars and turned it over to him.'

'Do you know whether Weston Hale was the man's right name or whether it was an alias?'

'I believe Weston Hale was the man's right name.'

'Do you have any idea why he took the alias of Montrose Dewitt?'

'No.'

'Did you know that he maintained an apartment under the name of Montrose Dewitt, and a separate entity and a separate bank account?'

'I know it now. I didn't know it then.'

'You gave this money to Weston Hale?'

'I did.'

'When?'

'On the third.'

'Where?'

'He stopped at the appartment we shared.'

'He came up to the apartment?'

'No, he asked me to come down and meet him on the sidewalk.'

'You did?'

'Yes, sir.'

'Was he driving his own car?'

'No, sir. He was riding as a passenger in a car which was being driven by the defendant.'

'Did he get out of that car?'

'He did not. He simply drove by, and I handed him the envelope containing the money.'

Mason frowned thoughtfully, then said slowly, 'I have no further questions.'

Marshall called the coroner and then the surgeon who had performed the autopsy, brought into evidence the existence of the wounds in the head and in the torso; wounds which had been made by a long, thin object 'similar to an ice pick.'

Then Marshall called the manager of the motel, brought out from her that each unit had been equipped with ice picks, that these ice picks were similar in appearance and design to the one that had been found in the automobile registered in the name of Lorraine Elmore, and that each ice pick had had stamped on its handle the number of the apartment in which it belonged, and that the number 16 on this ice pick would indicate that it had been taken from Unit 16.

Crowder looked to Mason for instructions.

Mason shook his head. 'No cross-examination,' he said. 'You've done fine so far. Just let these witnesses go.'

Baldwin Marshall arose and said dramatically. 'If the Court please, my next witness will be George Keswick Latty, and at the conclusion of his testimony counsel for the defense can cross-examine him to their heart's desire.'

'That remark is uncalled for,' Judge Manly said. 'If Latty is to be your next witness, call him and dispense with verbal flourishes.'

'Yes, Your Honor,' Marshall said, 'but in view of the fact that there had been an intimation that I was afraid to let the defense counsel interrogate this witness I simply want them to know he will be available for interrogation.'

'Well, you don't need to let them know anything of the sort,' Judge Manly said. 'They have a right to cross-examine any witness you put on the stand, and,' the judge added, his color deepening, 'in view of your declaration that they can examine him to their heart's content, the Court is going to take you at your word and the cross-examination will be virtually unlimited as far as this Court is concerned. Now call your witness.'

'Mr Latty to the stand,' Marshall said, apparently not in the least concerned with the Court's rebuke.

There was a moment's wait while all eyes turned expectantly to the doorway of the courtroom. Then Latty escorted by a police officer, stood dramatically in the doorway, his chin in the air, his pose that of a man fully conscious of the dramatic possibilities of the situation. Then, his chin still elevated, he strode down the aisle to the witness stand, held up his right hand, was sworn and was seated on the witness stand.

His eyes caught sight of Linda and he smiled, the gracious smile which royalty bestows upon a loyal subject.

'Your name is George Keswick Latty,' Marshall said, 'and you are engaged to be married to Linda Calhoun, who in turn is the niece of the defendant. Is that right?'

'Yes, sir.'

'Very well. Now, I will ask you where you reside.'

'In Massachusetts. Near Boston.'

'You are attending a university there?'

'Yes, sir.'

'When did you leave there?'

'On the morning of the third.'

'By plane?'

'Yes, sir. By jet plane.'

'And where did you go?'

'To Los Angeles.'

'Whom did you see in Los Angeles?'

'Linda Calhoun.'

'That is the niece of Lorraine Elmore?'

'Yes.'

'And did you discuss the affairs of Lorraine Elmore with Linda?'

'I did.'

'Now, I'm not going to ask you for that conversation because that would be hearsay and not binding on the defendant, but I am going to ask you if as a result of that conversation you took any action?'

'I did.'

'What?'

'We went to consult Perry Mason on the morning of the third.'

'Now, again without disclosing conversations, I take it that at the time you consulted Perry Mason the situation was, generally, that Linda and her aunt had quarreled over–'

'Just a moment, Your Honor,' Mason interrupted. 'I object to the question on the ground that it is obviously leading and suggestive and calling for hearsay evidence.'

'Sustained,' Judge Manly snapped.

'All right,' Marshall said angrily, 'if I can't prove it directly, Your Honor, I'll prove it by inference. What did you do after you left Mason's office, Mr Latty?'

'I rented an automobile.'

'And what did you do with that rented automobile? Where did you go?'

'I shadowed Lorraine Elmore in her automobile.'

'And where did that shadowing lead you?'

'She was joined by Montrose Dewitt. Then she put a lot of baggage in an automobile and they started south, after first stopping at the curb to receive an envelope from a man I now know was Ronley Andover.'

'What did *you* do?'

'I followed them until I lost them about ten miles or so before we came to Arizona.'

'And what did you do after that?'

'I continued on into Arizona.'

'Did you see anyone there whom you knew?'

'Yes. I saw Perry Mason and Paul Drake, the detective.'

'And then what happened?'

'Then I returned to El Centro. I telephoned Linda from El Centro, and she told me that she had heard from the defendant, Lorraine Elmore, and that Lorraine was staying at the Palm Court Motel in Calexico.'

'So what did you do then?'

'I had intended to return to Los Angeles, but since the motel in Calexico was only some ten or twelve miles from El Centro, I decided to drive down and look the situation over.'

'And you did so?'

'Yes.'

'What time did you arrive in Calexico?'

'I don't know the exact time. It was shortly before midnight.'

'And what did you do?'

'I drove to the Palm Court Motel. I checked on the cars in the parking place and found that Lorraine Elmore's car, with its Massachusetts license plates, was parked there in the motel.'

'What did you do?'

'I noticed that the car was parked in front of Unit Fourteen. I also noticed there was a vacancy sign so I registered and was given a unit nearer the street. I asked if there wasn't something farther back and was offered Unit twelve, which I accepted.'

'Now, where was Unit Twelve with reference to the unit occupied by Montrose Dewitt?'

'Montrose Dewitt was in Unit Fourteen and I was on the west adjoining his unit.'

'What did you do after you checked into your unit?'

'I explored the situation.'

'What do you mean by that?'

'Well, I looked the place over.'

'What did you find?'

'Apparently Unit Twelve and Fourteen were so designed that they could be rented as one double unit in case the parties renting the units wished to open them up into one double unit. I found that there was a door which was locked, but someone had bored a small hole in this door–a hole made with a very small drill, but it enabled one to see into the adjoining unit.'

'Could you hear through this door?'

'Not very well through that door. I could see through it and could see a very small section of the room on the other side. However, by going into the clothes closet and putting my ear against the wall of the clothes closet, I could hear conversation in the adjoining unit quite plainly.'

'What did you do?'

'I looked through the small hole which had been drilled in the connecting doorway. I could see a portion of the bed in the adjoining unit. I saw Montrose Dewitt and Lorraine Elmore sitting side by side on the bed. I could see they were talking but I couldn't hear what they were saying, so I left that door and went into the closet. By going to the extreme end of the closet and putting my ear against the partition, I could hear what was being said.'

'All of the conversation?'

'Not all of it, but nearly all of it.'

'Now then, just what did you hear?' Marshall asked.

'There was some discussion of a personal nature.'

'What do you mean by that?'

'Well, they were . . . well, what we call pitching a little woo.'

'You mean they were making love?'

'Well, not exactly love. They were doing a little necking and making a little . . . verbal love.'

'All right,' Marshall said, turning to smile at the crowded courtroom, 'now let's go on from there. Did you hear them discussing their future plans?'

'I did.'

'What did they say?'

'Mr Dewitt told Lorraine that Linda was simply trying to get her money, that she wanted to dominate Lorraine and force Lorraine to live the kind of life Linda wanted for her, a life of seclusion, a life of austerity, one that was barren of affection; that is was the sort of life that would lead to premature age and that Linda didn't have Lorraine's interests at heart.'

'Then what?' Marshall asked.

'Then Lorraine became indignant and told him that he had misjudged Linda, that Linda was impulsive but that when she once had a chance to get acquainted with him they would both like each other; Lorraine said she felt very repentant about having quarreled with Linda and that she had called Linda up and asked her forgiveness and told Linda that she would see her the next afternoon; she added that she and Dewitt would be married by that time and that she wanted Dewitt to meet Linda.'

'All right,' Marshall said, 'just go on from there. What happened after that?'

'Well, then Dewitt became very much enraged when he heard that she had telephoned Linda. He said, "I told you not to communicate with her. I told you that we were going to have to live our own lives, that we'd make this joint investment without letting anyone know we had done so and would cash in for a couple of million dollars within twelve months." Then, he said, Lorraine could let her friends know where she was and what she was doing. She'd be a rich woman by that time.'

'Go right ahead,' Marshall said. 'What happened after that?'

'Well, Lorraine was angry and hurt. She said that she was reasonably well fixed right now; that she didn't have to sacrifice her friendship with her family in order to make more money; that money wasn't everything in life.'

'And then what?' Marshall asked.

'Well, then he apologized for losing his temper and started using terms of endearment and she didn't respond very well. She said that she didn't see any reason why she should sever all connections with her family just because they were starting out again in life, and they talked for a while and then she said good night, that she was going over to her cabin.'

'And did she?' Marshall asked.

'She started for her cabin and got as far as the door and then Dewitt saw something in the parking place which alarmed him. He said something about a car. By that time they had moved away from the bed and were standing in the doorway and I couldn't hear very well, but he said something about a car and then there was a lot of motion and not much talk, and suddenly the lights went out and I heard Lorraine's car start.

'I dashed to the door and looked out into the parking area and saw the two of them in Lorraine's Massachusetts car, just pulling out of a parking space.'

'Who was driving?' Marshall asked.

'She was.'

'Who do you mean by she?'

'Lorraine.'

'And whenever you have used the word Lorraine, whom do you mean?'

'Lorraine Elmore, the defendant in the case, the person sitting there beside, and a little behind, Perry Mason.'

'So what did you do?' Marshall asked.

'I tried to follow them. I ran and jumped in my own car, started the motor. By the time I got to the street they had reached the corner and had made a turn. I knew I didn't have time to make any wrong guesses. I felt that they had turned to the left toward town, so I skidded into a left-hand turn and then found that I'd made a mistake. They weren't ahead of me. I was going to make a U-turn but saw a police car parked up the block so I had to make a run around the block, and by the time I got back to the intersection I'd lost all track of them. I cruised around for about an hour trying to find them and couldn't.'

'Then what did you do?'

'Then I took the road out of town and followed it as far as the junction with the Holtville road.'

'And then?'

'I couldn't find them so I returned.'

'Go on,' Marshall said.

'Well, I was very much chagrined. I felt I had made a complete failure of everything. I knew that Mr Mason would make some more of his sarcastic remarks and I was afraid of the effect he and his remarks would have on Linda. So I felt pretty low. I waited around for fifteen or twenty minutes, I guess, and then decided that they'd skipped out and the only thing to do was to get some sleep, so I went to bed and I was tired. I was asleep almost instantly.'

'What awakened you?'

'The sound of voices in the adjoining motel unit.'

'By the adjoining motel unit now, you are referring to Unit Fourteen, the one that Montrose Dewitt occupied?'

'Yes.'

'And what happened?'

'Well, I jumped out of bed and hurried to the place in the closet where I could listen.'

'You didn't try to look?'

'No, I could look through the door but I could hear through the closet and because someone was talking I wanted to hear what it was.'

'And what did you hear?'

'I heard Dewitt's voice saying how sleepy he was; that he had never been so tired in all of his life, and then he said something to the effect that "We're in the big-time now. We've got it made," or something of that sort, and then he started talking, mumbling, his voice sounding as if he might be talking in his sleep. I could hardly understand him.

"Then he started to say something about suitcases and I heard him pick up a suitcase and put it down on the floor and then I heard a heavy thud.'

'What do you mean by a heavy thud?'

'Like the sound made by somebody falling to the floor, collapsing.'

'And then what happened?'

'I was trying to account for that sound. At first I thought it might have been a suitcase. Then, while I was still thinking, I heard someone moving around and I thought that was Dewitt.'

'Never mind what you thought,' Marshall said. 'You heard the sound of a thud and then you heard someone moving around.'

'That's right.'

'And what did you do?'

'I continued to listen, hoping that there would be more conversation.'

'There was none?'

'No.'

'So then what did you do?'

'So then I left the closet and went to the door, hoping I could see what was going on, because with someone moving around I felt certain that that person would sooner or later come within my line of vision.'

'Did that happen?'

'No. Just as I got there the lights went off and everything was dark and silent in the cabin.'

'So then what?'

'I stood there thinking the matter over and finally remembered what Dewitt had said about feeling tired and decided he had gone to bed, and that Lorraine had gone back to her own–'

'Never mind what you decided,' Marshall said. 'That's not proper for you to state. Just state what you said, what you heard, what you saw, what you did.'

'Well, I went back to bed and lay there for ten or fifteen minutes but couldn't sleep and finally decided I would take a look and see if there was a light in Lorraine's cabin. So I got up and started to dress.'

'You say you *started* to dress.'

'That's right.'

'What happened?'

'I heard a door slam in the adjoining unit; in Fourteen.'

'You heard it *slam?*'

'That's right.'

'And then what?'

'I ran to the door just in time to see the taillight of an automobile turning from the parking space into the highway.'

'Could you recognize the automobile?'

'Not to be absolutely certain about it. I couldn't see the license number.'

'Well, what car did you *think* it was?'

'Objected to as calling for a conclusion of the witness,' Crowder said.

'Sustained,' Judge Manly said. 'The witness said he couldn't recognize the car. What he thought is of no importance in this case.'

'Well, what did you *do?*' Marshall asked.

'I finished dressing as fast as I could, again jumped in the car and went out and made a search. This time I didn't make such a long search. I swung around town but couldn't find any trace of Lorraine's automobile, so I went back to my unit, went to bed and tried to sleep but couldn't make it. Along about five or five-thirty in the morning I got up and dressed, took my car, and went to a restaurant and had breakfast. When I returned Perry Mason was there at the motel, and very shortly afterwards I went in and started to shave. It was about that time I heard a scream. I wasn't certain just where the scream had come from but I got to thinking things over and finally decided I'd better investigate. I went to the door of my cabin, standing there partially shaved, in my undershirt and trousers and then learned of the murder.'

Marshall turned to Mason with a bow. 'Now go ahead and cross-examine,' he said, 'and I can assure you there will be no objections from the prosecution. Just ask any questions you want.'

Judge Manly rapped on the desk with the tip of a pencil. 'Mr Prosecutor,' he said, 'the Court is not going to warn you again. I don't want any side remarks from counsel and there is no reason for you to make it appear that you are granting the defense a concession in connection with the cross-examination of a witness.'

'I *was* making a concession, if the Court please,' Marshall said. 'I was stating that I would make no objection to any questions they wanted to ask on cross-examination.'

'Proceed with the cross-examination,' Judge Manly said.

Mason rose to look searchingly at the witness.

For a moment Latty met Mason's eyes defiantly. Then he shifted his gaze and also shifted his position in the witness's chair.

'So you're engaged to Linda Calhoun?'

'That's right.'

'How long have you been engaged?'

'Something over five months.'

'Has a wedding date been set?'

'We're waiting until I finish law school.'

'Who is furnishing the funds to put you through law school?'

Marshall jumped to his feet. 'Oh, if the Court please,' he said. 'This is–'

'Sit down,' Judge Manly snapped. 'You said you weren't going to object to any questions defense counsel might ask. You said it several times under such circumstances that the Court feels it constitutes a stipulation. Any objection you want to make is overruled. Now, sit down.'

'But this is so manifestly improper,' Marshall said.

'It may show bias,' Mason said.

'I don't care what it shows,' Judge Manly snapped. 'The understanding was you could cross-examine this witness to your heart's content and there would be no objection. As far as this Court is concerned, you can go right ahead.'

'My fiancée is advancing the money that will enable me to complete my education and then I will repay it.'

'You'll repay it by marrying her?'

'I expect to, yes.'

'And then the monies that you earn will be community property.'

'I haven't given that matter any thought.'

'Now, when was the last time you saw Linda Calhoun before you came to court a short time ago?'

'I saw her on the third.'

'That was the last time you saw her until you walked into court today?'

'I–Well, I–That was the last time I spoke to her, yes.'

Mason, watching the witness's manner, said, 'I'm asking you when was the last time you *saw* her?'

'Well, I *saw* her very briefly on the street at Mexicali.'

'When?'

'Yesterday.'

'Did you speak to her?'

'No.'

'How close were you to her?'

'She was about half a block away.'

'Did you make any effort to catch up with her?'

'No.'

'What did you do?'

'I went to my hotel and telephoned the hotel where she was staying.'

'Did you ask for her on the phone?'

'Yes.'

'That was immediately after you had seen her on the street in Mexicali?'

'Yes.'

'Then you knew she wouldn't be in her hotel.'

'Yes.'

'And what happened? What did you say over the phone?'

'I asked for Linda and when I was told that her room didn't answer I asked if I could leave a message for her and was advised that I could, so I left her a brief message telling her not to worry about me, that I was all right.'

'So you put through that call when you knew she wouldn't be in her room?'

'She couldn't have been two places at the same time.'

'But you waited until you were certain that she was out of her room before you called.'

'Not necessarily.'

'You sent her that message because you thought she would be worrying about you?'

'Naturally.'

'It had then been some time that she hadn't heard from you?'

'Yes.'

'A day or two?'

'Yes.'

'And you sent that message telling her not to worry because you loved her and because you knew that she would be worried about you and wondering where you were.'

'Yes.'

'Then why didn't you send that message earlier?'

'Because . . . because I was told that no one was to know where I was staying.'

'Who told you that?'

'The prosecutor, Mr Baldwin L. Marshall.'

'And you obeyed his commands?'

'I prefer to state that I complied with his requests.'

'To the extent of letting your fiancée worry about you?'

'I just told you that I sent a message so that she wouldn't worry about me.'

'But you didn't send that until you were assured that she wasn't there so she could receive your call.'

'Well . . . yes.'

'So you did nothing to alleviate her worries for some twenty-four hours.'

'That's right. I've admitted that.'

'Just because the district attorney told you not to.'

'He said it was important that no one should know where I was. I asked him if I could let my fiancée know, and he said I could leave a message for her but he didn't want me talking with her. He didn't want anyone to see me.'

'Now, you went directly from your conference with the district attorney to Mexicali?'

'No, I went first to Tijuana.'

'To Tijuana!' Mason exclaimed in apparent surprise. 'And how long were you in Tijuana?'

'Overnight.'

'And then you went to Mexicali?'

'Yes.'

'By bus?'

'No.'

'By private car?'

'By chartered plane.'

'Who took you over there?'

'Mr Marshall, the district attorney.'

'And did Mr Marshall mention my name during the ride?'

'Oh, Your Honor,' Marshall said, 'this is going so far afield that it is ridiculous! What I talked about with this witness is completely outside of the issues. It has no bearing on the case. The conversation is not admissible. There has been nothing in the direct examination of this witness to warrant asking such a question and I object to it.'

'The objection is overruled,' Judge Manly snapped. 'You go right ahead, Mr Mason. You ask any questions you want to that would tend to show bias on the part of this witness.'

'If the Court please,' Marshall said, 'anything of that sort doesn't show bias. It simply shows that I was taking reasonable precautions to see that the defense didn't know all about my case.'

'We won't argue the matter,' Judge Manly said. 'A ruling has been made.' He turned to the witness. 'The question was: Did Mr Marshall mention Mr Perry Mason's name?'

'Yes.'

'More than once?' Mason asked.

'He discussed you at some length.'

'He mentioned my name more than once?'

'Yes.'

'More than twice?'

'Yes.'

'More than three times?'

'Yes.'

'More than ten times?'

'I didn't count them.'

'But it could have been more than ten times?'

'It could have been.'

'And you mentioned my name?'

'Yes.'

'And the district attorney told you, did he not, that he wanted particularly to have your story hit the defense in this case as a bombshell and that he was going to take every precaution to see that you didn't tell the story to anyone?'

'I believe so, yes.'

'And the district attorney went over and over your story with you?'

'Yes. We talked about what I had seen quite a bit. He kept asking me to think back and see if I couldn't amplify my testimony a little.'

'Oh, the district attorney wanted you to *amplify* your testimony, did he?'

'Well, he–Not exactly that.'

'You just said that he asked you if you couldn't amplify it a little bit.'

'Well, the word amplify was my interpretation of what he said.'

'All right,' Mason said, 'as nearly as you can remember what the district attorney said to you, the effect of it was that he wanted you to amplify your evidence, is that right?'

'Yes.'

'And he gave you money to do so?'

Marshall was on his feet. 'Your Honor, this a matter of personal privilege. I object to this. This is not proper cross-examination. This is a dastardly insinuation! It is a lie!'

'You object to the question?'

'Yes, I do.'

'The objection is overruled. Sit down.'

'Answer the question,' Mason said. 'Did Marshall give you money?'

'Not to amplify my testimony.'

'Did Marshall give you money?'

'Yes.'

'You were entirely dependant on Linda Calhoun for your spending money?'

'Well, I had a little savings account.'

'A *savings* account?'

'That's right.'

'Saved from what?'

'From my allowance.'

'What allowance?'

'What Linda gave me. I told you all about that.'

'And did Linda know you had put aside this little nest egg?'

'No.'

'Linda was working?'

'Yes.'

'And depriving herself of the little luxuries of life, the things that mean so much to a young woman, in order to give you money so you could put yourself through law school?'

'Yes.'

'And you were embezzling some of that money?'

'What do you mean, I was embezzling it?' the witness shouted. 'It was given to me.'

'It was given to you for a specific purpose, was it not?'

'I suppose so.'

'And you took some of that money and held out on your sweetheart. You deposited it in a savings account so you could use it for some other purpose.'

'Not for another purpose, no.'

'It was given to you to defray your living expenses while you were going through law school?'

'Yes.'

'And you didn't use it for that purpose?'

'I had more than I actually needed.'

'You didn't send the surplus back?'

'I did not. I made a lot of economies myself, Mr Mason. I went without things that I wanted in order to help out.'

'In order to help who out?'

'Linda.'

'Then you should have sent the surplus money back to Linda if you were economizing to help her.'

'I told you I put the surplus in a savings account.'

'In your name?'

'Yes.'

'Now, you saw me on the evening of the third in Yuma, Arizona?'

'Yes.'

'And told me you were broke?'

'Yes.'

'And I gave you twenty dollars?'

'Yes.'

'Then you immediately went back to El Centro and telephoned Linda and told her you were broke and asked her to wire you twenty dollars, did you not?'

'I asked her for funds so I could get home, yes.'

'And told her to wire you twenty dollars and waive identification?'

'Yes.'

'You told her you were broke?'

'Yes.'

'But at that time you had twenty dollars I had given you, did you not?'

'Well, that was a loan.'

'You intended to repay it?'

'Certainly.'

'But you had it?'

'Yes.'

'And you knew that I gave it to you to defray expenses?'

'No, you didn't give it to me for any such purpose.'

'I didn't?' Mason asked.

'No, sir. You did not. You told me to take that money and go to a motel in Yuma.'

'So you took the money and then didn't go to the motel?'

'I changed my mind.'

'But you had the money.'

'I considered that money was in trust for a certain specific purpose, Mr Mason. You had told me to go to a motel in Yuma. I decided not to do so. Therefore I didn't want to use your money. I telephoned Linda and asked her to wire me money.'

'So then what *did* you do with the twenty dollars I had given you?' Mason asked. 'Did you mail it to my office address, stating that you were sorry you–'

'No, of course not. I had it with me.'

'And how long did you keep it?'

'I . . . I can repay you now.'

'I'm not asking you to repay me *now*. I'm asking you how long you kept it?'

'Well, I still have it.'

'You didn't spend it?'

The witness hesitated, then said, 'No.'

Mason said, 'You were in Tijuana. You were staying at the best hotel there.'

'Yes.'

'Your expenses were paid?'

'I paid my expenses.'

'From the money Linda had sent you?'

'No, that was all gone.'

'What money did you use?'

'Money Mr Marshall had given me.'

'You looked around and saw the sights in Tijuana?'

'Yes.'

'Did you bet on race horses?'

The witness hesitated, then said, 'Yes.'

'More than once?'

'Yes.'

'Now, did the district attorney give you money to bet on the horse races?'

'He didn't say what I was to do with it.'

'He just handed you a sum of money?'

'Yes.'

'How much?'

'A hundred and fifty dollars the first time.'

'The *first* time!'

'Yes.'

'There was, then, a second time?'

'Yes.'

'How much was given you at that time?'

'A hundred and fifty dollars.'

'So you have received three hundred dollars from the district attorney?'

'Yes.'

'Any more?'

'Well . . . he okayed my expenses at the hotel in Mexicali. He told the hotelkeeper to give me anything I wanted and to charge it to the county here. He said the county would honor a bill from the hotel.'

'So you charged things in the hotel?'

'Yes.'

'And you used the money I had given you to bet on the horse races?'

'I did no such thing.'

'You used the money the district attorney had given you to bet on the horse races?'

'Well . . . yes.'

'And the district attorney gave you money for the purpose of betting on the horse races?'

'Certainly not.'

'Then why did you use the money for that purpose?'

'It was my money. I could do what I wanted to with it.'

'The money wasn't given to you for expenses?'

'I . . . I assume so.'

'What was said when the money was given to you?'

'He didn't say anything. He just handed me the money and told me that I'd be needing some money.'

'You paid your expenses out of this money?'

'Well . . . yes.'

'And then started betting on the horses.'

'I . . . I had to do something. I was shut off from all of my friends. I was forbidden to get in contact with anybody.'

'All right,' Mason said, 'now let's get back to the times the district attorney mentioned my name. What did he say about me?'

'Objected to,' Marshall said. 'Not proper cross-examination, no part of the issues.'

'Overruled,' Judge Manly snapped.

'He said you were a big-time lawyer and that he didn't want to have to be afraid of you and that he'd–Well, that he was going to get you down here in his county where the newspapers were friendly and give you a shellacking.'

'And he wanted you to help him do it?'

'He said my testimony was going to be of great help.'

'And he wanted to keep me from finding out what that testimony was going to be?'

'Well, he said he didn't want me to talk with anyone.'

Mason said, 'Now, you went to a curio store while you were in Mexicali, did you not?'

'Yes.'

'And you bought some curios?'

'Some souvenirs.'

'For your friends?'

'Yes.'

'And for yourself?'

'Yes.'

'And you bought a rather expensive camera, did you not?'

'Well . . . yes.'

'What became of the camera?'

'I have it with me.'

'Where?'

'In my suitcase.'

'Did you tell the district attorney you had bought this camera?'

'No.'

'What did you pay for the camera?'

'Two hundred and fifty dollars.'

'It was a bargain at that price?'

'Certainly. It was a camera that would cost five hundred dollars in this county.'

'Did you declare that camera in Customs when you brought it in here with you?'

'I didn't have to declare it. It had been used.'

'Did you declare the camera when you came through Customs?'

'No.'

'Did they ask you what you had bought in Mexico?'

'Yes.'

'And you told them nothing?'

'Well . . . I didn't.'

'You didn't? Who did?'

'Mr Marshall.'

'So you were staying in Mexicali and Mr Marshall went across to bring you over here this morning?'

'Yes.'

'And he told the customs authorities in your presence that you had bought nothing while you were in Mexico?'

'Yes.'

'Did you tell him any different? Did you interrupt to tell the Customs you had bought a camera?'

'No.'

'And where did you get the money with which you purchased this camera?'

'That was from my winnings on the horse races.'

'Oh, you won on the horse races.'

'I won very substantially.'

'How much?'

'I can't state, offhand.'

'A hundred dollars?'

'More than that.'

'Two hundred dollars?'

'More than that.'

'Five hundred dollars?'

'More than that.'

'You realize you are going to have to make a declaration of those winnings to the Collector of Internal Revenue and pay income tax on them?'

'No. This money was won in a foreign country.'

'That doesn't make any difference,' Mason said. 'You won the money and you brought it over to this country with you. Where is that money now?'

'It's . . . it's here and there.'

'What do you mean, here and there?'

'Well, I have some of it with me.'

'In your wallet at the present time?'

'Yes.'

'Suppose we count it,' Mason said, 'and see just how much you won.'

'That's none of your business, how much I have,' Latty shouted. 'It's my money.'

'I think defense counsel is entitled to find out where this money came from,' Judge Manly said, 'and whether the prosecutor gave you funds with which to attend the races.'

'He told me to have a good time and look around and enjoy myself.'

'And gave you money for that purpose?'

'Well, he didn't tie any strings on it. He just said I'd need some money.'

Judge Manly said, 'Gentlemen, it's past the hour of noon and the Court is going to take a two-hour recess. Court will reconvene at two o'clock.'

'May I ask one question?' Mason asked.

'Please be brief.'

'What horses did you win on?'

'Well, there was–There were several horses.'

'Name one. Where did you make your biggest winnings?'

'Well, there was a horse named Easter Bonnet.'

'You won enough money on that horse to buy your camera?'

'Yes.'

Judge Manly said, 'Gentlemen, it is now fifteen minutes past the noon hour. The Court dislikes to interrupt this cross-examination but it's quite apparent we can't complete it within the next few minutes and therefore Court will take a recess until two o'clock this afternoon.'

Judge Manly left the bench. Linda Calhoun hurried up the aisle to speak to George Latty, but before she could get there Marshall took Latty's arm and hurried him through the side door leading to the judge's chambers, leaving Linda standing there perplexed and embarrassed.

One of the newspaper photographers shot a picture of her as she stood there.

Mason turned hurriedly to Lorraine Elmore.

'Quick!' he said. 'Tell me, is his testimony true? Were you sitting on the bed? Did you discuss your telephone call to Linda?'

Lorraine Elmore tearfully nodded.

'Then did you come back with Dewitt to the cabin?'

'Mr Mason, as God is my judge, I am telling you the truth. I–How *could* I have got back? My car was stuck in the sand.'

'Anything else you talked about at that time?' Mason asked.

As she was searching her recollection, Mason noticed Duncan Crowder, who had moved protectively to Linda Calhoun's side and was doing his best to cover her embarrassment and humiliation.

'I said something about the money. I remember that.'

'What about it?'

'Well, when he wanted to go for a ride and–Well, I didn't think much of taking such a large sum of money in cash out in an automobile at night and I felt it would be dangerous. He laughed at me but I insisted that we should leave our money in the motel, that I was going to hide it. He laughed at me and said there wouldn't be any place to hide it where a person wouldn't look. I told him I was going to put it under the cushion of the overstuffed chair. I said that no one was apt to look in the unit of a motel, particularly when we were supposed to be sleeping there, but it was very easy to be held up in an automobile.'

'And what did he say?'

'Well, he thought things over and finally agreed with me.'

'Anything else you talked about at that time?' Mason asked.

'Not that I can remember.'

'But you think Latty is telling the truth? You think he–'

'Yes, oh, yes! Oh, Mr Mason, I'm so humiliated, so ashamed! I feel I could sink right through that floor. I just try to sit there and keep my eyes closed.'

'All right,' Mason said, 'you're going to have to remain in custody during the noon hour.'

She nodded tearfully, said, 'But Mr Mason, Montrose *couldn't* have gone back there! I saw him killed! I tell you, I saw him with my own eyes!'

Mason said, 'The question of the drugs hasn't come into it as yet, Mrs Elmore, but I think you're going to have to recognize the strong possibility that you *may* have an erroneous recollection as to what happened. However, we're going to check every possible angle of the case. Just don't worry. We've got detectives on the job and we aren't done with George Latty yet.'

'That man!' she said contemptuously. 'What in the world can Linda see in a man of that sort?'

'I don't know,' Mason admitted. 'Personally, I think the judge is thoroughly disgusted with him, but of course his factual testimony is something that we're going to have to overcome in some way, either by evidence or by some other means. However, don't worry about it. I'll see you at two o'clock.'

15

Lunching at a Mexican-style restaurant where they were able to get a small private dining room, Paul Drake filled Perry Mason in on details which he had picked up while court had been in session.

'We've been making like some income tax agents,' Drake said, 'snooping around, finding every place the guy has been, back tracking him on his purchases. To date we can prove that he spent eight hundred and sixty-two dollars and seventy-five cents. But I can tell you something else, this guy

Marshall is all set to file suit against you for defamation of character if you so much as intimate there was any question of bribery.'

'Let him file,' Mason said. 'I'll intimate and be damned to him! I'll go even further than that. When a man pays the expenses of a witness while he's living in concealment, that's one thing. When he gives him a flat sum of money and tells him to pay his expenses out of that, that's something else.

'This guy, Marshall, is an eager beaver, a go-getter, but he's relatively inexperienced. There's a lot he has to learn about prosecuting murder cases.'

'He's the darling of the county, however,' Drake said dryly. 'The guy is unmarried, an eligible bachelor, a smart cooky, and everybody's pulling for him.

'You're in a position where your reputation is assured. You can lose a case and it won't hurt, but if this guy wins a case against the great Perry Mason, it's going to make the whole community look good.'

'I know,' Mason said, 'He's clever in the field of public relations. He's used his newspaper friends to get that sort of a background and atmosphere.'

'What are you going to do?' Drake asked.

'I don't know,' Mason said, 'but I'm going to go in there fighting and I'm going to stay in there fighting.'

'And come out on top,' Della Street said.

'Look at the thing from a reasonable basis,' Mason said. 'A woman like Lorraine Elmore, somewhat frustrated perhaps, nervous, but eminently respectable, isn't going to come all the way across the continent, pick up with someone and then murder him for fifteen thousand dollars or whatever it was he was carrying with him. That woman has means of her own and–'

'And that's not the motive he's going to try to prove,' Drake interrupted.

'What isn't?'

'Money.'

'What is?'

'Jealousy, disillusionment, frustrated rage.'

'Go on,' Mason said.

'I picked up something this morning that I've been thinking over,' Drake said, 'and I guess I have the answer. It occurred to me just now. I should have thought of it sooner.'

'What is it?'

'This Belle Freeman.'

'What about her?'

'She put through a long distance call to the Palm Court Motel. She asked to talk with Lorraine Elmore. Apparently the call was completed. She told Lorraine things about her boy friend, and Lorraine, in a fit of jealous rage, doped him and then stabbed him with an ice pick.'

'How do you know about Belle Freeman?' Mason asked, his eyes narrowing.

'The manager told me that there was a long distance call for Lorraine Elmore from Los Angeles.'

'That probably was Linda Calhoun calling.'

'That's what I thought at first,' Drake said, 'but apparently this was another call.'

Mason said, 'I know the D.A. has Belle Freeman under subpoena. He caught her in this county and served a subpoena on her. Her boy friend lives here. I've been wondering what he intended to prove by her.'

Mason was silently thoughtful for nearly a minute, then he said, 'Find out about that horse, Easter Bonnet, Paul. See how much he actually paid off.

'The key figures in this case break out in a rash of gambling. Look at Howland Brent. He dashes to Las Vegas and starts plunging. He wins and quits. Then George Latty gets a little money and makes a beeline for the race track.'

'But he didn't go to the race track,' Drake said. 'He must have placed the bets with a bookie somewhere.'

'You haven't been able to get the bookie?' Mason asked.

Drake shook his head. 'That's one of the things that puzzles me. We had been tailing Latty all the time but of course when he's inside a house talking with someone, you can't just barge in there and have a man listen to the conversation.'

'No,' Mason said thoughtfully, 'but you *can* have a man go in there afterwards and find out what happened. Don't you have any idea where the bookie was?'

'We can make a good guess as to where he had to be, and that is in the curio shop, or the camera shop. Latty was in both places for a while.'

'He may have bought some of that stuff as a stall to cover up the fact that he was plunging on the horses,' Mason said. 'Of course, he was in a good position to take a chance. He had a hundred and fifty dollars for expense money. He could plunge with that and if he won he had something to work with. If he lost, he could always ring up his friend, the district attorney, and say, "I've been rolled and I have to have more money quick; otherwise I'll have to get in touch with Linda or Perry Mason." '

'I wonder if he didn't do just that,' Drake said, 'I wonder if he didn't put the bite on Marshall. There's something weird about this thing.'

'What about Brent?' Mason asked.

'Oh, it's the same old story–those thin walls again. Brent evidently had the idea that Lorraine was going to marry and from that time on her husband would be managing her affairs and there wouldn't be any room for him. So he was naturally concerned. It seems that the Elmore account was rather substantial and represented a fair source of income to Brent, so he did a little eavesdropping.

'Apparently he heard Lorraine tell you the story about her experiences, and Marshall is going to try to get his testimony in.'

'That's a confidential communication to an attorney, isn't it?' Della Street asked.

'It depends,' Mason said. 'It's priveleged as far as I'm concerned and as far as the client is concerned, but if some person happens to eavesdrop, that's another question, and probably a rather technical question. I'll have to argue the legal point. If it becomes important we'll ask for a twenty-four-hour continuance so we can dig into the authorities and see what the decisions hold.'

'Is it a close point?' Drake asked.

'We'll make it a close point,' Mason said.

Drake said, 'Let me do a little telephoning. I want to find out about that horse.'

Drake went to the telephone and was gone for some fifteen minutes. When he returned he cocked a quizzical eyebrow at Perry Mason.

'News?' Mason asked.

'News,' Drake said.

'Shoot.'

'The horse didn't win–he lost.'

Slowly a grin spread over Mason's face. 'What do you know,' he said.

'*You* seem to know something,' Della Street said.

Mason said, 'I know a lot and I'm beginning to get the picture now.'

The lawyer was silent for several minutes.

Paul Drake started to say something, but Della Street, with a finger on her lips, gestured him to silence.

Abruptly Mason pushed back his chair from the table, smiled, and slowly the smile broadened into a grin.

'Let's go on up to court and let Marshall pick up his little round pebble out of the stream bed.'

'What do you mean, his pebble?' Drake asked.

'David and Goliath,' Mason said. 'It's about time for Marshall to start putting his pebble in the sling and whirling it around and around his head. He might even make himself dizzy.'

16

Promptly at two o'clock Judge Manly took the bench, said, 'Court is now in session. We will resume the hearing of the case of the People of the State of California versus Lorraine Elmore. Mr Latty was on the stand. Come forward, Mr Latty.'

Latty resumed his position on the stand, and Judge Manly nodded to Perry Mason.

Mason said, 'How much money have you actually spent since the fourth of this month, Mr Latty?'

'I don't know.'

'Can you approximate it?'

'No.'

'Over a thousand dollars?'

'I don't think so.'

'Don't you know?'

'No.'

'All right, I'll go at it another way,' Mason said. 'How much money have you taken in since the fourth of the month?'

'Well, I had some money from Mr Marshall for expenses.'

'How much?'

'I believe around three hundred dollars in all.'

'And many of your expenses you charged at the hotel in Mexicali?'

'Yes.'

'Now, I'm not asking you about the things that you charged with the understanding that the county would pay for them later on, I'm asking you about how much actual cash you have received. You should know that.'

'Well, let's see. I had about three hundred dollars from Mr Marshall and–Well, that's about all, I guess.'

'You had some money in your pocket when you went across the border at

Tijuana? Money left from the twenty dollars I had given you and the twenty dollars given you by Linda Calhoun?'

'No, I was about broke at that time. I had to pay for the automobile I had rented, and with my necessary expenses I actually had to borrow money.'

'Oh, you *borrowed* money,' Mason said. 'And who did you borrow that from?'

'Mr Marshall.'

'I see. Any other source of income?'

'No.'

'Aren't you forgetting about your gambling?'

'Oh, yes, I made money from the horse races.'

'How much?'

'I don't know. I would win the money and put it in my pocket and then bet and pay out the losses, but pocket the winnings.'

'You didn't do this at the race track?'

'Well . . . I'm not sure.'

Mason said, 'You're sure whether you went to the race track or not. Now, did you bet at the race track or did you place your bets through a bookie?'

'I placed my bets through a bookie.'

'And you have no idea how much money you won?'

'No. It was a fairly good-sized amount.'

'More than a hundred dollars?'

'Oh, yes.'

'More than five hundred dollars?'

'It might have been.'

'More than a thousand dollars?'

'No. I wouldn't think it would be that much.'

'You wouldn't *think* it would be that much.'

'No.'

'More than two thousand?'

'No, I know it wasn't more than two thousand.'

'And what did you do with that money?'

'A good deal of it I spent.'

'But you haven't spent it all?'

The witness hesitated. 'I have a little.'

'You're planning to leave for Boston as soon as your testimony is completed here?'

'Yes, as soon as I'm excused I'm taking a plane back to Boston.'

'You have your ticket?'

'Yes.'

'Now, how did you purchase your ticket when you came out?'

'With cash.'

'You received the cash from what source?'

'Linda wired it to me.'

'You got a single ticket or a round-trip ticket?'

'Oh, Your Honor,' Marshall said, 'this is the vice of going into all of this extraneous stuff. It seems to be completely interminable, and it makes no difference one way or another.'

'Are you objecting?' Judge Manly asked.

'Yes, Your Honor.'

'Overruled,' Judge Manly said.

'Will you answer the question, please?' Mason said. 'Did you have a round-trip ticket?'

'No, a one-way ticket.'

'And do you now have a ticket on an eastbound plane, or just a reservation?'

'I . . . I have a ticket.'

'The plane leaves at what time?'

'At eleven-thirty tonight.'

'From Los Angeles?'

'From San Diego.'

'And that ticket has been paid for?'

'Yes.'

'Who paid for it?'

'Mr Marshall made arrangements.'

'In other words, he paid for it?'

'Yes.'

'So, not only has the district attorney of this county started loaning you money as soon as he found out that you might be persuaded to give favourable testimony, but he has been trying to keep you in isolation so that you wouldn't disclose what your testimony was going to be and now he wants to get you out of the jurisdiction of the court as rapidly as possible.'

'Your Honor, I object to that, I assign it as misconduct and I characterize the insinuation as a falsehood,' Marshall said.

'Well,' Judge Manly said, 'I think I'll sustain that objection. After all, the Court will draw its own conclusions. I don't think there's anything in the testimony *as yet* to justify this charge.

'However, the Court will state that it is very much interested in the peculiar financial status of this witness. He seems to have been getting money from somewhere.'

'From the horse races,' Marshall said angrily. 'He has been frank with the Court on that.'

'He seems to have been unusually fortunate,' Judge Manly said.

'That also can happen,' Marshall pointed out.

'Doubtless it has happened,' Judge Manly said.

Mason said, 'But your big winning was from this horse, Easter Bonnet?'

'Yes,' Latty said.

'You don't remember how much you won?'

'It was rather a large amount.'

'And you're sure you won it on that horse?'

Mason stood looking at the witness for a moment, then suddenly said, 'George, why don't you tell the truth? You didn't win that money in a horse race. That horse lost.'

'Lost!' Latty said.

'Lost,' Mason said. 'Now tell us the truth. Where did you get that money?'

'I . . . I–'

Mason said, 'You could hear the conversation in the adjoining unit there at the Palm Court Motel very plainly.'

'Yes.'

'And in that same conversation that you overheard, the parties were discussing what they were going to do with their cash. Mrs Elmore didn't want to take the money in the form of cold, hard cash with them when they went on that ride. She had something like thirty-five thousand dollars, and Dewitt had something like fifteen thousand dollars, all in cash. They discussed where they would hide it. That was part of that same conversation that you were listening to.'

'I . . . I didn't hear all of it.'

'You heard enough of it to know that they were concealing the money under the cushions of the overstuffed chair. Now, I submit to you, young man, that you tried to follow them, lost their trail, came back, started experimenting with the door which led through to the Unit fourteen which Montrose Dewitt was occupying, found that you could open that door by turning the bolt on your side, entered that unit and looked in the chair and found some fifty thousand dollars in cash. You had never had any money. You had been dependent upon friends for money. You had been placed in the embarrassing and humiliating position of having to ask your fiancée for money for every little thing you did. You couldn't resist that temptation. You took that money.'

'Oh, Your Honor,' Marshall said, 'that is absolutely absurd. There is no foundation for such a charge. This is not a question. It is an accusation. It is objected to as being not proper cross-examination.'

'Overruled,' Judge Manly snapped. 'Now, young man, *I* want you to answer that question and I want a straightforward answer. Remember, you're under oath.'

'I did nothing of the sort,' Latty said indignantly.

'All right,' Mason said, 'where's your baggage? You're all packed up to leave here and go to San Diego just as soon as you finish testifying. Where's your baggage?'

'In the district attorney's office.'

'Would you have any objection to having that baggage brought here and having it opened?'

'Certainly I would! I see no reason to subject my personal baggage to an examination by anyone.'

'Is there anything in there that you're trying to conceal?'

'No.'

'All right,' Mason said, walking two paces toward the red-faced witness. 'I'm going to look inside that baggage. I'm going to get a search warrant if I have to. Now, you're under oath. Remember that baggage is going to be searched. Is there or is there not money in it?'

'Of course there's money in it. I told you I won some money.'

'Is there as much as twenty thousand dollars in that baggage?'

'I . . . I don't know how much I won.'

'You don't know whether you won as much as twenty thousand dollars?'

'No.'

'Is there thirty thousand dollars in there?'

'I tell you, I don't know.'

'All right,' Mason said, 'I'm going to give you one more chance to tell the truth, and remember, you're under oath. Did you go into Dewitt's motel unit? Now, before you answer that question, remember that the police have testified there were some fingerprints in that room they couldn't identify but which were sufficiently definite to–'

'All right, I went in there,' Latty said. 'It's just as you thought. After I found I had lost them, I came back and started fooling with that connecting door and I found I could turn the bolt on my side and open the door. I found that the person on the other side hadn't turned the bolt to the position which locked the door on that side. So, by turning the knob which opened the bolt on my side, I could go in. I went in and looked around.'

'And found that money,' Mason said.

The witness hesitated for a long, uncomfortable moment.

Marshall got to his feet to make an objection, and Judge Manly motioned him to sit down.

Latty suddenly lowered his head. 'All right,' he said 'I got the money.'

'I thought so,' Mason said. 'Now, did you kill Montrose Dewitt?'

The witness raised tear-filled eyes. 'I swear to you, Mr Mason, I swear absolutely I know nothing about that. I did not kill him. The temptation as far as the money was concerned was too much. I intended first to take it and then get in the good graces of Lorraine Elmore by returning her money to her at the proper time. I felt that Montrose Dewitt was a confidence man and a potential murderer and I didn't know whether I'd ever return his part of the money. But I didn't kill him.'

Mason turned, walked back to his chair at the counsel table, seated himself and said, 'No further questions.'

Marshall stood looking first at the tearful witness, then at the stern face of the judge. He turned, walked over to the counsel table, whispered to his assistant, then said, 'Your Honor, this testimony naturally comes as a great surprise to me. . . . I . . . I'm going to ask the Court for a continuance.'

'You can't have one unless the defense attorney stipulates to it,' Judge Manly said. 'This hearing is supposed to be concluded at one sitting unless the defendant joins in a motion for a continuance. . . . Now then, I'm going to ask you, what do you intend to do about this witness?'

'I . . . I repudiate him.'

'I'm not talking about repudiating him. Here's a man who has been committing perjury and has just admitted to grand theft. What are you going to do about it?'

'I . . . I can appreciate the temptation but I suppose I will have to have him held.'

'I would certainly think so,' Judge Manly said.

He turned to Mason. 'What is the position of the defense in regard to a continuance?'

Mason said, 'I have no desire to take advantage of the prosecution's surprise, if the Court please. I am willing to consent to a continuance. I may state, however, that Mr Latty had not been concealed as far as we were concerned. We have had investigators keeping him in sight, knew where he was, and knew that he was spending a great deal of money.

'Under the circumstances, and knowing that he was entirely without funds when he had gone over into Mexico, it was only natural that I became interested in the source of his funds. At first I had formed the perfectly natural conclusion that this money must have been supplied by the person who was trying to keep him concealed. I am sorry I charged the prosecutor with seeking to bribe this witness.'

'The prosecutor has only himself to blame,' Judge Manly said.

Marshall, considerably chastened, said, 'I regret this entire situation. May we ask for an adjournment until tomorrow morning at ten o'clock?'

'Satisfactory to the defendant,' Mason said, 'but I would suggest that the defendant be released on her own recognizance until the hearing tomorrow.'

'I object to that,' Marshall said.

'Then I think we will object to the continuance,' Mason said.

'May I have a fifteen-minute recess to discuss the matter with my assistant?' Marshall asked.

'That would seem to be a very reasonable request,' Judge Manly said. 'Court will take a fifteen-minute recess. And as far as this witness, Latty, is concerned, I want him taken into custody. The Court is not satisfied in the least with the explanation of his conduct that has been made. If he went into that room, if he took that money, then I see no reason why he couldn't have used the murder weapon as well.'

'Then how did it get in the defendant's car?' Marshall asked.

'It got there because it was put there,' Judge Manly said. 'This witness was out a second time and that was after he had secured the money. How do we know where he went? We only have his statement for it.'

'I didn't kill him! I tell you, I didn't!' Latty protested.

Judge Manly said, 'You've told us a lot of things, young man. The court is going to insist that you be taken into custody. The Court is going to order you into custody for perjury and for grand larceny. Now then, Court will take a fifteen-minute recess.'

As Judge Manly left the bench, Lorraine Elmore squeezed Mason's arm until he could feel the tips of her fingers biting into the flesh. 'Oh, Mr Mason!' she said. 'Oh, Mr Mason!'

Linda Calhoun came hurrying forward. Her first objective was George Latty, but Latty, seeing her coming, hurried toward the exit door through which prisoners were taken from the courtroom and a deputy sheriff hurrying after him, said, 'Just a minute, Latty. You're in custody.'

Linda swerved over toward the defense group.

'Oh, Duncan,' she said, 'I feel so perfectly, utterly, absolutely terrible!'

'About what?'

'That heel,' she said. 'I made all sorts of sacrifices to keep him in law school and I *knew* how Aunt Lorraine felt about him. I . . .'

She blinked back tears.

Lorraine Elmore embraced her, said, 'There, there, darling. It's all right. *Everything's* going to be all right now.'

Newspaper reporters crowded around, asking for a story. Flash bulbs popped.

Mason said, 'I'm sorry, gentlemen. We only have fifteen minutes and we have to confer on some strategy. With your permission we're going to move over here to a corner of the courtroom.'

Mason beckoned to the others and they huddled in a deserted corner of the courtroom back of the judge's bench.

'Okay, what happens now?' Drake asked.

'Now,' Mason said, 'we begin to get the picture.'

'You mean Latty killed him?'

'Gosh, no,' Mason said. 'Latty didn't kill him. Latty hasn't the guts. He hasn't the initiative. He hasn't the determination. He's a jackal, not a lion.'

'All right, what did happen?' Drake asked.

Mason said, 'Dewitt had to have an accomplice.'

'What do you mean, an accomplice?'

'It's plain as day,' Mason said. 'He wanted to disappear. He had two entities, two separate identities. One was Montrose Dewitt, the other was Weston Hale.

'Weston Hale worked in a financial institution where he had an opportunity to handle a good many sums of money. I have an idea that the identity of Dewitt was taken for the purpose of enabling Hale to embezzle money and vanish without leaving any trace, but something happened to change the plans, and Hale was left with this alter ego of Dewitt on his hands.

'He found that by using this identity, he could victimize women and pick up quite a little money on the side.

'Now then, something happened to the Dewitt personality and Hale decided to kill off Dewitt, to get rid of the character, and he decided to do it under such circumstances that it would not only be profitable for him but so he would completely clean the slate.

'So he planned to let it appear he had been murdered. However, he wanted to do more than disappear. He wanted to take Lorraine's thirty-five thousand dollars with him.

'So he went out in the car with her to a predetermined destination and there his accomplice held up the car.'

'But how do you account for the terrific beating he took?' Lorraine Elmore asked tearfully. 'I saw it. I heard it.'

'That's the point,' Mason said. 'That's part of the game. He was beaten up with a rolled-up newspaper painted black so it looked like a club. The impact of the blows was terrific but had no more real force behind them than a good lick with a fly swatter.'

'And then what happened?' Drake asked.

'Then everything went according to plan for a while,' Mason said. 'The accomplice drove behind you, Mrs Elmore, until you got stuck in the sand. Then he turned around, went back and picked up Dewitt, or Hale, and returned to the motor court. That's when they intended to get the money and leave. And then something happened.'

'Such as what?' Drake asked.

'Such as the fact that the accomplice decided since Hale or Dewitt had been officially murdered and his murder was going to be reported to the police, it might be just as well to let Dewitt actually become a corpse, and the accomplice skip out with fifty thousand dollars.'

'But Latty has the fifty thousand,' Drake said.

'That was a fluke. They hadn't counted on Latty,' Mason said.

'Well, then–who was the accomplice?' Drake asked.

'Someone Dewitt was close to, someone he had done business with . . .'

'You mean Belle Freeman?' Linda asked incredulously.

The door from chambers opened, and Judge Manly entered the courtroom. Everyone hurriedly took their places.

Judge Manly said to Marshall, 'Has the prosecutor's office agreed on whether it wishes a continuance on condition that the defendant be released on her own recognizance?'

'If the Court please, we simply can't consent to that,' Marshall said. 'We would very much like a continuance but we can't consent to the release of the defendant on her own recognizance.'

'Well, I can appreciate the defendant's position,' Judge Manly said. 'Simply because the prosecution has been surprised by a very peculiar development in this case and desires time to meet the situation, is no reason why the defendant should stay in custody for another twenty-four hours. If you aren't prepared to make that stipulation, proceed with your case.'

Mason said, 'Perhaps, Your Honor, if I could ask two or three more questions of one witness, we might clear up the case to such an extent an adjournment wouldn't be necessary.'

'What witness?' Judge Manly asked.

'One who can tell us about Montrose Dewitt we may have overlooked,' Mason said, 'Ronley Andover.'

Judge Manly glanced at the prosecutor.

'I certainly have no objections,' Marshall said.

Judge Manly nodded to Andover. 'You will resume your position on the witness stand, Mr Andover. You have already been sworn.'

Andover took his place on the witness stand, his manner indicating puzzled surprise.

Mason approached Andover, watching the man's eyes as he advanced.

'Mr Andover,' he said, 'on the night of the third, where were you?'

'In Los Angeles. You know that. I was in bed with the flu.'

'Did you leave Los Angeles at any time during the night?'

'Certainly not.'

'Then,' Mason said, 'how did it happen that your fingerprint was one of the unidentified fingerprints found in the Palm Court Motel in Calexico?'

Andover stiffened with apprehension. 'It wasn't. It couldn't have been.'

Mason turned to the sheriff. 'Sheriff, I'd like to have you take this man's fingerprints,' he said.

The sheriff looked at Marshall.

'We object,' Marshall said. 'We feel that this is an attempt to intimidate the witness.'

'Ordinarily I would rule with you,' Judge Manly said. 'But in this case, Mr Prosecutor, there have been too many bizarre developments, and counsel for the defense has been able to call the turn so far. Let's have this man's fingerprints taken.'

'Now, wait a minute!' Andover shouted. 'You have no right to do that! I'm subpoenaed here as a witness. I'm not under arrest. I'm not under suspicion of anything.'

'Any objection to giving your fingerprints?' Mason asked.

'I don't have to.'

'Any objection?' Mason asked.

'Yes!' Andover shouted.

'All right,' Mason said, 'what's the objection?'

Andover, looking like a trapped animal, suddenly jumped up from the witness stand. 'I'm not going to stay here and be subjected to any abuse of this sort. I know my rights.'

'Now, just a minute,' Judge Manly said. 'Sheriff take that man into custody if he tries to leave here. Under the circumstances it would seem that this matter of the fingerprints may be of tremendous importance.'

Andover suddenly lashed out at the sheriff, turned and started running from the courtroom.

The sheriff shouted, 'You're under arrest! Halt or I'll shoot!'

Andover slammed the exit door in the sheriff's face.

The sheriff wrenched it open, pulling out his gun as he did so.

The courtroom went into an uproar as spectators struggled to get to the exit doors in order to see what was happening.

Mason glanced up at the bench and caught Judge Manly's eye.

'And now,' Judge Manly said, 'the Court will continue the case of its own motion, and of its own motion will order the defendant released on her own recognizance, unless the prosecutor wants to dismiss the case.'

Marshall hesitated for a moment, then threw out his hands in a gesture of surrender.

'Very well,' he said, 'the case is dismissed.' And without a word, either to the defendant or Perry Mason, stalked from the courtroom.

17

Mason, Della Street, Duncan Crowder, Linda Calhoun, Lorraine Elmore and Paul Drake gathered in Duncan Crowder's office.

'Well,' Crowder said, 'I guess the local David with his slingshot made a clean miss, and Goliath Mason is still with us.'

Mason said, 'Thanks to some darned good local assistance.'

Crowder bowed.

Drake said, 'Let's see if I get this straight, Perry. Andover was to be the accomplice. He went to the place that had previously been picked out for the holdup and where Dewitt had arranged to have Lorraine Elmore. He put a gun on Dewitt, ordered him out of the car, took him back a ways, beat him up with a newspaper rolled up and painted black to resemble a club; then came back, forced Mrs Elmore to drive to a point where she would be stuck in the sand; then went back, picked up Dewitt and they returned to the motel, apparently intending to stay just long enough to pick up the money and leave.'

'That was the idea,' Mason said, 'but when he was searching the car, Andover found that big bottle of barbiturates in the glove compartment. That gave him an idea. He hastily dumped the capsules into a whiskey bottle, waited until they had dissolved, gave Dewitt a drink in the dark, and by the time they arrived at the motel Dewitt was so groggy he hardly knew what was going on.

'In all probability he actually went to sleep almost as soon as they reached the cabin, and then just in order to make certain he wouldn't have any more trouble with Dewitt, and knowing that he had a perfect pigeon, Andover simply got rid of Dewitt by using an ice pick. Then he detoured back to the place where the stalled automobile had been left. He didn't take the road that Lorraine had taken, however; he went out on the Holtville road and drove south until he came to the sand patch. Then he put the ice pick in Lorraine's car and left a capsule on the front seat. By that time Lorraine Elmore was walking back toward the highway.

'Having done that job, Andover went back to Los Angeles, used an extract of onion or some other material to which he was allergic to start his nose and his eyes running, went to bed and pretended he was incapacitated with the flu.

'But the amateur criminal invariably overlooks some one important point. He forgot about leaving his fingerprints in the motel, and when he realized that he had done so he realized that the slip was disastrous–something he could never explain.'

'But why did he tear up Lorraine Elmore's unit?' Drake asked. 'Oh, wait a minute–I see. He thought the money was in the overstuffed chair in Dewitt's unit. When he looked for it there and didn't find it, he thought then it must have been in Lorraine's unit so he went in there and ransacked that.'

Mason nodded. 'He had the key,' he said. 'Remember he took everything from Lorraine, including her handbag. Incidentally that was a tip-off–that the handbag was found in the motel unit.

'At the time the holdup was planned, Dewitt had no way of knowing that Lorraine would insist on leaving the money in the motel. He naturally thought she would take it with her, but when he suggested the midnight ride in order to talk things over–which was, of course, all part of the plan which had previously been worked out with Andover–Lorraine insisted on hiding the money in the motel.

'At the time that didn't seem to make any difference, because Dewitt and Andover could take the money from the motel just as easily as they could take it from Lorraine.'

Della said, 'But what gets me, Perry, is how you figured it out. How did you know that the accomplice was Andover?'

'It was very, very simple,' Mason said. 'It was a point that I completely overlooked at the moment, and it's going to be a long time before I forgive myself for it.'

'What do you mean?'

'As soon as I realized what had happened,' Mason said, 'that is, what must have happened, I knew that Dewitt must have had an accomplice.'

Della Street nodded.

'So I started turning over in my mind the possibilities and wondering who that accomplice could have been,' Mason said. 'Then it suddenly became perfectly apparent. It had to be Andover.'

'Why?'

'Because,' Mason said, 'Andover got the fifteen thousand dollars for Dewitt, the fifteen thousand dollars that was to be the bait he was using in order to get Lorraine to take her thirty-five thousand dollars in cash. He stood on the curb and handed the envelope containing the money to Dewitt when Lorraine drove the car to the place which Dewitt had designated for the meeting.'

'Go on,' Della Street said. 'I still don't see it.'

'Remember,' Mason said, 'that Andover had only known Dewitt as Weston Hale, according to his story. And he didn't know that Weston Hale had an artificial eye. Yet at the time Andover handed over the money, Hale was masquerading as Dewitt and had the black patch over his eye.

'If Andover had been on the square and had been telling the truth, the first thing he would have mentioned was that he was surprised when he saw his friend to see the black patch over his eye.'

Drake snapped his fingers. 'Hell, yes,' he said.

'I guess that does it,' Della Street said, 'but I do wish somebody would explain to me what caused Howland Brent to suddenly make a beeline for Las Vegas and start plunging.'

'That,' Mason said, 'is puzzling.'

There was a moment's silence. Then Lorraine Elmore said, 'I am going to tell you the reason for that. I hope it won't go any further because I am satisfied Howland is thoroughly repentant and there is no danger of any future lapses.

'The fact of the matter is that Brent had some very urgent personal financial obligations. He had some money of his own coming in within a few weeks and knowing that I was out of town and had some funds which he could use, he dipped into my funds. Then, when he realized that I was about to get married, he knew that my husband would demand an accounting and his defalcation would be exposed.

'The man became absolutely desperate. He flew out here to try and see me. He wanted to confess, ask my forgiveness and arrange for a loan until he could make restitution.

'When he saw that I was being charged with murder, he realized that instead of getting out of the frying pan he had got into the fire. There was only one alternative as far as he was concerned. That was to stake everything on a last desperate gamble.

'So he decided to go to Las Vegas to plunge on the tables there. If he won the amount of his defalcations, he was going to quit and never gamble again as long as he lived. If he lost, he intended to commit suicide.

'I'm hoping that none of you will ever repeat this. I feel that you are entitled to an explanation. I am also certain that Howland Brent has learned his lesson and that he will never gamble again as long as he lives.'

'So that explains it!' Drake said. 'The guy certainly had me puzzled.'

'Well,' Crowder said, laughing, 'all's well that ends well, and this case hasn't done me any harm. Thanks a lot for having me associated, Perry.'

'Thanks to you,' Mason said.

Drake said, 'You sure gave Crowder the spotlight, Perry.'

Mason turned to Drake. 'Duncan told me there was a young woman in the courtroom whom he wanted to impress–'

Under Crowder's desk Della Street kicked Mason's shin so hard he winced with pain.

Linda Calhoun's face suddenly became a fiery red.

'Well, he certainly made a great impression on *me*,' Della Street said, laughing.

The ringing of the telephone gave Crowder a chance to turn to the instrument and to some extent recover his composure.

When he had finished the conversation, he turned to Mason and said, 'That was the press. They want a picture of us all taken together here in my office. I guess it's all right, isn't it?'

Mason nodded. 'Anything you want is okay, Duncan,' he said, '*anything*.'

LE STANLEY GARDNER
ARDNER ERLE STANL
LE STANLEY GARDNER
ARDNER ERLE STANL
LE STANLEY GARDNER
ARDNER ERLE STANL
LE STANLEY GARDNER
ARDNER ERLE STANL
LE STANLEY GARDNER
ARDNER ERLE STANL
LE STANLEY GARDNER
ARDNER ERLE STANL
LE STANLEY GARDNER
ARDNER ERLE STANL
LE STANLEY GARDNER
ARDNER ERLE STANL
LE STANLEY GARDNER